THE TALE OF
KHUN CHANG KHUN PHAEN

CHRIS BAKER formerly taught Asian history in Cambridge University and has lived in Thailand for over thirty years. PASUK PHONGPAICHIT is professor of economics at Chulalongkorn University, Bangkok. Together they have written *A History of Thailand*, *Thailand: Economy and Politics*, *Thaksin*, and published several translations.

MUANGSING JANCHAI, a native of Suphanburi, the cradle of the tale, was trained in Thai painting, and studied further in Tibet, India, Nepal, Burma, Laos, and China. He has executed several temple murals, including a series on the tale at Wat Palelai, Suphanburi.

The Tale of

Khun Chang Khun Phaen

SIAM'S GREAT FOLK EPIC OF LOVE AND WAR

TRANSLATED AND EDITED BY

CHRIS BAKER AND PASUK PHONGPAICHIT

ILLUSTRATED BY

Muangsing Janchai

SILKWORM BOOKS

This publication is funded by The James H. W. Thompson Foundation.

The Tale of Khun Chang Khun Phaen
© 2010 by Chris Baker and Pasuk Phongpaichit
Illustrations © 2010 by Muangsing Janchai

Jacket: From *Khun Phaen and Kaeo Kiriya*, oil painting by Chakrabhand Posayakrit, 1989–90.

First edition published in 2010

Silkworm Books
6 Sukkasem Road, T. Suthep
Chiang Mai 50200 Thailand

ISBN: 978-974-9511-95-4 (Main volume)
ISBN: 978-974-9511-96-1 (Companion volume)
ISBN: 978-974-9511-98-5 (Two-volume set)

info@silkwormbooks.com
http://www.silkwormbooks.com

Typeset by Silk Type in Minon Pro 10.5 pt.
Design by Trasvin Jittidecharak

Printed in China
10 9 8 7 6 5 4 3 2 1

CONTENTS

PREFACE

Khun Chang Khun Phaen is the great classic of Thai literature. The tale is a love story, set against a background of war, and ending in high tragedy. This is the first full translation.

The text is not the product of a single author or a precise time, but developed over centuries, with contributions from many poets and storytellers, all but a handful unnamed. Possibly the tale began from a true story around 1600, and grew with the telling as storytellers added dialogue, description, detail, and subplot. By the eighteenth century it had grown to a rambling epic of many episodes, and its recitation was highly popular entertainment.

The tale also intrigued Siam's royal court. Episodes were transcribed from storytellers into handwritten manuscripts. Court poets, including two kings, embellished the language, the meter, and the plot. Around the mid-nineteenth century, a collection of manuscripts telling the whole story was assembled in the Bangkok royal palace. In 1872, this collection was printed, becoming one of the first Thai literary works to appear as a book. In 1917–18, the great administrator and litterateur, Prince Damrong Rajanubhab, oversaw production of a standard edition that has been in print ever since.

In Thailand today, the tale is a source of songs, proverbs, and everyday sayings. Episodes have been adapted into novels, films, television series, and manga comics. The principal characters are used to name streets and temples, and represented in shrines and amulets believed to convey good fortune. The meanings of the story are constantly debated.

Like all great literature, *Khun Chang Khun Phaen* excites strong emotions. Critics have panned it as a paean to violence, obscenity, male chauvinism, and social disorder—even demanding it be banned or burned. Advocates celebrate it as a great story told in beautiful poetry, a unique essay in humanistic realism, and an unrivaled storehouse of old Thai culture.

We have based our translation on Prince Damrong's standard edition of 1917–18, but have retrieved around a hundred passages, ranging in length from a half-line to several pages, from older versions. We have not translated word for word, but have attempted to render the poem in its entirety, leaving nothing out.

Khun Chang Khun Phaen was composed in verse. We have translated the opening and closing paragraphs in an English-language approximation of the metrical form, as a sample. The remainder is in prose, but we have borne in mind that the original was composed for recitation and have tried to retain some of that character. Our text is laid out in two-line stanzas, which are the rhyming units of the original. This does not match any traditional layout but serves as a reminder that the original was a poem.

A handful of Thai words that appear often (e.g., wat, wai) have been treated as naturalized and are not italicized. A few terms, such as "sentinelle" for female palace guards, have been newly minted. These are all explained in the glossary. The remaining Thai words are transliterated by the Royal Institute system but with *j* used for *jo jan*, and some exceptions for words with conventional spellings.

In the back of this book, there is a pronunciation guide, a synopsis of the story, and maps showing places and routes. In an afterword, we explain the history of the tale and the text, some key features of the historical and social setting, and the approach of this translation.

The four hundred original illustrations by Muangsing Janchai show landscape, architecture, costume, weaponry, ritual articles, household goods, flora, fauna, and other details that provide background to the action in the text. Many of the drawings are adapted from old murals, manuscript illustrations, travelers' sketches, and early photographs.

Because the poem developed over a long period, there are alternative versions of several episodes, and many extra episodes extending the story. The companion volume contains a sampler of these additional chapters and alternative versions. It also has translations of Prince Damrong's two prefaces on the history of the poem, and details on the flora, fauna, dress, weaponry, and food in the text.

Khun Chang Khun Phaen was developed in oral tradition, and originally performed as recitation. Performances were usually of a single episode, roughly equivalent to a chapter. It was not originally written to be read cover to cover like a novel. Some readers might like a shorter approach. One suggestion is to cut chapters 14 and 15, a late addition, and put aside the Chiang Mai campaign in chapters 25 to 32 for a separate reading. An even shorter approach is to read the synopsis and then eight chapters which contain the key episodes of the love-triangle story and its tragic ending: 1, 4, 13, 17, 18, 33, 35, 36.

Old Thai literature is very little known outside its country of origin, largely because very little is available in translation. That is a pity. The great Thai linguist, William Gedney, wrote: "The quality of much of this work is superb, often entrancing for its elegance, grace, and vitality. One cannot help feeling that this body of traditional Thai poetry is among the finest artistic creations in the history of mankind." We hope this translation allows a few more people to enjoy a masterpiece of this literature.

PRINCIPAL CHARACTERS

Apson Sumali, queen of King Chiang In of Chiang Mai; mother of Soifa

Bun, abbot of Wat Som Yai, Kanburi

Busaba, wife of Phra Phichit; mother of Simala

Chaophraya Jakri, minister of Mahatthai at Ayutthaya

Chaophraya Yommarat, minister of the capital at Ayutthaya

Chiang In, king of Chiang Mai

Jiw, acolyte of Elder Khwat

Ju, abbot of Wat Palelai, Suphanburi

Kaen Kaeo, first wife of Khun Chang

Kaeo Kiriya, daughter of Phraya Sukhothai and Phenjan; wife of Khun Phaen

Kamnan Taeng, a village head in Suphanburi

Keson, queen of Lanchang, mother of Soithong

Khong, abbot of Wat Khae, Suphanburi

Khun Chang, son of Khun Siwichai and Thepthong; a rich man of
    Suphanburi

Khun Krai Pholaphai, a soldier in Suphanburi; husband of Thong Prasi;
    father of Phlai Kaeo, Khun Phaen

Khun Phaen Saensathan, title conferred on Phlai Kaeo after the Chiang
    Thong campaign

Khun Siwichai, head of the outer division of the elephant corps in Suphan-
    buri; husband of Thepthong; father of Khun Chang

Khwat, a monk and former royal teacher in Chiang Mai

King of Lanchang

Kloi, elderly neighbor of Khun Chang in Suphanburi

Koet, abbot of Wat Khao Chon Kai, Kanburi

Kueng Kamkong, a military officer of Lanchang

Laothong, daughter of Saen Kham Maen and Si Ngoen Yuang of Chom-
    thong; wife of Khun Phaen

Luang Ritthanon, friend of Khun Krai

Mai, maidservant of Soifa

Matho Thabom, a ferryman on the Song Phinong Canal, Suphanburi

Mi, abbot of Wat Palelai, Suphanburi

Moei, maidservant of Simala

Nu, abbot of Wat Takrai, Ayutthaya

Phan Chot, a village head in Suphanburi

Phan Sonyotha, a trader in Suphanburi; husband of Siprajan; father of Wanthong

Phanson, eldest cousin of Khun Chang

Phanwasa, king of Ayutthaya

Phenjan, wife of Phraya Sukhothai; mother of Kaeo Kiriya

Phim Philalai, daughter of Phan Sonyotha and Siprajan; later **Wanthong**

Phlai Chumphon, son of Khun Phaen and Kaeo Kiriya; later Luang Nai Rit

Phlai Kaeo, son of Khun Krai and Thong Prasi; later **Khun Phaen**; later **Phra Kanburi**

Phlai Ngam, son of Khun Phaen and Wanthong; later **Phra Wai** Woranat

Phon, servant in the house of Siprajan

Phra Kanburi, governor of Kanburi, title conferred on Khun Phaen after the Chiang Mai campaign

Phra Phichit, a provincial governor; husband of Busaba; father of Simala

Phra Thainam, a military officer, head of the six militia units (the standing army) at Ayutthaya

Phra Wai Woranat, lieutenant of the pages, title conferred on Phlai Ngam after the Chiang Mai campaign

Phramuen Si Saowarak-rat, one of the four heads of the royal pages at Ayutthaya

Phraya Falan, military commander of Chiang Mai

Phraya Maen, the Upahat (deputy king) of Chiang Mai

Phraya Sanbadan, deputy military commander of Chiang Mai

Phraya Sukhothai, a provincial governor, an old friend of Khun Siwichai; father of Kaeo Kiriya

Phya Suwannabat, a Lanchang envoy sent to Ayutthaya

Ratthaya, cousin of Khun Chang

Saen Kham Maen, headman of Chomthong village; husband of Si Ngoen Yuang; father of Laothong

Saentri Phetkla, a military officer of Chiang Mai

Sai, elderly neighbor of Khun Chang in Suphanburi

Saithong, foster-sister of Phim Philalai (Wanthong)

Si Ngoen Yuang, wife of Saen Kham Maen of Chomthong village; mother of Laothong

Simala, daughter of Phra Phichit and Busaba; wife of Phra Wai (Phlai Ngam)

Siprajan, wife of Phan Sonyotha; mother of Phim Philalai (Wanthong)

Soifa, daughter of the king and queen of Chiang Mai; wife of Phra Wai (Phlai Ngam)

Soithong, daughter of the king and queen of Lanchang

Sonphraya, cousin of Khun Chang

Thao Krungkan, a military officer of Chiang Mai

Thao Si Satja, deputy of Thao Worajan in charge of the inner palace guard at Ayutthaya

Thao Worajan, head royal governess in charge of the inner palace at Ayutthaya

Thepthong, wife of Khun Siwichai; mother of Khun Chang

Thong Prasi, wife of Khun Krai; mother of Phlai Kaeo (Khun Phaen)

Upahat, the second king of Lanchang

Wanthong, new name adopted by Phim Philalai

1: THREE BIRTHS

Respect to teachers has been paid,[1]	a start be made on this old saga,
Of when His Majesty King Phanwasa[2]	at Ayutthaya did power wield.
Paramount throughout the world,	his writ unfurled far afield,
A source of joy, like heaven revealed,	a shield and shelter of the commonalty.
Dependencies diverse within his power	did cower in awe of such authority.
All lands around the sacred city	in humility clasped hands, heads bowed.
The sovereign holder of the royal wealth,	perfect in health, with happiness endowed,
Ten Royal Virtues[3] duly avowed.	The common crowd as one was joyful.

This is the story of Khun Phaen, Khun Chang, and the fair Nang Wanthong. In the year 147,[4] the parents of these three people of that era

were subjects of the realm of His Majesty King Phanwasa. The story will be told following the tale. Please, listeners, understand it that way.

Putting other matters aside for now, let us relate the births of our various characters—how in the beginning a wicked spirit at the top of a tree brought them into a womb.

At night in fits of laughter, this spirit molds figures, picking them up, squeezing here and there without any pattern, molding and remolding, adding this and that to make them complete.[5]

---

1. The translation of this opening section mimics the layout and rhyming pattern used throughout the original. Prince Damrong explained that the customary prologue honoring teachers had been lost (*Companion*, 1363). The invocation of the king that follows was a standard part of court poetry in late Ayutthaya and early Bangkok (Nidhi, *Pen and Sail*, 21–25).

2. พันวษา, "thousand years," a conventional title for a king, not the name of a specific monarch. This name was given to certain major queens, including one of King Narai.

3. ทศพิธราชธรรม์, usually ราชธรรม, *thotsaphit ratchatham*. This code of conduct for kings, based on Buddhist principles, became important in late Ayutthaya and early Bangkok when some of the nobility promoted the application of Buddhist ideas in politics. The ten virtues are: munificence, moral living, sacrifice, honesty, gentleness, self-restraint or austerity, non-hatred, non-violence or not causing harm, patience or tolerance, and non-oppressiveness. According to the legend, a royal minister who had become an ascetic found a *thammasat*, law code, inscribed on a hillside. The code enjoined the king to follow these ten virtues and to practice the Buddhist precepts (Ishii, *State, Sangha and Society*, 44–45).

4. For the debate surrounding this date, see p. 882, note 4.

5. We have reordered the sections in this chapter. In the original, the three families are

One night when the molding spirit was in the treetop, beings still suffering pitiably and horribly in hell came to the end of their karma and were released from torment.[6]

Reborn from the form of netherworlders, suffering ghosts,[7] they rushed in turmoil to find happiness in heaven but were too late. The spirit shaped the beings, and slipped each into a womb.

∻

Now to tell of Khun Siwichai,[8] an officer in the provincial division of the Department of Elephants.[9] A diligent fellow, his home was in the city of Suphan.[10]

---

introduced; then the three dreams are recounted; and then the three births. Readers of the draft translation found this very confusing. Here, we have put the introduction, dream, and birth of each family together. This required no change in wording.

6. At death, a being with more bad than good deeds accumulated is sent to a hell. Time spent suffering there is set against this deficit, so at some point the account is balanced and the being is released (see below, pp. 938–39).

7. เปรต, *pret*, suffering ghost, is one form of อสุรกาย, *asurakai*, an inhabitant of the netherworld. In the Buddhist cosmology known in Siam, the universe is divided into three worlds, further subdivided into thirty-two levels. The world of sensual desire has eleven levels including the human world, six levels of heaven above, and four "realms of loss and woe" below. After death, any being with a deficit balance of good deeds is assigned to a particular hell to suffer until such time as the deficit has been paid off. The *asura* region is a netherworld immediately below the mundane world. A *pret* is the spirit of a dead person who still carries too much burden of wrongdoing from previous lives to be born into the human world and hence is stranded in the netherworld. A *pret* is as tall as a sugar palm tree, with long hair, elongated neck, dark body, protruding belly, and a mouth as small as a needle hole as a result of which such spirits are emaciated and constantly hungry (RR, 107–13; Anuman, *Phi sang thewada*, 59).

In the text versions of the Three Worlds cosmogony, rebirth is an automatic and natural process. The folk tradition has added the agency of a spirit that physically creates the new bodily form. According to Thai belief, when the spirit is feeling good, he makes his creations look beautiful, and when he is feeling bad, he makes them look ugly.

8. ศรีวิไชย, "glorious victory." The father of Khun Chang.

9. The forested hills beyond Suphan were one of the areas closest to Ayutthaya to hunt elephants for the palace and army. Prince Damrong noted that "Khun Chang" was not a personal name but an official title that appears several times in the Palatine Law, probably as a conventional shorthand for a senior officer in the Department of Elephants. Damrong speculated that Chang's father, Khun Siwichai, was probably known locally as "Khun Chang" because of his post in the Department of Elephants, and after his death the title was passed on to his son. The son would have had a personal name but possibly this had been forgotten by the time the story developed, and hence he is known as "Khun Chang" from the beginning (see *Companion*, 1375; KTS, 1:71, 83, 84, 86, 87, 92, 135).

10. Suphanburi, "town of gold," is a very ancient settlement on one of the main rivers of the Chaophraya Delta. It was a major town from the Dvaravati era, rising to special prominence in the twelfth century CE. The rectangular walls and moat are still clearly visible to the west of the

He was a rich man with masses of wealth and many servants. Together with his wife, Nang Thepthong,[11] he lived at Ten Cowries Landing[12] in Suphan.

adjutant stork

In her sleep, Thepthong tossed and murmured as she dreamed that a bull elephant died and rolled down a steep bank where its head became swollen and putrefied.

A baldheaded adjutant stork[13] flew over from the great forest, picked up the elephant in its beak, and set it down in the central hall where she slept.[14]

In her dream she called to the bird, "Please, bald lord, come over here." She clutched the hairless bird, and cradled both stork and elephant to sleep in comfort.

When she came to her senses, she retched at the foul smell of the elephant and bird lingering on her chest. With her body shaking uncontrollably, she quickly woke her husband, and begged him to hit the back of her neck.[15]

Khun Siwichai got a fright. He jumped up with eyes bulging and desperately clutched and kneaded her neck. She recovered and related the dream.

Khun Siwichai interpreted it. "Well, you'll be pregnant! Nothing to worry about. Our child will be a boy. That's the meaning of the big stork bringing an elephant in its beak.

Our blessings are complete, my love, but this child will be bald from birth. He'll bring shame on us, yet will be rich with more than five cartloads of money."

Thepthong did not want this blessing. She clutched her belly, still retching

---

river, and many Hindu and Buddhist artifacts have been found in the area. In the fourteenth and fifteenth centuries, Suphan was one of the network of towns from which emerged the state centered at Ayutthaya. In the wars with Burma in the late eighteenth century, the city was damaged and almost deserted but revived as a provincial capital a century later (see pp. 917–20; map 6).

11. เทพทอง, "golden deity."

12. ท่าสิบเบี้ย, *tha sip bia*. Cowry shells, *Cypraea moneta*, imported from the Maldives and the Philippines, were used as currency. There was a wharf with the same name in Ayutthaya, from which a ferry ran to the palace. The fare was five cowries each way, hence the name recorded the cost of a round trip (Boranratchathanin, *Tamnan krung kao*, 124). Perhaps the Suphanburi name had the same origin. The location of this landing is a matter of debate (see below, p. 857).

13. ตะกรุม, *takrum*, *Leptoptilos javanicus*, correctly called a lesser adjutant, has a dark grey head with a fringe of light grey round the back that gives the impression of a bald dome.

14. The house of any family of quality consisted of several separate buildings, grouped around a central terrace, all on stilts to rise above annual floods. The central hall, หอกลาง, *ho klang*, is a part of the terrace with a raised floor, roof, and no walls. She sleeps there to be cooled by the breeze.

15. A way to cure queasiness.

and queasy. "Mother's clan![16] Why do you make me sick? Why should I raise a bald baby?"

Thepthong's belly grew huge, jutting out front. She was so uncomfortable that she kept getting up, sitting down, shifting from side to side. She craved liquor and raw meat salad[17] so badly that her body trembled all the time.

She dribbled spittle like a hungry ghost,[18] wept, and complained to her husband. "I feel a spirit[19] has taken over my body. The more I eat, the more I want to eat."

She shoveled eels, chickens, frogs, turtles, butterfly lizards, giant spiders, and paddy frogs into her mouth in great handfuls, but there was never enough. Liquor jars emptied faster than they could be bought.

For many months, she was aching, queasy, uncomfortable, sickly, and shaky. After ten months,[20] the child kicked. Nearing delivery, the pain grew worse.

She writhed, called out to her husband and parents, and screamed uncontrollably. Her husband, parents, and all the servants rushed up into her room.

Some cast auspicious mantras on broken rice, or prayed while inserting masses of cowry shells between wall planks.[21] Some urged the midwife to hurry up. She straddled the belly and warned that the child was crosswise.

Someone sat behind Thepthong to support her back,[22] and others sat by her side. She cried, moaned, and rolled her head around. Trembling, Khun Siwichai clutched her hair and blew on her forehead.[23]

The midwife, squatted over the belly. Thepthong's mother helped to press until she shook, but nothing happened. The midwife said, "It's straight now. Push again!"

Granny Khong bent over and pressed. At a plopping sound, she fell off and collapsed against a wall. The baby wailed and the mother opened her eyes. At

---

16. A curse abbreviated from, "may your mother's clan be cursed."

17. พล่า, *phla*, a spicy salad made with raw meat or seafood flavored with chili, lime juice, fish sauce, basil and lemongrass.

18. ผีกระสือ, *phi krasue*, a female spirit, usually of an old woman, that likes to go out at night to eat dirt, rubbish, and feces. The spirit leaves its body at home, and takes only head, liver, and kidney, that appear as a flickering green circle. After eating feces, the spirit likes to wipe its mouth on drying laundry (Anuman, *Phi sang thewada*, 51–52).

19. (ผี)ตาหลวง, *(phi) ta luang*, a local spirit which needs to be fed regularly and which, if neglected, will possess someone.

20. Time periods are counted beginning with one rather than zero, so this is the same as nine months by Western reckoning.

21. An offering to the guardian spirits of the house to assist in ensuring a smooth delivery (KW, 6; Woranan, "Kan sueksa sangkhom," 215).

22. The person supporting the back helps the midwife to press on the belly.

23. There are standard formulas for blowing on a woman's head during delivery to ease any obstruction (PKW, 1:126).

that very day and time, a white elephant was brought.[24]

Thepthong turned and grasped the baby boy. Trembling, she turned him over, back and front. "Tcha! For shame! The spirit molded him like this—bald from the womb like the round moon.

He[25] looks shameful, like a suffering ghost with those two pitiful patches of straggly hair." She kicked him with her left foot to kill him, booting him down onto the floor of the room.

"What a waste of effort carrying him around. By mother's clan! Why raise a mangy puppy to be a laughingstock for the neighbors? Which side of the family does that head come from?"

Finished with cursing, she went to lie by a fire.[26] Wet nurses and servants looked after the baby—washing him, feeding him, rocking his cradle, and singing lullabies every day.

Because of the merit brought by this baby, the family's wealth expanded from the day of his birth, and the number of servants increased, both men and women.

Although the mother despised the child, the family became peerlessly wealthy. The grandparents on both sides were pleased, and gave an auspicious name to their grandchild.

"The mother had dreamed that a stork flew from the forest into the house carrying an elephant in its beak. From birth the child had a bald head but a hairy chest.

At the time he emerged from the womb,[27] a white elephant was presented to King Phanwasa. Let our beloved grandchild be named Khun Chang in commemoration of this event." [28]

---

24. See the fourth stanza of the next section.

25. This stanza is taken from WK, 1:8, absent from PD.

26. In the tradition of the Thai and many others in Southeast Asia, a postpartum mother went to lie beside a stove or fire constantly kept burning for a certain period, usually an odd number of days between seven and twenty-nine, as a preventive against infection or other complications. The bed was surrounded by sacred thread, yantras, tamarind thorns, and certain pungent leaves to repel malignant spirits. The beginning and end of the stay was usually marked by rites convoking protective deities. Medical manuals prescribed a complex formula of different woods to be used in the fire. Neighbors visited, bringing gifts (Anuman, *Prapheni nueang nai kan koet*, 39–57).

27. ตกฟาก, *tok fak*, "drop to the floor," the technical term for the time of birth as recorded for purposes of astrological reckoning (Woranan, "Kan sueksa sangkhom," 218–19; Anuman, *Some Traditions*, 53).

28. *Chang* means elephant. Elephants with unusual coloring, and especially those with albino characteristics, were deemed highly auspicious, especially for kings. Anyone finding such an animal was bound by law to present it to the king, and often was richly rewarded. In the

They had silver and gold made into a necklace for the darling grandchild's neck, lots of bracelets for both hands, strings of beads for both arms, and silver anklets so big that he walked with legs apart.

Around his waist he wore a soft chain with an engraved clasp, dangling with coral-decorated chili-shaped charms[29] that tinkled as they swung to and fro. He jumped around laughing loudly with his mouth open wide.

He[30] was not so tall but stubby like the pigs at Wat Kaeo.[31] His head and goggling eyes made people laugh. A whole pot of turmeric was not enough to anoint his body.[32]

Thepthong shouted at him, "Hey, you beggar, you dance up and down like a clown in the mask play.[33] You're like a big unruly monkey that can't stand still. What uncouth spirit molded you?"

bracelets
and anklets

She could not bring herself to cradle him. "You're like a miserable monkey making faces and causing me shame. You goggle your eyes like a dumb cat eating fish. Why don't you die of cholera?" She cursed him day in, day out.

"You[34] live to make me suffer in misery and be ashamed beyond reason. With that shiny head like a fishing cat,[35] you're so weirdly different from any of the kinsfolk."

Ayutthaya royal chronicles, there are records of a white elephant presented to King Trailokanat around 1471, of seven found and presented to King Chakkaphat between around 1549 and 1560, and one presented to King Narai in 1660 (RCA, 17, 27–31, 41–42, 246).

29. A law from the Bangkok First Reign (1782–1807) specifically banned this ornament for children on grounds it exposed the child to danger of robbery (KTS 4:287). This chapter probably predates that law.

30. This stanza is taken from WK, 1:9–10, absent from PD.

31. วัดแก้ว, probably the wat of this name in Thap Ti Lek village, around 5 kms due south of Suphanburi town center.

32. Powder made from the turmeric root, *Curcuma longa*, is applied to the skin to make it soft, to counter itchiness caused by heat and sweat, and to give a yellowish sheen, especially flattering for a darker complexion. "They account it very wholesome for their Children, to yellow the Body and Face therewith. So that in the streets there are only seen children with a tawny Complexion" (La Loubère, *New Historical Relation*, 36).

33. โขน, *khon*, a dramatic genre in which masked actors play stories from the *Ramakian*, the Thai version of the *Ramayana*. This genre probably developed in the middle Ayutthaya era, and was enthusiastically revived by the court in early Bangkok, as well as being performed in folk style. In a typical pose, actors stand with legs apart and knees bent, stamping alternate feet in time with the music (Mattani, *Dance, Drama, and Theatre*, 44–59).

34. This stanza is taken from WK, 1:10, absent from PD.

35. A stocky, mainly nocturnal cat with olive-grey fur and dark spots. It inhabits wetlands and lives off fish.

When Khun Chang was three and went off to play, other children took fright at the sight of him. "What's[36] that over there, Mummy? It's got a face and body like a big tomcat,

a humpback, a hairy chin, gaping mouth, hair all over its body and shoulders, white eyes, long feet, long hands, long navel, and rows of odd things round its neck."

Their mothers told them not to be afraid. "That's Khun Chang, son of the rich man with servants from Big Wall Village.[37] Don't get in his way. Let him through."

✎

Now to tell of Khun Krai Pholaphai,[38] a man of property and wealth from Ban Phlap,[39] and Nang Thong Prasi,[40] who lived at Wat Takrai.[41] They had become a couple,

dismantled their house, and brought it to build anew in the region of Suphan. Khun Krai was a skilled and sturdy soldier in command of seven hundred phrai.[42]

---

36. This hemistich and the next stanza are taken from WK, 1:10; PD has: opening its mouth and baring its teeth. Horrible!

37. บ้านรั้วใหญ่, Ban Rua Yai; the settlement of this name is now immediately west of Suphan town. At the time of *KCKP*, this name seems to have meant the area between the river and the old city wall (see map 6). Some believe the wall referred to in the name was the old city wall, once adjacent to the moat, now totally disappeared. On the location of Khun Chang's house, see below, p. 857.

38. ไกรพลพ่าย, "valiant vanquisher." This is the father of Khun Phaen. We learn in chapter 7 that Khun Krai was attached to the "six volunteer units," the main detachments of the guard under Kalahom (see p. 20, note 4). The name most similar in the Three Seals Law is Khun Krai Pholachat (พลชาต), an officer of the *lom wang* unit of the guard, *sakdina* 600 (KTS, 1:260).

39. พลับ, *phlap*, a tree in the persimmon family. Most likely, this is the Ban Phlap, 16 kms south of Ayutthaya on the west bank of the river opposite Bang Pa-in. The village used to be a fishing settlement, and got its name as a market for *phlap* sap used in the process of dyeing fishing nets. This stanza seems to say that this couple both came from Ayutthaya but moved to Suphan.

40. ทองประศรี, "golden holiness."

41. วัดตะไกร. There was a Wat Takrai in Suphanburi that was abandoned after the city was depopulated in the wars of the late eighteenth century. It was beside Wat Pratusan. A ruined stupa remained until 1952 (some sources say 1967), when it was pulled down and Wat Pratusan School built on the site. In his *Nirat mueang Suphan*, stanza 137, Sunthon Phu identified this as the wat mentioned in *KCKP*. However, this must be Wat Takrai in Ayutthaya, as Thong Prasi returns there in chapter 27 below. This wat is situated to the north of Ayutthaya, across the river from the palace, adjacent to Wat na Phramen on the north. (Manit Ophakun, personal communication; *Chiwit lae ngan khong Sunthon Phu*, 184, 263; Somchai, *Suphanburi*, 31; Winyu, *Tam roi*, 152; see map 6, map 8 and its accompanying note)

42. ไพร่, a commoner who was bound to work part of the time for the king, a noble, or a government department. Most men other than nobles, monks, and slaves fell into this category.

Courageous and invulnerable, he never retreated. No matter how many enemies he faced, he stood his ground and never fled the field.

Officials of Suphan shook their heads. From experience, they knew never to cross him. The king favored him to be a soldier of Ayutthaya, making him a dignitary in Suphan.

While Thong Prasi was asleep with her husband in the main room, she dreamed that the Thousand-Eyed Lord[43] flew in carrying a ring with a great diamond.

He offered her the ring, and she accepted it with delight. When the diamond's gleam flashed in her eyes, she started awake, flailing her arms, and roused her husband.

Khun Krai opened his eyes and asked what was the matter. She recounted the dream. Both got up, washed their faces, and found betelnut for themselves.[44] Then he interpreted the dream.

betelnut

"A special ring with a beautiful glittering diamond belonging to three-eyed Indra[45] tells us this is something auspicious.

You'll be pregnant with a boy. He'll be like one of Lord Narai's soldiers reborn—strong, brave, and daring, with the power to conquer all three worlds.[46]

A diamond of such dazzling color means in the future he'll be a great soldier, with the rank of phraya and many retainers. He'll be a favorite of the king."

Thong Prasi raised her hands in wai[47] to receive the blessing from her

---

In late Ayutthaya, a phrai of the king was bound to work six months for the king on a rotation system, though the system was widely evaded (see pp. 927–30).

43. ท้าวสหัสนัยน์, *thao sahatsanai*, the god Indra. According to the Mahabharata, Indra seduced the wife of the sage Gautama, and Gautama cursed Indra to have female sex organs all over his body but later relented and changed these into a thousand eyes. According to the *Ramayana*, Indra was always thousand-eyed but after Indra seduced his wife, Gautama cursed Indra to lose his testicles, and later relented and replaced them with those of a ram. According to the Mala Sutra, Indra was given this name because he could see a thousand things in an instant. (KW, 640; *Hindu Myths*, 94–96; Phlainoi, *Wannakhadi aphithan*, 324–25)

44. หมากพลู, *mak phlu*, areca nut, *Areca catechu*, and pan leaf, *Piper betel*, were habitually chewed as a mild stimulant. Strictly speaking, the nut is areca and leaf is betel but "betelnut" and "chewing betel" are used so commonly they have been adopted for this translation.

45. In Hinduism, the king of the gods. In the Buddhist Three Worlds cosmology, Indra presides over the realms of the gods (RR, 222–38). In Thai tradition, Indra sometimes has an all-seeing eye in the center of his forehead—an attribute of Siva, not Indra, in Hindu tradition.

46. On the three worlds, see p. 2, note 7 above. Here the phrase has a meaning similar to "the whole universe."

47. A gesture of greeting, respect, or worship made by bringing the palms flat together in front of the chest or face, or above the head, while maybe also inclining the head. The higher the hands, the greater the respect offered.

husband. Both slept the night overflowing with joy.

As Thong Prasi approached her time, she was truly beautiful. Her hair perfectly suited her face, her skin was as radiant as if burnished with gold, her face like the full moon,

wai

her cheeks like golden *maprang*, her breasts full to bursting, and her complexion fair and attractive. She glowed with health and was a delight for the eye.

She followed the precepts and prayed regularly with her mind composed and her hands joined above her head. She made offerings of lotus flowers, and had no fear of danger.

At ten months, her belly was fully swollen. Her merit indicated she would deliver a child to continue the family line. The karma wind blew,[48] turning the child's head down towards the opening.

Pains made her cry aloud. The grandparents created a hubbub all round the house. Crowds of relatives and servants arrived. The midwife fussed around getting things ready.

At an auspicious time without obstructions, Thong Prasi gave birth easily. The wailing child was a boy. Uncles and aunts came to take care of washing him, then gave him to a wet nurse.

He was rubbed with turmeric, rocked in a winnowing basket,[49] and laid on a little mattress covered with a blanket. All the grandparents happily admired his cute tuft of hair like a lotus seedpod.

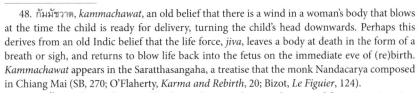

He was lifted into a cradle and rocked to and fro. His mother slept by a fire to be warmed all through. After one month, she came away from the fire without a blemish. She dressed him and applied powder and turmeric to look lovable.

cradle

The parents consulted the two grandmothers and grandfathers on what name to give their grandson. The maternal grandfather,

---

48. กัมมัชวาต, *kammachawat*, an old belief that there is a wind in a woman's body that blows at the time the child is ready for delivery, turning the child's head downwards. Perhaps this derives from an old Indic belief that the life force, *jiva*, leaves a body at death in the form of a breath or sigh, and returns to blow life back into the fetus on the immediate eve of (re)birth. *Kammachawat* appears in the Saratthasangaha, a treatise that the monk Nandacarya composed in Chiang Mai (SB, 270; O'Flaherty, *Karma and Rebirth*, 20; Bizot, *Le Figuier*, 124).

49. กระด้ง, *kradong*, a flat round basketwork tray with a raised rim, used for winnowing rice.

who was an astrologer, cast a horoscope for him.

"His birth time[50] is three by the shadow[51] on Tuesday in the fifth month of a year of the tiger.[52] The Chinese emperor has presented glittering crystal to the King of Ayutthaya

for placement on the pinnacle of the great stupa built since the time of Hongsa[53] and called Wat Chaophraya Thai in the past.[54] Give him the name Phlai Kaeo,[55] the brilliant."

A *baisi*[56] ceremony was promptly arranged with bananas, cucumbers,

---

50. *Tok fak*, see p. 5, note 27 above.

51. เวลาสามชั้นฉาย, *wela sam chanchai*, time measured by the shadow cast by the sun. The shadow of a standing man is measured in *chanchai* or foot lengths. One *chanchai* is subdivided into fifteen *nio*, นิ้ว, fingers, the modern word for inches; one *nio* into four *malet khao*, rice grains; one *malet khao* into four *malet nga*, sesame seeds; and one *malet nga* into ten *akson*, letters. The method is mentioned in the inscription of Wat Si Chum, Sukhothai. (Woranan, "Kan sueksa sangkhom," 218–19; Phlainoi, *Wannakhadi aphithan*, 93–95; Griswold and Prasert, *Epigraphical and Historical Studies*, 373, 400)

52. In the Thai lunar (Chanthrakhati) calendar, the year begins at the new moon after the rains, in November-December. Each month consists of a waxing phase of fifteen days, up to the full moon, followed by a waning phase which alternates between fourteen and fifteen days in odd- and even-numbered months. As the lunar month is actually 29.5306 days rather than 29, extra days or months have to be inserted every now and then. The fifth month falls in March-April. Years run in cycles of twelve identified by animals: rat, ox, tiger, rabbit, dragon, snake, horse, goat, monkey, cock, dog, pig. The system possibly originated from China but the early Tai substituted their own list of animals, which were translated into Sanskrit-derived versions, probably from the Sukhothai era (Diller and Preecha, "Thai Time").

53. Reference to the wars against Hongsawadi, Pegu, in the mid and late sixteenth century.

54. Now Wat Yai Chaimongkhon but called Wat Chaophraya Thai on the earliest Dutch maps of Ayutthaya from the mid-seventeenth century, and in the chronicles in 1659 (RCA, 248). This is a large wat to the southwest of the island of Ayutthaya (see map 8). According to Prince Damrong, this is the wat mentioned in the chronicles of the reign of Ramathibodi I, the first king of Ayutthaya, as Wat Pa Kaeo, the monastery of the crystal forest (RCA, 11). Later it was called Wat Chaophraya Thai because it was the residence of the *sangkharat*, the patriarch (SWC, 15:7254–56). Damrong speculated that the Chaiyamongkhon stupa was built to commemorate Naresuan's victory of 1593. This speculation has been challenged but the name indicates the stupa was built to commemorate a victory, and there is no other evidence on the timing of its construction. Although there is no historical record of such a gift by the Chinese emperor, it would be quite feasible around 1600 when the Chinese court was very concerned about the expansion of Toungoo Burma, and called on Siam and other countries to help contain it, promising rewards in return (see below, p. 884). Wachari surmises that the crystal would have been placed on this stupa at the time of its completion, and speculates this indicates when the composition of *KCKP* began ("KCKP roem taeng"). The first tiger year after Naresuan's victory was CS 964, 1602/3.

55. Phlai means a bull elephant, and Kaeo means gem or crystal.

56. บายศรี, general name for a ritual object used in many ceremonies among Tai groups. The word is of Khmer origin, meaning "auspicious rice," so the original was perhaps made with rice plants. *Baisi* are made mainly from bamboo, folded banana leaves, and flowers, and seem to be

incense, candles, and many kinds of flowers. They decked him with valuable silver and gold articles:

beaded bracelets with *sema*;[57] splendid golden bangles; gilt wristlets on both arms; a jewel-inlaid necklace made with a whole bar of gold;

a soft chain around his waist in a pattern of floating flowers, inlaid with bright emeralds, and dangling with golden chilies; and nak[58] anklets, dazzling to the eye.

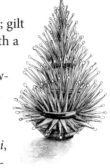

baisi

The guests sat round in a circle. All the clan was present including paternal grandparents. They raised the *baisi*, cheered three times, and passed it round the circle, cheering for good fortune.

> "On this sacred and auspicious day
> We call on the soul[59] of Phlai Kaeo not to stray
> Oh soul, stay with this body for joy and health
> Enjoy elephants, horses, servants, and wealth
> Oh soul, please come along and see
> Don't go hunting and wandering aimlessly
> Come and enjoy garlands of crystal and gold
> An abundance to make your happiness unfold."

They cheered three more times, extinguished the flames, wafted the smoke towards the infant, and daubed scented powder on his forehead. "May you live over ten thousand years, win victories, and be prosperous."

After the soul ceremony, all the clan members were in high spirits. By the time he was five years old, Phlai Kaeo could speak fluently and cleverly.

representations of trays of food offered to the spirits. There are both small versions a foot or so high, and larger ones of human height or larger (Anuman, "The Khwan and its Ceremonies").

57. เสมาปะวะหล่ำ, *sema pawalam*. *Pawalam* is a bracelet with beads or other items strung on a cord. *Sema* or *sima* are stones that demarcate the sacred space of an ordination hall in a wat. This is a bracelet in which the links have the inverted-shield shape of such stones.

58. นาก, an alloy of gold, silver, and copper with an appearance similar to silver and a slight russet tinge. The word probably originates from the Marathi *tuttinag*, which was converted into tutenague or tutenag by European traders in the seventeenth century.

59. ขวัญ, *khwan*, sometimes translated as spirit essence or life essence. In Thai traditional belief, the body and its various elements, usually numbered as thirty-two, all have a *khwan* or spiritual representation. In cases of illness or psychological trouble, the *khwan* is believed to have deserted the body for some reason. The ceremony of *riak khwan*, or soul calling, is performed for a wide range of occasions, including illness, travel, and life-cycle ceremonies such as birth and marriage (Anuman, "The Khwan and its Ceremonies").

Now to tell of Phan Sonyotha[60] who had a handsome wife by the name of Nang Siprajan,[61] a rich lady of good lineage.

They lived at Maids Landing[62] in Suphan. She had a loudmouthed younger sister called Bua Prajan, married to one Chot Khong,

who hailed from Bang Hia.[63] Once married and lost in love, Chot Khong gave no thought to his family and was interested only in stealing buffaloes.

At midnight, when Siprajan was asleep in her house, she dreamed that Phisanukam[64] flew across the sky, slid an ornate ring onto her finger,

and returned to his golden palace. She slept deeply and happily until dawn, then awoke and roused her husband with a smile. After washing her face, she blurted out the dream.

"Oh husband, last night I dreamed that Phisanukam, the great artificer, brought an ornate ring of captivating beauty and entrusted it to us,

then returned to his heavenly palace. Does this mean I'll fall sick? Tell me how bad it'll be. The dream is still clear in my mind's eye."

Phan Sonyotha, who was a loving husband, laughed merrily at his wife's account and told her what it meant. "You're going to be pregnant!

The ornate ring means the child will be a girl, and because the ring belonged to Phisanukam, the peerless craftsman, she'll be really beautiful, very special."

Siprajan laughed merrily at the news. "May it be as you say! If I have a child to treasure, I won't have to carry other people's children around, causing a lot of gossip."

When her pregnant belly was huge, Siprajan was cheerful and merry. At the completion of ten months,

the baby stirred and kicked to be born. The pain was unbearable. Siprajan tossed and turned, her cries echoing around the house, and then lost consciousness.

---

60. ศรโยธา, "military arrow." The title Phan, meaning thousand, indicates he has a minor official post but it is not specified. This is the father of Wanthong. We learn in chapter 2 that he trades in forest goods, and in chapter 4 that the family has land growing cotton.

61. ศรีประจัน, "glorious moon."

62. ท่าพี่เลี้ยง, *tha phi liang.* The origin of the name is uncertain. Some believe it is a reference to Saithong in *KCKP.* Others suggest it was a site for assembling provisions for armies against the Burmese (*liang* can mean "to feed"). The old location of this landing is a matter of debate (see below, p. 857).

63. บางเหี้ย, monitor lizard village, unidentified. As the monitor lizard is considered highly inauspicious, this place has probably been renamed.

64. A folk pronunciation of Wiswakam, Sanskrit Visvakarman, Indra's craftsman (KW, 640).

The parents, all the grandparents, a midwife, spirit medium,[65] other relatives and
servants all came together in haste.

Some threw cowries as offerings, made
wishes, and mumbled frantically. The old spirit
medium yawned and belched, "Hey! Why did
you summon me, my good fellow?"[66]

She swigged liquor, chewed betel, and got up
to dance, bobbing up and down, falling over,
raising herself up on all fours, clapping out
"dong ding dong," and dancing gracefully.

cowries

Becoming very drunk, she swayed to the four directions. "Great father has
come to protect us. Nothing bad will happen. All you grandparents, be happy.
Please, Father, I salute you, I'm just a small fry.[67]

Don't be impatient, listen to me." She got up, and took off her clothes. Siprajan had a contraction, doubled over, and cried out. The midwife squatted
down and pressed,

kneading busily until reaching an auspicious time without obstruction, when
the mother gave birth. The infant was a girl, pretty and adorable. She lay on
her back, wriggling arms and legs, and wailing.

She was bathed, rubbed with turmeric, given milk to drink, and put in
a cradle. Wet nurses and servants took care of feeding her and keeping her
happy all the time.

Time passed quickly, and she gradually grew bigger. The parents, who loved
her like their own eyes, raised her and kept her from danger.

The grandparents and elders came to hold a soul ceremony, and adorned
her with numerous gold rings. By late in her fifth year, she had become
beautiful and graceful.

Her figure was slender, elegant, and as peerlessly lovely as if sculpted. Her
hair was beautiful, black, and glossy. She was given the name Phim Philalai.[68]

She was taught to sew and embroider, and among girls of her age, no other

---

65. แม่มด, *mae mot*, in the next stanza called ออท้าว, *o thao*, possibly shortened from ท้าวมด,
thao mot. The medium and midwife may be one person. The spirit medium's role is to contact
local spirits and get their undertaking to assist in the birth in return for a promise of offerings.
The dance and the stripping are to attract the attention of the spirits away from the infant at the
critical moment of birth (Woranan, "Kan sueksa sangkhom," 217–18).

66. อ้ายขุนโรง, *ai khun rong*, possibly a variant of นายโรง, *nai rong*, a term for the lead male
players in a dance or drama (SWC, 11:5581).

67. ตีนโรง, *tin rong*, "court foot," a petty hustler who makes a living by hanging around the
law courts.

68. พิมพิลาไลย, "figure of beauty."

matched her skill. Morning and evening, she usually went to play and gather flowers beside Wat Khao Yai.[69]

Now to tell of Phlai Kaeo and Khun Chang. Both went out to play along with their servants. When they met, Phlai said amiably, "Let's go and buy liquor to drink together."

Phlai Kaeo took a swig. Khun Chang gulped until his head swam. "I fear I'm so drunk my eyes are bulging." He poured liquor into a bowl to swear comradeship,

and took Phlai Kaeo's hand to touch the bowl. "We will be faithful to each other until death. If either is traitor to his buddy, may the gods put him to death,

may the swords of the guardians of the four directions[70] not spare his neck, and may he be separated from his mother for five hundred eras." They dipped fingers in the bowl of liquor, and drew them across their necks.

Phlai Kaeo took a gulp of liquor. Khun Chang schlurped, rolling his eyes. Phim was bent over with laughter. "Serves you right, you outcaste."[71]

She played at cooking rice and curry, building a house and fence from sand, making merit and giving alms. "Let's invite the abbots. Quick.

Let Khun Chang be a Mon[72] abbot. No need for him to shave his head. He can hold a big prayer chanting. Phlai Kaeo can be a Thai abbot." Phim arranged everything for the occasion.

After the sermon was over and the monks fed, Phlai Kaeo made a funny suggestion, "Let's play at husband and wife." Khun Chang cried, "I like that!"

Phim said, "You vagabond with an ugly scraped head! I won't play." Phlai Kaeo said, "Let's play. It's nothing. Khun Chang can be the husband.

---

69. A wat close to the western bank of the river in the center of Suphanburi. Like many of this town's monuments, it deteriorated when the town was attacked and partially abandoned in the wars of the late eighteenth century. All that now remains is a ruined stupa, recently restored, in Soi Siwichai. Elsewhere in the story, this wat is called Wat Khao (see map 6).

70. See p. 42, note 64.

71. จัณฑาล, *janthan*; entry from Hobson-Jobson: chandaul, chandal, outcaste; "used generally for a man of the lowest and most despised of the mixt tribes" (Williams); "properly one sprung from a Sudra father and Brahman mother" (Wilson).

72. The Mon were and are a major component of the population of lower Burma. The Mon language, related to Khmer, was once probably spoken widely in the Chaophraya Basin, and is the source of many words in Thai. From the mid-sixteenth century, Mon groups often migrated to Siam, sometimes in rebellion against the Burmese rulers. Many settled in the west of Siam along the Khwae, Maeklong, and Suphan rivers. As *KCKP* is sited in this same area, many Mon figure in the poem.

I'll creep in and steal you from his side." The two boys begged her to join in, and gathered leaves to make a bed.

Phim artfully swept sand to make a house, with heaps for a mattress and pillow. She lay down on the ground and baldheaded Khun Chang lay beside her,

pretending to be asleep. Phim lay beside him, peeping out. Phlai Kaeo jumped in between them, hitting Khun Chang in the middle of his bare skull.

Khun Chang hollered, "A thief has stolen my wife away from my room!" He stood up, and walked up and down, shouting to his gang to come and help.

Children soon turned up in a noisy crowd. Khun Chang's gang gave chase fearlessly. When they caught up with Phlai Kaeo's band, all shouted at one another, and fell to blows.

Noses were smashed. Mouths split. Blood flowed. Some ran off shaking with tears, calling out to their mothers and fathers, shouting[73] and hitting at one another noisily.

One wild child picked up a huge stick and ran at the others, hollering. The crowd of children ran off in all directions, screaming noisily.

Phim cursed them, "Damn you![74] You naked skull! I don't want to play with you. You bald leper, you villain!" She took her gaggle of servants off in a rush.

Khun Chang, his head swollen, ran off in dismay. His servants hurried along, trembling. They rubbed casumunar on his wounds while he rolled his eyes, bared his teeth, and lolled his tongue, feeling almost all in.

Dear listeners, all of you, please do not suspect that this has been made up. No. Children's play is strange. Should it come true, well, the envoy of the gods makes it happen.

Whatever children play is not wrong. To call it bad is only a mouth speaking. This story comes down from ancient times, and there is a text in Suphan.

A time came when Khun Siwichai and his beloved wife agreed that their child Khun Chang was now grown up,

---

73. This hemistich and the next stanza are taken from WK, 1:17; PD has: Adults came and broke it up.

74. อ้ายตายโหง, *ai tai hong*, a common curse meaning roughly, "may you have a bad death," referring to *pi tai hong*, the spirit of someone who has died violently or in an inauspicious way as a result of bad karma. As the death was unprepared for, the spirit is unable to find refuge in any realm, and suffers continuously. Hence it tends to haunt, possess, and otherwise bother living humans. Adepts can adopt and feed such spirits in order to use them against others (YS, 415).

and should be taken to the court of King Phanwasa to be presented for entering royal service.[75] Failure to do so would have consequences.

They instructed servants to bathe him, wash his hair, rub him with turmeric and powder, pomade him down to the nape of his neck, and dress him up.

They put a pair of gold bracelets on both arms, and a diamond ring on his little finger. Looking like a fishing-cat cub with glazed eyes, he ran waddling into the central hall with his neck bobbing up and down.

Incense, candles, and flowers were set out on salvers in the usual way. Provisions were prepared for the journey. A bull elephant was harnessed up ready.

Father and son mounted and sat in the howdah. The mahout drove the elephant away from Big Wall Village, across streams and fields, heading towards the tree line. Servants followed along in a jumble.

salver

At Wat Thamma,[76] they stopped and dismounted from the elephant by the riverbank. Little Khun Chang and his father crossed by the official ferry[77] to enter the city.

---

75. Khun Siwichai intends to present his son as a royal page. The มหาดเล็ก, *mahatlek* or royal pages attended on the king; looked after the royal regalia; accompanied the king during ceremonies, travel, and processions; and conveyed royal orders to other officials. Membership in the pages corps amounted to an apprenticeship in court practice, and was a first stepping stone for a high-level official career. The elite of the pages were those with a regular appointment, บรรดาศักดิ์, *bandasak*. In late Ayutthaya, there were twenty-four of them (forty-four according to La Loubère), divided into four duty units, เวร, *wen*. The two duty units of the right attended the king at night, alternating every two days, while the two duty units of the left attended the king by day. Two other divisions of the pages, the *mahatlek khongkrom*, คงกรม, and *mahatlek wiset*, วิเศษ, took in recruits from sons of the minor members of the royal clan, and sons of nobles respectively. If these recruits displayed talent, they had the opportunity to be transferred into the regular pages, or moved upwards into departmental posts. The fact that Khun Siwichai presents Khun Chang with the hope of entering the *mahatlek wiset* is indicative of the family's background. Only an established family would have the opportunity to present a son to the king in this way. Although Phlai Kaeo's father serves the king as a soldier, he does not have the same status. Kukrit also notes that kings often selected only good-looking young men as pages, hence Khun Chang's family must have had considerable status to expect that an ugly son would be accepted. (KP, 27; *Rueang mahatlek*; La Loubère, *New Historical Relation*, 100)

76. A wat on the northwest side of Ayutthaya, across the river, almost opposite the "Jedi Suriyothai." The wat appears in the chronicles during the Burmese attack of 1569 as the site of an execution. In 1753, when Sri Lanka requested monks to revive Buddhism, King Borommakot sent Ubali and Ariya Muni from this wat. The wat was ruined in 1767 but restored in the Bangkok First Reign by Prince Anurak Thewet (Thong In), the king's younger brother. The building on the riverbank, now a scripture hall, was originally a kuti, remodeled by King Rama V. (RCA, 72–73; *Boranasathan*, 1:123–25; see map 8)

77. The river crossing from here to Wat Suan Luang (see p. 461, note 21) is used several times in the story. Ayutthaya was completely surrounded by water. Descriptions of the city from the

When local people caught sight of Khun Chang, they cried out, "Oh, what a shame! What kind of child has such a totally bare head?" They told their friends, "Looks so unreal."

"Was it some kind of monkey in a rush to be reborn?" "What wayward spirit molded that?" Bent over with mirth, they stared until father and son had entered the palace.

Nobles and others waiting to attend on the king burst out in crazed laughter as soon as they saw him. Little Khun Chang got flustered and did not know what to do. He crouched hidden behind his father's back.

Now to tell of the king, sublime ruler of the world, before whom the whole earth quailed in submission, every country and territory bowed down to pay respect in dread,[78]

and every land offered tribute and requested to be subject to Ayutthaya. His power provided perpetual protection, ensuring all the people were joyful,

with no hardship only happiness. His royal line was unbroken from the past, so the kingdom of Ayutthaya was eternal, and its populace prosperous and content.

The king walked to a jeweled throne, attended by a throng of fair maidens who knelt with heads bowed, waiting to perform every duty for the lord of the realm.

Each face was fair and alluring, fulfilling the royal pleasure. Like stars surrounding a full moon in the sky, they prostrated in attendance in groups,

while singers and musicians performed continuously to enhance the royal delight, and inner ladies[79] carried out their regular duties.

---

late eighteenth century list twenty-two ferry crossings into the city, including one from Wat Thamma to "the jetty of the house of Chaophraya Phonlathep," the head of the Ministry of Lands. This passage refers to ท่าคอย, *tha khoi*, a waiting landing, meaning a ferry that ran day and night to transport officials, but according to the late Ayutthaya sources the only two such ferries were on the northern side of the city, one between the main palace and the entrance to Sa Bua Canal, and another from the Front Palace to Wat Mae Nang Pluem (KLW, 173; APA, 92).

78. Whenever the king appears in the poem, there is a formal invocation of this kind. The authors ensured each was different in wording but the content is always similar: the king is all powerful; he lives in a splendid palace; he is attended by countless beautiful young women; he is bathed and dressed magnificently. This formula restates the political theory that the king, as the possessor of the largest stock of merit, naturally is surrounded by superlatives of every kind including the most resplendent dwelling, the most numerous and beautiful women, and so on.

79. นางใน, *nang nai*, "ladies inside." *Nai* or inside referred to the inner, private, forbidden area of the palace occupied by the royal family, the king's consorts, and exclusively female staff. A wall across the palace divided this area from the หน้า, *na* or "front" area used for public affairs (see map 9). At gates along this wall, "the *ja khlon* [female guards] guarded the inner side, and palace officials guarded the outer" (KLW, 205). Young women were presented to the king

victory drum

At a little after four in the afternoon, it was time for the king to proceed to the front courtyard. He was bathed in water flowing in a stream from a showerhead,[80]

anointed with perfumed scents, and attired in a lower-cloth with a prominent *kinnari* pattern.[81] Towards evening, holding a regal sword[82] with a lifelike face of a naga, he appeared at the front courtyard.

Horns and conches sounded forth. Gongs rang and victory drums boomed. The front guards and officials bowed and raised their clasped hands in salutation.

The king sat on an exquisite throne looking like a valiant Lord of the Lions.[83] Khun Siwichai of loyal heart crawled up with Khun Chang close behind.

---

by noble families, and became queen, consort, or servant depending on the presenting family's status and the king's preference. The number of queens and consorts is unknown and probably varied greatly from reign to reign. King Narai (r. 1656–1688) was reputed to have rather few, while King Borommakot (r. 1733–1758) had enough to sire forty-two or forty-eight children (Dhiravat, *Siamese Court Life*, 48–49). The terms *nai* and *na*, inner and front, were also used more broadly to mean the private and public affairs of the king.

80. สุหร่าย, *surai*, from the Persian *surahi*. The prominence given to this device in the invocation suggest this was a recent innovation, fit for a king. The fact that the term is in Persian hints that the chapter originated in the mid or late seventeenth century, probably the Narai reign (1656–1688), when the court adopted dress, architecture, and much else from Persia.

81. กินรี, one of many imaginary, hybrid creatures that live in the Himaphan Forest. Hindu mythology has only the male form, Sanskrit Kinnara, Thai กินร, *kinnon*, a mix of horse and human. They were born from the toe of Brahma, dwell on Mount Kailash, and attend on Kubera. Thai tradition has both males and females with the upper body of a human and the lower body of a bird. They are often portrayed as musicians.

82. พระแสง, *phrasaeng*, a double-edged short sword, part of the royal regalia. The royal practice of carrying such regalia swords can be traced back to Angkor, where it is portrayed in several bas-reliefs. The Angkor ruler conferred such a sword on King Lithai at his coronation, as recorded in Sukhothai inscription 2 (Prasert and Griswold, *Epigraphical and Historical Studies*, 381).

83. พญาไกรสรราชสีห์, *phya kraison ratchasi*, lord of the mythical lions in the Himaphan Forest, which are called *ratchasi, kraison, sing*, etc. There are four types, sometimes labeled as white, black, green, and yellow, and sometimes as grass, black, yellow and maned. The depiction of the *ratchasi* in the Three Worlds is based on the maned lion: "The body of a maned lion has red lips and the tips of his four paws are red as if they had been painted with a mixture of sticklac solution and vermillion pigment. His mouth and stomach are red in the same way, and there is a red stripe from his head on to his back and down toward his legs. His red mouth and back, along with the waistline, are as beautiful as if they had been purposely painted. His body has a mane that is so soft and delicate that it looks as if a cloth worth a hundred thousand tamlueng of gold had been draped over him. The white part of his body is very white and beautiful; it is like a newly polished conch shell" (RR, 86).

He raised a salver with incense, candles, and flowers, and placed it in front of him. Khun Chang prostrated close to his father, praying and shaking almost to death in fear.

The[84] king mused, "A shiny head with no hair on the pate, black, and fat as a barrel drum. What a disaster! His forehead bulges out in an odd-looking way." The king opened his mouth and spoke.

"Ha! Heigh! Khun Siwichai, whose child have you brought here? His head looks pitiful. Whose lineage is he from?

Or is he from your family? So bald it's unbelievable! Are you bringing him to present to me? Is that why you have the salver of incense, candles, and flowers?"

Khun Siwichai prostrated and said, "My liege,[85] Your Gracious Majesty, my life is under the royal foot.

Khun Chang is my own son. Please allow me to present him to be a soldier and seek the bo-tree shelter of the accumulated merit of the victorious lord.[86] His auspicious fate is to have great wealth.

Since the birth of this son, Khun Chang, money, valuables of all kinds, cattle, buffaloes, elephants, horses, and servants have appeared as never before."

The king listened and laughed merrily. "Eh, such a pitiful head but so much wealth, you say. That's curious.

At present, he's still a small child. It's no use presenting him to me now. You raise him first, and don't be impatient. Wait until he grows up and then bring him again."

He ordered attendants to arrange royal gifts including cloth. Father and child prostrated three times and took their leave, happy at the king's grace.

---

84. This stanza is taken from WK, 1:21; PD has: The king saw the offering of incense, candles, and flowers, along with Khun Siwichai and his son. He opened his mouth and spoke.

85. ขอเดชะ, *kho decha*, the standard opening for addressing the king, abbreviated from a fuller version meaning, "I appeal to the dust under the royal foot that covers my head." The person abases himself by verbally placing his life, his body, or his head, his highest part, under the dust on the feet or footsoles, the lowest part, of the king.

86. สู่โพธิสมภาร, *su phothi somphan*, a stock phrase which describes the ability of a king to shelter people under his power with the metaphor of a bo tree. The phrase is dramatized in the chronicles in a famous passage following Prince Naresuan's break with Ava in the mid 1580s. Several Thai Yai had fled from the control of Ava to Phitsanulok, and the Burmese king demanded their return. In response, Prince Naresuan sent a letter: "It is customary that a great king of kings, who upholds the Ten Kingly Virtues, be compared to the shelter of a great holy pipal [bo] tree and that people come to seek the protection of the King's accumulated merit with the hope of escaping various calamities" (RCA, 91).

2: THE DEATHS OF THE FATHERS

Having heard from Suphanburi that there were many wild buffaloes, the king announced he would go to the forest.

He ordered Khun Siwichai, "Go quickly to Suphan. Tell the valiant Khun Krai to have his phrai make the preparations.

Five days from now, I will leave to stay in the forest and round up wild buffaloes.[1] Have Khun Krai find a broad upland near a stream to set up a camp and a royal lodge.

Have about five hundred troops to chase the buffalo herd in to me." Then the king turned to give orders to the gallant Phraya Decho.[2]

"Organize this expedition immediately. Choose only men from your military units along with cavalry and elephant troops. Be ready to move in five days."

Phraya Decho acknowledged the command, went straight to a swordstore[3] of the palace administration, and issued orders for officials to convey the king's command to all their subordinates forthwith.

"The king will proceed to the forest to valiantly round up buffaloes." The duty officers of the palace administration wrote out orders in a flurry,

and sent for messengers to take them and get matters moving without delay. The orders were sent to the duty officers of Mahatthai[4] who immediately had them distributed to everyone.

---

1. กระบือ, *krabue, Bubalus arnee*, similar to the domestic water buffalo but a separate species, larger, fast-moving, and much more aggressive. Nowadays the only surviving colony in Thailand is in the Huai Kha Khaeng sanctuary and consists of only around fifty animals.

2. ออกพญาศรีราชเดโชไชย, *Okphya (phraya) siratcha dechochai*, one of two deputies in Kalahom, *sakdina* 10,000, one of two heads of the "six militia units" (KTS, 1:280; see p. 173, note 25).

3. ทิมดาบ, *thim dap*, literally a storehouse for swords but in practice working space for officials inside the palace walls. There were around ten *thim dap* scattered around the palace compound. The largest, sometimes called the "long brick building," is probably the building called "the Secretary's office" on Kaempfer's map of the palace from the 1680s. This was on the southern side of the courtyard marked (1) on map 9 (KLW, 201–9; Kaempfer, *Description*, 45).

4. With Kalahom, one of the two great ministries, probably established in the late fifteenth century to oversee manpower, public order, and defense. At the start, the idea of having two ministries was probably for counter check and balance. Later, the two developed regional portfolios with Mahatthai overseeing provinces and tributaries to the north of the capital, and Kalahom

The duty officers went to inform the head of Mahatthai, "According to orders received, in five days' time the king will travel to Suphan."

As soon as he learned of the matter, Chaophraya Jakri[5] summoned Phan Phut and Phan Jan to meet immediately at the inner official sala.[6]

He called Phan Phao and Phan Phan[7] to bring the registry rolls.[8] "Call up elephants, horses, and people all at the same time. Get everyone's minions here without delay.

Phan Jan, clear away the undergrowth and prepare a level path around eight fathoms wide. Be ready without fail within five days."

---

to the south. Later still, they divided along military-civilian lines with Mahatthai eventually converted into the Ministry of the Interior and Kalahom into the Ministry of Defense.

5. เจ้าพญาจักรีศรีองครักษ, *Chaophraya jakri si-ongkharak*, minister of Mahatthai, *sakdina* 10,000 (KTS, 1:224).

6. ศาลาลูกขุนใน, *sala luk khun nai*. The term *luk khun* was used both strictly to mean judicial officials, and in a broader sense to mean high officials in general (Vickery, "Constitution," 172–73). The *sala luk khun* were buildings for officials to conduct business. In late Ayutthaya, there was a *sala luk khun nok* or outer official sala for the use of judicial officers located outside the inner wall of the palace on the river side, while the *sala luk khun nai* or inner official sala for the use of civilian (*phonlaruean*) and military (*thahan*) officials was a group of three "twin" buildings in the northeast of the palace, with a pond in front for use in the ordeal by water (KLW, 200; APA, 65; see map 9). These are probably the buildings shown on Kaempfer's map as "houses where the mandarins meet to consult about the affairs of the Kingdom" (*Description*, 45). La Loubère described them as "inclosed with a Wall, no higher than one may lean over, and covered with a Roof, which bears only upon Pillars placed at equal distances in the Wall. These Halls are for the chief *Mandarins*, who do there sit cross-legged, either for their Functions of their Offices, or to make their Court, or to expect the Prince's [king's] Orders, viz. in the Morning very late, and in the Evening until the approach of Night, and they stir not thence without order. The less considerable *Mandarins* sit in the open Air, in the Courts or Gardens" (*New Historical Relation*, 33). These buildings were on the west side of the enclosure marked (2) on map 9. Another *sala luk khun nai* was built in the western part of the palace in the late seventeenth century when King Phetracha built the Banyong Rattanat Throne Hall (SWC, 13:6275; see p. 540, note 22). In early Bangkok, there were three *sala luk khun*: an outer one, outside the palace, used by judges; and two inner ones used by the civilian and military branches respectively. The inner *salas* were replaced in 1894 by a group of brick buildings that became the Kalahom and Mahatthai ministries (KW, 667; SWC, 13:6275).

7. พันพุทอณุราช พันจันทณุมาท พันภานณุราช พันเภาณุราช, Phan Phut-anurat, Phan Janthanumat, Phan Phannurat, and Phan Phaonurat were officials of Mahatthai directly under Chaophraya Jakri, all *sakdina* 400 (KTS, 1:225).

8. Every male of phrai status was bound to labor for the king or some other overlord. The obligation was six months a year, every other month, in the late Ayutthaya era, reduced to four months in early Bangkok. Censuses were taken periodically to compile registry rolls. This labor service was greatly disliked and widely evaded.

Khun Siwichai, along with his son, rode an elephant across the fields towards Suphan as the sun's rays sank behind the forest.

He directed the elephant towards his house, then briskly wrote out instructions for a retainer to take to the loyal Khun Krai.

The retainer received the order, ran to his destination quickly, and delivered the instructions.

Khun Krai took the instructions, read them, and ordered unit heads to chase down phrai and bring them forthwith.

Once the orders were sent, it was time to light the lamp. Khun Krai went into the house with his wife, Thong Prasi, and their talented son, Phlai Kaeo.

That night was filled with ominous sounds of spiders beating their chests[9] incessantly, scaring everyone until their scalps crawled and their hearts were gripped with a chill cold all night long.

In her sleep, Thong Prasi dreamed a fearful dream that made her body tremble and her heart sink. She started awake in a state of fear, and anxiously aroused her husband.

Khun Krai asked, "What's the matter?" She described the dream fully. "A tooth broke and flew out of my mouth. I don't think this is good. Please tell me what this dream means."

Khun Krai was devastated. "Oh no! Something big is going to happen. But if I give Thong Prasi too terrible an interpretation, she won't let me go off anywhere."

He said, "This isn't a bad dream. Something good will happen so don't get worried, believe me." But in his heart he thought, "This time I won't survive. I fear I'll die because of the wild buffaloes."

At break of dawn, he washed his face and picked up Phlai Kaeo. "It's light already. Why aren't you awake yet?" He cradled the child gently in his two hands, and kissed him tenderly.

Phlai Kaeo opened his eyes and flung his arms around his father's neck. "Papa, tell me where you're going. Why are you up when it's still not morning? It's like you're running away from me."

Khun Krai lifted his son above his head as his own tears flowed down. He hugged his child tightly with a sigh. "Papa doesn't want to go away at all.

But the king has commanded it, singled me out. There's nothing I can do,

9. A well-known omen, for which there is a ตำราแมงมุมตีอก, *Tamra maengmum ti ok*, Manual on Spiders Beating their Chests. If the omen occurs inside a house, it foretells a looming disaster such as things going missing or servants absconding. If it occurs in a bedroom, as here, it foretells death or serious injury (SWC, 11:5285).

dear Phlai Kaeo. Probably I'll be gone from now on. Things are strange and not to my liking."

Then he turned to talk to Thong Prasi. "This is our only child. He's still little. Take good care of him, day and night. Raise him well.

If he's naughty, set him right, but don't distress him so he runs away. Try to teach him whatever knowledge there is so he can carry on this military line."

Thong Prasi sensed her husband's instructions were different from anything in the past, and she was worried. The way he hugged and kissed the child betrayed a yearning. He seemed to be telling his wife something over and over again.

He had left many times before, but not in the same way. This farewell was strange and wrong. She embraced her husband's feet and raised them onto her head, with fires licking at her heart.

The more she thought, the more her heart cracked with trepidation. "My dear husband is going far away from home." She gazed into his face with her scalp crawling and sorrowful thoughts troubling her mind.

Brave Khun Krai quickly got dressed and picked up his sword. He stole out of the house full of concern and longing for his wife.

He look back to see Phlai Kaeo. "Father's pet, my heart is almost breaking." Tears welled in his eyes, and he felt very afraid, but he suppressed the love in his heart, and set off.

He led his men out of Suphan town to Phra Hill[10] just as the sun was setting. He gave orders to keep watch while waiting to receive the king.

Now to tell of the king, the fount of prosperity, the multiplier of the populace's wealth, who reclined on an ornate throne with glittering upholstery.

Surrounded by heavenly angel-like maidens who ministered to his needs, the upholder of the teachings listened to the singing of gentle lullabies, and felt contentment and joy in his heart.

Refreshed by the scent of flower garlands and the brilliance of shining crystal lamps, he pondered the affairs of state until he fell asleep in the night.

---

10. เขาพระ, *khao phra*, sacred hill, a common name for a hill with a Buddha image or other religious association. Perhaps this is the Khao Phra, 3 kms west of U Thong, that appears later in chapter 18. The distance of about 32 kms from Suphan is about right for a day's travel. The hill is sited on the fringe of the deltaic plain, and the buffalo hunt might have taken place in the hills beyond. There are remains of old elephant enclosures nearby in the forest at Phu Muang (see p. 368, note 25; map 2).

At dawn, attendants made preparations according to routine in every detail. The Department of Elephants prepared mounts of good form with a mahout assigned to each.

The armorers, right and left,[11] carried equipment out front for distribution. Elephant handlers harnessed their mounts, putting on saddle pads, fore harnesses decorated with stars,

yak-hair tassels on each ear, and forehead cloths checkered in gold.[12] Several royal mounts, both female and male, were drawn up in the elephant brigade.

Hibiscus, a royal mount for traveling, was harnessed and furnished with royal weaponry, looking awesome. The royal master mahout[13] of great skill wore a meshwork robe[14] and a patterned sompak.[15]

Another royal mount was harnessed with a golden canopied howdah[16] and a surrounding curtain drawn closed by

meshwork robe

---

11. Many departments, particularly with military or guard duties, had right and left divisions. This principle, designed to ensure no unit has a monopoly on a particular function, was found widely in Asian states.

12. The manual prescribed the attire for an elephant that the king rode into the forest as follows: a head cloth down to the shoulders; a square embroidered cloth on the back; front and rear harnesses of rope encased in red cloth; a page riding in the middle and mahout at the back; an infantryman at each foot (*Chang ratchaphahana*, 211–12).

13. นายทรงบาท, *nai songbat*; there were two such posts with titles Nai Jop-khotchasin-khwa and Nai Karin-prasit-sai, each with *sakdina* of 600, in a group of ten who manned the king's major elephants (KTS, 1:251).

14. ครุย, *khrui*, a light robe or tunic worn as a sign of office, especially on ceremonial occasions. The term probably derived from the Persian *khel'at*, meaning the bestowal of a robe of office or other regalia. This suggests the garment was introduced in the era of Persian influence at the Siamese court in the seventeenth century. The robe was often made of muslin or similar light fabric, knee-length with long arms and open down the front, perhaps with embroidery or other embellishment denoting rank on the collar, cuffs, and lower hem. (Floor, *Persian Textile Industry*, 290–95)

15. สมปัก, a form of lowercloth especially for nobles attending audience, sometimes called ผ้าเกี้ยว, *pha kiao*. The term derives from the Khmer *sombuat*, meaning any kind of cloth. Usually this cloth was presented by the king at the time of appointment, and the design and quality were marks of the noble's specific status. The *sompak* was generally made by sewing two narrow strips together resulting in a cloth much larger than normal, around 160 cms wide, and requiring a special and more elaborate form of wearing with pattern showing on both ends. A servant carried the *sompak* from the noble's house. There are murals depicting nobles changing into sompak outside the audience hall. "The *pagne* worn by the mandarins is much fuller and richer than any others, being usually of cloth of silver or cloth of gold or of the beautiful painted Indian cloth that is commonly called *chitte* from Masulipatam" (Gervaise, *Natural and Political History*, 77; SB, 300; *Kan taeng kai thai*, 214–15; CK, 473; Somphop, *Ayutthaya aphon*, 85).

16. กระโจม, *krajom*, a howdah with a semi-circular canopy open to front and rear; usually for royalty (Julathat, "Asawa-alongkan," 219, 221).

two cords, a pad with brilliant golden silk appliqué,[17] and a cushion to support the royal back.

Another royal mount was harnessed for the king to sit on its neck with a padded seat for comfort. Yet another royal mount was prepared for overnight travel. Many mounts for different purposes were all equal in magnificence.

The mahouts wore patterned lowercloths, shirts instilled with powerful lore,[18] sashes, and belts[19] cinched on top. Only the best men were chosen.

Behind them came the mounts of other nobles. Servants milled around noisily getting them ready. Each of the many fore elephants and many rear elephants[20] had a mahout aloft.

Ahead of these magnificent mounts came enough soldiers to make war on the heavens. Once the elephant brigade was ready, the cavalry was drawn up with fine steeds.

Phraya Si Saowapha[21] took care of the king's horses. Luang Songphon[22] arranged the whole column. The grooms harnessed the mounts, all nimble and swift.

The king's horses were outstanding, alert and spirited. Two magnificent black and yellow dapples stood about three cubits tall,

war elephant

17. หักทองขวาง, *hak thong khwang*, break-gold-athwart, an embroidery technique used on royal regalia such as fans and umbrellas. A pattern is made by laying cut lengths of golden silk thread perpendicular to the weave, and attaching them by overstitching (RI, 1280).

18. เวทมนตร์, *wetmon*, meaning supernatural or magic powers. The Thai word comes from Veda, or Hindu scriptures, and mantra, or Buddhist prayers. On the origins and scope of lore, see pp. 940–45.

19. เจียระบาด, *jiyarabat*, a sash tied with the ends hanging in front; and ปั้นเหน่ง, *pan-neng*, a Javanese word for a belt, now principally used for items worn as part of costumes for traditional dance; these belts are usually strips of brocade or other heavy fabric, around 10 to 15 cms wide.

20. ช้างดั้ง, *chang dang*, elephants placed at the front center of a column or procession, and ช้างกัน, *chang kan*, elephants placed at the rear center of a column or procession (*Chang ratchaphahana*, 359–63).

21. The head of the royal horse department, *krom pra asawarat*, or *krom ma*. The title is given in the Three Seals Law as Okya/Phraya Si Suriya Phahasamuha, ออกญาศรีสุริยะภาหะสมุหะ, but in the *Testimony of the Inhabitants of the Old Capital* as Phra Si Saowaphak (KTS, 1:256; KCK, 224).

22. หลวงทรงพลราชสมุหะ, Luang Songphon Ratchasamuha, head of the right division of the royal horses, *asawarat khwa*, sakdina 2,400 (KTS, 1:256).

with harnesses inlaid with French filigree, glittering in the foreign fashion; the king's guns placed to left and right of the gallant steeds; saddle pads embroidered with shining gold;

gilded stirrups hanging down, encrusted with jewels; bridles encased in shimmering velvet;[23] and reins exquisitely embroidered with gold thread. Everything was befitting for such beautiful mounts.

One royal horse was named Phalahok,[24] and the other Golden Ornament.[25] Grooms led them both attentively. Junior officers rode horses in the main procession.

Nobles were to ride elephants following the king. Everything was prepared down to the last detail. A junior officer[26] went around to check the numbers. When it was nearly time, all the troops were ready.

At the first light of the sun, the mighty king, before whose reputation all countries trembled, proceeded to a bathing place.

Water sprayed, sprinkled, and foamed from a showerhead, bathing the royal body in a delicate spray of fragrant rosewater like raindrops. He was anointed with perfumes and majestically aromatic unguents.

When the ablutions were finished, he was fanned by throngs of consorts from the inner palace. Grasping a regal sword at his side, he went out to a victory pavilion.

Promptly those in charge of the royal garments and headgear entered prostrate, one after the other, bringing the appropriate raiment to dress the king for entering the forest according to the planetary disposition for that day:[27]

---

23. Horse harnesses were made with rope or plaited leather thongs, encased in fine cloth for show in the case of important horses such as these (Julathat, "Asawa-alongkan," 202–5).

24. พลาหก, Pali *Balahaka*, meaning a cloud or thundercloud. In Hindu tradition, Balahaka is the name of one of the four white horses that drags the chariot of Lord Jagannath, and also the name of an ashen-colored horse among the four that pulls the chariot of Krishna when he abducts Rukmini in the Mahabharata. In the Three Worlds cosmology, Balahaka is one of the seven "gem" possessions of a Buddhist emperor: "a gem horse who is superb, who is fine, who is fast. . . . He is as beautiful as the color of the clouds or the white mist. . . . he can travel by air like the hermits who have magical power" (RR, 162–63).

25. กระหนกภูษา, *kranok phusa*, where *kranok* is an old spelling of กนก, gold, and *phusa* has its Pali meaning of ornament.

26. หัวพัน, *hua phan*, "head thousand." Ranking systems based on decimal numbers are known from ancient Tai states onwards. The numbers indicate rank, not command of men. Today, a trace of this rank survives in the Thai police where a major is *phan-tri* and colonel is *phan-ek*. The old usage seems to have been lower. Officers with *phan* or *hua phan* ranks mostly had *sakdina* in the range of 100 to 400.

27. Manuals of astrology prescribe what colors, gemstones, and other things are auspicious for wearing on each day of the week.

britches with curved ends and double cuffs; a kimkhab lowercloth with a gold stripe; a chemise[28] to be worn that day in shimmering indigo velvet,

cinched with a majestic sash in a flower pattern with a gold stripe; a short sword tucked on his left side; a ring with brilliant diamonds;

helmet

a royal helmet[29] decorated with yellow topaz against a black background; and the regal sword "Clenched in the Teeth to Destroy a City."[30] He walked elegantly to a mounting platform.

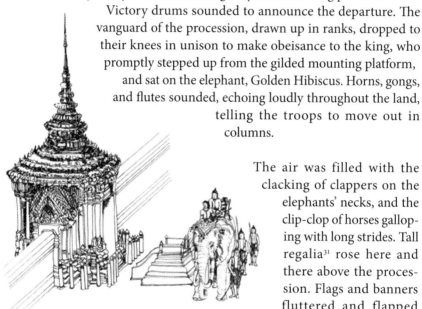

Victory drums sounded to announce the departure. The vanguard of the procession, drawn up in ranks, dropped to their knees in unison to make obeisance to the king, who promptly stepped up from the gilded mounting platform, and sat on the elephant, Golden Hibiscus. Horns, gongs, and flutes sounded, echoing loudly throughout the land, telling the troops to move out in columns.

The air was filled with the clacking of clappers on the elephants' necks, and the clip-clop of horses galloping with long strides. Tall regalia[31] rose here and there above the procession. Flags and banners fluttered and flapped overhead.

mounting platform

---

28. ฉลององค์, *chalong-ong*, outer shirt of a king in the royal language, *ratchasap* (Suwit, *Ratchasap*, 147).

29. พระมาลา, *phra mala*, a helmet with a straight stiff brim and an ornate crown.

30. พระแสงดาบคาบค่ายทำลายเมือง, *phrasaeng dap khap khai thamlai mueang*. According to the chronicles, when the Burmese attacked Ayutthaya in February 1587, Prince Naresuan rode out with only around 120 men, routed the Burmese vanguard, and began to scale a stockade with a sword in his mouth. He had to give up the attempt and return to the capital, but the chronicles report that the Burmese were greatly impressed, and abandoned the attack when the rains began shortly after. The sword subsequently became part of the royal regalia, with this name, and was believed to carry the marks of Naresuan's teeth. (RCA, 120; KW, 13; Damrong, *Our Wars*, 112; Damrong, *Naresuan*, 57–58, 147)

31. เครื่องสูง, *khrueang sung*, literally "tall articles," meaning ceremonial umbrellas and other regalia on tall poles, placed at ceremonial occasions or carried in processions.

The brave, robust troops rolled out in a rowdy, hectic, rumbling tumult that shook the earth as if it would soon collapse.

To front and rear of the procession marched the infantry units with shields, bucklers,[32] swords, pikes, and spears; the cavalry, spirited and imposing; the elephant brigade with both fore elephants and flank elephants;[33]

artillerymen carrying guns with bayonets; sword troops with their glinting blades held aloft; spearmen on the flanks of the procession; and shield bearers in red shirts[34] seemingly everywhere.

The noisy hubbub, along with the sound of gong, drum, flute, *shenai*,[35] and other instruments, echoed around the plain as they crossed a river and headed for the forest.

Seeing so many people, elephants, and horses, herds of animals took fright. Parrots flew off in fear, swooping this way and that through the woods, squawking loudly.

The king traveled through the hills, admiring the lofty, pristine, and shady peaks that blocked out the sunlight. Birds cried out their warning calls to the forest.[36]

Parrots prattled in *tumka* trees; bulbuls bunched on a big ivy gourd vine; magpies hid among the leaves of milkwood trees; red turtledoves cooed on laurels; wind-eaters[37] sat on the branches of giant *salaengphan* vines; rainbow

---

32. The passage mentions three kinds of shield: เขน, *khen*, round in shape; โล่, *lo*, oblong with a handle; and ดั้ง, *dang*, also oblong but longer. These would be made of wood or buffalo hide, and often decorated with protective yantra (SWC, 3:1164; Low, "History of Tennasserim," 319).

33. *Chang dang*, see p. 25, note 20 above; ช้างแซง, *chang saeng*, elephants placed along both flanks of a column or procession (*Chang ratchaphahana*, 359–63).

34. "'Tis a general Custom at *Siam*, that the Prince [king] and all his retinue, in the War or Hunting, be cloath'd in Red. Upon this account the Shirts which are given to the Soldiers are of Muslin dy'd Red" (La Loubère, *New Historical Relation*, 26).

35. ปี่ไฉน, *pi chanai*, a reed instrument with seven holes for fingers, one for thumb, and a flared end, emitting a distinctive "squawking" tone. It is probably of Middle Eastern origin and related to the Indian *shenai* and Malay *sarunai*, but has long been absorbed into Thai music as shown by mentions of the instrument in the *Traiphum*, *Khlong nirat Hariphunchai*, and *Lilit yuan phai* (Miller and Williams, *Garland Encyclopedia*, 233; SWC, 7:3703).

36. "Admiring the forest" is one of the main modes of Thai court poetry. These passages were probably inserted by court authors. They have some role in conveying the time and distance of a journey, but mainly they are occasions for the poet to show off skill. In the Thai original, much of the effect of these passages derives from wordplay, especially rhyme and alliteration, often of great complexity. The association of certain birds and trees in a line or couplet often has more to do with sound than any reality in nature.

37. วายุภักษ์, *wayuphak*, "eater of the wind," a legendary bird usually identified with the *karawek*, which, in the Three Worlds cosmology, has a voice so beautiful other animals cease whatever they are doing (RR, 175–76, where it is called a "fabulous nightingale"). The bird has never

lorikeets alit on jambolan in pairs; barred owlets
peered out from *mok*; imperial pigeons perched
up on a *phobai*;

doves cooed coyly from a paperwood; coels
called out from jambolan before taking wing; ibis
lined up on *hiang*; herons on *krasang* turned their
heads to look for fish;

partridges perched on the trunk of a *khondinso*;
quail fluffed up their feathers and chuckled; crakes
cried at the foot of the mountains; and egrets flew
with chammaliang fruit in their beaks.

Ranges of hills rose up in tiers with overhanging
rocks and curving cliffs. Streams flowed down, glinting brilliantly like diamond or black sapphire.

wind-eater

The cliffs of a gorge converged above them, ending in an overhang that they
craned their necks to see. *Teng, rang, pring, pru,* and *pradulai* trees sprouted
in rows at the foot of the slope.

Some bloomed in lovely sprays of flowers, their fragrant pollen wafting on
the wind. Some bore fruit that lay everywhere on the ground, pecked by flocks
of birds, and scrapped over by troops of monkeys.

Langur, lemur, monkey, and gibbon whooped and howled. A tiger crouched,
stalking *lamang* deer.[38] Rabbit, porcupine, and bear lurked. Gibbon and monkey gamboled, swung, and leapt away in fright.

The way led through hill and thick forest, twisting and turning through the landscape. Moving quickly, the troops reached a broad upland, and made a halt.

A royal lodge was erected in the forest for the king to spend the night. He
summoned Khun Krai. "Tomorrow you will drive the buffaloes in."

Luang Ritthanon was deputed to make a stockade of stakes driven into the
ground close together. Both received the orders, prostrated to take leave, and
hastened to make the arrangements.

---

been seen, but the feathers can be collected by doing a ritual and placing a bowl of water on a
platform in a treetop; the bird will bathe there and shed some feathers (Phlainoi, *Wannakhadi
aphithan*, 30–31). The bird was adopted as the symbol by the Ministry of Finance shortly after its foundation in 1890, and was translated into English as bird of paradise because the old
graphic representation of the *wayuphak* has a similarly spectacular tail.

38. ละมั่ง, *lamang*, Eld's deer, *Cervus eldii*, also called Thamin or Brown-antlered deer. The
species was discovered in Manipur, India, and named after a British officer, Lt. Percy Eld, in
1844. It is now virtually extinct in Thailand. In 2008, a thousand *lamang* bred using Burmese
deer and genes of the Siamese version from the Smithsonian Zoo were released into the western
forests in an attempt to reestablish the species.

Luang Ritthanon busily summoned the palace watch.[39] Unit heads checked off people in a rush, divided up the work of clearing, and supervised closely.

Orders were issued to clear bushes, level dense forest, and lop away thick brambles. Men shaped stakes, cut grass, set fire to the forest, and made paths.

They hacked, trimmed, dragged, pulled, cut, cleared, and chopped. Some dug holes, while others drove in the posts to form a stockade.

They fetched creepers and battens to bind the stakes tightly at intervals. Some ached and collapsed with exhaustion, but overseers beat them back to work.

Some were so tired they stopped work and fell asleep snoring, but woke with a loud thwack on the rear from a unit head, and ran off in fright. All shouted in unison, "Heave ho!"

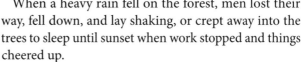

They hefted, hauled, and heaved to tighten ropes. A stockade of massive stakes took shape amid whoops and cries echoing through the woods.

Supervisors kept strict watch, handing each person a blow or two. Men raised their hands in wai, until they could stand it no longer, their tears fell, and they stumbled into one another trying to escape.[40]

When a heavy rain fell on the forest, men lost their way, fell down, and lay shaking, or crept away into the trees to sleep until sunset when work stopped and things cheered up.

hands raised in wai

Some went off to gather vegetables, break off firewood, and hunt down ducks and chickens, while others stood around peeing. They cooked rice and fell asleep around the stoves, bathed in sweat, and snoring from exhaustion.

At dawn, Khun Krai Pholaphai summoned his aides en masse, then led his five hundred militiamen[41] out with great fanfare to seek buffaloes.

---

39. ล้อมวัง, *lom wang*, "surround the palace," an elephant unit, originally with the duty to guard the king's elephant, but also deployed as an attacking unit in battle (*Chang ratchapha-hana*, 195; RI, 995; KTS, 1:77, 260).

40. Both Tachard and Gervaise described elephant hunts which are similar but larger in scale. Gervaise wrote: "But the enjoyment which the king derives from this hunting is dearly paid for by the thirty thousand men who are usually employed for it. Many of them die of exhaustion, some being obliged to run night and day in the forests to discover and take by force the strongholds where these animals take refuge, while others are ceaselessly occupied in constructing terraces and palisades to prevent them from escaping. In short, everyone has his special duties, to which he must devote himself wholeheartedly, for, if he slacks even a little or makes any mistake, he is sure to be punished there and then by the officials appointed to watch over his work" (*Natural and Political History*, 177; see also Tachard, *Voyage to Siam*, 233–34).

41. อาสา, *asa*, derived from Khmer meaning forward troops. The term was mainly used for

They slipped along paths through the forest, wending a way among the hills, their whoops and yells resounding around the woods and mountains. They set an arc of fire.

Murky dark smoke spread through the forest. Flames licked at the trees, burning them to the ground, killing cobras and turtles.

Deer, tiger, bear, boar, rabbit, and other animals had to take flight. Monkey and langur swung away from tree to tree. Throughout the forest, parrots took fright.

Scared by the forest fire and the shouts of people advancing, great numbers of wild buffaloes were seized with panic, and plunged around in all directions.

Some raised their heads and stared defiantly. Others used their horns to butt a way to the front. In a melee of mad excitement, the clamour of clashing horns echoed through the forest.

The buffaloes battered and buffeted one another. The forest was in uproar with men shouting, fire crackling, and a racket of gongs, clappers, and drums.

wild buffaloes

King Phanwasa looked out from his pavilion and saw the hordes of buffalo, packed together, and crashing into one another in confusion.

He called out, "Ha! Heigh! Khun Krai, why aren't you driving them into the stockade? Do you trust the phrai alone to chase the buffaloes while you swish your tail,[42] doing nothing? Useless."

On the king's command, Khun Krai leapt up, grabbed a spear, and rushed out to the front. The phrai roared loudly, making the herd of buffaloes ever more agitated and confused.

The animals plunged around in panic. A buffalo with curved horns, bold and enraged, charged forward, butting people wildly. Khun Krai rushed out to face the beast,

---

the "six militia units" (see p. 173, note 25), hence this translation. Here the word is possibly being used loosely as a substitute for phrai, conscripted men. Today it means volunteer.

42. ลอยชาย, *loi chai*, refers to a fashion for men to tie their lowercloth with the end hanging down one side as a long sash, and the phrase had become a derogatory epithet meaning casual or idle. The Palatine Law, clause 74, proscribed this and other improper dress in parts of the palace, to be punished by ripping the cloth (KW, 227–28; KTS, 1:101).

leaping, kicking, and stabbing like a windmill, his spear swishing and slashing. Buffaloes dropped down dead to the tune of around one hundred beasts.

The remaining herd, even more panicked, maddened, and hurt, broke away, and charged off into the forest in all directions, leaving only the dead strewn around everywhere.

The king was inflamed with rage, as if a black vapor had blown across his heart.[43] He bellowed like a thunderclap.

"Hmm! What are you up to, Khun Krai, spearing so many buffaloes? Do you mean to offend me? I saw it with my own eyes! Because of your fooling around, the buffaloes have all fled into the forest.

Heigh! Heigh! Bring the executioners here immediately. I cannot keep him. Off with his head! Stick it up on a pole and raise it high! Seize his property and his servants at once!"

Hearing the order, the fearsome executioners strode up and dragged Khun Krai away. They tied his hands behind his back, brought him to a stake driven into the ground, and told him to bow his head.

Khun Krai felt shocked, shattered to dust. His body trembled with fear. His soul left him,[44] as if he had been visited by a ghost. He yearned to preserve his life.

The blood drained from his face, leaving it white as a sheet. The spirits in his body fled away. Knowing his life would soon be extinguished, he shuddered in despair.

"Oh, pity, pity! Why did this have to happen? On the day before coming here, I had a premonition—those ominous noises in the house.

And my jewel, Thong Prasi, had a bad dream. I pretended to interpret it wrongly, but my bad karma has caught up with me, darling housemate. If you count the days waiting for me, they'll stretch into years.

Think of me no more, my jewel. I'll never come back to love you. It's my misfortune to be parted from you. I'm past hope because I'm condemned to death.

A great pity, my son is still small. Will he know his father came to such disaster?" Khun Krai collapsed on the ground, racked with sobs. Then he spoke,

---

43. ลมกาฬ, *lom kan*. An old Thai medical text, คัมภีร์ชวดาร, *khamphi chawatan*, describes six types of wind that are created by the body with fatal effects. *Lom kan (singkhli)* turns the face green, makes the heart palpitate, and creates difficulty in breathing.

44. ขวัญหนี, *khwan ni*, an idiom meaning feeling shocked or desolate.

begging the executioners. "Now that I'm about to die, please show me some kindness and consideration. Please inform Thong Prasi so she understands that my time was up, and the king ordered my execution. Tell her to look out and fear the worst." Then he again broke down in tears.

"Oh, oh, poor me! What did I do so bad that I have to come and die in a forest where my corpse will be prey for vultures and crows?

My dear son will not see my body. Thong Prasi will not see my face." He called his friend Ritthanon over. "Please tell my wife so she understands."

Luang Ritthanon could not contain his own tears. "Dear friend, don't get overwrought. Why be so upset? When the time comes, it comes. Try to concentrate and pray.

Who lives to prop up the sky, year in, year out? Even Lord Siva, Lord Indra, and the moon must be destroyed, and descend from the heavens, from the sky. Anything born cannot escape death."

Listening to his friend's instructions, Khun Krai gathered himself and began to control his grief. He put his hands together and concentrated on prayer.

He thought of the virtue of the Buddha and his teaching. He paid respect to monks who upheld the precepts. He honored his father and mother who brought him into this world and raised him.

"Grant me the power to proclaim to the gods that it be known throughout heaven and earth that I, Khun Krai, made a mistake and paid for it with my life,

yet died with integrity in the manner of one from a line of valiant and victorious warriors." He closed his eyes, composed his mind, stifled his fear, lowered his face, made a prayer, and signaled with a finger for the chop.

With one blow of the executioner's razor-sharp sword, the heart of Khun Krai stopped beating, and his life turned to dust. The jailers took the body away to impale on a stake.

After witnessing his friend's death, Luang Ritthanon straightaway wrote a secret letter, and gave instructions to Nai Mai.

"Hurry to Suphanburi. Tell Thong Prasi what I now tell you. The king has commanded she be seized. Tell the dear lady not to treat this lightly."

Nai Mai acknowledged the order and took his leave. He found a Lawa

executioner

sidebag,[45] grasped a big pike, strapped a knife on his back, and shambled off. In a short time he entered the forest.

King Phanwasa traveled in the forest and stayed in royal pavilions for many nights before resolving to return to the capital.

He ordered Phraya Decho to announce to the troops of all ranks that they would start back from this forest expedition at the first light of the sun.

Phraya Decho sent out written orders for all officers and men to make ready the procession, harness horses and elephants, and draw up in column order to await the arrival of the king.

At the break of dawn, the king left his bed, was bathed, dressed, and arrayed with jewels, and ascended a mounting platform.

Riding an elephant with a golden canopy and curtains tightly closed on both sides, he issued orders for the troops to move out, followed by flank elephants, post horses,

artillerymen, and infantrymen with swords and golden spears, all in ranks. The sturdy troops marched at a brisk pace, reaching the city of Ayutthaya in good time.

⁊

Nai Mai arrived at the house of Thong Prasi who immediately asked, "What are you here for? Come in to take some betelnut. Don't stand on ceremony."

Nai Mai opened his mouth to speak, but the tears welled up in his eyes and flowed down his cheeks. "I'm here on Luang Ritthanon's instruction. It's all here in this letter, everything."

The letter informed Thong Prasi, "Your husband and my good friend, Khun Krai, was condemned to death by the king, and stuck on a post in front of the buffalo camp.

The king has given orders to seize his property, wife, and child. Don't stay at home. Flee from Suphan. This letter sent to you today makes things clear."

Thong Prasi understood the letter. She wept, beat her breast with both hands as if grief would tear her apart, flailed around, and collapsed in a faint.

She lamented over and over in despair. "Oh my patron, you're lost and gone. You've died and become a spirit. Before you left, you weren't sick but hale and hearty. How can you have been chopped to death?

---

45. Lawa is the name of an ethnic group of Mon-Khmer speakers, found in the earliest chronicles of the north as inhabitants prior to the arrival of the Tai. Throughout *KCKP*, the Lawa appear as dwellers in the hills. A ย่าม, *yam* is a simple cloth bag, with a shoulder strap, similar to those still sold by various "hilltribes." A Lawa sidebag seems to have been large.

You were invulnerable, and nobody could defeat you, but now your power has gone. On that night I had a dream, a premonition. When I asked you to interpret it, you said the meaning was good.

Never before had you made such a mistake. Why were you so careless? Now that your time has come, and you've abandoned your wife and son, who would you have us turn to?

Our property will be seized. What a disaster! Where will your wife and son find a place to sleep? We're done for." She sobbed and sighed, again and again.

She turned to look at Phlai Kaeo. "Do you know your father is no more, and you're his orphan now, my jewel?" She hugged the child, racked with sobs.

Phlai Kaeo whimpered and sighed plaintively. He could not sleep until he had cried his eyes out. In grief, Thong Prasi lamented over and over, "Karma has caught up with us. What can we do?

The house will be cold as a graveyard. The servants will be scattered to the winds. Suphan officials will trample all over us. We can't stay here any longer, my jewel."

Hearing Thong Prasi, the servants could not hold back their own tears. They gathered together and wailed loudly.

All of them missed Khun Krai. They beat their bodies and lamented about him. "He never got angry or held a grudge." "We servants could always depend on him."

"Wherever we went, nobody dared bully us, because everyone feared Khun Krai. But now they'll all come and push us around." The servants wept and wailed in distress.

That evening, the city, palace, treasury, and land officials,[46] along with members of the left and right divisions of the guard and their retinues, arrived in strength, numbering almost one hundred men, and surrounded the fence of Khun Krai's house.

The governor of Suphan said, "It's sunset already, torch-lighting time. It's the wrong moment to make a seizure today. We'll draw up the inventory of goods tomorrow.

Light fires and quickly post guards all around to prevent anyone getting away overnight. We'll deal with this matter tomorrow."

---

46. เวียงวังคลังนา, *wiang wang khlang na*, the major ministries known as the "four pillars" of the administration in the capital (see p. 171, note 17). The names were also used for the chief administrators in each provincial town (see p. 537, note 8), but here probably mean men from the capital.

Thong Prasi saw crowds of people surrounding the house. In a panic, she got up, fell down, and stumbled around. She picked up Phlai Kaeo,

grabbed two bags of money, found an old basket with a hole, and lined it with a piece of cloth. In haste, she jumped down from the house, groped her way along a cat path, and hid in the shadows of the house pillars.[47]

Bending down, she spied through a hole in the fence, then squeezed through, getting her face dirty. She grabbed her son's hand, and ran off by the light of the moon. Meeting an old neighbor, she begged her,

"Oh please, I'm all out of rice and fish.[48] The whole house has been seized and we've got nothing to eat." The neighbor was kind enough to share what she had. Loaded with rice, vegetables, and fish, they set off.

Outside the village, they climbed a tree, looking for somewhere to sleep. She tried to comfort her son so he would not cry. "They want to truss both of us up and take us away." She hugged him and grieved.

"Oh my dear Phlai Kaeo, Mother's darling. Since birth you've never slept in the forest. Now you and your mother are in terrible trouble. You've lost your father, my husband, and I pity you.

That golden peacock calling[49] in the forest sounds like the spirit of Khun Krai. Oh Father, please look after us tonight. Don't let tiger, bear, or other animal chance upon us."

Sitting on a branch in the darkness, she had a hollow feeling of fear in her chest and throat. Worried that her son would fall out of the tree and kill himself, she tied one end of her cloth around his waist,

and made the other end fast to a branch of the big tree. There was no cloth to fashion a cradle. She caressed her son to sleep.

But Phlai Kaeo was too upset. His life seemed torn into a hundred shreds. He thought of his father and whimpered distractedly in consternation and self-pity.

He tossed and turned, scratched his head, and puckered his face in anxiety. Itchy red ants[50] scurried over every inch of his body. Midges and mosquitoes buzzed around.

---

47. Most houses were raised on stilts, mainly to rise above flooding during the rainy season, but also to catch the breeze and to provide security by pulling up the stairway. The area below was usually high enough for people to walk, and was used to keep animals or large equipment such as looms and rice pounders.

48. Rice and fish formed the main diet, and the phrase ข้าวปลา, *khao pla*, "rice fish," is used to mean food and generally here translated as such.

49. "A loud trumpet-like call, *kay-yaw, kay-yaw*, is uttered usually in the late evening and early morning" (King, *Field Guide*, 110, on the *nok yung*, green peafowl).

50. Red ants, *Oecophylla smaragdina*, have a very sharp, painful sting. They are known as voracious predators, viciously attacking other insects and other forms of life.

He yawned, "I'm so tired but I can't go to sleep. My bottom is so itchy, Mama. Come and do something. I'm being eaten alive by big bully ants, about five of them.

Papa's dead. We couldn't stay at home because those officials surrounded it completely. We only just squeezed through the fence. I had to follow you here and I'm scared.

It's impossible to sleep with the mosquitoes and midges buzzing around and the ants biting. Mama, come and slap them for me. As soon as it's light in the morning, let's get away from here."

Thong Prasi wept out of pity for him. "Dear child, this is karma. What can we do? There, I've chased the ants away, my jewel."

Both stretched out on the branch of the banyan tree. They soon nodded off from exhaustion, and slept through the night.

Promptly at dawn, the officials and guards from Ayutthaya, along with local officials of Suphanburi, went into Thong Prasi's house.

They seized cattle, buffaloes, elephants, and horses. All the servants, man and woman, young and old, took fright and ran around in shock and confusion.

They got the housekeeper, I-Phuean, beat her, and questioned her until she blurted out that the mistress had fled. Money and property, including the staff, were entered on an inventory.

Officials went up into Khun Krai's apartment,[51] seized the furniture from all around, carried it out to the terrace, and made a list so that the various officials would not get things mixed up.

Pikes, swords, tooled sabers,[52] nielloware bowls, silk, carpets, felt, velvet, nickelware, brassware, crockery, and anything of value was written down as found.

Five thousand in cash[53] was put in a chest and bound with a thread and

---

51. เรือน, *ruean*. A Thai house of someone of Khun Krai's status would consist of several units (*ruean*, apartment), all raised on stilts, clustered around a terrace.

52. กระบี่, *krabi*, a one-handed sword with a single-edged curving blade. The saber is คร่ำ, *khram*, tooled, meaning a pattern has been worked into the blade by scoring the surface and then casting and forging silver or some other metal into the pattern. This was for beauty, but also because the process amounted to another stage of annealing for hardness (SB, 89).

53. เงินตรา, *ngoen tra*, sealed silver. A minted currency was created in the seventeenth century and described by La Loubère as follows: "Their silver coins are all of the same Figure and struck with the same Stamps, only some are smaller than others. They are of the Figure of a little Cylinder or Roll, very short, and bowed quite at the middle, so that both ends of the Cylinder touch'd one another" (*New Historical Relation*, 72–73). In Thai, these coins became known as พดด้วง, *pot duang*, rolled beetle, because of the shape. Westerners dubbed it bullet money. Gervaise reported that the coins came in denominations of baht, salueng, fueang, and half-fueang

large seal. Two trunks of money were locked by key, and carried out to load onto elephants.

Looms for cotton and silk were put into carts. Mortars and pestles, pottery jars, and bowls were placed on rafts, taken for inspection at the provincial office, and then loaded onto elephants.

Within one night, the officials reached Ayutthaya and went to report to their superiors, "Handing over the goods seized from Khun Krai!" "Put them in the warehouse according to the inventory."

By break of dawn, Thong Prasi had resolved to take Phlai Kaeo to Kanburi.[54] She quickly dropped down from the tree,

her mind full of fear of danger. She carried the basket on her waist, and led her son by the hand. They skirted the edge of the woods, looking for paths, then pushed a way through the forest.

Phlai Kaeo caught sight of papaya and wild olive scattered all over the ground. In joy he pointed them out to his mother at once.

"Mama, look over there, wild fruit. Please go and get them. I really, really want to eat them all." She gathered them up for him.

Soon they reached a lake and stopped to rest and recover. She took out the cold rice, left over from the previous evening, that she had wrapped in cloth for the child to eat.

Phlai Kaeo broke off some with his hands and popped it in his mouth, but it was so dry and chewy that he lay down on the ground and cried.

"Where's the curry, Mama? Give me something to taste. The rice gets stuck in my throat." He screwed up his eyes, "I won't eat it."

Hearing him, Thong Prasi burst into tears. "Where can I find curry, dear Phlai Kaeo? We're on the run and desperate. The only thing left is some fish."

Phlai Kaeo said, "Cold rice and dry fish! How will we have any strength, Mama? If there's no curry, then just give me some fermented fish mixed in a bit of water. Quickly please!"

Thong Prasi hugged the child and wept. "Your mother doesn't know where to get it. Darling son, we're in bad trouble—so bad I'm at my wits' end."

At that, they set off along a path through the forest. Seeing her son so hot under the glaring sun, she wrapped a cloth around his head.

(*Natural and Political History*, 101).

54. กาญจน์บุรี, old Kan(chana)buri, "golden town," was around 18 kms west of the current site. It was a strategic town guarding the route up the Khwae Yai River and over the Three Pagodas Pass into Burma. The city was destroyed and the site abandoned in the wars of the late eighteenth century. There are remains of five wat and a fort beside the Khwae Yai River. (Sathaphon, *Mueang Kanchanaburi kao*, 109–13; SWC, 11:5048; see map 7 and accompanying note)

Phlai Kaeo walked behind, clinging onto her waist, in low spirits, with a face grim from hunger and thirst, and his feet burning from walking on pebbles and sand. He wearily pleaded,

"Mama, I've had enough. I'm fit to drop. My throat is so dry, I don't want to go another step. Walk slower, Mama, don't go so fast.

If I try to take long strides, I'll fall over. My feet are aching and all swollen. The ground is as hot as a furnace." She lifted him up and dangled him on her waist.

When she got too tired, she hoisted him onto her back, and raised the basket out front as shade. Then she got stiff, and lifted him up onto her shoulder, holding his legs with one hand.

Her feet swelled up with blisters, making her hobble slowly. When her attention wavered, she tripped and fell down, sending the child tumbling off her shoulder to roll along the forest floor.

Phlai picked himself up in a daze, and cried out, "I almost died! My legs are stiff and hurting. I'm all in. From here on, don't pick me up, Mama!"

Mother and son reached Kanburi. Thong Prasi said, "Son, there are people I know well in this town." They walked about asking for information.

Her husband had once told her that he had relatives owning land at Cockfight Hill.[55] They went there and found them. Without any delay, the relatives built a house for her.

Bit by bit, she began to earn a living, and to acquire some money and property. She redeemed some slaves and phrai so they could farm.[56] She bought land, elephants, horses, cattle, and buffaloes.

She acquired property through trading. People looked up to her with respect. She gradually established herself and settled down there with her son for many years.

---

55. Cockfight Hill is located north of old Kanburi. Many Thai towns are located beside a hill with sacred significance, and probably Cockfight Hill played this role. It is a standalone hill and, though not tall, totally dominates the site of the town. On the summit, there is the base of a large ruined stupa with a flat open space around 15 meters square in front. According to local legend, this was Khun Phaen's cockfighting arena. The army, however, has decided the stupa commemorates a victory over the Burmese at nearby Latya in 1785, and has erected a statue of King Rama I nearby. At the base of the hill, there is a shrine to Khun Phaen and Khun Krai with folk images made by local villagers in the 1940s. In 1995, the army built a much more substantial shrine, and added life-size bronze figures of Khun Phaen and Khun Krai. Dolls in the form of fighting cocks are available for purchase as offerings (see map 7).

56. Debt and slavery were closely interrelated. People could sell themselves into slave status to raise money, or be forced into slavery because of inability to pay a debt. *Chuai*, ช่วย, the word translated as "redeem," is the technical term for making a payment to release someone from debt slavery, perhaps to be their own slave (KW, 661).

Now to tell of Nai Janson, who had long been bold, invulnerable, and brave as a lion. His home was in Red Saltlick Village.[57]

His expertise was banditry.[58] He would burst in somewhere, make an uproar, and plunder everything. He attacked boats from north or south, and got worthwhile takings. He made allies in Kamphaeng.[59]

These thieves feasted together, got staggering drunk, and then played unruly games. They fooled around, slashing and stabbing one another day after day, with no cause for fear because of their invulnerability.

They loaded guns with shot, lit the fuses, and blasted away at one another. The shot never penetrated their bodies, and they all ran wild in uproar.

Janson said, "Hey, gang, I've got an idea. Today we'll go and raid Khun Siwichai at Big Wall Village in Suphan.

He's father of that Khun Chang, and his wife is called Nang Thepthong. He's a very rich man with many thousands. Let's help ourselves to about five loads.

They say a moneybags like that has lots of men, but our gang is enough to overpower them." The phrai agreed unanimously, and all got dressed up to look as fierce and fearless as possible.

They armed themselves with pikes, swords, flintlock guns, powder horns,

---

57. บ้านโป่งแดง, Ban Pong Daeng, in the north of Suphanburi province, above Samchuk, to the west of the Suphan River. In *Nirat Suphan*, written in 1841, Sunthon Phu described this area as thick forest with many wild elephants (see stanza 255 onwards, *Chiwit lae ngan khong Sunthon Phu*, pp. 210ff; see map 2).

58. The preamble of the Law on Theft, *phra aiyakan lakkhana jon*, states: "Bandits, โจรปล้น, *jon plon*, are defined as robbers who form gangs of ten, twenty, or thirty people to steal from houses by day or night by firing guns, shouting, and entering to shock the owners and steal all their property. Plunderers, โจรย่องสดม, *jon yong sadom*, are robbers who have knowledge of lore to put the owner to sleep and enter to steal" (KTS, 3:211–12). Through the nineteenth century, the Bangkok court became increasingly worried about rural banditry, which increased as the feudal systems of controlling people decayed. Here, Janson is portrayed as a professional bandit who approaches his craft in the same way as a soldier going to battle—calling on help from the gods and spirits, dressing to impress, enchanting weaponry. He also has a network of peers that extends over a wide area. Prince Damrong recorded the sophistication of bandit gangs and their use of lore in a famous "Conversation with a Bandit." Kukrit noted that such bands, which approached robbery as much as a sport as a means of income, continued to operate through to the Second World War, sometimes announcing in advance what houses they would ransack as a challenge to the owners and authorities (Damrong, *Nithan borankhadi*, 180–90; KP, 32–34).

59. Kamphaeng Phet, "walls of diamond," a strategic town on the east bank of the Ping River at the point where the northern hills finally subside into the Chaophraya Plain. The city is probably the place known as Chakangrao in the Sukhothai era. In the early Ayutthaya era, it was one of the "northern cities" and the target of several attacks by Ayutthaya armies. From the sixteenth century onwards, it figured prominently in the wars between Siam and Burma. Its massive brick fortifications still survive (see map 4).

fuses, and Ho spears. "Bring up the elephants now. Hey, don't hang about!" The servants grabbed their goads and brought the elephants along.

Nai Janson had climbed halfway onto his elephant, and was dangling there. A mate drove a pike point into his rump, and shoved him up into the howdah. The elephant trundled off.

They arrived at the edge of a forest near Suphan, dismounted from their elephants and left them among the trees. Nai Janson made an eye-level shrine[60] with a white cloth tied above as a canopy.

All the gang brought their bandeaus,[61] sacred threads, pikes, and swords to place on the shrine. They made offerings of liquor, rice, food, sweets, incense, bright candles,

krajae-sandal,[62] and fragrant oil. The robber gang gathered around. Nai Janson raised his clasped hands in prayer. "I call on the gods from all eight directions,[63]

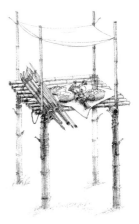

eye-level shrine

60. ศาลเพียงตา, *san phiang ta*. In *KCKP*, this term is used for a temporary shrine. The usual form is four wooden or bamboo posts of human height or higher, planted in a square of one meter or less, with a shelf suspended between them at roughly eye level to hold the offerings, and a cloth stretched over the top of the posts as a canopy. Such shrines are used to make offerings to the gods or to local spirits. The name implies height for respect, but the shrine can in fact be much smaller.

61. ประเจียด, *prajiat*, a piece of cloth inscribed with a yantra design (see p. 135 note 20), worn to convey invulnerability. It should be made with *bangsukun* cloth (see p. 828, note 46) that has been washed, impregnated with herbs, polished with a *saba* seed, inscribed by an adept using ink mixed with enchanted powder, and activated with further formulas. It might be tied around the neck, upper arm, chest, or head (PKW, 1:17, 39).

62. กระแจะ, *krajae*, a tree, *Ochna integerrima*, that grows in the north and northeast of Thailand. The wood and bark were steeped to produce a fragrant water that was applied to the skin. The term is also used for more complex skin preparations made by dissolving a powder containing krajae, sandalwood paste, musk, and saffron (*Kan taeng kai thai*, 226–27; SWC, 1:59–60).

63. The eight guardians of the cardinal and sub-cardinal directions come from Indian tradition: Kuwera, Sanskrit Kubera, north; Soma, Sanskrit Isana, moon, northeast; In, Sanskrit Indra, east; Akhani, Sanskrit Agni, fire, southeast; Yom, Sanskrit Yama, lord of the dead, south; Suraya, sun, southwest; Warun, Sanskrit Varuna, lord of the waters, west; and Wayu, wind, northwest. Kubera can be traced back to the pre-Vedic Puranic tradition in India, when he was a god of wealth, sometimes called Dhanapati. The others are Vedic deities, probably originating in early Indo-Iranian times, and having close equivalents in European tradition. These guardians have entered Thai tradition as part of the spirit world, slightly separate from the fourfold guardians in Buddhist texts (see note 64 below). (KW, 655; *Hindu Myths*, 70, fn.)

Lord Isuan, Lord Narai, Lord Brahma, Gautama, powerful yogis and rishis, teachers with expertise, the moon, the
sun, and other powers;

Wirunhok, Wirupak, Kuwera of the giants, and Tatarot,
all the four directions;[64] the gods of travel; Thorani, and
the Lord Krung Phali.[65] We call you to action!

Om, great lords of every land, empower the cow-
elephant tusks[66] on the shrine." As they prayed and
chanted incantations over the liquor, dark clouds and mists
shrouded the earth.

When the liquor was enchanted, each took a drink.
Hearts flashed, ears burned, flesh thickened. The power of
the liquor visibly invigorated them. Each dressed and decked
himself

Mae Thorani

with his own clothes and weapons. They tied bandeaus around their heads,
and hitched up their lowercloths to look barelegged and awesome. The able
Janson led the way off,

---

64. The guardians or "kings" of the four cardinal directions, as they appear in the *Three
Worlds* and the Maha-samaya Sutta, occupying the lowest of the six *deva* realms, are: Kuwera,
Pali Kubera, north, holding an umbrella, attended by giants, ยักษ์, *yak*; Wiru(n)pak, Pali Virul-
pakkha, west, holding a snake, attended by naga; Wirunhok, Pali Virulhaka, south, holding a
sword, attended by *kumphan*, Pali Kumbhanda, potbellied giants or devas; Tatarot, Pali Dhatta-
rattha, east, holding a mandolin, attended by *khonthan*, Pali Gandharva, celestial musicians (see
p. 343, note 29). Kubera also figures in the Brahmanic spirit tradition (see note 63 above). In
Buddhist texts he is sometimes called Vaisravana (Vessavana, Wetsuwan), with explanation that
Kubera was his name in a previous life as a rich Brahman merchant who gave prodigiously for
charity. The name Tatarot may have evolved from Dasaratha, ten chariots, the father of Rama.
(KW, 655; RR, 180, 219–21)

65. กรุงพาลี. In the Vayu Purana, Bali was a great demon who controlled the whole world
until conquered by Vishnu, bound with great cords, and sent to hell (*Hindu Myths*, 178–79). In
the Thai versions of Indian mythology, *Thewabang* and *Chaloemtraiphop*, Phali was formerly a
yak giant called Mulakini or Asuramulakini who made trouble for deities and rishis, so Isuan
(Siva) kicked him into the sea, gave him the name Phali, and cursed him to dwell in the human
world living from offerings. He became the spirit who presides over all the various spirits of the
place. Teachers of invulnerability have adopted the name for nine powerful gods with authority
over the world. In other versions, Krung Phali caused such happiness to people in the mundane
world that Vishnu (or Buddha) came down in disguise, encompassed the world in giant steps,
and forced Krung Phali to relocate to a forest in Himaphan. Also in these versions, Krung Phali
has become a place, possibly because the Khmer honorific *krong* was misinterpreted in Thai as
krung (city), and the Lord of Krung Phali has acquired the name Thotsarat, from Dasaratha,
who has many appearances in Hindu mythology. (SB, 352, 492–93; KW, 644; Terwiel, *Monks
and Magic*, 154–55)

66. Meaning the weapons.

with five hundred[67] robbers arrayed behind on both sides. They urged the mahouts to drive the elephants ahead, and soon arrived at Big Wall Village. All chopped at the gate with axes

until it splintered and fell with a loud thump. They rushed in whooping, "Let's go, tigers!", pounding loudly on the house, and firing off their guns. The uproar made the whole household tremble in fear.

Amid the hullabaloo, the robbers surged in one after another. The occupants woke up in a daze. "Grab them!" "Light the torches!"

While Thepthong and Khun Chang still had their heads down asleep, Khun Siwichai woke up with a start and jumped out of his house with no clothes on.

Robbers chased after him, beating left, thrashing right, throwing spear after spear, thrusting, stabbing, and waving torches. Others rapped loudly on the wooden walls,

or ran around catching people in the turmoil. At the sound of gunfire, the members of the household awoke quaking and ran off in all directions, breaking down fences, crashing into buildings and stunning themselves,

stumbling around in fright and confusion, picking up their children and grandchildren and taking to their heels, carrying baskets, bags, sidebags, and whatever they could.

Granny Lao started up with her lowercloth over her head, got in a tangle, and groped about for her husband. Granny Tao ran round in circles inside the fence crying, "Oh sirs, I'm afraid of you!'

Granny Mon fell down and her basket rolled away, "Oh, mother! Damnit! What's going on?"[68] Men and women ran wherever fate took them, naked and smothered in dust over their backs and shoulders.

Jek Kuai scrambled up a riverbank, lost his trousers, stumbled along naked, slipped, fell headlong into the water, and winded himself crashing into a fish trap.

He mistook the trap for a crocodile and cried out, "Mother, cunt, shit, help me, *aiya*!"[69] Ta-Fang, bumbling along blearily, got his neck stuck in the beams of a fish scoop.[70]

fish trap

---

67. This number comes from WK, 2:52, absent from PD.

68. She speaks in Mon: อุยย่าย, *ui yai*, mother; ตละกุ่น, *tala kun*, what's going on.

69. มะจิไบไซบวยซวยไอ๊ย่า, *ma ji bai sai buai suai aiya*. This and several similar passages spoken by Chinese characters contain scraps of Hokkien and Teochew dialect mixed up with Thai. *Aiya* is a cry of dismay.

70. ยอ, *yo*, a fish net suspended from a bamboo frame that can be swung out and lowered into the water. They are often seen in lines alongside canals.

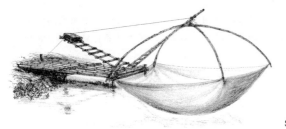

fish scoop

He thought the robbers had pincered him with their legs, and kicked out wildly with his eyes popping out. When a mulberry fruit dropped onto his back, he sat down, pleading, "Don't hit me. I've got a slipped disk."

I-Khaen ran and bumped into one of the robbers. Thinking it was Ta-Som, she grabbed his wrist and pulled. The robber said, "Eh!" and kicked her to the ground. She got up and ran off frantically.

The robber gang swarmed all over the place, searching everything, tapping the house walls,[71] breaking water pitchers and storage jars, whooping and hollering. They caught the mother and son and tied them up by their necks.

"Fear me, you hag. Had enough yet?" Thepthong cried, "Spare my life!" Khun Chang was so frightened that his body trembled and his eyes popped out. Thepthong begged them to punish her alone.

The robber gang hauled them to the center of the house. "Is this baldy your husband?" Thepthong cried, "This is my son. My husband took fright, abandoned me, and fled."

The robbers brought fire to burn her bottom. "Can you stand this, or will you tell us everything? Where are the money and valuables kept?" They tied her arms behind her back, arching her body. "Don't tell us lies."

Thepthong cried out, "I'm done for!" The robbers brought gunpowder. Khun Chang fell to his knees with hands clasped and begged them, "Excuse me, please spare my mother.

The money and valuables, five thousand worth, are in a chest. I'll show you." Whooping in glee, the robbers broke open the big chest and brought out

so much treasure they could not carry it all, and dropped stuff on the ground all over the place. Janson said, "Gang, bring the women over here. Get them to sing chicken-flapping songs."[72]

---

71. They are looking for valuables hidden in wall panels.

72. ปรบไก่, *prop kai*, also known as "wild chicken songs," a popular entertainment in which two groups of singers improvise alternating verses in a challenge-response style, often trying to outdo each other for innuendo and bawdy humor, while dancing and clapping with exaggerated elbow movements a bit like chickens flapping their wings. The response stanza often ends with a chant "ฉ่า ฉ่า ฉ่า ชะ ชา ใฮ้ *cha cha cha, cha cha hai!*" that is incorporated in the next stanza (SWC, 7:3499–3501).

Janson sat on an upended mortar.[73] The servants danced and jigged around energetically. People stood watching, holding torches to give light, and chanting "Cha cha, ha hai!" like the rhythm for a Manora.[74]

"Hey, mother and child, get up and dance. If you stay still I'll pound you into frogspawn. If you don't believe me, try it just once. I'll poke you with a pike butt and then you'll dance!"

Khun Chang and Nang Thepthong said, "We can't dance without a flute and drum." All the robber gang chanted a rhythm, and tootled like flutes.

Mother and son clomped around, looking forced and clumsy. The robbers said, "The boy is jiggling okay, but the mother is hopeless." "Her waist is stiff as a board."

Thepthong took fright. She jiggled and wiggled in all four directions, swaying her shoulders and bottom around to the rhythm, waving her arms clumsily like a mask-play actor so her droopy breasts swung and slapped against her body. Khun Chang jumped up and down frenetically like a big monkey.

Khun Siwichai had no intention of running away. He rounded up the villagers, altogether a troop of about two hundred. They staked out the paths and stood watch.

Carrying guns and crossbows,[75] fire ready to light gunpowder, and masses of pikes, staves, swords, and spears, they waited hidden in ambush in many groups.

crossbow

Nai Janson, with the assurance of a big boss, shouted out to his forest robbers, "Pick up the loads now. Let's get moving!"

The servants and phrai carried the loads all together. Nai Janson was out front. The mother and child, owners of the property, followed behind, roped

---

73. Robbers such as Janson often made their victims dance, strip, or perform in some fashion as an offering to the robbers' protective deities, entreating these deities to ensure the robbers would escape retribution.

74. มโนพรวด, *mano(ra) phruat*, the sound of percussion for Manora, a song and dance performance from the south.

75. หน้าไม้, *na mai*, meaning a trigger and also a bow released by a trigger. Captain Low in 1836 described the Siamese crossbow as "about five feet long; it is passed through a stock about three or four feet long, tipped with hard wood, or iron. The leaf of a palm supplies the place of a feather to the arrow. The bow-string is drawn to the notch by the united exertion of the feet and arms, and the arrow is shot off by a trigger" ("History of Tennasserim," 318).

by the neck. She was made to call out, "Anyone there, don't follow us,

or they'll kill us." The robber gang advanced in three rows, firing off their guns threateningly, and booming out loud whoops and cries.

Khun Siwichai and the villagers waited in ambush, watching the robbers approach. Then they too whooped, hollered, fired their guns, bellowed at the robbers, and rushed towards them.

Khun Chang and his mother slipped free. The robbers dropped their loads in surprise, then roared back at the villagers and leapt into the fray, slicing, slashing, and hacking.

Blades clanged and clashed. Guns boomed and banged. All was uproar and confusion. The villagers' thrusts were useless, not piercing the robbers' bodies but enraging them to hit and hack back.

Villagers fell dead in heaps. The injured, covered in blood, cried out pitifully. Khun Siwichai ran up, slashing around, and came upon Janson. The pair plunged into combat.

They thrust and feinted with their pikes; stomped around, windmilling their arms and feet; measured each other up; pulled back then charged into the battle, eyeball to eyeball.

Pike clashed with pike, sparks flying. Both were powerful and fearless fighters who stabbed and sliced wildly, using all their might and endurance.

One lost the advantage but closed, grabbed the pike and twisted it away, then drew apart, feinting and turning. Reaching the end of their strength, they grappled at close quarters, wrestling each other down rolling on the ground.

The robber gang gathered round and grabbed Khun Siwichai. They tried to chop off his head with a sword but the blade did not enter. They tied his neck and stabbed it like piercing a log but the blade bounced off.

They chopped at his shoulders but the sword crumpled and broke off at the hilt. The robbers said, "This guy is able!"[76] "Look what he's done to these weapons!"

They tied his feet together like a roasting pig, shot him, and stabbed him but still nothing penetrated. The robbers were getting frustrated. "Hey! What to do?" "Ah! I've got it!"

They took a stave and pierced his anus. Khun Siwichai's life was snuffed out. He died in the forest, eyes closed tight. The robbers celebrated by firing guns,

and whooping through the woods, dropping lots of goods without bothering to pick them up. The villagers were too afraid to follow. They crept into the forest to hide and sleep.

---

76. ดี, *di*, "good," is often used in *KCKP* with the special meaning of "adept in supernatural power." This usage is translated throughout as "able."

At break of day, Thepthong asked her people to go into the forest and look for her husband. Shivering and shaking, she and her son went to search along the forest rim.

When they came upon him, she cried relentlessly and beat her chest so hard her sagging breasts slapped against her stomach. "My friend in hardship, you've gone and left your wife and child all alone.

Truly, what karma made you die such a violent death, naked on the ground in the middle of a forest? Maybe in a previous life you skewered a fish, and so in this life you've been skewered to death too.

You look pitiful, dreadful. Someone please pull the stave out of him." Khun Chang hugged the corpse, whimpering, rocking back and forth in sorrow.

"Oh poor Papa, my friend in hardship, you're dead and gone from me. I won't see your face again. You've made me an orphan. Why should you be killed by forest robbers?"

The servants ran up in a great mass, and fell to crying floods of tears over their beloved master.

Their weeping and wailing wafted through the woods. Some went mad with sorrow, and beat their breasts, crying out in lament, "Our master came to the end of his merit!" "We've lost our protector!"

As their sorrow gradually abated, they carried the corpse back and buried it at a graveyard,[77] then returned to the forest to look for the property.

They gathered up all the goods that the robbers had left strewn around the forest, and carried them back.

Now to tell of Phan Sonyotha. He went to trade with the Lawa[78] and returned with a fever. Siprajan exhausted herself nursing him, but the fever abated only to return more gravely each time.

A spirit had possessed his body, making him crave pork, beef, spicy sausage,

---

77. La Loubère reported that the poor and victims of a violent or abnormal death were buried rather than cremated. "But they never burn those that Justice cuts off, nor Infants dead-born nor Women that die in Child-bed, nor those which drown themselves, or which perish by any other disaster, as by a Thunderbolt. They rank these unfortunate persons amongst the guilty, because they believe that such Misfortunes never happen to innocent Persons" (*New Historical Relation*, 125). In *KCKP*, Khun Siwichai, Phan Sonyotha, and Wanthong, who all have abnormal deaths, are buried first, but later a decision is taken to hold a cremation.

78. Sonyotha was probably buying forest goods such as timbers, aromatics, and lacquers that were exported mainly to China.

and spicy raw salad that he swallowed in huge mouthfuls, lolling his tongue, rolling his eyes, nearing death.

Siprajan was in great distress. She went to summon the abbot but it was too late. Phan Sonyotha breathed his last. The servants raised a loud lament.

Phim arrived in a rush, weeping and wailing, wiping her tears away with her hands. Siprajan collapsed to the ground, beating her breasts. "Oh my lord!

You gave no thought to young Phim. You made up your mind to abandon her. Poor, forlorn little child, your father has left his wife and daughter all alone.

Oh Father, in the past you went off in every possible direction but you managed to stay alive so we could see your face again. This time you've been careless and met your death. From now on, we won't see you ever again."

Phim was bent double with sobbing. She hugged her father's corpse in grief. "Dear Papa, we used to see each other every day. Even though you were down with a fever, that was all right.

I could still grind your medicine. But now that you're dead and gone to the land of the spirits, I can't do the job of fanning you. This evening, your dear daughter won't see you.

The house will be as cold as a graveyard. Your medicine pot will grow mold, I fear. Oh Papa, there'll be nobody to lay out the mattress, mat, and coverlet for."

The relatives of the clan wept and wailed too, lamenting together on and on until the sorrow finally abated.

They bathed the corpse, daubed it with turmeric, wrapped it in white cloth, bound it tightly in the prescribed way,[79] and placed it in a wooden coffin in the main room. Prayers were chanted every evening for many days.

Siprajan and Thepthong both pondered deeply and then had a discussion. "Our husbands have met their deaths. Doing nothing would be wrong.

We should have the bodies cremated in the best way possible so we don't make trouble for their spirits." Of like mind, they promptly asked Master Som, the abbot,

to arrange a cremation at Wat Khao. Craftsmen carved wood, split and wove bamboo, made frames and panels for the ceiling, raised a *meru*, hung curtains from the top,

---

79. ตราสัง, *trasang*. A raw cotton thread is tied in three places: around the face and neck; around the hands which are arranged in wai holding flowers, incense, and candle, and then around the body; and around the ankles and toes. The body is wrapped in white cloth, either a single large piece, or two pieces, lengthwise and traverse, or a long, narrow strip wound around. A finger-thick cotton thread is then tied around the wrapped body at five or eight prescribed places. In older practice, the face was left exposed and the coffin had no lid (Anuman, *Prapheni nueang nai kan tai*, 49–53; Pattaratorn, "Chanting for the Dead").

firework tower

and built towers[80] for fireworks. Cooks were laid on for feeding, with nothing stinted. Fireworks were provided including crackers, bangers, and firewheels to be lit and tossed, spinning and bobbling on the water.[81]

The crematory pavilion was made with English gold[82] in a pattern of repeating *kanok* motifs, inlaid with clear, glittering white and green glass, and decorated with flowers waving on wire stems.

On the front was fashioned a brilliant image of Lord Indra riding a three-headed elephant, wearing a beautiful crown of gold, surrounded by a *krajang* pattern combined with blooming lotuses.

When the work was finished, the two bodies were brought in procession[83] and placed on the grand *meru* while flute and drum played a dirge. At evening, fireworks were lit.

Bangers exploded. Firewheels and rockets whizzed in the air. Strings of crackers popped and

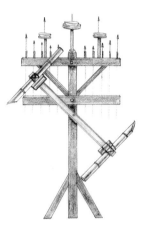

firewheel

80. ระทา, *ratha*, a square tapering tower with a peaked summit, used for mounting firework displays. Three large examples can be seen in photos of King Rama V's cremation. The use of such towers for royal cremations, to be furnished by Mahatthai, was specified in the Palatine Law (clause 171, KST, 1:149). King Phetracha's funeral in 1703 "had diverse fireworks and sixteen pyrotechnic towers lit to honor the Holy Paramount Corpse" (RCA, 380). More modest versions used in other cremations were generally constructed from bamboo and stood around four to five meters tall. The lighting of fireworks was considered a form of worship "equivalent to offering candles and incense," and the fireworks were sometimes lit at the same time as the pyre (see Anuman, "Akhinikritha," in *Prapheni bet set*, esp. 243–45, 258; Sittha, *Dokmai phloeng boran*).

81. พลุ, *phlu*, crackers, a thin cylinder, often bound with rope, filled with powder, and sealed with a plug; when lit, the powder explodes, making a loud noise and launching the lighted plug into the air. The word is often used as a general term for fireworks. ประทัด, *prathat*, bangers, fireworks designed to make a loud noise; usually a canister filled with powder and lit by a fuse. จังหันกล, *janghan kon*, firewheels, a piece of wood, pivoted at the center, with rocket-like devices at each end to make it spin like a Catherine wheel. Several varieties of fireworks were made to skip and skim on water (Sittha, *Dokmai phloeng boran*, 70–73, 82–87, 136–37).

82. ทองอังกฤษ, *thong angkrit*, a shiny thin metal used for cutting into decorative patterns.

83. ชักศพ, *chak sop*, "pulling the corpse," a procession to take the corpse from its resting place to the cremation ground, usually led by a monk holding a raw cotton thread attached to the front of the coffin (Anuman, *Prapheni nueang nai kan tai*, 112–13).

banged. To[84] the wailing sound of deer and tiger,
a call of "Pey, hey!"[85] and the beating of gong and drum,
prayer chanters sang a loud lament.[86] A Thai monk, started
the singing, waving a palm-leaf fan around.

"Da-ding, ba-boom, ding!
If you pound ginger and chili
to make a mad-fish curry,
and splash the chili in your eye,
A-choo! A-chaa! Whose fault is that?"

A Mon monk intoned,
"O-ra-nai.[87]

palm-leaf fan

---

84. The passage from here to "Disgraceful" on p. 54 is taken from WK 2:62–65, and other texts which have the same scene with variations in wording and spelling (SS, 77–79; CS, 55–57; TNA mss 33); PD has one hemistich, "Entertainments played at a row of screens." The passage describes a practice of humorous chanting at cremations that in various forms is known as the twelve-language chant, สวดสิบสองภาษา, *suat sipsong phasa*, monk clowning, จำอวดพระ, *jam uat phra, yike,* ยี่เก, or lay chanting, สวดคฤหัสถ์, *suat kharuehat*. In the past, relatives would invite monks to chant at the home of the deceased, rather than taking the body to a wat. Monks would chant the *aphitham* funeral prayer for two days, after which the hosts feared attendees would become bored, so monks would change the content of the chant to become entertaining. There were many variants of the practice. In one, the monks told a humorous version of the story of Phra Malai in which an *arahant* visits various hells and heavens, and talks to Indra and the Buddha Maitreya. In another variant, portrayed here, the performers mimicked "twelve languages," meaning various ethnicities, often including Chinese, Cham, Thai, Vietnamese, Mon, Khaek, northern Thai, northeastern Thai, southern Thai, Burmese, and Farang (probably English). The monks used costume, makeup, and wigs to fit the parts. This practice became widespread in the central region, but also raucous and obscene. King Rama I's Sangha Law of 1782 complained of "laypersons who invite monks to chant Phra Malai and monks who do not chant according to the Pali content but sing in the manner of Khaek, Chinese, Vietnamese, Mon, Farang. . . . When someone dies, it is forbidden for the host to invite monks to chant Phra Malai, but only the *aphitham* and in the normal way, not singing in the manner of Khaek, Chinese, Farang, or Mon" (Sangha Laws clause 10, KTS, 4:226–27). Subsequently, the same amusements were performed by lay persons, usually in groups of four, mainly but not exclusively male, sitting in the confined space of a low bench. They brought the props in a bag, and hid behind palm-leaf fans while making up. Despite the ban, the practice was still popular in Bangkok in the late 1930s, when two famous troupes were headed by a future police general and the father of the film director, Dokdin Kanyaman. The performance might include take-offs of prayers, exchanges of repartee, or passages from dramas or stories. In a nice piece of circularity, one of the standards of the repertoire had become spoofs of *KCKP*. (CS, 58–59, 197–98; Yai, "Suat kharuehat jam-uat"; Skilling, "Compassion")

85. เพ้ย, *phoei*, a shout that begins a mask play performance, and is also used for shooing away animals.

86. โอด, *ot*, a musical form played as background to weeping in a drama play.

87. อระนาย, *o-ra-nai*, a ululation to open a Mon song.

Your karma is to die.
I can't help you, sigh."

His partner said, "Oh sir, don't overdo it." He shook his body wildly and crooned,
"O-runny-high,
O-honey-lie![88]
I don't want to jump into a coffin.[89] I'm just a country monk. My skin doesn't grow as fast as the flesh inside.
One man went a-cutting cane, tried to eat a tiger.
One man went a-boating, dropped his pestle in the drink.
One man went a-diving deep, devoured a crocodile.
This dawdling spirit has died, but I don't give a blink!

A length of white cloth
That's what I'll nick.
A-hey diddle diddle, diddle diddle dee.[90]
These Thai are so thick,
Let's all take the mick!"

A pair of Vietnamese monks had tangled mustaches, white teeth, and tousled beards on their chins like forest langur.
One cried, "Dum-de-dum!" and the partner responded,
"*Khoan khoan*

monk clowning

---

88. His response, a nonsense play on the word *o-ra-nai*, means literally, "delicious, soft and slow, master."

89. This sentence is in Mon: อุมิด แลด (แลภ) ปาย ไพล่ ลง ใน กระบอก (หลาบอก), *umit laet (laep) pai phlai long nai krabok (labok)*.

90. ซาระโภ วา เฮลา ซาวะภา วา เฮโล, *sarapho wa he-la, sawapha wa he-lo*, a chorus to affirm the rhythm.

khoan ho khoan, khoan ho khoan.[91]
To the stars, no attention pay.
It'll happen anyway!
Bong, bong!
The bell sounds booonnnggg.
Jump up, dingle dangle dong,
End of the Vietnamese song!"

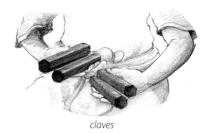

claves

    A pair of Chinese monks had beards like goats. One clacked claves,[92] and the other chinked cymbals in reply. They wailed to the rhythm through twisted mouths.

    "The Vietnamese monk has brought a secret weapon to scare me,
Six-six, dee-dee, six-dee-four![93]
The Vietnamese girl and I can still become lovers.
One fueang and two phai, one time can do!"[94]

    A Lao monk and his chanting partner then performed, opening their mouths wide, pinching their throats, and singing,

    "I'm not giving up.
Di-dum, di-dum, smart or dumb, it's all the same,
You're dead and I'm sorry, but that's the game.
Whatever the spirit molder will do,
It won't be quite the same as you.
Without whittling, a thorn is sharp.
Without shaping, a lime is round.[95]
We all end up like you, even me.
Day-da, day-da, day!"

    A pair of Khmer monks performed like toads, shaking their chins and croaking hoarsely.[96]

---

91. A chant that opens (or is the refrain in) several Vietnamese folk songs, sometimes meaning "slowly, slowly" and sometimes meaning "keep the rhythm" for rowing a boat.

92. กรับ, *krap*, two pairs of wooden cylinders, around six inches long, tapped together to provide rhythm and stress during the recitation of *sepha* and other performances. The wood is usually *chingchan, Dalbergia bariensis.*

93. *La-la, ding-dong, la-dong-su*, the Chinese equivalent of do-re-mi, in which some notes are sung as numbers and others as characters.

94. ไพ, *phai*, unit of money, one quarter of a fueang. The last clause is in Hokkien: จี ไป่ โต เอ, *ji bai to e.*

95. หนามแหลมไม่มีใครเสี้ยม มะนาวกลมเกลี้ยงไม่มีใครกลึง, *nam laem mai mi khrai siam manao klom kliang mai mi khrai klueng.* A saying with meaning similar to: A genius is born not made.

96. The next five lines, except for "White gold, yellow gold," are in Khmer.

"Hey you, dead you, lying up there,
You can't speak the lingo, you're just Khmer.
Where you came from, you tell me.
Where you're going, I'll go along to see.
White gold, yellow gold, everything in heaps.
Abbot, come and look! Mine's got a kink.
Mine's got a face—you see—that can wink."

A pair of Khaek chanters had tousled mustaches, beards on their chins, and teeth as white as Ai-Hu.

They drew on a hookah, gurgled and burbled, raised their big heads, and chanted on,

"Begat Parini[97] at my wat never eats pork.
I eat only Tani chicken.[98]
Parini is a spirit Thai.
With all support denied,
You closed your eyes and died.
All your parents and grandparents
Struggled with life until death.
You ran around, but in the end you join them!"

Up came two Farang monks, opened their mouths wide, rolled their eyes, and sang with heads shaking. They bashed their bottoms together, sat down, shook their bodies, fondled themselves for the audience to see, and sang,

"This Khaek monk Pari eats chicken only.
My thing eats too; pork additionally.
This fellow's captain is shorter than me.
I know how to solder constructively,
So mine's better than his!"

He took a swig of liquor, rang a bell, and the captain stood up and swayed to the music. He pulled down his trousers for the Khaek monk to see.

The Khaek monk's mouth dropped open, and he spat. "What are you showing me this tiddler for?" He waved a fan around to look fierce, and tried to hit the Farang monk.

---

97. เบกัด พะรีนี, variously spelled as ประวินี, *prawini* or พรรระนี, *phorrani* at different places and in different texts of this passage. The meaning is unclear, and may have confused copyists in the past. Perhaps the words were just meant to sound "Indian" (Begum Biriyani).

98. ตานี, *tani*, perhaps Pattani, maybe oily chicken. Other versions have ยานี, ยาลิ, *yani, yali*.

The Farang dodged, picked up a fan, clenched his fist, and raised it to fight
back. They went at each other crazily, one drunk on liquor, the other smashed
on ganja.

The host of the event hastily intervened. The Khaek monk shook his body
and growled. The Farang monk sat down immediately. "You hit me first."

The crowd watching in front roared in appreciation as the two Farang fought
with their fans. "Every one of these pairs is superb."

I-Kling said, "Really good. The Thai monk can play a Khaek so well. He
shakes his body, sings the chant, and dances. I like it. He sings really well."

Thepthong scolded, "Damn you! Liking these monks sounding off and rolling their heads! Where did this evil Khaek and Farang come from? Peeling off
their clothes for all to see. Disgraceful!"

As the golden light of dawn brightened the sky, the monks promptly stepped
down from the three platforms.[99] A mask play and puppet performance were
still going on merrily. Food, alms, and robes were offered to the monks.

After three days, the bodies were cremated in the presence of crowds of kinsfolk who paid respect to the remains, gave hampers of offerings to the abbot,
and returned to their homes.

mask play (folk style)

---

99. สร้าง, *sang*, a temporary dais erected at each corner of the coffin. By tradition, monks
occupy only three of the four while chanting the *phra aphitham* funeral prayer (Woranan, "Kan
sueksa sangkhom," 268).

3: PHLAI KAEO IS ORDAINED AS A NOVICE

Now to tell of the brilliant Phlai Kaeo. When his father died, his mother, Thong Prasi, fled with him to Kanburi.

They lived there until he was fifteen. He never stopped thinking of his late father, Khun Krai. For over a year, he had it in mind

that he wanted to be a valiant soldier like his father, so he begged his mother, "Please, I'd like to gain knowledge.[1]

Mother, please take me to a monk with good knowledge and ask him to ordain me as a novice[2] and become my teacher."

Thong Prasi had no objection at all. "If you want a teacher skilled in the inner ways,[3] the abbot of Wat Som Yai[4] is good.

You're thinking well, Mother's jewel. I'll take you to Master Bun. Once you

---

1. วิชาการ, *wichakan*, meaning the disciplines, or taught knowledge, including reading, writing, numerical skills, religious and ethical teachings, astrology, military arts, and supernatural practices with mantras and other devices. At the time of King Taksin of Thonburi (r. 1767–1782), and probably in the preceding Ayutthaya era too, there was a *krom wichakan*, a Department of Knowledge, among whose duties was looking after texts on warfare, and distributing charms and formulas for invulnerability to soldiers.

2. เณร, *nen*, Thai contraction of the Pali *samanera*, a "small monk." In traditional Siamese society, most male youths entered the novitiate, at least for a token period of a few weeks. For some, it was an apprenticeship before full ordination as a monk. For others, it was an opportunity for some education.

3. ทางใน, *thang nai*, meaning skills in tapping exceptional forces, believed to be latent within the individual, through various methods including meditation, formulas (mantra), and devices (yantra). These skills stem from a tradition of asceticism and self-mastery embedded in Thai Buddhism (see p. 943).

4. วัดส้มใหญ่, wat of the large citrus tree. In chapter 24, a วัดเชิงหวาย, Wat Soeng Wai, wat of the rattan thicket, appears as close to Thong Prasi's home. Probably these two are the same wat but the name was altered in the text during oral transmission. The true name is unknown because in the wars of the late eighteenth century, old Kanburi was abandoned and the names of its wat were completely lost. On a visit in 1888, King Chulalongkorn recorded: "There is still a derelict wat said to be built by Thong Prasi, mother of Khun Phaen" (Chulalongkorn, *Sadet praphat Saiyok*, 57). The remains of five wat have survived to the present. All have been renamed, three by reference to this poem. Possibly Wat Som Yai was one of these (*Phutthasasanakhadi*, 33–36; Sathaphon, *Mueang Kanchanaburi kao*, 56–72; see map 7 and accompanying note).

learn about the military arts and invulnerability,[5] you can carry on the line of your father, Khun Krai."

She gave orders to the servants without delay. "My most beloved son is going to be ordained. Go out and get some good-quality cloth

to make his *jiwon*, *sabong*, and *sabai*.[6] Also, find the right sort of sidebag and almsbowl.[7] Make a start on all of this today. Ai-Thi and I-La,[8] come and help me."

The servants went off to fetch betelnut, pan, and banana leaves. They all helped to stitch cones,[9] peel betelnut, coil and bind pan leaves, and roll wax candles.

They measured white cloth, cut and sewed it into a *sabong* with a nice flat hem. They cut out the *jiwon* and *sabai* neatly with scissors, and sewed the pieces together.

sabong and jiwon

They made a shoulder cloth from soft chicken-skin silk, and sewed on silk toggle buttonholes. They all sat round in a circle, making lots of noise but working busily with devotion.

Some went out to get turmeric, pounded it all up, then went back for more. "Oh, have you never done this before? You've dyed the cloth too light so it doesn't look good.

Pour some vinegar in. That'll make the ochre color deeper and brighter." "That's fixed it!" They laughed merrily. A clothesline was tied for drying the

---

5. คงกระพัน, *khong kraphan*. Khong means to remain or endure. *Kraphan* probably comes via Malay from Arabic, *cabal*, meaning invulnerability. Invulnerability means the ability to resist weapons through innate power and the use of various protective devices. According to Thep, *khong kraphan* originally meant resistance to blades and other sharp objects, achieved by ingesting some substance such as enchanted liquor. *Khong kraphan chatri* (ชาตรี, martial) was a superior form eliminating any pain as well. *Khlaeo khlat*, แคล้วคลาด, avoidance, means invulnerability to all weapons, including guns, achieved by wearing protective amulets and chanting formulas. *Maha-ut*, มหาอุด, great blocking, is invulnerability specifically to guns, achieved through wearing protective devices. *Niao*, เหนียว, tough, and *yukhong*, อยู่คง, survival, are other terms. In practice, both in *KCKP* and elsewhere these various terms tend to be used as synonyms. (PKW, 2: 31–51; see also Turton, "Invulnerability")

6. The three cloths of a monk's robes. *Jiwon*, จีวร, is the outer robe; *sabong*, สบง, is an inner lowercloth, from waist to shin; *sabai*, สไบ, is a breastcloth, today usually called *sangkhati*, สังฆาฏิ.

7. Theravada Buddhist monks are forbidden to work or handle money so that they are dependent on the charity of the lay faithful. The monks go out in the early morning to beg for alms. Laypersons gain merit by making donations, usually food. The bowl is for collecting these alms.

8. Ai- and I- are prefixes denoting commoners or subordinates, male and female respectively.

9. กรวย, *kruai*, cone, here a leaf sewed into a conical shape to hold incense, candles, and flowers to be presented as offerings.

dyed cloth, and then the triple robes were placed on a salver.

A team of the very best cooks steamed and boiled busily, their faces burned black from the stove.[10] They cleaned the rice and put it in pans;

fried and boiled; made *phanaeng*; curried river snails; mixed spicy salad; made sweets; arranged fruit for offerings; and set everything on many rows of trays.

When all was ready, Thong Prasi shouted at the servants to come quickly. "Ai-Mong, I-Ma, why are you so slow? Take the big bowl and fill it with water.

What have you done with the turmeric and whiteclay[11] powder? Yesterday I put them in the crock."[12] She bathed her son, getting rid of all the sweat and grime, then rubbed him with turmeric,

powdered his face, and combed his hair. Phlai Kaeo was dressed in a yok[13] lowercloth with a pleated front like folded leaves, a light robe[14] with gold embroidery,

a conical hat with waving flowers,[15] a belt embroidered in two rows, and a diamond ring with a beautiful glittering stone. He was given incense, candles, and lotus flowers to hold in a pouch.

Strapping Nai Dam was summoned to carry him on his shoulders with an umbrella overhead. Thong Prasi walked along beside. The gaggle of servants carried the offerings.

At Wat Som Yai, the offerings were placed in the front sala. Thong Prasi took bright-eyed Phlai Kaeo to pay respect to the abbot.

conical hat

---

10. เชิงกราน, *choengkran*, a portable earthenware stove with a tray for holding firewood and a raised platform to place a pot (CK, 178).

11. ดินสอพอง, *dinso phong*, a fine powdered white clay, used to cool the body, like talcum.

12. ถ้ำ, *tham*, a pottery or lead container used to retain fragrance and exclude damp, especially used for tea or medicine (KW, 656; CK, 231).

13. ยก, *yok*, means to raise or lift, and "is used to describe textiles on which the design has been made with supplementary threads, raised over a plain silk background" (Thirabhand, "Royal Brocades," 182). Throughout the poem, yok is used to refer to a smart lowercloth, generally of silk brocade.

14. See p. 24, note 14.

15. ลอมพอก, *lomphok*, a tall, tapering conical hat with an upturned brim decorated with golden flowers. It originated from Persia where it was known as *taj* and was formerly a royal headdress that later became a standard of court attire (Floor, *Persian Textile Industry*, 277–89). It became part of Siamese noble regalia during the reign of King Narai (1660–1688) as recorded by the illustrators of the French diplomatic missions in the 1680s. The ordinand is imagined as a prince renouncing his privileged life to enter the monkhood, just as the Buddha himself did, hence the wearing of a crown of some type is a common part of his costume in this procession.

"Your Lordship, I've brought my son to be ordained. Please teach him to be something of substance so he may make merit and share it with his father, Khun Krai, who had come to his time.

Also, teach him to read and write so he can learn young." Abbot Bun sighed heavily before he spoke.

"Such a pity Khun Krai passed away. His son, Phlai Kaeo, is very much like him. His looks make me think of his father. I'll take care of him, don't worry."

He turned to give instructions to Novice Khong. "Call the monks downstairs. Lay mats and arrange the seating. Shave Phlai's head and bring him back."

The abbot descended to the main sala, and the monks all came down together. Phlai Kaeo carried his triple robes and paid respect. Master Bun initiated him as a novice.[16]

When the ordination was over, Thong Prasi harassed the cooks so loudly her body shook. All the monks' bowls were lined up, and pots of rice were carried in.

Everyone helped place food into the monks' bowls and then present the usual offerings.[17] After eating, the monks chanted an offertory blessing. Novice Kaeo and Thong Prasi poured water on the ground.[18]

The[19] novice studied to read and write. With diligence, he soon mastered Khmer, Thai, arithmetic, the main scriptures, calculating the sun and moon, and translation of texts.[20]

The teachers were intimidated by his cleverness. Among all the many elders and novices there, none could match him. Within less than one year as a novice, he had things by heart,

could write perfectly, and could translate texts. The abbot had nothing left

---

16. For the simple initiation as a novice, after the head is shaved, the candidate makes an offering to the preceptor who chants a formula "giving the precepts and advice," after which the initiate dons the robe (Prachak, *Prapheni*, 33).

17. Offerings were everyday articles for the monks' use. Today this includes things like soap and toothpaste. Probably at that time it included candles, fire-making equipment, cloth, etc.

18. กรวดน้ำ, *kruat nam*, a way of sharing some of the merit made with the dead. The person pours clean water over an index finger while thinking of the intended recipient(s) of the merit. It may also be done while monks are chanting the concluding prayer, in which case the devotee pours the water from a bowl held in the right hand to one in the left while the first monk chants, and then pours the water onto the ground when the other monks chant the response. (KW, 656; Terwiel, *Monks and Magic*, 101–2; *Phojananukrom kham wat*, 21)

19. This stanza is taken from WK, 2:40; PD has: After the ordination, Novice Kaeo studied diligently. He had a quick and nimble mind. Whatever he studied, he got down quickly.

20. Probably Buddhist texts in Pali, and manuals of lore in old Khmer.

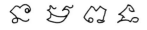

heart formula

to tell him. He patted Kaeo on the back and the head and said, "That's the end of my gut, my dear Novice Kaeo.

There's only the big treatise with the heart formulas[21] and mantras. I've been collecting them since I was a youth. Until now in my old age, I haven't shared them with anyone.

This is the extent of my knowledge. Because I'm fond of you, Kaeo, I'll pass it on to you. There's everything—invulnerability, robbery, raising spirits[22]—something for every occasion."

Novice Kaeo absorbed the master's treatise but he himself still wanted to study more. So one day he went to pay respect and beg leave to go to Suphanburi.

"I want to study further." The abbot was pleased and laughed heartily. "The abbot of Wat Palelai[23] is very able. He and Thong Prasi know each other."

Novice Kaeo took his leave and went to his mother. Thong Prasi rushed out to welcome him. "Why have you come, darling son?" "Mother, the abbot sent me.

My studies there are finished. He told me that Wat Palelai is very good. He said you've known the abbot for ages. Please take me and put me under his care."

Thong Prasi laughed with pleasure. "That's right, dear novice. As I recall, in Suphan there are two monks good at the inner ways—

---

21. หัวใจ, *hua jai* or heart mantras, were abbreviated forms used for purposes of memorization, and for quick application. Often these were two or three syllables, each of which represented a complete prayer. For example, อิสวาสุ, *i-sawa-su*, represented the *ittipiso, sawak-khato*, and *sapphipanno* prayers. These formulas are chanted as an aid for meditation, to activate a powerful object or yantra, to achieve invisibility or invulnerability, to induce love, and so on. A collection of 108 heart formulas, in which "108" is a powerful number, rather than the actual number of formulas, was well-known. (KW, 308; PKW, 3:136–42; Thep, *Khamphi hua jai* 108; Prachak, Prapheni, 159)

22. โหงพราย, *hong phrai*, spirits that are susceptible to control through mantras and other devices (see pp. 939–44).

23. Originally a forest wat situated 4 kms west of the river, outside the old town site of Suphanburi. Its massive main Buddha image, known as Luang Pho To, may date back to the Dvaravati or early Ayutthaya era as its Western-style sitting pose is rarely found from later periods. Initially the image was probably in the open air and went through repeated restorations. As a result, any trace of its old style is obscured. After Suphanburi was abandoned in the eighteenth century, the wat deteriorated. In 1844, the poet Nai Mi described it: "the walls are cracked, uneven-looking, patched up with lime. Whoever made the image in Wat Palelai, it looks pitifully dilapidated. . . . Both arms are broken. The gold covering the face is dull and tarnished… The roof is frightful. Rain leaks through and stains the image." The wat was restored by 1899 and adopted as a royal wat (third class) in 1909. Recently the main cloister has been decorated with a series of mural paintings on the story of *KCKP*. (Manat, *Prawatisat mueang Suphan*, 133–45; Phra Sithawatmethi, *Luang pho to; Nirat Suphan* by Nai Mi).

Abbot Mi of Wat Palelai and the master at Wat Khae.[24] I used to send food over there. He and Khun Krai loved each other greatly. It's no problem to place you under his care."

She immediately instructed the servants to bring elephants. "Harness cow elephant Bu for me and bull elephant Kang for the novice.

Put things in the howdah, including enough to feed the monks both morning and noon. Ai-Sen and Ta-Phum will go along to look after matters."

When everything was ready, they left the house at Cockfight Hill and crossed the grassland towards the forest. In three days they reached Suphanburi.[25]

Entering Wat Palelai, they went straight to the kuti[26] of Master Mi. Thong Prasi paid respect to him. "I haven't come to see you for a long time."

The abbot was pleased and laughed merrily. "I haven't seen your face for many years. Whose son is this novice? I don't know him." Thong Prasi said, "He's my own son.

Since Khun Krai passed away, I've been a widow on my own. I had my son ordained so he could study and make something of himself. He's now a gangling lad and it's not good I'm far away,

so I want to put him under your care, master. Please give him knowledge and look after him. If he's lazy and doesn't study, punish him with the cane."

The abbot said, "Don't be impatient. If he doesn't listen to the instruction, why should I look after him? But I'm not the sort of person to use threats. I'll teach him what his own mind can take.

If the child is good, he alone gets the praise; if he's bad, they blame the teacher. He has a respectable name and pedigree.

Wat Palelai

---

24. An Ayutthaya-era wat on the west bank of the Suphan River in the north of the old town of Suphanburi. It was abandoned for a long time but revived after the Second World War. To attract visitors, the wat built a "House of Khun Phaen" and shrines for Khun Phaen and Abbot Khong in the compound in the 1980s (Manat, *Prawat Wat Khae*; Winyu, *Tam roi*, 139–54; see map 6).

25. The distance by the modern road is 110 kms.

26. กุฏิ, residential quarters for monks in a wat. Often these were old houses, donated by devotees.

I don't think he'll disgrace the lineage."

Thong Prasi chuckled at the abbot's words. "Dear Novice Kaeo, remember this well." She entrusted her son to his care, took leave, and returned home to Cockfight Hill.

Novice Kaeo had an agile mind beyond compare, and was diligent without being told. After three months of practice, he had sermons down by heart.

Whether it was the Mahachat,[27] sermons on the teachings, or anything else, he spoke beautifully with a peerless choice of words, and a voice as charming as a cicada. Wherever he gave sermons, people loved to come and listen.

He soon gained such a reputation for his proficiency that villagers and townsfolk nearly went crazy about him. Elders and novices would skip the forenoon meal and sit waiting to beg for some recitation.

In[28] the evenings he went to the main kuti to pay respect, attend to the abbot, and take instruction: how to make a sword for war; how to transform a thorny branch into a buffalo charm; how to enchant dummy soldiers; how to charm a woman so that once their eyes had met, her heart would be captivated and she would never forget.

His master laughed. "Young Kaeo, I know you're interested in the stuff about being a lover. Don't do damage to people's wives but old maids and widows—take them!

buffalo charm

27. Mahachat means the "great birth" or "great Jataka." Jataka or birth stories are accounts of the previous lives of the Buddha before his final incarnation as Siddhattha, the historical Buddha. In the popular religious tradition throughout Buddhist Southeast Asia, Jataka stories were the main form of moral instruction, expounded in sermons, recited at festivals, dramatized in various forms of performance, and depicted in the decoration of religious buildings. The Buddha is said to have had 550 prior lives, and in the Jataka, these are presented as recalled and recounted by the Buddha himself. The last ten Jataka in the standard collection are of special importance for they are the stories of how the Bodhisatta or Buddha-to-be achieved the Ten Perfections, *thotsabarami*—giving, moral conduct, renunciation, wisdom, energy, patience, truthfulness, resolution, loving kindness, and equanimity—as a result of which he could be reborn as the Buddha. Most important of all is the very last and longest tale of Prince Vessantara (Phra Wetsandon), which illustrates the Perfection of Giving, and in the Thai tradition is known as the Mahachat. Annual recitations of the Mahachat were a major form of merit making in late Ayutthaya and early Bangkok. It was believed that those who listened to this Jataka were certain to meet the future Buddha, Metteyya, Maitreya, *phra si an*. (Anuman, *Thet Maha Chat*; Gerini, *Thet Mahachat Ceremony*; Jory, "The *Vessantara Jataka*"; Nidhi, *Pen and Sail*, 199–226)

28. The next two stanzas are taken from WK, 2:72; PD has: He studied hard on reading, writing, recitation, and questioning. He absorbed the major treatises on the arts of war, the sun and moon, auspicious times of day, / invulnerability, invisibility, and illusions used in fighting. He also liked studying love charms for captivating a woman's heart without any chance of escape.

I'll teach you everything about sacred mantras and formulas. You'll be a real gem." He spat out the betel he was chewing and passed it to Novice Kaeo to eat the remains. Then the master hit him with a pestle, almost chipping his skull. "There! It didn't crack or bruise. Like hitting a stone." The master rolled about with laughter.

Kaeo regularly waited upon the abbot and fanned him. The abbot, who loved Kaeo more and more, taught and tested the novice until his mind was quick. His confidence grew by the day.

Now to tell of Khun Chang. In his youth, his head was as bald as an adjutant stork, while his chin and chest were a mess of whiskers and hair.[29] His face looked like a forest monkey.

He fell for Kaen Kaeo, the daughter of Muen Phaeo from Big Wall Village. He asked the parents for her hand and they consented, so Khun Chang got himself a wife.

She came to live in his house as bedmate, sharing pillows side by side for over a year. Then she fell sick with a fever that lasted a long time, and developed into dysentery and piles.

She grew thin, her face turned hard and scaly, and her eyes became sunken. She had a huge craving for duck, chicken, and unwholesome things. Khun Chang was lonely and miserable.

Watching his wife ache with fever, he gradually lost heart. In desperation, he sent for Ta-Don, a doctor. He left money on a tray beside the bed, and pleaded with the doctor to give her medicine.

The doctor said, "The illness has passed into a fatal stage. Treatment would be useless. The fever is so severe she's close to death. Why didn't you send for me at the beginning?"

After the doctor took his leave, Khun Chang was glum and full of remorse. He felt he was burning inside, and did not know what to do.

Before long, Kaen Kaeo's life was snuffed out. Khun Chang sat and wept. He arranged a noisy cremation, and frequently made merit for her.[30]

---

29. In ancient Indian thought, hairlessness was associated with sterility, and a bald head often compared to barren earth. Hair had to be in the right place—on the head—to symbolize fertility, or else was a blemish (Jamison, *Ravenous Hyenas*, 153–54).

30. He may have held a feeding for the monks or performed some other deed or ceremony believed to make merit, and prayed that part of the merit be shared with Kaen Kaeo to improve her status in her next life.

Now to tell of Suphan-
buri at Songkran time.[31]
Everybody came to Wat
Palelai to make merit and
give alms with devotion.

Crowds of men and
women, young and old,
shuttled back and forth
with sand to build stupas
all around the wat.[32] The
monks, who would be fed
on the next day,

making sand stupas

chanted prayers in the afternoon. Everybody celebrated the sand festival
merrily, then returned home to prepare food for the monks. They got everything ready—grilling, roasting,

making *namya* sauce,[33] river-snail curry, plain soup, and chicken *phanaeng*.
They sliced gourd, carved marrow, baked *ho mok*,[34] made salty eggs, fried dried
fish, and prepared offal curry.[35]

They made jelly in syrup, sago, and sticky rice with pork topping. On benches
they laid out rice fritters,[36] young rice in syrup, oranges, and other fruits,

maprang, langsat,[37] rattan fruit, jambolan, pomelo, sharp orange, and finger bananas. Every house was busy until late at night when all fell asleep in a
trice.

At dawn, when golden sunlight lit up the sky, everyone got dressed quickly.
Young and old, men and women, crowded noisily into Wat Palelai.[38]

---

31. Thai new year, which falls around mid April, at the time the sun enters Aries according
to the Indic solar calendar.

32. Building a wat or other religious building is believed to result in a great gain in merit.
Building temporary stupas from sand became a custom practiced on the eve of the new year in
many parts of Buddhist Southeast Asia (Anuman, *Prapheni kiao kap thesakan*, 94–96).

33. น้ำยา, a curried fish sauce made with coconut milk, dried chili, galangal, lemongrass,
kaffir lime peel, ginger, shallots, garlic, coriander, several herbs and edible leaves, dried fish, and
snakehead fish, often eaten with *khanom jin*, a form of rice noodles (see p. 257, note 54).

34. ห่อหมก, "wrap and bury," originally a mixture of fish, herbs, and spices, wrapped in banana leaves, covered with mud, and baked with wood or charcoal in a hole in the ground.

35. แกงบวน, *kaeng buan*, an old dish made with pork offal and pork skin (SB, 26).

36. (นาง)เล็ด, *(nang)let*, sticky rice steamed, formed into disk shapes, sun-dried, fried, and
coated with syrup.

37. ลางสาด, *Aglaia domestica*, a berry-like fruit with fawn skin and translucent white flesh.

38. On normal days, monks went out to collect alms, but on Songkran, families cooked food
and took it to the wat in the morning to feed the monks. This was a chance to give the monks

Among them were Phim and her mother, followed by their servants carrying food to put in the almsbowls, and salvers with incense, candles, and flowers.

At the wat, they all sat down at the sand stupas and paid respect. The wat was full of people laying out mats to wait for the monks.

incense, candles, and flowers

Elders and novices donned their robes, came down to the main sala, and sat in order. The faithful paid respect happily.

Each monk was presented with a salver of medicines. The monks arranged their shoulder cloths properly. The request for the precepts[39] was made at once. Abbot Mi gave the precepts.

The monks paid respect to the Buddha with hands clasped. All the women scurried to fetch plates and bowls to prepare trays of food and set them out ready for offering to the monks in order of seniority.

The pupils, mendicants,[40] and novices placed food in the almsbowls, and lifted the offerings to place in front of the monks,[41] then watched to see who finished their *namya* curry so they could ladle out another portion.

Phim devoutly brought bananas, sweets, and sharp oranges on a large tray. Carrying a bowl of rice, she walked gracefully to give to the seniors and then down the line.

Coming to Novice Kaeo, she glanced at him and hesitated, remembering something from the past. "This novice and I seem to know each other." She ladled a big scoop of food

with a heap of fried pork, dried fish, chicken curry, halved boiled eggs, sausages, dried fish, watermelon, and a bowlful of curry—enough to fill him up.

Novice Kaeo had his head bowed and did not know who it was. Seeing so much food, he lifted his head with eyes opened wide. He saw Phim's face, smiling with her eyes averted. "Is she teasing me or what?"

---

a treat. It was also an opportunity for young girls to dress up and show off (Anuman, *Prapheni kiao kap thesakan*, 87–88).

39. อาราธนาศีล, *arathana sin*. To initiate the chanting, a leader of the lay attendees recites a formula requesting the monks to give the precepts.

40. เกร, เถน, *then*, an old person who stays in a wat in order to eat from the leftovers of alms donations. They may also choose to observe some of the precepts, and may wear a robe or other garment of similar color.

41. Women are not allowed to pass anything directly to a monk by hand (though they can place something in his bowl). Here the women prepare the sets of food and place them in front of each monk. Then a male lifts or pushes the tray forward for the monk to receive it.

"You're giving me so much my bowl is packed to overflowing. How can I eat it? There's too much, both sweet and savory, but you haven't given me what I really like."

Phim broke into a smile. "Oh Novice, when I saw the empty bowl, I thought it was an old mendicant, so I heaped it in. You accuse me of teasing. Would you rather have me lose merit?

In Suphan[42] it's hard to get the good stuff that will satisfy you. And it's expensive. You can go to two or three towns without finding any."

Phlai Kaeo thought for a moment with his heart thumping. "I can remember. I think she used to play with me. Her name is Phim Philalai. She's grown up so beautiful she makes my eyes hurt."

The monks finished eating. The abbot gave the offertory blessing, repeated by the other monks. The lay faithful poured water on the ground.

Everybody merrily bustled off home, noisily singing songs and dancing to celebrate the almsgiving.

Time passed. In the tenth month of the year of the cock, seventh of the decade,[43] just one day short of the Sat festival,[44] the Buddhist faithful in Suphan had the idea of staging a devotional recitation

of the Mahachat[45] in all thirteen episodes at Wat Palelai on the next holy

---

42. This stanza is taken from WK, 2:77, absent from PD.

43. ปีระกาสัปตศก, *pi raka sappata sok*, meaning a year of the cock which has a final digit of 7 in the Chula Sakkarat calendar. This is a form of counting using the intersection of a 12-base system, the animal years, and a 10-base system, the universal decimal system, to create a 60-year cycle. In the Ayutthaya chronicles, the year that the Burmese attacked the capital was a cock year, seventh of the decade (RCA, 495–96, 501). This was CS 1127, 1765/6. Other similar years were 1525/6, 1585/6, 1645/6, and 1705/6. The tenth lunar month falls in August-September.

44. สารท, a festival falling on the fifteenth waning of the tenth lunar month, usually in September. *Sat* is derived from a Pali word for season. A special sweet, *krayasat*, made from new rice, sugar, peanut, and sesame is presented to the monks. Some believe the dead return to the human world on this day thus merit made for them on this day is especially effective.

45. See p. 61, note 27 above on the Mahachat. In the usual form of these recitations in late Ayutthaya and early Bangkok, the whole story was recited over a single day in thirteen *kan* or episodes. Local dignitaries sponsored episodes to make merit and display their status. Sponsorship included decorating the wat with branches, sugarcane, and banana leaves to appear as Mount Wongkot in which the story is set, and making offerings to the monks. The thirteen episodes are: 1) *The Ten Blessings*. A prologue. 2) *Himaphan*. Wetsandon is born and ascends to the throne of Sonchai. When a neighboring city suffers a drought, Wetsandon gives away his rain-making white elephant, and as a result is banished by his furious subjects. 3) *The Gifts*. Wetsandon gives away his possessions to the needy before leaving, and then gives away his horses and chariot along the way. 4) *Entering the Forest*. Wetsandon and his wife Matsi travel to the Mount Wongkot and take up residence in a hermitage. 5) *Chuchok*. An old Brahman, whose

day. The lay elders held a meeting at the wat.⁴⁶

Certain persons agreed to sponsor the episodes of the *Ten Blessings*, *Himaphan*, and *The Gifts*. Someone with lots of children took over *Chuchok* for the daytime, and Siprajan was allotted *Matsi*.

The Great King of a Thousand Lives, which always had the audience rolling with noisy laughter, was scheduled for the middle of the night. Old Muen Si agreed to take on the nicely quiet and restful episode of the *Six Princes*.

Nang Wan took the *Small Forest*, to be recited by Novice On, a new and very accomplished performer. Monk Jai would recite the *Great Forest*, and Grandpa Tai immediately agreed to be the sponsor.

Grandpa Phae and Grandma Khli took on *Entering the Forest* by the abbot of Wat Khae. "Eh, who should we give the big episode to? It's not easy for just anyone of the faithful to sponsor."⁴⁷

"*The Children*? Yes, that's true. Give it to the bald fellow from Big Wall Village. Nai Bun, you know him well. Pop over there." Nai Bun went to Khun Chang's house and presented the request.

"The Mahachat in thirteen episodes will be performed at Wat Palelai on the next holy day. Sir, would you not like to show your devotion and make some merit?

Siprajan and Phim have the *Matsi* episode. There's still no taker for *The*

---

young wife is ridiculed by the neighbors for having to do all the housework, decides to go and ask for Wetsandon's two children to be his slaves. 6) *Small Forest*. Chuchok travels. 7) *Great Forest*. Chuchok travels and displays his bad character. 8) *The Children*. Chuchok arrives at the hermitage while Matsi is away. He asks for the children, and Wetsandon consents. Chuchok takes the children and beats them before Wetsandon's eyes. 9) *Matsi*. To prevent Matsi returning in time to chase after the children, Indra delays her return. 10) *The Powerful One*. Indra disguises himself and asks for Matsi. Wetsandon consents but Indra returns her to him. 11) *The Great King of a Thousand Lives*. Wetsandon's father sees the children and ransoms them from Chuchok, who dies from overeating on the proceeds. 12) *The Six Princes*. The children lead an expedition that finds Wetsandon at the hermitage. 13) *The City*. They return to the city, where Wetsandon is restored to the throne and rules until 120 years old.

46. The choice of sponsor and of performer was geared to the character of each episode. Some episodes performed during the daytime were suitable for sponsors with children. *Ten Blessings*, because it came first and was highly didactic, was often recited by the abbot of the host wat, as in this case. *The Children* was reckoned suitable for a young monk or novice who could approximate a young voice. The melodrama of *Chuchok* required a skilled and powerful performer. *Matsi* was often allotted to a young monk or novice who could imitate a female voice (SWC, 6:2679–80).

47. Traditionally, the scale of the offerings and decorations for each episode was in direct relation to the episode's length in verses. For example, the sponsor was expected to decorate the wat with the same number of flags and candles as there were stanzas in the episode. With 101 stanzas, *The Children* was one of the longest episodes and thus required heavy investment (Anuman, *Prapheni kiao kap thesakan*, 286–87).

Children." Khun Chang laughed with pleasure. "I'd be happy to have the great, great episode!

Don't spare a thought about the expense. Even if it costs me some five chang[48] I won't run away. I'll be born rich in my next life. I'm only too willing to make merit in such a way."

Nai Bun hastened back happily. Monks were asked to distribute the notice, "All thirteen episodes in sequence." The villagers began making preparations.

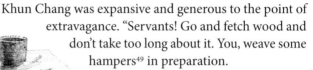

Khun Chang was expansive and generous to the point of extravagance. "Servants! Go and fetch wood and don't take too long about it. You, weave some hampers[49] in preparation.

And you, take this cash[50] and buy all the everyday stuff to offer to the monks. Find some good quality cloth to make triple robes. You women, go and find the offerings for the episode.

weaving basketwork

You pound the rice and sift the flour to make wheel sweets.[51] Do it straightaway. And don't stint. I want hundreds of everything. Don't worry about using lots of oil. Just go and buy some more,

and every type of orange and fruit. The cost is not a problem. Don't be stingy and create gossip. I'm considered gentlefolk."

wheel sweets

Siprajan called out, "Phim, come over and give some help." She shouted at the servants, "Get in here and lend a hand at once."

They mixed sweets, coated them in flour, and fried them in sputtering oil.

---

48. ชั่ง, *chang*, a unit of currency equivalent to 80 baht, sometimes called a catty, but different in value to an Indian catty: "Tsiani [chang], by foreigners call'd Katti, is understood of Silver, being two pound and a half, or twenty Thails, or fifty Rixdollars, that is, double the value of a Katti, as it is current at Batavia and in Japan" (Kaempfer, *Description*, 72).

49. กระจาด, *krajat*, a basketwork receptacle woven from bamboo with a small round or square base and much wider mouth. Those used for carrying offerings for the Mahachat were very large and ornate. The rim of the mouth was fashioned in the shape of lotus petals, decorated with colored paper, and hung with tassels (Anuman, *Prapheni kiao kap thesakan*, 286–87; SWC, 1:57).

50. In the Wat Ko version, Khun Chang here gives the large sum of five chang (WK, 2:79).

51. ขนมกง, *khanom kong*, formerly *khanom kongkwian*, cartwheel sweets. Paste made from green or yellow beans, flour, palm or coconut sugar, coconut milk, and duck's eggs is shaped like a Buddhist wheel of the law (*chakra*), and deep-fried (SWC, 1:6).

"Hey, this fire is too hot!" "Pull some firewood out." I-Khong scooped them up saying, "Done to a turn!"

The *chamot*[52] and wheel sweets were laid out neatly. *Thian* sweets[53] were molded and lined up so they would not get broken. Rice crackers and biscuits were tossed in Phetburi[54] sugar and placed alongside, looking good.

Young rice mixed with flour was deep fried, then hollowed out with a stick for inserting egg, coconut, and sweet palm sugar. "When they're done, pierce them on sticks, young Khon."

The crowd of servants milled around, scooping flour, helping one another with this and that, and making a racket like a mask play. Siprajan harassed and harried them, "Pass them over carefully! Don't throw those or they'll break!"

The sponsor of the *Ten Blessings* episode woke and got up before the cock. As dawn broke, he rushed over to Wat Palelai with all the offerings for his episode,

and laid them out on salvers in the preaching hall. He lit incense and candles to offer to the Buddha and left them smoldering. A monk chanted the precepts, spoke sharing the merit, and recited the Pali *junniyabot*.[55]

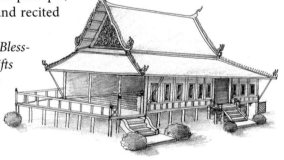

The episodes of the *Ten Blessings, Himaphan,* and *The Gifts* were soon over, and the stage was set up anew for the *Great Forest* by Monk Jai. When that was over, he returned to the kuti.

preaching hall

---

52. ขนมชะมด, coconut rolled in sugar, coated with flour, and fried. These sweets could be decorated with colored flour to make them attractive as festival offerings (Anuman, *Prapheni kiao kap thesakan*, 287–88).

53. ขนมเทียน, *khanom thian*, a dough of rice flour and sugar, rolled into a cylinder in a banana leaf, and steamed. Nowadays they are made in a pyramid shape and filled with various fillings.

54. พริบพรี, *Phripphri*, an old spelling. Then and now, Phetburi is famous for palm sugar.

55. จุณณียบท, phrases from the Pali version of the story, pronounced at the start of the episode and other break points. It was considered more meritorious to chant the Mahachat in Pali but few could understand it. Sometimes, all or part of the Pali text would be chanted by the monks prior to the Thai recitation. The *junniyabot* were probably retained in the Thai version to allow some listeners to follow the story in the Pali text, or just as a stylized reminder of the more meritorious Pali version (Nidhi, *Pen and Sail*, 204–7).

Now to tell of Khun Chang. He awoke late and washed his face in a panic. "Servants! Come over here everybody. Oh, I've forgotten the betel for the episode.[56]

I've been a widower for many years, and there's nobody to do these things. Shaping animals from papaya has me stumped. Is there anybody here who can do it?[57]

If there's no one in our household, we'll have to go and find some carvers elsewhere." Nang Mueang spoke up, "Me. I can give it a try. I'll soon get the hang of it."

They purchased a Chinese basket of papaya, and in no time she sliced them all and carved them into shapes. At the top were folded banana leaves[58] and bunches of mulberry seeds.

In front was a carving of an abbot riding on an elder, novices in the middle, and then vultures eating a corpse. Amora[59] flowers were slotted in among them, mixed up with marigolds. It all looked very odd.

Khun Chang was delighted. In reward, he gave Nang Mueang a ring made of brass that was not so expensive but worth several fueang. She took it and put it on her finger.

He then ordered the servants to carry the offerings for the episode in a noisy procession along the road so people would see. "Be careful with the offerings.

If you drop or lose anything, I'll kick you along like a ball." The servants carried the offerings to Wat Palelai, yodeling as they went,

and set them down in rows before the main sala. Everybody milling around

---

56. The "betel" here means a bowl or tray which the sponsor of the episode offered while paying respect to the Buddha image in the hall used for the chanting, and later presented to the reciting monk. This tray contained pan leaves folded and inserted in a leaf pouch, whole betelnuts, candles, and incense. Sponsors showed off by adding other decorations, such as the carved figures mentioned below, to catch the eye. The tray was displayed outside the wat until the time of its episode, then carried inside and placed in front of the pulpit. The sponsor(s) sat at the front with the offering tray, and kept candles and incense lit throughout the episode. At the close, when the reciter descended from the lectern, the sponsor(s) presented the offering tray to him. (Anuman, *Prapheni kiao kap thesakan*, 298; SWC, 6:2682)

57. Figures or flowers carved in papaya, pumpkin, or similar materials had become a customary part of the offerings at the festival. The papaya would be raw and green, or just turning pink. The point of this passage is to show Khun Chang's crassness in flaunting his wealth without understanding the aesthetics.

58. บั้งใบ, *bang bai*, rows of neatly folded segments of banana leaf used in making *baisi, kratong*, and similar decorations.

59. รัก, *rak, Gluta usitata*, a tree which is a source of lacquer; renamed in this translation because the Thai word also means love, and poets make use of that association. These two flowers are very different and would not normally be used together in decoration.

there in a noisy crowd had to take a look.

Phim Philalai summoned the servants. "Make the betel
for the episode for me. Go and fetch betelnut, pan leaf,
and cotton."

They brought many papaya to slice and carve, added
color to make the figures bright and attractive, and set
up the whole display as a mountain range.

The carvings included a lion with a full face, standing looking majestic; Lord Brahma in a votive pose; Lord
Indra soaring through the air holding a crystal;

and Lord Narai mounted on Garuda,[60] swooping across
the sky. "Carry them along for everyone to appreciate."
The servants set off immediately,

Narai on Garuda

and put them on display at the sala. The lay faithful crowded around to
look. "Oh, they did everything and so beautifully!" "All that hard work was
certainly not wasted!"

"The animals look real, both the standing ones and the sitting ones."
"Outstanding! As neat as a painting." "They know how to carve!" The whole
preaching hall was full of loud praise.

As the hour approached, Khun Chang ordered his servants to take turns
carrying water to fill a big tub to the brim.

He bathed cheerfully. Servants crowded around scrubbing him until the
grime flowed away, then rubbed his body all over with turmeric.

But his skin was still as green as water hyacinth. "Quick, the *Great Forest*
episode is almost finished!" Back in his room, he dissolved whiteclay powder
in water and patted it all over his body, making a pattern on his belly.

He scooped up pomade, shaped his
hair like a wing, then swept it across
to hide his bald pate, but the middle
was still as bare as a buffalo's water-
hole.[61] "My head's a disaster! I'm
so ashamed."

He put on a yok in a pattern of
kanok and golden swans, like a

buffalo's water-hole

---

60. สุบรรณ, *suban*, Sanskrit Suparna, "well-winged" or "golden-feathered," a name for Garuda, the mythical bird that is the mount of Vishnu who is called Narai throughout the poem.

61. Farmers often make a water hole in their paddy fields for buffaloes to keep cool. The
animals' wallowing denudes the surrounding area, creating a bald patch.

royal garment that nobody else could possibly have. He added a woolen[62] waist
sash embroidered with flowers in gold, and a pink handkerchief to dab away
perspiration.

"Today, I'll dress to the hilt. I'll show off to Phim and make her smile." On
his little finger, he put a snake ring and a wasp-nest ring; on his index finger,
a diamond ring;

and on his wedding finger, a ring decorated with rubies. "Like this, Phim
is almost mine! This set of rings with five jewels belonged to my father. The
people of Suphan will quail before such a rich man!"

He crept over to look at himself in a big mirror. "Ugh! My head is as hor-
rid as a shithole. Yet a ghastly head can still belong to a gentleman. Servants!
Come here and take the mats.

About ten of you, come with me. But follow my arse and don't go off anywhere. Ai-Jit, carry the flask and the nak betel tray, and don't give yourself
airs and graces."

Khun Chang came down from the house, and strutted along with his head
in the air, nodding in greeting to bystanders. Before long he was bathed in
sweat like a butting buffalo.

At the main preaching hall, the lay elders were gathered in front. They made
way for Khun Chang to enter. His servants laid a reed mat, and Khun Chang
sat down, striking a dignified pose.

A group of friends came over to greet him and chat. Some of them had big
mouths and talked too much. "Oh Buddha,[63] why are you sweating like this?"

Khun Chang was offended and snapped his face away. "People should not
pass remarks." He looked around and called for pillows, pointing his hand,
"Hey you!"

He ordered his servants, "Pile up the offerings for the episode—all the taro,
potato, white sugarcane, red sugarcane, watermelon, pomelo, *maduk, mafai,*

---

62. ส่าน, *san,* from the Persian word *shal,* and possibly further back from Syriac, *sa'r,* which
is the origin of the English word shawl. *Shal* meant a patterned twill-woven fabric made from
spun wool using a technique similar to European tapestry weaving. Earlier the word applied to
rough, thick fabrics but later was mainly used for cloth made from fine goat hair, such as those
known now as cashmere or pashmina (Floor, *Persian Textile Industry,* 296–97, 314). In Siam,
the term seems to have acquired more broad meaning as a fine, expensive fabric, generally made
from wool or similar material. In modern Thai, the word means wool.

63. พุทโธ, *phuttho,* an exclamation of dismay, shortened from พระอรหัง สัมมาสัมพุทโธ, *phra-
orahang samma samputtho,* a Pali invocation of the Three Jewels, especially for chanting at
the point of death to make merit for the next life (Anuman, *Prapheni kiao kap chiwit kan tai,*
25–26).

chamot and wheel sweets, red sticky rice, touchstone sweets,[64] clam sweets,[65] and big melons. Put things in order outside the sala! Don't muddle things up!

Bring in the monks' robes and bowls, the mats, mattresses, seats, and cushions! And don't hide away the betel tray for the episode! Place it out in front of the salver with the triple robes."

Incense and votive candles were lit. A monk made the recitation. The lay elders and faithful lit candles and offered flowers in worship.

Phim said, "It's almost time for our episode. Let's get going, Mother." She hurried off to bathe and change her clothes.

She dissolved turmeric, briskly rubbed it all over her body, shaped her hairline,[66] put oil on her hair, and powdered her face so it glowed like the sheen of a gourd.

She polished her teeth with *chi* [67] so they glinted shiny jet black in the mirror, and put on a yok with a *kanok* pattern on red in a shimmering and eye-catching golden cross-branch design.

cross-branch design

She wore a soft inner sabai in pink, overlaid by an elegant ruby-colored cloth with gold stripes and brilliant embroidered flowers, bound to delight the men.

She added a diamond ring decorated with rubies, and a snake ring with a moving tongue on her little finger. "Come here, servants. Bring the nak betel set and the nielloware bowl."

The servants powdered themselves, got dressed, combed and oiled their hair,

---

64. หินฝนทอง, *hin fon thong*, a round sweet with a dimpled top filled with some grated coconut, named for similarity to a goldsmith's touchstone.

65. ครองแครง, *khrong khraeng*, flour paste shaped as cockleshells, then either cooked in coconut milk, or dusted with sugar and fried.

66. Fashion at the time was to part the hair in a line running horizontally around the head about the level of the hairline on the forehead. This might be emphasized by plucking or shaving, and using color. La Loubère described current hairstyles as follows: "both sexes wear it so short, that all round the Head it reaches only to the top of the Ears. . . . The young unmarried [women] wear it after a particular manner. They cut with Scissars very close to the Crown of the Head, and then all round they pull out a small Circle of Hair about the thickness of two Crown pieces, and underneath they let the rest of their Hair grow down almost to their shoulders" (*New Historical Relation*, 28; KP, 172).

67. ชี่, an old toothpaste made from ground charcoal and salt. The fashion of the time was to blacken teeth. "To blacken their Teeth, they do theron put some pieces of very sowre Lemon, which they hold on their Jaws or Lips for an hour, or more. They report that this softens the Teeth a little. They afterwards rub them with a Juice, which proceeds either from a certain Root, or from the *Coco*[nut] when they are burnt" (La Loubère, *New Historical Relation*, 24).

and trimmed their hairlines. When everything was ready, they assembled in front of the house in good time.

When Siprajan saw her daughter, she said, "I'm already grey-haired and past it. Why should I get dressed up? A Tani[68] yok and an uppercloth with gold flowers are enough."

Her daughter laughed out loud. "Mother dear, aren't you ashamed you'll seem out of place?" Siprajan looked at herself and cried, "Karma, karma!" She changed into a lowercloth in black check, and a *phakhaoma*[69] as uppercloth.

Siprajan led the way with Phim following, looking as beautiful as a court lady. The ranks of servants brought up the rear, carrying the offerings for the episode.

The preaching hall was bright with incense and candles. Siprajan and Phim laid out their mats, sat down, and happily prostrated to pay their respect.

The monk finished recitation of *The Children* episode. The baldheaded sponsor rushed to make his offerings while a music ensemble played.

Phim and Siprajan had their servants carry in the offerings for their episode—almsbowls, sidebags, articles for everyday use, salvers, triple robes, oranges, many other fruits,

and various sweets.[70] Everything was set out in rows with the betel for the episode in front. The music ensemble played louder.

Now to tell of the abbot. He summoned Novice Kaeo and said, "I've been sick for several days, and I'm not up to it. You give the *Matsi* recitation instead of me."

Novice Kaeo paid respect and rushed off in a flap. He grabbed *Matsi* and began reading. He memorized the words and practiced reciting in the style of his teacher until he had got it down pat.

He even committed the Pali verses and *junniyabot* accurately to memory.

---

68. ตานี, probably meaning Pattani, an important port and Malay Muslim kingdom midway down the eastern coast of the peninsula. Cloth from Pattani was popular in the late Ayutthaya era. Near Wat Lotchong at the northeast corner of Ayutthaya on the opposite bank, there was a settlement of Pattani people who wove and dyed silk and cotton cloth. Alternatively, this might mean ยันตานี, *yantani*, a word probably derived from the Persian *jamdani* or *jamdari* but this was a fine-quality cloth brocaded with gold that seems not to have been the case in this reference. (Maxwell, *Textiles*, 249; KLW, 180; Wibun, *Saranukrom pha*, 232; *Pha phim lai boran*, 83)

69. (ผ้า)ขาวม้า, *(pha)khaoma*; the word probably originated from a Persian term for a waist sash, and was adapted to sound Thai. Now it means a general-purpose cloth, often used like a shawl, or worn while bathing, but in this reference it appears to denote a cloth of high value.

70. ขนมนมเนย, *khanom nom noei*, "sweets, milk, butter," a stock phrase meaning sweets of many kinds, not necessarily made of those ingredients.

Then he called Novice On. "Come and carry
the text for me."[71]

text

Novice On agreed and went off to arrange
his colored chicken-skin uppercloth. Then he
paid respect to the texts, wrapped them up, and waited ready at the stairs.

robe worn in open style

It was evening. To give the recitation, Novice Kaeo
changed clothes, wearing a robe in open style clinging
tightly to his body. He went to pay respect to Master Mi.

Leaving the abbot's room, he made a prayer, enchanted
beeswax, and rubbed it on his lips.[72] With Novice On
carrying the text in front, he walked from the kuti to the
sala.

He sat at a lower level than the monks and composed
himself. His eyes slid sideways and saw Phim's soft face.
She glanced up and their eyes met. Shyly, she bowed her head and kept still.

Novice Phlai repeated a Beguiler[73] formula several times to join their hearts
and eyes by special power. The force of the mantra made Phim succumb and
drew her gaze irresistibly to his.

As their eyes met, he nodded to her with love and desire welling in his heart.
"Please come closer. The abbot is not coming. He's sick,
so he had me give the recitation. As patron of this episode, what do you say?"
Phim smiled and replied, "Whoever does it, it's the same to me.
I'm not saying whether master or novice is bad or good. As long as it follows
the Pali."[74] While speaking, she smiled, and met his eyes. Then she pushed the
betel tray to Saithong,[75]

---

71. The text, written on *bailan*, usually called "palm leaf" but actually fiber from the trunk of
the *lan* tree, would be treated with great respect, and always carried to the recitation in front of
the reciter to emphasize its greater importance.

72. He applied the enchanted beeswax to his lips to enhance the impact of his words on the
listeners. Beeswax was regularly used as a lip cosmetic, especially by people who ate betelnut,
both men and women. The cosmetic was made by combining beeswax with coconut oil or coconut milk and the petals of flowers such as jasmine (SWC, 2:639–40).

73. ละลวย, *laluai*, to puzzle or confuse, a well-known love mantra (PKW, 2:207).

74. A stock phrase meaning as long as it is accurate. The Mahachat, as other Jataka, is written
as being related by the Buddha himself, and thus the words are considered especially sacred.
To approximate this sacredness, any translation from the Pali must be absolutely faithful. This
phrase probably dates from a time when the reciting monk read from a Pali text and improvised
the Thai translation on the spot.

75. Saithong appears here with no explanation of who she is. Over the next few chapters, it
becomes clear she is someone who has been adopted into the family to serve as a companion
to Phim—part foster-sister, part maid. In chapter 3 we learn that Phim's mother redeemed her

who knelt and placed it as an offering. The novice went up to the pulpit, picked up the text, cradled it carefully in his hands, and read faultlessly from the *junniyabot*

up to the passage when Queen Matsi comes across a lion and tigers on her path; she keeps on begging to pass by until night falls and a moon shines brightly;[76]

she reaches the hermitage, and is chilled not to find her beloved children; sobbing with grief, she sets out to search for them.

The sound of "*Sathu!*"[77] rose from the audience in unison as all were inspired to devotion. Phim took off her ruby uppercloth,

folded it, paid respect three times, and joyfully laid it on the salver. She remained prostrate with hands clasped, offering prayers full of devotion.

"I salute the almighty power. I offer alms. May I have rank and servants into the future, and be rich and joyful in every way." She sat up and listened attentively.

Khun Chang watched her offer the cloth. "Oho! Even a woman can do that! If I sit here quietly, I'll lose face by comparison. People will gossip.

If[78] a woman can show devotion by offering a cloth, as a man I could do the same, especially as a rich man." Aroused by this thought,

he turned to look at Phim with a smile, and took off his embroidered upper-cloth, folded it, raised it above his head in clasped hands, and made a prayer.

"I salute the almighty power who has a heart of loving kindness. Please grant fulfillment to my mood of love, quickly, as my heart desires, within this evening, without fail."

He[79] placed his cloth beside the ruby one. "May I have Phim as my wife to entwine our hearts closely, before too long, within the evening of this day."

---

from slavery, and in chapter 6 that she is twenty-two, six years older than Phim.

76. To test Wetsandon, Indra transforms three deities into two tigers and a lion that block Matsi's return until it is too late for her to chase after the children. Matsi pleads with the animals but they wait until nightfall before relenting. Arriving back at the hermitage, Matsi is distraught to find the children missing. Wetsandon refuses to speak. She searches around all night in despair, returning to the hermitage at dawn. She collapses, and Wetsandon believes she has died. After a time, she recovers and Wetsandon tells her the truth, which she accepts. This is one of the most poignant and popular passages of the story.

77. สาธุ, a Pali word meaning "good" or "I approve," uttered to show appreciation during sermons, recitations, etc.

78. This stanza is taken from WK, 3:51; PD has: He spoke out: "*Sathu mothana!* Such deep devotion! Even though I'm not the patron of this episode, I feel moved to great piety."

79. This stanza is taken from WK, 3:81; PD has: He placed his cloth beside that of Phim. "May the ruby cloth not escape me. May it miraculously float this way, before too long, by the evening of this day."

Phim felt disgusted and gravely offended. She clicked her tongue, spat in shame, and ordered servants to pick up the salver.

I-Phrom and I-Bu understood their mistress's feelings. They walked straight over, lifted up the salver, and passed it over the head[80] of Khun Chang in the middle of the sala. Khun Chang stared angrily into their eyes.

Saithong cried out, "Hey, I-Phrom! The end of your cloth brushed the gentleman's head. Didn't you see? Your manners are so wretched! Let's go, Phim. Don't listen."

Phim strode out. "I'm so ashamed. Really and truly. Oh dear me. He's worse than a farmer's son but knows no better!" She returned straight home, cursing Khun Chang.

After Phim left, Novice Kaeo was love-struck and in turmoil. He skipped through the rest of the recitation, cutting it short.

Reaching the final verses of the episode, he brought the recitation to an end, and came straight down from the pulpit. They launched quickly into the *Powerful One*,[81] and continued until all thirteen episodes were complete.

The lay faithful, male and female, poured water onto the ground from cups and bowls, expressed their appreciation of the abbot, and left at the second watch.[82]

Deep in the night, a gentle wind blew and a brilliant moon shone. In the quiet stillness of Wat Palelai, the little novice could not get her out of his troubled mind.

For over half the night, he did nothing but mope and moan. "Oh my soft, fair Phim, after you left, did you think of me at all? Or did you forget me without any feeling?

What must I do to have you?" His mind would not stay still. He whimpered, "I love you so much I want to swallow you, Phim. All the millions of other women don't interest me at all.

If we can share a pillow, I'll sweep you up and enjoy you so there's no single night without love. What must I do, precious Phim, to talk a word or two with you?

I don't even know where you live. When I met you it was almost dark. I

---

80. The head, the highest part of the body, commands great respect. Passing the tray directly over the head, especially of such a local dignitary, would be considered very rude.

81. สักรบรรพ, Sakkarabap, meaning the chapter of the Powerful One, *sakra*, sometimes a name for Indra, and sometimes, a different deity.

82. สองยาม, *song yam*. The night is counted in three-hour watches, the first running from 6 to 9 p.m., the second from 9 p.m. to midnight, and the third from midnight to 3 a.m.

saw your face only in the middle of my recitation. That accursed Khun Chang messed things up.

You took the servants off home in a boiling rage, and I lost my composure and blundered through the reading, making many mistakes. Since you disappeared, I've suffered misery. Tomorrow morning I'll figure out the way.

Even if you're hidden away in some hill or valley, I'll find you wherever you are." The more he thought of her, the worse he became, urging the cock to mark the passing of the night.

He hugged Phim's ruby cloth, kissing it, stroking it, and inhaling its fragrance to bathe his heart, falling ever deeper into turmoil throughout the night until the first streaks of the sun.

Near dawn, while gentle Phim was sleeping soundly, she began to dream. She and Saithong were swimming briskly across some water;

in the shallows at the shore, her feet touched and she stood up; Saithong handed her a golden lotus flower; she inhaled its fragrance, awash with joy, wrapped it in her uppercloth, and made her way back across the water.

As the dream ended, she woke up. Missing the golden lotus, she groped around. "Oh what a pity! It's gone."

She promptly shook Saithong awake and told her the dream. "What's going to happen? Tell me what it means, please!"

Saithong knew the meaning of Phim's dream without a shadow of doubt. "I've been noticing things for some time. Don't be worried, eye's jewel.

Dreaming about having a lotus means you'll gain a partner in love. It seems this man isn't far away, and perhaps you'll get him very soon.

The fact that you dreamed I picked the lotus and handed it to you probably means you'll depend on me in the time ahead. If you get what you desire, please be kind enough to let me have some benefit too."

Phim cried out, "Oh Saithong! Why do you come up with this interpretation? Where did you see any hint of such a thing in the years we've been together?

Have you ever seen me all restless and irritable? Is that why you're teasing me? I may have dreamed of a golden lotus and it may still be there in my mind's eye but I don't accept this means a man for me.

In the dream it was you who picked the lotus. If the man goes straight for you, I'll laugh. Please give an interpretation more to my liking and you'll get a pot of silver or pot of gold."

☙

Thinking of Phim, Khun Chang could not sleep. He tossed and turned, pined and longed. "Oh my Phim Philalai!

When you shouted at me, it sounded so mellow, so crystal clear. You're so elegant with your slender waist. Among thousands of girls, there's none other the same.

You were wearing a ruby uppercloth trimmed with gold over your green inner sabai.[83] Your arm is shapely, and your bottom enchanting. Your eyes were beautiful when you glanced my way.

What must I do to hold you tight? I'll raise you above my head. I'll fondle and caress you all day long. I'll place food in your mouth to eat,

provide you with an elephant to ride so the earth cannot irritate your body, surround you with perfumes while you sleep, and make you a shower spray to bathe.

inner sabai

I love you as much as my own life but I worry I'm wasting my thoughts as they'll come to nothing. I fear you'll hate my ugly body. Even if you loved me, you'd worry about your reputation.

Stop thinking about it! Why fret now? Let's find out first whether things turn out well or badly. If you're free, I'll find some way to plead my case and soften you up."

He opened his mosquito net. "Is it dawn yet? Oh, the moon's still high in the sky. This is a sign that I'll find my beautiful Ketsuriyong[84] for sure!"

---

83. Her sabai was pink but this passage is painting Khun Chang as a buffoon.

84. The heroine in a story titled *Suwannahong*, the golden swan, that was popular in the court in late Ayutthaya, and was composed as an outer drama by Prince Phuwanetnarit (1801–1856), a poet and son of King Rama II. Ketsuriyong is the adopted daughter of the ruler of Mattang. The hero, Suwannahong, flies a kite that comes down in the palace at Mattang. He follows the string, meets Ketsuriyong, and makes love to her. (KW, 658; Nidhi, *Pen and Sail*, 49; Mattani, *Dance, Drama, and Theatre*, 84–86)

4: PHLAI KAEO MEETS PHIM IN A COTTON FIELD

Now to tell of Novice Kaeo. As golden rays lightened the sky, he thought longingly of gentle, lovely Phim. He washed his face and quickly put on his robe

in open style, with a belt fastened around his waist. All ready, he picked up his almsbowl and went out. He searched every lane, alley, and bush. Before long, he arrived in Suphan town

and came to the quarter of Maids Landing. As he walked, he glanced around discreetly. Seeing a bench set out for almsgiving but unattended, he paused, and stood composing himself and taking his bearings.

Gentle Phim was inside with Saithong preparing food for almsgiving. No monk had yet come.

Phim opened a window and saw a novice standing with eyes lowered. The ochre color of his close-fitting robe made his skin glow like moonlight.

The power of lore made Phim feel unsettled. She put on an uppercloth, picked up the bowl of alms, and descended the stairs with Saithong.

Opening the door with a creak, she stepped elegantly down. Novice Kaeo heard and raised his face. Little Phim glanced long enough for their eyes to meet, and realized it was him.

She ducked and hid behind Saithong. "Oh! I'm not going down. Seeing Novice Phlai's face makes me shy." She passed her bowl of rice to Saithong,

and hid behind a wall. Saithong walked forward, breaking into a smile. Novice Kaeo used his knowledge to blow a Great Beguiler mantra onto Phim,

making her tremble with passion and arousal. She stood smiling, hardly able to restrain herself from rushing down. Saithong put down the bowl of alms and raised her hands to wai the novice.

He unhitched the almsbowl from his shoulder. "I'm late because I've come a long way. There were rows of other houses offering alms but I hurried past them and came specially here.

I'm worried. At yesterday's recitation, the sponsor of the episode dashed off. Maybe she's angry with me. I'd like a chance to explain. I'd also like to talk to you."

Saithong placed food in his almsbowl and invited him to come to the house after taking his midday meal some time. Suppressing the disquiet in her heart, she returned up the stairs.

Novice Kaeo went outside the fence and hid in order to spy for beloved Phim. She showed her face and saw him far away outside the fence.

He hugged his bowl close as if it were something else. Phim smiled, hid her face, and disappeared. He walked off with a spring in his step, unable to get her out of his mind.

The farther he got from the house, the more his heart was bursting. He looked back over his shoulder again and again. "Later on, Saithong will be waiting." He hurried to Wat Palelai,

and went to offer some food from the almsbowl to his teacher. Then he crawled away to take off his uppercloth, and waited attentively on the abbot. After eating, he went back to his sleeping quarters and moped.

Watching Saithong linger after putting alms in the novice's bowl, Phim had become agitated. "Why is she taking so much time?"

She beckoned Saithong into the bedroom, and spilled out her suspicions in an urgent whisper. "What took you so long down there? I saw your mouth chattering away with him."

Saithong replied, "I didn't say anything. It's getting late. Let's eat. Afterwards we can relax and spin some cotton. In the afternoon I'll take you to bathe."

"Food isn't going to pacify me. If you don't tell, I'll keep bothering you all day. I saw you standing there, all smiles, and speaking together for a long time. Why won't you tell me?"

"There's nothing. Do you want me to make something up? If there were anything, I'd tell you so that you wouldn't feel upset with me. He just said that he'd come a long way to get here. That's all. Then he went back."

"Right. That's it. Don't tell me. I'll probably find out in time because these things don't stay hidden." She left the room in a huff and did not eat with Saithong.

They had their meal separately. Phim took a spinning wheel into a room and sat spinning with a group of servants until two o'clock

when each had made a spindle of thread. Saithong advised Phim to hurry up so they could go for a refreshing bathe in the afternoon. Phim said, "I don't want to go."

Saithong tried to calm her down and bring her round. "Let's go to the landing, I've something to tell you." "Don't kid me. Why would you tell me anything? You're determined to keep it all to yourself."

spinning wheel

"I'm hot. Don't sulk and spite me. You're refusing to go for a bathe just to show me you're displeased. What am I determined to keep to myself? Is that Novice Phlai making a pass at me?"

"I'm not going. Don't insist." "I shouldn't leave it until late in the afternoon." Saithong walked slowly and gracefully out of the room with all the servants in tow.

I-Tai, I-Phrom, I-Sompaen, and I-Taen followed Saithong to the landing where they dived, bathed, played hide and seek, and chased one another around.

As the sun slanted down in the afternoon, Novice Phlai could not get fair, gentle Phim out of his mind. He knew from Saithong

that she and Phim by now would have gone to bathe, and he decided to go there to meet them. He put on his robe in open style, crept down the stairway, and went to Suphan.

Reaching Phim's quarter, he went straight to the landing, and spied from the bushes. "These people are all servants. I don't understand."

Seeing Saithong washing herself on the riverbank, he threw some earth and coughed to get her attention. Saithong quickly came over, and they stole away to hide from the others.

In a good spot surrounded by bushes, they sat down in the shade of a big heartache tree with sprays of flowers blooming overhead.

Novice Kaeo said with a smile, "Please forgive me. Don't think I'm being too forward. This little novice has fallen in love and into utter confusion. I've had to put up with this torture for days.

I can't concentrate. I can't relax. I can't stop feeling agitated. It's important for me to come and see you. I want to put my life in your hands.

I'm like a rabbit that wants to enjoy the moon. He's stuck on the ground because he can't fly. What he wants is so far away in the sky, he pines and mopes until his body wastes away.

Only Lord Indra can put him out of his misery by letting him romp with the heavenly rabbit in the moon. Little Phim is like the rabbit in the moon. Saithong is like Indra.[1]

---

1. The pattern on the moon is seen as a rabbit. In the Sasa Jataka a monkey, otter, jackal, and rabbit all resolve to perform an act of charity on a fasting day, believing the most generous act would earn a great reward. When an old man begged for food, the monkey gathered fruits from the trees, the otter found dead fish from a riverbank, and the jackal wrongfully pilfered a lizard and a pot of milk-curd from somebody's house. The rabbit was only able to gather grass, and therefore offered its own body instead, throwing itself into a fire that the man built. But the rabbit was not burned. The old man revealed himself as the god Sakra (Pali Sakka, sometimes

I'm counting on you. Don't let me down. Maybe two rabbits can taste the joys of heaven together. If you're kind, I'll
be enormously grateful for as long as I still have life.

Please help. Please make me happy. Get me out of this
darkness and gloom. Bring me back to life. Save me from
dashing to an early death. I'm not using words lightly.

rabbit in the moon

I'll help and support you from today until you die. I'll
always remember what I'm saying here. Once I decide something, I don't forget, and I never go back on my word."

Saithong turned her face away and said, "I'm not listening to this, Kaeo.
You'll get my back striped.[2] I've never acted as a go-between before. All your
hopes will be in vain.

The authorities[3] are terrible. If we put a foot wrong, the scandal will be as
loud as the troops in a mask play.[4] If I plead your case but she doesn't soften
up, I'll be putting myself at risk needlessly.

She'll shout at me, and I'll get my back caned, while you'll be dancing outside the curtain.[5] I shouldn't do it. I won't do it and suffer the consequences.
I'm not the person you should be asking, Novice Phlai.

Be a bit considerate to me. You talk as if Phim will play along so easily. Be
kind and don't make me ashamed. I'm dying and you're the murderer.

All that stuff about little Phim being like a rabbit in heaven is very clever. You
talk loads about relying on me. But I've never seen two rabbits in the moon.

If Indra went to the aid of a miserable rabbit, he'd be found at fault all over
the world. And the moon would be tarnished by the romping. I'm too scared,
Novice. Don't try to persuade me.

I won't get the meat to eat or the skin to sit on, only the bones hung around

---

confused with Indra), and drew a picture of the rabbit on the moon to be visible to all. This
story is retold in many places, including the Grimm Brothers tales and the Japanese collection,
Konjaku Monogatarishu. The Chinese, Hottentots in South Africa, and Tezcucans in Mexico
also have stories about a rabbit in the moon (en.wikipedia.org/wiki/moon_rabbit).

2. The Law on Marriage clause 89 specifies: "If anyone acts as a go-between without the parents' knowledge . . . the go-between shall be caned with a rattan for greedily taking a reward that
caused the woman to be despoiled" (KTS, 2:257–58; see also clauses 4 and 21).

3. ท่านเจ้าขุนมูลนาย, *than jaokhun munnai*, the nobles and overseers, the technical term for
those in charge of marshalling groups of phrai for labor service (see p. 7, note 42).

4. เขน, *khen*, the ordinary soldiers in a mask-play performance, who typically stand legs
akimbo, raising and stamping each leg in turn.

5. A stock phrase associated with the mask play mentioned in the previous stanza. Playing
"inside the curtain" means on the stage and thus subject to the scrutiny and criticism of the
audience, while "outside the curtain" is beyond such scrutiny.

my neck.[6] If you get Phim, you'll be all smiles. But it's me who'll suffer the shouting and the shame.

It's like killing a snake but not getting to eat snake curry because some hawk or crow swoops down and snatches it away. From now on, stop thinking and hoping. This is not something you nibble. One bite and you die."

"What a pity you have no sympathy. Every day I do nothing but pine and pray. My love for her isn't about to wane. You're abandoning me halfway.

But when a banana flower is picked, it still hangs on by a thread of stalk.[7] I'm relying on you so please do something. If I get Phim to love, would I abandon you? It's like broadcasting rice.

Even if the rain doesn't fall and the river runs dry, it's not a complete waste. You may not get rice to eat but you give alms to the birds.

If you do me a favor, and I then come to live in your house, the favor won't have been for nothing. I'll repay you before long. I'll share everything with you on par with the fair and lovely Phim.

Money, food, and everything else, I'll share half-half. Be kind to me, Saithong. Please persuade her. When I've got Phim, I'll bring you a reward.

One chang for Saithong. I won't bargain for even one fueang less. This evening, you must talk to her. I'll wait to hear at almsround tomorrow."

"Are you really in love or just pretending? One chang seems a bit heavy. I'm afraid that once you have her, this reward will vanish, and no amount of shouting and demanding will have any effect.

If you're really sincere in what you're saying, Novice Kaeo, you have to be ready to pay up on delivery. Keep your word faithfully. Tomorrow, come for the news."

Novice Kaeo listened to her words. He took his leave and went back to the wat. Saithong returned home with a throng of servants trailing behind.

After the sun had set, a white, haloed moon floated across the heavens, shining as bright as daytime.

Saithong invited Phim to view it. "Tonight the surface of the moon is so brilliant—dazzlingly beautiful like pure silver. Why does the moon care so much for the rabbit that it keeps her there?

She won't go anywhere in a hundred years. Why is she imprisoned up there?

---

6. An old proverbial saying meaning, "to do a work that yields no profit and leaves only a burden of troubles as reward" (Gerini, "On Siamese Proverbs," 218).

7. The trunk and stems of a banana are so fibrous that, when broken, some strands of fiber are left connecting the two pieces. This proverbial saying means that nothing is completely final.

Since we saw her, I don't know how many thousand days have passed. Looking at the moon makes me scared.

It's like us two sisters, stuck like the rabbit in the moon, having no partner. She stays in the sky without going anywhere, but the rabbit in the forest gazes at her all the time.

I've loved you and brought you up with care. Now you've grown up to be big and bold. Because your parents redeemed me, I'm like both a relative and a slave. I'm afraid of punishment, afraid of shame, protective of myself.

It's a pity to go through a whole life without knowing what it is to have a husband and children—like a brilliant, unblemished gold ring that lacks only a crowning gem.

I can accept the hardship because I love you. If I didn't, I'd probably have gone off roaming all over the place, maybe got myself arrested, or killed, or else survived unscathed. That's the way things go.

All this trouble is because of you, because you haven't made your own household yet and I have to continue looking after you. The fate of parents is to get older every day.

Like trees on a riverbank they'll fall down. I mention this because I'm worried what will happen if our mother, Siprajan, passes away. Everything will come apart.

Young men will sneer that this girl has no father or mother. I think about this day and night, and it sorrows me. What do you think should be done?

If you get married while your mother is still alive, then she'll see the wealthy line continue unbroken. How many years do people live? What do you think about what I'm saying?"

Phim listened without wavering in the least. She answered the arguments of her companion. "I don't think about this at all, Saithong.

As a woman it's normal that a man will come to ask for our hand, for better or worse. A mother makes every effort to bring up her daughter with the aim of setting her up in a household.

Well, we're said to be gentlefolk. Mother is wealthy enough for her children not to be ashamed with the neighbors. It would be disobedient to do something hasty without Mother's consent, and it would bring shame on her.

If it turns out Mother dies before I'm married, that's fortune. Doing anything hasty without her would be improper. It's not as if I don't have men to pursue me.

If you're ugly, cancerous, leprous, or just no match for your friends, there won't be any suitors. But if you're good-looking and have money, they queue up to come after you.

Fruits are raw before they become ripe. It's better to avoid the sour and wait to enjoy the sweet.[8] Meanwhile just powder the face to look pretty. Why are you so impatient that you question me all the time?

A big worry is like a fire in your breast. If you cover it up, it shows in your face. Had I a craving just like hunger, your words would be fitting.

Admiring the moon together is relaxing, but your saying such things is unsettling me. If you'd love my fair face to stay fair, don't fret me with such words. I don't like it."

"Now, who's harassing you to have a husband? I'm thinking of you, not acting as a go-between. In the past I've never been impatient. Have I said anything about this before?

You're yawning. Why not go to sleep." She took Phim's hand, led her inside, hugged and fanned her. "Go to sleep. I'll sing you a lullaby.

Oh, have pity on the poor young boy
why does he roam like a vagabond
trying to forget that he fell in love
now far from home, from everything fond

hopes dashed, love was not what he thought
wishing for a sweetheart, finding only heartbreak
so he runs away to wear the robe
ordained but tortured, weary with heartache

the wat and her home are so far apart
so far away yet he goes to seek alms
sees her, returns to his lonely cell
thinking of nothing but her tender charms

the sad little novice comes after noon
hides at the landing, pines and mopes
no one to talk with, no one to share
came such a distance, with only his hopes

wasting away with love's dire grief
how long must he suffer enough to die
Oh gentle Phim, go to sleep, go to sleep
La la, la la la, dear Novice Phlai

---

8. Both these sentences are proverbs warning against impatience.

Are you asleep? Then I can get some sleep too." As she sang, Saithong fanned Phim, and spread her arms to hug her, smiling sweetly.

"Oh Saithong, you put the novice into my lullaby. When you went down to give alms, did you fall for him?

When I asked you this morning, you wouldn't reply. I didn't see it then but now it's clear. You met him again when you went bathing and hit it off. Did you come back later than usual because you floated downstream?

Don't sleep near me. Go outside the mosquito net. I'm too lazy to interpret your dreams before dawn. You're going to get mixed up about today. You'll scare me by talking in your sleep and hugging me."

Saithong listened with her face drawn. "Lightning strike! How come it turned out this way? Really hateful of me. I made a mistake. Now I'll tell you the whole story.

When I went to bathe today, Novice Kaeo came and hid in the pussbosom bushes at the back. I angrily told him he was hateful, and asked whether he'd come to make fun of us.

Even if I didn't tell you earlier, I don't regret it. I met him by chance. I've got nothing against him. But while I was giving him alms, something was strange. He was talking away with me but his eyes were somewhere else.

His mouth was smiling at me but he was only pretending to look at me. Even while giving the recitation, he was still making eyes. I can't look into his face.

Really, it's true. When I met those sharp eyes, it quite took my breath away. I'm grown-up but it made me feel shy. He's a smart fellow.

He said to me, 'The other lady won't greet me. Maybe it's because I'm poor and down on my luck. When we were both tiny, we were playmates and saw each other a lot.

But because of troubles, I had to leave our home in Suphan. She should at least say a few words in greeting. These days, I'm at a loss. I can't hide it. My home was a long way from her, a night's travel.

If it hadn't been necessary, I wouldn't have made the effort to come. In Kanburi there are wat all over the place. But I couldn't stay there like a cock evading a trap. I made the effort because of love.

I feel so hurt I have to talk about it. Was it right for her not to acknowledge me? I can't bear it so I'm barging in to greet you. If you rebuff me, then never mind.

Your mother, Siprajan, is good friends with my mother, Thong Prasi. That's well known for better or worse. So please be kind to this poor novice Kaeo."

Even if you don't accept this business of love, he begged to see your face and talk, just once. He asked me to plead with you to consent. He's risking his merit to create something important.

On the day of the recitation, he felt he saw a sign. In his own heart, he was absolutely certain that he could fly in the air, walk on the clouds, pick up the stars,

and swallow them. He woke up with his mouth still full of them. He thought this meant his wish would be fulfilled. So he blundered off on almsround, desperate to find how things would turn out, for better or worse.

He set out at first light to get here. He asked me to plead with you. I tried to put him off several times but he kept on at me to persuade you.

I was at a loss. I didn't know what to think. But after some reflection, it made sense. If he were fooling around and playing tricks, why would he trek from Kanburi to Suphan?

On the day of the recitation, he saw a sign. Luckily it inspired you to dream too. That means you could be a happy couple, for sure. Don't have doubt and suspicion."

As she listened, Phim was falling into the trap and setting her heart on love. Since her eyes had met those of Novice Kaeo, she had felt as if her body were attached to him by a diamond bolt.[9]

Even without Saithong's attempts at persuasion, her mind was already bent on love with no wish to escape. The novice had been in her thoughts day and night, and Saithong's words pleased her.

Yet feminine instinct made her dissemble. She kept her feelings inside, put on a sullen face, and left a long pause before turning to reply.

"I thank you from the bottom of my heart, dear Saithong. You have always loved me and protected me. You carried me around so I didn't have to touch the dust. You taught me everything so considerately—

how to sit, stand, sleep—everything, even how *not* to look at anything while walking. Now that there's someone after me, you're there to be my protector. I can put my life in your hands.

But why are you offering me the novice on a plate? Whether it will be for better or worse, it's tempting. Or are you scheming something together?

You and Novice Kaeo have hit it off, isn't that so? That's how I became involved. What you two get up to doesn't bother me, but why are you leading me to dream?

It's not as if every other man in the world has died. People will sneer and gossip about me all over Suphanburi. I won't know where to hide my face.

---

9. See p. 318, note 12.

You're in love with him so let it be you alone. I'll help you cover it up. I'll keep the knowledge to myself. Don't doubt me, Saithong."

"Oh what a pity, dear Phim. You're really thumping me around. I feel bruised all over. You've never made fun of me like this before. Dear me, with this lad, younger than me, the novice?

Am I a slave who wants to be on par with her mistress? I know the difference between salt and *phimsen*.[10] Do you think the novice doesn't know that too? Why would he plunge into mud? Even if I put myself on offer, I'm poor,

and my body is all wrinkles. I'm like this lead ring—no use as the setting for a diamond. Fortune doesn't favor me. If I'm fired up over this, it's because I love you.

I can see you looking down in the mouth. I can sympathize and I can't stay quiet. If there's no point, why prolong the matter? Enough! I won't discuss it any further.

Remember your dream? You got a golden lotus because of me. If I take offense and don't help you, let's see if this doesn't end in tears.

In the future, you can consult me about this. I won't go and tell your mother. I'll leave you in torture for a bit, until swallowing rice is like taking medicine—it brings tears to your eyes.

For better or worse, I've been in hot water before. I cradled you from childhood to teenage. Things don't remain hidden so it'll all come out in time. If there's not a scandal, then I'm not Saithong."

"Ha, ha! Really funny, big sister. Don't go on. I'll give in to you readily, make no objection. But you're covering things up. Though there's nothing wrong, I can make accusations so Mother beats you.

Now. How many chang has he offered as reward for you to stick your neck out and be so insistent? Do you truly think the novice is good? Where did you get such assurance

that you believe it body and soul? Did he really promise not to abandon me, and so you undertook to come and talk with me? In the future I may get badly hurt.

Should I be spoiled just because I fear you'll be angry? When I look at this care-

10. พิมเสน, *Pogestemon patchouli*, borneol, Barus camphor, a crystallized herb used like smelling salts. It is much more expensive than salt, hence an old Thai saying for a foolish bargain, "like bartering phimsen for salt." The saying appears in the Ayutthaya chronicles, around 1590: "King of Hongsawadi asked his generals, 'King Naresuan's coming forth and acting like a soldier in this fashion is comparable to bringing patchouli to trade for salt'" (RCA, 120; Gerini, "On Siamese Proverbs," 174).

fully, I don't see the point. If I trust in Novice Kaeo's word, I'll end up shamed. The more I think about it, the more worried and wary I am.

If he goes back on his word and abandons me, what can I do to you, Saithong? Best to go slowly, think carefully before anything happens, and ask questions to winkle out whether he's serious.

If he's true to his word, he must send a betel tray to ask for my hand.[11] If he just wants to be my lover, I fear it'll end badly. We're born for only one life. If I make a careless mistake, I'm done for."

betel tray

"Oh Phim, my dear gentle sister, don't be afraid. I'm not like that. Why are you worried and reproachful? You are Saithong's best beloved.

If he weren't good, would I drag you into spoiling yourself and being tarnished, eye's jewel? I think he's a perfect match for you in status and beauty, my golden Phim. You should be a couple.

Comparing you in rank, both are esteemed. Comparing you in wealth, both are equal. The scales are evenly balanced in all ways.

In looks, you're both lovely—young, bright-faced, like the sun nestling beside the moon. If you marry, I'll earn merit.

I'll admire you sitting or lying, every night and day. I'll arrange a soul ceremony for you two soulmates. I'll have you sit beside each other on a golden bed, and fan you when it's hot.

My job will be to furnish and decorate your home. Mattresses and pillows kept neatly on a bed. Folding panels to act as screens.

A fine, silky-looking mosquito net trimmed with gold, beautiful and neat, hung with flower tassels and garlands. The spittoon and betel tray set out in a row.

A cosmetic set in gold, decorated with gems and glittering little mirrors. I'll depend on your merit. I'll eat and sleep happily without a care.

Don't be hesitant. You two should be a couple. Be agreeable, not suspicious. I'll cushion you like a pair of shoes. That I promise, darling Phim.

If Novice Kaeo doesn't keep his word and things turn out dif-

flower tassel

---

11. ขันหมาก, *khan mak*, a proposal of marriage. An emissary is sent with two containers, one containing eight betelnuts and an even number of pan leaves, the other with money and various auspicious objects. Accepting the gift signals acceptance of the proposal. The containers are usually large, round, footed trays.

ferently, you wouldn't want me around. You'd shout at me, beat me, and send me off to the kitchen

to carry water and pound rice day in, day out. You'd drive me hard and never give me a break so I'd feel my body was chopped into pieces. If I led you astray, why would you keep me?

At dawn, Novice Kaeo will come to beg alms. Dearest, come down to offer them with me. I'll make arrangements with him to meet you in the fields and make matters clear.

When he's talked with you for just a little while, you can accept his love in your heart for certain. Or else you can put your nose in the air every day, and take fright at any man's approach,

then the burden will fall on your servant again, and see if I don't complain. Go to sleep, my eye's jewel. It's late. Let me give you a hug."

She stroked and soothed Phim to sleep, repeating the novice's name over and over until Phim gave in to her cajoling. As the moon slipped across the sky and slid from sight, they fell asleep.

Dawn brightened the sky and bathed the whole earth in gentle early sunlight. Birds twittered, and took flight.

The wind wafted a soft golden dust of fragrant pollen, suffused with refreshing scents. Novice Kaeo's thoughts harkened back to Phim.

"If I sit around, the sun will get too bright." He got up, came to a window, washed his face, put on his robes in open style, and descended the stairway.

Arriving at Phim's house, he composed himself, and intoned a mantra in his mind in the hope it would make her come down.

Phim and Saithong were in the house preparing food, tobacco, betelnut, pan leaf, and medicine to place in the novice's almsbowl.

Fearing their mother would see, they wrapped these things and hid them under the bowl. "Why is Novice Kaeo slower than the other day?" Phim opened the window and saw him.

She hid and nudged Saithong. "Look. The little novice is as composed as an abbot. I'm not going. I'm scared." They smiled and giggled together.

Saithong prompted her to go down. Phim cradled the bowl, hid behind Saithong's back, and timidly stepped down the stairway.

She crouched, set down the bowl, and paid respect, unable to look at his face. In a fit of nerves, she almost overturned the bowl. Then she put tobacco, fish, betelnut, and pan leaf into his almsbowl, all mixed up.

With face bowed and heart thumping, she went back up the stairway to the hall and sat hiding behind a door. Saithong glanced around to check there was nobody nearby,

then whispered to the novice, "After the forenoon meal, early in the afternoon, I'll bring darling Phim out to the cotton field. Hurry back to the wat and then come again. Where is it, novice? Give me the money."

Novice Kaeo smiled and replied, "I haven't forgotten the agreement we discussed. If the cotton field is a success, I'll reward you.

If I get her but don't give it to you, you can create an uproar at my kuti. I've been ordained to study and gain merit. I observe the precepts and I won't go against my word.

Allow me to take leave. I'll come around to the field in the early afternoon." Saithong crept away, glancing around warily. Novice Kaeo went to Wat Palelai.

Phim and Saithong had their meal in a very cheerful mood. Then they went to talk with their mother.

"Today I'm going to the north field. The cotton bolls have burst and a lot have been scattered around and wasted. I want to take a look with my own eyes. I don't trust the servants.

They steal and sell to buy food and gamble, the whole lot of them. I saw it with my own eyes just recently. I tell them off but it's no use."

Siprajan scolded the servants and all their forebears. "Those thieves have stolen too much from me. You hurry off and look, Phim.

If you catch them, beat them with a big stick so they cry out like a Jek pork vendor. It has come to my ears many times that those tricksters not only steal but gossip about me too."

Phim shouted to summon all the servants, who arrived in a rabble, hoisted wicker baskets, and jostled one another descending the stairway.

Phim and Saithong went down from the house and hastened to the field with the throng of servants in tow.[12]

They halted and sat down by a big bushy *krathum*. "We'll stay here. You lot go off. Don't laze around and play about. Do a proper job, and come back here at four o'clock."

wicker basket

---

12. By local legend, this cotton field was located near the current site of the Suphanburi city pillar. The road leading past the city pillar is now called Cotton Field Road.

I-Mao-Tao-Hap, I-Phlap-Thet, I-Tan-Pret, and I-Khwai[13] picked up their baskets and carried them off. Once far from their mistress's eyes, they sang wild chicken songs while picking the cotton.

After the forenoon meal, Novice Kaeo slipped away downstairs, slung some clothes in a bundle on his shoulder, and cut across to the preaching hall in a merry mood.

He spoke to Monk Mi. "I'm running away from the abbot. Please allow me to disrobe, and re-ordain me when I come back."[14]

The monk complied. "Off you go. Bring me back some betelnut and tobacco." Novice Kaeo prostrated, took his leave of the monk, and disrobed.

He grabbed his lay clothes, shook them out, and put them on. Setting off at a fast pace, he soon reached the field.

He hid in the bushes, peering out until he saw Saithong, and greeted her with a friendly smile. "Have you been here long?"

Saithong glanced up to see him standing a little way off, no longer in his robes. She smiled softly and said, "We came after the morning meal and have been waiting a while.

I looked around but couldn't see you, so I'd almost concluded you wouldn't come. Then I heard a rustle and thump in the bushes. If you'd arrived just a bit later, we'd have missed one another.

You can't stay here by the path. Go and hide over there. That *krathum* with the low-hanging leaves is suitable. I'll bring Phim to talk with you."

Saithong crept away and disappeared from sight. Peering ahead of him, Phlai Kaeo made for the leafy tree.

Near the place, he detoured to avoid some thorns, and crept through a gap in the thick foliage, coming upon his darling Phim.

She was sitting plaiting a flower garland. Her whole body seemed to bloom. She looked like a beautiful angel dancing gracefully on air.

Love surged in his chest, and he wanted to greet her, but was nervous because he had never done this before. Thinking what to say made his mouth tremble and his heart shrink. He moved his lips but was overcome with nerves.

---

13. Miss Box-Turtle, Miss Persimmon, Miss Tall Sugar Palm, Miss Buffalo, and (later on their return) Miss Banana Flower. These names, different in sound and meaning from those of the servants who accompany them to the bathing, seem designed to identify them as the agricultural crew.

14. The procedures to disrobe and be re-ordained require only simple verbal formulas, and can be performed by any monk in the wat. The disincentive of disrobing temporarily for a regular monk is that his seniority in the monkhood counts from his last ordination.

Love triumphed over fear. He moved gingerly to sit near her, and greeted her with a smile. She started, and her body stiffened with shyness.

"Did you come from home a long time ago? It's a pity you have to come for the cotton picking. You have masses of servants. It's a burden to have to follow along with them.

I fear the strong wind and fierce sun will spoil your fair face. You must be stiff and weary from walking. How good of you to make all this effort.

I followed you here because I love you. Did Saithong tell you that? Since the day of the recitation, I've been missing you and moping without any relief.

At night my eyes are awake through all four watches. I feel a fire is licking after me, and I can't escape. I'm sick with desolation and yearning. How is it with you?"

Phim's chest shook with shock and consternation. She turned her face away, shy and dumbfounded. She had never had such a conversation.

She shifted farther apart. Her face trembled. She glanced this way and that without meeting his eyes. She spoke not a single word.

"What's this, my eye's jewel? You don't say anything. Are you cross? Have you forgotten, my beauty? Please think back to the past.

When we were little children, we played together in all sorts of ways, and loved each other very much. Remember playing 'bridal house'? I took you and ran away from Khun Chang.

He followed, picked a fight with me, and hit you by mistake so you cried. Why are you shy with me now? Please say just a couple of words in friendship.

It's a waste of effort to hope Saithong could convey my message to you. Why are you afraid? I won't do anything rough to hurt you, believe me."

Phim knew that Phlai Kaeo's words about the past were all true. She turned to look at his face.

Because they had once been close neighbors, the sound of his voice came back to her. Her fear receded and her trembling heart calmed. She replied, "Honestly, I'd forgotten you,

though I recognized you on the day of the recitation. But I'm a woman. I couldn't greet you first. That doesn't mean I dislike you. I'm just worried that people will gossip.

I know you complained to Saithong that I didn't greet you. Were you so angry that now you want to complain to my face? Look, why have you disrobed? What brings you through the forest to our field?

Have you finished your study and disrobed to go home? Or have you fallen in love with Saithong? Look for her over there, by the big *matong* tree."

After listening, Phlai Kaeo replied, "I came here for a reason. I ran away from the abbot because I knew you would come here.

If I go back and get found out, I'm not concerned, not afraid of being punished. Let me tell you the whole story, from then until now, clearly and honestly.

Some merit made me think of looking for you, and then I couldn't stay with my mother. I was unhappy, incredibly unhappy, like being burned by a blazing bonfire.

I had the idea of leaving my mother and being ordained. As quick as I could, I moved away to another wat. It's a long way to Suphan, at least a night's travel. I had to make the journey on my own.

I met Phim, but no smile, no greeting, so I became even more unhappy. I ran into Saithong and that gave me a channel, so I sent a message to my eye's jewel to ease my heart.

We came face to face when you gave alms, but you were still very nervous and wouldn't greet me. Today we meet with nobody around. I want to offer my love to gentle Phim.

I'm not spinning a story to get my way. In truth my mind's made up a million times over. Let me be your partner and cherish you. This isn't a passion that will pass once we part."

"It's a pity you talk like all the others. You see the face of an old playmate, and show no restraint. The way you're going will ruin any friendship. If I object, you'll take offense.

Because we're old friends you believe you can snag me as a lover. I don't know what I should think. You seem to imagine we've been in love forever. You're fantasizing, no doubt about it.

It's not proper, and I forbid it, Phlai Kaeo. This time let it go but don't do it again. We've been sitting too long. The servants will come back. I'll say goodbye." She stood up immediately.

Phlai Kaeo got up and calmly tried to pacify her. "Your coolness is based on a misunderstanding. Please think again, sit down, and don't rush off. I'm not making things up to seduce you.

I'm deeply in love and I'm terribly miserable. I feel there's a great mountain weighing on my chest. I've prayed to Brahma, Indra, the moon, the whole lot of them, everything in the heavens.

If they don't turn to give me some help, I'll surely die. I've got no thoughts for anyone except you, my gentle heartmate. You alone can ease the burden."

"You speak eloquently, pouring out your heart. If I were naïve, I'd be carried away by your words. Such pleading can befuddle someone. You thought out what you were going to say here, didn't you?

This is just the beginning of love, and you can already die for it. You're telling me you'll never desert me until your dying day. You braved the forest because of love. You live in constant melancholy.

Human beings are too full of greed. We shouldn't be led by desire. It's like with food, there's never enough. We always have to find something else, salty or sour,

boiled, curried, fried, grilled, raw, or cooked—any and every way. We get tired of anything we eat too often.

Just think. You yourself couldn't bear eating one thing alone. Lovemaking is thrilling. When a love is brand new, you want to entrust your lives to each other.

It's the same with the clothes we wear. We like something newly bought because it looks splendid. If times are hard, we have to wear the same thing, day in, day out.

Then when we get something new for a change, we put it on and strut around. This new cloth makes us feel good, and we wear it to show off all the time.

That love meant to be eternal is the same. Once it's old, you can't drag yourself to look at it. If you do look, you turn away every time. It's become like an old cloth used for bathing.

Wash and wash, bash and bash, until it's shreds, rags for wiping, nothing left. Even sewing the bits together wouldn't make the fabric as it was before.

In the same way, a man and a woman say they'll die together, but how long does that feeling last? Tongue and teeth are together all the time but sometimes they get in each other's way.

You've come to pour out your heart. You're talking in the hope I'll soften up. I think I do care for you a little so I won't reject your feelings completely.

Go to my mother and ask for my hand. If she's kind enough to fall in with your intentions, I'll consent without any objection. If another man asked for me,

and Mother gave me over to him but he wasn't to my liking, I'd tell her to kill me rather than force me against my will. I wouldn't beg for mercy.

If you ask my mother and she agrees, I'll be happy to have you as husband. But chasing after me to be your lover frightens me. People will gossip about our wrongdoing, and I won't be happy with that.

You've come after me because of love. I know that clearly now. So why waste time carrying on this conversation?

Another thing, the servants will see us, and weave a story to repeat in the future. When it suits you, on whatever day, come and ask for my hand in the proper way.

The sun is going down, and evening is approaching. Please return to the wat and I'll go home. Don't delay until evening comes, or I'll be annoyed. If you have any further fantasies, I'll be shamed."

"What a pity, my eye's jewel. Why rush to chase me away so easily? I love you enough to beat myself to death. The only reason I didn't do it today was because I was meeting you.

To go away until I can come and ask for your hand, still not knowing whether we'll be a couple—and what if your mother doesn't consent?—every day apart from you I'll fade from your memory.

With days passing and so many other diversions, you'll forget me, my beauty. Were we to run into each other in the middle of a road, things would be different and you'd probably be irritated.

If you've definitely decided to love me, don't run away from it. Let me entrust my heart to you. Please be merciful. Just this once, don't be stubborn.

You made a comparison about the human heart—that desire is limitless, just like our hunger for different kinds of food is endless. That's the nature of people in general.

It's a bit of this and a bit of that that makes the taste delicious. But take the example of rice. It's always there—like passion's turmoil, the impatience inflamed by love.

An old cloth, already sadly the worse for wear, shouldn't be washed again and again until it's threadbare and torn. Take an attractive golden yok, worth cherishing, not just something with a peeled-lotus and sesame-seed pattern.[15]

Such a cloth is not easy to make. Before it can be worn, a lot of money and effort has been spent. Even when it's old, we try to take care of it for lasting enjoyment.

We store it carefully in a fragrant chest.[16] When there's a suitable occasion

---

15. ตาบัวปอกและเมล็ดงา, *ta bua pok lae malet nga; ta bua pok* was a printed cloth with a square pattern, popular in the court; *malet nga*, sesame seed, was an intricate flower pattern on dark cloth. This cloth was imported from India but also brought to the city by cart traders from Khorat. (SWC, 8:3769; KLW, 177)

16. Clothes were kept in chests and impregnated with fragrance by interleaving the clothes with flowers or, because the moisture in flowers could cause mold, with pieces of cloth steeped in floral water and then dried (*Kan taeng kai thai*, 235–36).

like a big festival, we take it out and unfold it so the cloth can be admired, and the fragrance is pleasing too.

Even though we have many other new cloths, we don't treat them with the same care. Let me say goodbye. It's nearly evening. I won't force you even though I'm reluctant to be parted from you."

He stroked and kissed the end of her sabai. "Let me enjoy this a bit. Don't be upset. It's very pretty, and suits your fair complexion. Did you weave it yourself or buy it somewhere?"

She tugged the sabai away from him. "Don't waste your praise. Mother gave it to me. You're acting like a bully with no consideration. What is this, Kaeo? It's not proper.

You love me and want some result. Because we're in the middle of nowhere, are you going to force yourself on me? You don't want to marry so you'll risk creating a scandal. You're selfish and in too much of a hurry.

If you get your satisfaction by making me miserable, then you won't find love. I might very well lose out to you, Kaeo, but don't fool yourself you'll get me this way.

It's like being so hungry that you eat uncooked rice even though it's still hard and not tasty at all. Please drop it. If you insist on annoying me, we're finished."

"Gentle Phim, have a care. You're cutting off my love at the first try. Please calm down and stop accusing me." He kissed her, saying, "Don't take offense, precious.

I love you honestly with a heart of love. I'm not forcing myself on you." With passion rising at the thought of parting, he pushed her hand away and pulled the end of the sabai.

"Stop punishing me, please, for merit's sake. Don't be so angry and protective. Your breast curves beautifully like molten silver. Let me caress you a little. Don't take offense."

He embraced her and lifted her onto his lap. "Why are you pushing and trying to slip away?" He tried to peel away her uppercloth but she hung on with a firm grip.

"It's a pity you don't listen. Are you going to kill me here in this field? Making love to me in the open will make people talk. I don't think this is loving me.

It's wrong because we're not married. You should make it official, arrange a bridal house for me, then I'll consent and drop my objections.

My body is not something that's for sale, something to be laid out in the middle of nowhere. Please consider what's fitting first. Go home, Kaeo.

You die from no food, you don't die from no lovemaking."[17] She lowered her face onto her knees and wai-ed him, pleading to be let down.

He tenderly kissed and stroked her hair, then admired her face. "You're so lovely. Your skin is so fair, so soft. Your eyes are brimming with tears. Please give me a little smile, heartmate.

I'm touched by your pleading to let you go but I love you so much I don't want to be apart. Lugging my love away from here will be torture."

He picked up her hand and pressed it to his chest. "See, my heart is bursting. Take note of this. In the evening I'll come to the house to find you."

He lifted her chin, kissed her,[18] and hugged her tightly to his body, feeling her full, firm breasts budding against him. He caressed every part of her body.

He took her hand and looked at her fingers. "So beautiful, these ten fingers, so lovely." She bent her face over her lap and said nothing. "I'll say farewell, Phim. Please turn your face towards me."

At that moment, with the sun dropping and the light fading, I-Tao-Hap, I-Phlap, and I-Pli returned from picking cotton with baskets well stuffed, sing-ing songs as they came.

Saithong was keeping watch on the path. Seeing the servants, she cried out twice to warn the couple, "Let's go, let's go, it's almost evening."

Phim prostrated and wai-ed Phlai Kaeo. "They're coming! Please go. They'll see us. Do you want to kill me? Have mercy and go quickly!"

Phlai Kaeo embraced her on his lap, still reluctant to let her down. But as the sound of the servants came close, he was forced to stand up, hide behind a tree, and slip away.

Phim stood up at once. "How are the cotton bolls, you girls? The sun is set-ting so it's time we went." She left the bushes and walked off.

Saithong fell in beside her with a smile. She nudged Phim and whispered teasingly, "Dear Phim, what happened today? Your back and shoulders are soiled."

Phim smiled back out of the corner of her eye. "Don't speak so loud that they can hear." Then, for Saithong's ears only, "I'm happy enough to fly.

Yesterday I seemed miserable all the time. Now I've found a friend to die for. But don't say anything. Nothing happened. Just a little speck of dirt."

---

17. A famous line, often quoted.

18. จูบ, *jup*, kissing was usually lip or nose to cheek or other skin, or perhaps lip brushing lip, or cheek against cheek and inhaling the partner's fragrance, the "whiff-kiss," now known as หอม, *hom*, a word that does not appear in *KCKP*.

Saithong smiled quietly. Phim flashed her a sideways glance with fiery eyes. They returned home followed by the servants carrying the cotton.

All went up into the house as dusk gathered and shadows lengthened. By the time the cotton bolls were stored, darkness had fallen.

Saithong led Phim into the bedroom where they lay on pillows, whispering happily. Saithong teased her, "Now fair Phim, how was it today? Don't hide anything."

Phim gave her a cool look, and rolled over onto her side. She was in turmoil. She pinched Saithong and said, "Because you'd advised him what to do,

as soon as we'd spoken a couple of words, he jumped all over me, just like that. Did you intend to make me ashamed, Saithong? I wanted to cry out loud enough to shatter the field into pieces.

I felt very hurt and I burst into tears. We went two rounds with me bent double and him trying to raise my head and pull the clothes off me. I'd rather die than go on living.

Really, he wanted to jump on me for fun. I was angry but it had no effect. Today I'll take a knife and stab myself to death to erase the shame.

I have a little consideration since you brought me up. Lightning strike! Otherwise, I'd blurt everything out to Mother so I can see your face, Saithong.

Luckily, in the thick of it, the servants came. Any later, one thing would have led to another. You complained that I wasn't cooperative and showed no gratitude for your efforts.

But all he wanted was to impale me on his sharp sword, and it's shameful to be killed by a wooden sword.[19] He even wants to prolong matters. He says he'll come back at midnight tonight."

batten

She slammed the door shut, closed the windows, barred them with battens, and sat rigid, gripping a knife, looking angry enough for blood to drip from her eyes.

"If he comes today, have no doubts. If I don't stab him, you can call me terrible. Leave the room. Don't tell anyone. Tonight, I'll wait through to dawn without sleeping."

Saithong soothed Phim. "Don't be so angry.

---

19. ดาบทองหลาง, *dap thonglang*, a toy sword of *Erythrina fusca* wood; a metaphor meaning a beginner or duffer.

Examine your heart first. Love and longing make the heart feel hot, tight, bursting.

Phlai Kaeo is a young man and very virile. He can't restrain his love. He's aroused, besotted, carried away because he's never met a woman before.

My darling, listen to me. Men have very little shyness. But a woman, even when stirred up with lust, still has her feminine instinct.

Don't rush to think all this is unseemly. What he's saying is not far from the truth. There's still promise for the future. You must think things over carefully.

Phlai Kaeo is a virgin, of that there's no doubt. You're a virgin too, and beautiful. Since you came of age, nobody has touched you.

You've only just met Phlai Kaeo but already you want to drive him away. You don't want to let him fondle you a second time because you think deep down you'll feel tarnished.

But suppose someone else romances you, and then you run into the old flame. You won't know where to put your face. A bad deed sticks with you until death. Don't snap this off hastily and leave yourself alone.

Stop worrying for now. If you don't go to sleep, you'll wake late tomorrow and Mother will be concerned. Phlai Kaeo wouldn't dare come.

Get some sleep so I can too." Saithong walked to her room and went to sleep. Phim continued to mope and moan.

"Oh Phlai Kaeo, my eye's sparkling jewel, have you forgotten me already? Are you so furious you'll fling me away and leave me lonely?

If you won't love me, better not to love me from the start. Now that you've made me moody and miserable, will you dismiss me? I remember you promising you'd come to the room where I sleep.

It's the first watch already, dear Kaeo. You're not here, and my heart feels empty." As Phim lay pining, the moon sank out of sight, and she fell asleep.

Phlai Kaeo arrived at the wat in the evening but was not re-ordained. He looked for an auspicious time to make a move, and found one at the end of the second watch.

The moon slid across a star-spangled sky. Phlai Kaeo stood gazing at the shining clouds and the glitter of the Milky Way.[20] He dressed, prepared himself, made calculations for the Iron Spear and Great Spirit,[21] and was heartened

---

20. The shining clouds and Milky Way are both good omens (Prachak, *Prapheni*, 143).

21. หลาวเหล็ก, *lao lek* and ผีหลวง, *phi luang* are inauspicious directions that change according to the day. There are several methods for discovering them. In a 3x3 grid, the numbers 1 to 8, meaning 1=Garuda, 2=tiger, 3=lion, 4=dog, 5=rat, 6=goat, 7=naga, and 8=elephant, are written clockwise around the rim, beginning in the northeast. The Garuda, lion, naga, and elephant (1,

to find a conjunction of great success.[22] He carefully and expertly considered the breath through his nostrils,[23] and strode off in the given direction.

At Phim's house, he enchanted rice, scattered it around to make everyone sleep soundly, and used a Loosener[24] mantra to unlock the doors and spring the bolts throughout the house.

3, 7, 8) are considered dangerous, and the others benign. The positions are then changed by an arcane series of transpositions ending up with the second diagram, which serves for Sunday. This diagram is then rotated by another arcane series to produce a diagram for each day of the week. It is inadvisable to travel in a direction signaled by all four of the dangerous animals but especially the lion, which, over the seven days from Sunday to Saturday, is found in the NW, E, NE, N, S, W, and SE (Eade, *Calendrical Systems*, 111–14). In a slightly different version, the inauspicious directions of the Great Spirit are: on Sunday, the horse, in the northwest; Monday, the cow, in the east; Tuesday, the lion, in the northeast; Wednesday, the *yaksa* giant, in the north; Thursday, the buffalo, in the south; Friday, the pig, in the west; and Saturday, the elephant, in the southeast (*Tamra phichai songkhram*, 261). Identifying the inauspicious direction of the Iron Spear is usually simpler. In one version, it is in the west on Sunday and Friday, east on Monday and Saturday, north on Tuesday and Wednesday, and south on Thursday (SB, 127; KW, 155–57). In another, it is always diametrically opposite the Great Spirit (Thep, *Horasat nai wannakhadi*, 89). Another method is to examine a chicken in the act of laying eggs as she will always face towards the direction of the Iron Spear to protect her eggs (SWN, 14:7477).

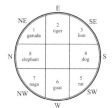

basic Iron Spear diagram

Iron Spear diagram, Sunday

The legendary origin of the term is as follows. During the Buddha's lifetime, Phra Thewathat, a Brahman, annoyed everybody, including the demons. One day an infuriated demon shot him with three *lao lek* arrows. Phra Thewathat went to the Buddha, who told him to recite the three jewels. Phra Thewathat recited the first two, celebrating the Buddha and the Thamma (the Buddha's teachings), and two arrows fell out. But he refused to recite the third, celebrating the Sangha (the monkhood), on grounds he did not believe in the specialness of monks. The third arrow remained sticking in him, and eventually killed him. This arrow continues to exist, changing its direction (SWN, 14:7477).

22. ปลอดห่วง, *plot huang*, the same as *mahasitthichok* (Prachak, *Prapheni*, 129; see p. 319, note 23).

23. Breath flowing more through the left nostril, called จันทรกลา, *jantharakala*, the moon wind, is favorable, while more through the right nostril, สุรยกลา, *surayakala*, the sun wind, is unfavorable. If the flow is equal, he should delay and focus his mind before proceeding. He should hold his weapon in the hand indicated by the stronger breath, and step off on that foot. (SB, 127; Prachak, *Prapheni*, 126–30)

24. สะเดาะ, *sado*, meaning to move something that is stuck, by supernatural means. The formula can be used for a child in the womb, or a lock, bolt, or shackle. A simple form is: มะอะอุ โออุโอ อะมะมา *ma-a-u o-u-o a-ma-ma*. Modern manuals have more elaborate versions entitled "The Great Loosener Formula of Khun Phaen." (PKW, 1:22; *Khamphi khatha 108*, 167; Thep, *Wicha athan*, 109–10)

He rolled a mortar to stand on, and climbed up into the house. Tiptoeing quietly, he made straight for his goal and entered Phim's room.

Lanterns lit the room and its many contents: a footed tray, salver, betel box, and bowl; a beautiful cosmetic set; an elegant half-moon seat with a carved pattern;

footed tray

a looking glass with two side mirrors; handsome gold ornaments; several betel sets made from nak; and a curtain strung across the room,

made from silk, embroidered beautifully in gold, displaying Phim's workmanship. It depicted the story of Sinsuriya when he took Nang Rattana across a wide ocean and they became separated.[25]

Rattana carried Singhara through the forest to the sala of a rishi of the ten teachings.[26] She paid respect and begged the teacher to let Singhara remain there and to look after him. She took her leave and went with the two brother princes to stay at their grandparents' house, where she gradually recovered.

looking glass

The embroidery showed Sinsuriya traveling in search of Rattana without success until nightfall when he stayed in the garden of Thao Kuta.

"My darling, how clever! No mistakes. Your skill is excellent." He carefully drew the curtain, walked forward, opened the mosquito net, and saw Phim's sleeping face.

He came close and kissed her while she slept. "You smile as if inviting me

---

25. The curtain is embroidered with scenes from the story known in Thai as Sangsinchai, สังข์ศิลป์ชัย, which appears in Thai, Lao, and Mon versions with variations in plot and character names, and which is best known as an outer drama by King Rama II. Thao Kuta, a ruler, has seven sons by seven sister-queens and another by a slave girl. The youngest son, Sangsinchai, is born with a sword and conch, and the son of the slave girl is born as a lion, Singhara. Fearing that these special qualities will give these two advantages in the succession, the other six conspire to have them banished to the forest. But when Thao Kuta sets out to rescue his sister, who has been abducted by a neighboring ogre king, Sangsinchai and Singhara are called in to help. Despite further trickery by the jealous siblings, Sangsinchai eventually recovers the lost sister, and is installed as Kuta's heir. In this extract, Sangsinchai is called Sinsuriya, and Rattana seems to be the sister, known in the outer drama as Sumantha. In the outer drama, there is a lot of searching in the forests, a visit to a rishi, and a trip across an ocean but the plot does not match the story as told here. Perhaps this extract comes from another, earlier version. (*Bot lakhon nok*, 485–566)

26. ทศธรรม์, *thotsatham*, probably the same as the Ten Perfections (see p. 61, note 27).

to share your pillow. Lovely smiling cheeks. Eyes so beautiful when you peep at me admiring you.

Slender neck and sweet little chin. Fingernails long and polished to look beautiful. Breasts full and firm. Faultless." He gently touched her breasts,

then blew a charm onto her to undo the sleeping formula and revive her. "Please don't have suspicions I'm deceiving you. Wake up now, my love."

With a little touch, gentle Phim started from a deep sleep. She turned over and peered upwards to see Phlai Kaeo's face.

She glanced around in fright. "What? You came in here even though the door's locked? Now, this is forcing yourself on me. It's not seemly. You got no satisfaction in the field so now you come to the house.

But that's not all that's hateful. You've almost, very nearly, shamed me in front of people. I fought you off and pleaded with you to ask my hand from my mother but you glossed it over and changed the subject.

Do you think this is love, to practice housebreaking? Don't try to patch things up. I'm angry beyond belief. In the field you jumped on me, made me feel ashamed, and got itchy cotton fiber all over my body.

Tugging at my clothing with your heavy hands is so rude. Having such a fine fellow as a husband, I'd be afraid of being in the same house. I might not die but my back would be dripping blood.

Just grabbing my hand or holding my arm, you hurt me. You've got sharp fingernails that draw blood. Just teasing, you leave lots of scratches. Please go away at once. I don't care for you."

"Oh my beauty, my utmost love, now that I've come, please don't chase me away. I'm ready to fight to the death without a care for my own life. My jewel, please don't go on so.

I was wrong so I came to apologize. Calm down and don't think I'm rough. I admire your beauty and I caress you with a good heart. It was you, poor dear, who needlessly tried to escape,

and my fingernail grazed you accidentally when you swiped me away. You were shoving, pinching, and hitting out. I'm sorry you got scratched.

I came after you here because I love you. I'm afraid you'll be unhappy because I've hurt you. If some cloth's been torn, I'll sew it back together.

Give me your hand and let me look. Does it hurt a little? More than my arm does? Let me kiss and caress where it hurts." He stroked and tickled her sensually.

"Who asked you to be here? Even if my hand is hurt, I didn't ask you to come. Why should you take care of that? The wounded can look after themselves.

You grab my hand and arm so easily. You're not shy about playing husband-and-wife. This is a house, not a field. I'm not afraid because here, for better or worse, I have the neighbors as witnesses.

If you carry on like this and don't leave this room, I'll scream out loud. If you don't release my arm, I'll be angry. This isn't right! You can't act like you did in the field."

"If you have no mercy, then kill me. Go on, cry out loud and clear. Fetch a knife and slash me. Don't think I'm afraid to die.

Make a racket so your mother catches us. I'll stand my ground and not run away. I want to hug gentle you, be close to you—whatever kindness my heartstring will allow."

He embraced her tightly. "Don't squirm. You can't get away. Both your cheeks are smiling happily. May I kiss one? Please have mercy."

He stroked her, kissed her, caressed her ardently. "These cheeks and breasts, did you buy them?" "Lightning strike! You're playing with me as if I'm your war slave. You don't listen to me at all.

However much I pinch, you don't hurt. If you grab with your fingernails, I'll break them clean off. Ow! Don't touch me there. Aren't you ashamed to batter me?"

"Breaking my fingernails shows you don't really love me. Even with one chang of money, you can't find love equal to that fingernail."[27] He smiled sweetly, moved closer, and hugged Phim to his chest blissfully.

Pushing her down on the pillow, he put his face against hers, whispering softly, rocking her to and fro. Dark clouds gathered in the sky above.

Storm winds hummed and howled. Great clouds, glutted with rain, swirled and swung around the sky. When a first gust of rain broke from the heavens, nothing endured throughout the three worlds.[28]

Fair Phim was thrilled with love, her heart churning with passion. They lay close together on her bed with faces touching.

She did not want to move from his side. She fanned him, hugged him, whispered sweet nothings, mopped his sweat with her delicate sabai, and

---

27. For adepts in lore such as Phlai Kaeo, the integrity of the body is important. Damage to a bodily part may imply damage to his powers.

28. บทอัศจรรย์, *bot atsajan*, "wondrous scenes," describing sex through metaphors taken from nature or human activity, were a literary convention of the era. Nidhi argues that old court literature used literal descriptions but later absorbed a tradition of elaborate and sometimes outrageous metaphors found in the courting songs of common oral tradition (*Pen and Sail*, 21–32).

mixed krajae-sandal water to cool him.

chariot of the sun

She begged him to eat some sweets. She set up tables on both sides of the bed, and happily gave him betel and tobacco. They whispered sweet talk,

back and forth, kissing and hugging, on fire with love's ten thousand passions. Neither was interested in sleep.

The god king, seated on his heavenly throne, drove his chariot aloft to extinguish the bright shining light of the moon and stars.

Birds sang. Cockcrows echoed around. Flowers bloomed on the touch of dew. The caress of bees wafted pollen. The sun's chariot soared into the sky.

As the light spread in all directions, Phlai Kaeo's heart lurched. He said sweetly, "Leaving lovely Phim is terrible. Parting is like dying.

When evening comes and the sun goes down, I'll come back for sure. Have no doubt. Stay well. Let me say goodbye. My heart will break any minute."

Phim sighed and softly sobbed. She hugged Phlai, listless with great yearning. "You came to lie here to make my heart ache.

I deserve to be miserable for my stupidity. I love myself but I don't love my own well-being enough. From now on I'll be miserable from morning to night. When will this agony end?

You love me, I love you, Phlai Kaeo. But this is planting a tree of love and then cutting it down, leaving us in torture. Will this love break because we're far apart?

Will Mother beat me and Saithong scold? Who can I talk to? When my breast feels as hot as lying in a bonfire, how can I let you know so far away?

If there's some unhappiness at the house while you're at the wat, I won't be able to come and find you. In the evening, Kaeo, please return here. Seeing your face every night will lift my heart."

Phlai Kaeo comforted and caressed her. "I love you. I don't want to be apart and unhappy. But the cock is crowing and I must get away. Don't worry. I'll come to see you every night.

At sunset I'll escape to come to your room and caress away your sobs and sorrows. Parting from Phim is like being shot by a gun. Come and send me off just beyond the room."

He tenderly lifted her up and carried her to the door, his face pale and streaked with tears in the dim moonlight. "This is like karma, suffering and pain in the heart."

The sky was already turning golden but he could not walk away from her. He sat down, racked with longing. They kissed and hugged in a daze.

"Go inside and close the door, my love. Don't be miserable." He got up and moved off, his love multiplying a hundredfold. The more he looked back, the more he yearned.

Little Phim forlornly closed the door. Phlai Kaeo steeled his heart and walked away from the house. At the wat, he evaded the abbot, and went to pay respect to a monk to re-ordain him.

5: KHUN CHANG ASKS FOR PHIM'S HAND

Now to tell of Khun Chang. He was smitten. Ever since the day of the recitation, the fair, gentle Phim was going round and round in his head without relief.

Morning and evening, day in and day out, he moped over not seeing her face. In his sleep he dreamed of her and babbled drunkenly all through the month without a break.

He had no peace of mind in any position. He lay on the bed feeling miserable and hugging a pillow with eyes closed. When he got up from sleep he felt groggy, and had no appetite for food.

Nothing sour nor sweet passed through his stomach. His heart thumped in distress. He did not hear what people said to him. He was obsessed with Phim.

None of the many servants around the house dared to face him. One day before sunrise, I-Krim was standing happily on the stairway.

Khun Chang was in the room, in turmoil. Just before first light, he poked his head out of a window. Imagining he could dimly hear the voice of gentle Phim, he went to open the door and look.

Peering around, he saw nobody so returned to his bed and moaned, "Oh Phim, your soft skin shines like moonlight!" I-Krim thought he was calling her so she answered him and went in.

Khun Chang was overjoyed to hear a sweet voice in reply. With still bleary eyes, he got himself ready. I-Krim crawled up to the mosquito net.

Khun Chang embraced her neck, laughing with joy. "My darling, why did you come just before dawn?" He hugged her, kissed her, and caressed her belly. "Why are you taking fright and wriggling around?"

I-Krim was happy that the master loved her. She did not push him away or say anything. She lay still and let him have his way. Khun Chang fondled her up and down.

In ecstasy, he squeezed her breasts, surprised to find they hung so very long and pointy, not at all like the lovely Phim who entranced him. He stopped and asked, "Who's come here under false pretences?"

I-Krim replied with a happy smile, "It's me, I-Krim, master. You called me, and I was afraid you'd beat me in anger if I didn't obey. Why do you now accuse me of false pretences?"

Khun Chang froze, dumbstruck. "Wha-wha-what is this? I call for Phim and get I-Krim! Well, one good thing, she got here in no time.

I-Krim, I called out to Phim but you came. I was feeling randy—no time to look at the face. Well, a knife in the house is like a machete . . ."[1] He grabbed her and caressed her feverishly.

Wonders burst into a river. A boat pitched and yawed. Spume broke over the gunwales, splashed against the housing, and streamed down from the upper decking over the sides.

Khun Chang was carried away in ecstasy. He caressed Krim and beamed at her, imagining she was really Phim. He lay back in his mosquito net with a grin on his face until dawn broke.

Khun Chang walked out of the room to wash his face at a window. I-Krim brought a betel tray with a smile. His mood darkened.

He put betel in his mouth and stood with jaw open and chin resting on his chest, completely engrossed in thoughts of Phim. He left his apartment and went to pay respect to his mother.

Thepthong saw Khun Chang's gloomy face and sensed his mood was abnormal. She raised both her hands to stroke him.

"You seem out of sorts. Your face is as black as a sooty pot, and your neck is grimy. You're wasting away like a skinny bamboo. Tell me, don't hide things from your mother.

What's the cause of this distress? You're much too gloomy. Do you have a headache or eye ache? Why don't you answer me?"

Khun Chang wanted to reply to his mother but was too bottled up with misery. Instead, he burst into loud sobbing.

Wiping his tears with a hand, he said, "I'm enormously miserable. It's like my chest is infected and swollen with pus. I feel as if a bo tree were felled across my body,

shattering my bones. I'll ache for a hundred years without relief. If things get worse, I may die. Only you can save me.

I've been unhappy since Kaen Kaeo passed away. I grieve for my dear wife so much. Morning and evening I eat nothing but tears. I've been a miserable widower now for more than a year.

---

1. One of the *Suphasit Phra Ruang* (Sayings of Phra Ruang), an early-Bangkok collection of proverbs and didactic sayings attributed to a legendary hero king of the Sukhothai era, runs, "Iron in the house is like a knife, a slave in the house is like a wife." Khun Chang alludes to this saying but gets it mixed up (KW, 661).

I have heaps of money but who knows whether this will remain or disappear. Why should I keep check on it when I have no one to look after it?

There are millions of women but I can't find one suitable to be mistress of the house—to live together, and to help look after the property. I've been all over Suphan looking.

The only one is Phim Philalai, daughter of Siprajan, from the big house at Maids Landing. We've been in love for a long time.

She's begging me to ask for her hand in marriage. If she's pregnant, there'll be shame in front of the neighbors. She bothers me about it morning and evening. I feel utmost pity for her and can't ignore this.

Mother, please do something kind for your son. Please ask for her hand. If her mother doesn't consent, I'll abduct Phim from their house.[2]

But if she's agreeable, I'm ready to make a generous settlement so there'll be no shame with the neighbors. Once she promises for sure, no need for delay. The first waxing of this month is a good day,

an auspicious time[3] of the first order. I'll enchant some beeswax for you to put on your lips.[4] Mother, please have mercy on me. Today would be a fine day to go."

Thepthong listened to Khun Chang, not believing a word. She replied, "Young Phim is very beautiful,

more than anyone else in Suphan province. You look like a Lawa's cloth sidebag.[5] It'll be a waste of effort to try. Let me make a comparison to help you understand.

Phim is as captivating as the moon. You're like a field turtle down below wanting the moon far away in the heavens. Do you really think you can get her, my son?

You have heaps of money so why not use it to redeem somebody.[6] Listen to your mother.

sidebags

---

2. For a marriage to have status in law, the parents of the bride had to give their prior consent. Alternatively, the man could abduct or elope with the woman, and subsequently make a formal apology to the parents. Given the *fait accompli*, the parents might then consent but only after demanding recompense in money or kind. This latter method avoided the expense of a formal ceremony.

3. เอกะปาสัง, *ekka pasang*, the first noose, an astrologers' term for an auspicious time for any matter (KW, 661).

4. So that her words will be persuasive.

5. In other words, shapeless, bulging, untidy.

6. See p. 39, note 56.

Go to the city of Ayutthaya and choose a pretty thing who suits you,

someone with a slender figure like a *kinnari*. Stop being unnecessarily miserable. With all your money, you'll have no trouble. Why go begging after someone who doesn't want you?

In the past you and Phim knew each other as playmates. Even when she was a child, she used to make fun of you. Every time she opened her mouth, it was the bald head. Her speech is too overbearing. I don't like it."

kinnari

Khun Chang replied, "But when we're man and wife, won't she be afraid to talk to me like that? Kids play like kids, and I'm not bothered about what happened then.

But now we're grown up, manners matter. If we live together and are intimate with each other, love and fear will prevail. Why worry about this issue?

I'm concerned for Phim. I've promised her, with my word as my bond, that we'll be married within three nights.

Phim said that if I don't come to ask for her hand, she can't face life so she'll hang herself. If she dies, don't imagine I'll want to carry on living.

I'll split my head open with a cleaver and chop my whole body into pieces. If you are not kind to me, I'm stuck, Mother. I don't know who else to turn to."

He lifted his mother's foot, placed it on his head, and rolled around, weeping floods of tears and clumsily punching his bald head with his fists.

Thepthong shouted at him, "You're like a naughty schoolchild who won't listen to the teacher. You sound off with these lies about being her lover and seeing her for a long time.

You don't think. Take a look at yourself, you airhead. You look like an unlovely basket of kapok. I don't see how anyone will go for you. And Phim Philalai is a beauty.

She's got the soft slender figure of a *kinnari*. Is she going to couple with a pig-dog and make the neighbors gossip? You're a big liar, all guesswork.

I don't want to walk over there and get a headache and sore feet for nothing. You pretend to cry and plead but you're a big fibber. Go to your own apartment. Get away from me."

Seeing his mother's mood, Khun Chang got up and left. He went into his own apartment, opened the mosquito net, and threw himself down on the bed.

"Oh my fair, gentle Phim! When will I have you lying beside me on the bed?

My chest feels on fire. I'll pummel my body to death in constant grief.

I've never loved anyone like I love Phim. You're beautiful—beautifully grace-ful, beautifully good, beautiful in every way—appearance, manners, allure, so perfect.

My body is awful. My head looks as if a herd of elephants trampled across it! If I came across a rishi or a monk or a Brahman, I'd have him transform me to be like Lord Ram,[7] ruler of the realm.

Then when I walked past Sida,[8] she'd see my face and fall for me. But this body of mine is an ugly mis-take. Nothing good about it at all. Terrible!

I'm no good at courting. I'm built for wrestling and that's all. But I don't have to stay here with my face buried in the bed, torturing myself.

rishi

It's late in the afternoon and the sun is easing. Phim will go out to romp in the water along with the servants. I'll take my retinue and go down there.

Through the power of the merit I've accumulated, I should be able to bribe someone. Nine or ten chang—who cares! Invest a little to achieve success."

No sooner had the thought come to him than he got up and looked at the sky in dismay. "Oh dear! Damn! It's rather late." He called his servants, who appeared en masse.

He got up and sat down in a dither, grabbed a bag and put in five chang of cash, threw on a yok and a woolen uppercloth, and doused himself in sandal oil so the scent suffused the air.

He cinched his waist with a belt but his belly bulged out like a balloon, quite out of keeping with his lowercloth. His chest hair straggled down to his belly. He quickly marched down from the house.

The gaggle of servants followed behind. Seeing several people watching them, Khun Chang scolded the servants to follow their master attentively. "I'll thrash your backs till you wail!"

Reaching the landing where Phim bathed, he turned and whispered to the servants to hide in the bushes and watch from a distance. "If anyone comes, don't let them see you."

Khun Chang hid in some *chingchi* bushes. He unfolded a cloth, wrapped it round his head, and waited for Phim with his face beaming and gleaming like a lotus leaf.

7. Hero of the *Ramakian*, the Thai version of the *Ramayana*.
8. The wife of Ram, heroine of the *Ramakian*.

Phim and Saithong were indoors embroidering silk on a frame. As the sun began to drop, they set off to bathe,

along with a crowd of servants. At the landing, they changed clothes, gaily went down into the water, and scrubbed themselves clean.

I-Ma, I-Mi, I-Si-Siat, and I-Khiat went off to play hide-and-seek together. Some went to hide, some gave chase, and others just stayed put.

They ran around hiding and catching rowdily. Crying "Gotcha," Nang Jan as seeker found I-Khok, who leapt into the water, dipping and diving.

I-Ma, I-Mi, I-Si-Siat, and I-Khiat dived into the water and I-Khok chased after them. I-Rak was not so nimble because of her big tummy, and I-Khok pounced and caught her every time.

Ai-Hong went to squat in a clump of sugar reed. As he pee-ed, his head stuck out with a vacant look on his laughing face. Khun Chang angrily hit him with a stick. Ai-Hong pointed out to him,

"Look, there's Mistress Phim on the riverbank, washing herself. Really, really big breasts." Khun Chang scolded, "Don't talk about her. She belongs to me, and that crab of a woman belongs to you."

Ai-Hong was happy to hear his master's words. "Since I first came down here, I've been thinking what a firm body my love has, worth one chang,

a figure like a barrel drum. Just now—using a charm a teacher gave me—I raised my eyebrow, and she plunged into the water and turned over on her tummy twice."

I-Khok chased after I-Rak, grabbed for her leg but missed and got the end of her cloth. They plunged under the water wrapped together, and came up with eyes bulging, shaking off the water.

barrel drum

I-Rak spewed out enough water to fill a big bowl, crying "Horrors! I almost drowned." She lay on the ground with no lowercloth on her body.

Ai-Hong straightened himself up, clapping his hands. "Oh, it's huge,[9] mistress! It looks like the mouth of a horse fish.[10] Horrible!" He threw back his head and shook with laughter.

On the riverbank, Saithong and Phim laughed so much they rolled around helplessly. Khun Chang stood up feeling irritated. Phim's cloth slipped from under her armpits.

---

9. "It's huge," ออ อือโตถนัด, *o ue to thanat*, is taken from WK, 4:155; PD has: Oh dear.

10. A kind of croaker, common in the Suphan River. There is a Bang Pla Ma, Horse Fish Village, around 12 kms south of Suphanburi down the river.

Khun Chang saw her round, sculpted breasts. He half-squatted down, grasped his shins, and rocked from side to side like a *tukkae*.[11] "Oh Mother, today I die!"

Phim and Saithong called the servants, "Let's go. The sun is dropping." They all climbed up, changed clothes, and trooped off in order.

Khun Chang emerged from the *chingchi* bushes, followed by his noisy gaggle of servants. He caught up with Phim on the path, and walked beside her, shoulder to shoulder, with a broad smile on his face.

tukkae

Saithong and Phim stepped off the path and let Khun Chang walk on ahead. As he passed them, he pretended to recite a love poem[12] within their hearing.

"Oh, heavenly *montha*[13] flower by the flowing leat . . . "

Ai-Hong thrust his neck out and continued his master's verse.

" . . . I saw your breasts and took them for a sweet,
Whopping palm fruit wobbling in syrup for me to eat . . . "

As Khun Chang walked past, Phim burst out angrily, "Your mother! You old baldy, shiny pate!" She took a shortcut to the house with the servants following.

Khun Chang stopped at some distance from the compound, his face puckered in the beating sun. First he told his servants to wander around and kill some time.

Then after a while, he instructed them to keep quiet and walk in an orderly fashion to the house of Siprajan.

At the gate, he inquired of a servant, who said her mistress was in. "Please be kind enough to inform Siprajan that we are here."

The servant climbed the stairway up to the house, sat down, and relayed to her mistress that Khun Chang had come to visit.

Siprajan came to a window and saw Khun Chang. Her heart sank. His forehead was damp and shiny with running sweat. "Why did he come like this in the sun?"

---

11. ตุ๊กแก, *Gekko gecko*, a house lizard, named after its distinctive call. The lizard characteristically rocks its body to and fro. Khun Chang has adopted a characteristic pose of *yak* giants in the mask play.

12. เพลงยาว, *phleng yao*, literally "long song," a poetic genre, which often took the form of a love letter, rendered in a variant of the *klon* meter.

13. มณฑา, *Talauma candollei*, Magnolita, a tree of the Magnolia family with large yellow flowers and a strong morning fragrance. In some Thai versions of the Buddha's life story, *montha* flowers fell from the heavens as an offering when the Buddha was close to attaining enlightenment, and Kusinarai was strewn with them again after his passing away. Hence the flower is often used in offerings, and much beloved by poets.

She invited him up to the house. "You've been out in the sun. You look drawn and drenched in sweat. Wash yourself, there's water." She bustled around shouting at the servants.

front terrace

Khun Chang stepped up to the terrace, and entered the main apartment on his knees. He sat on a mat and raised his hands to wai Siprajan.

She reciprocated and invited him to take betel. Once he had accepted, she asked, "Why did you come in the hot sun?"

Khun Chang coughed and spluttered without a word coming out. Gradually he managed to mumble something. "This is all beyond me." He lowered his face and sat there, saying nothing.

Siprajan watched Khun Chang struggling to mumble something. She asked over and over what the matter was.

"What's making you talk in circles? Get it off your chest. No need to be hesitant, we're not formal here. Why have you come?"

Khun Chang bent forward to pay respect until his head met a pillow, and said, "Please, first, my dear lady, this is all beyond me. I've no one to talk to.

Kaen Kaeo died many months ago. I have heaps of money but there's nowhere to keep it, and unfortunately it's getting stolen. One pair of eyes is not enough to watch over it.

Today a large amount disappeared, and this was not money that was buried in the ground but kept in chests. They broke the locks and took it in broad daylight. Cloth also gets stolen from time to time.

If there were someone to look after all my money and property, I'd hand over paddy lands, house, and servants, and make her the mistress of the household.

I wouldn't mind a penniless widow as long as she had manners enough not to cause shame with the neighbors. I need someone to help look after property, run matters, and give advice. Someone just like Phim Philalai."

As Siprajan listened to Khun Chang weaving his story, greed rose in her breast, and she could not restrain herself, bursting out, "If you have silver, why should you go without gold?

Just select a good person, someone meticulous who knows how to look after things, manage your affairs, and hold onto your servants and lands.

A man like yourself, Chang, can easily find a good wife who's a suitable match, who won't make you ashamed in front of Khaek and Thai who come and go, and who can talk nicely in the manner of gentlefolk—

someone equal in social rank, who knows how to sew and embroider. But around Suphan, I don't see anyone on equal standing with you, Chang.

In truth, young Phim is almost an adult but her status is no more than middling, comfortable, not like some in Ayutthaya."

Khun Chang's face brightened into a smile. "Finding someone else like Phim would be impossible. I think constantly of having her as my partner.

When I consulted my mother, Thepthong, she was reluctant to agree. Because Phim and I used to play together like brother and sister, she thought it was not good, too close.

At the cremation of my father, we talked about having this childhood friend as my bride. But my mother was afraid you wouldn't consent so she didn't pay you a visit.

If you don't think this is improper, I'll get some elders to talk with you. I'll hand over cattle, buffaloes, paddy lands, money, cloth, and everything."

Phim was listening with Saithong in the next room, growing angry and agitated over what her mother and Khun Chang were discussing. "That old baldy! How rude! What a liberty!"

Phim opened a window and pretended to call a servant. "Ta-Phon! Where have you got to? Come here, you evil, hairy-chested baldy. There's work still to do but you pay no attention."

Baldheaded Ta-Phon replied, "What's all the confusion, mistress?" He came out of his hut with his head gleaming, and strode up the stairs.

hut

Khun Chang heard Phim's abuse and felt ashamed in front of the servants. He quickly took leave of Siprajan and stumbled down from the house.

Ta-Phon passed him in the middle of

the stairway, stepping aside with his body trembling. Khun Chang held his head up high, and said awkwardly through bared teeth, "We meet again after a long time."

Ta-Phon shakily raised his hands to wai. "This sin is the result of a cock-fight in the past."[14] Khun Chang ignored him, and lurched off with an angry look on his face.

⤷

In the west, the last rays of the sun disappeared behind the hills. A moon of great power moved across the sky in its brilliant celestial carriage,
    adorned with thousands of heavenly maidens, drawn by the Phalahok horse capering powerfully round the rim of Mount Yukhanthon.[15]

The world were bathed in the sublimely beautiful moonlight of this majestic, haloed, celestial body.

Little Phim was missing Phlai Kaeo. For many days there had been no sign of him. She moped morning and evening. She went to consult Saithong, who was older and wiser.

"Phlai Kaeo has disappeared for many days now. I'm disappointed because he made promises and things are not turning out as he said.

I can't blame you alone. I must blame my own heart for being too careless. I was taken in by his good looks and eloquent words, and now I've wasted my love.

I don't know what to do. I'm hurt, worried, almost heartbroken. If he were honest, he wouldn't skulk but would come round to show his feelings.

Whether those are hot or cold, we could at least talk. Since he hasn't come, what can I do? I don't know who to turn to. Didn't you see, Saithong?

Khun Chang dared to come and visit Mother, and sneakily ask for my hand, just like that. Mother's inclined to consent because she's totally bowled over by his wealth.

Are we just going to sit around here, watching? I don't think I can go on living. Saithong, please think of something and tell me what to do."

Saithong hugged Phim tightly to her own face to comfort her. She lifted Phim's chin and helped wipe away her tears. "Don't be sad. There's still time.

Phlai Kaeo means to love you till his dying day. He's not just trying to lure you as a plaything. He's serious and has made many promises.

---

14. He attributes his baldness, a physical abnormality, to some karmic misdeed.

15. One of the mountains surrounding Mount Meru, the center of the universe in the Three Worlds cosmic geography (RR, 276–78; see p. 2, note 7).

Perhaps he's suddenly sick, or too tired, or is tied up by many important matters, or word has got to the abbot, who's making trouble. Perhaps this is why there's no sight or sign of him.

But why be upset and impatient? Tomorrow I'll find him and clear up any doubts, for better or worse. Don't be so quick to torment yourself.

If he's well and has no commitments, I'll bring him here for you to cherish. So lighten up and be patient, or else you'll waste away and lose your figure.

Powder your face and wait for Phlai Kaeo. Tomorrow evening the fever will vanish." With these comforting words, she fanned Phim to sleep.

Once Phim had nodded off, Saithong went to her own bed, lay on the pillow, and slept soundly, waking promptly as dawn broke.

In the early morning sun, Saithong got up from her bed, rinsed her mouth, washed her face, and went to see Siprajan.

She sat down and said, "Last night Phim had a very strange dream that seems bad and rather worrying.

In the dream she was asleep at midnight in some other house when it caught fire and collapsed to the ground. She was burned and blistered by the flames.

Phim is shocked almost out of her wits, not knowing what it means. I'm going to Wat Palelai to relate everything to the abbot."

main kuti

Siprajan burst out, "Go quickly. Don't delay. Tell the abbot the whole story from beginning to end.

Take along some betelnut and pan. Oh, dear Phim! And lots of sweets and fruit as offerings. Soon it'll be too late. Go in time for his early morning meal."

Phim smiled broadly. "Mother's in the dark." She briskly peeled betelnut, rolled pan leaf, and put in treats including lots of sweets and oranges, along with rice and bottle gourd curry, taking only good things.

Saithong left the room to bathe. Wearing a black silk uppercloth with a colored lining, she hurried down from the house with servants in tow.

Reaching the wat, she took all the servants to pay respect at the main kuti so that nobody would be suspicious. Then she told the servants,

"Go to the preaching hall and collect the pupil flowers[16] that have bloomed and fallen all over the ground." The servants went off, leaving Saithong, the senior, in the kuti.

She offered rice, curry, and sweets to the abbot. She hid the betelnut, pan leaf, and tobacco to give to Novice Kaeo,

and also arranged oranges and various dried fruits for him. All the monks were sitting in a circle eating. Saithong waited for a good moment.

When the monks finished and went to their rooms, Saithong looked carefully to check no one was around, then slipped into the novice's room.

She gave him the betelnut, pan, and tobacco, and spoke to him in a rush. "Little Phim has been waiting for you many days. She's desolate with worry.

This evening, she orders you to go to her. She's been waiting and waiting but all in vain. It looks as if you seduced her for your enjoyment, then abandoned her to misery.

She's suspicious and uncertain. She doesn't know the real reason why you're dawdling so she asked me to find you, Novice Kaeo, to see if you're sick or in some other distress.

Yesterday when we went to bathe, that vile Khun Chang acted very coarsely. When he walked past her, she lost her temper and poured all sorts of abuse on him.

After that, Khun Chang went to see our mother, Siprajan, and went too far. He dared to ask for Phim's hand. He thinks everything will fall into his lap.

That's why I've come. Phim says she can't stand it. She says I acted as a go-between, persuaded her to give herself to you, and now she's heartbroken.

You said all kinds of good things but they seem to be getting lost and forgotten. She thinks I deliberately made her suffer. The poor thing is in a pitiful state.

She's worried she's done wrong, and you seem to be easing away. She's anxious about the future. Bad news will spread far and wide.

On top of that, Khun Chang has come to ask for her hand. She doesn't know what to do. She's your lover and she intends to be your partner but she can't talk to you when she needs to.

So she asked me to come and find out what's up. She suspected there was something wrong from the start. You said you wouldn't make her suffer shame. What can be done to improve matters?

---

16. พิกุล, *phikun, Mimusops elengi*, a tree whose small white flowers have a lasting fragrance. The tree is often found in wat. The name derives from Bakula, a disciple of the Buddha, who was swallowed by a fish as an infant, rescued by a fisherman, became an adherent of the Buddha late in life, helped cure him of illness, and lived for 160 years (Malalasekara, *Dictionary*, 261–62).

Are you going to face up to this or just save yourself? Tell me now without any delay. You're happy because you're far away, but I'm close to her so I'm the one suffering.

It's like trying to fry peas with sesame. When the sesame's hot, the peas are not ready. By the time the peas are cooked, the sesame is ruined.[17]

Staying here at the wat is like playing outside the curtain.[18] I'm at the house so I'll get all the blame. Think what to do and tell me. It's late now, almost time I must go."

Novice Kaeo smiled knowingly to reassure her. "Everything you say is true. I made a promise to you.

Fair, gentle Phim and you are the two nearest and dearest to me. My heart is pledged and will never weaken. I'll fight to the death. Don't imagine my love will fade.

Let's talk this through slowly, Saithong. You're my elder. There's no need to be cross. Keep the matter quiet, and don't let it reach the ears of others.

Every day I long for her terribly, and can't get her out of my mind. The problem is the abbot. He makes me study and practice recitation from after breakfast until midnight, the third watch, or beyond. The night I went to see Phim, the abbot angrily reprimanded me, tied me up, and beat me.

You're worried about getting flayed because of me, but you undertook this task so please see it through. I'll repay you, don't worry. Please plead my case with Phim.

The day I can escape the eye of the abbot, I'll come straightaway. I've kept my word many times in the past. Remember that. Don't be suspicious of me."

With these words, he blew a Beguiler mantra. "Please be my supporter, Saithong. Is your mouth sour?[19] Have some betel." He enchanted a piece and gave it to her.

Saithong put the betelnut in her mouth and chewed. The love charm multiplied a hundred thousand times, making her hair bristle and nerves tingle with desire. "Now things fall on me, Saithong,

a poor person who has to put up with nothing but hardship. While you have fun, I sit quietly in my room. I'm like a banana leaf for wrapping sweets.

The sweets are unwrapped and eaten, and the banana leaf discarded

---

17. An old saying meaning, "ere all is in readiness the opportunity will have passed" (Gerini, "On Siamese Proverbs," 217).

18. See p. 82, note 5.

19. A standard question when offering betel.

without a care. Because I'm poor I have to go through misery in order not to lose both of you."

"Make merit and you'll see the results later, Saithong. First things first—tell her I'm a good person.

As for your earlier complaints, please be less angry. Forgive me. Every night I feel concern. Where did you get beaten? Open your uppercloth so I can see."

Saithong was taken aback and pretended to be cross. "What is this, pulling at my clothes to peek at my breasts? Are you a sham monk, a bad novice?"

on almsround

At that moment, Elder Thai was returning from almsround. He heard a muffled female voice, spied through a gap in the wall, and saw them pulling at each other's clothing.

"A curvy waist and big breasts like balloons! Damnit, she's a meal for the novice. Young Kaeo is bad but daring too—in broad daylight, not afraid of anyone!

This is improper behavior in the monks' quarters. I'll tell the abbot to come after them." Still, he watched for a long time, feeling excited, before walking away in agitation, looking straight ahead.

Some distance away, he shouted out, "Novice Kaeo is sparking a fire![20] Oh Lord Abbot, I saw him bothering a woman. They're tugging at each other's clothes!"

The abbot gnashed his gums, rolled his eyes, and quivered in anger. He got up, seized a walking stick, strode shakily over, and opened the door with a crash.

Just in time, Novice Kaeo and Saithong ducked behind a water jar. The abbot loped around, thrashing about with his stick, shouting at the top of his voice, "Damn you! Goddamn you!"

Saithong slid down a trapdoor and hid. The abbot cried out, "I'm sick of this misbehaving! You were attending to me in every way up to the forenoon meal." The novice ran round and round evading him,

jumped out of an open window, and galloped away, his robe streaming behind him. The abbot ransacked the kuti, finding nobody. Still in a rage, he bellowed,

"Ugh! That dog-faced novice and his ghost woman have defiled our kuti." He sat down to pound some betelnut but the pestle remained motionless while he ranted until satisfied.

---

20. สีไฟ, *si fai*, a wat term meaning consorting with a woman (KW, 662).

Saithong slipped down the trapdoor and scurried away from the abbot and the kuti. She turned to find Novice Kaeo had disappeared, and had no way of knowing whether this was good or bad.

She stopped in the middle of the wat and straightened herself out. Still worried about the abbot, and wanting to get away, she called out to the servants, "I-Mi! Quick, I'm going."

The servants recognized their mistress's voice, gathered up the pupil flowers in a cloth, and were ready in an instant.

pattern of pupil flowers

Saithong passed her basket to a servant. "I-Mi, take this." She hurried back to the house, and went up to Siprajan's room, smiling brightly.

Siprajan saw Saithong arrive. "Why were you so late coming back from the wat? Wherever you go, you take so long. Did the abbot interpret the dream as good or bad?"

Saithong replied, "I was slow because the abbot went off on almsround for ages, and we had to wait however long he took to have his meal and say the blessing.

His advice is that this is a very bad omen for Phim. She must be very wary for the next three days. After that he says things will be fine."

She took her leave, went up to the room, and huddled whispering with Phim. "Novice Kaeo says he'll fight to the death. His promises are all sincere.

He'll find a way to disrobe and come. Even if there's a sword waiting to cut his throat, he won't retreat. He should be here soon, as promised. Please listen to me and don't be downhearted."

Novice Kaeo had fled from the abbot and could not return. The more he thought, the more his mind spun. "I've been at Wat Palelai for a long time

but I'm certainly not yet expert in various branches of knowledge. There's still Wat Khae[21] which is said to be excellent. My mother, Thong Prasi, told me a long time ago that the abbot named Khong[22] is a good man,

and was a close friend of my late father. She told me to seek him out when in

---

21. See p. 60, note 24.

22. In the old Ayutthaya-era preaching hall at Wat Khae, there is a large statue of Abbot Khong, and a smaller one of Khun Phaen. Writing in 1996, Winyu related that these images were created within the past thirty years (*Tam roi*, 151).

Suphan to study further and be knowledgeable. Yet I'm also concerned about Phim to the depths of my heart.

She'll complain I broke my promise and ran away. But if I disrobe now, my knowledge is not yet powerful. Though I value being true to my word, I must stifle my longing for her." Having made up his mind, he wrapped himself in a sabai and hurried off.

He crossed the fields and made for a path through the dense trees. Reaching the elephant enclosure,[23] he made inquires about the wat. People pointed the way and he hurried to the sala without stopping.

A lone elder sweeping the wat turned with a start on seeing him. Novice Kaeo asked, "Please be straight with me. Where is Abbot Khong?"

Elder On pointed the way, "Beyond the three kuti, there's the scripture hall."[24] Novice Kaeo happily rushed across.

At that moment Abbot Khong came out to a terrace. Novice Kaeo paid respect and crawled up to him. The abbot asked, "Where have you come from, young novice?"

Kaeo replied, "I'm the son of the late Khun Krai. My name is Phlai Kaeo, a loyal fellow. My mother is Thong Prasi.

She told me to seek you out as a teacher so I came to Suphan and asked around. May I request to study knowledge further."

The abbot said, "Oh yes! Right, I haven't forgotten. I used to be a good friend of Khun Krai. I'm still disappointed that he died without putting up a fight.

He'd lost his knowledge. Why didn't he come to see me? If anyone dared come after me, there'd be no match. I'd cut them down and win fame as a killer of Lao.

Even if they raised an army of ten thousand from all over the land, I'd conjure up dummy soldiers[25] and defend myself famously. Before even one night passed, they'd flee, waving white flags and abandoning thoughts of victory!

I'm very disappointed. I miss him every day, like losing my own right eye, you could say. I'd even intended to entrust him with my cremation."[26]

---

23. The enclosure was on the west bank of the Suphan River, just south of the old bridge on what is now Malai Maen Road (Manat, *Prawat Wat Khae*, 30; see map 6).

24. หอไตร, *ho trai*, literally a place to keep the Tipitaka or Triple Gem; a library.

25. ผูกพยนต์, *phuk phayon*. According to Thep Sarikabut, making dummy soldiers by enchanting grass is the most advanced department of lore and very difficult to master. He had never seen a successful example. Phrakhru Wimonkhunakon (Suk) of Wat Makham Thao, Chainat, a most famous practitioner who had studied the art, only managed to transform the legs and feet (PKW, 2:24–25). Later in the story, Khun Phaen and his sons display mastery of this art.

26. A stock saying meaning the abbot had hoped Krai would remain as his acolyte throughout the abbot's life.

He turned to examine Phlai Kaeo. "You're a puny thing, not tough looking at all. Yet you made it the long way through the forest from Kanburi to Suphan to find me.

Is Thong Prasi well? We're all scattered far apart in different places, and never know if one another is sick or anything. Stay with me. I'll give you knowledge.

I have a duty to Khun Krai who died. You're exactly like him. Don't[27] worry, I'll teach you knowledge. I won't let you get killed like your father, the able fellow."

Novice Kaeo told the abbot, "Father had no thought of running away. He had drunk the water of allegiance[28] and was not tainted by thought of revolt.

He was ready to die to uphold the family name in a line of soldiers. In order not to break his oath dishonorably, he renounced his superior powers so that all his lore was lost. If the king would no longer keep him then that was his merit.

For this reason, they could easily slash him to dust. If Father had totally broken his word and turned against the land, there would have been turmoil. Don't feel bad about this.

As for my mother, Thong Prasi, she gets older and older but she's still strong, not ailing, and hasn't lost her memory. She's happy and well."

---

27. The next three stanzas, down to "lore was lost," are from WK, 5:174–75. PD has: Don't worry, I'll teach you all the texts. I won't let you get killed like your father." / Novice Kaeo told the abbot, "Father had not lost his powers and had no thought of running away. He had drunk the water of allegiance, and was not tainted by thought of revolt. / He agreed to die to uphold the name of a family line of soldiers and not break his oath. Thus all his lore was lost.

The WK version describes Khun Krai as an "able fellow," คนดี, *khon di*, with knowledge, วิชา, *wicha*, who voluntarily "renounces his powers" ตัดใสย, *tat sai*. These three key term are missing from the PD version. *Sai* (usually spelled ใสย) is a Khmer-derived word meaning "greater than, more excellent than," and the root of *saiyasat*, the modern term for lore. *Tat sai* is the technical term for renunciation. The WK version implies that Krai had the ability to resist a royal order. In the PD version, this is no longer clear.

28. An oath of loyalty to the ruler. It is first mentioned in the chronicles after King Naresuan put down a revolt by Phichai and Sawankhalok in the mid 1580s. The description of that occasion has formed the pattern for the ceremony ever since: "Then he was pleased to command the head priest to assemble the Brahman professors to bring water from the well of the Self-Created Protector and from the Phoi Si Well, to hold the rites according to the proper ritual forms for the Water of Allegiance, to invoke the Triple Gems to preside, and to have all the high-ranking nobles, generals, ministers, and soldiers drink the Water of Allegiance" (RCA, 92–93). King Mongkut made the ceremony an annual event for all officials. Water was collected from several sacred sites, and enchanted by a Brahman immersing a regal sword. Officials assembled in the palace at the capital, or in a major wat at provincial centers, recited an oath, and drank the water.

The abbot said, "Oh, Thong Prasi's getting old, is she? I haven't seen her face for about ten years. You stay here. I'll teach you the military arts.

In the future, don't boast about keeping your word. And don't overdo things and risk becoming dust.[29] You're tired from walking through the forest. Go stay in the kuti next to the central hall."

Novice Kaeo took his leave and went to a room where there was a bed, mattress, and pillow. His thoughts turned to fair, gentle Phim, and he grew miserable.

In the evening, the longing worsened. He lay in his room thinking only of her. At the last rays of the sun, he went to the inner room to pay respect,

fan the teacher, and serve him in other ways so that the abbot would be well-disposed towards the novice. The abbot promptly began to instruct him on everything:

putting an army to sleep and capturing its men; summoning spirits; making dummies with power to fight courageously; writing *pathamang*;[30] concealment;[31] invulnerability; undoing locks and chains;

all the arts of victorious warfare;[32] all knowledge for overcoming enemies with no hope of resistance; calculating auspicious times for any action; enchanting tamarind leaves to become wasps;[33]

---

29. This line is taken from WK, 5:175; PD has: "Honor must be preserved without fail. Because your father wasn't careful, he became dust."

30. ปฐมัง, from Sanskrit *pathamam*, first or primary, name of a text in old Khmer which relates the history of this era from the re-creation of the world through the life and death of the Buddha. By writing out each verse with a whiteclay stick on a blackboard, the student learns characters, words, and symbols that are components of yantras (see p. 135, note 20). The used whiteclay powder, now considered powerful, is collected, enchanted with formulas, and put to various uses such as smearing on the forehead for protection or invisibility.

A whiteclay stick is made by dissolving fine whiteclay in water, pouring it through a cloth sieve, drying the powder, mixing it with ground herbs and water thickened by boiling rice, and forming it into a stick like a piece of chalk as thick as a thumb and four inches long (KW, 56; YS, 489, 493–94; Natthan, *Lek yan*, 99–103).

31. กำบังตน, *kambang ton*, the power to pass someone by without being recognized or remembered (KPW, 2:22).

32. พิชัยสงคราม, *phichai songkhram*, victorious warfare, name of a treatise first mentioned in the chronicles in 1516/17, and believed by some to derive from sixteenth-century Indian prototypes. Several texts were assembled in the First Reign, and a last recension made in 1825. The manual covers troop formations, omens, astrology, and other matters (RCA, 19; Battye, "Military, Government and Society," 9, 52; *Tamra phichai songkhram*).

33. At Wat Khae, there is a massive old tamarind tree, reputed to be five hundred years old, now legendarily associated with this line.

expertise in all covert war tactics; commanding troops in hundreds of thousands; defeating whole territories; the Great Beguiler mantra to induce strong love;

stunning people; invisibility; gaining the strength of a lion; withdrawing *athan*[34] protective powers and preventing their replacement; and keeping spirits to act as spies.[35]

He studied all branches of knowledge, reciting both old and new repeatedly to commit to memory. He thought of Phim but did not go to her because he had fallen in love with gaining knowledge.

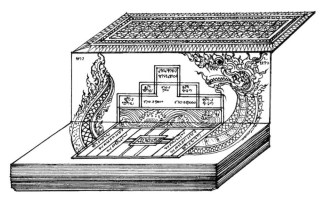

Manual of Victorious Warfare

34. อาถรรพณ์, *athan*, sometimes pronounced *athap*, from Atharva-veda, the Fourth Veda. This Sanskrit text, dated to 900 BCE, is a collection of formulas to combat disease, enemies, weapons, and sorcery, along with prayers and other devices for protection, blessing, love, long life, successful childbirth, and so on. Probably this catalog was compiled by the authors of the Vedas from the practices of the local population in India (Witney, *Atharva-Veda Samhita*). In Thai usage, *athan* had come to mean protection provided by the spirits, especially protection of a city or palace.

35. Literally, to whisper everything, meaning to act as a sort of secret service, spying on the enemy and providing intelligence.

6: PHLAI KAEO GOES INTO SAITHONG'S ROOM

Now to tell of Khun Chang. After returning from Siprajan's house, he pined for little Phim all the time from morning to night.

He would not eat or sleep but burned with love, as if his heart would break. For many days, he was unwell and felt like holding his breath to die. He could not stop thinking of her.

He stayed in his room. Whatever time of day, he lay sobbing, sighing, and simpering. "What must I do to be close to my gentle Phim?

On that day you bathed with your servants and I went to hide and peep at the landing, what a pity you did not see me making eyes. You turned your face away without looking.

After you came up from the river, I followed you home and went to talk with your mother, Siprajan. I think things will work out for sure.

Tomorrow I'll ingratiate myself and plead for your hand, using all the tricks at my disposal, both money and other things in support. Even if I look awful and have a bald head, she should be considerate."

He continued in this agitated state until dawn broke and the sun rose in the sky. He opened his eyes to the brightness, washed his face, and got dressed.

When he picked up a mirror to look at himself, his head made his heart sink. He used soot to darken the pate, and smothered his whole body with powder.

He put on a yok and a meshwork[1] uppercloth with glittering gold thread, left the room, and called his crowd of young servant boys to accompany him.

Reaching Siprajan's house, Khun Chang went up in a merry mood. Siprajan saw him coming and welcomed him in.

She pushed over a betel tray, inviting him to take some, and they chatted like neighbors. "What have you come for? Speak freely. Is your mother well?"

Khun Chang grasped the opportunity to reply. "Please let this son be your

---

1. กรอง, *krong,* also known as ถักตาชุน, *thak ta chun,* or ถักสไบ *thak sabai,* loosely woven fine cotton, woven or embroidered with gold thread, usually in a ตาข่าย, *ta khai,* mesh, pattern. Reserved for auspicious occasions, it was worn by men draped over the left shoulder or tailored into a long tunic, and worn by women over the sabai (KP, 317).

humble servant, to serve Mother as shoes or as a bowl.[2] My mind is full of thoughts but I'm too nervous,

because I'm sincerely in love with gentle little Phim. Please settle her with me, my dear lady. If she is mine, I'll cover her body with gold. I'm not afraid. I have piles of money.

She will walk only inside a room. Even moonlight will not be allowed to touch her body. Why live in fear of poverty and hardship? I wai you, Mother. Please accept me as your son."

screen

Siprajan listened to everything Khun Chang had to say with a beaming smile. She would be very happy to have a rich man as a son-in-law.

She said, "My dear Chang, whatever merit and karma decree, whether the horoscopes match or not." She called her daughter to come immediately.

"Phim, oh Phim, where are you? Why don't you come out to greet him and get to know each other. Come quick, my darling."

Phim had seen Khun Chang arrive, and had hidden behind a screen close to the wall, overhearing his story. She was furious.

"It was because of this fellow I couldn't listen to the recitation and the teachings on that day." She called back to her mother, "I'm not coming, however much you call me."

She pretended to cry abuse on one of the servants. "Hey, Ai-Phon! Where are you off to, you baldy? How come you think you're such a big shot? Can a pandan flower pass off as a forest *phayom*?[3]

You're so puffed up, boasting about money. I don't have any desire for that, you louse. You're the laziest of all the workers. The water jars are all empty because of your slacking.

What a great lover! You take too many liberties, you numbskull. You swagger about swishing your tail to court dogs. Ugh! All that powder and sandalwood oil, and your hair parted on two sides like pigtails!

phayom flower

---

2. This phrase signals he is asking to become a son-in-law.

3. The pandan reed has an insignificant flower while the *phayom* is a forest tree with spectacular yellow flowers.

A dog was due to be born but you arrived in its place. Go to hell, you cheap-skate! With a face like that, who'd marry you? You don't know your place, you dog-licked mango!

You're like a dragonfly boasting you can race Garuda across the ocean, a little rock that thinks it's mighty Mount Meru, a forest firefly that wants to rival the sun.[4]

You look terrible. You're like an adjutant stork wanting to embrace a swan that would rather play on Mujalin Lake.[5] You think so much of yourself but really you belong in a swamp."

Khun Chang understood this abuse was meant for him. He felt ashamed in front of the servants and had to get away. He took leave of Siprajan, and quickly went down from the house.

Now Siprajan was furious. She got up, grabbed a stick, chased after Phim, and beat her. "You're uncouth, terrible, too much!

Do you think all that noisy eloquence was nothing? If you're like this, who'll have you?" She beat her again and again until Phim's back was soaked in blood, her face bathed in tears,

and her body striped by the blows. "I'm afraid now. I won't say any more." With her entire body in pain, she fled into the kitchen,

closed the door, shot the bolt, and sank down on the floor, whimpering. "I'm so hurt and ashamed!" Her whole back was marked and flowing with blood.

She called out to Saithong through her tears. "Come and look. Where have you got to? Why don't you help me? I've been beaten almost to death. Saithong, please help me!"

Saithong heard Phim's distress and anxiously went to find her. She saw the door closed and bolted, so came close to the wall and asked, "What did you call me for?"

"Dear Saithong, I'm so upset. Against my will, Mother is going to give me to that half-headed fellow that I don't like. Let's run away from her and go to the wat right now.

I'll tell the novice and see what he thinks. If I delay, I'll be destroyed for sure." She opened the door but was still too scared to come out.

Seeing other people, she ducked back inside and waited, popping her head

---

4. The comparisons of both the dragonfly and Garuda, and the firefly and sun, are old sayings with several variants (Gerini, "On Siamese Proverbs," 175).

5. In the Three Worlds cosmogony, Mujalin, Pali Muchalinda, is a lake or river in the Himaphan Forest where the *hong* mythical swans live.

out to look, until the coast was clear. Then she crept out, and went off with Saithong.

They hurried along a shortcut with Phim weeping. "Oh dear, it hurts and it's too shameful. Why is my mother so unkind?"

They reached Wat Palelai. "As I remember, the novice's kuti was that one." Saithong crept up and saw that the kuti was empty. Their hearts sank further.

She whispered to some other novices there, "Is Novice Kaeo still here? If not, where's he gone?" They replied, "The abbot beat him. He ran away to stay at Wat Khae."

"Really? Or are you trying to deceive us?" The novices assured them Kaeo had been beaten and run away. "Karma, karma! Bad news multiplies. Sorrow piled upon heartbreak."

With the pain in her back and the worry about the novice, Phim wilted into misery and gloom. She went down the stairs and asked around.

"Does anyone have news of Novice Kaeo? Even just a word? Even if he's at the ends of the earth, I'll go looking for him." They went to Wat Khae and asked the monks, "Please, where is Novice Kaeo?"

At the sight of women, the monks crowded around and stared. Some greeted them. Others shouted out, "Are you court ladies?" "Where did you come from?"

Heads poked out of windows and doors. "We've never seen these two ladies before." They called others to come. "There, over there. See?" "Women. Come and look!"

After the forenoon meal, Novice Kaeo was making whiteclay powder and diligently practicing writing *pathamang* for his teacher. Hearing the noise, he poked his head out and saw the two of them.

"Oh, that's Phim and Saithong! Come over here. You took the trouble to come looking for me? Why this sad face? What brought you here?" Seeing Phim's swollen eyes, he was taken aback.

At the sight of Novice Kaeo, Phim managed to break into a smile. She came up the steps with Saithong, sat down close to him, and started speaking.

"Tcha! What is all this, Novice? You seduce me then you skip off. I want to think you have a good heart, but what about those many things you said to me?

You gave all sorts of promises about everything. I'm a woman, what can I do? You said you'd ask for my hand but I'm still waiting. Now, something big has intervened.

Khun Chang has asked for my hand, and my mother has consented. I was so cross I could die. I objected, and she beat me until my back nearly caved in.

This is the mother who raised me from childhood and never once before left a mark on me with a stick, but now she has no feelings. I'm thankful you have a good heart.

I want to think you wouldn't go back on your word, on all those things you said to me. What do you have to say? Speak up, right now. Or else I'll curse you until I feel satisfied."

The novice saw Phim's dark mood. He stroked her hand soothingly and wiped away her tears. "That Chang is a terrible troublemaker. Because of him, you were abused and beaten.

This is no trifle, striping you with a stick. Did she tie your hands up against the wall?[6] Is that why you're marked all over? Lightning strike! Even your little finger is scored."

He felt devastated by what had happened to his darling Phim, and broke down in streams of tears. "This is beyond belief, my jewel, but don't be disheartened.

After the abbot beat me, I fled to my mother. She doesn't want me to leave the monkhood. Because we're poor, I'm at a loss what to do. Where could I find the money for a nest egg?

So I don't dare disrobe, yet I'm fed up and miserable. My love and longing for you is unbroken. You're never out of my mind whatever I'm doing.

Raise your face, dear Phim. Your cheeks are dirty. I'll wipe the tears. Don't be so miserable. My heart doesn't forget my promises."

Phim shot back, "How come you're so slow? Why can't you get some money? I'm afraid it means you don't really love me.

Oh, this is my karma! Why was I born a woman? I fell for your sweet words, and now it looks as if I've really fallen. I'm afraid you'll abandon me to sorrow and heartbreak.

This evening, please come to the house, Novice. I'll find some money to give you. On second thoughts, maybe I shouldn't go back home. I fear Mother will beat me again.

Whatever will be will be. I won't go. I'll stay at this wat. I feel enormously hurt and resentful. If I stay with you, what would happen?"

"Oh eye's jewel, it's a pity but you can't stay here and eat from the alms." He caressed Phim to cheer her up but she still cried tears of complaint and anger.

---

6. An old practice when beating children.

"This evening I'll take leave of the abbot and disrobe. Late at night, I'll come to your house. If I pay respect to take leave but the abbot refuses, I'll run away to you anyway."

With these words, he shifted so his body touched hers. "Your skin is soft, silky soft. You look so beautiful, like something made in a mold, like a lotus bud bursting out behind a leaf.[7]

Raise your face and give me a little kiss, Phim. I'm only a novice, it's not against the rules." "What is this! You make me feel hurt. Soon you'll be chased out of here like that other wat.

The more someone tells you not to do something, the more you do it. You're acting rudely and people watching will complain. If anyone comes to make a fuss, we'll have to jump out of the kuti, but this one is too high to jump.

I truly have to go. If Mother finds out, things will get blown up." She went out, but still feeling lovelorn, came back to speak to the novice again.

"Disrobe and come this evening. No more lies and evasion." With that, she strode out and returned home with Saithong.

They cut through to the house, then detoured round to hide at a corner of the wall. Once they were sure Siprajan was not looking, they crept up the stairs,

and hid behind a door on the terrace. Ducking behind a doorway going up to the main apartment, they tiptoed ahead, glancing around, and darted into the room.

At dusk, the sun weakened and slid behind the hills. The world was about to slip into darkness. As the twilight sun began to set, the forest came alive with the calls of animals.

Sounds of roaring and trumpeting echoed round. Deer cowered in fright with hair standing on end. Novice Kaeo trembled with fear and longing.

He sighed and sorrowed out of concern for gentle Phim. His breast ached and shivered as if pierced by an arrow.

Unable to find any peace of mind, he went to see the abbot. Kneeling to pay respect, he said, "I'm greatly troubled. I feel there's a bonfire raging in my breast, making me unsettled, listless, and lonely.

deer

Because of past sins, I have no merit to enter the monkhood. The yellow robe

---

7. A bud sheltered by leaves from sun, rain, wind, and insects is believed to result in a fresher and more perfect flower.

pack baskets

is too hot for me to wear. I beg the soles of Your Lordship's feet to allow me to leave. Without your blessing, I'll be burned to death in this blaze."

These words made the abbot sore at heart. "I'll miss you badly. I was hoping you'd look after my cremation. Now you want to run off mid-way, without any feeling left for me.

As a lay person, life will be tough. Do you want to disrobe and get yourself tattooed?[8] Once your wrist is black, it's all hard times—carrying pack baskets on your shoulder until you collapse.

If the overseer likes you, things are a bit easier. He can look after you and find work that's not too heavy. But if he hates you, he'll use you until you ache—sawing wood, dragging big logs, anything.

With a body like yours, slender as a sculpture,[9] do you think you can manage that? Or are you disrobing in the hope of being a chaophraya? Listen to me. Don't rush to disrobe and leave."

"Your Lordship, my beloved patron, you're absolutely right. I can't argue. But don't stop me. I no longer wish to be here. Please look for an auspicious time."

The abbot saw he was beyond restraint. He picked up his slate and checked the date by the lunar calendar. He wrote in the day, month, and year of Novice Kaeo's birth, and made calculations according to the manual.[10]

calculating slate

---

8. Phrai, subject to corvée labor, were identified by a tattoo on the wrist or back of the hand specifying their name, father's name, place of residence, and their *munnai*, foreman or overseer. In early Bangkok, when there was a pressing need to marshal manpower for war and reconstruction, attempts were made to register all phrai at the start of each reign. In late Ayutthaya, and again by the mid-nineteenth century, the system was less rigorous, and widely evaded (Englehart, *Culture and Power*, 36–44; Akin, *Organization*).

9. For a noble male of this era, a slender body was considered elegant. Muscle bulk was associated with manual labor.

10. A common technique in Thai astrology is to cast one chart of the time of birth, and another of the present time, and make comparisons between the two. The background of the chart divides the heavens into twelve signs, ราศี, *rasi*, based on stars. Nine bodies, เคราะห์, *khro,* from Sanskrit *grava*, seizing, holding, i.e., influence or force, orbit through this map. These bodies include the sun, moon, five planets, and two imaginary planets, Rahu and Ketu, which are located at the two points where the paths of the sun and moon cross. The mathematics for calculating the orbits were based on observations but made complex by the fact that the planets

horoscope diagram

He entered the results and saw the meaning as certainly as with Indra's eye. "Your fate is good—to be a soldier, my son. But I can also divine that you've been lying to me.

I understand now why you're in such turmoil. I didn't realize before you're having a love affair. Listen to my words and remember them well. After disrobing, you'll marry as you intend,

set up house together, and build up some wealth, but it won't last. You'll be separated and kept far apart. She'll discard you and have a new husband.

When you reach the critical age of twenty-five,[11] a misfortune will occur. You'll be clapped in irons and locked away. At the age of forty, you'll do well."

The words of Abbot Khong made Novice Kaeo's heart lurch. He knelt to pay respect and left, shaking with fright and stifling his sorrow. He entered his kuti, prostrated three times, and disrobed.

He tied on a subduing charm[12] and a mercury amulet.[13] He dressed in a yok with a kanok-and-vine pattern and Garuda flying with Wasukri[14] in his claws.

Garuda and Wasukri

move in ellipses rather than circles and actually orbit the sun rather than the earth and hence, as seen from earth, may speed up, slow down, or even reverse at certain points of the cycle. The horoscope is shown in a round diagram with each planetary body depicted by a number located in one of the twelve signs. The abbot may have been using the fully fledged system, based on the Jyotisha system originating from India, in which case the calculations are quite complex, or alternatively, some simplified version.

11. เบญจเพส, *benjaphet*, distorted from Pali *panja wisa*, five and twenty. In astrology, a life is divided into phases of twenty-five years: a "first age" from one to twenty-five; "second age" from twenty-five to fifty; and a "third age" from fifty to seventy-five, after which the "first age" recurs. *Benjaphet* is a point of transition.

12. ลูกสะกด, *luk sakot*, a seed-shaped amulet made with metal left over from casting a Buddha image, threaded on a string tied round the waist (Noranit, *Sanuk kap KCKP*, 17).

13. ปรอท, *parot*. Because mercury is a metal that acts unnaturally (like a fluid), it is one of the most common substances considered ขลัง, *khlang*, of intrinsic power. A *parot* amulet is usually a small enclosed metal cylinder filled with mercury. It is believed to convey invulnerability by flowing to any part of the body that is threatened with piercing (SB, 180–81).

14. A naga king used as the rope for churning the ocean of milk to create the world in the Mahabharata (*Hindu Myths*, 275). The rivalry between Garuda and Naga, bird and snake, is found in Hindu mythology with several legendary explanations, and is thought to symbolize rivalry between mountain dwellers and plains dwellers. In Buddhism, the Garuda is huge,

He flung across his chest a black silk uppercloth with tassels hanging from the end, infused with fragrance. He put on a belt cinched good and tight, and inserted a kris with a crow's head handle.

He arranged a fine set of offerings, cast a powerful mantra over rice, and set off with victory candles in his hand. A bright moon lit the way.

It was the second watch. The sky glittered with stars. In the center of the firmament, brighter than the others, shone the moon with an aura like a royal parasol.

He hastened to a graveyard and built an eye-level shrine with a white cloth as a canopy. He lit candles that flared brightly in the darkness, walked around the shrine making a protective circle with sacred thread,

kris

then entered the circle, sat cross-legged,[15] and summoned up the powers. In every direction, the lofty forest trembled. A storm wind thrashed through the bushes. Trees bowed over and came crashing down.

Under the power of the mantra, thunderbolts exploded like the thumps of a giant pestle. Lightning flashed and wind howled, as if to shake the earth and shatter it into fragments.

The ground on which he sat quaked as if being shaken apart. A swarm of spirits, sprites, and spectrals rose up, and all ran towards him, their bodies transforming into different shapes.

Once close, they were in awe of Phlai Kaeo's lore and could do him no harm. They all bowed, prostrated, and beseeched him, "Lord, what do you desire here?"

One[16] bold, adept spirit with a huge form was the leader. Hearing Phlai Kaeo's mantra, he found it intolerable.

He roared loudly enough to collapse the earth, and extended his body

---

powerful, and intelligent ("like the *devata* in heaven they know basic principles") and feeds on the almost-as-powerful naga: "Whenever a *garuda* snatches a *naga* from the middle of the ocean, the splash extends for 100 *yojana* in every direction. He grasps the tail of the *naga* tightly in his talons, flies away through the air leaving its head dangling down below, and takes it to his dwelling place where he eats it" (RR, 88, 89). The Garuda carrying one or two naga in its talons is a very popular image. It was used for the first national emblem of Siam, designed in 1873, later modified to show Garuda alone.

15. นั่งพับแพนงเชิง, *nang phap phanaengchoeng*, an old Khmer-derived word for a crossed-leg pose, now surviving in the name of Wat Phananchoeng in Ayutthaya because of the massive Buddha in such a pose (Noranit, *Sanuk kap KCKP*, 17; KP, 71).

16. The next three stanzas down to "pulverize you" are taken from WK, 5:190, and were condensed in PD into one stanza: The chief spirit arrived last, in a rage. He jumped up and down shouting "Who is this? If you don't get out of here, I'll come after you, beat you, pulverize you!"

upwards, with stretching noises, almost as tall as a mountain, looking awesome with two rolling, flashing eyes.

Holding a club, he screeched stridently, "Hey! What's this? If you don't get out of here, I'll come after you, beat you, pulverize you!"

Phlai Kaeo yelled so loudly that the sound echoed around the forest and sky, then scattered rice,[17] striking the spirit's body, which reeled, and shrank as small as a bee sting.

Phlai Kaeo by now was expert with the powers of lore. He asked, "Hey, are you or someone else in this graveyard the boss around here, or is there nobody in charge?"

As if they were listening to a command from Indra, the spirits quailed and longed to disappear into the ground. "I'm master of this graveyard," said the spirit, "I'm the boss of these spirits, the demon in chief.

Wesawan[18] granted me this territory as a servant of the fearless god king.[19] I've been here a long time. As for you, what business brings you here?"

"Me? A big matter." He slashed at the spirit with an enchanted nettle vine and bellowed, "Will you go with me or not? Answer quickly!" The spirit prostrated and consented to take him.

Phlai Kaeo enchanted a Trinisinghe yantra,[20] and called the spirit, who

---

17. Scattering rice is a means of control or suppression, often used in conjunction with the Subduer mantra (see p. 282, note 2). The rice used should be grains that stuck to the pestle during pounding, dyed with a potion of leaves and herbs including leaves of tamarind, pacifier, *hinghai*, and *chumhet*, a cassia, enchanted with 108 repetitions of a formula, and thrown while standing on one leg (Prachak, *Prapheni*, 159).

18. Vaisravana, a name for Kubera, guardian of the north, king of the *yaksa* giants (*Hindu Myths*, 119; Anuman, *Essays*, 278; see p. 41, note 63).

19. เทวราช, *thewarat*, Sanskrit *devaraja*, perhaps referring to Indra.

20. (เลข)ยันต์, *(lek) yan*, yantras are mystical diagrams which originated in the Hindu tradition but also are prominent in Buddhist cultures, especially tantric Buddhism. Chawdri defined a yantra as "an instrument, an apparatus, a talisman or mystical diagram" (*Secrets,* 3). They probably originated as aids to meditation but later acquired many uses, especially to ward off enemies and bad events. Yantra have to be drawn by an adept and are energized by chanting a mantra. In the South Asian versions, the diagrams consist primarily of geometric shapes and numbers, all of which have specific symbolic meanings. In the Southeast Asian versions, the diagrams also incorporate abbreviated mantra, written in Pali, sequences of numbers written in Khmer, and images of Hindu gods, disciples of the Buddha, and mythical animals. Yantra can be tattooed on the body or inscribed on various materials that can be worn on the body or used in ritual. In the Thai tradition, their main purpose is to convey invulnerability. (See PKW, especially vol. 4)

Trinisinghe, ตรีนิสิงเห, three lions, is one of the most well-known yantra diagrams. The simplest version has one square with another square positioned diagonally inside it, and numbers

staggered towards him. Phlai promptly placed the yantra
cloth over its head, and slung his things on its back.

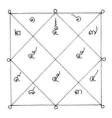

He jumped up onto its shoulders, and they glided
away as if borne by a strong wind. They flew through
lofty woods, crossed grasslands, and cut through dense
forest, aiming straight into Suphan town.

The spirit soared speedily to the house of Siprajan,

Trinisinghe yantra

crossing the fence and landing in the flower garden. The
wind wafted a fragrance of soft pollen.

Phlai Kaeo got down from the spirit's shoulders. "You stay waiting here in
the garden until I come back." He walked quickly to the stairway.

Now to tell of Phim and Saithong. Neither was feeling happy. As the rays of
the sun were hidden by the forest, little Phim's heart yearned and grieved.

She felt sorry for herself. She regretted giving herself away, and fretted about
the shame. She feared the novice had deceived her. Her eyes welled with tears,
her mind swirled, and her chest felt choked.

Night came and there was still no sign of Phlai Kaeo. "I think he's tricked
me. If he doesn't turn up tonight, I'll say farewell to Saithong and hang
myself."

Saithong was greatly worried about her. She chattered away in an attempt
to cheer her up. "He's despicable, this Novice Kaeo. It's late and there's still no
sign of him.

Maybe he's come and is lurking around outside for fear someone will see
him." She opened the door. "I'll go out to look around."

She soon came upon him. "Now, my rich fellow, why have you been dawdling?
Phim has been waiting until late. And I want the reward you promised me."

Phlai Kaeo smiled and replied to Saithong. "Please let me postpone a little.
Take me to her for one more night. Tomorrow I'll give it to you. Honestly."

Saithong spread out her seamed uppercloth to hide Phlai, and he walked
eagerly up into the house, hidden behind her. Pretending it was accidental, he
touched her breast.

When she did not react, he grasped with his full hand. Saithong felt ticklish

---

written in the chambers. More complex versions have concentric strings of numbers. It serves
as an all-purpose tool for subduing or countering the power of other spirits, and for protecting
against dangers such as disease. Here, Phlai Kaeo probably has a cloth drawn with the yantra,
and pronounces a mantra to activate it. (Anuman, *Essays*, 310–11; PKW, 1:157)

and embarrassed. She pushed him away. "Hey! You're not worth helping. This is a breast, Phlai Kaeo. It's not proper."

He saw she was angry. "I only touched it a little. Forgive me. I thought it was Phim—soft, nice and soft. May I have a kiss? Oh, I forgot."

"Hey! Mistaken, huh, Phlai? Has there been anyone who thinks so much of himself? If you create a scandal here you won't get what you want. You're too full of yourself. I'm keeping quiet for your sake, but you just take liberties.

That's her room. Creep in yourself. I don't want to see her. I'd better go to sleep." She snatched back her uppercloth, tossed her head, and flashed him an angry look.

After Saithong left, Phlai Kaeo wasted no time. He crept to the inner bedroom, found the door open, and went in.

He carefully parted the curtains and mosquito net, and peered in. "Poor thing!" She was sitting with head bowed. In the glow of a lamp, her complexion shimmered as fair as the moon.

Pretty curls framed her sad face. Her figure was beautiful, her complexion radiant, her bearing adorable. He could barely restrain his desire to embrace her.

Instead, he teased her by clearing his throat, "Ahem!" Phim looked up and came forward with her eyes still lowered. Her cheek collided with his nose, and his hand with her breast. Phim jumped away, stumbled, and uttered a squeal of shock.

Glancing up, she saw Phlai Kaeo. "Oh! You've come. What are you skulking around for? Just now I thought it was a ghost. You scared me. Haven't you had enough of fooling around?"

Phlai Kaeo doubled over laughing. He hugged her and guided her into the room. They sat on the bed side by side, fondling. "Eh, were you waiting for me?"

"So what if I was waiting? I was miserable from thinking about you. If you didn't come tonight, I was going to say farewell to Saithong and hang myself."

"Oh Phim, how could you abandon me so easily? I'd have to stay in the monkhood until death, with no one else from now onward,

just praying every evening and telling my beads[21] to make some merit for you. It wasn't that I was never going to come but I had to take leave of the abbot.

I told him all sorts of lies but he knew. A real teacher can see the truth. He made lots of objections so it was this late by the time I could come."

---

21. (ลูก)ประคำ, *luk prakham*, a string of small beads worn as an ornament or as an aid for counting the recitation of prayers.

beads

While speaking, he caressed her with his hands, kissed her left cheek, then the right one, hugged her tight to his chest, pressed his face to hers, and gently guided her to lie down.

Hearts thumped. Passions multiplied. Chaos approached. On the ocean, winds whipped up waves that crashed on the shoreline, recoiled, and crashed, over and over again.

A Hainanese junk sailed into a small canal. The sky shivered with thunder, and rain sluiced down. The captain lost his way and turned the helm. The ship faltered, grounded on the shallows, and broke apart.

Phlai Kaeo sat up and said, "My love, it's very hot. Let's go and bathe." Phim did not hesitate. She took his hand and led him out.

As they crept along, floorboards creaked. Siprajan called out, "Who's there?" Phlai Kaeo nudged Phim to reply. "Just me. I'm going out to bathe."

They went to a bowl placed on the terrace and sat happily on a low bench beside it. She released water to spray and splash from a lead nozzle.

He tugged at her sabai. "Hey, don't play around. I'm shy about my breasts and I've never bathed with nothing on. People will see. Don't embarrass me, please."

"Go on. There's only you and me—nobody else to see us, dear Phim. Bathing with your clothes on is not as cooling." With those words, he peeled the sabai away from her breasts.

In the light of the moon floating through a hollow sky, her breasts shone full and fair. The gush of water splashed on them like a shower of diamonds.

Phlai Kaeo smiled. "Darling Phim, they rise and shine at the touch of moonlight. Let me wash you to feel good. I won't be rough on your skin but soft as a spider's web."

Phim sat close to him with a smile and stretched out her arms. Phlai Kaeo hugged her tightly to him and caressed her gently with his hand.

"Hey, what's this! Didn't you have enough just now? To scrub my arms do you have to squeeze me like this? I'm very ticklish and you're annoying me. Take your hands off. You're really too much."

"Forgive me. I was a bit lost. You get irritable and make me beg forgiveness for everything. Please don't be so sulky. It's chilly. That's enough bathing."

They got up, dressed, and powdered. Phim poured krajae water for him. "Give me a little kiss. What fragrance is this?" She was shy, hid her face, and did not speak.

"Turn your face here. I'll powder it for you. Why should we be needlessly shy of each other. Your right cheek has to be powdered just so." "Don't fuss over my cheeks. I'm a poor person."

"Oh Phim, you're always hurt so easily. You keep finding fault with everything." He guided her gently back onto the bed where they fooled and fondled.

Phlai Kaeo began to think about Saithong asking for her reward. "I could find the money for her somehow but that would be a waste of my talents as a lover.

There's an old saying that hits the nail on the head: If a thorn pricks, use another thorn to pry it out.[22] That's the way. Money is not what she's after." With these thoughts, he turned to Phim with a broad smile,

and cunningly questioned her with hidden intention. "I'm really worried, gentle Phim. I'll come to ask for your hand from your mother but if she refuses, I'll die of a broken heart."

With no idea of the ruse he had in mind, tender Phim turned and bantered with him. "Don't worry. I won't make you ashamed.

If our horoscopes don't match, I'll probably run off with you. Whether it's for better or worse, I'll think about that later. What I'm really afraid of is that you won't ask for me."

"Eh? How so? Why do you say that? You pick at me in advance about everything. Please don't fret that I'm delaying matters. But tell me really, dear Phim, what's your birth year?

Then if I'm asked, I can tell them a year that comes to the same place on the naga.[23] Don't believe that

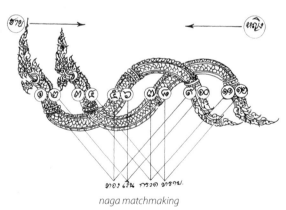

naga matchmaking

----

22. An old saying meaning "like cures like" (Gerini, "On Siamese Proverbs," 162).

23. The compatibility of a husband and wife depends on their birth years. A common method for checking on this compatibility uses a picture of two entwined naga with twelve points marked along their length. The man starts at the head, taking that place to denote the year of the rat, and then counts forward until he reaches his birth year. The woman does the same, starting at the tail. If both end at the same place, then compatibility is at its most perfect, with some added qualifications given whether they end up at the head, foot, or other location on the naga

stuff in the manual about predicting whether we'll be good or bad for each other.

There are lots of people who elope. Do they look at their horoscopes, dear Phim? What counts is the merit we've made from the past. If there's karma, better not to talk about it at all, Phim."

"Me? I'm the year of the rat. This year, I'm sixteen, just blooming." "Younger than me by two years, tender Phim. How about Saithong? What year is she?"

"She's the year of the horse—twenty-two, as I remember.[24] Why are you asking for her year? Are you in love with her and hoping to marry her too?"

"Oh Phim, you always say such odd things. What a shameful idea! Enough of that. There's no way she's going to be my lover or wife. You're always having a dig at me."

With these words, he encircled her again, pressing her tightly to him, and kissed her, inhaling her krajae powder. Her breasts felt taut and proud enough to burst. He caressed her to sleep in no time.

Once he saw Phim was asleep, Phlai Kaeo's turbulent thoughts turned to Saithong. He had in mind to go and offer his love.

"She's neither old or young but youthful enough and good-looking. Her breasts I felt just now aren't flabby yet, but nice and firm. She's only four years older than me.

Fine. I'll sneak out to find her. Even if she doesn't like it and calls me a bully, she dare not cry out noisily because she herself let me into the house."

With these thoughts, he stepped down from the bed and tiptoed slowly away, glancing around. At the sound and tremor of his footfalls, Phim turned over. He edged back to her side,

hugged her close to his chest, rocked her back and forth, and cradled her back to sleep. "Don't you want to nap, Phim? Though we did it until the sweat flowed, still you don't sleep."

He opened a sandalwood fan and fanned her. "Relax and have some rest,

---

(Wales, *Divination*, 54; Hora Purajan, *Tamra phrommachat*, 77–78). In the graphic, the words at the top are male and female, numbers 1 to 12 are written along the nagas, and the positions are labeled as gold, silver, gravel, and sand.

24. The Thai sequence of animal years is: rat, ox, tiger, hare, dragon, snake, horse, goat, monkey, cock, dog, pig. Phim was born in a rat year and is now sixteen. Saithong was born in a horse year and is now twenty-two. This matches. Phlai says he is eighteen, which means he would have been born in a dog year but chapter 1 states Phlai was born in a tiger year. In chapter 3, the Mahachat festival was held in the year of the cock, and the current scene is probably in the following year (dog). But this works with neither age sequence. If Phlai was born in a tiger year and is now eighteen, the current year is a goat year. And if Phim and Saithong's details are correct, the current year is a hare year.

dear Phim. It's late now but you're still awake." Under his caresses, she lapsed into slumber.

Once she had dropped off as he wished, he left her room and crept directly to Saithong's.

He blew a Great Loosener formula, making the bolts spring and slide out. He stole into the inner bedroom, sat down beside Saithong, and embraced her.

He kissed her cheek. He nuzzled and pressed her breasts that lay round, proud, large, and exposed. Lying down close beside her, he blew a mantra while caressing her back to arouse her.

Saithong came to her senses at once, and turned to see Phlai Kaeo. Her heart felt full of a craving for love.

She was touched by a God-Arouser mantra[25] that made her tremble with excitement and confusion, but her female modesty made her dissemble. She called out, "Who is this?"

Phlai Kaeo smiled and replied, "Please don't cry out. I've come to find you because I couldn't swallow the love that's weighing down my heart. Forgive me. Don't think of yourself as Phim's elder sister.

You're not many days older than me. Making love together isn't wrong. There are lots of lovers older than this. Please don't stop me and leave me yearning."

"This is embarrassing, Kaeo, you big bully. You're a kid standing on tiptoe to court a grown-up. You're too used to getting your own way. You've come to wheedle me so you can take liberties.

You're a good and thoughtful person so why are you giving me this trouble? If Phim finds out, it won't be pretty. She'll think I made a date for you to come here.

It'll be bad for you too, Phlai Kaeo. Coming to see me and making me upset is karma already. You may end up not tasting the cream. Think carefully. Please leave this room."

---

25. เทพรัญจวน, *thepranjuan*, the deity that excites. The mantra should be chanted while inscribing the name of the loved one on the petal of a *jampa* flower. The petal should then be shown to her, and if she asks for it, she will be captivated. Alternatively, a doll is made of the woman with her name inscribed on the chest. The doll is then hugged while chanting mantras until sleep comes. The mantra may also be used to enchant a cloth worn by the target. (PKW, 2:198–99; examples of the formula are in Thep, *Wicha athan*, 30–31; *Phra khamphi khatha 108*, 254–55)

"What a pity. My heart felt you loved me so I dared to come, but you still complain. Even if Phim finds out, don't worry. I'll patch things up so you don't get any of the blame.

You've already been kind to me. Please keep on being so. Don't complain and make a loud fuss. You're not listening even though I've fondled you this much already."

"Are you really so insistent? Do you want to raise a scandal all over the house, sir? I've talked to you nicely, but you still pester me. I don't know what to do. Here, I'll scratch you so it shows, right now!

Oh, who would want to be in my place? All this pinching and teasing is uncouth and shameful. I thought you were a good fellow, not a wicked one. You shouldn't be sitting here bullying me.

Go, go! Please leave the room. If you stay, I'll scream and you'll get what you deserve for coming here to play around and seduce me. I'll tell Mother to come and catch you."

Phlai Kaeo edged closer with a broad smile, chanted a mantra, and blew it onto her body, arousing her to passion.

He pleaded, "Have pity, Saithong. If you aren't kind, you can be certain I won't live long. I'll probably hang myself. Just wait and see."

With that, he teasingly picked up a cloth, tied it over a beam in the wall, and wrapped the end around his neck. Saithong shrieked, "Don't do it, Phlai Kaeo!

Come here. I've something for you to hear. Are you mad enough to kill yourself so easily? It's very difficult to be born a man.[26] Won't you miss Phim?

She's young and she's got the figure of a *kinnari*. She's the one you're in love with. I'm old already and my figure is not beautiful."

Phlai Kaeo smiled. "You're like Phim in every way—manners, talk, elegance. Your body and your breasts are just right. I've seen the lot.

Being a bit older, you must have more skill, more tricks, all the various games. That can't be bad." He edged up next to her and lightly touched her breast without pressing hard.

They embraced and lay down side by side on the bed. He kissed her head very gently, and hugged her tightly against his chest. "Please don't be stubborn. Be kind. Don't resist and try to wriggle away."

---

26. Being born female meant having too little accumulated merit to be born a man. This is not explicitly stated in the Three Worlds cosmology but is implied by the fact that all the divine forms higher in the scale than humans are male. In an inscription of 1399, a Sukhothai queen mother begged, "By the power of my merit, may I be reborn as a male in the future" (Griswold and Prasert, *Epigraphical and Historical Studies*, 65).

Saithong answered, "Don't be rough with me. I'll let you stay. I'm just worried you'll play the loverboy act. Once you've coupled with me, you'll throw me away.

If what you're after is love, don't use force. And please give me your word on one thing. Be clear that you really love me. Then I'll lie back, stay still, and let you do what you want."

"It's a pity you need my word, Saithong, but I don't object. I can swear—let lightning strike me down—I won't lie to you and I won't cheat on you. I don't rock back and forth, really."

With that, he blew a *pathamang*[27] onto her breast. Saithong lapsed into a drowsy stupor. Her eyes fluttered and drooped. Phlai Kaeo lay down covering her on the bed.

Little by little, he edged closer and closer, touching very gently. Raindrops pattered, lightning flashed, thunder rumbled, wind howled. Waves battered a junk that heeled over, and sought refuge by slipping along the riverbank.

In the heavy storm, the sail was reefed to half mast, yet the ship still pitched and yawed, wallowed and rolled. Several times it had to throw anchor and heave to for a while.

Making love with Phim was like being in the shallows at a river's edge with no waves, only some splashing ripples. With Saithong was like being hit by a kite storm.[28] As soon as the ship left the bight, it sank to the bottom.

Now to tell of gentle little Phim. She woke and sleepily reached out for Phlai Kaeo. He'd gone. Her heart sank. "What's going on?"

She sat up and saw the door standing open. "Where has my love run off to? He can't have gone to find someone he knows. And the time now is very, very late.

Maybe he's playing a joke on me." She parted the curtains and looked around but could not find him. Her heart sank further and tears flowed. "What a pity you didn't tell me where you were going.

Maybe you're angry at me for something, but I don't see I've done anything wrong. I'm surprised you've run off. Maybe you left word with Saithong. I'll go and ask."

She crept to Saithong's room and heard the muffled sound of conversation

---

27. Here it means a love mantra (see also p. 124, note 30).

28. พายุว่าว, *phayu wao*, more commonly *lom wao*, the "kite wind" which blows from the north at the start of the cool season in November-December, a popular season for kite flying.

inside. Listening hidden behind the door, she knew he was in the room where Saithong slept.

Saithong was feeling gloomy, listless, and full of uncertainty. "Because you're strong, you tend to be a bully.

Now that I'm tainted, you have to look after me. If you neglect me, I'll be shamed. If Phim finds out, she'll bully me too. I'll be the minor wife and I won't be able to avoid paying respect to her, truly."

"What's up? Why do you say that? I'll love you equally and not put one above the other. Raise your face. I'll tell you the truth about who I've loved for some time.

Remember when you came to talk about the reward for Phim? Because I loved you, I acted the part. If I'd tried to court you then, I was worried you wouldn't talk to me. But I love you more by five to one."

Listening behind the door, Phim felt choked and burned up with anger. When she could stand no more, she pushed the door open with a bang, and stamped up to the bed.

Opening the mosquito net, she peered in to find them in each other's arms. She glared at them in rage. Saithong jumped up from the bed. "Kaeo forced me, Mistress Phim!

I tried to fend him off but he wouldn't budge. However much I protested, he just smiled. If I made any noise, I worried I'd get you into trouble. I felt blood was almost spurting from my eyes.

Because I love you, I accept what comes, bitter or sweet. Do you take me on my word? I didn't know this Kaeo of yours would be like this. Just thinking about it, I feel hurt."

curving shafts

She put on a show of modesty, lowered her face, and burst into tears. Feeling choked with anger and disgust, Phim spoke with acid sarcasm.

"I thank you for having such a good heart. You're kind and considerate in every way—straight, really straighter than a chariot's curving shaft.[29] It's all of us who are crooked."

---

29. *Ngonrot* (this assumes that อนรถ in the original is a misprint for งอนรถ), the curving up-swept shaft of a chariot, often depicted in mural painting and similar illustrations.

Then she turned on Phlai Kaeo. "Do you think it was good to come and bully her? She's older than you and she raised me from childhood but you have no qualms.

You don't think carefully. You're just out for what you can get. It's beyond a joke, really. Were you grown-up, you wouldn't bully a child. You're like an over-exuberant little monkey, like a pushy Chinese Jek who's bent on riding a cow elephant.

Good thing I came in time to disturb things, otherwise you'd probably have speared her again. It's like when Rahu swallows the moon. Only when people ring bells does he shit it out."[30]

Rahu swallowing the moon

"It's not like that. Don't make so much of it. Please calm down. There's no need to be so angry and make things confused. Creating a row will only bring scandal and shame.

The truth is I came to ask Saithong if I could postpone paying the reward that I'd promised her. Really. I'm not like that, eye's jewel. It's a pity you're so cross with me."

"I'm more hurt than you can imagine. My ears are full of it, everything. I heard it all. You're not telling but I saw the truth. Not just a reward, you tossed her the full ding-dong bar of gold!"

Phim's sarcasm cut Saithong to the quick. She could not hold back and turned on Phim in anger. "Tcha! It's like we don't know what's going on here.

It's you who has the whole bar of gold. Yes, definitely, enough of them to fill a chest. Probably over a hundred. Even if you shared some with me, I wouldn't take it.

This is already the thinking of a wife. You coached him to go back on his promise, right? You're worried you'll lose the reward money to me. We both know what's going on here.

This is the first husband you've fallen for, and now you won't have any use for me until the sky caves in. I worked hard at bringing you up, night after night. Is this how you repay me, beloved?"

"Tcha! You're not bad yourself, Saithong. You string words like a braided

---

30. According to the belief, an eclipse happens when the demon-god Rahu swallows the sun or moon. People ring bells and make other noise to frighten Rahu into releasing it.

necklace. They sound wonderful. But laughable, ha-ha! You worked hard at getting him to fall in love with you.

And like this, why shouldn't he be smitten? Loved to stupefaction. So I'm not the same. Inferior by five to one because I can't match your pace and style.

I thank you for bringing me up—and bringing both me and an in-law into this room. There's an old saying: Sisters from the same womb are like each other's hands and feet."[31]

Saithong shot back, "You've so many complaints, and no consideration. What will be will be, according to karma.

Your tongue is sharp so keep scolding. Soon I'll beat you and knock you down. This is deep. Are you going to stand still and let me do it? Don't believe in sheer bulk. I may be small but I can be fearsome."

"If that's the way it is, you can hit me and I won't complain. I think of him as my lord and husband. You're the minor wife taking liberties and not knowing your place. I'll grab your hair and bash you with a coconut shell!"

"Tcha! What a speech! I'll have to beat this sharp-tongued girl." Phim's anger rose. "Don't you dare hit me, Saithong!"

Alarmed over the rising level of noise in the room, Phlai Kaeo jumped up and stood between them, spreading his arms to shield Saithong. "Don't, Phim!

Hold off. Have a care for your elder sister. Noise will only create trouble, my tenderness. Saithong, you're not being conciliatory with Phim but throwing more fuel on the fire and making matters worse."

Three voices made even more noise. Siprajan woke from her sleep in alarm. "What's that racket? Deafening. Like a gunshot. What are you all doing at this late hour?"

Saithong had a smart idea and called straight back, "Phim's reprimanding me. I went to sleep and let a dog eat the fat." Siprajan called out, "Good. You deserve it."

Phim smiled and contributed to the lie. "I came to chase the dog away or else the whole jar of fat would've gone." She glared at them angrily and went back into her room.

Phlai Kaeo could see how angry Phim was. He followed her, sat down beside her, and tried to make things up. Gently he hugged and laid her down,

kissed and caressed her, trying to soothe away her anger. "Please forgive me, my tenderness." Still feeling hurt, Phim shoved him away. "Don't come and sleep in this room, my dear sir.

---

31. Meaning that they share everything.

Why come to touch me? It's a waste of your hands. Don't fondle me, I'm not fragrant, not like Saithong. She's perfect. Is it true you've fallen for her?"

"Oh what a pity, dear Phim. All the time now you distrust me. You get at me for everything you can. Though I'm weighed down by problems, you don't see.

What if I come to ask for your hand tomorrow but your mother doesn't consent? My darling, that's the problem upsetting me, so I went to talk it through with Saithong.

I hadn't even chewed the betel into bits when you burst into the room. There wasn't enough time to get mixed up with Saithong. You're concerned about nothing. Don't be upset."

"My, my! You're quite something. Lightning strike! A real big liar. I was hiding there listening for a long time. Don't try to talk your way out of it.

If things are like this, will we love each other in the future? You say you'll ask for my hand but I'm still waiting. Even on something like that you can't stop fibbing. It's second nature for you to lie about everything.

I've fallen in love but it's all one-sided. You just tell lies, twist and turn. I made a mistake, and the more I think about it, the more disappointed I am. Oh dear me, I'll be shamed.

I didn't listen to the sayings they teach us. I was too easily persuaded by a sweet tongue. It's said really smart men have about thirty-two tricks.

By comparison, this fellow has at least sixty-four. You speak as beautifully as a gong circle playing but you don't love. I won't believe in promises from now on."

gong circle

"It's a pity you don't believe I love you. Don't hate me. Don't think like that. I love you as much as my own heart. I want to hug and caress you all the time."

The cry of a coel announced it was close to dawn, making them start. "Oh! It's almost first light!" He got up, opened a window, and saw the early glimmers with stars still shining.

The sun's chariot would soon chase away the darkness. The thought of leaving made his heart churn. Sadness welled in his chest, and his eyes filled with tears. He felt his heart was being plucked away.

"Parting from you is such sadness, my sweet. Our jealous friend has created a big problem. Look after yourself. Your husband[32] bids farewell. Be wary of danger and don't meddle with that ruffian.

I'm scared your mother will give you to that creature. As her daughter you can't resist. She'll beat and abuse you and make you miserable.

Stay here, my blossom, light of my life." The sun's chariot was fast approaching. He got up, already feeling the pangs of parting. Phim clung on to him not to go,

in despair that he had to leave, her heart falling apart at losing her love. "Late in the night I'll always be thinking of how you came to talk with me.

My bed will be cold at that chilly hour. My heart will feel cracked and clouded, as if the Lord of Darkness is coming to annihilate me. From now on, my eyes will be flooded with tears.

Lord of Darkness

Will you make it all the way to Kanburi? The wild animals will give you terrible trouble. Walking on your own will be lonely. Your poor fragile feet will ache.

When the sun is high, the heat will be unbearable. The more I think, the more your wife[33] is concerned about you in every way. Along the way it's all *yang*[34] forest where it'll be cold and you'll see no one.

In the evening you'll hear only the gibbons. When they swing around and whoop-wheet, it sounds so lonely and desolate, like the cries of the spirits. Oh beloved, I'm desolate too."

---

32. This is the first point where Phlai Kaeo refers to himself as ผัว, *phua*, husband. Later in the scene Phim refers to herself as เมีย, *mia*, wife. In the argument above, Phim has already used this vocabulary, and referred to Saithong as the minor wife (see p. 144). The marriage is already established by the sexual relationship. This is reflected in the Law on Marriage, พระไอยการลักษณผัวลักษณเมีย, *phra aiyakan laksana phua laksana mia*, literally the law on *phua* and *mia*, where the sexual relationship creates the legal relationship, although marriage ceremonial affects the detail of that legal relationship (KTS, 2:204–84). In other trysts in *KCKP*, the couple start using the vocabulary of *phua* and *mia* immediately after the first lovemaking. Phlai Kaeo and Phim have been more tentative. They have continued to address each other as พี่, *phi*, elder brother and น้อง, *nong*, little sister, everyday forms of address, while she has occasionally addressed him as พ่อ, *pho*, father, often used for a husband or patron. From here forward, she also sometimes addresses him as หม่อม, *mom*, lord, an element of several royal titles, used in *KCKP* to address a husband.

33. See note 32 above.

34. Throughout the story, "*yang*" or "*yang* and *yung*," *Dipterocarpus alatus* and *Dipterocarpus grandiflorus*, are used to refer to deep forest with tall dipterocarp trees.

She got up with her eyes full of tears, opened a chest, and took out five chang of money wrapped in a ruby colored cloth. "This is mine. Please take it.

Pay for an elephant to ride there. If they want ten tamlueng, just pay it. Believe your wife, don't walk." Phlai Kaeo took the money, his face flooded with tears.

He rested his chin on her shoulder and whispered, "Take care of yourself. Stay in your room. Don't even poke your head out of a window. Don't go down to the ground."

On the point of leaving, the heartbreak seemed infinite. "If I could divide myself in two, I'd leave one half here to keep you company. But that's beyond me. I don't have the powers of Lord Narai."

Almost dawn, the sound of monks tolling a bell and a coel's haunting cry in the forest made his heart sink. On the point of parting, tears welled in his eyes and spattered onto Phim's shoulder.

He stood up and moved to a window. "Wait for me, my gentle darling. Within seven days, I'll come to ask for your hand." He stood on the window ledge and called to the spirit.

Stepping onto its shoulders, he tied the money round its neck, and turned back for a final aching farewell. "My heart stays here but I have to say goodbye."

Phim raised her hands to wai him with tears streaming down her face. So pent-up she could scarcely speak, she sobbed out, "Safe journey."

Phlai Kaeo returned her wai, his heart breaking apart and his tears falling on the spirit's shoulder. Each was already yearning for the other. The spirit whisked him away.

She stayed looking until he slipped from sight. When he had finally gone, her misery multiplied. She closed the window, went into the room, and collapsed crying on the bed.

She ached and pined, softly sobbing herself into a stupor. "Oh my Phlai Kaeo! When will you come back to lie on this pillow?"

7: PHLAI KAEO MARRIES PHIM

As soon as Phim disappeared from his sight, Phlai Kaeo longed for her. The spirit sped unwaveringly across forest and grasslands,

soaring and swooping like the wind, past lakes, hills, and landings. They happily arrived at the house in Kanburi. The spirit disappeared promptly as the light came up.[1]

Phlai Kaeo entered his mother's house and peered around. His heart was still in Suphan, and his thoughts dwelt gloomily on Phim.

"Oh Phim, my friend for life, by now you'll be forlorn and tearful because we're far apart. How I miss you, Phim of mine!

If you'd come with me, you could wai Mother. You must be suffering beyond belief, my darling. Who'll cheer you up?" He walked straight into the house,

and embraced his mother's feet with tears flowing. Thong Prasi looked at his face, surprised to see him. "Oh Kaeo, why did you disrobe?

What happened to you, my dearest? You can't stop crying and won't raise your face. Where did you get this money?" Her own tears fell for her beloved son.

Phlai knelt and paid respect at her feet. "Mother, I'm going through a very bad time. Worse than bad—unbearable. Phim and I are in love.

The money came from her. When I left, she gave me five chang as capital so I can travel to ask her mother Siprajan for her hand. If she won't consent, Phim will follow me anyway.

Please be kind to your son, Mother. Phim is miserable waiting for me. Pity her for having to eat only tears. Don't be unfeeling."

Thong Prasi said, "Karma comes, karma goes! Oh Kaeo, my eye's jewel, be ordained as a monk first. Don't take a wife yet. Let your mother admire you in the robe.

Your father died a long time ago. Make some merit for him first by being a monk for just two rains retreats.[2] Don't worry; after you disrobe, I'll allow you to get married.

---

1. Such spirits cannot tolerate daylight and appear only during darkness.

2. Phlai Kaeo is currently only a novice. By being ordained as a monk, a man makes merit for his parents. This merit is especially important for the mother who does not have the chance to enter the monkhood herself. If a man has already married, the merit will go to the wife

I'll make you the son-in-law of a chaophraya. Listen to me and forget all this. Someone like Phim isn't suitable for you." Wearily she sobbed and soothed her son.

"There are girls more beautiful than her. If you want a palace lady, I'll ask for someone's hand for you. I'll offer a silver and gold plate to the king,[3] and get you an attractive court lady."

court ladies

Phlai Kaeo paid respect at his mother's feet. "I have no desire for some heavenly maiden. The only beautiful thing about court ladies is their manners. They're no match for my lovely Phim.

Her face, her breasts, her mid complexion[4]—she's perfect. And she's sharp and witty too. There's nobody in Suphanburi who can rival her beauty.

Oh beloved mistress of your child, there's no bar on entering the monkhood after marriage. Please don't raise these objections. If I can't follow my heart, I'll surely die."

Thong Prasi was very cross but she had pity on him too. Soothingly she said, "Don't be miserable, eye's jewel. If you won't listen to me, then I'll fall in with your wishes.

If I ask for Phim's hand, Siprajan can't refuse because we were old neighbors. Stop worrying and don't weep. You'll have Phim as your wife. Have something to eat."

These words made Phlai Kaeo stop grieving and cheer up. He went down to the jetty to bathe, and then had his meal. Thong Prasi called the servants, "Come here quick!

bathing jetty

rather than the parents (KW, 65). พรรษา, *phansa*, sometimes called "Buddhist Lent," a period of three lunar months from July to October when forest monks "retreat" to a wat because of the rains. Monks use this unit to count the number of years they have been in the monkhood.

3. Kukrit notes this was the practice for requesting to marry a palace lady down to the Fifth Reign (KP, 80). In Kukrit's novel, *Si phaendin*, Four Reigns, the hero, Prem, sends a relative to present a gold and silver tray to the king to ask for permission to marry Mae Phloi.

4. สองสี, *song si*, two-colored, between fair and dark.

Take these three chang and go to the timber wharf. Buy what's needed for building a new house, and bring it all back here.

Get the posts and everything to build five rooms." The servants fetched buffaloes, yoked two carts, and went off to make the purchases.

Thong Prasi organized buying quantities of sugar, savories, sweets, betel, and coconut. By sunset, ten carts were loaded and ready.

Thong Prasi assembled all the servants and gave orders delegating duties for going and for looking after the house.

Men were assigned to stay and watch over the house and its contents. "Look after things properly, Nang Mi and Nang Muean." Thong Prasi went into her apartment. Phlai Kaeo wandered through the central hall,

entered his room, and closed the door. Alone, his thoughts turned to gentle Phim, and he embraced a side pillow in a fit of passion before falling asleep.

cart

At sunrise, Thong Prasi came down from the main house. Some fifty servants, male and female, loaded up the goods.

Phlai Kaeo mounted a cart and led the way off into the forest, all creaking noisily along. In the heat of the sun, they rested the buffaloes.

From evening until dawn, they forged ahead, then ate and continued until late morning. At midday they halted and relaxed. In the afternoon they harnessed the buffaloes and drove ahead.

When the sun again beat down, they lay inside the edge of the forest until the sun had almost dropped behind the mountains. Birds called through the forest. Cicadas trilled loudly around the *lamduan* trees.[5]

Phlai Kaeo listen to the plaintive, lonely-sounding whooping of the gibbons. "That little baby gibbon clinging on a *rang* branch reminds me of Phim hanging onto me when I said farewell."

A pair of langurs sitting side by side made him think longingly of sitting and chatting close to little Phim. "Eye's jewel, what is happening to you right now?"

They reached a cart stop and rested the buffaloes. The servants fetched wood to build a fire. They slept beside a pond.

---

5. ลำดวน, a tree with a fragrant light yellow flower that appears often in poetry more for the soft, melancholy sound of the word than the attributes of the tree.

After traveling and sleeping another night in the forest, they soon reached Suphan and halted the buffaloes just beyond Siprajan's garden. The servants were ordered to build lodging.

They cut wood in the forest, dragged and carried it out, set it down with a bang, trimmed it to shape, and dug out postholes.

They drove in posts, hung floor beams, fastened a ridgepole, raised rafters,[6] cut vetiver grass for the walls, and thatched the roofs of five houses. Thong Prasi went to stay happily inside.

In the evening, Phlai Kaeo was in a very happy mood. His thoughts turned to Phim. "She must be unhappy at being apart and waiting for me for so long.

The doubt and insecurity must make the poor thing miserable." With this in mind, he set off. A bright shining moon

floated across a star-spangled sky, flooding the earth with light. He walked across to Siprajan's house.

Wild animals called out of the surrounding silence as he slowly crept to a side of the central hall, rolled a mortar over, and climbed on it. He cast a Loosener formula, springing the bolts,

and clambered in through an open window. By the light of hanging night lamps,[7] he arrived outside beloved Phim's room. Everyone in the house was fast asleep,

snoring, talking in their sleep, scratching a rash, or lying with legs raised and uncovered. He found the door bolted, chanted a Loosener to slide the bolt out, and walked in.

He quietly drew the curtains apart and saw her sleeping. He sat down beside her and hugged her awake. "Don't stay asleep. Please get up."

Phim awoke with a start. In the dark, she panicked that a thief had got in. She screamed and tried to get away.

Phlai held tightly onto her hand. "Why are you squirming and trying to escape? I'm here, eye's jewel. Don't be alarmed. I've come because I'm concerned about you.

Since the day we parted, I've been buried by worry over whether you'd wait. As soon as I got home, I pleaded with my mother to come. She was cross but I wouldn't listen.

---

6. พรึง, *phrueng*, the tie beams that form the oblong frame between the posts under the floor of a house, and on which rest the wall panels; อกไก่, *ok-kai*, the ridgepole running along the peak of the roof; and กลอน, *klon*, rafters (for these construction terms, see CK; Anuman, *Prapheni nai kan sang ban*).

7. ชวาลา, *chawala*, usually a round bowl filled with oil and a wick.

I cried and cried myself senseless, and then she gave in, as I'd hoped. We came from home through the *rang* forest and arrived here today."

Listening to this, Phim's doubts disappeared. She smiled brightly and moved close to him, leaning against his chest. "If your mother hadn't been kind, I'd have died.

If you weren't sincere in your words, I wouldn't have wanted to see anybody's face again. I couldn't have lived with the shame. Please have mercy, Phlai Kaeo."

Happy to hear this, Phlai Kaeo caressed her gently. "I love you, dearest darling. Don't doubt my heart is true. If I could, I'd cut open my chest to let you see it.

But it's beyond my power to pluck out my heart. Though my body was far away, my heart was still here. I was worried because Khun Chang is our enemy. I tried to come quickly to arrange the wedding.

Forget your sorrows. Tomorrow it'll be fixed for sure. My mother will come to your house and ask for your hand in the ancient way." With these words, he tugged at her shoulder cloth,[8]

peeled it away, and lifted her onto his lap. They cuddled closely together, wrapping around each other with passions surging. A storm wind arose, strong enough to destroy an era,

howling and booming as if it would erase the world. Oceans churned. Forests shuddered. Mountains heeled over, cracking apart. Sun and moon were obscured by chaos.

Flowering trees along riverbanks came crashing down, trunk and branch. Thunder rumbled and rolled around. Only when rain fell did the storm subside.

After it was over, he went to open a window. "Oh, the light's up already." He put his arms around her. A cock flapped its wings and crowed loudly.

stairway

---

8. สะพัก, *saphak*, an elevated word for the sabai or uppercloth, used especially when worn by ladies of the court at ceremonial events. The basic form is wound once round the torso, covering to just below the waist, with one end thrown over the shoulder, leaving the other shoulder and midriff bare. The more elaborate form is a longer cloth wound crosswise over the breasts with the two ends thrown over the two shoulders (*Pha phim lai boran*, 74).

The piercing cry of a coel announced the approach of the sun, reminding Phlai Kaeo to leave the house. "Stay well. I must say goodbye. Please come to see me off at the stairway."

Phim took him by the wrist and walked to open the door out to the central hall. The pair walked past the female servants sleeping quietly.

They reached the terrace and opened the gate. Phlai turned back, reluctant to leave. "Stay well. I must say goodbye." He turned and hurried down the stairs.

The moon faded from sight as he left the house. In the dim before dawn, he went out through the main gate in the fence, and soon reached the lodge, feeling jubilant.

As dawn lit up the world, Thong Prasi opened her eyes. She washed her face, pounded betel, put a piece in her mouth, and sat chewing while pondering what to do.

She called on the neighbors, Grandpa Son, Grandpa Sao, Grandma Ming, and Grandma Mao.[9] "I would like to request you to help me ask for the hand of Siprajan's daughter."

coral-pea pattern

The elders agreed and quickly went off to get dressed up smartly in lowercloths with a coral-pea[10] pattern and uppercloths in attractive embroidered silk.

Thong Prasi wore a lowercloth with a peeled-lotus check and an uppercloth with a white gardenia pattern that suited her well. As soon as all were ready, they set off with servants carrying baskets with a betelnut set, mortar, and pestle.

Phlai Kaeo enchanted beeswax with a Karani heart formula.[11] The elders accepted it and spread it on their lips. Thong Prasi led the way.

In a short time, they reached Siprajan's house and nervously called out for someone to take care of the dogs. Opening a window and seeing them, Siprajan shouted at the servants,

"Hey you, and you! Why didn't you tell me guests have arrived, you slaves?" Shaking with fear, servants tumbled down the stairs to escort the guests up into the house.

---

9. Elders brought in to help argue the man's case.

10. ตามะกล่ำ, *ta maklam,* a dark-colored cotton cloth with a small woven pattern resembling the seed of a *maklam ta nu, Abrus precatorius,* a vine with long pods containing seeds of brilliant red with a black spot.

11. หัวใจ(พระ)กรณีย์, *hua jai (phra) karani,* a well known abbreviated heart formula with several variations. A common form is: จะ ภะ กะ สะ, *ja pha ka sa.*

Mats were laid and a tray of betel and pan hastily prepared. They all sat around in a circle to talk. Siprajan opened the conversation.

"I've been thinking and thinking of you, Thong Prasi. We've been apart from each other for many years now. You look thinner and paler than before. Your hair is white and many teeth are broken. Things must have been hard.

When the king was angry at your husband and punished him by death, where did you and your son disappear to? We meet again after eleven years.[12]

How are things now, good or bad? Are you settled down and making a living? Or are you in any difficulty or trouble? What brings you to my house now?"

Thong Prasi answered Siprajan. "Every day, we face hardship not happiness. You must have heard that we were ruined and in great difficulty.

When Khun Krai passed away, all our property was seized—cattle, buffaloes, paddy fields, home, everything. Disastrous. We fell on hard times and had to leave Suphan.

I put some money in a basket and fled in fear into the wilds with my dear son. We staggered around the forest for over a month. Then we found some friends who helped us out.

They welcomed us, gave us a house to live in, and were all so kind. Times were hard beyond belief. I've blazed a path through the elephant grass, holding my face high. [13]

I ask you for seeds of squash, marrow, cucumber, and bottle gourd to plant in my field. As we're poor and short of cash, I've come to sell you young Kaeo so you may use his services.

Think of him like a pair of leather shoes. If you don't trust me, I'll find guarantors.[14] After the toil and trouble of coming to your house, don't turn me away. Do I get this or not? Tell me."

Siprajan laughed. "So you've come here specially to go through these motions! We were neighbors for a long time. Why should I be possessive about my daughter?

---

12. This would make Phlai Kaeo seven in chapter 2. Chapter 8 says he was five when Khun Krai died.

13. With this sentence, Thong Prasi shifts from her account of the past into the formula for a marriage negotiation. The imagery for this negotiation is drawn from pioneer cultivation. She struggles through the wilds and trades her son to borrow seeds. He is accepted as long as he has the machete needed to clear new land.

14. Meaning someone else to give a character reference for her son, like the four elders accompanying her.

Even if your son's poor, it doesn't matter. As long as he comes with a big knife slung on his back, I'll give her to him. He can work to make a living. He either knows what to do already or can learn easily.

The money given by parents soon vanishes if someone doesn't know how to look after it. Let me ask the elders one thing: in what way is this son of yours any good?

Does he gamble, drink liquor, or get giddy on ganja? Does he smoke opium at all? Is he tall or short, dark or fair? So far I haven't seen him with my own eyes. Tell me the truth."

opium smokers

At this point Grandpa Son, Grandpa Sao, Grandma Mao, and Grandma Ming spoke up. "In the future you'll be able to rely on him." "This son of Thong Prasi is a very good lad."

"He's clever, easy to teach." "He looks smart and handsome." "He's a nice well-mannered young boy." "There's not one bad thing about him."

"When he was a novice, he recited *Matsi* so well and eloquently it was captivating. Last year, you yourself were sponsor of the episode. On that day Phim listened and liked it.

She took off her cloth as an offering for the recitation of this episode. It created an incident because Khun Chang did the same thing. He took off his cloth and put it down over Phim's. Don't you recall?"

Siprajan was pleased and replied, "I do remember now. We felt annoyed for a long time. Because Phim's my only child, she's like my own heart.

I want to see her married, and share out the property with my own eyes. I'm getting old, and I tend to get sick. How long will I live? I'm not so rich but I'll provide according to what I have.

I'll give my daughter fifteen chang. I'm not fussy about the size of the dowry.[15] One set of cloth[16] for offering is about right. The bridal house should have five rooms and timber walls.[17]

---

15. ขันหมาก, *khan mak*, literally "betel tray." Technically this is a bride price.

16. This would consist of one uppercloth and one lowercloth which Phlai Kaeo will present to his new mother-in-law (KP, 84).

17. ห้อง, *hong*, room, is the space between two pairs of pillars inside a house, not necessarily enclosed by walls. Each would be around four meters square, so this would mean a unit of four by twenty meters (KP, 85). Timber walls are more substantial, expensive, and prestigious than

Please give some thought to Saturday the ninth waxing day of the twelfth month[18] as the date." Thong Prasi accepted immediately. "Up to your judgment. I've no objection.

It's time for us to take our leave." Thong Prasi went back to where they were staying and told her son the outcome.

abbot

Siprajan instructed the servants to get busy preparing food and other things. They purchased betelnut, coconut, and palm fruit, and busily made sweets and savories.

They arranged betel and pan on trays. Siprajan called all the servants to board a large boat. At Wat Khae, they disembarked and entered the kuti. Siprajan sat down, paid respect, and started talking.

The abbot was sitting with his back turned, enjoying a game of chess. He picked up a bishop[19] and banged it down. "Lured into checkmate, right in the middle square!" Siprajan called, "Your Lordship,

I came to invite . . ." "It's not mate," said the abbot. "The king can escape!" Siprajan said, "I wish to make merit . . ." "The rook attacks," said the abbot. "Checkmate!"

He turned to see Siprajan, tried not to laugh, and asked her to repeat why she had come. Siprajan replied, "I wish to ask for ten or so monks to chant prayers.

Young Phim Philalai is getting married. The date is fixed so don't muddle it up. I'm getting old and I want her married now so I can see it with my own eyes."

The abbot said, "Is she old enough to have a husband? Only last year I saw her coming to bathe, taking off her cloth, eyes red from crying.

I saw her running around the wat with a *jap-ping*[20] tied on her. They dashed

the alternative of woven bamboo.

18. Around late October.

19. He is playing the Thai form of chess, หมากรุก, *mak-ruk*, and this is the โคน, *khon*, equivalent to a bishop. In the following lines, the king is the ขุน, *khun*, and the rook is the เรือจุน, *ruea jun*, ship. The board layout and principles are similar to Western chess. The major differences are that the bishops and queen may move only one square, and that the pawns start on the third rank.

20. จับปิ้ง, a protective ornament tied on a chain or cord round an infant girl's hips. The form may originate from south India where it is known as *mudi-thagadu*, and the Thai name may come from Malay where it is *caping* (Untracht, *Traditional Jewelry of India*, 90). The implication is that he remembers her as a small infant.

around after one another and broke the trees. Every day I cursed them and chased after them with my walking stick.

I haven't seen her face for a couple of years and now she's to have a husband! You and I have to think about ourselves. You're getting on bit by bit. We're both growing older."

Siprajan said, "You and I are the same, Abbot. In old age, health is never really certain. In a little while, we'll all be dead.

jap-ping

The appointment is fixed. Please remember it. I'll take my leave." She descended from the kuti, and soon returned home. She went up the stairs and busied herself arranging a great quantity of food and other things.

Nearer to the appointed time, Phlai Kaeo organized his male friends to come to Siprajan's home to help build a house.[21]

All the materials for the construction were brought and left at the site. Holes were dug to the right depth to plant the doctor posts.[22] At an auspicious time in the eleventh hour[23]

house building

---

21. Traditionally, the groom went to reside with the bride's family, and a "bridal house" was built for them, usually as an extension of the existing building. This was used for the wedding ceremony, and then for them to live, at least temporarily.

22. เสาหมอ, *sao mo*, an extra post to act as "doctor" in case the main post deteriorates, often inserted first to serve as support for erection of the main post (Woranan, "Kan sueksa sang-khom," 59).

23. This means 5 a.m. The counting starts from 6 p.m. (as is still practised with *sam thum* as 9 p.m. etc.). Traditionally a house was built in a single day, with the help of fellow villagers. On the prior day, offerings are made to ask permission from the spirits of the place, and the holes dug for the posts. One hole is identified as the "first post" by astrological principles, and the most beautiful length of wood is selected for this position. On the appointed day, the first post is raised at an auspicious time around sunrise. Before raising this post, more offerings are made to the spirits of the place. A young banana plant and young sugarcane are attached to the post, which may also be decorated with yantra and other auspicious marks. As the post is raised, someone intones a long drawn-out call. The ceremony may be a lot more elaborate but given that no monk or ritual specialist is mentioned, and the time is given as seven minutes, it was probably as simple as this.

nearing dawn, they held a soul ceremony for the posts, finishing in seven minutes.

With the banging of gongs and hollering, the posts were raised and put in place. The floor beams and roof beams were shaped to fit snugly and fixed with nails.

Hammer beams were set to support the purloins, and kingposts placed to bear the central roof ridgepole. Rafters were nailed on, thatch busily passed up, gable ends raised, and the walls fixed in by men shouting and wiping their faces.[24]

With all of them drilling, hewing, planing, cutting, chopping, piercing, and arguing in a noisy swarm, the task was completed successfully in one day.

Siprajan called servants to bring both sweet and savory to feed all the workmen. When they were full, they went home.

Dawn broke on the auspicious day. Thong Prasi arranged a large canopy boat and supervised the loading of the dowry.[25] A *mahori* ensemble was installed at the rear of the canopy.

dowry boats

(Terwiel, *Monks and Magic*, ch. 7; Anuman, *Prapheni nai kan sang ban*)

24. This passage relates the sequence of building. The postholes are dug, and the posts erected; beams are inserted between the posts at the level of the floor, พรึง, *phrueng*, and at the base of the roof, ขื่อ, *khue*; เต้า, *tao*, hammer beams are set from the posts outwards to support the bottom edge of the roof; แปลาน, *paelan*, purloins, are set lengthwise along the roof to support the rafters; จันทัน, *janthan*, kingposts are set up to support the ridgepole, อกไก่, *ok-kai*; กลอน, *klon*, rafters are placed along the sides, running upwards from the roof edge across the purloins to the ridgepole, and thatch placed on top; finally, จั่ว, *jua*, the triangular gable is set on each end, and ฝา, *fa*, wall panels are inserted.

25. ขันหมาก, *khan mak*, betel tray. Usually there would be three containers, one containing the agreed bride price, and the others containing betelnut, sweets, and other gifts. "Peoples who take betelnut seem to use betel and pan as a welcome and display of friendship. When guests arrive, a betel tray is offered, meaning they are welcomed with friendship and intimacy. If no tray is offered it implies the host is not welcoming. . . . It is not surprising that betel which signifies friendship has been incorporated into marriage ritual" (Anuman, *Prapheni kiao kap chiwit taeng ngan*, 12, 17; KP, 84).

An attractive woman was chosen to carry the first dowry tray. She wore yok and sabai that went well with her complexion. The boat set off, soon reached Siprajan's landing,

and moored in front of the main wharf. Ta-Phon came down with a big stick to obstruct the procession.[26] Money had to be paid before they could pass and the dowry be carried up the stairway.

Grandma Pao, an elder in the house, counted the cash and cloth, which matched the promised amounts. Everything was then carried into the house.

As reciprocation, food was brought in, and all ate their fill. The party returned to the boat moored at the wharf and departed.

In the afternoon, Phlai Kaeo fetched jars of liquor. Snacks and curries were already prepared. He called Ai-Thai,

"Go quickly and find Khun Chang. Tell him I'm inviting him to be part of the groom's party."

Ai-Thai took off, rushed to Khun Chang's place without stopping, and walked straight up into the house.

Khun Chang was sitting relaxing. Ai-Thai raised his hands in wai and said, "Phlai Kaeo has asked for the hand of Phim Philalai in marriage.

He's short of people for the groom's party. He sent me to pay his respects in friendship and beg you to go over today. Don't delay, sir, please get dressed."

Listening to Ai-Thai, Khun Chang felt someone had split open his head with a sword. Tears flowed down in anguish over Phim, and he turned to the wall to hide them.

"Oh what a pity, my eye's jewel! Things haven't turned out as I hoped, but I won't give up trying, regardless. Even though you're his wife, it doesn't matter."

With these thoughts, he bathed and dressed in a golden yok that Phraya Lakhon had given him,[27] and an uppercloth of wool embroidered with gold.

---

26. This clowning is part of the ceremony, and was known as the "gold and silver gateway." The groom has to pay a "fine" in order to meet the bride (KW, 86).

27. This is a reminder of Khun Chang's court connections. The reference is to the governor of Nakhon Si Thammarat. In his preface to the poem, Damrong suggests this chapter was written in the Second Reign as this officer held a chaophraya rank in the First and Third Reigns but phraya in the Second. Damrong seems to have got this wrong. Phat, the ruler of Nakhon from 1784 to 1811, held chaophraya rank. So did his son Noi, who ruled the city until 1839 (and who by legend was actually the son of King Taksin of Thonburi by a wife presented to Phat when already pregnant with Taksin's child). Throughout this era, Bangkok was concerned that Nakhon might attempt to gain its former near-independence, or even collude with the British in Malaya. When Noi was succeeded by his son Noi Klang in 1839, the rank was reduced to phraya. So

The servants followed in a gaggle.

At the place where Phlai Kaeo was staying, the members of the groom's party had already gathered and were sitting around eating, pouring liquor, and chatting in a tipsy hubbub.

Phlai Kaeo said, "My buddy, don't hold it against me that I love Phim. Knowing she was your wife,[28] I should defer. But please give her to me."

Khun Chang listened, looking uncomfortable. "It's a pity. If you weren't my buddy, I wouldn't give her to you. If you don't love her, I'll take her." He knocked back liquor and got merrily drunk.

Late in the afternoon, Phlai Kaeo left the house and boarded a boat to go to Siprajan's house together with his friends.

Accompanied by the groom's party, he walked up to the bridal house. Monks were calmly waiting to chant. The bridal party gathered around Phim and came out of the apartment.

The couple sat down in front of the abbot who placed a sacred thread on their heads.[29] Khun Chang saw Phim looking elated and stared at her dolefully.

He picked up a tray meaning to take betel but missed his mouth and put it in his ear. He chewed and chewed wondering why he had only leaf. Others in the groom's party saw him and burst out laughing.

Monks chanted prayers to a slow rhythm, then sprinkled water all around.[30] Nang Mun, a loudmouthed old maid, butted in to get splashed. Khun Chang barged in too and took her wrist.

She gave him a knock on the head. "Don't be pushy, you savage.[31] Let me

---

this reference suggests the chapter may have been written in the latter part of the Third Reign. The Nakhon governorship was elevated back to chaophraya rank at the next succession in 1867 (Munro-Hay, *Nakhon*, 167–219).

28. Phlai Kaeo is referring to their childhood games (see ch. 1).

29. A cord of white raw cotton made into two circles with a connecting strand. The two circles are placed on the heads of bride and groom, and one end of the string is attached to a bowl of sacred water.

30. Phya Anuman believed that the water sprinkling originated from a cleansing ceremony to purify the bride and groom. Here it has become a blessing for the couple and the guests, with a chance for some horseplay. By the mid-twentieth century, it had changed again into a rite in which guests pour water over the hands of the couple as a blessing (Anuman, *Prapheni kiao kap chiwit taeng ngan*, 108–25; KW, 68).

31. เงาะ, *ngo*, name of a negrito hunter-gatherer group, also called Sakai, who live in the forests on the hills of the peninsula. Both names are derogatory as Sakai means slave and *ngo* is Thai for the rambuttan, drawing a comparison between the spiny fruit and negrito hair. They call themselves Samang. The court was intermittently fascinated by them. One appears in *Sangthong*, a drama written by King Rama II (see p. 258, note 56). King Rama V adopted a Ngo boy and wrote an adaptation of *Romeo and Juliet* set in a Ngo village.

monks chanting prayers

go!" Khun Chang grabbed at her cloth but instead poked her in the navel. "You don't give up, you rascal!" She rapped his head again.

The chanting of prayers came to an end. Tea was offered to the monks who took their leave as planned and descended the stairway to return to the kuti.

Siprajan had sweets and savories brought to feed the groom's party. After they had eaten their fill, gifts were produced as mementos.

Jars of nielloware plated with gold and leaf baskets of fermented tea were laid out in rows to be given to everyone. As the light faded and evening came, Khun Chang left to return home.

Phlai Kaeo took the groom's party to see Thong Prasi, and said sweetly to his mother, "Now that the marriage is over today, why should you stay here?

There's nobody looking after the elephants, horses, cattle, lands, and house." Thong Prasi replied, "I'll go by and by, maybe in about five days.

It's only just over. Everyone's tired from working hard. There's no need to set out immediately. You go over to eat and sleep in Siprajan's house, Phlai."

In late afternoon, Phlai Kaeo got dressed up smartly and walked to the house of Siprajan.

He climbed the stairway into the bridal house, and at sunset went to sleep there, pining randily for Phim through the prescribed period.

After three days, Siprajan talked soothingly to her beloved daughter about the devices of being a wife.

"My fair and gentle Phim, you've never experienced a man's love. You must listen to your mother's words, my precious. He's your partner from previous lives.

Hundreds and thousands of people didn't inspire you but specifically this Phlai Kaeo. I brought you up not letting anything bother you. The cane has never once touched your body.[32]

Now you're grown up and leaving my bosom, I'm concerned because you have to look after a husband. I fear you'll do something wrong or speak rashly. You must make no mistake that moves the man to malice.

A cool head is mistress of the house. Follow what I've always taught you. Both inside and outside the house, in whatever situation, be careful to pay respect to your husband and heed him.

Don't be jealous and make accusations that cause a scandal. Don't go ahead of your husband;[33] it's not appropriate. I brought you up in the hope you'll do well. I pray you'll be blessed with constant happiness.

I've given you instruction until late. Now Phlai Kaeo is waiting and pining for you." She embraced Phim and encouraged her to go into the bridal house to see him.[34]

Hearing a footfall, Phlai Kaeo got down from the bed. Phim hid behind her mother, peeping out. Her fair face seemed to float in the lamplight. When their eyes met, she lowered hers demurely.

They sat down and Siprajan said, "I'm bringing Phim to you. Please live in harmony and look after each other forever until the ends of your lives.

Whatever mistakes are made, talk it over first. It's not good to beat or berate each other. Stay here, my dear. Your mother is taking leave." Phim hung on and would not release her mother's hand.

"Is Mother abandoning me here?" They pushed, pulled, and circled around until Siprajan persuaded Phim to drop her hand. Then she opened the door of the room, and walked out.

After Siprajan left, Phlai Kaeo became more cheerful. He smiled broadly at Phim, went to sit close beside her, and said pleadingly,

"Precious, why are you sitting so still? Please join me on the pillows inside the mosquito net. Are you hot? I'll fan you to sleep. I've been here three days waiting for you."

He slid to sit touching her, put his arms round her, squeezed, stroked, and kissed. "Why are we sitting here? Let's go and lie down together." He tickled to make her heart jump.

fan and whisk

---

32. Of course this statement conflicts with chapter 6.

33. Meaning, walk behind him, eat after him, go to bed later, get up earlier in order to prepare things, etc.

34. Kukrit claimed to remember another version of this advice (KP, 92–95; see *Companion*, 1207–8).

Phim squirmed and giggled. "Hey, don't play around like that. I can't stand all that pinching and tickling. Go to bed if you want. I'm not sleepy yet."

Phlai Kaeo got up and went inside the net. "Lots of mosquitoes! Light a candle and bring it in here." Phim stood up with a smile and unbolted the door. "It's too hot. I'm going to sit in the cool."

Hearing her footsteps, he got up and grabbed the end of her cloth. "Lightning strike! This Kaeo always makes trouble. You're good at that. Always pestering. It's not that I'm running away, not consenting,

but you grab my hand. You're so rough and pushy. Are you hungry like starving for rice, sir? It's so hot and sweaty, I'm wilting. I'm going to freshen up with scented powder and fragrant water."

"Oh good. Let's put it on together. When you're nice and cool, you'll feel better." He pulled the cloth off her breasts, round and full like lotuses in bloom. Even in the dim light, they shone.

"If you're looking for the powder, why are you tugging at my uppercloth? What is this? Is dawn here already?" Earlier in the evening she had been listless and drowsy. Now she tossed her head and ran across the room on her own.

She opened a pot of scented water, releasing the aroma, and poured a lot to give him. Phlai Kaeo crept up behind her back. "Oh, are you pouring it all away, Phim?" She smiled sweetly.

"It's no business of yours so don't interfere. If it's spilt, there's more. Go away and don't bother me. I'll put it on myself, and then come over."

"Bring it here. I'll do it for you. What's the problem with doing it for each other? Trust me." He dissolved the powder. "Turn your face here. I'll make you even fairer."

He picked up a fan and fanned the powder dry. "You look as fair as the sheen on a gourd shaded by a leaf from the sun." He hugged and stroked to arouse her, and powdered her breasts, making her heart jump.

"For pity's sake, you're too much. I can't even sit and powder myself. What's wrong with wanting to cool down? It's irritating to be bathed in sweat."

"The sweat is not the problem, is it? Not at all. You're really a big tease. Let's go and lie down. Don't make me beg for so long." He hugged her to his breast and kissed her very softly.

Phim smiled but shot him a sharp look. "Hey, your sweat has smeared my cheek." "What sweat? You're just guessing. Look in the mirror. There's nothing.

The net is full of flying mosquitoes. Let's go and see to it, or we won't be able to sleep." With that, he swept her up in his arms but she kept on pushing him away.

He lifted her onto his lap so she could not struggle, and pressed her close with his heart bursting. Phim continued to twist and squirm until they entered the curtains, when she prostrated to him.[35]

Phlai Kaeo nuzzled her and smiled passionately. He caressed Phim as his heart flooded with love. He kissed her hair—elated, giggling, and carried away.

Hugging and stroking, he told a tale.[36] Lord Ram, the avatar, followed Sida into the depths of the forest, crossed the ocean to Lanka island, and devastated a whole clan of giant demons.

He suffered countless hardships for his beautiful lady, wasting away and turning yellow with suffering. Only fourteen years later did he bring her back to the city. At the end of the story they fell asleep together.

Lord Ram

---

35. According to traditional noble etiquette, a wife should prostrate to her husband every night before sleep.

36. The *Ramakian*, which is of course a very long story.

8: PHLAI KAEO IS CALLED UP FOR THE ARMY

Now to tell of King Chiang In, who ruled the royal city of Chiang Mai,[1] with a full complement of officials and royal poets, and abundant ladies in his inner palace.

In wealth, he lacked nothing. His reputation spread far and wide among the people. Smaller cities willingly submitted and presented golden gifts in tribute.

One day he appeared in audience before his nobles, lords, generals, Lao[2] chiefs, and troops, prostrate all across the palace courtyard. He was pleased to see his principal officials.

At that moment two Lao brought a missive that Chiang Thong,[3] unmindful of the king's power and surpassing merit,[4] had switched allegiance to Ayutthaya,

and sent tribute to the southern city, adding to the glory of the Thai capital. "Chiang Thong is getting too big for his boots, and will cause the Thai to attack our city."

At this news, the King of Chiang Mai was as angry as if seared by fire. "Mm! This Chiang Thong is arrogant. He has no fear of siding with the Thai.

Before, he was subject to us. Now, he's puffed up like a two-headed bird. Heigh! Conscript ten thousand fighting men, and requisition everything for war—

guns and other weapons of all kinds. Have everything assembled within seven days. Get moving today with the preparations.

Prap Mueang Maen will be commander of the vanguard with five thousand

---

1. Founded in 1296 according to its chronicle, Chiang Mai became capital of the Lanna kingdom in the north of the Chaophraya River system. On the relations of Ayutthaya and Lanna, see below, pp. 934–37.

2. In Ayutthaya and early Bangkok, the peoples of both Lanna/Chiang Mai and Lanchang/Vientiane were referred to as "Lao."

3. The location of Chiang Thong has been a matter of debate but most likely it was a little south of the current site of Tak/Rahaeng. In the poem, it is imagined as further north, beyond Thoen (see below, p. 853).

4. บารมี, *barami*, merit accumulated from good deeds in the current and previous lives, especially the unmatched accumulation by a king, which is what qualifies him to be a king.

phrai to crush them on the spot. Saen[5] Kamkong will be good as his deputy.

Falan will be chief of the main army and in overall command. He has fought well in the past. Sanbadan, as his deputy, will expedite the conscription of five thousand troops.

Let them appoint a full complement of junior officers for the left and right wings,[6] and many quartermasters,[7] a commissariat, ambush brigades, and signals brigades.

Arrange food and other supplies including elephants and horses for transport." After issuing these orders, the king left the audience and went up to his resplendent golden residence.

The lords and chiefs set about conscripting troops. They beat, bribed, and badgered people into the army. If a man could not be found, they impounded his wife and children.[8]

Supplies of food, pikes, swords, guns, elephants, horses, cattle, and buffaloes were arranged in large quantities. The various units were assigned their places in the column.

On a day calculated as auspicious for victory, the main army moved out with great fanfare, bristling with swords, pikes, guns, flags of victory, and pennants inscribed by teachers.

The elephants and elephant troops marched packed together. The cavalry hastened into the lofty forest. The soldiers[9] moved rapidly ahead with their shouts echoing through the trees.

When the column halted to rest and eat, the liquor jars were quickly raised. At night they camped with bonfires burning. The march through the forest lasted many days.

When they reached the region of Chiang Thong, the villagers trembled like stricken fish. They did not wait to show their faces but closed up their doors

---

5. แสน, *saen*, hundred thousand, is a rank in a system of decimal-based ranks found widely in Tai societies.

6. This translation assumes there is a misprint in the original: ขาว *khao* should be ขวา *khwa*.

7. ยกกระบัตร, *yokkrabat*, a name for several officials, mostly in the Ministry of the Palace. Here it means officers in charge of equipping the army.

8. In early Bangkok, each phrai registered on the roles had to nominate a guarantor, usually a wife, relative, or close friend. If the phrai evaded call-up, the guarantor was liable for imprisonment. Here a similar "prison guarantor" system, ขังเร่งประกัน, *khang reng prakan*, is being imagined in Chiang Mai (Battye, "Military, Government, and Society," 19–20).

9. จัตุรงค์, *jaturong*, from Sanskrit *caturanga*, literally four-limbed, here meaning the four divisions of an army: elephant troops, chariot-born troops, cavalry, and infantry; a poetic term for troops in general.

and windows, and scattered in panic into the forest.

Neither big villages nor small put up any resistance. People hid, or scrambled and staggered away in flight. The Chiang Mai troops gave chase, shooting the villagers down to roll in the dirt.

At Chiang Thong, they set up camps surrounding the whole city in siege, and fired guns constantly to induce fear. "We'll capture the ruler and then see his face!"

Every gate was blocked by units of guard. "If anyone comes out, seize them and slash them dead. Don't let anybody escape."

Seeing the Lao chiefs in such force, the ruler of Chiang Thong sat and wept. "They've set up camps to surround us. We can't get out. We'll die for sure."

He trembled and lost heart. "We can't match them in any way. There's nobody we can call on for help. All Chiang Thong will fall to them and be captured."

They conferred and reached an agreement. They would pretend to submit without any resistance, wave flags, ask for conciliation, request to pay respect, and offer gold and silver flowers.[10]

gold and silver flowers

They would beg forgiveness and plead that the small people be spared without having to flee. If Chiang Mai planned to attack and annihilate the southern city,[11] they would volunteer to fight alongside Chiang Mai until death.

"This should convince the Chiang Mai people. Then if a Thai army comes, we'll join with them and pulverize this lot. We'll fool them so our troops survive." Having agreed on this tactic, they all mounted the walls,

waved flags, saluted, and shouted to the army officers, "We cannot match you, sirs." "Don't be suspicious. Please inform your superiors."

"We beg you not to attack and slaughter us." "We volunteer to help you pulverize the Thai." "Allow us to make amends this once." "Please be merciful and don't put us to the sword."

The Lao chiefs and their troops were glad. They escorted the Chiang Thong people to inform Phraya Falan.

Phraya Falan heard their proposal and accepted it. "If Chiang Thong now

---

10. Among the traditional forms of tribute that a subordinate ruler presented to his overlord were models of trees, sometimes of gold, sometimes in pair of gold and silver, and usually one to three feet high. The practice probably began in the Malay world where they are called *bunga mas*. The reference here signifies subordination.

11. Meaning Ayutthaya.

begs forgiveness and wishes to submit and become subject to the Lao,

the city ruler and officials must come out and drink the ceremonial water of allegiance again, open the city gates, and allow us to come and go at will,

deliver all necessary food and supplies for our army, draw up a complete inventory of arms, and hand them over. Then we'll trust in their loyalty."

The officials of Chiang Thong accepted these conditions and took leave to return to their city and pass on the orders.

The ruler of Chiang Thong made no objection. He ordered the city gates opened, and led his officials out.

After the water oath, the Lao officers and men ceased being suspicious of the Chiang Thong people. The Lao traveled around freely all over the place.

They went to court country girls, toured around scavenging, swaggered about, singing and dancing, or got boisterously drunk on liquor.

✧

Now to tell of the governors of Thoen and Rahaeng.[12] When they heard that the Chiang Mai army had come in force and taken Chiang Thong easily, they were incensed by news that the city's ruler had put up no resistance,

but defected to Chiang Mai and agreed to stand and fight against a Thai army. The two governors had all the details written up in a missive and sent in the early evening by post horse

to Kamphaeng Phet.[13] Once informed of the whole affair, Phraya Ram[14] understood this was a critical matter for government, and thus dispatched a fast boat downriver.

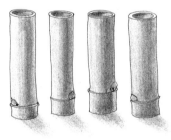

At Ayutthaya, the missive was promptly delivered to the sala where a duty officer broke open the message cylinder[15] and inquired about the details.

message cylinders

---

12. Two towns on the Ping River. Rahaeng was historically the crossing point for an important route westwards into Burma (see map 4).

13. See p. 40, note 59.

14. The title of the governor of Kamphaeng Phet was Okya/Phraya Ramronnarong Songkhramphakdi, *sakdina* 10,000, indicating a first-class city (KTS, 1:320). This sequence suggests that Thoen, Rahaeng, and Chiang Thong were all cities subordinate to the provincial center of Kamphaeng Phet (see map 4).

15. Messages were sent in a wooden or bamboo cylinder, closed with clay and marked with a seal for security.

When senior officials arrived, the duty officer informed them of the matter, and they immediately went to the audience hall in an angry mood.

Nobles of all ranks and departments from the various ministries gathered to wait at the front of the audience hall, and entered at the appointed time.

The almighty king came to sit on a jeweled throne at the front. Officials and courtiers prostrated to pay respect.

At his turn, a senior official opened the message and read it to the king. "Recently, Falan and Sanbadan, soldiers of Chiang Mai, brought an army and set up camps surrounding Chiang Thong. The city's ruler did not fight but submitted and agreed to drink the water of allegiance. He appears to be in revolt.

Hearing of this matter, the governors of Thoen, Rahaeng, and Kamphaeng Phet have promptly dispatched this message. Whatever Your Majesty commands. My life is beneath the royal foot."

The almighty king was enraged. He spoke to the lords and courtiers in audience, "Discuss this matter among yourselves today.

Should we send a major army? Who will volunteer? Return here tomorrow to report." With this order, the king left and returned to the palace where he slept.

Both sides, military and civilian,[16] left the audience together and went to sit in the sala to discuss the war as ordered.

The four pillars[17]—the ministers of the palace, capital, treasury, and lands—discussed and argued vociferously, but nobody volunteered and the meeting broke up with no full agreement.

The nobles went home. The army chiefs were highly disappointed. Because of their official position, they feared punishment arising from the lack of any volunteer.

---

16. In a pattern widespread in Asia, Siamese government was split into two divisions to provide counterbalance. These were called ทหาร, *thahan* and พลเรือน, *phonlaruean*, and the original meanings of these words is a matter of speculation. These fell under the two great ministries, Kalahom and Mahatthai respectively. Over time these two ministries evolved into interior and defense, and the two terms came to mean "military" and "civilian" (see p. 20, note 4).

17. จตุสดมภ์, *jatusadom*, a collective term for the four leading ministers: city or capital, *mueang* or *nakhonban*, headed by Chaophraya Yommarat; palace, *wang*, headed by Chaophraya Thammathibodi; treasury, *khlang*, headed by Chaophraya Kosathibodi; and lands, *na*, headed by Chaophraya Kasetrathibodi. In the original, palace does not appear in the following phrase but has been inserted for clarity.

The king of the city of Thawara[18] Ayutthaya, a world like heaven, resided in a brilliant jeweled palace surrounded by all his consorts and court ladies,

like Lord Indra of mighty power ensconced in the resplendent Wetchayan,[19] surrounded by heavenly angels, and regaled by his booming drums.

The king pondered about the border regions and the provinces surrounding the sacred city of Ayutthaya. "Chiang Mai has sent an army to trample the ground up to Chiang Thong.

The ruler of Chiang Thong put up no fight but went over to Chiang Mai easily. He has become insubordinate and seems intent on revolt against the holy city.

Kamphaeng Phet, Thoen, and Rahaeng acted with appropriate loyalty in sending the information. Officers and troops must be sent to attack and recover Chiang Thong."

With that resolve, he went out to preside on a resplendent golden throne at the front, surrounded by his leading officials.

The four pillars, other ministers, officers of various ranks, court poets, and servants of the dust beneath the royal foot all prostrated flat and raised their clasped hands.[20]

prostrating at audience

---

18. ทวารา, Sanskrit *dvara*, gate, refers to the kingdom of Dvaravati that may have existed in the Chaophraya Basin before the Ayutthaya era. Reference to this kingdom was incorporated into the official title of Ayutthaya as a claim for historical depth and continuity. Historical sources on Dvaravati are scant, and there is no agreement on where or what it was.

19. เวชยันต์, Pali Vejayanta, a name for Indra's palace and chariot. "In the middle of this city [on Mount Meru] of the thirty-three *devata* there is the Vejayanta castle which is 25,600,000 *wa* high. This castle is most exquisitely beautiful and is covered with the seven kinds of gems, which are 2,400,000 *wa* high. This Vejayanta castle, which is covered with the seven kinds of gem, that are gloriously beautiful beyond anything that can be conceived, has been provided for Indra; and he is lord of this Vejayanta castle" (RR, 223–24).

20. According to the members of the 1685 French embassy to King Narai, nobody was allowed to stand in the king's presence at audience, or talk except when addressing the king. The courtiers would arrive beforehand, enter the hall on their knees, and remain prostrate throughout. "The most respectful, or to say better, the most humble posture, is that in which they do all keep themselves continually before their King. . . . They keep themselves prostrate, on their knees and elbows, with their hands joined at the top of their foreheads, and their body rested on their heels; to the end that they may lean less on their elbows, and that it may be possible (without assisting themselves with their hands but keeping them still joined to the top of their forehead) to raise themselves on their knees, and fall again upon their elbows, as they do thrice together, as often as they would speak to their King." The king appeared at a window set into the western end of the hall above head height. Before the window was opened, music played as a warning (La Loubère, *New Historical Relation*, 57).

Amid a thunder of gongs and drums, and a fanfare of conches and horns, the king looked as sublime as Lord Indra seated on his immense glittering throne,

Bantukamphon,[21] the seat of stone, with all the gods arrayed around, under the resplendent Parichat tree[22] and the many-tiered ceremonial umbrellas[23] of Indra.

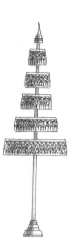

The king spoke with the roar of a lion.[24] "Officers of all ranks, I am enraged because Chiang In has acted in an insolent and contemptuous manner towards me.

Chiang Thong belongs to Ayutthaya, yet he sent an army to lay siege and convert it into our enemy. We know because of information from the three cities.

Will we sit and take this quietly? No! They will exult and become yet more insubordinate. They will believe I fear their power, as if we had no soldiers in Ayutthaya.

tiered umbrella

Such things have happened in the past, and we sent Khun Krai who has now been dead and gone for many years. This time, who will go?

I ask you officers here in audience whether or not Khun Krai had children. The commanders of the six units[25] should know because Khun Krai was in their department."

---

21. บัณฑุกัมพล, Pali Pandukambala, pale yellow woolen stone, the throne of Indra. In Hindu mythology, this throne is yellow marble. In the Three Worlds, "Under this [Paricchattaka] tree there is a dais of gem stone, which is called Pandukambala and is 480,000 wa long. . . . The color is deep red like that of the flower called *sa-eng*, and it is soft as a cloth cushion or the comb of a royal golden swan. Whenever Indra sits on this stone slab, it is soft and he sinks down to his navel; but when Indra gets up and leaves the stone, the stone fills in just as it had been before" (RR, 233).

22. ปาริชาติ, Pali Parichhattaka, a tree of great beauty in Indra's Daowadueng heavenly garden. In Hindu mythology, Krishna stole it because his wife liked it, prompting a massive war between Krishna and Indra. In the Three Worlds, it is a wishing tree that shelters the Pandukambala throne (RR, 233).

23. Umbrellas are a major article of royal regalia in Southeast Asia, symbolizing the ruler as protector. Early examples can be seen in the bas-reliefs of Angkor. Both size and, more particularly, the number of tiers, are signals of rank. At the French ambassador's audience with King Narai in Ayutthaya on 16 October 1685, there was a nine-tiered umbrella immediately over the window where the king appeared, and a seven-tiered umbrella on each side.

24. สิงหนาท, *singhanat*, the roar of a *singha*, a mythical lion-like creature; a metaphor for a royal command.

25. จางวาง, *jangwang*, a name for several senior officials, especially in the palace; "the head official of a palace, or one in charge of some governmental work" (MC, 243); "steward of the princes; head of public office" (PAL, 83); an official immediately below a minister.

อาษาหกเหล่า, *asa hok lao*, the six militia units, a collective term for six permanent units whose

Phraya Ram Jaturong[26] prostrated and spoke without delay, "My liege, Your Majesty, my life is under the royal foot.

I have information on these matters. At the time Khun Krai lost his life, he had one son recently born, aged almost five years.

Thong Prasi fled from Suphan with the little child and disappeared. I do not know whether they are alive or dead but I heard they are in Kanburi."

Hearing about Thong Prasi, the king immediately asked Khun Chang, "Your home is in Suphan.

You should know about Thong Prasi. Is her son still alive or dead? Tell us whatever you know at once so he may be sent to Chiang Thong."

Khun Chang had been a page at court since childhood[27] and was fluent at talking with royalty. He saw a way to possess Phim Philalai as he had long intended.

He would make sure the king sent Phlai Kaeo off to war, and then he would court Phim again. With this thought, he addressed the king. "My life is under the royal foot.

The son of the late Khun Krai is called Phlai Kaeo, a brave fellow. He has a wife and lives in Suphan but his mother is in Kanburi.

He is brave, skilled in lore, and knows everything about raising spirits. He is about seventeen years old. Let me inform the dust beneath the royal foot."

The king, ruler of the world, heard Khun Chang out and said, "You, Chang, go and fetch him here. Duty guards will go with you."

A department head of the royal guard took the order and backed out immediately. He assigned junior officers, and gave orders for Khun Chang to lead the way.

---

main role was to guard the city. They were: the militia of the left and right, อาษาซ้าย/ขวา *asa sai/ khwa*; golden shields of the left and right, เขนทองซ้าย/ขวา *khenthong sai/khwa*; and golden spears of the left and right, ทวนทองซ้าย/ขวา *thuanthong sai/khwa* (KTS, 1:280–82). *Asa*, derived from Khmer, means forward troops, and was converted into the Thai equivalent, ทหารหน้า, *thahan na*, in the nineteenth century. These units became the core of a permanent standing army formed in the early twentieth century.

26. One of the two heads of the six militia units (see note 25 above), often called Phraya Decho (see p. 20, note 2). In late Ayutthaya, the title of Phraya Ram Jaturong was given to a leading Mon, and subsequently was passed down as the title of the head of the Mon units in the army.

27. At the end of chapter 1, Khun Chang's father presented his son at court but the king said he was too young and should be brought back later. Here we learn that this did indeed happen.

They left Ayutthaya and arrived in Suphan at dusk. Without speaking to anyone, Khun Chang went up into his house to bathe and make himself comfortable.

Then he went to the house of Siprajan and called for someone there to light a torch. Saithong saw the palace guards. "Hey, why did Khun Chang bring them here?"

In trepidation, she informed Siprajan, who invited the guard officer up into the house. "Officer, please come up to sit and have a talk. Please take some betel—such as we have."

The guard officer told Siprajan the details of the royal order. "His Majesty the King wishes to attack Chiang Thong.

He is looking for an able person with knowledge.[28] Khun Chang said that Phlai Kaeo is very capable and suitable for what the king needs so we have to fetch him to the palace."

Siprajan trembled with fear at the guard's news. She got up, left her apartment in a fluster, and went straight to her daughter's bridal house.

She sat down and collapsed sprawling against the couple. With tears flowing and chest pounding, she cried, "Oh, my dear children!"

Phlai Kaeo and Phim did not know what all this weeping was about. "Has someone dropped dead? One of our relatives?" "Who has a problem? Is that why you're crying?"

Siprajan beat her breast. "That Khun Chang could do something like this! He told the king that you, Kaeo, are clever and equipped with knowledge.

And the king has ordered you to war, to catch and kill Lao. What do you really know about such things, about going to war to fight enemies?

Your waist is as slim and elegant as a painting. Just a flick would snap it. You look in need of care. Where would you have got knowledge!"

Phim's chest felt so tight she thought she would lose her mind. Tears trickled from her eyes. She wiped them away and angrily cursed Khun Chang, "The villain!

The interfering, uncouth troublemaker! How can he do this with no fear of sin and karma? Because he's frustrated in love, he's truly going to do us in.

---

28. วิชา, *wicha*, knowledge, especially in the sense of the military skills and supernatural arts that Phlai Kaeo has learned. This Sanskrit word, at the other end of the Indo-European spectrum, is the root of witch and wican. In this line, "an able person," คนดี, also means a person with such skills.

He wants to separate us and send you off to suffer in the forest. From now on we'll be far apart. In a few days, you'll be gone, my jewel!"

Phlai Kaeo saw his beloved wife weeping and his heart went out to her. He steeled himself to speak. "Why get worked up, curse, and cry when it's no use?

This is about royal service, army work. It's been like this since my father's time. If we take an army up there, we should be able to attack Chiang Thong successfully.

Listen to me and don't cry. The guards have come all the way to our house. Calm down and make some food. If they don't have anything to eat, they'll say hurtful things."

He gave orders to the servants. "Saithong, you're in charge of the main kitchen." He went out to sit with the guard officer and Khun Chang.

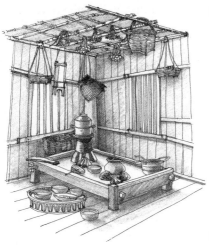

He greeted them and led them out of the main hall, along the terrace and central walkway, up to Phim's bridal house.[29]

The three dropped their bottoms on a mat, and Phlai Kaeo called for a betel tray. Phim was so angry she would not go out but pushed a betel tray through the door.

Seeing her hand, Khun Chang raised his head, smiled, and gazed long at her little finger with a snake ring. Though a mosquito bit him, he did not brush it away.

kitchen

Saithong and the servants found everything to make prawn patties with chili, lime, galangal, and lemongrass.[30] They cooked aromatic *kaeng-om*[31] and *tomyam*.[32]

---

29. Here it is clear that Phim's bridal hall was built as a new wing of Siprajan's house, extending out from the terrace.

30. ทอดมันกุ้ง, *thotman kung*, prawn meat pounded with herbs into a paste, kneaded into small flat patties, and deep-fried.

31. แกงอ่อม, a characteristically northern curry of deer, buffalo, beef, chicken, or offal made with bitter gourd, chili onion, garlic, galangal, lemongrass, coriander root and seed, fish paste, and kaffir lime leaf (SWN, 1:489).

32. ต้มยำ, the classic Thai hot and sour soup made with lemongrass, chili, fish sauce, and lime.

When ready, sets of dishes were arranged. Women dashed in and out. Finding Khun Chang hateful and vile, Phim called baldheaded Ta-Phon

to carry the footed trays of rice and savories over. As old Ta-Phon walked in front of him, Khun Chang stared with his mind seething. "Not this accursed fellow again."

Phlai Kaeo smiled innocently and invited them to eat. "This is all we have, sirs. It's dark now, not daytime, no time to do anything." Khun Chang picked up a metal drinking cup to wash his hands.

The food was eaten and cleared away. They chatted together openly. "I'll truss up the Lao and bring them back. Make a name for myself." Khun Chang saw he was serious, and made agreeable noises.

chatting

They talked till late. When they yawned, mattresses and pillows were arranged for the two officers to sleep comfortably. Phlai Kaeo went into his bedroom and bolted the door.

He hugged Phim tenderly with his heart breaking into fragments. They whispered together lovingly. Khun Chang craned his neck in frustration,

shifted to lie close to the wall, and heard the sound of boards creaking. He clapped his hands to his face and kicked his feet in the air. Sweat ran down his face. His eyes bulged.

Phlai Kaeo hugged her tightly and would not let go. They kissed, caressed, and nuzzled. "When I'm gone, you'll be gloomy. We won't pleasure each other for many days."

Phim's tears fell on his chest. "I fear you'll fall fighting the Lao." Phlai Kaeo soothed her, "Don't fret." He caressed her breasts tenderly, and kissed them passionately.

Khun Chang heard the kiss and rolled over face down. "A spirit has possessed me! Oh Buddha! The spirits of this house are very fierce! I'm new here and they haven't possessed me before!"

By sunrise, Phlai and Phim were more troubled. They washed their faces and went to Siprajan, trying to swallow their grief.

"The king has sent for me. Whatever the outcome, I first have to go to the city to discover how matters lie." Phim found clothes for him to take.

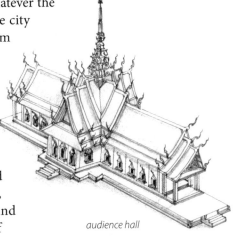

Phlai Kaeo and servants went down from the house. The guard officer warned, "Don't be late." By afternoon they reached the forest edge, entered Ayutthaya, and went straight to the sala.

Phlai Kaeo sank down, paid respect to the royal officials there, and talked with them. They found him good-looking with signs of being capable.

audience hall

He talked well, using words appropriately, and had round, black eyes befitting a soldier. "If you go, conclude the war, and return, it should be good for you. You'll be able to enter royal service."

The almighty king was pondering the affairs of the realm. When golden rays lit the sky, he walked out to the audience hall of victory.

The commander of the six militia units bowed, prostrated, and addressed the king. "We have the son of the late Khun Krai.

His name is Phlai Kaeo. We have talked and he will volunteer. He seems an able person with knowledge, who speaks boldly and fears nobody."

The king said, "Bring him here quickly." A palace guard called Phlai Kaeo to crawl in and pay respect.

The king examined him for a while. "Appealing. His appearance is appropriately good-looking. Eyes round and bright. Skilled in knowledge and lore."[33]

He called out, "Ha! Heigh! Phlai Kaeo, you were born to a line of soldiers. Do not dishonor your deceased kin. Perform royal service in succession to your father.

If you gain victory over Chiang Thong, I'll bestow on you money and cloth. Ponder carefully and be certain. Can you do it or not?"

Phlai Kaeo prostrated and replied, "My liege, lord over my head, my life is beneath the royal foot. I beg to volunteer, Sire,

---

33. There are manuals for predicting a person's character and future from facial and body features. A famous example is attributed to Phra Mahamonthian and dated to the Bangkok First Reign (Hora Purajan, *Tamra phrommachat*, 217–54).

to attack Chiang In and Chiang Thong and fulfill Your Majesty's wish without fail. As long as I live, I will not shrink from battle."

The king, ruler of the world, slapped his thigh. "Ha! Crush them to dust! Make sure they're annihilated. Don't let the arrogant Lao come to attack the Thai!"

The king commanded rapid conscription from both military and civilian departments,[34] to be fully completed in good time.

He bestowed cash and clothing on Phlai Kaeo to encourage his martial spirit. Phlai Kaeo received the royal gifts, prostrated, and addressed the king.

"Your humble servant will return home first to enchant the equipment to be taken along, and hasten back here in three days."

"Good! Go home but don't stay long. I'll arrange the troops to wait for you." Phlai Kaeo prostrated to take leave. Servants wrapped the cash and followed him out.

A senior noble on royal command[35] went to sit in the main official sala, and summoned Phan Phut[36] to conscript phrai, both military and civilian.

officials in the palace

"Issue call-up notices by units. Get masses of royal conscripts. Send orders to round up both those on and those off this month's rota.[37]

If any hide and abscond, reprimand their parents and overseers. The sick must hire a replacement for cash. Find many elephants and horses.

Requisition guns, other weaponry, and various war materiel. Have the food supplies lined up all together. In three days, they leave for Chiang Thong."

Arriving home, Phlai Kaeo saw Phim's face but walked straight into the

---

34. See p. 20, note 4.

35. A roundabout way of saying Chaophraya Jakri. He oversaw the north, and Phan Phut is a direct subordinate.

36. See p. 21, note 7.

37. Phrai were organized on a rota system. Here the order is to conscript both those due for corvée service this month, and those due on other months, นอกในเดือน, *nok nai duean*, out and in the month.

house without even a smile for her. The servants deposited the cash and cloth in piles. Phim saw her husband looked dark and distracted.

She followed him headlong into the room. Phlai Kaeo saw her face and rushed into her arms. Wearily, he hugged her with tears welling. "King Phanwasa is sending me to war,

because Chiang Thong is in revolt. It switched sides and conspired with Chiang Mai. If I disobey the king's order, my back will be crushed, so I've steeled myself to volunteer.

The king was deliberately told that I'm invulnerable and strong on lore, so if I go, they don't have to fret because the enemy will be pulverized in the blink of an eye.

I'm not so anxious about the fighting but I'm worried about missing you. Every night I'll be far from my love. Till I return will be almost a year.

Tonight I can still hug and caress you, but in two days—misery. The side pillows will replace me. When you think of me, you'll clutch them close.

Who will you be able to talk to? You'll have to tell your troubles to Saithong, woman to woman, but talking can relieve misery only a little. At sleeping times, you'll lie and mope.

At midnight, I'll be awake, eyes open, beating my breast in worry about little you in a hundred ways—not sick but heartsick that you'll waste away, lose your figure and your fairness.

At mealtimes, you'll look for me but I won't be there. Even water will be harsh and hard to swallow. The old peace of mind will peter away. Every night will leave another trace of wrinkle.

Your hair won't know the tweezers.[38] A hundred days won't see mirror or comb.[39] The krajae powder will stay dry in its pot all year round. Turmeric will go unused and your face will lose its sheen.

The soft warm pillows will be cold to lie on. Your chest will crack from longing. Your lovely smiling cheeks will become dull and sunken.

Your heart will imagine all sorts of disaster. The more you brood, the more massive the sorrow. Pining so much will make your proud breasts droop. I'm worried about you."

Phim, too, was distraught over her husband leaving, and lost her composure completely. She doubled over on her chest, sobbing and sobbing so the tears splashed down.

---

38. Meaning she will not bother to pluck her hairline (see p. 72, note 66).

39. "They have Combs from *China*, which instead of being all of a piece like ours, are only a great many Points or Teeth tied close together with Wire" (La Loubère, *New Historical Relation*, 29).

"Can you walk to Chiang Thong? Your soft feet will blister from sole to heel, swell up, and collapse. And my heart will collapse along with my beloved.

My pining will pass beyond heartbreak. Who'll help pry out thorns in your flesh? If I went along, I could pull them. I pity you sleeping in the forest.

Your tender skin is used to a soft mattress, not the hard earth. The dust in the woods will make your body itch. Who'll help scratch your back? I think about these things.

My love, I've been making your food, morning and evening. You don't eat like other people, just a little fish and vegetables.

With three full meals a day, you don't put on even a little weight. Now all you'll have, raw or cooked, will be plain and tasteless, just arum[40] and wild yams.

You won't be full and satisfied. Thinking about this makes me pity you so much. So slender, with hunger and exhaustion you'll faint away, my slight husband, your wife's only one.

Late at night you'll think of little me. Far apart from the wife you used to hold, you'll be lonely, randy, and sad. Wherever you look, you'll see only men.

In the dawn chill, when the gibbons whoop, you'll think it's my voice.[41] The blazing sun and brute wind will batter your body. In fatigue, you'll sleep soaked in sweat.

You'll bathe in stream water so cold you shiver all through. Who'll put on the krajae powder, whose scent used to refresh you?

Oh Phlai, my heartstring, you're not used to being far from love. You came to lie with me in the bridal house twice a day. You talked with me

about this and that, chatting playfully, teasing, and not letting me stray from the pillow. You let me cushion on your left arm. When you saw I was hot, you fanned me.

You whispered sweet nothings, hugged me, lifted my chin

gibbon

---

40. บุก, *buk*, low forest plants in the Amorphophallus family that in the rainy season sprout fleshy leaves and flowers, some of which can be eaten, including *Amorphophallus rex*.

41. Part of the gibbon's plaintive call sounds like "phua, phua," similar to the Thai word for husband, ผัว. According to legend, the female gibbon is calling for a lost husband. In a story taken from a Jataka tale and adapted into an outer drama by Sunthon Phu, Janthakhorop and Nang Mora travel through the forest, and Nang Mora falls in love with a robber, giving the robber her husband's sword to kill him. Mora is then cursed to be reborn as a gibbon that laments for her husband with this call.

to kiss, ran your fingers through my hair, without a break all through to dawn without sleeping, too blissfully in love with me to lie apart.

You held me so close, so lovingly, never rolling over with your face turned away, or ever saying you were a little tired. When you're gone, who'll hug me to sleep?

When eating, you always waited for me to sit with you. If I took nothing, you'd plead, knead the rice, place it in my mouth, and try to please me.

I've seen many other couples but none loving each other like you love me. Now my love must be severed away from me. How to bring it back to enjoy again?

Going along is impossible. I fear trouble. All you can do is take my coverlet to clasp in the forest when you toss and turn in loneliness.

How will I survive sleeping alone? Who'll hug me to sleep against the cold? You used to be so close beside my body. Husband, lord, and master, your wife will die."

Phlai Kaeo stroked and soothed her. "Don't be so sad or you'll waste away and lose your figure. All that sobbing and sighing will make you weak, listless, and fretful.

Being forced apart is heartbreaking but nothing can be done about a troubled karma. If it were possible, I'd take you along to see the forest in bloom.

You could pluck the flowers you love, pulling down those dangling on high. We'd bathe happily in the streams and ride horses through the trees.

Though tired, seeing your face close beside me would lift my spirits on the way to Chiang Thong. If a Lao army mounted an attack, we'd dress you as a man,

with a tight shirt to flatten your chest, and a Farang hat to hide your hair under the brim. You'd ride carrying a sword with magnificent power, and a kris tucked in your waist.

I'd mix and enchant herbs[42] to make you invulnerable to all weapons, and I'd slash the Lao down into dust. If you could go, I'd take you.

But it's beyond my power to imagine getting away with it. I can't stay here to hug you to sleep either." He felt desultory, sad, and desolate till the cock's crow echoed around.

He opened a window a crack to glimpse golden rays lighting the sky. "Oh, dawn is here already, my jewel." He hugged her with his face against hers,

caressing tenderly, warming her against his chest, kissing long and passionately. "Kiss me again to give me heart."

---

42. ว่าน, *wan*, a whole category of medicinal herbs, and more generally a catch-all term for herbs believed to have supernatural powers (KW, 158).

Dawn lit the world. Neither could overcome their grief. Phlai Kaeo soothed her. "Let's go and tell Mother."

They crept out of the mosquito net, still locked in each other's arms, and walked out of the room leaning together, cheek to tearful cheek. By the time they reached Mother, both were sobbing.

Seeing the two crying, Siprajan asked, "Eye's jewel, what's the matter? What's making you weep until your eyes are red?

After you came back from court last evening, you didn't explain things to me clearly, only that Khun Chang knifed you with the king. Are you going off to war?

You didn't say whether you are or not. Ever since you came back from court, you've been crying. Look, this is very tedious. Both of you are smothered in tears."

Phlai Kaeo told Siprajan the whole story from beginning to end. "The king has ordered me to war up north to destroy the Lao of Chiang Thong.

Right now an army is being conscripted and the capital is teeming with troops of every kind. I was upset and took leave from the king to come home, but it's fixed that in three days the army will march.

I'm worried about Phim. When will the war be over and I return? In truth, your son's fate is bad—only three days in the bridal house.

I leave early tomorrow morning and go away to suffer in the wilds. Don't count the days because they'll surely stretch into months. Who'll be companion for Phim?

When I think about this, I'm furious at Khun Chang. He's been in love with Phim forever. He intends to get her for himself so he dug up a story to tell the king,

hoping I'll go and probably die. He's clever, crafty, and silver-tongued. He'll try to gradually steal away fair, gentle Phim. I'm sure of it.

Though my body goes, my heart stays here. But I don't see anybody who can protect Phim except you, Mother. Look after her until I return.

If anyone says I've died, don't believe them and become confused. Make inquiries in the capital to be sure. Don't simply believe it's true.

Phim is like my own heart. Don't forget that. Protect her well until I can return to the city.

Humans are not sincere to one another. They rock back and forth, in and out. Even if anyone comes to talk with gold in their mouth, don't be carried away and comply, Mother."

As Siprajan watched them weeping, her own tears flowed like water. She rubbed her eyes, face pale, sighing, sobbing, murmuring, and mumbling.

"Don't be worried about Phim, young Kaeo. When you're gone, nothing will happen. I've looked after my daughter for a long time, not letting even a beetle or spider touch her.

Prepare yourself to go without worrying about her at home here. Don't treat royal service lightly. Don't stick your neck out when you shouldn't.

Make sure forts and moats are built securely. Don't be too sure of yourself and get lured into a trap. Hang back, play clever. At night don't think of sleep.

Sit guard. Set lights. Have gongs ready. Keep a company hidden and waiting. May you win victory and take the city. Try to bring back cattle and buffaloes for plowing.

Servants! Come here quick! At dawn tomorrow, young Kaeo is leaving. Mill some rice so it's white with no husk,

and tie it up in sacks. Help one another to arrange matters, and get a move on. Grind chili and salt. Make all kinds of sweets.

Where's Saithong disappeared to? May the wretch be mauled by a tiger! When something's urgent, she wanders off somewhere to hide.

The betelnut, pan, and lime paste are not ready. They're scattered all over the place." While Siprajan harried the servants, Phim and Phlai Kaeo went sadly back to their apartment.

I-Mi and I-Rak scooped out handfuls of fermented fish. It stank like maggot droppings. Siprajan scolded loudly, "You jailbirds! What's the matter with this fish? It's come out full of worms." [43]

I-Dam pounded chili like the thunder of horses' hooves, then added galangal, ginger, chili, and salt, and mixed until it was ground fine and well blended.

Ai-Mi and I-Kuai took baskets to measure rice from the granary for milling. After pounding, they filled sacks and lined them up in rows.

Dried fish and huge giant snakehead fish were grilled with onion and garlic, and packed away. Sugarcane juice and cake sugar were prepared. People bustled to and fro, in and out.

pounding rice

43. This hemistich is taken from WK, 7:268; PD has: I put in the right proportions.

To make caramel, dehusked coconuts were broken open with a thwack, and shredded on a rabbit-grater.[44] The coconut milk was squeezed out and put to sizzle in a hot pan.

rabbit-grater

Flour was mixed and sifted, and added to the big pan along with sugar. At first the mixture was runny and easy to whisk, but with heat and stirring it thickened.

People took turns stirring. "What's up? Is your shoulder tired?" "My arm's stiff enough to die!" "Here, it's sticking to the pan and getting messy." "Use a paddle to scoop it onto a banana leaf."

"You taste it from the edge of the pan. I'll taste it too." "Mmm, good, sweet, and nutty—yummy." When the edge had gone, they scooped tastes from the middle. "Half the pan's disappeared." "Really sweet!"

Siprajan said, "Phim, why are you sitting doing nothing in the room? Your husband has to go away but you don't stir yourself. Come and help somehow.

You haven't arranged the betel, pan, or tobacco. How long is the princess going to keep on crying? You're like a water primrose that puts out shoots but won't bloom. You're not paying attention to his clothes, either.

Is this what you call loving your husband, just putting your face down and weeping? If I wasn't here to take care of things, he wouldn't have even one piece of fish to eat,

nothing but salt to crunch his teeth on. You're sitting still there hugging your knees while I'm the person making all the effort, as if I were the minor wife, not the mother-in-law.

The only noise from you is boo-hoo and Oh Buddha. You're not even lifting a finger, like some lady of leisure. The more I scold, the more your eyelids droop. I'll have to slap you so your cries echo through Suphan."

Phim felt too pent up to lend a hand. She hugged Phlai and tried to swallow or stifle her tears but they flowed even more.

Yet her mother's scolding got to her. She left Phlai's side and began to peel the betelnut, put it into a bowl, and tie rolls of pan leaf. She glanced over at Phlai as if her heart were on the point of breaking.

She looked down, whimpering, her chest feeling cramped and her head in

---

44. A traditional grater was in the form of a stool with the grating teeth protruding in front. These stools were often shaped like rabbits, or other animals, hence the name.

a daze. She tried to roll the pan leaves but failed. A ball of cotton[45] lay forgotten in her hand.

Phlai Kaeo saw his wife's distress and moved to sit beside her, stroking her soothingly and wiping away her tears. "Don't cry so much, my darling. I'm here with you. Please roll the pan so I can have some in the forest. Try to stop crying. Here, I'll help put the lime paste."

He kept on stroking and fondling her until his closeness made her tears gradually subside. He teased her playfully, "There, Phim, your chest is so bruised it's swollen."

peeling betelnut

Phim smiled through her tears. "Don't say bruised. It's completely collapsed." She quickly gathered up all the betelnut and pan into a betel box, and put the leftover in a cloth bag with a drawstring.

"Husband, lord, and master, come back to me before my pan leaves dry out and wilt, while the Phetchabun[46] tobacco is still pungent, and the banana leaves still green."

She felt a little better after Phlai Kaeo had cheered her up, and her sobbing subsided. She crawled over to fold his clothes into neat little pleats, and put them into a chest for going into the forest.

She packed a trunk with clothes, mirror, and comb as she could remember doing before. When she picked up his pillow and little mattress, the sadness returned. "Oh, you'll be far from my bed, sleeping alone."

Her own pillow was embroidered in gold with a pattern of Garuda grappling at a naga with its claws, the pair intertwined.[47] The sight of it made her tremble in panic, and she lay down sadly on the bed.

As Phlai Kaeo's wedding had only just taken place, his mother Thong Prasi was still in Suphan, and she would see her dear son off to war.

She summoned the servants to carry all the food supplies laid out in her house down to load onto a canopy boat. "I-Jan, don't forget anything!"

---

45. Cotton wool rolled between the fingers to make thread to tie the pan leaves.

46. A town in the upper Pasak valley, surrounded by low hills. At Ayutthaya in the eighteenth century, "Boats from Rahaeng, Tak, and Phetchabun came loaded with lac, benzoin, iron, rattan, *yang* oil, and tobacco" (APA, 126; see map 4).

47. See p. 133, note 14.

Male and female servants bustled about. A stove and rice pot were sent down. Thong Prasi tottered up the stairway to talk with Siprajan.

"Everything is ready, including the food. Are we all going, Jan? Will you see your son-in-law off? Seeing his face will give you some peace of mind."

Siprajan replied, "The house needs looking after and there's nobody else. Things are still piled up outside. You take Phim to see him off."

Thong Prasi ordered the servants to load the boat. Phlai Kaeo came out and wai-ed his mother-in-law, Siprajan.

He arranged for Thong Prasi to go and wait at a rendezvous. "Ban Maen.[48] Make sure you don't miss it. I'll go overland to the capital

to take leave of the king. We'll meet on the day after. You go off by boat first, Mother. Look out for the mosquitoes at night. I'll follow tomorrow."

Thong Prasi replied, "Yes, I can remember that rendezvous." She boarded the canopy boat with the servants. Phim went along too,

sitting in the middle seat with her mother-in-law. The oarsmen paddled the bow away from the landing, slapping their oars and crying out, "Long, long, short, short. What's up?

Ai-Dam, you're turning the bows. I can't keep up, I beg you." The helmsman was not practiced and turned too sharply. "Hey, paddle a bit at the bows!"

They could not correct in time. The prow hit a bank. The stem post collided with an underwater stump. The whole hull was bashed hard. Some people fell in the water. Thong Prasi picked up a mat and covered herself in fright.

Phim crawled into a sack far enough to hide her head. The oarsmen looked frightened and helpless. Water poured in where the boat was holed by the stump.

canopy boat

48. Around 5 kms north of Ayutthaya on the main water-borne route northward (see map 3 and its accompanying note).

An oarsman dived into the river, pulled the boat free from the stump, scooped up mud, and pasted it over the hole. Everyone shouted at everyone else. By dawn, they were near Bang Lang.[49]

on the river

<hr />

49. See p. 190, note 5. The route by water from Suphanburi to Ayutthaya went down the Suphan River to Ban Yihon, then along the Jao Jet Canal and Mahaphram Canal (see map 2).

9: PHLAI KAEO LEADS THE ARMY

After his mother and wife had left, Phlai Kaeo readied his various gear, herbs, and medicines for warding off weapons.

He prostrated to take leave of his mother-in-law, mounted an elephant, and left Suphan along with many servants and phrai. On arrival at the city of Ayutthaya,

he hastened to find the minister,[1] lodged overnight, and after sunrise went to royal audience.

britches

The almighty king came out to sit in the Suthasawan[2] Throne Hall. High officials all entered together and prostrated, packing the audience chamber.

Looking around and seeing Phlai Kaeo, the king's face brightened with pleasure. "Make haste to move the troops out. May you meet with success.

Grind the Lao into fine dust! Have the powers and strength of a lion! I present you with this sword. The hilt contains a spirit."

The king also gave him a fine, bright-colored yok, britches, a brilliant sash, and a fringed helmet.[3] Phlai Kaeo prostrated to take leave,

and went out to the official sala. Soldiers and militiamen were milling around. After inspection, he received his orders under seal, and took leave of the nobles, who gave him their blessing.

---

1. ผู้รับสั่ง, *phu rap sang,* the person who received the king's order, a term used to mean the official for implementing a certain order, usually a minister (see for instance KTS, 5:106, 142, 160). Probably in this case it means Phraya Decho.

2. สุธาศวรรย์, may be the nectar of heaven or of Siva; not known as the name of a building in the Ayutthaya palace but the name of a favorite residence of King Narai in his palace at Lopburi, set in a beautiful garden with many fountains.

3. ตุ้มปี่, *tumpi,* from the Sanskrit *topi,* meaning hat, which is the root of (solar) topee; a general word for military headgear of no particular shape.

troops marching

At an auspicious time to march, the massed hordes of elephants, horses, and military units of various ranks and types marched out of the capital.

Lumphli Plain[4] was awash in magnificent red shirts, bristling with weapons of all types, fluttering with flags and pipe flags, echoing with the sound of gongs and war cries for a long time.

They marched to the mouth of the Bang Lang Canal[5] and crossed over to the side with houses. Porters dropped loads that had bounced up and down until the frames loosened, and untied the shoulder poles to take a rest.

As soon as they had eaten their fill, Phlai Kaeo ordered the troops to march on to the start of the route they would travel.

"Unharness the elephants and horses, and wait for me at the sala of Wat Pa Fai."[6] The troops saluted their chief and moved off immediately.

---

4. The area immediately to the north of the city, close to Wat Phu Khao Thong (see map 5). The word is a distortion of Lumphini, the Buddha's birthplace.

5. There was a customs post at each of the cardinal directions from Ayutthaya. As the main northward route by water passed along the Bang Lang Canal, the post for the north was located at Bang Lang, on the east bank of the canal around 1.3 kms south of Three Bo Trees (APA, 89–90; see map 3 and accompanying note).

6. วัดป่าฝ้าย, the wat of the cotton place. ป่า, *pa*, usually meaning forest, is a local word meaning place or market found in many Ayutthaya place names (APA, 103, note 134). Wat Pa Fai was around 2 kms north of Three Bo Trees, close to where the Bang Lang Canal meets what is now the Lopburi River. The wat has now disappeared. All that remains is an old Buddha image, heavily renovated and now revered as Luang Pho Khok, หลวงพ่อโคก, sheltered by an open sala, around 300 meters north of Route 32 in Hua Hat, หัวหาด, on the right of the road 50 meters before the road crosses the Lopburi River (see map 3).

Left alone, Phlai Kaeo looked around and saw the
boat with Phim and his mother at a mooring. He went
down from the sala to meet them, and the three talked
together.

As he was going far away to war with consequences
unknown, they would plant three bo trees[7] and pray
that if disaster struck any one of them, the bo tree of
that person would be disfigured in the same way.

After a short discussion, they went off to look for
bo tree shoots, and dug them up, taking care not to
snap the roots by wrenching them sharply,
and to keep a nice clump of soil.

They loaded the saplings on the boat,
crossed the river, and dragged the bows up the

bo tree sapling

bank. They got down and carried the bo trees to a site marked by a big tree.

After making offerings to the deities that resided in that spot, each of them
dug a hole, planted one of the saplings, and made a prayer.

Thong Prasi made the first prayer. "If I pass away and cannot survive, may
this bo tree of mine die. If I'm sick, may the bo tree sicken in the same way.

If I'm hale and hearty with no suffering, may this bo tree be leafy, lush, and
shady for all to see."

With these words, she lifted the bo tree into the first hole. Next, Phlai Kaeo
prayed to the gods. "I'm going off to war.

If I gain victory over the enemy, may this bo tree sprout profusely. If I die,
may this bo tree die too.

If I'm not sick, may this bo tree be healthy and flourish. If I have success in
war, may it be beautifully green, leafy, and lush."

With this wish, he lifted the bo tree along with its roots into the hole, pushed
in some soil, and tamped it down. Phim's tears spattered down.

She raised her hands and paid respect to the guardian spirits of the place.

---

7. โพธิ์, *pho, Ficus religiosa*, pipal, the tree under which Buddha sat in Bodhgaya when attaining enlightenment. The village of Pho Sam Ton, Three Bo Trees, is on the banks of the Bang Lang
Canal (see note 5 above; map 3). Locally it is believed that the name of the village is derived from
this passage of *KCKP* (SWC, 10:4654). This area was chosen to settle Mon who migrated away
from Burmese oppression in the seventeenth and eighteenth centuries, partly so they could
guard the customs post and the northern approach to the city. During the siege of Ayutthaya in
1766–67, the Burmese troops established their headquarters at Three Bo Trees, partly in order
to make use of the Mon residents in the area. Wat Khai Raman, the wat of the Mon camp, and
the surrounding area are today full of bo trees, though there is no place with a triplet.

Racked with sobs, she cradled the little bo tree in a sad daze. "Oh lords, gods of great power,

with this golden bo tree of mine, I pray that, if at home my body should die and life be snuffed out, may this bo tree likewise sicken and die. As long as I remain alive,

may it grow happily to be so lush and shady that even the nectar of the gods bears no comparison. Should my body sicken, wilt, and waste away, may the leaves of the bo tree wither unnaturally."

With this wish, she planted the sapling, while tears bathed her face and trickled down. They heaped earth around the three holes and poured water. Each took off their sabai,

folded it, and gently wrapped it around their respective tree. "We call on the gods that the cloth tied on each bo tree is a sign that, though we three

will be far away from one another, on return may we succeed in meeting together again. Should any one of us die, may that person go happily to heaven above,

to be born again in the next life. May we meet together with certainty for hundreds of ages and thousands of eras into the future until attaining nirvana."

Having wrapped the three bo trees, they left the wishing place and boarded the boat, which the servants poled out and paddled away.

They moored at Wat Pa Fai at the end of the embankment, and gave orders for goods to be loaded onto elephants. Phlai Kaeo wai-ed his mother.

Thong Prasi gave him a blessing for success. "May the future be auspicious and prosperous." Phim wai-ed while trying to hold back her tears, and sobbed out, "Safe journey."

Phlai Kaeo said to her, "Save your heart, save your love, wait for me." Then he bottled his love, steeled his heart, and stepped up from the boat to go.

Thong Prasi, Phim, and the servants pushed the bows of the boat around. Husband and wife craned their necks to look at each other, trying to hold back the tears until they were out of sight.

The servants joked merrily among themselves. Phim sat with face lowered, unable to speak. Her mother-in-law tried to console her and cheer her up on their return to Suphan.

Phlai Kaeo began missing his wife and mother as soon as they left. Everything was ready on time—elephants, horses, and porters.

Baskets and panniers swayed to and fro. Fish heads poked out with mouths jutting open like bamboo bracts. Boxes of chili and crates of ginger bounced, swung, and clattered together as the porters walked in file.

playing saba

Some men dragged their feet with fatigue and stiffness. Some stopped and played *saba*,[8] ignoring the reprimands. Some paused to take medicine or rub oil but were pushed to keep moving.

Some sat down to smoke ganja, closed their eyes with a drowsy yawn, and fell asleep. When their clothes were burned, they jumped up blearily, still trying to strike a flint. The army crossed the plain heading for the forest.

Phlai Kaeo rode an elephant named Khotchasanghan[9] that stood lofty and commanding in the forest. After one day, they reached Pretty Plain.[10] "Oh what a pity, my beautiful Phim!"

At Ban Kratong, they crossed to Bo Landing,[11] "Oh, our three bo trees are still so young." In the evening the army halted and was allowed to sleep. At dawn, the soldiers marched across the river.

They passed by Nakhon Sawan[12] through the forest, and cut their way along

---

8. คัดลูกสะบ้า, *khat luk saba*, pick a *saba* seed, a group of games possibly of Mon origin but also found in Isan, originally played with the seeds of the saba vine, *Entada pursaetha/rheedii*, disks around 10 cms in diameter. The simplest game resembles lawn bowls with one seed placed as the target, and others rolled in an effort to get as close as possible (SWC, 14:6609–10).

9. Meaning "killer elephant."

10. The next section is in the style of a *nirat*, นิราศ, "parting," a genre of poems in which the author on his travels is constantly reminded of his loved one by things seen along the way, especially plants, animals, and place names. Here ทุ่งโสภา, *thung sopha*, meaning plain of beauty, reminds him of beautiful Phim. Many of these allusions depend on wordplay and are difficult to translate. *Thung sopha* was probably in present-day Singburi, where there is still a Wat Sopha in Amphoe Tha Chang. This means they marched to the west of the Chaophraya River (see map 2).

11. Ban Krathong is in the north of Chainat province, near Amphoe Wat Sing. Bo Landing, also called Paknampho, the river mouth by a bo tree, is where the Ping and Nan rivers join, now in the town of Nakhon Sawan (see map 2).

12. The old site of Nakhon Sawan was 8 kms northwest of its current location along the Ping. The site was moved in the early Bangkok period after the old town became separated from the river by a bank of muddy silt, and the new site, formerly Paknampho, was becoming important as a center of riverine trade (Pornpun, "Environmental History," 22).

the river in the shade of bushes and flowers. Phlai Kaeo missed his beloved wife.

"Oh my fair, gentle Phim! Your breast will be aching enough to break apart. You sent me off to war and went back home to pine with pale face and mouth unspeaking.

If you'd come with me through the cool forest in this cruel time, I'd point out things to see, all the different pretty trees and the birds perched twittering on their nests.

That pair of doves nestle close on a paperwood yet I'm sadly parted from Phim. Cottonteal geese are making a nest in a *khae* but I had to forsake our bridal house and come to this far forest.

cottonteal goose

The imperial pigeons pecking at a bunch of rose apples remind me of my love's pink cloth. The scent of the *phayom* lifts my heart like the fragrance of your sabai that still lingers with me.

The aromas of so many forest flowers are like the scent on the cheeks that I yearn for. Parrots are prattling together on that gem jasmine but who can *you* talk to, my poor eye's jewel?

There's an oriole flying up to a *maduea* fig. Oh my Phim Philalai, your skin will lose its luster because you're too forlorn to trouble with turmeric.

Along our route are so many plants. Those *maprang* are like your two cheeks. *In-jan*, *phrom*, angelbreast, and sandal are everywhere but I have no krajae or sandal at all.

That *krathum* puts out shoots as thickly as your beautiful, wavy hair. I'm lonely and my heart feels cold as ice. When will I see you again?"

Pining sadly, he spurred the troops ahead, through the woods and into the wilds of the great forest where trees grew thickly together. Bark on trunks had split and peeled away.

Stands of lofty *yang* and *yung* trees swayed and bent in the breeze. Gusts of wind battered and broke branches with resounding cracks that disturbed the nests of bandicoots.

Limbs were heavily stained with lichen along their whole length. A treeshrew chased a squirrel which escaped into a hole. A green snake slithered along to the tip of a branch.

Fallen trees stood propped up with their roots exposed, broken, and parched, piled in a messy, dead tangle. Overhead the shoots of rattan canes inter-twined like a canopy.

treeshrew

Below was dank and marshy, a tangled, dilapidated mass of decomposition and decay. A disheveled fluff cloaked rattan fruit.

Some trees looked naked and shiny where herds of elephants had scratched their flanks and stripped the bark. Others were lush and leafy but carpenter bees had hollowed out cavities.

Monkeys and langurs leapt along the way, breaking off small branches as they swung ahead. Lianas hung intertwined, as if fashioned that way from the ancient past.

langur

They entered a gorge. Overhead, the cliffs rose up into shady overhangs. Directly in front they could see through a gap like a cave. Looking up from below, their eyes were dazzled

by sunlight sparkling off striations of red and green. Misty purple quartz seemed to have been daubed in five colors.[13]

Red shone out like rubies in an exotic and elegant bracelet. Black gleamed like jet fashioned into the shape of luxuriant foliage.

White sparkled like diamonds. Water surged and splashed, throwing up a dancing spray that smashed against the cliffs, shaking the forest.[14]

They walked through the trees down to a big rocky stream where the water flowed calm and clear over a bed of pebbles. "Oh Phim of mine,

if you'd come, I'd collect many lovely pebbles so you could play with them with your pretty fingernails. It's a pity you're far away.

You love to play with things, and if you see anything pretty, you can't leave it alone. If you'd come with me into the forest, you'd sit plaiting garlands on an elephant's back,

and hang them around the howdah as fresh, fragrant braids. The more I think, the more I can't help being disappointed that my heartmate didn't come, close by my side."

---

13. เบญจรงค์, *benjarong*, five colors—black, red, white, yellow, and green or indigo—the name of a style of Siamese pottery painted with five colors, popular in the court.

14. The poem seems to set this landscape along the Ping River between Nakhon Sawan and Kamphaeng Phet but the river there runs through a very flat plain. There are some limestone outcrops, especially Khao No, which rises out of the plain like the petrified skeleton of a giant lizard, but this is not close to the river or any water course. More likely, this location is above Kamphaeng Phet where the Ping River enters hilly country. Possibly this is a description of the Kaeng Soi rapids that were situated in a gorge and had multicolored rocks. The rapids are now submerged under the reservoir of the Bhumibol Dam.

They cut across to Kamphaeng, Rahaeng, and Thoen. "If we dawdle around admiring the scenery, people will talk." He presented his orders to the governors,

who organized troops from the three cities, and held a big, rowdy feast. Then at an auspicious time for victory, gongs were rung and shots fired as a signal.

The army marched off, shouting and hollering, brandishing their weapons, with throngs of elephants and horses, up to the boundary of the Chiang Thong region.

They[15] rushed into villages, shouting wildly, creating chaos, slashing people dead in piles, seizing property, and then hurrying on.

Masses of men and women ran off but were captured by the soldiers, who danced up and down in glee. "Who stabbed you? There's still a hole."

A soldier seized a Lao girl, and lifted her cloth to look at the bush. She bent over and cried out, "Please have pity on me! I don't know anything. It hurts to death."

Ai-Mak dragged off silver in sacks. Lao were stripped of everything but their buffaloes, and ran off panting with their cloths slipping off. Those who stayed behind were in just as hopeless a state.

The army forged ahead without stopping until within earshot of Chiang Thong. Many Chiang Mai units could not organize their defenses in time. The Thai troops cut them down or chased them away.

Since Chiang Thong had not put up a fight but waved the flag of surrender and changed sides, the Chiang Mai Lao had become careless and overconfident. Officers and men had wandered around the town,

or gone off to forage for fish and vegetables far away from camp. The Thai stabbed them to death in large numbers. When the Lao realized an enemy had arrived, they frantically called their troops

to return to camps around the moat. The Chiang Thong people saw their confusion and understood this was because a Thai army had come. In joy, they closed the gates immediately.

The ruler of Chiang Thong, along with his people, was exuberant that a Thai army had arrived to help in time. "I'll chop off the heads of Chiang In's people!

Have the head monk go out to explain to the Thai army that we didn't rebel against the king, lord of the land." The nobles and chiefs agreed.

---

15. The next four stanzas down to "just as hopeless a state" are taken from WK, 8:285, condensed in PD into one stanza: Forward units were sent ahead to locate the Chiang Mai troops. They fell on any hideout they found, cutting the enemy down in great piles, and seizing their rice and equipment.

The patriarch, who was learned and fearless, left from the rear of the city, accompanied by two other monks.

Seeing they were holy men, the Chiang Mai soldiers did not attack and kill the monks, who walked to the Ayutthayan army encampment and called out for the gates to be opened to admit them.

Surprised to see these courageous monks, the Thai opened the gates, took them prisoner, and brought them before the commander and the assembled army hierarchy.

The governors of Kamphaeng, Rahaeng, and Thoen said, "These Lao monks have overstepped the mark." "We cannot let it go. The penalty for spying on an army is death." Phlai Kaeo told them to desist,

and asked the monks, "Why did you come so near evening? Tell the truth now and don't hide anything. Who told you to come?"

The brave and clever patriarch managed the situation with his quick wisdom. "*Sathu*! I'm a monk.

The ruler of Chiang Thong sent me. You have come wielding royal authority. May you be blessed with success. I'll tell the story of the conflict from the beginning.

The city of Chiang Thong was besieged by a very large force. There were several bloody engagements but their army did not withdraw.

In the city, food supplies were exhausted, and it was impossible to go out to forage, so we pretended to side with Chiang Mai in order not to be killed.

Everything was in short supply. We wanted to send word to Ayutthaya but the Lao guarded the city tightly. Today we're happy to see the Thai have come.

I've been sent to convey that we'll help you surprise them with a joint attack from front and rear. Let me give a promise to the Thai commander that if there's an auspicious day

for the Thai army to launch an assault, we'll attack also and cut them down dead. Do not doubt our sincerity. These words are the truth.

If we harbor thoughts of deception or revolt, then kill us all—man, woman, and child, even infants no larger than a cotton bud. We will not beg to be spared."

Phlai Kaeo smiled at the patriarch's words. "We from the southern army are not afraid. Even if Chiang Thong treacherously turns against us,

we'll still crush this Chiang Mai army. For certain, we'll capture them, truss them up, and chop them to pieces. Now you monks have come to negotiate.

Because you're monks, you should be straightforward and not lie, so we find you credible. Please return to the city, and inform the ruler of Chiang Thong that tomorrow afternoon we'll destroy the Lao army for sure. He must get his troops organized and be ready when the auspicious time comes."

The patriarch promptly took his leave, hastened back inside the city walls, and relayed the message entrusted to him.

At dusk, the ruler of Chiang Thong acted according to the patriarch's words. Guns were hauled up to the ramparts, and weapons of all kinds were made ready.

People enchanted their equipment with auspicious formulas, and poured sacred herbal water to instill courage. The men of Chiang Thong were in good spirits. Gongs and drums were beaten loudly all over the city.

Chiang In's two army chiefs, Falan and Sanbadan, discussed the military situation along with Prap Mueang Maen and Saen Kamkong.

"Now that the Thai have come and surrounded our army, the ruler of Chiang Thong has recovered his courage. They've closed the gates and are busily hauling guns into position, ready to stand and fight.

The Thai army has trapped our troops in the rear and won't let us escape. If we stay still, we'll be at a disadvantage. They'll attack our position hard.

But why should we fear the Thai? However many ten thousands have come, we'll attack swiftly, scatter them into the foothills, then capture the whole army, and send it to Chiang In!

As for that arrogant Chiang Thong, we'll truss up his wife and children and put them to the sword, and chop little infants into pieces!"
Prap Mueang Maen and Saen Kamkong received their orders.

"You two defend the side towards the city wall against the Lao from Chiang Thong. Shoot, stab, and block their passage. We two will attack the Thai.

They have only a few handfuls of soldiers. The fighting need last no longer than one blink of an eye." With this agreement, they went off to prepare their troops.

The courageous, strong, and capable cavalrymen wore red tunics with tight pink sashes, and carried their swords slung across the chest, ready to unsheathe and slash. Each also carried a golden spear,

and a pike for hurling from horseback. Their saddles and bridles looked brilliant. Each had enchanted his equipment with his own herbal medicine. The gunners looked sturdy in their crossbelts.

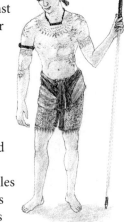

spearman

Some boosted their morale by reading powerful mantras over their kit for might and courage. All were experienced in combat. The army was fully prepared.

At an auspicious time for victory, a great cry went up and echoed around. The troops poured out of the camp in columns.

The two commanders mounted horses. With swords flashing and spear points glittering, they drove ahead almost to the Thai camp where they planted their flag.

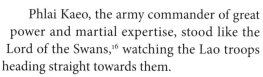

Phlai Kaeo, the army commander of great power and martial expertise, stood like the Lord of the Swans,[16] watching the Lao troops heading straight towards them.

He ordered the three city governors to quickly inspect their troops, draw them up ready, extend them protection,[17] and prepare all the martial equipment.

Lord of the Swans

He enchanted oil for the three governors and troops to rub on themselves. He dressed impressively for achieving success at that particular time.[18]

At a very auspicious time for victory, the army moved out in a great uproar, hollering, yodeling, banging gongs, and firing volleys of shot.

The din shook the world, cloaked under smoke, as dark as midnight. The Lao were scared enough to scatter in panic. Closing on them, Phlai Kaeo halted to survey the position.

Now to tell of the ruler of Chiang Thong and his men, readied in full array. When they heard the guns and saw the Thai army launch its attack,

they opened the gates and poured out of the city in a tight mass along with

---

16. พญาราชหงส์, *phya ratchahong*, from the (Maha)Hamsa Jataka, known in Thai as Suwannahong, the golden swan. Buddha is incarnated as Dhatarattha, a *hong* swan with beautiful golden feathers who lives in the Chittakuta mountains as king of ninety thousand other swans. One day he is caught in a snare, and only one follower remains with him. By a combination of his stunning beauty and humble manner, he persuades the hunter to release him, and then instructs the local ruler, who had ordered the trap set, on the proper virtues of kingship. The story is alluded to in the Three Worlds (RR, 293) and found as No. 502 in Cowell, *Jataka*, IV:264.

17. แต่งตน, *taeng ton*, extending one's own powers of invulnerability onto other people, often using enchanted oil (Prachak, *Prapheni*, 162–63; PKW, 2:43–44).

18. Meaning he chose colors and ornaments appropriate for that day according to a military manual.

mobile forts.[19] The army alone counted around five thousand, and more city people came out to join the battle,

both masters and men, with guns and pikes in profusion. They broke into the Lao camps, wrenched up the defensive spikes[20] in the ground, hauled away the guns to use, and torched the camps, leaving a pall of smoke.

Seeing the Chiang Thong forces closing on them, the troops of Prap Mueang Maen and Saen Kamkong fired off guns in volleys, and plunged into close combat with spears

and bamboos sharpened to serve as pikes and javelins. With heads held high, they stabbed this way and that. Some fought at close quarters, slashing with swords. Others dashed ahead, lunging to left and right with pikes.

The Lao camp was riddled by fierce gunfire from both sides. People fell dead in droves. Legs were severed and scattered around.

The Chiang Thong men were defended by their mobile forts, impervious to gunfire. The uproar of battle echoed through the forest but neither side yet had victory.

The troop commanders, Falan and Sanbadan, saw a handsome, fine-looking figure driving the Thai army forward.

He was agile on a high-spirited horse, and bold as the Lord of the Lions. They wanted to question him and trick him into revealing how good his knowledge was.

They shouted out, "Hey, little Thai! You're still a child, not even old enough to be ordained. Seeing you, we think you must have studied only the devices of love,

Lord of the Lions

19. ปิหลั่น, *pilan*, sometimes *wilan*. A Portuguese soldier described something similar in Pegu around 1600: "he [Banha Dala] constructed many huge cars of three or four storeys, supported on strongest axles, with enormous wheels, to be pushed along, or pulled with ropes, by a great number of men protected by long shields to enable them to lay the machine close along our Fort wall in spite of carbines and burning powder-jars" (Ribeyro, "A brief account," 128–29). Probably the devices meant here are simpler—perhaps a ring of men holding palisades or long shields.

20. กวาก, *kwak*. Captain Low in 1836 described these as follows: "crow's feet, made of bamboo sharpened, and then hardened by fire, or of iron, and so constructed that on being cast on the ground one spike remains nearly upright. They are carried in bags, and during a retreat are strewed in the path and amongst grass to impede pursuit. They also . . . use spikes of bamboo similarly prepared, from six inches long and upwards, for the same purpose and also as a defense to a town or stockade. These are generally concealed in grass and weeds, and inflict very bad wounds, penetrating even the thick sole of a leather shoe" ("History of Tennasserim," 319).

and just a little bit of mastery.[21] It seems inappropriate for you to be in a battle. Maybe your friends provoked you so you volunteered to blunder up here.

What's your name? How come the Thai king puts such faith in you? Please tell us truthfully who you think the city of Chiang Thong belongs to.

The domains of Lao and Lao border one another. This Chiang Thong ruler is crooked. He lied and placed his city under the Thai, and thus our lord Chiang In sent us here

to capture and kill this Chiang Thong rebel along with his wife and children. It's no business of the King of Ayutthaya to invade this area for any reason.

You have only a handful of troops, not as many as the army of the city of Chiang Mai. We'll just stamp on you and everything will be quiet. No need for a real engagement."

Phlai Kaeo smiled and shouted back, "Who am I? I'm the Lord of Darkness, the principal soldier of Ayutthaya!

My name is Phlai Kaeo. I'm tried and tested, and so I volunteered. The two-faced, dubious, and traitorous ruler of Chiang Thong irritated the royal foot.

He presented his city to Ayutthaya but then reneged and became subject to Chiang Mai. Kamphaeng Phet and Rahaeng informed my king who sent me to fight.

When we arrived, the city of Chiang Thong agreed to return to the old position and not waver. They said they'd been besieged and failed to flee in time, so tricked you into believing them.

Now that they've come out to fight on our side, you'll be destroyed for sure. Don't be so bold as to underestimate the Thai. If we weren't good, why would we have come?

What's your name? You talk big, rant around, and boast a lot. But in one blink of an eye, you'll die.

All those who marched here will meet their life's end. Nobody will be left to return. I'm telling you this to earn merit and peace of mind. Please submit to the Thai and survive."

Phraya Falan clapped his hands and laughed his head off. "Damnit! You're a good talker, and fearless. It's known in every region of the three worlds,

that the city of Chiang Thong has been subject to Chiang Mai since ancient times. If Chiang Thong harbors thoughts of revolt, it will be dangerous for that city.

---

21. อิทธิฤทธิ์, *itthirit. Itthi*, Pali *iddhi*, are "special powers in conformity with nature possessed by certain people who are able to accomplish acts beyond the powers of ordinary men" (Tambiah, *Buddhism and the Spirit Cults*, 49). This translation plays on the dual meaning of mastering oneself and mastering a skill, as in the original.

Chiang Mai and Chiang Thong treat each other as lord and servant. It's not your business so don't interfere. If you act too big for your boots, I don't think you'll survive.

You ask my name. I am Phraya Falan. That colleague is Sanbadan. Have no illusions!" With that, he stopped talking and ordered all his troops to advance.

The Thai hollered, fired guns, and brandished pikes. The Lao charged in a teeming mass. "Hey! Take them!" "Fear nobody!"

Hit by gunfire, the Lao wavered. Some staggered and fell, unable to rise again. Others were knocked headlong by bombs[22] thrown to explode in their faces, searing their eyes.

The Lao replied with gunfire, killing and wounding large numbers of the Thai who fell back, giving the Lao the opportunity to recover ground.

Phraya Falan and Sanbadan led their troops to attack the Thai, brandishing swords and pikes. The forest echoed with shouts and hollering.

Phraya[23] Chiang Thong, spattered red with blood of the Lao, fired his gun. Phraya Kamphaeng fired his gun also, and rushed to slash the defending Lao.

The Lao and Thai approached to grapple at close quarters, cloaked in noise and dust, slashing at one another fiercely. Some fell dead on their backs with their necks broken. Soldiers daubed with protective medicine war-danced bravely into battle. Horses came to surround them, circling around like windmills. Men grabbed one another round the neck and fell chaotically. Some retreated and then rushed back, hollering.

When the Lao attacked, the Thai withdrew until they had a good position, and then engaged the enemy hand to hand. The Lao cheered and the Thai hollered, creating uproar. Horses were stabbed and fell in the forest.

The rear cavalry swarmed over the battlefield, whips urging their steeds into the attack. Pikes were hurled, flashing in the sun. Those that missed were picked

cavalryman

---

22. หม้อดิน, *mo din*, "earthen pots" filled with gunpowder and lit with a fuse.

23. This whole section down to "Thai cheers echoed through the forest" is taken from WK, 8:296–97, absent from PD.

up and hurled back.

The two vanguards engaged, hacking and slashing at one another wildly. The left and right wings streamed in, slashing people down from horseback with necks severed.

swords

A Thai grabbed the reins of a Lao's horse and whirled around. The Lao circled back at him, slashing and stabbing, but the blade did not pierce the flesh. The Thai wrenched the sword away and cut off the Lao's hands and feet,

so he could not unsheathe his sword. The Thai troops attacked en masse, forcing the Lao to flee, gnashing their teeth and looking back over their shoulders. Thai cheers echoed through the forest.

Phlai Kaeo, brilliant and bold, gripping the war sword presented him by the king, spurred his horse into a gallop straight towards the division commander, Sanbadan.

He slashed but the Lao turned the blow with the end of his spear. Sanbadan lunged but Phlai Kaeo dodged away nimbly, the blow missed, and the Lao toppled forward, eyes bulging, crying out, "The dog dies! Come here quick, Mother!"

Phlai Kaeo slashed at him with a loud thwack, cutting him open from shoulder to waist. At this sight, Falan spurred his horse straight towards Phraya Kamphaeng Phet.

He slashed but did not penetrate, only knocking him from his horse. Phlai Kaeo barged in and slashed Falan who shat himself as his severed head fell, and his body dropped from the horse to the ground.

Seeing their leaders killed, the Lao troops broke into flight, running in all directions with the Thai in pursuit. Countless fell to the ground dead, with others wounded and streaming blood.

Many of the fleeing Lao were chased down and dispatched by the Thai troops, while others scattered and disappeared, abandoning elephants, horses, weapons, and families along the way.

Lampang put up no fight.[24] The city's people fled in droves. Lamphun's inhabitants took off to the forest. The Thai army camped comfortably.

---

24. Sujit interprets this as meaning the Lamphun and Lampang contingents in the Chiang Mai army fled the battlefield (Sujit, *KCKP*, 89). It may also be read to mean that the Thai army chased the Lao troops back towards Chiang Mai, taking these cities along the way. The translation allows for both interpretations.

They detoured to cut off the route back towards Chiang Mai, looting along the way. But at Chomthong village,[25] they gave protection and the troops harmed no one.

The gods induced Phlai Kaeo to have this idea so he would get Laothong to love. So by chance, here the troops were kind and helpful. They passed in and out freely.

Many soldiers found a wife, old or young according to fate. While waiting to return to Ayutthaya, they enjoyed themselves the whole time.[26]

---

25. Throughout *KCKP*, the geography of the north is vague and faulty, in strong contrast to the geography of the central plain. The authors knew place names in the north but had little idea of their relation to one another. Chomthong is in the southwest of the Chiang Mai valley, and way off the "shortest route" from Lampang/Lamphun to Chiang Mai (see map 4). Chomthong is also the site of an important relic stupa. The fact this is not mentioned during the account of Chomthong is another indication of the limited knowledge of the north.

26. There is a story in the chronicles which may be the origin of this Chiang Thong episode. In 1660, an envoy came from Chiang Mai begging for Ayutthaya's assistance to fend off an attack by the Ho (Yunnan Chinese). Chiang Mai, currently under Ava, had heard that the Ho were attacking Ava, and decided to submit to Ayutthaya and ask for military help in case the Ho continued their attack into Lanna. King Narai clearly saw this as a chance to wrest Lanna away from Burmese control, and thus proceeded north personally leading a large army. However, Ava rebuffed the Ho attack, and Chiang Mai now feared Ava would re-impose control and extract some retribution, so it recalled its envoy from Ayutthaya. The Ayutthaya forces realized they had been tricked. In anger, Narai resolved to take Lampang and Thoen as revenge. On the approach of the Ayutthaya army, most of the inhabitants of these towns came out "to ask to become vassals" of Ayutthaya. As the Thai army approached Lamphun, a delegation of four monks "wise and clever at negotiating" came out to meet the Ayutthaya commanders. They blamed the incident on the Chiang Mai envoy, promised to send tribute to Ayutthaya, and begged the armies to spare the people. The army commanders referred this request down to Ayutthaya. At this point, a Burmese army attacked through the Three Pagodas Pass, so Narai withdrew the army from Lanna. Although there are differences from the Chiang Thong story in *KCKP*, there are enough echoes to suggest this incident may have been its inspiration. A border town flip-flops in its allegiance. Ayutthaya sends an army. The Phraya of Kamphaeng Phet has a leading role. "Clever" monks come to negotiate a delicate subterfuge. One town mentioned in the chronicles story is Chiang Ngoen (=silver) which echoes Chiang Thong (=gold). Thoen and Lampang also figure in the chronicles story. (RCA, 250–65)

10: PHLAI KAEO GETS LAOTHONG

Now to tell of Saen Kham Maen, the district head of the big village of Chomthong, and his beloved wife, Nang Si Ngoen Yuang.[1] They had loved each other for a long time,

and had a daughter, Laothong, who they had brought up protectively to become a flourishing and totally lovely young lady, now at the end of her fifteenth year.

She was as radiant as a lotus bloom on the water's surface. Having never felt the harsh late-morning sun, her face was without mole, freckle, or other blemish. Her shoulders were wide and her waist curvy as if cinched.

No man had touched her because her two proficient and experienced nursemaids, Nang Wiang and Nang Wan, looked after her hidden away in a bedroom.

When Nai Phlai Kaeo came to attack, villagers ran off and hid in the forests and hills, and many were hunted down and rounded up by the Thai.

Kham Maen's Chomthong was the sole exception. It survived because Phlai Kaeo gave it protection, and so the place still teemed with people.

As the warring had now subsided and peace returned, Phlai Kaeo would soon return to Ayutthaya. Ngoen Yuang and her husband pondered over the goodness of the army commander.

"Hundreds of villages and thousands of cities felt his wrath. Many had to flee, kicking up the dust. Men and women fell dead. Others were captured. Only our village was happily spared.

Now that he's going to return to the southern city, we don't know what he'll do. If we just sit around waiting and doing nothing, he might sweep all of Chomthong away with him.[2]

That would mean ruin for every household." The two discussed and agreed on a plan. "Our daughter Laothong is very dear to us,

but we'll give her to the army commander as a token of our respect. He looks as if he'll love her. Even if our child goes to the Thai capital, she should be able to hold her head high and not feel ashamed.

---

1. Their personal names are Mr. Golden Angel and Mrs. Pure Silver.
2. People were one of the main spoils of war.

If the army commander keeps her as his wife, then we won't have anything to fear from the Thai army. Our kinsfolk won't be scattered to the winds. The villagers will be happy."

The two agreed and summoned their beloved Laothong. Wiang and Wan came along too. The two parents sat close beside her and spoke sweetly.

"Now, our darling Laothong, you're a pure and attractive girl. Soldiers have come from north and south to fight around here. Rice, betelnut, and everything else is running scarce.[3]

Hundreds of villages and thousands of cities have felt their wrath. It's been hard to keep you hidden. Soon the army units will return to the Thai capital, and we expect them to round up people to take along.

Property will be lost, husband separated from wife, and wife from husband, with not a stitch on their backs. I'm afraid this is how it will be for us too.

Their army commander looked after us and stopped his men from chopping us down. That's why we still enjoy each night and day. But I'm worried now that he's leaving.

There's an ancient saying about digging a pond and fooling the fish to feel safe. Feed them. Don't eat them yet. Don't damage the lotus in the pond.

And don't let the water get murky. Left to themselves to feed, the fish will multiply. In the same way, they're letting us alone, doing nothing. But when they leave, they'll corner us.

There'll be no way to escape. We must deal with this thorn before it pricks us, not allow ourselves to be trodden underfoot like grass. You're like a candle giving us light.

Your old father and mother feel we're in a dark thorny forest and can't see a way out. But there's one ray of light, and that's your radiant beauty. We put a lot of thought and effort into bringing you up.

When you were tiny, you depended on your parents, my precious. Now that your parents are old, they must depend on you. We'll give you to the commander to love. My dear child, don't be angry or upset.

He's a top soldier and skilled fighter. He should doubtless do well, and you'll be able to depend on him in the future. Chiang Mai and Ayutthaya

will probably be at war with each other for some time yet. People will come from this way and that to trample all over us. You're a fair and attractive young woman.

If you stay in Chomthong, everyone who comes will swarm around, trying to court and seduce you, and very likely you'll end up as someone's wife.

So, tough or easy, the rest of your life will be spent far from here. This way

---

3. An idiom meaning times are hard.

nothing bad will happen to you, our darling. He's a young lad and you're a young woman, roughly the same age. Your fate should be good.

Wan and Wiang will go along to protect you and look after you until death. As for servants, Mother will give you what we can. Don't let your face cloud over and start weeping."

Laothong raised her two hands above her head and burst out crying, flailing around and trembling all over.

She embraced the feet of her mother and father with tears flowing down her face. She wiped them away but they welled up and fell again. Forlornly she pleaded,

"My lord and master, do you no longer protect your child? If you hadn't sheltered me so closely, I wouldn't exist.

You washed and fed me, morning and night. You never failed to look after me and answer my every need with kindness. That's why I'm still alive today.

I had meant to die at your feet to repay my debt of gratitude to you and Mother until death. Every night I think that I'll never be far away from you, even if I have a husband and children.

But those thoughts were useless and my hopes are dashed. I'll have no chance to repay your kindness. We're all together now but soon I'll leave and never see you again.

Being forced apart will be terrible. If I could be close and just see your face passing by each day, that would be enough to keep me from sorrow.

But I'll be miles away, and for years! It's like the other end of the earth, of the whole three worlds! I don't know when I'll be able to visit. I'll truly be wretched all the time.

I won't know whether you're hurt, sick, dead, or alive. Day in, day out, I won't see your faces. Who'll help me get over difficulties and dangers, like you used to do with such kindness and sympathy?

Even if he loves me greatly and is good to me, even if he tries to look after me and please me in every way, a husband is not the same as the mother and father who brought me up.

He's truly a stranger, Mother. Why should he care about me? If I displease him, he won't pay me any attention. It's not as if he's still a virgin.

It's like I'm closing my eyes to follow a torch, not knowing whether I'll bash into a stump and break my neck. He'll already have a wife and children that he's happy with, so I'll run into jealousy everywhere.

The Thai have sharp tongues. He'll talk about all the help he has bestowed on my family. How can I respond? If I talk back, he'll get angry.

Being a minor wife has hundreds of problems. I won't be able to open my mouth to argue. The husband will be close to the wife. If his love for me lasts, then I can just about survive,

but he can't keep watch the whole year round. There'll be times when he's away, and then she'll bully and intimidate me with words. If I'm stubborn, my head will flow with blood.

And it won't only be the mistress—the servants will try to trample me down too. When he comes back, they'll make up stories, and if he believes them, he'll beat me more.

So I'll be crushed whichever way, reduced to the level of a servant fighting with his other servants. The more I think about it, the more my heart sinks. I was born to die for nothing."

Saen Kham Maen and Ngoen Yuang felt dejected. Both feared the future would turn out as their daughter was saying. Their hearts shivered and their tears fell.

But they suppressed their own sadne concern, embraced their daughter, a tried to console her. "We've looked at your horoscope. Nothing will hap- pen, Father's jewel. In adulthood you'll be gentlefolk.

I've already looked it up in the manua It says that this year you'll have a partner. horoscope falls on the beautiful Sida,

after she's been kidnapped by the ten-f giant, when Ram follows, attacks fearle and brings her back.[4] Don't worry. Yo have someone to depend on.

Sida captured by Thotsakan

---

4. This is a form of divination known as the Three-Tiered Umbrella, ฉัตรสามชั้น, *chat sam chan*. Legendary episodes, mainly from the *Ramakian*, the Thai version of the *Ramayana*, are assigned to the cells of a 3x3 diagram. A man starts at Ram and counts clockwise for his age, less one year. A woman starts from Sida and counts the same, counterclockwise. In the resulting square, the inner, middle, or outer position is chosen depending on whether the subject's birth month is 5–8, 9–12, or 1–4 respectively. Each of these positions corresponds to a certain literary episode. In this case, the position is probably the outer 4 in the middle-lower square for Sida, which corresponds to age seventeen for Laothong. This refers to the time when Sida was released from her captivity by Thotsakan, the "ten-faced giant," in Lanka and returned to her husband, Ram. It is considered a very good portent (Wales, *Divination*, 36–39).

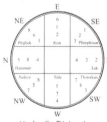

Umbrella Divination

When you arrive there, it'll be rough, but only a little. Wait for some time and from then on, you'll float through the air like a bubble, without a care.

You were born with this fate so please stop crying. Bathe, and we'll go over there near evening." The maids and servants came

to console her and lead her to her room. They filled a bowl with water, scrubbed her, changed her clothes, applied krajae-sandal, and powdered her face to look fair.

waving flowers

They swept her hair into a neat chignon, decorated it with waving golden flowers, inserted a beautiful jeweled hairpin, tucked in shimmering golden aubergine blossoms,

and hung pendants of diamonds and crystal. She wore a breast chain[5] and waist chain glittering with gold inlay and gems, bracelets on both wrists,

rings of diamond, jet, and emerald, and a sabai of ripe yellow[6] color, full of fragrance. Her mother and father escorted her down from the house, surrounded by their servants

carrying many gifts. All their relatives came to accompany Laothong without needing to be told,

bringing whatever they had as gifts for the army, carried along in a jumble of covered trays.[7] They reached the camp and were received by people from the army,

who turned out in droves to gaze at the Lao girls. "Wow!" "Really something." "Immaculate face." She walked in the middle with her curvy waist, stacked breasts, and complexion glowing like the moon.

"She jiggles along like a dancer." "Fair skin, curvy waist, she looks like a sculpture." Eyes glazed over at such a truly fine figure. Ai-Mun said, "If I got my hands on her, I'd never let go."

breast and waist chains

---

5. สังวาล, *sangwan*, long chains or sashes worn either around the neck, looped over the shoulders, or crosswise on the breast, as a mark of status for gods, kings, or nobles. They probably originated from India, where they were called *sankal,* and appear as the regalia of several gods, especially Ganesh (Untracht, *Traditional Jewelry of India*, 209, 224, 275; CK, 480).

6. สีสุก, *si suk*, "ripe color," bright yellow with a touch of orange, the color of ripening rice, mango, or betelnut.

7. ตะลุ่มทับ, *talum hap*, a large tray made from wood or basketwork and probably lacquered, with a cover (KW, 667; Wibun, *Phojananukrom hattakam*, 168).

They came to Phlai Kaeo, and sank down quietly and politely with hands raised in a respectful wai to the army commander as the gifts were set down in piles.

Phlai Kaeo returned the wai of the two parents and invited them to come up and sit on a carpet. Laothong also shifted, and sat demurely with her hands in wai.

Phlai Kaeo glanced at their fair daughter. "She's lovely. Very much like my Phim." The parents met his eyes. He picked up a betel tray and talked about something else.

The two parents spoke in the manner of elders. "We've come to see the Thai noble to thank him very much for his protection.

Hundreds of villages and thousands of cities met disaster and didn't survive. They were cut to pieces like fish on a slab, until the water flowed so thick it was undrinkable.

But our little Chomthong village wasn't destroyed because the soldiers respected us. They did not create resentment by looting whatever property we have.

We thank you sincerely. Even the merit of our parents is incomparable. Now you'll march the army down to the Thai city. As you don't have anything to take back with you,

we've brought whatever poor gifts we can for provisions along the way. We don't have much money or other things to give to all the troops who came up here.

We have only our daughter, Laothong, and a few little things that we thought of bringing to you. We offer you Laothong, our dear and charming daughter, to be your servant until death.

She'll leave her parents to go along with you, and will be without any kin, sir. We entrust her to you. Please don't abandon her.

We're afraid of what will happen when she's out of our sight. If you don't take care of her, she'll lose her head. But if you're kind, it won't be bad.

This old couple will be far away. When would we go down to see her? If in the future you come up here again, kindly pay a visit to give us peace of mind."

Phlai Kaeo replied with a smile, "Don't be too sad. I understand what it means to be far apart and out of sight.

If you're offering me the daughter who you love like your own hearts, it must be because you love me. Perhaps it was some merit accumulated from the past that made me be kind to Chomthong.

Every other village we smashed but here we gave protection and did no harm. This wasn't because someone told me that you have a lovely daughter.

I honestly didn't know. I was sitting quietly and found out just now when you brought her here. I'm happy beyond comparison, even beyond getting heaps of silver and gold,

and thousands of men and women. This is something I didn't expect. No woman came to lie with me here. I resolved to sleep alone and didn't care.

As you've presented Laothong to me, you need have no doubt that I'll look after her in a manner that befits her dignity. I won't want to part from her in a hundred years.

I'll cherish her and be beside her until death. I'll not weary of her and let my heart wander away. Whatever wealth I acquire, I'll not share with anyone else as much as with her.

From all the spoils of war, even down to the level of little things, I'll give to Laothong. You don't need to worry about that."

With these words, he ordered servants to prepare clothing, silver, gold, cattle, buffaloes, elephants, horses, and people to be given to the parents.

The villagers responded by presenting their many gifts in a joyful spirit. "*Sathu*! You've been like a father to us."

"You should be taking the silver and gold you have back home but you're giving lots to us little people." "The more you're a big brother, the more a little brother looks up to you." "Definitely you should be our lord."

The parents paid their respects to the army chief to take leave, and both entrusted their daughter to his care. Laothong was distraught thinking of her mother.

She prostrated and wai-ed, racked with sobs. "When will I come up to see you?" All of them were bathed in tears. The two parents tried to bottle their feelings.

The money, clothing, and other things given by Phlai Kaeo were carried away. Some people chatted happily but the two parents were already missing Laothong.

Servants lamented over their mistress leaving. When they reached the house in the afternoon, the father and mother went into their room, distraught and tearful.

When the sun took leave of the sky and dusk fell, Phlai Kaeo as army commander had candles lit to give light,

and assembled his troops along with the lords, chiefs, and overseers from the provincial cities. All prostrated in respect for his power.

They discussed the conclusion of the war with Chiang Thong. Clerks drew up an inventory of the massive number of captured families,[8] and unit heads were assigned to check them.

The large volume of weapons and equipment, abandoned by the Lao when they scattered, was marked with seals as royal property. Fine silver,[9] things of value,

good elephants and horses were entered on an inventory. Cattle and buffaloes were distributed to the troops. Trays, tables, salvers, and other household articles were given to whoever won them in battle.

"Don't try to conceal things and don't get into jealous fights over them. Everything is above board. In five days we march back to the city.

The ruler of Chiang Thong is liable to a major royal punishment. He'll be escorted to Ayutthaya to hear the king's order on what is to be done.

If the king wishes to punish him, we'll plead his case. Kamphaeng Phet and Rahaeng will also go along to give evidence to the king in his favor."

These orders were passed on by word of mouth, and promptly implemented. People made their farewells.

After the nobles left towards the end of the first watch, the phrai in Phlai Kaeo's camp folded up the carpets.

Servants fell asleep. Candles were extinguished and darkness fell. Phlai Kaeo glanced around and then made towards Laothong. He drew back the curtains

but found she was not there. He asked Phromma, a Lao in her service, who said she had been crying since her parents left. She had gone to stay in another room with her maids looking after her.

"We went there for a chat but she's still too upset." Phlai Kaeo ordered, "Go back down there right now,

and tell the maids, Wiang and Wan, to bring her up here because I want to talk with her about her future."

Phromma received the order, got up, and went straight into Laothong's room and sat down close beside her.

She told the three of them who were sitting together that Phlai Kaeo had asked her to go up for a talk. Then she took leave.

Knowing that Phlai Kaeo wanted her to go up to the bedroom, Laothong clung to the two maids, sobbing

---

8. ครอบครัว, *khropkhrua*, the modern word for "family," is used in *KCKP* exclusively in the sense of people captured and swept away as prisoners of war.

9. เงินขาเกวียน, *ngoen kha kwian*, "cartwheel silver," a term for finely grained white silver (KW, 667).

and trembling with trepidation. "Wan and Wiang, go up first." She raised her hands in wai and pleaded, "I'm no good at talking with nobles.

I was brought up to this age with no young man ever setting eyes on me. My parents fed me morning and evening. Day and night I saw no one.

Now the army commander wants me to go and talk. What'll I say? I don't know anything at all. I'm not going to survive, Wan."

The maids Wan and Wiang tried to comfort her. "Mistress, why do you think that you won't like him?

Your mother and father sent you to be his servant. Why be stubborn? You must learn how to please him and curry his kindness. Then you'll do well.

If you annoy him and spoil his mood, he won't be friendly and might be cruel. Our friends and neighbors will suffer the consequences, and your father might too.

He offered us protection and that's why you were given to be his servant. You're meant to be the face of the family now. Your mother and father will depend on you until their dying day.

You've forgotten everything and you're not listening to us. You'll bring disaster on your mother and father. Please have a care for your old relatives. They sent you to be his wife so they can depend on you.

Don't make a fuss. We'll go as your companions. Wipe away the tears smudging your cheeks. It's a pity you're so gloomy and listless. Let us put on powder to freshen you up."

Laothong desperately tried to evade them but the two maids on either side walked her up to the curtain and knelt down to crawl in together.

Laothong hung back and sank down on the floor. The two pulled her in by the hand. The curtains parted and a blinding light illuminated the sheen of her skin.

Laothong bent forward, burying her face, and crouched hidden in turmoil behind the curtain. The maids tried to draw back, leaving her alone at the front, but she cowered down behind them.

Phlai Kaeo saw her hiding at the back and understood she was still nervous and flustered. Even behind the maids, she looked lovely.

He gazed at her radiant skin and beautiful face and could not help falling in love. Feeling exuberant and eager, he addressed her with a broad smile.

"Precious, sit up. What's the matter? Don't hide in the shadows. Please sit in the light. Let's talk together calmly. May I ask what problems you've had in the past?

The day the army came to Chomthong, were you frightened? Other villages fled in fear, so how come your village took the risk of staying put?

Or did someone tell you I'd be kind and not round everyone up? Or was there an able person of some sort,[10] and that's why you didn't run off and abandon the village?"

Crouching and looking up with their hands raised in wai, Wan and Wiang nudged Laothong to respond. She did not say a word.

The two of them smiled at Phlai Kaeo and burbled answers to his questions. "The day the Thai army attacked? We didn't run away in time because we didn't know what was going on!"

"Besides, we're under Lamphun. There's no cause for war. Everywhere's peaceful so people stayed put to protect their property and families. They feared they'd die if they ran away."

"We thought we'd keep quiet and not make a stir. People hid away in their houses. The headman told us not to flee but stay in our homes and not get concerned."

"Even if the army captured the whole village, we wouldn't be separated from our families. Thanks to your merit, you gave us protection and so Chomthong still exists."

"Even then, we're still anxious. So Laothong has been offered as your servant. She's meant to be the face of us all. May we rely on your protection until death."

Phlai Kaeo replied with a smile, "Perhaps I'd made a lot of merit, and that induced the officers and men not to harm Chomthong.

But really, I didn't expect to get a beautiful wife to share my room. This evening I saw a lot of faces coming, and the two parents brought Laothong.

She's exactly what my heart desires. Even capturing Chiang Thong means less to me. Why isn't she talking? Is she unwilling?

You two maids close beside her, please ask her this question to dispel my doubts. If she's not willing to love, it doesn't matter. But she shouldn't cry. It dulls her cheeks."

Wan and Wiang thought up a ploy, with good intentions. They nudged Laothong. "Dearest, why are you keeping silent and not talking?

If you do well, we two can depend on you. If you resist and don't listen to us, you'll have to go to Ayutthaya but you won't see our two faces because we'll

---

10. Perhaps this means the village had someone versed in lore who was able to protect it, or who predicted that Phlai would not sack it.

run away back here."

"We brought you up and expect to rely on your merit. If we can't, we'll have to go elsewhere. It's a waste of effort to instruct you day and night when you just whimper and don't listen to us."

Laothong heard what her maids were saying but found it difficult to open her mouth because she had never spoken in Thai.

Talking to a man also made her so shy that she was trembling all over. But she was afraid the two maids might really abandon her, and there would be no one else.

She tried to force herself to speak but still turned her face away in shyness and embarrassment. The maids pinched and prompted her. In a tremulous, timid voice, she said,

"I agree to be your servant. I'll go to the southern city. But I'm worried to breaking point about what I'm leaving behind. I'm at a loss and don't know what to say."

Phlai Kaeo watched her speaking without raising her face and knew she was still so nervous that further conversation would take a long time.

He reached out and took a betelnut from the tray. Holding his breath, he recited a formula. Knowing she had trusted the maids for a long time, he passed it to them.

"Please offer this betelnut to Laothong. You both take from the tray. We've talked until late. Please go now and come again tomorrow."

The maids took the betelnut and offered it to Laothong who received it without raising her face. She feared he would not let her go unless she ate it, and so put it into her mouth. The mantra thrilled her.

Since arriving that evening, she had not once looked at Phlai Kaeo's face. Now, under the influence of the mantra from chewing the betelnut a little, she stole a glance at him.

The sight of the army commander made her break into a smile. She wanted desperately to crawl over to him. Phlai Kaeo saw her manner and knew she was excited by the God-Arouser formula.

He turned to address the two maids. "Please go now and come again tomorrow. Laothong is already yawning. It's time to extinguish the lights and go to sleep."

The two maids left, closed the door, and hurried away. Laothong could not tear her eyes away from him. She did not leave and wanted to be his partner.

Phlai Kaeo got up from the bed and walked over to close the door of the room. His hands groped around and found Laothong. She stayed still and did not cry out.

He sat down close to her. "Who is this? Nothing comes out of her mouth at all." She pushed his hand away from her breast in surprise. "I know who this is now—Laothong.

Precious, why are you sitting here. It's not suitable. The time is getting close to dawn." He stroked, kissed, and fondled her, then lifted her onto the bed in his arms,

and lowered her gently onto the mattress. "Don't get alarmed when I embrace you." He smiled as he caressed her feverishly, and breathed in the fragrance of her krajae-sandal.

Her skin felt velvety soft. Her breasts were pointed like lotuses with petals on the point of bursting apart. She was fragrant, sweet, and very lovable.

A storm rumbled, and fierce clouds gathered. Dust swirled in a monsoon wind. Thunder crashed across the universe. Beyond resistance, waters flooded the whole three worlds.

The storm subsided, darkness dispelled, and the moon again shone brilliantly. Both were bathed in bliss. He struck a flint and lit a lamp.

Laothong lay limp, face down on the bed. Phlai stayed close beside her body, and went on gently kissing her, keeping her heart spinning.

He raised her chin and made her sit up and take some betelnut. "Isn't your mouth sour? How can you stand it?" He lifted her onto his lap. She was listless, languid, lissome, lovely.

He kissed her hair and pressed his face against hers. "Open your eyes. I want to ask you a question. This is the truth, I tell you. I love you very much and I'll follow your desire.

If I didn't have my official army duty, I wouldn't go back down there. I feel sorry for you. Leaving your parents will be a source of unfailing sadness.

Even though I'll be there to caress you, thinking of your parents will make you weep. I feel sorry for them too because they'll be miserable. With them staying and you going, it'll be heartbreaking.

But if I were to abandon you in Chomthong, I would never lose you from my thoughts. To gain a wife[11] and then leave her would be a great loss. Thinking about this is perplexing,

because either way a love has to be broken. Don't cry. We can go down

---

11. See p. 148, note 32. Phlai Kaeo here addresses Laothong as *mia*, and refers to himself as *phua* in the next stanza. Laothong reciprocates in the next speech. In the case of Phlai and Laothong, there is no marriage ceremony. She is given to him "as wife," and the marriage is confirmed by the sexual bond.

together, or you can stay here—it's up to you. Your husband won't complain and make you miserable."

Laothong shyly averted her face. Her passion had not yet subsided. She clung close to Phlai Kaeo's chest, not wanting anything to change.

"My old parents are lovely. They took care of me until I'd grown up, and I haven't repaid their kindness very much yet. I'll miss them more than I can describe.

Leaving their care to go with a husband, I worry about how things will be. At the beginning, we'll say we love each other but I'm afraid about what will happen once we get to the southern city.

If you're quick enough to have two loves, I'll be in difficulty because your wife is your ruler. If you love me and look after me, I'll just about survive. But I'm worried it won't work out with your wife.

Don't imagine that I'll stay home here. Out of love I agree to follow wherever you go. Though love makes me an outcaste, I'll face it until I die before your eyes."

Phlai Kaeo smiled, soothed her, and replied, "I love the beautiful Laothong with more love than a hundred of other people's loves combined.

Even though I have a wife, don't worry. It won't be as you think. I look after everyone, big or small, on equal level.

Eye's jewel, though you're now an orphan with no kin, don't be afraid and miserable." He soothed her with insistent caresses that stirred her full of passion.

They fondled and whispered sweet nothings. He nuzzled both her cheeks, caressed her breasts, and gently lay his cheeks between them, lighting flames of desire that scorched her heart.

They went on fondling without a nap or feeling sleepy until almost dawn. When the sun rose brightly, sprays of fragrant flowers burst into bloom,

bees caressed their petals, and the coel uttered its sweetly melodious call, they still clung close in ecstasy for a long time. Then Phlai Kaeo drew the curtain and went outside.

War prisoners prostrated. A salver was brought with water and facecloth. A betel set was placed inside the room. Phlai Kaeo went to sit outside and receive the nobles.

In the room, Laothong thought up a plan. "As I'm going to be away from here forever, I'll leave a record so my skill is well known."

With this idea, she called the two maids. "Wan

coel

and Wiang, come here. I've had this idea.

I'm going down to the southern city and who knows when I'll return home. I'm good at embroidery so I'll make a tapestry,

and offer it to the wat in Lamphun to serve as a record in the future. The two of you go off and find some good cloth and all the other things."

They ground, mixed, and boiled dye to make the silk a glossy bright purple. The fabric was put in a frame and stretched evenly. She sat, intent and joyful,

with the two maids on either side to thread the silk. She embroidered the lord of the demons leading his army

to do battle under a great bo tree.[12] He was angrily kicking his elephant to charge, and his soldiers were transforming their bodies into various shapes. Some wore glinting armor,

and others held clubs across their chests. He rode an elephant as high as Mount Meru, and carried poison arrows, a glittering short sword,[13] shining crystal discus, mace,

trident, throwing knife, bow, dagger,[14] and shields for his arms and body. His valiant elephant had upcurving tusks. A tall and powerful lion followed behind.

A magnificent steed like the Phalahok horse, decked in beautifully ornate harness, high-stepped elegantly across a field. People riding great oxen over-flowed from a troop column.

She embroidered the army's standard waving against a pall of clouds obscuring the sun, while the gods of every direction fled away. The scene shimmered with gold,

lustrous bright purple, and red like vermilion. She embroidered luxuriant trees with leaf and branch, and parrots swooping after one another,

looking lifelike, in a flock pecking, peeping, and flying away. She embroidered Suthat, one of the seven ranges, and also Winantok, Karawik, and Yukhanthon,[15]

---

12. While the Buddha was meditating under the bo tree at Bodhgaya, he was attacked by Mara, the personification of illusion, and his army of demons. The Buddha remained supremely composed and thus rendered their assault harmless. Finally he touched his fingers on the earth, summoning Mae Thorani, the earth goddess, who wrung from her hair all the water poured after meritorious deeds in the Buddha's previous lives, and this torrent washed away the demons. This scene is a favorite subject for mural painting in Thai wat, usually on the end wall opposite the Buddha image.

13. ขรรค์, *khan*, a double-edged short sword with a short handle, wielded by gods and kings (CK, 86).

14. กันหยั่น, *kanyan*, a double-edged dagger or sword of Chinese origin.

15. สัตภัณฑ์, *sattaphan*, the seven hills or ranges surrounding Mount Meru are Yukhanthon, Isinthon, Karawik, Suthat, Neminthon, Winantok, and Hatsakan; in Pali, Yugandhara, Isadhara,

beyond them, five bands for the ocean,[16] and the river
Ganga, crystal clear and full of rippling, splashing water,
with crowds of *kinnon* and masterminds[17] coming to
bathe and drink.

She embroidered attractive lotuses in bloom, bees
gliding and hovering, masses of four-legged beasts
on the ground, and *kinnari* flying throughout the
scene.

Little Laothong sat from morning through until the
sun dipped and disappeared. Phlai Kaeo came to take a
look. Entering the room, he was dazzled by the tapestry,
and stood watching her embroider. "So lovable and so
skillful too. Sitting humbly with her head lowered, she's
beautiful from head to toe. Her face is just like Phim."

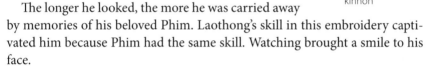

kinnon

The longer he looked, the more he was carried away
by memories of his beloved Phim. Laothong's skill in this embroidery captivated him because Phim had the same skill. Watching brought a smile to his
face.

He sat close to her but got excited and had to leave. He stood up, went
into the room, and lay down on Laothong's bed, lost in thought until he fell
asleep.

Laothong and her two maids lit lamps and went on embroidering without
sleep. At the first streaks of the dawn sun, the tapestry was complete as she
intended.

They cut it from the frame. The two maids bathed her, powdered her face,
and perfumed her with krajae-sandal. Then they went to see Phlai Kaeo.

The three prostrated beside one another. Phlai Kaeo came and sat close
to Laothong. Still thinking about Phim, he said, "Your embroidery is very
skillful.

You're more knowledgeable about the story of the war of the demons than
any woman in the capital. Even in Ayutthaya, nobody can match the skill of
Phim—oops!—Laothong."

Karavika, Sudassana, Nemindhara, Vinataka, and Assakanna (RR, 275–78).

16. The Sithandon Ocean, Pali Sithantara, which surrounds Mount Meru, is often depicted
in pictures as five bands (RR, sixth color plate).

17. วิทยา, วิทยาธร, *withaya, withayathon,* Sanskrit *vidyadhara,* "upholder of (special) knowledge," non-human beings, ranked below *thewada,* with very sweet tongues and the ability to fly
through the air, variously described as attendants on Indra or Siva (Childers, *Dictionary of the
Pali Language,* 606; Phlainoi, *Wannakhadi aphithan,* 302–3). The translation is invented.

Hearing him slip up over the name, Laothong stretched out her hands and nudged the two maids. She thought before answering very deliberately. "This tapestry of mine,

I intend to offer to Wat Chedi Luang.[18] Please come with me. Because I'm going to the southern city, I'll also have my statue made.[19]

It will lessen my old parents' suffering from missing me. Our home and the wat are close enough to pass by. I'll have the statue inscribed with the name *Phim*."

"Oh! Look here. What's making you apprehensive? Your mouth is as thin as if painted with vermilion. So you think my wife is called Phim." He smiled and stood up.

They went to the wat in Lamphun. Laothong and the two maids traveled behind Phlai Kaeo, followed by the servants and a mass of men in the rear.

They prostrated and paid respect, and then went over to arrange for Nai Sa to mold the statue. Servants pounded the mortar, and added water steeped with cinnamon tree bark and cattle hide.[20]

When the mixture was the right consistency, the couple sat together watching him mold the statue. It was exactly like her, beautiful from head to toe.

The figure was inscribed with the name Laothong. She called the two maids who happily prostrated before the tapestry, and threaded a cord to hang it up.

She sat and offered a prayer: "Oh lord, may this tapestry I have embroidered completely in one night and one day, and hung as an offering to the holy Buddha image,

help me towards nirvana and wealth without decrease. Should I die, may I go to the heavens.

May this statue and tapestry remain for a hundred years. If and when Lam-

---

18. The name of a wat in Chiang Mai, not Lamphun. Another mistake in northern geography. The Wat Ko version calls it Wat Mueang Lamphun, also nonexistent (WK, 9:328, 330).

19. This idea is very strange. In old Siam, the only images made were of the Buddha, gods, and other religious and mythological figures. There was reluctance about making images of living people for fear they would be subject to lore. Some images were made of past kings, including a statue of U Thong in the Ayutthaya palace, and there were some Buddha images made with a king's features and royal regalia. King Rama V was the first king rendered in sculpture, and the practice is still effectively confined to prominent historical figures, especially royalty, politicians, and monks. Perhaps this statue making was intended to portray Lanna as exotic.

20. โมง, *mong*, local name for *Cinnamomum iners*, usually called อบเชย, *opchoei*, or เชียด, *chiat*. Water in which the cinnamon-scented bark has been steeped hardens the plaster (KW, 667). "They do likewise make better Mortar than our's: by reason that in the water which they use, they do boyl a certain bark, the skins of Oxen, or Buffalo's, and Sugar" (La Loubère, *New Historical Relation*, 12).

phun disappears, let them disappear together."

After this prayer, she prostrated to take leave and called Phlai Kaeo to return. They arrived at the army camp in good spirits.

That evening, Phlai Kaeo and Laothong lay together in the room in blissful happiness. After Laothong went to sleep,

late at night when the moon shone brightly, Phlai Kaeo's thoughts turned to home. "My gentle Phim must be waiting forlornly for me every night and day.

The war is over. As soon as I get the military order, I'll go back to enjoy my darling love. How many more days now?"

He was too pent up to sleep soundly. The more he thought, the more unsettled he felt, but had to bottle it up in his heart.

11: PHIM CHANGES HER NAME TO WANTHONG

Now to tell of Phim Philalai. She slept alone and lonely in the bridal house, straining for news of the army, but no news came.

Every night, she missed Phlai Kaeo so much she could never fall fast asleep. In the daytime, she lay engrossed in lifelike dreams, sleeptalking as if possessed by spirits.

For no reason, she would rush out of her room, laughing, crying, and babbling deliriously. She contracted a fever that would not go away but became progressively worse.

Saithong tried to console her but Phim had no ears for listening. "Oh my brilliant Phlai Kaeo, don't you care for me at all?"

Watching her daughter wasting away, her old mother, Siprajan, was overcome with grief. Many doctors came but their medicine had no effect.

All the servants bustled around providing the doctors with whatever they wanted. The whole household prayed, at a loss to know what was the matter.

On consultation, one doctor said she was not dying. Another said he could find no problem. Another said tetanus had entered her heart. Another said the fever was caused by menstruation.

Yet another said the spirit of the house was running in and out of her body. Siprajan rolled her eyes and did not know what to do. She berated the doctors, "You're no good. You sit around happily eating and eating.

When the patient cries out like a mooing cow, you don't take a look—you just laugh. Why should I let you treat her? Get out of my house!"

The doctors left with Siprajan's scolding echoing in their ears. "Sending for doctors to see my daughter is just a waste of betel and pan. I'm fed up with it.

doctors

She's so thin her eyes are bulging." She hugged her daughter, weeping. "I've been tending to you for a long time without my attention wavering for a minute.

I don't know what sickness you have. The more I think, the more upset I am. The doctors have given you every medicine in the book. It's cost a fortune already.

Please try to eat something. Set your mind to wait for Phlai Kaeo. But since the army left, we haven't had a whisper of news about what's happened."

She stroked her daughter to console her. "Would you like some rice gruel? I'll boil it for you. How come you don't say anything? Has some spirit taken possession of you? Tell me.

Why did it choose my dear daughter? Is it the spirit of Phan Son, my husband? Oh Husband, I didn't realize it was you. Please don't take offense. I'll make an offering of liquor, rice, turtle, and fish.

Please help our daughter recover, and then I'll feed the monks and send the merit to you. Why are you sticking out your tongue and rolling your eyes? Phim has a fever. Please help her."

Phim was angry. "What spirit has come and from where? My father gets blamed for so much. I'll die within days.

My heart is so very, very heavy. Don't bother about tending to me, Mother. It won't go away." She hugged Saithong close and whimpered. "What to do to see the face of Phlai Kaeo?"

Siprajan's body trembled and her tears flowed to see her daughter so disturbed. Her thoughts turned to the abbot.

She got up, came out of the room, and called the servants. "Where have you got to? Put some betelnut and pan on a salver." They hurried off to Wat Palelai.

On arrival she went straight to offer betelnut to the abbot. "Phim has some kind of fever. None of the doctors in Suphan can cure it.

She's babbling without making sense, as if possessed by a spirit. She's wasting away with so much grief I don't think she'll survive. Master, please look at her stars."

Abbot Ju promptly examined the horoscope. When the meaning was clear, he spoke. "Phim's luck right now is bad.

She's on the position of Sida being abducted by Thotsakan.[1] If she doesn't

---

1. This uses the Three-Tiered Umbrella method of divination, and probably accords to the middle 7 in the west segment (see p. 208, note 4). This corresponds to the passage in the *Ra-*

separate from her husband, she'll die. But if we act, it can be cured.

She must change her name to Wanthong,[2] then she won't die, her sickness will disappear, and she can look after all the property."

Siprajan took leave, happy that the abbot said Phim would recover. Arriving at the house, she cried out, "She won't die! The abbot says so, for sure."

Rice, fish, bananas, sugarcane, several little sweets, and everything else was prepared to do a soul ceremony for Phim.

Siprajan did a soul-scooping[3] for her daughter, getting some of it right and some wrong.

"Oh soul! Don't wander into woods alone.
On your own the forest will be lonelier.
Don't stray after mole, rhino, bear, lion,
Treeshrew, porcupine, rabbit, kingfisher.
Don't get lost over deer, elephant, and tiger.
Gibbon, langur, and lady ghosts[4] will haunt you."

She scooped up rice and fish and threw them on Phim. "Away with all diseases and dangers, thorns and splinters!" She tied a black thread round Phim's wrist, extinguished the candles, and changed her name to Wanthong.

tying thread on wrist

Before long, Wanthong began to eat, to sleep soundly without dreaming and sleeptalking, and to put on weight day by day. Siprajan gradually cheered up too.

❧

---

makian when Sida is captured by Thotsakan and taken away to Lanka. The portent is very bad (Wales, *Divination*, 36–39).

2. Thai systems of divination lay great store on choosing a name that suits the astrological disposition at the time of birth. Manuals describe in detail what letters, and what sequences of letters, match what planetary conditions, days in the week, and so on. Failure to have obeyed these principles could be a cause of misfortune. In addition, a name may be a signal that attracts the attention of malevolent spirits. Changing a name to improve fortune remains common to this day. In Phim's new name, *thong* means gold and *wan* probably comes from วรรณ(ะ), meaning color, derived from the Sanskrit *varna*. Phim would have been auspicious only if she had been born on a Tuesday. (See the naming manual in Hora Purajan, *Tamra phrommachat*, 258–90).

3. ทักขวัญ, *thak khwan*, usually one part of a *khwan* ceremony (see p. 11, note 59). Someone uses a ladle to mime scooping the *khwan* into a bowl which is then covered with a cloth (Anuman, *Essays*, 237–38).

4. นางกราย, *nang krai*, "walking lady," name of an orchid, an obscure poetical meter, and a dance performed by elephant mahouts. But here WK 9:337 gives พราย, *phrai*, ghost or spirit.

Now to tell of Khun Chang. He heard that Wanthong's fever had gone. "Phlai Kaeo has disappeared off to war with no news, neither good nor bad.

He'll never come back. What powers of lore does he have? If he'd taken Chiang Thong, he'd have returned by now. The Lao have probably slit open his liver and left him rolling in the dirt.

Well! I'll take this opportunity to plead for Wanthong's hand. It'd be better for me to take care of her in my room. I'll talk to her mother, Siprajan, and tell her Phlai Kaeo is dead."

He gave orders to his servants, "Quickly go over to tell Granny Kloi and Granny Sai that I invite them to my house." The servants ran off

and gave the invitation to the two old ladies, who promptly scurried over to Khun Chang's house.

He entreated them. "I need your help. Whatever money it costs, I'll pay without a thought. Kindly go with me to ask for Wanthong's hand.

Her husband, Phlai Kaeo, went off to war. They were defeated and the Lao stabbed him to death. Nobody survived. Now, about Phim Philalai.

Her mother changed her name to Wanthong, and the astrologer foretold she'll be able to look after the property. Kindly help by going with me to ask for her hand."

Granny Kloi and Granny Sai did not know that Khun Chang was being devious. They were taken in by the thought of getting cash so they agreed and took leave.

They bathed, powdered themselves, combed their hair, and put on new clothes. Khun Chang selected a servant that he knew from experience could be trusted,

and whispered his orders. "I've put my faith in you before, and now I have some important business. Hurry over to the wat,

collect some bones from the bodies in the graveyard, and put them in a new earthenware pot." Ai-Bao hastened to the graveyard and arranged a pot of bones as ordered.

Khun Chang took the new pot and put it in his room. He dressed in a golden yok and a woolen uppercloth. When he lifted up a mirror to look at his head, he was upset by the sight of his bald pate.

"I'm so angry I could bash it myself. It's foul, hopeless! Nothing at the front, nothing at the back. Awful!" He slapped on a couple of handfuls of soot,

and smudged it over his head like a child playing. Though he spread the hairs with a comb, they still did not hide the smooth patch. He used a small stick to arrange

earthenware pot

the hairs in rows, then daubed on lots of pomade.

"This straggly little bit of hair is not enough to cover the vacant patch. It's the hair of a slave, so ugly I can't be bothered to comb it. What a shame! I've enough money to redeem over a thousand slaves,

and buy over a hundred elephants or horses, so why can't I have enough hair to cover my head? If only I could buy some, what fun it would be to have a haircut and admire the styling!

If I'd known I'd be bald from birth, I wouldn't have wanted to be born. Such an outcaste!" Burned up with frustration, he plunged into an inner room,

picked up the pot of bones, and tied it up in paper. He summoned a servant that he could trust from all those gathered kneeling around, gave him the pot of bones, and set off.

They came down from the house around noon with the two old ladies walking in front. They arrived at Siprajan's house and asked for her.

Servants said she was inside and ran off to tell their mistress. "Khun Chang has come. He's waiting at the bottom of the stairway with an oily glint in his eye."

Siprajan opened a window and called out a greeting to Khun Chang. "Your face is bathed in sweat. What have you come for? Please come up."

Khun Chang walked up the stairs with the two old ladies close behind. They sat down with their eyes rolled up, raised their hands and wai-ed repeatedly, one after the other.

Siprajan returned the wais but could not keep up. She turned and pushed a betel tray towards them. "Why have so many of you come? What brings Granny Kloi and Granny Sai here?"

Khun Chang screwed up his face and pretended to sob. Wiping away the tears trickling from his eyes, he brought out the pot of bones, and set it down.

"These are the bones of Phlai Kaeo. They were brought to me. He was stabbed dead by a Lao. The ruler of Chiang Thong was two-faced. He sided with Chiang Mai but then switched and pretended to side with Phlai Kaeo. They marched the army through the forest, halting to sleep several times. One day at dusk,

the ruler of Chiang Thong crept up and stabbed him. There was blood every-

preparing a betel tray

where, right into his lungs. He cried out but the assailant fled, and Kaeo died quickly.

His men returned to the city and were clapped in prison. Many people are suffering badly. Ai-Mak sent the pot of bones." After these words, Khun Chang put on a sorrowful face.

"He was so young! Just thinking of Kaeo, I'm devastated. He shouldn't have volunteered so boldly that he died and left Phim a lonely widow."

Siprajan listened to Khun Chang spinning his tale. " Phlai Kaeo is dead? Oh no! I've been waiting, and counting every day.

Wanthong was overwhelmed by bad luck, grief, and sickness. She had a fever but didn't die, and now Phlai Kaeo has died before her. They were in the bridal house such a short time.

Wanthong cried endlessly, beyond consolation." She shouted out to Wanthong, "Mother's jewel, your heart is broken!"

In her room, Wanthong had heard what Khun Chang was saying. At the sound of her mother wailing, she came out, saw Khun Chang's face, and spoke angrily.

"Who says my husband is dead? Who's making up this bad news? You cobra, you big trickster, you just bought this pot for ten cowries."

She stamped her foot down hard in the doorway. "A curse on your mother's clan! I can't be bothered to shout at you." She went back into her room with tears welling, and collapsed crying on the bed.

"Oh my Phlai Kaeo! I don't believe this baldy. He's making things up. It was his deviousness that got you sent off to war.

Now the wheedler turns up with a story and a pot of bones to fool us. How can he say these things, damn his mother! He's so shifty and sly.

Thinking about it makes me lose heart. You've only just gone, and people are getting at me. If you'd stayed, no one would dare. I'm at my wits' end, dear Kaeo."

Siprajan was very cross at her daughter's cursing. "Oh good people, please pay no attention to her. She wasn't like this before.

Since she had the fever, she's a bit crazy. Whatever I say, she takes no notice but complains and makes a big row. I can't be bothered to beat her. She won't ever see Phlai Kaeo's corpse now."

Granny Kloi and Granny Sai saw a clever way to intervene. They fluttered their eyes and whispered, "Well, my dear Siprajan, for ages the law has been that anyone who dares volunteer for war and comes back defeated gets the chop." "That's the law laid down by the ministry."

"And if anyone dies in war, his wife is seized to be a royal widow,[5] and the children too." "And the troops who come back defeated are rounded up and sent to the inner jail."[6]

"Wanthong will have to be a royal widow." "It'll be tough, and that's a cause for concern." "You must do something about it." "Let Khun Chang take her as his wife."

"He'll think of a way to fix things in the capital. He's got bags of money that he's ready to use." "Don't let this blow up like a big fire. Find a compromise before it's too late."

Siprajan was racked by floods of tears. "Wanthong's a widow. Her husband's dead. We won't see his face. Who'll protect us?

Khun Chang's a very rich man. He can shell out money without a thought, and we can depend on him in the future." With this in mind, she said,

"Wanthong's husband has just died. We can't sit still and let her become a widow. If there's a law case, it'll be a bed of thorns. If Chang asks for her hand, I'll do the clever thing.

But the plain is wide and the road is long. I don't know where to begin. If Phlai Kaeo isn't dead and comes back, there'll be trouble between him and Khun Chang in the future."

Granny Kloi and Granny Sai spoke up. "Phlai Kaeo died for sure." "The phrai are all in jail." "Even if he did survive and comes back,

you can say you didn't know and it won't matter. We'd be the ones who might get fined." "If you consent to the match, make an agreement now. It'll be dangerous to delay."

"If they seize her and take her off, it'll be the talk of the town." "Fix things up right now. Have the ceremony in the waning phase of this month."

Siprajan agreed and said, "On the third of the waning moon, come to the

---

5. A woman taken into the palace and employed in some service. Originally a way to support the widows of deceased nobles, in this case it is a punishment.

6. They are exaggerating a little for effect. The Law on Revolt and Warfare, พระไอยการกบฏ ศึก, *phra aiyakan krabot suek*, has several clauses prescribing that deserters will have heads and feet cut off and be stuck up on poles. No law prescribes penalties for defeat, though Clause 43 is worded to make defeat and desertion virtually the same: "Anyone employed by the king in war is assumed to give his life in defense of the royal power and thus should not retreat at all in the face of the enemy but be intent on victory. Should anyone flee and the army be lost, he shall be executed as an example to others, and his wife, children, and goods be seized as royal property" (KTS, 4:144–45).

house. Hurry and don't delay. I agree for sure and won't change my mind."

In her room, Wanthong heard her mother giving her away. She leapt up, shaking her head in anger, and shouted at the servants.

"Where's my Saithong? Go and call Ta-Phon[7] to me. He doesn't take care of his duties, morning or night. A curse on his mother's clan! What's he thinking of?"

Saithong heard Wanthong calling her, and shouted to Ta-Phon, "Quick! Come with me to Mistress Wanthong."

Bald Ta-Phon responded and came out of a room. He sank down humbly, looked up, and asked, "What did you call me for?"

Wanthong waggled a finger at his face and shouted, "A curse on your mother, you useless baldy. Don't you have any sense? You're a servant but you don't look after the house.

The only thing you're good at is lying. You deserve to be slapped down into a pile of dogshit. You were supposed to be watching the gate but you closed your eyes and let a pack of dogs stray in.

They went around pissing and shitting all over the place. The mangy dog is making a row barking, and the bitches are howling and whining. Why do you let your mother's ancestors make such a racket?"

Hearing Wanthong's cursing, Granny Kloi and Granny Sai sat with grim faces. Khun Chang pretended he was deaf and did not know what was going on, until it became too much to bear.

He said to the two old ladies, "Time's getting on. Let's go." He wai-ed Siprajan who repeated, "Don't forget. What we've agreed must happen quickly."

Wanthong shouted out loudly, "Hey! Where have you got to, Grandma Mi? You don't do your duty morning or evening. Wherever there's chitchat you'll be sitting there,

wagging your tongue, you slave. Your head looks like a scraped coconut, as weird as wild waterfern boiled in coconut milk. You're descended from a bunch of lying fish-owls."

Kloi, Sai, and Khun Chang hurried out of the central hall, down the stairs, and away from Siprajan's house.

Granny Kloi and Granny Sai spoke up. "We've lost face." "I don't wish to come here ever again to have my ancestors dug up and reviled." "I wouldn't

---

7. In the original, the baldheaded servant is named Phrom in this chapter but the name has been changed in the translation to Phon as found in earlier and later chapters.

come for a pile of gold."

Khun Chang said, "It's not like that. Wanthong was speaking in riddles. She told me it's a woman's ploy. She wants my mother Thepthong to pay a call.

That's why she talked about my mother's ancestors, meaning: Please ask your parent to come. I should certainly get her as wife! Don't fret. Nobody like my eye's jewel can be found anywhere."

In her room, Wanthong yearned. "Oh my brilliant Phlai Kaeo, how could you really be dead?

On the day your life ended, I should have dreamed a little something but there's been nothing, no bad omen giving the news. The men who went with you haven't returned.

They're saying that when a commander dies, the men are jailed. But it's beyond poor me to find out. There are so many obstacles, checkmate on every square. I don't know how things are in Ayutthaya.

Ever since I was born I've never once been to Ayutthaya. The day I went to see my husband off, all I can remember is the Bang Lang Canal.

The bo trees! We planted them together so that if anything happened there'd be a sign. If Phlai Kaeo is dead and gone, the middle bo tree will be dead too.

The more I think about it, it's awful of Mother not to find out for certain. She's fallen for that villain's story and consented to give me to him.

Oh what a pity, poor me! Why am I so badly troubled? Am I suffering without relief because of some karma created in the past?

I was married and within two or three days my husband disappeared out of sight. The day he left the bridal house, he said with tears in his eyes that he was greatly worried about me.

In his heart, he thought he'd return. He said it over and over again, despite the sorrow. He entrusted Saithong to look after me, then left because he had to."

At that moment, Saithong crept in to find Wanthong with her face bathed in tears. Wanthong flung her arms round Saithong's neck and cried and cried. "Oh Saithong, I don't want to live."

Saithong soothed her, "Don't weep. I'm tired of seeing you getting ever sadder." The two clung together, sobbing and sighing in floods of tears.

"Oh my dear Wanthong, how come you can't find even a little happiness, just because this villainous Khun Chang has been smitten with you ever since you came of age?

He was maneuvering to snag you at the house and at the wat. This outcaste is too much. Even when you married Phlai Kaeo, he kept poking his nose into everything.

He got the king's ear and had Phlai Kaeo sent off to war, leaving you crying as if to die. Now he's going on all the time that Phlai Kaeo is dead.

I think it's just a trick by this toady. He brings along a pot of bones to claim that Phlai Kaeo is dead so he can ask for your hand.

He says he's a rich man and ready to spend money like water. Our old mother has given her consent, and now we two are at our wits' end.

This is ill fate. What shall we do? Where can we run away and hide? Your mother-in-law lives far away in some unknown place in Kanburi.

Why don't you and I go to Wat Palelai to see Abbot Ju? He foretells the future well. Mother Siprajan will go to sleep soon.

Stay in the room and don't cry, while I find some betel and pan." She found them and put them in a bowl. Around dusk, whispering and signaling with their eyes,

the two left the room and quietly stole down from the house. At the wat, they went up to the abbot's kuti,

and handed the betel and pan to a novice, who in turn offered them to the abbot. He peered out, shading his eyes, and asked who it was. Then he recognized her and laughed. "Oh, Wanthong!

I changed your name to make the fever go away. What's the matter? Are you still not well? You look unhappy but you've put on some weight. That's good. Why have you two come?"

Wanthong and Saithong prostrated and raised their hands in wai. "I've been terribly upset because my husband went to war and has not returned.

People are spreading bad news that he's dead. Master, please check by the manual. Is what they say true?"

Abbot Ju examined the positions of the sun and moon. He was confident there was no problem, and so he said,

"Divining by the three-eyed time,[8] whoever told you this is lying. Don't believe

8. ตรีเนตร, *trinet*, from Sanskrit, three-eyed, originally an appellation of Siva, later transferred to Indra. This form of divination for deciding binary decisions was supposedly passed on to humans by Indra. In the calculation, his central eye is the sun (ใส, *sai*, 1), right eye is the moon (ปลอด, *plot*, 2), and left eye is Mars (กำ, *kam*, 3). Starting from the sun, count counterclockwise round this triangle during a waxing moon, and clockwise in a waning moon for the number of days plus one. From this spot, then, keep counting in the same direction for the number of three-hour *yam* plus one. In general, Mars indicates a negative result, while the moon is positive, and the sun is neutral. However, the result depends also on the activity concerned, and the whole sequence of eyes. For example, in warfare, if the calculation alights on the moon with Mars

them. Your husband won a victory, took the city, and pulverized the enemy. He's acquired money, goods, and people in large numbers. In a little while, he'll return. Don't worry, and don't believe anyone sowing confusion."

Listening to these words, Wanthong and Saithong felt their sorrow disappear. They wiped away their tears in relief, prostrated to take leave, and hurried home.

Going up into the house, they joyfully told Siprajan everything the abbot had seen.

abbot divining

"I went to see the abbot. He divined that nothing's the matter. Phlai Kaeo attacked and won a victory. He's captured families and will soon return."

Siprajan shook her head. "I don't believe it. How can these divinations based on some tricks with time compare to seeing with your own eyes?

He boasts he knows for sure. Oh child! Sometimes these divinations are not even a little bit right. Don't be naive and believe him. Every one of the soldiers has been jailed.

They'll seize you as a royal widow. You'll sit there hugging your knees, moaning and groaning, all alone. Nobody will be on your case because you're poor. Accept things as they are without anger.

It's not that I'm not fond of Phlai Kaeo. But he's dead and won't return home. The only thing wrong with Khun Chang is his skull. And even though that's bald and shiny, what's inside is good."

Wanthong felt as if her mother's words were killing her. She collapsed, crying in distraction. "If you talk like this, I'm done for.

All you can see is his money. Even if he were a pig or a dog, you'd give me to him. The abbot makes a divination but you ignore it. You're not kind to me.

You might not be ashamed before other people, but you should be ashamed before the spirits. Sixteen years old and two husbands! Even if you give me to him, I won't consent. Nothing has happened to my husband.

If the seer's advice is wrong, then the bo tree is an important sign. Let's go there to look and make sure. If Phlai Kaeo is dead, then so is the bo tree."

ahead (i.e., next in sequence) and the sun behind, then victory will be gained (Thep, *Horasat nai wannakhadi*, 470–76). The method is known colloquially as จับยามสามตา, *jap yam sam ta*, three-eye prediction, and used by children rather like eeny-meany-miny-mo.

Siprajan was frustrated at not getting her way. "Don't prolong matters, you abomination. You'll create trouble for me too. Will you love being a widow?

It's not a short hop to check the bo tree. It's a long way and I won't go. If you keep crossing me, I'll give you to Khun Chang today."

At this, Wanthong collapsed in grief on the spot and screamed out loud, "This is not right! Beat me to death, I don't care.

When I'm born again in my next life, I've no desire to enter your womb. Not ever! Not for hundreds and thousands of eras. What kind of mother is this?

All you can see is money. It's obscene. You'd give a person to a ghost. Please kill me and let me have done with life." She beat her chest, boxed her head, and collapsed down flat.

"If that shiny head ever comes near me, I'll whack him with a stick so he bellows out loud. I don't want to live any more."

Siprajan jumped up and grabbed a stick. "Your mother's clan! You've got a foul and catty mouth. I'll beat you into dust." She lurched up the stairs to the bridal house,

and hit Wanthong on the flank with a big thwack. Wanthong shrieked and turned sideways. Siprajan pinched her repeatedly, and thrashed her with the stick until the welts showed.

Wanthong asked for no forgiveness. "My husband's dead so I'll follow him. That vile Khun Chang has no more hair than a pygmy owl. I'll have nothing to do with this tribe of shiny skulls."

Siprajan pinched Wanthong's lip. "You difficult child! I'll flay your back into stripes. He's a very rich man. He'll slap you till your teeth all fall out in a pile.

You've got a coarse tongue and a hard chin. Your words are crude and vulgar, you arrogant girl. Khun Chang is like a goldmine." She beat her back mercilessly while delivering her tirade.

Wanthong wept but did not stop arguing. Under the blows, she shouted wildly, "Even if you beat me until you're worn out, I won't listen, I won't listen.

You won't even check the bo tree we planted. Why do I want to live like this? Tomorrow when the sun comes up, I'll take leave of you and die."

These words made Siprajan afraid that Wanthong really would hang herself and create a commotion. She suddenly felt pity and could beat her no more. "Don't cry, dear daughter.

If you want to see the bo tree, that's up to you. Go tomorrow. Listen to me.

I carried you in my womb and I don't want to stand in your way."

Wanthong replied, "Bringing me up was a waste of your efforts. Even if Phlai Kaeo's dead and breathes no more, I won't consent to be given to that baldy.

How could I sleep with someone with such a mucky mouth? It's like tossing me away in a forest. Don't you love your daughter any more?"

Siprajan tried to console and appease her. "Don't say that. I don't really want to give you to him. I love you like my own eyes. Why should I force you?

It's late now, my jewel. Listen to your mother, and don't cry." She slept with Wanthong in the inner room for fear her daughter would hang herself if left alone.

✥

Khun Chang's love for Wanthong had not waned. Feeling upset and unsettled at home, he stole over to the house of Siprajan

and heard the uproar inside—Siprajan hitting Wanthong, Wanthong crying, then the reconciliation, and the plan to make sure by going to see the bo trees.

Khun Chang took note of the place and rushed back home. He summoned servants and ordered them to harness an elephant.

After finding several hoes and spades, he mounted the elephant and set off across the paddy fields. By dawn he had reached Bang Lang landing.

He dismounted from the elephant and figured out the site, then hurried across the river and found the bo trees planted in a line with their foliage green and bushy.

He grasped the central tree and wrenched hard. Phlai Kaeo had made a prayer for the local guardian spirits to protect the trees and deflect any hoe, spade, machete, or knife,

but the tree was still very young and could not withstand such a wrenching. The leaves shriveled and fell as if touched by fire. Khun Chang and his servants returned home.

✥

When dawn came up and the sun lit the sky, the fair and beautiful Wanthong promptly went to remind her mother.

Siprajan summoned the servants. "Quickly now, don't delay. I'm going off. Find some fish, rice, betelnut, and pan. Where's the boat? Bring it here.

Hey, you men, you'll do the rowing in the bows. Get dressed quick, you slaves." She hitched up her lowercloth, stood with legs akimbo, and cursed their mothers' clans loudly.

Wanthong and Siprajan boarded the boat together, "Cast

hoe and spade

off! What are you hanging about for?" The servants cast off and paddled the boat away,

dipping their oars in time with their singing. When they didn't paddle together, Siprajan scolded, "The boat's rocking. Are you having an argument?" They sang,

"Lightning strike! We're used to riding buffalo.
Just wiggle a leg, or waggle a leg, like so.
This way, that way, the beast knows how to go.
But paddling a boat is deathly boring, oh!
We miss the stroke, we don't know how to row."

Siprajan raised her eyes to the heavens and shouted at them. "You're not paddling in time, you clan of slaves. You're good only at making a merry racket. I'll break your necks with this punt pole.

Over here you're rowing light, over there heavy, all so uneven. With this rocking we can't sleep. And you're making a racket arguing, damn your mothers." She picked up a stick to throw at them, creating more argument.

After racing along for one night and one day, they arrived at Bang Lang and moored the boat. The servants dived in the water and splashed around rowdily.

Wanthong did not bathe but got down from the boat and walked straight to the bo trees. Seeing the fallen leaves, she sprinted ahead, beating her chest and screaming out loud.

She fell prostrate at the tree, "Oh, Phlai Kaeo is dead and won't return! Now that I've seen the bo leaves strangely shriveled, I'm certain it's true.

Under the tree, the leaves are newly fallen. Seeing this sign, I'm very sure that Phlai Kaeo is dead. Something in his fate has caught up with him.

oarsmen

They told me the news but I didn't believe. Now I can't block my mind and stifle the grief any more. You won't return so we see each other's faces again. Each day will bring only pain in the heart.

I've enemies all around. Khun Chang is the main one. Were you still alive and well, you could shelter me completely,

like having a diamond wall seven layers thick to ward off any enemy's bad intentions. But who'll protect me now? Mother Siprajan is like a stick planted in buffalo dung.[9]

Even though she didn't know a thing, she was going to give me away to Khun Chang so easily. By dying alone, you leave me lonely. I don't think I can survive.

If I stay alive, Khun Chang will persist in asking for me. I'd rather die and follow you." She wept until she collapsed, her heart still throbbing,

lying under the central bo tree without stirring, sighing once in a while, and streaming with sweat, motionless as if on the point of death.

Siprajan waited a long time and then felt it strange that her daughter had not returned. She did not know what had happened,

and began to imagine Wanthong had tied a rope around her neck and hung herself. She rushed frantically in pursuit and found Wanthong lying in a faint. In shock, she embraced Wanthong,

but her body was motionless. Distraught, she cried out loud and burst into floods of tears, hugging her daughter to her own heaving chest.

"Wanthong, oh Wanthong!" No sound came in return. With body trembling, she shouted, "Servants! Come to help, quick!" The servants all came up in a rush.

They propped Wanthong up. They wept. They massaged both her legs. They pressed between her eyebrows to open her eyes. Siprajan cried out, "Softly now!

Why don't you massage her jaw?" She sat with a kaffir lime in her hand, staring vacantly. "Do everything you can, everything." Someone bit Wanthong's big toe, and then she murmured.

Siprajan stroked her and carried her back to the boat. Ai-Duea poled and paddled away from the landing. Wanthong came round with her eyes still blurred. She grieved along the waterway.

"Oh my beloved bedmate! You shouldn't have been plucked away to lose your life in Chiang Thong. I should die too.

I had the misfortune to be born with bad fate. I was married only a moment and now I'm a widow. I'll slit my throat and follow you so we may meet again in the next life.

---

9. Meaning the stick will easily lean or fall down.

Oh my dear lord and master! You abandoned house, abandoned home to go to heaven. You abandoned wife, love, everything. Even the flame,[10] my eyes did not see.

If I could have laid one piece of kindling to repay your goodness, I wouldn't complain. I just saw the bones in a new pot, and it was too pitiful.

To deny it, I'm uncertain. To accept it, I'm unable. If anyone else had brought the bones, I'd believe it, but Khun Chang is evil.

Oh pity me! Why is everything strewn with obstacles? I was born with bad fate. When I was still little, my father died.

I lived with my mother until I had my own house. Too few days passed to make a month, and I was a widow. If I go on living, I can't escape shame. That abomination has meddled and messed up everything.

My husband died far away, out of reach, and now I've nobody to rely on. I'm at my wits' end what to do. Eye's jewel, I yearn for you."

Siprajan was overcome with pity. In the boat, she hugged Wanthong with tears streaming down her face. "Oh dear, Phlai Kaeo is dead!"

In her grief, she slipped into pining over her own husband's death. "I used to take care of him and humor him. He wanted to eat chicken boiled with fermented fish every day.

I wished to die and follow him but I was afraid of ghosts. I worried I wouldn't be able to breathe after I died. I was going to jump into the water and drown but I was scared a crocodile would bite me.

Several times I wanted to slash my throat but I was afraid it would hurt. I prepared a rope to tie my neck but it was so big I feared I'd throttle myself.

Oh my beloved husband, father of Phim! I worried I might die but not meet you again. I thought and thought again, and kept putting it off. I'll just have to live on into old age."

Then she recovered herself and could think straight again. "The brilliant Phlai is dead. Now what will we do? Oh dear! What a pity Phlai Kaeo is dead."

Hearing her mother babbling made Wanthong sob even more. Siprajan blundered around, beating her chest and mumbling on in distraction.

"The more I think, the more awful matters are. Other people don't suffer this way. They live together in the same house into old age, friends in hardship, friends in difficulty, never apart.

This is truly a case of karma causing hardship. Fortune is so unkind. He lived with Wanthong only two days, not long enough to know how things are.

Because of the dispute with Chiang Thong, he had to go to war. I can still

---

10. Meaning his cremation pyre.

remember giving my word when he said: I entrust Phim to you, because I intend to return."

Wanthong cried her heart out. Siprajan moaned and mumbled on. The faces of both mother and daughter were awash with tears. When the boat moored at the landing, they were still grieving.

In her room, Saithong heard the sound of weeping. She opened a window, saw the boat mooring at the stairway, and rushed down to meet them.

Wanthong called out to her, "My head's truly been lopped off. The central bo tree has almost no leaves, while the other two still look fine."

Saithong's heart sank. Her face fell and she flailed around. The two of them stayed in the boat weeping until sunset.

Saithong consoled her. "Don't cry. Let's go up to the house." Saithong helped her into the bedroom and they talked and grieved together.

Saithong said, "I'm sure Phlai Kaeo isn't really dead. Abbot Ju divined everything with no doubts and he's never once been wrong.

When you had a fever, if it hadn't been for Abbot Ju, you'd have died. After you changed your name, you were fine. The day before yesterday he said nothing was the matter with Phlai Kaeo.

I think someone is fooling you about the middle bo tree losing its leaves. I don't believe it. I fear that oily-headed Khun Chang who brought the pot of bones is up to something evil.

He wheedled your mother into giving her consent. That day when you shouted at him, we had a loud argument with Mother in the house and begged her to go to the bo trees.

At dawn next morning that villain disappeared. The lowlife must have done something to the bo tree for sure. This evening I saw him skulking around with his servants.

Please keep quiet about this for the time being but I think I'm right. If Phlai Kaeo had fallen dead, surely there would have been some bad omen."

Wanthong said, "I think you're right but I'm still afraid and uncertain. The more I think, the more my heart feels choked." She sobbed on the bed until she fell asleep.

When dawn whitened the rim of the sky and birds broke into song, Wanthong opened her eyes feeling forlorn, and went to talk over her troubles with Saithong.

"Whether Phlai Kaeo is really dead or not, we shouldn't be attached to his things. My beloved husband is not using them. I think I'll make merit for him.

I'll take his possessions to earn merit and send it all to him. If he survives and comes back, we can acquire things again.

Today I'll go to Wat Palelai—also to question the abbot. We still have some betel and pan in the store. My dear, please bring them along."

She went to find Siprajan and mumbled to her between sobs. "Now that my husband is dead, I'm taking leave to go to the wat.

I'll take his clothing and anything else remaining—money, cloth, everything—to make merit and send it to him." Siprajan said "Go. Please go.

I've no complaint about you making merit. I intend to pour water and send the merit to him. Why should we keep the belongings of a spirit? Khun Chang has heaps of money."

This made Wanthong angry. She tossed her head, got up, and left the cross-hall. In her own room, she arranged things in piles and summoned servants to carry them.

Wanthong and Saithong took only a short while to walk to Wat Palelai. They went up the stairway to find the abbot.

Seeing Wanthong, Abbot Ju said, "Eh? What are all these things you're carrying here? Why are you crying and looking hopeless? Did someone at home say something's up?"

Wanthong and Saithong knelt and raised their hands to wai him. "I saw the bo trees where we made the prayers. Oddly, the leaves have dropped,

so I can't be sure that Phlai Kaeo isn't dead. I think something's very wrong. I've brought all these possessions to make merit.

If my husband still survives, we can acquire things again. They all belong to him, and all the merit is to be sent to him."

Abbot Ju listened and laughed. "Whether it's true or not, your thinking isn't bad. Make the merit, send it to him, and don't be afraid. It'll help him to return quickly."

He picked up some cloth of good quality. "This can wrap texts and cove Buddha images. The *attalat* cloth can be cut into flags.[11] We'll keep the gold and silver for making Buddha images."

---

11. อัตลัด. "Atlas or qotni . . . is a mixed silken-cotton fabric, often also referred to as satin" (Floor, Persian Textile Industry, 134). In Persia, the term covered plain, striped, and sumptuously brocaded variants worn in the court. In Siam, *attalat* usually meant a satin fabric from Persia or Bengal with gold and sometimes also silver brocade motifs placed in the weave at intervals. A popular design used an oval motif representing a mango tree. "This type of brocade does not have borders or end panels and is used for making trousers, shirts, or other items."

Then he said to Wanthong, "Make a prayer with these gifts of yours. Pray for your husband to come quickly. Ask to meet him tomorrow."

Wanthong laughed through her tears. "Your Lordship, what did you say just now? If my husband hasn't lost his life, I promise I'll build a kuti as an offering to the wat."

"Is that right? You'll give it for sure? I'll make certain you're not disappointed. If he doesn't come as I've said within this month, please come and burn the wat down. Really!"

Wanthong and Saithong listened to the abbot challenging her to be sincere in her promise. Their sorrow lifted and doubts diminished.

The servants who had accompanied them also heard what the abbot said and felt happier. With their troubles lightened, the two took leave.

Back home, they went to see their mother and related the abbot's words while the servants crowded around. Siprajan cried out, "I don't believe it.

The abbot has his eye on the donation, on everything you carried over there. He's just saying things to please you. I don't believe a word of it."

kuti

(Thirabhand, "Royal brocades," 191; *Thai Textiles*; Chira, "Jewellery," 129; Chandra, "Costumes," 14; Farrington and Dhiravat, *English Factory*, 1392)

Flags made from scraps of cloth attached to thin sticks stuck in the ground are used to decorate a wat, especially on festivals. People attending cremations make merit by constructing small temporary stupas of sand and adorning them with such flags. Flags made from *bangsukun* robes (see p. 828, note 46) are especially favored. The practice continues in Laos and northern Thailand but is now rare in the central region.

Khun Chang's love for Wanthong had not waned. He ordered his servants who were skilled craftsmen to fashion a bridal house quickly in time for the wedding.[1]

They sawed, chiseled, and hammered, making a racket through the whole village. "A grand house with nine rooms and wooden floors, as big as a preaching hall, is what I have in mind."

Women soaked flour to make sweets. Bananas, sugarcane, oranges, rose apples, coconuts, palm sugar, betelnut, pan, chicken, pork, prawns, and fish were purchased in large quantities.

sawing wood

As the time approached, Khun Chang was counting the days. He asked his elder cousin, Sonphraya, to accompany him to Siprajan's house to report that everything had been arranged.

"I've come to consult you. I'd like to pull down Phlai Kaeo's old bridal house and offer it to a wat so the ground can be cleared.

My bridal house will be huge, like Lord Indra's golden abode.[2] There'll be nothing comparable anywhere." Siprajan doubled over with laughter.

"So! My daughter's bridal house will be massive. Thank you so much, sir. Whatever you want, just ask with no hesitation. Build the bridal house well, my son.

We'll take the old one to a wat. Whatever you think fit, I won't complain. A huge new bridal house suits our standing. Bring it over here without delay!"

Siprajan got up and went to speak with her daughter, sweet-talking her so she would not know her mother's wiles.

---

1. The house is crafted elsewhere, probably at Khun Chang's residence, and then carried to Siprajan's compound for final assembly.

2. Probably meaning the Wetchayan Palace (see p. 172, note 19).

"Dear daughter, I've been thinking. I'm very sorry about Phlai Kaeo. We don't have any idea whether he's dead or still surviving.

I think his bridal house should be taken to make merit that can be sent to him. If by the power of this merit he returns alive, then we can rebuild it.

If we offer the house to a wat as a kuti, certainly there'll be some merit. If he returns, we'll rebuild it even bigger. My darling, what do you say?"

Wanthong did not understand her mother's subtlety and fell for the trick. She turned and replied, "Just what I've been thinking, Mother.

Take it to make a kuti or sala. I agree without reservation. There's nothing better than making merit through good deeds. It'll help my lord and master survive."

Siprajan was pleased by this response and hurried over to tell Khun Chang. "I fooled Wanthong.

She didn't see through my tricks. You must go away from this house quickly now. Get only your own servants and relatives to come and pull it down."

Khun Chang was happy to hear this, and quickly crept away. He gave orders to his servants to dismantle the bridal house without delay and offer it to the monks in Wat Klang.[3]

Siprajan promptly arranged to store goods in the cross hall. Then Khun Chang's servants and relatives came to pull the house down and take it away.

They quickly carried it out of the compound, offered it to the monks in Wat Klang, reassembled every plank, and all returned home.

⨪

Now to tell of Thong Prasi. At Cockfight Hill in Kanburi, she had been waiting for her son for many days. "It's a long time since I've seen him.

I feel sorry for Phim Philalai. She's very determined to wait for him. When they were first parted, before I left, she was missing him so badly.

I don't know how she is now. Is she well or sadly wasting away with fever? Tomorrow I must go down there to visit her and see for myself."

With this thought, she ordered her servants to

buffaloes

---

3. This large wat, on the east bank of the Suphan River to the north of the market, is now called Wat Suwannaphum (see map 6).

arrange everything. "Go and round up buffaloes with good hooves and hitch them to the cart at dawn tomorrow.

I'm going to visit my daughter-in-law. Don't be late or you'll be flogged." She ordered I-Thap and I-Thian, "Look after the house and don't steal when my back's turned."

With that, she went in to sleep. Very early as the dawn broke, she rose, washed her face, found betelnut and pan, and checked on the people loading the goods.

When everything was stowed, she mounted the cart and set off. At midday they slept until the sun eased. After two nights they reached Suphan.

At Siprajan's house, Thong Prasi was shocked not to see her son's bridal house. She quickly went up inside, and Siprajan came out to welcome her.

Servants brought a betel tray. Thong Prasi sat down with a thump, and Siprajan said, "There's been a disaster. Phlai Kaeo fell dead in the war."

She spoke with tears flowing. "He left my daughter a widow. It's bad fortune but it's all true. Phim almost died too.

She had to change her name to Wanthong and got a bit better because of the abbot. Then she heard the news her husband had died and she became even sadder.

She cried her heart out all the time and almost went mad. The bridal house has been pulled down and offered to a wat. All the clothing has been cut up for flags."

As Thong Prasi listened, her eyebrows furrowed and her face puckered in anger. "Look, who came to tell these tales? It's untrue, all of it.

If my son had died in the Lao country, some news would've come for sure. What about all those phrai who went with him? I've not seen a single one return."

Siprajan said, "The phrai that escaped death were all clapped in jail. Khun Chang went to the city and brought back the news.

Even then, Wanthong didn't believe it. She was so hopeful she got in a boat and rushed off to see the bo trees where you all made a prayer. For some reason, the leaves had fallen."

Wanthong, who was still grieving day and night, was glad to hear her mother-in-law had come.

She came out of her room, sank down, and wai-ed her with tears streaming. "Thanks to merit, you came quickly or else you might not have seen me alive.

Khun Chang has been sowing confusion. He wheedled my mother to give me to him in marriage, and she consented. I almost hanged myself.

The abbot of Wat Palelai divined that Phlai Kaeo defeated the enemy and is still alive for certain but my mother doesn't believe it.

Khun Chang fixed the wedding date for the third day of the waning moon. I'm desperate because there's nothing to give me hope. I'd have run away but I hadn't the faintest idea where to go.

Thanks to merit, you've come, and I feel as if I've been raised from the dead. Please shelter me from danger. I'll come to live in the house in Kanburi."

Hearing this, Siprajan was livid. "Look at her! She talks without shame. She's arrogant enough to accuse her mother so as to excuse herself. Let's see if I don't shame you with a beating!

Do you think it's nothing to make insinuations about me like this? You don't know anything, do you? Ai-Mak brought the bones for us, and Khun Chang just helped to deliver them,

and tell us Phlai Kaeo met disaster on campaign. He's dead and gone so I'm concerned about you. They'll haul you away by the ear and you'll suffer.

Being locked up morning and evening as a widow in the palace will be no fun. Khun Chang can help get you out of this problem by spreading his money around

to make the royal punishment disappear, so I agreed to give you to him. If you want to go to Kanburi, fine, off you go. But if I don't beat you with a stick, I'm not Siprajan."

Thong Prasi was now angry too. "You can speak well but my ears aren't listening. You believe this dirty old man so easily. You didn't check for certain.

Someone just comes to fool you and you happily give away your daughter so quickly. If Phlai Kaeo isn't dead and comes back, how are you going to deal with it?"

Siprajan cried out, "My dear lady, don't believe in ghosts. He won't come back. Besides, even if he does defeat the army and return victorious, what can we depend on him for?"

These words hurt Thong Prasi so much she shook with rage. "What is this? You'll see how good he is. I'll pursue this until I hit my head against a wall."

She went down from the house and asked around to see the village headman. She found Phan Chot and Headman[4] Taeng, and told them the story.

"My son Phlai Kaeo volunteered for the army. It's not yet time for him to

---

4. กำนัน, *kamnan*, a word, originally meaning a manager or protector, which acquired the more specific meaning of a village head. In the modern administrative system, a *kamnan* is the head of a group of villages or a subdistrict.

return but that mischievous old woman is out of control and believes people who claim my son's dead.

She hasn't checked the news but has simply given her daughter to be married. It'll create a big issue. Please come to be a witness."

Phan Chot and Headman Taeng responded. "He volunteered to go to war on royal service. It's our duty

to tell Siprajan to do the proper thing. If she won't listen, then that's her own issue but we'll avoid any blame." Saying that and no more, they hurried over

to Siprajan's house and were invited up. They sat on a bench placed for conversation, and said, "For sure, Grandma,

Phlai Kaeo volunteered for the army and received orders from the king. It's not known yet whether he's alive or dead. You shouldn't be too hasty and create confusion."

"Think carefully before giving your daughter in marriage. It could blow up in a dispute, and we'd have the bother of sending her back to Phlai Kaeo."

Siprajan said, "Enough! Don't go on. My daughter has to be married off. Whatever will happen, I'm not afraid. Gold and silver will take care of it.

People don't see the good in others, even make up things which aren't there. Even if Phlai Kaeo returns from war victorious, what can we depend on him for?"

Thong Prasi was so hurt her body shook. "What will be will be, let's see. I've made my case for you two to hear.

You're sure, are you, Siprajan? If I'm lying, may I not live to see the sunset. I love my son and I warned him but he wouldn't listen.

He was just a youth and he fell in love—so besotted he didn't look where he was going. He pleaded with me so sincerely I was forced to follow his wishes.

Now you're going to snatch Wanthong away from Phlai. Well, I'm not a bit disappointed because with her lineage, there's nothing to be sorry about. I'm saying that because you forced me to. Enough!"

She hurried down from the house. Wanthong rushed after her. Siprajan grasped a stick, blocked her daughter, and dragged her back towards the house.

Thong Prasi grabbed Wanthong and tried to pull her away. Siprajan called the servants who came in force and hauled Wanthong up into the house. Thong Prasi returned home angry, with a scowl on her face.

On the appointed day for the ceremony, Khun Chang bustled around

organizing matters. He ordered his servants to carry the
materials for the bridal house
        to Siprajan's compound. His relatives went in large
numbers including Sonphraya, Phanson, Ratthaya,[5]
and Khun Chang himself.
        "Invite[6] old Khun Chot, the astrologer. He knows the
ancient stuff about making offerings." Phanson went to
fetch him immediately. "Please come to help with an
auspicious event, sir."

        Khun Chot, the old holy astrologer,[7] called
for incense, candles, six salueng of money, a
washbowl for offering sacred water, and a
banana plant. He stripped off the stalks
and leaves,

shrine

        and made squares[8] for offerings to Krung
Phali, and a square leaf tray[9] for holding a pair of large pig's heads to offer to

---

5. Khun Chang's three cousins. See the start of chapter 20.

6. The passage from here to "in time for the auspicious day" on p. 251 is taken from TNA mss 131, starting at 29 front; PD has four stanzas: At the spot, they assembled the house rapidly. They dug holes to place the doctor post, laid the floors, fitted the walls, and thatched the roofs. / Siprajan laid on food including rice and sweets, all of good quality. The whole crew feasted noisily. / Wanthong looked at Khun Chang's edifice in sadness and distraction, murmuring to herself as if losing her mind, and cursing him badly. / The building was quickly complete. Khun Chang took leave of Siprajan, returned home, and bustled around preparing the dowry.

7. พรหมาโหร, *phrommahon*. He is not necessarily a Brahman but the name recalls that this ceremony has Brahmanical roots. The procedure here is very close to that described by Bas Terwiel, based on fieldwork in Ratchaburi in 1967. The principal difference is that in Terwiel's description, the preliminary ceremony and digging of the post holes takes place a day earlier but here it starts in the darkness before dawn. The main post has to be raised at sunrise. The ceremonies are designed to: assuage the spirits of the place for the intrusion; apologize to the earth for making the post holes; and apologize to the spirit of the forest for using the wood. In addition, there is a general call to spirits and gods for protection. But the ceremony does not seem to include placing articles under the main post for *athan* protection (Terwiel, *Monks and Magic*, 142–52).

8. In Terwiel's description, these "rectangular pieces of plant material cut from an inner layer of the trunk of a banana tree" are placed on a twig driven into the ground at the place for each post, and a small portion of the offerings "such as a tiny piece cut from a banana or a minute piece of sugarcane, sometimes accompanied by incense" is placed on each little platform. This is an offering to Phaya Nak, the serpent lord of the earth, asking forgiveness for making the post holes (Terwiel, *Monks and Magic*, 143–45, 157).

9. บัตร, *bat*, a flat tray fashioned from banana flowers, pandan leaves, or banana leaves for holding offerings.

Lord Phum, the spirit of the place, and the deities.[10]

Various sweets, banana, sugarcane, and other bits and pieces were all provided, and, importantly, young coconuts to offer to Lord Indra, Brahma, Yama,

the gods of wind and fire, and Lord Narai of great power, for success at this auspicious time and place. Altogether eight leaf baskets were quickly prepared with vegetables, citrus, spicy fish salad, and ancient articles for offering.

Khun Chot called for white upper and lower cloths and scents. Everything he requested was quickly supplied. All the offerings were placed in the leaf baskets according to the way he had learned from his studies.

He changed into the white cloths, bowed, prostrated, and pronounced sacred verses inviting the deities to come and create an auspicious time of happiness and good fortune.

He enchanted water for appeasing the earth,[11] and sprinkled it on the ground to dispel any obstacles and obstructions, and to prevent bad fortune, evil, and danger.

They staked out the plan, buried the offerings, set up a doctor post,[12] and busily dug holes for all the pillars of the house, telling one another to throw the earth on the paddy fields. The auspicious main post was lifted up, waiting by its hole,

with its head pointing directly east.[13] Cow dung was smeared on each of the posts, and the hammer beams were inserted. Lotus leaves and pink cloths inscribed with yantra to ward off dangers were placed over the tenon[14] atop each post.

10. พระภูมิเจ้าที่ศรีวิไชย, *phra phum jao thi siwichai*. *Phum*, Pali *bhumi*, means earth; *jao thi*, lord of the place; *siwichai*, is a flourish meaning "holy victory." This is a general title used for the guardian or tutelary spirits of any location.

11. ธรณีสาร, *thoranisan*. Mae Thorani is the goddess of the earth. *San* is shortened from *san-thi*, peace. "The *thorani san* ceremony is held in order to prevent the earth from opening up under a person's feet, namely when something terrible or a deeply polluting event occurs. . . . The ceremony itself consists of the sacralization of a bowl of water with very intense and difficult chanting by a chapter of monks, and the rinsing of the object or person with this purifying liquid" (Terwiel, *Monks and Magic*, 156).

12. See p. 159, note 22.

13. The hole for the first post must not be dug where it would penetrate the head, tail, or back of Phraya Nak, the serpent lord, as this would have disastrous consequences such as deaths in the family or community. The right place is his belly. As Phraya Nak shifts around, tracking the sun, so does the best direction for the first post. His belly is to the east in the first three lunar months of the year, roughly November to February. The earth mentioned in the previous stanza should be thrown in the opposite direction to his head (Terwiel, *Monks and Magic,* 145–47; Wales, *Divination*, 77).

14. หัว(หัว)เทียน, *wua (hua) thian*, "candle head," an extension protruding from the top of a post to slot into a hole in the beam.

cone pattern

Banana and sugarcane plants were tied to each pillar. There was a lot of shouting. "Hey, change that post. It's wrong. See for yourself, Ta-Thian. Lend a hand to carry over that timber in its place."[15]

The commotion went on until four in the morning "That one's wrong. Look at the holes. Hurry, dawn's almost here. Go and fetch Ta-Rak to do the soul ceremony on time." He called for a yok with a cone pattern[16] embroidered in gold,

trimmed in ruby color, and a *baisi*. "There's some little sweets, bring them too, and strong liquor, duck, chicken—whatever you can afford. Plus krajae, sandal oil, and scents."

Candles and incense were tied on each post with a cloth, and a golden ring was attached too.[17] They quickly pronounced *namo*[18] three times, and invited the lady tree spirit from the forest.[19]

They called out the name of the great Gem Treasurer[20] to ward off fire and danger. For the auspicious main post, several timbers had been cut in readiness, and one was chosen for its knots.[21] They set up a lamentation.

---

15. The shapeliness of the post timber, and the number of knots in the wood, are important, especially for the principal posts. An ideal timber will have one, three, five or seven knots (Wales, *Divination*, 77).

16. กรวย, *kruai*, cone, often กรวยเชิง, *kruaichoeng*, a common border pattern on cloth and elsewhere, such as the bases of wat pillars, with rows of elongated cones or triangles.

17. The candle and incense are fixed on every post that supports the roof, and some jewelry is placed on the first post, and perhaps the second, as a gift for the wood spirit (Terwiel, *Monks and Magic*, 149; see note 19 below).

18. นะโม, a *hua jai* heart formula, นะ โม พุท ธา ยะ, *na mo phut tha ya*, in which each syllable represents one of the five Buddhas of this era (see p. 483, note 42). In Theravada tradition, the five Buddhas are named Kakusandha, Konagamana, Kassapa, Gotama (the "historical" Buddha), and Metteyya (the future Buddha). This is an invocation for general use.

19. ผีนางไม้, *phi nang mai*. "Nang Mai is the spirit of the wood, which can be heard crying and protesting when a tree is felled. She can be expected to have become very unhappy during the cutting, transportation, and erecting of the timber" (Terwiel, *Monks and Magic*, 152).

20. ขุนคลังแก้ว, *khun khlang kaeo*. In the Three Worlds cosmogony, an emperor has seven gem or crystal attributes: a gem wheel of the law, gem elephant, gem horse, gem woman, gem knight, gem treasurer, and gem son. "As for the decorative gems, silver, and gold on the land, under the land, as deep as sixteen *yojana* under the land, or even in the depths of the ocean, this [gem] treasurer is able to see them wherever they are. If at any time the treasurer wishes to obtain jewelry of various kinds, the silver, gold, and decorative gems come up to the treasurer of their own accord and grant the treasurer's wishes' (RR, 168). This treasurer is able to supply the emperor with limitless revenue. The name was later used in various ways associated with wealth and good fortune. In the nineteenth century, kings dubbed favorite nobles with this nickname. Nowadays it is used to name amulets. Here it has become a protective spirit.

21. " . . . the ritual specialist examines the general shape and the position of the knots in

At dawn, the main post was daubed with krajae-sandal, and its soul called to come quickly. A gong was beaten, and people shouted and hollered in plaintive tones.[22]

They raised the first post and staggered forward. Khun Chang called out, "Help carry it with all your strength! Use your left foot to guide it straight!" Phanson stood legs apart, looking up and carrying the design.[23] Sonphraya held a staff, waiting to receive.

gable end

When the post was placed upright in its hole, they crowded around to fill in soil. The posts were all raised, one after another. The beams were placed, floor joists hung,[24] gable ends set, riser posts attached to the roof beams, ridgepole raised, purloins fixed, floor beams inserted, and flooring laid so they could stand on it. They trimmed and shaved where there were gaps until everything fitted snugly.

The wall bases[25] were installed, and walls placed for all five rooms. They busily put in windows and door frames, raised gable boards,[26] attached rafters to fit snugly, and called for thatch to be passed up to cover the roof.

Khun Chang cried, "Be careful! Don't mess it up, young man! You'll have to do that corner again. Tie the top of the thatch neatly on the corner beams.[27] Hurry up. It's getting late, you lot."

Roof panels were passed up to cover the ridgepole, and then they worked downwards. Their faces looked weary and stomachs ached terribly from a desire to get drunk. They cried out for liquor and food to eat.

Siprajan ordered servants to bring liquor and food. They polished off everything, both savory and sweet. "That's not enough! Bring some more." They finished off two hundred trays and still kept crying for extra.

---

the wood of each of these pieces of timber," and chooses the most attractive for the main posts (Terwiel, *Monks and Magic*, 149).

22. As the main post is raised, someone calls out "Ho," held for around five seconds, and others present respond "Hiw." The chant is repeated several times to scare away evil spirits (Terwiel, *Monks and Magic*, 149).

23. แผน, *phaen*, probably meaning a yantra cloth to place on the post.

24. รอด, *rot*, timbers running between the beams to support the floor.

25. ล่องตีนช้าง, *long tin chang*, "elephant's feet," oblong wood panels at the base of the walls.

26. ปั้นลม, *panlom*, "wind spoilers," boards on the two sides of the gable end.

27. เต้ารุม, *tao rum*, the hammer beams supporting the roof at each corner of the house.

Siprajan complained. "What a pestilential lot. I've never seen such a set of hungry ghosts. Hey, I-Sa and I-To, don't be stupid. They're so drunk, we can give them anything.

Use that rotten old mat, coat it in flour, and fry it in fish oil as a snack. Give them five pots of fermented fish sauce as a dip. They're so drunk, anything'll taste good." All five pots were demolished.

Khun Chang and Sonphraya sat together eating dry prawn curry,[28] *masaman* curry,[29] *tomyam*, chili paste, fish, fried prawn, turtle in sour salad,

pork curry, fermented fish soup, grilled snakehead fish, cured fish[30] and raw vegetables for dipping, three softshell turtles fried with *rakam* palm fruit, an enticing mixed spicy salad, chicken *phanaeng*,

deer meat made into *lap*,[31] and curried weaverbirds which the cook deliberately left with the heads on.[32] Khun Chang got very angry. "What ghost made this?" He and Sonphraya cursed the cook for doing it on purpose.

They washed their hands to eat dessert—pine nuts in syrup, pretty multicolored jelly very sweet to eat, golden pinch[33] made very fine,[34] golden puffs[35] in syrup,

golden spray, golden drops, *chup-chu*, underripe tamarind, sandal fruit fragrant and as yellow as if dyed with turmeric, egg custard, water peony and earth flower—every possible kind of sweet.[36]

---

28. ชูฉี่(ฉุฉี่) กุ้ง, *chuchi kung*, a dry curry made with kaffir lime leaves.

29. มัศมั่น, nowadays มัสมั่น, a name clearly derived from Mussulman, Muslim; a sweet, rich curry, probably with remote Arabic origins.

30. ปลาจ่อมเจ่า, *pla jom jao*. *Pla jom* is made with small fish and prawns mixed with salt and rice, and left to cure until sour. *Pla jao* is river fish cured in the same way and then cooked in coconut milk with garlic and chili.

31. ลาบ, a preparation with raw or nearly raw meat, finely chopped and heavily spiced.

32. The heads of weaverbirds look rather bald.

33. ทองหยิบ, *thong yip*, golden pinch, a mixture of beaten egg yolk, sugar, and flour, dropped into boiling syrup in disk shapes, then creased by the fingers into a mold in the shape of a small flower. This and similar sweets probably originated from early Portuguese visitors to Siam in the sixteenth century. *Thong yip* is probably based on Fatias de Tomar, though the original recipe precooks the egg yolk in a larger mold and then drops it in slices into the syrup.

34. ทองโหย่งโปร่งทำ, *thong yong prong tham*, perhaps another sweet called *thong yong*, unidentified, but probably meaning the strands are made very fine.

35. ทองพลุ, *thong phlu*, a stiff batter of wheat flour, butter, eggs, jasmine water, and salt, formed into small balls and deep fried to be crisp and hollow. Originally of French origin. All of these sweets are favored at ceremonies because they have auspicious names.

36. ฝอยทอง, *foi thong*, golden spray, beaten egg yolk squeezed from a banana-leaf cone into boiling syrup as a mat of yellow strands. *Foi thong* is based on the Portuguese sweet, Fios de Ovos, though the Thai version has slightly finer strands made as a mat rather than a pile. It is served at weddings in the belief it aids a long married life, probably because of the length of the strands and the auspicious association of gold.

When full, they washed their hands, and Khun Chang took leave of Siprajan, who said, "Go and bring the dowry without delay!"

The three cousins went down the stairs with all their servants following behind. Arriving home, Khun Chang reminded his mother to arrange things in time for the auspicious day.

Siprajan and her servants walked the short distance over to Wat Palelai and went up the stairs to find the abbot.

She handed over an offering of betelnut and pan and asked him to come on that same day to chant prayers at the house. "Now that Phlai Kaeo has died, I'm marrying Wanthong to Khun Chang."

Abbot Ju was worried this was a mistake. "But Phlai Kaeo isn't dead. Hold off and listen to me before there's a problem.

Do you know for certain he died? Later this could create big trouble. Listen to my words, and don't be easily led. I think this will turn out badly."

Siprajan lost her temper. "Your Lordship, you're losing your mind. What you're saying isn't true. It's not believable, just nonsense."

Abbot Ju said, "Look here, Siprajan. You came in here quivering to talk. This shouldn't be any business of mine, but it is because I helped to bring Phlai Kaeo up.

If you don't listen to my advice, that's up to you. I fear Kaeo will come back, and complain that I knew about this yet still let it happen. It'd be better for you to invite other monks."

Siprajan took leave and lurched off. She went straight to Wat Klang and then Wat Phlap[37] to ask them to chant prayers that evening.

Thepthong was busily arranging the dowry, shouting at the servants until the tendons on her neck bulged. "Would you run around and help a bit?

ทองยอด (หยอด), *thong yot*, golden drops, adapted from the Portuguese sweet, *ovos moles*, soft eggs, made with flour, sugar, egg yolk, and jasmine water mixed into a paste, cooked until the sugar melts, formed into balls, and served coated in syrup.

ชุบชู, *chup-chu*, miniature imitation fruit made from bean paste, dipped in coloring, and served floating in syrup.

ดอกจอก, *dok jok*, water peony, a paste of rice flour pressed in a mold in the shape of a water peony, and deep-fried.

ดอกดิน, *dok din*, earth flower, a sweet made with the herb, *Aeginetia indica*, sometimes called forest-ghost flower. A paste of flour, sugar, banana, and the herb is steamed in leaf baskets and served with coconut. The herb gives an unusual deep purple color.

37. Now Wat Phihan Daeng, on the west bank of the river 4 kms north of Suphanburi.

Hey, tell Granny Kloi and Granny Sai that it's almost
afternoon and the sun's high in the sky. How come
they're so slow and not dressed yet?"

dowry procession

Granny Kloi and Granny Sai
frantically changed their clothes and
combed their hair. The servants
got one another dressed up prettily. When the whole dowry procession was ready, they set off.

In[38] front came a bottle-drum band, followed by Jek Jo on a
big horse with a Chinese ensemble playing loudly, then a flutist
tootling along with a Lao *khaen*.

The first dowry tray was carried by Nadda, the daughter
of Ta-Chen, dressed in a lowercloth of Khmer *pum*[39] silk and
a brocade uppercloth, with wasp-nest rings on all eight fingers. She walked with her chest thrown forward, looking like a
puffed-up Garuda.

The second was carried by Nang Mei, the daughter of a Mon,
dressed in lower and upper cloths of *attalat*, with her hair put

flute and khaen

---

38. From here to "They arrived close to the house of Siprajan" on p. 255 is taken from TNA
mss 131, starting at folio 7 rear (CS, 165); PD has two stanzas: Those chosen to carry the four
trays with the dowry were all fair, attractive teenage girls from respectable families of good status, and all dressed splendidly. / The very best *mahori* ensemble had been found to accompany
them. At an auspicious time, the dowry was hoisted aloft, and the *ranat* and gong started playing. The Wat Ko version is similar to PD, except that those carrying the trays are not "attractive
teenage girls" but: Nang San with blind eyes, Nang Rot with a bad leg, Nang Mak with a cleft lip
and Nang Ma with a squashed nose, all dressed splendidly, walking in pairs. (WK, 10:387)

39. ปูม, *pum*, a silk with a floral pattern made with *ikat* weaving, originating from Gujarat
where it is known as Patola, adopted into Siam from Cambodia, presented to nobles by the king
as a mark of rank.

up in a chignon bound with a gold band and decorated with sparkling waving flowers.

Her waist was slim, her bottom curved like a *norasing*,[40] and the cleft of her bottom like the monkeys at Granny Kaeo's beach. The third tray was borne by Sida, daughter of Ta-Aeo of a Lao lineage from Vientiane.

She had her hair in a tall chignon, and was dressed in a *sin* lowercloth[41] and uppercloth in ruby-colored silk of good quality and bright red hue. She wore a *phirot* ring[42] next to a golden spiral ring, a *takrut*[43] with a yantra, and gold chains on both wrists.

With a flat bottom, bandy legs, sunken eyes, bulging belly, and flat chest, the bearer of this third covered tray[44] looked like a hungry ghost. Although not so beautiful, she was known to be the daughter of a rich man.

takrut *before and after rolling*

Fourth came Nang Bu-nga, daughter of Ta-Chet, a Javanese who came from overseas, from Bali,[45] to sell articles of good quality in the city. Khun Chang had spotted this rich man and requested his daughter to come.

---

40. นรสิง(ห์), a mythical creature with a lion's head on a human body, derived from a story in which Vishnu transforms himself in order to defeat a *yak* giant (*Hindu Myths*, 170). However, in Thai tradition the term is also used for a figure with the upper body of a man and the lower body of a hoofed animal like a deer, similar to a satyr. Probably that is the form meant here.

41. ผ้าซิ่น, *pha sin*, a tubular lowercloth worn in Lanna and Laos.

42. พิรอด, *phirot*, a ring made from some soft material on which a yantra design has been inscribed by an adept while simultaneously pronouncing a mantra. The material, usually cloth or paper, is then rolled, plaited, tied with thread, and sometimes coated with lacquer. Large ones are worn as a belt, or on the upper arm, and smaller ones on the finger. (PKW, 1:17; YS, 29; KW, 672; Anuman, Essays, 324)

43. ตะกรุด, a type of amulet usually made from a thin plate of soft metal like tin or gold, rolled into a cylinder around a cord, and tied round the arm, neck, shoulder, or waist. The size may vary from about 3 to 15 cms long. Its power comes from the yantra inscribed on the metal by a teacher while simultaneously intoning formulas. Sometimes the yantra are so complex they are spread across several *takrut* worn as a set. The principal benefit of wearing *takrut* is invulnerability. (Anuman, *Essays*, 304–5; PKW, 1:17; Terwiel, *Monks and Magic*, 60; Textor, *Patterns of Worship*, 630)

44. เตียบ, *tiap*, a form of covered tray that, for such ritual purposes, was woven from strips of wood, lacquered, and inlaid with mother of pearl (CS, 62; Anuman, *Prapheni kiao kap taeng ngan*, 79–80).

45. Bali is of course not in Java but the term *khaek chawa*, แขกชวา, is used generally for what today would be Indonesian.

She wore a kimkhab lowercloth, a two-layer embroidered uppercloth, a decorative ring with good and valuable diamonds, rubies, and splendid emeralds, and a pair of pendant earrings like fancy tassels.

Her hair was in a chignon woven with garlands, fixed with a hairpin, and trailing braids of *kruai* flowers.[46] She was dark and beautiful like a bright-eyed crow, short and roly-poly but with a fine bottom.

The money for the dowry was carried by a child of gentlefolk with a good name, dressed as for an outing in a yok lowercloth held by a sash embroidered in shining gold in quatrefoil pattern,[47] and a belt cinched on the waist,

flower braid

with many bangles, beads, and bracelets, rings with yantra, fine choker[48] embroidered with filigree in a flame-*kanok*-in-vine pattern,

quatrefoil pattern

overlaid with a breast chain of several soft strands with a *banphap* pendant, a carved topknot ornament, and a hairpin. All four[49] walked along together in their different dress, bearing the golden trays with the dowry,

along with tiered trays laden with offertory cloth to pay respect to the parents and grandparents of the host. They all carried themselves in the dignified manner of gentlefolk with great merit. The trays of the secondary[50] dowry were hoisted along in a jumble behind

by young girls, servants, and neighbors, wearing dazzling lowercloths and colored uppercloths, and talking excitedly because of the great occasion. In total they numbered 101 persons,

---

46. อุบะ, *uba*, flowers threaded on a string as part of a garland. กรวย, *kruai*, is the name of several trees in the Myristicacae family, especially *Horsfieldia irya*, which has masses of small, very fragrant, yellow flowers.

47. ประจำยาม, *prajam yam*, literally "usual for the time," a pattern based on a flower with four leaves, often used in borders, found in decorative design reaching back to the Dvaravati era, nominally reserved for royalty (*Pha phim lai boran*, 117; KTS, 4:286–87).

48. สร้อยนวม, *soi nuam*, alternatively called *nuam nang* นวมนาง or *krong so* กรองศอ, a neck ornament formerly worn by royalty and nobility, now sometimes in stage costume.

49. According to wedding manuals, the procession should have two trays for the bride price, or at the most three, but Khun Chang has four (CS, 62; Anuman, *Prapheni kiao kap taeng ngan,* 74).

50. เลว, *leo*, here meaning ordinary or secondary. These were trays lined with red paper for carrying fruit and sweets. According to manuals, the number ranged from ten up to a maximum of one hundred but again Khun Chang has more, 101 (CS, 63; Anuman, *Prapheni kiao kap taeng ngan*, 75).

carrying tables of sweets and fruit—bananas, plantains, and young coco-nuts, already peeled. They shouted and hollered back and forth. Some walked quickly, while others lingered along in groups.

At the rear came a mass of retainers, and the *mahori* ensemble of Ta-Phu, playing music without a break. They arrived close to the house of Siprajan.

At Siprajan's house, they made a racket shouting and beating gongs. Baldheaded Ta-Phon leapt out to close the door and prevent anyone from entering.

The elders dug out money to offer him so he would open the door to let them into the house.[51] They led the way up and sat on carpets. The dowry trays were set down in rows.

The elders inside the house welcomed them and counted the trays and big baskets with sweets, pork, chicken, strong liquor in full round bottles, bananas, oranges, and hundreds of things as promised.

The elders from both sides chatted together. The dowry cash and cloth was counted and placed on three-legged tables, then everything was carried into the house.

The customary presents were distributed. Food and sweets were brought out and everybody merrily ate their fill. The elders returned home.

In the evening when the heat of the sun had faded, Khun Chang bathed, changed his clothes, and patted sandal powder on his unruly chest hair.

"I'll dress to the hilt." He placed a mirror and looked at himself from differ-ent angles. "Why is this beeswax as sticky as toffee?

I'm fed up with this beard. Why doesn't it run up and sprout on my head but teases me by growing on my chin? The more I shave it, the heavier it returns.

But on top of my head, there's not a trace! All my hair has run away to shame me." He put on a good, pricey yok, recently purchased inside the palace,[52]

an uppercloth of good wool in a bright color, and a belt worth over ten chang. Descending from the house, he waddled along with his servants fol-lowing en masse.

The bridegroom's party and villagers came to have a look at his finery, but when they saw his face and body they laughed, winked, and whispered among themselves. "Hey, look at this fellow with bulging eyes and a gleaming face—both back and front!"

---

51. See p. 161, note 26.

52. Inside the palace of the eighteenth century, "along Iron Flower Street, women from Sand Landing and Khaek Landing come and sit at stalls selling various kinds of cloth" (KLW, 204–5). This street probably ran east-west across area 5 on map 9 (*Boranasathan*, 1:226).

verandah

When Khun Chang reached Siprajan's house, Ta-Phon slammed the door shut. Khun Chang lost his temper. "Who are you making fun of, you damned bald fraud?"

Ta-Phon said, "My lord, Khun Chang, I was bald since I was a baby, and I'm not making fun of anyone. You're such a rich man, give me some money and I'll open up."

Khun Chang handed money to Ta-Phon and they went up into the house and sat in lines on the verandah. When the time came, all the monks arrived from Wat Klang and Wat Phlap as arranged.

They entered the room and sat waiting, holding a twin sacred thread and gazing around. Meanwhile, Siprajan told her daughter to put on a white lowercloth and white uppercloth.

Wanthong angrily refused. Siprajan smacked her back loudly. "You difficult, foulmouthed child." She wound a cloth round her. They wrestled together. Siprajan dragged her daughter by the hand.

Wanthong clung tight onto a door bolt. Siprajan put her foot against the wall and tugged with body trembling. Her hand slipped and she flew backwards and fell down. Boiling with anger, she got up bellowing

and called out to the monks, "Chant the prayers now. It's coming to lamplighting time. The bride is sick and in pain. She can't come for the water sprinkling, Your Lordship.

When the chanting is over, please let me have some lustral water. The pouring can be done inside here." Khun Chang looked on awkwardly. The monks were invited to start the prayer chant.

After water was sprinkled, the monks left, and the food was busily carried in. The groom's party changed their clothes and sat in rows on the verandah to feast.

Everyone ate their fill and returned home happily, except Khun Chang, who was overjoyed that he did not have to go anywhere. He had *sepha* recited with a *mahori* ensemble.

Next morning after the sun had risen, the abbot and monks got dressed and left their kuti carrying bowls and trays.

At the new bridal house, the cooks had prepared food, ready and waiting. The monks filed up in order, the novices set down their bowls, and the monks chanted prayers.

Khun Chang picked up a scoop to ladle rice, and called out to Siprajan, "I beg your kindness, please get Wanthong to come out here

so we can give alms together.[53] She's my wife now." Siprajan was wondering why she had not come out,

when Wanthong wailed angrily, "I have no desire to give alms and be shamed in front of pigs, dogs, and servants." She doubled over in tears.

Siprajan groaned. "Khun Chang, please don't take offense. Since she was very ill in a year of the dog, she's been a bit crazy."

Khun Chang said, "I can see that. Wanthong had a severe fever. She can dig up my ancestors as far back as she likes but I won't take offense, don't worry."

After the chanting was over, the monks and novices were fed from five big earthen pots of *khanom jin namya*.[54] "The abbot knows how to eat. Give him a full helping!"

Servants carried in the sweets, golden pinch and golden spray, all excellent. They were put on plates for each of the monks,

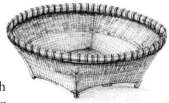

hamper

then offered to them. When everyone was full, the trays were cleared away, the monks chanted the offertory blessing, and returned to the wat, with novices carrying many hampers.

At dusk as the sun faded, Khun Chang went to sleep in the big bridal house. Overexcited with longing for Wanthong, he paced up and down distractedly for three days.

He tried hugging a long pillow and imagining it was her. At the dead of night, he sat driven almost mad by fantasies. The mattress was bathed in sweat from his fevered body. Even in his sleep, he babbled about Wanthong.

He got up and recited *sepha*, beating claves to keep time.

---

53. Jointly giving alms to the monks is a customary part of the marriage ritual. There is a belief that the partner whose hand is on top during the ladling will dominate the household, hence this part of the ceremony can be something of a tussle.

54. ขนมจีนน้ำยา, thin round noodles, like angelhair spaghetti, made from slightly fermented rice, eaten with a curry of fish pounded to a smooth paste. The Thai term *khanom jin* comes from a Mon original, *hanom jin*, meaning cooked by boiling. In Thai the opening consonant was hardened and the "i" lengthened to produce a term that seemed familiar, "Chinese sweet." In chapter 25, the Thai is spelt หมมจีน, closer to the Mon original (SWC, 2:519).

"Oh little Chim, my own true bride,
say when will I lie by your side,
be gratified, dessert of mine?
When we meet I'll slurp the pot!
I pine, hot tuna boiled in brine.
Oh turtle, come to drink moonshine.
Dear Mother fine, please send her quick!"[55]

Siprajan listened and praised him to the skies. "Dear me! It's like Jao Ngo[56] reciting *sepha*!" She tried to pacify her daughter. "Don't delay. You've already been in a bridal house so don't be hesitant."

Wanthong was so pent up that she shouted out loud and made a racket pounding the walls of the room. "I don't wish to see that hateful baldy's face. If you want him, have him yourself."

hitched up Khmer-style

Siprajan could not tolerate her daughter's sarcasm. She hitched up her lowercloth Khmer-style and danced up and down. "Look here, Wanthong, you have a bad mouth and show no respect." She grabbed a stick and beat her many times.

Wanthong cried out, "Oh Father and Mother, I've never experienced anything like this here. I don't love this baldy so you hit me. Though not ashamed before other people, you should be ashamed before the spirits."

"You won't stop arguing, will you?" Siprajan grabbed a rope from the wall,

---

55. This rendering mimics the eight-syllable lines, rhyming scheme, and Khun Chang's clumsy rhymes and nonsensical meaning in the original. A more literal translation would be: Oh my true bride, I-Chim / when will you let me enjoy you / dear *krim*-fish dessert of mine / when we meet I'll slurp the whole pot / my dear anabas fish boiled in salt I long for you / I want to drink liquor with a field turtle / Mother please send her to me. ขนมปลากริม, *khanom pla krim*, is made with rice flour rolled into a fish-like shape around 5 cms long, cooked in thick coconut milk and palm sugar, and garnished with fried sesame.

56. Jao Ngo is a character in *Sangthong*, Golden Conch, a non-classical Jataka found in several collections of the so-called Panyasa Jataka, "fifty birth stories," adapted into an outer drama by King Rama II. The hero is a divine being who is born as the son of Queen Janthewi in the form of a conch. When Janthewi discovers the child can come out of the shell, she breaks the conch. Because of conflict between Janthewi and another queen, he is abandoned in the forest. While in the care of a giantess, he discovers a golden pond, dips himself in it, and becomes golden. To escape the man-eating giantess, he disguises himself as a Ngo. When he is in the guise of Jao Ngo, he becomes a fool. However, he eventually marries a princess, proves to have knowledge that is valuable to the kingdom, and is restored to his princely status and his golden form (*Bot lakhon nok*, 1–222). The joke here is that, if Jao Ngo were to recite *sepha*, it would be awful, and Siprajan may be assuming that Khun Chang does not know this.

tied Wanthong's hands up to the ceiling, and circled round thrashing her with the stick.

"Are you going into the bridal house or not? Answer quick! I won't untie you until you reply." Wanthong writhed and shouted as if she were dying, "Where's Saithong gone? Why don't you come?

Help me please or I'll die this time! Please save me, Sister." Saithong heard and burst into tears. She ran up and snatched the stick away to stop the beating.

"Mother! Don't try to break a machete handle over your knee.[57] Let the hard work fall on me. Leave her be. I'll help bring her round to going into the bridal house willingly."

Saithong untied Wanthong's hands and led her into the room, still crying. She quickly ground some casumunar and applied it to the welts on her back and shoulders.

Wanthong lamented over Phlai Kaeo. "Is he dead or alive? We don't know what's happened. If he's dead, there should have been a sign. Now I'm at the end of my tether.

I'd go to Ayutthaya to find out the truth but I don't know my way around the capital. As a woman, how can I travel through the forest where there are so many wild animals?

But if I do nothing, I have this threat close at hand. It looks like I'll die. Truly, karma is catching up with me." She lamented on and on till she collapsed into sleep.

---

57. A proverb somewhat like, "Don't beat your head against a brick wall," with the meaning, don't hurt yourself trying to do something impossible.

13: KHUN PHAEN AND WANTHONG QUARREL

Now to tell of Phlai Kaeo. After sunrise, he came out to sit in front of his quarters. Thai and Lao nobles prostrated to pay respect.

They were discussing that the war had been completed according to the royal wish when a duty officer of the guard rushed into the camp, sank down, and greeted them with a smile. "I carry the king's orders. Without delay, close the campaign and return to Ayutthaya." Phlai Kaeo was very happy. He gave orders to the Lao chiefs and lords to stay and look after their territories.

He instructed phrai to harness his elephant with an elegant black howdah, and to load up food, gold, silver, and other goods. He had the captured Lao families sent on ahead.

At an auspicious time for the troops to march, the columns set off to the sound of gongs and shouting. Files of elephants and horses swarmed across the plain.

Phlai Kaeo rode his elephant in a howdah. The mahout drove the mount swiftly into the forest. A breeze fluttered the flags and wafted a fragrance of flowers.

Laothong rode on a cow elephant, Yot, along with her maids, all clinging tightly together. She still wept despondently at the thought of her aged parents.

"I won't know whether they're sick or well, dead or alive. Who'll look after them? Nobody is the same as one's own child." Her loud weeping resounded along the way.

Phlai Kaeo overheard the sound and felt sorry that Laothong was still forlorn. He ordered his mahout to slow down so her elephant came alongside, and then asked her to come over.

He lifted her in his arms into his howdah. Curtains were arranged to conceal them at front and rear. With his arms round her lovingly, he urged her to enjoy the plant life in the forest.

Leaves and flowers sprouted from every branch. Buds bloomed in bunches all around. Pollen sprinkled down from on high along the way, suffusing the air with scent.

As they sat embracing cheek to cheek, Laothong's sadness began to subside. Love lulled away her tears and longing. Passion smothered her pining.

He pointed out herds of wild animals, tigers loping along, gibbons, lemurs, langurs, and monkeys on the branches of a banyan. A male monkey grabbed his mate,

swung up to the treetops, and stood bent over, hugging her. A big monkey chased after her, but they bounded away up high. Phlai Kaeo said to Laothong, "Look at that dirty monkey!" She shyly hid behind him, averting her eyes.

The governors of Kamphaeng, Rahaeng, and Thoen marched ahead through the outposts of Nan and Phrae.[1] The ruler of Chiang Thong was kept under arrest. At a river landing, they made rafts and boarded the captive families.

Phlai Kaeo embarked on a large sleeper boat, with Laothong staying close by his side. A full crew of oarsmen boarded and took their places. They strained their necks and loudly sang a slow boat song.[2]

With the oarsmen pulling hard, churning the water into eddies, they pounded ahead for seven days. Swept along by the current, they passed many places, great and small,

and reached the city as the dawn came up. Phlai Kaeo bathed, changed his clothes, and escorted the four lords to enter the palace and sit in the inner official sala.

They met senior officials who greeted them and asked to be told tales of the victory. On a command, they were escorted into the audience hall.

Now to tell of the almighty king who resided in a golden palace surmounted by a spire.[3] When the sun had risen to the second hour,[4] he came out to the

palace and spire

---

1. This would be a strange route from Chomthong to Ayutthaya as it would start with a trek northeast, away from Ayutthaya, across three ranges of hills. A much more obvious route would be straight down the Ping River that flows through Chomthong, or back down the Wang River via Thoen, as they came up, or cross to the Thung Saliam route used in chapters 27 and 32. This routing reflects the authors' hazy grasp of northern geography (see map 4).

2. โยนยาว, *yonyao*, a song with a slow rhythm to accompany paddling.

3. The word for palace here is ปราสาท, *prasat*, meaning a building in which only a king or god can reside, and the "spire" is a ปรางค์, *prang*, a Khmer style of corncob-shaped tower.

4. 8 a.m. by modern reckoning.

ranat

resplendent audience hall.

Throngs of ladies of the inner palace brought regalia in procession. He sat on a throne made of a slab of stone.[5] Officials clasped hands and bowed to pay respect.

An ensemble of *ranat*, drum, gong, conch, and horn played loud and joyful music. The king, upholder of the teachings, spoke on affairs of state.

Each officeholder made statements on various matters without giving offense to the dust beneath the royal foot. Pages read reports. The royal pleasure was absolute.

A senior noble had his turn to address the king. "My liege, Your Sovereign Majesty. Pray allow your servant to report. This matter arose when a Chiang Mai army went

to besiege Chiang Thong. The ruler was unable to put up a defense and agreed to cede the city. Your Majesty graciously allowed Nai Phlai Kaeo

to go up there in command of phrai to attack on your behalf with the help of three cities. Through the power of Your Majesty's accumulated merit, the attack was comfortably successful. Families, cattle, and buffaloes were captured

along with pikes, swords, guns, other weapons, and masses of materiel including clothing. All has been sent to the capital under an inventory with a seal. May it please Your Majesty."

The almighty king clapped his hands loudly. "You Chiang Thong are a rogue with thousands of ruses. Heigh! What were you thinking?

You switched sides, back and forth. You didn't honor the water oath of allegiance.[6] Did you believe you had sufficient merit not to depend on anyone?[7] Tell me what you were thinking!"

---

5. In 1833, Prince Mongkut, the future King Rama IV, discovered a stone slab in Sukhothai and assumed it was the Manangkasila throne or stone platform mentioned in Sukhothai Inscription One, dated 1292. There is no reference to a stone throne in documents on the Ayutthaya era, so perhaps the stone throne in this passage was inspired by the discovery of the Manangkasila. The authenticity of Sukhothai Inscription One, the role of the Manangkasila in the inscription, and the likelihood that the discovered stone is the Manangkasila, have all since been thrown into doubt.

6. See p. 123, note 28.

7. A king theoretically became king by having accumulated more merit from previous lives than anyone else. King Phanwasa is asking Chiang Thong whether he believed he was powerful enough not to be subordinate to Ayutthaya.

The king's questions made the ruler of Chiang Thong hot and flustered. He stuttered, "My liege, please have mercy! I face a charge with a penalty of death.

I'm not dissembling or concealing matters. I did not revolt against the royal footsoles but acted in fear of danger. If I had not submitted to the Lao, I would be dead.

The Chiang Mai army numbered in tens of thousands. The Lao soldiers were numerous and valiant. Their commanders, Falan and Sanbadan, had invulnerability and expertise as warriors.

Yet on the day that the Thai army arrived, I immediately made a secret agreement with them. The enemy fell for our trick, and we attacked them hard at the same moment.

They did not realize in time, and so could not avoid being defeated, scattered, and pulverized. If you fail to show me favor, my punishment is death. This is the sincere truth. Have mercy."

The king responded, "I still have doubts about what you say. Heigh, Phlai Kaeo! Tell us what you know about this.

He looks to me like an evil two-headed bird. Chiang Mai comes so he sides with Chiang Mai. The Thai arrive so he submits to the Thai. He sways this way and that like a stick planted in mud."

Phlai Kaeo prostrated and related what had taken place. "Chiang Thong did indeed shift this way and that. Probably he was maneuvering to save his own skin.

But if he truly went along with Chiang Mai, why then did his people charge the enemy camp, and not retreat one pace, neither officers nor men? Even a very bad action can be erased by a good one."

The king listened and ordered Phramuen Si[8] to present caskets, sabers, cloth, and other gifts as tokens of royal appreciation.

casket

---

8. This is Phramuen Si Sorarak, who has an important role in the story. The main corps of royal pages was divided into four six-men units who attended the king by day and night on a two-day rotation (see p. 16, note 75). The head of each of these units had the title of *jao/hua/phra muen, sakdina* of 1,000, and was addressed colloquially as *phra nai*. The four were: Sanphetphakdi, Si Sorarak, Samoe Jairat, and Wai Woranat (*Rueang mahatlek*; KTS, 1:223; KCK, 222). La Loubère noted, "All four are very considerable *Nai*, having a great many subaltern Officers under them; and though they have only the Title of *Meuing* [*muen*], they cease not to be Officers in chief" (*New Historical Relation*, 100). In the poem, his name is variously given as Jamuen Si, Phramuen Si, or Muen Si but has been standardized in the translation as Phramuen Si.

Phlai Kaeo was appointed to the title of Khun Phaen,[9] and assigned to guard a remote frontier region in command of five hundred phrai. He was also presented with a boat nine fathoms in length.

For action beyond the call of duty, the rulers of Kamphaeng, Rahaeng, and Thoen were rewarded with betel boxes, golden flasks, and other articles. They took leave of the king,

left the palace, and boarded a boat immediately, taking the ruler of Chiang Thong with them. In fifteen days they reached home happily.

flask

✦

Now to tell of Phlai Kaeo, raised to noble rank by royal appointment with the name Khun Phaen. He took leave of the king and went to board his boat.

He escorted Laothong and her two maids to sit in a row in the sleeper boat. They left the landing with the oarsmen loudly singing boat songs.

A haloed moon shone serenely in a cloudless sky strewn with shining stars, highlighting the fairness of Laothong's face.

Late at night, when a breeze came up, Phlai Kaeo's thoughts turned longingly to little Phim. "Right now, is my jewel waiting forlornly? Is she lovesick or ailing? I don't know.

With me so far away, she must have faced many obstacles. There's an old saying: If you sleep on high, it's smart to lie face down so you'll spy anything that happens,

but if you sleep down low, lie face up. A man with a beautiful wife shouldn't entrust her to a mother-in-law. Oh my heartstring, you've been so far away,

sleeping alone and lonely. And Khun Chang has jealous intentions." With these thoughts, he urged the oarsmen to hurry. In the bright light of dawn, they arrived at Suphan

and moored in front of the landing just as Saithong was coming down. She happily went straight back to tell Phim that Phlai Kaeo had returned.

---

9. The full title seems to be Khun Phaen Saensathan, which appears sixteen times through the poem, though the text plays with the name, using Saensongkhram, great warrior, eleven times, Saensanit great friend, thirty-nine times, Saensakda, great power, fourteen times, and other variants according to context. The nearest equivalent to this title in the Three Seals Law is Khun Phlaeng Sathan, ขุนแผลงสท้าน, *palat* of the left in the royal guard, *tamruat phuban*, *sakdina* 600 (KTS, 1:226). This name is mentioned three times in documents dated around 1600, hinting that there may have been a prominent figure holding the title around that time (see below, p. 883).

Wanthong, who was still pining sadly from morning to night, was overjoyed to hear Saithong's news.

She grabbed a cloth to put round her shoulders, opened a window, and saw the sleeper boat moored by the main jetty. "Phlai Kaeo has come! It's him!" She came down the stairs and walked quickly

to the sleeper boat.[10] She noticed the mattresses, pillows, and curtained partition. Khun Phaen saw her coming and stuck his head out of the curtain to greet her.

At the sight of his face, her tears fell. She raised her hands to wai her husband but her face clouded over. She struggled to speak because her heart was bursting. She embraced her husband's feet, sobbing.

Seeing her grief, Khun Phaen thought, "What's up with my beloved bedmate, Phim? She looks thin and her figure has changed. Has she been sick with fever and grief because I took so long?

Her mood seems very out of sorts, swallowed up by such sorrow. She can't speak for crying as if someone had made trouble for her.

Seeing the face of her returning husband should make her happy but she's weeping in utter misery." At a loss for an explanation and growing suspicious, he asked,

"What's the matter? Why are you so sad, Phim? Don't cry. Listen to your husband." He lifted her chin and wiped away her tears. "What's troubling your heart?"

Wanthong spoke through tears. "I feel a thorn is stuck in my breast, making it swell up, fester, and ache. It's hard to speak because my heart is bursting. You protected your wife like a bird

that looks after the nest so no eggs fall and no hawk or crow can swoop down to steal them. But when you leave your wife's side, before even a month has passed

with the nest left empty, hawk and crow swoop down, clean out the nest, and scatter it to pieces. Our bridal house has disappeared because a friend had tricky, treacherous ideas.[11]

---

10. Simmonds recorded a recitation of this passage in Wiset Chaichan, Ang Thong, in 1950. Most of the oral version followed the Damrong text, though with many differences of detail. At this line, however, the female reciter replaced the action of Wanthong descending the stairs and walking quickly with her crying out, "Oh! If I had wings and could fly, I would swoop gaily down to him" (Simmonds, "Thai Narrative Poetry," 288).

11. From here on, Wanthong gets the story recounted in chapter 11 a bit muddled (her sickness and name change preceded Khun Chang's ploy that Phlai had died), but whether this is because she is overwrought or because the compilers of KCKP made a continuity error is not clear.

Khun Chang came to tell my mother that you wouldn't return from Chiang Thong; the army was defeated, slaughtered, and scattered; and you'd been stabbed by the Lao and left in the uplands.

He brought some bones wrapped in a cloth to show me. When I heard this, I cried endlessly, lying on the bed with Saithong. My heart ached all the time.

I went to see the three bo trees. The leaves were yellow and fallen. I felt dismal, depressed, devastated—powerless to do anything but grieve. So I went to make merit and pour water.

I had flags made and sent the merit to you. I couldn't stop grieving day in, day out. Because of this terrible heartache, I sickened with fever almost to the point of death.

Mother nursed me for a long time but the fever wouldn't go away. So she went to ask the abbot at Wat Palelai and he divined that my stars were behind it.

If I didn't separate from my husband, I'd die. Nothing could overcome this misery except changing my name; then the sickness would ease,

and I'd be able to manage the property as before. So my name was immediately changed to Wanthong, and after that I began to get better. Then that lackey Khun Chang turned up.

He brought some elders to the house to speak with Mother. They said my husband was dead, I was a widow, and the ministry has a law

that if a man goes to war and dies, his wife is kept as a royal widow. So they asked for my hand for Khun Chang. Mother didn't know this was a lousy trick.

She got greedy at the thought of wealth, and consented. The old house was taken down and sent to Wat Klang. A new bridal house was built and a prayer chanting held.

It's seven days now and I haven't gone in there. Mother shouted at me, beat me to a pulp, and tied my hands to hang me up for people to see. I'm so ashamed but I've borne it and borne it until today."

She peeled off her thin white uppercloth, "Look at my back and shoulders. Like flayed meat. I'm deeply, deeply hurt. If you don't believe me, I'm done for."

Khun Phaen, great romancer,[12] felt angry enough for blood to flow from his

---

12. This is the first place where Khun Phaen is introduced with a mini-invocation that plays on his given official name, Saensathan. *Saen*, แสน, is a superlative. In each of these mini-invocations, *saen* is yoked with another word such as *sanit*, สนิท, friend, lover, or *songkhram*, สงคราม, war, or *sakda*, ศักดา, power, often but not always retaining the s-s alliteration, and usually related to the context. These are translated with phrases of the form "great romancer," "great warrior," and so on. Probably the use of this device originally began after chapter 16 when Khun Phaen equips himself with a special sword, horse, and spirit, but there are a few appearances in earlier chapters.

eyes. "Tcha! Can a friend be so disloyal? Let's see what will happen today.

The whole place knows you're my wife but this baldy thinks he can wreck everything. And that old mother thinks she can pull your hair and beat you to her heart's content.

They're in league to take my wife—saying I was stabbed to death by the Lao and wouldn't come back, saying all kinds of bad things, cutting the bo tree roots as a bad omen.

What a liberty to pull down a bridal house and simply build a new one over the remains! If I don't repay him, then I'm not a man. If it means the king won't keep me, well that's the way it is.

And you, Wanthong, not going into his bridal house for seven nights like this—you're the best in Ayutthaya! Any other woman would have lost her honor.

If he snatched any one of thousands of other women away from me, I wouldn't complain a bit. But snatching the lovely Phim is like cutting open my breast and plucking out my heart.

Hey men, why are you sitting around doing nothing? Surround the house!" He drew his sword and brandished it furiously. "I'll slash down the whole of Suphan!"

From behind the curtain, Laothong saw him shaking with rage. Fearing he would kill someone, she opened the curtain and came out to block his path.

"Hold off and think first. Please listen to this wife. Why all this noise? There are laws[13] in the land, and wherever you go you won't escape them.

Right or wrong, think it through. Why not report the matter to the king? If you rashly attack and slash people, later you'll be in trouble.

You've heard only one side and lost your temper. You don't yet know the rights and wrongs of the matter. How come this fellow had the nerve even though you two were already married?

Was there some kind of consent that made him dare to seize her and your bridal house? What's really behind it? You must think carefully. Listen to me and don't get carried away like a drunk.

He doesn't have a steel neck or an iron spine,[14] nor is he some baby child. And the mother-in-law gave her consent. That's why he had the nerve to do all this."

---

13. มีขื่อ, *mi khue*, shortened from มีขื่อมีแป, *mi khue mi pae*, to have beams and rafters, an idiom meaning to have a framework of rules and laws.

14. คอทั้งสันหลังเหล็ก, *kho thang sanlang lek*, to have a steel (literally, anvil) neck and an iron spine, meaning to have no fear for the law of the land.

Wanthong felt a thunderbolt had broken her head into seven pieces. "How come you float your face into the middle of this, raising your voice and flaunting your body like a flying swan!

Cutting me off. Telling my husband what to do. Knowing the rights and wrongs of the matter so perfectly. Suspecting something fishy. Flirting and flaunting to get my husband to fall for you.

Is this your wife, sir, or is her ladyship some palace consort? Is that why she followed a torch, blundered into a stump, and broke her neck?[15] Or perhaps she's a relative of yours? Or a stray Lao kid you abducted along the way?"

"This wife of mine is from Chomthong. I'm not hiding anything. Her parents gave her for me to marry and bring down here. She's the child of a headman from a big house, and her name is Laothong.

I was bringing her to wai you,[16] but then things blew up and got in the way, so I failed to introduce you in time. Please show me some consideration, the two of you.

Laothong, wai Phim first. Phim, calm down and don't take offense. Please show forbearance to each other without prejudice. If there's any problem, we can talk it over later."

"Enough, sir! This is shameful already. I have no desire for a wai from her. I only find out that you have a lover when she comes and shows her face here and now.

I was telling you what happened to me when she butted in, spitting out these contemptuous insinuations to hurt me and create confusion. But perhaps you agree with everything she said.

Her words warning you were slanderous,[17] sowing suspicions about me in many ways. Shouldn't I feel insulted? She's crafty, subtle, and sharp as nails.

What's right or wrong, the husband can judge. But does she flare up and attack anyone she sees? Does she just like flaunting her body, and isn't *really* following you to be a wife?"

---

15. Alluding to a saying, จุดใต้ตำตอ, *jut tai tam to*, light a torch but get pierced by a stump, meaning doing something which has unintended and hurtful consequences.

16. The minor wife gives a wai to the major wife to indicate subservience, and if the major wife returns the gesture it signifies acceptance of the minor wife into the household.

17. เป็นครามทา, *pen khram tha*, daubing with indigo, meaning tattooing. A woman found guilty of persistent adultery was liable to be tattooed with a picture of a man or woman on her cheek, and a palace woman found guilty of sexual misbehavior was liable to be tattooed on the face and paraded around the palace grounds (KTS, 1:270–71; KTS, 3:207).

Hearing this made Laothong almost mad, crazed, off her head. She felt as angry as if licked by fire. "You pick and poke at me about everything.

I didn't know in time that you're his major wife. I didn't intend to give offense. I saw Phlai Kaeo was wild enough to kill someone, so stopped him to let him cool off.

I just said, be patient, everything comes to him who waits.[18] But did my intervention leave you dangling? I don't sway around like a stick stuck in mud. Seeing my husband thundering on, should I let him continue?

If I didn't stop him, who would? You were too worked up and not likely to back down. If a fire's flaring and you carelessly fling on more firewood, it flames up even fiercer.

You don't wish to receive my wai but I'm not a bad, hard-headed little thing. Phlai Kaeo ordered me to wai, and I was intending to comply. It was not that I feared my wai would not be returned.

I didn't wai you in time because of this confusion between us. I'm just a simple-mannered Lao from the forest. I didn't know the situation here in any depth, not even the name of his major wife.

If I'd known beforehand that he had a wife, I'd have brought good presents like eaglewood[19] and ivory. That's the custom among forest people.

Now I'm at a loss because I came empty handed, and it's too late to bring anything to give you. So let's just greet each other for the time being. There, let me wai you. Don't be angry."

palanquin

"Tcha! This little upland Lao can weave hundreds of words full of wiles! If you'd brought wood and ivory, I'd have brought a tusker out to receive you,

so that Lady Laothong would not have to walk on the ground.

I'd have sent up a palanquin so soldiers could take turns carrying you along the way, and people could admire you among the troops.

That would be fitting for the Chomthong family with its rank and its big

18. ช้าช้าจะได้พร้าสองเล่มงาม, *cha cha ja dai phra song lem ngam*, literally, go slowly and you'll have two beautiful machetes (Gerini, "On Siamese Proverbs," 161).

19. ไม้กฤษณา, *mai kritsana*, agarwood. The tree *Aquilaria agallocha/crassna* secretes a fragrant resin to counter a parasite that may kill the tree. The resinous wood was highly prized as an aromatic, especially in China, and was a major export from Siam for centuries. The word eaglewood is a corruption of the tree's Sanskrit name, *aguru* via Portuguse *aguila* meaning eagle (Farrington and Dhiravat, *English Factory*, 1392).

house. I'd have arranged food in advance and rushed up as soon as your litter was set down.

I thank you for being careful about creating trouble. When Phlai Kaeo was growing aggressive, you thought quickly and jumped up like a windmill to stop him, or else things would be even more confused today.

Because of your ladyship's action, we now have absolute peace and quiet. You grasped the firebrand and dunked it in water—but your face looks as sour as if you just ate a gherkin.[20]

No, you're no stick stuck swaying in mud. You're thick clay so firm that a boundary post can be rammed in nine spans deep all day long—until Phlai Kaeo falls flat on his face.

If that weren't so, how would you dare come? Here at Ayutthaya you'll be a sensation, talked about every day and night as unlike any other woman in the whole land.

Hundreds of villages and thousands of cities with no exception will celebrate this one lady. Nay! Not only the humans who walk this earth, even Lord Indra will probably come down too!"

Lord Indra on Erawan

"In truth, good people are not celebrated and evil people become popular. It's shameful. I'm like a post planted in stone. But I didn't see that it was muddy in front of the landing.

When the boat moored, I put out my foot and got filthy because there wasn't a hair's breadth to stand on. Rice husks, feces, and duckweed all mixed up in a gooey, muddy mess like sap. I'll have to wash it all off and dry in the sun. I thank you for wanting to bring an elephant to receive us because Phlai Kaeo and I don't have one.

You have plenty in reserve, both real elephants and man elephants,[21] enough to pull down a house and build a big new one, all of them in musth and with splayed tusks!

I heard you were sick and wasting with fever because you were separated from your husband Phlai Kaeo. You didn't have any servants so you had to ride on an elephant all the time.

---

20. ตะลิงปลิง, *talingpling*, fruit of the cucumber tree, *Averrhoa bilimbi*, which looks like a small cucumber and is very sour.

21. A pun on *chang*, which means elephant.

The elephant broke the house pillars so you built a new one over the top. The astrologer said you had bad fortune from the past—Venus entering, Saturn stuck, Mars intervening.[22]

The bad fortune was averted in time, yet you still almost fell to pieces. So you changed your name and shaved your head so your husband wouldn't recognize you. Though broken, you'll be back together again."

"Even so, whose affair is this? Did an elephant stab you all the way up to your throat? Tcha! You little forest Lao who floated your face up here, I'll beat you and use the blood to bathe my feet.[23]

I'm deeply hurt, like someone sliced my body into pieces with a sword. Saithong, I-Pli, I-Jin! Climb down to the boat and help me!

Whatever happens, I'm not letting you get away with it." Khun Phaen blocked Wanthong. Laothong hid behind him, peeping out. Saithong and the servants rushed up, ready to deliver a slap.

"Don't! Don't make more trouble, Saithong. How come Wanthong is like this? You should calm her down. Don't, Wanthong. Please restrain yourself."

"No sir, I won't listen to you at all. Even if Lord Indra comes down to forbid me, I won't listen. If you don't want to keep me, so be it. Just slash me down in this boat.

Shout at me as much as you like, I won't argue. Bash me into ten pieces, I won't complain. But this little upland Lao, this clever talker, this eater of lizards and frogs, is getting a slap!"

She grasped Laothong's arm. Khun Phaen cried "Don't! Don't!" and blocked her with his hands. Laothong dodged away. The slap came too late and caught Khun Phaen full on.

"Eh! Look here! What's this? Don't you fear me one little bit? I say don't but it just fans the flames. Fine. If you defy me then let's see."

"If you want to beat me then beat me, Phlai Kaeo. Strange, you didn't have a temper like this before. Now you're so smitten you can soar.

Why is the sight of me as hateful as the sight of a tiger? Have you been dosed, my dear husband? Did she cut open your body and eat away all the innards so the potion would seep into your body hair and blacken your bones?

---

22. Mars and Saturn are unfavorable planets, while Venus is neutral, meaning its influence is determined by the planets it is currently in conjunction with. So the indication is very unfavorable.

23. On his accession in 1590, King Naresuan swore to attack Cambodia and "wash our feet in the blood" of its king. In the chronicles for 1594, this threat is carried out, but there is strong proof that the passage is apocryphal (RCA, 122, 153).

Your face is covered with freckles, all over the nose and lips.[24] Before long, you'll be crawling on the ground, and she'll ride on your neck like an ox."[25]

"Eh! Enough! Too much, Wanthong. You show no respect for your husband. You're stubborn, wrongheaded, thoughtless. Even if you don't fear me, at least show me a little respect.

For better or worse, I'm your husband, but you don't seem to want me to be. Don't overdo it or I'll get angry. Don't lose the fish by beating the water in front of the trap.[26]

If you love yourself and fear shame then calm down. Don't make a row or you'll lose face. If you don't listen to me and keep on, you'll be shamed in front of the townsfolk. Wait and see."

"I know now you don't love me. If you want to kill me, kill me. You brought her home to slight me. Now we're wise to Mr. Silver Tongue.

This scourge[27] is all you've got, and yet you're already making up stories to batter me. If you get someone better than this, will you expect me to receive her like a public footbath?

If you leave me now, before long you'll be like a board used for chopping fish morning and night, and this little Lao will chop you to shreds. Our merit and karma is finished from today."[28]

Wanthong leapt up onto the jetty. "So no stain is left, I'll scoop up river water to wash the house, scrub it with my feet,

even spread some oil and krajae powder, and leave it to dry as a crust. To get this liar out of my life, I'll even dig his feces out of the ground so there's not a trace left behind.

I cut myself off from you completely from today. I won't miss you in even one joint of my little finger. Even if Lord Indra comes down to scold me, don't wait around for me to go back on my word!"

"My, my! You're full of yourself, Wanthong. And you want to put the blame on me, don't you? When I arrived, I thought things were good. I didn't yet know your trickery.

---

24. A dark face, freckles, or eyes rimmed with green are signs that someone has been subjected to a love charm (PKW, 1:24).

25. A stock saying implying the wife will dominate the husband, in reversal of convention.

26. An old saying, included in the "Sayings of Phra Ruang," meaning don't be unnecessarily disruptive to spite someone (Gerini, "On Siamese Proverbs," 151).

27. กาลีเมือง, *kali mueang*, someone who brings bad fortune to a place; derived from Kali, in India a fearsome representation of Uma, the wife of Siva.

28. Meaning that she is breaking with him.

You pretended to weep and wail but you were hiding a lot away, you little schemer. I've caught you out, you tricky tongue. You were scared I was about to go up

and slash Khun Chang in the house. You couldn't stay still because you love your baldheaded husband. To conceal the truth, you shouted at Laothong, then quarreled with me and severed the relationship.

You don't wish to be friendly, you devious, thick-faced, wicked, shameless piece. I wasn't even out the door and you were stuck with your lover very willingly.

A nettle vine is horribly itchy but not as bad as you. With ringworm, mange, or flukes,[29] the itch can at least be soothed with medicine.

But this lowlife is as bad as the worm that bores its way in and gives one the shakes. Even if I looked for a cure all over Suphan, I'd exhaust the medical manuals in one day.

You're going to die, Wanthong. You cannot live." He drew his sword, raised it to strike, and stamped his foot on the boat. "I'll grasp you by the hair and cut you dead!"

In shock, Wanthong ran up into the main house, threw herself down on the bed, and flailed around in utter despair.[30] "Oh my Phlai Kaeo!

It was a waste of effort to preserve myself untarnished like a gold ring that lights up the sky, trying to hide even from bugs and mites, like an egg buried in stone.

---

29. พรรไน, *phannai*, a disease with parasitic worms under the skin, possibly schistosomiasis.

30. At this point Damrong's edition omitted a scene that was retained in folk versions performed as drama and *li-ke*. In the drama version, Wanthong comes to her room and writes a letter for Saithong to take to Khun Phaen, pleading for him to come and collect her in a palanquin. Khun Phaen replies that he will come in three days. Khun Chang sees Saithong returning with this letter, suspects something, and grabs it. He takes it for his younger brother Janson to read, and there is a comic scene where Janson demands payment on grounds Khun Chang cheated him in the past. Khun Chang then changes the letter to berate Wanthong for being two-minded, and urging her to go and live with Khun Chang since Khun Phaen will not come back. Wanthong reads this and hangs herself in despair. Siprajan declares she will give Wanthong to anyone who can revive her, and Khun Chang succeeds in doing so. Three days later Siprajan sends Wanthong to Khun Chang's room, and on that night Khun Phaen appears with a palanquin. He slashes the curtain and takes Wanthong away, as in chapter 17 below. In the *li-ke* version, Khun Phaen is able to reconcile Wanthong and Laothong on the riverbank, and Wanthong returns to live with him. Khun Chang thinks up the ruse of faking a letter in which Khun Phaen breaks with Wanthong because he knows she has been living with Khun Chang. Wanthong believes the letter and goes to live with Khun Chang. In these folk versions, Khun Chang is much more clearly the villain who destroys Khun Phaen and Wanthong's love. In this version, all the characters bear some of the responsibility. (Sukanya, "'Khun Chang plaeng san'")

My body was untainted. Even the breeze had no chance to brush me. I saved myself and waited for you but as soon as we met again, trouble flared.

I can't blame you at all. I deserve it for being so insulting. I'm the one with guilt on my face.[31] You tried to stop me but I was still rash and didn't see the danger.

Now, because of my carelessness, everything is severed, snapped, cracked, and crumbled into dust. The tallest tree with no neighbors to lean on gets blown down in a gale.

Oh, poor Wanthong! I shouldn't be shattered into dust. How can I put things back together? I'm like a swan with a broken wing that falls into mud,

loses its glittering gold,[32] and becomes like a crow. Because of bitterness, of clever words that provoke anger, a whole tribe of swans is drowned.

Oh my lord and master, my partner at the table, partner in bed, friend in sickness, friend in health, you've gone and I won't see you again, night or day.

Since our love began, this is our first quarrel. You came in time and I rushed down to meet you. You still loved me and meant to live together as before. Then the demoness of jealousy brought disaster.

Feeling slighted made me so mean, hasty, and stubborn beyond reason. I should've borne things for half a year and let you beat me to your heart's content.

But I've slipped up and you've cast me away. How can I escape Khun Chang now? I'm heavy-hearted that Mother will give me to him, even though I've no feeling of love.

Only this old, and already two husbands! So much badness, so much evil, in every strand of hair! I'll suffer only shame and endless grief. When I'm dead and buried, my name will still be notorious.

The pain won't lessen, and the shame will never disappear, like a tattoo on the back of a hand. Why should I love this body?

Death is finer." She dragged over a rope, raised her hands, and prostrated three times. "In this life, I've lost you, Phlai Kaeo.

In fear of shame, I'll die and wait for you. May we meet again in the next life. Don't let Khun Chang have even a hint." She ducked behind a curtain, reached up,

grasped a pillar, and climbed onto a roof beam. With two hands, she tied the rope tightly round her neck, and let her body swing, making the roof sway. Coming in at that very moment, Saithong was shocked.

---

31. หน้าทาคราม, na tha khram, with face painted in indigo (see above p. 268, note 17).

32. This is a hong, หงส์, Pali hamsa, a mythical swan, hence the golden color. This passage seems like a Jataka, which are often full of swans and crows, but is using the imagery rather than telling a particular story.

She shrieked, took the weight of Wanthong's body, grabbed a knife to cut the rope, and cried out loud, "Mother! Come quick! Wanthong has hanged herself!"

Siprajan cried out, "I'm done for too!" She jumped up, fell flat on her face, and rolled over. Khun Chang leapt up too with bleary eyes, tripped over his mother-in-law, and crashed down with a thud.

In pain, Siprajan complained, "You old elephant! You blundered into me and almost broke my spine." Khun Chang wailed, "My eyes were so bleary. I fell on my shoulder blade and nearly died."

The servants in the house were in uproar. They massaged Wanthong but failed to bring her round. Saithong cried out, "Wanthong has really hanged herself, Phlai Kaeo. Come and look."

Khun Phaen was angry as if seared by fire. "I won't miss Wanthong." He ordered servants to harness elephants to go to his mother's house at Cockfight Hill.

When the elephants were ready, they quickly loaded up much of the goods. Khun Phaen mounted an elephant with Laothong.

Her maids, Wan and Wiang, rode a big cow elephant. With the servants and phrai following behind carrying goods, they reached Kanburi in two days.

Seeing the many people, elephants, and horses coming, Thong Prasi recognized him and cried out happily, "My son has come! Over there!"

She shaded her eyes and peered out from the stairway. "Servants, come quickly to receive Phlai Kaeo. There are two of them. It must be Wanthong." She hawked and said, "Why ever did young Kaeo bring Wanthong?"

Khun Phaen dismounted from the elephant, and brought Laothong along to prostrate at the feet of his mother, who said, "It's not her." He told his mother the story from the beginning up to the quarrel with Wanthong.

Thong Prasi said, "Oh my son, no need to tell me. Siprajan is full of herself. When she gave Wanthong away to Khun Chang in marriage, I went and shouted at her, made a big commotion,

and severed relations completely from that day on. We can't keep Wanthong." Then she turned to speak to Laothong. "I trust you to look after me in sickness and death, dear child.

Whatever we have, poor or plenty, I give to you. Come to live with us from now on. Love yourself, protect yourself, and fear gossip." She ordered the servants to carry their things up into the house.

The servants tethered the elephants and horses, and put everything away neatly. The many Lao who had arrived with them went off to build new houses around the village.

᠊ᢏ

Now to tell of Khun Chang. He spent fifteen days in the bridal house in utter misery, curled up, wide awake, mumbling to himself, and hugging his pillow.

Up to the second or third watch, he could not sleep. When he dropped off, he dreamed and sat up in his sleep with eyes wide open and hands pressed on the mattress hard enough to break it apart.

A creaking sound made him get up to look around. "Have you come? Don't go away!" The only reply was a *tukkae*'s call. He lay down again, stood up, sat, and went back to lying again—

first face up, then face down, then turning on his side. His legs felt as stiff as blocks of wood. He got up to recite a love poem.

"My love, this bed is cold as ice.
What must I do, where can we meet,
To eat palm sugar and young rice.
I miss you darling club of wood,
But must refrain this holy day.
From dearth may riches come to rule.
At Bang Kaja, where whirlpools play,
I'll drool and suck it all away.
Please say we'll meet or else I die."[33]

Siprajan[34] heard the tail end of her son-in-law's recitation and praised him to the skies. "It's so eloquent, so poetic, I'm truly enthralled."

Khun Chang laughed distractedly. "Oh, Mother dear! Today may warmth dispel the chill. Be kind to your tormented son. Spirits of my grandmothers, come and help.

Grandfathers too—everyone. I'll give you strong liquor and roasting pigs.

---

33. Khun Chang is not a very good poet. This rendering mimics the eight-syllable lines, the rhyming scheme, and Khun Chang's clumsy search for rhymes found in the original. More literally it translates as follows: Oh lady, my bed is cold as if soaked in water / what should I do and where / to eat young rice and fresh palm sugar / I miss you darling club of *jan* wood / but I restrain myself as it's a holy day / may I overcome poverty and become rich / may I find a whirlpool at Bang Kaja / suck bowl sink whirl to the bottom / may I meet you for a while as I almost die from waiting. Bang Kaja is at the southeast corner of Ayutthaya on the west bank of the Chaophraya opposite the fort Pomphet (APA, 126–7; see map 8). The "whirlpools" are the disturbed water where the Pasak and Chaophraya rivers meet in front of the fort.

34. This stanza is taken from WK, 11:423, absent from PD.

Please urge her to come here quick. Anyone who can persuade her will be richly rewarded.

Oh loverboy spirits and spirits with fearless tongues, come and help me! In reward, I'll offer you a hair quill befitting my wealth, Tani oil, and a comb."

Seeing her son-in-law frustrated and miserable, Siprajan tried to bring Wanthong round. "Don't sit there doing nothing. Flesh of my flesh, don't delay.

Today, fifteen days are up. Precious child, please go into the bridal house. Khun Chang has been straining his neck waiting so long, food sticks in his throat. Don't be so reluctant."

"Oh Mother, mistress of your child, do you want to murder me? My husband went to war and just came back. You saw him with your own eyes too.

If he hadn't survived, had met his death, I'd live with Khun Chang without hatred. But Phlai and I have been parted for only a couple of days. Will you force me so hard I'm throttled to death?

If you can kill me so easily, it was a waste of effort to carry me in your womb. If I go on living, I can't escape shame on account of this bothersome baldy."

"You're mixing up right and wrong, you arrogant child. Don't you want to have a husband of silver and gold, and sit eating in comfort until your dying day? Why make so much of his bald head?

You're[35] moaning on about Phlai Kaeo but he's gone off with that woman, hasn't he? Khun Chang will give you so much money, you won't be able to sew sacks fast enough to hold it all.

If you won't listen to me, you can get out of this house. Whether times are tough or easy, whether you live or die, don't look to me." She grabbed Wanthong to drag her out.

Wanthong dodged her. They pushed each other and fell against the wall. Khun Chang blundered up, rubbing the sleep from his eyes, opened the door, and waited.

Siprajan kept on dragging her. "You little abomination, you'll make your mother lose face. All tears and snot like a toddler." She grappled, tugged, pushed, and pulled.

---

35. This stanza is taken from WK, 11:425; PD has: You're moaning on about Phlai Kaeo but he's got a new wife, hasn't he? He insulted you loud enough for all Suphan to hear. He's broken it off with you and doesn't care.

Her hand slipped, and she fell against a wall, ripping her cloth, and cracking her head. Wanthong too fell face down with a bang. Siprajan pushed her, rolling her head-over-heels,

and beating her remorselessly. "Are you really not going? Well I'm not listening to that." Wanthong shouted out, "You're bullying me. Hold off, Mother! Oh villagers, come and look!"

Baldheaded Ta-Phon, who lived in a house close by, took fright that robbers had come to spear his pigs. He grabbed a pike, came out to his doorway, and cried out, "To battle! No retreat!"

Siprajan shouted angrily at old Phon, "Why are you jumping up and down and shouting, you hairy-chested old baldy? Nobody's spearing your pigs."

Khun Chang thought his mother-in-law was shouting at him. "Heavens above! I haven't speared anything yet. Why are you slow at sending Wanthong to me?" Siprajan cried angrily, "You sex maniac!"

She turned away and dragged Wanthong further. Her cloth slipped off and she staggered about in a rage. By a fig tree, she stepped on a bowl that broke and cut her foot.

She screamed, "I'm dying!" picked up her foot and waved it around, red with blood. "You're dreadful, you bully!" Wanthong got a grip on a bamboo bench and hung on tight.

Siprajan pulled shards of the bowl out of her foot, climbed onto the bench, and grabbed Wanthong again. Wanthong lost her grip on the bench and was hauled clumsily by her mother up into the new bridal house.

They went through the door in a tussle. Dragged along the floor, Wanthong lost her uppercloth. Khun Chang's eyes glazed over. He leapt across, missed Wanthong, and kissed his mother-in-law twice.

Siprajan reeled away, pushing against his chest. "You dirty baldy, you ghost's skull!" Khun Chang cried, "Ay! Damn! Riding your wife's mother is a big mistake!"

He released Siprajan, grabbed Wanthong, and dragged her into the room in high excitement, clumping along on his knees like a turtle. "I'm going to heaven today!"

Inside the room, Wanthong shouted, "Khun Chang is forcing himself on me, Phlai Kaeo! This pestilence is going to kill me. His eyes are bulging like a big ugly tomcat.

Get away from me, you lowlife! Your head's like a dried old coconut!" Panting, Khun Chang reached out his hands to grab her shoulders and push her into the mosquito net.

bamboo bench

Wanthong kicked him in the chest, and he fell off the bed with a thud. Scrambling up, he lay across her stomach. The string of the mosquito net broke. As she squirmed desperately,

the net wrapped round her like a coating of egg white. "I can't breathe, you abomination!" With bleary eyes, Khun Chang groped around and got the net totally tangled.

"I'm really furious with this net. First thing tomorrow, I'll throw it in the shithouse." He ripped the net and screwed it up in his hands but Wanthong was still tangled up.

Khun Chang lifted the net from her body, leaving only her head in the tangle, giving himself an opening. In[36] delight, he jumped up in a frog-like pose, found her little belly with his hands, and rocked.

Wanthong struggled to get up, her eyes popping out. "You winded me, damn you." She kicked Khun Chang who fell down doubled over. He leapt up, hopping back and forth,

and kicked over a water bowl, drenching his legs and making him shiver. Wanthong freed herself enough to sit up, still wound up in the net. Khun Chang stumbled over, grabbed her by the throat,

and wrestled her down onto the bed with a thump. Wanthong struggled and pounded on the wall, eyes staring wide. Wondrously, the sky burst and rain sluiced down in an unbroken babbling stream, bathing the earth.

Fish and shrimps jumped happily up from the water. Huge ones slipped over rocks. Catfish, looking for food, swam down and wriggled into the ground,

scraping[37] their heads and scuffing their barbs on the undergrowth at the riverbank. An eel nosed into a hole but stuck, rose to the surface, and careened about. Two fighting cocks struck, sinking in their rear claws to the hilt.

---

36. The next three hemistiches down to "hopping back and forth" are taken from WK, 11:428; PD has: Stuck in the folds, Wanthong was at her wits' end. She struggled to get up, crying her eyes out.

37. The next stanza and a half, down to "bristled in bliss," is taken from WK, 11:428–29; PD has: Wanthong was despondent, feeling only sorrow. Khun Chang was ecstatic.

Naked and alone, Wanthong sobbed in the dead of night. Khun Chang's body hair bristled in bliss. "I love you enough to swallow you up. Thousands of other women mean nothing to me.

I'll give lots of money, at least a hundred baskets, to you, my lady luck. No matter where you go, I won't let you get tired. You can ride on the neck of your loving husband instead of a bull elephant."[38]

Wanthong harrumphed and tossed her head. She could not stop being angry at herself for doing wrong. Her thoughts turned to her husband and she wanted to die. She was too ashamed to let anyone see her,

and stayed in the room for two days, grieving enough to lose her mind. She was now forced to live with Khun Chang but behind his back she pined for Phlai Kaeo.

She ate nothing, neither rice nor fish. She woke in the morning but lay in bed until late, heartbroken enough to pass away, hands wiping away her flooding tears.

---

38. Another pun on his name and *phlai*, meaning a bull elephant.

14: KHUN PHAEN STATES HIS CASE

Now to tell of Khun Phaen, great romancer, whose mastery made enemies quail. He had been living together with Laothong for two nights

when he woke at midnight in their room.[1] The earth was bathed in bright moonlight. The voiceless silence was broken only by the lonely sound of birds calling through the forest,

and the relentless trilling of cicadas. A cool dew lay on the ground, and a refreshing breeze blew. His thoughts turned to Wanthong.

"Oh, I was really rash. Should I have thrown away a loving wife? On the day I arrived back, the jealousy between her and Laothong made it a very dark day.

On top of that, she was so quick-tempered. Khun Chang had already built a bridal house, ready and waiting. The longer I leave her there, the more chance he has to fulfill his desires. That thought is disturbing.

Oh pity, pity! I was so full of hopes but now this demon has smashed them all. While I was away, he was just waiting to grab her. I rushed back but it was too late.

We met face to face but still came to calamity—like having a jewel in your grasp but then dropping it exactly where a thief can attack. Perhaps now she's already tarnished.

tiger feeding

When a tiger gets a juicy chunk of meat, does he dally before devouring it? I've left her with him for two days already. What's happened to my eye's jewel?

---

1. This chapter 14 probably began as an alternative version of the abduction in chapters 17–18. It opens in the same way (thinking of Wanthong, journey, spirit ceremony, climbing into the house, cutting down a curtain), and ends very abruptly with Khun Phaen returning to Kanburi for no obvious reason. Possibly the alternative (Kaeo Kiriya) version of the abduction became very popular but the comedy in this version was felt too good to discard, so this version was recycled as a separate episode, earlier in the story.

The more I think about this, the more I feel choked with concern, boiling with anger and frustration that won't subside. Tomorrow I'll go to Suphan.

By midnight on the day after tomorrow, I should know how things are. I'll use a Subduer mantra[2] to enter and see for certain. If Wanthong is sleeping with him, I'll slash both their throats,

and those of Siprajan and Thepthong too. They were involved and I won't let them live. I'll treat them like dogs with crooked tails, as they deserve. Those old ladies who asked for her hand too."

With this in mind, he pushed open a window and saw the golden light of early dawn at cockcrow. He quickly got up and washed his face as the sun came up.

Summoning his servants and phrai, both Thai and Lao, he made up a story. "Get things ready quickly. Put enough rice in your waist pouches for about four days.

Prepare horses for everyone, and ready the weapons you usually carry." He chose by name twenty of those with skill.

"I'm making a patrol to the frontier. It doesn't pay to neglect royal service. You men have already been to war and survived so now I trust you to follow my arse."

He went back into the room and talked to his beloved Laothong. "I'm going on patrol on the king's orders. I'll be back shortly."

He got dressed, decked himself with devices of lore, picked up his sword, and walked away from the house. The phrai and horses were ready and waiting. They mounted,

carrying their weapons, along with food and torch sets in their waist pouches. They cut across the plain and reached the Suphan area after two nights.

They halted and dismounted at the fringe of the forest where they ate steamed rice and grilled fish. At sundown, they made a shrine,

lit victory candles to initiate it, pronounced extraordinary formulas to instill their equipment with power, and used mantras to enchant rice and limes.

When this was quickly done, they got dressed, harnessed the horses, and all grasped their weapons. At an auspicious time, Khun Phaen made a prayer,

brandished his sword to flash as bright as a jewel, strode off quickly, and leapt on his horse. His men followed behind.

Around the second watch, under a glittering starlit sky, they reached the

---

2. สะกด, *sakot*, to suppress, immobilize, restrain; name of a mantra for immobilizing people or putting them to sleep, used many times by Khun Phaen.

house. Khun Phaen dismounted and scattered enchanted rice

to drive away all the spirits of the place, and to ensure nobody would wake up. He hastened to Khun Chang's bridal house, lit a candle, and fixed it to the first post.[3]

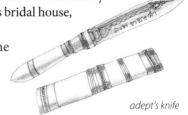

adept's knife

With an adept's knife,[4] he hacked at the post, splitting its top into four, and used a Loosener mantra to spring the bolts and open the windows. He scattered rice mixed with bones of the dead,

ensuring that all in the house were overcome with drowsiness and fell asleep instantly, curled up and tumbled over one another. He climbed up to a big window,

and jumped down onto the floor inside. A dim light illuminated faces. He cut down a curtain into a pile on the floor, and moved ahead to open a mosquito net. He saw the face of Wanthong,

asleep on the bed beside Khun Chang with their arms around each other. "Mm! How dare you, my good woman! So confident in this husband you don't fear me at all.

All the promises we made still stand but I was not out of the door when you took a lover in full public view."

He stepped up onto the bed, pushed them apart to see her face, and lifted the cloth covering her chest. "Tcha! It'll serve you right, my fair face.

I didn't realize such a figure would have no heart. You're so beautiful—your breasts and your alluring ways—I wanted to swallow you whole. But I shouldn't have put such store in looks.

Your body is beautiful but your kiss is not sweet. Your face is as black as a sooty pot yet you raise your neck like a swan." He kicked them off the bed, one after the other. "Why should I let you live?"

He raised his sword to cut them in two but a *jingjok*[5] called out a warning close by. He stopped himself, held back his anger, and did not strike. "Your

---

3. This post would have been the subject of ritual during construction to enshrine powers to protect the house. By ritually damaging this post, Khun Phaen is removing this protection over the house's inhabitants.

4. มีดหมอ, *mit mo*, a knife that has been made with special materials, inscribed with yantra, and instilled with power by an adept. Typically the blade is 5 cms wide and 10 cms long. Kept in the house, it offers protection from danger. In battle, it conveys invulnerability, and can penetrate even people who themselves have invulnerability. Steeped in water, it creates medicine that cures sickness. During ceremonies to overcome spirit possession, the knife is placed on the subject's head. (PKW, 1:17–18; YS, 766–67; SWN, 4:5176)

5. จิ้งจก, common house lizard. There is an old belief that when a *jingjok* calls out close at hand, one should stop whatever one is doing or saying (KW, 669–70).

fortune is good. You'll survive.

Otherwise you wouldn't live to see tomorrow morning. Both your heads would be off. But within today I'll make you pay for daring to do this without any fear."

He pulled a cord out from a curtain. "Although I've decided not to put you to death, you'll still get what you deserve, you scourge. I'll fix you with this rope."

With his foot, he pushed the two of them together, and wound the rope tight around their prone bodies. He trussed them with lengths of the rope, tightened the bonds with splints, and tossed the end of the rope up onto the roof.

Then he wrapped them in cloth like a corpse. "Tcha! You vile lot, that's what you deserve." With dawn almost brightening the sky, he hurried down from the house,

and pulled the adept's knife out of the post. He called his phrai and had each of them bind a torch and light them all so it looked like a royal procession.

torches

Then he released the Subduer mantra and in an instant everyone in the house awoke at the same time. Khun Phaen remounted his horse and beat on the walls with his sword.

He had his men shout loudly, "Is Wanthong there?" "Where is she?" "Is anyone awake in there?" "Lower the stairway to receive Khun Phaen!"

Saithong heard the noise. "Eh? Whose voices are those?" She rushed out and saw many people on horseback

and torches blazing brightly all around. She took fright and hid herself. Peering around, she saw Phlai Kaeo. "Now we're in for it!

Darling Wanthong is already spoiled and now Phlai Kaeo has come back to find her. I must go down to talk with him and try to calm things."

She got up to open the door but sensed his anger and was unnerved. "If he lashes out, I'll die. But he's not bad at heart so it should be all right."

She pushed the stairway down and steeled herself to descend. Arriving in front of Khun Phaen, she burst into floods of tears, and said, "I'm in despair, Phlai Kaeo.

How come you abandoned Wanthong so easily? On that day when she hanged herself, you weren't concerned and wouldn't even look.

Siprajan forced her to marry that baldy. They had a big fight, pushing and pulling, and Siprajan beat Wanthong until her blood flowed.

Because the journey across the plain is very far, I couldn't go there to tell you. She was spoiled by force just two days before your arrival now."

Khun Phaen, great valiant, boiled with rage. "Saithong, there's no need to say anything else. I understand the trickery.

I don't have wealth and good fortune so Siprajan sees no benefit in me and wants to separate us. Khun Chang is richer than anyone else. I have to accept this, and bear it somehow.

I came with the intention of fetching her, and would love her if she were still good and not ruined. But now she's tainted, why should I take her? You can't wash this away however hard you try.[6]

But why talk about Wanthong? Even you won't escape his clutches in the end. When he doesn't have her, he'll take you instead because you're the same in flesh and spirit.

This one or that, that one or this—he'll make use of you. I fear you'll be spoiled too, and often. Don't deny it. It was a waste of effort to love and make promises. I want to see the faces of his lackeys.

I thought of bringing charges but it's a waste of time. I'll just slash the whole house so nothing's left! The couple will be hanged, and I'll have fun and games with those who went along to ask for her hand.

Even you, who are also my wife, how come you fell in with them? Now you're cornered and scared, you'll tell me only things that put you in a good light."

Saithong cried out, "Oh no! Don't talk like this, I won't listen. It's like looking in a basket of fish and seeing only the one that's rotten.

It's almost light, Phlai Kaeo, sir. Please come up to the main house." She went up the stairs and into Siprajan's room.

"Get up quickly, Mother. Khun Phaen's come. He's downstairs in the middle of the compound with lots of people, pikes, horses, swords, and everything."

Siprajan's body shook, her mouth trembled, and her neck palpitated. She wanted to disappear into the earth. "What shall we do, Saithong?"

People were in uproar all over the house. "Has he come to arrest me? I'm

---

6. ถึงจะใส่ตะกร้าล้างไม่มีเกลือ, *thueng ja sai takra lang mai mi kluea*, literally, even though put in a basket and washed, there's no salt. If a woman had sex before marriage, the parents could จับใส่ตะกร้าล้างน้ำ, put her in a basket and wash with water, i.e., pretend that her virginity was still preserved and go ahead with a marriage. Marinating in salt was used to remove the strong smell and taste of fish. Probably this line combines these two ideas.

cornered, and my head's swelling. He'll beat me into the ground!"

"Mother, this time he's on top. He's utterly in the king's favor. I heard him talking with the phrai that he'll rip us to pieces.

They've brought swords, pikes, and rope. Someone will be hanged for sure. He named Thepthong and Siprajan. He said he'd slash and leave the results for people to see."

Siprajan trembled like a chick. Sweat flowed down her face and dripped from her ears. Tears gushed down in floods. "My time has come to die!"

In despair, she went back into her mosquito net, covered herself with a mattress, and wound cloth round herself. "Saithong, please shout out to Phlai Kaeo that I fainted down dead several days ago."

"Where will you hide from him? You think he won't come in and search?" Saithong went out and pushed on Wanthong's door,

but found the bolt closed tight so she could not enter the room. She returned to look out of the doorway, and called Khun Phaen to come up.

Khun Phaen ascended with his big crowd of servants and phrai. He questioned Saithong, "Why don't I see my mother-in-law?

Is Wanthong here or not? Where's she gone? Why is she still sleeping so late?" He made a show of shouting loudly and pounding on the walls with a stick.

Khun Chang and Wanthong were scared by all the noise of people outside the room but could not get up because they were trussed tight with rope

and wrapped in a curtain. They rolled their heads around, trying to breathe. Their hearts pounded and bodies trembled with fear. They[7] had no lowercloths,

and were bound together face to face. Khun Chang got hard and laughed in amusement. Wanthong shouted, "You villain! We're tied up like corpses but you're still happy."

Khun Chang said, "We're done for. Who can get us out of this? Hands and feet are tied so tightly we can't breathe. If you can get up, then get up, I don't mind."

Khun Phaen called out, "Wanthong! Aren't you coming out of your room? Don't you get up until midday? Come and talk. What's up?"

Wanthong recognized her husband's voice and shivered in growing panic.

---

7. This hemistich and the next two stanzas down to "I don't mind" are taken from WK, 12:449; PD has one hemistich: In fear, they could do nothing but stare at each other.

With the two of them tied together, she felt helpless, and was too ashamed to call out.

They[8] could not move hand or foot but could roll over from front to back. Khun Chang called out, "Whee!" with eyes flashing, and tried to scramble on top of her.

Wanthong was furious. "Why is your body covered in hair? It irritates. Why don't you lie still, you corpse. Why are you butting me with your knee?"

Khun Chang protested, "You think it's my knee but it's not. Who called you just now? It sounded like a man's voice."

Khun Phaen shouted, "Hey, Khun Chang! Its late now. Why don't you put my wife down? Today you meet your death. Don't give a thought that you'll survive.

I don't know whether you're in there, but if you are I'm coming in to cut your head off." Shaking with aggression, he grabbed his sword and kicked the wall to make them panic.

Khun Chang heard it was Khun Phaen. His mind was full of anger and despair at being trussed up like a corpse. Wanthong felt more and more ashamed and would not open her eyes.

Saithong called out, "Mother Siprajan, he's going to slash Wanthong for sure. Why are you skulking in there? How do you think you can escape?"

Siprajan was too scared to come out but also afraid he would slash her daughter to death. Steeling herself to go and face her fate, she lifted the big mattress off her body but was again overcome with panic. She tied the mattress round herself with string like a dummy. "Even if he slashes me, it'll only hit the kapok."

She folded a cloth into five, wrapped it thickly round her head, completely covering her ears and eyes, and thrust her hands inside the mattress.

With the cloth covering her face and eyes, she walked blindly off in the wrong direction and tumbled over, snorting from her nose. "Saithong, come and help me!"

Saithong ran up, found a bulky roll of bedding stuck in the doorway, and burst out laughing.

She wrestled with the cloth and mattress, but Siprajan blundered this way and that, and was too big to go through the door. She pushed and pushed, then slipped and fell down with a thud.

Khun Phaen's men craned to look and cackled with laughter. "See the

---

8. The next three stanzas down to "a man's voice" are taken from WK, 12:450, absent from PD.

terrace

masked raider!" "The horses have seen and are bucking about in fear. They think a spirit of the saltlick will eat them!"[9]

Saithong guided Siprajan out onto the terrace. Trying to contain his anger, Khun Phaen called out, "What's this wrapped in a mattress? Is Saithong making fun of us?

Where's Siprajan? I don't see her yet. She won't escape being killed." Siprajan thought he did not realize it was her, so she leaned against a wall and said nothing.

Khun Phaen, great romancer, pondered very carefully, and sent for Phan Chot because he was an important man in the district.

"You're headman of the village. I went to Chiang Thong on royal service. You were aware that Wanthong and I were married and for how long.

When I came back from the war, my bridal house was nowhere to be seen. Who does this new house with nine rooms belong to? If you know, tell me."

Phan Chot the headman told what he knew with no falsehood. "When you were away up there and had not yet returned, I was a witness

that Khun Chang brought Granny Kloi and Granny Sai[10] to say that you were dead, and to arrange a date for a marriage ceremony.

Before the day when the dowry was brought to the house, Siprajan and Thong Prasi had a big, long argument over whether you'd died.

Thong Prasi told her not to hold the ceremony but Siprajan was highhanded and didn't listen. Before she went home, Thong Prasi informed me so I know the truth."

Khun Phaen, great valiant, listened to everything the headman had to say, then sat quietly and pondered the truth of the matter. "I still love my beloved

---

9. ผีโป่ง, *phi pong*, a type of forest spirit that lives near saltlicks, perhaps a *phi pong khang*, which appears in the shape of a langur with a short tail and upper lip drawn back to expose the teeth, and which likes drinking blood (Anuman, *Phi sang thewada*, 107).

10. In the original, her name is spelled Sa in this chapter, but this has been changed in the translation to Sai, the spelling used when she first appeared in the previous chapter.

wife Wanthong

as much as my own life. Khun Chang made up stories to break us apart. He's intent on being hostile. He used trickery in order to ask for the marriage.

Wanthong tried to wait and save our relationship until the war ended and I came home but when I arrived, we got into a quarrel and stupidly wrecked it.

I was too hotheaded—just blundered in and put the blame in the wrong place. Regrettably, that allowed Khun Chang to close in. On the one hand, should I think about taking her back?

Yet I've doubts about her love. Now that Khun Chang has enjoyed her, it'd be like drinking water and seeing the leeches and everything else. Reviving our love won't feel right.

To report matters to the king would affect Wanthong and make her shamed in front of a law court. She was spoiled because of an evil man. What use would it be to let the king see?

On the other hand, should I think about the loss of face? Khun Chang dared do this with no respect for me because his money makes him arrogant. If I let things go, he'll trample over me even more.

Up to now, I haven't done anything to him. If I let things ride, he'll just play more tricks. I have to teach him a lesson." With these thoughts, he said,

"Phan Chot, you're an important person around here. Please summon all those involved, including Thepthong, Granny Kloi, and Granny Sai."

Phan Chot ordered Nai Son to go off immediately. Son rushed over and went up into Thepthong's house.

Thepthong called out, "Why have you come with a face covered in sweat and eyes screwed up? What business brings you to the house?" She pushed a betel tray over and invited him to take some.

Nai Son said, "Oh, Grandma, things have blown up. Our village has a case as big as the earth on fire."

In fright, Thepthong asked, "Where? Servants, fetch the machetes and protect the house!" She got up and bustled about frantically. Nai Son said, "It's not a fire."

Thepthong cried, "Then it's robbers come to steal. Robbed ten times you don't lose everything like a fire." She sat back down and asked with her mouth trembling in apprehension, "What case?"

Nai Son said, "The case concerning Wanthong. Her husband has come to that house. He's now in royal favor. He's got a title and thousands of men.

He's been appointed Khun Phaen Saensathan. He's shouting threats at the headman. He wants to arrest people, take them to the city, and ask the king to execute them.

Phan Chot sent me to fetch you—along with Granny Kloi and Granny Sai. As for Khun Chang, Wanthong, and Siprajan, they're tied up already."

In the middle of pounding betelnut, Thepthong dropped the pounder with a thud.[11] "Oh damn! Really? I beg of you! Karma, oh karma, karma! What have I done? How can we to talk our way out of this?

betel pounder

From birth to old age and broken teeth, I've known only how to keep gardens and paddy fields, how to plant taro and cassava, how to till the earth. Now almost at death's door, I'm being taken to court

trussed crabs

because that lackey Khun Chang with the beard on his chin didn't listen to his mother. Sai and Kloi spun a tale and now he'll have them tied up like wat cattle."

She cried out to Granny Kloi and Granny Sai, "That damned Khun Chang has fixed you good. Khun Phaen came back to arrest him but he's shifted the blame onto you. Khun Phaen will truss you up like sea crabs."

In panic, Granny Kloi fell down the stairs, and limped along with her sagging breasts slapping on her unruly belly. The pair tottered over to Thepthong's house.

Granny Sai said, "Let's go up there," but did not spot a gap in the stairway, and fell in. She eased herself up, eyes bulging, and staggered up the stairs, dragging her leg and feeling very stiff.

Thepthong said, "What's up, Granny Sai? Does your leg hurt? Did you blunder and break your hip?" Thepthong jerked her head. "It's late. Let's go and find out how bad things are.

Grab some cloth to cover those droopy dugs. Hurry up now, we have to give evidence." Servants came along behind en masse, eyeing one another's faces with apprehension.

The closer they got, the more scared Thepthong became. She turned and said, "Dear Nai Son, help me. I'm not going, sir.

Please pacify him, I beg of you. Don't let his anger get out of hand. I'll give you money. Make merit by helping me. Tell him Khun Chang's mother has gone far away—

---

11. Betelnut was pounded either in a mortar or in a ตะบัน, *taban*, consisting of a metal cylinder enclosing a piston usually made of brass.

took the family and moved elsewhere so there's nobody left at the house. Granny Kloi and Granny Sai, please go along and sort this out. Help to get me off."

Nai Son said, "Why are you asking me this? Am I to tell him lies? For better or worse, let's all go. This is a serious matter. Don't beg me."

They walked along together and soon reached the house. Seeing people swarming all over the place, the three became even more terrified.

Nai Son went up to the terrace first. Thepthong would not follow but skulked at the foot of the stairs, peering around. Phan Chot said, "Why aren't you coming up?"

The three then rushed headlong up the stairs. Khun Phaen was sitting holding his sword and looking down. He stood up and called out, "Who's come?" Thepthong shrieked and fell down with a bump.

Sai and Kloi tumbled after her. A stair rail crashed down on top of them, pinning their necks so they were unable to get up. People roared with laughter.

Thepthong called out, "Why put us in the stocks, sir? I'm ready to give evidence though I've never done it before." Then she raised her head and realized she was pinned down by a stair rail.

They all got up, feeling as battered as if chopped with knives. They helped one another put the stair rail on the terrace, and stood craning their necks looking for a place to hide.

Thepthong steeled herself to step forward. Kloi and Sai followed her in dread. When a *tukkae* called, they dropped to their knees, and Thepthong called in reply, "It's only me!"

She stumbled into a door, and a batten thumped down on her head. Saithong cried, "What a shambles!" People laughed uproariously.

Thepthong tottered up to the main hall with Kloi and Sai following. Catching sight of Khun Phaen, she timorously crawled away to the wall to avoid him.

She saw the mattress wrapped around Siprajan. "Heavens, I've met a ghost!" She scrambled to her feet and bumped into the mattress, knocking Siprajan down flat.

Siprajan cried out, "Spare me. I'm terrified, sir." She poked out her face with eyes bulging, then extricated her trembling body from the mattress. "Sir, please forgive me."

Khun Phaen, great romancer, furiously demanded answers at once. "Now, you, Wanthong's mother,
I came to ask for your daughter's hand in marriage and you consented. When I went off to distant Chiang Thong, the bridal house was still there as evidence.

I entrusted my Wanthong to you. I never abandoned her, yet you gave her to Khun Chang. What have you got against me?

Perhaps you thought I had only low rank and little of any kind of property so you could act highhandedly and I wouldn't have the standing to pursue you in court.

Your new son-in-law is such a big fellow, overflowing with so much property, and so many elephants and horses, that you conspired together to treat me roughly with no respect.

You knocked down the old bridal house to rebuild in a wat, and brought a new one in its place. You think I deserve to be cut to pieces like this just because I'm poor."

Siprajan's mouth went dry with fear. Her skin crawled and her lips trembled. In utter panic, she lifted her bottom but then dropped it crashing down on the bamboo floor.

She heaved a great sigh and her body was racked with sobs. She buried her tearful face in both hands, then sat up, wiping away snot like a chick. She boxed her own head repeatedly, saying, "Yes, yes, sir!

Granny Kloi and Granny Sai came to sow confusion by bringing bones that had just been cremated and saying that you were dead. They asked for her to marry Khun Chang.

I was worried that I couldn't prevent Wanthong being taken as a royal widow, so I consented. Wanthong complained every day and cried her eyes out—tears as big as cowry shells.

For fifteen days she refused to go into the bridal house. She only gave up and went in two days ago—not time for her to be worn away *that* much. Don't hold it against her. Take her back."

Hearing Siprajan's words, Kloi and Sai could not remain silent. "No! No! Why are you saying this? It was Thepthong who asked us to come

and say that Phlai Kaeo had gone to war with Chiang Thong and been stabbed by the Lao in the forest. Whether that was true or false, have mercy on us. She coached us to say it, so we did."

Thepthong reeled around, beating her breast. "It was Khun Chang who told you to say it! I beg of you. I was completely in the dark. I'm at my wits' end. Please spare me."

Khun Phaen, great master, saw them speaking in such frantic confusion, and had to suppress his laughter. "It was wrong from the start. The whole of Suphan knew, but you had no fear.

My mother, Thong Prasi, came to the house and objected to the marriage, the bridal house, everything. But Thepthong and Siprajan stubbornly went right ahead.

In effect, you challenged me to take you to court. With all your money that was no worry. Why are you afraid now? Today it'll all come out.

Where's Khun Chang, where is he? Why is he hiding his head? Come out here! If you speak rashly, I'll beat you to death. But if you're good, I'll think of you as a friend."

Siprajan and Thepthong called out, "Why don't you come out to meet him?" "Are you having fun sleeping over half the day, you lowlife with a head girdled down to the nape?"

However much they called, there was no answer. Khun Phaen said, "My anger's rising up to my throat . . . " Khun Chang called out blearily, "I've been tied up, my whole body."

Siprajan pushed on the door of the room. "Why are you lying in there, you lowlife? Just because you're inside there means you have no fear? Thepthong, let's haul him out by his ear."

Thepthong and Siprajan shoved on the door but it was locked tight and would not open. Khun Phaen held his breath and blew a formula.

The door opened with a click. Siprajan and Thepthong went into the room, shrieked, and collapsed, trembling. "Who brought Jek Khong's corpse in here?"

Khun Chang cried, "Mother, don't be scared. It's not a corpse. Help untie me." Thepthong screamed in greater panic, "Oh! This corpse can speak like a live person!"

Siprajan cried, "Too much! And I've never seen twin corpses before." Thepthong shouted, "He died just this afternoon, and his dreadful wife made such a performance she fell down dead too."

Khun Chang hissed, "It's me!" The two old ladies leapt about frantically and fell down on their backs. Siprajan's cloth slipped off except for the very end. The two grappled with each other noisily.

With a thought, Siprajan turned to take a closer look. "What's this? He doesn't have a pigtail." Thepthong shouted, "There in the middle at the crotch, that's a pigtail."[12]

Siprajan said, "The other one's Wanthong!" Thepthong said, "No, it's Mistress Ai-Bia. How come both husband and wife died? Why haven't they been cremated? Who brought them here?"

pigtail

---

12. Thepthong's words are taken from WK, 12:464; PD has: "Really? Isn't that a pigtail?"

Khun Chang shouted, "It's me!" The two ladies jumped wildly in fright, banging their heads on the wall. Covering their eyes with both hands, they started praying loudly. "Saithong, please help."

Saithong called, "What's up?" and rushed in, colliding with Siprajan and knocking her over. Siprajan said, "What are you shoving me for?"

Thepthong cried, "Help me too! Isn't that the Jek's corpse? Though the hemp rope is tied too messily for a shroud. Surely it can't be Wanthong and Khun Chang."

Saithong looked closer and beat her chest in shock. "Eh! Why are you lying there groaning, tied up without any clothes on?" Then she turned and said, "What is this?

Who told you it was Jek Khong? You're talking blind nonsense. You see a live person and bawl out it's a corpse." She felt ashamed for them and walked out.

Siprajan and Thepthong got down to look, and wanted to die of shame. "Why are you lying in here with your eyes shut? Did you let a robber strip off your clothes and wind you up in rope?"

The mothers of the pair frantically fetched a betelnut knife. "It may nick your flesh a bit." They severed the ropes, stripped them away,

and[13] cut the splints used for tightened the binding on the corpse but one hit them in the mouth, bringing tears to their eyes. The couple sprang apart. Khun Chang had only a handkerchief.

He tried to hide his rear, leaving the front bare. Thepthong cried, "Tcha, cover yourself!" Khun Chang rolled over on his stomach. Wanthong covered her face in disgust.

Siprajan picked up clothing to give her daughter. "How scandalous! I'm shamed." She said to Khun Chang, "Khun Phaen has come to make trouble.

He'll ask the king to have us executed. You and I face disaster. The property will be scattered. Just now he said,

if you're good, he'll look on you as a friend; but if you're obstinate, he'll kill you. You must go out there to wai him, ask for his pardon, and make him calm down.

Just don't be stubborn. Go along with what he wants so the case disappears. He's got a new wife close by his side. I don't think he's upset about Wanthong.

He's come here to complain that we acted highhandedly. Ask his forgiveness and I think it'll come to nothing. Just don't answer back. Go out there now."

---

13. These two stanzas down to "in disgust" are taken from WK, 12:465, absent from PD.

Khun Phaen, great master, seeing nobody had appeared, shouted a warning, "What's up? Why don't you come out to talk?

If you come nicely, nothing will happen. If you're too stubborn, I'll slice you up." Thepthong's eyes rolled up in their sockets. Siprajan shouted, "Khun Chang,

you're still lying here, you blinking abomination!" She shoved him in the side with her foot. Thepthong cried, "Get out there, you thinhead!" Khun Chang stiffened his body and shook his head.

Thepthong thumped him. "It's worse than trying to drag Jao Ngo,[14] damn you. You've no lowercloth and your belly's hanging out. You'll turn this house into a coffin, you villain."

Khun Chang pried open a chink in the wall and peered out. "Wanthong, please come out with me. Even if he's angry enough to kill someone, he'll soften up if you come."

Wanthong said, "Forget it! Even if Lord Indra comes down, I'm not going. I'm happy for him to strike me dead right here. Don't dream that I'll go out there."

Khun Chang said, "If you won't come, why should I go out to get killed? I don't want to die apart from you. Right or wrong, we should die looking at each other.

If we're slashed dead beside each other, we'll be born again beside each other in heaven." He jumped up with his eyes rolled up and hugged tight onto Wanthong. "I'm not going out there."

Thepthong and Siprajan were shaking with fear. "Tcha! *You* did this, you beggar! You've got nothing on, you villain." She seized a block of wood and bashed him in the midriff.

"Don't hit me! I'm going out. Why do you hurt me like this, Mother dear?" Khun Chang grabbed a cloth and wound it round his trembling body. Scared to distraction,

he hid behind the door and peered through the wall for a way to escape. Eyes screwed up with effort, he started to climb up the wall. Siprajan grabbed his foot, "Come down from there!"

Thepthong berated him, "You clown!" She grabbed the other foot and pulled him back down. His cloth slipped off but he hung onto the end. He picked up a lantern and went out with it on his head.

---

14. Jao Ngo is a character in the outer drama *Sangthong,* The Golden Conch (see p. 258, note 56). When the hero takes the form of a Ngo forest dweller, he acts as a buffoon, and has to be dragged to meet his bride who is a princess.

He raised his two hands to his forehead. "Please have some betel, dear Phlai." He prostrated on Khun Phaen's lap and raised Khun Phaen's foot onto his head. "I'm so happy,

Your Fragrant Excellency, Lord Kaeo. They said you were dead but you've came back! Your stock of merit was enough to bring victory. Your innards are as beautiful as lotus flowers."

He lifted Khun Phaen's lowercloth, made a grab, and begged to kiss. He stroked his hands here and there, and then rubbed them on his own head. "As fragrant as krajae!" People around shook with laughter.

Khun Phaen said, "Don't! Don't, Khun Chang!" He pushed him away and quickly drew his cloth closed. Khun Chang went on busily kissing and stroking. Thepthong and Siprajan looked away.

Khun Phaen, great romancer, ground his teeth in anger and disgust. "Hey, Khun Chang! What were you thinking, my friend? Phim Philalai here is my wife.

I was still away at war. I did not abandon her or sell her to you, yet you knocked down my house to build a replacement, said I was dead,

turned up at the house with some bones wrapped in cloth, and dug up a bo tree so it withered. You were bent on being her lover and husband. What were you thinking? Tell me."

The question made Khun Chang's scalp crawl. He embraced Khun Phaen with eyes closed, and said nothing.

Khun Phaen posed the question three times. Khun Chang did not answer. Khun Phaen's temper rose. "I'll ask Wanthong first.

What's up, my dear? I'm coming to find you. Why are you lying in the room hiding your face? When a guest comes, you should welcome him properly.

It's good manners among both rich and poor to offer the betel and pan tray, and give whatever you have for guests to eat, not discriminating between rich and poor.

Here there's no sight of any betel from dawn to dusk. My mouth's sour. All I can see is a lantern. Are you not coming out because you're ashamed to talk about something in front of others?"

In the room, Wanthong heard this furious summons. She was so miserable and resentful that she truly found it difficult to open her mouth to talk.

Terrified he would storm into the room, she darted forward to close the door tight shut, and shoot the bolt on the inside so even if he pushed it, the door would not even give way a little. She sat down, lost in fearful thoughts, heartsick almost to death.

"Aren't you coming out, Wanthong? Do you think I can't get in there? Have you bolted the door tight? Are you playing with me, Wanthong?

Or are you luring me into a secret place where you'll catch me and eat my liver? Life or death, I'm going in there, even if I end up crying for help."

He drew his sword and raised it aloft. Khun Chang embraced his feet, whimpering. Khun Phaen kicked him away. Khun Chang grabbed at Khun Phaen's cloth that slipped down.

Khun Phaen clutched at the waistband, and raised his sword to strike. Thepthong cried out plaintively. Siprajan stumbled on top of Granny Khong.[15] Khun Phaen bellowed,

"I'll kill you, both man and wife! Look out for yourselves, all four or five of you! Wanthong loves her room and won't leave it. She's afraid her fair face will lose its luster in the wind.

The name Wanthong[16] really suits you now. You're grade eight on the royal scale.[17] You're afraid if you speak, *jampa* flowers will pour out of your mouth.[18] You severed things completely on that day.

It was you who were rash. You went back on your word and wanted to cut me off. When I came to your house, I was still naïvely thinking how we were before.

My heart felt you still had some thoughts for me. I didn't know you'd ditched everything. When you cut a banana flower, it hangs on by a strand,[19] but for you, the memory was already faded and forgotten.

At the start, I believed you were a genuine ruby, but you turned out to be a paste gem. A crow disguised as a swan deceived me because I didn't look at the crest first.

You faked it so completely and cleverly, I was fooled by the camouflage and thought you really were a swan that loved the Mujalin land. But out of sight of

---

15. The name of the midwife from chapter 1. Probably this is a continuity error and should be Kloi or Sai.

16. See p. 224, note 2.

17. In the system for grading gold, grade eight meant one unit of gold was worth eight units of silver (KW, 670).

18. In an old folktale, whenever Nang Jampathong and Nang Phikunthong speak, golden *jampa* and *phikun* flowers spill from their respective mouths. This gave rise to a saying that someone who refuses to speak is afraid such flowers will appear from their mouth (KW, 670).

19. See p. 83, note 7.

mask play actor

the flock of swans, you played in the mud,
    and got covered in stinking filth. You swap heads
like an actor in a mask play. If the audience likes dancing, you arrange barrel drums. If they like bawdiness,
    you give them bawdiness.
        The time you spent in learning and rehearsal
    was not wasted. You're really proficient, stylish,
    unmatched—a tribute to your clever teachers.
When I was here, nobody came to give you a job.
    But now you have a new teacher who puts you to
    good use. In competition, everybody loses to you,
    and your name is mentioned everywhere. Before
    long they must come to ask you to dance,
        and will likely insist you dance all through, not
    taking off your headdress until nightfall. Today I
    came to find you to make a booking, and then go
    back to prepare the theatre.
        Stay well, Lady Hibiscus-behind-ear."[20] In anger,
he left immediately, mounted his horse, and led his
men through the forest back to Cockfight Hill in
Kanburi.

Now to tell of bald Khun Chang. He did not run away but stayed with his
mother-in-law, on the lookout for danger. After things had been quiet for
about a month,
    he respectfully took leave of his mother-in-law to go home. "If I stay too
long, elephants and horses will go astray, and money will go missing. I'm taking leave to go to my house."
    Khun Chang and Wanthong went to live happily as husband and wife in the
house in the middle of the compound, looking after his lands and property.

---

20. The Law on Marriage stated that if a man took a beggar woman or prostitute as his wife
and she was proved to have been unfaithful, the woman and her lover were to be punished by
being yoked to a plough to till the fields for three days with the woman wearing a straw star,
เฉลว, *chaleo*, on her forehead, a red hibiscus behind each ear, and a garland of red hibiscus round
her head. Those sentenced to death wore hibiscuses behind their ear while in procession to the
execution ground (KTS, 2:210; Anuman, *Essays*, 333–34).

This chapter will stop here and, before resuming, tell about the governor of Sukhothai[21] who had to remit revenue from fines to the treasury.[22]

He had sent a portion but still owed a balance of fifteen tamlueng and so was suffering as a prisoner in the guardhouse.[23] He talked with his daughter, "My precious Kaeo Kiriya,[24] please save your father's back."[25]

She willingly consented. "Who will you sell me to, dear father?"[26] He replied, "The son of my friend in Suphan."

The governor bailed himself out and took his daughter to meet Khun Chang. Seeing their gloom, Khun Chang asked, "What's the matter? Why have you come, along with your daughter?"

The governor said, "I must deliver the fines revenue and I don't have enough. This is a big matter that has made me suffer. I've brought my daughter to mortgage to you.

You're a son of my friend and like a son to me. Please help. I need fifteen tamlueng immediately. I'll write a deed for you to keep."[27]

Khun Chang called to Wanthong, "Bring money, count it, and hand it over. There's no need for a deed. I'll look after her like my own sister from the same womb."

The governor took leave of both of them. "I leave this young lady in the care of you two. If she does anything wrong, please be kind. Stay well, Kaeo Kiriya.

Be their humble servant. Pay careful attention to your duties. Help them to protect their property. Avoid trouble and don't get yourself tainted.

---

21. The center of a Thai kingdom in the thirteenth and fourteenth centuries, Sukhothai became one of the "northern cities" subject to Ayutthaya and declined in importance, probably because of a shift in the course of the Yom River. In the Three Seals Law, it is listed as a second-class town, and its governor titled as Okya (Phraya) Sithammasukarat, *sakdina* 10,000 (KTS, 1:320).

22. Many officials, especially in the provinces, were expected to support themselves by taking a share of the money they collected on behalf of government, including taxes and fines imposed by the courts.

23. The original has no unit of currency here but Kaeo Kiriya specifies fifteen tamlueng in chapter 38 when she is relating the story to her son. A tamlueng was equivalent to four baht, or one twentieth of a chang.

24. แก้วกิริยา, "fine manners."

25. Meaning saving him from punishment with the rattan or lash.

26. Selling oneself or a dependent into slavery was a common form of raising money. A household head had the legal right to sell himself, his wives, or his children. The law required that the sale contract should be recorded in writing. The slave could redeem himself or herself, or be redeemed, by payment of the original sale amount. The contract usually identified a guarantor who would be liable for the same amount if the slave fled. (See the Law on Slavery in KTS, 2:285–343; several subsidiary laws in KTS, 5; and Lingat, *L'Esclavage privé*)

27. กรมธรรม์, *krommathan*, a document required under the Law on Slavery (KTS, 2:288–96).

As a servant, don't let your clothes smell of sweat. Be polite, humble, and likable. Don't sleep late. Fear your master. Prepare his rice, water, vegetables, and fish.

Losing money is better than losing your dignity.[28] Don't associate with those lower than yourself. Maintain your status, treasure your rank, avoid shame. In three months, I'll return."

Kaeo Kiriya listened to her father's advice, prostrated to wai him, and sadly said, "Don't let me stay here too long after you've gone. Come in three months, Father."

The governor of Sukhothai left his daughter, but being very attached to her, could not avoid thinking of her and quickly went to Ayutthaya to pay the balance due.

---

28. One of the proverbs in the collection known as the "Sayings of Phra Ruang" (Gerini, "On Siamese Proverbs," 195).

15: KHUN PHAEN IS PARTED FROM LAOTHONG

Now to tell of the king, ruler of the world, to whom every country from both north and south submitted, who resided in his golden-spired palace of victory, where inner consorts prostrated and bowed with clasped hands,

rendering the royal pleasure complete. Towards afternoon, as the sun descended and softened, His Majesty walked out to the jeweled audience hall, handsomely attired and arrayed in superlative regalia.

He pronounced upon affairs of state, with nothing to disturb the royal humor. Turning his face to look for the astute Phramuen Si, he spoke.

palace ladies prostrating

"That Phlai Kaeo who took the Lao territory, returned safely, and was made Khun Phaen, is brave, daring, and still young. If he's put to work, it'll pay off in time.

But right now he's sent to patrol the forests. We've never had him come to serve at court. If we leave him there for too long, he'll not get to know the work of the capital.

He doesn't have any relatives but you're good at training people, Phramuen Si. Bring Phaen to serve in the corps of pages, and I'll entrust him to your care as his teacher.

Also that Khun Chang from Suphan, the one with a bald skull like a Jek. His father came to present him when he was still only a child.[1]

Let me place him with you too. Train them and see how they turn out. Send to Kanburi and Suphan to have them both brought here immediately."

Jek

---

1. In chapter 1.

Phramuen Si took the order, crawled back out, and told a department head to arrange a group of palace guards to go forthwith.

They arrived at Cockfight Hill, entered the house, and informed Khun Phaen, "His Majesty the King has ordered you to the city

to be trained on royal service in the palace." Khun Phaen was very happy to hear this, and went to tell his mother. "I'm taking leave to go to the city tomorrow morning,

on the orders of King Phanwasa, to attend at court to be trained on royal service of various kinds. Let me leave Laothong in your care, Mother.

When I'm settled in a house, I'll come to fetch you so we can be together. Meanwhile the city is not far away so I can go back and forth. I won't abandon you."

Thong Prasi was so happy at her son's news that she wept freely, and patted him lovingly.

"Go, and don't worry about your wife. Leave her here and I'll look after her and make sure nothing bothers her.

Put your heart into training for royal service.[2] Make an effort to put up with sourness now so you can taste sweetness later. If you do well, you'll get rank to show for it, and that will repay the debt of gratitude to Khun Krai, your father.

But it's very hard to be accomplished at royal service. In the old days, they laid down four qualities for a king's servant.

First, he must be gentlefolk with lineage, and have proper manners, showing his gentility. Second, he must study and gain knowledge as the basis for supporting himself.

Third, he must be of mature age, and understand all his responsibilities. Fourth, he must be quick-witted to distinguish good from bad in the course of his work.

They say servants of the dust beneath the royal foot must have all four qualities. You seem to have them all and are suitable to come under the royal grace.

But don't be too sure of yourself and carelessly do something rash that won't escape the royal wrath. Remember your mother's words, dear Phlai Kaeo.

There's an old saying that servants of the king have to study diligently the principles laid down in manuals that have long existed from the past.

---

2. This whole passage of instruction is missing from the Wat Ko version, meaning it was probably inserted in the mid-nineteenth century when several manuals of proper behavior were composed.

One, whatever knowledge and capability you have, don't hide it from the king but let him know everything. Two, be courageous in any task and determined to bring it to its proper conclusion.

Three, don't neglect any royal duty, and always study deeply what is right or wrong. Four, be honest, reliable, and ethical, as if following the precepts faithfully.

Five, adopt a modest attitude and don't stray into boastful arrogance and overconfidence. Six, when close to the king, do not abuse his graciousness by acting as his equal.

Seven, don't sit on the throne, as that is an act of great wickedness and villainy. Eight, when at court, pay attention to the business at hand, and don't be more close or distant than is appropriate to the matter.

Nine, don't meddle, flirt, or fall in love with any palace woman. Ten, show love and loyalty to your royal master, and even if he is angry, bear it and never answer back.

These are the ten principles of royal service which you must commit to memory. Keeping your word is the most important of all. You must be dedicated, Phaen of mine.

Go well, win success, and overcome all obstacles so you gain royal favor to be raised to the rank of phraya."

She left the room and summoned servants. "Khun Phaen will take Ai-Tao and Ai-Ma along with him."

Khun Phaen took his mother's blessing then went to Laothong. Finding her forlorn, he stroked her back and consoled her over his departure. "Why keep on crying?

My leaving doesn't mean I'm abandoning you. Whenever I'm free, I'll come home to be with you." He comforted her and asked her to prepare things for going away.

At dawn, Khun Phaen and the guard left the house together and went straight to Khun Chang's house in Suphan.

When Khun Chang saw Khun Phaen coming, he jumped up and slammed the door shut. Going inside, he lay down hugging a pillow, and said tremulously to Wanthong,

"Khun Phaen is coming up to the house, bringing lots of guards with him. Why? I think a court case is going to flare up. Would he have come without the king's orders?"

Wanthong was flustered and very afraid. "Oh dear! What can I do? Where can I hide my face?

If word spreads, it'll become a big issue like licking fire. But if enough money is spent, there won't be trouble. I fear being arrested and taken to court, which would be bothersome. What do you think, your lordship?"

"Truly, this is our karma, Wanthong. If he brings charges, then it'll be complicated. I don't care how much money it takes, I beg only that I can keep you.

If it were only me, I'd face up to the royal law court but my concern for you makes me downhearted." In tears, he embraced Wanthong and fell into a funk, moaning and groaning.

The guard cried out, "Hey, you rogue elephant! Have you gone to sleep inside there? We're calling and calling but there's no reply. Are you going to remain stubbornly lying in there?

We have the king's orders to fetch you. You can say whatever you like but let's go today, in time. If you delay, we'll drag you off."

Khun Chang trembled in terror, dripping with sweat. In reply, he called out, "I can't even sit up, my dear sir.

The doctor says it's a severe fever[3] and I'll die this afternoon. Just now, I couldn't move. Don't bother me, I beg you."

The guard said, "Just now I saw you sitting there, but you closed the door and hid. You're lying. If you don't come out, we're coming in to get you."

In fright, Khun Chang nudged Wanthong, "Bolt the door, my dear wife!" She walked across on shaking legs, and shot the bolt in time.

Khun Phaen and the guard rushed up to shove the door but found it would not open. Realizing it was bolted, Khun Phaen

blew a Great Loosener formula, and the bolt sprung as if someone had pulled it. They crowded into the bedroom. Khun Chang picked up a pillow, and adopted the pose of a *yak*,

swaying his body, rolling his head, and saying, "A spirit has possessed me. I'm the Lord of Phrapradaeng[4]

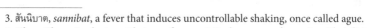

yak

---

3. สันนิบาต, *sannibat*, a fever that induces uncontrollable shaking, once called ague.

4. Khun Chang is playing at being a fierce spirit. ประแดง, *pradaeng*, is a Thai distortion of *kamraten(g)*, a Khmer term for a "big person" meaning a king or noble, and is used in Thai for powerful spirits. The Lord of Phrapadaeng was a famous spirit in the lower Chaophraya River. In the 1510s, during dredging work, "The images of two guardian spirits, cast in a gold alloy,

from a broken wall."⁵ He rolled his eyes, stuck out his neck, waggled his head to and fro, and cackled with laughter. "Do you know me or not, officer?"

The guard shouted, "Khun Chang, you clown around too much, damn you." Khun Chang jumped up and down. "If you insult and threaten me, I'll break your necks!

Where do you mob come from? Do you have the temerity not to fear me?" He raised an eyebrow, blinked his eyes, and scowled. "If you make fun of me, you'll get what you deserve!"

Khun Phaen was scorched with anger and truly wanted to kill Khun Chang. He was angry at Wanthong too. "The despicable scourge! If I had a sword, I'd cut her in half."

He pretended to take fright that the spirit possessing Khun Chang would break his neck. He danced up and down, deliberately treading on a curtain, and ripping it in two when it fell. He kicked Wanthong who tumbled

flat on her face, doubled over and winded. She clutched her stomach, unable to get up. Khun Chang shook with fear. He hugged his wife saying, "Karma, karma."

The guard said, "So the spirit possessing you has gone already? Why didn't it stay all day? Is it a forest fever that's making you mad and sunken-eyed, or

---

were dug up at the spot where Samrong Canal and the Thap Nang Canal come together. One of the images was inscribed with the name of Lord of the Hundred Thousand Eyes (พระยาแสนตา), and the other with the name of the Lord Holding a Conch Shell (พระบาทสังขกร). So the King had offerings made to them and then they were taken out of the canal, a building was erected, and they were enshrined at Phra Pradaeng" (RCA, 19). Since that time, the area around the mouth of the Samrong Canal has been called Phrapadaeng. The images were carted away by a Khmer naval invasion in 1575 (RCA, 79) but the shrine remained. Phraya Trang described the shrine in *Nirat thalang*, written in 1809: "At the shrine to the fearful Lord Phra Pradaeng / I felt greatly afraid of the Lord Phra Pradaeng / on the shrine was the head of a crocodile / all except for Indra would pass this stretch with their heads down / the Lord of Phra Pradaeng is so fierce" (*Nirat thalang*). The poem specifies the location of the shrine between Chong Nonsi and the Phrakhanong Canal, hence around today's Khlong Toei port. In his memoirs, Prince Damrong (b. 1862) recalled, "When I was a child, I saw the spirit possession rites, that were secretly performed inside the royal palace several times. During that time, there were three widely regarded spirit lords, namely, *jao pho ho klong* (the lord father of the drum hall), *jao pho nu phuk* (the lord father of the white mouse), and *jao pho phra pradaeng*" (Damrong, *Khwam songjam*, 158).

In the Bangkok Fifth Reign, the name Phrapadaeng was transferred to a provincial headquarters 12 kms to the south. In 1946, this town was renamed as Samut Prakan, and Phrapradaeng became the name of a district. The fate of the shrine is unknown.

5. กำแพงหัก, *kamphaeng hak*, "broken wall." In the past, earthenware tablets with several rows of small Buddha images were sometimes used as decoration in wat. Later these images were rescued from ruined wat and made into amulets known as "broken-wall amulets."

is some internal disorder giving you the shakes?

We came today on the king's orders to fetch you forthwith because your father presented you at court but you haven't yet been employed on royal service.

You're to be taken for training. Now, why are you so worked up, and why are you putting on this chaotic act of being possessed, and acting like a monster or demon to deceive us?"

Hearing he was not being taken to a law court, Khun Chang breathed easily and calmed down. "If I'd known from the start there'd be no trouble, why would the spirit lord have possessed me?

I'm not one little bit lazy at the prospect of entering royal service." He promptly ordered Wanthong to call the servants and phrai to go down from the house.

Khun Phaen, Khun Chang, and the guard cut through the forest to Ayutthaya and went straight to find Phramuen Si.

Phramuen Si Saowarak greeted them and said, "His Majesty the King has ordered me to train you both.

Anyone who does royal service for a long time and with dedication is rewarded." Khun Chang quickly said, "I'm stumped. I don't know anything about royal service.[6]

I'm only used to shouting at buffaloes in the fields. I'm not acquainted with any royalty. I know only how to play humming sticks.[7] How does one go on all fours in court, sir?"

Phramuen Si cackled with laughter. "If all you're good at is raising buffaloes,

6. Chapter 8 states, "Khun Chang had been a page at court since childhood and was fluent at talking with royalty." Perhaps Khun Chang is playing around. More likely, this episode is a late addition to KCKP and not well integrated to other parts of the story.

7. ไม้หึ่ง, mai hueng, a children's game played between two teams of three to ten persons, especially at Songkran or other festivals. A short stick is placed over a hole in the ground. One player uses a longer stick to flick the short stick into the air, and then places the longer stick over the hole. If the opposing team can catch the short stick before it lands, or throw it to hit the long stick, the player is out. If not, the player then throws the short stick into the air and hits it with the longer stick, and the fielders again try to get him out by catching or throwing. If they fail, the player faces away from the fielders and hits the short stick over his head. When one team is all out, the members of the winning team take turns at trying to keep the small stick in the air as long as possible, counting the number of taps with the long stick. The short stick is then hit with the long stick, picked up and hit again, with each winning player having as many hits as he/she was able to keep the short stick in the air. Finally, each losing player has to run back over this distance, humming loudly and continuously (SWC, 11:5311–13).

you're going to be a big problem, you abomination. Just don't cause trouble and it'll be alright.

You won't be put to work immediately. You'll have time to learn." They began training together every day.

Khun Phaen was dedicated and easy to teach. Khun Chang was quite hopeless. He crawled into audience like a field turtle. It was many days before he could go on duty.

playing humming sticks

The other pages laughed and nicknamed him the wat mendicant. But after long practice he gradually became accomplished, and both went on duty together.

One day, Khun Phet and Khun Raminthra[8] called at the learned Phramuen Si's house to dine and drink liquor.

Along with Khun Phaen and Khun Chang, there were five of them. They drank until they were all drunk with eyes glazed over, and then poured more liquor with salt to take an oath

to be loyal to one another at all times. They sat around, drunkenly shooting their mouths off, until the liquor was finished, when each went merrily home.

Now to tell of the beautiful Laothong. While living with her beloved husband's mother, she collapsed with fever and was at death's door for several days. Doctors were summoned to give her medicines,

but to no effect. Thong Prasi tended her as best she could. She also prayed anxiously and made many propitiatory offerings but these did no more than keep death at bay.

So Thong Prasi sent off a servant. "Make sure you find Khun Phaen and tell him quickly." The servant raised his hands in wai, and descended from the house.

---

8. Officials of the guard under Mahatthai but not found in the listing in the Three Seals Law. The titles were later used by the police department. Raminthra Road in Bangkok is named after a director-general of the police department who owned the land on which the road was built (Prachak, *Prapheni*, 200; KP, 132).

Arriving at Phramuen Si's house where Khun Phaen was staying, Ai-U promptly sought his master out and told him everything.

The servant's news made Khun Phaen very concerned about Laothong's fever, but he kept himself calm and examined the horoscope down to the minute.

"On Saturday in the morning at the time of the moon,[9] the fever will be almost fatal. But fevers at a moon time are predicted to abate. The place where the messenger sat is not bad.[10]

In addition, the Iron Spear[11] is wrong, and Rahu is moving above the arrow, indicating a quick recovery.[12] The manual indicates she will not die but I know my eye's jewel will be distraught.

Because her husband is far away, she'll be gloomy and the fever will overwhelm her. Even the treatment of ten doctors will not be the same as just seeing her husband's face.

As I'm on duty today, I must first find someone to take my place." He anxiously got up and went to sit beside Khun Chang, loosing a big sigh.

"My buddy, a servant has come to tell me that my wife is suffering from a high fever.[13] Can I ask you to take care of all my royal duties?

I'll be grateful to you far into the future until my dying day. We're gentlemen and friends to each other. If you need to go somewhere, you can always ask me."

Khun Chang replied, "No problem. I can easily take your place. Go off as you wish and don't be worried." Khun Phaen left with his servants, wrapped a *thompak*[14] haphazardly round his belly, and rushing through the

---

9. Time can be counted in ยาม, *yam* of one and a half hours each, with night and day sequences beginning at six o'clock, and the *yam* named after heavenly bodies. Moon is the fourth in sequence in the morning, running from 10:30 a.m. to noon.

10. When Ai-U delivered the news about Laothong, the position where he was sitting was not inauspicious according to some system of divination.

11. See p. 100, note 21.

12. Each day is ruled by one of the nine planets, เคราะห์, *khro*, of the Thai astrological systems. Saturdays and Wednesdays are split, with one planet ruling in the morning, and another in the afternoon. As a result, these are believed to be days on which large changes are likely. On Saturday, Ketu rules in the morning, and Rahu in the afternoon. Ketu is a gentle, passive influence, and possibly not powerful enough to combat the illness. Rahu, however, is powerful and aggressive. Often Rahu's impact is malevolent but his aggression is favorable for warriors and those using lore.

13. ไข้เหนือ, *khai nuea*, northern fever, malaria (KW, 671).

14. ถมปัก, an alternative spelling of *sompak*, the formal lower cloth for attendance at court. This is not appropriate wear for travel, but he is in such a rush that he leaves without changing.

forest to Cockfight Hill.[15] Going up into the house,

he prostrated at his mother's feet. She told him, "Your wife's back there with fever. I've tended her, called the doctors, and offered prayers, but the sickness has not eased, and I'm losing heart."

Khun Phaen went in to find Laothong. "Don't be sad. I've come. Your fragrant flesh is wasting away. Can you eat something or nothing at all?

When one of the servants came to tell me, I rushed here. I wasn't neglecting you." With her husband's attention, Laothong felt a little better. She raised her face, showing her fair cheeks. "I've taken nothing but medicine.

I've been at the point of death countless times but hung on patiently waiting for you. If you'd delayed your return a few more days, I'd have stopped taking those bitter medicines.

Seeing your face I feel the fever has retreated, even more than if Lord Indra had come to be my doctor." Khun Phaen rocked with laughter, hugged her, and begged her to take her medicine.

He tended her for many days. The fever quickly disappeared, and her health gradually improved. Khun Phaen pondered that he should return to Ayutthaya on the following day.

That night he slept with the lovely Laothong, and both tasted bliss with no thought of what the future held in store.

❦

Now to tell of the king, ruler of the world. He went out to the front to preside serenely over the audience of his senior officials.

On seeing Khun Chang, he asked, "Where's Khun Phaen? Isn't he on duty with you? This fellow usually does his work properly."

The past entered Khun Chang's thoughts like a raging fire. "Khun Phaen harbors resentment and in the long term he'll probably bring a case against me, if he can,

to take Wanthong from my side. He intends to destroy me. Well, I'll slaughter him like snake venom, have him demolished in an instant like chopped fish."

With this thought, he raised his neck and said, "My liege, I can tell no lie. We had been on duty together for many days, and I heard him moaning about his wife every day.

Yesterday, he said he would go home. Your humble servant advised him against such a rash move but he just complained, cursed, and threatened me.

---

15. On foot, the journey of about 160 kms by modern roads would take at least three days.

Then late, around the end of the third watch,

Khun Phaen climbed over the palace wall, an exceedingly insolent and uncouth act. I berated him but he threatened to kill me. I think he went to his wife's house."

palace wall

The king, ruler of the world, was enraged at hearing this. He stamped the royal foot and bellowed, "This fellow turns out to fear nobody.

Khun Chang reprimanded him, but he arrogantly dared to climb out over the walls. He is condemned to execution.[16] Skewer his head on a pole as an example to others!

But let me ponder a little. He's gained royal favor. Otherwise he would be put to death. But why can't he bear to be apart from his wife? Did she float down from heaven and make him forget he should be fearful?

Heigh! Ratchamat,[17] go right now and bring this Laothong away from her husband. I don't want to see Khun Phaen. He did wrong, and must stay in Kanburi.

Let him take phrai to patrol the frontier. If Ayutthaya should be embroiled in a war, he can be called back to royal service to fight. Go quickly within tonight!"

---

16. The Palatine Law, clause 66, lays down: "For kicking the palace wall, sever the foot. For pushing the palace gate with one's own hand, twenty strokes of the cane. For climbing the outer palace wall, sever the foot. For climbing the inner palace wall, execution" (KTS, 1:98).

17. ราชามาตย์, a deputy in the left division of the guard under Kalahom, *sakdina* 800 (KTS, 1:284).

Ratchamat took the royal order and assembled a group of the palace guard. They mounted horses and left the capital in the night.

᭣

Now to tell of the beautiful Laothong who had gradually recovered from the fever that had laid her low. That night she lay close beside her husband, bathed in joy until falling asleep on the bed.

She dreamed a big monster entered the room, tied her up, dragged her from the pillow, put her in an iron cage, and made her suffer greatly all year round.

In the dream, her husband came after her but fell into a mountainous ravine and also faced enormous hardship. Then a man of great power

came and carried both Laothong and Khun Phaen in his arms out of the land of the monsters. At the end of the dream, she woke in fright and aroused her husband to interpret it.

Khun Phaen, great romancer, sat pondering to himself over Laothong's dream. "Eh, both auspiciousness and evil are coming at the same time. Tomorrow, there'll be danger.

Laothong and I must be parted, and some huge problem will arise. In the long term, someone will bring us back together and events will turn out happily.

I should warn her but I fear it'll make her sad." So he covered up and spoke reassuringly, "This dream is neither good nor bad.

Because of your fever, the elements[18] in your body are unstable, so the dream is confused and meaningless." He distracted his beloved wife by talking about something more cheerful.

When the sun's chariot rose in the sky, brightening the earth with golden light, the calls of coels echoed through the forest, and cicadas trilled in their nests without a break.

Fragrance wafted on the breeze. Bees swarmed and buzzed. Khun Phaen nudged Laothong to listen but the sounds were eerily lonely.

jingjok

Mice clacked.[19] *Jingjok* chattered. Spiders beat

---

18. ธาตุ, *that*, the four elements or humors—earth, water, air, and wind—that control the state of the body.

19. There were manuals of prediction based on the calls of mice. "If the mouse calls *kuk-kuk*, good fortune; *si-si*, a death; *khik-khik*, siblings will fight; *khuk-khuk*, an argument; *khit-khit*, good fortune" (quoted in Prachak, *Prapheni*, 116–18).

their chests incessantly.[20] He knew these strange sounds foretold something unusual.

At dawn, the palace guards arrived, dismounted, and came towards the house with sullen faces. Seeing them, Khun Phaen felt as if someone had plucked the life from his body.

There were crowds of them but he steeled himself to go out and meet them. "What business brings you here, sir? Is there some trouble or war?"

In reply, Ratchamat informed Khun Phaen in full detail. "At audience, Khun Chang told the king that you had climbed out over the wall.

Khun Chang said he tried to stop you but you threatened to chop him dead. This is a capital offense but the king has been merciful because you took Chiang Thong.

You're banned from the palace, and we're under orders to remove your wife from the house. Your arrogance alone is the cause of all this. We'll take your wife away with us."

Khun Phaen's heart shuddered and he felt feverishly cold. Going inside, he lay down on the bed with a sigh.

Covering his face with his left hand, he embraced Laothong with the right. "Oh pity, pity! We're going to be parted just as if someone had cut us in two with a sword. Khun Chang has killed me this time.

When I left, I asked him to take care of my duty but he spoke to the king very cleverly. I had no inkling of the offense. I feel as if I'm trapped in a forest,

like a bird flying in the sky that carelessly gets blown off course and seeks shelter, but is forced by the gale to fly down straight into a menacing snare.

I thought it was a branch not a snare, got my feet caught, and am now squirming helplessly until death. The king angrily condemned me to die but I've escaped because I had something in my favor from the past.

He reprieved me and will only take you away. Oh, where will I see your face again, dead or alive? I'm in despair and desolation to be distant from you, my eye's jewel."

Laothong felt her breast had been slit in two by a sharp kris. Sobs escaped from her mouth and tears flooded her eyes. "You have possessed me for less than a year.

To leave you is like falling from a golden mountain and rolling along, dead and broken, bones cold as ash. Nowhere under the sun can I escape sorrow.

During the waning month, I'll wane like the moon. When it waxes, my con-

---

20. See p. 22, note 9.

fusion and sadness will increase. Until the end of the savage[21] Kaliyuga, I'll be struggling against a sadness that never subsides.

Oh, what karma made this happen? You two are bent relentlessly on revenge. Even if a war broke out and you were killed, the feeling would not ebb away.

I'm saddened that some karma made you forget your quarrel with that man. He'd done you wrong before but you were too complacent and didn't see the crooked kris in his heart.

He'd already grabbed Wanthong, destroyed a bridal house, and stolen everything. He's like a scorpion whose curved tail shows he's wild and never straight.

Yet you still trusted him, giving him the opportunity to fulfill his desires. You saw a clear path and wandered off into the forest, only realizing it was the wrong way after you were lost.

You're cornered now as a result of your trust, and I have to be parted from you." She wept from a broken heart, flailing about until she swooned away in the middle of the room.

Khun Phaen turned to console her. "We'll be far apart, my jewel. Leave me well, even though my coming is the reason we're being parted.

My love for you has dragged our love to disaster, as if I'd thrown you away in a great ocean. Oh, this is the result of some karma we've made. I'll cry until blood spurts from my eyes.

Your breast, my breast will swell and collapse, but nobody will see how we feel inside. Look after yourself all the time. Do no more bad deeds,

and through the merit we've made in the past, there should come a day we overcome this misfortune. Recalling good memories will help you endure until this karma eases.

If any senior noble wants you as servant, you must consent, ingratiate yourself, and be deferential. Take care over what you say. Always be true to your word.

Don't be too sad. The palace guards are impatient to leave. Get your things ready and don't take long." The pair of them went to see his mother,

and prostrated at her feet with tears flowing. "The king has ordered me to be parted from Laothong. This matter has blown up like a fire, and Khun Chang is behind it.

---

21. มิคสัญญี, *mikhasanyi*. RI (860) glosses the word as an age of conflict and warfare, but more likely it is an adjective qualifying Kaliyuga, combining the Pali *miccha* and Thai *sanyi*, meaning a time when people act like animals. According to the texts, at the end of the Kaliuga, people will have lifespans of ten years, lose the ability to speak human languages, fight over food, and have no capacity for conceptual thinking.

Laothong has to go and stay in the palace." He told his mother all the details. Laothong wept and wept. "Since I had to leave Chomthong[22]

and be far away from my parents, I've depended on you. Your generosity has made me happy since the first day I came. I hope I can repay your kindness.

When I was sick with fever, you nursed me morning and night, took the trouble to give me medicine, fed me morsels of food and water, and helped me to recover.

How can I repay you? We'll be far apart, not knowing whether each other is dead or alive, each with her own life and problems. Will I ever see you again?"

Thong Prasi felt so sorry for her that sad tears streamed down in an endless torrent. "Tcha! Karma is truly dragging you off. Where will I find someone like Laothong.

You absorb everything I teach you, and never grumble. But now you'll disappear from every room of this house." She hugged Laothong sadly in floods of tears. "I'd hoped you'd look after my cremation,

but now you're leaving and that won't be. You'll be far away and out of sight. After several months have passed, if it's permitted, please come to see me some time to raise my spirits."

She counted out three chang for Laothong to take. "When it's finished, send for more. I-Si and I-Sa, also the elders, Nang Wiang and Nang Wan,

go along the five of you and make sure you get on well together." She went out to speak with the guard. "Sir, please be kind.

She's only a forest Lao. She doesn't know about things. If she makes a mistake, please just put her right." The officer replied, "No problem. Khun Phaen and I are friends.

You stay here but she can't delay." He went off. Laothong prostrated to take leave of her mother-in-law, then turned sobbing to take leave of her husband.

The more she put on a brave face, the more her heart was in turmoil, as if the ground under her feet would collapse away. Khun Phaen was devastated. Laothong sobbed sadly.

"I feel sorrow for myself, sorrow for you, sorrow for the house, sorrow for your sobbing mother, sorrow for this garden and its fragrant flowers, sorrow for the servants, sorrow for us all."

Khun Phaen said sadly, "I feel sorrow for you, sorrow for our room, sorrow for the bedding and pillows where we sleep." He watched her until she disappeared into the forest, then went into the room and lay weeping on the bed.

---

22. The text says Chiang Thong, perhaps a copyist's slip.

Along the way, Laothong sobbed unstoppably on the elephant's back. They reached Ayutthaya in two days and one night. The servants promptly returned home with the elephants.

The officers entered the palace with Laothong following behind. She was presented to the king who turned to observe her.

"Is this her, Khun Phaen's wife? Trim, curvy waist, attractive face, good complexion, nice chin and eyebrows, good-looking. She wanted to stick beside one of my lads.

Was it for this that Khun Phaen neglected his work and couldn't be stopped from climbing over the wall?" "Head governess,[23] keep an eye on the gates to make sure she doesn't leave the palace.

Put her to work embroidering silk." The head governess took the order. Laothong was billeted in a swordstore beside the treasury. She sat embroidering every day,

and grieved for her husband morning and night. She concentrated on her work, ingratiated herself with all the palace governesses, and was intent on acting modestly and avoiding punishment.

palace ladies embroidering

---

23. เจ้าขรัวนาย, *jao khrua nai*; this is Thao Worajan, the head royal governess, *thi somdet phra phi liang, sakdina* 1,000, head of the administration of the inner palace. Often this position was occupied by a former consort of a prior king (KTS, 1:221; KW, 444).

16: KHUN PHAEN FORGES A SWORD, BUYS A HORSE, FINDS A SPIRIT SON

Now to tell of Khun Phaen, great romancer, whose famed mastery made heads bow and tremble in every city, as much in awe of him as of a fierce lion.

While asleep in his bed at midnight, he started awake with an unsettled heart. He had been sleeping alone for many days and felt randy thinking of his wife.

"What a pity that Khun Chang separated us! He was intent on plucking my heart away. He had sworn friendship yet treacherously wronged me over my wife.

Not content with that, he led the king to believe that I'd climbed over the city wall. Now my fortune's bad because karma caused the king to forego making proper inquiries.

He became enraged and found me guilty. Laothong was detained in the palace. I'm forbidden to attend court, barred from entering the palace, and condemned to patrol the forest.

The more I think about this, the more I'm losing my mind. This accursed Khun Chang can do all of this! If I can't repay him to my satisfaction, it'd be better to die than continue living.

I'll go and kidnap my Wanthong. If Khun Chang comes after me, I'll kill him. The only thing I fear is that the king will send troops after me.

If they show no mercy, I'll be slashed dead. How can I protect myself? If I make a mistake and I'm on my own, I may be crushed to dust.

In the forest there'll be no one to rely on, only my spirits and spirit dummies,[1] and they're getting old and losing their powers. They probably can't put up as good a fight as I expect.

I'll forge a sword, buy a horse, and find a spirit son[2] to give me the expertise

---

1. หุ่นผี, *hun phi*, some material molded into human shape and then enchanted so that a spirit resides in it. Often these are doll-like creations that people carry on their body as protection. Later in the story, Khun Phaen creates armies of such figures from grass (KW, 130–31).

2. กุมาร, *kuman*, from Sanskrit *kumar* meaning son or prince, and here meaning a spirit son. The spirits of infants that die in the womb are believed to be specially potent, perhaps because they contain all the energy of the unlived life. The most common form of these infant spirits is ลูกกรอก, *luk krok*, a stillborn baby, small and not fully developed, dried and kept as power-

and knowledge to overcome my enemies. If I can find these three things to my satisfaction, whatever commotion arises, I won't be afraid."

This thought made him seethe with excitement. In the murky light just before dawn, he washed his face, looked over all his personal equipment, and called in old Ta-Bua.

Karen

"I'm going to the forest frontier on royal duty. As the senior, you'll be in charge of the house. I'm going alone and I don't know how long I'll be away."

He gave orders to pack his kit in a side-bag, and thirty pieces of silver[3] in a waist pouch. He stuck a kris enchanted by a teacher in his belt, and left at dawn for the upland forests.

In search of what he needed, he delved into every nook and cranny, passing through villages of Karen, Kha, Lawa, and Mon,[4] and sleeping along passes through the mountains.[5]

In preparation for forging a sword for subduing his enemies,[6] he gave thought to finding the correct metals according to the great manual on weaponry.[7]

---

ful protective charm, nurtured or enchanted so it will love and hence protect its master (YS, 521–24; KP, 141–42).

3. The unit is not given but is probably tamlueng, making this equivalent to 120 baht (KW, 134; KP, 137).

4. Karen is a general name for several related ethnic groups that live along the hills that separate Thailand from Burma. Kha is a homophone of a word for servant, and is a pejorative term applied to many non-Thai groups. Lawa is the name of a Mon-Khmer ethnic group but the term is also used more generally to refer to non-Thai peoples in general. Strung together like this, these four words become a catchall term for the various non-Thai groups who live in the hills on the western edge of Siam.

5. The sequence here follows the WK text—sword, spirit son, horse—with the sword and horse sections taken from PD and the spirit son section from WK. The alternative PD version of the spirit son story (Buakhli), the WK version of the sword story, and Khru Jaeng's alternative version of the horse story are in the *Companion* volume.

6. The procedure for creating Khun Phaen's sword follows in basic outline the method for making a *mit mo*, adept's knife, which has the following stages according to one manual. 1) Collection of various metals including fitments from a palace, city gate, battlement, coffin, and stupa. 2) Smelting together using various different auspicious woods to make the fire, and chanting formulas. 3) Inscribing the blade with letters and yantra. 4) Filling the handle with various powerful substances. 5) A final set of rituals to sacralize (YS, 764–65).

7. The metals listed below mostly imply some kind of special power or protective ability.

Metal from the peaks of a relic stupa, a palace, and a gateway.[8] Metal fastening for the corpse of a woman who died while with child.[9] Metal binding from a used coffin.[10] Fixing for a gable board.[11] Diamond bolt.[12]

Bronze pike. Copper kris. Broken regal sword. Metal goad.[13] Bolt from a gateway.[14] Mushroom nail.[15] Five-colored smart metal.[16] Household metal.[17] All genuine articles. Fluid metal.[18] Ore cast at the

elephant goad and mushroom nail

peak of a stupa

Several come from the highest point of sacred places. Some have been through rituals that instill power. Some are associated with gates or fastenings that are difficult to undo, implying protection. The two mines mentioned are the sources of metal for making royal swords. "Fluid metal" is used to make protective amulets.

8. The highest point of a *prasat* is the นภศูล, *nopphasun*, "hollow spear of the sky," a finial. See the Wiset Chaisi Gate of the Bangkok Grand Palace as an example of a peaked gateway (KW, 147). These three metals would obviously be very rare and difficult to come by. In addition, they have special power, coming as they do from the highest point of buildings with sacred power.

9. เหล็กขนัน, *lek khanan*, a nail or other fastening, enchanted by an adept before being used to close a coffin, as a means to prevent the spirit from escaping to haunt or disturb people.

10. เหล็กตรึงโลง, *lek trueng long*, literally "metal to tighten/secure a coffin"; as with the previous item, a special term for a fastening used in crematory rites (SB, 78; KW, 147–48).

11. Fixing for a ปั้นลม, *panlom*, the decorative boards edging a Thai roof, probably here from an ordination or preaching hall in a wat (KW, 148).

12. สลักเพชร, *salak phet*, a bolt or wedge inserted to prevent movement of a door or window, with the end filed round so it is difficult or impossible to remove.

13. ปฏัก, *patak*, a straight stick with a sharp metal tip, used for riding any animal.

14. สลักประตู, *salak pratu*, a large bolt, probably from a city gate or similar major entrance.

15. ตะปูเห็ด, *tapu het*, a large-headed nail, often used on doorways.

16. เหล็กเบญจพรรณกัลเม็ด, *lek benjaphan kalamet*, possibly the same as เบญจโลหะ, *benjaloha*, a blend of metals used for casting Buddha images, namely gold (five parts), silver (four), copper (three), lead or mercury (two), and iron or tin (one) (Phlainoi, *Wannakhadi aphithan*, 193). Quaritch Wales suspects this may mean metals from different places, as used in India and the Malay world for the making of special weapons (*Ancient South-east Asian Warfare*, 150).

17. Knives and other household implements.

18. เหล็กไหล, *lek lai*, a naturally occurring metal-like compound that becomes malleable under a little heat such as a candle, and is believed to convey invulnerability to piercing by making blades bend, or by making the skin elastic and impenetrable. According to one account, the "male" variety is greenish-black, and the "female" is reddish-black. To test for genuineness, a lit candle is held under the metal. A sap-like fiber should ooze out and shrink back into the metal when the candle is removed. It is found as lumps of whitish ore in the forest or caves but can

Phrasaeng mine. Iron ore and metal from Kamphaeng[19] and Namphi.[20] Gold. Bronze. Nak from Aceh.[21] Genuine silver. Forest copper.[22]

All were collected and combined into an ingot that was heated red hot, beaten, dipped in a solution, left for three days, then beaten again. The ingot grew smaller but still looked fine according to the manual.

In all, it was doused and beaten seven times. Then on an auspicious day, the fifteenth of a month in which the first waxing fell on a Saturday,[23] wood was cut to make an eye-level shrine, and many offerings prepared—

pairs of golden candles, pig's head, duck, chicken, and a *baisi*. The bellows, anvil, and some of the charcoal used were brought in for the ceremony.

---

only be collected by an adept. It is used as an ingredient for making amulets, or inserted under the skin. (Textor, "An Inventory," 63; YS, 21; SWC, 15:7217) In another account, there are twelve varieties differing in color, texture, and powers. The ore is found in caves, and is believed to have come from the deep core of the earth in ancient times. It possesses both life and spirit, and hence can move of its own accord, shrink and swell, and change its weight. It "eats" honey and sheds droppings. There are several methods to prove its genuineness. Matches brought into contact will not strike, and guns will not fire. Only persons with the right spiritual quality are able to find it, keep it, and put it to use, with the help of exacting ceremonial. (Daeng, *Leklai mi jing*)

19. Phrasaeng is a famous mine in Uttaradit from which iron was taken to make the king's swords. Kamphaeng Phet (see p. 40, note 59), meaning "diamond wall," continues the theme of protection. The place has long been famed as a source of protective amulets. One of the most famous monks of the twentieth century, Abbot Phutthajan of Wat Rakhang, used ore from Kamphaeng Phet to make highly prized amulets.

20. A twin mine of Phrasaseng (see note 19 above) in Uttaradit, believed to have a protective spirit, who ensures that swords made with metal from the mine will render their owner invulnerable and invisible to their enemies. Namphi swords are used in ceremonies to combat *athan*, and steeped in water to cure diseases (SWC, 15:7416).

21. A territory on the western tip of Sumatra which was a trading partner with Ayutthaya since at least the sixteenth century, and a source of silver and other metals.

22. ดง, *dong*, forest, here meaning the Dong Phaya Fai hills on the border between the Chaophraya Plain and the Khorat Plateau (see map 5). These hills have many mineral deposits.

23. This is a form of divination supposedly originating from an ancient treatise, อธิไทยโพธิบาทว์, *athithai phothibat*, Overcoming Eight Evils, and more popularly found in ตำราวง, *tamra wong*, the Treatise on Circles. Certain days are defined as auspicious, and others as inauspicious. The calculation depends on intersections between the solar and lunar calendars—between the day of the week on the one hand, and the date in the lunar month on the other. This intersection can be shown by diagrams of interlocking circles, by tables for each lunar month depending on the day in the week of its first day (as here), or by a series of verses for memorization. The day identified in this passage would be มหาสิทธิโชค, *mahasitthichok*, a conjunction of great success, one of three auspicious days identified by this method, the others being อมฤตโชค, *ammaritchok*, conjunction of eternity, and สิทธิโชค, *sitthichok*, conjunction of success. A *mahasitthichok* day occurs on a Sunday 14th of either waxing or waning phase, Monday 12th, Tuesday 13th, Wednesday 4th, Thursday 7th, Friday 10th, or Saturday 15th. In addition, the days in the latter part of the waxing phase when the moon is brightest, and especially ปูรณจันทร์ *puranajan* when the moon is full, are the most favored. The day here would be *puranajan*. (Thep, *Horasat nai wannakhadi*, 61–68; Wales, *Divination*, 127–30; Phanomphon, "Khwam ru thang horasat," 34)

The metalsmith's skills were famed throughout the city. He dressed handsomely in white lower and upper cloths, made a circle of sacred thread, blew onto a yantra, and waited to find an auspicious time.

They found a time of kingly power with the sun at midday in the house of the lion.[24] Khun Phaen worked the bellows to heat the metal bright red. The head smith beat it to shape the tapered end,

straight, one cubit and one fist long, and three and a half fingers wide in the middle.[25] The haft had the face of a chick. To temper it, the blade was heated and doused three times, then filed until suddenly it became smooth and glossy,

with not a single cat's hair scratch, looking razor sharp. Catching the sunlight, it flashed green like the wings of an emerald beetle.

A handle, made with victoriflora wood, inscribed with a yantra of the Buddhist wheel of the law, was fitted over the metal stock. The hair of a fierce and evil spirit was put in the handle, and dammar poured in to seal it.

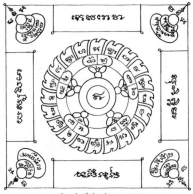

wheel of the law yantra

When it was finished, Khun Phaen picked up the sword and brandished it, flashing. The heavens darkened and swirled. Great powers clashed in earsplitting sounds. Rain fell. The sky rumbled,

and burst in echoing bolts of thunder. Khun Phaen listened, his heart surging to have the good omen of thunder like a gunshot. He named the sword Skystorm,[26] the mighty.

He placed it on the center of the shrine and intoned a prayer. The sword

---

24. The time of the sun's growing power from dawn to midday is considered most auspicious for rituals, including the casting of Buddha images. Midday, the highpoint of the sun, is always associated with the king, here appearing also through the symbolism of the lion, and the Buddha, here expressed as victory (Jina). The time before midday belongs to the monk but after midday, the power of the monk wanes, and that of the king rises, making it a good time for making a weapon. In addition, the sun is in the fourth of the twelve houses, ราชสีห์, *ratchasi*, Leo (Thep, *Horasat nai wannakhadi*, 24, 67–68).

25. The length is ศอกกำ, *sok kam*, the length from elbow to tip of middle finger (*sok*), plus the width of a clenched fist (*kam*), around 50 cms plus 10 cms. A "finger," นิ้ว, *nio*, is usually reckoned as 2.5 cms, making the width around 9 cms.

26. ฟ้าฟื้น, *fa fuen*, thunder before rain. Khun Borom, the hero ancestor of Lao legend, was given "a pike called Fa Feun" among the regalia at his coronation (Souneth, "The Nidan Khun Borom, 126).

showed its power by jiggling about. Seeing this evidence of sacred might, he was pleased he had got what he wanted.

A sheath was made from medicinal pacifier wood,[27] coated with glossy lacquer made from powder, and decorated top and bottom with one baht weight of gold from Bang Taphan.[28]

Khun Phaen poured out fifteen pieces of silver to give to the head smith, saying, "Your craft is supreme, beyond estimation. I reward you at once."

Catching sight of a fine *rang* tree three fists wide, he slashed it to the ground, hardly feeling a thing at his shoulder, like cutting a banana flower.[29]

He hurried away, making for the forest. After a long time traveling in search of spirits, he came upon the grave of a dead woman, I-Ma.

He chanted a mantra and put himself in a trance. The earth trembled and split apart. The spirit of I-Ma rose through to breast level with hair disheveled, tongue lolling, body twisting upwards,

eyes sunken, and huge head towering aloft. From a mouth as hollow as a cave, the spirit roared and shrieked in his face, then collapsed face down, waied, and asked,

"Sir, where are you going? What business of revenge do you have? Do you desire anything from me? I pay respect at your feet."

Khun Phaen, great master, told the spirit truthfully, "I want the child from your womb according to the manual." He used a chisel to pierce her belly,

and took the child.[30] He went to a graveyard where bodies were buried, and found a long oblong pit where a spirit named I-Phet-khong was buried.

He chanted the potent Great Collection mantra, put a fresh egg in a leaf basket, and concentrated to summon I-Phet-khong.

---

27. ระงับ, *rangap*, *Barleria siamensis* or *Breynia glauca*, a Phyllanthus whose leaves are used to treat fever, here named "pacifier" to reflect the Thai word's other meaning: to pacify or suppress.

28. A gold mine in Prachuap Khirikhan, discovered in the early nineteenth century, in the place today called Bang Saphan.

29. In the PD version, this segment of the story ends as follows: He promptly returned home. / He now had a sword made according to the manual and thus as mighty as the weapons of the gods. Arriving home, he placed the sword on the place of worship, and began thinking about looking for a horse.

In the Wat Ko version, reproduced from here to the end of the spirit son story, he does not return home. This segment, from here down to "Eventually they came to Phetburi" on p. 325 is taken from WK, 13:495–501.

30. The story here is not clear why he now goes to find a second child. Perhaps the first one does not suit the manual because it does not wail when taken from the belly.

The spirit of Phet-khong was greatly enfee-
bled under the effect of the mantra. She turned
her head, and her body swung upwards. The
earth and sky resounded with thunder,

leaf baskets

crashing and crashing as if the world would
collapse. An unnatural storm raged. The spirit
hollered angrily.

She had hollow eyes, a huge white glistening head, sunken chest, short neck,
white teeth, lolling tongue, flashing eyes, long hair, great height, and bloated
belly.

Her womb was split open to reveal the intestines. She stood with feet apart,
lolling a tongue as long as a *pheka* tree, peering from sunken eyes, and growling, "You crafty fellow, why do you come to the graveyard?"

Hearing Phet-khong, Khun Phaen hurled rice and chanted mantras. "I want
to take the child in your womb according to the manual. I want to raise it."

He chanted a Great Suppressor[31] mantra, creating as much fear as a thundering sky. The spirit shrank down to the size of a bullet, hid its body away,
and peered out.

Phet-khong was so confused and frightened that her body shook and she
fell down flat. Pulling her belly open, she took out the child and offered it,
"Here."

The child came out of her belly wailing. Khun Phaen plucked the mother's
hair by mantra, cut her tongue, and took the infant as his Goldchild.[32]

Carrying Phet-khong's child, Khun Phaen walked away from the graveyard. In one day he arrived at Bang Jara[33] and went around looking for spirits
all day and night.

Searching continuously, he came to the forest of Ban To Khwan,[34] and found
the graves of important spirits, full of choice bodies.

He strung a sacred thread around the graveyard, placed liquor, rice, and
fish as offerings, held his hands in wai and chanted mantra, while standing on
one foot and looking around.

Spirits from bad deaths rose up through the earth, and ran around shouting
loudly, cloaked in a pall of smoke,

---

31. มหาปราบ, *mahaprap*, presumably similar to *sakot* (see p. 282, note 2), meaning suppression.

32. กุมารทอง, *kuman thong*, "golden son/prince," a particular form of the spirit of a child that
died in the womb (see p. 316, note 2 above).

33. บางจะรา, unidentified.

34. บ้านต่อขวัญ, extending-soul village; possibly Lao Khwan, now an amphoe, in the uplands
west of U Thong.

sugar palms

making strange noises, poking their tongues, and rolling their eyes like mechanical dolls. Many transformed themselves into tigers or elephants and bounded fiercely around. One appeared as a cobra with a body as big as a sugar palm.

They swarmed inside the ring of sacred thread, and invited one another to drink the liquor for bravery. Khun Phaen watched the mass of spirits, and scattered rice at them while pronouncing mantras.

Hearing him, the spirits came to prostrate before him, shaking with fear, and asked Khun Phaen, "What is your desire?"

Khun Phaen replied to the female spirits, "I came here to feed you handsomely so I may make use of your services to fight and gain victory. I'll give you liquor, rice, duck, and chicken to eat."

The crowd of spirits laughed happily. Every one of them was pleased at the words of the accomplished Khun Phaen. He cut the tongue from every one of them,

and now had his own spirits. Extremely pleased, he hastened away, arrived home, and prostrated to his mother.

"May I request two chang of money to purchase a brave and powerful horse. Mother, stay here and look after yourself happily with the relatives and servants."

Thong Prasi heard her son's request, and saw that he would not listen to any opposition, so she quickly counted out two chang.

"Go and don't take too long. I'm old, sick, and near death. I'll wait for your return every night. Go well and return quickly."

Then she summoned servants. "Hurry to get things ready. Fetch chili, salt, the leftover deer meat, rice, vegetables, and fish.

Also put *thian* sweets, pork sausage, rice cakes,[35] crisped rice, sweet-in-attap,[36] and sweet bananas in a shoulder sack to eat on the long journey." She hauled out a large sidebag and put in betelnut, mortar,

chili, salt, lime, and tamarind with both hands. Her head and body shook as she bustled about. Eventually she sank down in a heap.

I-Yu tumbled over her, sending a mortar and pestle crashing down, and calling out "I'm done for!" Thong Prasi scolded, "You didn't look."

The servants carried the supplies and set them out in rows. Thong Prasi shouted endlessly. Seeing retainers sitting all around, she said, "You'll go along too, about ten of you."

Hearing the order, the servants hitched up their lowercloths and danced around happily, holding machetes behind their rears. The supplies were prepared for everyone. Each found a sword or pike, and waited for the master.

Thong Prasi gave her son a fine blessing. "May enemies and dangers not approach you. May you achieve your purpose, dear son."

Khun Phaen, great valiant, prostrated at his mother's feet to take her blessing on his head, then went down from the house.

His servants and porters assembled in a crowd, and quickly walked away from the village. In the evening they halted and relaxed. At dawn they ate and set off.

They went to Phae, Bo, Nan, Taphan Saeng,[37] and many other places. They traveled as far as Khorat, Phutthaisong, Nakhon Chai, Phiman, and Nang Rong,[38]

visiting all places, great and small. They came upon more than one thousand two hundred horses but none matched what he wanted, and so they traveled onward without buying.

---

35. ข้าวตู, *khao tu*, a sweet made with leftover rice that is dried and pounded, sugar, grated coconut, coconut milk, and a jasmine flower, cooked and then pressed into shapes with a mold.

36. ขนมห่อใบจาก, *khanom ho bai jak*, sticky rice, sugar, and grated coconut, wrapped in an attap leaf and grilled.

37. The places chosen are far away, the ends of the earth. This group are in the far north (see map 4): Phae must be Phrae; Bo is probably Bo Kluea (salt mine), now an amphoe in the east of Nan province; Taphan Saeng is unidentified.

38. This group are all in the lower northeast (see map 5). Khorat is Nakhon Ratchasima; Phutthaisong is now an amphoe on the Mun River in the very north of Buriram; Nakhon Chai is now Prakhon Chai, an amphoe in the southeast of Buriram; Phiman is probably Phimai, the ancient Khmer city to the northeast of Khorat; Nang Rong is now an amphoe in Buriram.

They looked all over Ayutthaya, the districts of the capital region, and all the provincial centers without success. Eventually they came to Phetburi.[39]

Now to tell of Luang Songphon and Phan Phan.[40] They had been sent to Tenasserim[41] on the king's orders. Along with thirty-four accompanying phrai, they stayed in Mergui for half a year,

because Luang Siworakhan[42] had gone to the western lands[43] to buy horses and had not yet returned. He had to wait for the season of the wind for the ship to sail back from the western lands.[44]

Luang Si brought back a total of sixty-five horses, both Thai and foreign. They were joined by a bay from Mergui, who was said to have mated with a water horse,[45]

and had a foal called Color of Mist,[46] born on Saturday the ninth day of a waxing moon. The foal had a formidable presence and black eyes. He saw the royal horses crossing the water and tagged along.

---

39. From here to the end of the chapter is the PD version, which differs only very slightly from WK. In PD, the transition from the horse passage, as translated above, is as follows: He put five chang of silver in a waist pouch and set off. Day after day he could not find a horse he liked so moved on, ranging all over the country through Ratchaburi, Suphan, and Phetburi.

40. Luang Songphon Ratchasamuha, head of the right division of the royal horses, *asawarat khwa*, *sakdina* 2,400, who already appeared above in chapter 2. Phan Songphonphan is a deputy in the same department (KTS, 1:256).

41. Tenasserim or Tanaosi is the name of a river on the western side of the upper peninsula, and a town on its mid reaches. It is also used for this area in general. The route from Singkhon on the Siamese side, over the watershed, and down the river to the port of Marit/Mergui was the most northerly portage across the peninsula. For a long time, Ayutthaya controlled these towns and the portage route, and thus was able to act as an entrepot between the trade of the Indian Ocean and the South China Sea (see map 1).

42. The name ending in -khan suggests a Khaek, probably a Muslim from the Indian subcontinent, possibly an official in the right division of the port department that looked after westward trade. The WK version names this character Luang Si Marathon, มะระทน, and explicitly calls him a Khaek (WK, 13:501–2).

43. เมืองเทศ, *mueang thet*, a general term for westward countries from Arabia to the Indian subcontinent. Here it could mean India but more likely Persia, which was a favored source of horses from the mid Ayutthaya era onwards.

44. Because of the monsoon in the Bay of Bengal, ships had to make the eastward crossing by August-September, or wait until the following February.

45. The term nowadays is used for a seahorse, but possibly at this time there was a mistaken idea that there was an aquatic variant of the horse. Kukrit noted, "Saying the father of Color of Mist was a water horse is not so strange because the Thais who started telling the *KCKP* story seem to have had little knowledge of zoology and still believed there were both land horses and water horses, and that they could mate together" (KP, 154).

46. On the origin of this name, see *Companion*, 1203.

At Singkhon,[47] the men stopped to rest and released the horses to graze. Officials from Kui and Pran[48] came to accompany them. They passed Cha-am and reached the landing at Phetburi.

The horses were feeding at Sala Ban Taeng Ngae[49] by the brick staircase next to the holy hill,[50] when Color of Mist made a show of strength by biting one of the foreign horses.

Luang Songphon angrily had his phrai chase this devilish horse away. "He's mischievous, abnormal. Whenever he turns up, chase him away."

Color of Mist would come to find his mother, and had to be hustled away again, but as soon as they sat down, he would return immediately. After running around in circles, the whole team was fed up with him.

Khun Phaen, great romancer, famed and feared in every direction, saw Color of Mist acting boisterously and knew he had found what he wanted.

The horse was spry and nimble. His features matched the manual completely, as if he were a gift from Lord Indra. Khun Phaen promptly went to find Luang Songphon.

"Is this colt, Color of Mist, yours? Do you want to sell? If you would be so kind, I'd like to buy him."

Luang Songphon informed him, "That horse, Color of Mist, over there? He's not one of the king's horses under our care.

He's the foal of a Mergui horse and came from Mergui with his mother. His appearance and bearing are good but he's so mischievous we're fed up with him.

When we were off guard, he bit one of the king's horses. That's a big concern. If you buy him, we'll drop the price. You can take him for fifteen tamlueng."

---

47. A pass over the Tenasserim range, one of the major portage routes running from Mergui to just south of Prachuap Khirikhan (see map 1).

48. Now Kuiburi and Pranburi, on the coast of Prachuap Khirikhan (see map 1).

49. The "pavilion for dressing" before entering Phetburi town. Formerly such pavilions were found outside many towns. The sala still existed when Khun Wichitmatra was writing in the 1950s, but subsequently it collapsed and the adjacent pond for washing was filled in. The restored sala is on the north side of Route 3171 about 700 meters west of the Phetburi bypass.

50. Wat Bandai-it, wat of the brick staircase, is sited on a hill on the outskirts of Phetburi, about 2 kms west of Khao Wang, palace hill. Sala Ban Taeng Ngae is close to the foot of the staircase. According to legend, a rich man built a stupa in the wat, while his major wife built the ordination hall and his minor wife, the preaching hall. The stupa later leaned towards the preaching hall (SWC, 2:705).

horse and harness

Khun Phaen had what he wanted. He counted out the money at once, and walked towards Color of Mist.

Enchanting some grass with a Great Beguiler formula, he approached Color of Mist and said, "If you will come with me, move closer." He proffered the grass,

which Color of Mist took, chewed, and swallowed. The horse became frisky, high-spirited, and attached to Khun Phaen, loyally following along behind him.

Khun Phaen stroked his back, and put on a saddle, bridle, bit, and pretty crupper, all brand new with attractive gold trimming.

He put his foot in a stirrup, and swung himself up. The horse reared up, set off at a fast gallop then slowed to a trot, with the mass of servants following behind.

They traveled through the forest for three days. As the sun disappeared behind the hills, they reached the old village at Cockfight Hill. He ordered the servants to make a stable for the horse.

Khun Phaen,[51] great romancer with powers as strong as a lion, had now acquired his spirit son, weapon, and horse. He was happy and well pleased.

"I must think of taking revenge on Khun Chang, reducing him to fragments, seizing Wanthong, and taking her away into the forest. If he chases after me, I'll attack him.

With Goldchild, my beloved son of sacred power, I have a spirit of brilliant and expert capabilities. With Color of Mist, this exceptional horse, even if I have to flee, he's so fleet none can give chase.

And with Skystorm, sharp and shiny as a diamond sword, I can sever seven necks in one. Even if an army of five thousand were raised to pursue me, they'd be slashed down into dust."

The more he thought, the less he was able to sleep peacefully. When the world was bathed in golden light, he opened a window, quickly washed his face, and went to the room of his mother, Thong Prasi.

---

51. The next five stanzas, down to "and went to the room of his mother, Thong Prasi," are from Khru Jaeng's version, published in Sujit, *KCKP*, 249.

He went in and told his mother everything. "I've got a spirit son, a horse, and a good weapon." Thong Prasi saw her son was happy.

She invited him to eat his fill. Khun Phaen was feeling very merry. He went up to the sitting hall and gave orders to Ai-Jan, "You and Ai-Kliang work shifts to look after my horse."

Ai-Kliang and Ai-Jan rushed around arranging a stable, feeding Color of Mist with grass, setting a bonfire at the door,[52] and taking care of the horse as required.

towards Kanburi

---

52. To drive away insects with the smoke.

17: KHUN PHAEN ENTERS KHUN CHANG'S HOUSE

Khun Phaen, great romancer, was now unmatched in mastery, with skill, courage, and knowledge that made his enemies' hair stand on end.

Pondering how Laothong had been parted from him disturbed and darkened his mood. He had young Thai and Lao women in his service but he was not happy with anyone. He pined for her.

He slept alone, lonely, and doleful through each season of the year. In the hot season, his heart burned like fire. In the rainy season, he grumbled like the sky.

In the windy season, a draught blew through his heart, and swaddling himself in a shawl still left him soulful. Not seeing her fair face for over a year made him long for her and fret in frustration.

In the dead of night, he sobbed softly, lying awake in ever-deepening melancholy, tossing and turning and never sleeping deeply. "How many years before Laothong returns?"

Listening to cicadas shrilling around the house drew his thoughts back to the forest when he brought Laothong down. "I showed you how to enjoy the forest, my eye's jewel.

Dear heart, I'm not used to being apart. I pity the room left chilly without you, the bed and pillows now somber and sad. Do they sorrow because you're sick with fever?

The lamp languishes unlit longer than a year. My jewel, do you think of me when the side pillow rolls far away from your body, like you away from me?

Powders and perfumes lie unused. Mirrors are cracked or closed. The mosquito net is frayed and fallen. The oil has lost the fragrance that used to scent your clothes.

My heart aches as if pierced with a poisoned arrow." He grieved and groaned until almost dawn. "At this moment in the city, Laothong will awake to sorrow."

Too fretful and too unsettled to slip back to sleep, he turned over, parted the net, and went to look outside. Hearing a coel's clear call, he pulled open the door,

but she was not out there walking up to the little house, only a dipping moon, shining so dazzlingly bright he felt even more wistful. A cool wind rustled banyan leaves,

bathed in a chilly dew. "Sadly, you're far away from my sight, though this dew reminds me of your trickling tears. Morning, evening, or night, you'll lie lost in thought.

When eating, you'll taste only tears. Late at night, you'll lament. From morning to evening, you'll mourn." The deeper he dwelt on this, the darker he felt.

"Oh, what store of karma made these troubles arise? A friend can do such wrong to a friend. When I let that pass, he bullied me again.

I resent Khun Chang and want revenge. He has a hard heart and evil mind. The blackguard grabbed Wanthong from me. I haven't said one word to annoy him.

Yet he went so far as to mislead the king into having Laothong seized and taken away. He could do all this! Why does he wreck my loves every time? If I don't take revenge, I'll harbor this resentment till death.

There's a saying: With someone crooked, oppose him in every way, with someone honest, be honest till your dying day. This bad fellow broke the rules of friendship.

If I'm condemned to punishment, that's karma. Let's see what the future has in store. I'm known as an able person. Tomorrow I'll go to Suphan,

split open his chest to secure my revenge, and kidnap Wanthong away into the forest." With this thought he leapt up in excitement,

and burst out, "I'll go directly at dawn!" His chest felt as hot as a raging fire. By first light, he had arranged everything, and went to his mother's house.

Thong Prasi was pounding betel. She stopped with pestle raised, and looked up. "Oh, Phaen of mine, where are you going so strangely early in the morning?" Her heart shivered with trepidation.

Khun Phaen, great gallant, prostrated to his mother and said, "I've been mournful for so long I can't stand it any more, so I've to come to take my leave.

I'm going to get even with Khun Chang, give him what he deserves for all he's done. I'll take Wanthong off into the forest. If he follows, I'll slash him dead."

Thong Prasi tried to calm him down. "I don't think you should. I hate him too but aren't there any other women in this town?

If she were beautiful in both body and mind, I wouldn't object. If she were worth running after, then you should do it. But Wanthong is beautiful in body, not in mind. You shouldn't chase after her.

She's ruined, like a diamond ring whose gem is broken into two or three. Even if you put the pieces back together, the ring doesn't regain its beauty. I warn you that you'll only get hurt."

Khun Phaen replied, "What you say is right, and I can't contradict you. If you want to call her bad, then she's bad through and through. But I've thought it over and come to the conclusion she's good.

The day I reached Suphan, her jealousy was proof that she hadn't deserted me. What she said was all true but I made the mistake of accusing her, of trying to hurt her,

and walking away in anger. Wanthong felt battered, bruised, and broken-hearted. She cried endlessly, and tried to hang herself.

Even then she was still in love with me, still true to how we were. Saithong pointed all this out to me but I wasn't thinking.

While I had Laothong sleeping in my room, I forgot Wanthong completely, but then Khun Chang treacherously had me separated from Laothong. I lost a friend. Now let us test our powers for all to see.

Mother, please give me your blessing. I'll succeed, don't you worry. Even if they raise an army of three thousand to chase me down, I'll slash them into dust."

Seeing opposition was pointless, Thong Prasi fell in with his wishes and gave him the blessing he wanted. "May your mastery and martial powers be sufficient for success in your aims.

When you find Wanthong in her bedroom, may her heart agree to go with you. Don't be fooled by wiles, or waylaid by love. Reap success and return to this house."

Khun Phaen was buoyed by this blessing. He circled his mother to the right three times,[1] and took his leave.

Going up to a prayer room,[2] he composed himself, made offerings of candles and incense to both left and right, ground sandal on a stone, and mixed it with oil to anoint himself so anyone seeing his body would be charmed.

He put on inner britches of purple with a bird pattern, a yok with bright golden cross-branch design, tightly pleated around his body, a short inner shirt with yantra designs, and an outer shirt with floral patterns embroidered in gold. He tied a sash round

inner shirt with yantra

---

1. ประทักษิณ, *prathaksin*, circling somebody or something, such as a stupa, in a clockwise direction, considered a form of worship or respect.

2. หอพระนารายณ์, *ho phra narai*, a hall for Vishnu, probably used here as a poetic name for a prayer room where Buddha images and other sacred items are kept.

his waist, fixed with a medallion,[3] and put on a plaited *phirot* ring and a breast chain with amulets interleaved with the hair of spirits.

Carefully he tied a bandeau round his forehead. Finding the conjunction of great success[4] he needed, he stood holding Skystorm aloft, and turned away from the direction of the Great Spirit[5] and the Lord of Darkness.

Descending the stairway, he mounted Color of Mist and summoned all his spirits. With them following rowdily behind, he left Kanburi and entered the forest.

They passed Huai Rong and Nong Taphan,[6] crossed Crocodile Stream,[7] reentered the forest, and arrived at the shimmering pond of Ban Phlap. He hurried close to Khun Chang's house,

cut wood to build a shrine, made some quick offerings, and marked his forehead with krajae-sandal powder. At an auspicious moment, he lit candles and incense,

summoned up powerful deities, and concentrated his mind to make a prayer. "May the gods be my witness. Let me destroy Khun Chang, this bad friend,

who snatched my wife away for his own pleasure. Grant me the power to overcome him as I hope. If I have ever disloyally caused calamity for a friend, do not let me succeed in this endeavor."

Then he took up Skystorm and stood, hardening his mind to be brave and ruthless. He saw that the stars shone brightly, and he checked the direction his breath flowed easily.[8] Then he urged his horse to gallop ahead.

Arriving at the open space by Khun Chang's house, he saw a strong embankment and surrounding moat with guards sitting by fires. He reined in Color of Mist to take his bearings.

---

3. ตระพอง, *traphong*, usually the frontal lobes of an elephant but the context here suggests a belt with clasp in a diamond shape, similar to the elephant's lobes, probably embroidered with a floral pattern.

4. มหาสิทธิโชค, *mahasitthichok*, see p. 319, note 23.

5. See p. 100, note 21.

6. Now Ban Nong Rong and Nong Saphan, earlier Ban Huai Saphan, shown on the nineteenth century maps as Ban Hoi Taphan (Santanee and Stott, *Royal Siamese Maps*, 102; see map 2).

7. Now known in full as *than jorakhe sam phan*, Three Thousand Crocodile Stream, which now runs parallel to the Kanchanaburi–Suphanburi road to the south of U Thong. There are several stories explaining the name. One tells of a man who bought a baby crocodile from a Mon fisherman for three thousand cowries, only to be eaten by the crocodile when it grew up, giving the name Three Thousand Cowries Crocodile, since shortened. Another explanation claims the area used to be the home of three *species*, พันธุ์, *phan*, of crocodile but this phrase was later distorted to the homophone, three *thousand*, พัน, *phan*. In another tale, a king ordered a census of crocodiles in the area but the three clerks deputed for the task each could count no higher than a thousand and hence arrived at this total (SWC, 3:1340–41).

8. See p. 101, note 23.

Now to tell of Khun Chang's five female spirits[9] who were patrolling around the boundary. One said to the others, "Enemy! Let's have fun beating him and chasing him away."

They soared through the air, bellowing, scattering sand and earth, dangling their heads, twist-

guards

ing their bodies to and fro, lolling their tongues, and pulling fearsome faces.

Khun Phaen's spirits responded by rushing at them, hurling rocks, swooping down, and lashing out with nettle vines. The two sides were well matched and the battle was fierce.

Khun Phaen, great romancer, drew Skystorm and stood looking slim, handsome, powerful, and imposing. He scattered rice grains to weaken the opponents,

then opened a packet of herb-coated fragrant rice[10] and flung it to hurt like hard gravel. The five spirits jeered, and hid themselves to consider the situation.

They could see he was young, fair-faced, handsome, and obviously well-versed in lore, so they transformed their bodies into lady attendants of the palace and walked out to meet him.

Approaching him, they made eyes and retreated, walked up to touch him and then acted scared. One cocked her head, peered out of the corner of her eye, and asked, "Why are you standing here blocking the way?"

Khun Phaen, great romancer, knew very well they were spirits transformed. He stood smiling at them and said, "I'm not a villain or thief.

I have business here, and I've run into you by chance. I was feeling grievously upset but I'm a lot better since you came to greet me. Still, love will have to wait a while.

I'm Wanthong's husband. Khun Chang took Wanthong away to keep for himself. Without her, I've been lovesick and miserable. Now that I've met you five lovely ladies,

---

9. Like any householder, Khun Chang would propitiate any spirits residing at that place and ask them to help provide protection. He might also use some lore to invite other more powerful spirits to strengthen the defenses.

10. See p.135, note 17.

please help me by opening the door. I'll be grateful to the end of my days." At the same time, he blew a mantra to command their attention and said, "Don't hide. Come and have a mouthful of betel each."

The spirit ladies turned their heads away and hid their faces with coy smiles. One answered, "Khun Chang looks after us.

Even if he's done you wrong, you shouldn't come sweet-talking us about love and wanting us to help you. It's trickery, and it won't do.

Khun Chang feeds us well, and we should repay his kindness. You don't have any love for us at all. You'll never give us satisfaction.

You're not wanting for spirits of your own. You've got crowds of them. Yet the first thing you mention out loud is love, and your mantra went extremely deep."

"Now, now. Don't complain and get sulky. If you were human I'd take care of you truly well. But as to love, what can I do? I could enjoy only your false bodies.

If you'd return to true human form, I'd couple with you for sure, and pleasure you to the full. But now please show me the way to Wanthong."

He scattered more rice, making the spirits flee in all directions, and urged Color of Mist along a dike across a moat.

He drove away the lady spirits, and chanted a Subduer mantra to send people to sleep, snore, mumble, and dream. He sprung the locks, bolts, and battens, then urged Color of Mist to bound ahead again.

All the sentries guarding the house nodded off and lay motionless. Axmen standing at guard posts hit the ground already asleep and snoring.

Around stoves, people cooking rice and grilling fish dozed off, heads drooping, eyes closed, and mouths mumbling. One held a pot lid against another's rear.

A fellow who had been chopping ganja dozed off with one hand wiping the sleep from his eyes. Another napped with his head flung backwards while a rice pot boiled over.

They looked pitiful. Khun Phaen urged Color of Mist ahead through two gates. All around, people slept quietly.

One lay naked, mumbling, with his cloth slipped off his body. Another was dreaming and trying to climb up a post. A drinker with a mouthful of liquor waved his cup drunkenly and lowed like a buffalo.

Khun Phaen entered a third gate and crossed another moat. The moonlight was dim and hazy. People slept motionless here too. "That fine house must be Sonphraya's,

and this must be the house of that toasted turtle with the smooth bald skull.

rich man's house

He has some lovely lush plants with beautiful blooms.

Tomorrow morning, Khun Chang will lie hugging only a pillow and groaning in misery. He took my Wanthong to sleep by his side, and today I'll take my revenge."

He put a yantra cloth over Color of Mist's face. "Don't go prancing off on your own. Hide here in the shadow of a pillar, and be careful." Then he gave orders to his spirits.

"Keep the whole house asleep. When I tell you, fly away from here." He intoned a mantra, and scattered enchanted rice
over the roof of the house, making it tremble. A pack of guardian spirits swarmed out. People murmured and crawled about in their sleep. He threw limes around, making the house shake.

All the bolts and locks sprang open. Khun Chang hugged Wanthong and dreamed madly as his soul took off into the wilds. Khun Phaen climbed onto a wooden post, and stood on the top.

He leapt down onto a terrace tiered with flowers planted by Khun Chang. Even past midnight, the fragrance of pollen wafting on the wind was fresh and pleasing.

basin with fish

Rows of pots were planted with gem jasmine, damascene, milkwood, pupil tree, and lightleaf, all elegantly shaped;[11] wild olive neatly tied and sweetly trimmed; pecking plum and paperwood artfully arranged together;

ebony fashioned into branches ending in leafy orbs;[12] orangegold jostling among *phrom, in-jan*, and angelbreast, shooting up floral sprays to catch the moonlight magnificently;

damascene, double jasmine, rose, and hidden lover with sensuous scents; *lamduan* that lured him on, and waitinglady that stayed him to stare in admiration.

Beyond, he found a basin[13] with goldfish swimming, slip-sliding side by side, blowing bubbles, diving down, gliding along in pairs like loving couples,

nudging through water peony, tunneling through rocks,[14] jostling to nibble on waterweed, wheeling around and waving their tails sublimely. Further on he found a yoke and plough of curving wood;

animal bells, elegantly carved and polished smooth, lying under a felt blanket patterned with bright stars; coils of rope, placed in piles;

horse harness and elephant equipment, all neatly arranged; goads with tooled handles, and staves ringed with gold. He passed along, glancing around,

sprung the locks by mantra, drew a screen aside,[15] and saw throngs of young women. Walking past their sleeping forms, he arrived at the room of Kaeo Kiriya.

On a low bed, a slender body slept silently, looking lovely, lissome, and fresh. Her eyebrows were fine and softly bowed, her hairline neat and pleasingly shaped.

hairline

---

11. Kukrit noted that most of these are large trees that must have been trimmed bonsai style (KP, 162). มะสัง, *masang, Feroniella lucida*, lightleaf, a tree with glossy, fleshy, composite leaves, is now popular worldwide as bonsai. Khun Chang was ahead of his time.

12. ตะโก, *tako, Diosporos rhodocalyx*, a type of ebony which is often trimmed so each bare branch ends in a round clump of leaves, as described here. Such trimmed trees are common in wat and public gardens. These clumps are described arcanely as ประกับ, *prakap*, earthenware disks used as coinage in the Borommakot reign (1733–1758).

13. An ornamental pond, probably a large Chinese ceramic pot.

14. The pond has a miniature artificial mountain with tunnels through the base.

15. Phraya Komankulamontri (Chuean Komarakun na Nakhon, 1891–1961) wrote a description of Khun Chang's house based on this chapter. He imagined this screen would have been "of the old type, painted gold, with glass and pictures painted on each side" (Chotchuang and Niranam, *KCKP*, 63).

Features[16] similar to a foreign face. Cheeks as fair as karaket. Mouth breaking into a smile or speech. Neck like a kinnari gliding to land.

Fingers, hands, and arms as neatly drawn as a fine portrait. Slender waist as if sketched to please the eye. Bosom sweetly spread open.

Hair fell loosely down over her shoulders, curling up prettily around her face. The bed was small, soft, and snug, with a pair of pillows nestling either side.

She had a little mirror with limpid glass, and a hairpin with a handle of pellucid ivory. Screens were arrayed beside the bed, and a row of half-moon tables stood along the little room.

Though the space was small, it was arranged to seem uncluttered. Her spittoon, water bowl, and cup were as petite and pretty as their owner's figure.

"This isn't Wanthong. Maybe a sister, but I doubt it. Her manner is not that of a poor person, and her betel set belies that too.

Is she a minor wife of Khun Chang? But why wouldn't he put her in a room worthy of her status?" He examined her face, finding it fair and lovable. "If a man had enjoyed her, she'd have lost that sheen."

He stole in close to her, touched her breast, and wanted to enjoy her. Pressing close against her, he drove away his spirits[17] and chanted a Beguiler mantra to excite her.

Kaeo Kiriya, who had been sleeping soundly, started awake in shock and surprise. "Oh! What's this apparition?"

She wanted to cry out but was held by the lore. She trembled with fear and recoiled from him, sliding down from the bed and looking at the handsome figure, clearly no villain.

She hid behind a screen, mouthing words, and nervously thinking what to do. "If I say nothing, I'll never know what's happening." She summoned up the courage to question him.

"Sir, please don't think I'm complaining but who invited you to stray in here? Your slight figure, spruce looks, and fine bearing are not those of some bad fellow."

Khun Phaen, great romancer, listened quietly to her voice, which was sweet, clear, and commanding. "I'm a skilled soldier.

16. The next two stanzas are taken from SK2, 121, absent from PD. The petals and bracts of the young flowers of กระเกด, karaket, Pandanus tectorius, have a curved shape and pale yellow color, which are the basis of the simile with cheeks.

17. To wake her, he drives off his own spirits who are keeping her asleep.

The king bestowed on me the name of Khun Phaen Saensongkhram according to the royal wish. I came to find Wanthong because Khun Chang brought her here to keep and caress.

He and I were friends but he broke an oath of loyalty over this wife. I thought you were Wanthong so I peered in here, came to sit beside you, and only then knew it was someone else.

But you're exactly like her. Thinking it was her, I'd already had no qualms about kissing and caressing you all over. I've taken liberties with the wrong person. Don't be cross.

You're not Wanthong but please excuse me. Don't turn your face away so shyly. Tell me honestly what connection brought you to be in Khun Chang's house?"

Kaeo Kiriya was falling in love, but shyly stayed still and thought, "This must be Khun Phaen for sure. His slender, slight figure is very lovable.

His gentle manner is sweet. How come Wanthong did not stay with him? He's gained great powers from a good teacher. Khun Chang would be no match in a contest.

He's walking around all the rooms here at will!" Her mind raced, her hair bristled in fear, and her heart skittered. "This is Wanthong's husband for sure.

If I don't answer his question, he might get angry and turn nasty. Fighting him or fleeing away would be as futile as flinging money into the wind."

She said, "This is laughable. You get the wrong person and the wrong room. It won't do. I'm furious you sneaked in here and now try to flatter me so contemptuously.

A low turtle can't grow long legs. I'm no peacock and it's not amusing to paint me as one. A firefly can't compete with moonlight, and water won't be molded as a statue. It's illusion.

I'm not Wanthong, I'm a slave, and this is just a little bedroom, as you can see. Don't get mistaken, I'm not the person you're seeking. I'm the daughter of the Sukhothai governor.

My father was imprisoned over some difficulty and so mortgaged me into service here for fifteen tamlueng.[18] My name is Kaeo Kiriya.

You're a freeman. Don't consider consorting with a slave. I shouldn't be so bold as to sit on the same level. Whatever is making you angry from the past, please take your revenge in the manner of gentlefolk."

---

18. The original says only fifteen at this point but Kaeo Kiriya specifies fifteen *tamlueng* in chapter 38 when she is relating the story to her son.

"It's no small thing to speak coyly in sweet-sounding words, and with sarcasm too. I'm quite captivated by what you say. I feel sorry for you not having a lover yet.

Any man who could possess you would hold on tight. I'm after love, not a one-night affair. I'm not trying to deceive you so don't be upset.

You can't be in this spot because of only fifteen tamlueng! I can redeem you, even if it were five chang. Some merit I made in the past has caused me to meet you by chance."

He snuggled close to her. "Heart's delight, don't shy away from me." He took out a packet of money to give her, and said soothingly, "Don't be cross, I beg you."

Kaeo Kiriya turned to hide her face and pushed him away to forestall his fondling. "I know you talk of love and being kind,

and say you'll give me heaps, cartloads of money. I raise my hands above my head in gratitude for your goodness. But I still think of my father's words of warning. Out of kindness, he instructed me repeatedly on several matters:

suffer poverty with humility; don't make mistakes for pleasure; love your back and beware the lash. I gave my word to my father.

If you love me truly and won't throw me away, don't be hasty. Hold back now for future gain. Don't make me break my promises. Please speak to my father in the proper way.

You love me. It's not that I won't return your love, but to have a secret affair, I fear a thousand wrongs. I love myself, and shun shame and ruin. I absolutely won't give in so don't plead."

"Your words are truly sweet, my jewel. Your skin is as fresh and fragrant as cinnamon. Raise your face. I'll tell you everything.

I've enjoyed you this intimately already, please show some mercy. I pledge my love to you, Kaeo Kiriya. Don't feel suspicious and angry.

Should I deceive you by breaking my word, let me suffer endless misfortune, and let all my fine learning go to waste. Your skin glistens as if gilded with gold."

He took off his belt with all its gear, and hung it over a screen.[19] Lifting her up in his arms, he lowered her into his lap, breast to breast, then laid her down, and covered her gently like a nugget of gold.

A breeze blew through blossoms, strewing their pollen and bathing the room with fragrance. The end of her embroidered sabai rippled in the wind. A shimmering moon bounded into the sky.

---

19. His amulets and charms would lose their power if worn during lovemaking.

The sun vied but the moon shone more brightly. Stars sparkling alongside were snuffed out. Flickering fireflies frisked among the trees. The tread of tramping beetles made tall trees tremble.

Kaeo Kiriya was lost in passion. Love left her drained and drowsy. She clung to him, weak with rapture,
softly sobbing and sighing, tears falling onto his lap. "I resent the way you force yourself on me. And now you'll leave and steal Wanthong away into the forest.

For you it'll be all joy and laughter, while I'll be counting the nights sadly waiting. How many years will pass until you've enjoyed the forest enough to return? Meanwhile Khun Chang will take it out on me.

You came here to find her, not me, yet you've brought me karma and turmoil, made me worry that I'm tainted." She shot him a pleading look from the corner of her eye.

Khun Phaen comforted her. "Don't be afraid. I won't forget what's happened. I'll feel for you greatly until the end of my life, from today until my dying day.

There'll be a time I'll return to couple happily again and chase away your sorrow. Cheer up, and please make plans to recover your freedom.

Even[20] if the gods were to fly down to forbid me, I wouldn't give you up. Don't be so quick to doubt and suspect me." With these words, he embraced, kissed, and caressed her again.

"Hey! You're just using my cheeks like a war slave. You're so happy, but I'm bruised black as a boil. Please have some mercy. Don't go too far. You're not letting poor me open my mouth."

Khun Phaen said, "Oh my eye's jewel, you protest too much. I love you greatly. Don't resist and make me angry. No matter how you object, I won't listen."

With these words, he hugged her tightly to him, with arms encircling her like a naga, breast to her breast, hand caressing her feverishly.

Passion stirred turmoil in their hearts as the pair clung together in ecstasy, wrapped around each other, each experiencing the joy of their first lovemaking.

A breeze gently wafted pollen as if inviting them to love. Bees circled among flowers, caressing the blooms,

---

20. This stanza and the next two sections, down to "clung to him in grief," are taken from SK2, 126–27, absent from PD.

releasing their aroma to mingle with the scent of her cheeks, cloaking the pair in the fragrance of petals and pollen. He embraced her closely, feeling a warmth that urged them to lose themselves in love.

The first taste had left Kaeo Kiriya enraptured. She clung tightly to him, the pair entwined around each other, both blooming with love.

But it was approaching dawn, and any further lovemaking would cause delay. Ruefully, she had to suppress her love. She hugged, kissed, caressed, and then spoke,

opposing what he had come intending to achieve. "Give up your plan. Be cautious. Just thinking about it makes my whole body fearful.

If you get caught, you'll die, and I'll wish to die along with you. I'll be too sad to continue living." She clung to him in grief.

He hugged her, wiped away her tears, and took off a diamond ring. "Don't cry. Look at this ring instead and brighten up." He slipped it on her finger,

put his arms round her neck, and began to leave the room. They were locked together, breast to breast, hearts pounding, and reluctant to move. Yet he lifted her arm and asked, "Please help me by pointing the way to Wanthong."

Kaeo Kiriya yearned ever more deeply, yet steeled herself to point out the room. "Go straight that way. Don't look to either side. Pass two partitions and go into the inner room.

The house is lit with lanterns and there are people sitting and lying everywhere. Avoid the light. Please, for my sake, don't go at all. Your wife[21] feels her heart is breaking in fright."

"Don't worry, Kaeo Kiriya. You're nervous because you've never seen your husband's powers. Would I have come here alone if I couldn't handle it? It was wrong of me to abandon Wanthong.

Take heart, and go to sleep. Close your room tight, put out the light, and stay still. Don't be tempted to come out for anything. I'm going into the inner room."

He soothed her then crept away, peering ahead to find the room where Wanthong lay. Watching him disappear and reappear, Kaeo Kiriya yearned too much to hold herself back.

She ran after him because of love. "You'll soon forget me for sure. You can't find her room because you don't know the house. Pass the hall and then enter. It's right there."

---

21. See p. 148, note 32. He reciprocates by referring to himself as "husband" in the next stanza.

Khun Phaen turned to look at her face. "You told me already but I couldn't quite see it. I can find the way. Don't make so much noise. I was afraid I might mistake it so I was being careful.

It's late, my jewel, and you haven't slept. Don't worry. I won't take long." He led her back into the room and soothed her to sleep on her little bed,

embracing her closely, with his arms round her neck. "Why don't you sleep?" He began to move away but saw she was still half awake, eyes winking and fluttering. "Though the sweat trickled down, you still don't slumber."

He blew a powerful formula to put her to sleep, and got up to leave. Still concerned, he stood waiting with heart pounding.

He saw her turn over. Fearing she would run after him again, he went back and endlessly hugged and fondled her until he saw her slip into a deep slumber.

Then he disentangled himself, arranged the side pillows to support her, tiptoed softly from the room, and bolted the door, feeling very happy.

Holding Skystorm, he walked up to the central hall, newly built by Khun Chang. A sitting area[22] was furnished with folding screens, and a hill myna in a fine golden cage.

A large frame held a picture of a seated Farang, looking out sideways in a pose that suited the face.[23] He admired it in passing but hurried on to find Wanthong.

sitting area

---

22. The central hall would be a sala with a roof but no walls. Phraya Komankulamontri imagined that the "sitting area" was a part of this central hall with a raised floor (Chotchuang and Niranam, KCKP, 67).

23. This picture has provoked much discussion. Kukrit thought immediately of the Laughing Cavalier (KP, 176). Atsiri Thammachot argued it was probably the picture of a woman because the word for "looking out," ค้อน, is usually used with women (Atsiri et al., *KCKP*, 61). Khun Wichitmatra noted that the picture also figures in the *Samnuan kao* version of this chapter which, he argues, from internal evidence was written by Chaophraya Phrakhlang (Hon). Hon was *phrakhlang* in 1786 when a Portuguese envoy arrived from Macao bearing a royal letter from Lisbon—the first diplomatic contact with the West in the Bangkok era. Khun Wichitmatra surmised that Hon would have received gifts destined for the king and probably for himself too, among which might be a picture inspiring this passage, perhaps a likeness of the Portuguese king (KW, 166–69). When in 1690 Kaempfer visited the house of Kosa Pan, who had earlier been on embassy to France, he found that "the hall of his House . . . was hung with the pictures of the Royal Family of France" (Kaempfer, *Description*, 38).

Seeing slave girls asleep on the floor of the central hall, he blew a Loosener formula and walked past them into a room full of glittering crystal, double screens,[24] curtains, and blinds.

"This curtain is Wanthong's handiwork.[25] My mind's eye remembers it perfectly. Her silk embroidery is very precise. Such workmanship can be hers alone."

She had embroidered a forest scene. Around the borders were mountains wreathed in lush greenery. Plants of all kinds, profuse with budding foliage, flowed elegantly across the tableau, a wealth of rich blossoms scattered prettily among them.

A peacock glided down to cavort on a tall mountain peak, spreading its tail and extending its wings voluptuously. Gibbons hung from branches, glancing sideways.

The Himaphan Forest[26] was shown in all its grandeur, with the splendid form of holy Mount Meru, surrounded by Winantok, Hatsakan, Karawik, Isinthon, and Yukhunthon,[27] the heavenly rivers,[28] Mujalin Lake with all its five streams, and Mount Kailash standing out magnificently. Throngs of *kinnon* and skillful *khonthan*[29] dived and disported in the clear, chill waters of Anodat Lake.[30] Beside a cliff, a posse of dragons tossed a

khonthan

---

24. Screens placed inside and outside a doorway (KP, 183).

25. On the historical significance of the curtain in this passage, see p. 893.

26. In the Three Worlds cosmology, Himaphan, Pali Himavanta, snowy, is the area beyond human settlement, inhabited by animals, including many mythical species, and sometimes visited by gods. "In the land which is the Jambu continent which extends for 10,000 *yojana*, the place where humans live extends for 3,000 *yojana*; the place where the water has flooded and there is sea extends for 4,000 *yojana*; and the place of the Himavanta forest extends for 3,000 *yojana*. In this Himavanta forest there is great enjoyment. The Himavanta mountains are 500 *yojana* high, extend for 3,000 *yojana*, and have 84,000 peaks" (RR, 290). The Himaphan is the site of five great lakes, five great rivers, and five mountain ranges. As the geography of the Three Worlds is a mythologized version of northern India, this clearly is based on the Himalayas.

27. Five of the seven mountains or ranges surrounding Meru (see p. 218, note 15).

28. อากาศคงคา, *akat khongkha*, the systems of waterways around Mount Meru, a mythic description of the five rivers of the north Indian plain, including the Ganges (SB, 146; RR, 295–96).

29. คนธรรพ์, Sanskrit Gandharva, heavenly musicians. In Hindu mythology, they are nature spirits born from the body of Brahma as he sang, and become husbands of the Apsaras, heavenly nymphs. In the Three Worlds cosmology, they are minor deities that attend on King Dhatarattha, lord over all the deities to the east of the Yukhanthon range, and perform music for Indra with various instruments (*Hindu Myths*, 45, 342; RR, 220, 230–32; SWC, 2:847).

30. อโนดาต, Anottata, "unheated," one of the seven lakes in Himaphan. In the Three Worlds, it states that the sun's rays never penetrate to this lake "and thus this water is extremely cool as well as clear. It is the source of the five rivers, including Ganga" (RR, 292–96).

crystal ball from mouth to mouth. As he admired the scene, he thought of Wanthong,

and slashed the curtain to ribbons. He stepped through into a second partition. "Adorable! Exquisitely embroidered. Oh my dear, your skill is superhuman."

She had embroidered the illustrious Phra Lo[31] when he reached the Kalong River, became sorrowful thinking back to his mother, and asked the waters to give him an omen.

Pining over his mother, the queen, Phra Lo saw the waters as red as sappanwood. Laksanawadi[32] was left at the palace. His thoughts turned to the two sister princesses.

Old Lord Tigerspirit used a gem cock[33] to lure Phra Lo, who gave chase and lost his way. He arrived at a garden,[34] feeling ever more distraught. Phra Phuean and Phra Pheng were embroidered in gold,

entering the garden of love where Phra Lo caressed, coupled, and tasted bliss with both of them, while the ladies-in-waiting, Nang Ruean and Nang Roi,[35] waited on either side to give service.[36]

"Your efforts aren't wasted, Wanthong, but why did you get lost in lust with Khun Chang?" In rage, he cut down the curtain, ripped it to shreds, and tossed it aside.

---

31. ลิลิตพระลอ, *Lilit Phra Lo*, a courtly romance, maybe one of the oldest works of Thai literature, though the date of composition is widely disputed. Phra Lo is ruler of Suang, and exceptionally handsome. Phuean and Phaeng are the beautiful princesses of neighboring Song, a city defeated by Phra Lo's father. Hearing songs in praise of Phra Lo by balladeers, the two sisters fall in love with Phra Lo and decide to use magic to lure him. Under an ascetic's spell, Phra Lo leaves his home and wife in Suang to travel to Song to find Phuean and Phaeng. In stanzas 296–97, at the Kalong River, he misses his mother, and asks for an omen whether he should continue or return. "As soon as his words had passed from his lips, the waters circled, / And turned deep red, as though mixed with blood. / His heart was beset with a terrible suffering, / As though crushed by a tree a hundred spans in girth." Even so, he goes onwards, meets Phuean and Phaeng, and enjoys their love in a garden pavilion (Bickner, *Introduction*, 23, 58–59).

32. Wife of Phra Lo.

33. แก้ว, *kaeo*, gem, crystal, is used here, as in the Three Worlds cosmology, to mean something of unusual quality or value. *Pu jao samingphrai*, Old Lord Tigerspirit, the ascetic who works magic for the two sisters, summons all the cocks of the forest and chooses the most beautiful to entice Phra Lo.

34. The royal pleasure garden of Phuean and Phaeng.

35. Ladies in waiting of the two sisters.

36. In *Lilit Phra Lo*, the servants bathe the feet of Phra Lo and the two sisters but then withdraw before the lovemaking. Later, they help smuggle Phra Lo into the palace so he can stay with the two sisters. When this menage is eventually discovered, the king's mother arranges for all three to be assassinated in revenge for her husband's death when Song was defeated. The king is so appalled at this assassination that he has his mother cruelly killed. Subsequently the two cities are reconciled.

He found a third curtain. "Beautiful! I recognize Phim's handiwork." He stood admiring her curtain, captivated. She had cleverly embroidered the story of Khawi[37]

as he made his way through a forest to the holy city of Janthaprathet, and killed the eagles, spattering the ground with their red blood.

Khawi was portrayed playing in a river with the exquisite Jansuda, whose fragrant hair was placed in a golden casket and floated away.

Bold old Thatprasat was depicted coming to lure Jansuda from her home to be presented for the lord of another city to possess. The story reminded Khun Phaen of Wanthong and inflamed his rage.

"That hag of a mother, Siprajan, is no different from this bold hag." The more he looked at the lord, the more he was maddened with anger. "It's like Khun Chang seizing Wanthong from me.

That lord would have no difficulty getting ten thousand women. Khun Chang is a rich man too—loaded." Looking at the curtain, his heart raged like a roaring fire. Suddenly he raised Skystorm, slashed the curtain to ribbons,

and chopped it into a heap of hundreds of shreds. Cutting the drape and mosquito net away from the bed, he saw Khun Chang's stout form lying with his arms around Wanthong. He was filled with black feelings of disappointment, anger, and hatred.

"Little Wanthong, the one and only! Beside him you're not even half the size." He drew his sword. "Lay bare his neck. I'll slice it to pieces!"

Goldchild intercepted the sword, and then prostrated in apology. Growing ever angrier, Khun Phaen kicked Goldchild off the bed, but the spirit came between them and would not yield.

"Hold off! Cool down. Don't kill him, Father. Don't you fear the power of

---

37. A non-classical Jataka, found in the so-called Panyasa Jataka, *panyat chadok*, the "fifty lives" of the Buddha, which has been adapted into Thai in various forms as the tale of a tiger and cow. King Rama II composed part of the tale as an outer drama entitled *Khawi*. Khawi is a calf transformed into a human by a rishi who recognizes Khawi's qualities. Khawi travels to Janthaprathet, a place that is being terrorized by two giant eagles. He kills the eagles, rescues the king's daughter, Jansuda, who was hiding inside a drum, and falls in love with her. While they are swimming in a river, she sheds some of her fragrant hair which she collects from the water, places in a golden casket, and lets the casket float down the river. King Sannurat of Phathawisai opens the casket and falls in love with the owner of such special hair. Thatprasat, an old female retainer of Jansuda, offers to find the owner for the king. Thatprasat almost kills Khawi and abducts Jansuda to present to the king but Jansuda's body proves too hot for the king to touch. Eventually Khawi is revived, the king is killed, and Khawi replaces the king on the throne. (*Bot lakhon nok*, 387–482)

the Lord of Life?"[38] Khun Phaen ground his teeth and growled back, "No! I don't fear his power.

The wrong Khun Chang did me deserves a response this dire. I'll split open his chest with my sword. Back off and don't interfere! This is not your business. If I kill him secretly who'll catch me?"

Goldchild replied, "Don't make him die, just so hurt and ashamed that blood flows from his eyes. If you slash him dead, the gods may ensure you're arrested, and the story will spread around."

Khun Phaen's anger cooled. He stood looking at Wanthong despairingly. "You black woman, you feel even less shame for your own body than there's dirt under your fingernails.

You float your face over to be with your lover, Chang. Scouring your forehead with a ray skin would probably not hurt you at all.[39] To embroider those curtains, you sat leaning elegantly on your elbow, making such lovely little stitches.

Is he a good match for your figure? Now that you're enthralled by him, you don't look at his head. With a new pleasure, you forget me. Such a perfect couple!

I look at your cheeks but they've lost their sheen. I see no fairness of turmeric in your complexion. I gaze at your breasts but they're flabby. I can't find even a little firmness.

You've lost your old beauty, my crooked lady. I can't stand this any more, dear Wanthong. If I didn't complain, I'd be remiss." He drew his sword and raised it, but Goldchild jumped forward.

Khun Phaen angrily swatted the spirit aside. "Don't get in my way. I'm going to finish them off." Goldchild seized the sword and would not let go. Khun Phaen hurled the weapon away in anger and regret.

"Oh my Wanthong! I didn't think it could come to this—that you could sacrifice your rank and your dignity to this extent, like a jewel ending up with a monkey,[40]

who just lets it drop in the dust and bats it around. I'd like to slice your body into a hundred pieces and feed them to crows and vultures in the hills. I'll enjoy slashing Khun Chang too.

And Siprajan—all this happened because she looked down on me and didn't fear my sword. I'd like to slice her skin, slit open her chest, and sprinkle it with chili and salt!"

---

38. เจ้าชีวิต, *jao chiwit*, a conventional reference to the king.

39. The skin of the ray, a flat fish, is so hard that it is used to make armor and as a whip.

40. Throwing jewels to a monkey is a Thai proverb equivalent to casting pearls before swine (Gerini, "On Thai Proverbs," 164).

He grabbed Khun Chang's head. It was bald on top with a straggly fringe round the bottom, like a pond snail. The hair was shaped with pomade into a single circling wing, like the tasseled umbrella of a Mon noble.

topknot

He tried to gather Khun Chang's hair together into a topknot. "You jailbird, the middle of your skull is a wasteland." He combed the hair upwards into a curving wing, and plucked a track two fingers wide round the base with tweezers.

He held the hair up, inserted a stick, and bound it with cotton. "Damn you, your empty skull makes fleas go hungry." With soot he drew a scissortail fish, a turtle riding on his neck,

and a catfish poking out of the water at the top of a leg. Standing back, he laughed at his handiwork, then kicked Chang off the bed face down in a heap on the floor, and found two pots to tie round his neck.

Finished with Khun Chang, he stepped onto the bed beside Wanthong and loosed a deep sigh. "Oh Wanthong, you've lost your luster." He stroked her softly.

"My hand alone should feel your soft flesh this way. I alone should love and cherish you this gently, and touch you with my palms like pressing gold leaf.[41]

It's pitiful that your flesh and breasts are sad and wasted. That vermin has squeezed you sore already." He kicked Khun Chang in the stomach. "You're just an evil monkey that's drunk on riches."[42]

He was angry enough to cut off Chang's head and toss it away, but Goldchild intervened again. "Don't kill him, Father. Chop him up enough for his just deserts and your satisfaction but if you kill him, the wrong will cling to you."

Hearing the spirit, Khun Phaen calmed down and stood looking at Wanthong, hating Khun Chang ever more. He drove off the spirits and chanted a mantra to revive her. "Wake up and take a peek at your husband."

Wanthong, who had been asleep under the mantra, started awake with a shock. With eyes drowsily closed, she cuddled up to Khun Phaen and lay still.

A shiver of fear ran though her body, and she pinched what she thought was Khun Chang to wake him. "Let me tell you my horrible nightmare. You built a fire in the mosquito net.

---

41. One form of worship is to affix small squares of fine gold leaf, especially on Buddha images.

42. This translation assumes that ราย *rai*, a qualifier, in the original is a misprint for รวย, *ruai*, rich.

It flared up and caught the tips of the thatch that burst into flames and collapsed down, burning your gut and belly. I jumped down onto the floor.

The curtain, pillows, and mattress went up in flames, and I was blistered in several places. There was no one to help me beat it out. I was terrified.

Please tell me what this dream means. I've never had one like it. What terrible thing is going to happen?" She hugged him tight with eyes still closed.

Khun Phaen was angered by her words but replied, "This is a good dream, eye's jewel. Don't feel dismayed.[43]

When you dreamed that fire consumed the mattress, pillows, and curtain, it means someone else will bring these things to you. As for feeling upset, it means you'll hate some bad, besotted person.

Dreaming you cried out means something loved and lost will return. An old friend will hug little Wanthong and lighten her troubles and woe.

You and I will be happy, my cool one. Don't be afraid, don't be sad." He chucked her chin to amuse her. "Let me give you a little kiss."

Wanthong did not recognize the voice. His whispering made her even more nervous. She felt the smoothness of his chest and the slimness of his waist.

Surprised that he was so smooth and slight, she was too scared to say anything for fear of provoking him. She wondered why the chest was hairless, and the chin too. The fragrance of krajae-sandal heightened her suspicion.

"Is Khun Chang this slim? I can't even get my hand round his wrist." She sprung awake in alarm. Groping around, she found Khun Chang.

"Beloved husband, why are you lying down there on the floor with your eyes closed?" In panic, she tried to shake him awake with tears trickling from her eyes.

Angered by her words, Khun Phaen said, "Wanthong, my love, open your eyes and look what's happening.

I'm not some bandit so don't jump up and start shouting. Why are you shaking him awake? He doesn't have to get up so leave him be.

You're shaking a sleeping person awake while making a waking one feel unwelcome. Do you hate me or do you just not know me? Raise your face and greet me. Stop pushing and squirming.

It's a pity, Wanthong. I can remember every inch of your face and body but to you I'm a stranger. You feel me with your hands but you have no inkling.

You've forgotten us lying under a low *krathum* tree in the cotton field, and

---

43. Khun Phaen's interpretation reverses each of the messages of the dream.

picking a caladium leaf to scoop water. I was chewing betel and you wanted some, so I gave it. My left arm went stiff because you lay on it.

You've found yourself a good husband with lots of property, and forgotten the old house and a poor friend. You fell for the ploys of this pestering Khun Chang, and now you're hugging a log that looks like a person.

If he wakes up and sees me kissing you, I'll die for nothing with my throat shredded. If you manage to shake him awake, he'll get up and knock me down dead—really."

These words made the beautiful Wanthong's heart lurch and her doubts disappear. She felt as hurt as if pierced by a poisoned arrow. "He's sharp at using words to wound me,

dragging up the cotton field to sow confusion. This can only be Khun Phaen, for certain. He's so stubbornly sure of himself and fears nobody. With his powers, he'll create havoc.

His playfulness and sarcasm are unbearable. Stay still and think! What will be will be, according to karma. He may trample me to pieces but I'm not afraid of him."

She turned again to shake Khun Chang awake. "Get up, my lord and husband. Why are you lying there, eyes closed and oblivious? Don't you fear the Lord of Darkness from Kanburi?"

She batted over a betel tray, got up with tears in her eyes, and stood behind a screen in fury. "Tcha, that's enough! I thank you.

You're true to your word in everything—but in reality, never in full measure.[44] You can even spit saliva out of your mouth and swallow it back again. You're *really* good."

Khun Phaen replied angrily, "Tcha, you can say anything so cleverly. Trumpeting away, so truly sharp and so eloquent. Don't stop. Today let's hear each other out.

Just now you said I wasn't true to my word. You make lots of insinuations, and you're very self-righteous. But when it comes to keeping one's word, it's you who gives short change.[45]

You broke your promise first with bad intentions, and so I've come after

---

44. This is a complex metaphor about measurement. *Sat*, สัตย์, honest, true to word, is a homophone of *sat*, สัด, a volume measure, equivalent to twenty liters. At the time, *sat* and *thang*, ถัง, were both used as volume measurements, with *thang* only four-fifths the volume of a *sat*. She says: You're *sat* (honest), yes *sat* (measure). But in reality a *thang* is not a *sat* (measure) (KW, 174–75).

45. Continues the measurement metaphor: Your hand fails to fill the measure.

you to balance the account.[46] It's you who are clever at being honest in short measure but shift things around to look nice.

As soon as you had Khun Chang, you weighed matters up and became very, very light with the truth.[47] Your eloquence is truly biting. You're flaunting your fair face to provoke me.

You've no qualms about waking your lover to fight with your husband. You don't have a trace of fear. Why do you want to shake him awake? How many days has he been allowed to enjoy you in my place?

Aren't you sated and satisfied yet? Do you still consider him your heart's jewel? Does he still make you shake, shudder, swelter, and swoon? If you don't listen to me, your back will be striped."

Wanthong was cut to the quick by this angry assault. "Say what you like, I'm not afraid. It all comes down to calling me bad, over and over and over again.

You're taking one tiny little hair and slicing half of it into seven strands. You're the one who's so self-righteous. I've never experienced anything like this in my life.

Why are you pointing the finger at me? Only recently you came after me with a raised stick and a clenched fist. I still remember the past perfectly. You told that woman to slap me with no respect.

You even sent a letter full of abuse, breaking things off,[48] wanting to rip open my old mother's breast, saying you wouldn't support me, like Kaki.[49]

I was livid that you sent a letter accusing me of being lewd, destructive, bad through and through. It was like scratching a crab to draw blood.[50]

I tried to stop Khun Chang making love to me. He's ugly, and it was shameful. I didn't want to be here but my mother cried floods, and forced me into the bridal house,

so Khun Chang had the opportunity to do the damage. When I've been

---

46. More of the metaphor: I came to check the scales.

47. More of the metaphor: You repay each *sat* with only twenty-five (when it should be eighty) (SB, 159).

48. This is a remnant of an episode omitted from the PD version (see p. 273, note 30).

49. Kaki is the heroine of the Kakati Jataka, no. 327 in Cowell, *Jataka*, 4:60–61. The tale was adapted into a poem by Chaophraya Phrakhlang (Hon) in the 1790s, and then into an outer drama by Chaophraya Mahasak Phonlasep during the Second Reign. In the tale, Kaki is a very beautiful woman. Her fragrance lingers for seven days with any man who makes love with her. She is first married to King Phrommathat of Benares, and subsequently has five other lovers. The name Kaki is used to refer to a woman with many lovers.

50. The simile is similar to "trying to draw blood from a stone." She is accusing him of over-doing his invective.

through this much, don't you come back and carp at me. I'm spoiled because you didn't care. If you'd had some mercy, nothing would have happened.

When things are going your way, you soar. You get a good new wife and have no complaints. All lovey dovey. You even teach her how to abuse me terribly.

Now Laothong has left you, hasn't she? That's why you blunder up here in a blaze in the night. Things aren't going your way so you've lost your head. Starved for water, are you now turning to drink mud?"

"So eloquent and so self-righteous. I can see changing your name hit the mark. You must like the name Wanthong.[51] Before long your cheeks and breasts will be gold.

Yes, that's it. You don't want me to say anything—just stay at home with my eyes closed like an idiot while you do as you will. When I complain a little, you claim you've never experienced anything like it.

But that's not enough for you, is it? You're just getting into your stride, hammering away, dragging up the past to help you. Just who did I call to slap you, as you say?

You were in such a black fury with Laothong that you insulted her to her face and then leapt down from the boat. You were very abusive that day. No one could restrain you.

Who wouldn't take offense? You were in the wrong and that's why you ran off. Because I had mercy, I didn't slash you dead. I was angry with you, yes, but I didn't break it off.

Two nights later, I came to the house and found this wild elephant all over you in bed. I was as angry as if burned by fire, and on that day you nearly died.

If I'd used my kris, by now you'd be ash. Though I was angry, I still loved and missed you so I stopped thinking about it and forgave you.

At dawn when I kept asking you to come out of the room, you wouldn't look at my face for even a second. I'm still wavering and thinking of our love but you're twisting everything to blame me.

If you still loved me, you wouldn't say these things. But now that you don't, you make matters up. What are these letters I sent? The handwriting was Khun Chang's!

Because your lover pleases you, you invent anything to stab me and sow dissension. Our house built at the side has been torn down, thrown away, and his house built on the spot.

You got caught by his bait. Once you were in the cage, you couldn't wriggle

51. See p. 224, note 2.

free so you decided to turn against me. On reflection, this is all the fruit of fate.

It's like the story of Kaki. That bird Khun Chang flies off with the lady, and I'm cast as the *khonthan*, but don't sweet-talk me so you can go back to the palace.[52]

It's a waste to have loved you. I can see clearly what's really been going on. I come to find you but you act as if you hate me. And you want to wake your lover to try out his power.

For pity's sake, Wanthong! How can you cut me off like snapping a stalk? No queen to give cover. A rook taken without warning. A knight lost too. The position hopeless.

Two pawns lost in a sacrifice. Promoted pawns slashed and scattered. A knight marching up, and a rook falling. Now that I'm in check, the bishops will come under assault.[53]

When I think, it's pitiful—a tragedy, like a story from the mask play. Sida, alone and lonely, goes off with the villain, and Lord Ram trails after her with a heavy heart.

If only you were a little honest and true to your word like Sida, but you're not. You've lost every trace of principle or precept. In the past you said

that you'd rather die than let another man touch you, that you'd keep your love only for me. Why do you now let this fellow feel and fondle you? Is he your lover or not? You tell me!

This is already too much but you still want to rouse him to kill me. Where are his pike and sword? Bring them in! But don't wake him just yet.

If he opens his eyes to see me kissing you, then I'll die easily, topped at the neck. If he can do it, then let him. It's not every day that a good man dies.

In olden times, they said women had three hundred wiles, and they weren't making it up. I'm learning how true it is. I'll mold a statue of you for all to see,

as an example—to be remembered in every detail—of how good looks can go with a bad heart, how such round black eyes hide a sharpness inside."

Wanthong was sorely hurt by this verbal pounding, and tears welled up in her

---

52. See page 350, note 49 above on the Kaki tale. The mythical bird, Garuda, disguises himself, abducts Kaki from King Phrommathat, and flies away to his palace at the foot of Mount Meru. A *khonthan*, King Phrommathat's musician, goes along, disguised as a midge hidden in Garuda's feathers. When Garuda leaves the palace, the *khonthan* becomes her next lover. He later returns her to King Phrommathat's palace to win the king's favor.

53. Queen=เม็ด, *met*; rook=เรือ, *ruea*, ship; knight=ม้า, *ma*, horse; pawn=เบี้ย, *bia*, cowry; bishop=โคน, *khon*. These chess analogies were common in the literature of early Bangkok when the game was popular at court. They are found in *Rachathirat*, and *Ramakian* (SB, 160).

eyes. She tossed her head and said, "So, you don't remember your own words.

On the day of the quarrel with Laothong, you roared and bellowed on and on, blocked me from getting to her, and even chased after to slash me dead.

I was so angry I went to hang myself. When Saithong told you about that, you cursed, mounted your elephant, and took Laothong off like Phra Suthon with Manora.[54]

I'm sleeping with Khun Chang, it's true. But I put up a huge fight first. I wasn't spoiled with my eyes open. His spirits came and put me to sleep.

If my husband had had mercy and protected me, who could've done this to me? You just cast your net and take whatever fish is in front of the trap.[55] Because your heart has no mercy,

you mounted your elephant and went off with little Laothong, while I could only wait and pine. Your new wife clung tight and wouldn't let you come—and you have the nerve to say *I* don't keep my word.

You say I have three hundred wiles and you want to make a statue as an example. Why didn't you do it before? Because you were fondling *her* to your heart's content and didn't open your eyes.

Now you think I'm bad and won't support me. Nobody will argue with you that I'm good. If someone is bad, people run a mile. If someone is good, who doesn't love them?

You're ashamed you made the mistake of becoming my husband. You were as blinded by smut as if you'd fallen into a pit. Because you were dosed with a love potion, and mated with a bad woman, it detracts from your manliness.

Back when you loved me and lived with me, your complexion turned dark and blotchy as if affected by something in my body.[56] I apologize. But now

---

54. Another tale from the Panyasa Jataka that was adapted into an outer drama in the late Ayutthaya period under the titles of *Manora*, or *Manora and Phra Suthon*. Suthon, Pali Sudhana, a Bodhisatta, is a prince looking for a bride. A hunter comes across a group of *kinnari* bathing and manages to capture one of them, Manora, by taking away her wings, which she had removed before bathing. He takes her to court where she marries Suthon. When Suthon goes off to war, a counselor persuades the king, Suthon's father, that Manora is inauspicious and will bring disaster to the city. She is condemned to death but the queen gives her back her *kinnari* wings, allowing her to escape. Suthon returns from war, and sets off to search for her. With help from a hermit, he travels for seven years and seven days, crossing mountains swarming with monsters and rivers blazing with fire. When he reaches his goal, Manora's father sets him three tests to win her hand, the last of which is to identify her among seven identical girls. He succeeds when a golden butterfly alights on her.

55. A saying meaning you always take the easy route, like a fisherman who catches fish just where they are being driven by the current into a trap (SB, 161).

56. It was believed that someone subject to a love charm would develop freckles and blotches on the face. Wanthong is sarcastically saying that she must have used a love charm to get him to fall for such a bad person as herself.

those freckles have disappeared.

Since you went with Laothong, your skin gleams like a glittering diamond, your complexion glistens as if tinged with gold. So why flip-flop back to philander here?

This Wanthong is so evil, so terrible, that you couldn't keep her. Aren't you afraid to sit close to such an evil person? Oh! Are you leaping away?

It's not right for you to eat leftovers. It's beyond the call of duty, not befitting your status. Don't keep circling round and round. I release you like giving freedom to a bird.[57]

If you want money, maybe a couple of baskets,[58] I don't mind giving it to you. Or is it losing Laothong that's making you gloomy? I'll find a squeeze to cheer you up.

Would you prefer a Thai or a Lao? Should the young lady have a chignon or a topknot? I prostrate and beg you to stop pestering me. Don't get mixed up with me, or you'll be miserable."

"So sharp, so eloquent. Bang! Bang! Full of hidden meanings. I'm furious you accuse me of distorting things. Please look out for your head!

You float your face to challenge me on and on, and use such biting eloquence as if nobody knew what's behind it. You're weaving quite a tale, Miss Storyteller.

You think I'm poor and penniless so you can just mock and tease me. Don't float your face to abuse and hurt me. Don't question my words to cause me pain.

lady with chignon

I know your lover is a rich man with heaps of money to give whenever you wish. You keep saying how good he is to you.

This Khun Phaen has nothing—no gifts to bring you, no means of support. Your husband has wealth in millions. He's a real aristocrat.

You say you'll find someone else's daughter for me. You go on about it in a hundred ways. You want to foist someone on me to fill my loss so you can cuddle Khun Chang in comfort.

---

57. A common way to make merit, especially on festival days, is to release birds, fish, turtles, or other captive animals.

58. สัด, _sat_, a basket used as a measure (see page 349, note 44 above), perhaps a pun as the word also means mating among animals.

Don't bother thinking that I'll give you up. Even a lady from Dusit heaven[59] won't make me waver. My passion will never cool. If I can't have you alive then I'll have you dead.

Don't bother imagining that I'll give you up. This goes too deep to change easily. You can say anything without shame, even claiming you went bad because spirits possessed you.

You're good at lying and making things up. Your mother had a part in it too. She dragged you in with Khun Chang. Although I was far away, I know everything.

My spirits told me it all. Though your body was squirming, your heart was right in it. My love is still sincere and hasn't faded. Don't pretend otherwise. I've come to take you away.

Though you're spoiled and fallen now, it doesn't matter. I don't care. It's almost dawn and time to go. If you won't come, I'll cut you in two."

"Why are you bullying me, going on at me in a hundred ways? I'm spoiled and fallen because I was put to sleep, but you say I'm hiding things. Your spirits are intent on false accusations.

I squirmed and screamed enough to break the house apart. I got up to flee but he dragged me back. I ran into my mother who beat me over and over. Your spirits ducked in to look and thought I was willing.

Because I'm a woman, I was cornered. Who could I stagger after for help? I'm spoiled and fallen because he forced me. Your badmouthed spirits are good at mudslinging,

good at making false accusations, just lying rascals. They deserve to be smacked with a durian thorn and knocked senseless.

You say if you can't have me alive you'll have me dead. Strike me down, I'm not afraid. Whatever I say you don't believe so, why should I bother to live and put up with this?

Don't grind your teeth and growl for nothing. Do it! Why don't you kill me, slash me to death?" She pushed, pinched, and scratched him relentlessly.

"Just a moment! Don't do that. Are you really so stubborn? I'll draw my

---

59. ดุสิต, Pali Tusita, the "heaven of joy," fourth of the six heavens or "realms of the gods" in the Three Worlds cosmology. "In this heaven full of joy gem castles, silver castles, and gold castles provide the abodes, and there are gem walls surrounding them . . . and there are all kinds of activities, and all sorts of places such as lakes and parks. . . . The devata who live in this heaven full of joy know merit and know Dhamma. What is more, the Lord Bodhisatta who have built an accumulation of merit and will descend to be Enlightened and become Lord Buddha live in this level of heaven" (RR, 239).

356 | 17: KHUN PHAEN ENTERS KHUN CHANG'S HOUSE

sword and cut you to pieces, and then what will be will be.

You abuse my spirits to hit at me but it hasn't knocked me out. I came to take you back but you won't go. Aren't you scared to put up a struggle?

Today I'm not listening to you say you won't come." He clenched his fist, hit her, pulled her over, and drew his sword as if to cut her dead. "Why are you still nudging your lover? Be careful."

He brandished Skystorm, and blew a Beguiler mantra into Wanthong's face. "Don't underestimate me. Quickly. Get up. We're in a hurry."

Hit by the Beguiler breath, Wanthong felt drowsy. Her anger ebbed, and she stopped struggling. The sword made her heart skitter in fright, and each time he raised it, she squealed.

"What is this, my lord? Don't force me. I'll fetch some things. I'm going, understand? I'll take some savings—rings, money, cloth."

The more she twisted, the more he tightened his grip on her wrist. "Both my arms will break if you don't let me go. Why raise your sword to kill me? I'll leave quietly, so let go of my hands."

"Are you losing your biting eloquence? No more sounding off and waving your hands around? Good. If you're still stubborn, I'd like to hear it now.

Go and pick out some clothes and come back here." He blew a mantra onto his hands and stroked her back. "I love you, really I do. I teased you only because I was angry."

Hit by the mantra, Wanthong forgot her anger. She sat next to him with one hand on the floor and her head bowed. "Did I say I wouldn't go? I'll fetch some clothes and then leave with you."

She walked into a room to collect things. When she unlocked a chest, fragrance billowed out from the silk and cotton, all new and in many colors.

She picked out pieces and folded them neatly, then quickly opened another chest of cloth dyed in bright colors and scented with sandal oil and floral bouquet.

chest

She wrapped everything in a Farang silk handkerchief, and unlocked another chest full of gold, sparkling sapphires, elegant emeralds, *phirot* rings, and rings sparkling with diamonds.

She picked some out and wrapped them tightly in a shawl. "I'm taking time and Khun Phaen will be waiting." She put her cloth bundles in a little basket, and walked out.

Coming to the bed, she sat next to Khun Chang's sleeping form. As the mantra was weakening, she began to feel regret. "Leaving you, I feel like a kite that's lost its wind. Don't wait expecting me to still be alive."

She bent down and embraced his feet but he did not move. "Oh, your merit has run out, my lord. However much I shake you, you don't stir. How can you sleep and abandon your wife?

How can I let you know that Khun Phaen suddenly turned up and would have chopped off my head if I hadn't gone—that I didn't run away because I'm unfaithful?"

She wrote a letter relating everything. When finished, she folded it tightly, and stuck it on the wall of her beloved husband's room.

Again she tried to shake him awake, crying "Oh Chang, why are you sleeping so deeply? Are you under the control of bad spirits? I'll make offerings to them.

Please let my darling husband wake up. I'll prepare turtle salad, fish salad, duck, chicken, strong liquor, and sweets, along with silver candles, gold candles, and dazzling things."

One female spirit listened with her mouth watering, ravening for duck and chicken. But Goldchild called out in a fearful, forbidding tone, "I'll lop off your head right now. Don't even think about it."

The female spirit knew to fear Goldchild. She came up and kicked Khun Chang away, grabbed his arms and legs and bent him over backwards so that he slept on, oblivious.

Wanthong hugged him again but he did not respond. "Oh my lord, your merit has really run out." With her heart trembling in fear, she blacked out and fell unconscious.

Khun Phaen, great romancer, waited unusually long for Wanthong's return. Greatly concerned, he went into the inner room to find her.

Coming upon her crying and still groggy from fainting, he enchanted some water with a powerful mantra, and sprayed it on her face,

blew into the palm of his hand, and stroked her back. Wanthong revived and got up. "Why have you taken so long to pick out your clothes? You've kept me waiting."

She excused herself by saying blearily, "The basket has gone missing, and the hairpins too." Khun Phaen said, "Don't waste time over them. I'll carve you a hundred."

Wanthong lowered her face, and peered up at him. "Do you think I don't want to leave?" She tossed her head in annoyance and stood up. "Let's go. Run quickly and I'll follow."

"Oh love, I'm not used to this wooden floor. If I take you by the hand and run, I'm afraid I'll get a splinter or trip over a bowl and be stuck with the shards. Don't run."

She replied, "Why are you so tense and angry that you keep mumbling complaints, my lord?" She quickly left the bedroom, not raising her face.

Again she thought sadly of Khun Chang. "Oh pity! In sleep you roll far away from the pillow. When the dew is cold and clammy, who'll draw a coverlet over you?"

Seeing the remains of the curtains scattered in the middle of the room, she beat both hands on her breast hard enough to shatter. "What outcaste did that? I'm so hurt." She walked on, sobbing.

The central hall was full of female slaves asleep, motionless, on the floor. She looked at them with regret, then walked to Kaeo Kiriya's room and felt even sadder.

"I say goodbye, dear Kaeo. Look after Khun Chang and console him. You can remember how I did things. Prepare his food as when I was still here."

She came to the cages, hanging by a low seat,[1] with a pair of hill mynas and a lory. "Oh birds, your strong, sweet songs lifted my spirits.

Oh myna, you mimicked Khun Chang calling me 'Mistress Wanthong,' but now I won't hear you morning or night." She followed behind Khun Phaen, grieving.

On the terrace she stopped and turned to look back at the house with pangs of regret. She walked to the fish pond, leaned over and slid in her hand to feel

the smooth, round, sculpted shapes of the fish as they wheeled and whirled. She glanced her eyes over the pot plants, paired in couples with pretty blooms,

and a hollow-trunked tamarind, bent like an elbow, its seedpods parched, split, and peeling. "I say farewell, my fragrant sandalwoods.[2] Stay and flourish, double jasmine and hiddenlover.

Oh *lamduan*, I lament having to hurry away. Milkwood, gem jasmine, pupil tree, and damascene, I'll miss the scent of your falling flowers. Dear *jampi*, till I see you, how many years?

Oh fragrant friends, your flooding scent will sadly fade and fail. Oh flowering friends, your blooms will wither, wilt, and fall.

Little bushes hung with fruit, I'll see only tall trees from today. I leave this house to live in a forest where mosquitoes and midges will swarm over me.

Tree roots will replace my pillows, and I'll sleep pitifully. The stars will serve as torches, and I'll despair." She descended the stairs streaming tears as if about to die.

Khun Phaen consoled her, "Don't cry. Come with me for a bit and then I'll bring you back. Be my companion in the forest and enjoy seeing the birds for a month, then I'll bring you

stairway

---

1. เตียง, *tiang*, a flat seat on low legs.

2. จันทน์, *jan*, is used as the name of many trees distinguished by fragrant wood, bark, or fruit, including nutmeg and sandalwood. This line mentions two, จันทน์หอม, *jan hom*, and จันทน์คณา, *jan khana*, both members of the coffee genus. But the point here is the sound of the word and its associations (*jan* is also a homophone for the moon), not the species. This is one of the most famous passages of *KCKP* for its poetry.

back here, and come to fetch you again a month later. Why are you crying? There'll be times with him and times without.

With him, you can relish a house, and with me, revel in a forest. Both will be delightful. You can take turns at being rich and being poor, and find out which is best."

"Oh shut up! Don't keep annoying me with these fantasies. I'll go anywhere with you for the long term. Are you intent upon destroying me?

I didn't beg you to come and fetch me. Taking me away then bringing me back would cause me shame and misery, again and again. I won't go, won't go! Don't insist."

"Can't I tease just a little? Why are you so touchy, Wanthong? I love you and will take you to enjoy. Don't imagine I'd really give you back to anyone."

He led Color of Mist over, decked out in a saddle and bridle so fine he looked fit to soar on the wind. "Don't worry. Come and mount the horse."

He put his arm around her soothingly and whispered, "This is Color of Mist, a magnificent animal. My tenderness, please beg his pardon so he won't feel offended."

Wanthong was too frightened to go close to the horse but raised her hands in wai. "Oh my Color of Mist, don't put us in peril. Please allow both of us to ride you."

Khun Phaen stroked the horse's back to calm him while drawing Wanthong close and gently taking her hand to pat him. Color of Mist licked the hand, making her squeal in fright.

"What's this? Why are you scared for nothing? It's a pity you don't trust in my love. Jump onto his back and don't be afraid." He gathered her up in his arms and put his foot in a stirrup,

but she shook with fear and could not mount. Khun Phaen restrained the sure-footed Color of Mist from prancing around friskily. Once in the saddle, Wanthong clung to Khun Phaen in fright

with both her arms tight round his body. Khun Phaen smiled, nudged her teasingly with his elbow, and turned to say, "That's nice and close. Give me a little kiss and we'll be off."

He called out to the five lady spirits, "Please follow us into the forest," then urged the horse to leave through Ta Jom Gate.[3]

---

3. ตาจอม, eye peak, name of a gate at the southwest corner of the old wall and moat of Su-phanburi (see map 6).

They passed Wat Talum by a lake and saltlick, and Kamyan Mound by a fragrant pond.[4] With her arms around Khun Phaen, Wanthong's sadness gradually slipped away.

After cutting fast across the plain until they were clear of Suphan, Khun Phaen reined in the horse to trot towards the paddy fields of Plaek Mae in the distance.

Leaving the plain, they skirted a broad ditch lined with clumps of bushes. Reaching the river at Ban Phlap,[5] he reined the horse to a halt and wondered what to do.

"I'm worried about Wanthong crossing this deep water at night, either on horseback or by swimming, because of the fierce crocodiles. She's cheering up but this will unsettle her.

What shall we do to avoid crossing this river, Color of Mist? I seem to remember there's a ferryman for hire."

He told Wanthong his idea, and rode Color of Mist ahead to the ferry landing, where he shouted in a loud and intimidating voice, "We're here on orders from the king

to investigate whether a herd of elephants has come to the saltlick. There are important[6] elephants in this forest. Fetch us across without delay."

Matho Thabom[7] was fast asleep, and his ferryboat was stuck in the mud. Khun Phaen's call started him awake. "Eh? Who's shouting and what for?

Are they coming from south or north? The ferryboat's stuck fast in the mud and needs to be hauled out. Maybe it hit a stump and is leaking. If I step on both gunwales, it'll split.[8] That's my karma."

---

4. The sequence is slightly wrong but the places exist. Khok Kamyan, now Don Kamyan, "mound of the benzoin tree," is 7 kms south of Suphanburi, and appears on early Bangkok maps where the road crosses a canal (Santanee and Stott, *Royal Siamese Maps*, 104). The large pond still exists and is famous for leaf fish, *pla salit*. A further 7 kms south is Phai Plaek Mae, ไผ่แปลกแม่, "the bamboo different from its mother," i.e., different from before. Wat Talum is another 3 kms to the southeast, and is shown surrounded by lakes on the military maps of fifty years ago, though now the area is all under paddy (see map 2).

5. Ban Bang Phlap, is around 25 kms south-south-west of Suphanburi, on the Song Phinong Canal (see map 2).

6. Elephants with certain characteristics, including large size, shape of tusks, coloring of hide, and genital features, were considered "important" as military equipment or as ceremonial possessions of the king. The "white" or albino elephants were merely one subset in a much more elaborate system of classification, defined in manuals (see p. 410, note 27).

7. The name in Mon means "round gold," and the text suggests he has a broad Mon accent.

8. Maybe there is a pun here. "To step on both gunwales of a boat" is a proverb similar to "Run with the hare and hunt with the hounds," meaning taking both sides.

Khun Phaen cried out, "Get a move on. I'm on royal orders to follow up the news about big elephants. Don't dally."

Catching the part about a royal order, Matho Thabom stirred himself. He took off all his clothes and waded through the mud to push and rock the boat. It would not budge.

He went round to the stern and heaved, spattering mud up to his shoulder blades. Feeling so cold his teeth were chattering, he got into the boat, picked up a paddle, and quickly splashed off.

Seeing a horse and two people at the landing, he lifted his rear and levered himself up clumsily. "That's odd. Is he fooling me? Looks like he's kidnapped a palace lady,[9] and spun a tale to get me to bring the boat." He paddled along, stark naked. Wanthong shyly shut her eyes. "Oh! Look, this fellow goes too far!"

He had the paddle raised high and his feet placed wide apart. Khun Phaen cried, "I'm fed up with you. Put a cloth on first, boatman! And wash off the mud before you come up here."

Matho Thabom glanced down at his belly. "Who took my cloth?" He sank down on his heels, covered himself with both hands, and stared around vacantly.

Edging along to find his cloth, he quickly wrapped it round his belly. "I think you're fooling me. You've kidnapped one of the king's ladies."

Khun Phaen knew that delay would bring disaster, so he chanted a formula, leapt down from the horse, and blew it into the boatman's face.

"I'm asking you nicely, good boatman. Don't turn us away. Please send us safely across and I'll reward you for your trouble."

From his little finger, he took a ring with a lustrous pearl that glistened in the light, and proffered it with no hesitation. "It's nearly sunrise. Please take us across quickly."

Matho Thabom looked down at the ring, then raised his head with mouth fallen open. He cupped his hands to receive the beautiful thing, and quickly wrapped it in a cloth.

"I'll[10] sell this to redeem a slave I can hug in bed. I'm in love with I-Khlai at the end of the village, and I-Phon with the dangling breasts, the wife of Phan Son. You're like a patron who has brought me a mattress to lie on.

---

9. Matho has reason for concern. According to the Palatine Law, anyone abducting a woman from the palace was liable to death, and anyone helping such a person's escape was liable to have the throat cut and property seized (clause 123, KTS, 1:121).

10. This stanza is taken from SK2, 148, absent from PD.

horse with flanchard

Come along quick. Before long the sun'll be up. You must cross the fields and get clear of the village. Once people wake up there'll be trouble, and you'll be the death of me too."

Khun Phaen turned to find Wanthong, then went over to Color of Mist, took off all his gear, and led Wanthong down to the boat.

They sat side by side on the central seat, smiling happily. He picked up the reins and pulled the horse. "I'm sorry, Color of Mist, you have to swim.

We're greatly indebted to you. You must be angry at having to travel at night through the wild forest. I'll take care of you as well as I can, my hardworking friend."

Reaching the other ferry landing, he released the horse to shake himself dry in a clearing. Wanthong helped to carry the horse tack over,

and they put all of it back on Color of Mist including stirrups, leather flanchards,[11] saddle, bridle, and pretty tassels.[12] He lifted Wanthong in his arms up onto the horse,

held her to make sure she would not fall, then dug his heels into Color of Mist, who set off at a thundering gallop. They went like a streak until they reached Ban Kluai Yung Thalai.[13]

He scraped a tree with his sword, and

rice barn

---

11. แผงค้าง, *phaeng khang*, side flaps. The standard Thai military saddle, adopted from Burma, had a wooden seat covered with thick cloth, and panels of cow or buffalo leather hanging down each side to protect the horse's flanks. These panels were often painted (Julathat, "Asawa-alongkan," 195–201; Robinson, *Oriental Armour*, 218).

12. พู่, *phu*, tassels made of cotton or cowtail hair in the shape of a banana flower, hung from the bridle just below each ear (Julathat, "Asawa-alongkan," 205).

13. บ้านกล้วยยุ้งทะลาย, the Village of Banana and Cluster of Rice Barns, 4 kms southeast of U Thong. There is a legend about the village's name. Grandpa Khun Thong was a metalworker and alchemist able to convert ore from a local mine into pure silver. He hid his output in rice barns and swore his daughter to secrecy on pain of death but she eventually revealed the truth to her pestering husband in a riddle. Khun Thong killed her, was arrested, refused to reveal the secret of his alchemy in return for a pardon, and was executed (KW, 187; SWC, 7:3345–46; see map 2).

wrote with charcoal. "If that shiny-head follows me, he'll meet disaster. Let them all come, grandpas riding on grandmas, I'll hurl them down on the ground so their hearts tremble.

Then I'll slash them with this sword till they writhe to death, turn them face up to split open their chests, and chop them into chunks to my satisfaction.

Even if it results in a court case, I'm not afraid. When they're dead, what can they do? I'll slash them; hang the consequences. Where are his grandparents? I'll dig them up.

I'll make those slaves, the three miserable cousins,[14] feel a ghost scraping down the nape of their necks. I alone will kill the cowardly Ratthaya and Sonphraya. Just wait and see.

Don't ever imagine I'll run away. If that buffalo-head follows, I'll fight. The big baldy, little baldy, and the whole crowd, if they come after me, I'll kill them stone dead.

I'll hug Wanthong with my left hand while I slash them to pieces with my right. Let them dare come and test their powers, one on one!" His eyes suddenly blazed blood-red.

In a fit of aggressive rage, he drew Skystorm, raised the sword high in a powerful pose, then slashed, sliced, and stabbed about himself wildly.

His elbow hit the chest of Wanthong who cried out, doubled over, and almost fell. "Oh karma! You really got hit." He hugged her.

"I'm sorry, I was babbling. Where did I hurt you? Please forgive me. I truly was carried away, Wanthong."

He caressed her and calmed down. They mounted the horse and set off, both smiling happily. They had left Suphan as intended. A brilliant moon bounded above.

They reached Phra Hill[15] where he had earlier come to worship. He pointed out to Wanthong, "From here, Venus looks like a firefly." The moon was fast dipping down.

---

14. On Khun Chang's family, see p. 392.

15. เขาพระ, *khao phra*, sacred hill, is a rocky outcrop on the edge of the Tenasserim range foothills, 3 kms northwest of U Thong. It has clearly been a sacred site for a long time. There are remains of a brick stupa on the peak, and of a Dvaravati-style stupa at the foot. Fragments of many Buddha images, rishis, Hindu images, tablets, and amulets have been found at the site. Formerly, there was an open-air Buddha image on the site but this collapsed. Around 1912, a reclining Buddha was made in one of the caves facing U Thong town, and this still exists (this is probably the location marked as "Ban Tham Phra," sacred cave, on the early Bangkok maps, see Santanee and Stott, *Royal Siamese Maps*, 92–93). In 1964, a Buddha's footprint found at the site was moved to the peak. In 2000, a new pavilion was built over the footprint, and in 2002

The fresh fragrances of many flowers mingled merrily with the perfume of her cheeks. Peeping through the mist, a red-tinged moon

shone on splendid sprays of flowers. A patter of pollen softly suffused the air. Blossoms bloomed voluptuously. He pulled down a branch, picked a posy for Wanthong,

put it behind her ear, and gaily inhaled the scent. "Let me savor the flower. Don't stop me. Just a little taste." He hugged her. "Hey! Don't touch. My things will bruise."

"I'm touching very softly, just enough to drive away the weariness of the night. Me, I'm never rough. That's an old bruise you got in a row."

Wanthong cried, "Oh, what's this? Even now, you're making fun of me. You're so cutting." A loud cockcrow announced the approaching dawn.

The shrill of cicadas and drone of crickets rang through the forest all around them. When golden light lit the earth,

birds burst into song. A gibbon, hanging from a branch, whooped plaintively at seeing the light of the sun, tinged strangely red like dripping blood.

Swaying in a treetop, the beast let forth chilly whoops and wails as if crying pitifully for her husband.[16] At the sight of people, she swung away, followed by her young, worried their mother was abandoning them.

Gangs of monkeys hung among the limbs of a *langling* vine,[17] swinging madly in strings, and scrapping with langurs. Crows[18] dived dizzily into the branches of a *kalong*,[19]

clung to every twig of a *pheka*, jostled to peck at the night jasmine, and careered down to nest in creepers in a cacophony of cackling and cawing.

---

two flanking sala were added, one of which has a mural depicting Khun Phaen's flight with Wanthong. (*Wat khao phra sisanphetyaram*, 1–7; KW, 187; see map 2)

16. See p. 181, note 41.

17. ลางลิง, more often กระไดลิง, *kradai ling*, *Bauhinia scandens/anguina*, a large hardwood vine. The plant appears often in Thai poetry, e.g., *Nirat Than Thongdaeng*, *Lilit Phra Lo*, and in manuals of versification, because it is alliterative on its own, because it is a homophone of the Thai for "some monkeys," and because it links easily by rhyme and alliteration to words for run, jump, play, etc. This stanza is a riot of wordplay, barely approximated in the translation, with repeated play on the sound "ling" (=monkey) conveying the impression of crowds of monkeys scampering around.

18. In the thirty-five syllables of the following five hemistiches, there are thirteen repetitions of the syllable *ka*, the Thai name and the call of the crow, plus six other *k* initial letters, interleaved with six repetitions of the sound *long* in various tonal forms. Crows caw loudly through the passage (Atherton, "Space, Identity, and Self-definition," 45–47).

19. กาหลง, *Bauhinia acuminate*, a small shrub with pretty white flowers, sometimes called a dwarf white bauhinia, originating from Malaysia. It is scarcely big enough to have the "branches" imagined by the text here but lends itself to alliteration and wordplay both here and elsewhere in Thai verse.

A tiger slunk behind a tiger-eye tree, stalking a herd of sambar deer sheltered in the shade
of a broad deer's-ear tree. Elephants flattened a
stand of elephant cane. Magpies fed on the branches
of a pupil tree.

Doves, buttonquails, and imperial pigeons cooed in
couples. Partridges harrumphed[20] among the trees. Rose-
finches fretted and frenetically flapped their wings. Orioles
perched on cinnamon trees at the for-
est fringe.

sambar deer

Passing through the edge of the forest by the
bank of a pond, Khun Phaen saw a lone adjutant
stork,[21] wading and bobbing its head. He whispered
to her, "What's this? Khun Chang has chased us down
already. Look!"

buttonquail

partridge

Wanthong's heart skipped a beat. She peered around for a
moment but saw only a stork catching crabs. She kept quiet and
said nothing.

"Oh, it's a bird, Wanthong. From a distance I couldn't see clearly and thought
it was your husband giving chase. Now that we're close I can see it's a stork.

Why has it got no hair on its head? There are people with heads like that
too. Why are there lots of such birds that cruise around catching nice fresh
prawns to eat?

I thought your husband had followed us, and I almost spurred the horse to
gallop away. What if he really had come? Where could we hide? If he got too
close, I'd hand you back to him.

If he had mercy and didn't kill me, then there probably would be no court
case. But if he sued me in the inner sala, I'd defend on my merit.

I'd give evidence that I didn't break in and take his lordship's wife by force,
but went there on other business, and she fell in love with me and took the
lead. She latched onto me and raced in pursuit.

Seeing me on my horse, she ran behind, begging to come along. Even though
I refused, she grabbed the horse's tail and wouldn't listen, all the way past Ban
Phlap Yisae.[22]

---

20. ปักก่อ, *pak-ko*, an onomatopoeic rendering of the Chinese francolin's call, described as
"harsh, grating '*do-be-quick papa*' or '*more beer, hah* or *come to the peak, ha-ha*'" (King, *Field
Guide*, 100).

21. See p. 3, note 13.

22. The same Ban Phlap where they made the ferry crossing earlier in the chapter. Yisae is

She was so tired, I took pity on her, and let her mount and ride. Next thing, she was begging to sleep with me but I didn't agree to lovemaking."

"Oh right! I'm a bad person. I leave the husband I hate, and run off with the lover I love. I'm so excited by this fine fellow's charms that I'm smitten.

You[23] notice only that great adjutant stork. But further on, don't you see that mound, that's a *soithong*[24] bird on a *satue* tree? Is that Laothong following us?

Somewhere I heard she went into the palace. You can't have her any more, that's why you came after me. Oh, are you annoyed? Let me down from the horse. I'm not going."

"Hey! Do you want to jump off? So brave! Aren't you afraid you'll lose your way? It's a long, windy way across a great plain. Can you walk through the forest?

Don't give up, my jewel. Come with me, and I'll fulfill your desires. Now that we've come here clasped together, my feeling for you has returned, Wanthong.

Besides, who'd believe me saying all those things? When has a rich man's wife ever come just like that? If I lost the case, that'd be normal. I've touched you too much already. That's the truth.

Whether we live or die is up to fate. I'll take you all the way, my lucky charm." He hugged her, kissed her, and stroked her back lovingly. "Calm down. I love you. Don't be angry."

Wanthong scratched, pinched, twisted, and squirmed. "Stop making love to me. I won't let you have me. Why should I be bruised for nothing? It's not a fee for the horse ride.

You're all sweet talk and playing around. I'll give you what you deserve. Let go of my hand. Why are you holding me? I won't fall from the horse. Take your arms off!"

"Earlier you seemed scared so I was protecting you, but now you're complaining again. An expert rider already are you, Wanthong? I feared you'd fall off because of inexperience. Raise your face and don't be angry."

---

another name for the Song Phinong Canal (see map 2).

23. The next two stanzas down to "I'm not going" are taken from SK2, 150; PD has: Why am I following you for no use? You can't say one little good thing about me. I'm ill-fated, as worthless as a speck of dust. Why am I going? Stop the horse. I'm getting down.

24. สร้อยทอง, golden necklace, a bird that appears in poetry and modern song but appears to be mythical.

With that, he dug his heels into Color of Mist who galloped off, full tilt. Khun Phaen turned back to watch over Wanthong while the horse streaked ahead, wind whooshing out of his ears. Wanthong clung on tight with her face down. "Lightning strike! I'll fall off and die. Please rein him in!"

"I thought you said you weren't afraid of falling off. How come you're hugging me so tight now, pinching so hard you'll leave a mark? We've reached a place to stop and rest."

They had come to a mound and cliff at Banyan Landing.[25] Pools brimmed with crystal clear water. A stream poured over rapids in a torrent. Overhanging cliffs soared above. A beautiful place.

Lovely lotus flowers, peeping from behind leaves, loosed their scent into the stream. A

banyan tree

thicket of tall trees screened the bank, and the ground was strewn with petals of blooming flowers.

A fresh breeze blew cool fragrance through the lofty forest. The shrill of cicadas rang through the trees. He lifted Wanthong down from the horse's back,

and released Color of Mist to drink water. He scrubbed the horse, chanted a mantra, and splashed water on his face. He urged Wanthong to change clothes and plunge into the stream.

They splashed around in the water, merrily ducking and diving, laughing and joking. Blooming lotuses released their soft pollen.

---

25. Suphon suggested that Phu Muang, ผุผ่อง, purple fountain, was the site of this scene (SB, 208). The Phu Muang Forest Park now makes the same claim. The park is around 6 kms southwest of U Thong, with the entrance a few hundred meters along the Bo Phloi road, Route 3342, from its junction with Route 321. The site would be 6–7 kms from Phra Hill, the last identifiable place on their journey, by a route skirting the base of the hills. A wide, shallow stream comes down from Khao Khok, with three small waterfalls in its rocky bed. However, the area has had low rainfall in recent years, resulting in the stream running dry, and the surrounding vegetation becoming so parched it is difficult to identify with this scene. The park also has some pits claimed to be elephant enclosures dating back to the Dvaravati era, and the remains of a laterite preaching hall.

Limpid water lapped over rocks. "Look how really clear it is!" Gleefully he swam close to her, smiling, laughing, teasing, and tickling.

He stretched out his arm, and asked her to wash him. "Hey! Why are you squeezing me there? I didn't ask you. Hands off!" "Well, there's some dirt or something—

something black on your breast." He stroked it and laughed. "Oh, it's a mole!" He gaily splashed water on her breasts. "Hey! Too much! I'm getting angry.

And I'm cold. I can't bathe with you." She got out and sat laughing on the bank. Khun Phaen changed his clothes and said, "It really is cold." He led her under the shade of the banyan.

He ordered his spirits and Goldchild to keep watch and not let anyone approach. He cut banana leaves, and laid them on the ground for Wanthong under the tree's shade.

Then he took off all his gear. He removed his bandeau, raising hands to his forehead to pay respect. He took off his shirt dyed with powerful herbs, golden beads, hat, waist sash,

belt embroidered with letters in gold silk and cotton thread, and single *takrut* heavily inscribed. Carefully he laid out everything,

then snuggled up and hugged her blissfully. "Let's ask forgiveness of this holy banyan together. It's broad daylight and he might not approve."

"Don't get carried away so, my lord, Khun Phaen. It's not the end of the day yet. Where can I flee in this forest? I came with you because of such great love.

I've abandoned house and home to be your friend to death. I've allowed myself to be carried off to this forest. My love is plain to see. Aren't you ashamed in front of this banyan's spirit?

Even though times are hard, let's make a hut. How can I close my eyes and sleep here? If you don't look after me, I'll become gloomy. Don't make me embarrassed."

"We've got nothing. No curtain, no mosquito net, no home. It's like old times at our beginning. Remember going to the cotton field?

This lofty forest should make your heart bloom. My cool one, have some sympathy for me. Don't be shy of this heavenly banyan."

He hugged her tightly with desire. Thunder rumbled, and rain splattered heavily down, drip-drip-dripping through the banyan until the leaves were soaked sopping, shiny wet.

A breeze rippled through the forest, swaying the tree and setting its branches trembling. The pair fondled passionately, and found happiness in the shade of the banyan.

The coupling greatly satisfied Wanthong. She tasted the love she had missed while they were apart, and her passion for Khun Phaen was rekindled.

She picked a *yang* leaf to fan him, swatted away bothersome gnats and mosquitoes, and watched over him attentively until he fell fast asleep from great fatigue.

Sitting alone beside him, she became quiet, lonely, and wistful. As the mantra faded, she realized her predicament, and sighed with anxiety.

"Oh pity, pity, look at me now. I've come to stay in this great forest where I'll be prey to its wild animals. As a home, the forest will be like a graveyard.

I can't see how I can survive here. Dead or alive, I'll probably be crushed in this forest. I thought only of coming, without thinking of myself. I didn't know it'd be like this.

Khun Phaen brought me because of love. That's obviously true and I can't ignore it. But, goodness, I've never experienced this kind of hardship since the day I was born.

Before, I couldn't even imagine it; now it's sadly real. Before, I knew nothing; now I'm an expert. Before, I'd never met buzzing bugs and crawling caterpillars; now I know them all.

How will things be tomorrow? Even worse?" Her thoughts made her heart heavy and her tears fall. She began to worry about Khun Chang again.

"Pity, pity. I was happy in that house. He was very protective, let nothing upset me, and cuddled me every morning and evening without fail. Life was easy and sweet.

When it was time to sleep, I had a bed and a net to fend off the mosquitoes and flies. When it was hot, I had a fine couch and someone to fan me.

When I bathed, there was someone to scrub me and put turmeric on my skin, a fine bright mirror to admire myself, tooth powder to polish my teeth to gleam,

perfumes with rich floral aromas, krajae-sandal to make me pretty, cloths and silks by the thousand. Now all is lost and gone.

From here on, there'll be only dust and wind, grime and gloom. Before long we'll have to weave leaves to wear. Day by day my misery will mount."

She shivered and sighed in self-pity, turning to look at Khun Phaen, fast asleep. "I'd like to rest my back but how can I lie on nothing but pebbles and sand?"

She picked up a tree root to use as a pillow, then stared at it in utter despair. She felt the ground, finding it rough and rock hard. "I miss the house where I was happy.

Now everything's a disaster. I left my home to come and sleep in the wilds where there are no lights, only the moon, no roof, only the shade of a tree.

Oh, the misfortune of being born a woman! I should be happy but I cannot be. I went astray in love's pleasures without thinking of shame. Because I wasn't strong-willed, I now suffer.

It's a waste to have beautiful looks, a pretty name, and a gentle manner if you have a terribly wicked heart. The good in me is the best in the land; the bad, nobody can match."

She shuddered, heaved a deep sigh, and lay sleepy, lonely, and sad. To stop her mind racing to and fro, she thought of love. "The damage is done. Whatever will be follows from there.

I can't be angry at Khun Phaen. He truly loves me deeply. We'd been apart a long time and he had another wife. He could have become distant.

Out of love he had the nerve to come after me and spirit me off to the forest, unafraid of the clamor of a court case. He offered his life in exchange for me, Wanthong.

I can't quit now. I have to go with him. Whether I die is down to fortune." She stretched out, slipped her arms around him, and wept. Lying still, her face nestling against his, she fell asleep.

Now to tell of Khun Chang. He could not wake up until Khun Phaen's mantra had worn off. When he revived and opened his eyes, there was a bare track across his skull.

His head hurt. He felt where the hair had been pulled out. "It shouldn't be bare like this. My whole body is covered in soot. Eh! How did I come to be under the bed?"

He got up, saw Wanthong was missing, and shouted out for her at the top of his voice. "In the evening I asked her to sleep beside me. Just at midnight, I turned over and gave her a hug."

He saw the door standing wide open and leapt over to look out a window. There was no sign of her around the central hall. Seeing the ruined curtains scattered about,

he gathered a pile in his arms and roared, "It must be Khun Phaen who came and took her away!" He summoned the servants and shouted at them, "You hid your faces and let this villain come up here!"

The house servants cried loudly in alarm, "A tiger came to maul the dogs." Khun Chang lashed at them with eyes closed. They shouted, "A wild tiger came to eat people."

Ai-Thong opened his eyes and said, "What's that? A tiger? Couldn't be, it had no coat. Maybe a spirit or a butting goat? But it had hands and feet like a person. Oh! An abbot."

He raised his hands in wai. "*Sathu saja!*[1] What is your wish?" Khun Chang angrily chased him away, and went round looking for Wanthong, even getting down on hands and knees. He was surprised to see salvers scattered around.

When he opened a chest and found many pieces of cloth had disappeared, he lost his composure and began sobbing. He discovered many rings had also gone. Looking round, he saw a letter on the wall.

In the note, Wanthong said, "I'm sad and miserable. Make haste to follow me into the forest. At cockcrow, Khun Phaen

---

1. สาธุสะจะ, a formula for giving thanks as the opening of a prayer or invocation, especially famous as the opening of the invocation to teachers in Sunthon Phu's *Kap phrachaisuriya*, a passage adopted into literary and language manuals as a model for such invocations.

put people to sleep, came up to the house, and entered our room. I tried hard to shake you awake. I resisted him several times but he raised his sword to kill me.

I'm just a helpless woman with no one to help me so I had to go with him, not because I'm tired of being here. Don't abandon me to die. Hurry after me at once."

Khun Chang raised the letter reverently above his head and writhed around in distress. "Why was I unconscious? I'm a bad husband, eye's jewel.

How come I slept through all this? Khun Phaen shaved my head, playing with me like a dog. You shook me but I didn't wake. Those five spirits were a sham.

It's a waste of effort feeding them offerings of liquor, rice, turtle, fish, chicken, and pork. They did nothing to protect us but let that villain take us by surprise.

I'm going to drown you five spirits,[2] the whole lot of you. May you die bad deaths." He called Sonphraya. "Why did you hide away and sleep?

Khun Phaen came right into the room and kidnapped Wanthong. Why didn't you bolt the gate of the house? Money and cloth have disappeared too."

Sonphraya said, "Why are you getting angry with me? I was in the other house. You didn't even wake up when he was plucking your head bare.

Why did you fall for her, sir? Why are you shouting angrily like this? And why are you so upset about her going? She doesn't love you so she ran away from you."

Khun Chang replied, "I'm not besotted with Wanthong. I'm angry because she stole my money. If I catch her, I'll carve here so the blood flows.

As for Khun Phaen, I'll chop him into piles of little pieces with my sword, reclaim all the property, and bring back Wanthong—Oops! I forgot."

Sonphraya laughed uproariously. Khun Chang turned to order the servants. "Go and talk to the forest people we've had dealings with in the past,

those Karen and Lawa who come to sell eaglewood from the deep forest. Send people to bring them here. When there are five hundred, we'll march."

Once the Lawa men had arrived en masse, Khun Chang gave orders to feed them. He had liquor poured for his elephant, Phlai Kang, until he was fully satisfied with a hundred liters.[3]

---

2. To dispose of a spirit, it must be trapped in an earthen pot, the lid closed and sealed by a mantra, and the pot submerged in a river.

3. The elephant is given five ไห, *the*, an old unit of roughly twenty liters. Liquor was believed by some to make elephants (and people) fight more strongly. "One day, seeing that they were

Then he hurried over to his mother's house, prostrated at her feet, and told her everything openly. "Last night Khun Phaen came,

put people to sleep, and entered right into our room. He stole a lot of property and kidnapped Wanthong too. I'm taking leave to go after them.

If I catch him, I'll slash him dead and bring Wanthong back. In war I'm not afraid of anyone. Please give me your blessing for success."

Thepthong replied, "Why are you in love with her? She's wicked, gone off with another man. It's not fitting to chase after her so why do it?

You can choose from all Suphanburi. There are plenty as good as her. Listen to your mother and don't run after her. She won't come back, my son."

Khun Chang answered plaintively, "Wanthong is not wicked, Mother. She did her best to wake me but he raised his sword to kill her,

and she's just a helpless woman so she really had to go. She wrote a letter telling me everything so I'm very upset. Don't stop me, Mother. Give me your blessing."

Thepthong knew she could not restrain him so fell in with his wishes. "May you have victorious power like a poisoned arrow. May you find Wanthong in the forest, and get her to return with love in her heart.

If Khun Phaen resists, may he lose to your power in every direction, and meet his death. May your hopes and wishes be fulfilled." Khun Chang received the blessing, took leave, and went out to the central hall.

tuck-tail style   He[4] dressed in a yok, worn in tuck-tail style[5] and secured

---

already outmanned, they thereupon decided among themselves to take liquor and pour it down [the throats of] their elephants and people. Consuming it beyond capacity, they fought while disoriented and tipsy" (RCA, 495, explaining a Thai army defeat by the Burmese at Ratburi in 1765).

4. In TNA mss 59, the next three stanzas are substituted with a more comical description of Khun Chang's dressing: Khun Chang got dressed and prepared. He combed his hair and powdered his face to look handsome. He put on an elegant golden yok, and an uppercloth edged in yellow, gentlemanly stuff, / and tightened a belt round the waist, making him bulge. He was roly-poly and lovely in every detail. He grasped a highly polished sword and went to the shrine room to cleanse himself. / He enchanted water and washed himself three times, took a big sacred thread to bind round his head, smeared his face with krajae powder to frighten enemies, dabbed sandal all over his thighs, and wobbled out. / He gave orders to Kaeo Kiriya, "All of you here, look after my house well. I'll be far away for several days." He left the house immediately.

5. โจงหาง, *jong hang*, more often โจงกระเบน *jongkraben*, "hitch tail." The lowercloth is wrapped with a long "tail" that is passed between the legs and tucked in the waist at the back, giving a pantaloon-like appearance. The style was fashionable at court in the nineteenth century.

high on his chest by a belt. He tied around his body a cord hung with auspicious amulets, mercury charms, a sacred thread,

a single copper testicle like a diamond wall,[6] a turmeric-colored stone from a duck egg,[7] and a single *takrut* from Master Khong.[8] In his mouth he put a Phakhawam[9] amulet to make his speech stun.

On the back of his neck, where his hair was sparse and curly as a conch, he put a yantra cloth. Picking up a lance-goad,[10] he stumbled over to mount the neck of his elephant, Phlai Kang.

Sonphraya rode swaying behind him, looking as fine as a molded doll. The servants, all merrily drunk with glazed eyes, waited together in front of the stairway.

Phakhawam amulet

---

6. ลูกไข่ดันทองแดง, *luk khai dan thongdaeng*, a metal lump believed to be a "copper" or single testicle, one sign of a man with lore, that was not burnt by a cremation pyre.

7. ไข่เป็ดเป็นหินขมิ้นผง, *khai pet pen hin khamin phong*; a stone, usually light green, found in the egg of a duck or chicken. When placed on a shrine and worshipped, it will fulfill any wish. "Khun Chang may be rich because of this one article" (Prachak, *Prapheni*, 171).

8. Perhaps the same abbot of Wat Khae who instructed Khun Phaen in chapter 6. With the exception of the *takrut*, these are objects found in nature that are considered powerful, คลั้ง, *khlang*, in themselves because they appear to defy the usual laws of nature—a metal that behaves like a liquid, a stone that looks like an egg, etc.

9. พระภควำ, a small metallic figure of Gavampati, an early disciple of the Buddha. In the canonical literature and early commentaries from Sri Lanka, Gavampati is mentioned among the second group of disciples of the Buddha, associates of Yasa, but with no detail. Probably on account of his name meaning "Lord of Cattle," other early texts gave him a background as an ox herder, and a quirky trait of chewing the cud. He also displayed supernatural ability to hold back a river that threatened to swamp the Buddha and a group of disciples. From around the fourteenth century onwards, texts appeared in Southeast Asia that celebrated eighty early disciples and gave several of them substantial biographies, including Gavampati. He is described as so beautiful in appearance that he was often mistaken for the Buddha, and as a result used special powers to make himself ugly—hunched, potbellied, flat-faced. When he was approaching death, he set himself the task of converting Somphon, Sanskrit Sambala, a Brahman who stubbornly rejected Buddhism, by delivering a series of sermons on impermanence in which he stated that the human body was a "public place" because its nine orifices (two eyes, two ears, two nostrils, mouth, urethra, anus) served only to emit impure excretions, and to admit impurities from the outside. Somphon was converted instantly, and went on to achieve nirvana. Gavampati achieved nirvana, underwent a magnificent funeral ceremony presided over by the Buddha himself, and became an *arahant*. Since the Sukhothai era, Gavampati has been depicted in statuary as a potbellied monk, often known as Sangkachai or Mahakaccayana. In lore, images of Gavampati are credited with strong powers to convey invulnerability. Apart from the Buddha himself, Gavampati is the figure most often depicted on amulets, usually with hands over eyes, and sometimes extra pairs of arms for other orifices. Many such amulets are small, almost spherical balls of metal. Often these images are mistaken for representations of the Buddha. (Lagirarde, "Gavampati"; Lagirarde, "Devotional Diversification"; Strong, "Gavampati"; SB, 353; KW, 682; YS, 31–39)

10. ของ้าว, *kho ngao*, a lance with an elephant goad fixed to the haft just below the blade.

At an auspicious time for victory, they struck gongs to signal to the Lawa, and set off into the forest, waving banners, firing guns, and shouting rowdily.

The Karen and Lawa carried crossbows with bolts dipped in powerful poison. Khun Chang drove his elephant forward at a jog trot, and the troops made a good pace.

After leaving the city of Suphan, Khun Chang was anxious and uncertain about the direction to head. Seeing a forest hunter coming towards them,

he called out, "Have you seen anything? Two people fleeing on horseback? A villain has kidnapped my wife."

Hunter Rot paid respect. "I saw them. I'll tell you about it." Khun Chang dismounted from his elephant and happily poured liquor for them to drink together.

Rot sunk nine cups of liquor, and dizzily told him the whereabouts. "I definitely saw them crossing the river at cockcrow.

They were riding a horse, laughing and flirting. He grabbed her breasts. I couldn't look. The woman had very beautiful, soft arms and they rode in the saddle with legs intertwined.

A while ago they went to sleep at Banyan Landing. I'll take you there." Khun Chang was seething with rage and bathed in a cold sweat.

He grasped his goad and mounted back onto the neck of his tusker. Rot led the way through the deep forest almost up to Banyan Landing, then pointed out the spot.

Now to tell of Khun Phaen's Goldchild and other spirits who were keeping watch. Seeing this huge horde arrive, they ran over to wake their master.

Khun Phaen, great romancer, excellent in mastery, was lying in the shade of the glossy banyan, happily snuggled up to Wanthong, cooled by a fresh breeze.

The gentle afternoon sun slanted through the trees. Crickets chirped and churred all around them. Both were fast asleep but Khun Phaen woke on Goldchild's arrival.

He rolled over and gripped his fearsome sword. Seeing such a mass of troops coming through the forest, he softly stirred Wanthong. "Eye's jewel, please wake up,

wash your face, and get dressed. You're about to see the battle of your lover versus your husband. If you're unhappy and afraid, reveal yourself to him. It's up to you.

Khun Chang has a huge force with hundreds of men. I have only little me. Though famous for my powers, this could be my dying day.

I'm concerned for you. Khun Chang is very upset because you crossed him.

That's why he came after you in this thick forest.

Now that he's found you, if you don't reveal yourself but try to get away, he'll be furious. Should he catch you, he'll slit you open and leave your flesh as prey for the crows.

Think again about how things are. He followed after you because he loves you, so if you speak to him nicely, he should welcome you and take you back to enjoy.

I won't fight but will make good my escape in this forest and save myself. What do you think? Will you stay or go? Don't be upset."

Wanthong gave him a black, wounded look. "Do you no longer love me? I intend to entrust my life to you. I've no regrets over leaving Khun Chang.

How come you don't think of the past? You're famous everywhere for having enough power and knowledge to turn the world upside down,

and he has just these troops who've followed him here. With all your powers, aren't you ashamed to run away so easily? As for me, I'm not going back. I'll fight to the death, come what may.

Whatever happens, my name will last. Don't imagine I'll return to die in that house. If you're afraid, hide in the banyan and hand over Skystorm for me to fight."

"Oh! These words I like! I'll dress you up properly with a shirt, cloth leggings, and a helmet dyed with herbs. I'm just a bit worried that you're not used to riding a horse.

You'll have to master the rhythm of spear play, because Khun Chang's timing is expert and his spear is huge. If he stabs you, it'll pierce.

I'm a man. If I die, that's commonplace. But why trouble yourself, my jewel?" He quickly prepared himself for battle in the way he had done before.

He chanted formulas, blew on his palms, raised his clasped hands reverently to his forehead, and grasped Skystorm in his right hand. He intoned a powerful mantra to make Wanthong invisible to anyone who came,

and concentrated her mind to ensure no enemy weapon would touch her. Then he leapt on Color of Mist and galloped off with Goldchild and his spirits in train.

He sent the spirits to cut couch grass, then composed his mind and intoned a formula that transformed the grass instantly into people, all equipped with lances and spears.

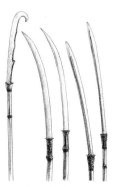

lance blades

He gave them orders, "Stay here and keep out of sight in the forest until I give the signal, then come out and fall upon Khun Chang's troops."

He spurred Color of Mist away. The spirits surrounded the enemy on the front and flanks. Seeing the horse racing towards him and Skystorm flashing, Khun Chang called out, "Prepare to defend!"

His men drew their swords, readied their pikes, raised their guns, shouted and hollered. They pulled the triggers but there was no flash, no bang. Khun Phaen rode up in front of Khun Chang,

and bellowed a mantra. Some men took fright and ran away, abandoning their guns. Others stood stunned, their swords slipping from their grasp. Khun Chang was frozen in a defensive posture.

Everybody was befuddled by the mantra and fearful of Khun Phaen's mastery. Seeing him almost on top of them, Khun Chang took fright, fired his gun, and urged his troops to advance.

Gunners and pikemen moved en masse, sending a rumbling sound through the forest. They swarmed around the horse, loudly triggering their crossbows.

Color of Mist wheeled around, kicking and biting. A man tried to dodge but was kicked on the chin. A Lawa said, "This is a mighty animal!" and clumsily tried to catch hold of the horse,

but Khun Phaen shouted and slashed with his sword, sending a head tumbling along the forest floor. Khun Chang did a war dance on the back of his elephant, crying out, "Forward! No retreat!

Why be afraid? There's only one of him. Soon I'll dance over and slash him in two like a banana stalk. Sonphraya, advance the elephant so I can stab him."

Sonphraya said, "Eh? If we blunder over there, we'll get knocked down and buried in the dirt. Don't you think it's a good thing our elephant is far away from him? There's no need to go closer."

Khun Chang saw this was true and quietly offered no argument. Instead, acting brave with his voice, he urged his troops forward. "Hey! Split up and form crow's wings abreast.[11] Shoot him off his horse!"

pikeman

11. ปีกกา, *pik ka*, a military formation with both wings spread like a crow. The term is used today for a curly bracket (}) which gives an idea of the shape. The idea was to drive the enemy

Khun Chang's Lawa troops poured forward in tight formation like an army of ants, swarming around Khun Phaen, stabbing and firing gunshots that echoed around the forest.

They attacked Goldchild and his spirits on the right and left, but none of their slashing and thrusting met its mark. Khun Chang backed his elephant further away, crying, "Forward! Don't let up!"

Khun Phaen could now see the size of the Lawa force so signaled to his spirit dummies to attack Khun Chang's troops in the middle of the battlefield.

The dummies joined the fight, shouting, yelling, and stirring up clouds of dust. Lawa dead piled up on Mon corpses. Some stabbed back,

but the dummies were elastic and nothing pierced them. They responded by slashing and chopping. Khun Chang's men broke and scattered in defeat. Khun Chang turned his elephant and fled.

Khun Phaen spurred Color of Mist to give chase. "Where are you going on that elephant, you slave?" Khun Chang replied, "Why do you ask?" and drove the elephant pounding into the thick forest.

The howdah got caught on thorns, teetered, broke apart with a crack, and slid down the elephant's side. Sonphraya jumped off and ran into hiding. Ratthaya could not remain so leapt after him.

Khun Chang fell from the elephant with a thud, and ran, bent double, straight into the thorny undergrowth, snagging and grazing his flesh so the blood flowed. In panic, he blundered ahead without stopping.

His leg tangled in a vine and he fell rolling on the ground. "I'm caught in a trap! Release me. You dumb dogs all abandoned me! Oh dear, I'm done for!"

He[12] collapsed panting on a log. The dummies spun and chased after the Karen and Lao, who raced away in uproar. Burmese, Khaek, and Chinese were all mixed up together.

Mon stumbled on Thai, with hearts pounding. Thai collapsed on the ground, able to go no further, crushed together with their flesh split open and blood flowing.

Others ran headlong, careless of the thorns and branches, crying noisily

---

into the center, and then pincer him from both sides, as described in the Chiang Mai chronicle around 1300: "When we have wedged our body in, we will [sandwich and] smash them in and push them into our crow's-wing. When they have been pushed down into our crow's-wing, the governor of Fang should press them [from the other side]. Have all the cavalry volunteers fight the enemy, and all the footsoldiers' first ranks shoot arrows into the enemy" (Wyatt and Aroonrut, *Chiang Mai Chronicle*, 48).

12. The next five stanzas down to "He hid away" are taken from WK, 15:588–89, absent from PD. With some poetic exaggeration, the author seems intent on portraying the extent to which armies were made up of foreign mercenaries, war captives, and recent migrants rather than the local Thai population.

for their mothers and fathers, not knowing in what language, Lao mixed with Chinese mixed with Thai,

Thai mixed with Khaek mixed with Mon, all calling out to one another in a noisy confusion that echoed around without a break, Mon muddled with Meng[13] muddled with Mon,

Burmese muddled with Karen. Khun Chang could not make out a word of it. "Is something coming to eat my liver?" He hid away,

sitting exhausted in a thicket with his blood spattering down like raindrops. "This time, I won't live. If he catches me, I'll probably be crushed to death.

Because I love my wife, I lose my life. What a pitiful thought! There's not a scrap of clothing left on me. I came to die for nothing, absolutely nothing."

Khun Chang's men who had fled away realized the enemy was not following them. Ratthaya came to find Sonphraya, and they each called their servants to search for their master.

They fanned out through the dense forest, cutting away the thorny rattan. It was a long, weary time until they found their master, looking as if he had been mauled all over by a tiger.

They hugged him and wept affectionately. "Such bad fortune, lord and master. If your wounds disappear, we'll kill and grill a couple of monkeys as offerings."

The rattan thorns had stripped him of his shirt, hat, and everything else. He was spattered with blood like drizzle. They brought clothes for him,

mopped away blood with their uppercloths, washed off mud, and pried out thorns. Many Karen, Lawa, and his own people went off to find medicines from the forest to treat him.

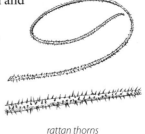

rattan thorns

Khun Phaen's anger cooled and he did not give chase. Thinking of Wanthong, he told his spirits to keep watch and hurried over to her.

Close to the shady banyan, he dismounted. Pretending to have an injured leg, he walked forward, intending to test fair Wanthong's feelings. "What will she say?"

Hiding in the shade of the big banyan, Wanthong was happy to see him return. She rushed out to greet him lovingly.

Khun Phaen leaned his arm on her shoulder and whispered, "I'm badly

---

13. Meng is a synonym of Mon.

wounded. I got shot in the side, and it hurts. Please walk steadily."

Wanthong was shocked and saddened. Under his weight, she could hardly walk. At the banyan tree, Khun Phaen pretended to collapse as if on the point of death.

He said, "I was shot at the top of my leg and nearly fell off my horse. Pitiful! Khun Chang had countless men. They followed and nearly finished me off.

He stabbed me so hard, my innards almost spewed out. His spear play is good. Please staunch the blood for me a bit."

He picked up Wanthong's hand and put it on his belly. "There's blood or something dripping down here. Please staunch it. This damn muscle is twitching. Press it hard."

Wanthong now knew he was fooling. She turned aside, withdrew her hand, and shoved him away. "What's this, my good fellow? Too much! You must be tired. What is there to eat?"

Khun Phaen replied, "The rice crackers aren't finished yet, my sweet. If we loved each other like we did in our house, you wouldn't be thinking about food.

If you loved me like I love you, then you'd overlook your stomach pangs like I do mine. I brought supplies from Kanburi but I forgot them when we left last night.

Just looking on your face, my stomach pangs disappear in an instant. I think only of holding you close with unending love.

I'm full to bursting with love for you. I hope you feel the same." Wanthong exclaimed, "What a talker! You're very smart, lord of a hundred tricks!"

Khun Phaen, great romancer, famed everywhere for his powers, turned to look at the sun about to disappear behind the mountains,
    its light softening and turning bright red as it was hidden by the trees. He suggested to Wanthong, "My love, let's go and bathe to cool down."

Wanthong tossed her head in annoyance and replied, "My legs ache. I can't walk. All those lies about being shot hurt me a lot. I'll go down to the water in a while."

Khun Phaen said, "Don't take long, my love, or you'll shiver with cold on the approach of evening. I know why you're hurt. It's because you went to war no holds barred,
    fighting with me so urgently in the shade of the banyan. Do you have to lean on me to walk? I'll carry you. Let's try. Come on, I'll pick you up."

"I dislike this, I really do. I'm not some hunchback who can't walk. When have you ever carried me before?" She got up and strode off in a huff.

Khun Phaen coaxed her to enjoy the stream. A breeze rippled the water. Buds rose elegantly from lotuses. Blooming flowers sprinkled their pollen.

Bees bunched around blossoms, buzzing and bathing themselves in pollen. Wind rustled the leaves, and blew ripe petals to fall into the stream.

Their fragrance suffused the water like refreshing celestial nectar. With her fingernail, Wanthong nipped off a lotus leaf and flower, and fashioned them into a little boat.

Khun Phaen pulled up a lotus stalk and coiled it round her like a necklace. Wanthong gathered floating lotus petals and gently blew them to fly on the wind.

Fish swam under the limpid water, threading through lotus stalks, hiding near the banks, foraging in the mud, looking lovely. Khun Phaen and Wanthong watched them, then went down to play in the water,

both laughing and giggling, merrily teasing each other. Khun Phaen suggested they play hide-and-seek. Wanthong cried, "I'll be it.

Don't go so far away I can't follow because I'm scared of crocodiles." Khun Phaen said, "It's not yet time for you to come chasing after me. Hide your face. If you cheat, I'm not having it.

If you don't fear a poisonous snake and chase after me without closing your eyes, may you run into a puffer fish or get nipped by a scissortail[14] that sucks all your flesh and blood."

Wanthong said, "Playing like this is very scary to me. I've never played with such cursing. You come back and close your eyes.

I'll go off and you seek. If I manage to touch base, I'll have a good laugh. If[15] you peek, may a rat bite your leg and drag you off to devour. Don't look."

Khun Phaen said, "What's this? Now you're cursing too. I've never heard such cursing either. Let's stop picking at each other.

If I can grab anything of yours, I'll hang on tight." Wanthong said, "Fine. Grab what pleases you." She swanned off, glancing around, then plunged in and swam to hide among the lotus leaves.

Khun Phaen looked up and could not see her. He swam right past where she was hiding in a lotus clump, spying on him.

He glanced all around and called out, "Wanthong, little Wanthong, where are you hiding?" His nose touched her cheek and he laughed. "Ah! This is Wanthong's cheek."

He grabbed hold of her and squeezed her breasts with both hands. Wanthong

14. ปลาซิว, *sio*, general term for fish in the Rasbora family, small fish that cluster in shoals, including highly colored varieties found in aquariums such as the harlequin fish. *Rasbora trilineatea* or scissortail is one of the most common of the family in Thai waterways. They are all toothless and harmless so it is surprising that they appear here as predators.

15. From here to "pleases you," two stanzas down, is taken from WK, 16:596, absent from PD.

pried off his hands and cried, "If you catch both sides, the eggs are broken."[16]

Khun[17] Phaen said, "I don't know, I'm afraid you'll run away so I'm holding onto you tight." Wanthong said, "I didn't realize in time that you're so full of tricks.

It's cold. Let's go up." Khun Phaen said, "Scrub my back, please." Wanthong looked at him askance. "I just want to bathe but you're so demanding."

She peeled the uppercloth from her body. "Shift over here and I'll wash you." Khun Phaen looked at her, making her feel shy. Wanthong picked up her sabai and covered her front.

Khun Phaen said admiringly, "Your breasts in the open are as firm and full as these sacred lotus buds." Wanthong said, "Now that you've had a good look at my breasts, you make fun of me."

Khun Phaen was blissful. He sat close beside and kissed her. "I'll scrub your back. Let's take turns." Wanthong turned away, flashing him a sharp look.

She sat beside him, shoulder to shoulder, and stretched out her arms. He slipped his arms around her immediately and softly massaged her breasts.

"Why aren't you scrubbing my arms but squeezing there instead?" "I thought there was a spot of dirt so I scrubbed and was about to blow it away but the bump turns out to be just you."

Wanthong cried out, "Now, now, don't be sarcastic. It's not fitting. So this 'bump' doesn't please you? It's not like the time you climbed the palace wall.

That was a divine *montha* flower but now it's floated away. How maddening for you! The heavenly flower has gone into the palace so you have to admire a grassflower instead."

Khun Phaen, great valiant, was stung and embarrassed. He mumbled, "Don't pick at me. There's no woman I love as much as you."

He suggested they go up and get changed. They walked back shoulder to shoulder, went under the shade of the holy golden banyan, and tasted bliss together.

Khun Phaen, great romancer, skilled and masterful soldier, slept with Wanthong under the shade of the banyan. At the end of the third watch, he woke, chilled by the cold dew, and hugged Wanthong's sleeping form. He raised her chin and coaxed her to admire the full moon. Filtering through the banyan leaves, moonlight fell on her breasts,

---

16. In the old Thai version of hide-and-seek, if the seeker tags two people at the same time it is called "breaking eggs," and the seeker loses (KW, 207–8).

17. The next four stanzas down to "make fun of me" are taken from WK, 16:596–97, absent from PD.

full[18] and firm as the buds of red lotus. Heavenly water spattered down, collecting on her bosom like a lustration of liquid gold.

Dew drenching the little leaves of the holy banyan fell in drops like diamonds, scenting the air softly like a garland of sweetpassion, pattering on Wanthong's breasts,

as if the holy banyan itself wished to caress her. Moonlight caught the bloom of a nymph lotus. Cicadas chirped cheerfully. Crickets shrilled in reply like a lamenting chorus,

ringing and singing softly and mournfully, lilting in lament like a young girl grieving. He nudged Wanthong to listen to the plaintive sound.

As dawn streaked the sky he said to her, "I can't hold you close here for too long. For better or worse, that villain Khun Chang will go back and accuse me before the king,

and make His Majesty angry enough to send an army to arrest us. The matter will blow up like a raging fire, and I think a huge force will be dispatched in support.

We must leave this holy banyan and go deep into the forest." He prompted Wanthong to take leave of the holy golden banyan,

and quickly went off to find Color of Mist at a path beside a marshy stream. He harnessed the horse and rode off with Wanthong through the forest.

Goldchild led the way, wending through the hills. Wind wafted pollen far and wide, dusting the forest with fragrance.

At a clearing among rocks, blossoms bloomed all around. He pointed out to Wanthong, "Look at the flowers. They're captivating."

The light of a bright moon illuminated the sweet sight of blooming sprays. "There's a smilinglady smiling in the forest fringe, just like you smiled in the cotton field;

an elegant spray of hiddenlover, just like us two hiding away as young lovers; a secretscent, perfuming the air, like the fragrance of your delicate cheeks when you were sent to me in the bridal house;

a lady's fingernail with its tiny petals open, like your fingers fan and comb for me; and an eveningbloom all over the bank of a lotus pond, like I'm all over you, evening and morning too.

There's climbing jasmine twined round miseryplum and parting palm. After

---

18. The next four stanzas down to "plaintive sound" are taken from WK, 16:599; PD has: that looked like a pair of red lotus buds. Drops of chill dew scattered on them, glittering like diamonds. He hugged her and stroked his back and forth. / In the dead of night, animals made no noise. Only the ring of cicadas echoed around like the playing of java flutes. The more he listened, the bleaker he felt.

only three days, karma parted us in misery. There's a *jampi* beside a heartache tree hanging with braidflowers. For more than two years, heartache and gloom were hanging over me.

Fragrance from a cinnamon tree mingles with the scent of a happyshade. Enjoying you today sent me such happiness. The air is bathed in the aroma of roses and waitingladies. Little lady, let's wait a little—and enjoy a kiss."

Wanthong cried, "Oh, you're hateful! I was enjoying listening to you spinning words. When it comes to joking around, you're the expert. Please let me listen to you admiring the forest a little more."

"There's nothing to admire as inspiring as you. It wards off the loneliness of the third watch." The moon slid down and hid in the forest, followed by the stars as the dawn came up.

Golden light tinged the foliage a hazy yellow as the sun strode into the sky. Packs of animals opened their eyes. Birds left their nests in a chorus of calls.

Monkeys scampered away in all directions. Female gibbons loosed plaintive whooping. Pairs of rabbits leapt after one another exuberantly. Khun Phaen urged the horse to canter through the forest.

They came to a valley among the hills where a broad area had been cleared for cultivation next to a lofty forest. Lawa houses clustered at the foot of a hill. He took Wanthong straight through a field of gourds.

hill village

Lawa woman

Many lines of bamboo fences surrounded areas where the Lawa were planting sweet potato and taro. On the hilltops were fields of gourd, aubergine, chili, dry plantain, and sparrow's brinjal.

Some wild Lawa, a race of forest people, were walking in file. All were young women who wore shirts and applied turmeric to make their skin yellow.

Others were sitting, smiling and joking together beside some rocks. When they saw people coming on horseback, they ran away. Khun Phaen rode over to halt by the terrace of a house.

An old Lawa woman who was looking after the house was agitated by the sight of people riding up on horseback. "What are officials coming to my house for?"

Khun Phaen and Wanthong dismounted and greeted her. "We've come looking for the medicinal herbs and roots said to be in these hills.

Where have all your menfolk gone? Just now we saw only women tending the vegetables. May we please stay in this village for about five nights, and then we'll move on."

Wanthong gave her a bead wristlet appreciated by the hill people. The old lady was pleased, and called the young women to come back.

They stood looking shy and peeping furtively. When they too were given beads, they laughed gaily and their shyness disappeared. They promptly arranged a hut and brought sweet potato and taro in gratitude.

Khun Phaen flirted with the young women. "Later I'll come back and give you necklaces, earrings, bracelets, and *phirot* rings to put on both hands."

Wanthong put a smile on her face. "So you're going to be a Lawa son-in-law, are you?" She stretched out her hand for the old lady to read her palm. The old lady went on and on, relating many, many things.

phirot ring

Khun Phaen ordered Goldchild to be on the alert for an army coming. "Come and inform me when they're still far away." The spirit wai-ed to take leave and went off immediately.

༄

Now to tell of Khun Chang.[19] After the battle, he lay in the forest, aching badly and whimpering. After sunset and nightfall, his men collected wood, lit fires,

and made shelters to sleep in the wilds. The injured lay around groaning. Some went off in bands to gallivant around the forest. Late into the night, many cocks crowed in the wilds.

Khun Chang wept and wailed through the night. At dawn he was reunited with several servants, and retrieved the hat and clothes he had lost.

He was nursing revenge. "Khun Phaen really did me in. I'll inform the king and get an army sent to arrest him."

With this in mind, he ordered Sonphraya to harness his elephant and hustle everybody to get ready to leave.

Sonphraya rushed off to harness the elephant. Porters followed behind, along with the injured, leaning on one another.

Khun Chang mounted the elephant and lay groaning, his arms and legs shaking with aches and pains. He had the elephant hurry along by the shortest route.

In the howdah, he lay with a fever, feeling the wounds all over his face, streaming with tears. "Oh, karma did this, Wanthong.

Now you'll be in a pitiable state, eye's jewel. Are you trekking through the forest, even across streams and bogs? Your legs will ache and feet will blister. You'll have to exchange gold rings for sweet potato and taro.

Khun Phaen has a lot against you. Maybe he's killed you already, my heart, taken all the gold rings, and left your corpse in the woods,

with your blood spilling over the forest floor, and your bones scattered piteously. Who'll cremate the body?" He sobbed heavily.

Sonphraya consoled him. "Don't cry. Why are you so very concerned? Wanthong ran off because she doesn't love you. On top of that, she urged her lover to slash you.

After she's done all that, don't you feel bad? Why do you have such a tearful face? The fact you almost collapsed and died from thousands of rattan thorns was because of Wanthong, wasn't it?

If you just say you don't love her and break it off, then you can sleep happily at home. There are lots of servants at the house. Aren't they as much fun as Wanthong?"

---

19. In the original, the next two stanzas appear earlier, after "tasted bliss together" on p. 383.

Khun Chang said, "I'm not in love with her. I'm crying over the property that's been lost. He stole gold rings and cut curtains to shreds.

I want revenge. If I find Khun Phaen I'll leap on him and slash his people to death, man or woman, for taking the property. All I want back is Wanthong—Oops! Forgot."

Sonphraya doubled over with laughter. "Oh, really? You said you weren't in love. The mouth and the heart seem to have a slight disagreement here." He urged the elephant forward,

crossing field and forest, rivers and rapids, pond and plain. Making good time, they reached home just as the sun set.

Arriving at the house and not seeing Wanthong there made Khun Chang even more dark and desolate. He strode up into the house in a daze. "I'm going to hang myself here."

He went into a room and looked around. Ruined curtains were still scattered about. Mattresses and pillows were strewn everywhere. Betel boxes, bowls, trays, and salvers lay in disorder.

"She's been gone only a short time and nobody is looking after things. Wanthong's merit is used up so why bother hanging onto possessions? I'll smash them to pieces now."

He grabbed a pike and raised it above his head. "I'll stab myself to death. May it enter easily and may I die well! Have all the goods here put in my coffin."

He threw the pike down and ran out to the kitchen, picked up a pestle, and bludgeoned some fermented fish. He ran around throwing pots all over the place. "May I die and follow my wife."

He went back to his room, found a rope, tied one end to a roof beam, the other round his waist, and swung out into space, shouting "Help! Untie me!"

Sonphraya was alarmed. He looked up, saw the rope tied to a beam,[20] and thought Khun Chang's neck must be broken. He pushed open the door and found Khun Chang hanging by his waist.

"Eh? People usually hang themselves by the neck but this fellow thinks he'll die hanging by the waist!" He pushed Khun Chang's hands and feet so he spun, flailing around, and left him there, tied up.

Now to tell of old Siprajan. On that day she had heard the news that her son-

---

20. The room probably has a *chong lom*, ช่องลม, "wind passage," an opening at the top of the wall, that allows Sonphraya to see the roof beams.

in-law had lost the battle and returned injured. "I-Tai, come along with me."

They went to the big house, entered the main apartment, and saw Khun Chang swinging from the roof. She asked Sonphraya, "What's going on here? Come and look. What *is* Khun Chang doing?"

Sonphraya said, "Haven't you seen this before? Khun Chang is playing crow hatching eggs."[21] Khun Chang called out wearily, "Don't believe him." He managed to untie his waist, got down,

and raised his hands to wai his mother-in-law. "This is the end. Khun Phaen wronged me beyond belief. He's kidnapped Wanthong and taken her into the forest,

and stolen valuable gold and silver articles including a great amount of cash and cloth. I followed and caught him at a banyan tree where he was staying with Wanthong.

He had several hundred forest bandits under his control, hiding in the woods in ambush. I stabbed piles of them to death but I wasn't in time to seize Wanthong.

Because my elephant was stabbed and ran amok, they were able to speed away on a horse. I gave chase and had almost caught them when my elephant veered off trumpeting into the forest.

I was caught by the undergrowth, knocked off, and bloodied by many thorns. Khun Phaen's horse galloped away through the forest so I couldn't bring Wanthong back."

Sonphraya tried to interrupt but Khun Chang added further untruths. "I gave chase without any thought for the thorns sticking in me, and let off a warning shot. If I'd been in time, I'd have seized Wanthong,

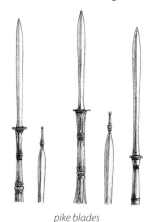

pike blades

but he was protected by his forest bandits. They stabbed me maybe twelve hundred times. There were about five piles of pikes broken because of me." Khun Chang cried out, "This is the end!

For better or worse, I'll see him dead. He fled because my men are able—all invulnerable warriors. Stabbing them nine or ten times does nothing."

Siprajan pursed her lips. "I don't believe you. No one beats you at lying. Khun Phaen is a skilled and experienced fighter. Anyway, what are you thinking of doing?"

---

21. A common children's game. Each player gives one article (stone, stick, etc.) to the "crow" who sits inside a circle, and then all try to snatch the articles away without entering the circle.

Khun Chang said, "I still want revenge. I intend to follow after Khun Phaen and kill him. I'll attend on the king and ask for a great army to chase him down.

Lightning strike! Why don't you believe me? I'm daring and fearless. If you'd seen me in the fight, you'd have admired my fine spear play."

He gave orders to Sonphraya, "Harness my elephant quickly. It's urgent. I'm so concerned about Wanthong that I'm going straight to Ayutthaya."

He went to bathe and change clothes. Inside the room, he took up a mirror to look at himself. He was bathed in blood, and his face looked as if it had been minced. In the furrow hoed through his hair, new shoots were just sprouting.

"Oh, how long will it take for my hair to grow back? If only I could exchange this head for someone else's, but it's mine so I'm stuck.

Even if it cost ten chang, I wouldn't complain. I'd bow my face and hand over my head in exchange. Oh, who else is like me? No wonder Wanthong is in two minds."

He left the mirror and put on a brand new golden yok that cost twelve[22] to buy, and an uppercloth of yellow wool. He walked over, mounted the neck of his elephant, and jogged off.

They crossed field and forest, rivers and rapids, taking shortcuts through the thick forest undergrowth. He reached Ayutthaya in one day, left the elephant beside the graveyard of Wat Na Phramen,[23]

and walked down to find a ferry. People addressed him as if he were an old wat mendicant. He crossed to the city at the time of the forenoon feeding. Wearing his lowercloth in

Wat Na Phramen

---

22. No unit given.

23. On the north side of Ayutthaya, opposite the palace on the other, northern bank of the river. It is sometimes assumed this wat was founded in 1491 as the chronicles mention King Ramathibodi II building a stupa for the ashes of his predecessors, but the wat appears by name for the first time in records of 1549 as the site of negotiation between King Chakkaphat and Burmese attackers. Several times it became a site for besieging armies to bombard the palace, and it was here in 1760 that a cannon exploded, fatally injuring the Burmese general Alaunghpaya. After 1767 the wat was abandoned but repaired and repopulated with monks in 1835. Just beside the wat at the mouth of the Sa Bua Canal was a ferry to take officials to the palace (RCA, 18, 483; KLW, 159, 173; SWC, 14:6975; *Boranasathan*, 443–44; APA, 92; see map 8).

tuck-tail style, he stumbled along in a daze with his head down.

At the sight of him, children danced around in excitement. "Mummy, mummy, what's that coming over there with a red head like a vulture in a paddy field? Will it eat my liver?" The child's eyes gaped wide.

ferry

The mother shouted, "You slave, fancy coming to frighten my child, damn you!" Khun Chang looked away and walked on, shaking his head, making for the inner sala.

Seeing him enter, a noble friend was startled. "Sir, my bushy-haired department head, where have you been? What's happened to your skin and your head? You look like you've been mauled by a cat.

Your chest hair has been plucked out.[24] Did you go on a romantic escapade and get bitten by a toad?[25] Your yok and wool uppercloth are a mess. What problem brings you here?"

Khun Chang doubled over in tears and said, "Sir, this time it's the end. Phaen has gone too far. He kidnapped my Wanthong,
and stole gold rings and other valuables including much cash and cloth. I went after him and caught him at a banyan tree, but Phaen had made friends with lots of forest bandits
who swarmed out, all carrying spears, pikes, shields, staves, and javelins. I charged with my elephant and scattered them, killing hundreds of them dead like rain.

I would've caught Khun Phaen but he galloped away and hid in the deep forest. I followed but couldn't find him before nightfall so I've come back to attend on our king.

I'll ask for an army to arrest him. Sir, please help me. I don't care about the money and other things. If he's caught, all I want is Wanthong."

---

24. In older versions of the abduction scene (see *Companion*, 1147) but not in chapter 17 of this version, Khun Phaen also shaved Khun Chang's chest hair.

25. A toad bite can result in itchiness. This is a metaphor for contracting disease.

Now to tell of the king, ruler of the world, unmatched in excellence on earth, who resided in a golden palace with a gilded spire, contemplating affairs of state.

As the sun descended in the afternoon, he was bathed and arrayed in magnificent raiment, glittering with gold and gems, while throngs of inner ladies sat with clasped hands.

He came out to sit on a throne, and the mass of senior officials in attendance prostrated. He heard cases concerning the populace and gave judgments of life or death according to the crimes.

Then he looked around. "Who is that prostrate at the back? Is it Khun Chang? Where have you been to get your chest and shoulders striped with welts,

your face and forehead scored with scratches, and your hair hacked about? Your head bald down to your ears looks awful. Did somebody beat you up?"

For a moment, Khun Chang was nonplussed, and left the royal question hanging without any reply. So the king roared, "Khun Chang, who did this to you?"

Khun Chang twitched and trembled until Phramuen Si hit him in the chest. "His Majesty has issued a command so why do you remain silent?" Still trembling, Khun Chang addressed the king.

"My liege, your humble servant's name is Khun Chang from Bigwall Village. My father's name was Khun Siwichai, and my mother is Thepthong.

My elder cousin, Phanson, was born before me, son of my aunt. Next came Sonphraya and Ratthaya, and then myself, your humble servant.

I had a wife called Kaen Kaeo, daughter of Muen Phaeo from Bigwall Village. She sickened with piles, became hollow-eyed, and died many years ago . . . '

The king became very angry. "Who asked you to recount your household census details?" Khun Chang was shocked to his senses. But, prostrate before the king, he was still flustered,

and got everything upside down and back to front. "Wanthong disappeared away to the forest on horseback . . . many, many forest robbers . . . weapons scattered everywhere . . .

Khun Phaen, son of Thong Prasi . . . a great deal of money and valuables . . . with Wanthong, the two of them, at a banyan tree . . . the elephants and horses panicked and charged off . . .

officers and men lacerated by rattan thorns . . . a sacred thread around the house . . . wanted to hang myself . . . Sonphraya jumped off the elephant into the undergrowth . . .

hundreds died . . . little things fell off . . . he charged away on his horse, Mist . . . set up a shrine near the gate . . . '

The king said, "I hear but I don't understand. Everything's topsy-turvy. What's the matter? Phramuen Si, whisper in Khun Chang's ear to speak without panicking."

Phramuen Si followed the king's order. "Relate what happened from the beginning." Khun Chang calmed down, and wove a story of fact and fiction.

"I was asleep in the house with Wanthong at the third watch when the villain put people to sleep, plucked my head drawing blood, drew patterns on my body in soot,

and chopped three beautiful curtains to shreds. Cash and property are missing. He wound a sacred thread around the house and made many offerings to an eye-level shrine.[1]

My wife, Wanthong, disappeared. I followed after them with my people and found Khun Phaen and his horse with my wife Wanthong in the shade of a banyan.

Khun Phaen had several hundred bandits under his command. They ambushed us, and slashed my men down dead all over the place. I was caught, beaten,

and lacerated with rattan thorns up to my neck. Then he shouted at me provocatively, saying it was not a good idea to kill me; if he released me, I would go to Ayutthaya and tell everything;

then, were the king to come out, he would engage the king in an elephant duel, win a famous victory, and seize the city as ruler. These were his vile words.

---

1. With these words, Khun Chang is accusing Khun Phaen of using supernatural power with malicious intent, which was an offense under the law. "Should anyone accuse another of being a *chamop* [a female spirit], knowing the use of knowledge, herbal potions, and methods to cause death, if the accusation is examined and found false, the accuser will be fined a multiple of his price according to the severity of the offense, and if the accusation is proved, the person knowing about herbal potions, spirits, *jakla* [a spirit with the form of a cat], and knowledge will be executed to prevent any future application, and all property will be seized into the royal treasury" (*Phra aiyakan bet set*, Miscellaneous Laws, section 157, KTS, 3:174; KW, 217).

He has built a royal lodge in the forest and a camp fortified with spikes. Very mischievously, he has constructed a toilet.[2] Before long, he will become a threat to the city."[3]

King Phanwasa pondered over this story. "Mm! This Khun Phaen makes me angry. But is this fellow Khun Chang embroidering the tale?

I can't make out what is fact and what is fiction. There's something wrong about his account of getting into a fight en route. I think some is true and some is false.

Khun Phaen took his wife away. Khun Chang chased after him, and so Khun Phaen fought back. Khun Phaen has knowledge and courage while Khun Chang is as slow as a crab so he got beaten.

He probably blundered into the rattan in flight but he accuses Khun Phaen of lacerating him. Listening to one side is misleading." The king spoke to Phramuen Si and Phramuen Wai.[4]

"You will go as military commanders of the troops. Conscript five thousand select men, and arrange everything for a military expedition.

Put Khun Phet on the right wing and Khun Raminthra on the left.[5] Go and

---

2. The lodge, fortifications, and toilet are the evidence that Khun Phaen is in revolt. The phrase for the lodge, *tamnak phlap-phla*, specifically defines a building that is built for a king. At this time, a constructed toilet was also one of the privileges of royalty. The law specified, "Wherever the king travels, overseers are to organize phrai to dig deep holes, and to cover them up after use. If anyone is seen violating them, they are to be bound and delivered to the judicial authorities who will administer five strokes of the rattan" (*Phra aiyakan aya luang*, Code of Crimes against Government, section 115, KTS, 4:85).

3. Khun Chang has accused Khun Phaen of five offenses: robbery, abducting his wife, using supernatural power with malicious intent, murdering Khun Chang's men with the help of bandits, and appropriating the privileges of royalty and planning revolt. The latter three were capital offenses.

In the court sources of mid and late Ayutthaya, revolt means any challenge to the authority of the king. It is applied to: breakaways by subordinate cities or tributary rulers; dynastic challenges, especially during or after disputed successions to the throne; attempted military coups; and uprisings that may have millenarian aims. The word first appears in the later chronicles to describe a challenge for the throne by an alternative dynastic line around 1540. Revolt is covered by a specific law, พระไอยการกระบดศึก, *phra aiyakan kabotsuek*, the Law on Revolt and Warfare, sometimes called the law on treason, dated 1434. The penalty is a form of execution that takes seven days to complete, imposed on up to seven generations of the offender's clan. (KTS, 4:115–64; RCA, 20)

4. Jamuen/Phramuen Wai Woranat, one of the four heads of the royal pages, along with Phramuen Si (see p. 16, note 75).

5. Khun Phetinthra and Khun Raminthra were two senior officers in the guard, who appeared in chapter 15 swearing an oath of friendship with Khun Phaen. These and the two heads of the royal pages were all officers close to the king, indicating the importance given to this expedition (KP, 203).

find out where Khun Phaen is hiding, and whether Khun Chang's words are true or false.

Ascertain whether Khun Phaen is living in a royal lodge. Listen to his words for any guile. See if he fears me or not.

Tell him that I sent for him, and that I will hear the case on any dispute between him and Khun Chang. He need not be afraid. If he comes, he will not be executed or beaten,

but if he resists, he will be captured, executed, and his head stuck on a stake in the forest. Take the army quickly right now."

Phramuen Wai and Phramuen Si received the king's orders, prostrated to take leave, and promptly withdrew on all fours. They sent a requisition order to Phan Phut[6]

to organize conscripts and supplies. Recruiters were dispatched with call-up papers to drag and dragoon people in by any method, and to haul off their wives and children en masse.

Soldiers and civilians[7] were quickly recruited in large numbers. Horses and elephants were organized, and silk flags distributed. Swords and pikes were seen everywhere.

Provisions were laid out on the parade ground along with many helmets and shirts of different sizes. The astrologers found an auspicious time to march on the following day at four in the morning.

The troops were ordered to assemble in units at Wat Chai Chumphon.[8] The officers went home. "Come in time tomorrow morning, Khun Chang."

Khun Phetinthra returned home where provisions, organized by his wife, were laid out everywhere. Khun Ram also went home promptly and sum-

---

6. A Mahatthai official responsible for conscription (see p. 21, note 7, and mention in chapter 8).

7. See p. 20, note 4.

8. The name indicates the function: "the monastery for assembling victorious forces." There was a Wat Phra Chai Chumphon off the island around 1.5 kms east of the Ho Rattanachai Gate. It is now abandoned and buried in undergrowth, to the east of Route 3061, almost opposite Wat Ayodhya, immediately south of the Juvenile Detention Center. There are remnants of a large stupa, fragments of sandstone Buddha images, and many brick foundations. However this location would not suit an army preparing to march north as the route would require crossing the Pasak River. Below in chapter 27, the troops assemble at Wat *Mai* Chai Chumphon, and this is probably the same wat mentioned here. This may be the wat labeled as Wat Mai on Phraya Boran's map of Ayutthaya, and now known as Wat Mai Pak Khlong, the new wat at the mouth of the canal. The wat is on the northern bank of the river, just east of the palace, and just east of the mouth of Sa Bua Canal. Now, the remaining ruins are small and undistinguished but the wat has a large courtyard that could have served to assemble an army (see map 8).

moned his people
    to lay out provisions, and harness horses and elephants in the proper fashion. As evening fell, he and his wife went into the house to sleep.

Khun Phetinthra's wife dreamed that her husband was sliced in two, his chest slit open, and his heart discarded in a forest. She woke trembling with fear
    and aroused her husband to tell him about the dream. "I had a strange dream like never before." In consternation, she recounted the story from start to finish. "I'm very frightened."

Khun Phetinthra was shocked by what he heard. "If I say this is a bad dream, there'll be sorrow and confusion."
    So he covered it up. "In your sleep, your mind is racing and uncertain. Don't be upset." He urged her to go back to sleep.

Khun Raminthra's wife dreamed a tooth broke into three pieces. In alarm she clutched her husband. "I've had a bad dream.
    You're going with the army to arrest Khun Phaen. This strange omen signifies danger. Your wife will suffer for you. I'm desolate." She lamented, her eyes brimming with tears.

Khun Raminthra listened to her and could not remain silent. He hugged and reassured her, "Don't be worried and frightened.
    Because I'm going far away, you're having dark and fearful thoughts. I'll bring back Khun Phaen." With these words, they went to sleep again.

When dawn brightened the sky, Khun Phetinthra promptly bathed, changed his clothes, and went to fetch his trusty sword.
    As his wife raised her hands to wai him, she saw him with no head, only shoulders. In alarm, she ran up to him, wailing, "Listen to your wife. Don't go.
    As you were walking just now, I saw you with no head. I think this is important. It fits with my terrible dream." She embraced his feet in the middle of the house.

His wife's words turned Khun Phetinthra's face ashen. Such an abnormal thing was a warning. He turned to look at his wife and became even more disturbed,
    his breast full of foreboding. He stood, rigid with fear. He had been with an army many, many times but had never experienced anything like this.

"Oh dear! Will I return? Probably I'll die in the forest, but if I don't go, I'll be in danger from the king." He shooed his wife away and steeled himself to leave.

Khun Raminthra got dressed, strung on many amulets, and picked up his trusty sword.

His wife walked behind him lovingly. As he descended from the house with a heavy heart, the stairway swayed and splintered. Five steps snapped off and fell to the ground.

His heart shuddered in surprise. "This time, my life will come to its end. I'll die separated from my housemate." He turned to see his wife looking ever more upset.

The troops were already drawn up ready in front and behind. They immediately set off surrounding him, and met up with Khun Chang, who was followed by his own servants and phrai.

The roads were jam-packed with crowds of people. The wat was a hive of organization. When both army commanders were ready,

the units were inspected and organized into a column with pikemen, lancers, archers, and units bristling with swords and guns. Prudently they waited for an auspicious time to march.

archer

When an auspicious time came, gongs were beaten, guns fired, and shouts echoed around. Swords and pikes glinted in the sunlight. Riders sat tall on their horses and elephants.

Phramuen Si rode an elephant in the middle of the army, while Phramuen Wai led the vanguard, and Khun Phet and Khun Ram came at the rear of the column, all riding tuskers with howdahs.

Khun Chang sat gloomily in the howdah on his old elephant, Kang, with his head bobbing up and down. Sonphraya rode on the neck holding a goad, and Ratthaya sat on the elephant's rear.

People catching sight of them broke into laugh-

elephant with three riders

ter. "Those bald elephants go very well together!" They shouted at others to come and see. Khun Chang hid his face and looked away.

They passed the Don Fak customs post beside Pak Khu.[9] Many people came to look at the throng of elephants and horses. The column made for the plain towards Talan.[10]

Some seized dried fish, fresh fish, or whatever they could find from every house. Keeping up a good pace, they reached Sam Ko[11] by evening.

They halted, set up the pots, prepared food, ate, and went to sleep. After the morning call, they hastened along to Bo Landing,[12] with panniers and baskets bouncing on the porters' shoulder poles.

panniers

When they reached Banyan Landing, Khun Chang became apprehensive. He said to Phramuen Si, "Right here is where I charged and slashed him.

The dead were scattered all over the place. His people were completely finished off. They ran scrambling off into the thorny rattan." Phramuen Si cackled with laughter.

"Oh, really? I can see the rattan thicket has been demolished, but your story doesn't hang together. Was it your handiwork chopping this up, or did your servants clear it to get you out?

Where's Khun Phaen? I don't see him. Think it out and tell me quickly." Khun Chang summoned his servants, who told him they had seen the tracks of a horse.

They decided to follow the trail. The army swarmed noisily through the forest

---

9. ปากคู, *pak khu*, meaning the mouth of a moat or ditch, is 3 kms northwest of Ayutthaya along the main Chaophraya River at the entrance to the Wat Lat (Mahaphram) Canal that led westward from Ayutthaya to join the Chaophraya River, which at that time flowed southward from Wat Julamani to Bang Sai along what is now the Bang Ban Canal. Pak Khu was the site of the westerly of the four customs posts around the city. "Each customs post had two officers and twenty men, who rotated every fifteen days. They checked for goods forbidden by law and unusual weapons, and challenged strangers entering or leaving to explain themselves. Each was equipped with horses and fast boats to report to the city" (KLW, 171; see map 3).

10. Just south of Phak Hai (see map 2).

11. "Three cows," now an amphoe in the west of Ang Thong province. This route was often used by armies as it led to a shallow ford on the Suphan River. The Burmese army marched this route in reverse when attacking Ayutthaya in 1548/49 (Damrong, *Our Wars*, 18; see map 2).

12. ท่าโพธิ์, *tha pho*, probably modern Ban Pho Phraya, 5 kms north of Suphanburi on the Suphan River. It is shown on the early Bangkok maps (Santanee and Stott, *Royal Siamese Maps*, 98, 104; see map 2).

to Three Thousand Crocodiles, where they waited for everyone to catch up.

Then Phramuen Si called out, "Hey, hairy chest! There's something odd here. Send some people out to spy."

Khun Chang dismounted from his elephant, called Sonphraya over, and they both climbed a tree to look around.

They saw Color of Mist eating grass, Wanthong lying asleep, and Khun Phaen all over her, hugging, kissing, and stroking her breasts.[13]

The sight made Khun Chang almost fall out of the tree but Sonphraya grabbed him just in time. He stood back up, and shaded his glazed eyes with a hand, shaking and growling with rage.

Khun Phaen's spirits saw people coming, and rushed over to intimidate them by leaping and wriggling around, lolling their tongues, growling, and bellowing menacingly.

Khun Chang staggered backwards in alarm, slipped out of Sonphraya's grip, and fell crashing down flat on the ground. He picked himself up and ran over shouting,

"I've found Khun Phaen! He's hugging Wanthong tight over there. My wife's cheeks are as flushed as if powdered red. Phramuen Si, please help. Have some mercy."

Phramuen Si and Phramuen Wai replied to Khun Chang, "You're off your head. You see your wife and all you say is her cheeks are flushed red!

If she were a bit of land, she wouldn't dry out by the end of the year.[14] It seems a beetle boring towards the red core of a tree has right now eaten away about two fathoms."

Orders were given to the army units to pick up their weapons and get ready. "Surround him but stay out of sight. Don't approach and attack.

---

13. In the previous chapter, Khun Phaen and Wanthong traveled deeper into the hills, yet here they are still at the edge of the plain. This clash with Khun Phaen probably began as an alternative version of the battle at the start of chapter 19. The pattern of the battle, the role of Wanthong, and the result are exactly the same in the two episodes. Later in the chapter, Wanthong says she has been in the forest only "five or six days," which seems too short after the excursion to the Lawa village. Also, Khun Phaen's teasing after the battle seems to fit with their early days in the forest, prior to the renewed intimacy achieved towards the end of the last chapter. Just as chapter 14 seems to be an alternative of chapter 17, so this episode was probably an alternative version of chapter 19 that compilers were reluctant to throw away when all the episodes of *KCKP* were assembled in sequence in written form in the mid-nineteenth century.

14. Probably a reference to the proverb, คอยให้น้ำบางกอกแห้ง, *khoi hai nam bangkok haeng*, waiting for the Bangkok river to dry up, meaning waiting for something that never comes (see Gerini, "On Siamese Proverbs," 222).

Post guards in every direction so he can't escape, and then make a racket with guns and gongs." The spirits told their master Khun Phaen that they were surrounded.

Seeing masses of soldiers approaching, Wanthong clung to him trembling with fear, tears flooding her sad eyes.

"How are we going to survive this? What do you think, my love? Their army is all over the forest. They have us completely surrounded.

Can you fight them? If each of them rips you a little, you'll be dust. There's no way you can defeat a whole army on your own.

You and Color of Mist could escape but there would be me left behind to worry about. What shall we do? Think about it."

"Listen to me and don't be afraid. If ten times this number had come I could win. They're like mosquitoes and midges that carelessly fly into a flame.

Though there's only one of me, I'm as fierce as a lion, and they're a tribe of pigs. Don't be afraid, my jewel. Their heads will be pulverized.

First, I'll take you away to hide in the forest." He promptly raised his hands in wai, chanted a powerful mantra,

lifted her onto the horse's back, and rode Color of Mist out of the trees. He audaciously galloped the magnificent steed with the two of them across in front of the troops

with his spirits swarming around them. As Color of Mist came out on Khun Ram's flank, Khun Phaen pronounced a formula and blew it to stun the troops and make them fear his powers.

The artillerymen and pikemen, who had been advancing en masse, stopped stock still. Khun Phaen rode outside the encircling troops, and nudged Wanthong to look.

"Over there's your husband in the elephant's howdah, showing off his fine figure and his head bald down to his ears. Sonphraya's riding on the neck, brandishing a goad. All three baldies came to give chase.

You and I are just two people. How to stand up to the power of these valiants? Because I love you, I have to engage them. Whether I live or die will depend on merit.

If you were anyone else less dear to me, I'd hand you over without a second thought." He kissed and caressed her gently to mock Khun Chang, and then sped away.

They came to a banyan and sheltered under its dense foliage where the light did not penetrate. He helped Wanthong down from the horse. "Eye's jewel, stay in the shelter of this banyan.

I'll see what Khun Chang has in mind. If he's good, he can live a little longer, but if he attacks me, he'll be dead.

When I've finished with the army, I'll come back to fetch you. It won't take long for them to disappear into the forest." He chanted a mantra to focus Wanthong's mind,

and scattered enchanted sand around to form a diamond-hard barrier. He cut grass, tied it into the shapes of dummies, and placed a thousand of them around in a chain.

When he pronounced an incantation, fire flared up as if burning the grass dummies. He threw sacred water over them, extinguishing the fire and leaving the dummies changed into people

dressed as sturdy soldiers with weapons in hand. The dummies all paid respect to him, and he gave them their orders.

"Wait until I give you a signal, then attack their troops and annihilate them." He spurred his horse to gallop out of the trees.

The troops from front to rear had all been equally stunned, and it was some time before they came round and fell to questioning one another.

Phramuen Si said, "How come nobody moved a muscle just now? Khun Phaen rode across right in front of your faces, and went out on your flank, Khun Ram."

Khun Ram said, "I wasn't afraid but he froze my whole body and rode across on his fine steed without a trace of fear. We'll chase him down and chop him dead."

Khun Chang said, "I'm furious. He galloped his horse right up close here, kissing my wife however many times, all to mock me." The mass of troops was ordered to advance.

The crackle of gunfire echoed through the forest. Spearmen advanced with flags flying. Khun Chang urged them forward from his tusker. "Charge for victory!"

Khun Phaen bellowed a Power of Garuda formula,[15] stopping the men frozen in their tracks. The troops became confused and uncertain. Military discipline broke down.

The main army became the vanguard. The left and right wings swapped over. The forward strike troops went on the defensive. Khun Chang rode his

---

15. อำนาจครุฑ, *amnat khrut,* a stunning mantra that immobilizes the enemy, often used in the battle scenes.

elephant into the middle of the army.

Banging a hand gong, he overtook Phramuen Wai, shouting wildly, "Capture and kill him!" Then he hid himself in the howdah and ordered, "Take my elephant over to seize Wanthong."

hand gong

Phramuen Si and Phramuen Wai rode their elephants across and rebuked him loudly. "Don't interfere, Khun Chang. We two are in command of the army."

They rode their elephants out front and waved their hands to call Khun Phaen to ride back. "We're here on the king's orders to bring an army after you."

Khun Phaen, great romancer, whose reputation for powers of combat was unequalled, spurred his horse across in a bellicose manner, and asked, "Why did you come out here
with all these troops, weapons, and war materials? Where are you going? Has some enemy appeared somewhere? Please explain what the matter is."

When Khun Phet and Khun Ram advanced, Khun Phaen said, "This forest is swarming with your troops. There's an elephant hiding on another elephant around here. It's like following the faint red light of a flickering lamp.

You have to stare for a moment before you can recognize him. Why is he hiding his face away? This fellow has been banging a gong. Who picked this scum to lead an army?"

Khun Chang was burned up with rage and his skull drenched in sweat. He smacked his knee, gnashed his teeth, and seethed. "Enough! I'll arrest you.

You're puffed up with arrogance, shouting and showing off and making fun of me." He banged a gong and cried, "Advance and arrest him!"

Phramuen Si and Phramuen Wai rebuked Khun Chang angrily. "Instead of speaking nicely, you only provoke him. You act brave and daring because you have lots of allies and no need to fear.

You talk a load of rubbish! It's because you're such a fool that he shaved your head." He turned to reply to Khun Phaen. "I'll answer your questions so that you may understand.

At present His Majesty the King, who offers protection to the great and small throughout the world, has commanded us to bring an army in order to investigate the truth—

whether you abducted Khun Chang's wife, escaped from the city into the forest, associated yourself with bandits, set yourself up as royalty,

built a royal lodge as your residence, fortified it with many spikes, installed a toilet like royalty, mischievously imitated the Lord of Life,

killed over a hundred of Khun Chang's men, created trouble without fear of the consequences, behaved drunk with power, acted as if you were planning a revolt,

captured Khun Chang, lacerated him with rattan thorns so he suffered shame before the whole city, and hoped to provoke the king to engage you in an elephant duel.

When His Majesty knew of this case, he thought deeply about the criminal charges against you, but remained suspicious, and so sent us

to investigate on the spot first. If we're certain of the truth, we are to arrest you. If there's no case to answer, we still have to take you and Wanthong back.

The king will hear the case about your dispute over the woman, and give his judgment. He'll not pursue the case about the killing of Khun Chang's men in the forest.

As far as we can see, nothing that Khun Chang told the king has any reliable basis. You have no need to fear. Let's go together. Where's Wanthong? Bring her here."

Khun Phaen replied to Phramuen Si. "There's a lot more in the past but it's no use to tell you. Is she my wife or is she really Khun Chang's?

Please forgive me. We're all buddies here. It's totally obvious who's being crooked. This whole big matter arose out of rivalry over one woman—that alone is the cause.

Khun Chang brought his troops into this forest and ordered them to surround me in large numbers. I spoke to him nicely but he wouldn't back down, and instead came blundering on his elephant to stab me.

I had the choice to fight or to die, to act like a man or to run away. I rode my horse full tilt to break through his troops. They stabbed at me, breaking six or seven spears.

Because of my past merit, they failed. Khun Chang's men were gutless cowards. They broke and fled off into the forest in confusion, but I didn't chase after to slash them down.

Khun Chang scraped his sides and scratched his head because he was bent on running away, yet he went back and told the king I beat him up. Really it was two sides fighting tit for tat.

I'm telling the whole truth with no deceit. You say you're on the king's orders to take me and Wanthong back.

I'm in a tight corner. I fear royal authority but I've nobody to help me. Sir, please take the army back and report to the king, setting matters right.

I'll wait for the king's anger to cool somewhat, and come later. Please have mercy on me and help to stall this matter by reporting the truth to the king."

Phramuen Wai and Phramuen Si listened to Khun Phaen. "You're an able person with knowledge but what you just said shows you're thinking wrongly.

The king will be angry that we found you but failed to bring you back under arrest. Your past deeds will be forgotten, and the king will side with Khun Chang.

Why not come along with us and clear everything up? If you continue to resist, I'll order the elephants and horses to charge and seize you."

Khun Phaen, great romancer, thought quietly, grinding his teeth and shaking his head. "A good friend is issuing threats to frighten me. If I were no good, I'd have been crushed on the Lao campaign."[16]

He forced himself to restrain his anger, knowing that if anything major happened, it would go to the king. He answered evasively, "I said just now that I fear royal authority.

I could go with you, and it'd probably be all right. I'm not going to run away and hide. If you had no mercy, you'd just slash me dead rather than talking.

You'd charge the elephants, stab me, and take me. Although I'm fearful, how will you make me go with you? A single person is like a lone fly that soars up, attracted by a light,

only to fall down dead. If you have no mercy and kindness, then I'm done for. But if you want to take me back under arrest, I won't die quietly."

Hearing this, Phramuen Si and Phramuen Wai angrily gave orders to their troops. "Hey, men! Take him alive. Don't kill him." The officers and men swarmed forward with guns and pikes,

firing volleys and hollering. Khun Chang stood up banging a gong and shouting, "Take him!" Swords and pikes flashed and glinted. Khun Phaen boldly chanted a mantra,

and bellowed a Power of Garuda formula. The troops were stopped in their tracks with hair standing on end. Khun Phaen spurred Color of Mist away from an engagement. "If I act first, I'll be a traitor."

---

16. Meaning the Chiang Thong campaign.

On the left and right wings, Khun Phet and Khun Ram saw that all the guns and troops had fallen silent. "Mm! Phaen may have crooked ideas to revolt and seize the country."

They directed the elephant troops to split into a crow's wing formation. Khun Phet wagged his finger and said, "Hey, Khun Phaen, you're acting insolently, as if I don't have a clue. Your lineage is nothing.

Defying royal orders is a grave matter. You're full of ambition for kingship. You think you're able and have powers enough to take the territory,

but who's going to pay respect to *you*? Everyone knows your merit is insufficient. I knew your father and mother from way back. Your father's name was Khun Krai.

Your mother's that crone, Thong Prasi. That year the king went to round up the big buffaloes, he had Khun Krai executed and his head stuck on a stake in the hills.

Your property was seized, and all your clan's too. Your mother sneaked out of the capital with you and went back to hide in Kanburi.[17]

You stayed with your old mother at Cockfight Hill, and were ordained at Wat Som Yai, you fugitive. You went to fight at Chiang Thong, made a reputation, and became Khun Phaen.

You did well, but within less than a year, you slunk off with ideas of revolt. You had an affair with your lover, kidnapped her, and took her into the forest. I can no longer associate with you as a friend.

The king loves you but you don't love him in return. You gain royal favor but then you turn bad. Don't imagine you'll escape alive." He drove his elephant up close.

Khun Phaen was flaming with anger. He brandished Skystorm, flashing in the light. "You big mouth, you barge your way in here and slander someone already dead and in his coffin for no good reason.

You won't remain standing for eternity. Today, I'll give you a bad death, falling from your elephant to roll on the ground. Your wife will be a widow and I'll take her naked as my wife."

He chanted a formula, and summoned his mass of grass-dummy troops who swarmed out of the *rang* forest, whooping and shouting in uproar.

Khun Phaen swooped down on horseback and burst upon the vanguard, slashing with his sword. The grass-dummy troops ran like the wind, encircling his horse on both sides in an instant.

Under the power of mantra, the sky grew overcast, darkness shrouded the

---

17. They fled from Suphan, not from the capital (see ch. 2).

heron-leg gun

scene, and the earth trembled as if it would overturn.

Troops of the six militia units fought back with necks straining, arms at full stretch, and lungs gasping for breath, but their weapons broke and shattered as if they were slashing stone. Not pierced, the grass-dummy troops turned and slashed back,

their swords and pikes flailing and flashing. Weapons were broken down to the hilt. Heron-leg guns[18] were raised and fired but the shot bounced back,

hitting the ranks of artillerymen. Unde-
terred, they charged forward in a tumult,
until their weapons were exhausted. A[19] Jek
grasped a pike, closed his eyes and slashed.

machete

A Mon, brandishing a big machete, cried out and fell on his face. A Thai and a Jek died, writhing. A Jek gritted his teeth in pain, and toppled sideways, strength gone.

A Khaek was slashed, his head fell, and his body tumbled over. A Mon, shot by a gun, cried out "Oh, mother!"[20] A Lao was stabbed and screamed "I'm dead."[21] A Khmer fell flat on his back crying, "Help me!"[22]

Khun Chang drove his elephant off into the forest in panic. His cloth slipped off. The elephant charged straight into a grove of cowitch.[23] Sonphraya scratched himself, yelling "Ouch!"

The elephant kept hurtling into the trees. Khun Chang lost his helmet, and his head burned like a torch. He fell off and scurried along, bent over double. The panicked elephant ran away, shitting floods.

Khun Chang climbed on a tree stump. Without a cloth, he was as naked as his pate. Khun Phaen slashed masses of people until he suddenly came upon Khun Ram face to face.

---

18. ปืนขานกยาง, *puen kha nok yang*. "Pun khá nok yang, is a short piece which one or two men can carry. When it is to be fired, it is supported on a sort of tripod of wood. It is either a wall or a field-piece" (Low, "History of Tennasserim," 317). The gun had a barrel over a meter long and a bore of around 20 cms. It was fired from warships as well as on land.

19. The next two and a half stanzas down to "Help me!" are taken from WK: 17:639–40; PD has: Then the volunteers scattered away.

20. อุย ย่าย, *ui yai*, in Mon.

21. ค่อยตาย, *khoi tai*, in Lao.

22. ซุมจุย, *sum jui*, approximation of the Khmer *soum cuay*.

23. หมามุ้ย, *mamui, Mucuna gigantea*, cowitch, cowage, horse-eye bean. Cowitch are vines that snake through the forest canopy. The seedpods, which hang from the vines on long ropelike stems, are covered with very small hairs that itch and sting, particularly if entering the eye.

Khun Ram thrust with a long pike but landed only a glancing blow on the shoulder that spun Khun Phaen around. Khun Phaen lunged forward into the fray, and slashed Khun Ram down from his elephant onto the ground.

Khun Phaen leapt down from his horse, and hacked Khun Ram's shoulder, felling him, doubled over. Khun Phaen slashed again, and Khun Ram tumbled forward, convulsed, and died in a pool of blood. "One down, you meddler!"

Khun Phetinthra came to help with his pike raised in challenge. He thrust into Khun Phaen's chest but it was as impenetrable as iron or diamond.

Khun Phaen leapt onto the elephant and swung at Khun Phet's neck, which severed like a plucked flower, staining Khun Phaen's sword red with blood. He remounted his horse and galloped into the thick of the army.

His grass-dummy troops charged forward, hollering wildly, scything down the army row by row. Phramuen Si rode into the fray on his elephant with the howdah slipping and slapping.

Khun Chang caught sight of Phramuen Si's elephant and called out, "Help me, I beg you!" When the elephant brushed past the tree stump where he was standing, Khun Chang scrambled up on its rear.

Phramuen Si turned to look. Through blurred eyes, he dazedly thought Khun Chang was a tiger, and poked him in the side with the handle of his goad. Khun Chang cried out, "Damn you! It's me!"

In alarm, Phramuen Wai thought it was Khun Phaen, and hit him with the handle of a pike, cracking his skull and drawing blood. Khun Chang dangled from the elephant, scrambling to climb back up, and almost falling to his death.

Phramuen Wai spurred the elephant to charge ahead with its tail up, straight into a thicket of rattan. The troops broke and scattered, running away in a chaotic mass.

Khaek,[24] French, English, and Dutch galloped away on horses and elephants, hoping to preserve their lives and return to their wives, shouting at the tops of their voices, losing shirts and hats that disappeared in the brush.

People scattered across the plain, shedding the weight of pack baskets, panniers, and canisters, wheezing and panting, faces pinched with hunger, legs giving way. "For the merit of my wife and children, come and help me!"

Those who loved themselves and feared death scurried off, flinging away their guns anywhere, ducking to hide crouching in the undergrowth, and frantically stuffing back their innards.

One begged a ride from friends but got abuse in return. "You slave!" "Get

---

24. The next two stanzas down to "come and help me" are taken from WK, 17:642, absent from PD.

lost!" "Villain!" Another dropped to the ground and crawled along like a cat, saying, "That bald lackey deceived us."

Others shouted and screamed, spewing spittle. "I'm not going to survive!" "Oh Buddha!" Some collapsed flat out with exhaustion but figured they would be abandoned and managed to run on.

Others fled, crashing into one another, moaning and groaning over their bruised heads. Some feared they had met Khun Phaen, and raised their hands to wai and plead, "Oh sir! Don't do it! Spare me!"

Phramuen Si drove his elephant through the thick, lonely forest. Rustling sounds made him jump with fear. By dusk, he was almost to Sam Ko.

Horses and elephants were exhausted. Men were filthy, weak with hunger, hollow-eyed with exhaustion, and low in spirits. Phramuen Si caught sight of Khun Chang beside a bo tree, and cried, "Oh Buddha! How did you get here?"

Khun Chang replied, "I got up on the rear of your elephant, and you hit me in the side. Don't you remember? People shouted 'Tiger!' and scattered away. Khun Phaen attacked us in strength.

Please have mercy. My wife is still in dire straits. She has to put up with lying on the hard ground, and eating *jaeng*[25] roots rather than rice, with moonlight instead of lamps."

In fury, Phramuen Si came up and elbowed him. "Are you still thinking of her, damn you?" He kicked Khun Chang down on the ground. "Hey! You broke my ribs."

Phramuen Wai said sharply, "You're vile, Khun Chang. Stop moaning. We just got thrashed because of you." Officers and men carped and complained, loudly and wildly. They dug up taro or sweet potato and ate whatever there was.

᭡

After the army fled in retreat, Khun Phaen's anger cooled. He galloped away on Color of Mist, and happily went down to bathe.

Taking off his devices, he walked down to a stream where beautiful lotuses bloomed and a refreshing fragrance hung in the air. He scrubbed away the dust,

washed his victorious sword, sheathed it, and slung it over his shoulder. He changed clothes and went to find Wanthong. Snuggling up to her, he gradu-

---

25. แจง, *Maerua/Niebuhria siamensis*, a shrub whose root is used in Thai herbal medicine to treat headache, muscle cramp, arthritis, and gout.

ally relaxed in weariness.

"Did you see what a great army your husband brought here, Wanthong? I killed Khun Phetinthra and also Khun Ram, two officers in all.

If they'd behaved well, I wouldn't have killed them. But they used insulting words about me, and so brought disaster on themselves. Several thousand troops died.

They were led to their deaths. Others ran away, abandoning lots of gear. Except those two officers and Khun Chang, I didn't go after anyone to kill them.

Your husband, Khun Chang, stabbed me in several places, and my innards almost spewed out. I would've slashed him dead but I feared you'd be angry.

I restrained myself because I thought it through. If I hadn't been mindful of darling Wanthong, I would've pulverized him.

Come to the battlefield. You'll probably find your husband's clothes. You can gather them up in a bundle and keep them for merit. Hugging them while asleep will keep your face warm and heart happy."

"Oh dear, when will you stop harboring resentment? It's too much, all this cattiness. When did I ever refer to him? I'm really very hurt by your insinuations.

In the five or six days since I came here, I haven't mentioned even his name, yet you still pick at me relentlessly. It's really become a habit.

Do you think I don't love you? Is that why you maul and bite me so much, and the only thing you haven't done is swallow? Your anger is making you unreasonable.

We're starving. There's no betel, no pan. We have to forego not only sour but salty, sweet, and savory too.[26] The fighting went on so long the food is all finished—both fresh and dried."

"My blossom, my eye's jewel, don't be so troubled. We've been through much hardship already. Sometime we can probably be happy and carefree.

There's still fruit in the forest. We can make do in a forest sort of way. Why mention these things when it serves no purpose. Make an effort not to be sad."

He cuddled up to her and touched her breasts, exciting passions, like picking the right celestial medicine to lighten her heart. The breeze blowing through the budding leaves wafted them to sleep.

In the cool of the evening, when the soft light of the falling sun flickered on

---

26. This is a pun on the saying, อดเปรี้ยว ไว้กินหวาน, *ot priao wai kin wan*, literally forego eating the sourness (of an unripe fruit) to enjoy its sweetness later.

the leaves, animals moved through the woods and hills. A herd of elephants[27] forged a path through the thick forest,

moving in groups of both males and females, Niam[28] and Nin,[29] looking magnificent, Khobut, golden[30] Sangkhathan, Amnuaiphong, and Supradit, majestic and beautiful,

27. Khun Wichitmatra argues this passage on elephants suggests the dating of this chapter. While only one white elephant was found in the Bangkok First Reign, three were found in the Second Reign—in 1812, 1816, and 1817—provoking a lot of writing about elephants, including *Khlong Tamnan Chang*, Poem on the history of elephants, by the Front Palace Prince Mahasenarak in 1815. The chronicle of the Second Reign recorded, "Acquiring three white elephants of first class in one reign has never occurred before in either Siam, Burma, or the Mon country. King Chakkaphat had seven white elephants but how many were of first class is unknown" (Damrong, *Phraratchaphongsawadan*, 213). If this chapter was composed by the future King Rama III, it was probably in the period between the finding of the white elephants and his ascent of the throne in 1824 (KW, 211–14).

There were manuals of elephantology that described the various lineages of elephants both in the celestial and terrestrial realms. Vishnu (Narai) arranged that a lotus flower be born from a womb with eight petals and 133 pistils, and presented it to Siva (Isuan) who shared it out among Vishnu (Wisanu), Siva, Brahma (Phrom), and the god of fire, Agni (Akhani). The gods then arranged that the petals and pistils be born as elephants in the terrestrial world. From these origins arose the four main lineages of elephants associated with these four deities. Each of these lineages is then subdivided into several sub-lineages, usually eight, for the eight directions, including those named here, each with distinctive characteristics described in the *Tamra chang*, elephant manual. The manual used here dates from the reign of King Rama I. Khobut, โคบุตร, is a sub-lineage of the Isuanphong lineage of Siva (but sometimes classified in the Wisanuphong). Khobut are born from a cow, have a cow-like yellowish hide, tail like a cow, mooing voice like a wild cow, curved tusks, and a gentle manner. They are powerful, auspicious, and good protection from all dangers, hence of great benefit to kings. Sangkhathan, สังขทันต์, is also of Siva's lineage (or sometimes, Vishnu's) and has two variants. One is black with pure white tusks curved like a conch. The other is golden-yellow, with small tusks curved upwards to the right, and a cry like a cock, bullfrog, or animal horn. Amnuaiphong, อำนวยพงศ์, is sometimes classified in the Brahma lineage, or as a hybrid born from crossbreeding between elephants from the four main lineages. Supradit, สุประดิษฐ์, meaning "beautiful form," is in the Wisanuphong/Phisanuphong lineage of Vishnu (or sometimes classified in that of Brahma), has hide the color of evening clouds or red lotus or ruby, stomach folds like a snake, white tusks, long mouth hair, and a soft penis. (*Tamra chang*, 49–63; SB, 204–5, 212–13; KW, 675; SWC, 4:1899–1919)

28. เนียม, *niam*, technical term for an elephant with tusks that are naturally short with tips that look as if spiked with a lotus bud. There are three levels: first, with tusks less than two inches, shaped like a coconut heart; second, with tusks between two and five inches; third, with tusks longer than five inches, shaped like a banana shoot. They are usually placed in the Akhani lineage. Most of the titled royal elephants appearing in the Ayutthaya chronicles are *niam* (*Tamra chang*, 61, 68).

29. นิล, *nin*, blue, a division of the Amnuaiphong lineage with several subcategories: *nilathan*, with pure dark blue tusks; *nilajaksu*, with pure dark blue body; *nilnakha*, with pure dark blue toenails (*Tamra chang*, 61, 68).

30. คันทรง, *Colubrina asiatica*, latherleaf, a bush with yellow flowers, here used as an epithet indicating one of the two varieties of Sangkhathan (see note 27 above).

all lineages born in the Ton Forest.[31] Droves of big-tusked Ekkathan, Phinai, and Si-do[32] hurried along in file, stepping humpbacked over fallen logs, foraging as they went.

A tiger stalked *chaman* deer,[33] crouching to pounce, then springing forward, throwing up dust, sending the deer bounding away into the hills in high leaps.

A serow sprang from a cliff and fell but licked its broken bones to heal them with saliva.[34] Wild buffaloes with elegantly curving horns recognized a scent and scattered away, thrashing through the grass.

serow

Flocks of birds flew to nest in a noisy chorus, milling around prey, sharing the food while their cries floated away on the wind.

A little gibbon hanging from a tree lamented in lonely whoops, then looped lithely away. Cicadas chirped and churred from the branches of a banyan, and crickets crooned in response like singing counterpoint.

---

31. There is a saying: ช้างป่าต้นคนสุพรรณ, *chang pa ton khon Suphan*, "Elephants of the Ton Forest, Suphan people." ต้น, *ton*, can mean "primary," sometimes referring to attributes or possessions of the king, including elephants. Suphon suspects there was an area known as the Ton Forest that was a known haunt of "important" elephants, and was used for royal elephant hunts. She surmises it was in the vicinity of U Thong where these scenes of the poem are set. The saying is interpreted to mean that Suphan people are as distinguished as royal elephants (SB, 205–8; Sithawatmethi, *Luang pho to*, 6–7).

32. Ekkathan, เอกทันต์, is from the Akhani lineage (sometimes that of Siva), has a single tusk from birth, and strength equal to a hundred, sometimes a thousand elephants, and thus was placed by the god Khotchanat in the Wanwihan Forest rather than the human world. Si-do, สีดอ, is a name for bull elephants with large body, small face, and small or nonexistent tusks that tilt downwards at the tip, sometimes classified among the eighty variants of *chang thuralak*, ช้างทุรลักษณ์, ill-omened elephants with some form of disfigurement, from the Akhani lineage. Phinai, พินาย, another ill-omened *chang thuralak*, has a single, left tusk and is boisterous. (*Tamra chang*, 59; *Chang surin*; Wira, *Sapthanukrom chang*, 98; SWC, 4:1899–1919)

33. ฉมัน, *chaman*, *Cervus schomburgki*, Schomburgk's deer, a deer with spectacular antlers that used to live in herds in the plains of the Chaophraya valley but was decimated by hunting and the advance of rice farming. The last specimen in Thailand is believed to have been killed in 1938, and the species was declared extinct in 2006. Schomburgk was the British consul in Bangkok in 1857–64.

34. เยียงผา, *yiang pha*, more often *liang pha*, *Naemorhedus (capricanus) sumatrensis*, the southern serow or Sumatran goral, a small goat antelope found mainly in steep limestone terrain. These animals were believed to have bones filled with powerful oil, enabling them to climb steep cliffs and perform other remarkable feats such as healing themselves with their own saliva, hence the animal's carelessness about leaping around limestone crags because it could always repair itself after a fall (SB, 216, 631–32; Parr, *Large Mammals*, 180).

The sun set and the moon shone brightly through the leaves of the holy golden banyan, highlighting two breasts like heavenly lotus buds.

Dewdrops gathering on the holy banyan leaves were blown by the breeze to plop gently down. A chill wind brushed Wanthong's body, coaxing the couple to cling together, whispering.

They gazed at the moon and listened to the crickets' chorus. He covered her, nuzzled her breasts, pressed her close, kissed to raise her passions, and caressed her softly until they slipped into sleep.

ॐ

The defeated army waited in the forest at Sam Ko by the big bo tree for two days until all the survivors had straggled back.

They numbered in total around five hundred, far fewer than those who had died. Khun Phet and Khun Raminthra of the left and right wings were among the fallen.

"All because of that pestilential Khun Chang." "He led us this way and that so we got thrashed." "Parents will collapse in grief by the cartload." "No need to find candles and offertory robes."

"If not slain, then the cane." "One time more and the clan's done for." "Anyone who came back must have a lot of merit." "What a scandal because of your woman, Khun Chang!"

They had been stripped of their cloths and weapons and were fiercely resentful. "You abandoned your love to hug a tree stump, and climbed onto my elephant to escape death."

Khun Chang said, "You can't blame me. If people run off and fling things away, they get lost. What am I to do? I'm still upset over my wife. If it were Phramuen Si's wife, I bet

you'd run after her roaring out loud. If you don't believe me, try it and see. You'd be leaping around blaming everyone in sight. We saw who did the fighting and who ran away.

Khun Phet and Khun Ram were on the left and right wings but I was in the vanguard, wasn't I? When Khun Phaen was slashing around, I stabbed him eight times.

When he chopped Khun Phet and Khun Ram down dead, I turned and saw Phramuen Si driving his elephant to escape. There was nobody to call upon. We were done for so I fled too."

Phramuen Wai cursed. Phramuen Si said angrily, "You lowlife with a head shaved by a ghost! You turn everything around so I fled before you. When

Khun Phaen charged and slashed those two,

where were you to be stabbing Khun Phaen? You still dare to say this, you hairy face. You? You were at the rear of the troops. Who ran to climb on the back of my elephant,

someone with a head just like yours? When you clambered up, I hit you with the goad, kicked and elbowed you many times, but you wouldn't let go and swung yourself up on my mount, you mother."

Ratthaya said, "My brother Son and I slashed and stabbed Khun Phaen before you, sir. We meant to haul him in by the ears but the elephant carrying us ran off so we lost the chance."

Phramuen Wai laughed. "Ha! What you say is true. If the elephant hadn't run off, your liver would be slit." When all were ready, the chief commander, Phramuen Si, ordered the army to march.

Khun Chang, Ratthaya, and Sonphraya rode on an elephant with their heads bobbing and glistening in the sunlight. Phramuen Si rode a bull elephant.

When they passed the customs post at Pak Khu, many people came to look. The troops hurried along in shame, cut into a wat,[35] and entered the city quickly.

As they rowdily dismounted from their horses and elephants, the two heads of the pages felt apprehensive. The evening sun had almost set behind the forest. As there was no further audience on that day,

they all went home. Friends, wives, and children came to meet them and ask what had happened. They told them sorrowfully.

The wives of the fallen wept and flailed around in distress. Some fainted and would not get back up. Others milled around massaging, stroking, and hugging them to revive.

The wives of Khun Phet and Khun Ram heard the news from their servants. They wept, their heads swollen in horror, stretched out on their beds in thought.

Khun Phet's wife beat her chest. "Oh my lord and master, you shouldn't have died in battle. When you interpreted my dream, the worry made my breast tremble, and I've been fearful from that day on.

Didn't I tell you I saw you without a head? Didn't I tell you not to go with the army? You didn't believe in the karma that you'd made. You insisted on going, and you lost your life.

Others came back home but you went to die unseen in the wilds. The servants and men who went with you have returned, but the light of your wife's

---

35. Probably Wat Thamma (see p. 16, note 76).

life has gone out.

Your corpse will decay in the undergrowth, with no cloth as cover, prey to wild animals, left to rot in pustules. Pitiful![36]

Your flesh will spill on the dust, and swill around the edges of the marsh. Your bones will be scattered in piles. None of your kin will see you again.

Your merit was finished. So be it. But had you died at home, your body could be cremated with a balustrade, tiered umbrellas, all the adornments appropriate to your status,

krajang *design*

the bright light of lamps, incense and candles on display, clusters of golden stars hanging down, layered wreaths with delicate tassels,

a coffin carved with a frieze of magnificent *krajang* designs decorated with gold, a canopy with scattered stars in *benjarong* pattern, monks invited to chant sweetly,

and the patter of twin Malay drums. Late at night all your many relatives could gather to sing your praises in harmony.

scattered stars pattern

Oh my lord and master, why did you die, a broken life, as if fleeing your wife to deny her the chance to make your corpse look fine?

No umbrellas, only great trees. No pipe, drum, and gong to mark time, only the sound of animals in the forest undergrowth. No incense and candles, only the moon and stars.

No lofty canopy, only the sky murky with clouds and mist. No curtains, only the surrounding hills. Nothing but the bare ground to support the body in place of a pyre.

You lie left lonely in a forest with no one to cremate your corpse. Many are scattered and lost. Many have died, never to be seen again."

She beat her head and breast, her lament echoing through the rooms of the house, grieving until her voice tailed away into a sad silence.

---

36. Suphon notes this passage is similar to two other famous laments (SB, 217). The first is from the Matsi episode of the Mahachat (see p. 61, note 27). After Wetsandon gives away his children, Matsi searches for them throughout the night, then returns to the hermitage and faints from fatigue. Wetsandon believes she is dead and gives vent to his grief over her ill fortune to meet her death in the forest. The second is the "Kap nang loi," floating princess, episode from the Ramakian. In an attempt to prevent Ram from attacking Lanka, Thotsakan arranges for his brother's daughter, Benyakai, to assume the appearance of Sida and be washed up, apparently dead, on the shore at Ram's camp. Ram discovers the body, is fooled by the disguise, and laments over his love's death until Hanuman arrives and unmasks the deception ("Benyakai plaeng pen sida," in Premseri, *Ramakian*, 259–66; Cadet, *Ramakien*, 126–30).

In the bright light of dawn, Phramuen Si and Phramuen Wai set off along with Khun Chang.

Senior officials inquired what had happened. Once they knew the story, they feared the king's anger. At the appropriate time, they entered the audience hall.

palace ladies with regalia

Now to tell of the almighty king, whose reputation made the world quake in all ten directions. He resided in a palace of victory under a golden spire, surrounded by throngs of inner ladies,

rejoicing in the royal pleasure, refreshed by the measured strains of orchestra and chorus. At the appointed time, he emerged from his golden room,

was bathed and dressed in glittering attire, and walked elegantly forth holding his regal sword to preside in the resplendent audience hall, while a succession of consorts carried in regalia.

A curtain was drawn aside to reveal the royal presence.[37] Nobles prostrated with faces bowed. Those who had returned from the campaign prayed feverishly and fearfully.

The almighty king looked around and saw Phramuen Si and Phramuen Wai but not Khun Phet and Khun Ram.

Noticing Khun Chang prostrate beside Phramuen Si, he asked, "On the matter of Khun Phaen Saensongkhram, did you bring him in or not?"

---

37. Seventeenth-century European visitors described two tableaus of the king in audience. In the first, he appeared seated on an elaborate throne on a raised platform. In the second, typified by the audience with King Narai in October 1685, "The King . . . appears at a kind of Tribune or Window, raised six foot higher than the first Court," set into the end wall of the audience hall at above head height (Tachard, *Voyage to Siam*, 155). The plinth on which the king sat behind this window can still be seen in the remains of the Lopburi Palace, and less distinctly in the remains of the Sanphet Prasat in Ayutthaya. Forbin wrote, "The same drum beat again several times, with certain intervals between, and at the sixth beat the king opened the window, and showed himself." At the close of the audience, "the king shut the window" (*Siamese Memoirs*, 53–54).

The sharp, clever, and wise Phramuen Si Saowarak-rat promptly addressed the king. "My life is beneath the royal foot.

The army marched to Banyan Tree Village, which is still far from Ton Forest.[38] Khun Chang said that was the place

where he had found both Khun Phaen and Wanthong staying under a holy banyan. We looked and found nothing, neither a royal cloister nor royal lodge.

Even if such buildings had been taken down, the elephant grass would have been flattened. What we saw did not fit Khun Chang's description at all. So we marched further into the forest to Three Thousand Crocodiles stream,

and had people climb a tree to spy around. They saw a horse released in the forest, and Khun Phaen with Wanthong, just the two of them.

No forest bandits. We sent men to poke and pry about, both in the vicinity and farther into the forest. Nothing.

No royal lodge. So troops were ordered to surround the place. Khun Phaen and Wanthong mounted their horse and broke through our ranks.

I thus ordered the troops to give chase and catch them. Wanthong and Khun Phaen sped off but we followed and surrounded them.

Wanthong hid away out of sight but Khun Phaen was in our encirclement. When the left and right wings were ready, I spoke with Khun Phaen

about the points that are at issue. I told him that His Majesty had given orders that he be found immediately, and that he would be given a fair judgment on the matters under dispute.

Khun Phaen replied that Wanthong was definitely his wife; he had asked for her hand and built a bridal house where they lived together until Khun Phaen went to Chiang Thong;

Khun Chang had deceitfully said that Khun Phaen was dead, and Wanthong's mother had given her to Khun Chang in marriage; Khun Phaen returned and took Wanthong away;

Khun Chang led troops to find them at the big banyan, and ordered his men to charge and kill Khun Phaen, who angrily fought back.

As for Khun Phet and Khun Ram, they insulted Khun Phaen and spoke inappropriately.[39] They raked up matters and made accusations at length, say-

---

38. See note p. 411, note 31.

39. In the Law on Conflict, พระไอยการลักษณวิวาทตีด่ากัน, *phra aiyakan laksana wiwat ti da kan*, literally the law on quarreling, beating, and cursing, Clause 36 prescribes punishments for various acts of provocation which lead to quarreling and violence. It specifies that "cursing someone's whole lineage" merited specially severe punishment. By detailing the tirade of Khun Phet and Khun Ram, Phramuen Si is giving evidence in Khun Phaen's defense. At the trial below, the king is quick to absolve Khun Phaen of guilt over the killing of Khun Phet and Khun

ing he had done wrong in kidnapping Wanthong.

In addition, they accused him of treason, revolt, and acting highhandedly. They raked up many matters about deceased members of his family. They said, 'Your father was called Khun Krai

and your mother is old Thong Prasi. You ran off to be ordained at Wat Som Yai. Your father died badly long ago. You're arrogant and not submissive.'

They charged forward with men and elephants to close in on him and cut off his head. Khun Chang kept on shouting he'd arrest him. The troops were intent on slashing him.

Khun Phaen escaped three times but the army persisted in trying to chop him down.[40] So Khun Phaen rode into the confrontation, slashed Khun Raminthra dead,

and Khun Phetinthra as well. Many troops were killed, and the others broke and scattered, leaving their weapons behind.

We set out with five thousand. Over four thousand five hundred have died. The remaining troops who have returned to the city number only four hundred and fifty-five persons."

Having heard this account of the battle from its beginning, the almighty king raged like a roaring fire. He stamped hard enough to bring the audience hall crashing down,

as if a bolt of lightning had lashed Mount Meru so hard that the peak bowed down to earth before snapping back upright. "What? The army commander, his deputy, and the troops have been wiped out—

elephants, horses, and weapons in thousands? Only one person and you can't defeat him? You're that cowardly and hopeless? You shamefully ran off and hid like women.

It was a waste to have kept you for no result. What a toll on the conscript rolls and rice supplies! You deserve to be flogged and sent down to prison, yet you still have the nerve to come in here to tell me.

If this isn't the truth, then why come? If you were sent off to fight other distant enemies, you wouldn't get close enough to see their footprints. You'd flee in terror at the sight of the dust they raise.

What a tribe of evil curs! If you saw some tiger droppings you'd run off into the elephant grass without looking back. There's only one thing you're good

---

Ram, possibly because the two engaged in provocation considered unreasonable and unlawful. (KTS, 3:201; Woranan, "Kan sueksa," 169)

40. Again Phramuen Si is offering a defense by emphasizing that the troops attacked first and Khun Phaen entered the fray only in self defense.

at—strutting around and swishing your tails to flirt at Din Gate,[41]

combing your hair and making up your faces. You're sex mad! Fighting wars doesn't interest you at all. You're only good at cheating your own men for corrupt gain, and using fancy words to get blood out of a crab.[42]

You deserve to have your heads lopped and your clans obliterated. Bad people should not live. Why should I keep you to bring shame on me? First off, Kalahom and Mahatthai,

urgently send out arrest warrants under seal to the guard posts and customs posts in all the regions and cities, great and small, to all the provinces under our control, to cities of the first, second, third, and fourth classes.

Wherever Khun Phaen is found, arrest him but do not kill him; remember this well and deliver him here. In the order under seal, give his name and reputation,

appearance tall or short, dark or fair, how old he is, so he will be recognized." Having given this order, the king retired to his bedchamber.

Senior officials busily assembled clerks to write out warrants, affix seals, and send them to the guards

to be taken to all major cities, ordering the arrest and delivery of Khun Phaen. Guards took the orders urgently to north and south,

to cities of the first, second, third, and fourth classes, to guard posts and all the lairs of forest gangs, complete with full information and the stipulation to follow the official order in every detail.

---

41. Din (earth) Gate was the colloquial name for Udom Nari or Bowon Nari Mahaphopchon Gate on the western end of the north wall of the palace (see map 8). The name came from the *Thanon din*, earth road, leading up to the gate on the outside. This was the gate used by inner ladies, especially to "go out to the market for fresh produce in the mornings and evenings" (KLW, 200, 206; APA, 70). It was also a gathering place for men who wished to flirt with them, hence the term, "Din Gate lovers." The name of the gate was carried over to Bangkok, and referred to the gate leading to the market later known as Tha Tian. "Swishing your tails," see p. 31, note 42.

42. See p. 350, note 50.

21: KHUN PHAEN GIVES HIMSELF UP

Now to tell of Khun Phaen,[1] great romancer, renowned for his splendid powers, who was living in the forest with Wanthong, just the two of them.

He enjoyed the hills and the forest, the absence of any threat from their enemies, and his intimacy with fair and gentle Wanthong. Though their bed was logs, their life was bliss.

No mattress cushioned Wanthong's soft flesh, yet she slept as if on a resplendent golden bed, lulled by the soothing strains of cicadas, the forest orchestra playing for the wilds.

In the lightless night, their lamp was the lustrous moon. Blossoms bathed the air in lightly scented pollen. Plants jostled to sprout new young leaves and blooms.

The wind wafted soft perfumed pollen and the sweetly scented fragrance of flowers as they drifted to sleep in each other's arms.

Wanthong dreamed in a deep slumber, and awoke as soon as the dream ended with it still fresh in her mind. In alarm, she aroused her husband to interpret it.

"I dreamed that I reached up into the sky and amazingly could pluck the sun like a flower. When I put the sun in my mouth and swallowed, my whole body shone brightly.

Then a strong man came along, boldly gouged out my right eye, and threw it away, so I was constantly in the dark and in dismay.

He didn't return the old eye but offered me another one that was not as good, less bright. Please tell me if this dream is good or bad."

Khun Phaen felt anxious because he could see good and bad in the dream, both in great measure. "Oh my heart, you'll have a child. That's the meaning of the sun in the dream.

This will overcome our hardship and misery, make all our problems disap-

---

1. Khun Wichitmatra speculated that chapters 21, 22, and 23 were revised by Krommuen Mahasak Phonlasep. He was a son of King Rama I, a half-brother and close associate of King Rama II, served as Kalahom, and became the Prince of the Front Palace in the Second Reign. He composed several *nirat* and outer dramas, including one based on *KCKP* (KW, 267–81).

pear. The child in your womb will have powers, and will be a partner we can depend on."

But the part of the dream where Wanthong's eye was gouged out meant great difficulty in the future. He worried that telling the full meaning would make Wanthong miserable,

so he suggested instead they bathe and wash their faces to feel refreshed. They boiled yams and sweet potatoes, and went looking for fruit, rambutan, persimmon, water chestnut, and lotus in the forest.

Dwelling on the dream made Wanthong apprehensive. She agreed she must be pregnant, as he said, and winced at the thought of the hardship from earth, dust, and wind.

"We have nothing as it is, so being pregnant too is going to make everything worse." Multiplying their hardships weighed heavily on her heart.

"If we were living safely in a house, a child would be like a jewel, and we'd be only too happy to look after it. But when I think matters through, giving birth here worries me.

The child will be born like a condemned person. This is not something to be a bit happy about. How to bring up a child in a forest?" These thoughts made her miserable.

Khun Phaen, great romancer, was surprised that being pregnant made her weep, but on reflection he could understand. He comforted her and urged her to get dressed.

"We can't stay here any longer. The source of our danger hasn't gone away. The king will be angry, and I don't think he'll give up the idea of sending troops after us.

We have to leave the forest where we're living now and make for the hills. There we can hide where nobody will find us until matters eventually simmer down."

He summoned his spirits, harnessed Color of Mist, and prompted Wanthong to take leave of the forest. They mounted and went off through the trees.

In the shade, the ground was carpeted with colorful flowers, pretty and pleasing to the eye. Khun Phaen drove the horse ahead and before long they came to Thammathian Hill.[2]

---

2. เขาธรรมเธียร. Khun Wichitmatra suggested this is เขาธรรมามูล, Thammamun Hill, a low flat rocky elevation that rises up from the deltaic plain about 7 kms north of Chainat town. However this seems improbable. More likely they went deeper into the western hills rather than crossing the plain (see map 2; KW, 238).

Among the hills, many species of fine trees swayed in the wind:[3] *rokfa,*
khanang, yang, takhian, kankrao, trabao, trabian, chingchan,
   son, sak, krak-khi, kamyan, chanuan, chanan, khla, khlak, jakajan, prang,
pru, pradu, duk, mukman, hiang, han, kraphrao, sadao-daeng,
   teng, taeo, kaeo, ket, inthanin, roi-lin, tatum, chumsaeng, khwit, khwat,
rachaphruek, jik, jaeng, samun-waeng, thaengthuai, kluai-mai,
   krapho, ngo, rangap, krajap-bok, krathok-rok, kalampho, samo-khai, phak-
wan, tan, dam, lamyai, mafueang, fai, khai-nao, sadao-na,
   sai, sok, ulok, phokphai, phobai, krai, krang, oi-chang, wa, phlap, phluang,
muang, man, janthana. Birds twittered and trilled in a noisy chorus.

A laughingthrush pecked at grubs while her young implored her with gaping mouths. A coel landed on an ivy gourd vine, spied the ripe-red fruit, and
took a peck.

An oriole perched on a cummin vine and flew away with a beak full of prey
for its young. A flock of magpies fluttered around the sky. Doves cooed in twos
in the cool of a wood.

A partridge poked around looking for a mate, clucking, chucking its neck,
raking its wings, and flicking its tail. Barbets burbled back and forth. Quail
flapped and flew off in a flurry.

Wild cock scratched for bamboo
seeds on a patch of ground, and
crowed loudly through the forest.
Done with feeding, they called out to
their mates and flew off cackling to find
a nest.

wild cock

barbet

At dusk as the sunlight faded,
Khun Phaen and Wanthong
rode down beside a flowing stream until they reached a landing. He asked
Wanthong to dismount,
   unsaddled the horse, shed his own gear, and walked her down to the landing. They drank the cool water and washed their hair among the blooming
flowers.

He plucked lotus pods, and pulled up a lotus root that popped out of the
earth in naked coils. He stripped the skin, leaving it white and curly, and begged
her, "Try this, my love."

---

3. The next nine lines are a tour de force of the "admiring the forest" genre, with the names of
seventy-one trees or shrubs fitted into the metrical pattern, and only two other words: *lae*, and;
ton, tree. Since the point of the passage is the sound, rhyme, and rhythm, here it is given pho-
netically. Only คลัก, *khlak*, is not identifiable, while ฉนาน, *chanan*, is probably *khanan*, ขนาน.

"Oh, I've never eaten the root. I'm afraid it'll make my mouth itch and my tongue sting. I'll just eat the seeds." "Try it. Believe me, it's delicious. I just fear you'll be capti- vated once you know the taste."

"There's only one lotus root and you're giving it to me? Oh no, you shouldn't go without. If you're not hav- ing any, nor am I." "There's more lotuses, don't worry."

"In that case, you dive down to pull them up while I pick the pods. They're easy to pluck." They flirted happily while collecting the lotuses, both gradually shedding their fatigue.

They left the landing and went up to find somewhere to sleep in the forest. At dawn they set off again. Life was hard but they were free from danger.

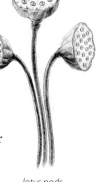

lotus pods

One day, Khun Phaen, great valiant, realized it had been many months since he had brought Wanthong to the forest, and this was the end of her seventh month.

He faced a sad dilemma. They had been forced to live in the forest because it was remote, but medicines for giving birth would be hard to find, and there was no one to turn to for help.

Weighing up the options made him heavy-hearted. He was very concerned about the child in her womb. "This could be a disaster." He sobbed sadly in the forest.

Puzzled by his misery, Wanthong asked him straight out, "What are you thinking? Tell me.

Why are you crying? Do you have doubts about our love? Will we not stay together? Have you had enough of me? Tell me."

"Oh my utmost love, don't have such thoughts about me. You are equal to my own heart. There are no doubts. Don't stab me like that.

I love you as much as when we were first in love. Because I now know you well, there's not a single reason for doubt or worry. I'll tell you the truth but don't be upset.

I'm crying with heartbreak for the difficulty we're in. I keep looking at your growing belly. You'll give birth before long, and there's no one to nurse you.

We've got nothing, no place to live. Finding a cradle will be hard away from home. Many medicines can't be had in a forest. There's no mattress, no pillow, no mosquito net, no curtain, no bedding or anything else for the child. I'm saying this infant will be unhappy—will have to brave the rain and endure the sun throughout the year. We alone are already starving.

The baby will wail for food. These thoughts are what bring tears to my eyes." Desolate enough to die, the couple clung together and wept.

As they gradually got over their sadness, Khun Phaen pondered and said, "Did you ever hear people talk of Phra Phichit[4] and Busaba as kind people?

Anyone who is poor can go to them for help. Anyone condemned to death can rely on their mercy. Let's go there.

I'm someone who's able, someone with knowledge, so I don't think there'll be a problem. Don't worry, eye's jewel. Even if he sends us down to Ayutthaya,

the king will probably hold an inquiry. My past reputation is still very good, and I have hope because of the powers of my knowledge." He harnessed Color of Mist, summoned his spirits,

and lifted Wanthong up onto the horse. They rode out of the forest late in the morning. He kept the horse to a steady gait so as not to cause her belly any discomfort.

Out of concern for her awkward condition, he hugged and stroked her gently to keep her spirits up. They took a direct route, stopping every now and then at a stream or pond,

digging up such sweet potatoes as there were for each other, and resting among the trees. After ten days' travel through hill and forest, they rode into Phichit,

and reached Wat Jan[5] at dusk. They went in to pay respect to the Buddha image, then stayed in a big sala beside the kuti. At lamp-lighting time, they set off.

Buddha image and kuti

---

4. Meaning the governor of Phichit, an old provincial center on the Nan River in the north of the Chaophraya Plain. Phichit in *KCKP* is the old town, now the site of a small historical park about 9 kms to the south of the modern town along route 1068. It was a third-class town under the aegis of Mahatthai. The official title of the governor was Okya Thepathibodi Sinarong-kharuechai, *sakdina* 5,000 (KTS, 1:321; see map 10 and its accompanying note).

5. The monastery of the moon, which features again later in chapters 28 and 31 when Khun Phaen billets his army in the wat. There is no sign or record of a Wat Jan near old Phichit. Possibly there is some confusion with a wat of this name to the south of Phitsanulok. More likely, the site referred to is the wat now called Wat Sama Bap, วัดสมาบาป, the monastery to atone for sin (see map 10 and its accompanying note).

Khun Phaen enchanted powder with many devices, and daubed it on their foreheads as a charm to induce love. Then he made them all invisible, including the horse, and went straight to the residence of the city governor.

Now to tell of Phra Phichit. After the sun had fallen to earth and the light had disappeared, he was happily sitting in his house under a bright luminous moon.

He had his young servants come to play chase, giggling and enjoying themselves. His wife and heartmate, Si Busaba,

was at the end of the fifth month of pregnancy. She came out to sit with him and laugh along with the children. "Hey, kids, come and play chase." The house was merry under the moonlight.

children playing

Khun Phaen and Wanthong went without challenge, delighted at their skill in becoming invisible.

They dismounted and tethered Color of Mist at the gate of the house. Khun Phaen released the formula of invisibility, and they entered on all fours to pay respect.

Prostrate in front of the pair, Khun Phaen intoned a mantra and blew it hard towards them, while believing in his lore and thinking of the virtue of his teachers.

Phra Phichit and Busaba peered at this couple coming to pay respect, and guessed they were from another city. To find out, he asked,

"Here, young man and beautiful lady, who came together, where are you traveling to? Where is your home? Are you man and wife or brother and sister?"

Khun Phaen, great gallant, prostrated along with Wanthong, and replied, "This young child's name is Wanthong

and mine is Khun Phaen Saensongkhram. We have made our way here through the forest. I'll tell you the whole story. In the past, Wanthong was called Phim Philalai.

Khun Chang seized her from our bridal house so I kidnapped her away into the great forest. After I defeated, killed, and dispersed an army, we were forced to live in the forest for many months.

Wanthong's pregnancy is now advanced, and we're concerned something could happen in the wilds. Going back home would create karma for our mothers.

I know that you, sir, are kind to people, so we made our way straight here through the forest. We put our two lives in your hands. Sir, please be merciful."

Phra Phichit and Busaba were touched by this story, and also affected by Khun Phaen's expertise in lore, which made them love the couple like their own children.

They called servants to take the horse to tether, and led the couple by the hand up into the residence.[6] "Listen to me. You have no need to fear. For better or worse, I'll try to ease things."

He ordered servants to prepare a large meal. Khun Phaen and Wanthong bathed happily.

Si Busaba gave them clothes to change, and sent over some krajae powder. They went to sit in the central hall, and Phra Phichit invited them to eat.

When the four had finished, Phra Phichit arranged for the couple to stay in an apartment beside the central hall. Khun Phaen and Wanthong grew more cheerful.

Khun Phaen, great romancer, lived in the new apartment beside the residence, enjoying the affection, protection, and support of Phra Phichit. But after a full month he began to worry.

"Phra Phichit and Busaba let me stay here and love me like their own true son. But how long can things stay covered up when the king is still enraged?

He's ordered officials of the guard posts to keep a tight watch on all hideouts. Anyone who catches me must send me to the capital for the offense of killing several thousand people.

Phra Phichit has been like a father, having the mercy to look after us and let us live here, but before long this will expose him to punishment. He says he'll plead our case to the king,

but as long as the king is still angry, he'll not favor us with a pardon. If we stay quiet but news reaches the capital and an order arrives for me to be sent down, I'll be at a disadvantage."

He consulted Wanthong about these thoughts. "My love and life partner, I

---

6. จวน, *juan*, the technical term for the residence of a provincial governor. Typically, this was a large walled or fenced compound with three main parts: an open sala at the front that served as office and law court, a cluster of residential buildings, and a jailhouse at the rear (Pornpun, "Environmental History," 105–9).

fear that staying here in Phichit will create trouble.

I'll ask Phra Phichit to order us sent down to the capital, Ayutthaya. I must confess guilt and think of how to counter Khun Chang's charges.

If I give myself up rather than being captured in the forest, the punishment should be light. Besides,[7] I can create obstruction with the power of my knowledge.

If I could fly in the air, I'd ride a horse across the sky, take you to the city, and let all our difficulties be known.

But I'm at a loss because I'm the king's servant. When he showed me favor, I was very happy and drank the water of allegiance several times. Fleeing from a hard taskmaster doesn't matter,

but the king has appointed me and fed me. It's unthinkable to consider going anywhere else. Whether heavy or light, life or death, let matters fall according to the karma I've made.

I love you and I'll give my life for you. If I'm destroyed this time, I won't complain. I'll find a way for you not to face punishment. Let's bow our faces and go without sorrow."

The beautiful Wanthong listened with tears flowing. She made an effort to swallow her sadness and said, "I've also considered everything.

We've committed a capital offense because so many officers and men were cut down dead. We disobeyed a royal order and on top of that we fled like criminals.

The defeated army probably went back and told the king that we're in revolt. Even though we had nothing treacherous in mind, it won't do to sit on the matter.

It's grim but necessary to go and find out whether we'll live or die. I don't cling to life. If the king is not merciful, then we'll die.

There's only one thing I'm afraid of—that he'll send me back to Khun Chang. I couldn't stand the shame and I'd much prefer death." She sobbed on and on.

Khun Phaen cradled little Wanthong, wiped away the tears that bathed her face, and said, "Why are you sad?

If the king isn't merciful and has us executed, we must bow our faces and

---

7. Three stanzas from here to "consider going anywhere else" are taken from WK, 18:673; PD has: I think there'll be ways to ask for a pardon. / If the king wants to punish me in some way, that's up to him because I'm his servant and I drank the water of allegiance. There's no reason to run away and hide. / As the old saying goes, "Swim towards the great crocodile."

This saying means, "when there is no other way of escape, better to take refuge with the mighty, however perverse and cruel they be, than to suffer total ruin" (Gerini, "On Siamese Proverbs," 233).

be born again well.[8] In this life we've made some karma.

If he sends you back to Khun Chang, I'll not fail to come after you and kill him before he can have you. Don't be upset. Please cheer up."

He consoled Wanthong and prompted her to scoop water for washing away her tears. Then they went into their patrons' room and paid respect at the couple's feet.

Puzzled to see them so sorrowful, Phra Phichit and Busaba inquired, "What has suddenly happened since this morning to upset you?"

With his head bowed, Khun Phaen, great romancer, explained as they had planned. "I'm afraid I'll bring punishment upon you.

Because there are arrest warrants to stop me at every guard post, the district officials are on the alert. You've hidden me for many days and I fear it's risky.

The deputy governor, magistrate,[9] and other officials will talk and pass on the news, which will be bad. You'll be an associate of criminals, and that will bring down the king's anger on you.

Sir, it would be better to avoid this risk. Send me down. Just help by explaining in your report that I gave myself up properly,

and convey my testimony including my wife's words in full. That will help me to confess and beg the king's favor. Beyond that, it's up to the karma I've already made."

Phra Phichit saw the truth in Khun Phaen's words, and pondered quietly. "At first I thought I'd make a request—

on grounds that you're expert in warfare and have defeated enemies from all directions—for you to take charge of the guard posts on the forest side. But then I realized this was not appropriate.

Because you're under charges, the king would say I'm siding with a criminal. But I was extremely concerned about sending you down, so I was truly stumped and did nothing.

But your thinking is exactly right. Your whole approach to the matter is very good. Because you came to confess to me, it's clear you had no subversive ideas of revolt.

If the old case comes to be examined, matters appear to be greatly in your

---

8. Meaning to be reborn in human form and of good social status, as a result of the accumulated merit (karma) mentioned in the following sentence.

9. ยกกระบัตร, *yokkrabat*, originally an official of the Ministry of the Palace, sent to major dependent cities as a magistrate or legal advisor but also more generally as a representative and spy for central authority. Later the term became more widely used for officials with judicial duties (Akin, *Organization*, 86, 91).

favor. When you went with the army, stories were made up that you were dead, and your mother-in-law took away your wife, so you were very upset.

Who wouldn't get angry? There've been many worse reactions. All you did was take your old wife back. Who can say that's seditious?

Only your battle with the royal army lays you open to charges of revolt. But an army of thousands came and surrounded you, a single person.

You restrained yourself from attacking, and they acted first, giving you no option but to stand your ground. The fact the army couldn't match you but broke and scattered is not your fault.

When you go down, the king will be angry but should submit you to questioning before punishing you on the major issue. Don't stay quiet but tell him the truth, and I think that'll overcome his anger and suspicion.

The royal order is very insistent that, if you're caught, both of you must be imprisoned with no clemency and sent to Ayutthaya.

Along the way, things needn't be so strict, but if you're not under restraint when reaching the capital, I'll be in the wrong too. I feel as bad about this as if licked by fire but don't be despondent, either of you.

It's not difficult to make your case in the report because there's a lot in your favor. I'll just give evidence that's true in every detail, and it won't prejudice either of you in any way.

Clothes and food will all be arranged. Shed your worries. I think you'll get clemency. After that come and live up here with me."

Busaba hugged Wanthong tearfully and expressed her regrets. "I love you like a child of my own womb. It's a pity you're being parted from me.

Oh my dear Wanthong, you're going away even though we love each other. I'm very worried because your pregnancy is so advanced. If you're convicted, there'll be no respite.

I'm distressed enough for my heart to break because I don't know what the future will bring. By the power of your merit, may you survive. When the case is over, please come back here."

Wanthong put her arms around Busaba and shed tears of parting. "Though my body leaves, my heart stays here with you. I won't find anyone like your ladyship.

Even though we're criminal suspects, you helped us by not putting us in jail but looking after us and loving us like your own children. We slept cozily, ate fully, and had no anxiety. May you earn merit.

At the capital there'll be no mercy. We'll have bricks and stones from the road in place of pillows, and the bamboo mats and slats of the jail instead of a mattress.[10] There'll be no one to bring us water to bathe and drink, no relatives to send food to fend off starvation. We'll be subject to questioning in the city, and we won't have a gnat's wing of money. They'll demand judicial fees,[11] and truss us up for public shaming. Awful. If we lose, we'll probably be loaded with heavy fines, and have only our own flesh and blood as money."

The more she thought about it, the more she became downhearted and miserable in every way, flailing around in floods of tears, her cries echoing through the house.

When their sadness subsided, Busaba gathered goods together in piles all around, and sat giving instructions to the servants, "Don't be so slow. Arrange what they need—

mattress, pillows, mosquito nets, soft mats, the good clothes we have in the house, pots and pans, jars, stove, food supplies, plates and bowls,

a betelnut set in nak and gold, a nielloware container for lime—put everything in sidebags. Facing a court case is expensive." She gave them three chang of silver to take for food.

stove

Phra Phichit came out to the central hall and sent for all the nobles to assemble. He composed his report and read it aloud to them so it would have no mistakes.

The testimony of Wanthong and Khun Phaen was tied, sealed by fingernail,[12]

---

10. " . . . nothing is more cruel than the Prisons of Siam. They are Cages of *Bambou* exposed to all the injuries of the Air" (La Loubère, *New Historical Relation*, 85).

11. ค่าฤชาตุลาการ, *kha ruecha tulakan*. Fees were levied from both plaintiff and defendant in court cases. These fees were the main source of income for many officials, as well as revenue for the royal treasury, and could be very high. A schedule of fees for parties undergoing ordeal by water ran as follows: "1) Fee for clerk reading the case summary, 3 baht; 2) fee for the registrar summoning the gods and administering the oath, 3 baht; 3) cost of posts, 3 baht; 4) fee for presiding judge, 6 baht; 5) fee for removing bamboo collar from plaintiff and defendant, 1 baht; 6) fee for four guards, 3 baht; 7) fee for preparing bank, 5 baht; 8) fee for ringing gong, 1 baht; 9) fee for pushing underwater, 1 baht; total, 16 baht." (KTS, 2:113–14, as summarized by Kukrit in *Sirindhorn, Banthuek*, 114; see also *phraratchakamnot kao*, Old Laws, clause 16 in KTS, 5:10)

12. Documents such as records of testimony were folded flat, pierced with a hole, threaded and tied with string, and the knots sealed with clay and marked with a fingernail (KW, 247). The Law on Judges, *phra aiyakan laksana tralakan*, clause 77 specified that after evidence was recorded "the plaintiff shall mark with fingernail first and the defendant following; if the defendant marks first, the fine is 64,000 cowries" (KTS, 2:166). When the site of the inner court sala at Ayutthaya was excavated in the early twentieth century, they "found clay seals for evidence with fingernail marks, baked hard by fire. Now they are kept in the Ayutthaya museum" (APA, 65,

put in a cylinder along with the written report, and handed over to a warder.

A boat was brought to moor at the landing, and servants carried everything down. Phra Phichit summoned the warders and ordered them, "You're in charge of escorting Wanthong and Khun Phaen.

Don't lock them up until you get close to Ayutthaya. If they want to visit somewhere on the way, let them do so. Look after them well."

Khun Phaen and Wanthong prostrated and took their leave in floods of tears. Phra Phichit and Busaba cried equally in sympathy.

In a miserable state, the couple left the residence and descended the stairway with the governor and his wife following. They went to find Color of Mist and tell him what was happening.

"Color of Mist, the governor is sending us down, and we don't know whether we'll live or die. We've come to say farewell. If we don't die this time, we should meet again."

Wanthong said, "Oh my Color of Mist, you went through hardship with me in the forest, getting eaten by gnats and mosquitoes for many days. You allowed me to ride you all the way.

You had to push through thick forest and dense thorny thicket, going without grass or straw for many days and nights.

When we reached this place, there was somewhere to stay, but having to part now brings tears to my eyes. You've been our friend in trouble, friend to death, through many travails. Leaving you, my heart will collapse."

Khun Phaen said, "Farewell, friend in trouble. We may die apart or meet again some day. While I'm still alive, I'll never stop thinking of you, even from jail.

If a time comes that I'm released, whether sooner or later, I'll come to find you at Phichit. I'd like to take you with us but I realized that, if our lives ended suddenly,

you'd be used as a workhorse, tethered tight, left without water or grass. If our merit came to an end in death, I'm worried there'd be nobody to love you."

Because he was affected by a mantra, Color of Mist understood. He shed tears, shook his head from side to side, shuddered with sadness, and lowered his face onto the couple's feet.

Khun Phaen made a request to Phra Phichit, "Sir, please have some consideration for me. I'm very concerned about my faithful horse, and I wish to leave him in your care."

Phra Phichit replied, "No need for concern. We have plenty of boys to

---

note 58). The site of this excavation is now under a new statue of U Thong.

look after him, and plenty of grass, straw, and water. Don't worry about the horse."

They set off. Color of Mist felt heavy-hearted, and both Khun Phaen and Wanthong were in floods of tears. They boarded the boat and entered under its canopy.

Phra Phichit and Busaba made their farewells. Khun Phaen and Wanthong wai-ed Phra Phichit. After the boat left the landing, they stayed staring at one another thoughtfully until they were far distant.

Phra Phichit and Busaba returned to the residence, grieving sadly. The boat floated along quickly past villages and towns.

They stopped at places to levy supplies of rice and other food. They forked at Bang Phutsa[13] and passed in front of Lopburi.

Beyond that city in the early evening, they saw a settlement with lush trees. Seeing it was almost night, the warders halted the boat there.

Khun Phaen picked up Skystorm and disembarked. Walking up through the thick bushes, he saw a hollow under a big banyan tree. Placing the sword inside, he chanted an *athan* concealing formula,

prostrated, and prayed to the guardian deities to look after the sword. "When I return, let me make no mistake. In the future if a village is established here,

let it be called Village of the Sword and Drawn Bow[14] because Skystorm is

big banyan tree

13. The old name for Singburi which was formerly located on the Noi River some 4 kms to the southwest of the current site. In the late Ayutthaya period, Wat Phra Non Chaksi, a wat in Singburi with a famous reclining Buddha, was threatened by river erosion. To the north of the town, a canal was dug to divert excess water away from the Noi River into the Chaophraya. This strategy was too successful as the old course of the Noi River dried up. The wat was saved, and King Borommakot presided over the rededication in 1750, but the town had to be relocated to the site of Ban Phutsa (Pornpun, "Environmental History," 28–29; RCA, 453). This fork takes them eastward along the Lopburi River (see map 2).

14. Ban Dap, บ้านดาบ, and Ban Kong Thanu, บ้านก่งธนู, are now two adjacent places on the east bank of the Lopburi River in the south of Amphoe Mueang Lopburi. Local legend on the

hidden here." He went back aboard and they continued the journey, alerting one another as they neared Ayutthaya.

The warders prostrated and asked his pardon. "Please don't be angry with us." Khun Phaen let them apply the restraints. They stretched out their legs to be put in chains fastened by bolts.

Feeling sorry for Wanthong, Khun Phaen wound a cloth round her. When they landed, he carefully supported her, and tied a string so she could lift her chains to walk.[15]

She carried a little basket on her waist, and lifted her feet gingerly. Her hands trembled holding the string. She accidentally took too large a pace and fell down,

spilling the contents of her basket with a shriek. Khun Phaen picked her up, and dusted her off. Tears of sympathy streamed down his face.

Now to tell of Kaeo Kiriya.[16] She had redeemed herself from Khun Chang with the fifteen tamlueng that Khun Phaen gave her. She lived in Ayutthaya,

in the house of a friend from her old home who helped look after her. Any man who saw her was attracted but she made a point of saying discreetly that she had a husband.

She did good business selling low-priced goods like fruit, sweets, oranges, and lychees from a dry goods store with signs for "good astringent betel," "Phetchabun tobacco," and "fresh banana leaves."

She had been miserable waiting for her husband for almost a year, and did not know he was coming.

As that day was the fifteenth, a holy day,[17] she went as usual to hear a sermon.

---

origin of the name differs slightly from the version here: On release from jail, Khun Phaen passed this way carrying a sword which he buried in order to avoid making people fearful; nearby he found a bow already strung for hunting which he took with him (www.thaitambon.com/tambon/ttambon.asp?ID=160104; see map 2).

15. Kukrit notes that this passage uses a special term, สายหยก, *sai yok*, for the string used by prisoners to lift leg chains to allow walking. Kukrit believes this and other evidence shows that the authors of the *sepha* knew about prison life, and that the *sepha* was originally a genre developed in prison (KP, 208).

16. In the original, the next three stanzas appear earlier, after "Khun Phaen and Wanthong grew more cheerful" on p. 425.

17. วันพระ, *wan phra*. In the lunar month, the holy days are the 8th waxing, 15th waxing, 8th waning, and either the 14th or 15th waning depending on the length of the month (see p. 10, note 52). On these days, the Buddhist faithful believe they should attend a wat to make merit or hear a sermon. Strict practitioners will observe the eight precepts, abstaining from: killing, taking something not given, sex, incorrect speech, intoxication, eating after noon, entertainment

She bathed, powdered herself, oiled her hair nicely, and dressed

in a lowercloth in sesame-seed pattern and a quilted uppercloth. The clothes were not cheerful because she was unhappy to be without a husband,

and did not want to offend him should he return. Also she was far from her family with no friends to think of her.

She descended from the house, carefully holding her uppercloth not to expose her breasts. In her hand she had the sort of betel basket that the poor carry with flowers, incense, and candles.

Arriving by the end of a wall at the top of a street, she saw a big crowd of people. She stood craning her neck from a distance and spotted Khun Phaen and Wanthong.

Yet she did not recognize them because their faces were dark with freckles. Both seemed strangers. She noticed Wanthong was pregnant and in great difficulty.

Khun Phaen looked over, saw her, and was not sure whether he knew her or not. She looked familiar and he was tempted to greet her but was afraid she would be angry if it was not his old love.

Wanthong glanced sideways at Kaeo Kiriya and wanted to greet her because they had known each other some time ago, but she was shy and apprehensive so kept quiet.

Then Kaeo Kiriya heard someone say, "They've got Khun Phaen!" and her doubts disappeared. She pushed her way through the people, and sank down to wai them with tears streaming down.

She clasped the feet of Khun Phaen and Wanthong. "Oh pity, pity! You look so different I almost missed you. Then I heard what people were saying and knew for sure. You disappeared into the forest as if you had died."

Khun Phaen recognized her voice. "I thought it was you, Kaeo." Wanthong stroked her with her hand and said, "When your name was called, I knew it was you."

After speaking, she turned her face away, embarrassed because of their misery and poor circumstances. Khun Phaen walked off in his chains, leading Wanthong. Kaeo Kiriya followed along behind.

They soon came to a swordstore of the palace guard[18] where many nobles were gathered. Phramuen Si saw Khun Phaen coming and happily called him over.

(including dancing and self adornment), and lying on a high or soft bed.

18. ทิมดาบใน, *thimdap nai*, inner swordstore, probably the *thim dap tamruat nai*, the headquarters of the palace guard, at the northeast corner of the palace (KLW, 203; APA, 68; see area 1 on map 9).

He broke open the cylinder, took out the report, and read it in full. Then he spoke in a friendly tone. "The king is unbelievably angry.

But now that I've examined this report that you gave yourselves up to Phra Phichit, put your lives in his care, and admitted guilt, I think it'll be all right.

You went to the forest with Wanthong alone so where did you get this spare seat[19] from? Oh friend! Even as a prisoner in extreme hardship, you arrive with something in reserve."

Khun Phaen said, "She's my wife from a long time back, before we went to the forest. I left her with Mother.[20] While coming back, I met her on the road."

Phramuen Si was kind enough to give them a big meal. They chatted away like old times, with no bad feelings.

Towards eleven in the late morning, nobles went into the audience hall. Phramuen Si changed his clothes and went to attend on the king.

---

19. ที่นั่งรอง, *thi nang rong*, colloquialism for a minor wife (KP, 210).

20. A continuity error or a white lie by Khun Phaen? She was left as a slave of Khun Chang.

Now to tell of the gracious king, resident of a jeweled palace that illuminated the world. When the sun was bright, the time had come to proceed to the front.

Phramuen Si Saowarak-rat bowed his head, made obeisance, and reported on the case. "We now have Khun Phaen."

The king raged like the heavens on fire. Not yet knowing the details, he angrily stamped his foot in the audience hall.

"This trickster believes he has powers and thinks I can't match him. He abducted Khun Chang's wife away into the forest, and slashed dead the people sent after him.

If he's so able, why didn't he fly away instead of coming here on foot with head bowed? Give a reward to whichever city arrested him. Was he locked up on the way here?"

Phramuen Si raised his clasped hands in homage, bowed his head, and addressed the king from the contents of the report. "My life is under the royal foot.

Khun Phaen went to Phra Phichit and gave himself up to face the charges. He was securely restrained, and a report was sent. He claims he acted sincerely with no seditious ideas.

Khun Phaen and Wanthong were questioned and gave evidence that tallied with each other, claiming Khun Chang wronged Khun Phaen and thus Khun Phaen took reprisals. He had no thought of treason or revolt.

In the past, when Wanthong's name was still Phim, Khun Phaen asked for her hand from her mother, who consented. They built a bridal house, and Wanthong was sent in. This is generally known. After living together for three days,

he had to go up to Chiang Thong with the army. He did not divorce, reject, or sell her. Khun Chang told the mother-in-law that Khun Phaen had died on campaign.

He asked for her hand, built a bridal house, and had a marriage ceremony. When Khun Phaen returned from royal service, he did not sue his wife or her lover for the property[1] but lived with Laothong thereafter.

Then, when on duty at the palace, out of hatred and jealous rivalry, Khun Chang told Your Majesty that Khun Phaen had climbed the palace wall. This lie resulted in Khun Phaen being wrongfully charged.

He had no way to tell Your Majesty the truth because he was barred from audience. He became a miserable fugitive, and Laothong had to go and live in the palace.

Khun Phaen wanted revenge on Khun Chang, and hence abducted Wanthong. He knows that the fact he killed officers and men in the forest carries a death penalty.

He was not arrested but gave himself up to clear himself. If Your Majesty does not spare him, he begs to surrender his life calmly in grateful recognition of Your Majesty's virtue." Ending the report, Phramuen Si made obeisance.

The almighty king, eminence of the excellent city, heard the report and his anger eased.

"Bring both Khun Phaen and Wanthong here immediately for me to see their faces." A guard took the king's order, backed out, and brought Khun Phaen and Wanthong in.

They made obeisance with clasped hands but the king was still too angry to look at them. Khun Phaen intoned a mantra he had decided on in advance, and blew it with faith in its lore.

The king's mood relaxed, and he turned his face towards them. "This couple is beyond fathoming—stealing off into the forest, not fearing anyone.

Now they come back and give evidence shifting the blame onto the mother-in-law for giving Wanthong away to a new husband. Is she really your wife as you claim? Did you come back because you think you can fight the case?"

Khun Phaen, great gallant, prostrated and said, "It is as Your Majesty states. If

---

1. Under the Law on Marriage, the wife was the property of her husband, and adultery was analogous to theft. In the event of a separation, any bride price had to be returned to the husband (Clause 68). If the couple had children, there was a more complex division. If the husband left in anger, and cut the house post with a knife, he forfeited the right to sue for return of the bride price (Clause 51). In this case, however, Wanthong had funded the marriage so there was no question over the bride price. But the law went further: "If a wife takes a lover, and the court rules the man and woman guilty and subject to fines, the cattle, elephants, horses, boats, slaves, servants, and whatever other property in total shall be given to the former husband. Should he no longer wish to keep the wife, he may leave her with only one uppercloth and one lowercloth" (Clause 10). The adulterer would also be liable to a fine, and if the infidelity took place while the former husband was absent on military or other government service, the fine was doubled (Clause 3). (KTS, 2:208, 211–12, 232–33, 242)

investigation shows that Wanthong is not my wife, as my testimony claims,

I willingly surrender my life. Do not waive the execution such guilt demands."
He made obeisance and remained prostrate before the king.

Having listened to these points, the king said, "I will see this matter contested. Whoever loses will be executed as deserved.

On the killing of Khun Phet and Khun Ram, I absolve you of guilt because you had no thought of revolt. Release them so they may contest the case."

Phramuen Si made obeisance to take leave, and led the couple away. He promptly had the chains removed,[2] and ordered a guard to hasten

to Suphan and bring Khun Chang. The guard rode rapidly by horse to the vicinity of Khun Chang's house.

Now to tell of Khun Chang. He had been moaning and groaning gloomily in his room since Wanthong left almost a year earlier. With no bedmate, he suffered.

He slept less than half the night and woke with a start before the cock could rouse him at dawn. Touching mattress and pillow was like being licked by fire. His stomach felt cramped and queasy day and night.

Yet on the day Wanthong arrived in the capital, he slept through to dawn, and also had a dream. On his way to cut firewood, he waded through shallow water, found a huge lake,

and saw a brilliant blooming lotus, yet the stamens had wilted and the petals were hollow inside. He wanted to pluck it but a bo tree got in his way. He woke with a start at dawn.

Thinking about the dream made his chest tremble and his thoughts race. "Is this about Wanthong—the stamens fallen and the bloom hollow because a lover is enjoying her?"

This would make him unsettled for many days. That evening as the sun sank and shadows lengthened, he came out to sit in the hall in the evening breeze, thinking longingly of Wanthong.

The guard officer reached Suphan and hurried to the house. He dismounted in front of the gate and looked up at Khun Chang, who was sitting reciting *sakkrawa*[3] verses

---

2. As the king has absolved Khun Phaen of the charge of rebellion, there is no reason for him to be restrained. He and Wanthong now face only the "civil" case brought by Khun Chang but this case is special because it is to be heard "on royal command."

3. สักระวา, a verse form consisting of eight lines of seven to ten syllables with a strict rhyming scheme. Each verse always begins with the word "*sakkrawa*" and ends "*oei.*" Improvising these

in lament over Wanthong. He spoke a couple of words but then made a mistake in the verse, over and over again. He was about to reach the "oei" at the end but wandered off many times. The guard officer got tired of waiting for him to finish.

He went in, and Khun Chang greeted him. "Why are you here?" The guard shot back, "Khun Phaen and Wanthong have been brought in.

They gave evidence both solid and barbed. There'll be a trial in the palace. The king has sent for you. Come along with me now without delay. Hurry."

Knowing Wanthong had been found, Khun Chang felt reborn. He bounced up and down in joy, ran into the house,
and unlocked chests to find upper and lower cloths. Feeling as bright as the moon, he summoned his gaggle of servants and turned to give them orders.

"You stay behind here and look after the house and possessions attentively!" He went off immediately, mounted his elephant, and made for Ayutthaya.

On arrival he dismounted, took a bath, merrily changed his clothes, and scurried along behind the guard to the inner official sala.

Looking around, he saw all the nobles but could not see Wanthong. He pushed his way through the crowd and pay respect to the accomplished Phramuen Si.

Dashing to the front, he sank down to wai and asked, "My dear sir, where is my wife?" Khun Phaen and Wanthong were close at hand.

Phramuen Si indicated, "Just here! Isn't that Wanthong?" Khun Chang looked round and grabbed hold of her in glee.

She shrieked and clawed at his chest. Khun Phaen punched, elbowed, and kicked Khun Chang away, then stood shielding her. Khun Chang cried loudly,

"Oh pity, Wanthong! You have your lover elbow me and push me around too. I've missed you and never forgotten you for one moment, but you don't love me any more and throw my love away.

What's this? Are you with child, Wanthong? This means you were pregnant in the forest. When you were living with me, you missed your period for more than a month.

I dreamed I got a wasp-nest ring that sparkled like pure, undying fire. That means our child will be male. When you left me, I had morning sickness,

verses back and forth, between groups of male and female singers, either on boats in moonlight, or with the backing of an ensemble, was a traditional entertainment especially important in the Bangkok First Reign when the Mahanak Canal was dug, partly for this purpose (SWC, 14:6606–8; Phlainoi, *Wannakhadi aphithan*, 328–29).

and couldn't eat or drink anything. Because of you, I was upset and had a craving for tamarind and pickled thornweed. I'm overjoyed to see your face today.

Come back to the house at once. I won't beat or berate you." He grabbed her wrist. "Don't resist." Wanthong struggled to escape his grip.

Phramuen Si raged like a roof on fire, bellowing fiercely and fearsomely, "You lowlife! You wheedle and blather shamelessly.

Didn't you say you were angry at Wanthong? You followed her because of your possessions and had no interest in her. If you got her, you wouldn't love her but chop off her head. Now that you see her face, your eyes glaze over and you forget your anger.

This is the way you rock back and forth, you slave. That's why you got kneeed and elbowed down on your back. Your talk is drivel, dribbling on and on about taking her away.

Don't you know you have to answer a case on royal command? How are you going to possess the woman in dispute? Find yourself a guarantor[4] quickly. Hey, guards! Hold all three of them."

At the appointed time, the judges assembled, and the guards brought in the plaintiff and defendants. The plaint was written down, and the examination began.

"Khun Chang stated that he asked for Wanthong's hand, and her mother consented. People were aware that they held a prayer chanting and sprinkled holy water." Khun Phaen objected, "I did not know."

Khun Chang cited as witnesses the many villagers, male and female, who had seen this. "Next issue. Khun Chang stated that he had

sprinkling water

---

4. Once a case was in process, both plaintiff and defendant had to be detained at the court. A plaintiff or defendant of noble status could name a guarantor, ผู้ประกัน, *phu prakan*, to be detained instead. The guarantor was liable to pay the costs of detention (food and clothing while in jail), fines, and judicial fees if the defendant absconded or was unable to pay. When a guarantor was named, the court would visit his home to appraise his property and to gain the consent of his wife and children. A large body of law laid down what happened if both defendant and guarantor defaulted on the liabilities, if the guarantor died, and other related matters. See the Law on Judges, *phra aiyakan laksana tralakan*, especially clauses 1, 2, 11, 12, 13, 29 (KTS, 2:132–36, 143).

lived with Wanthong and supported her

for about two months when she disappeared, taking a large amount of property including money and cloth.

He went after her and found her at a banyan tree. He saw her sleeping beside Khun Phaen and hence knew her lover had abducted her. Khun Phaen had many forest bandits under his command."

Under questioning, Khun Phaen objected, "Not true." Khun Chang cited his witnesses and proceeded to another matter.

"Next issue. Khun Phaen and his forest bandits launched a murderous attack in which Khun Phet and Khun Ram died." Khun Phaen admitted this was true.

"Next issue. Khun Phaen and his bandits mischievously constructed a royal lodge. When they saw Khun Chang coming, they attacked him with guns, tied him to a tree,

and lacerated his body all over with rattan thorns." Khun Phaen objected, "Not true." Khun Chang began to go round in circles and get lost. He stated there were no witnesses to call

because the army ran and scattered in defeat. Yet he cited the marks on his back that were still visible. He pleaded for a decision through ordeal by water. With this, the plaintiff rested his case.

The case involved many issues. A copy of the testimony was quickly made. Khun Phaen used his skills to chant an anus-stuffing mantra,

and blew it onto Khun Chang's chest. His face reddened. His scalp crawled. Sweat streamed down. His mind swam. "I beg your pardon, I'm not well.

My head is spinning, my bowels are churning, and my stomach is swollen full of gas. I don't think I can answer the case today. Please grant a recess until tomorrow, Your Honor."

Phramuen Si said, "This is a case on royal command. Are you trying to delay the trial to create confusion? Nobody will grant a recess in your favor. Don't listen to this pregnant woman."[5]

Khun Chang shouted out with eyes bulging, "I'm going to shit myself. I can't hold it, I'm bursting. Please delay for just one day." "Overruled. Continue with the questioning."

Khun Chang jumped up, "For life or death, please let me shit." Khun Phaen said, "Objection, Your Honor. The plaintiff will abscond."

Khun Chang was angry and frustrated. As soon as he took a step, the shit burst out onto his clothes and splashed down in bowlfuls in the middle of the

---

5. แม่ตั้ง, assumed to be an abbreviation of แม่ตั้งครรภ์, *mae tang khan*, a pregnant mother, probably in reference to Khun Chang's big belly.

sala. People laughed and scattered.

The judges ran off to all points of the sala. "Smellier than dogshit, you commoner face." Khun Chang looked at Wanthong and felt even worse. The shit flowed out even while standing.

"Oh Wanthong, my jewel! The shit has ruined the whole cloth. Please support me to delay for one night. Now that you're happy, you won't support me."

He lunged to grab Wanthong and out came another pile. "Oh my jewel!" Phramuen Si called out, "Ha! Heigh! Guards, why aren't you doing something?"

Guards rushed in, grabbed Khun Chang round the waist, and pushed him out of the sala in front of the crowd. He ran off spraying shit around.

Reaching the riverbank, he descended to a quayside, and jumped into the water, submerging and surfacing like a porpoise. He got out and ran up to the landing of Granny Mi,

who shouted, "What's this? A hungry ghost? It stinks of shit!" Khun Chang cried back, "You evil old woman!" and rushed back to the inner sala.

He changed his clothes and went to sit beside the defendants. The judges looked up. The stench was still unbearable. They sat holding their breath. Clerks were instructed to record the proceedings.

"On the first count, Khun Phaen testified that he and Wanthong were lovers since the time she was still called Phim. He definitely asked for her hand from her mother, Siprajan, who gave Wanthong to him in marriage.

They lived together happily as a couple until he left on the Chiang Thong campaign." Khun Chang responded, "Your Honor, as to this count, I do not know."

Khun Phaen cited as witnesses several villagers who had seen the events. "On the next count, when the army returned to Ayutthaya,

Khun Phaen went back home and found Khun Chang had highhandedly asked for Phim in marriage and built a bridal house." "He made love to my wife as well, hence my anger."

Under questioning, Khun Chang objected, "Not true." Khun Phaen cited several witnesses. They proceeded to a new issue.

"On the next count, although Khun Phaen did not press charges, Wanthong was certainly his wife. He came to take her back but did not remove any of the property cited."

Khun Chang turned with fiery eyes and objected angrily, "Not true!" Khun Phaen asked to proceed to the next issue about what happened in the forest.

"On the next count, Khun Chang came after Wanthong and wanted to slash Khun Phaen down dead. Khun Phaen was provoked into joining the fight, and they exchanged blows with each other in the forest."

Khun Chang denied everything. Khun Phaen said he could present further evidence on this point for entry into the court record. He indicated that the two matters which the prosecution

had already entered into the court record should be adjudicated. He withdrew any further counts, and requested to proceed to the witnesses. The record was folded, tied, and sealed by fingernail.[6]

Then Wanthong's testimony was recorded. It concurred entirely with Khun Phaen's except for one variation. "Mother forced me to marry against my will.

When I refused to enter the bridal house, she grabbed me by the neck and beat me, as could be heard all over the village. When Khun Phaen went on royal service, Khun Chang came to say that Khun Phaen was dead.

He brought bones wrapped in cloth to show, as several people saw." Khun Chang cried out, "Shameless! You change everything, Wanthong.

Now that you've got someone new, you've forgotten the old, and you brazenly change your evidence, you trickster." He jumped up with eyes bulging, and tucked up his lowercloth. "I'm going to kick you down, you evil woman."

Wanthong appealed to the judges. "This baldy is making a fuss. If I give evidence, the villain will beat me. Khun Chang, how much did you pay to ransom me?"[7]

Khun Chang was furious but the guards obstructed him. He jumped up and down and his cloth slipped off. Phramuen Si shouted, "Beautiful! You shameful slave,[8] you blind idiot!

Your cloth has slipped off and we can see your whole belly, you abomination." Wanthong called out to Phramuen Si, "Khun Chang is making trouble because of what I said."

Seeing his own thighs, Khun Chang felt ashamed. He sat down, pulled up his cloth, and grumbled to himself, "It's a pity I can't kick her over. Even if it cost me a bowlful of money, I wouldn't mind."

Phramuen Si said angrily, "You scum, this case will bring problems down on your head. You can't see what's serious and what's not. Simmer down and be more careful."

Wanthong's testimony was taken down but ruled as inadmissible.[9] Phram-

---

6. See p. 429, note 12.

7. Meaning, how much did he pay her mother, but she uses the verbs for ransoming a slave, ช่วยไถ่, *chuai thai*, to make the barb more pointed.

8. งามทั้งห้าไร่, *ngam thang ha rai*, "beautiful the whole five rai." One interpretation is that the curse meant roughly "beautiful as a slave," as five *rai* was the *sakdina* of a slave, the lowest rank. Another theory is that it was a purely verbal riff on งามหน้า, *ngam na*, "beautiful face," meaning "shameful" (Phlainoi, *Wannakhadi aphithan*, 24–26).

9. The Three Seals Law includes a detailed Law on Witnessing, พระไอยการลักษณะภญาน, *phra aiyakan laksana phayan*. This code listed thirty-three categories of people barred from giving evidence without the consent of both plaintiff and defendant, and classified all other people into

uen Si said, "This woman in the middle is impetuous. She finds herself in the wrong but has no fear.

She loves her lover so she sides with him. She lives with her husband and so she sides with him. The evidence is muddled and hence inadmissible." The papers were tied and sealed by fingernail.

At dawn the three parties went to take evidence from the various witnesses. They walked to Siprajan's house,[10]

and Khun Chang pointed to Siprajan, who tottered out trembling and took the oath. Khun Phaen promptly lodged an objection.

"She's the mother-in-law of the plaintiff,[11] very badly disposed towards me, and completely prejudiced. It was she who separated me from Wanthong

and gave her for Khun Chang to enjoy. She's deceitful and without scruples. She likes talking to her son-in-law in private. She had him massage her stomach in the house

so much that an unwanted baby[12] popped out, yet he still went on massaging her from dawn until he was red in the face. She's such a shriveled old fraud even vultures issue warnings. She volunteered to act as a witness[13] though they were cohabiting."

Listening to this objection, Siprajan so shook with anger that her sagging breasts slapped against her chest. She wagged her finger at him, "My oh my, you foul slanderer!" The judge commanded, "Order in court!"

Siprajan admitted she was the mother-in-law but denied all the other claims. They passed on to take depositions from all the remaining witnesses.

The evidence tended to support Khun Phaen's position. The witnesses for the plaintiff touched on some points but did not make a tight case. The documents were tied and sealed by fingernail, and then they left. The witnesses'

three categories of witnesses graded according to credibility. Possibly Wanthong's evidence is judged inadmissible because she is "someone in dispute with parties to the case" (KTS, 2:68–104, quote on 69).

10. According to court procedure, witnesses were not called to the court but the court traveled to interview the witnesses at their homes (Seni, *Pathakatha rueang kotmai*, 43–46). The case is being heard in Ayutthaya but Siprajan's house is in Suphan. Below they seem to return to the court by afternoon. This slip hints that the location of this trial may originally have been in Suphan, not Ayutthaya.

11. In the Law on Witnessing, relatives and friends of the parties to the case were forbidden from giving testimony unless both the plaintiff and defendant gave their consent (KTS, 2:74–75).

12. มารหัวขน, *man hua khon*, a hairy-headed devil, a colloquial phrase for an unwanted baby but also a dig at Khun Chang.

13. He is implying she has been coached. Several clauses in the Law on Witnessing instruct judges to disregard such evidence, and prescribe penalties (e.g., clauses 41, 64, KTS, 2:93, 103).

depositions were copied out,

and a summary made to put in the record of the defense.[14] Discussion was held on how to present the matter to the court. In the afternoon, everyone assembled including Phra Maharatchakhru,[15]

Luang Yanprakat, Luang Theprachathada,[16] and both sentencers.[17] All sat and listened to the record of evidence.[18] A legal code was produced and consulted.

The case was taken to be presented in royal audience, and the parties to the case were detained under guard in the palace. Siprajan was sent for and arrived trembling with confusion.

She turned to look at Khun Chang and muttered abuse. "You abomination! You bald lowlife! You got me into this." Khun Chang warned his mother-in-law, "Don't make so much noise."

Just before the hour for audience, all the nobles assembled. At the time, Phramuen Si led the way in, followed by the parties to the case.

Old Siprajan tottered along, open-mouthed and gasping, looking pitiful. The guards escorting them said, "Come along, you old crone, you rotten fish dropping, hurry up."

Siprajan trembled and mumbled delirious nonsense. A clerk shouted, "Tcha! Why are you so slow?" She hurried along behind, feeling flustered.

When they reached the palace swordstore and saw people, she took fright and her stomach churned. She fell down in a faint and crawled along with her bottom in the air. Khun Chang leapt over and grabbed her round the throat.

14. กระทงแถลง, krathong thalaeng, a record of the defendants' evidence, point by point (KW, 676).

15. The royal court had two sets of supreme judges, each headed by someone with the tamnaeng of Phra Maharatchakhru and sakdina of 10,000, on par with the "four pillars." Their titles were Phra Ratcha Mahithon and Phra Ratcha Phrarohit. Their role was not to deliver judgment but to give advice on points of law (KTS, 1:265; KW, 265; Ishii, "Thai Thammasat," 167).

16. Phra (Luang) Yanprakat was the athibodi horadajan of the first set of judges, and Phra Thepratchadabodi Siwasuthep was the palat phrarachakhru prarohit in the second set, each with sakdina of 3,000. These titles indicate the intermingling of ritual and judicial duties. The holders would have been Brahmans. The post of athibodi horadajan originally belonged to a head Brahman who led prayers and appeals to the gods in offering rituals, while a prarohit was a Brahman adviser to a king. (KTS, 1:265; KW, 265)

17. The judges decided on the issue of guilt or innocence but the sentencing was the responsibility of two other officials: Phra Kasem Ratchasuphawadi Simonthatularat, head of the department of civil peace, krom phaeng kasem, and Khunluang Phra Kraisi Ratchasuphawadi Simonthatularat, head of the central civil department, krom phaeng klang, both sakdina 3,000 (KTS, 1:266; KW, 265).

18. ใบสัตย์, bai sat, meaning they listened to a reading of the record of evidence (KW, 676).

kaffir lime

"You're not listening." He grabbed her by the shoulder blades. She burped and retched with her mouth open and eyes staring blankly. She got up, hitched up her cloth, grimaced, and called out, "Give me a kaffir lime. Did anyone bring one?"

Wanthong chewed a piece of betel and put it in the mouth of Siprajan who angrily looked the other way. Wanthong called out, "She doesn't deserve pity." Khun Phaen walked past with eyes averted.

Nobles of all ranks entered the audience in clusters. At the royal pleasure, the king, ruler of the world, came out to preside.

The king roared his question. "Phramuen Si, how is the case?" Phramuen Si promptly replied, "My life is under the royal foot.

On Friday of the eighth month, the plaintiff Khun Chang laid charges as follows. He had arranged for elders to ask for the hand of his wife named Wanthong.

Old Siprajan gave her daughter to him, and he assembled a large dowry. They lived together as a married couple for about two months.

Then at midnight, Khun Phaen Saensathan put people to sleep, boldly came up to the house, made love to Khun Chang's wife, Wanthong, and stole her away.

Khun Phaen does not accept the charges. He states that Wanthong was not the wife of Khun Chang. Previously she was named Phim Philalai, and she and Khun Phaen were lovers.

Khun Phaen asked her mother for her hand, and happily took care of her as his wife. They had slept together in a bridal house for two days, when he had to go on royal service with the army.

When he returned from Chiang Thong, he found Khun Chang living and sleeping with her. He did not sue for his property, but missed his wife and came to take her away.

In support of his claim, Khun Phaen has offered evidence that has been confirmed by the testimony of neutral witnesses. Khun Chang called Siprajan as witness but Khun Phaen objected on grounds she is the mother-in-law.

The judges have conferred and found the mother-in-law guilty of acting with folly and negligence in giving away her daughter to two men. She, rather than Wanthong, will be subject to public ridicule[19] for severe guilt.

---

19. ประจาน, *prajan*, public shaming. In the case of adultery, the law imposed a fine on the man, and public shaming on the woman: "As for the guilty woman, mark a stigma on her fore-

Khun Chang was intent on marrying Khun Phaen's wife, and hence stated that Khun Phaen was dead. He rashly dismantled Khun Phaen's bridal house, and married Wanthong. Under the legal code, Khun Chang is liable to pay a fine,

as well as compensation for adultery, calculated using the *sakdina* of Khun Phaen.[20] Siprajan and Khun Chang are guilty and will pay fines and commutation fees[21] in place of Wanthong.

In addition, Khun Chang, Siprajan, Kloi, and Sai are sentenced to be flogged.[22] Finally, if Khun Phaen fears for his own karma and does not want to invoke the full force of the law, he will be awarded compensation according to the code.

But if Khun Phaen does not fear for his own karma and is so disposed, he may execute Khun Chang. Wanthong is returned to Khun Phaen.[23] By royal decree."

---

head, put a red hibiscus behind both ears and a garland of hibiscus on her head or neck, and have her led around by a drummer for three days of public ridicule" (preamble to the Law on Marriage, KTS, 2:206).

20. *Sakdina* was used to calculate certain punishments, especially fines and compensation payments, resulting in higher punishments for those of higher rank, and higher punishments for those who offended against those of higher rank. In the case of adultery with a woman who had been through a marriage ceremony, compensation was calculated as follows: Assume there had been eleven dowry trays at the betrothal and fifty trays at the marriage; calculate one fueang for each betrothal tray and one salueng for each marriage tray; multiply the total according to the *sakdina* of the offended party; split the resulting sum evenly between compensation paid to the husband, and fine paid to the treasury (Law on Marriage, clause 107, KTS, 2:268–69).

21. The public ridicule (see note 19 above) could be avoided by paying a commutation fee "calculated according to the age of the wife" (preamble to the Law on Marriage, KTS, 2:206).

22. Clauses 106 and 122 of the Law on Marriage stated that if parents or other family members gave away their daughter in marriage to one man, then took her back and gave her to another, the second man and the woman would be fined for adultery and given thirty lashes. In similar laws, though not these particular clauses, the parents and any other intermediaries were liable to half the number of lashes as the man and woman. All flogging could be avoided by payment of a commutation fee. (KTS, 2:267, 275–77)

23. A wronged husband had the right to kill the adulterer, or have him executed. "If a husband apprehends a man who has committed adultery with his wife and kills him in anger before investigation, and investigation proves that adultery did take place, the husband shall not be punished" (Clause 9). "If the husband kills the adulterer, he should kill the wife also, not the adulterer alone. If he kills the wife alone, the husband shall be fined according to his *sakdina*" (Clause 8). "If the husband fails to kill the wife because she runs away, the wife shall become royal property (คนหลวง)" (Clause 9). If the husband chose to spare the adulterer, the adulterer was subject to a fine, half due to the husband as compensation and half due to the treasury (see p. 436, note 1 above). Under a law amendment dated 1755/56, the fine ranged from thirty chang for a chaophraya with *sakdina* of 10,000 and above, to four chang for someone with *sakdina* of 200 to 400. Assuming Khun Phaen had *sakdina* of 600, the fine would be six chang. The right of the husband to kill the adulterer was abolished in 1782. (Law on Marriage, KTS, 2:210–11; Old Laws, clause 65, KTS, 5:190; Ishii, "Thai Thammasat," 187; New Laws, clause 37, KTS, 5:343–45)

After listening to the judges, the king said, "Heigh! Khun Phaen, what do you think of that? Will you execute Khun Chang or not?"

Khun Phaen prostrated. "I do not want vengeance. Impose only the compensation and fines, as Your Majesty wishes."

The king said, "Yes, there'll be vengeance for certain. You're straight and may think you and he are friends but this baldy of bad birth has an evil heart.

Close the case and impose the judges' sentences. Phramuen Si, hurry back to the court." Phramuen Si made obeisance, and backed away on all fours from where he had been sitting.

He had guards escort the parties to walk along together including Khun Phaen, Khun Chang, Kloi, Sai, and Siprajan.

They reached the sala where the guards were gathered, and the sentences were read out for all to hear.

Khun Chang counted out the money. He could pay commutation fees for his flogging without difficulty, but Siprajan, Sai, and Kloi trembled in distress.

They counted out money as if their hearts were breaking. Their tears plopped down. "He's a rich man who floats on water like cottonwool, but he lets poor people like us almost die."

After parting with their money, they set off home. Khun Chang was annoyed at not achieving his intent so he crawled in to see Phramuen Si. "Sir, please find a way round this for me.

I can spend money without a thought as long as I'm alive. Have mercy on one point—please let me have Wanthong back, sir.

I'll repay your kindness with twenty chang, with great respect, as long as you can make it lasting with no subsequent change and disappointment."

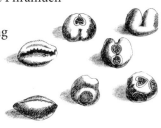

cowries and bullet money

The formulas for calculating the fine were specified in the *phra aiyakan phrommasak* (KTS, 1:197–218). Khun Wichitmatra calculated all these fines, as follows. The fine on Khun Chang would have been two chang and eight tamlueng, a significant sum (Khun Wichitmatra must have used a rate that existed before the amendment cited in the previous note). Next came the commutation fee for public shaming, transferred from Wanthong, which was calculated on the basis of Wanthong's age. If this was twenty-two or twenty-three, the fine would be twelve tamlueng. The commutation fee instead of twenty strokes of the lash would be eight tamlueng. Siprajan was due around one chang for commutation for the public shaming transferred from Wanthong plus the commutation for flogging. Kloi and Sai would each be due eight tamlueng for commuting the flogging (KW, 266).

Phramuen Si said angrily, "You fool! Nobody can overturn a royal order. Don't bother me. Get out." Khun Chang backed out, feeling helpless.

Overwhelmed with love and craving, he sat down with a big sigh beside Wanthong, and his thoughts slipped out of his mouth, "Oh heavenly flower[24] of mine!"

People around laughed. "Please sing some more, my good sir." "It's so beautiful, so captivating." Khun Chang ignored them and left.

The faces of Khun Phaen, Wanthong, and Kaeo Kiriya were shining from having won the case. Phramuen Si suggested they leave and hurry home.

---

24. ดอกฟ้า, *dok fa*, a metaphor for a palace lady or other high-status lady.

23: KHUN PHAEN IS JAILED

Khun Phaen, great valiant, stayed happily in Phramuen Si's house for many nights before the day of the incident.

Khun Phaen, Wanthong, and Kaeo Kiriya were sleeping peacefully in the house under a sky lit by bright moonlight and scattered with stars.

A breeze wafted the soft refreshing scent of flowers. Khun Phaen awoke on his bed thinking of Laothong.

"Oh my friend in hardship, you left your hometown to come south, and then were forced from our room. I now possess Wanthong and Kaeo Kiriya but I feel concerned for you. It's as if I didn't care.

Losing your husband, you will face difficulties. Confinement is miserable. If the news has reached you in the palace, I expect you're waiting for me to come and fetch you.

I undertook to look after you and I won't evade or go back on that promise. Out of consideration for the two wives I love, I could just do nothing and let you stay hidden.

But there's an old saying: Sacrifice money but not morals, sacrifice anything but your word.[1] You haven't done wrong by being unfaithful. The reason we parted was because of Khun Chang.

He made false accusations to the king to get me punished, and had you taken away from me. That matter is now closed, yet you're still confined in the palace.

Because the Lord of Life has forgotten, you can't come out, heart's delight. I'll have to petition the king but I fear it could turn out badly.

The king has just pardoned me and it might be an improper imposition if I dare to approach him again. If he's not merciful, I could lose what benefit I've gained.

But neglecting a wife is pitiful. The thought makes me very concerned for you." The matter spun round and round in his head until sunrise when he washed his face, left his inner room,

went straight to find Phramuen Si, and said, "I have a big problem. The case

---

1. A proverb, with several variants, that appears among the "Sayings of Phra Ruang" (Gerini, "On Siamese Proverbs," 195).

ended successfully because of your assistance and protection, sir.

But now my only concern is Laothong, who is still confined in the palace. Please help address the king to let her out."

Phramuen Si promptly replied to Khun Phaen, "You're an able person and a clever one. Wouldn't it be better to wait about a year?

A fire not fully extinguished can flare up easily. Hastiness can make things worse in the future. It's not as if she's far away, but close by here in the palace, a forbidden lady,[2] confined by gates all the time.

No lover, husband, or anybody else can go in and out as they do elsewhere. Why are you so agitated? Waiting a while won't matter."

Khun Phaen replied to Phramuen Si, "I've no doubts about her character. What's making me concerned and upset is that she herself did nothing wrong.

It was me the king was angry about. Laothong was confined because of me. Now that I'm happily free again, it might seem I'm selfishly satisfied with the wives at my side.

That's bothering and unsettling me. Though lightning may strike, I want to know. Sir, please see what you can do to help. I think the king will have mercy."

Phramuen Si saw no use in opposing. "If you don't listen then it's up to your fortune." They spoke together until almost time for audience, when Phramuen Si summoned his people to go to the palace.

A crowd of retainers[3] followed. Khun Phaen walked at the rear and sat outside,

behind the screens

---

2. ห้าม, *ham*. In the nineteenth century, women of the palace were commonly called *nang ham*, forbidden ladies, meaning forbidden to anyone other than the king. This appears to be the only appearance of the term in the PD edition of *KCKP*, though it is used several times in the WK edition.

3. หนาย, *thanai*; when a case entered the law courts, both plaintiff and defendant had to be detained by the court but someone with *sakdina* of 400 or higher was allowed to send a *thanai* as substitute (*Phra aiyakan laksana tralakan*, clause 92, KTS, 2:121–22). Subsequently the word *thanai* was used more widely to mean an agent or retainer. Here and elsewhere in *KCKP*, it is used loosely for a member of a noble's retinue. In modern Thai it means a lawyer or advocate.

hidden behind the screens, waiting to hear what the king would say.

Now to tell of the mighty king, eminence of continents great and small, who resided in his palace of victory under a golden spire, attended by throngs of inner ladies.

He administered affairs of the palace until the sun shone strongly, then walked out to the jeweled audience hall which was opened for courtiers to enter.

Everyone prostrated and clasped palms, arrayed in accordance with their position. Those with government business reported to the king.

The astute Phramuen Si Saowarak-rat pondered matters apprehensively until he had his opportunity to address the king. "My life is under the royal foot.

At present Khun Phaen Saensathan has requested your humble servant to address Your Majesty. In the past he faced charges but has been pardoned by royal grace.

He is inestimably pleased and, to make amends, requests to do royal service until the day of his death to please the royal foot.

Laothong has been confined in the palace for a very long time. May Your Majesty graciously release her so that she may be manpower for royal service."[4]

On hearing Phramuen Si's statement, the king's face turned white with rage. "This fellow dares to presume on my kindness!

When Khun Phet and Khun Ram went after him and were rashly killed, I waived the punishment of execution. On top of that, I gave Wanthong back to him.

He still dares to pursue Laothong! He forgets he's in trouble up to his neck. He arrogantly speaks his mind with no deference. Because Laothong has to stay in the palace,

out of his sight, he distrustfully fears I'll have her behind his back. This talk is abominable! Were he to set his mind to do royal service

and perform well, then we wouldn't talk of Laothong alone—I'd give him another two or three. If I do nothing, this will go to his head. If I let this pass, it'll get worse and worse.

Were I to agree to his wish for Laothong, he'll become even more bold and presumptuous. He'll think he can get away with anything and has no need to fear anybody.

---

4. กำลังราชการ, *kamlang ratchakan*, a phrase which appears often in the Three Seals Law, meaning state resources, particularly phrai labor. A male released from prison, slavery, or such like would become available for corvée. A woman was not liable to corvée, but probably this was a stock phrase in petitions for release.

five irons

Heigh! Clap him in jail,[5] and apply the full five irons.[6] Weld the rivets in his leg chains too, as he deserves."[7] The king retired inside to his bedchamber.

Phramuen Si was shocked. He backed out with a crazed look on his face and spoke to Khun Phaen through tears, "I told you but you didn't listen to me."

On the king's order, officers of the Ministry of the Capital[8] surrounded Khun Phaen front and back, and led him out of the gate under guard. Phramuen Si tried to help by calling out to them.

"I entrust him to you, sirs. Morning and night, put on irons only as required." The capital officials took Khun Phaen straight to the main jail.[9]

---

5. Fulfilling the abbot of Wat Khae's horoscope from chapter 6, "When you reach the critical age of twenty-five, a misfortune will occur. You'll be clapped in irons and locked away." Seni Pramoj pointed out that jailing was rarely used as a punishment in the Ayutthaya era, only as detention before trial. In the laws, the only instance of jail as a punishment is for violating the royal prerogative (Seni, *Pathakatha rueang kotmai*, 8; Code of Crimes against Government, *phra aiyakan aya luang*, clause 1, KTS, 4:6).

6. In his *Description of Siam* published in 1854, Bishop Pallegoix described the five irons as follows: "Ordinary prisoners only wear irons at their feet consisting of two great iron rings riveted below the calves and linked with the other by a chain a cubit long which does not prevent him to walk but only to run. Major criminals wear what they call the full five irons, i.e., an iron collar around their neck, handcuffs at their hands, irons on their feet, and a chain around their waist. Moreover, they put on a cangue sometimes consisting of two long pieces of wood arranged around the neck by means of two crossbars. The cangue is more or less heavy according to the seriousness of the crime. Besides the problem of its weight, it also hinders all movement and especially prevents resting" (Pallegoix, *Description*, 192–93; see slightly different descriptions in *Prachum phongsawadan phak thi 39*, reports from foreign missionaries, part 6; La Loubère, *New Historical Relation*, 105; SWC, 2:651–52). The five irons are mentioned several times in the Three Seals Laws including in the Criminal Code, Law on Theft, and the Palatine Law. The use was not finally abrogated until the post-absolutist criminal code of 1936 (SWC, 2:651–52).

7. Prisoners could pay to have all irons removed except the leg chains, and could pay to ensure the rivets on the leg chains were hammered so as not to be too tight. As Khun Phaen is not convicted by a court but jailed on royal command, such leniency is impossible. Welding the leg chains implies a life sentence (KP, 226; KW, 284).

8. นครบาล, *nakhonban*, sometimes called *mueang*, city or capital, one of the "four pillars," the major ministries.

9. There were eight jails in the city in late Ayutthaya but the main jail was to the south of Wat Phra Si Sanphet. The site is now occupied by the tourist attraction known as "Khum Khun Phaen," Khun Phaen's residence. This teak house, built in 1894, was formerly the residence of the provincial governor, located near the provincial office on Loi Island across the river from the Front Palace in the northeast corner of the city. After the 1932 revolution, one of its lead-

They brought fetters, chains, and cangue, and put them on his feet and hands in the usual way. The governor of the jail made a strict inspection. Phramuen Si went home in distress.

He called Kaeo Kiriya and Wanthong, and told them the whole truth with tears streaming down in floods. "Your husband has been locked up tight on royal command.

He had me ask the king for Laothong. I tried to stop him but he wouldn't listen. As soon as I'd addressed the king, it was like the city was on fire. To prevent this happening was beyond my ability."

On hearing this, Wanthong and Kaeo Kiriya felt choked with sadness, as if their breasts would break apart. Wanthong said, "He should have been less hasty and done it properly.

We just started to be happy and now there's more hardship. Probably this man is just trouble. Somehow he never makes life easy. We never seem to be together for long.

We got off to a bad start—a hundred different houses a year, a hundred different villages a month. Even when doing his duty on royal service, he still climbed over the wall.

When will he cut loose from this young Lao woman? I feel choked with sorrow and anger." She sobbed sadly.

When the two got over their grief, they rushed off. Poor Wanthong's pregnancy was almost full term, and she carried herself along awkwardly.

They reached the jail and fiddled their way in. Seeing Khun Phaen's face, they fell down at his feet, shaking and flailing around. "Husband, you never tell me anything.

If you'd consulted me, I'd have stopped you asking the king for Laothong. Bad karma has now put you in jail. When we came out of the forest hideout,

and were sent down from Phichit under guard, you weren't put in a cangue like this. The court case was a threat but it turned out in your favor in every way.

You shouldn't have acted hastily, thinking only of another gain. You acted wildly and rashly, and now you'll be separated from all your wives, old and new. Oh, from now on, we'll all suffer.

You're in irons and the rivets welded to boot. Do you think you'll ever be

---

ers, Pridi Banomyong, a native of Ayutthaya, had the building moved to its current site and renamed, clearly as a reference to Khun Phaen's sojourn in the jail on this spot. (KLW, 197; *Boranasathan*, 1:51; see map 8)

happy? Will you die in jail, or can you bear it until release?

What karma have I made? I can never raise my face on a level with others. Being both pregnant and in such trouble is awful. With no servants,

sending you food every morning and night will be troublesome.[10] There's nobody I can speak to for patronage. Even though I'm pregnant, I can come every day, but I worry that I'm about to give birth to a child.

While I'm lying by the fire,[11] there'll be nobody to bring you food and water every morning and evening. Looking around I can see only Kaeo Kiriya.

If she comes to stay in the jail, she can cook, and that'll make things easier. I feel I'm almost dying." The two women were smothered in tears.

lying by the fire

Khun Phaen sorrowed together with the two women. Tears bathed his face. "I misjudged things and so ended up in this cangue. A time of bad karma brought this on.

The reason why I asked for Laothong is because I have you two close beside me, while she alone still suffers hardship. Abandoning her would be unjust on my part.

I didn't think the king would be so angry as to impose a severe penalty of imprisonment. This time, the punishment is almost unbearable and there's an equal chance I'll live or die.

Even if they doubled these irons, I could still escape but I'd sacrifice my good name. That's the bind. If I run away, nobody will reckon me a man.

It's like the time my father was punished. When the king gave no pardon, he didn't try to escape. I'll suffer even to death if that's the penalty.

Wanthong, you're pregnant and terribly uncomfortable. Stay at home and come just once in a while so I can see your face and know you're well.

Kaeo Kiriya is not pregnant. If she can steam rice and make curry here, and circulate back and forth, it'll be all right. When precious you are at home for a long time

to give birth, I won't see you, but Kaeo Kiriya can be my companion. She

---

10. Jail provided no food. Families had to send it, or the prisoner relied on charity.

11. See p. 5, note 26.

can find firewood and make the evening meal until you're back on your feet and can come again.

I'll have to suffer for several days until I know the guards have some respect for me. Then I can ask them to let me out to visit you. Don't be sad.

If you stayed here now, how could you give birth? It's almost evening, Wanthong. Time to go. Please don't cry. Stop being angry.

Make an effort to put yourself under the patronage of Phramuen Si and the wives and children at his home. Act humbly and timidly. And be patient. It'll be a long time before I'm released.

Kaeo Kiriya, take Wanthong back home, and organize things to bring back here—food, clothing, and so on, appropriate to the dire straits I'm in."

Kaeo Kiriya and Wanthong sobbed and sighed, their faces bathed in tears. Reluctantly, they took leave of him and walked away.

Arriving back home, they quickly arranged betel, tobacco, clothes, mattress, pillow, and mosquito net, such as they had.

It was too much to carry, so they went to ask Phramuen Si's servants to take it to the jail. The prison governor was considerate,

and had some convicts help build a shelter for Kaeo Kiriya to live outside the slip gate.[12] At sunset, all the gates were closed and double bolted.

In the still silence of the night, in the light of a brilliant moon, Khun Phaen was greatly distressed. His body was fastened by a cangue

and the full five irons. He was tormented by stiffness. He wanted to shift his body but it was held tight. Over time, the discomfort got worse.

"Oh all you prisoners here, how can you stand it the whole year through? As for me, I'll serve my time but I don't have to endure this.

Just keeping to my word that I have no thought of escape will be enough to benefit me. If I show no bad intentions towards the lord that raised me up, the world will accept me as an excellent person."

With this thought, he chanted a Loosener mantra. While others slept tight, the irons slipped off his hands and feet, and the cangue fell. Invisibly he left the lockup.

At the shelter he found Kaeo Kiriya still awake, sobbing and grieving. He went inside to cradle and console her. "Why are you sad?

Weeping won't make you happy. You're already suffering terribly so why suf-

---

12. หับเผย, *hap phoei*, literally, "shut open," probably the gate between the inner portion of the jail where the cells were located, and the outer portion where the warders stayed. It is mentioned in *Khamhaikan khun luang ha wat*: "in front of *hap phoei* there is a patrol unit to look after incidents in the capital and the jail" (KLW, 198; KP, 230; KW, 285–88).

fer more? I'm concerned that crying will make the suffering heavier and you'll get sick, eye's jewel.

Listen to what I say, Kaeo. I'm here now so it'd be better to forget your sorrow." He embraced her and wiped away her tears. "Lift your face and give me a little kiss, sweetheart.

Don't sob and grieve, my beauty. Go to sleep. I'll sing you a lullaby." He hugged her compassionately to his chest, and both fell asleep.

The jailors and inner wardens awoke and took a roll call, shouting each name in sequence.

All responded "Here!" without fail except Khun Phaen. "Is he asleep and unaware or what?" His name was called again but still no response came.

The inner wardens lit torches and went to look. "There's only a pile of chains, sir. He's got free of everything, even the cangue." The cry went up to give chase and catch him.

"I woke and saw him just now. Where's he sneaked off to?" They all went together to see the prison governor, stumbling along and looking around.

They came to the shelter at the slip gate but passed it by. In growing panic and confusion, they swarmed around looking behind doors, up on the roof, and in every nook and cranny.

"How come we can't find him?" The governor had an idea. "His wife's in that shelter, right? Hey, take a torch and have a look."

Finding Khun Phaen and Kaeo Kiriya, they called out to one another, "He's here!" The jailors were angry. "Why didn't he tell us?" They dragged Khun Phaen out roughly.

Khun Phaen jumped up, growling. "Why are you lowlife manhandling me—pushing and pulling, dragging and grappling? Do you think I'm trying to escape?"

The governor and jailors came up and all reviled him without any fear. "Flog him until his back caves in." "Why listen to him?" They surrounded him to take away under guard.

Khun Phaen bellowed a Power of Garuda mantra. Hands lost their grip. Heads toppled over and banged against the wall. The warders were stunned for some time. Khun Phaen shouted, "Leave me alone!

Are you thinking of placing me under restraint? Do you think you can lock me up? If so, then try." They fetched the irons and clad him up to the ears in chains.

Khun Phaen chanted a Loosener mantra, and everything fell off in a tangled heap. He beckoned to them "Hey, you, come and lock me up."

The governor and jailors saw he was truly able. They sank down in silence and raised their hands to wai him repeatedly. "Forgive us for what we did." "For your own karma, please be kind."

"If you escape, we'll be punished." "Our boss will reprimand us terribly." "We'll all have our backs flogged hard."

Khun Phaen said, "I'm kept by the king. I've sworn not to deviate from my word. If I wanted to escape, I'd escape. I could simply go off in broad daylight.

Hey, please watch this for fun." With these words, he held his breath and made his body disappear. The governor and jailors were panicked. "Sir, we're dead now."

"Please come back." "Don't worry, we won't lock you up. Just don't escape." Khun Phaen relaxed the mantra's power. In relief, the guards sank down to salute him.

They sat talking until dawn broke and the sun soared into the sky. The governor walked out of the jail and went to see Phraya Yommarat,[13]

who asked, "Why have you come so early?" "Sir, Khun Phaen's expertise is like the power of the wind. All the irons slipped off him.

When we reprimanded him, he said he wouldn't escape but we can't trust his word alone. As his guard, I fear a disaster. Sir, kindly help."

Phraya Yommarat said, "Bring him here quickly." The governor took his leave, rushed back to the jail,

and said, "Phraya Yom has sent for you. Let's go immediately." He led the accomplished Khun Phaen over. They both sank down and wai-ed.

Phraya Yommarat said, "What's this, Khun Phaen? You're already in a huge mess. You've being convicted under the law but you still dare to break the locks and chains.

Do you believe you're able, and have the powers and the lore to escape? Are you trying to create trouble for us? Do whatever you like,

but if word gets to the king, he'll punish you with death. What do you have to say? Speak out freely. Do you think you're so able you can just stay quiet?"

Khun Phaen replied to Phraya Yommarat, "On my honor I won't escape. But I can't stand being placed in irons, including the cangue.

You have authority by the grace of the king, sir. I won't run away. I'll die

---

13. Head of the Ministry of the Capital with the title Phraya Yommarat Intharathibodi, *sakdina* 10,000, often shortened to "Phraya Yom" (KTS, 1:229).

keeping my word, and I swear I won't put you in the wrong, sir."

Phraya Yommarat responded, "If that's so and you don't make trouble from now on, I'll follow your wishes for nothing. Don't forget the virtue of the king who keeps you.

You must take an oath that you won't escape. Do it openly before us now as a promise, and then I'll be agreeable to your wishes."

Khun Phaen prostrated, wai-ed, and spoke the oath. "If I escape, may I fall into a hell below Aweji.[14]

Should I die, I'm ready to die in jail until the king graciously releases me. I'll not think evil, treacherous thoughts from now until my dying day."

Phraya Yommarat listened and then gave orders to all the guards. "Don't make trouble by putting the irons on Khun Phaen. Let him be comfortable.

Khun Phaen, don't go out gadding around. Anyone seeing you will report you. Off you go. Take him away at once." The governor prostrated, wai-ed, and led Khun Phaen off.

From then on, none of the jailors reprimanded Khun Phaen, who lived happily with Kaeo Kiriya in the inner jail.

Wanthong took the trouble to visit even though she was very uncomfortable with her pregnancy. When the guards were not around, Khun Phaen sneaked out to see her from time to time.

He behaved very humbly in fear of punishment on account of the king's anger. The governor and guards were considerate, and Phraya Yommarat was not concerned.

❧

Now to tell of the bald demon, Khun Chang. Since the court case, when he had to pay out ruinously, he could not come after Wanthong but he lay thinking of her.

There were masses of servants in the house but he had no desire to couple with them—and the servants would not consent anyway. Every night he lay face down with an aching belly.

He dreamed of Wanthong all the time. He felt miserable. He could not eat.

---

14. อเวจี, Pali Avici, is the lowest of all the eight great hells, described in the Three Worlds cosmology as "the great hell of suffering without respite." It is surrounded by iron walls nine *yojana* thick and has constant fire that torments but never kills. This hell is the destination of those who break the five precepts and commit major crimes such as killing their own mother or father (RR, 66).

He sat down, felt restless, and stood up again. As soon as he dozed off, he woke with eyes open wide.

He could not sleep without seeing spirits everywhere, and he started awake like a dancing prawn every time.[15] From cockcrow until evening, he had no relief.

His belly ached and he cried fretfully. "Oh, Mother and Father, I'm going to die for sure! When Wanthong was here, I wasn't like this. I've never been this bad.

Maybe a little from time to time but never so terrible as this, day in, day out. Why? If this goes on for a year, I'll die."

He jumped up, rushed out of the room, and called to Sonphraya, "Where've you disappeared to? Come up and play chess to get rid of my misery." Sonphraya walked up with his head in the air.

The chess pieces were set out. Khun Chang, eyes bulging, moved a knight directly forward two squares, recklessly taking Sonphraya's king.[16] "Oh sir, I beg your pardon. Please take that back."

chessboard

Khun Chang laughed, "I won't!" Sonphraya begged, "My lord and master, I can play only tiger eat ox.[17] I'm afraid of chess, sir.

Not even the abbot could match you. It's stupendous to take something on the king's rank. My moves are so clumsy and slow. Eh! There's a rumor going round from the inner palace

that Khun Phaen asked the king for Laothong, and the king angrily locked him up in the main jail. Wanthong is on her own and maybe lonely. We should go for a chat to see how she is.

She didn't leave you because she was angry but because Khun Phaen took her off. Now that he's in jail and in big difficulty, she should agree to come back without any sulkiness."

---

15. กุ้งเต้น, *kung ten*, a dish made by pouring lime juice, chopped chili, and other ingredients over freshly caught live prawns, causing them to twitch or "dance."

16. A knight should move two squares forward plus one to left or right, and a king cannot be taken.

17. เสือกินวัว, *suea kin wua*, a board game with two players. The tiger has four counters, initially placed at the corners. The ox has twelve placed elsewhere. The tiger attempts to "eat" the oxen by jumping over them, as in draughts, while the oxen try to corral the tigers by boxing them in on all four sides.

Khun Chang listened to Sonphraya. "Is that really true, Son?" He got down on his haunches and began reciting from a play.

The king made camp in the great forest,
to hunt the noble white elephant
but scant he found, a fruitless quest
and marched back to the city, unblessed.[18]

Today I'll get Wanthong.

Ai-Di and Ai-Thai, go and harness an elephant." He went off to change his clothes, descended from the central hall, and mounted the elephant. The servants tagged along en masse.

As dawn streaked the sky, he reached the city and dismounted beside Wat Thamma Yai. A little later, he sent his servants into Ayutthaya.

"Seven of you go along. Keep a lookout on all sides. If you meet Wanthong, grab her and bring her here. Don't be afraid of anyone."

The servants took Khun Chang's order and went off together, slipping through the city until they were close to the front of Phramuen Si's house.

When the sun shone brightly, the beautiful Wanthong came down from the house with the intention of going to see her beloved husband.

As she walked along a cross street,[19] Khun Chang's servants recognized her but deliberately walked past without any greeting. Wanthong hurried along with head bowed.

When she reached the middle of the Elephant Bridge quarter,[20] far from the

---

18. A reference to ไชยเชษฐ์, Chaiyachet, a story taken from the Jatakas, adapted into a drama during the late Ayutthaya period, and recomposed by King Rama II. Princess Suwitcha is banished by her father for raising a crocodile that kills people. She wanders in the forest and is adopted by King Singhon. As she is fated to become the wife of Prince Chaiyachet, Indra sends a deity down to earth disguised as a deer that lures Chaiyachet to find Suwitcha, and take her back to his city where she becomes pregnant. Out of jealousy, his seven other consorts encourage Chaiyachet to go hunting for a white elephant, and then substitute a log for Suwitcha's newborn son. On return, Chaiyachet chases Suwitcha out of the palace for giving birth to a log. She finds the son, who had been hidden by the seven consorts, and returns to live with her adoptive father. Seven years later, Chaiyachet meets the son by fate, all is resolved, and Chaiyachet and Suwitcha are remarried (Bot lakhon nok, 223–97).

19. Meaning one of the north-south streets in Ayutthaya's grid pattern (see map 8).

20. Elephant Street ran eastwards from the palace. "On the canal running from Paddy Gate to Chinese Gate there is a bridge crossing that canal made of laterite and called Elephant Bridge" (KLW, 188; APA, 104). This canal ran north-south through the western part of the city, and crossed Elephant Street northeast of Wat Ratburana, close to the current intersection of Chikhun and Pa Maphrao roads, in front of Wat Phlabphlachai. There were stables for eighty elephants ranged along both sides of the street between the palace and this bridge. Perhaps

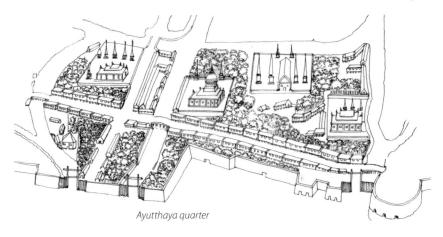

Ayutthaya quarter

house where she stayed, they suddenly surrounded her. "Where are you going? We haven't run into you recently.

You borrowed five chang from our master, and since then both you and your husband have been hiding. Now that we've chanced upon you, we're taking you away." Trembling with fear, Wanthong cried out,

"I didn't borrow any money. No, no! Where are you taking me? Oh townspeople around here, help me! I beg all of you!"

The people in the neighborhood thought this was all about government money. "Why should we get involved?" "Not our business." "That lot are detaining her."

They went out of the Wat Suan Luang Gate.[21] Nobody in the crowds gave any help. The regular ferry was ready to take them immediately. They boarded, crossed to the other bank,

landed, and dashed up. Khun Chang was so happy his body quivered. "Don't cry. Come along with me. I came to collect you and take you back."

He summoned the elephant, Jamlong, and lifted Wanthong up into the howdah. She angrily showered him with abuse, pushing and pulling, tugging his hair, and spitting at him.

Khun Chang consoled her as he drove the elephant along. "Don't cry and make such a fuss. I love you almost to death, and I'll never stop doing so."

because it had to accommodate elephants, this was one of the largest bridges in the city (KLW, 196; Boranratchathanin, *Tamnan krung kao*, 87–88; Thawatchai, *Krung Si Ayutthaya*, 78, 81–83; see map 8).

21. Wat Suan Luang Sopsawan was in the northwest of the Ayutthaya island, right opposite Wat Thamma from where people took the ferry to enter the city. The name of this gate was shortened to *Pratu suan* (gate 26 in KCK, 199; see map 8).

Wanthong raged and sobbed. "Don't expect me to make up with you. Chop my head off. If you take me by force,

as soon as we reach the house, I'll die. Don't expect me to last for even three days. I don't want to live lovelessly with you." The sound of her crying continued along the way.

Khun Chang was happy to have found her, and hugged her close. "Oh excellent lady! Come to reside in my palace, Theplinla.[22]

The property is all given over to your keeping. I am Sophin, lord of the monsters, and Khun Phaen, who is in jail, is like those two animals in human form.[23]

How many years till he can come to find you? Return home and be happy with me. Please overcome your sadness." He hugged, kissed, and climbed all over her.

Wanthong wept with lowered head. "Your mother's clan! I'm disgusted." She cursed and abused him through the forest. Nearing dawn, they reached Suphan,

and halted the elephant at the stairway. Khun Chang carried Wanthong up into a room, and put her down on the bed. "Why are you wriggling and whining?

The first time, when you were young and not pregnant, you couldn't fight me. Now you're pregnant and clumsy, so why wear yourself out struggling for nothing?"

Khun Chang coupled with her, fulfilling his most eager wishes. She was forced to give her body in tears. At the last light of the sun, she fell asleep.

Khun Chang kept on climbing all over her, making love, and blissfully kneading her breasts—as jubilant as if he had chanced upon a gold mine.

---

22. This is a reference to an episode of *Khawi* (see p. 345, note 37). Thao Sophin, lord of the *yak* giants kidnaps Nang Thepli(n)la. Honwichai and Khawi, a tiger and a cow transformed by a rishi into human form, try to help her. Khawi was an old tale known in the Ayutthaya era. This episode does not appear in the Second Reign version of *Khawi* but was developed as an outer drama in the Fourth Reign when outer dramas were written with themes and characters similar to the *Ramakian* because the performances were taxed less than inner drama performances, based on the *Ramakian* (KW, 267–68; Mattani, *Dance, Drama, and Theatre*, 86).

23. Meaning Honwichai and Khawi, a tiger and cow; see previous note.

24: THE BIRTH OF PHLAI NGAM

Living in the house with Khun Chang made the beautiful Wanthong miserable. Because her pregnancy had reached the tenth month, she was unhappy and tearful all the time.

The birth pangs were very painful. Her pelvis was distended, her thighs stiff. She felt so fatigued that she saw fireflies flickering before her eyes, but was loath to call out to Khun Chang.

Instead she massaged herself, tossing and turning, until the pain became intolerable. Cradling her belly, and with tears streaming down her face, she cried out to the servants, "I'm dying! Help me!"

Khun Chang awoke and raised his head. Alarmed at the sight of his wife, he leapt up, hugged her, and prayed to preserve the capital.[1] "Don't lose heart. Please steel yourself."

He looked at her belly and exclaimed, "Eh! It's coming out! Compose yourself and I'll press." Wanthong cried out and tossed around. Khun Chang found a pillow to support her neck,

and called out frantically to the servants. Women rushed out onto the terrace and were sent to fetch the midwives, Granny Sai and Granny Yo, who arrived amid the uproar.

They felt her belly and said the child's head was pointing downwards and the face twisted to the right. They made a correction as her time approached. Medicine was pounded, oranges squeezed,[2] and water boiled.

boiling water

---

1. บนเอาต้นทุน, *bon ao ton thun*, meaning that in childbirth, the mother is the capital and the child is the profit, so if there is danger in the delivery, it is better for the mother (capital) to survive as she can give birth to another child (profit) in the future.

2. ส้ม, *som*, a term used loosely for various sour things including tamarind. Wenk suggests this might be ส้มกุ้ง, *som kung*, *Rubus moluccanus*, a wild raspberry whose leaves are also used for medical preparations (*Studien zur Literatur der Thai*, 83). More likely this is what La Loubère described: "Amongst the sweet Oranges the best have the Peel very green and rough; they call them *Soum-keou*, or Crystal Oranges. . . . . They give of these *Soum-keou* to their sick" (*New Historical Relation*, 23). ส้มแก้ว, *som kaeo*, is probably *Citrus nobilis*, king orange or temple orange.

Wanthong wept as if her heart would break. The karma wind came and went. As dawn broke and the sun rose, her womb loosened and she gave birth without fatality.

The infant emerged from her belly and promptly wailed. Wanthong screamed, her face pale, her breast palpitating, and her soul lost. Khun Chang took a look and called out, "The kid's a boy!" Both grandmothers came to look and give medicine.

Wanthong went to lie by a fire[3] with no fever or pain. To cut a long story short, the child was raised to be of good character until he had grown to the age of nine years.

pounding medicine

He looked exactly like his father, Khun Phaen—plump and handsome, with fair blonde skin, a nicely rounded head, and a topknot. He was talkative and well-spoken.

Wanthong thought about Khun Phaen. Because the child had inherited his family likeness, she told the servants to call her beloved son by the name Phlai Ngam.[4]

Khun Chang was disappointed and resentful. "He's Khun Phaen's son for sure, not a shadow of doubt. At first I thought he looked like me, but in the end the ungrateful Thoraphi[5] has turned out like his father.

Wanthong, the two-minded woman, fittingly named the son Phlai after this clever fellow, his father." Every night he thought about killing the child.

Wanthong had the misfortune to fall sick and become especially miserable. Khun Chang listened until she fell sound asleep in the middle of the day. Phlai Ngam was sitting with him in the central hall.

He saw the child had no companions so invited him to go downstairs and

---

3. See p. 5, note 26.

4. พลายงาม, beautiful bull elephant. His father's birth name was Phlai Kaeo, crystal bull elephant.

5. ทรพี, Thoraphi is a buffalo in the *Ramakian*, and the name has become proverbial for a child who is ungrateful or harmful to parents. Thoraphi's father, Thorapha, used to be a giant guarding Siva's palace but, after playing around with one of Siva's female servants, was cursed by Siva to be reborn as a fierce albino buffalo. He became lord over five hundred female buffaloes, and killed any male rivals. One of his consorts gave birth to a male calf, Thoraphi, who survived because the forest deities hid him and protected him from his father. When Thoraphi grew up, he challenged his father and killed him in combat. Thoraphi then became arrogant and challenged everybody, including the deities who raised him. He was killed by Phali, a monkey king, son of Indra (Premseri, *Ramakian*, 116–20).

have a ride on his shoulders. Then he said, "Let's go look at the many elephants, deer, and other animals,

peacocks and flocks of swans. We could catch some wild cock to raise and hear their crowing." As they walked through the forest, he went on speaking to keep the child's spirits up, distracting him to look at coveys of crows,

barbets, darters, and cockatoos,[6] and treeshrews gamboling in the branches and leaping away in fright. While Phlai Ngam asked a stream of questions, Khun Chang led him on a winding route until they came upon some logs.

Seeing this was a remote and quiet spot, Khun Chang hitched up his lowercloth Khmer-style, swung Phlai Ngam down with a thump onto the ground, and laid into him with kicks, punches, pokes in the stomach, slaps, and elbow jabs, delivered with loud grunts.

Phlai Ngam cried out but Khun Chang stopped up his mouth with both hands. Phlai Ngam wriggled, wept, wailed, and slipped out of Khun Chang's grasp, shouting, "Wanthong, help! Father's beating me to death!"

When his mother did not appear, he burst into tears. Khun Chang punched and pummeled him mercilessly until he himself was exhausted and soaked in sweat. Panting, he straddled the child and wrung his neck.

Phlai Ngam squirmed until his cries died away and his breath slowed. He raised two hands in wai. Khun Chang said, "Stop crying." Phlai Ngam paused and pleaded, "Don't kill me, dear father.

Spare a thought for my mother, Wanthong, oh kind father, Khun Chang, sir! Please keep your child to service you as before." He raised his head but was slapped back down, stunned.

Khun Chang pinched Phlai Ngam's nose, covered his mouth, and dragged him bumping along the ground until the child spluttered and passed out. Khun Phaen's spirits came to embrace their master's son so nothing could touch him.

Khun Chang thought he had crushed the child till his liver ruptured. He made a pile of elephant grass and earth to hide the body, rolled logs over the top, and sauntered home blithely enjoying the forest.

Khun Phaen's spirits were furious at Khun Chang. They dragged away the big logs so Phlai Ngam could move, and blew on his wounds to make them fade away. The boy stirred and revived like waking from sleep.

A female spirit said, "We're servants of Khun Phaen. We came to act in his stead by cushioning the blows when that fellow dragged the logs over you. Don't worry, eye's jewel, you're not dead. Wait here and don't be disheartened.

---

6. This unlikely list appears because the Thai names rhyme: *phoradok nok ngua kratua*. Cockatoos are not native to Southeast Asia.

We'll tell your mother to come and fetch you." They disappeared in a flash, as was their nature. Until evening, Phlai Ngam saw nobody. He wandered around, crying and craning his neck to see his mother.

He could not remember the way home through the forest, and that thought brought on more tears. He watched the sun slanting downwards and smarted at the way his father had tricked him.

"Loving him and relying on him was a waste of time. What made him so furious? None of my friends has a father who'd lure him off to wring his neck.

After this I don't want to call him Father. I'll tell my mother, Wanthong, to lay charges." Looking around and seeing nobody, he felt cold and forsaken, and tears welled up.

Around him the forest was dark, dense, and still. No branch swayed or twig trembled. Only cicadas droned, and crickets shrilled.

When a coel called, he thought it was his mother, and stood up, craning his neck and straining his ears. "I'm here, Mother. Please come and get me." Fretfully he ran round in circles.

With their exceptional powers, the spirits could travel anywhere like a puff of wind, enter Wanthong's room, and slip into her dreams so she would seem to see her beloved child.

At the time her darling son was about to die, her eyebrow twitched as an omen,[7] making her anxious. She yawned sleepily even though it was only midday,

dozed off, and immediately saw little Phlai Ngam being covered with logs by the vile Khun Chang. She started awake in shock, with her breast trembling.

At that moment a pregnant spider beat its chest,[8] and she looked up at the sound. Perturbed by the omen, she thought immediately of Phlai Ngam.

She came out and looked around but could not find him anywhere. When she went to inquire where he usually played, the slave I-Duk told her he had seen Phlai Ngam following his father into the forest.

She suspected Khun Chang had taken her son off to kill him. With tears streaming down, she went out of the fence and walked along on her own, peering around and calling out forlornly.

The dim shapes of bushes in the evening gloom made her heart falter. "Oh Phlai Ngam, my heartstring! Where have you gone? Why don't you come to

---

7. Any involuntary twitch is an omen, the message depending on the part of the body (Wales, *Divination*, 84).

8. See p. 22, note 9.

me?" There was no sign of him at the mound where he used to play.

"Has he fallen dead—gored by a buffalo or bitten by a poisonous snake? Why has his corpse disappeared?" As the evening turned murkier, her cries grew more desperate.

Crows careered around, cackling and cawing. Jackals howled as they sought a lair. The trilling of crickets rang through the branches.

The faint sound of a grebe's song floated from afar.[9] Cicadas shrilled like a conch and horn. Wanthong searched around in desperation. "Have some spirits hidden him away from sight?

jackal

I'll offer a pig, liquor—anything. May I find my beloved child!" She wound this way and that, peering everywhere. "Oh my eye's jewel, this is very strange."

As dusk fell, she walked on, feeling lonely and desolate, sobbing and shouting the name of her beloved Phlai Ngam, as birds went to roost in nests all through the forest.

Seeing a flock of birds nestling with their young deepened her misery. "Oh son, I don't know where you are." The plaintive whoops of gibbons brought on a flood of tears.

Several times, she thought she heard a faint sound of someone calling, and felt the hair on her neck stand on end. Then, looking around a dense thicket, she saw him standing, sobbing, and staring around.

In joy she threw her arms around him. "Your mother's here now. Don't be afraid, my love. What happened? Why did you wander away from the house? I've been looking since this afternoon when I found you'd disappeared."

Little Phlai spoke sorrowfully. "Father led me in circles to get me lost. Then he hit me, kicked me, pinched my nose, and piled logs on my throat. I almost died.

People belonging to someone called Khun Phaen came to help me so I didn't die, thanks to my beloved mother's great merit. But I'm battered and bruised all over." As he spoke, tears of hurt trickled down.

---

9. เป็ดผี, *petphi*, can mean either a large grasshopper, *Holochlora siamensis* or *Eleandrus titan*, which calls "wit, wit" at night, or a little grebe, *Podiceps ruficolis*. The word used for the cry, ปี่แก้ว, *pikaeo*, is a type of song.

Wanthong cried as if to die. "Oh, what can be done about our karma in this life? I'll tell you the whole truth. You're not his child and that's why he hates you.

Your father's name is Khun Phaen. He and Khun Chang are enemies from the past." She told him about the old problems. "Khun Phaen is now still suffering in jail.

We're in dire straits because we have nobody to depend on. Khun Chang can be so rough because we're poor. We can't lay charges against him for the same reason. If you don't run away, you'll be in danger.

I know Granny Thong Prasi lives in Kanburi at Wat Soeng Wai.[10] If you go there and depend on her, you'll be safe and sound from now on.

But it's a day and a half to get there, and you may get lost walking through the far forest. Oh, who could take you?" She sobbed, swallowing her own tears.

Now that Phlai Ngam understood the situation, he said, "Mother, I'm so angry. If this man isn't my father, then let me go to stay with my granny in Kanburi.

But I'm worried about you, Mother. If I go away, I don't know if we'll see each other again, dead or alive, because this stepfather is crafty and cruel. But if I stay here, I'll die.

I'm ready to face death or whatever the future holds. Because we're born with karma, what else can we do? Let me take leave of you for a long time." Then he wept, thinking of his real father.

"Oh Father, Khun Phaen, when will your son see your face? Having to suffer in jail is painful and pitiful." He grieved sorely over his loss.

Wanthong wept in desolation, hugging little Phlai Ngam and already missing him. "Oh eye's sparkling jewel, you're leaving me. You've never been on a track through the forest.

Will you find the way or will you wander astray and get lost? Oh, what trouble we're in! Maybe in the past we made some karma by forcing animals apart,

and now you must be parted from me. Not seeing you will break my heart." She hugged him close, unable to stop her tears from streaming down.

As darkness gathered and dew glistened on the ground, she soothed her beloved little son. "If our enemy finds out, he'll come after you. I'll take you to Master Nak."

They cut through to Wat Khao,[11] saw the abbot, and went in on all fours

---

10. วัดเซิงหวาย, the monastery of the rattan thicket (see p. 55, note 4).

11. Wat Khao Yai where Phim played as a child in chapter 1, and where the fathers of Khun

to pay respect. She told him the whole story. "Your Lordship, please favor us with your assistance.

Take the young lad and hide him in a room. If that man's people come looking, don't let them find him." The abbot said, "Fine. Leave the matter to me. Don't be afraid of your husband.

If he comes up to look in my room and I don't give him the elbow, you can complain. I've never heard of anyone trying to kill a poor fledgling stepchild under their care. Don't worry. I'll help the young fellow."

Wanthong despondently coiled her son's topknot with tears flowing. Knowing it was nearly dark, she had to depart despite her concern. She descended the stairway and quickly walked off.

As she entered the fence, she hurled blunt abuse at Khun Chang. "Trying to break his neck, damn you! I don't want to see you! I must have made some karma in this life to have such a man as a husband."

She went up to the house feeling her heart would desert her body. The sight of Khun Chang was so hateful that she turned her back and ran into her room, beside herself with misery. Seeing the empty bed deepened her sorrow.

The thought of her beloved child made her breast tremble and tears trickle down. "Oh my son, here's where you slept until you were ten.

Now you're being parted from me and your bedding is all I'll see. Oh Phlai Ngam, my heartstring, I'll miss the sweet sound of your voice." Wanthong was awash with tears.

Khun Chang, the bearded trickster, was standing by a wall, beaming drunkenly. Hearing Wanthong crying, he lit a lamp and went to sit beside her on the bed.

Feigning innocence, he inquired jokily, "Is there a thorn hurting you? I'll help pull it out." To cheer her, he sang a line from a drama, "What agony is making you so aggrieved?"

Wanthong tossed her head in anger. Khun Chang struck a dance pose and approached to grab her. She pushed him away, scratching and pinching. "You're annoying me. Hey! Why are you pestering me?

My son's disappeared. Dead or alive, I can't find a corpse. Don't shamelessly cover up the tiger's tracks.[12] Why did you take him into the forest and not bring him back?"

Chang and Phim were cremated in chapter 2.

12. A saying meaning to cover up an evil deed (KW, 677).

Khun Chang made excuses. "I got drunk on liquor and passed out asleep. Who told you I took him? Lightning strike! You didn't follow me.

At midday I saw him playing humming sticks[13] with Ai-Ueng and I-Duk, children of I-Pi. You were sitting in a daze. I've told you before not to let him go down to the ground.

He's loaded with bracelets and bangles. Probably he ran into an opium smoker who beat him to pulp like a midge, and stole the bangles. It's karma."

bangles

For show, he stumbled out of the room, cursed the servants, and went down to the landing to make inquiries. Finding nothing, he came back home, pretending to sigh.

He poured liquor and lapsed into a drunken stupor, putting on an act of crying like nobody had ever cried before. He went up to the cross hall in the moonlight. "Oh friend for life of your father!"

He pretended to weep and wail, covering the whole register of lamentation[14] from high to low, before wandering into a forest ode,[15] "Your soft wing fluttered down into the pandan fronds."

Then he came to his senses in fear of his wife, and sang another song. "You were forced far apart from your father, precious child." He lay spread-eagled on his back, mumbling thickly, until he dozed off from drowsy drunkenness.

Wanthong crept out to find Khun Chang asleep as she wished. She sobbed, thinking she had to be parted from her son because of this demon of a husband.

She sewed a little waist pouch and put in things her son would need—sweets, dried mango paste,[16] candied fruit,[17] Chinese brittle,[18] sweet persimmons, and

---

13. See p. 306, note 7.

14. โอด, *ot*, a singing style, often accompanied with tears, mainly for death laments.

15. เดินดง, *doen dong*, "walk in the forest," a passage of poetry admiring nature. The imagery of the line is of a young bird whose wings are still weak but who tries to fly and falls into a thorny type of bush.

16. ส้มลิ้ม, *som lim*. There are various interpretations of what this could be, including *mamuang kuan*, dried mango paste, a small candied orange, or a *yam* salad made with raw mango or gooseberry fruit and dried prawns mixed with fish sauce and sugar (SB, 281; KW, 667; RI, 1125).

17. แช่อิ่ม, *chae-im*, a fruit or fruit peel so thoroughly soaked in syrup for preservation that the sugar may crystallize on the outside.

18. จันอับ, *jan-ap*, chow chow, a Chinese sweet made with flour, bean, sesame, sugar, and oil, left to dry to a brittle texture. Usually it is made in five varieties—bean, sesame, puffed rice, gourd, and sugared peanut. It may be used as a ceremonial offering, in which case it is usually colored red. In late Ayutthaya there was a Chinese settlement in the Nai Kai quarter of Ayutthaya that specialized in making *jan-ap* (SWC, 3:1432; APA, 112).

a ring of Bang Taphan gold worth five chang.

"Going to live in his grandmother's house will have its difficulties. Should he ever go hungry, he'll have some spending money." She sat lost in tearful thought, waiting for sunrise.

Now to tell of poor little Phlai Ngam. Under the abbot's care, he sat crying inside a room while disciples, novices, and elder monks helped to grind casumunar and apply to the wounds where he had been beaten.

After the abbot fell fast asleep and quiet reigned, the crowing of a cock chilled Phlai Ngam's heart to the core. Because mother and son were thinking of each other, he kept dreaming that he saw her coming to him.

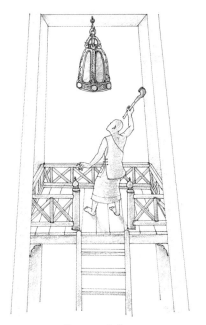

tolling a wat bell

When a coel sang loud and clear, he thought Wanthong was calling. His heart leapt even though his eyes stayed closed, and he shouted back at the top of his voice even though it was midnight.

Then he came to his senses and felt sorrowful. He lay quietly sighing and sobbing until the wat bell was hit with a merry clang. The abbot woke up and reminded the monks to chant prayers.

Near dawn when a heavy dew fell and the sky was streaked with red, Wanthong wept. She knew Wat Khao well as she once went there often. She secured her lowercloth in tuck-tail style, and wore an uppercloth in black.

Carrying some clothing and the waist pouch with the sweets under a coverlet, she came down from the house and sauntered along as if making for the landing, then quickly strode straight into a sugar palm grove.

Arriving at Wat Khao in the early dawn, she saw her little child sitting waiting, and looking pitiable. Not wanting to waste time talking, she took leave of the abbot and led her son off to the *sakae* woods.

She gave him the sweets and fruit. "I feel so sorry for you having to be parted from your mother. The way to Kanburi is right here. Remember it well. Don't get lost and go round in circles.

Try to reach there on the route I tell you. Follow the cart track to the open plain, then cut into the forest by the flat clearing. Let your grandmother teach you how to read and write."

She tied his topknot, fastened the waist pouch she had packed, gave him the gold ring and other things, and wished him luck. She hugged the child who would now be far away and, with sobs escaping her mouth, entrusted him to the gods.

"Oh lord spirits of the forest, I pay respect. Please subdue the tigers, buffaloes, and other wild animals. Oh spirits of the hills, please guide him to his grandmother without him losing the way.

And Father, Khun Phaen, master of lore, begetter of our eternal eye's jewel, help your son Phlai Ngam in this time of need so he may overcome danger and evil to reach Kanburi."

She sobbed with tears falling as if her breast were an aching abscess. "I carried you in my womb and brought you up till over ten years old but now we lose each other.

You're used to eating and sleeping close by my side. In the forest, you'll be alone and lonely. Who'll coil your topknot and shave your hairline? I'll tally the days and months you're out of my sight.

For countless years you won't see your mother's face—as distant and unseen as a moon that's set. Oh, I'm so bad I don't deserve to have been born! I have a foul fate to be so battered and fraught.

I had a husband but the husband was forced away, bringing such heavy hardship. On top of that, I have a child, but the child is parted from me. Such troubled karma!" She sobbed and sadly grieved.

Phlai Ngam felt distraught for his mother. He looked at her face streaming with tears, and prostrated to her with yearning. "When I'm grown, I'll come to find you,

but at present our karma is to part. I have to leave you because of that man. May I have the power of merit to travel and find my father. I won't forget my mother's goodness, and I'll return.

You love your child and your child knows he's loved. Among thousands and millions, no one else is the same. You raised and guided me with loving care. I leave home and I leave you, but only in body.

Mother Wanthong, please go home. That evil fellow will make trouble for you. I must make my farewell, bow my face, and go without fear. Don't be miserable, Mother. Please be brave."

She hugged and kissed him, stroked his back, and gave him advice. "Blessings on you, little Phlai. I weep for you. May you travel safely and remain unharmed. When you grow bigger, be ordained to study.

A gentleman's handwriting shows his rank. You must make the effort to practice regularly." She led him down to the cart stop. Parting was tearing at their hearts.

Son looked at mother, and mother at son, both feeling so overwhelmed they could weep blood. They sobbed their farewells. Then he steeled himself and walked away from her along the track.

Son turned to look back and saw mother still gazing after him. Mother looked towards son with great yearning. The path twisted, each slipped from the other's sight, and their hearts lurched. "Oh, gone!" Both stood, stunned and sobbing.

Wanthong was darkly fearful about Khun Chang. "He's terribly jealous, like no one else in this world." She quickly skirted the fields and arrived back at the house feeling miserable.

She missed her beloved Phlai Ngam so much that she cried with sorrow every day and night. She had no taste for food, and her flesh wasted away day by day.

Phlai Ngam made his way across the plain towards the hills, sobbing as he walked. Beyond Ban Tan,[19] the woods loomed around him in the dim light— rows of shady *rang* and ironwood,

lush stands of *khae, khang, krang,* and *krathum* with sprays of flowers as pretty as a painting. He walked along the cart track, lost in thought, cooled by a gentle breeze.

He passed Gong Mound,[20] Saphan Pond,[21] and a Karen village. Left and right, he saw shelters beside the cotton fields, bright flashes of chili and yellow eggplant, and green magpies[22] which ate them and flew off cawing.

Spotting bantams scratching for bamboo seeds, he sprinted zigzag after them. Coming across a big bevy of peacocks, he chased them to whoosh up into the sky, honking in alarm.

---

19. บ้านตาล, Sugar Palm Village, of which there are several. Probably this is Ban Hua Tan, around 18 kms almost due west of Suphanburi, as it falls on the route from Suphanburi to Kanburi in the early Bangkok maps (see map 2). The journey is rather foreshortened (see note 24 below).

20. โคกฆ้อง, *khok khong,* unidentified.

21. หนองสะพาน, *nong saphan,* probably Huai Taphan, near Phanom Thuan. The name is marked on the early nineteenth-century maps (Santanee and Stott, *Royal Siamese Maps,* 102; see map 2).

22. สาลิกาแก้ว, *salika kaeo,* probably *salika khiao,* the common green magpie, *Cissa chinensis.*

He grew sleepy and his spirits slumped. His thoughts strayed to his mother and he started to sob. The sun slowly slid down the sky, and his heart sank too.

Close to dusk, he came upon a pack of little jackals and ran after them, but their howls made his hair stand on end. He reached the upland forests bordering Kanburi,

and saw an old abandoned wat beside a hill.[23] All that remained was one Buddha image but the doors of the ancient ordination hall were still standing. At nightfall, he prostrated to pay respect, and slept there.

At dawn, he ate his fill of the sweets and dried mango paste, then walked through the hills to Ban Krang.[24] On the way he met hill people hefting goods on poles, and boys busily herding buffaloes.

Not know-ing where Thong Prasi's house was, he asked the locals. A village boy explained, "She's in the fields over there, out of sight.

At her house, there's a big gooseberry tree[25] with unusually sweet fruit. We often go to steal them, but she lies

old wat beside a hill

---

23. Perhaps Khao Noi, 3 kms northeast of modern Kanchanaburi, or Khao Meng, 4 kms further towards Suphan, both of which have a wat at the foot of a hill. Khao Meng appears on the early Bangkok maps (Santanee and Stott, *Royal Siamese Maps*, 102).

24. บ้านกร่าง, 5 kms northeast of modern Kanchanaburi on the road to Cockfight Hill (see map 2). The distance from Suphanburi to Cockfight Hill by the modern road, which follows a slightly more direct route, is 110 kms. The journey has taken only a day and a half, too short even for a strong young lad. In *Nirat Mueang Klaeng*, Sunthon Phu takes four days to go roughly the same distance overland from Chonburi (Bang Plasoi) to Rayong, and arrives exhausted after a long final day. The same Kanburi–Suphan journey takes three days by elephant in chapter 3, and two days in chapter 13.

25. มะยม, *mayom*, a tree originating from Brazil with a fleshy sour fruit which resembles a gooseberry, resulting in the name. The fruits, which ripen from green to pale yellow, grow in dense clusters along the main branches. They are usually very sour and are used in curries and *som tam*, but here the text specifies that this tree's fruit is unusually sweet.

gooseberry tree

in wait and if she catches you, she'll grab your prick and pinch it hard. She's awful, like an ogress.[26]

If she sees any kid playing there, she'll catch him and slap him round the head with her droopy breasts. Why are you asking after her so fearlessly? Granny Droopy Dugs will nab you and bash you to death."

Phlai Ngam boldly asked, "Please take me to see this sweet gooseberry tree. I'll climb up and steal enough for all of us to eat together."

The kids said happily, "Let's go!" They packed rice and fish, released the buffaloes, and set off, tucking up the front of their lowercloths or tying them round their bellies. They laughed among themselves. "I'll collect as much as I can bundle up!"

When they arrived, the boys pointed out Thong Prasi's house and went to hide. Phlai Ngam began to feel uneasy. He crept forward and surveyed the place from a distance.

It seemed quiet with no sign of the fearsome old lady. He slipped round the end of a fence, came to a closed gate, stopped, and listened. From inside came a squeaking sound.

He knew that someone was upstairs spinning cotton. He thought up a plan for telling Thong Prasi what was going on. He'd climb the gooseberry tree and bounce up and down noisily to make her come to catch him,

then tell her the whole secret story, and live with his grandmother from then on. He peeped around, pushed through the fence, climbed up the tree where he could not be seen,

and beckoned the kids over. Wary of the garrulous old granny, they sneaked in with their heads down, and picked up the fruit while whispering and winking at one another.

Thong Prasi was in the house with Granny Pli and Granny Ple. The servants had been sent to the fields following the practice of Kanburi folk.

Since Khun Phaen was jailed, Thong Prasi had been miserable. She stayed in her room all alone, weeping. Over the years, she had become shrunken and somber.

---

26. ผีเสื้อ, *phi suea*. The idea of an ugly giantess with oversized droopy breasts is found in the *Ramakian* as Phi Suea Samut, the Ocean Ogress. Sunthon Phu expanded this into one of the most memorable characters in his picaresque fantasy, *Phra Aphaimani*.

Her ears pricked up at the sound of gooseberries falling. She looked through a chink in the wall and saw the boys slipping in. Picking up a cudgel, she peeped out.

As she descended the stairs, the little boys ran away. She chased after them scolding loudly. They teased her in return. She cursed their mothers' and fathers' clans to the full. Hearing a sound up in the gooseberry tree,

she looked up to see a boy with a little topknot, and shouted at him, "Mm! You little forest thief! Stop hiding up there like a squatting god. Come down and let your back have a taste of my cudgel!"

Phlai Ngam was frozen with fear like a timid mouse. He replied, "I'm your grandson, I tell you, the one who lives at Wanthong's house in Suphan."

Thong Prasi waggled her finger and said, "Really! This fraud of a grandson deserves my elbow. Come down here and 'grandmother' will give you some stick." She waited to punish him to her satisfaction.

Phlai Ngam trembled, rooted to the spot, not daring to go down. But then he thought, "Why should I be afraid of my grandmother?" He jumped down and prostrated at her feet.

Thong Prasi thwacked his back. "I'll tie you up rather than having you fined for theft. Where do you come from? A Thai lad or Chinese? You thieves keep breaking the branches on the gooseberry tree."

Little Phlai tried to dodge the blows while wai-ing her. "I'm hurt badly already. Have mercy on your grandson. I'm the child of Khun Phaen Saensathan. My mother's name is Wanthong.

I came to find my grandmother called Thong Prasi. Don't keep beating me. I'll tell you the whole sad story." Thong Prasi saw it was true and threw away the cudgel. She hugged and consoled him while swallowing her own tears.

She scolded herself for not believing him and thrashing her beloved grandson so much that he hung his head. "Oh, poor you!" She took him up into the house and shouted to Granny Pli.

"Help grind some casumunar paste—quickly! I-Ple, bring a washing bowl out here!" She scooped water over him, scrubbed the dirt away, applied a whole bowlful of turmeric,

and put casumunar on his wounds, feeling very concerned. They sat on a fine reed mat to talk, and she asked, "What's your name? Tell me why you came to find your grandmother."

Phlai Ngam sadly told the story from the time they were in Suphan. "Wanthong brought me up close by her side. She gave me the name Phlai Ngam, her heart's jewel.

She made me pay respect to Khun Chang just like a father. Then he played a crafty trick on your grandchild. He took me on a winding route into the forest, and piled logs on me so I nearly died.

Mother then told me that my father was called Khun Phaen, and that Khun Chang was jealous of him. I couldn't stay in Suphan so I came here. Let me depend on your merit and kindness like a pauper."

Thong Prasi beat her breast. "Tcha! That hairy-faced animal, Chang of a slave race, son of old Thepthong from Khlong Namchon![27] To kill someone without any mercy!

He's acting like the Lord of Life. I'd like to lay charges against him and have him punished till his ears wilt." She reeled off a flood of curses. "You've reached your grandmother's house now so don't be afraid.

Even if that troublemaker comes to claim you're his child, he'll get slapped around the skull by my droopy dugs." She called I-Mai in the kitchen, "Bring some thick curry,[28] rice, and fish for him to eat."

In the late afternoon, the Lawa, Mon, and Lao servants came back from the fields. They lit smoky fires to ward off the mosquitoes and midges, as was the custom upcountry among the paddy fields.

At dusk, a gong was struck and Thong Prasi called Granny Pli and Granny Ple into the house to make a *baisi* with pussbosom flowers,[29] water peony, and gem jasmine. They placed rice, fish, sweets, and savories on salvers,

along with candles, flowers, boiled eggs, rice, and coconuts. The whole room was scented with fragrant oil and powder. Thong Prasi brought out a pile of bracelets and bangles, saying, "These belonged to your father from childhood,

and now we'll put them on our poor grandson because you're flesh of our flesh and dearly beloved. You're exactly like Khun Phaen, handsome and brilliant."

She called the servants up to the house and had them sit next to one another in order. When the *baisi* was set up, they all bowed to pay respect and chanted for the benefit of Phlai Ngam's soul.

---

27. คลองน้ำชน. In chapter 1, Thepthong's home village is not mentioned but seems to have been in Suphan. *Khlong namchon* can mean an intersection of two canals. There were several canals leading westward from the Suphan River, including one to Wat Palelai. Only small parts are traceable now. Perhaps this was a location on one of these.

28. แกงคั่ว, *kaeng khua*, a curry thickened with rice that has been dry-fried and then pounded.

29. นมแมว, *nom maeo*, here meaning an artificial flower made with four pieces of banana leaf folded into triangles, used in constructing *baisi* (Phlainoi, *Wannakhadi aphithan*, 158).

"Soul of Phlai Ngam, beloved, come
behold these brilliant golden trays,
scented sandal and garland sprays.
Soul, don't stray to forest, hill, and lea
with lion, monkey, sambar, tiger.
Don't wander, all alone and lonely.
Come to grandma's home, be merry,
and prosper in safety a hundred years."

soul ceremony

A candle was lit and circulated around the servants, each taking a turn to hold it and pass it on, while they yodeled so loudly the place shook. The candle was extinguished and the smoke wafted towards Phlai Ngam.

A young coconut was sliced and fed to him along with rice from the ceremony. His face was daubed with krajae-sandal to look radiant. Lao Wiang[30] girls with good voices came to play the fiddle and flute, and sing for the soul of their master.

"Under the forest's dome,
no home, only the wood,
no food, not rice nor fish,
famished, your soul strayed.
Your soul, weak, bereft,
has left your body lonely,
lives lofty in the *yang* trees,
grass leas, and paddy fields.

---

30. Lao from Vientiane. After being heavily depopulated in the wars of the late eighteenth century, the west of Siam was resettled with war prisoners including many Lao and Khmer. Several thousand Lao were brought after the destruction of Vientiane in 1828–29.

Oh soul, now in flight,
we invite you, come near
to hear fiddle and song,
to belong to our beloved.

A basket full of sticky rice,
a coppice full of berries,[31]
soul, please come to be
with the body of Phlai. Oei!"

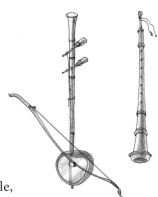

fiddle and flute

Next, a Mon played a strain on the fiddle,
and announced, "This is how a *thayae*[32] is sung,
ladies!"

"Oh! Master Phlai Ngam, beloved of all.
Oh soul, we call you to return here,[33]
to live well, be well, have a young bride.
Soul, don't hide in wild forest and mere.[34]
One, two, come back, soul, to enjoy good cheer.
Three, four, come near to join us again."[35]

All around, Thong Prasi saw only a throng of slaves. She happily gave them
money. The time came for Phlai Ngam to go to bed, and enjoy having a mattress, pillow, mosquito net, and curtain.

Phlai Ngam asked his grandmother, "Why does my father Phaen have to
suffer such hardship? I'm not acquainted with him at all. Would you please
take me so I can see his face."

---

31. ป้อม, meaning *makham pom, Phyllanthus emblica,* emblic myrobalan, a tree with sour,
juicy fruits eaten to moisten a dry throat.

32. ทะแย, an old song form from the Ayutthaya era with alternating bars of four and six beats,
played by a *mahori* ensemble or as accompaniment to a *khon* mask play. A variant known as
thayae hongsa, believed to be in Mon style, is played to accompany *lakhon* drama (SWC, 6:2482;
Narongchai, *Saranukrom phleng thai,* 120–21).

33. กกกะเนียงเกรียงเกลิง, *kok kaniang kriang kloeng,* in Mon.

34. เนียงกะราวกนตะละเลิงเคลิง, *niang karao kon tala loeng khloeng*; in Mon. As the translitera-
tion from Mon to Thai in the original only approximates the sounds, and as copyists may have
stumbled over words they do not understand, it is impossible to be sure of the original Mon
phrase, and there are alternative translations. Some people think this line means: Oh soul of the
young master, please return.

35. จะเปิงยี่อิกะปิปอน, *ja poeng yi ika pi pon,* in Mon. Some people think this line means: come
to eat rice and three or four fish

At her grandson's words, Thong Prasi dissolved in tears. "My darling, whatever I said to your father, he didn't listen because he was besotted with a Lao wife who was taken into the palace.

He petitioned the king, who lost his temper and had your father imprisoned as punishment, though not in irons. It's ten years now and he's still not been released.

At dawn tomorrow, I'll take you to find him at the shelter beside the slip gate. Your father will be delighted to see you." They talked until dropping off to sleep.

Seeing the golden light, Thong Prasi thought dolefully about her son. She ordered the servants to harness an elephant with a big howdah, and pack fish, rice, clothing, torches, gourds, melons, sugar,

sago, medicine, betel, pan, and lime paste to give to poor Khun Phaen. A Kula[36] called Ta-Lo acted as mahout. She took her grandson to mount the elephant and set off.

They went down to Bang Kham, and passed Ban Saphan Khlong.[37] Going out to the open plain, they turned towards the right, and in two and a half days reached Ayutthaya. They dismounted and she walked with Phlai Ngam along the road.

Now to tell of the unfortunate Khun Phaen. Since his imprisonment, he had been low in spirits. Although he used to take good care of himself, in the shelter at the slip gate he had let himself go, wasted away, and now looked a mess.

His hair, which could not be cut because of his invulnerability and mantra lore, was long and coiled up on his head.[38] As he was idle and desperately poor, he worked at weaving small baskets.

---

36. A branch of the Shan or Tai Yai, now mostly resident in upper Burma. They were known for their expertise in mining and processing precious stones. Some were brought as war prisoners and settled in Kanchanaburi, Chanthaburi, and Battambang, where they gained a reputation as hunters and itinerant traders.

37. บางขาม, possibly Ban Tha Makham, tamarind landing, between Cockfight Hill and modern Kanchanaburi. บ้านสะพานโขลง, Ban Saphan Khlong, herd bridge village, perhaps a bridge for bringing elephants captured in the forests, unidentified but perhaps near the site of modern Kanchanaburi where they would have branched eastward away from the river—a right turn from the Suphan road.

38. Because of his invulnerability, Khun Phaen's hair would resist a blade. Before cutting his hair, Khun Phaen would always have done a rite, enchanting water and immersing the blade (see ch. 27), and presumably this was inconvenient in jail (SB, 286).

Khun Phaen plaited the frames tightly with rattan, and Kaeo Kiriya painted them with lacquer. They could easily expect one baht each, and many were hung for sale around their dwelling.

When his mother arrived at the shelter, Khun Phaen welcomed her inside along with all the things brought for him. Spotting Phlai Ngam, he asked, "Whose child is this? He looks lovable."

baskets

Thong Prasi explained, "This is your son. Come on, wai your father." She told the story about their enemy. Khun Phaen consoled Phlai Ngam, smothering his own tears.

He hugged and kissed his son, and stroked his back while his own tears came in floods. "I hate Khun Chang so much I could writhe to death. He gets his way so often it's become a habit.

He dragged Wanthong off to partner and possess. Because I've given my word that I won't escape, he thinks I can't cut his head off. Now he's tried to kill my son like an ox or horse. Does the villain think I'm scared of him?

This evening I must go to his house and chop his head so the blood flows. A man dies where he dies." He gnashed his teeth and worked himself up into an aggressive rage.

Thong Prasi said, "My son, I beg to oppose you. It would be better to kill a ghost rather than Khun Chang. Why go on creating karma by bad deeds?

Your own child has come to see you. What other descendants do you have? Please listen to your mother alone. Let bygones be bygones. You must pray to stay alive.

I'll bring your child up, educate him, and have him presented at court so the king may calm down and relax your punishment. In a time of bad fortune, you must act humbly.

There's an ancient saying that mortal humans can rebound from hardship seven times. All these difficulties will pass. You should survive beyond your sentence."

Khun Phaen, great gallant, prostrated to his mother in tears. "I have only my mother's kindness to warm my heart. Please teach Phlai Ngam to study knowledge.

cupboard

All the manuals, both my father's and my teachers', are kept arranged in order in the cupboard. If you forget anything, unlock it and bring them out to consult."

Then he stroked little Phlai Ngam's back and instructed him. "Please study how to write formulas. No pursuit surpasses the pursuit of knowledge.[39] In the future when you grow up, you'll reap the benefit.

We're in trouble, eye's jewel, and you must tread carefully. We've no kinsfolk to support us, only the kindness of your grandmother. I'm relying on her to raise you.

Please think of her as your mother and father. However much she scolds you, don't answer back. I can't be close at hand to help bring you up, eye's jewel."

He hugged Phlai Ngam tearfully to his chest. "Oh, what karma did we create in the past? I've just seen my child's face and now we'll be parted again.

You came to visit me but I've nothing to give you except these beads. Take them as a present. They'll make you invulnerable to pikes and guns, and protect you from now on."

Phlai Ngam felt so distressed for his father that tears streamed down his face. He accepted the beads and spoke his feelings, "I want to live with you and help

draw water, pound rice, make the fire, and find vegetables every morning and night to help you overcome your difficulties. I'll try to study by and by."

Khun Phaen, great romancer, was overwhelmed. "Where would you find another tiny fellow who knows how to speak like this?" Thong Prasi also gave vent to her feelings of pity, and her tears flowed.

Khun Phaen said, "You cannot stay here to look after me. In this main jail there are so many difficulties, it's like hell on earth. I haven't been released from my punishment for a single day.

But Minister Yommarat allows me to stay in this shelter by the slip gate, and I'm on good terms with all the overseers so they leave me alone and don't put me in irons.

Phramuen Si provides my food every day, and that lightens the burden of having to fetch water and pound rice. His goodness overflows the sky.

If you can study knowledge, I'll put you under the patronage of Phramuen

---

39. A very famous line that has become a well-known proverb. Sunthon Phu repeated it in slightly modified form in *Phra Aphaimani* when the rishi is instructing Sudsakhon: "No pursuit surpasses the pursuit of knowledge / knowing how to survive is the ultimate" (SB, 287).

Si, and he'll present you to the king so you'll be a man of rank in the future."

Little Phlai Ngam replied sorrowfully, "Sir, I'll study hard." They grew happier, chatting together until almost dusk.

Thong Prasi said, "It's evening. I have to leave you, dear Kaeo." Khun Phaen wai-ed his mother. Phlai Ngam took leave of his father with regret,

and followed his grandmother away from the shelter at the slip gate. He turned to cast a tearful look back at Khun Phaen who was nearly heartbroken. Both felt their souls skip with yearning as they passed from sight.

They mounted the elephant beside Wat Tha Ka Rong.[40] With the moon shining brightly in the middle of the sky, they set out across the plain of Ayutthaya and hastened back to Kanburi.

Now to tell further of little Phlai Ngam who studied assiduously with Thong Prasi as his teacher. He happily mastered both old Khmer[41] and Thai, and studied texts on Buddhism and mantra lore.

He knew all the *pathamang* texts beginning with *na* characters,[42] and practiced correctly how to become invisible. He studied the abbreviated heart formulas, *itthije* texts, [43] making charms, pronouncing mantras, enchanting

---

40. The monastery of the landing of the cawing crow, to the northwest of Ayutthaya, around five hundred meters up the Chaophraya River on its southern bank. On the map of old Ayutthaya compiled by Phraya Boranratchathanin, this is shown as two wat, Wat Tha and Wat Ka Rong. All that remains of the latter is a mound with one image in a sala. The modern Wat Tha Ka Rong is on the old site of Wat Tha. At the riverbank, there is a lovely wooden sala, claimed to date from the Ayutthaya era, with two rows of inward leaning pillars. The wat appears in the chronicles' account of the Burmese attack of 1563/4, but this might have been a geographical insertion by later chroniclers. According to the Religious Affairs Department, the wat was founded in 1732 (*Boranasathan*, 1:113–14; see map 8).

41. Many texts, especially on lore, were written in old Khmer, ขอม, *khom*, script.

42. นะ, นะปัถมัง, นะปัดตลอด, *na, na pathamang, na pat-talot. Pathamang* is a text for learning elements used in composing yantras (see p. 124, note 30). Each verse begins with the Khmer character *na*, the first character that appeared in the world. In the Three Worlds cosmology, each era ends with the world consumed by fire and then flooded by rain. A *brahma* (spirit from the upper levels of heaven) called Mahabrahmadhiraja then looks at the flood, sees a certain number of lotuses, and predicts that the same number of Buddhas will appear in the approaching era. In the current, "most fortunate" era, he spotted five. In each of the lotuses, he saw a character, "*na-mo-phut-tha-ya*," representing the five Buddhas of this era, Kakusandha, Konagamana, Kassapa, Gotama, Metteyya. The basic form of *na*, known as *na pathamang, na pat-talot*, or *na phinthu* is written with five strokes while pronouncing a formula. Many more elaborate variants are formed by adding extra strokes while pronouncing further formulas, for a specific purpose such as inducing love or becoming invulnerable. (RR, 311–14; KW, 307, 677; PKW, 2:149; Thep, *Khamphi na 108*; Prachak, *Prapheni*, 156–57; Natthan, *Lek yan*, 199–203)

43. อิทธิเจ, "complete form," is a Pali text copied by students to learn writing and pronouncing Pali. The initial Khmer "u" character, in simple and complex forms, is used like the *na* device (see note 42 above) to induce love or successful trading. The characters are written with

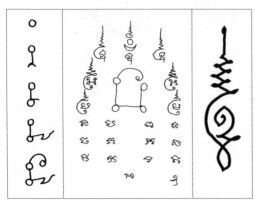

drawing the basic na character, complex na character, and itthije character

turmeric, and drinking oil.

As children do, he tried out his knowledge in his room, stabbing himself repeatedly until a sharp blade was blunted because of the Great Awesome[44] formula for invulnerability. He was able to draw yantra designs without error.

He knew the abbreviated *itipiso* formula,[45] the Loosener to unlock chains, and the Sub-duer mantra to stun people or conceal himself.[46] He applied himself diligently to learn omens from the clouds[47] and from breath in his nostrils.[48]

In addition, he studied self-control and meditation, the Formulas on Extinction for summoning and suppressing spirits,[49] and methods to animate grass dummies as warriors. Thong Prasi taught her grandson to be expert.

---

whiteclay powder that is then collected and used to daub on the forehead or in other ways. Such "*itthije* powder," made by famous monks, is now a popular ingredient in amulets. (KW, 308; YS, 483–91; Natthan, *Lek yan*, 104–6)

44. มหาทะมื่น, *mahathamuen*, an adjective for something dark and tall, and the name of a long formula, โองการ, *ongkan* associated with invulnerability (*Phra khamphi khatha 108*, 109–12).

45. อิติปิโส, *itipiso*, an abbreviated heart formula, consisting of 108 syllables, condensed from the Dhajagga Sutta, a canonical text. The Buddha tells his followers that the king of the gods once instructed his troops during a battle to concentrate on the top of the banners of himself and three other gods to overcome their fear, but the Buddha's followers should rather recall the Buddha, Thamma, and Sangha as "For those who have thus recalled the Buddha, Thamma, and Sangha, there will be no terror, horripilation, or fear." The name *itipiso* is taken from the line, *Itipi so bhagavaa araham sammaa-sambuddho*, "He is a Blessed One, a Worthy One, a Rightly Self-awakened One." The formula is considered a powerful mantra for invulnerability. (YS, 107–57; Bizot preface in Becchetti, *Le mystère dans les lettres*, 13–14)

46. จังงังกำบังกาย, *jang-ngang kambang kai*. With this device, "someone seeing us opens his mouth to talk but stands stunned with no sound emerging," or "someone seeing us, even if he knows us from the past, will not recognize us . . . this is called concealment not invisibility" (PKW, 2:22).

47. Omens in the clouds are important in warfare, and are extensively described in the *Tamra phichai songkhram*, the Manual of Victorious Warfare (see notes and examples in ch. 29).

48. See p. 101, note 23.

49. นิพพานสูตร, *nipphansut*, the teaching on nirvana, is a section of the Anguttara Nikaya in the Tipitaka in which the Buddha briefly describes the stages of obtaining release from the world. The name has been adopted as a collective term for four short formulas for summoning, activating, attaching, and ordering spirits, especially for use in war.

When Phlai Ngam was aged thirteen, he looked robust with a fair complexion. Reaching adolescence, he was an attractive lad with a smiling disposition, reserved manner, and good looks.

His eyes were round, black, keen, and handsomely bright. Everyone he met liked him and enjoyed asking him questions. Thong Prasi happily looked for an auspicious time. "You're thirteen now, my dear grandson.

On Friday the tenth of the waxing month,[50] we'll shave your topknot."[51] The day before,[52] she made *namya jin* and boiled pigs' trotters. Neighbors brought betelnut and pan, and helped to sweep the floor and lay mats, carpets, and rugs.

Silver and gold pots were brought out of storage, conches filled to the brim with sacred water, a half-moon dais prepared for the monks, and gongs and drums readied to celebrate the almsgiving in accordance with custom.

On this auspicious day, old Master Koet was invited from the nearby Wat of Cockfight Hill[53] with ten monks. An ensemble played a *sathukan* salutation.[54]

The monks sat chanting prayers until dusk, then sprinkled sacred water. Young men jostled together with young Lawa women, cheering rowdily during the water sprinkling.

The women pinched the men pestering them, and there was a lot of noisy pushing and grappling. I-Hang aimed a crazy kick at Ai-Dam, and the two leapt up and began wrestling uproariously.

Thong Prasi gaily said, "Ai-Dam wrestling I-Hang will be fun for sure! Who's going to lose?" She sent her grandson to change his clothes. He went shyly to prostrate before the abbot.

Master Koet looked at Thong Prasi and asked, "Whose child is this little one?" Opening her mouth and dribbling betel juice, Thong Prasi told the story from beginning to end.

"Currently Khun Phaen is still in jail. When we've shaved this lad's topknot,

---

50. A *mahasitthichok* day (see p. 319, note 23).

51. A coming of age ceremony, traditionally performed when a boy is around thirteen, and a girl is eleven. On the day before, the monks come to the house to chant prayers, and guests are entertained. At dawn, the boy is dressed all in white with no shoes. The presider (monk or Brahman) divides the hair into three tufts, each with a *madum* leaf and a nine-jeweled ring. At an auspicious moment, the presider rings a gong, chants the *chayanto* prayer, and cuts the first tuft. An elder of the family cuts the second, and the father the third. Then the remaining hair is shaved, and all the attendees anoint him with sacred water. The boy then changes into new clothes, and the monks are fed (Prachak, *Prapheni*, 31).

52. สุกดิบ, "cooked-raw," a term for the eve of a festival but also here a metaphor for Phlai Ngam between youth and maturity.

53. There is no wat of this name today (see map 7 and its accompanying note).

54. สาธุการ, a piece of music played at the start of many ceremonies.

I'll take him to present at court. Master, please look at the horoscope of Phlai's father. Will his bad fortune disappear somehow?"

Having heard the story, the abbot was angry. "Tcha! Phaen is hopeless. After all the knowledge I taught him, he ran off to jail. What fun!

I told that loverboy his weakness for women would get him into trouble." The abbot laughed, reclined comfortably, and examined Phlai Ngam, thinking to himself,

"This lad looks a clever and lovable type. He'll have the good fortune to ride on palanquins. If he strikes it really lucky, he has the attributes to be rich.

As for women, a big mess. This fellow's weakness will be a beautiful young lady with fair skin. He'll easily fall head over heels and be influenced by greed, lust, and passion."

The abbot laughed, "This young lad, this grandson of yours, is going to be a loverboy beyond belief. But at eighteen years old, he'll become an official with a title as Muen or Khun,

and a young wife, a northerner from a long lineage. This lass will bring disaster. Young Phlai's father, Khun Phaen, will be released at the end of the second month in a year of the pig.[55]

From then on, all will be happiness not hardship. He'll have a bed for sleeping and a chair for sitting as an official." Thong Prasi happily wai-ed the abbot. "Please share your merit[56] so Khun Phaen gets back on his feet."

The abbot acknowledged her and went back to the wat. A music ensemble played. Thong Prasi's family and friends had sought the very best masters of *sepha*. Ta-Mi, a firecracker maker, excelled at fight scenes,[57]

his throat swelling with sound as he recited. Old people liked to hear him and declared he

sepha performer   knew everything. Ta-Rongsi was good at being

---

55. As Khun Phaen was born in a year of the tiger, he will be thirty-four in a year of the pig. This matches with him being around twenty when jailed and spending a period in jail described as "over ten" or fifteen years.

56. If a person with much merit, such as the abbot, shares it with someone, then the receiver benefits greatly (SB, 290).

57. The figures who appear here were the great *sepha* players of the Second Reign. The reference here means that Mi was famous for reciting Phlai Kaeo's expedition to Chiang Thong, and Khun Phaen and Phra Wai's campaign in Chiang Mai (*Companion*, 1351–53, 1377–78).

funny, and knew every trick. He clacked the claves while clowning around and rolling his eyes.

Nai Thang, with a loud booming voice, made the quarreling scenes very amusing. Nai Phet had lots of tricks, and dragged the choruses out to three fathoms and two cubits, as long as a long gun.

As for Nai Ma from the retinue of Phraya Non, he was a comedian good at bawdy improvisation who made people laugh heartily. Ta-Thongyu knew how to recite in Lao[58] and sing background music in a drone.[59]

At dawn, Phlai Ngam's topknot was shaved. He felt free of hardship and slept peacefully. After his hair grew long, he had it cut in Mahatthai style.[60] He thought about entering royal service

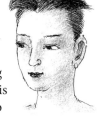

Mahatthai style

and relying on the power of his merit to petition the king for Khun Phaen's release. It would be a fine way to repay his father. He sat quietly pondering until nightfall, then went to his grandmother's bedside with tears flowing.

He stroked her and spoke pleadingly in a soft, sweet voice, "Tomorrow, I'll leave to visit Father. I'll enter the service of the Lord of Life and, when I gain enough favor, I'll ask pardon for Father's punishment."

Thong Prasi was happy to give her consent. "You come from the Phlai lineage. Helping your parents get over this will be a fine display of filial duty. Please go.

I'll have you sent to see your father, and then be delivered to Phramuen Si. From there you must depend on your merit and fortune. As for me, I'll die some day.

Having a child has been an added burden. I've always known tears rather than happiness, always suffered sickness, injury, coughing, and wheezing. Who'll cremate my corpse, I don't know.

Remember everything I've taught you, and you'll rise steadily in rank. I'll give three people—Ai-Phlat, Ai-Pat, and Ai-Pu—to attend you,

---

58. Thongyu was a famous actor, teacher, choreographer, and *sepha* reciter during the Second Reign. He specialized in the episodes of *KCKP* with Lao characters such as Laothong and Soi Fa (*Companion*, 1351).

59. กราวเชิด, *krao choet*, rousing background music, now associated with Thai boxing matches, formerly used also to accompany marches and dramas.

60. A style initially fashionable among officials of the Mahatthai ministry, and later more widely among officialdom. The hair was parted along a horizontal line circulating the head at the level of the hairline on the forehead, and this line was emphasized by shaving and applying powder. Below this, the hair was cut short. Above it, the hair was parted in the middle and combed into two sideways wings (KP, 173).

carry your sompak[61] and umbrella, draw water, steam rice, and prepare all sorts of food." They talked together until late at night and then slept until the sun shone brightly.

When she awoke, Thong Prasi packed silver and clothing in a chest along with various sweet and savory foods, and loaded everything in an elephant's howdah.

Phlai Ngam took leave of his grandmother and received her blessing. At an auspicious time with no obstacles, he mounted a cow elephant and jogged off along the road, crossing the plain to the capital without an overnight stay.

He went to find his father, crouched down, and paid respect. Khun Phaen asked what was the matter, and little Phlai explained to him, "I would like you to have Phramuen Si present me at court."

Khun Phaen, great romancer, gave his consent. "Those of the Phlai lineage are destined to be fearless warriors. Please make an effort to maintain the family name, my dear son. I'll take you to Phramuen Si."

He grilled Phlai Ngam on what he had learned, and made him recite passages. His expectations were fulfilled, and he went on teaching his son other devices and stratagems until dusk.

When the gong and drum sounded at nightfall, Khun Phaen told his son to follow behind. Even though they met people on the way, nobody saw them. They arrived at Phramuen Si's house on the canal bank,[62]

and went up the brightly lit stairway. They inquired of servants and were relieved to hear that all was well. As they waited at the hall, Phramuen Si called out, "Come on in, my friend."

Because he honestly loved Khun Phaen and considered him a friend, Phramuen Si always treated him well and never turned his face away. Khun Phaen took his son to wai him. Phramuen Si asked, "Who's this young fellow?"

Khun Phaen said, "This is the son of Wanthong who was heavily pregnant when we came from the forest." He related matters from the past. "I wish to place him under your care, sir.

Ever since my conviction, I've had nowhere else to turn, and you've kindly given me such help and support. You're my patron so I've come to ask a favor. I have to depend on your merit because now I have none.

---

61. A patterned lowercloth worn by nobles at royal audience. A servant carried the sompak from home to the audience hall. There are murals depicting nobles changing outside the hall.

62. See p. 554, note 43.

His grandmother has taught him the disciplines, and he seemed well versed when I drilled him. If there's an opportunity that you deem propitious, please kindly find a way to present Phlai Ngam at court."

Phramuen Si was pleased. "He looks sharp, the true son of a seasoned soldier. Don't worry about him becoming a servant of the Lord of Life. When there's a war, he should do well.

Leave the matter with me. I'll present him and do the talking so your beloved son is raised to a position of status. He can lodge in this house. We have space, people, and food. Don't worry.

Khun Phaen, you know I love you. We've narrowly avoided being speared to death together many times. I love you as a friend even though you're poor. For me, your neediness is no barrier.

It's beyond me to help you because your punishment is by royal command. There has to be an opening before we can expect relief. In truth, I think about you every morning and night, and I'll help you until my flesh fails."

Khun Phaen felt exhilarated, and joyfully raised his hands in wai. Trying to smother his tears, he said, "You're helping me overcome hardship just like a parent.

Even though I'm in great difficulty and facing severe punishment, you still send me food as solace. Though I'm in jail, I make sure I show my gratitude. It cheers me just to prostrate to you every single night.

As for my son, Phlai Ngam, his future is now in your hands. Let me pay respect and take leave. I can stay no longer." He stroked his son's back lovingly and advised him, "I'm leaving, eye's jewel.

You'll stay here and depend on his kindness from now on. Do well, get established, and fulfill my hopes." He went down from the house in the bright moonlight, and returned to his usual sleeping place at the slip gate.

Phramuen Si summoned Phlai Ngam for instruction. "To be a king's servant, you can't lie around doing nothing. It won't do.

There are many volumes of royal laws and decrees filling the big cupboard. Bring them out and read them. Then there's the treatise on punishment and compensation,[63] the penal codes, the royal household law, royal court judgments,

---

63. กรมศักดิ, *kromsak*, more usually พระไอยการ พรมศักดิ, *phra aiyakan phromsak*, a legal code on the calculation of punishments and compensation according to age, *sakdina*, and severity of the offense (KTS, 1:197).

the royal language,[64] and royal orders. You should know the sayings of the learned King Ruang,[65] and study the responsibilities of various ministries. Once you know all of this, you'll be ready.

Those who don't pursue knowledge as child or adult remain royal pages[66] through three generations—father, son, and grandson—the family ruined, eclipsed, or disregarded for being as lazy and blunt as a Mon cleaver.[67]

You have good family on both your mother's and father's side. Don't go astray. Try to remember what you're taught." He arranged a room for Phlai Ngam to sleep. Knowing Phramuen Si would bring him up in a fair way, Phlai Ngam was free from worry.

Phlai Ngam was sharp, good at figures, wise, and diligent. He lived happily in Phramuen Si's house, and every morning and night followed his patron into the palace.

While Pramuen Si went into audience, Phlai Ngam sat behind the topiary,[68] listening to the king's words and studying his disposition. He gradually acquired an all-round knowledge of court affairs and responsibilities. He did not make friends and go gadding about.

At the house, he read legal treatises and texts on royal warfare. He matured into a smart looking youth, and many young women were interested in meeting him.

They sought him out but he knew nothing about courtship. If he turned round and saw a young woman, he would run away and hide. He applied himself to studying hard so that he would know everything, and by understanding the customs, would conduct himself humbly.

On an auspicious day, Phramuen Si was cheerful because he had an opportunity to take Phlai Ngam for presentation at court. He prepared incense,

---

64. ราชาศัพท์, *ratchasap*, vocabulary derived from Khmer, used when addressing the king or when describing royal matters (Suwit, *Ratchasap*).

65. A literary work of the early Bangkok era that purports to be a collection of aphorisms attributed to a legendary king of the Sukhothai era (see Gerini, "On Siamese Proverbs").

66. Meaning that they do not rise from the status of page to a higher office.

67. Suphon speculates that Mon here is used to mean blunt because Thai metalworkers at that time had better command of the techniques of forging and annealing metal to be harder and sharper, and hence others' workmanship was inferior (SB, 296).

68. This description is probably based on the Amarin Winitchai Audience Hall in Bangkok. The hall was a wooden building with no walls, open to the breeze. Ranking nobles assembled inside, while their retinue stayed outside behind a screen of pruned plants placed between the hall's pillars. Such topiary was especially popular in the Bangkok Second Reign. The hall was replaced with a walled, brick structure in the Third Reign (SB, 297; KP, 240).

candles, and flowers,

and put on a sompak with a pleated front. When everything was ready, he got in his palanquin. With servants crowding along behind carrying a salver, and Phlai Ngam bringing up the rear, they entered the palace.

At the courtyard they inquired of palace attendants who responded courteously. The gold salver with incense, candles, and flowers was carried inside and placed as required.

Phlai Ngam came behind and sat by the salver, following exactly the procedure that Phramuen Si had told him. Close to the time, the chaophraya and other courtiers ushered one another to the front of the audience hall.

They wore sompak with tucked tails, tied prostration cloths in the front, and walked grandly along, flourishing their fingernails.[69] At four o'clock to the minute, the officials entered the hall.

The almighty king, crown of the capital of Ayutthaya, resided in a crystal residence as majestic as the palace of a heavenly city,

attended by throngs of beautiful ladies with gracious manners who sang in the style of the inner court, making the royal pleasure complete.

At the daytime hour, the king came to the jeweled audience hall. He spoke and laughed merrily, in very good humor because the people were content, no enemies were approaching from north or south,

and, as a result of the king's merit and power, there was only good fortune and growing tax revenues. Courtiers who had performed well were presented with golden salvers.

Phramuen Si Saowarak-rat made obeisance to the royal foot, and addressed the king. "My liege, pray favor from the dust beneath the royal foot. These flowers, incense, and golden candles belong to Phlai Ngam,

the son of Khun Phaen Saensathan and grandson of Thong Prasi. He is properly educated and well-mannered. May I request that he endeavor to be a servant of the dust beneath the royal foot."[70] Phramuen Si prostrated three times and waited attentively for the king's words.

King Phanwasa looked at Phlai Ngam's face. He felt pity and was about to pronounce a pardon for Khun Phaen but karma was destined to influence the king's disposition.

---

69. กรายกรีดเล็บ, *krai krit lep*, suggesting they show off long fingernails like a dancer.

70. ขอรองมุลิกาพยายาม, *kho rong mulika phayayam. Mulika* is a shortened form of the formula for describing oneself as dust beneath the royal foot, บาทมุลิกากร. This is a set formula for requesting admission as a page.

His mind veered to a verse from an outer drama[71] that he could not recall. His head spun and his thoughts drifted away. He forgot to make the announcement as intended, and instead returned inside to the royal bedchamber.[72]

Phlai Ngam was now a royal page. He lived with the astute Phramuen Si, attended audience every morning and evening without missing a day, and gradually grew in confidence.

The nobles were all kind to him. None disliked him. He placed himself under the patronage of the two superintendents of the pages, and acted timidly towards all.[73]

---

71. ละครนอก, *lakhon nok*. Plays based on the *Ramakian*, *Inao*, and *Unnarut* were reserved for performance at court, and known as *lakhon nai*, inner dramas. Others, known as *lakhon nok*, were mostly based on Jataka tales. Several were composed in King Rama II's literary salon.

72. This scene may be modeled on King Rama II, who, as the chronicle of his reign reports, was more interested in literature than administration. Sunthon Phu (see next note) was very devoted to Rama II, whom he served as a court poet. But Sunthon Phu also disliked the arbitrary use of power under the monarchy and *sakdina*, and had a talent for gentle lampoon which blossomed in his picaresque epic, *Phra Aphaimani*.

73. This chapter was composed by Sunthon Phu (1786–1856), a poet famed for his mellifluous and seemingly effortless verse. He was born in Thonburi and his mother was a wet nurse (and possibly a relative) of the queen of the Rear Palace. His father split from the family and entered the monkhood in his family home of Klaeng, now in Rayong province. His mother remarried. Like Phlai Ngam, Sunthon Phu grew up with his mother and a foster father. Like Phlai Ngam, he met his natural father much later—by traveling to Klaeng, an experience he described in a nirat: "My head bent low, I bowed at his feet; / Not without pangs of grief / that some past sin had separated us / and kept me from my father and relatives." (Sunthorn Phu, *Nirat Mueang Klaeng*, 58, lines 775–78). Pinyo Sijamlong speculates that, in this chapter, Sunthon Phu drew on a trip he made to Klaeng as a child; that Thong Prasi's role in Phlai Ngam's education is modeled on Sunthon Phu's mother; that Phlai Ngam's training and presentation at court follow Sunthon Phu's experience of becoming an alak scribe around 1816 under the patronage of the Rear Palace; and that Khun Phaen's anger at Khun Chang was inspired by an incident in which Sunthon Phu was jailed by the king for drunkenness because of scheming by an elder relative (Pinyo, *Thong lok kawi*, 108–16).

25: THE KING OF LANCHANG PRESENTS SOITHONG TO
KING PHANWASA

For now we will set this matter aside, and relate a new story about King Chiang In.[1]

The king resided in a jeweled palace, surrounded by his resplendent queens and palace ladies, scented with refreshing and inspiring fragrances, bowing their heads to pay respect to the monarch.

Every one was adorable and fair of face, with beautiful breasts, hair in chignon, and radiant complexions which alone were a feast for the eye and an invitation to love.

They wore uppercloths of *tat* silk[2] with gold stripes and embroidery on the front. Their hair were embellished with waving flowers. At dusk, the evening gong sounded, and the king entered his bedchamber.

---

1. The King of Chiang Mai who appeared in the war over Chiang Thong in chapters 8 and 9. Chiang In (อินทร์, Indra) is a synonym for Chiang Mai. It is used for the name of the king but also in the original is very occasionally used to refer to the city. To limit confusion, in this translation Chiang In is reserved for the king while the city is always referred to as Chiang Mai.

In the preface to *KCKP*, Prince Damrong quoted a version of this story from the *Khamhaikan chao krung kao*, the testimony of Ayutthaya war prisoners taken to Burma after 1767. He then dated the event to around 1500, and suggested this was the root of the *KCKP* story. However, there is no trace of such an incident around 1500 in the Ayutthaya, Lanchang, or Chiang Mai chronicles. This incident does echo a story that appears in the Ayutthaya and Lanchang chronicles in 1564, with the roles of various cities altered. In the version in the Ayutthaya chronicles, Lanchang sent a missive asking for the hand of Princess Thepkasat, daughter of King Chakkaphat of Ayutthaya. As Ayutthaya was under pressure from Pegu and wanted Lanchang as an ally, Chakkaphat agreed, and invited Lanchang to send an escort to collect her. Thammaracha of Phitsanulok, who at this point was allied with Pegu, intercepted the party on the way back to Lanchang and captured the princess to present to the King of Pegu. Ayutthaya and Lanchang both sent armies with the aim of capturing Thammaracha and retrieving the princess. From this point, the story in the chronicles diverges from the version here. With help from Pegu, Phitsanulok defeated the Ayutthaya and Lanchang forces, and subsequently Phitsanulok and Pegu besieged and took Ayutthaya in 1569. The Lao version claims the original match between Lanchang and the princess was a consequence of a 1560 treaty of friendship between Lanchang and Ayutthaya recorded on an inscription found at Dansai in Loei province. (RCA, 49–56; Stuart-Fox, *Lao Kingdom*, 81)

2. ตาด, *tat*, from *tas* or *tash*, a Middle Eastern silk brocade, considered of high status and reserved for senior nobility. "The textile used in making supplementary patterning is made from flat metal strips of gold-plaited silver or gold-plaited copper or silver and silver-plaited copper" (Thirabhand, "Royal Brocades," 192; Chandra, "Costumes," 37; *Pha phim lai boran*, 82).

A *mahori* ensemble played a lullaby as beautiful as celestial music, while the king, upholder of the teachings, quietly pondered and daydreamed.

He had heard stories, spreading to cities far and wide, about the captivating beauty of Princess Soithong, who had just reached fifteen years, the blossoming age.

She was daughter of the King of Lanchang,[3] and so superlatively handsome that no other lady in a hundred and one cities could compare.

"How can I secure her as my partner in love to embrace tightly and keep by my side? Should I send a missive to the King of Lanchang to ask for her hand in the proper way?

Or should troops be dispatched to besiege her city and seize the princess? How should I get her, by good means or bad?"

He could not decide, and pondering over this problem plunged him into turmoil, unable to sleep during the night.

He lay with his hand flung across his forehead. "How can I arrange this romance? What will be the best tricks and tactics? I can't see the way to bring her here."

With nobody there to consult on the rights and wrongs, he agonized over the issue until he dozed off at the first watch and slept through to dawn.

The king rinsed his mouth and bathed his face. Carrying his splendid regal sword, he went out to the audience hall and commanded officials to call the nobles to audience immediately. Guards took the order, raised hands in salute, and ran off in all directions.

"Sir, please hurry to audience. I don't know how weighty is the matter at hand but the king will be angry if you arrive late so please don't delay."

The nobles arrived at the screens and peered in. The king's voice was so loud and fierce that their hair stood on end. They made obeisance together and crawled in with hearts pounding.

Inside they prostrated, and the king spoke immediately. "Now that you're all here, I want to hear your opinions so please speak out.

At present the King of Lanchang has a charming daughter called Soithong. How should I secure this princess? Should I compose a missive in a spirit of friendship to ask for her hand in the manner of royalty? Do you think this might be

---

3. "Million elephants," usually spelled Lan Xang when transliterated from Lao. The main territory of the Lao, and the forerunner of modern Laos. The capital was earlier at Luang Prabang, but moved to Vientiane in 1560, partly to facilitate relations with Ayutthaya.

refused? Or should troops be sent to besiege their city and seize her?

In my opinion, these are the alternatives. Whoever has a view, speak up immediately. Consult among yourselves on what's best."

The Lao lords and officials all made obeisance there and then, and conferred together on the king's request.

The Upahat[4] and senior officials came to an agreement, and the lesser officials gave their consent. All affixed their names to a document in order, and together presented their response to the king.

"I, Phya Maen, the Upahat, along with Saen Thao Krungkan,[5] the military commander, the mighty Phya Kanji, and all the senior officials are in agreement

on the issue that Your Majesty has raised over this princess of Lanchang. As she is also of royal lineage, it would be proper to make a request first.

This will be correct according to royal practice. If the request is refused, once that is known, then troops may be sent to besiege the capital and seize her.

None of the Lao countries and cities would express disapproval. A missive must be sent to ask for the hand of this charming princess."

Hearing his officers' address, the king slapped his thigh. "That's the nub of it! Prepare a missive along those lines in the style of royal friendship,

and send it along with golden flowers[6] and other articles of tribute. Arrange everything to arrive at their capital within one month. Don't delay. Go quickly."

The Upahat had the missive prepared on a sheet of gold, and had articles of tribute assembled.

The military commanders, Thao Krungkan and Saentri Phetkla,[7] were assigned to guard the tribute along with five hundred phrai and full equipment, including horses.

---

4. Northern version of *uparat*, the deputy king or viceroy. In Lanna under the Mengrai dynasty (1296–1558), the king usually appointed a capable son to this role. When Lanna subsequently fell under Burmese suzerainty, the title was occasionally applied to the Lanna rulers in their position as tributaries. In Vientiane and other Lao states, the three seniormost officials below the ruler were the *upahat*, *ratchawong*, and *ratchabut*. Generally these posts were occupied by sons or other relatives of the ruler. (Sarassawadee, *History of Lan Na*, 84, 112; Paitoon, "Social and Cultural History," 81–85)

5. The great lord of the black city.

6. See p. 169, note 10.

7. "Valiant diamond." Saentri is a rank, meaning roughly, of the hundred-thousand rank, third class.

When everything was ready, the commanders came to report to King Chiang In. After they had read out the contents of the missive, the king gave his approval and ordered them to depart at once.

Thao Krungkan and Saentri Phetkla made obeisance to take leave, mounted their horses, and hastened away with all the tribute.

They cracked the whip and made a fast pace without resting the horses. In the evening, they halted, lit fires, ate, and rode onward until the third watch, when they slept.

At five o'clock in the early dawn, they set off again. At midday, they halted the troops to steam rice. After eating, they remounted and continued their journey. Sleeping at night and setting off promptly each morning,

they reached the Lanchang customs post in ten days. There they presented a report to the officers of the post, who fed them and then escorted them to the city of Lanchang[8] in seven days.

On arrival, they dismounted and entered the city, guarding the tribute and missive. The Upahat and nobles[9] of Lanchang gathered at the front of the palace courtyard,

seated in state. The envoys from Chiang Mai made a report on the contents of their royal missive, and were promptly taken in for audience with the city's ruler.

Now to tell of the King of Lanchang, who resided in his holy palace, contented and untroubled, attended by consorts and palace ladies,

all excellent and numbering in thousands, on duty throughout the palace to fan and minister to the monarch. Those carrying the regalia were as dazzling in their beauty as ladies in the heavenly palace of Indra.

Around the monarch, their appearance was refreshing, and their fragrance uplifting. They wore their hair in chignon, entwined with flowers and fastened with a pin.

lady attendants with fans

---

8. Vientiane.

9. เพี้ยกวาน, *phia kwan*. *Phia* is an alternate spelling of Phya, lord. *Kwan* is an official title for a noble or village head used in the Lao states but never in Ayutthaya, so here employed to give some local color (SWN, 1:146).

arm elegantly bowed

They were clad in uppercloths woven in dazzling colors and rimmed with gold thread. They prostrated all around with charming faces that inspired love.

When they knelt in attendance, their arms were elegantly bowed,[10] and their lofty hairstyles matched the beauty of their faces. As the sun descended in the afternoon, the king went to bathe

in fragrant waters, and be dressed in royal garments infused with sweet scents. Arrayed in brilliant royal regalia, he proceeded to the audience hall

and sat on a nine-jeweled throne under a large and lofty tiered white umbrella.[11] He conducted the affairs of the capital, with palace officials presenting matters one after another.

The king beamed with pleasure. When all his courtiers were gathered together in audience, a wise and senior minister bowed in obeisance and spoke.

"My liege, my life is under the foot of the lord of power and creation. Whatever pleases or displeases[12] the lord upholder of the teachings. Today Chiang Mai has sent a missive,

brought by a royal envoy along with golden flowers and many articles of tribute that are under guard outside." He read the missive to the king.

"This royal missive states as follows. The mighty King of Chiang Mai, by name Chiang In, is paramount ruler over cities and territories,

and pillar of the populace of many millions. Every territory submits without opposition, and his power is feared by every locality and every country throughout the earth.

As for the city of Si Sattana Nakhanahut,[13] crown of the world, unrivalled in

---

10. They knelt on the ground, feet tucked behind them, leaning on one arm with the elbow slightly bowed inwards to make an elegant curve.

11. เศวตฉัตร, *sawettachat*, white royal umbrella or parasol, one of the symbols of royalty.

12. ควรมิควร (แล้วแต่จะโปรดฯ), *khuan mi khuan (laeo tae ja prot)*, "should, should not, (according to the king's favor)" an abbreviated version of a formula acknowledging the absoluteness of the royal power. In current Bangkok court practice, this formula is pronounced to conclude an address to royalty (Suwit, *Ratchasap*, 27–30).

13. Si Sattanakhanahut, a Pali rendering of Lanchang. In this name, *nak* means elephant while *sat* and *nahut* are numerals that together mean ten million so the Sanskrit is similar to *lan* (million) *chang* (elephants). Here in the original it appears in the abbreviated form Nakhanahut,

splendor, both cities enhance the earth and are equal in renown.

News has come to us of a princess who is beautiful, graceful, brilliant, of resplendent lineage, and suitable to be presented in marriage to a monarch.

Ten thousand other kings of a hundred other countries are unfitted to be partnered in happiness with such a royal lady. Unsuited in face, and in rank lower than dust, they would besmirch and belittle your royal authority.

Thus I solicit the hand of the princess, jewel of the eye, to be a royal lady of the right. Please grant the beauteous Soithong to be a servant of the foot[14] of King Chiang In.

If, once you have received this missive, you will grant this jewel of beauty to be a bridge of gold and silver to my capital,[15] our two cities will rejoice." Finishing the missive, the minister prostrated three times.

After listening, the King of Lanchang was furious. He stamped his foot loudly and roared, "Lords, listen, all of you.

He already has wives and children in abundance yet he has these intentions towards our tiny child. We all heard how arrogant he is. He sends this missive without thinking properly.

This king did not examine the situation first. It's laughable that he's so unafraid about people gossiping and criticizing how shameless he is to ask for my daughter."

Then the king said to the listening nobles, "His words do not respect my feelings. Send an army at once.

I will besiege the city of this Chiang In and annihilate him. As for the people who brought this missive, have their heads chopped off and stuck up in public."

He raised his sword as if to execute them himself, and angrily stamped his foot so loudly that the sound echoed round the audience hall. All the nobles and officials kept their faces down and mumbled prayers.

The Upahat prostrated and said, "Your Majesty, please stay your hand. Over the fact that the King of Chiang Mai sent this missive,

---

and later in the story is rendered as Si Sattana, Nak city, and other variants. For simplicity, all these subsequent mentions have been standardized as Si Sattana.

14. The king uses a term, บาทบริจา *batborija*, that literally means "a maidservant to please the royal foot." In this context it probably means a consort, not a high-ranking wife.

15. The idea of a "gold and silver" road or bridge connecting two realms was a staple of diplomatic language in the region. Perhaps it stemmed from an old ritual of mixing water from gold and silver bowls while negotiating a treaty of alliance, as in a 1563 treaty between Siam and Lanchang (Griswold and Prasert, *Epigraphic and Historical Studies*, 794).

do not get too angry. Envoys should not be executed. They are mere servants of whoever sent them, and every country would find this inappropriate.

The correct thing will be to order them to return to their city, and find a way to reply to the missive. Don't be indignant but reply in a judicious and moderate way that the princess is not yet suitable,

still young and not ready for marriage. Don't be aggressive and he'll accept your words, thinking we are not irredeemably opposed. Meanwhile begin amassing troops to attack him.

This Chiang Mai is piffling. He's like a firefly imitating the sun.[16] With just a finger, he can be smashed to dust. When we attack, success will come in an instant.

Let that be the duty of your humble servants. The nobles, officials, and military all agree. Do not allow any irritation to the sole of the royal foot. My liege, reply with such a missive."

The king listened to this reasoning and calmed down. "Have a missive prepared and return all the tribute.

As for the envoys, give them presents of money, food, white liquor, duck, chicken, and toasting spirit, and order them to return home."

The envoys bowed in obeisance to take leave and went out to a swordstore. They loaded all the goods on horses and set off. Pushing their steeds at a good pace

through the forest, they reached Chiang Mai in fifteen days along with the tribute and missive of reply. The lords were summoned immediately.

The tribute was placed at the front of the palace courtyard while all the courtiers entered into the audience hall at the appointed time.

When the king came to the audience hall, the nobles and officials prostrated. "My liege, Your Majesty, Lanchang has sent this reply.

In this missive, the King of Lanchang, father of the charming Soithong, acknowledges the missive brought from Chiang Mai asking for the hand of the beauteous princess.

The mighty King Chiang In desires our daughter, the gracious Soithong, the object of our highest concern, but this princess is only fifteen years old.

It is not yet seemly for her to marry and become an exalted queen of the first rank.[17] She is still a child who has not been apart from her mother for a

---

16. A proverb from the "Sayings of Phra Ruang" (Gerini, "On Siamese Proverbs," 204).

17. เอกอรรคราชมเหสี, *ekakharatcha mahesi*. In the Palatine Law clause 50, detailing the regalia

single night. In our opinion, this is not correct.

Every country will criticize, and we fear such reproach. The golden flowers and other presents are returned to King Chiang In.

Proceed gradually so no issue will arise. It is better not to make the Lao reproachful." Having read the reply to Chiang In, the official prostrated.

After hearing the royal missive, King Chiang In pondered. "The contents sound noble but they're subterfuge." He spoke out,

"We made our request in friendship in the proper way but he did not grant us his daughter. We'll now take troops and, if it comes to battle, we'll reduce them to dust.

We'll besiege their city, slash them dead, and bring Soithong back here." With these words, he went straight inside.

Now to tell of the King of Lanchang. He sat on his glittering crystal throne, still brooding angrily

over Chiang In's words. "This Chiang Mai king is very arrogant." As his anger persisted, he summoned the queen and asked her opinion.

"Chiang Mai has sent a missive asking for Soithong as a consort. I replied with a refusal, though done in the proper way.

I said our daughter is still a young child, and it's not fitting to arrange a marriage now. But if we ignore this matter, there'll be trouble. He'll come to besiege and attack our city.

My jewel, what do you think? The prestige of the Thai monarch is known far and wide. If we ask to depend on his protection, I think our plea will be well received. Don't they talk about the reputation of the King of Ayutthaya, upholder of the teachings,

and how his power extends in ten directions over all countries and languages?[18] If we present Soithong to him, and Chiang Mai ever attacks,

---

of royal consorts in hierarchical order, *akha(ra) mahesi*, "exalted queen," heads the list. Normally this title would be reserved for wives from the dynasty itself or other recognized ruling families, especially from tributary states. Here the title also has the prefix, *ek-*, meaning first. Chiang Mai had proposed only to make her a *batborija*, servant of the royal foot, a consort of significantly lower ranking. The concern for differentiating the status of queens dates from the late seventeenth and early eighteenth century (KTS, 1:132–33; Busakorn, "Ban Phlu Louang Dynasty," 155–57).

18. Up to the mid-nineteenth century, the conventional way to refer to different peoples was as people of different languages.

the Ayutthaya army will come to our aid. They won't leave us to die because their illustrious king is just. Tell me what you think."

Queen Keson[19] raised her clasped hands and bowed her head. She pondered the matter and then said, "I agree with what you say. There's a problem.

This King of Chiang Mai is headstrong, and too boldly overrates his own status, but there are no bad tidings about the King of Ayutthaya.

According to tradition, a tree dies because of its own fruit.[20] We raised Soithong to be someone of substance. A royal missive must be sent to offer her to Ayutthaya.

Ask them to come here to receive the princess and to arrange the marriage. If we sit on this matter, there'll be trouble. I think your idea is correct."

The king, ruler of the world, paramount of Lanchang, smiled and laughed merrily at her agreement. He promptly went to the portico out front,

and gave orders for the Upahat, senior officials, and all officers to come to audience. After they made obeisance, he commanded them to arrange articles of tribute,

and to inscribe a sheet of gold with two matters. "One, that we present our first-ranked princess to seek the bo-tree shelter of the accumulated merit of the Thai monarch,[21]

because King Chiang In sent a missive asking for her hand but we declined. Two, that these articles of tribute are presented to the King of Ayutthaya."

Officials took the orders and hastened away. They arranged a great many articles of tribute and a gold sheet inscribed with the missive, along with elephants, horses, and troops.

When all was ready, they attended on the king, ruler of the world, paramount of the Lanchang capital, who commanded that the tribute should go immediately to Ayutthaya.

The senior officers made obeisance to take leave, and crawled back out. They boarded a boat and crossed the river to the main landing at Pak Mong.[22]

There they mounted horses and hurried through forest, over hill, and across

---

19. เกสร, pollen or stamens of a flower.

20. A saying meaning that parents are prepared to sacrifice themselves for their child, even to death, in the same way that certain plants die after giving fruit.

21. See p. 19, note 86.

22. Now Ban Nam Mong, slightly downstream from Vientiane on the opposite bank in Amphoe Tha Pho (see map 5).

plain to the customs post at San Hill,[23]

where they halted the horses and let them graze and overcome their fatigue. In a sluggish wind, they remounted to journey onward. At midday, they stopped to sleep in the forest, then continued past Sam Mo[24]

to the Chi River,[25] then further through the forest, spurring the horses and cracking their whips, to the customs outpost for the territory of Khorat.[26] They entered the outpost to find Muen Wai,

and informed him about the royal missive. The officials from the outpost escorted them straight down to Khorat where they tethered the horses to rest and entered the city.

The Lao went up into the central sala and made a report to the local officials. They and the tribute were placed under guard.

The governor arranged for them to be lodged, looked after, and fed with rice, savory, sweets, water, and liquor to their satisfaction.

Understanding the content of the missive, the governor of Khorat[27] and local officials promptly wrote a report, and commanded some Thai from there to carry it down.

The report conveyed the contents of the missive, adding that many Lao nobles, officials, and men had arrived bringing golden flowers and other tribute to present to the King of Ayutthaya.

A deputy commissioner[28] was assigned to carry the report. He prepared phrai, servants, swords, pikes, and well-bred horses, then set off through the forest.

---

23. The Khao San gap, 60 kms southwest of Vientiane, is a narrow pass through a steep ridge that divides the Mekong Plain from the valley of the Chi River. Khao San appears as a customs post on the early Bangkok maps (Santanee and Stott, *Royal Siamese Maps*, 131; see map 5).

24. Now Chong Sam Mo in Amphoe Khon Sawan, Chaiyaphum, slightly north of the Chi River. Here there is a narrow pass through a ridge. According to an old history of Vientiane, the Lao territory of Jao Anou extended "to Sam Moo, frontier of Khon Lat [Khorat]" (Mayoury and Pheuiphanh, *Paths*, 145, 197; see map 5).

25. Given here as ลำพาชี, *lam phachi*, horse river. Perhaps this reflected a Bangkok belief that this was the derivation of the river's name but that belief appears faulty.

26. It seems the frontier between Lanchang and Ayutthaya territory was between Khorat and the Chi River. There are two villages, Dan Khla and Dan Jak, which were probably old customs posts, ด่าน, *dan*, on their possible route, both around 24 kms north of Khorat.

27. Khorat or Nakhon Ratchasima, city of the royal boundary, was secured by Ayutthaya during the Narai reign (1656–1688) as a strategic outpost for expeditions against Cambodia, and as a collection point for forest goods destined for export. It was a first-class town, and its governor was Okya/Phraya Kamhaeng Songkhram, *sakdina* 10,000 (KTS, 1:320).

28. รองปลัด, *rong palat*, an assistant deputy-governor.

They passed Phu Khao Lat, Sung Noen, and Khok Phya,[29] then dismounted to rest the tired horses. In the afternoon, they remounted,

crossed the Khuenlan Hill,[30] galloped ahead to the Dong Phya Fai,[31] and in five nights reached Kaeng Khoi.[32]

In the evening they bathed and ate, and at dawn mounted and continued at a gallop. In six nights and seven days[33] they reached the capital,

delivered the report to a duty officer at Mahatthai, and explained its contents in detail. The duty officer escorted them to inform Phraya Jakri about the contents of the report from Khorat.

The nobles discussed the report and the fact that Lanchang wished to present tribute. Then all went to attend on the king.

The king, crown of the city, resided in a glittering crystal palace, in a state of superlative bliss

and perfect contentment, surrounded by ten thousand consorts of exquisite beauty who presented their faces and attended on the monarch.

Arrayed in magnificent raiment, with a shimmering diamond crown on his head, ornaments of gems and gold hanging on his breast, and a short sword in hand, the king walked forth.

Guards unbolted the door. Horns were blown. Gong, drum, *shenai*, Khaek drum, and Java flute played brightly. Nobles bustled about in alarm.

Chaophraya and phraya took up their positions. Lesser people sat hidden behind screens, hushing one another to silence. Some trembled, bowed their faces, and prayed.

The curtain was swept aside. Nobles prostrated, their hearts fluttering as if singed by the Lord of Darkness. When

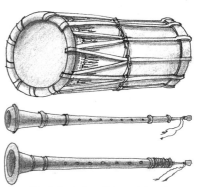

Khaek drum, Java flute, and shenai

29. Phu Khao Lat is now on the northwestern edge of Khorat city; Sung Noen is 25 kms to the west along the Mun River; and Khok Phya is a village in Amphoe Sung Noen (see map 5).

30. Now at the eastern tip of the Lamtakong reservoir (see map 5).

31. The forest-clad escarpment separating the Khorat Plateau from the Chaophraya Plain. The name can be translated as "forest of the lord of fire," alluding to its reputation for malaria and other forest fevers (see map 5).

32. At the foot of the escarpment, on the Pasak River, now a congregation of cement factories (see map 5).

33. This would be the total time from Khorat to Ayutthaya, a distance of about 220 kms.

the king spoke, they saw he was in good humor, and they relaxed somewhat. Those with important business addressed him.

"The rains and the river flow are good." "The first and second crops of rice are plentiful." "The people are happy every day." The king laughed heartily at these reports.

Chaophraya Jakri[34] addressed the king. "May I beg royal blessing on my head. A report has come from Khorat that some Lao have arrived there from the forest.

They are servants of the King of Lanchang bearing a missive to present a princess, and a great quantity of tribute. They are being held at Khorat.

This is the report that has come from Khorat to inform the foot of King Phanwasa, upholder of the teachings."

Ratchasi seal of Mahatthai

The king, paramount ruler of the world, was supremely pleased. He turned to ask his senior officials what they thought about this.

"A foreign city has come to present a princess. Do you think this is genuine or a military stratagem that should arouse our suspicion? Whoever has an opinion, speak."

The nobles bowed with clasped hands and replied that Lanchang's approach on this occasion

did not seem to be underhand. The princess was presented in the hope of being able to depend on the king's illustrious merit. Hence the Lao should be escorted down.

The king agreed and laughed jovially. "Heigh! Palace guards, go up to Khorat at once

to receive the envoy carrying the missive, all the troops, the tribute, gold salvers, and everything. Prepare good boats to transport them."

Jamuen Ratchamat[35] crawled back out to organize the boats. Oarsmen boarded and rowed off.

---

34. The text calls him Chaophraya Ratchasi, part of his official title and the name of the mythical lion on the Mahatthai ministry's seal (KW, 321–22; KTS, 1:174–76).

35. *Palat* (deputy) of the left division of the department of the palace guard, *sakdina* 800 (KTS, 1:284; KW, 324).

In one night they arrived at Rap Landing.[36] Conscript porters landed with their shoulder poles, and walked through the forest, reaching Khorat in five nights.

When they presented their sealed order and explained its contents, the local officials bustled about in noisy confusion to assemble the tribute. They set off by elephant and horse

to the landing where they boarded boats. The troops rowed nonstop, urging one another to hurry, and reached the city in one night.

As soon as the boats moored, the royal missive was invited[37] to be placed on a ceremonial salver, and borne along in procession with drums sounding loudly and people crowding around noisily.

At the palace, the missive was invited up to the hall where a scribe received it and passed it on to senior officials for translation into Thai, with each point copied.[38]

The envoys were lodged, and fed each day with a feast of duck, chicken, and white toasting spirit, all provided by the king.

The almighty king, ruler of the joyful abode of Ayutthaya, proceeded out to the front. All government officers entered

and made obeisance to the foot of the supreme ruler. All the many courtiers who usually attended audience were present according to their position.

Chaophraya Jakri raised his hands pressed together above his head, and addressed the king. "My life is under the royal foot.

As to the royal order to go to Khorat, Jamuen Ratchamat and his troops went to escort the envoy, tribute, and royal missive to Ayutthaya.

They have been lodged, fed, and looked after. I will now report under the foot of the king, upholder of the teachings, on the contents of the royal missive."

"In the missive, the King of Wiang,[39] ruler over the royal wealth of the city of Si Sattana, upholder of truth and religion, pays respect to the King of Ayutthaya,

---

36. Flat Landing, in Ton Than village, Amphoe Sao Hai, just west of Saraburi on the bank of the Pasak River (see map 5).

37. In the custom of such embassies, the missive is treated with the same respect that would be shown to its author, in this case, the King of Lanchang.

38. The official translation hall, หอแปลพระราชสาส์น, *ho plae phraratchasan*, was on the eastern side of the palace opposite Wat Thammikarat (see area 1 on map 9; KW, 324; KLW, 200; APA, 65).

39. เวียงจันท์, *wiangjan*, "city of the moon," Vientiane. In 1695, the King of Vientiane offered a daughter to the King of Ayutthaya in order to gain Ayutthaya's military aid against Luang Prabang. The missive on that occasion, has many similarities to this one (RCA, 363).

the great, who resides under a tiered white umbrella loftier than that of any monarch in all directions. He begs to present tribute of gold to the king of the capital of Si Ayutthaya,

who has such renown that every country quails and submits, who protects the mass of the populace and soldiery so they are joyful,

who upholds the Ten Royal Virtues, and who governs with justice and honesty. As the King of Lanchang wishes to request the protection of your royal power until his dying day,

he begs to offer his daughter as a servant to the royal foot of the great and glorious king, descendant of a brilliant royal line. Your humble servant pays homage.

The princess has not yet been sent as it is not wished that she pass through the forest for fear that she may be seized by brigands and lost completely.

It is requested that troops from Ayutthaya escort the princess so there will be no danger of her being waylaid in the forest.

Also it will convey great honor, which will spread by word of mouth to other cities to north and south, that the Thai city went to receive the princess.

If this is not to the royal liking, reply to this missive accordingly. We beg to entrust our daughter and ourselves to you until death.

This matter is not a military stratagem. Do not be wary and suspicious. We have spoken as a king and will not go back on our word." Each point was read aloud to inform the king.

The monarch of the holy city and royal domain of Ayutthaya immediately ordered that preparations be made to receive official guests.

"Conscript soldiers and militiamen, both front and rear. Prepare the palace and set up regalia. Harness the elephants and horses which dignify the city." The king walked back inside the palace.[40]

Palace officials quickly went off with the king's commands. Duty officers wrote out orders. "Raise conscripts according to official position as previously.

---

40. The description of the reception of the envoy has many close parallels with the account of the reception of an envoy from Tavoy in 1791 in the chronicle of the Bangkok First Reign, leading to speculation that the author was a noble present at that event. In 1791, Tavoy sought the protection of Ayutthaya and presented a princess and tribute in exactly the same way as this account. The envoy was halted at Kanchanaburi while a message was sent ahead, in the same way this embassy is halted at Khorat. The procedure and officials involved are very similar (KW, 323; Flood and Flood, *Dynastic Chronicles*, 1:176–82).

Requisition bows, bucklers, shields, lances, and spears according to the procedure of the left and right divisions of sentinels.[41] Have everyone send their attendants. Be ready by dawn tomorrow."

The military units, all carrying weapons and furnished with martial equipment of various types, were drawn up in close formation according to custom.

The archery unit wore leggings and helmets wound with cloth. The palace watch[42] sat in a row carrying shields, some with swords slung over their shoulders on a length of patterned cloth.

The spear unit carried their weapons and looked skilled. Many well-built phrai, drilled in bearing firearms, sat in ranks wearing red shirts and red helmets, some carrying bucklers.

Phrai of impressively solid physique, drilled in the Farang way, sat in groups wearing the appropriate shirts and helmets, each carrying a gun with a bayonet.

Bands with victory drum, horn, and conch wore striped leggings and hats of a distinctive type. Large numbers of people, segregated into different groups, lined the route.

In the audience hall, carpets were laid, smart new screens and curtains were provided, and lofty regalia[43] were installed in front of the curtains, including three-tiered umbrellas spaced in rows.

lofty regalia

The various articles of tribute were set out in front of the screens. Places for the official guests were arranged according to rank directly in front of the royal throne.

Pages and palace officials crowded in, dressed in finery. All the nobles entered and arranged themselves according to rank as usual,

wearing sompak and embroidered robes, with golden salvers and caskets placed in front of them. The four-pillar ministers of capital, palace, treasury,

---

41. กะลาบาต, *kalabat*, a division of the guard defined as those who stand watch by the lamps, with a duty to stand posted along the routes of royal processions (CK, 42; KW, 679).

42. See p. 30, note 39.

43. เครื่องสูง, *khrueang sung*, a category of regalia including banners and ceremonial umbrellas on tall poles (listed in Suwit, *Ratchasap*, 156).

and lands entered with the left and right divisions of the palace guard.

Khaek and Farang filed in dressed in turbans, tailored shirts tucked in the waist, and sashes over inner belts. Their presence was an honor to the city.

Ten thousand gallant, robust, and battle-hardened troops were arrayed in columns. In the middle of the courtyard, pavilions were set up for standing elephants and many fine royal horses.

Sentinels were seated at front and rear. The fore-part of the main courtyard overflowed with Khaek, Farang, Chinese, and Cham,[44] arrayed according to royal command.

Khaek

The king, ruler of the world, paramount above monarchs of all other territories, went to bathe in the flowing waters of the stream of the golden lotus.

After washing away all dirt and dust, he was anointed with fragrant scents, and attired in a yok with a flying *kanok* pattern and Garuda clenching in his beak a naga that wound round his body, and a robe with an elegant pattern of intertwined vines, dazzlingly embroidered in gold, with vine flowers done in floating appliqué.[45]

He held a great regal sword named Diamond Heart[46] with a twined and tasseled sash, and a handle embellished with many magnificently glittering jewels.

Farang

---

44. Descendants of the people of the Champa Empire in central Vietnam from the seventh to fifteenth century CE. Originally Hindu, most subsequently converted to Islam. Under pressure from the Khmer and Vietnamese, many groups of Cham migrated to Siam, and others were seized as war prisoners, especially in the early Bangkok era. There are still communities of Cham resident in central Bangkok.

45. ฉลุดอกลอย, *chalu dok loi*, "floating flowers," embroidery cut so the flowers "float" above the surface of the fabric.

46. พระแสงองค์ใหญ่ใจเพชร, *phrasaeng ong yai jai phet*, a regalia sword that is mentioned in an elaborate account of the coronation of King Ekathat in 1758. It also appears in Bangkok-era accounts of royal weaponry as a secondary regalia sword, part of a set called *phrasaeng rai tin thong*, used in processions and in the water-oath ceremony. (KLW, 136; KW, 326; *Phrasaeng ratchasastra*, 32–34; *Rueang mahatlek*, 69–70)

He went through a passage-way[47] to the throne hall which was decorated with shimmering crystal and gold. Victory drum, horn, and conch waited in line. A head drummer beat to announce the king's entry. Curtain attendants pulled back the curtain.

palace passageway

The crowd of nobles trembled. Luang Ratchamanu[48] raised the insignia of golden flowers. Horn and conch played loudly.

All the officials bowed and prostrated in obeisance. The king immediately sent for the official guests.[49]

Phra Ammat[50] passed the royal order to Jamuen Ratchaban[51] to fetch the guests. Palace guards rushed off, and attendants brought them into audience.

insignia of golden flowers

---

47. มุขกระสัน, muk-krasan, an enclosed passageway connecting two buildings in a palace complex (KW, 679; CK, 387). The king entered the audience hall from the western end.

48. Head of the department of victory drums, sakdina 1,000 (KTS, 1:300; KW, 327). The insignia of the golden flowers is a representation of a bunch of flowers in gold on the end of a staff, carried ahead of the king to announce his arrival. A twin officer, Thepmanu, had the duty to raise a silver version. In the Khamhaikan chao krung kao, these two are described as "officers to receive envoys" (Prachak, Prapheni, 202; SB, 314–15; KCK, 226).

49. This scene closely resembles historical accounts of the reception of envoys at Ayutthaya. The building used for such receptions was the Sanphet Mahaprasat, built by King Trailokanat at the start of his reign in 1448. The plinth of this audience hall still exists, but nothing else. In Tachard's description of the reception of French ambassadors in 1688, probably in this hall, the envoys walked through the outer courtyards, drawn up with troops, horses, and elephants in all their finery. Immediately outside the audience hall were lesser officials, kneeling on mats or carpets. Around fifty senior nobles were inside the audience hall. The envoy's presents were placed at the front. The king appeared at a window, raised "seven or eight foot" higher than the hall, to the sound of "Trumpets, Drums, and many other Instruments" (Tachard, Voyage to Siam, 161–68; see also La Loubère, New Historical Relation, 109 and 111, 113 for a sketch of the interior of the audience hall; Choisy, Journal, 160–62; Forbin, Siamese Memoirs, 51–54; and Kaempfer, Description, 45 for the entry route; KLW, 202; Boranasathan, 1: 229–30).

50. อำมาตย์, ammat, probably Luang Maha-ammatyathibodi, sakdina 3,000, a senior post in Mahatthai with responsibility for the north, including the recruitment of phrai (KTS, 1:184, 225; KW, 327; Sirindhorn, Banthuek, 5).

51. A deputy of the left department of the outer guard, sakdina 800 (KTS, 1:290; KW, 327).

Arrayed in front of the throne in order of rank, they all made obeisance, raising their clasped and trembling hands, while prostrating to pay respect.

Luang Ratchanikun[52] addressed the king. "My liege, upholder of the teachings, over my head, the envoys have come to attend on the footsoles of Your Majesty."

The almighty king looked around to see the envoys making obeisance, along with the golden tribute,

and said, "How many days did you travel through the dense forest to reach the city, and was the journey easy or hard?

At Si Sattana, is the rice season good, or is drought making rice troublingly expensive, and are enemies to the north and south satisfactorily quiet?

Are things well in Vientiane and is its king healthy and content, untroubled by disease?"[53]

The envoys responded, "My liege, Your Majesty, the journey here took forty days and was comfortable. Our city is happy and untroubled.

The first and second crops of rice are excellent, with no cause for shortage. Neither army nor enemy has approached the city.

The king, upholder of the teachings, ruler of the city, whose power spreads in all directions, is constantly happy and untroubled by disease."

The king was pleased by these answers. He made gifts of clothing and good silk, and ordered pleasant lodgings.

Seven days later, all the officials again gathered to make obeisance, and the king commanded the envoys to return home. "Conscript five hundred men immediately.

Phra Thainam[54] will lead the escort. Prepare reciprocal presents of colored silk, silver, gold, other valuables, and a royal cow elephant with a gold-roofed howdah.

---

52. Khun Ratchanikun Nityaphakdi, *palat thun chalong thoe sakdi* in Mahatthai. A *palat thun chalong*, ปลัดทูลฉลอง, literally an officer who can address the king, was the immediate deputy to a full minister with the duty to attend audience in the minister's stead. In the 1791 Tavoy embassy (see p. 506, note 40 above), this same official read the embassy's missive (KTS, 1:224; KW, 327; Sirindhorn, *Banthuek*, 3–4).

53. This is a diplomatic formula known as พระราชปฏิสันถารสามนัด, *phraratchapatisanthan sam nat*, the three royal greetings—asking after the journey, the situation in the envoy's country, and the health of the envoy's ruler. The three positive responses are likewise a formula (KW, 328).

54. Along with Phraya Decho, one of the two military commanders in Kalahom, each with a *sakdina* of 10,000 on par with Kalahom himself, in command of the six militia units. His full title was Okphya Siharat Dechachai Thainam (KTS, 1:280; KP, 254; KW, 329; SB, 306).

howdah

Prepare a missive on gold with no dreary mistakes in wording. Take pikes, lances, javelins, and golden spears to guard against danger."

Officials took the orders and backed out of the audience. They arranged many phrai and militiamen, excellent and glittering articles of tribute, magnificent elephants and horses, fine gems, pikes, lances, javelins, and guns. They also prepared the royal missive. After attending on the king, they were commanded to depart.

The envoy, Phra Thainam, led the troops out of the capital with crowds of elephants and horses amid a noisy tumult from gunfire and hollering.

At dusk, they drove in spikes to set up camp and dragged logs from the forest to make fires. From morning to evening, they traveled without rest, reaching their destination in one month and ten days.[55]

On the riverbank at Phan Phrao[56] opposite the city of Si Sattana, they halted the troops and sent Phya Suwannabat ahead.

He greeted the Upahat and local officials, and informed them of their arrival from the southern city. The king and all the courtiers convened in the audience hall immediately.

When the almighty king looked around and saw Phya Suwannabat, his face lit up like the moon shining in the sky.

"You went down to the southern city. Tell me quickly what happened. Is the King of Ayutthaya's reply good or bad?"

Phya Suwannabat made obeisance. "The king of the Thai city of Ayutthaya asked after Your Majesty's royal foot,

and gave presents including a great deal of clothing and fine silk. He sent Phra Thainam with troops to present tribute and receive the princess."

For the king, the Phya's confident address was like celestial waters. He

---

55. The distance by road today is 580 kms.

56. Across the Mekong River from Vientiane in Amphoe Si Chiangmai. On early nineteenth-century maps, it is marked as Mueang Phan Phao (Santanee and Stott, *Royal Siamese Maps*, 131, 137; see map 5).

ordered officers to erect a pavilion beside the sala

to receive Phra Thainam and the many troops brought with him. He specially commanded that the troops from the Thai capital be well fed and looked after.

He turned to command the Upahat to arrange the reception of the southern envoys, then went into the elegant and sumptuous inner palace.

Officials called up both the main guard and royal phrai to erect the pavilion ordered by the king within three nights.

The Upahat issued notices to commandeer a large number of boats and conscript oarsmen for crossing to the other side of the river. Arriving at Phan Phrao, he went straight in

to invite Phra Thainam to bring all his officers and men. They arrived at the palace, lodged in the pavilion, and were fed by royal cooks.

They ate in groups, waited on by Lao who brought sticky broken rice to ease their aching legs and backs,[57] five or six chili dips, *namya* fish curry with *khanom jin* noodles,

and chili paste with *makhaen*[58] fruit and Mekong giant catfish roe. "We wanted to make it spicy. Is there any problem?" After eating, they were escorted to the pavilion for official guests.

tattooed legs

The King of Lanchang was bathed, attired, and proceeded to the elegant audience hall which was packed with officials in attendance.

He sent for Phra Thainam. Lao guards with tattooed legs ran off and said, "Sir, we invite you to the audience hall."

Phra Thainam ordered his men to carry the tribute over. He entered the audience of the ruler of Vientiane, presented his missive, and made obeisance.

Senior officials received the missive, unfolded it, and read it out. "In this royal missive, the King of Ayutthaya,

who lives under a tiered white umbrella in a radi-

---

57. Among the Lua of Nan, broken rice is believed to be healthier (information from Chonthira Satyawadhana). Perhaps there is an old belief in the special efficacy of sticky rice with broken grains.

58. หมากมาด, *makmat*, better known as มะแข่น, *makhaen*, *Zanthoxylum budrunga*, a tree with green-brown berry-like fruits used in cooking.

ant holy golden palace, has learned that the city of Si Sattana wishes to present a beauteous princess.

The king will take great pleasure to be joined in matrimony with her as an exalted queen.[59] He sends for the princess to be escorted down."

After the missive was read, the Lao nobles bowed and raised their clasped hands to pay respect. Phra Thainam addressed the king. "As to this tribute of many types,

I am under royal command to present under the foot of the royal lord protector." He paid respect and waited for the king's response.

The King of Si Sattana was well pleased, and so said to Phra Thainam, "In fifteen days, we shall send the princess down."

He left the audience hall of royal victory. Phra Thainam paid respect, took leave, and went to stay in the lodging with his troops.

---

59. The missive employs the term อรรคมเหษี, *akkamahesi* (see p. 499, note 17 above).

26: THE KING OF CHIANG MAI SEIZES SOITHONG

Now to tell of the King of Chiang Mai. Pondering over the King of Lanchang's reply, he wondered whether it was straightforward, and suspected some trickery.

"We sent to ask for Soithong's hand but he did not say whether he agreed or not. He only replied that his daughter is still a child. And he returned the tribute.

When someone asks for a lady's hand, the response should be clear. Replying in this misleading fashion suggests there's subterfuge of some kind.

He's afraid we'll turn into an enemy, and he won't be able to resist if we attack, so he's thought up some underhand plot. Sitting on this will achieve nothing."

With these thoughts, he gave orders to Kwan Mahabat. "You're smart and daring. Without delay, go under cover to Lanchang and investigate what's going on—

what are their thoughts on political matters, how are things in the palace, and has anyone else made contact to ask for the hand of their beautiful princess."

Kwan Mahabat prostrated to take leave of the king forthwith. He dressed, put some crisped rice in a waist pouch, harnessed a horse,

and left Chiang Mai at the break of dawn. He galloped through the forest without stopping, eating handfuls of rice on the way.

After traveling from morning until around midday, he rested the horse, then set off again in the late afternoon, and galloped through the moonlit night, striking a flint to smoke tobacco while still in the saddle.

When the horse tired, he gave it a rest and a drink of water. Once the fatigue lifted,

forest hunter

514

he thundered ahead until the moon went down, and then slept beside the way. At first light, he mounted and hurried onward.

Slipping through the forest, he met no one, not even hunters. He kept to the banks of streams and fringes of woods, avoiding all villages along the way.

He entered the territory of Vientiane. Two days before reaching the river landing,[1] he learned from a Lawa village that Ayutthaya people had come to the capital.

Mahabat stopped to think. "I have to hear things firsthand." He dressed himself like a Thai, and went into Vientiane.

He walked along amid Lao and southerners without fear of anyone in the city, listening to what officials were saying. He arrived at the inner official sala

and saw a big pavilion, nineteen rooms long, with people and goods coming and going. The people spoke Thai and were obviously from Ayutthaya.

Also there were many Lanchang nobles and officials milling around, talking about the Thai coming to their capital

to escort a princess down to the southern city to be queen of its ruler. Having got the news that she would leave in fifteen nights, Mahabat set off home.

In seven days he galloped to Chiang Mai,[2] dismounted, entered the front of the audience hall, prostrated elegantly three times, and addressed the king. "I have been to Vientiane.

I went to the official sala and saw lords and nobles milling around. There were many Thai in the city, and rumors everywhere

that five hundred Ayutthaya soldiers had come and were waiting to collect Soithong and escort her to Ayutthaya in fifteen nights' time."

The King of Chiang Mai raged like the sky on fire. "Mm! The King of Si Sattana is playing around perfidiously with no fear of me.

I asked for the hand of the princess properly. He did not grant her to me and secretly contacted the Thai to come up. Fine! Let's see what happens. I'll not have an enemy show contempt for me.

Heigh! Conscript an army immediately. Select about five hundred thousand brave troops. I'll march this army into their territory to take revenge on the King of Si Sattana.

I'll attack the city of Lanchang and leave not even one blade of grass standing." The king's rage echoed around the audience hall, alarming the lords in audience.

---

1. Presumably Phan Phrao on the Mekong opposite Vientiane, as in the previous chapter.
2. The distance by modern roads is around 820 kms.

Two senior officials, Phraya Maen the Upahat, and Saentri Phetkla, promptly bowed and addressed the king. "My liege, by your grace.

The way to Lanchang is very long. An army of phrai cannot be organized to march and besiege the city of Lanchang in time before the princess leaves.

As Phya Mahabat said, they are about to depart for the southern city. If we want to bring the princess here, an army must leave at once

to intercept and ambush them along their route. We should be able to capture the Thai and Vientiane Lao people, and bring the princess to our city."

The King of Chiang Mai greatly appreciated this response. "Raise an army immediately. Saentri Phetkla will be in command.

Intercept them, ambush them, and bring them here. Don't kill their troops as it may upset Soithong. Go quickly."

Saentri Phetkla took the order and made obeisance three times. Five thousand soldiers were selected, all brave, invulnerable, and equipped with knowledge.

Guns, crossbows, spears, elephants, and horses were prepared. At the first light of the sun, the army set off,

and quick-marched through the great forest, skirting the high hills, to Phu Wiang.[3] Knowing for certain the princess would take this route, they halted the army and set up an ambush beside the hill.

Saentri Phetkla ordered the soldiers, "Don't go around the villages looking for bananas and sugarcane. When the Thai army approaches, we'll get wind of them. Wait to hear a gunshot as the signal.

Split up into detachments of eighty. Creep up to surround them. Capture them alive, don't chop them dead." The soldiers hid in the forest.

≼

Now to tell of the King of Lanchang. As the day approached for his daughter to leave, he could not stay still. He went to the audience hall to oversee all the preparations.

He ordered a militia brigade as escort under the command of Kueng Kamkong, a royal retainer, and assigned the lords, chiefs, and heads of ministries to make the arrangements.

All had to be ready at dawn on the day of departure—lady attendants from

---

3. ภูเวียง, "circle hill," a site discovered in the eighteenth century by a hunter from Vientiane, and established as a border outpost, now an amphoe in the northwest of Khon Kaen province. A circular ridge of hills encloses an oval plain of around 10 kms' diameter with an exit to the east (SWI, 10:3400–3402; see map 5).

the palace, guards, doctors and masseurs in various posts, and militia units to be placed at the front, rear, and throughout the column.

The king told the queen, "My jewel, you take care of ordering the attendants from the inner palace to prepare the princess for her journey."

Queen Keson came to the residence of the princess with tears streaming from her eyes. She embraced her daughter and gave her instructions.

"Oh my Soithong,[4] Father is sending you to the southern city. In three days you will leave, my darling, and your mother's heart will break from sadness.

Being parted from my precious daughter is like dying. From now on, I'll be deeply distressed. Nobody is like one's own beloved child. Sending you away is like gouging out my eye.

We're accustomed to seeing each other every morning and evening. Just the sight of you lifts my spirits with love. Since your birth, we've never been separated, and we've shared our happiness every day.

When I carried you in my womb, I cared for you with love, went without spicy food, kept to the precepts, and prayed all the time.

By the time I gave birth, my jewel, I'd already been carrying you, and had to cradle you from then on. You suckled your mother's milk every day until you'd grown up many years.

From now on, I'll be out of your sight, as if both your eyes had been struck blind. If I could, I'd go with you." She grieved at her loss.

The beautiful Soithong embraced her mother's feet, sobbing. "It's a pity Father does not care that I'll be parted from your breast.

Being forced to go is heart-rending. I'll probably lose my life in the forest. How can I reach Ayutthaya when my heart feels so completely bruised?

Since birth, I've not been separated from you. Who else can I turn to? I'm going to be terribly sad, and I'll probably die.

Oh, I was born to have ill fortune, to suffer miserably. You and Father cherish me like your own hearts but we're parted in the blink of an eye.

I had hoped to make you and Father happy but it turns out I'm the cause of your suffering. The country was splendidly content but I was born to be a demon of destruction.

I am the cause of so much grief, gloom, and turmoil for the whole city. Why should I stay alive?

---

4. In this speech in the Wat Ko version, the queen says: When you were born, someone came to present a golden chain, and hence you were given the name Soithong. (WK, 21:824)

Mother, please tell Father to have me slashed dead to remove the cause of these troubles." Soithong sobbed on and on.

Queen Keson put her arms round her daughter to console her. "Don't be too upset, my dear child. It's not that your father doesn't love you.

The King of Chiang Mai asked for your hand in a manner he found high-handed and threatening—as if we were his vassal. Your father thought this slighted our honor, and so did not give his consent.

His refusal means the King of Chiang Mai will be angry, and will bring an army to attack and humiliate our city. Our cityfolk fear that if war breaks out, it will bring defeat.

We'll lose our beloved daughter, our honor, and our capital. And if the city falls, the common people will suffer becoming war prisoners.

Affairs of state can create this much trouble and strife, my darling. Were it not for this, we'd never let you be parted from us.

But you alone can release your parents from this suffering, like a junk carrying us across a great ocean. The common people, too, will be freed from danger all because of you, my beloved daughter.

The King of Ayutthaya has the power to conquer all three worlds. That you should become his loyal servant befits our status and rank.

This king is considerate. He sent word with his royal retainers that he'll look after you and make sure nobody can impugn your honor.

Moreover, he won't allow anyone to browbeat Si Sattana. Go, eye's jewel. Don't be reluctant. This is a way to repay your parents' kindness.

Your reputation will spread across the world. Sorrow will give way to joy, and you'll be happy every night and day. Don't grieve and feel wronged."

The queen soothed away her daughter's sorrow, and arranged articles to go with her. She summoned the princess's four maids to help select what was needed.

A queen's regalia. Glittering jewelry. A crown of shining crystal, diamonds, and gold. Earrings and necklaces. Breast chains and *banphap* pendants.

Sets of hairpins. Bracelets. Sparkling rings encrusted with gems. Several sets of sapphire and zircon. Every kind of jewelry.

Next they selected clothing: everything for nightwear, yok embroidered with gold, and various silks of good quality.

Then gold and silver vessels for dining, perfume sets, golden bowls, betel boxes—all the objects that the queen liked, she gave to her beloved daughter.

hairpin

Female attendants were chosen from among those who had good appearance and status, who were already on intimate terms, and who were loyally committed to serve the princess.

In all, thirty-five ladies were selected, headed by four maids, with royal retainers of the second rank below them, and many slaves and sentinelles.[5]

Ladies-in-waiting on service in the palace were summoned for several to be selected. One of the maids was appointed superintendent in charge of a detachment of male attendants.

sentinelles

The queen organized all these matters, including the distribution of money as allowances to all the persons going, so that none of them should feel aggrieved.

When the arrangements were complete, the queen returned to lamenting over her dear daughter's departure. She summoned Soithong and her maids to her inner room,

hugged her daughter to her trembling chest, and gave instructions. "You're leaving the palace to go to the southern city. You will be among the Thai and must be careful, my beloved child.[6]

You must study the customs of the southern country and learn to understand them. The women you'll meet will be important people in the palace.

Show your respect to those you should respect. Don't turn your back on those you should be friendly and intimate with. Don't be heartless so people dislike you, but don't make the mistake of befriending those who are worthless.

Such people tend to poke their noses in your affairs and curry favor with various ruses. As soon as you fall for such a person, they turn round and take your property by the armful.

---

5. โขลนจ่า, *khlon-ja*. *Khlon* were female guards for the gates of the inner palace, and *khlon-ja* was an officer of this guard (PAL, 298). The term sentinelle is an invention.

6. This speech does not appear in the Wat Ko version, suggesting it was inserted in the mid-nineteenth century. The instructions recall manuals of etiquette that were a popular literary form of the mid-nineteenth century. They also reflect a view of monarchy as somehow intrinsically different ("solar lineage"). This ideology had been absent in early Bangkok when the dynasty's antecedents as a noble family that took power by coup in 1782 were well known. King Mongkut (r. 1851–1868) aimed to reestablish the idea that the right to rule depended on qualities passed down in the blood of the lineage. Possibly this indicates that this revised version of the whole Chiang Mai campaign was composed in the Mongkut reign.

Bad people and good people are all mixed up together. Wherever there's one, there's the other too. The Lao country and the Thai country are no different. Since this is so, remember this well, my precious.

Among ladies of fine appearance, there are both gentlefolk and commoners. The real difference lies in the heart, and how they have been brought up.

Queens are taken to be exemplary because of their solar lineage. They uphold the truth, the teachings, and morality, and they speak with politeness and elegance.

Their character is a result of lineage, and is continuously passed down by upbringing so no exceptions are ever found among them. For this reason they are generally admired.

The royalty of various languages and locations do not differ in behavior. If you keep up the traditions of your own lineage, even the king of the Thai city should show you due consideration.

But don't forget yourself and become overconfident. You're presented to him as a servant. Even though the king is gracious, don't get puffed up and carried away.

There's an ancient saying to instruct a bride that details the seven good and bad points of a wife's behavior.

These are what make a terrible wife: One, harboring bad intentions towards the husband; two, becoming intoxicated with greed; and three, being lazy over her duties.

As for a good wife, the text lays down four qualities: One, looking after her husband with kindness; two, sharing hardship and happiness equally;

three, paying respect and obeisance to her husband; and four, giving her body willingly for his use. These will make for peace and contentment every night and day because the husband is trusting of his wife.

But there's a difference between a queen and the wife of a commoner. You must be loyal and deferential, recognizing that you are a servant of the dust beneath the royal foot.

You must be committed to support him so that he graciously returns the kindness. Though at times you may be disaffected and discontented, you should never anger him,

because if the king is badly disposed, it may give rise to risks of many kinds. If the king shows favor to you, he will keep you in splendid state,

so that you will be happy all the time, your kinsfolk will be able to depend on you, and all the slaves and freemen will be happy too. Remember what I've told you."

Then she turned to the four maids. "You've helped to raise Soithong with love as if you were her younger sisters from the same womb. Now you'll be her friends in need in the difficult task of going to a faraway city.

Every day you'll see one another's faces. Whether she's bad or good, you four must take care of her. You've already raised her through many difficulties. Don't let her fail when she's passing out of your hands.

And Soithong, if you do well and become famous, you must always trust your four maids. Seek their advice. They've been loyal and caring for a long time.

May you go with happiness and succeed. May you not fall sick traveling through the forest. Once you're at Ayutthaya, may you be happy every day and night."

Soithong and the maids made obeisance in a row with clasped hands to receive the blessing of Queen Keson. Their distress gradually diminished.

At dusk, the queen took her daughter up to the main residence where the two grieved over their parting until they fell asleep in the bedchamber.

On the auspicious day, troops of both the left and right divisions were drawn up in columns all over the riverbank opposite Vientiane on the Phan Phrao side.

There were militia groups carrying arms, some displaying green and white pennants, and officers and men both Thai and Lao. Long boats were brought alongside a landing in front of the palace.

The front squadron, rear squadron, and royal barge[7] were moored in line, with troops in readiness. Boats carrying porters crossed in succession. Royal pavilions were set up on both banks of the river.

Lao high officials and various nobles gathered and waited. Men and women from the city crowded the paths on both banks.

In the palace, court relatives and other ladies assembled to send the princess off, some sadly lamenting the departure.

As the dawn sun streaked the sky, Queen Keson, still sad over the parting, arranged ablutions for Soithong.

She was anointed with rosewater, and turmeric powder was applied to her skin. All dirt was scrubbed and rinsed away, and her fair skin polished to gleam.

She was anointed with perfumes and the fragrant scent of krajae-sandal. Her skin was powdered to be fine and fair but only moderately as she was distracted with grief.

Her hair was coiled in regal style, fastened with a brilliant diamond hairpin, and decorated with flowers. She was arrayed in valuable jeweled earrings,

---

7. เรือประเทียบ, *ruea prathiap*, a boat specifically for women of the palace (KW, 680).

a *sin* yok in a golden *kanok* pattern, a soft-textured embroidered sabai covering her shoulder, a delicate necklace, dazzling breast chain, gold bracelets on both upper arms,

rings on both hands, and a girdle tightly cinching her waist. She looked radiantly beautiful in every way, befitting a queen.

Once Soithong was adorned with royal regalia, Queen Keson took her darling daughter out of the sandalwood residence.[8]

The royal kinsfolk, waiting to send her off, swallowed their sadness and gave blessings to the lovely princess. They all went to pay respect to the city's ruler.

kanok

In tears, Soithong walked to where her father was seated. She raised a salver with incense, candles, and flowers, and crawled to place it in front of the king.

She raised her hands to wai her father, prostrated at his feet, and buried her face on his lap, shaking, sighing, and sobbing. Then she controlled her feelings to take leave.

"I make my farewell to the royal foot. I'm going very far away. I hope to repay your goodness by offering my life under the dust below the royal foot.

I don't know whether the future will be good or bad, whether I'll return or not. I pray only that my father and mother be blessed with eternal happiness.

Whatever mistakes I've carelessly made, and whatever annoyance I've caused you in the past, please grant me your pardon, Father, so that the karma won't stay with me when I leave.

Though I go to face hardship, I'll not lose heart, though I'll be extremely concerned about the queen, my mother.

She's accustomed to seeing me morning and night but now I have to be taken very far away. She'll be so distressed and disturbed that I fear she may soon fall sick.

So I humbly request you, Father, to take it on yourself not to let her depart this life." Sobbing sadly, she prostrated at the king's feet.

His daughter's piteous farewell pierced the King of Si Sattana's heart like a powerful arrow. He shivered and sighed in distress.

His pent-up sorrow brimmed over in floods of tears. Striving to steel himself and swallow his sadness, he caressed and consoled his beloved daughter.

"Oh my sweetheart, don't be distressed at leaving. It's known that we're born to be governed by fate, eye's jewel.

---

8. ตำหนักจันทน์, *tamnak jan*, originally a royal residence constructed from fragrant sandalwood, later a term for any royal residence (CK, 218).

I'm very concerned for you but your marriage is at the will of the fortune that created this current situation whereby you have to be parted from me.

You are not leaving to face hardship but to reside in a place of honor at Ayutthaya, and you should be happy all the time.

Please suppress your feelings, my beloved child. Help to raise the honor of the solar lineage and strengthen the city of Si Sattana so that the people may be content.

Don't worry about your mother. I'll look after her. Please go safely with my blessing to live in Ayutthaya."

After giving his blessing, the king invited the queen to take their daughter out to the terrace at the front of the palace.

The three each sat in a royal palanquin and were carried down to the river landing, with masses of officials ahead and behind. Many palace ladies followed although their presence was forbidden.

The three stopped at a royal landing stage close to the riverbank, boarded a boat, and sat under its canopy. They crossed the river, followed by a water procession, and arrived at a pavilion on the shore.

Among groups of senior officials and masses of ordinary people, the three walked gracefully up to a royal pavilion.

A chaophraya brought Phra Thainam and the senior royal retainer Kamkong to bow, prostrate, and crawl in to pay respect and take leave.

The King of Lanchang spoke. "May you journey well. I entrust you, Phra Thainam, with the task of informing the King of Ayutthaya

that we offer our obeisance to the great king, upholder of the teachings, and beg to place our beloved daughter under the royal footsoles.

She is still young and inexperienced in duties. I beg His Majesty to give her instruction and training, including on the customs of the southern city with which she is not acquainted. May he please pardon any error that may arise.

Now the city of Si Sattana and the great capital of Si Ayutthaya are joined as one magnificent sheet of gold, two kingdoms like a single territory.

We will protect the northern side. Should any enemy encroach on our joint territory, let us cooperate to mobilize our forces so we may defeat any city.

We offer wishes of victory with sincerity. May the King of Ayutthaya's fame spread, and may he eternally enjoy great happiness, free of any irritation or oppression."

The King of Lanchang presented gifts of jewelry, silver, gold, and cloth. He gave orders for Phra Thainam to lead the vanguard column ahead of the princess's convoy.

Next he summoned Kueng Kamkong to receive his orders. "Keep careful watch all around. Inspect and check the route. The great forest on the way to Phu Khiao[9] is very remote.

There, the territories of the Thai, Lao, and Chiang Mai people meet. Keep a close guard at front and rear. When you halt at night to rest, prepare the main guns and light fires for security.

Proceed past the Chi River to the Khorat territory. Then you are released from your duties. From there onwards, Thainam will lead the troops and place the surrounding guards.

Go well and return well with my blessing. Overcome all troubles, threats, injuries, and disease. When the princess is finally delivered to the Thai city, return to Vientiane without delay."

Phra Thainam and Kueng Kamkong prostrated and went to take up their positions in the front and rear of the column, waiting for a drum to signal the march.

Robust-looking Lao from the outpost of Nong Bua[10] Village were stationed at the front, followed by the Thai of Ayutthaya, and a militia brigade ahead of the elephants.

Detachments of Lao militia walked in file on both left and right. The princess's convoy was at the center of the column, guarded by troops.

Kueng Kamkong came next behind to keep close watch over the princess, followed by the rearguard and the supply train, with militia stationed at the tail.

Troops, elephants, and horses were present in great numbers. The entourage of the princess, including servants, was distributed through all the units of the column.

At an auspicious time for victory, the clouds parted and the sun's rays streamed through. The astrologer promptly ordered the beating of gongs. Drums thundered out a signal.

---

9. ภูเขียว, "green hill." Both Phu Khiao and Phu Wiang are on the route from Vientiane to Khorat, with Phu Khiao further south. But in this chapter, the two names seem to be confused. Similarly, in the early nineteenth-century maps, the place labeled Phu Khiao is sketched with the distinctive circle of mountains that must be Phu Wiang (Santanee and Stott, *Royal Siamese Maps*, 130–31, 136; see map 5).

10. Currently Nong Bua Lamphu. It is situated on their route, at a pass through a steep ridge that divides the Mekong Plain from the valley of the Chi. It is first mentioned as a border outpost of Vientiane in the Lao chronicles when Fa Ngum attacked and settled Vientiane, probably in the 1360s (Souneth, "Nidan Khun Borom," 188; see also 299 and 313). It "was traditionally given as an appendage to the crown prince of Lan Sang" (Mayoury and Pheuiphanh, *Paths*, 198). On the early nineteenth-century maps, this route first goes eastwards along the Mekong to Wiang Khuk, then south through the Khao San gap to Nong Bua Lamphu (Santanee and Stott, *Royal Siamese Maps*, 130–31; see map 5).

The Lao King of Lanchang led his daughter forward to mount an elephant, and ordered the troop column to move.

Seeing their daughter depart, the king and queen were in a pitiable state, unable to suppress their sadness. When she disappeared from sight, they returned to the inner palace and wept inconsolably.

Queen Keson beat her breast in lamentation. She remained sad and forlorn for many nights before the pain of parting eased.

Now to tell of the beautiful Soithong. She too could not stop weeping. Her maids caressed and consoled her by suggesting she enjoy viewing the forest trees.

"Please be more cheerful, mistress. Over there, look at the entrance to the forest with magnificent tall *yung* and *yang* trees. They say ahead is a thick forest,

so densely overgrown that many tigers and wild elephants live there. If people go in small groups, they'll be afraid of coming across animals and perhaps being savaged.

But we're going in there with many elephants, horses, and troops. The animals will all run off and hide away from us in the forest.

We'll be able to enjoy the plants. There are endless numbers of them to see—those with succulent fruits, sweet and sour, and those with flowers whose fragrance floods the woods.

Though there are trees in the royal garden, they're not the same as those in the lofty forest. In a short time, we'll reach the entrance. Mistress, please wait to see the woods and hills.

Here at the edge of the forest there are still villages because it's close to an outpost. Lawa come to plant crops on the uplands, including bananas, sugarcane, custard apple, galangal, and lemongrass. Look at the house by that clump of bamboo

with a group of little children standing looking, and a lot of old folks by the copse. They'll draw river water and bring it over without being asked. Living in the wilds, they're very goodhearted.

That house is right at the edge of the fields. It seems there are beautiful houses and gardens along here. They plant coconut, betel, mango, lychee, orange, and longan.

The pan garden looks so lush and dense. Along the fences, they're growing white mulberry to raise silkworms. Because this is a village of forest folk, they have to plant enough to live on."[11]

---

11. This passage, which does not appear in the Wat Ko version, is similar to a famous entry in Prince Damrong's journal on a visit to Udon in 1906: "Each village household has a house

They reached a remote area with no inhabitants. The maids pointed out different birds. "On that sandalwood tree, there's a magpie. Flying over there is a black drongo.

That loud bok-bok noise is a coppersmith barbet,[12] and the clear cry is the call of a coel. A kingfisher is dancing up that *taeng* tree, and the echoing din is a posse of parrots on the wing.

A partridge is prattling in search of a partner, and an imperial pigeon is laying eggs in her nest. There's a magpie robin flicking its tail among the trees, and that flapping is a wild cock flying off.

The koo-kuk-koo is a dove, and there are hill mynas billing and cooing at the top of that *krathin*. The *kot*[13] swooping around is looking for food, and an oriole has just flown down onto that *phobai* tree."

There were animals all around but they ran off shyly at the sight of so many people coming. Young deer gamboled up the slopes. Moles and rabbits scurried off to hide in thickets.

The party was disappointed not to get a better view of animals that disappeared in a flash as soon as they caught a glimpse. Just as the sun began to beat down, they reached the entrance to deep forest where a cool wind blew under the shade.

Fine tall *yung* and *yang* trees formed a thick canopy that blocked out the sun. Dew still lay on the leaves, dripping down. The route was like a tunnel, just big enough to pass.

Both sides were thick with undergrowth. Even in the center of the road, their heads almost touched a tangle of vines. It looked frightening, and Soithong was afraid.

They heard only the plaintive sound of gibbons whooping in the big trees, and golden peacocks calling to one another. She felt lonely and sad at heart.

---

with enough space for living and a granary to store enough rice for one year. In the yard of the house they plant chili, eggplant, galangal, and lemongrass for making curry. Outside the house they have a garden for fruits such as banana, sugarcane, betel, and coconut. And between the garden and the paddy field, there is a space to plant mulberry for raising silkworms. . . . . Villagers around here make all their own food and scarcely have to buy a single thing" (Quoted in Chatthip, *Village Economy*, 69–70).

12. ค้อนทอง, *khon thong*, "golden hammer," crimson-breasted barbet. "Call: a hollow, resonant *took* or *tonk* repeated about 80 times a minute" (King, *Field Guide*, 497).

13. นกกด, a bird that appears in Thai literature including the Mahachat and *Prapat Than Thong Daeng*, Visiting the Thongdaeng Stream. Pallegoix identifies it as *Mycteria asiatica*, which is the black-necked stork, now named *Xenorhynchus asiaticus* (PAL2, 412). Others identify it with กะปูด, *kaput*, the coucal (SWN, 1:9). The *kot* that appears below in chapter 27 seems more like a bird of prey.

They came to a stream where many sorts of butterflies of myriad colors fluttered prettily in and out of the forest.

Everywhere around, plants were in bloom—happy-shade, angelbreast, tasselfern, per-simmon, *phluang*, camphorwood, sandal, *satta-ban*, orangegold, orchids,

milkwood, pupil tree, eaglewood, gem jasmine, and *jampa* smoth-ered with beautiful blooms. The maids at her side urged the princess to cheer herself by looking at the flowers.

through the forest

Soithong shed her melancholy. They slept fifteen nights in the deep forest before emerging at the village of Phu Wiang beside the hills.

There they released the elephants, and set up camp in a circle. Troops milled around noisily. The maids suggested Soithong go down to bathe in a river

that came from the foot of the mountains. Its cool water gushed down to a basin, and then flowed over an overhang in front of a cliff. The rocks were dazzling,

striated with the red of uncut ruby and the green of clear emerald. The stream wound captivatingly through the hilly landscape.

In the late afternoon, a refreshing breeze blew the scent of mountain flowers along the line of the hills as they walked up to their forest pavilion.

⤚

Now to tell of Saentri Phetkla who had assembled his troops in the deep forest. Scouts came to report that the Lao, Thai, and princess were at Pang Kha.[14]

At dusk Phetkla assigned his men to surround them on all sides. The troops split up and advanced, crouching down and spying around. Saentri Phetkla intoned a mantra,

held his breath, and exhaled seven times. The sky flashed. The moon was obscured. A stormy rain streamed down. All around, villages were cloaked in darkness. A strong wind buffeted

the tall *yung* and *yang* trees, which splintered and fell this way and that. A dust storm darkened the sky. Thunder echoed around the forest as if the earth were about to overturn and collapse.

The Thai and Lao were white-eyed and trembling with fear. Both officers and men lost their heads.

Kamkong took fright. Phra Thainam shook as if a ghost had possessed him. "What's happening in this forest?" The bonfires went out, plunging all into darkness.

Saentri Phetkla fired a gun as a signal, and his troops immediately loosed a thundering volley.

They swarmed forward, hollering loudly, and surrounded the column. Phra Thainam saw the Lao storming upon him but stood staring stock-still in shock.

In the pitch dark, he could see no faces and was uncertain of the enemy's position. Fighting back was useless because the attackers were almost upon them and the column was lost. Both officers and men took to their heels as best they could.

The Chiang Mai Lao chased after to cut them off. The Thai fled in confusion, falling down, scrambling up, crawling, and running chaotically. The Lao horde took them captive and tied them up.

Saentri Phetkla captured the commanders, Phra Thainam and Kueng Kamkong. His phrai chased down the troops and caught them all with no deaths.

Hearing the sound of men shouting, Soithong and her entourage of ladies ran around screaming in confusion.

---

14. In his modern Thai prose version of *KCKP*, Premseri changed this, without explanation, from ปางคา, Pang Kha, to ปากคา, Pak Kha, the Kha mouth or gap. Perhaps this refers to the narrow entrance into the Phu Wiang circle of hills. The stream flowing through the gap is now called the Bong but it originates at a Kha Lake (Premseri, *KCKP*, 352).

Everything was dark, both earth and sky. They could not see the faces of the enemy anywhere. In great distress, they wept loudly inside the pavilion.

Once all the officers and men had been captured, leaving only Princess Soithong to be dealt with, the commander, Saentri Phetkla, chanted and blew a formula

to dispel the darkness. He had men surround the pavilion, and went inside accompanied by a few trusted troops carrying torches.

Seeing Saentri Phetkla, Soithong felt as if her head had been lopped off. She swooned with shock. The four maids supported her

until she regained command of her senses. Saentri Phetkla said promptly, "Your Highness, don't be upset. We're not forest bandits come to ravage you.

King Chiang In, king of kings, has sent me to invite your gracious self to possess the city of Chiang Mai. There's no reason to be sad."

He ordered horses and elephants to be harnessed, and escorted her to set off, along with all the other palace ladies. Soithong sobbed and wept along the way.

The[15] seven hundred Thai and Lao were clapped in yokes[16] with their arms tied. They cried out loudly. Kueng Kamkong and Thainam were placed under full restraint. The Lao beat them while fitting them with shackles and cangues.[17]

shackle

Ai-Ma shouted, "I'm done for really. Mistress I-Kling will wait forever but I'll not return. Loosen my arms to give some relief." Shit stained his cloth and hands.

Ta-Lo said, "I'm done for! My grandchild I-Kaeo will be as cold as a hungry ghost. Now that my arms are tied up tight, please loosen the hands." He shouted fearfully and laughed like a drunk.

Ai-Sang took to his heels and got away. Lao ran after him, grabbed his hair, and hauled him back, elbowing him over and over, but he still ducked his head and struggled. Even laid out flat on the ground and beaten, he continued to resist.

---

15. The next seven stanzas, up to "dragging them along," are taken from WK, 22:853–54; PD has a modified version of the first stanza: The captured Thai and Lao, both officers and men, were put in yokes. Even Phra Thainam was put in a cangue. They trailed along in file through the forest.

16. โตงก, ตะโหงก, *ta-ngok*, a crude form of cangue made with two pieces of wood clamped around the neck. It allowed the prisoner to walk but made it impossible to run away. The word is also used for the yoke of a draught animal.

17. ขื่อคา, *khue kha*, literally cangue and shackle, which can mean restraints on hands and feet, rather like the stocks but here probably means that the wrists are poked through the cangue and inserted in a shackle.

Ta-Lo cried, "This is too much." He was hit by a stick, and fell rolling on the ground like a cookie.[18] His cloth slipped off totally but he walked along with his head in the air. When he looked down, he said, "It's shrunk!

Dear Father, I'm done for now. This dead, crumpled thing will never get to see a young Thai girl's. I can't poke out my head and chat with a darling." Ta-Kae shouted, "Your mother, you villain!

You're about to die yet you're showing off, wishing to put it in a hole. Well, that's tough." The Lao drove them without mercy, beating them to walk or dragging them along.

Mortified at being imprisoned by the Lao, Phra Thainam hauled himself along in tears. In despair, he thought to himself, "How could it have come to this?

I was badly careless. It was incautious and inappropriate of me to trust the Lao. I thought that Kueng Kamkong was good. I wholly believed he was trustworthy,

and I didn't take sufficient care of the princess, not thinking there'd be a major incident. Our enemies took us by surprise. Will I ever return to Ayutthaya?

I'm not unhappy if they kill me. It would be better to die. Now that they've imprisoned me, with a cangue to boot, where will I be able to hide my face?

Besides, news will spread that they managed to capture Ayutthaya soldiers! The more I think about it, the more furious I am." Along the way he avoided looking into anyone's face.

Some of the phrai were so upset they trembled, sighed, and hung their heads. Others were boisterous, singing merrily and playing around boldly with no fear of anyone.

The army quick-marched to Chiang Mai and entered the city. The local Lao people came out in droves to look.

Young women, old women, and widows scrambled over. Men and women crowded together in groups. "Who's this coming here, all trussed up like crabs?" They asked if anyone knew what had happened.

"They say they're southerners, Thai from Ayut-thaya." Others were called to see the sight. Word circulated. Ta-Lo gyrated to tease the Lao, making girls turn away in embarrassment.

Lao couple

---

18. ขนมหนา, *khanom na*, probably ขนมหน้าแตก, *khanom na taek*, a mixture of flour, sugar, oil, eggs, and lemon juice shaped into disks and baked.

"Why[19] are their heads like that, some pointy, some curly, some flat, all different?"[20] Seeing Ta-Lo with his big head and hollow eyes, children cried out, "You're a dead man, old fellow!"

A young girl threw him a banana, saying, "Eat and enjoy, Grandpa, I beg you." Ta-Lo picked it up and stuffed it in his shoulder bag. He swaggered along, shaking his legs,

and opened his cloth for the Lao girls to see. "Short or long?" A Lao girl shouted, "Damn this fellow!" Ai-Mak bent over, exposing his arse, with his equipment dangling like a bunch of bananas.

"You've never seen me dance. Come and look. The cat will catch the mouse for sure." Lao girls spat on the heads of the Thai. "Can't look at them." They went off home.

The column arrived at the inner official sala where all the nobles had gathered. Kueng Kamkong and Phra Thainam entered in chains, followed by the troops roped together.

Princess Soithong remained on her elephant in front of the inner sala, awaiting orders from the king.

The senior lords and nobles asked questions, and Saentri Phetkla related the whole story. Then they interrogated Phra Thainam. "How did this come about from the beginning?

Tell us why you went up to collect the princess. Was she presented to the King of Ayutthaya, or did he ask for her hand? Which?"

Furious at being imprisoned, Phra Thainam reasoned with himself, "Telling them or not telling them won't make any difference.

They'll probably slash me dead anyway. I'm not afraid to lose my life, and it would be improper to beg for mercy." He remained quiet, saying nothing.

The nobles were infuriated. "Why don't you speak, damn you?" "These Ayutthaya Thai are the most arrogant people." In the evening, they took

Phra Thainam and Kueng Kamkong and left them under guard at the front of

---

19. The next four stanzas, up to "They went off home," are taken from WK, 22:854–55; PD has: Old folks threw bananas at them. "If any of you Thai guys are hungry, eat 'em up!" Ta-Lo collected them, stuffed them in his shoulder bag, and swaggered along in front, rolling his eyes. / "You want to see Thai or Lao, long or short?" Lao girls cried, "Damn that guy!" Ta-Rak pulled up his lowercloth and stuck his arse out. "Here we are, the fierce tigers from the Thai country! / You've never seen us before. Dance up for a look. Do you want a cat or a mouse? I'll give it to you." Young Lao girls spat on the heads of the Thai. "Can't look at them!" "They're shameless."

20. บักแบ่นหรือแลหวา, bak baen rue lae wa, in Lao.

the main terrace. All the nobles entered to attend on the King of Chiang Mai.

King Chiang In, eminence of the world, ruler of Chiang Mai, saw Phra Thainam in chains and Saentri Phetkla.

He laughed loudly and clapped his hands. Leaping up, he grasped his regal sword, waved it above his head, and asked Saentri Phetkla, "Did you get Soithong?"

Saentri Phetkla made obeisance and said, "My liege, Your Majesty, this man here is called Phra Thainam, commander of the Ayutthaya Thai army.

That is Kueng Kamkong, the commander from Lanchang. They were guarding the column escorting the princess through the forest. Soithong is here, at the inner official sala

with several hundred palace ladies and a great quantity of silver, gold, and jewels. Seven hundred troops, both Lao and Thai, are all imprisoned."

King Chiang In did not wait for him to finish talking. Not seeing Soithong as he desired, he impatiently scolded his commander.

He ignored Phra Thainam and Kueng Kamkong, showing no interest in questioning them. Instead he shouted, "Here, what are you doing, officer?

What kind of custom is it to let phrai stare at a princess? Why didn't you take her inside? Wouldn't that be right, or what do you say?

You know this princess is my love. You officials are all hopeless. You're interested only in face, nothing more. You should be flogged to the point of death. Bring the cane!

Don't we have a palace? Where is the lovely Soithong? Why do you leave her at the sala? Who does the crystal palace belong to?

Or are you of the opinion she should not be my spouse, and hence cannot live there? Why bring me this Thai rabble? Fling them in jail, the lot of them."

The courtiers were shocked by the king's thunderous outburst. City officials escorted the Thai away at once. Palace officials backed out in confusion,

and went inside to tell the palace governesses[21] that the king had ordered them to receive the princess at the front. "He's very angry. Please don't delay." The governesses were all alarmed.

Sentinelles and retainers dashed around everywhere in confusion. The governesses came to the inner official sala and prostrated.

---

21. ท้าวนาง, *thao nang*, "noble lady," general term for those in charge of administering the inner palace. Many were consorts from a prior reign (Chatraphon, "Kan borihan," 156).

They invited Princess Soithong to descend from the elephant, and enter a golden palanquin to bring her to the front terrace of the audience hall.

The King of Chiang Mai saw the palanquin approaching and flew into a rage. He stamped his foot and shouted, "Why are you bringing her in here?

This place is full of oarsmen! You want them to stare at her too? Why do all of you behave as if we had no palace? You lot should be flogged to the point of death."

The governesses trembled with fear and despair. They all rushed into the palace and waited for the king's order to present Soithong.

King Chiang In smiled broadly at the achievement of his desire. His craving for Soithong had not diminished one bit. He went up from the audience hall

to the golden palace bedchamber in an unbearable frenzy of anticipation. He whispered to the inner palace servants, "Where's Soithong? Summon her here."

The inner ladies hurried to tell the governesses to bring Soithong. They all helped to dress and prepare her, and then escorted her up to the golden royal residence.

They prostrated beside a screen at the entrance to the room while a head governess made the formal announcement to present Princess Soithong.

At the sight of her, King Chiang In fell madly in love. He stared transfixed, unable to take his eyes off her. Everything about her was beautiful—

except one. "She still looks like a child." Her figure was slight. She was not ready for lovemaking. He[22] was disappointed that she was still so young but his heart was breaking at her soft, swan-like figure.

He approached to embrace her, with his thoughts wavering back and forth, as if his mind were being seared by the fire of an era and his body were being burned away.

He sank down unmoving beside her body, and closed his eyes. He felt embarrassed at what the palace ladies would think but his craving remained and he was torn two ways.

"Don't! You must restrain yourself. It won't be long to wait. Meanwhile, the King of Ayutthaya will be furious over the matter of this princess, and will send an army up here.

---

22. The next two stanzas, up to "closed his eyes," are taken from WK, 22:860, absent from PD.

I must concentrate on the war first. By the time that irritation has been dealt with and the enemy finished off, the princess should be ripe and I can enjoy her as I crave."

After debating with himself, he greeted her. "My charming lady, don't be sad. I'll keep you in state in a golden residence as possessor of the royal property.

In the future, should you think of your father, our two cities are not so far apart. You may go to see him and return. My beauty, don't be fearful."

He ordered that two golden residences be prepared along with furnishings, servants, and everything to please and delight her.

Soithong was troubled and miserable. Every day without fail, she stayed in her room, weeping morning and night.

"Oh pity, pity! When I left my mother to go to the southern city, we wept because we loved each other so much. I never reached Ayutthaya but was captured midway and brought to Chiang Mai.

Mother and Father will mistakenly think that I'm happy now. They expect I'll do well, and hope they can depend on me.

If they find out I've been captured and taken to Chiang Mai, they'll be furious. With luck, they should bring an army to attack and take me back.

I'm past thinking about it." Every night, her tears streamed down in misery. "This is the fruit of karma I have made."

27: PHLAI NGAM VOLUNTEERS

Now to tell of the King of Chiang Mai. Since bringing the princess to his capital, he had never stopped thinking of his enemies. He realized there would be war before long,

because both Lanchang on one side and Ayutthaya on the other were enraged. "If both sides bring an army at the same time, it'll be difficult to fight back.

I must concentrate on defeating the Thai first, and get it over with quickly. If I can gain victory against the Thai on the southern flank, Lanchang should be too scared to attack."

He pondered quietly until the sun shone brightly in the sky, and then went to the resplendent audience hall where all the lords made obeisance.

He asked the senior officials in audience, "What do you think? The Ayutthaya king unjustly came to seize my intended wife.

On orders, our people laid an ambush, seized the princess, and captured the Ayutthayans. If news reaches the Thai city, they'll send a large army.

Should we prepare to repel them here, or should we go down and attack them first? Consult together and decide how to deal with this."

The Lao lords and high officials conferred together and then addressed the king. "The enemy Thai forces are strong.

If we go down, we don't think we'll win. But if we're slow in making preparations and they bring a large army, we can't hope to match them either.

We need to think up a stratagem. We must challenge the Thai and provoke their anger so they rush up here unprepared. Then we can smash their army easily."

The King of Chiang Mai agreed that this approach would achieve his aim. He had a deliberately insulting missive prepared to incite the Thai to anger.

It was placed in a cylinder and given to Saen Kamkong and Saentri Phetkla to take with a hundred phrai on horseback and deliver to the border post of the Ayutthaya territory.

Saentri Phetkla and Kamkong took the royal missive, and called up the required number of phrai from the rolls. They mounted their horses and set off in file.

The men slung bags of crisped rice across their chests. The harnesses, bright red shirts, and tasseled spears looked dazzling in the forest. They forded the river to Lamphun,

and crossed the Mae Tha stream[1] to reach Lampang. Without halting, they galloped through the forest and reached the Thoen region in the evening. Bright moonlight lit the sky.

The horses and riders were becoming weary, out of breath, and hungry. They ascended the hills, passed through the defile,[2] and descended again into the forest. In the heat of the day, they stopped to rest and allow the horses to graze and recover their strength.

As soon as their tiredness passed, they remounted and set off, cracking the whip and making long strides without looking back. After three days without a break, they reached the outpost of Ban Tha Kwian.[3]

Nai Bun, who had the title of Khun Krai, saw the Lao coming and suspected they were enemy troops. He summoned the old phrai on guard duty to stand across the road at the gateway,

holding arms at the ready. "That group coming on horseback are Lao for sure. They're dressed in red with heads wrapped in pink. There's red all over the place."

They closed the gate of the outpost, and scrambled to load cannons, set them in position, and ready a flint set. "Who goes there? Hey! Answer immediately. Friend or foe?

If friend, advance with just two horses. If foe, come on, I'm not afraid." Some of the guards came out and stood with swords raised and guns ready, while the rest prepared for a full attack.

Seeing the outpost detachment boldly standing to block the highway, the Lao reined in their horses and spoke in reply.

---

1. Amphoe Mae Tha is located where the Lamphun–Lampang road (Route 11) crosses this stream (see map 4).

2. The pass over the hills west of Thoen towards the Yom valley, now Route 1048 (see map 4).

3. Cart Landing Village, on the watershed between the Wang and Yom valleys, now in the south of Sukhothai province. Apparently this was the frontier between Lanna and Ayutthaya, and is still marked as such on Route 1048, actually the border between Lampang and Sukhothai provinces. They are following the Thung Saliam route that is used several times in the story and appears to have been the major overland route between Ayutthaya and Chiang Mai. The distance from Chiang Mai to Tha Kwian is 250 kms by road today (see map 4).

"We're just little people bringing a missive. We'll come to tell you about it at the outpost." Saentri Phetkla and Kamkong alone advanced to deliver the missive and explain

about Phra Thainam and his troops being imprisoned in Chiang Mai. "Our king is sending a missive to the Thai city. Forward it for presentation to your king quickly."

The outpost guards received the missive and followed out to look at the horsemen in the forest. Seeing there was no army, they returned. Nai Phun, a unit head, was assigned to guard the outpost.

Khun Krai took the missive, and mounted a post horse. Cracking the whip, he galloped into the forest, crossed Saliam Plain,[4] and made straight down to the local headquarters.

Reaching Sawankhalok,[5] he dismounted and hurried along, leading his horse. Nobles and local officials were sitting in a court, discussing the case of I-Mei Thong.

The old Chinese offered no defense and agreed to pay a fine, saying "Oh shit![6] I'm ready to accept the guilt." Seeing someone from the outpost, the officials called out, "Why are you standing out there staring? Come on in."

Khun Krai went into the central sala and pushed his way through. He prostrated, crawled up to deliver the cylinder with the sealed letter, and explained the whole affair.

The governor[7] discussed the matter with all his officials of the city, palace, treasury, and land departments.[8] "This is a major incident.

---

4. The plain reached on descent from the watershed between the Wang and Yom valleys, now in the west of Sukhothai province. *Saliam* or *sadao*, *Azadirachta indica*, is the Siamese neem tree.

5. Now an amphoe on the Yom River; here called Sangkhalok, but regularized to Sawankhalok throughout the translation (see map 4).

6. ไสบวยพวย, *sai buai phuai*, in Chinese (see p. 43, note 69).

7. The text says "chaophraya," implying a first-class city. In an old list of provincial cities, purportedly dated to 1440, Sawankhalok is a first-class city. In the Three Seals Law, Sawankhalok is a second-class city and its governor had the rank of phraya, as he appears later in the chapter (Suphawat, "Phra aiyakan kao," 335; KW, 349–50).

8. The "four pillars" in the central government were replicated in the major provincial centers. The city officer judged serious criminal cases, supervised district officers, and organized the watch. The palace officer was in charge of protocol, ceremonial, and civil justice. The treasury official oversaw tax collection and cases concerning debt. The land official registered land, managed state granaries, and judged cases concerning land. First-class and second-class towns also had a *palat* (deputy), *khunphon* (garrison commander), *mahatthai* (overseeing manpower, issuing writs, keeping records), *yokkrabat* (magistrate, see p. 427, note 9), and *satsadi* (keeper of

Seizing a princess, and capturing soldiers to boot, is bold and aggressive. And the missive is rash—like a midge flying unawares into a flame.

But the first thing to get trampled will be the grass.[9] An army will have to be raised and that will create trouble for the phrai. Don't treat this lightly. We must forward the missive quickly. If we do nothing, there'll be trouble, maybe fatal.

Those damn Lao have done it. Write a report and seal it straightaway." When the report was ready, it was put in a cylinder, tied around with string, closed with hot wax, and a seal applied.

Phan Mano was placed in charge of taking the report to the capital along with twenty-five phrai carrying panniers and pack baskets, creaking along. They boarded a nine-fathom canopy boat,

untied the bows, and rowed away from the landing with each oar pulling strongly, churning the water into white foam under the moonlight, and hollering loudly.

At dawn they reached Tha Kasem,[10] where they cooked a meal and ate happily, both officers and men. Once full, they hurried briskly onwards. The commander, Phan Mano, sat rocking back and forth.

They passed Wat Mai,[11] Ban Tru, and Tha Kong,[12] then went down the Phing[13] to reach Phichit Wang Jan[14] on the strong current. Someone sang out, "Hey! The prow has hit a Jek's boat."

"Ah! The boat's selling liquor. Let's grab some." "Knock you dead, sir.[15] Grab some-

liquor boat

---

the rolls). (Akin, *Organization*, 87; KW, 349; La Loubère, *New Historical Relation*, 84; Suphawat, "Phra aiyakan kao.")

9. Alluding to the saying, "When elephants fight, the grass gets trampled."

10. Ten kms south of Sawankhalok on the Yom River (see map 4).

11. The new wat, a generic and often temporary name, unidentified. Possibly this means the modern site of Sukhothai town, which was moved to the east of the ancient site after the course of the Yom River shifted.

12. Now Amphoe Kong Krailat, on the Yom River in southeast Sukhothai (see map 4).

13. A waterway that crosses from the Yom River to the Nan River where the two are only 3–4 kms apart, just below Phitsanulok. The Nan is a bigger river with a stronger flow, and thus faster on a southbound journey. If they continued down the Yom, they would not join the Nan until much further south around Chumsaeng (KW, 350–51; see map 4).

14. Wang Jan is now a village adjacent to old Phichit (see map 10 and accompanying note).

15. พะซี้ไปใส่บวย, *phachi*, a Teochew phrase meaning "beat you dead," used especially by children as a playful threat; *bai sai buai* (see p. 43, note 69). The soldier mocks the liquor merchant

thing, fellows!" They lifted a sizable pitcher over to their boat, and pushed the Jek's boat away with their feet, shouting loudly.

"A glug for you and a glug for me. Pass it on." The prow of the canopy boat ploughed into a clump of bamboo. To cut a long story short, in seven days they arrived at their destination.

As soon as the boat moored at a landing, Phan Mano hurried off, followed by his men. He spotted a young palace lady[16] and took a liking to her.

Clicking his tongue and smacking his lips, he inhaled her scent, raised his face like a staring buffalo, and swaggered along, glancing at her with twinkling eyes. Flirting and forgetting himself, he wandered off course,

and stumbled across the porch of Din Gate.[17] Ta-Thin, the gatekeeper, grabbed Phan Mano's cloth, and the waistband came undone. The gatekeeper laughed, "You madman! Sauntering along with something under your waistband.

Oh dear. It's a country bumpkin bringing a report. What are you hiding under your cloth? It looks like a basket of birds' eggs. You dirty northerners[18] are hopeless."

Phan Mano paid a salueng to be released. Looking crestfallen, he retraced his steps along with his men, and asked for the inner official sala. It was pointed out to him straight ahead.

Seeing supervisors, duty officers, and reserve governors,[19] Phan Mano sat down right at the entrance. When a duty officer came out of the sala, Phan Mano promptly prostrated and presented the report.

The duty officer cracked open the cylinder on a balustrade, and extracted the report and royal missive. He read the contents and, knowing it was government business, hurried off to tell the palace officials.

When the senior minister, Chaophraya Jakri, knew about the royal missive, he was troubled. He ordered a copy[20] made quickly to present to the king.

---

by mimicking sing-song Chinese.

16. In the Wat Ko version she is a "lady of the waterfront" (WK, 22:871).

17. See p. 418, note 41.

18. "Northern" here refers to the area of the "northern cities," including Phitsanulok, Sukhothai, and Sawankhalok. It does not mean Lanna.

19. These are all Mahatthai officials. There were four posts of supervisor, หัวพัน, *hua phan*, *sakdina* 400; four posts of duty officer, นายเวร, *nai wen*, *sakdina* 200; and four posts of reserve governor, เกณฑ์เมืองรั้ง, *ken mueang rang*, *sakdina* 400. The latter were posted temporarily to minor cities. Phan Mano probably dealt with นายควรรู้อัฏ, *nai khuan ru-at*, a duty officer with responsibility for correspondence (KTS, 1:225, 227; SB, 332–33).

20. The letter from Sawankhalok was addressed to Chaophraya Jakri so the procedure was to make a copy before presenting it to the king (SB, 333).

Now to tell of the almighty king, paramount in wealth and power, who resided in a room of glittering crystal and lapis lazuli, enjoying perfect and continuous contentment,

because the gods were ever-present to protect the king, upholder of the teachings. But he did not yet know about the royal missive that would greatly disturb his disposition.

He remained inside the palace until three o'clock[21] when a gong sounded for him to go to the audience hall. He went to bathe

in fragrant rosewater, and was anointed with floral scents. Lady attendants crawled in to present his splendid attire.

Once dressed, he took up a short sword with brilliant diamond filigree. Loyal inner lady attendants prostrated to present a betel tray.

After partaking of betel, he walked elegantly up to the Banyong Rattanat Hall, looking as splendid as the Lord of the Swans.[22]

The curtain was drawn back. The audience was so crowded with senior officials, nobles, and judges[23] prostrating on their knees that the place looked about to burst.

Horn and conch sounded. Nobles made obeisance in rows and groups. Palace guards drove away people waiting around the doors to see what would happen as a result of the report.

Chaophraya Jakri had the floor. He made obeisance and addressed the king. "My life is under the royal foot.

Chiang Mai has sent a royal missive, delivered to the outpost guards at Tha

---

21. Probably meaning 9 a.m.

22. บรรยงก์รัตนาสน์, "seat of the jeweled chair," built according to the chronicles by King Phetracha at the start of his reign in 1688, but more likely slightly earlier during the Narai reign as it must be the building that Gervaise, who stayed in Siam from 1683 to 1687, described as the "king's apartment . . . newly built . . . in the form of a cross. . . . . it looks out on to a large well-tended garden" (Gervaise, *Natural and Political History*, 32; RCA, 324; *Boranasathan*, 1: 233–37; Choisy, *Journal*, 170).

This audience hall was on the west side of the palace, in an area formerly part of the women's quarters. The building had a cruciform pattern with a nine-tiered spire at the center and four wings in the four directions, each wing containing an audience hall. It was surrounded by a pool twelve meters wide, watered from the canal running along the western edge of the palace, and spanned by bridges in the four directions. The inner official sala was relocated to the northeast rim of the pool. The boundary of the inner (female) section of the palace was relocated behind a wall built to the north of this sala. This hall was used for major royal occasions from 1688 to 1733, then repaired by King Borommakot and used again from 1744 to 1758. (KLW, 200, 205–8; KCK, 207; APA, 59; *Boranasathan*, 1: 233–37)

23. ครู, *khru*, teacher, but here probably an abbreviated reference to Maharatchakhru, the two chief judges (see p. 444, note 15).

Kwian to forward onward. Phraya Kaset Songkhram Ramnarong[24] assigned
Phan Mano to bring it here.

The matter concerns Phra Thainam, who has been captured by Chiang Mai
but not killed." Before the missive could be read, the king flew into a rage,

and stamped his foot hard enough to shake the golden royal throne. "Mm!
These arrogant, uppity Lao. What do they have to say? Tell me."

"My liege, the missive reads as follows. The great king, ruler over the territory of Chiang Mai, a monarch of great splendor, cleaves to truth, honesty,
and the teachings.

His power extends over all regions of the realm. Before him, enemies quail
and submit. A royal household text inscribed long ago on a golden sheet

described him as a warrior king, the unparalleled eminence of the world,
like an avatar who destroys all enemies so he may be free of any irritation.

An envoy was dispatched with a missive to request the hand of the gracious
Princess Soithong, daughter of Lanchang, according to ancient royal custom,

in the expectation she would be consecrated in marriage as a wife of the first
rank, though, since she is still young and unfit to possess with joy, she would
not be entertained close to the royal side.

In the past the Thai city was honest, but now has become woefully vain and
besotted with power. Phra Thainam was sent to lead troops across the forest
to infringe on our territory

with no respect for us as ruler. This was insolent and imprudent. In addition he took away the Princess Soithong, our love.

Hence an army was conscripted and sent in defense. It was able to defeat
the enemy and seize the princess. The Thai army commander, Phra Thainam,
and his men have been imprisoned but not killed.

If we did not so advise, you might suspect that we had abducted this gracious
princess but in fact she has been received in a sandalwood residence.

If you wish for this princess, leave home and fearlessly bring an army. I invite
the King of Ayutthaya to a duel by single combat on elephant back.

Whoever wins will have Princess Soithong to partner and caress without
restraint. In the meantime, Phra Thainam will remain in prison as surety for
the Ayutthaya side.

At the end of three months, all five hundred will be killed. We await your
response. Whether you stake your glory to be known forever, or shirk coming
from fear, is up to you.

---

24. The governor of Sawankhalok who appears in the Three Seals Law as Okya Kraset Songkhram Ramrat, *sakdina* 10,000 (KTS, 1:320).

This war will be decided according to past examples.[25] The princess will not be joined in love until the battle with the king of the Thai city has shown whose power is ascendant.

Then the royal marriage will take place, and the honor of him who fought on elephant back and won a queen will spread far and wide." Finishing the reading of the missive, the minister prostrated.

The king was choked with fury. His breast burned as if an era-destroying fire[26] would reduce his life to ashes.

After a moment, he roared like a lion, stamped his foot so the hall shook, drew his sword, and brandished it above his head. All those in audience shrank back

in alarm, faces pale and bodies trembling. Some could not stop betelnut spilling out of their waistband.[27] Others hid crouching and curled over behind the pillars of the audience hall. The whole palace trembled with fear.

Some were terrified enough to disappear into the earth. Others scrambled to crawl out backwards. Inner palace ladies huddled together in alarm. The king again roared like thunder.

"Hmm! This Chiang Mai is evil-minded. He captures my troops and insolently challenges me to a fight. Such bluster is improper.

This piffling country makes bold to fight with *me*! It's like a lone young deer coming to confront a lion and die.

Me, the pillar of the city, whom no country dares oppose. This fellow is deluded and ignorant. His karma has led his thinking astray.

Chiang Mai is no bigger than one handful. It's not fitting for a Thai army to engage them. His whole dynasty will be wiped out. He boasts he will fight an elephant duel with me.

So he doesn't look shameful, he makes up stories that he asked for the princess's hand and that they granted her to him. But it's generally known that the envoy came to present the Lanchang princess to me.

If he had the power that his missive claims, Lanchang would have feared

---

25. Legends of wars decided by kings dueling on elephant back are a staple of the Thai royal historical tradition, especially a battle between King Naresuan and the Burmese Uparat in January 1593 (RCA, 130–31).

26. ไฟกัลป์, *fai kan*, the fire that consumes the world at the close of an era (*kalpa*) in the Three Worlds cosmology. The fire starts after seven suns rise in succession, and burns not only the realm of mankind, but all four realms of loss and woe below, and ten of the realms above, up to the second *jhana* (RR, 305–11).

27. "The other end of the *Pagne* [lowercloth] hangs before, and as they have no Pockets, they do frequently tye thereunto their purse for the *Betel*, after the manner that we tye any thing in the corner of our Handkerchief" (La Loubère, *New Historical Relation*, 26).

his authority and not resisted. But because they know he's evil, they presented the child to this city.

He has shamefully seized the princess in the forest. He has captured Thainam in order to kill him. Why allow this king to remain a burden on the earth? Heigh! Phraya Jakri, raise an army immediately.

In three days, I'll lead it to Chiang Mai. If I can't take the city, I won't return. Conscript untold numbers of troops from the dependent cities, great and small. Squeeze them to the last man.

Don't spare this Chiang Mai rabble. Wherever they're found, slash them to dust. Lay waste their city and leave it deserted. Raze its walls and fortifications!"

For the four pillars, listening to the king's outburst was like being pierced by arrows. Trembling, they nudged one another, and had Chaophraya Jakri make a reply.

"My liege, Your Majesty, eminence of the city, great monarch whose abundant merit is so perfect that it enhances the royal guardianship.

If Your Majesty is thinking of war, we see there is good cause and have no objection. But I crave Your Majesty's pardon for saying that it will weigh upon the royal advance to enlightenment[28] in the long run.

For an official matter as small as this, it is not fitting that the king should go to battle with the Lao of the forests. Are there no military officers for such purpose?

Your royal dignity may be impaired, while Chiang Mai will gain in glory by proclaiming this is a duel between the kings of the world. It is not fitting to bring the sky down to the earth.

At the time of Lord Ram, Hanuman volunteered, and accomplished the dispelling of the demons and the restoration of Sida to the city.[29]

What if, on this occasion, the king were to go to Chiang Mai and lose all the capital's troops? I beg Your Victorious Majesty to preserve his honor by emulating the time of Lord Ram."

Hanuman

---

28. โพธิญาณ, *phothiyan*, the enlightenment of the Buddha. In the political theory of late Ayutthaya, the king had qualified to become king by accumulating more merit than anyone else, and was thus similar to a Bodhisatta, a Buddha to be, or en route to becoming one himself (Nidhi, *Pen and Sail*, 323–30).

29. A one-sentence summary of the plot of the *Ramakian*.

The almighty king, eminence and pillar of the world, pondered quietly on what he had heard,

and then asked the officers and courtiers, "What do you think? Now that they have come to challenge me, who will volunteer to go? Tell me!"

The high officials were at a loss because they had no volunteer. Not knowing how to answer the king, they remained silent and prostrate with their heads bowed.

The king angrily stamped his foot and roared like thunder. "When I want something important, you just sit in stunned silence with no answer. You're all chatter and no substance.

You're good only at cheating your own men out of money by using your clever tongues. I don't have to support you with allowances.[30] Your property and rank are a burden on the realm."

Still angry, he went into the inner palace. All the nobles went home feeling tarnished and fearful from hearing the king's warning.

⚛

Now to tell of the lovable Phlai Ngam, clever, courageous, diligent in acquiring knowledge, and equipped with exceptional powers. His fearless aim was to go to war.[31]

He had lived with Phramuen Si for over a year, making efforts to be of service so that Phramuen Si loved him and raised him like a son to be happy and comfortable in every way.

On the day that news came of war, he hoped that this was a chance to achieve his aim. He would ask for Phramuen Si's patronage in maneuvering for him to be accepted as a volunteer.

Then he would somehow find a way to address the king on behalf of his father. Thinking of him made tears well up in his eyes. "Oh, what karma did you make, Father, that you must bear such terrible hardship?

You've been jailed since I was in the womb. Somehow my mother, Wanthong, is not concerned. She shared your hardship for a long time but once she went home she paid no attention.

It's many years since she took an interest. She doesn't seem to think of the

---

30. เบี้ยหวัด, *biawat*, annual allowances paid to members of the royal family and senior officials.

31. Phlai Ngam is fifteen or sixteen. He was thirteen (twelve by Western counting) at his topknot ceremony in chapter 26, and has spent over one year in Phramuen Si's household. According to the horoscope in chapter 26, he will be eighteen (seventeen) on return from the campaign which takes a little over a year.

past with you, yet I almost died because of that devil, Khun Chang."

As he sobbed, his thoughts turned to the Buddha. "Oh Lord, I sincerely pray that I may think up a way to ask pardon for my father.

May I achieve what I hope. May my keen desire not be disappointed." He prayed and made obeisance. At dusk, lamp-lighting time,

he found Phramuen Si in the central hall with his wife and children seated all around amid bright candlelight. Phramuen Si was unhappily

relating the king's anger over the army. "The king finally gave orders for call-up papers to raise a royal army, officers and men. The city is in uproar."

Phlai Ngam hid listening to Phramuen Si. When an opportunity came, he crawled in, chanted a formula to gain mercy, made obeisance, and asked,

"You seem unhappy, Pa.[32] What's the matter? I hear the whole capital is in uproar. They're conscripting people and it's chaotic. I'd like to know what's going on."

Phramuen Si said, "Oh Phlai Ngam, we're not used to war. Today the king posed a question to everybody.

Total silence. No volunteer. The king was thunderously angry. He'll come to audience tomorrow but we're at a loss. It's up to our merit and karma.

If nobody volunteers, I think it'll be terrible. Death and chaos will follow. Everyone's face is black with gloom."

Phlai Ngam knew this situation suited his aim. He crouched close to Phramuen Si and said, "Don't be worried, Pa. Please make a petition on my behalf in the proper way.

I'll volunteer to crush Chiang Mai to dust and capture this good fellow, its ruler, so troops don't have to suffer.

Everything that I've studied from teachers at great effort has not been put to use. Let me volunteer to fight this time so my name may be known throughout the world as the descendant of a valiant military line."

The astute Phramuen Si was dubious about Phlai Ngam daring to volunteer. "I cannot agree.

You're still a very young child. It's not fitting to address the king about you volunteering. I've never seen what powers of lore you've acquired from study.

Oh Son, warfare is a deep matter. You can't fight with fine words alone. If

---

32. คุณพ่อ, *khun pho*. Phlai Ngam addresses Pramuen Si as his father, and Pramuen Si reciprocates by calling Phlai Ngam his son. This vocabulary was common between patrons and dependents (see pp. 923–25).

you were like your father, than I could have faith in you. Did he give you his manuals to study?

If I petition the king and it turns out well, we'll gain face. But if it goes badly, we'll be taken off to be flogged. You'll suffer a setback and all your efforts at study will go to waste. If you fail, we'll all be dead.

Think carefully, beloved child. Making a bold petition isn't a simple matter. I care for you like my own son and I intend to establish you to be something.

I'm not standing in your way because of prejudice. I just fear you'll go and not survive. Don't be so fearless that you're careless. Please look at this matter from all angles."

Phlai Ngam bowed and answered humbly. "You oppose me out of love because you don't yet know my ability, Pa. I'm not speaking rashly.

I've been the student of teachers with authentic knowledge and unparalleled powers of divination. If you want evidence, I'll demonstrate so you can see for sure with your own eyes."

With these words, he raised his hands to pay respect to his teachers and summon their powers, then chanted a formula. In full view of everyone there, his body instantly disappeared.

Phramuen Si took a moment to recover himself, and then laughed heartily. "Oh, that's good! You'll do well. You're no blight on the lineage. Release the formula so we can talk."

Phlai Ngam released it and reappeared, then turned himself into an aged striped tiger, drawing its body up into an awesome pose as if about to pounce on the people there.

Phramuen Si's wife and children fled in fright, but Phramuen Si understood the artifice and was bent over with laughter.

Phlai Ngam relaxed the power of the mantra, transforming himself back into human form. He sat down and wai-ed Phramuen Si who smiled broadly while patting Phlai Ngam on the back.

"You'll succeed for sure, my son. You're better than a common ruffian, have no fear. At first I had my doubts and so didn't agree, but now I've seen how good your knowledge is.

With this, the king should be pleased, and not get enraged a second time. All the officers and nobles will gain face because you alone will get them off the hook."

The two of them talked without sleeping until dawn came and sunlight caught the hilltops. They prepared to go to audience, and walked away from the house at the appointed time.

Phramuen Si boarded a palanquin and Phlai Ngam walked behind him to the official sala. The senior nobles were all there.

Chaophraya Kalahom, Chaophraya Jakri, and the four pillars were engaged in discussion. The astute Phramuen Si led Phlai Ngam over
to tell them the news. "This able fellow will volunteer. He's the son of Khun Phaen Saensathan and grandson of Khun Krai. His name is Phlai Ngam. He's swift, of good character,
and accomplished in knowledge. He can make himself completely invisible." The ministers brightened up when they heard this. Chaophraya Jakri said, "Excellent!

He has the bearing of a brave soldier, definitely. There are signs this can work. He's both son and grandson of soldiers, and with powers of lore he can probably succeed.

He's good-looking like his father, Khun Phaen, and also has the same brave heart. If you enter royal service and you're as expert as he says, you've nothing to fear.

We'll help raise you to have rank and a reputation known everywhere. If you take Chiang Mai, you'll acquire many families, cattle, and buffaloes to make you comfortable."

After their discussion, it was almost time for the king to appear in audience. The ministers prepared to enter in rank order at the appointed time.

Now to tell of the king who resided under a brilliant jeweled spire. In the dawn light of the sun, he was bathed and dressed,
and went out to the Sutthasawan Hall[33] with his mind full of anger at his foes. The sound of horns echoed through the palace as the nobles prostrated.

The king looked at his officials, his face pale with anger almost to distraction. "Why are you quiet? I'm waiting to hear who will volunteer. Or is there nobody?

Perhaps some slaves from some department or other will volunteer, and I can get rid of you lot at once and make room to give them appointments in your stead."

---

33. สุทธาศวรรย์, "nectar of heaven," name of the building in the Lopburi Palace where King Narai is supposed to have died, and also of a building in the Bangkok Grand Palace, built at the start of the Third Reign and known as *phlapphla sung*, the tall pavilion. In Ayutthaya, processions and entertainments were staged on the parade ground on the eastern side of the palace, and the king viewed from the Chakkaphat Phichaiyon Throne Hall (see p. 794, note 17). In this passage, the entertainment is located inside the palace wall, requiring entry through a gate, as was true in Ayutthaya, but the name of the throne hall comes from Bangkok where entertainments were staged outside the palace in Sanamchai Road (KW, 357–58; see map 9).

Phramuen Si Saowarak-rat made obeisance to address the king without any fear. "My liege, upholder of the teachings, my life is under the royal foot.

I went to make inquiries and found Phlai Ngam to volunteer. He's the son of the mighty Khun Phaen and has studied to be expert in knowledge.

I myself had my doubts so I tested him and he is indeed accomplished, able, bold, and well-equipped with knowledge. His forebears went to war in the past."

Hearing Phramuen Si, the king said brightly, "Aha! Where is he? Summon him quickly so I can see if I like his face."

Phramuen Si turned to pass on the summons. Phlai Ngam, who had been paying attention, promptly crawled past the minor royal pages[34] as duty officers cleared his way.

In front of the royal throne, he prostrated, composed his mind to chant a formula to gain royal mercy, and remained prostrate, praying in his heart.

The almighty king looked round and liked what he saw. He roared, "Heigh! Phlai Ngam, bold young fellow!

Your lineage are soldiers. Try to acquit yourself well on royal service. If you can fix these Lao as wished, you'll be rewarded with money and rank.

Tell me whether you can do this or not. I see your face is handsome, and your character is like your father's. Why are you quiet? Speak out!"

Phlai Ngam raised his hands above his head to receive the royal order, and responded, "My liege, Your Majesty, my life is beneath the dust.

May I volunteer, under the protection of Your Majesty's power, to capture the impetuous ruler of Chiang Mai so that phrai troops need not be troubled.

May I request a royal pardon for my father so he may accompany me as partner, and I may consult him and draw on his assistance in case of difficulty in countering the stratagems of the enemy.

If I can join forces with my father, may I request to volunteer until death. If I fail against Chiang Mai, may I offer the lives of all living members of my lineage."

---

34. หุ้มแพร, *hum phrae*, "silk wrap." When pages joined a royal procession, they walked in file holding a manila rope to ensure they looked orderly, and used a piece of silk to guard their hands against chafing by the rope. *Hum phrae* became the name of a junior post in the royal pages. Each of the four units consisted of one *hua muen*, one *nai wen*, one *ja*, and three *hum phrae*. The term *phrae* was originally applied to silk from China but subsequently was used more loosely for any silk (*Rueang mahatlek*, 1, 24; KP, 243).

Wreathed in smiles, the king clapped his hands loudly. "Oh, you present yourself well!

It's a pity that Khun Phaen was unfortunate, fell on hard times, and almost died. He's festered in jail for many years. It was wrong of me to forget him.

Did something block me thinking of him? Only when Phlai Ngam came with this request, did I recall him. When Khun Phaen asked for Laothong, I was angry and imprisoned him for a long time, up to this day.

Look here, you nobles, it's not right for you all to remain so quiet. He's suffered for fifteen years because not a single person liked him enough.

As he had no wealth, his case lay hidden, isn't that so? If he were rich rather than poor, all you fellows would be asking on his behalf every single day.

We're looking for the right kind of person to go to war but nobody thought of him because you're jealous that your own knowledge doesn't equal his, and because he attacked you when you went with Khun Chang,

and you all ran off in fright, heads nodding like flowers. You knew about his skills but you didn't seek him out. Phraya Yom, you heard. Why delay? Have Khun Phaen released and brought here."

Minister Yommarat prostrated in delight, and left the jeweled audience hall. He gave orders to a sheriff[35]

to release Khun Phaen forthwith and bring him quickly, in time for the royal audience. The sheriff scurried away

to the jail and had the warden make the release immediately. He brought Khun Phaen back to the palace, sank down, and wai-ed the minister.

Phraya Yommarat greeted them and explained matters to the bewildered Khun Phaen. "Phlai Ngam asked the king on your behalf as a favor, and the king graciously granted a pardon.

It's a pity your hair is all the way down to the ground and your appearance is pitifully changed, but go into the audience without delay." He took him in on all fours.

The king beckoned with his hand and called Khun Phaen to come closer.

---

35. นรบาล, *noraban*, Sanskrit *narapala*, man in charge. For security, the city was divided into four zones which met at the *ho klong*, the drum tower by the *talaengkaeng* crossroads (see map 8): "from the drum tower to Jao Sai and Yot Market is the quarter of Khun Thoraniban (ธรณีบาล); from the drum tower to Pratu Chai and Jao Sai is the quarter of Khun Thoraban (ทราบาล); from the drum tower to Pa Maphrao, Tha Chima, and the end of Bang Iyan is the quarter of Khun Lokaban (โลกบาล); from the drum tower to Bang Iyan and the palace is the quarter of Khun Noraban" (Palatine law, clause 16, KTS, 1:76). This divides the city roughly into quadrants, with Noraban in charge of the northwest including the jail.

Khun Phaen crouched down in front of Phlai Ngam and prostrated three times.

The king spoke, "Eh, Khun Phaen, this isn't right. You particularly have suffered a bad fate for many years. Today that's ended because of your son.

We currently have a war on the Chiang Mai side. Your son will go to attack for me. He requested for you to go as a companion-in-arms and advisor.

I found you trustworthy in the past. Nobody can counter your skills. It was wrong of me to keep you in jail—out of forgetfulness, not anger.

How many thousand troops do you want? I'll have them conscripted day and night with no trouble. Would you prefer men from the capital or the provincial cities? Oxen, royal elephants, and other equipment will be requisitioned."

Khun Phaen, great gallant, prostrated and answered. "My liege, Your Majesty has graciously allowed me to go on campaign with Phlai.

I and my son, request to volunteer to take Chiang Mai and present it to Your Majesty. There's no need to bother many phrai. The call-up will be troublesome and create delay.

May I request only enough military phrai to transport food supplies and cook. For battle troops, may I request some convicts from the jail.

There are thirty-five men, all tough, invulnerable, capable, and brave. They've studied everything about warfare and have every kind of knowledge from various teachers."

The king, upholder of the world, heard Khun Phaen through to the end and found him amusing. "Heigh! The Chiang Mai territory is big, with many people from several cities.

You want to take just these few men? Even though they're able and proficient, and will do their utmost to fight and kill, I think you'll come back defeated.

The day after tomorrow, bring these men to show off how able and skilled they are for us to see. Phraya Yom, what d'you think? Release all thirty-five to him without delay."

With this order, the king returned inside in good humor. The nobles left the hall together. Khun Phaen wai-ed everybody.

Some greeted him and spoke as friends. All happily praised him in various ways and offered him moral support, blessings, and advice. "Your bad fortune and unhappiness are now over."

Minister Yommarat called the father and son over. They went with Phramuen Si, and gave the minister a list of the convicts that the king had granted to them.

An officer was sent to secure their release. The convicts were brought over and drawn up for inspection and roll call in front of Khun Phaen. Each gave testimony on his background in turn.

"My name is Ai-Phuk from Luk-kae. My wife's name is I-Tae, sir. I was convicted for robbery, forcing the victims to dance a forest dance, and making I-Ma dance naked single-handed."[36]

"Next!" "Ai-Mi from Ban Yilon, wife's name I-Phon. I robbed Ta-Khiao, and stabbed I-Chang while she was pissing. She grimaced and fell down flat, slobbering."

"Next!" "Ai-Pan from Ban Chi-hon, wife I-Son. I robbed Bang Plakot, tied Ta-Jai and Granny Rot by the neck, and singed off all their hair."

"Next!" "Ai-Jan Samphantueng, wife I-Ueng, from Ban Mueang Mai, in the gang that robbed Khun Siwichai and shoved a stick up his arse so he died."[37]

"Next!" "My name's Ai-Khong Khrao, wife's name I-Tao, from Ban Nong Wai. Last year I robbed Ban Bang Phasi, taking buffaloes and property."

"Next!" "I'm Ai-Siat, wife's name I-Kongrat, sir. I fell in with some Thai and robbed a Lawa village, then murdered Ta-Pan from Ban Tan-en."

"Next!" "Ai-Thong from Chong Khwak, husband of I-Mak. I killed a Lao called Thao Sen, crept in to steal an almsbowl and shoulder cloth from a novice, thumped an old monk, and had a wrestle with the abbot."

"Next!" "Ai-Chang Dam, from Ban Tham. I burgled a tax collector and took all his money and property—good stuff and no small amount, including jewels."

"Next!" "Ai-Bua Hua Kalok, convicted for robbing Monk Khok at Pak Kret, hitting Ai-Duk with the flat nose, and stabbing Ta-Sai the duck vendor at Ban Tuek Daeng."

"Next!" "My name's Ai-Taengmo, wife's name I-To, from Ban Chumsaeng. I robbed Chi Dak Khanon, taking all I could carry, and killed Khun Thipsaeng, owner of the goods."

"Ai-In Suea Luang from Chainat town, wife's name I-Pat from Ban Khanai. I've robbed and killed about a hundred people, and stolen countless buffaloes to kill and eat."

buffalo

<hr />

36. Probably with one hand covering her modesty. On making victims dance, see p. 45, note 73.

37. Presumably he is the same Janson that appeared in chapter 2, and must by now be over fifty (Phlai Ngam is sixteen; Khun Phaen was around twenty-three when Phlai Ngam was born; Janson must have been at least eighteen when he killed Khun Krai, while Phlai was five; 16+23+18-5=52).

"Ai-Mon Mue-dang from Bang Chalong, wife's name I-Khong, a northerner. I've stolen just about everything including mortars and pestles, and robbed boats."

"Next!" "Ai-Thong from Nong Fuk, wife's name I-Duk, daughter of Ta-Jop. In daytime, I kept the house closed like a female spirit,[38] but at dusk went off alone to burgle."

"Ai-Mak Saklek. I robbed Jek Kua and his slit-eyed wife named I-Sao." "Next!" "Ai-Kung from Khung Taphao. I stabbed I-Mao's husband and seized her as my wife."

"Ai-Song, husband of I-Khong, from Kongkhon. I killed a Mon and stole cloth." "Next!" "Ai-Krang from Bang Hia. I couldn't find a wife so I robbed boats."

"Ai-Kling, husband of I-Klak. I barricaded roads, stole buffaloes to sell, and robbed boats from the north." "Ai-Phao, husband of I-Phan from Ban Na-kluea. I poisoned Luang Choduek[39] and cleaned out his house."

"Ai-Jua, husband of I-Prang, from Bang Namchon. I burgled Muen Thon, picking him clean." "Ai-Maeo, husband of I-Ma, from Tha Kwian. I went to Ban Phitphian to rob and steal.

Under questioning, I put the blame on someone else. Then I took goods from Nang Thong Kramip." "Next!" "Ai-Man, husband of I-Janthip, from Namdip. I robbed Abbot Phao,

but did not stab him as accused. The sheriff's examination found it was an old wound." "Ai-Jan, husband of I-Jan, from Ban Kaphrao. I was convicted of robbing Chinaman Kao and burning his shop.

I fired a gun, hollered, and hit the head of a child with the back of a big machete." "Next!" "Ai-Sa Noklek, from Khung Thalunglek, husband of I-Di.

I barricaded roads to rob cattle around Khorat, and stabbed Ai-Chua, husband of I-Pat, who fell down in the dirt." "Ai-Mak Nuat, husband of I-Khuat, from Bang Phli. I was convicted of daylight robbery in Doembang."

"Ai-Koet Kradukdam, husband of I-Khamdang, convicted of burgling the Department of Elephants with mahout Man, and robbing a forest Lawa. I'm invulnerable with a single testicle and twisted scrotum."[40]

---

38. ชะมบ, *chamop*, an old word for a shadowy, malevolent female spirit, capable of possessing people. Spirits do not like to go out in daylight. (Anuman, *Pi sang thewada*, 50–51; KW, 681–82)

39. The official title of the head of the Chinese community in the capital, usually a very rich and influential person.

40. Both signs of a man with powerful lore. The places mentioned by the thirty-five soldiers are scattered all round the Chaophraya Plain.

Luk-kae, on the Maeklong River at the border of Ratchaburi and Kanchanaburi.

The thirty-five pardoned convicts were all daring, strong, invulnerable to sword and spear, capable of withstanding anything.

For their karma, they had been imprisoned a long time. But now the ending of that karma caused a change for the better. Phlai Ngam asked the king for the release of his father, and so all of them were pardoned too.

After the inspection, the thirty-five were entrusted to Khun Phaen. Phraya Yommarat gave his blessing.

"May you defeat demons and kill enemies so the king's reputation spreads far and wide. And son, Phlai Ngam, may you take the city of Chiang Mai as we hope."

Ban Yilon, in Amphoe Sam Ko, Ang Thong.

Ban Chi-hon, unidentified.

Bang Plakot, Catfish Village, just outside Pa Mok, Ang Thong.

Ban Mueang Mai, New Mine Village, possibly in Amphoe Amphawa, Samut Songkhram.

Ban Nong Wai, Rattan Pond Village, possibly in Amphoe Bo Phloi, Kanchanaburi.

Ban Bang Phasi, Tax Village, in Amphoe Bang Len, Nakhon Pathom.

Ban Tan-en, Leaning Sugar Palm Village, in Amphoe Bang Pahan, Ayutthaya.

Chong Khwak, possibly Ban Khwak in Amphoe Samchuk, Suphanburi.

Ban Tham, Muen Han's lair in Kanchanaburi, from the Buakhli story (see *Companion*, 1174).

Pak Kret, an island in the Chaophraya River, now just to the north of Bangkok.

Ban Tuek Daeng, unidentified.

Ban Chumsaeng, now an amphoe, 30 kms northeast of Nakhon Sawan (see map 4).

Chi Dak Khanon, on the east bank of the Chaophraya River, north of Chainat (see map 4).

Chainat, now a provincial headquarters on the Chaophraya River (see map 4).

Ban Khanai, possibly Ban Wang Khanai in Amphoe Tha Mueang, Kanchanaburi.

Bang Chalong, possibly in Amphoe Bangphli, Samut Prakan.

Nong Fuk, Kapok Pond, unidentified.

Khung Taphao, Fieldrat Bend Village, elsewhere called U-Taphao, now Khung Samphao, in Amphoe Manoram, Chainat (see map 4).

Kongkhon, unidentified.

Bang Hia, Monitor Lizard Village, once probably a common name, but now almost disappeared as the animal is considered inauspicious.

Ban Na-kluea, Saltfield Village, of which there are many, but none in the probable region.

Bang Namchon (see p. 477, note 27).

Tha Kwian, on the route from Sawankhalok to Thoen (see above p. 536, note 3).

Ban Phitphian, in Amphoe Maharat in the north of Ayutthaya (see map 3).

Namdip, Freshwater, possibly in Amphoe Mae Sot, Tak.

Ban Kaphrao, unidentified.

Khung Thalunglek, Ironsmelt Village, just west of Amphoe Khok Samrong, Lopburi.

Bang Phli, in Amphoe Bang Sai in the south of Ayutthaya.

Doembang, now Amphoe Doembang Nangbuat, in the north of Suphanburi (see map 2).

Then he turned to give orders to his retainers. "Select patterned cloth from the swordstore[41] along with many oranges and other fruits, and distribute them to all the war volunteers."

Retainers carried over piles of goods, and Phraya Yommarat invited them to choose. Khun Phaen organized the distribution to all the men.

They changed and threw their old cloths away. "Tcha! It didn't cover my arse. I shamed my wife." Some took off strange-looking clothes made from sacking. They had been extremely poor until this escape from hardship.

They called one another to eat, whooping with joy. "From now on, times will be good!" "If Pa[42] hadn't asked for our release from prison, we'd have festered hopelessly in jail until death."

"We'll be your servants until the end of our days, to be of use in whatever way you want." The proficient Khun Phaen paid respect to the high officials and took leave.

Phramuen Si rode his horse home.[43] Khun Phaen followed on foot with Phlai Ngam behind him and then the big crowd of thirty-five men.

Phramuen Si arranged places to stay and had food prepared. The thirty-five made merry in high spirits until the sun dropped down at dusk.

Now to tell of Kaeo Kiriya, who had remained beside her husband when they stayed in the shelter at the slip gate. She was now ten months pregnant and big.

When her husband was able to leave the jail, their house was strewn with pots and pitchers and piles of raggedy cloth. These were her old friends in hardship, but now she would be parted from them.

She donated them as alms to other convicts, and cheerfully set off after her beloved husband. Phramuen Si gladly said, "Live with us. Don't worry that your husband is going off to war."

He invited Khun Phaen and Phlai Ngam to sit together with him in a circle, and called the minor wives to serve the three of them food. When they were finished, Phramuen Si pointed out,

"My friend, your hair is such a mess it's shameful, like a ruffian. You don't

---

41. ตึก, *tuek*, a building of durable materials, most likely brick, probably the *tuek lang yao*, the long brick building, a name for the swordstore used by officials.

42. The thirty-five look upon Khun Phaen as their patron and address him as their father. He reciprocates by sometimes addressing them as his children (see pp. 923–25).

43. In the Wat Ko version at this point, it specifies that they go to Khan Landing, which was situated outside the northeast corner of the palace, suggesting this was the location of Phramuen Si's house (WK, 22:889; KW, 361; see map 9; KW, 361).

look like a Jek, and I doubt you're a Thai. You look suspiciously like a Lawa. It's comic."[44]

Khun Phaen made a request to Phramuen Si. "Now that this lad has determined to volunteer, I'm concerned over my mother. She's getting older and ricketier every day.

Living in Kanburi, she'll be miserable thinking about her son and grandson. If we could bring her to live with us, we'd have some peace of mind even though we go off to war."

Phramuen Si replied, "Happy to be of service. Bringing her here is no problem. I'll have her fetched tomorrow."

The three talked until late. At midnight, they went into the house and all slept until sunrise.

Now to tell of King Phanwasa. He summoned Laothong. "Phlai Ngam bravely volunteered, and asked for his father to be released from jail.

You've suffered for over ten years. I can see you're not happy here. I'm pardoning you to end your sorrow. No more embroidery. Leave quickly."

Laothong was exultant at the king's pardon. She quickly prostrated to take leave, and went to make her farewells to the senior palace women.[45]

Her close friends exclaimed that she had had a stroke of luck. Others whispered, "She found a loophole." She said farewell to her many good friends including Si, Phrom, and Mae Som-O,

and then to the head governess.[46] She went into her own room, combed her hair in a mirror, put on oil, and doused herself with krajae-sandal in the hope of being attractive at close quarters.

She wore a yok with aporosa flowers, upper-

votive-deity pattern

---

44. At this point in PD, Khun Phaen cuts his own hair. The following two stanzas have been removed here, so as not to conflict with the hair-cutting scene below, taken from WK: Khun Phaen laughed. "Sir, you're very eloquent." He got up, enchanted some water in a bowl, wet his hair, cut it in the Mahatthai style, and oiled it. Then he bathed himself, / applied powder, and dressed neatly in a cheerful patterned cloth. He came back to the front of Phramuen Si's hall, and the three continued chatting.

45. หม่อมป้าโต, *mom pa to*, lady great aunt, probably a colloquial term for senior women in the palace administration.

46. เจ้าขรัวนาย, *jao khrua nai*, a term for the chief palace governess (see p. 315, note 23).

cloth in light purple, and another cloth with an elegant votive-deity pattern over the top. With thoughts racing, she looked herself over, set her mind, and walked out, looking beautiful.

She packed a chest with betelnut sets in nak and gold, trays, and water bowls made for palace ladies. She put in all her sparkling jewelry, then went out a side door and through Din Gate.

I-Thueng hurried along behind her mistress carrying the chest, with five others walking behind in a

chest

crowd, lugging the rest of her things. They[47] came through Din Gate towards Khan Landing

and saw Khun Phaen gazing around. "Over there! Who's that? He looks similar but thinner, and his hair is long enough to sit on."

From a distance they peered across but neither mistress nor servants could recognize him. He resembled the sort of madman who throws dirt around. I-In called out, "Poor fellow,

my mistress is looking for her husband, but this fellow sitting and staring around turns out to be the husband of the lady with the heavily pregnant belly." I-Suk got up to look. "What?"

Khun Phaen almost failed to recognize Laothong but figured it out. He called out happily, "Don't you know me? Why don't you come over?"

Hearing his words, Laothong could remember the voice. Going closer to him, she recognized his face and clasped his feet, brimming with tears. "I just heard the king gave you a pardon,

so I came to find you. You look so strange that I didn't recognize you, and I was standing there not daring to come. Your appearance is so wasted and different.

Oh my dear lord and husband, it's as if you'd died and been born again to reunite us. Ever since I was confined in the inner palace, I've cried all the time without missing a day.

At mealtimes, I couldn't eat a mouthful without being forced to swallow tears of sorrow. At night, I'd sleep thinking of love. I felt like holding my breath until I died.

I embroidered silk endlessly, beyond thinking when I would see you again.

---

47. From here to the end of the section, "What?" is taken from WK, 23:891–92; PD has: Friends greeted Laothong, but she did not hear them. She reached the house and went up the stairs.

embroidery frame

I was miserable morning and night, and the suffering has lasted an age."

The[48] crowd of people walking past stopped to look at them and tut-tutted to one another. "Oh good lady, you have a very lovely face. In every respect you look like a palace lady.

But falling in love with someone who's lost his mind is not befitting. Aren't you ashamed, I beg of you? Don't good people like us please you? Hanging around to consort with a madman is despicable."

Someone else said, "Hey! You crazy fart. Don't be so arrogant. When a tiger falls on hard times, nobody pays him attention. That's the mighty Phaen who has just been released.

Behind is Phlai Ngam who has volunteered to go on military service. And that's Phaen's wife Laothong who was punished but has been released to rejoin her love."

Laothong looked around and asked, "Who's sitting back there?" Khun Phaen said at once, "Her name is Kaeo Kiriya.

I got her as a wife when I fled away with Wanthong. While I was in jail, she looked after me. That's my son who asked the king for my pardon. His name is Phlai Ngam. His mother is Wanthong."

He took Kaeo Kiriya into the house, and piled up her belongings in a room. They all talked together, getting on well without jealousy.

Kaeo Kiriya[49] and Laothong stayed with the grandmother while Khun Phaen and Phlai Ngam went in one day to Suphan to pay respect to the abbot of Wat Palelai.

They took offerings of incense, candles, betel, and pan. The abbot scrutinized them and asked, "Where are you from?" "My name is Phlai Kaeo. My son petitioned the king to have me released from punishment.

---

48. This section, down to "rejoin her love," is taken from WK, 23:892–93; the scene is absent from PD where the reunion takes place inside Phramuen Si's house.

49. This whole visit to Suphan, down to "They received this blessing, prostrated, and left" on p. 558 is taken from WK, 23:897–99; the scene is absent from PD, where Khun Phaen cuts his own hair in an earlier scene (see p. 555, note 44 above).

My wife's name is Wanthong. After I abducted her, she became pregnant in the forest." The abbot laughed, "Oh, that's right. I thought it was somebody else, some madman.

After I'd taught you everything, it was unnecessary for you to face such hardship. You can unlock manacles and any kind of restraint, disappear, be invulnerable or invisible, and hold your breath.

Yet you still got yourself locked up in chains and cangue. What was up? Didn't you have faith in your knowledge? Or was it fun lying in jail? Why didn't you escape to find me?

If they'd come after you, I'd have put on a yantra cloth and fought back. Why did you sit doing nothing, not following what I taught you? You've got knowledge up to your neck yet you're still afraid of people."

abbot giving takrut

Khun Phaen prostrated on the ground to the teacher. "I was not lacking in power but I'd sworn to Phraya Yommarat, and would not go back on the word I'd given.

He trusted me, and as a result I was not placed under restraint. It was unbefitting for me to disobey and put him in the wrong. I would rather die keeping my oath. You're disappointed because you're unaware of this.

I'm going to attack and take Chiang Mai. My hair is as messy as a lunatic. May I ask the master to cut it for me, and wash it so I'm comfortable.

After hearing Khun Phaen, the abbot changed his robe, picked up scissors and comb, parted the hair, and gathered it up with the comb.

However hard he tried, the hair resisted[50] until Khun Phaen enchanted some water and wet it, after which the cutting was quickly done. Then the abbot had a fire made to bathe Khun Phaen's body.

Khun Phaen clasped his hands in prayer while the flames whooshed up to cover his head. When the fire went out, his body was not burned but looked as beautiful as a freshly blooming lotus.

The abbot anointed him with water. Father, son, and their phrai were happy.

---

50. On account of Khun Phaen's invulnerability.

"Be victorious over Chiang Mai without fail!" They received this blessing, prostrated, and left.

∽

Khun Phaen came out in front of the sitting hall, and commanded the thirty-five soldiers to have their hair cut. "Prepare upper and lower cloths to look smart.

If you need anything, ask Phramuen Si. Tomorrow we go to test our skills before the king." Khun Phaen, his son, and Phramuen Si talked into the night.

At dawn they ate and hurried over to enter the palace just before the time for audience. On that day, word had spread around the city

that the knowledge of the volunteers would be put to the test. Everybody came in a raucous, excited crowd—Thai, Chinese, Mon, Burmese, Kha, Lao, and Lue[51]—dragging their children and grandchildren by the hand.

As they squashed through the gate, breasts were slyly pinched and squeezed. Young lads, puffed up with excitement, groped at young girls and larked about.

Some tugged at uppercloths and grabbed for a breast. The guards whipped as hard as they could. Anyone caught was clapped pale-faced in a cangue. Those who could dodge, escaped into the palace.

Crowds of people filled the outer courtyard.[52] At the appointed time, conch and horn sounded, the king emerged, and everybody prostrated together.

The king went to sit in the Sutthasawan Throne Hall. When the curtain was drawn back, he looked like the sun god riding in his chariot.

He summoned Khun Phaen and Phlai Ngam. All thirty-five soldiers entered and crawled up to make obeisance to the king at the front of the palace courtyard.

Boxer guards[53] made a circle by stretching a leather cord around the fore courtyard in front of the throne. Officials sat inside the circle, and ordinary people outside.

---

51. ลื้อ, a Tai ethnic group from the region of Chiang Rung, now in southern Yunnan, China.

52. This would have taken place in the area in the southeast corner marked as "parade ground" on map 9, with the king presiding from the Chakkaphat Phichaiyon Hall (see p. 794, note 17 above). The plinth of this building still exists, including a semicircular terrace looking out onto the parade ground.

53. ทนายเลือก, *thanai luek*, a unit of skilled boxers and swordsmen that acted as bodyguards for the king, especially when in procession. Usually they were unarmed or carried lances for show. They were left and right units within the palace guard, headed by Khun Phakdi-asa and Khun Yotha-phakdi respectively, each *sakdina* 600 (KTS, 1:294; KW, 682; Sirindhorn, *Banthuek*, 61).

The noisy crowd of all ages sat jammed together. Some squatted, glancing around. Others shifted, fidgeted, and poked one another.

Around the whole field, lines of guards carrying canes kept strict order. The king commanded Khun Phaen to bring the first man on.

Nai Bua Hua Kalok from Ban Khok Kham[54] prostrated and came out front. He lay face up, chanted a mantra, and had someone hack at him many times with an axe.

The axe bounced off while he lay there winking. Uninjured, he got up with a bright red face. Nai Khong Khrao came in, sat down, and entered meditation. He was struck with a pike full in his chest many times, without even bruising. He sat nodding his head and laughing until the handle of the pike gave way and broke.

Nai Mon lay down naked while a saw was brought. They sawed at him but the teeth bent and broke. The sawing team was changed many times but after several attempts the blade had not penetrated at all.

Nai Chang Dam, strong as a great elephant, prostrated and crawled in with no fear. He jumped three fathoms high with his eyes shining, showing off his strong black muscles.

Nai Siat, who had always escaped injury, had seven pikes thrown at him but they just slid off and fell to the ground. Nai In held his breath and disappeared.

Nai Thong stood still while a gun was fired and he caught the shot. Nai Jan amazingly lifted an ox. Nai Bua transformed himself into several people.

Nai Taengmo made himself grow to giant size, then leapt around goggling his eyes and screwing up his face. Nai Jua, with his funny-looking head, showed he could withstand a flaming fire.

All thirty-five displayed their respective disciplines to the king, one after another. Then they all came to prostrate in a row for the king to present rewards.

Each received five tamlueng in cash, a set of cloth, and bonuses according to whether their skill was of first or second class.

"There's still Phlai Ngam, the volunteer. Is he really able or just boastful?" "His body doesn't look big but his heart is huge." "Hey, Phaen! Show us a contest with your son."

Khun Phaen and Phlai Ngam prostrated in turn. The crowd swarmed to their feet to watch the father and son test each other's skills.

---

54. Tamarind Mound Village, a common name, now found in Nakhon Sawan and Samut Sakhon.

Phlai Ngam asked forgiveness from his father, then picked up a spear and stood with arms stretched, looking funny. Khun Phaen stood with a sword in each hand, struck a pose, and advanced to engage with the spear.

Khaek drums pounded out a rhythm. The pair strutted and struck through several rounds, trading maneuvers of equal proficiency, with neither giving ground or backing away.

Phlai Ngam looked the more agile but Khun Phaen had the style and strength. When one gained the advantage and attacked strongly, the other parried and thrust. They exchanged slashing blows

yet none of them penetrated. Phlai Ngam turned and walked away as if retreating. As soon as he was some distance apart, he put his spear down on the ground, made a wai, and chanted the formula of the Era-destroying Fire.[55]

A blaze exploded in the middle of the arena in an echoing whoosh of licking flames. As the fire spread, people in the audience ran away en masse.

Everyone blanched in alarm. Khun Phaen chanted a mantra, and rain poured down, dousing the fire in a flash. From the audience, the sound of "Aaah!" echoed around.

cobras

"That's good!" "This father and son are the real thing!" "Superb skills!" "Unmatched." Khun Phaen made yet another formula and instantly turned into a snake, rearing up and swaying,

a big fellow as large as a tree trunk with a hood and eyes as red as red lead. As he slid along, some two thousand attendant snakes appeared, swarming around, spreading their hoods,

slithering everywhere. The watchers frantically looked for somewhere to hide. Women ran off in all directions, pale-faced, shuddering, and shrieking.

Cloths slipped, and people tripped over, trampling one another underfoot, and skidding around. Phlai Ngam promptly hurled a *takrut* amulet that turned into a big *kot* bird[56] that chased the snake,

clutching with its talons and pecking with its beak. The snake wriggled and struck. The bird parried with its wings, and pecked back. People crowded around to watch. The bird lifted the snake in its bill and flew away.

All the attendant snakes disappeared without trace. Phlai Ngam enchanted a lump of earth and the bird disappeared, transformed into an elephant

55. See p. 542, note 26 above.
56. See p. 526, note 13.

with two long white tusks, ears flared, and trunk raised. Secreting oil, the elephant raised its head, swayed from side to side, and trumpeted. Khun Phaen stood before it, flourishing a goad,

then stepped on the end of a tusk and climbed astride the beast's neck. The elephant squirmed violently but Khun Phaen hacked with a goad, slashing at the beast's forehead until it collapsed and fell back onto the ground with eyes closed.

The elephant disappeared but Phlai Ngam leapt up with some knowledge still in reserve. He uttered a formula to transform his body into a buffalo.

Khun Phaen disappeared and became a tiger. He bounded over with curved fangs bared, and then drew back, enticing the buffalo towards the king's throne. The tiger slapped with its paws and the buffalo went to gore with its horns.

They thrashed around wildly with the tiger pouncing and the buffalo tossing its horns, slashing at each other without backing off until they were bathed in sweat. Then both transformed again in the same instant.

The father became a squawking parrot and the son a magpie. They flew up to a tree, perched beside each other, and displayed their ability to speak several human languages.

The audience loved it and praised the pair all around. "What powers of lore!" "No enemy will be able to stand up to them!"

The king smiled broadly, laughed merrily, and loudly clapped his hands. "These two fellows are all right! No slouches. Equal in their powers.

We've heard that Chiang Mai fellow boast about his might and power but I'd like to see him fight with my fellows! Before a day is out, he'll flee into the forest.

Is this the end of your repertoire?" The parrot and magpie replied, "My liege, Your Majesty, we have not exhausted our teachers' manuals."

The two relaxed the mantras, returned to human form, and prostrated at the front of the courtyard. In delight, King Phanwasa had the royal gifts moved closer, and said,

"Ha! Heigh! Khun Phaen and Phlai Ngam, you had a good fight, father and son. Your faces look hungry and tired. Eat something to recover your strength."

Then he ordered the Cardinal Treasury[57] to prepare foreign *mot*[58] cloth in a

---

57. คลังวิเศษ, *khlang wiset*, used to store cloth, in the charge of Phra Ratchaprasit, *sakdina* 3,000. The building was between the Sanphet Mahaprasat Audience Hall and Wat Si Sanphet (KTS, 1:271; KLW, 203–4; APA, 68; see area 3 on map 9).

58. โหมด, originally a textile of Indian origin, principally from Rajasthan. Cloth is rolled diagonally and tie-dyed to give a striped pattern, then untied, re-rolled on the other diagonal, and dyed with another color to create a checked pattern. The term comes from *moth*, a lentil, in reference to the usually small checks. In Siam, this term seems to have been applied to Indian fabric woven with silk, silver and gold thread, and silver and gold paper, probably first imported in the early Bangkok era. (Murphy and Crill, *Tie-dyed Textiles*, 19, 72, 90–91, 200; SB, 347; *Pa phim lai boran*, 51)

cross-branch pattern, Chinese silk with a cottonrose hibiscus motif, red wool, and sompak appropriate to the position of palace nobles.

hibiscus motif

The Great Treasury[59] provided five chang, which the king presented to them. "You two are to use this until you receive rewards[60] when the war is over."

Khun Phaen and Phlai Ngam prostrated in the middle of the courtyard, happy to be in the king's good graces. The whole palace was overflowing with spectators.

King Phanwasa summoned an astrologer and commanded him to calculate an auspicious time for the army to march.

The astrologer sought an auspicious time, then addressed the king. "The seventh of the waxing moon has a remainder of five,[61] an auspicious time to open a campaign at 4:09 in the morning.

It's free of both the Great Spirit and a daily circle.[62] This time corresponds to the position where the rishi became enraged and tied the hands of the terrible monkey.[63] If you go to attack a country, victory will be gained."

---

59. คลังมหาสมบัติ, *khlang mahasombat*, the treasury of the great wealth. Conventionally there were twelve treasuries, as listed in the *Three Seals Law*, though a few more are mentioned in later Ayutthaya sources. The Great Treasury was used to store gold, silver, gems, and articles for royal use (ราโชปโภค, ราชูปโภค, *rachupaphok*). The officer in charge was Phraya Ratchaphakdi, *sakdina* 5,000. Gervaise wrote in the 1680s that the king had "eight or ten warehouses . . . that are of unimaginable wealth," piled "to the roof" with jewels, metals, exotic goods, and "great lumps of gold-dust." Originally the treasury was on the western side of the courtyard housing the main audience halls (area 4 on map 9), behind the Sanphet Mahaprasat. The foundations of two brick buildings divided into many small rooms have been excavated. After King Prasat Thong's expansion of the palace area, an annex was built in the next courtyard to the south (area 5 on map 9). (KTS, 1:267–72; Gervaise, *Natural and Political History*, 183–84; Kaempfer, *Description*, 45; KLW, 203; APA, 68; Boranasathan, 1:225; SWC, 14:6767–68; KTS, 1:267; Woraphon, "Kan borihan," 30–31)

60. บำเหน็จ, *bamnet*, money discretionally granted by the king as reward for some action.

61. This form of divination starts with calculating the astrological position (สมผุส, *somphut*) of the moon for the assigned month and converting it into minutes (ลิบดา, *lipda*, the sixtieth fraction of a degree). This figure is then divided several times, finally by seven, leaving a remainder in the range of 0–6. Among these 0, 1, 5, and 6 are favorable, and the others unfavorable. A remainder of 5 is สิทธิโชค, *sitthichok*, a conjunction of success (see p. 319, note 23). Further arithmetical manipulation will have produced the time of 4:09 (Thep, *Horasat nai wannakhadi*, 73–74).

62. The passage as a whole seems to mean that the day is neither auspicious nor inauspicious, while the time is auspicious. The march should not set off in a direction currently occupied by the Great Spirit (see p. 100, note 21). Nor should it leave on a day among the twelve types considered inauspicious according to the *Treatise on Circles* (see p. 319, note 23; Thep, *Horasat nai wannakhadi*, 75–81).

63. This is another use of the Three-Tiered Umbrella divination (see p. 208, note 4). The posi-

The king promptly commanded that the army be ready on the auspicious day. "They've requested phrai for porterage only. Conscript seventy for them."

The king went into the palace. The nobles got up in a tumult, so weak from hunger it was almost unbearable, and rushed off home in a happy mood.

All the spectators, Thai or Chinese, child or adult, exclaimed out loud, "They're really able!" "Best in the capital!" "They can transform their bodies like gods."

"Nothing like this was seen in my parents' time." "I've watched lots of fighters in my life but what we saw today was a feast for the eyes." "It was worth being born for this."

Khun Phaen, great valiant, returned to Phramuen Si's house. In the morning he went to pay respect and report that he had news from a servant

that his mother, Thong Prasi, had come from Kanburi and was at their house. "By your grace, my wives, son, and I will take our leave, sir."

Phramuen Si kindly ordered his servants to help carry their belongings over. The father and son took their leave and departed, followed by the wives, servants,

and thirty-five soldiers. Walking along, they filled the street to overflowing. Market traders who saw but did not know about them whispered to their friends, "Who're they?"

Others replied, "They're the lot the king pardoned to take Chiang Mai." Khun Phaen came to the house at Wat Takrai,[64] went in, and prostrated to his mother.

Thong Prasi was very happy to see her son. She stroked him back and front with tears flowing. "Oh, meeting is like being born again.

I thank you, Kaeo Kiriya, for making the effort to follow your dear husband. You must be sisters with Laothong. Don't dislike each other and cause trouble.

---

tion is at number 8 in the North/Hanuman square. This refers to an incident in which Inthorachit, son of Thotsakan, calls on the nagas to donate their poison for an arrow, *nakabat*, Rope of Snakes, which trusses up Hanuman, Phra Lak, and their monkey troops. Ram arrives to release them by summoning Garuda to scare away the rope-snakes, and subsequently Inthorachit is defeated (see the chapter "Suek wirun yamuk" in the *Ramakian*). The omen foretells eventual victory after initial hardship. In this episode, however, there is no rishi. Perhaps the astrologer is using a slightly different version of the Three-Tiered Umbrella diagram, as this seems to be a story later in the Ramakian in which two sons of Ram, born to Sida after their estrangement and brought up by a rishi in the forest, start to make a stir because of the powers they have inherited. Ram sends Hanuman to find out what is happening. They beat him and tie him up (see the chapter "Song kuman jap ma upakan khi" in Premseri, *Ramakian*, 606–30).

64. This must be the house where Thong Prasi lived before her marriage (see ch. 1, and on Wat Takrai, see map 8 and accompanying note).

Oh dear, here's smart Phlai Ngam. You managed to petition the king for your father. There's an ancient saying: To be a man, do not look down on another man."

Then she turned to Khun Phaen. "Now that I've seen you I'm even more distressed. Even though you didn't die in jail, you look so thin, wasted, and changed.

Your bad fortune and sad troubles are now at an end, my jewel. From now on, may you have only joy for a hundred years, no suffering for a thousand, and remain happy until you enter nirvana."

Khun Phaen received his mother's blessing, then went out and gave orders to arrange the house. The belongings were carried up and piled on the terrace. A bamboo shelter was built for the soldiers to sleep in.

The old house was rickety and about to collapse so they shored it up for the time being with timber. They worked together until the sun dropped at dusk and then rested, happily forgetting their past suffering.

The heads of the Department of Rolls[65] busily sent out call-up papers to unit heads. As the matter was urgent, they limited the conscription to villages close by.

In some cases, wives and children were tied up and dragged in.[66] Pleas for remission were ignored. All of the seventy required were found.

The chief record keepers[67] were ordered to deliver the whole contingent to Khun Phaen. The wives and children of the recruits rushed around to find rice and get organized within the day.

They asked people to donate however little or much rice they could. People trembled and handed over what was demanded. The space in Khun Phaen's house became overcrowded. Everything was ready to go in three days.

tall baisi

---

65. กรมสัสดี, *krom satsadi*, which kept the records for conscription, had left and right divisions, each with a department head, *jao krom*, Okphra Thephathibodi and Okphra Sisurentharathibodi respectively, *sakdina* 3,000 (KTS, 1:249).

66. Each phrai on the rolls had to name a guarantor, usually a close relative or friend. If the phrai evaded call-up, the guarantor would be imprisoned. This hostage system was an attempt to combat widespread evasion (Battye, "Military, Government and Society," 19–20; KTS, 5:205–6).

67. นายสมุหบาญชี, *nai samuhabanchi*, "chief secretary" (PAL, 708), a post associated with record keeping in several departments.

Khun Phaen, great master, and his son had the idea of instilling their devices of lore with power. They took everyone out to a graveyard,[68]

and had the soldiers build a shrine and place three-level *baisi* to the left and right. Pig's head, duck, chicken, liquor, and other offerings were arranged in rows.

A white cloth was spread as a roof. They paid respect, lit incense and offertory candles, and made a sacred area circled with thread where only men could enter.

The father and son sat in the circle and chanted mantras and divine prescriptions to convoke all the gods of all channels and levels. "Lord Indra, Lord Brahma, Lord Yama, *yak* giants, Lord of Fire, Lord of the Winds, Krung Phali, the mighty guardian spirits of the place, the spirits of the forest, Lord Narai the discus bearer, Siva the sun,[69] Lord Ganesh of the left,[70] Phinai of the right,[71] we call on you to come down to grant holy powers. Also the supreme Three Jewels,[72] our eternal fathers and mothers,

Lord of Fire

Lord of the Winds

---

68. A graveyard was where dead bodies were deposited temporarily before cremation, or left for other reasons, especially after epidemics. It was considered a good place for such ritual because the quietness helped to compose the mind (SB, 353).

69. ศิวาทิตย์, *siwathit*, unusual because elsewhere Siva is usually referred to as Isuan. The word appears in the chronicles, early in the reign of King Narai (1656–1688) when the king had four images of Siva cast to make merit including "one statue of Siva the Sun standing up, a little over a *sok* [cubit] and a *khup* [span] in height," all covered in gold and "reserved for worship in the performance of the holy royal ceremonies" (RCA, 243).

70. พระคเณศร์, the elephant-headed son of Siva, who appears in the *Ramakian* under the name Phinet or Phra Kanetkuman. Tripuram, King of Solot, had ambitions to overthrow Vishnu. Siva gave him special powers which he abused to rape many heavenly ladies. Siva thus summoned Indra, Brahma, and Vishnu to help attack Tripuram. Siva transformed Vishnu into an arrow and shot it at Tripuram but it failed because Vishnu fell asleep in this role. Siva then incinerated Tripuram with fire from his third eye. Phinet played a bit part blowing a trumpet when the attack began. In the Valmiki version of the *Ramayana*, this episode does not appear, and Ganesh does not appear at all in the work. (Premseri, *Ramakian*, 17–20; Olsson, *Ramakien*, 12; SB, 353)

71. In Indian tradition, พินาย Phinai, Sanskrit Vinayaka, is another name for Ganesh, particularly his "malevolent form . . . who causes all forms of problems: madness, nightmares, etc." (Bunce, *Encyclopaedia of Hindu Deities*, 639). In the Siamese tradition, Phinai has become another son of Siva who blows a trumpet alongside Ganesh in the incident described in the previous note.

72. แก้วสามประการ, *kaeo sam prakan*, a Thai version of the Pali-derived *phra rattanatrai*,

our teachers and preceptors, and the royal command,[73] please assist by giving your blessings and disseminating your powers into all these."

They chanted a potent formula to instill special power in all their protective gear including auspicious bandeaus impregnated with herbs, and powerful single *takrut* amulets with oil.[74]

The power of their expert incantations made their devices move as if someone were turning them over. They made bonfires in all four directions, and placed their devices in the midst of the fire.

Lord Ganesh

The flames flared up but the sacred thread did not burn and break. They brought a Phakhawam image, placed it in an enchanted bronze bowl,

added fragrant oil, chanted a formula, and blew down on the bowl three times. When the seated image promptly floated up, they applied the oil to make themselves invulnerable,

capable of invisibility, able to stun others, and equipped with all other tricks and artifices. Having enchanted their devices of lore, they paid respect and pronounced a mantra to summon up spirits.

"Spirits of those who died by lightning and plague, all the various spirits who live in cavities and coffins, spirits who died in childbirth or from hanging themselves, spirits of officers and men, hasten here."

Because of these powerful formulas, all the spirits became hot and agitated, and could not hide away. They arrived together at the ceremony in droves.

People sitting in the circle saw the spirits swarming all around. Phlai Ngam and Khun Phaen poured white liquor into a skull as an offering,

along with raw meat salad and fish salad[75] that they had prepared. The swarm of spirits came down to eat ravenously. Those spirits still sitting around outside were all invited to eat too.

Those that were starving so much that their lips burned and guts ached, happily feasted on the offerings. They gathered around the food, rolling

---

meaning the Buddha, Thamma (his teachings), and Sangha (corpus of Buddhist monks).

73. พระโองการ, *phra ongkan*, a circumlocution used for referring to the king without using his name (SB, 353).

74. ตะกรุดโทนน้ำมัน, *takrut thon namman*. A yantra is inscribed on a small sheet of soft metal. The sheet is rolled up and inserted in a small vial which is filled with spirit oil (see p. 795, note 18) and sealed.

75. เนื้อพล่าปลายำ, *nuea phla pla yam*. Both ปลา, *pla*, and ยำ, *yam*, are spicy salad-like preparations using chili, lime juice, and fish sauce. *Pla* is usually made with raw meat or fish along with basil and chopped lemongrass. *Yam* has a cooked or par-cooked base along with coriander and chopped spring onion.

up their eyes, opening empty mouths, and swigging the liquor repeatedly. "Delicious!"

When they had finished, father and son commanded the spirits, "Today, all of you please volunteer to accompany us to war. Be ready to go at the auspicious hour of the forenoon feeding."

The spirits were pleased. "We'll go, sir!" "We beg to be your servants to sing the shield cheer."[76] "With an army of spirits, there's no need to bother with things like conscription and who's on rotation duty."

Khun Phaen and Phlai Ngam felt pleased when they had completed the rite. They distributed the enchanted devices to the soldiers and phrai to gain their affection.

All the men were happy. "Knowing things are like this, Pa, we're very confident." "We'll go wherever you send us, and fight hundreds or thousands of men without fear."

They went back to the house, and Khun Phaen called the soldiers over to choose their weapons. "Take whatever you're good with."

Some took swords and tried their cut and thrust. Others picked up twin-edged daggers. Some took guns and stood taking aim. Others asked for long pikes.

Ai-Choei said, "I'm only used to a wooden stave." Ai-Ma said, "I'm good with just a javelin." Ai-Phet said, "A machete's enough for a Lao throat." Ai-Thitsa took a lance and went off to try out his moves.

They milled around choosing their weapons until evening, when cloths, medicines, water carriers, bags and waist pouches for food were distributed.

The porters searched for wood to make carrying poles, and stripped bamboo to weave into baskets, panniers, and cases. Those appointed as unit heads carried out inspections with a lot of boisterous laughing and joking.

Thong Prasi bustled around from the morning busily arranging food supplies—chili, salt, rice, fish, everything. Anyone slacking got a tongue lashing without any discrimination.

Kaeo Kiriya and Laothong packed goods for their husband, chatting together happily and harmoniously for fear he might be upset.

stave

---

76. กราวเขน, *krao khen*, a martial song sung in the mask play, and a metaphor for serving in the front line.

A chest of betelnut, a nak set in a betel chest,[77] a case of tobacco, a big sidebag packed with folded cloths, sleeping gear, mosquito nets, pillows, and everything else

were carried out and piled up in front of the apartment. Servants bustled around. As for Phlai Ngam's gear, Phramuen Si arranged everything.

In the morning, they went to take leave of the king. Khun Phaen and his son prepared a salver of incense, candles, and flowers, and went to meet the high officials in the palace.

At four o'clock, horns sounded. The king came to the outer audience hall, sat on the royal throne, and interrogated many cases.

Chaophraya Jakri got his turn, bowed his head, and addressed the king. "My liege, I am governed by the royal foot.

These flowers, incense, and golden candles are offered by Khun Phaen and Phlai Ngam who have come to take leave of the dust beneath the royal foot, and go to war in response to a royal command."

The king smiled and laughed. "Heigh! Khun Phaen and Phlai Ngam, it pleases me that you two volunteered. I thank you.

Go well and return safely. Avoid trouble, risks, injury, and fever. Make sure the enemy loses to your might. Win victory, take the city of Chiang Mai, and return."

He commanded attendants to present various royal gifts including insignia of rank, cloth, sabers with gold-tooled hafts,[78] cash to be used for the war,

royal horses for each of them with saddle and bridle, and a set of cloth for each of the phrai. The king returned to the inner palace.

They[79] led the horses out through the palace gate. Crowds of people sat to watch. Khun Phaen galloped off merrily. Phlai Ngam and the phrai rode in pursuit,

all carrying their particular weapons at the ready. Young women crowded around to look. "Oh sir, this young and going to war already."

"So slight I can't take my eyes away." "Such a pretty body, I'd not go to sleep at

---

77. กลี่, *kli*, a container usually for betelnut, usually square, often divided into separate compartments for betel, pan, etc. (MC, 62).

78. กระบี่บั้งทอง, *krabi bang thong*, a short sword with a gold pattern worked into the handle, part of the regalia presented by the king to someone of phraya rank.

79. The next six stanzas, down to "you evil horse," are taken from WK, 23:913–14, absent from PD.

all." "I'd love to go to war with you but the action would make my clothes filthy."

Widows fluttered their eyes at Khun Phaen. He still looked brisk, galloping along with his legs in the stirrups powerfully urging the horse ahead. "I'd like to jump up in his saddle for a ride."

The thirty-five volunteers struggled to control unruly horses. One pranced sideways, frightening a Mon woman who fell down with a bump.

"Tcha, you slave horse, you trumpet flower! Damnit, lord fuck me,[80] a pot of shrimp paste has broken." A fish vendor was knocked aside and her cloth fell open. "Don't bash me, you evil horse."

vendor

Khun Phaen and his son arrived home. They found incense and candles to put on a salver, crawled in, and prostrated to Thong Prasi.

"Your son and grandson have come to say goodbye. Please look after the house and be good enough to take care of Laothong and Kaeo Kiriya.

If there's any problem before I return, there's someone you can depend on for sure—Phramuen Si and I are true friends. If you're sick, please ask his help.

If the house collapses, I've left enough money to fix it. Just make sure you're happy, Mother. Even if I go for a long time, don't be anxious."

Thong Prasi listened to this farewell with tears falling. She stroked him back and front, saying, "Don't worry about things here.

Those wives of yours, leave them to me. I'll look after everything, including the house and what belongings we have. It's good we can rely on Phramuen Si.

If I have any difficulty, I'll visit him. Set your mind to it, my dear son. Avoid hardship, sadness, sickness, and danger. Be radiantly happy all the time.

Defeat demons and kill enemies. Don't let anybody match you. Young Phlai Ngam, don't get separated from your father. You're still a child, and your grandmother's concerned.

Don't be so brave in battle that you're careless. Your grandfather, Khun Krai, from youth to broken teeth, never looked down on an enemy, or got into a rage. Whether it's a big matter or small, think what you're doing.

---

80. ดอกขมิอ่าง, *dok khami ang*, in Mon.

Also, if any of the troops going with you have any difficulty, help them. Don't look down on them but make an effort to treat them in a fine way, then they'll fight as if they're following you to death.

If you can unite them as one mind, though few you will not lose against many. They say a forest depends on its tigers, and a boat on its oarsmen. As a commander, you must depend on your troops.

Also, be grateful to the king. Think on this every morning and evening and it'll do you good. May you succeed through your powers and lore. Please remember your grandmother's words and heed them."

Khun Phaen and Phlai Ngam happily received these blessings from Thong Prasi, and prostrated to wai her. Khun Phaen went to give orders to his men, then entered the room of the two ladies.

"Laothong and Kaeo Kiriya, please try to get on well without any unhappiness. If there's dissension at home, it may be a bad omen for those who go to war.

Look after Thong Prasi's food and comfort. Don't let there be any problem. Kaeo Kiriya, your pregnancy makes you very clumsy. Please take care whatever you do.

And Laothong, after Kaeo Kiriya gives birth, please look after her clothing and make the fire for her. Get the servants to squeeze oranges, boil hot water, bring a cradle and blanket for the child, and sing slow lullabies.

As for the ceremonies for the child's soul, leave those to Grandmother as she's the senior and has done these things in the past. Also she understands everything about medicines.

Another thing has occurred to me. On this trip, I'm likely to meet your parents as we'll journey not far from Sukhothai and pass Chomthong on the way to Chiang Mai.

Do you two have anything to send? Would you like to leave it with me? I should get a chance to see them, and I'll take what you wish."

Laothong and Kaeo Kiriya listened with their hearts in turmoil. They feared that crying would be a bad omen for the journey, and so struggled to suppress their sorrow. They spoke,

"Don't worry about us. We'll get on and love each other." "We'll do whatever Mother wants us to." "We've made up our minds to behave properly."

"If you meet our parents, just say their daughter is well." Then the husband and wives talked with the love and intimacy of parting.

Khun Phaen, great master, woke at dawn, rinsed his mouth, washed his face, and went to fetch his son to get the army ready in the vicinity of Wat Mai Chai Chumphon,[81] an auspicious place laid out according to the manuals. The area was packed with people. Khun Phaen and his son made inspections.

Thong Prasi, Laothong, and Kaeo Kiriya followed to arrange the food supplies. Relatives of the phrai, who had come to see them off, swarmed all over the wat grounds.

Phramuen Si was truly helpful. He could not stay still, and took along his major wife, all his minor wives,[82] his children, and his mass of staff. He provided all sorts of things that were lacking, and helped to organize the baggage.

Big items were put on elephants while the food supplies were loaded on oxen, and light materials needed along the way were carried by phrai porters accompanying their masters.

porter

When everything was ready, they waited for the appointed time. The astrologer paced out the sun's shadow[83] to determine exactly the auspicious minute after four o'clock for the column to move off.

Kaeo Kiriya had been rushing around since morning arranging the food. Her belly was now swollen beyond tolerance. The pains came and she screamed, "I'm dying!"

Thong Prasi frantically called Khun Phaen, and rushed over to support her shoulders. Khun Phaen quickly made some loosening water.[84] Immediately after swallowing, she gave birth to a boy,

right on the auspicious time for the army to march, the most excellent moment according to the manuals. Thong Prasi lifted the child, hugged him

---

81. See p. 395, note 8. At this point in the Wat Ko version, the text editorializes: "Don't be concerned about them staying at this wat. It is a wat with a good name for the arts of war, with good *chaiyaphum* according to the manual" (WK, 23:914–15). *Chaiyaphum*, literally a location that delivers victory, means a good location of a town or building for environmental, military, religious, and other reasons (Pornpun, "Environmental History," ch. 1).

82. The major and minor wives appear in the Wat Ko version (WK, 23:915); in PD, it mentions only his "wife."

83. See p. 10, note 51.

84. น้ำเสดาะ, *nam sado*, is usually made by steeping a *takrut* in water while pronouncing a Loosener mantra. Other methods include pouring water over the husband's toe, throwing water on the roof and collecting it, or enchanting the water with a comical and obscene mantra, which may be effective by making the mother laugh. (Woranan, "Kan sueksa sangkhom," 214; Anuman, *Some Traditions*, 49)

close to her body, and gave him the name Phlai Chumphon Ronnarong.[85]

Then she summoned a boat to take them home. She was concerned about the grandson and did not stay for the sendoff. Phramuen Si said, "Don't worry. Leave the arrangements here to me."

Khun Phaen, great master, looked at the sky and saw it was bright and clear, right at the auspicious time according to the manual. He ordered them to beat the victory gong as a display of power.

They marched from Wat Mai Chai Chumphon out to Three Bo Trees Plain with all the troops hollering, and monks chanting a Chayanto prayer of victory.

Gongs chimed and troops hollered. Nai Jan Samphantueng led the vanguard, and Si-at Ratchanya the rearguard. All the thirty-five soldiers marched.

Some hefted a sack of ganja on a shoulder pole, and a hookah in their side-bag, making the sweat flow. Some had a bamboo cylinder of liquor hanging from their pike. Whenever they felt tired, they took a quiet swig.

Others had packs of *kathom* leaves[86] slung across their shoulders. If they craved the drug so much their faces felt dry and tight, they took enough *kathom* from the pack for a hit, and soon had the strength to catch up with their mates.

kathom *leaf*

Arriving[87] at a junction on the river, the soldiers came upon a liquor boat and called out loudly, "Hey! We must get some." They poled and paddled over at speed, and collided with a Mon boat on the way.

The Mon shouted, "You sons of slaves, you tangerine flowers!"[88] Ai-Phut and Ai-Ngok elbowed him. I-Tasoi cried loudly, "Hey, robbers!" They rushed towards the Jek, hollering,

grabbed pitchers of liquor, and put them in their own boat. Northerners in the army went off to catch girls. Others took a whole field of cabbages from a

---

85. ชุมพล, *chumphon*, a gathering of troops or concentration of forces; รณรงค์, *ronnarong*, battle.

86. กระท่อม, a narcotic from *Mitragyna speciosa*, a plant of the coffee family native to Southeast Asia. The leaves are chewed as an antidote to the stress of hard exertion, and to enable the user to last for a long time without food. It is used mainly in Thailand and somewhat in Malaysia (MC, 34; http://www.murple.net/yachay/index.php/kratom).

87. This section, down to "beat their gong and watch," is taken from WK, 23:918, absent from PD.

88. มะจุก, *majuk*, a dialect word for ส้มเขียวหวาน, *som khiao wan*, *Citrus reticulate*.

Jek, Chinaman Lek, who ran up to ask, "What are you up to?"

The Thai grabbed hold of his pigtail. "Knock you dead. Oh shit,[89] please help me!" Elephants, horses, and people swarmed across the river and out to the plain.

Guards at the customs post[90] rang a gong, called in their troops, and raised lances and swords to attack, but the robbers bounded away with flaming eyes, and all the guards could do was beat their gong and watch.

Khun Phaen and Phlai Ngam rode their horses in file across the plain towards the forest. They left the home territory as the sun went down, and stopped to rest at Ban Phitphian.[91]

Without any forcing, the headman had villagers carry lots of food over. People came to see the army, bringing firewood, torches, and candles.

The troops ate the food that the villagers brought. The headman arranged a place at the wat for them to sleep.

In the morning, they ate again, and set off without delay across the plain and into the forest and upland.[92] The heat of the sun made them hot in the face, weak, and weary.

At the village of Dap Kong Thanu,[93] they rested in the shade. Father and son sat relaxing and enjoying the comfort of a cool breeze.

Khun Phaen called Phlai Ngam to walk over to a big banyan tree, taking along betel, pan, incense, and candles. He prostrated at the tree

and said, "My sword, Skystorm, has been buried here since the time the governor of Phichit sent us down. This sword has the power to win battles. It's buried by the branch on the east side."

Phlai Ngam dug into the earth and was very happy to find the sword. As he passed it to his father, the blade gleamed and glinted. Khun Phaen raised the sword above his head with great love.

Phlai Ngam[94] asked his father, "But it's been buried for a very long time, up to fifteen years. It's odd it should have no rust. How can that be?"

Khun Phaen told his son, "Hundreds and thousands of swords cannot com-

---

89. พะชี้ใบใส่บวย, *phachi bai sai buai*, see p. 43, note 69 above.

90. Probably the customs post at Bang Lang (see p. 190, note 5).

91. On the Lopburi River north of Ayutthaya (see map 3).

92. Not hills, but the text correctly pinpoints the area between Ban Phitphian and Ban Dap where they climb slightly out of the floodplain onto the fan terraces that fringe the delta.

93. Where Khun Phaen buried his sword in chapter 21.

94. The next four stanzas, down to "carpenter bee," are taken from WK, 23:919, absent from PD.

pete with this. Many metals were collected to make it good. At each stage, years ago, an auspicious moment was found.

It was anointed with 108 herbal waters and spirit oil. The haft was filled with a diamond, jet, yantra, and mantra. Once made, it was activated in seven graveyards. A damned spirit was inserted for protection,

and it was entrusted to the care of the gods and Krung Phali. How could it ever get rusty? The metal is good and has martial power. The fluid metal lends it the greenish sheen of a carpenter bee.

In the future, I'll give you this sword to be your main weapon in battle. This Skystorm is superb. Tens and hundreds of thousands of other swords are not as good.

Even the king's regal sword is not equal to mine. I'll train you to get accustomed to using it." They walked along, admiring the weapon.

Returning to the camp, they rested until the afternoon sun fell into the forest. Then they woke everyone up, had a meal, and marched at dusk when the wind dropped.

regal sword

In the night, they halted to sleep at Lopburi, and left in the morning for another long haul. They passed Bang Kham, crossed to Ban Dan Pho Chai, and entered the region of U-Tapao.[95]

Further along they came to the district of Phu Khao Thong and Nong Bua[96] where a stream ran aslant down the side of a hill. They cut along the edge of the uplands where it was very hot, and reached Thung Luang[97] at dusk.

Khun Phaen gave orders to stop and rest. The soldiers lit a circle of bonfires.

---

95. Bang Kham in Amphoe Mi, Lopburi; Ban Pho Chai on the Lopburi River near Inburi; U-Taphao, probably the place called Khung Taphao earlier in the chapter, and now Khung Samphao, Amphoe Manoram, Chainat (see maps 2, 4; KW, 364).

96. Khao Thong in Amphoe Phayuhakiri, Nakhon Sawan; Nong Bua in Amphoe Chumsaeng, Nakhon Sawan (KW, 364; see map 4). The army seems to have swung eastward, away from the course of the river. Most likely this was because areas near the river were flooded. The huge wetland of Bueng Boraphet to the immediate north of Nakhon Sawan is probably the remnant of a much larger expanse in former times. The swing eastward takes the route up onto the fans beyond the edge of the floodplain. It is unlikely that the march would have been undertaken at the height of the wet season because it would have been impossible. But this detour, and the description of the lakes in Phichit in the next chapter, suggest that the march may have been at the tail end of the rainy season when water was still lying in the area around Nakhon Sawan. In the next chapter, some of the lotuses in the Phichit lakes are blooming, and some already have seedpods.

97. "Great plain." No sign of the toponym today, but it is generic. North of Nong Bua, is a fan plain which is still fairly arid, with a broken line of hilly outcrops to the east.

Exhausted ones collapsed into sleep. Some looked for a log to chop ganja, and sat smoking a hookah until their heads fell backwards.

Those who had ganja sat taking turns to chop it, load the pipe, and light it. Those with none asked to buy at three handfuls a salueng, chopped it, lit up, and inhaled the smoke.

When giddy, they wanted something sweet, and bent over searching in their belongings for some jujube paste.

The opium smokers stretched a cloth to screen themselves from view, lay next to a fire, and busily filled their pipes. When the drug was almost used up, they tried to save the dregs that were left.

Mates asked to share them at one baht a *hun*,[98] but the owners refused to sell, fearing they would die when all was gone. The real addicts moaned and groaned until they got some secondhand dregs to stave off death.

They offered to exchange their sword or pike, or even sell their washing bowl, for the opium dregs. Once their craving was satisfied, they ate their fill and fell asleep.

troops in camp

---

98. หุน, *hun*, a unit of weight of Chinese origin, a fifth of a fueang, fortieth of a baht, equivalent to 0.375 gm.

Now to tell of Phlai Ngam. At the third watch,[1] when he was asleep on his pillow, troubled by the randiness of youth, the gods sent him a premonition.

He dreamed of a young woman, just come of youthful age, faultlessly beautiful with fair skin and a pair of breasts like plump lotuses. She stood smiling alluringly, then walked towards him.

When he greeted her in a friendly way, she turned as if to flee. He ran and caught up with her but when he grasped with his hand, she disappeared.

Dozily he reached out and hugged his father, saying, "Don't you have any mercy?" Khun Phaen woke up and pushed his son's hands away, crying, "Hey Phlai Ngam, what are you doing?"

Phlai Ngam's heart trembled in fear of his father. He said, "I dreamed I saw an extremely beautiful, fair, young woman but she ran off. I got carried away. Sorry. Forgive me."

Khun Phaen said, "Eh, you have very funny dreams. There's an ancient saying about dreams like these: The dreamer gets a good wife.

Maybe a governor's daughter, huh?" With that prediction, he walked off and told everyone, "Today we'll reach Phichit before evening."

They called one another to eat, and hastily set off on the march, not stopping in the heat though covered in sweat. When the city came in sight, they turned into Wat Jan.[2]

On that same night, Simala[3] dreamed she went down to play happily in a lake and saw a lovely lone lotus flower
pushing prettily above the water. She plunged gaily in, picked the flower, and swam back feeling happy. She sniffed it and snuggled it close to her breast.

---

1. Midnight to 3 a.m. Dreams at this time were known as เทวเทพสังหรณ์, *thewathep sanghon*, divine premonitions, meaning they were contrived by the gods and thus credible.

2. See map 10 and accompanying note.

3. The daughter of Phra Phichit and Busaba, who was five months pregnant when Khun Phaen and Wanthong arrived in Phichit in chapter 21. She is two to three months younger than Phlai Ngam.

lotus blooming

Opening her eyes, she groped around but the lotus had disappeared. "What a pity! I'm so disappointed." In consternation, she woke I-Moei to interpret the dream. I-Moei said, "Mistress, this is a good dream.

The lotus can only be a husband. If not tomorrow then the day after, he should turn up here. If things are not as I predict, you can thrash me. I've interpreted dreams like this for many people."

Simala said, "Hey, you lousy Mon! Saying a husband will turn up is nonsense. That's a silly, indecent interpretation. If anyone turns up, even a god,

with the cheek to court me, it'll be in vain. Don't spin fantasies. I'm fine on my own and have no desire for a man to come along. They say they're lords of your heart."

I-Moei cried perkily, "Oh mother![4] Don't say that, mistress. I don't believe you. You haven't met him yet so leave off talking until you've seen him."

Mistress and servant taunted and teased each other. Next morning, Simala went off to see to household affairs as she did every day, but could not escape feeling uneasy at the thought of her dream.

Khun Phaen, great warrior, rested in the wat until late afternoon, then called his son to go to the governor's residence. They walked along followed by their crowd

of servants and phrai, carrying a betel tray and flask as marks of rank. Phlai Ngam was unsettled thinking about his dream. They went into a market for a look around.

All[5] the woman vendors—young, old, and widows—liked what they saw, and smacked their lips. "Just perfect! Figures good enough to eat."

The widows fancied Khun Phaen. "I think we would be just right for each other." The young women thought Phlai Ngam was a dish. Their hearts were in turmoil.

When the men looked over, a young woman wriggled her shoulders to make her uppercloth slip down, and left it there with breasts bare, then jiggled her eyebrows as she turned her body away.

Shops selling cloth had barrels out front with bundles of patterned Surat[6]

---

4. อุยย่าย, *ui yai*, in Mon.

5. The next three stanzas, down to "turned her body away," are taken from WK, 23:923, absent from PD.

6. A port and weaving center in Gujarat, western India, which became a major supplier

cloths and uppercloths. Other shops were full of crockery, pretty silk, and sundry goods

including rows of brassware and glassware. Lines of people crowded around to look. The daughters of the shopkeepers were youthful, well-built, and forceful in the manner of people from the capital.

They were in every shopfront, some sewing sacks, all with fair and charming faces. They used yellow turmeric, shaved their hairlines, put on perfume that wafted along both sides of the street,

wore cheerful patterned lowercloths and colored uppercloths, and powdered their faces and applied soot just like people down below.[7] One with a girlish figure and an attractive fair complexion looked like the lady Phlai Ngam had dreamed of the night before.

He went for a closer look and found she was only similar. She was not as slender as the young woman in the dream, and her breasts drooped a bit—and besides that, really was different in all sorts of ways.

The dream woman was imprinted on his mind, and he was becoming ever more distracted and disturbed. He tried to walk along looking straight ahead and not thinking about it. They left the market and went into the governor's residence.

Phra Phichit sat relaxing in the cross hall, and was disturbed to see a crowd of people walking towards him. "Eh! Why are so many royal retainers coming here? The one at the front looks like a phraya."

Then he recognized Khun Phaen, and happily rushed down, dragging him by the hand up to the residence to talk. Khun Phaen and his son wai-ed him.

Phra Phichit called Busaba, "Khun Phaen has come! Where have you disappeared to?" Busaba stuck out her face, saw the two of them, and came out wreathed in smiles.

She sat down and asked about their problems. "Since you left us, it's been all tears. We didn't know who to ask for news. Because you were so far away, we had no idea

for many years whether you were living or dead. To this day we hoped you were still alive. Seeing you again is like being given a jewel because we love you like our own beloved child.

And Wanthong? When you left here, she was heavily pregnant. Was the

---

of printed cotton textiles designed specifically for the Siamese market in the eighteenth and nineteenth centuries. The goods were mostly white cloth of English origin, hand-printed with wooden blocks. "Surat cloth and white cloth" were sold in a market in the Takrai Yai area in the southwest of Ayutthaya (KLW, 195; APA, 115; Guy, *Woven Cargoes*, 151; *Pha phim lai boran*, 84).

7. Meaning Ayutthaya.

birth easy or painful? Was it a son or daughter? Where are they now? You haven't brought her?"

Khun Phaen told the story. "When we were sent from here, it was fine. They were lenient with us until Ayutthaya. The king pardoned me from execution.

There was a case against Khun Chang that I won. I went to live in Phramuen Si's house but then karma caught up with me. I had a bad idea that I stupidly thought was good.

I asked the king for Laothong, and was jailed. I suffered punishment almost as bad as execution. Wanthong was left on her own, heavily pregnant and in terrible difficulty.

Khun Chang boldly seized her, and there was nobody to object. She gave birth to a son—this fellow. When he was ten,

Khun Chang took him off into a forest to kill him but my spirits saved him from death. He fled to Kanburi where my mother, Thong Prasi, brought him up and educated him.

When a war broke out, he dared to volunteer. I was still in jail and he took the opportunity to petition the king for my release. The king had reason to be kind

so he granted Phlai Ngam's request and appointed me to act as his adviser in the war. The king gave us thirty-five convicts who have knowledge, and seventy porters.

We came here on our way to Chiang Mai to capture the Lao and thrash them to dust. I thought of your kindness during my hard times so I called by to pay respect."

Phra Phichit and Busaba felt sorry for Khun Phaen. "Oh pity, pity, such bad fortune you almost died! What a long time to suffer."

"Your dear son hoped to repay the debt of gratitude to his father, and took his courage in both hands. If he hadn't dared to petition the king, you'd have died in jail. He made his father happy. That was worth the effort."

Phra Phichit and Busaba lavished praise on Phlai Ngam. "He's good-looking and brave, a military type exactly like his father." They liked him, admired his slender looks, and kept talking to him.

"I'm annoyed that when Busaba was pregnant, the child was a girl. I was desperately disappointed. Now I'm thinking it's a pity because, if the child were a man, I'd send him along with you."

He called to his daughter, "Simala, why are you sitting in there? Come out to meet your brother. Don't be shy." Simala hid and peeped out in consternation.

"Are these some relatives I don't know from somewhere?" She slowly pushed the door open and looked through the gap. She saw two people, a father and son she did not know. The young man with a fair face thrilled her.

I-Moei came and stood beside her, nudged her teasingly, and giggled. "What's the matter? Praying to the gods? I predicted this already. Don't say I was wrong."

Simala said, "Hush, you lowlife! What nonsense you speak. If you say anything else, I'll give you a tongue lashing." She glared at her, then turned her face aside to conceal a smile.

When Phra Phichit called again, she replied, "Yes, sir." Embarrassed about walking in, she sank down, slid slowly forwards, keeping her face bashfully lowered, and sat hidden behind her mother.

When she raised her hands to wai Khun Phaen and Phlai Ngam, her heart leapt and she quickly lowered her face. Looking from the corner of his eye, Phlai Ngam returned her wai. Their eyes met and he felt a tremor of excitement.

"This is the one in my dream, I'm sure. She looks exactly the same. Oh, how lovely! Even ladies in the capital can't compare.

Like a full moon shining pure, clear, and brilliant. Her cheeks smile as if alluring me. She has the beauty and poise of true gentlefolk.

Her manners are proper too. She looks clever in a feminine way, and delicate, as if begging to be cared for. When she smiles, her eyes make her even prettier.

Wherever you look, there's nothing out of place. Is this the one destined to be my partner? When our eyes met, I felt she was cutting out my heart to take away.

I've seen thousands of other young women but none that captivates me like this. If I could make love with her for just one breath, I could face death without a thought."

Simala's[8] heart was trembling and she was overcome with shyness. Seated beside her mother, she saw lovable Phlai Ngam looking intently at her.

She turned away and shifted behind her mother. After a while, she looked at him again. "So this is the knowledgeable Phlai Ngam, sitting with his father and looking as if made from the same mold.

He has a bright face and cheeks like nutmeg. His lips look as if painted with

---

8. The next six stanzas, down to "went up into the residence," are taken from WK, 23:927–28; PD has: Phlai recited a formula, caught her eye, and blew it to entrance her. Touched by the mantra, Simala felt her hair stand on end. She glanced across in a fluster. / When their eyes met, her heart leapt. The longer their eyes were locked, the more she fell in love. Her heart felt it was melting with fire. She could not stay, and went into the room.

rouge. His black teeth gleam prettily. When he smiles, you can see a glimpse.

Hair as cute as a lotus pod. A rounded neck in proportion like a molding. Eyebrows curved like a bow. The black pupils of his eyes gleaming like jet.

A strong chest and curvy waist. Everything looks perfect. If he came to lie with me for one night, I'd gobble him up." They looked at each other without any shyness,

both with the same hope and intent. Then she came to her senses, felt shocked and shy in front of him, rose, and went up into the residence.

Simala hid inside, looking through a chink. The more she stared, the more her heart yearned. Love was arousing her and befuddling her like madness. She could not tear her eyes away.

"This man is no waste of time! Like an image cast with no blemish. His face and figure look like they're painted with gold. Handsome to perfection."

She was overwhelmed by shyness, and slipped away to hide in her room. I-Moei followed with a big smile on her face and asked, "Today you don't look well. What's up?

You go out to wai the men from the capital then run back into your mosquito net as if you had a fever. Has some evil spirit alarmed you with a greeting? If so, I'll make some offerings for the spirit to eat.

Oh spirit, do you come from the city or the provinces? Please don't haunt her, just make yourself scarce. Wait a bit until sunset. Then I'll swat the mosquitoes and make offerings here inside the net."

Simala thumped Moei's head. "Stop going on, it's shameful. This here is a phrai of the worst kind. Making offerings to a spirit in a mosquito net! You evil Mon!"

They teased each other until the sun cooled. Simala was getting further carried away. Busaba saw it was late and asked, "Why aren't you arranging the food?"

Simala got up and went to help supervise the servants preparing a fine meal including soup and curry. The food was put under red covers and taken in.

Simala carried the bowl of rice while servants brought trays of food. Her heart was thumping and she did not want to pass the partition. Once outside, she put everything down on her father's side without raising her head to look at Phlai Ngam's face.

Phra Phichit invited them to eat. Phlai Ngam was seething with excitement. He gazed at Simala with only an empty bowl in his hand. Swallowing rice felt like thorns in his throat.

In panic that others would notice, he stole glances at Phra Phichit and his father. Phra Phichit knew what was happening and pretended to complain.

"What's up? You don't seem to be enjoying the food.

Is nothing to your taste? We northerners can't match the skills down there. Is the taste of our cooking too mild?" He laughed while teasing Phlai Ngam.

Then he invited the two of them, "Spend the night here. It's more comfortable. Don't stand on ceremony. You have a house here so why stay in the wat? Come and sleep as you please in that hall."

When they had eaten their fill, he told Simala to arrange mattresses, coverlets, everything. "Get out those two little velvet mattresses and the soft double mats."

Khun Phaen asked Phra Phichit, "Is Color of Mist well, sir?" Phra Phichit replied, "The horse is well but very old.

His hide is wrinkled with age. He gets plenty of grass and water, morning and evening. I go to see him on my rounds, and I've assigned Ai-Jan to look after him."

Khun Phaen called his son, "Let's go and visit the horse together for a moment." They went out the door and arrived where Color of Mist was stabled.

Ai-Jan saw them and raised his hands to wai. "I feed him well so he's good and plump." Khun Phaen and his son went up to the horse, and Khun Phaen enchanted grass for him to eat.

Under the effect of the enchanted grass, Color of Mist could recognize the words spoken to him perfectly. He tapped a hoof on the ground and jiggled with so much joy he almost escaped his stall.

He licked and sniffed Khun Phaen all over. Khun Phaen hugged the horse with tears flowing, and stroked his back, saying, "I had a royal punishment and was only just released.

I was in jail until my son asked for a pardon. After the king freed me, I came to see you. Phlai Ngam, here, is the son of Wanthong who you carried into the forest with me."

Color of Mist looked round for Wanthong, and seemed sad at not seeing her. He had no way to ask so just kept looking at the two of them with tearful eyes.

Khun Phaen said, "I'm going on campaign. I'd like to take you with us because you were of assistance in the past. Will you come or has your strength gone?"

Color of Mist was glad to go with the army. He pranced around, stretched his legs, and whinnied as if saying, "I'll go, have no doubt." Khun Phaen understood perfectly and was pleased.

He picked a handful of grass shoots, enchanted them with the Great Collection formula, and gave them to the horse to lessen his infirmity.

With the power of the lore, Color of Mist's old strength returned. Khun Phaen decked him in a fine, glittering harness, and trotted him out.

He put the horse through his paces by galloping back and forth, fast and slow. His speed and agility were perfect in every way. Even a young horse could not compare.

harnessing a horse

Khun Phaen dismounted, feeling well pleased. He called Ai-Jan over and commanded him, "Make sure he's well fed and content. I'll ride him tomorrow at dawn."

Khun Phaen, great master, called his son and said, "I fear if we're slow it'll look negligent. We march at dawn tomorrow.

It's neither a day of the Obstructive Sun or of Yama's Portion,[9] but a splendidly auspicious time with the ninth constellation on a Saturday.[10] With determination we'll defeat our enemies. What do you think?"

Phlai Ngam was thinking of Simala and could not accept leaving Phichit, but he feared his father would not be sympathetic if he told him the truth, so he tried to manage the situation with subterfuge, saying,

"The troops are still tired and weak. Why are you in such a rush to march? Let the soldiers rest for a bit. When their fatigue has gone, then we can leave."

Khun Phaen said, "Look here, Phlai Ngam, we can hang around here enjoy-

---

9. ทักทิน, *thakthin*, and ยมขันธ์, *yommakhan*, are two of the inauspicious days defined by the "circles" method of divination. The first is a day when any endeavor will meet repeated obstructions. The second is "a day when it is like being in the fires of hell" (Thep, *Horasat lae wannakhadi*, 75–76; see p. 319, note 23).

10. This is a method of divination based on the twenty-seven นักษัตร, *naksat* or constellations that identify divisions of the sky through which the moon passes over its orbit. Each of these constellations is assigned to one of nine categories of influence—poverty, wealth, etc. The ninth category is สมโณ, *sommano*, the calm one or monk. This category is usually examined on matters to do with religion. The *naksat* constellations in this category are: number 9, อาศเลษา, *atlesa*, Hydra in Leo; 18, เชษฐา, *chettha*, part of Scorpio, with Antares as the principal star; and 27, เรวดี, *rewadi*, which includes parts of Andromeda and Pisces. A further dimension of divination is added by combining the influence of the *naksat* with the influence of the day planets. The moon's passage through a ninth or *sommano naksat* (especially 18, *chettha*, part of Scorpio) on a Saturday is considered very auspicious. (Singto, *Horasat thai*, 344–54, 365)

ing ourselves and not bothering about the king's orders but what place is the same as one's own home?"

"Nowhere," replied Phlai Ngam, "but I want to enchant our devices one more time. The power is still weak. Let's rest the troops and enchant the gear a bit."

Khun Phaen said, "If we want to be in time, tomorrow is both a day of great power for enchanting the devices and an auspicious day for setting off.

It's better to do the ritual for enchanting the equipment in a forest. At a house is not the same because crowds of people in town are not conducive to composing the mind."

Phlai Ngam said, "The powers from enchanting in a forest are not as effective as in a graveyard. In town there are graveyards that are quiet enough."

Khun Phaen was angry because he knew Phlai Ngam was hiding something. "Why are you concerned about staying in this town? What business makes you want to delay? You're not listening to anything I say."

Phlai Ngam was afraid of his father and did not argue but said evasively, "I've no business here." They went into the governor's residence, with young Phlai in high excitement over Simala.

Khun Phaen, Phlai Ngam, and Phra Phichit chatted happily together about warring, routes for travel, and various matters—talking and laughing on and on.

In the evening when the sun sank from sight, a flawless moon edged above the mountains and slowly floated across a clear, cloudless sky.

A breeze wafted a soft, refreshing fragrance of flowers. Simala lay moodily hugging and stroking her side pillow.

"Oh Phlai Ngam of mine, how can you know that I'm thinking of you, that I feel an arrow has pierced my breast, and that I'm miserable?

When your eyes met mine, did you know for sure or have doubt in your heart? You seemed to want to be my friend. Or did you wrongly think I wouldn't care?

It's hard for me because I'm a woman. I have to sit quiet and hide my love. If I were a man and you were a woman, I'd seek you out tonight, come life or death."

She lay shaken by sighs, clotted with uncontrollable tears, her mind in a troubled turmoil of burning and yearning, until she finally fell asleep on the bed.

Phra Phichit, Khun Phaen, and Phlai Ngam talked without a break until the first watch. Then Phra Phichit said, "You two are leaving in the morning. Please get some rest."

He got up and went into the house. Phlai Ngam was very agitated. He suggested to his father that they should turn in. "Father, isn't it late?

Somehow today I'm not well. I feel very tired and my back's stiff. I'll make it an early night to get my strength back ready for the march tomorrow morning."

Khun Phaen thought to himself, "What a loverboy! He thinks I don't know. Karma, karma! How's this going to turn out? Will he set us adults at odds with one another?"

Worried about what his son might do, he decided to play a trick. He closed his eyes and lay perfectly still, waiting to discover his son's plan.

Phlai Ngam lay still on his pillow as if asleep though his heart was on fire, his stomach churning, and his patience gone. He fretted with randy passion. "Oh my plump breasted Simala!

Right now are you fast asleep, my tenderness? Or is your heart feeling love? By the look of it, you'll have mercy on me, but you're staying quiet because you're a woman.

My heart is bursting with love, but do you know that or not? I'd guess you're thinking of me and I shouldn't face a setback if I seek you out.

They say that if you feel in love then you should not fail in love. I love you like my own life. How to make this happen?

I'd go round in circles trying to put it in words. It's difficult to be intimate because time is short. Tomorrow I have to go away and there's nobody to act as a go-between.

If I delay asking for your hand until the way back, I think I'll die. This love weighing so heavily on my heart will get worse by the day till I collapse.

I must think about getting close to you, as I desire, and worry about making war later. If I don't get my sweetheart, Simala, I won't go to Chiang Mai for sure.

It's in the lap of karma, my jewel. Now that everyone's asleep, I'll sneak in to find you. If you don't have mercy on me, then let fate take its course."

The more he thought of her, the more he fretted. A bright shining moon and the gleam of the dew cloyed his heart. The crow of a cock signaled time was pressing.

He listened to his father and went over for a closer look. Still suspicious, he called out a question. Knowing Phlai Ngam's game, Khun Phaen did not answer, but quietly waited.

Phlai Ngam concluded his father was asleep. He slowly got up and walked away. Once outside the room, he felt happy, and moved away from his father, hiding in the shadows.

Khun Phaen looked up, walked after Phlai Ngam, and asked, "What did you come out here for?" Phlai Ngam mumbled an excuse. "I'm going out to pee on the terrace.

All today I've been aching to pee, and I've been many times already. I've got groin ache[11] and it's killing me. I was going to wake you for some medicine." Khun Phaen said, "No use, Phlai.

This kind of groin ache is terrible. Hundreds of doctors could give treatment but it wouldn't go away." He pulled his son's hand, and walked pointedly back into the room.

Phlai Ngam felt frustrated. He lay down, then got up and sat. He resented his father so much that his chest felt it would burst. "Why's he pushing me around with no mercy?

So he wasn't asleep, he was just waiting to catch me. No problem!" With that, he chanted a sleeping mantra, meditated to compose his mind,

and blew the mantra onto Khun Phaen. His father grew drowsy under the formula, and fell fast asleep, flat out, as Phlai Ngam hoped.

He crept out of the room into the bright moonlight where a breeze wafted pollen and a fresh fragrance of flowers.

He came to Simala's apartment, and hid in the shadows, full of uncertainty. "Is this the one?" As he stood weighing things up, the light of the lamps flared up.

He decided to chant a Subduer mantra, putting everyone to sleep, leaving perfect quiet. He used a Loosener to spring the locks, peered around, and crept into a room.

Hanging lanterns shed light. "You have a lot of furniture." There was a powder set on a horse-stool; a washing bowl on a salver as used by gentlefolk;

two betel sets, one in nak and one in gold, placed neatly in a row; jars for beeswax, face powder, and Tani oil, with a comb stand set beside them;

footed trays, salvers, and chests all piled up; cloth all neatly folded; equipment for worshipping a Buddha image on a half-moon table; a looking glass with Brahma's face carved from ivory;

and hairpins by a big clear mirror hung with flower tassels looking fresh and beautiful. Every-

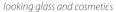

looking glass and cosmetics

---

11. กล่อน, *klon*, a disease in old medical texts caused by impurities in the scrotum; "a condition characterized by infiltration of serum into the tissues of the scrotum" (MC, 59); "lumbago, rupture, swelling of the testicles" (PAL, 339). The modern medical term is hydrocele.

thing was neat, tasteful, and attractive. He admired a curtain hanging beside the bed.

The curtain was silk embroidered with gold in a delicately executed design. It depicted Raden in a fever of passion for Busaba,

burning the city, disguising himself as Joraka, and sweeping up Busaba in his arms to abduct her away in a royal chariot.[12] Busaba was shown sobbing helplessly,

while the prince drove his chariot at speed into the hills and entered a jeweled cave to enjoy her. After the prince and princess had made love, he left her at dawn

to return to the city and deceive the others. Although he had to part from Busaba because of karma, he ordered the maids to stay close by her. As it happened, Busaba had the idea

of going out in a chariot to admire flowers. A great celestial being[13] was shown making a storm wind howl through the trees, blowing the princess's chariot

far into the depths of the forest. Busaba grew increasingly sorrowful from thinking about the prince, and almost died of grief.

Raden was shown traveling in search of her from place to place, disguised along with his kinsfolk as forest bandits, roaming around many localities.[14]

"You embroider so well it's beautiful. The main thing is I can make out

---

12. This is the Inao story, part of the Panji tales that originated in Java some time before the sixteenth century, and came to the Ayutthaya court in the eighteenth century, possibly via Pattani, transmitted by Malays taken to Ayutthaya as servants or war prisoners. The stories were probably greatly transformed in the process. They became one of the most popular sources for court literature, second only to the *Ramakian*. King Rama II was responsible for the most famous version but this passage may be based on an earlier composition by Chaophraya Phrakhlang (Hon) that excerpted only this episode. Inao (here called Raden, a Javanese title) is a prince. Busaba is his cousin from another of four great royal clans. The two are destined to be married but have never met. Inao falls in love with Jintara and rejects the match with Busaba, whose father angrily agrees to marry Busaba to an ugly prince, Joraka. By chance Inao then sees Busaba for the first time, falls desperately in love, and decides to prevent the marriage by disguising himself as Joraka and abducting her away to a cave. (Robson, "Panji and Inao"; Dhani Nivat, "Siamese versions of the Panji romance")

13. ปะตาระกาหลา, *patarakala*, a great deity. The word comes from Javanese but presumably derives from Sanskrit Bhadrakala, meaning an auspicious deity. Prince Dhani suspects this figure is based on an actual Javanese king transformed into an ancestor spirit ("Siamese Versions of the Panji Romance," 98). The deity is incensed by Inao's abduction and bent on separating them in punishment.

14. Inao and his brother and sister disguise themselves and set off in search of Busaba, accompanied by many servants, all disguised as forest bandits. However, the great deity has disguised Busaba as a man and decreed she and Inao will not recognize each other again until the searchers have visited all families of the four clans. This will take a long time.

the story without any mistake. If I think about it, Princess Busaba is just like Simala,

and Raden Montri's heart is just like mine, yearning for you. We're exactly like Raden and Princess Busaba. The only difference is that we have no Joraka.

If someone like Joraka interfered, I wouldn't disguise myself like Raden here, I'd just grab Joraka's head and chop it off." He laughed and turned to look around.

Her Chinese bed was magnificently gilded with feet shaped like lions and prettily carved paneling along with various accoutrements. The mosquito net was in yellow silk with a pattern of scattered flowers

and a frilled opening in many colors—the sort of net used by gentlefolk. A horsetail whisk hung beside. He opened the net and stared at her sleeping form, his heart racing.

Her pretty face seemed to smile in sleep, and the lamplight caught it alluringly. "You sleep so gracefully, like no other." The more he thought, the more he seethed with excitement.

He gently embraced her and planted a kiss as she slept. Her fragrance made his heart leap and tumble over. When he touched her breasts, he trembled in utter confusion. He kissed and caressed her, mesmerized.

He picked her up, then put her down, growing ever more tormented. He was young and had never been with a woman. He worried that if he woke her up, she would cry out and run away. But he released the mantra, and coughed to wake her.

horsetail whisk

Simala came to, hearing the sound. She opened her eyes, saw a man at the end of the bed, and recognized Phlai Ngam.

Thinking it was a dream, she smiled unguardedly and greeted him. "What's this? You dare come in here. This will result in shame and embarrassment."

Phlai Ngam came close and embraced her. She realized it was a real person and panicked. Shocked enough to writhe to death, she screamed and fainted.[15]

Sleeping on the balcony, I-Moei recognized her mistress's cry. She got up in alarm, went into the room, and looked towards the bed.

---

15. Kukrit notes that Prince Damrong probably edited this part under the influence of Western literature, as Thai heroines do not usually faint in this way (KP, 266–67).

She saw a young man lifting Simala onto his lap. She knew it was Phlai Ngam, as expected. Realizing what had happened, she took a washbowl over to him.

"Take this cloth, soak it, and wipe her face until she revives. Then console and comfort her, make her happy. If you force her, she'll die in the blink of an eye."

I-Moei walked off and closed the room. Out of concern for Simala and Phlai Ngam, she went and sat out front, smiling sweetly and keeping watch for people coming.

Now to tell of Phra Phichit, who was startled awake from a deep sleep by his daughter's cry. Not knowing what was happening, he called out to I-Moei, "Hey! What's up?

I thought I heard Simala's voice. Did you wake up and hear it or not?" I-Moei replied at once, "My mistress called me to go and swat mosquitoes.

While I was swatting, I didn't see there was a *jingjok* hidden in there. I swatted it down from the net onto her tummy, and she cried out loud."

Phra Phichit said, "You lousy Mon. Next thing, she'll have ringworm. Busaba already reminded you but you didn't take care of this during the day."

In the sitting hall, Khun Phaen started awake and listened with apprehension. "Young Phlai's gone off, that's for sure. The beggar's probably in her mosquito net.

The accursed child is making trouble. I think this'll be a mess tomorrow." He lay through to dawn, not going back to sleep but racking his brains to think up a solution.

Simala slowly revived, still feeling weary and weak. When she finally came to and opened her eyes, she found Phlai Ngam wrapped round her whole body,

with one hand bathing her face. Her hair stood on end in fright, and her heart skittered around with fear. She was still dizzy and did not know how to escape.

Slowly she slid down from his lap, lay there shyly, and loosed a long sigh. Then she turned over with her back to him so he could not look at her.

For a moment, Phlai Ngam did not know what to say because he did not yet know how she felt. Watching her lying there so quietly, he gradually gathered up courage.

He picked up her fishtail fan and softly fanned

fishtail fan

her. "Lie still and I'll fan you. Just now I was so worried. If you'd died, I'd have died too.

I prayed to the gods for help. You survived because of them. They are kind towards the beauty and Phlai Ngam because they can see the love I have for you.

Since our eyes met when I first arrived, I've felt like a fish caught in a creel. I'm burning with love and craving. If you're not willing, I'll die.

I'm so sick and sad and lovelorn. Please give me some care as a cure. Please turn your face towards me and say something to give me heart."

Listening to this, Simala fell ever deeper in love but feminine manners forced her to say, "I'd like to know who gave you permission to come here.

You're a gentleman but you have no consideration, no respect for my parents at all. We've only just met, not even a day, and you come to kill me with an excuse about love.

If you truly love me, why not inform my parents and ask for my hand? You've already gone too far and now you beg me to talk. Who would agree to it?"

"What a pity you speak like this, eye's jewel. Don't you see I'm in love? I dare come with no fear of death because I love you more than life itself.

If I can, I may ask for your hand from your parents. For sure, I'll ask Phra Phichit. He should be agreeable because he's long been a friend of my father.

When we were eating this evening, didn't you see? He was teasing me like a son. But it's hopeless because I'm on royal duty. I have to leave tomorrow in command of troops.

If I part from you lovelorn and brokenhearted, my misery will persist day and night like a running sore. I'll probably die before we have a chance to be lovers. Don't think that I have bad intentions.

Because of the obstacles, I could see no other way so I had to come and see you. If you're not kind, I'm willing to die. Let me entrust this body of mine to you in this room of yours."

Simala pondered everything Phlai Ngam was saying. It seemed sincere but she worried that she would be blamed and shamed for inviting a man into her room.

Now that he had come so close, he would not leave. It would be difficult to delay his advances, and love was tugging at her heart. She got up and turned to give Phlai Ngam a disdainful look.

"So young men from Ayutthaya are like this—smart with tongues as sharp as thorns. Whatever you say, they have an answer. No wonder young women run after them in droves.

You come up to Phichit and fall for a young woman but can't ask for her hand because you're going off on military service. You haven't left with the army yet so you wait till the parents are asleep and slip into her room.

If I'm not friendly, you say you'll die. Country bumpkins are the same everywhere. If any young woman is softhearted enough to let you enjoy her, in less than a month you chuck her away and go to war.

The woman is left behind with nothing, and she could wait a hundred years for your return. She's spoiled and ruined because she fell for the deceitful romantic trickery of an Ayutthaya man.

I thank you for helping tend my sickness. Now go, please go. It's near dawn. If my parents find out, this will blow up in anger and confusion, and you won't get what you want."

"Don't imagine I'm leaving. I'll die in this room. I'm not deceiving you. I'll possess and protect you as your partner until death.

Be kind to me. Don't stay so stubborn. Now that I've felt you like this, I'm not fleeing away." Phlai Ngam moved close against her and touched her to see how she would react.

Simala tried to fend him off. "I've told you already but you won't back away. Promises with words alone are easy. Don't be impatient for gain. Please hold off and weigh things up.

If you're sincere, give me your word that you'll definitely be honest with me into the future. If I believe you, then I'll agree to be lovers. But if you're lying, don't waste time on more pleading."

"Is that true, my jewel? If so, I won't make you tell me off again. I'll give you my word on oath. Let the gods come to hear me.

If I should abandon you and not look after you in the future, may I for certain descend alive into hell, right down to the Lokanta depths.[16]

There! I've given you my word on oath. Do you still have any doubts? Please accept my love. There's no further need for fear."

"I can see you love me. I'll probably consent to be lovers, but now I'm still shaking with fever. Please wait for some time and I'll follow your will."

Phlai Ngam understood feminine "fever." With no delay, he hugged her

---

16. โลกันต์, *lokan*, the very last hell in the Three Worlds cosmology. It exists in the gap between universes, and hence is totally devoid of any light. Each person there can see no others and believes himself the sole inhabitant. Those who have harmed their parents, monks, or Brahman teachers are reborn in the Lokanta hell (RR, 80–84).

tightly, kissed her, and slipped his hand inside her sabai. She pushed and pulled until they collapsed on the bed.

He[17] was young and had just been taught to mount a horse. Neither had the filly ever been ridden before. She bucked and swirled at full force. They fell and rose, locked together.

When he cracked the whip, the filly slowed to an unsteady trot, and the rider clung on with legs trembling in fear of falling off such a bumpy ride. Then the filly got stirred up and stampeded, panting heavily.

He went to whip her hard but had to slow down. The track was not yet as smooth as a stiff chopstick. The rider was unskilled and kept losing the timing, gripping onto the mane to steady the pace.

They bucked against each other wildly for a time. Then the horse calmed and the rider found a rhythm. With strength undiminished, the filly pranced and reared in fine tempo.

Once she knew the way, she was as good as a trained steed. Now that they knew each other, there was no limit to their energy, no need for him to urge her onward, just follow the rhythm until the sweat soaked down to her hooves and he unharnessed her.

Simala was swept away by passion. She snuggled close by his side and used her sabai to swab the sweat that soaked his skin.

She fanned him and, fearing he was fatigued, asked, "Are you famished? I'll find something." Phlai Ngam wrapped himself around her. "Just holding your soft flesh, I'm divinely full.

No need to talk of food. I went up to heaven and saw a palace flash before my eyes." They fondled and whispered secretly together until they slipped off to sleep.

---

17. The next five stanzas, down to "unharnessed her," are from KW, 375, and attributed to Khru Jaeng. Prince Damrong used Khru Jaeng's version for this section but claimed in the preface, "the original manuscript of this version is missing the passage where Phlai Ngam goes to the bed of Simala. This passage had to be composed at the Library." The substituted passage ran as follows: For both of them, it was the first time to make love. They had not experienced passion before but now their lust heated beyond tolerance, and when they came together on the pillow it was wondrous. / A fierce storm arose. The sky rumbled and raged, flickered and flashed, crashed and smoldered. Heaven and earth shook and shivered in chaos. Waves swelled. / Streams were thrashed into foam. The sky streamed with rain. The world throbbed and shook. Both felt the taste of love in their hearts.

Khun Wichitmatra quoted the Khru Jaeng version in full, and then commented. "Oops! Sorry. Careless of me. I put in the old version by Khru Jaeng." This passage is very similar to Khru Jaeng's version of Phra Wai's later tryst with Soi Fa in chapter 33, and the last five hemistiches are almost the same.

Approaching dawn, pink glimmers lit the sky and the crow of a wild cock hastened the break of day. Simala woke first and sighed at the thought they had to part.

She washed her face, powdered herself, and combed her hair. Then she nudged and shook him. "Wake up. The sun's almost up. If you linger here with me, we'll be shamed."

Phlai Ngam awoke, intent only on kissing and caressing, loath to leave, saddened at having to be severed from her. Listlessly he got up and washed his face.

Simala took him to her powder table, and made him up with powder, floral water, and krajae mixed with sandal fragrance.

Once he was all dressed and powdered to leave, Phlai heaved a deep sigh. He sat down again and lifted her onto his lap. "I'll miss you so much. I don't want to go."

powder set

Simala sobbed softly in sadness. Having an idea, she turned to plead with him. "Think about this. You're going far away from me.

The parents don't know about us. We must think how to drag brambles to cover the hole.[18] Suppose someone asks for my hand after you've gone, I might have to go against my father's word.

Though I could have some difficulty, it won't matter. I'll wait for you. When your military service is over, please come back, and don't delay so I get mired in misery."

Phlai Ngam was already despondent over the parting, and her words made it impossible to smother his tears. "I'm terribly concerned about you. I'll tell my father to ask for your hand.

If at least we got betrothed it would prevent anyone else getting involved. If Father doesn't cooperate, I won't go to war even though he cuts my throat.

Don't get burned up with worry, my jewel. Though I go away, you'll not go missing from my mind. Remember I gave you my word. As soon as the war ends, I'll hurry back here.

Don't cry. Please listen to me. If anyone sees you today, they'll think some-

---

18. A saying meaning: If you have done something wrong, don't leave the opportunity for someone following to repeat the same wrong (SB, 363).

thing's up." He helped wipe her tears, kissed her on the left cheek, then the right, and walked away.

Simala felt heartbroken. She would not see his face as before. After he left, she went back to her bed and lay grieving with her face buried in the pillow.

Phlai Ngam looked forlornly back towards her, desperate to return to her inside but desolate because the sky was already light.

He suppressed his feelings, walked away from the room, and crept along the wall in the shadows, intending to lie back down in the sitting hall. He was shocked to see his father awake.

Khun Phaen, great master, asked Phlai Ngam, "Where have you been?" Acting innocent, Phlai replied, "I had a bellyache. I went downstairs to the privy."

Khun Phaen said, "Which privy in this city has a powdering service? Your face is covered in it. I know a lie when I hear one. Don't try to deceive me.

We came to stay in Phra Phichit's house. His kindness has been enormous. Yet you've had the bad manners to take liberties with the daughter of someone of such kindness.

If we didn't have this little matter of the army, I'd take you under the house for a thrashing. You're lucky not to get striped by the cane. What do you have to say for yourself for causing this mess?"

Phlai Ngam did not argue with his father's rebuke but thought for a moment and saw a happy opportunity. He prostrated and said, "It's true, I did wrong,

but only because my heart was overflowing with love beyond endurance, and I was completely besotted. I didn't know how to get over it. If I kept quiet and went to war, I felt I'd die.

I thought, well, I won't live forever, so I climbed into Simala's room. I depend on my father's favor to please ask for her hand. By afternoon we'll be gone.

She agrees to be my heartmate, there's no doubt. You can see the powder on my face. I gave her my word that I'd get you to ask for her hand.

If at least we could be betrothed, it'd guard against falsehoods. Leave the proper marriage until the way back. Father, please consent so I can go to war with a still heart."

Khun Phaen, great romancer, watched his son's distress, thinking quietly to himself. "The whole thing has come to this! To abandon her would be unjust.

Phlai Ngam got besotted and befuddled. If I don't help, there'll be trouble down the road. If you stumble on the stairs, leap and trust your luck." He pretended to be angry at Phlai Ngam.

"You've caused trouble, you ungrateful child. Why didn't you ask me earlier? A young heart is never satisfied. Now that it's happened, why come begging me?

If I didn't love Phra Phichit like a father, I couldn't find a way to talk with him on your behalf. He loves his daughter like his own heart but you ravish her like some villain.

Now we have to find a solution that doesn't make him lose face. If you ever abandon Simala, I'll kill you or else I'm not worthy to be considered a man."

Phlai prostrated and wai-ed his father in delight. "I won't disappoint you on this." They both washed their faces and walked out to the front of the apartment.

Now to tell of fair Simala who was missing Phlai sadly beyond compare. Hugging her pillow and heaving heavy sighs, she lay listlessly until mid morning without rising.

I-Moei noticed her mistress was not to be seen, and crept in to wake her. She found Simala looking limp and forlorn. I-Moei dumped herself down beside her mistress with a thump to shake her up, and feigned a sigh.

"What a pity! I'm so poor and can't find anything to put in my mouth. I dreamed that a god came last night,

and departed just before daylight. On his way, he'll want betel and tobacco. I haven't even a hundred cowries. Where can I get offerings for the god?

When you get up, you must give me an advance because I'm very worried about this god. It was nice of him to fly down and if my mistress has no mercy, he'll be disappointed."

Simala was not paying attention to anything, but I-Moei's interpretation of dreams was more than she could bear. She got up and thumped the troublemaker. "Don't you have anything better to do than poke your nose in others' affairs?

Don't talk so much, sweet mouth. Sit here and help for a moment." They sliced betelnuts and made rolls of pan leaves. "The tobacco's in the cupboard. Bring it out and pack it."

They stitched leaf baskets, put in betelnut, pan, and tobacco, and added snacks to eat along the way, packed in a jar capped with a cloth carrying a seal.

Everything was placed in a basket and covered with a cloth. "Take this carefully." I-Moei received it. "Offerings to the god who came to visit you . . ."

Until around half past seven, Phra Phichit and Busaba were busy giving orders to feed the troops. When that was done, they came to find the two commanders.

As soon as she sat down, Busaba called out, "What's up with Simala? Where's she disappeared to? Khun Phaen is leaving this morning. It's already late and she hasn't brought food."

I-Moei came out with her heart in her mouth. "Dust got in my mistress's eye while she was washing her face. It's still stinging badly. I saw her rubbing her eyes." Busaba said, "You're just a chatterbox.

You leave your mistress and come out here with your sweet talk. Any moment her eye will swell up. You only grin and think about food, you lousy Mon. Why don't you give her eye drops of turmeric water?"

Phlai Ngam was amused. "This girl is quite something. She must be in league with Simala. I recall her face from last night.

She came to lend a hand when Simala fainted, and now she helps by fibbing to her parents." He sat quietly waiting for an opening, and then said to Busaba,

"Mother, to cure dust in the eye, opening the eye underwater and fluttering the eyelid is good. If you do that, the irritation disappears."

Busaba laughed. "You're very considerate. I-Moei, remember this method, and tell Simala what Phlai Ngam said."

Then she turned to speak to Khun Phaen. "I'm eternally annoyed with myself that I have a child but no son. I'm still disappointed, and would like to have one."

Khun Phaen, great master, saw the opening, picked up the thread, and ran with it. "I depended on you when I was in dire straits, and you showed kindness in countless ways.

I've thought and thought about every possible way how to repay your kindness, but couldn't see any means until I came up to Phichit.

I've been dwelling on this since we arrived yesterday evening and have now found something fitting. As the two of you have no son, I'll offer young Phlai Ngam here to be at your service,

to repay the kindness I've received from you both. Beat or scold him at will, I'll not complain. How do you feel, sir? My son loves and respects you."

Phra Phichit was delighted to give his daughter. He smiled and replied with the gist, "No need to go through the formalities.

As you say, I can see them as partners. In truth, to my mind they're perfectly suited. But I have some apprehension that my daughter, being provincial, doesn't know anything.

She's just a straightforward girl, not stubborn but not up to city people. If in the future my daughter doesn't please you, whatever you do, don't cause any shame."

Khun Phaen replied humbly to Phra Phichit. "I've given considerable thought to this point. Only after I'd extracted a promise from Phlai Ngam that made this concern disappear did I speak to you.

As for Simala, even in the capital, no match for her can be found, either in appearance or manners. I liked her on sight.

Even if young Phlai Ngam were to become a chaophraya, she could entertain anyone as guest. As long as I'm alive, I'll make sure no shame will attach to you."

Phra Phichit said, "If that's so, we can trust each other. But Busaba will say I'm too easy. Simala is her child so you must ask how she feels."

Busaba was sitting listening with a smile on her face. "I was eager to tell you how pleased I was. But second thoughts make me a little ill at ease. We're parents. Rushing into something will look suspicious.

I have only one child, and I've cared for her since she was little. When she's gone, what will I have in her place? You came specially to make this request, Khun Phaen,

and because I love you like my own flesh, I can't oppose it and must fall in with your wish. But if I'm to speak straightforwardly, I'm still a bit concerned about Phlai.

He has business far away in the Lao country. There are plenty of young women there. If he falls for the daughter of some lord, whatever we've said today will be meaningless.

That would cause distress and disappointment for the parents. I may be called an addlebrained oaf who doesn't know how to judge a man,

but what I'm saying is not that I want to break it off. I've loved you greatly for a long time. But if I'm to gouge out my darling eye and give it to Phlai, some means have to be found to make matters secure."

Phlai Ngam gave it some thought and said, "If you parents can all agree, have no doubts about me.

Even if I stray beyond the sky to the Himaphan Forest, have no suspicion that I will go astray and be unfaithful. If you want a pledge with a red seal, I'll sign with a cross.[19]

---

19. "Particular Persons, instead of a Signature, do put a single Cross; and tho' this kind of

Though I'm young, I know of your kindness in the past because my parents told me a lot about it. Allow me to be a golden shoe to support your foot.[20] Please don't be anxious."

Khun Phaen took up from Phlai Ngam. "What he's promising is fitting, and I believe he's not lying. But going away for too long isn't good.

I think if they were betrothed, though far away, his thoughts would be here—in body somewhere else but in heart with his partner. This would be prudent.

Today is a very auspicious day. Please accept a gift of betrothal. All the business of fixing a day and making a bridal house, I'll leave to you, sir.

Because we must go with the army as we volunteered, my son's future is still unclear. Please have the mercy, kindness, and warm consideration that you both have shown me in times past."

Phra Phichit and Busaba agreed with delight, and accepted the betrothal gold[21] at once. Phra Phichit said, "There's no problem.

If the war to take Chiang Mai goes smoothly, I think it'll be over around the second month. Then you'll have to bring the army back here so the marriage can be around the fourth month."[22]

Everyone was pleased with this agreement. As food was ready, they sat round in a circle to eat, chatting merrily.

After the meal, Khun Phaen and Phlai Ngam took their leave. Phra Phichit came to send them off at the foot of the stairway. They left the residence and went to Wat Jan.

I-Moei intercepted them on the way from the house. After Khun Phaen had walked past, she coughed as a signal to Phlai, who looked round and understood.

He slipped off the road into the trees and asked, "Why did you come here?" I-Moei said, "This basket of goodies is for sale to Phlai Ngam."

He smiled and said, "I'll take it. There's no need to ask how cheap or

---

Signature be practiced by all, yet every one knows the Cross which is under his own hand" (La Loubère, *New Historical Relation*, 71).

20. A formula phrase for a prospective son-in-law, or similar dependent.

21. ทองหมั้น, *thong man*; by tradition, the gift at a betrothal should be gold, but in practice the phrase is used conventionally for any gift.

22. Most likely these are lunar months so the second month would start in December, and the fourth in February.

expensive it is." He passed the basket for a phrai to carry, and gave three tam-lueng to I-Moei,

whispering to her, "Go straight back to the house. If your mistress is still sadly crying, you're the person who's been serving her regularly,

so you must console her and cheer her up. Please look after her. Keep her happy morning and night until I return and I'll give you more cash in reward."

He hurried after his father in a joyful mood, and helped to organize the troops at Wat Jan.

The men were summoned for inspection. The head and rear of the column were assigned. Phra Phichit came to give his blessing, and the troops moved off.

When a gong chimed, the vanguard under Nai Jan Samphantueng led the way, hollering. Next came the main division, commissary, convict troops, and rearguard.

Villagers and market people rushed up in crowds to see them. As they passed a wat, monks sprinkled them with sacred water. Outpost guards escorted them until they passed the frontier.

Now to tell of Phlai Ngam, who was riding his horse behind Khun Phaen. He was very sleepy and swayed in the saddle, feeling both very randy and very miserable.

"Oh Simala, my eye's jewel! Right now you must be grieving sadly, just as I'm thinking of you. Who'll soothe my beauty's sadness away?

After what we said this morning, if you know that I've asked for your hand and your parents agreed, then I think that'll overcome your fears. Sit and count the days until the ceremony.

Remember me morning and night. When you have a chance, give some thought to decorating our house. That'll take your mind off things and cheer you up.

Thinking on this, I'd like to know how my partner feels. In what style would you decorate our bridal house? Who will you talk to about it?

I think there's only I-Moei. She's just a phrai and probably never contradicts you. She'll suggest you buy everything new and forget about the old, some of which is good.

Lots of the furniture in your room is fine. I saw it with my own eyes. There's no need to find new stuff.

The bed is a bit narrow for sleeping but that's good for love. In the hot season or the cool, we'll not sleep far apart. There's no need to find a new bed, my beloved.

The curtain that you embroidered in gold and many colors has the story of Raden Montri, which is just like our own story. There's no need to make a new one.

If you want to embroider some more, do another curtain with the episode about disrobing the nun.[23] Your powder and makeup things are peerless. The bowls, salvers, and little bottles are so sweet.

I still remember late last night when you took me to sit beside you there. The betel sets in nak and gold are charming. They're all still in my mind's eye.

I'll build a big new bridal house for you where we can put both your things and mine. I've got lots of different things—good weapons and arms,

charms, amulets, and yantra cloths. But perhaps you don't like these for fear of spirits. No problem. I'll keep them somewhere else. I'll make a little shrine hall.

In our own room, we'll have a carpet and a pair of pillows placed neatly alongside for lounging where I can hug and caress you morning and night.

When we dine together, it's better not to let anyone see so we can fool around and chat while we eat our fill.

Who needs furniture anyway? With just a soft mat, a pillow, and our love, we should be happy every night and day."

Phlai's sleepy mind began to wander. He became befuddled, as if dreaming, and imagined his lover was there with him. He grew excited and giggly, and began to talk with her.

"I'm still a bit upset. Can't think it out. Suppose you have a child in the future. I've seen the belly pains and the screaming. Will you be like that, eye's jewel? I don't know.

They say midwives tend to be careless about massaging, and do it in a rush if you don't watch them. They've killed many people by just yanking.

I'll stand over them with a stick. If they get up to their tricks, I'll thrash them like *this*." Dozily he swung his horsewhip and carelessly hit the rear of his father's mount at full strength.

betel set

---

23. After the deity separates Inao and Busaba, they meet several times but Inao fails to recognize her as she is disguised as a man, Unakan. When her gender is eventually discovered, she and her attendants become nuns and hide away in a nunnery. However, Inao recognizes her, forcibly disrobes her, and discovers a cloth and ring which he had given her, proving her identity. Inao takes her back to his kingdom.

The horse got a fright and Khun Phaen almost fell off, but he had a good seat and clung on. When he got the mount back under control, he turned round, face red with anger. "Did you mean to do that, or what?"

Phlai Ngam was shocked. He told his father quickly, "Honestly, I was dozing and dreaming of Simala. She was giving birth, groaning with pain,

and I thought the old midwife was taking the easy way by pulling the child carelessly when it was sideways, so I feared it would be dangerous to let it happen and struck at her, but I hit the horse.

It was because I was dozy and dreaming, not because I meant to hit him. Honest. Color of Mist has been good in the past. Father, please forgive me."

Khun Phaen, great romancer, heard his son's words and his heart softened. "See! Love brings anxiety, awake or asleep, night or day."

He pondered quietly to himself. "Phlai Ngam is lost in dreams about Simala because he's just known love for the first time and sees everything from the good side.

Oh Son, you don't yet know the bad taste when love changes and takes flight. The worst pain in the world can't equal the pain and woe of love.

Why talk of others far away? Your mother herself gave me great misery. Several times I had to suffer badly enough for blood to spurt from my eyes.

When young people are lovers, they feel quite seriously that they could swallow each other up. They live together and spend all the time in lovemaking with no thought they'll ever part.

When I came back from the army and saw her for just a moment, she wrecked our love. I almost writhed to death trying to suppress my anger, and suffered nothing but misery for over a year.

Then I went after her and we fled away into the forest. We had to put up with poverty and hardship, but we didn't care about life because of love.

Just when I thought we were out of danger and could be happy together in peace and safety, troubles arose as the fruit of karma. That demon destroyed our love.

I was hurt and vengeful but didn't know what I could do. I had to suffer miserably in the inner jail for over ten years.

Oh Wanthong, my jewel, you've probably forgotten me because we've been constantly apart for so long. Now you'll be carried away by the merit of Khun Chang.

Or do you still think of me, your long-lost friend in hardship, like I think of you, day and night, all the time?" He sighed, and grieved on and on.

❧

The army left Phichit and had to skirt lakes that lay across their path. Some were huge, and home to many kinds of fish.

Seen from horseback, the water teemed with them—jumping and diving, surfacing and ducking back down. Giant snakehead, catfish, and red catfish glided past. Schools of sweetlip could be glimpsed in the dark depths.

pelican

Blackear catfish, giant catfish, snakehead, whisker sheatfish, mud carp, striped catfish, leaf fish, grey featherback, java carp, and spotted featherback—many species swam in the lakes.

In places where fish were abundant, crocodiles chased after them, thrashing their tails as if in a rage. When they heard the sound of people above, they dived down and lay low in the depths.

All around, many different kinds of birds sought fish to feed on. A golden pelican floated in the current, its food sack hanging from its beak, open to scoop the water.

darter

Darters plunged underwater to catch fish. Storks bustled about. Egrets stood staring intently. At dusk, night herons croaked.[24]

Flocks of hawks hovered above, swooping down to eat fish from the lake. Baldheaded adjutant birds waded on long legs, looking for a catch.

Painted storks and openbills scooped up shellfish. Flocks of birds of many different species were scattered all around as far as the eye could see.

The plant life was just as full, varied, and unusual. So many species sprouted leaves and flowers around the lake that the sight was a joy to see.

egret

Some spots were prettily carpeted with an unbroken cover of red lotus, some blooming, some turning to seedpods and their leaves wilting. Looking beyond, the red flowers stretched as far as the eye could see.

Clusters of star lotus were scattered everywhere. In the streaks of dawn, the opening blooms looking dazzling. Water chestnut, turtleweed, ottelia vine, and many other species colored the lake.

stork

---

24. แขวก, *khwaek*, the black-crowned night heron. "Call: a throaty *kwok*, often heard at dusk when going from daytime roost to feeding grounds" (King, *Field Guide*, 37).

In the early morning, bees flew around with a sleepy hum, probing into the flower stamens for their specially sweet taste.

A light wind blew the water into ripples that glistened gloriously in the light. Though the sun was hot, the breeze refreshed their spirits. Both officers and men walked along, entranced by the view.[25]

Leaving the region of lakes and waterways, they turned to cut through the forest. To both left and right, the path was screened by dense thickets of sugar reed, giant reed, and clumps of lalang grass.

There were no animals of any sort to be seen, only weaverbirds[26] carrying material in their beaks for building nests. The forest path was difficult with many water crossings but they marched quickly.

Leaving the forest, they followed a path on the riverbank. At Pak Phing[27] they crossed over to the right bank, and entered the forest. Arriving at Phitsanulok-Okhaburi,[28] both officers and men went to Wat Mahathat[29] to pay

---

25. Phichit today is still surrounded by lakes, though there would certainly have been more in the past before the canal building of the modern era. The biggest is now Bueng Si Fai, just south of the modern town of Phichit. Khun Phaen's route from the old town of Phichit towards Phitsanulok would have started alongside this lake. It still teems with fish, birds, and plant life. Close to the city this is not so obvious as it has become more like an open lake. But around the perimeter, there are large expanses of lotus that, in the wet season, match the poem's description. Also in these remote areas, the sky can fill with flocks of birds, mostly various kinds of egret, heron, darter, and duck. The passages of appreciating nature in other chapters are exercises in the *nirat* genre in which the sound of the words and the cleverness of the associations are more important than the reality of the scene. Some passages in this chapter have a different feel, and are clearly based on the author's experience of actual places (see map 10).

26. กระจาบ, *krajap*, a name used for many different types of small bird, especially the Ploceus genus of weaverbirds but also bushlarks, neither of which likes a forest habitat.

27. The end of the shortcut canal mentioned in the previous chapter, on the Nan River around 20 kms south of Phitsanulok (see map 4, and p. 538, note 13).

28. In a preamble to the Ayutthaya Chronicles, British Museum version, which reproduces several early legends from the *Phongsawadan nuea*, Northern Chronicle, Phitsanulok was founded by a king from Chiang Saen. "And when the King was about to bestow a name on the city, he asked the Brahmans, 'What name shall we give it?' The Brahmans answered, 'Your Majesty arrived today during the watch of Vishnu.' So he gave it the name of the City of Phitsanulok [Vishnu's World]. And the King said, 'As the lord Buddha came here to gather alms, the western part of the city is to be called Okburi and the eastern part is to be called Canthabun.'" *Okha* means an expanse of water, probably the wetlands to the west of the river but also a reference to the waters which, after an era has been destroyed by fire, flood the world and make possible the regeneration of a new era. (RCA, 6–7; *Phongsawadan nuea*, 21; RR, 311–27)

29. Wat Phra Si Rattana Mahathat, the temple of the great holy jeweled relic, one of the oldest Thai temples still in everyday use, and one of the most honored. In 1482/83, King Trailokanat, then ruling in Phitsanulok, "held a great festival for fifteen days to celebrate the great and glorious, holy jeweled reliquary" (RCA, 18). This is usually taken to mark the construction of the stupa, though it might equally have marked a renovation or some other event.

Phra Chinnarat

respect to Phra Chinnarat and Phra Chinnasi,[30] and ask for victory and well-being. Then they proceeded to the main sala to present their sealed orders.

Chaophraya Phitsanulok[31] and local officials busily arranged food and other matters. When the soldiers had rested enough to lose their fatigue, they marched onwards to Phichai.[32]

At every city on the way, the governor and officials welcomed them and made themselves busy. From Phichai they crossed to the other bank, marched to Ban Krai and Pa Faek,[33] then branched off

and reached Sawankhalok[34] in one day. All the senior local officials welcomed them and

---

30. Two of the most renowned Buddha images in Thailand. According to the *Northern Chronicles*, they were cast by Phrajao Sithammatraipidok, a ruler from Chiang Saen, when he founded Song Khwae (Phitsanulok). The king summoned craftsmen from Satchanalai, Sang-khalok, Hariphunchai (Lamphun), and Chiang Saen. The casting of the Chinnarat failed three times and succeeded only after the king and his queen had prayed long and fervently, per-suading Indra to intervene. The Chinnasi image was brought to Bangkok and installed in Wat Boworniwet in 1829. The Chinnarat image remains in Wat Mahathat at Phitsanulok but King Chulalongkorn had a copy made to install in Wat Benjamabophit in Bangkok in 1901. (*Phong-sawadan nuea*, 22–24; RCA, 7; Chatri, *Phraphutthachinnarat*)

31. The governor's title was Chaophraya Surasi Phisomathirat, *sakdina* 10,000 (KTS, 1:317). Phitsanulok was a first-class town, and for strategic and historical reasons the most important political center in Siam after the capital.

32. The old site of Phichai is on the west bank of the Nan River, 2 kms from the current town. However, it seems unlikely that the army would have come this far north, as their next desti-nation of Ban Krai and Pa Faek is far to the southwest. In the Wat Ko version of this passage, the governor of Phichai appears while the army is in Phitsanulok (WK, 24:941). In the past, town sites often moved permanently because of shifting river courses, or temporarily because of drought and flood. The town was wherever the man appointed as governor chose to reside. The site of Phichai has shifted several times over history, largely owing to the vagaries of the Nan River. Perhaps at the time of the Wat Ko version, the Phichai governor resided in Phitsanulok. When this version was developed from the Wat Ko text, the authors misunderstood and in-serted a visit to Phichai on the route (Pornpun, "Environmental History," 13, 20–1).

33. The two tambons, Krai and Pa Faek, are just north of Kong Krailat. This was a common route. The Burmese army camped at Pa Faek en route to attack Ayutthaya in 1775 (Sujit, KCKP, 127; see map 4).

34. Here in the text, the town is called Satchanalai but it is clear from the next stanza this means Sawankhalok, not the modern amphoe of Si Satchanalai further to the north. In the Wat Ko version, they stay at Wat Pa (Khoi) which is on the south side of Sawankhalok town (WK, 24:940).

looked after them as instructed in their sealed orders. They stayed three days in the town.

Marching from Sawankhalok, they crossed an upland and entered the forest. Phlai was extremely randy, thinking of Simala.

"If my eye's jewel could come with me, I'd invite her to admire the forest trees." He mused as he made his way along the path, crossing hills, streams, and rivers.[35]

He looked up at cliffs with shadowing overhangs towering above. A funnel of water surged down from the peak and splashed through a ravine, sending crashing sounds echoing through the forest.

The mountainsides rippled in hollows, promontories, spurs, and caverns. Everywhere was rock, some as magnificent as black jet, some like garlands with rows of hanging tassels.

He craned his neck to gaze at an overhang jutting out like the rock roof of a lean-to shelter. In the valley, the stream ran through a deep gorge of crumbled rocks, gouged with pools and shallow caves in a haphazard pattern.

In some places, rugged rocks were piled up in jumbled mounds. Stalactites began as uneven bulges and narrowed down to points dripping with water, some looking sharp and glistening with many colors.

Stalagmites stuck up like barbs, some rounded, some swollen in a mass of knobs and lumps, some flat and thin in clusters. In the distance, the gorge opened out to a distant view of nothing but mountain peaks.

Auspicious banyans and heartache trees stood on the bank of the stream. Wind blew their leaves to fall in the water and float on the current. The water was clear enough to see the stream bed. The air was suffused with scent from dangling sprays of flowers.

White and red lotus blooms poked up among their seedpods, with many plants woven among

water peony

---

35. As with the wetland above, this description has the feel of real life rather than poetic wordplay. The site is hard to locate. It should be on the Thung Saliam route which is the route used by all the other comings and goings from Chiang Mai in the poem, and is still the only road (Route 1048) crossing the watershed between the Yom and Wang valleys in this area. There are some fine crags around Thung Saliam. The Huai Mae Mok that flows through the Thung Saliam gap is a modest stream, possibly because it has been dammed for water supply. The Mae Mok waterfall cascades over a large convex rock formation, but lacks the overall grandeur of this scene. Further north, none of the three waterfalls in what is now Satchanalai National Park meet the description, and there is no route from any of these falls over the watershed to Thoen. Perhaps the author described a scene that is not on this route at all.

their stems. Water primrose shoots tangled with ottelia vine floating on the water along the stream.

Pondweed intertwined with water chestnut and water peony. Water spinach sprouted in neat clumps. Bees browsed around, caressing the blooms. The stream seethed with scintillating fish.

Admiring the view along the way, they walked into the hills. Dense foliage offered refreshing shade as they viewed the birdlife. Magpies chattered in a relentless hubbub.

The squawking of quails and cooing of doves echoed through the trees. A heron sang out loudly from a *krasang*. Parakeets peered out from perches on the branch of a *pralong*.[36] Cottonteal geese sat under a *khang* tree beside the path.

Coppersmith barbets perched up in a *kathin*. Parrots sat eating on an orange jasmine, and flew away. Peacocks spread their tails and strutted on a *yang*. Golden pelicans settled on a santol, gently swaying their heads.

Weaverbirds babbled softly on a *krajao*. Plain black drongos perched on a pine with woodpeckers, pheasants, and peacock pheasants. Bulbuls whispered lovingly on the branch of a *jan*.

Pairs of doves caressed on a steep hillside, cooing ju-huk-koo, ju-huk-koo. Crakes clung to the branch of a blackwood. Giant parrots perched quietly on a jewel vine.

Junglefowl dashed around cackling boisterously, the males calling out ek-i-ek plaintively, scratching for bamboo seeds beside their mates. Seeing people, they darted away to hide in the bushes.

A partridge spread its wings, warbled, and pecked around, chuckling non-stop. Seeing its mate eating a cricket, it went over to strut around in a courtship dance, looking lovely.

They traveled along admiring the thick forest, guiding the horses under the shade. The sun descended to hide behind the hills. Just as the wind dropped, they came out onto a level path.

New grass shoots were sprouting after a recent forest fire. The bare, open ground stretched away to the distance. Many animals were roving around. Some played together, turning to look for their partners.

gaur

---

36. ประโลง, *Ceriops decandra*, a shrub usually found in mangroves, displaced to the upland forest in the service of rhyme and alliteration.

A powerful tigress loped along, thrusting its legs to spring and pounce. Timorous deer watched with bodies stooped, or ran off helter-skelter to hide.

Golden deer stood on tiptoe beside the path, looking innocent, and bleating brightly. A sole young gaur forged through the forest. Wild buffaloes chased one another through the trees.

Porcupines, bears, and civets prowled. Mouse deer stared, looking poised, ready to flee. *Lamang* deer peered warily out from a thicket. Gaur scattered away from a rhinoceros.

A growling leopard stalked the deer. A cow elephant noisily tugged at clumps of bamboo. Sambar peered out from bushes before coming out to taste a saltlick.

They cut across the Rahaeng region and through Thoen district without entering the towns. After fourteen days' travel through forest and hill, they were within two days of Chiang Mai.[37]

They halted at Khok Tao Lake.[38] They did not enter the village but made a camp to rest the troops at the edge of the lake, driving in a boundary circle of stakes to prevent anyone wandering in.

Khun Phaen, great warrior, called his son Phlai Ngam over to talk. "We're close to the city of Chiang Mai. It's not a good plan to rush into battle.

They've captured Phra Thainam, and if we go straight in, they may cut off his head. We should sneak into the city and look for some way to bring the Thai out.

After that, we can attack the city. This roundabout way is better. You and I, just the two of us, will go to find where the Thai are.

We must disguise ourselves as Lao locals. We'll find clothes from a village. We must hurry in there now. Or do you have any thoughts?"

---

37. The route from Sawankhalok onwards is not clear. Most likely they followed the route across Thung Saliam towards Thoen taken in the other direction by the Chiang Mai message carriers in the previous chapter, though they do not seem to pass the outpost at Ban Tha Kwian. Since there is no mention of Lampang or Lamphun, they possibly then took one of the passes into the south of the Chiang Mai valley, such as modern-day Route 106 through Li. The distance from Ayutthaya is around 600 kms by today's roads.

38. หนองโคกเต่า, *nong khok tao*, turtle mound lake. There is a Ban Nong Tao, Turtle Lake Village, on Route 1033 just to the east of Amphoe Pa Sang in Lamphun province. There used to be a large lake with many turtles to the northeast of the village but it has since been filled in (see notice in Wat Nong Tao). The village site is raised slightly above the plain, and might with some imagination be seen as a mound. The location is on the route from Chomthong to Chiang Mai along the Ping River. It is around 30 kms from Chiang Mai, which would fit with two nights' cautious travel (see map 4).

Phlai Ngam agreed with his father and replied, "I don't find fault with what you say. If we take the troops in, as soon as the Lao see any Thai, they'll raise the alarm.

The news will spread all over the city. Before long the prisoners will be in danger. Their jailers will get nervous and execute them all, and we'll have failed.

If we sneak in and find the prisoners first, we can release them and then we'll have about four to five hundred people, Thai and Lao[39] combined, to fight against the Chiang Mai Lao."

The two agreed and went back to give orders to the troops. "Stay hidden, rest up, and keep a good look out for people coming and going."

When all the troops had their orders, the father and son dressed splendidly, decked out with charms, daubed with herbs, and heads tied with bandeaus infused with power.

Phlai Ngam gripped his sword and stood up. Khun Phaen grasped Skystorm of exceptional power. They turned their faces in an easterly direction and set their minds to killing Lao.

They stood with eyes closed, praying according to an ancient teacher's manual, and examined the sign of their breath. As it flowed from the right nostril, they set off on the right foot.[40]

They cut through marsh and bushes rather than turning onto a road. When they saw a field of gourds, they hid in the woods. Some Lao farmers were walking beside the road.

Now to tell of this Lao father and son. They had been to plant a field at the edge of the forest with many different vegetables including gourd, cucumber, beans, sesame, plantain, and banana.

As their time of death was approaching, they felt uneasy and thought of returning home even though it was still daytime. They called each other to walk together.

The father carried a fine sword and a cloth bag slung across his back. The son had a spear on his shoulder and a bottle gourd stuck on a pole. Their pink headcloths stood out as they walked along.

The old father led the way and the young son followed close behind. By fate it was the day of their death. The son dreamily took up his fiddle, and the father raised his *khaen*.[41]

---

39. Meaning those from Lanchang who were captured along with Phra Thainam.

40. See p. 101, note 23.

41. The *khaen* is found throughout the Lao world as it is known today, meaning Laos and Isan, but not in Lanna, the old kingdom centered on Chiang Mai. This is one of many mistakes

"Oh young lovely golden girl,
I want a whirl[42] with a Chiang Saen maid,
a fine foreign lass to gaze on undismayed.
My life laid down, oh my beauty.
Listen, ancestor spirits of the hill,
please will this city girl to favor me.
Pig, liquor, chicken, I'll offer gladly
In ceremony so I invade her heart."

The Lao father and son came singing towards the wood where Khun Phaen had been watching them from afar. Khun Phaen whispered to his son to look.

"Don't you see? The Lao with the fiddle has no head. He's reached the time of his death. Don't be afraid. Grab their heads and chop them off at the same time."

Ongkot

They both unsheathed their swords and hitched up their lowercloths. When the Lao walked up, they burst upon them as boldly as the warriors, Ongkot and Hanuman.[43]

Khun Phaen slashed and Phlai Ngam struck. The heads of the Lao father and son were lopped off, and blood spurted from the necks in a torrent as they fell to the ground dead,

eyes rolled up, faces blanched, and blood streaming out. Khun Phaen and Phlai Ngam were pleased as could be. They picked up the heads, stuck them firmly on the necks, and sat composing their minds.

Khun Phaen scattered rice and chanted a mantra. The spirits of the Lao rose up in front of them and made obeisance at their feet. Khun Phaen said, "What are the names of you two spirits?"

Already prostrate, the spirits flattened themselves on the ground. "I am Khanan[44] Mano Yai. This is my son, Noi Siwichai. What brings you up here?"

---

committed by the Bangkok authors as a result of calling both Lanna and Lanchang "Lao."

42. เซ้ย, soei, a northern Thai word meaning to tease or flirt.

43. Two monkeys whose martial exploits make up much of the Ramakian.

44. ขนาน, a former monk, especially one who takes a leading role in ceremonies at the wat. The word may derive from a term for a raft, and refer to the old Lanna practice of ordaining monks on rafts mid river (SWN, 2:537).

Khun Phaen said to Khanan Mano Yai, "We came with the aim of taking the city. Help lead us in there."

The spirits paid respect and consented, then dropped back down flat. Khun Phaen and Phlai Ngam stripped off the spirits' clothes, cut off their hair with a sword, and took the pink headcloths.

They put on the upper and lower cloths, attached the hair pieces, and wrapped the headcloths like Lao from the forest. Khun Phaen took the big sidebag and put it over his shoulder. Phlai Ngam grasped the spear.

black belly

The two of them laughed loudly. They walked off together and reached Khok Tao at dusk. The volunteers were alarmed.

Thinking these were Lao farmers, some went to hide in the bushes nearby. Khun Phaen strode in with no hesitation. The volunteers thought they really were Lao.

All looked at them without recognition, and all kept themselves quiet and hidden. Khun Phaen called out, "Why is nobody moving?" The soldiers recognized him, and rushed out to salute.

"Sir, with those clothes and the long hair, you really look just like a Lao." "We hid to take a good look at you, and you were truly unrecognizable disguised as black bellies!"[45]

Khun Phaen and Phlai Ngam took off the hair and clothes, and gave orders. "We'll go at nightfall. If we delay, the Lao will tumble us and spread word to the city."

The soldiers caught and harnessed the horses and elephants, and marched across the plain. To prevent word spreading to people in the city, they went into the forest shortly before dawn, dismounted from the horses and elephants,

and slept hiding in the bushes until evening. In the night, they forged ahead until nearly light. After traveling for two nights and two days, they reached a broad lake.[46]

---

45. The Siamese liked to call the people of Lanna the *lao phung dam*, black-bellied Lao, on account of the male custom of profusely tattooing the abdomen, and in distinction from the white-bellied Lao from Lanchang who tattooed only their legs.

46. The only lake of any size found today in the Chiang Mai valley is Nong Sariam, just to the southwest of Sanpatong, around 22 kms from the center of Chiang Mai. In the next chapter, a horseman rides out from Chiang Mai to spy on the camp, and returns by nightfall, so Nong

Their goal was only another half day away. They halted the army, cut timber, and drove in a boundary of stakes beside the lake. The army stayed there quietly.

Elephants and horses were fed grass and water. Soldiers relaxed and slept. Howdahs and saddles were arranged side by side for the two army commanders to rest.

Sariam's distance from Chiang Mai is about right. But this lake has survived because of community protection and government investments in dredging and bounding. In the past there were probably many others. Other elements of the geography, such as a defile between the lake and the city which appears in the battle in the next chapter, cannot be matched to Nong Sariam or to any site within a similar radius.

Now to tell of Phra Thainam, who had been imprisoned by the Lao under full restraint for half a year without seeing daylight.[1] He was almost mad from misery,

starvation, and discomfort. He wept constantly and was wasting away. No water had touched his grimy body. He was forced to endure, night and day.

"Oh my lord father protector, have you abandoned your child to suffer this torture for so long? Why has Your Majesty not sent anybody?"

Phya Kueng Kamkong, who had escorted the princess, also grieved and groaned at having to suffer so pitifully. Every day they both ate their own tears instead of rice.

Phra Thainam's complaints were heart-rending. "This is just terrible, like falling into hell while still alive, with absolutely no respite.

Hey Ta-Lo[2] and Sa, my merry fellows, come and cheer me up a bit. You're always so playful, with a grin on your faces. How can you be so unconcerned and not at all distressed?"

Ta-Lo said, "Sir, you're in jail. Though it's tough, you can't do anything about it. You've got to put up with it so you should try to be cheerful. Moaning and groaning won't get you out of here."

Phra Thainam said, "Oh Ta-Lo, they've left us here to die. It's odd the king

---

1. The story of Thainam's release has several parallels with an incident recorded in the royal chronicles. In 1662, during a Siamese army's advance on Ava, Phraya Siharat Decho was captured but escaped being killed because of his powers of invulnerability. He and five hundred soldiers were imprisoned in a stockade. A relief force under Phraya Surin Phakdi arrived and began to attack the stockade. "Meanwhile, Phraya Siha Ratcha Decho, bound in fetters, thereupon examined the clouds and shadows in the sky, saw a propitious omen, and recited a holy Buddhist mantra spell and magically managed to make all his fetters fall off from his body." He freed the other prisoners who proceeded to kill their guards, and take other stockades. "The Thai army gained a victory and, the Burmese prisoners, elephants, horses and weapons they had captured being numerous, had them sent under escort to [the king of Ayutthaya], and reported all of the details of their royal service for his benefit" (RCA, 280–81).

2. Probably not the same Lo who appeared as a Kula mahout in chapter 24. In the original, he is sometimes called Ta-Lo, and sometimes Ai-Lo, but in the translation these have been standardized to Ta-Lo.

doesn't bother to send someone up here with troops to storm the place and release us."

Ta-Lo said, "Sir, don't strain yourself. That could turn out well or badly. Even if an army came to attack, we've seen with our own eyes that the Lao are no pushovers.

Soi Dao, Thao Krungkan, Prap Mueang Maen, and Saentri Phetkla are skilled warriors. If they sent anyone except Khun Phaen, it'd just be hastening our own deaths.

When we came up here, Khun Phaen was still in jail. We've no idea whether he's alive or dead. The other Thai nobles, all thousands of them, are not on par with the Lao of Chiang In."

Phra Thainam replied, "Yes, I agree that's all true. I can't see anyone in the land who's better than Khun Phaen.

Oh almighty god under the great white tiered umbrella! Please end our suffering by inducing the king to send Khun Phaen."

The two of them chatted to ease their pain until nightfall. As the sun sank from sight, warders made their tour of inspection, putting chains and cangues on everywhere.

Phra Thainam, Kamkong, and the troops were put in all five irons with no remission. The warders had prisoners hit a wooden triangle while they sat awake at the lamps on watch.

Kamkong and Thainam were manacled in a seated position. They leaned their backs against the wall and let their heads loll forward over the cangue, praying and yawning until they dozed off.

That night, troubled Phra Thainam dreamed about a splendid Brahman with hair coiled neatly up on his head and a powder mark on his forehead.

The Brahman carried a sacred conch with a right spiral,[3] and wore an elegant seven-stranded breast chain, earrings,

Brahman with conch

3. ทักขิณาวัฏ, *thakkhinawat*, more usually *thaksinawat*. The right spiral is a sign of Vishnu. Khun Wichitmatra related this story. An ogress called Sangkho Surani, who had the power of flight, flew up and stole Brahma's text called the Wethangkha-sat, เวทางคศาสตร์, knowledge of the Vedas, so that the gods would not be able to use the knowledge in the text. Surani swallowed it down to her stomach and flew back down to the ocean. Siva sent Vishnu down to deal with her. Vishnu wrenched Surani's mouth open with his hands and pulled the text out. He then cursed Surani to become a conch shell, and ordained that humans should use the conch to blow and hold sacred water in auspicious ceremonies. The spiral pattern on the conch is the trace of Vishnu's hand (KW, 683).

an uppercloth tied crosswise, and a sumptuous lowercloth of white linen, neatly pleated and tucked in on one side with a flap. His complexion was a radiant yellow. He flew down at the back of the city, opened the jail, and walked up to Phra Thainam.

When he poured medicine from the conch over Phra Thainam's head, all the chains fell away. He repeated the pouring with all the other Lao and Thai whose chains also slid off.

Then the Brahman disappeared in a flash. Phra Thainam promptly woke up with a start, thinking his chains were gone, but as soon as he moved, he found his body was still constrained.

Lying quietly, he realized it was a dream. "This must be an important omen." He whispered to wake Ta-Lo. "It's me. Get up and help interpret my dream."

Ta-Lo asked, "What was the dream, sir?" Phra Thainam related it all. "Please interpret it well. This is a superb, powerful omen."

Ta-Lo smiled as he gave his interpretation. "We definitely won't die here in Chiang Mai. We should be out of jail in a few days. The meaning is that some able person is coming.

By my calculation, it's a time of Saturn, which is favorable.[4] We're going to get out of here alive for sure." The two whispered together until the roll call was held for the second watch.

Each name was called, according to the offense, and they quickly replied, shouting in succession along the row. Those who failed to respond were flogged to writhe and howl.

When it was finished, a triangle was beaten noisily. The prisoners took turns staying awake and keeping watch through until the light of dawn.

Prison warders of junior officer[5] rank came to the jail to distribute the prisoners to various tasks.[6] "Ta-Lo, Ta-Rak, and Bak Jandi, your group is cutting grass. Find sickles and shoulder poles."

sickle

---

4. This time period, ยาม, *yam*, is governed by Saturn, which is generally favorable for travel and warfare (Thep, *Horasat nai wannakhadi*, 461–70).

5. นายร้อย, *nai roi*, literally head of a hundred. The term is preserved in present-day military ranks from lieutenant to captain.

6. In late Ayutthaya, prisoners and their families were used for public works. "In front of every jail is a camp for putting the wives and children of convicts. Light offenders are chained by the neck in teams of ten and taken to do government work all over the city. Heavy offenders are chained by the neck in teams of twenty or thirty. . . . Their wives and children are taken out to work in two levels of chains and tied by rope round the waist" (KLW, 197).

Thinking of Phra Thainam's dream, Ta-Lo sang and danced along merrily. The warders followed behind them as they walked through a market to loot.[7]

They grabbed raw betelnut and put it in their baskets. People tried to hit them but missed. They grabbed some finger bananas, snatched anything they could find, and ran off,

with their chains clanking and scraping along the road. Whatever shop they entered, the women shouted and sometimes cursed them at the top of their voices. They jogged across a bridge over a long reach of the river,

arrived at a meadow, and went down to the edge of a lake.[8] They cut the grass, boisterously singing the sickle song,[9] while the warders laid out cloth behind jujube bushes and went to sleep in the cool.

Now to tell of Khun Phaen, great valiant. He ordered all the soldiers to stay together in their hiding place and take turns keeping watch.

"Don't stray off. Wait for us. We two will go into the city and find a way to rescue the Thai and Vientiane Lao imprisoned in the jail.

We'll get out of the city quickly and should be back here tomorrow evening." The soldiers acknowledged with salutes, and repeated the orders to one another for certainty.

Khun Phaen and his son dressed up in finery. They wore bandeaus formerly worn into battle, shirts with Buddha images,

and lowercloths like a Lao farmer. They attached hairpieces with a pink headcloth, strung on powerful amulets, and tied spirit-skull belts[10] round their bodies.

Khun Phaen grasped a sword and hung a sidebag over his shoulder. Phlai

---

7. The jail provided no food. The warders took the prisoners through the market to give them this chance to steal. In late Ayutthaya, "On holy days at the 5th, 8th, 11th, and 15th of the month, those under heavy punishment were chained up in groups of twenty or thirty, with their wives attached at the back by chains or rope round their waists, and taken out to beg for food" (APA, 132–33; see also KLW, 197).

8. This may be the lake that used to exist to the northeast of the city, in the area between the city walls and the Ping River. It is shown on the map of Chiang Mai made by James McCarthy, probably in the 1880s, as "Nawng Bua," หนองบัว, lotus pond. It was filled in for land development after the Second World War.

9. รำเคียว, ram khiao, the sickle dance, an old harvesting song, now performed with dance poses wielding a sickle (KW, 685).

10. ปะขมองพราย, pa khamong phrai, a belt made by digging up the corpse of someone who died a violent death, sawing the skull into strips, weaving the strips into a belt with a checkered pattern, and inscribing formula. Later in the chapter these are called ขมองโขมด, khamong khamot (YS, 39; SB, 374; KW, 684).

Ngam carried a sturdy spear. Looking like two formidable lions, they walked into the city.

They strolled among the Lao cityfolk without exciting any suspicion because the power of their spirits and mantras made people believe they were Lao farmers come to town.

In the outskirts, local young girls eyed up charming young Phlai Ngam. Their hearts fluttered and they could not take their eyes off him. He walked with his face averted, looking at nobody.

Young women, widows, and old ladies greeted him, "Where are you going, young fellow?" "Why not relax here a while? I'll give you betelnut, pan, and good tobacco."

The spirit of Noi Siwichai, who had come along with them, replied to the young women in Lao. "Dear ladies, please forgive me, I've got business in the city.

My heart loves you very much but right now I must take leave. After going into town, I'll come a-courting on the way back home to sleep this evening."

He kept walking along. Even the market ladies were good-looking. They thought little Phlai Ngam was a Lao from the forest, and found him very handsome.

One called out, "Hey, sir, you walking at the back and not talking, going along in a daze. If you want anything, come and sit down." She offered a flower to Phlai Ngam.

He accepted it and gave her hand a squeeze. The young Lao woman brushed his hand away, feeling excited. "Where's your home? I want to know. I'll follow along to sleep with you."

Phlai Ngam looked at her sideways, and said, "I like you." The young Lao woman uttered a sigh, and coyly loitered there, making eyes. She smiled, lowered her face, and peered up at him.

Widows selling betelnut called out to him boisterously and with no shame, "You good-looking young fellow in pink, if you want some betel and pan, I've got them."

Miss Ong called out to Miss Fak. "He doesn't love widows. He'll run away because your body can't compete. Aren't you ashamed to be bothering him?"

Miss Fak replied, "Don't interfere. Young things like you can't compete with me. You've never made love so what do you know? You young girls have got as much inner rhythm as a Lao corpse.

Just because you're breathing, who's going to love you? When it comes to the tricks, watch out for us widows. A young chap like this is a pushover. Just tug his string and he'll tremble."

Khun Phaen and Phlai Ngam kept moving. Wherever they went, the vendors talked to them. "Where do you two live?" "What business have you come for?"

The spirits who went along with Khun Phaen spoke in their stead. "We're forest people. There's talk that some Thai have been captured and held in the city. I've never seen the face of a Thai fellow.

I'd like to know what they're like. Where are the prisoners being kept?" A Lao told them the truth without suspicion. "They're locked up in the jail beside the stables.

The officers are confined and don't get dragged off for hard labor but the men are taken under guard to cut grass. If you want to see some Thai fellows, go to the meadow. They'll return as the sun sets."

Khun Phaen was pleased to get what he wanted. "In that case, I'll bid you goodbye." The two of them hurried off to the meadow.

They caught sight of the Thai chopping grass in the middle of a marsh, and scurried over to find them. Seeing that the guards were asleep with eyes closed and heads covered, they rushed across to the Thai.

Ta-Rak and Ta-Lo looked up. "Where do this couple of good-looking fellows come from?" When the two came close, Ta-Lo turned his head to examine them.

At first he thought they were Lao forest villagers. Then he looked again and recognized a face. "Eh! That's Khun Phaen for sure." He took Ta-Rak over towards them.

When they got close, Ta-Lo said, "Pa!" He rushed to clasp Khun Phaen's feet, burying his face, and shaking with tears. After a short while, he recovered himself.

Khun Phaen said to Ta-Lo and Ta-Rak, "Don't make too much noise or the warders will wake up. However upset you are, try to swallow it. If they see, this won't work out."

Ta-Lo and Ta-Rak wiped their tears, and talked softly to him. "Pa Phaen, it's been torture." "Jailed and manacled." "Very painful."

"They use the cane on our backs." "We're all in." "The morning rice has to last until evening." "My back's got over a hundred terrible stripes." "Phra Thainam is locked up day and night."

"He's bruised in body and soul beyond description." "He's been thinking of killing himself." "By the power of merit, you've come in time, sir." "Whose son is this young fellow, Pa?"

Khun Phaen, great warrior, told them, "This fellow is none other than my first born son with Wanthong.

Phramuen Si presented him as a page. Though his body is still that of a boy, his heart is huge beyond compare. He had the nerve to volunteer to the king. I was released from jail because of him.

I asked for thirty-five convicts, all brave fellows, and the king granted them. We've come to rescue you from death. Tell your commander, Phra Thainam,

and the Vientiane Lao, and also all our men. Tonight we'll come for sure. Wait and help chop off the warders' heads.

Don't fall asleep and cause delay. We'll come around eleven o'clock. No more talking. If someone sees us, we'll be arrested. Where's a good place to hide during the day?"

Ta-Lo said, "No problem, Pa, sir. Wat Nang[11] behind the jail is a good spot. There's a dilapidated kuti with no monks on the edge of a pond. I haven't seen anyone coming and going there the whole year."

He gave directions. "Go straight to the rear of the city and walk to the right. You'll see the jail beside the horse stables. Wat Nang is right behind the sala."

Once he knew the place, Khun Phaen said, "We can't hang around talking." He and Phlai Ngam went off across the meadow towards a clump of *yang* trees.

Seeing a lot of people on the road, they veered to the right and passed through a district with a cross bridge.[12] They stayed off the roads in order to avoid people. Past the jail, they found the dilapidated wat,

completely overgrown with brambles. "This must be Wat Nang for sure." They went into a kuti which was crumbling away but still had walls. They sat and slept while waiting for the time.

In the evening the sun dropped below the treetops. Warders shouted to the prisoners to leave. They all quickly picked up their shoulder poles and baskets,

and tramped along in a group, carrying the grass. The warders chased them along with canes. Their chains clanked loudly all along the road.

When the vendors saw the prisoners entering the market, they lifted baskets away and closed awnings[13] to guard their cloth. Those in shops selling fish and prawn gripped the wicker trays and kept a sharp eye out.

---

11. วัดหนัง, perhaps the wat with a screen, for puppets. There is no record of a wat of this name in Chiang Mai.

12. Or perhaps the name of a district: สะพานขวาง, *saphan khwang*.

13. กระชัง, *krachang*, awning outside a shop, a weather shield on the front of a market stall. The term probably comes from the Malay term *kajang*, cadjan, palm leaf used for making thatch, mats, and other articles (MC, 24; KW, 684; Farrington and Dhiravat, *English Factory*, 1395).

At the head of the group, Ta-Lo scooped up eels, and Ta-Rak snatched some sweetlip. The others behind scrambled after some little fish. The vendors hit at them and cursed when they dodged away.

wicker tray

Ta-Lo laughed uproariously. "What shall I order today?" The vendors slapped them but they dodged and grabbed oranges, bananas, and papayas until they had enough.

They clanked off in their chains. One woman planted herself stoutly out in front of her house, and tried to hit them with a pole. Ta-Lo caught it and hit back. She grabbed for the pole but missed and fell over in a heap.

The vendors shouted angrily. "What's up with the prisoners today?" "Why are they so high-spirited and making such a disturbance?" "I'll petition for their backs to be flogged to ribbons."

Ta-Lo said, "I'm not afraid. If you want to lay charges, go ahead. You don't scare me, funny face. If you try coming over here, I'll lay you out, groaning."

At dusk they left the market and ran along the road, clinking and clanking, carrying the grass and fish. At the jail they deposited the grass and went to prepare food.

They put on the rice pot and grilled catfish. In a short while, when everything was cooked, they scooped some rice into a small basket for their commander to eat. At sunset,

junior officers counted all the prisoners, checked the manacles, threaded them all on a big chain, set lighted lanterns at three places, and locked and double-bolted the doors.

When the three guards had gone up to their platform, Ta-Lo crawled to see the commander, Phra Thainam, and whispered, "Sir, your dream has come true for sure,

exactly as you told me. Khun Phaen has really come, sir, with his son. They were disguised as Lao. I was cutting grass when they turned up.

They had long hair just like the Lao, but me and Ta-Rak recognized them. He asked about you, sir, and the Thai. I told him everything.

He had me inform everyone to get prepared. They're coming tonight for sure. He'll use mantras to put the whole jail to sleep, spring the locks, and get us out."

Listening to Ta-Lo, Phra Thainam felt he was being anointed with celestial water. He was as encouraged and excited as if he had gone to Indra's palace.

"Hey, Ta-Lo, you loudmouth! The chain is long. Get them to whisper the message along to everyone. Don't let the Chiang Mai people hear. He'll come to fly us away tonight!"

The message was passed on in whispers to all the Lao and Thai along the chain. The prisoners happily prepared themselves. Nobody slept.

Khun Phaen, great romancer, along with Phlai Ngam his beloved and talented son, looked for a time with no obstructions.

They saw the stars had all gone out and the waning moon had left the heavens. Finding an auspicious timing late at night, they dressed and prepared themselves carefully.

They took off the Lao clothes and put them in a sidebag, then donned *pha-muang*[14] lowercloths in a fine indigo, awesome-looking spirit-skull belts, bandeaus infused with power,

and shirts enchanted with yantra and dyed with herbal medicine. They enchanted sandal paste and put it on their foreheads. Picking up their swords, they walked off in the appointed direction, looked at the clouds,[15] and saw an omen in the shape of a person.

Detecting the breath emerging from the left nostril,[16] they stepped off on the left foot along the road. They chanted a formula to stun others into not seeing them, and walked quickly to the jail. It was brightly lit.

Khun Phaen chanted a mantra to put people to sleep. Immediately the jail resounded with the sound of snoring. He whispered orders to his spirits to make sure all the warders were asleep,

---

14. ผ้าม่วง, silk woven with stiff yarn in dark colors (blue, purple, or green), generally worn in tuck-tail style. It was made locally but the most popular, and probably original, type came from China (SWC, 8:3769, 3779).

15. ยกเมฆ, *yok mek*, inspecting the clouds to see an omen. This is originally a technique for predicting the outcome of a battle, and is dealt with extensively in the Manual on Victorious Warfare. In the simplest form, the observer looks for shapes and patterns in the clouds. A four-armed Narai (Vishnu) in battle pose, or a two-headed crocodile, are notably good omens. Before his victory in the 1593 elephant duel, King Naresuan saw a white tiered umbrella. A headless man is bad. Clouds moving from north to south or west to east and obscuring the sun are a bad omen, but the omen changes to good if the clouds then clear. And so on. The method also includes more complex techniques which can be deployed to predict the likely outcome of any enterprise, not just warfare. The observer focuses his mind, meditates on his own shadow, and then slowly raises his face while mentally projecting his own shadow onto the clouds. The omen is then read in the same way. In another variant, the observer keeps his eyes closed so that the projection onto the clouds takes place entirely in the imagination. In more complex versions, the exercise is preceded by making an offering with flowers of seven colors, or by preparing sacred water and imagining the clouds in the water. (KCK, 88–89; Prachak, *Prapheni*, 132–36; SB, 374; PKW, 2:23, 248–52)

16. See p. 101, note 23.

then relaxed the mantra for the jailed Thai who came to as if waking up. He
chanted a Loosener to spring the locks. Doors opened wide on both stories.
The two hurried in.

Khun Phaen enchanted rice and scattered it around. The manacles fell off
everyone—feet, hands, and cangues. The Lao and Thai leapt up on shaky legs.

Phra Thainam and Kamkong came out. The officers and men saluted Khun
Phaen. Some were so hurt and angry they wanted to slash their tormenters.

"Those three warders are evil." They cut the warders to pieces, bathing
swords in blood and gore. "There! Slashed them. They pushed us around cruelly, cursed us, and flogged me almost to death."

"That governor is in the outer shelter, too. The slave flogged me with two
canes." Ta-Lo went up to the shelter, smashed down the wall, and swung his
sword to drop the governor down dead in an instant.

Ta-Rak wanted revenge on the fire inspector.[17] "He flayed my back into
chopped meat. Why should this villain be left alive?" He slashed him down
and left him rolling in his shit in the room.

The prisoners rampaged around, lopping off the heads of those they hated.
Those spared the sword dreamed, mumbled, and snored on, spattered with
gore like a graveyard.

Once outside the jail, Ta-Lo told Khun Phaen, "We've been trussed up so
tight that many people's legs are weak or lame.

We can't run or fight well, and if they cut us off, we'll be crushed. We must
steal horses for everybody so we can keep up with you.

We'll go because we know the place. The right-hand stable has the strong
procession horses. The left stable has the royal steeds. If we take them all, we
can mount everybody."

Khun Phaen said, "Slow down, old fellow. I don't think you can do it on your
own. You'll run into some Lao and the whole city will be in uproar. They'll
chase you down and crush you till you die shitting yourself."

He ordered Ta-Lo to lead the way and all the rest to follow. At the stables,
he scattered rice and commanded his spirits to conceal everyone.

The Lao guarding the horses, along with their wives, fell asleep, hugging
one another and snoring loudly. The Thai opened the doors and swarmed in
without any fear. They went around poking into everything,

grabbing cloth and silk, stripping people of their lowercloths, snatching

---

17. In charge of torches and bonfires to provide light.

wives' purses, stealing waist pouches, and picking up money and valuables that caught their fancy. They took everything they could lay their hands on without mercy.

Khun Phaen shouted, "Hey! Don't waste time!" They all came to untie the horses and harness them to mount and ride off together.

For the four commanders, Ta-Lo chose good horses—smart, trained mounts with firm saddles. Phra Thainam rode at the front, with Kamkong in the middle,

and Khun Phaen and Phlai Ngam at the rear. They dug in their heels and trotted off to a place where four roads met. Khun Phaen used his sword to cut wood from a coral tree to make a post.

He wrote on it in charcoal to tell the cityfolk the true story. "Whoever finds this writing, take it straight to your master."

When it was finished, they erected the post, leapt on their horses, dug in their heels, and followed one another at a brisk trot to the route out of the city.

Ta-Mo came with Ta-Ma and Ta-Lo to say, "Pa, don't rush off yet. In the hills the Lao keep some thirty elephants, all fine tuskers.

We have a battle to win. It'd be good to have elephants to ride. At the least their tusks will look formidable. I know all the places around here."

Khun Phaen called, "Old fellow, if we know the location, I think it's a good idea to take the elephants. We don't have that many people.

Several fine elephants will add to our strength. We've got many good mahouts who can smash their camps and destroy their armies.

Here Ta-Lo, take about a hundred men. Surround those puny Lao and seize the elephants along with their howdahs and everything else, and ride them back here."

Ta-Lo counted off over a hundred people. They cut through the forest to the place he remembered. There they halted, hollered three cheers, stormed in, and captured the elephant handlers,

scaring them but not killing them. They tied their two elbows together, and rushed around noisily seizing everything they could carry—

howdah belly straps, front and rear leather harnesses, stirrup ropes, tooled saddles, howdahs, side straps, and goads. They collected enough for their needs, then mounted the necks, and hit the animals with bolas.[18]

---

18. ประคน/กระคน, *prakhon*, a strap from the howdah passing under the belly just behind the front legs, usually made with plaited leather thongs; พานหน้า, พานหลัง, *phan na, phan lang*, a

Feeling the bolas, the elephants set off, jostling for the road. Some trumpeted and crashed noisily through the forest. The Thai and Lao, known for their skill as mahouts, rode the elephants fast.

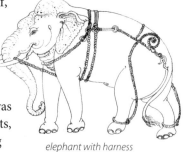

elephant with harness

Ta-Lo followed the tracks to find Khun Phaen, and quickly reached where he was waiting. Ta-Lo said, "I've brought the elephants, Pa. They're all big, fast, and fierce, with long tusks down to the ground."

Khun Phaen laughed heartily, and ordered all the elephants and horses to march. Late at night under bright stars with dew falling, they arrived in the area of the lake.

The thirty-five soldiers heard a racket coming through the forest, and thought it was Lao from the city. They rushed to get kitted out.

Phromson and Sammayang ordered the men, "We'll wait for the army here and cut them down. If you hear the small drum, retreat; if the gong and horn, attack."

They picked up their weapons, strung on *takrut* amulets, and tied on bandeaus. Phromson led the volunteers on the right, and Sammayang led the phrai on the left.

bandeau, takrut, beads

They went to a place where the road passed through a defile, and hid in the bushes. They were all firmly resolved not to give way before the enemy.

When the leader, Phra Thainam, rode his horse unawares past the place, Sammayang ordered three cheers, and the men rushed out of the thicket to attack.

Sammayang leapt onto an elephant's tusks, raised his weapon, and hit Ta-Lo hard enough for blood to ooze like sap. Ta-Lo raised his goad in defense, and swung a blow that found its mark so Sammayang slipped and fell off with a thump.

---

strap passing round the neck then over the back to hold the front of the howdah, and a strap from the rear of the howdah under the tail; ชะนัก/ชนัก, *chanak*, strap or rope passing around the neck of the elephant with metal pegs inserted to hold a stirrup made of rope for the mahout to get a grip with his feet; กระแชง, *krachaeng*, a leather side strap that runs horizontally from the *prakhon* howdah strap round the back haunches, for the mahout to grasp in case of emergency; ลูกดิ่ง, *lukding*, bolas, two balls of metal attached with a cord. (Julathat, "Asawa-alongkan," 215–16; Natthaphat, *Chang ton*, 288, 477; Wira, *Sapthanukrom chang*, 2)

He jumped up and rushed at the horsemen, hurling his sword at Phra Thainam and hitting him square. Phra Thainam's shirt ripped, and he lost his balance, but dug in his heels and galloped after the elephant.

The Thai and Lao did not know what was going on. In fright, they ran off, abandoning their swords. Thinking some Lao had blocked the road, Khun Phaen spurred his horse into the thick of it.

Phlai Ngam raced after him, slashing left and right with his weapon. Thammathian rushed up with a group of soldiers who swarmed around Khun Phaen and Phlai Ngam.

Khun Phaen bellowed a Power of Garuda mantra. Swords slipped from hands and dropped onto the grass. Phromson and Sammayang assumed an attacking pose with legs astride, then stabbed,

hitting Khun Phaen in the chest, but their pikes broke without piercing him. Khun Phaen drew a stiletto[19] and stabbed old Phromson who fell writhing on the ground

but his skin was not pierced. Sammayang slashed Phlai Ngam in retaliation but it was like striking stone. The sword did not penetrate even his outer shirt, and crumpled to pieces.

Nai Dot and Nai Suea brandished their pikes and threw them at Khun Phaen but they glanced off. Sammayang and Thammathian were perplexed. "How come they're invulnerable, beyond our powers?"

Sammayang rushed angrily back into the attack, waving his sword, but caught sight of Khun Phaen and so backed off. "Who's that? Is it you, Pa?" "Eh? Is that Ai-Sammayang?"

The soldiers recognized Khun Phaen. In shock, they dropped their swords and prostrated to wai him. "We didn't know it was you, Pa." "Please forgive us." "We thought it was the Chiang Mai Lao bringing an army."

"I stabbed you, Pa, and Phlai Ngam several times. I'm guilty of a capital offense." Khun Phaen was pleased rather than angry. "It's good you're this brave."

They milled around getting to know one another. The horse and elephant troops followed along, calling out to one another rowdily.

Kamkong and Phra Thainam had trembled with fear through the whole journey. They all dismounted from horses and elephants, and stayed together happily by the lake.

As the early streaks of dawn touched the mountaintops and dissolved into daylight, Lao officials of the capital went to unlock the prisoners for work.

---

19. กระเบา, *krabao*, a dagger or short sword with a very narrow blade.

They walked up to the door, oblivious, and saw headless warders all around the area. In shock, they ran around in turmoil, finding several who were still barely alive.

The governor's house had been smashed and looted, along with other houses nearby. The officials went to the prison upstairs and discovered that the Thai and Lao had disappeared.

Warders were lying tumbled over one another with heads off, eyes rolled up, and faces blanched. Chains were piled up on both sides. Cangues and manacles were scattered around.

The manacles were locked and the chains unbroken, with no sign of cutting. "These cangues are still intact. How did they slip out of them?" In amazement they raced around the prison.

The Lao superintendent of horses and his wife awoke and sat up drowsily, stripped of their clothes. As the mantra wore off, they looked around and saw that pillows, mosquito nets, and baskets had disappeared.

The wife looked at her husband and realized he was naked. "Eh? Who took your lowercloth?" The husband shamefully looked at his wife. "Where've all your clothes gone?"

They beat their chests in consternation. The naked wife grabbed a rattan mat. The husband groped around in confusion until he found a sack he could wrap round himself like trousers.

In both the north and south stables, there were no horses. The ostlers rushed around, some of them with no clothes on and dangling. "They've all gone from my stable." "We're dead!"

The ostlers rushed out in panic and ran into the prison officers. They talked together in confusion like drunks. Then the old elephant keepers ran up.

They all got together at the head of a road and shared their stories. Setting off towards the sala, they came across a post with writing in the middle of their path.

They could see the message was Thai handiwork so they uprooted the coral-wood post, read the message to know for sure, and carried it along to the inner sala.

Nobles and high officials were sitting in the main official sala discussing the government business of the capital when they saw an unruly crowd running up.

Some were panting along wearing sacks and mats. Others were stumbling stark naked. The officials called out. "What's going on? Who are these outcastes, galloping up here scandalously with no clothes on? Did someone rob them, hit and run? Are they madmen? What have they come for? Duty officer, go and ask them what's happened."

The group entered the sala, prostrated, and crawled clumsily over with their mouths trembling and necks shaking in fear. Hearing the questions, they explained.

"Hail, lords, merit over our heads! We're guilty of a major offense. Late last night, some able people came. They put us to sleep, killed many warders,

unlocked the chains by mantra, and released the Thai and Lanchang people, who've all disappeared. They killed the governor and wardens. Sirs, please have mercy."

The elephant keepers paid respect. "They tied us up, flogged us, and stole around thirty big elephants along with their gear."

The ostlers explained through trembling mouths, "Hail, masters and protectors. They put us to sleep and stripped the clothes off every one of us.

They chose the good and powerful horses, and also took every bit of saddle and harness. By estimate, the total number of horses missing is almost five hundred.

We found this wooden post set up in the middle of the road with a boastful, rude, provocative message that they're going to destroy Chiang Mai completely."

A Lao phraya said, "Those damn Thai are creating trouble." They picked up the message and all stared at it, feeling as angry as raging fire.

Once they understood its contents, they all went to change clothes quickly, walked off in a crowd with the minor nobles following, and soon entered the audience hall.

King Chiang In, eminence of the black bellies, resident of a brilliant golden palace, possessor of profound power to shake the earth, was in the resplendent jeweled audience hall

with his nobles and officials, giving royal orders and pronouncements, when he saw courtiers enter in a frenzy. "Heigh! What's that wooden post you're carrying?"

The nobles prostrated and said, "Hail, power above our heads. Last night some arrogant bandits came to rescue the Ayutthaya people.

They also stole five hundred horses, picking the tallest and best, and went off to seize some thirty of the finest elephants in the forest.

All the Lanchang Lao prisoners escaped too, my liege. They posted a fearless and provocative message. We searched for them everywhere but it was too late."

The King of Chiang Mai listened as if fire was raging. He summoned an official interpreter. "Heigh! Read this message and explain the meaning. What challenge does it make?"

Phan Jam, the interpreter, crawled over, picked up the message, and read it out. "The eminent monarch of the Thai city has sent me, a diabolical soldier, by name Phraya Phaen Phikhat.[20] I have marched here with my powerful son and thirty-five *athamat*[21] conscripts to destroy your city.

Because the Lao seized Soithong from our king, and imprisoned several Thai, we have come to rescue these Thai along with the Lanchang people who escorted the princess.

We are not running away or hiding to escape a fight. Will you wait there for us to come and defeat you? Or will you come out after us at the lotus lake?

If you love life and care for your colleagues, please deliver Princess Soithong to us, and bow to show your fear, so you may survive without death."

The King of Chiang Mai blazed with anger like the sky on fire. "Mm! These arrogant, leprous Thai. Their bragging is provocative and truly insulting.

Heigh! All you nobles, is what they say true? Or are they scared that we'll follow after them and so are issuing these threats to delay us?

There's only a handful of them, thirty or so. Those who broke out of jail aren't capable of putting up a fight. We can round them up and chop them down in less than an eye blink. Who has an opinion on what I've just said?"

---

20. Khun Phaen has promoted himself to phraya for effect, and given himself a second name พิฆาต meaning "the killer."

21. อาทมาต, probably a word used to describe spies, especially those working across the border into Burma. The word appears only once in the Ayutthaya chronicles, in a listing of various scouts and spies during a campaign in Kanchanaburi in 1660 during the Narai reign. An *athamat* department came into being during the military reforms of the 1890s, and was staffed by Mon. Several writers have imagined that this department existed earlier but there is no good evidence. More likely the word was used to describe certain people acting as spies. The meaning and derivation of the word have been the subject of much debate. Some have suggested a Mon origin but have been unable to come up with a convincing derivation. Others believe it may have come from a Tamil word meaning "secret." Kukrit believes this was the department to which Khun Phaen was assigned when he received his title, and that here he simply accredits the thirty-five to his own unit, but there is no basis for Kukrit's surmise. Khun Phaen is claiming association with *athamat* for effect, just like he is claiming rank as Phraya and a fearsome name. (RCA, 264; Suphon, "Chao mon nai prathet thai," 96–114; KP, 276; Prachak, *Prapheni*, 211–12; Naritsaranuwittiwong and Damrong, *San somdet*, 12: 306, 315)

Phraya Jantharangsi,[22] minister of the army, promptly addressed the king. "The words of his challenge are important.

If he weren't able, he wouldn't issue such a challenge. This commander must be tough. If we march against them, there'll be a battle because he's pretty full of himself.

But the thirty-five followers, however able they are, can't do much. The five hundred Lao and Thai that he's spirited away are half-starved.

Like a herd of deer once attacked by a tiger, they won't come back for more. Even if these thirty-five are top class, the starvelings will make them all run away.

Let a rider be sent out to look. If they're still at the big lake, take an army and crush them to dust."

King Chiang In, eminence of the world, heard him out, pondered, and agreed. He ordered a cavalryman, Mung Kayong, to choose a good horse and ride out

to investigate. "Have they fled, or are they still at the big lake? If they're there, hurry back. We'll conscript an army to attack them."

Mung Kayong Monglai took the order, and rushed off to saddle up the horse, Phon Thorani Sijan.[23] He mounted and galloped off,

giving the horse its head and racing along. As the sun weakened, he arrived at the big lake and dismounted. He stole through the bushes and climbed a tree to spy.

He estimated that there was a total of over seven hundred men, and that their disposition was to fight, not flee. Looking around, he saw no sign of a fort or moat.

Climbing down the tree, he remounted and rode back through the forest. At sunset he dismounted and entered the audience hall.

Arriving at the front, he made obeisance and gave his report to the king. "I crept up and saw the Lao and Thai sitting and standing all around.

Officers and men together number over seven hundred. Their disposition is to stay and fight but I saw no sign of them making a fort or moat. They're at the lake, half a day away."

The king roared, "Mm! These brave Thai! Isn't seven hundred too few to come and fight?

22. จันทรังสี, "moon beam"; there is no trace of such a title in Chiang Mai history.
23. โผนธรณีสีจันทร์, "moon-colored earth leaper."

That won't match the skill of the Lao of Chiang Mai. In one breath, they'll be trussed up like frogs. If each person just breaks off a branch and tosses it over them, they'll all be buried completely."

He commanded Thao Krungkan and Saentri Phetkla to quickly take an army. "Bring me back their heads.

Phya Prap Mueang Maen and Saen Kamkong, who have both shown skill as leaders in the past, will command the left and right wings. Krungkan will be the army chief.

Saentri Phetkla, an excellent horseman who acquitted himself well in the capture, will command the cavalry.[24] Have everything ready tomorrow before four o'clock in the morning."

Phraya Jantharangsi took the order and went to sit in the sala, issuing call-up notices for troops, both officers and men, and allocating elephants, horses, and weaponry.

The cavalry had five thousand stout men of the most indomitable spirit, trained and battle-hardened. The men of both right and left flanks could all ride wildly.

They were equipped with bows, spears, and throwing knives. These five thousand strong and tough militiamen, with their officers in charge, were ready as the vanguard.

Phetkla was mounted on a powerful, hard-working, and nimble royal horse called Hem Rasami Sijan[25] with a harness of filigree inlaid with jewels, flanchards decorated with dancing *kinnari*, stirrups inlaid with gold, a saddle tooled and engraved with patterns, and tassels hanging from its ears. Its regular ostler led the horse to wait for the march.

Leaving aside Krungkan of the main army for the moment, now to tell of the commander of the cavalry, Saentri Phetkla, a man with powers, invulnerability, and skill in the arts of war.

cavalryman with spear

His right arm carried a gamboge tattoo of Lord Narai,

---

24. สินธพ, *sinthop*, originally a breed of horses from the Indus River region but used poetically for horses in general.

25. เหมรัศมีสีจันทร์, "golden brilliance of the moon."

his left arm a vermilion[26] tattoo of a lion, his right leg an ink-black tattoo of a tigress, and his left leg, a powerful bear.

His chest was tattooed with a picture of Phra Mokkhala,[27] his back with a Phakhawam image with eyes closed, and his flanks with a *na*[28] formula for stunning. He had a jet gem[29] embedded in his head,

golden needles in each shoulder, a large diamond in the middle of his forehead, a lump of fluid metal[30] in his chest, and herbal amber and cat's eye[31] in his back.

His whole body was a mass of lumps and bumps in ranks and rows. Since birth he had never been touched by a weapon, and did not carry even the scratch from a thorn.

He was tall and broad like a tiger, very powerful, with firm and invulnerable flesh. His moustache was twirled to curve upwards.

tattoos

na *character for stunning*

---

26. The colors have symbolic significance. รง, *rong*, gamboge, yellow, symbolizes greatness, and ชาด, *chat*, vermilion, signifies power (KW, 390–91).

27. พระโมคคลา, Mokkhalana, Moggallana, was a Brahman from Rajagriha who became one of the two chief disciples of the Buddha. He was renowned for his supernatural powers, including the ability to transform himself into any shape or form. When the Buddha sent him to cure a schism in Kalasila, the heretics hired five hundred brigands who beat him until all the bones in his body were crushed. This lapse in his power was explained by an incident of cruelty towards aged parents in a previous life. He was still able to drag himself to the Buddha to ask leave to depart the world. Mokkhalana's name is used for formulas and amulets to guard against injury, and to repair broken bones. (KW, 391; PKW, 1:106)

28. See p. 483, note 42.

29. The various items embedded in Phetkla are *khot*, คด, materials found naturally with some strange characteristic which suggests a miraculous origin. Other examples include petrified seeds, and stones believed to be petrified forms of various eggs. Such objects have power of themselves, without the need to be activated by a teacher with knowledge, and their main benefit is to provide invulnerability by moving to block the entry of weapons. Black is the color of Saturn, and signifies supernatural power, so embedding this in the head signifies an abnormally powerful person, and will make an enemy afraid to fight. The needles will fly to any part of the body to block any piercing but if they are inserted without the proper ritual they may cause blindness. Diamond is the hardest stone and hence a symbol of invulnerability, which accounts for its appearance in headgear in both Western and Eastern traditions. (KW, 391; SB, 378–79; Textor, "An Inventory," 60–64; YS, 15–19; Prachak, *Prapheni*, 163–64)

30. See p. 318, note 18.

31. "Herbal amber" is an invented term for เทียนคล้า, a hard, apparently metallic core naturally occurring in *khla*, shrubs of the Calathea genus (SB, 378). แก้วตาแมว, *kaeo ta maeo*, is a semi-precious stone believed to be the eye of a dead cat, miraculously transformed. Usually green, translucent, and sparkling, it conveys invulnerability and other benefits (Textor, "An Inventory," 62; YS, 16–17; SWC, 10:4607).

His teeth were white, and his mouth green like a giant leech.

His eyes were black like a tiger's, and rimmed with red as if daubed with vermilion. His beetling eyebrows and reddish moustache gave him a fierce look. His hair was coiled like a yogi.

He never slept with his wife for the entire year. From youth until adulthood, he did not bathe but applied a paste of medicinal herbs. The only exception was times prior to battle,

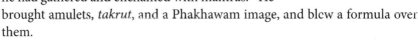

when he bathed in medicine made with herbs he had gathered and enchanted with mantras.[32] He

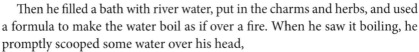

coiled hair

brought amulets, *takrut,* and a Phakhawam image, and blew a formula over them.

Then he filled a bath with river water, put in the charms and herbs, and used a formula to make the water boil as if over a fire. When he saw it boiling, he promptly scooped some water over his head,

took out the charms and herbal mixture, stepped into the bath, paid respect, and washed himself. Next, he looked for an omen in the water.

If he were in mortal danger, the water would be reddish like sappanwood. If he would neither win nor lose but something in between, the water would have the color of dissolved gamboge.

If he were to have victory over the enemy, the water would have the brilliant luster of crystal. On this occasion, he was fated to die. The omen in the water was red.[33]

Phetkla stared at it, knowing the meaning exactly. "Water colored like sappanwood is a terrible sign." He sighed in apprehension.

Devastated, he got out to change his clothes, unable to steady his body, but thought, "Even though I die, my skill as a valiant Lao warrior will still be known."

In a foul mood, he got dressed. As it was a Monday, he wore a yok lowercloth with a white base.[34] He put on a *takrut,* glistening mercury charm, diamond ring that sparkled like a star,

---

32. ถมถนำ, *thom thanam,* a synonym for mantra or yantra. Khun Wichitmatra suggests the herbs might include *wan hanuman, Haemanthus multiflorus, wan saeng athit, wan kamphaeng jet chan* (KW, 393).

33. The same omen appears in *Lilit Phra Lo* (see p. 344, note 31).

34. One list of auspicious colors by days runs as follows: Sunday, red; Monday, white or grey; Tuesday, pink; Wednesday, red or orange; Thursday, green or yellow; Friday, purple or dark grey; Saturday, black or dark blue.

bandeaus tied crosswise on his chest, brilliant breast chains and girdle, headcloth in white with scattered stars, and golden belt embroidered with lettering.[35]

He put a string of golden beads round his neck, and daubed enchanted whiteclay powder on his fore-head.[36] Picking up his lance, he strode forward to leap on the back of his magnificent horse.

He looked as bold as a lion, befitting his skill on the battlefield. He examined the inner clouds for an omen,[37] found it was an auspicious time, and ordered three cheers to begin the march.

breast chain and girdle

A ceremonial parasol[38] was spread for the army officer. The ground shook with the sound of horses' hooves, and the forest echoed with the boisterous shouting of the troops.

Now to tell of Thao Krungkan, the valiant army commander. He pressed forward with the preparation of the troops, giving orders for harnessing tuskers.

The Department of Elephants provided robust and powerful military elephants with good harnesses, first-rate mahouts for the neck and rear, one soldier to sit in the middle of each elephant, and a full complement of weapons. They formed two lines along the road. The men all wore shirts, bound auspicious threads around their heads, and made themselves invulnerable against weapons—

some by using herbal roots,[39] some by chanting formulas, some by wearing yantra designs and applying oil, some by drinking liquor subjected to incantation,

parasol

---

35. อักขรา, *akkhara*, term used in Thai *saiyasat* to refer to lettering in old Khmer characters, usually of *na* or similar formulas.

36. He would have written some device such as a *na* symbol (see p. 483, note 42) on some surface with a stick of whiteclay, wiped it off to become powder, then used his finger to daub the powder on his forehead (KW, 394).

37. This passage specifies เมฆใน, *mek nai*, "inner clouds," suggesting this is the method of seeking a cloud omen by imagining the sky, rather than looking at it (see p. 621, note 15 above).

38. สัปทน, *sappathon*, a long-handled ceremonial umbrella.

39. Suitable roots include: casumunar; turmeric; มะตูม, *Aegle marmelos*, baelfruit; and กระเช้าผีมด, *krachao pi mot*, *Aristolochia tagala*, "witch's basket." They are enchanted with formulas and eaten (Prachak, *Prapheni*, 163; PKW, 2:49).

some from fangs, tusks, or animal eyes,[40] some from *kamjat*,[41] copper, or stone, and some from hide embedded with diamond or jet.[42] All were able to withstand weapons.

Phya Prap Mueang Maen, a great warrior and commander of the right wing, rode on the neck of a majestic tusker, wearing a headcloth in ruby color edged with gold,

and a bright pink shirt trimmed with shot-gold brocade on both upper arms. Nai Kamkong of the left wing wore the same ruby headcloth edged with gold,

a shirt of light leaf-green velvet, and golden beads round his neck. He looked formidable. Both wore yantra for invulnerability. Each commanded a thousand troops,

all battle-hardened, and carrying weapons of many kinds. Nai Soi Dao, who commanded almost a thousand men as the rearguard,

rode on the elephant Phlai Kaeo Ming Mueang,[43] arrayed with protective amulets and sheltered by a parasol. He wore a pleated shirt in wrinkled chicken-skin silk of moon yellow and a helmet of *mot* cloth instilled with yantra. The army was ready.

The King of Chiang Mai presented his army commander with a royal mount named Phlai Phlik Thorani[44] to ride into battle. The beast was in musth.

He stood six cubits and one fist tall,[45] and had tusks hooped in gold, a broad forehead,[46] a lower rear end like elephants in statues, long tail, large ears, a brave heart, and auspicious dual frontal humps on his head.[47]

---

40. Meaning stones such as cat's eye, believed to be the petrified form of a cat's eye (YS, 30; see p. 631, note 31 above).

41. กำจัด or กำจาย, pieces of ivory broken from the tusks of elephants in musth charging through the forest, and embedded in trees, rocks, or ant heaps. These are considered to have great intrinsic power without need for further enchantment. They are collected by hunters and sold to adepts who shape them into images of Buddha, Gavampati, or Ratchasi, and who add other lore to enhance their power (YS, 19).

42. The hide would be taken from the forehead of a tiger or buffalo (YS, 30).

43. แก้วมิ่งเมือง, "crystal charm city."

44. พลายพลิกธรณี, "earth overturner."

45. ศอก, *sok*, like a Western cubit, is the length from fingertip to elbow, usually reckoned as 50 cms; กำ, *kam*, is based on the fist and has several variants; this is probably based on a clenched fist, measured crosswise (from thumb to little finger), and usually converted as 10 cms. Hence this height is three meters, 10 cms. Chaiyanuphap, the elephant ridden by King Naresuan in the famous duel with the Burmese Uparat in 1593, is reported in the chronicles as six cubits, one span (คืบ) and two fingers/inches (นิ้ว), slightly taller than the elephant here (RCA, 128).

46. ตระพอง/กะพอง, *traphong/kaphong*, the domed forehead of an elephant (Natthaphat, *Chang ton*, 145).

47. โขมด, *khamot*; these humps are believed to be the nerve centers of an elephant (Natthaphat, *Chang ton*, 145).

He walked nimbly with poise, and under gunfire did not tremble but whisked the rounded hairs of his tail around his heels. He had thick hide, a giant face, and wrinkled skin.

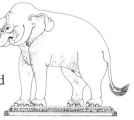
elephant statue

He was decked with a sash across his forehead in gold thread, fine-looking tassels hanging from his ears, front and rear harnesses spangled with aporosa flowers, and both flanks clad in gold and pure silver.

clashing-circles pattern

He had a stirrup strap of embroidered silk, and padding on the middle of his back. The goad had a lance blade, sharp and glistening white. The mahout looked vigorous in a red shirt of clashing-circles pattern,[48] and a hat of purple *mot*.

The expert soldier, Krungkan, raised his devices of lore to his forehead, and put them on. He wore a Lao-style yok lowercloth in white with red flowers, a meshwork shirt with a fighting Garuda embroidered in gold thread, breast chains, a Phakhawam image, beads around his neck, a gold ring inlaid with a ruby, *takrut* amulets, an inner shirt with yantra to protect against weapons, and an embossed spirit-skull belt.

He inserted a kris enchanted with a Discharger mantra,[49] then tied on top a sash in jackfruit-spine pattern.[50] He wore a hat embroidered with gold silk meshwork, and slung a Japanese sword across his shoulder in a sheath plated with gold.

Having sprinkled his body with water used to wash an image of Lord Narai, he walked from the room. The mahout brought an elephant beside a platform for him to mount. He walked up to the neck, and grasped a goad.

He prayed, peering intently, and saw a strange omen in the shape of a man with no head. On a second look, the arms and neck were not attached to the

---

48. แย่งชิงดวง, *yaeng ching duang*, also called *kaeo ching duang*, a pattern based on adjacent or overlapping circles, usually combined with floral motifs.

49. ประจุขาด, *prajukhat*, "shedding the load," a formula for disrobing from the monkhood, which may also be used to cancel the powers of an enemy. The formula consists of a list of weapons used by Vishnu and other Hindu gods. By conveying the power of these weapons to resist attack, it provides invulnerability (YS, 28; SB, 392–93).

50. หนามขนุน, *nam khanun*, jackfruit spine. This may be a checkered pattern, produced by tie dye or batik technique, used on cloths imported from India or Japan and worn by nobles, but here probably refers to a method of weaving silk to produce a stretchy, bobbly fabric used for sashes. In Ayutthaya, belts or sashes in this pattern were supposedly reserved for the families of the senior ministers (Mahatthai, Kalahom, four pillars) but this rule was widely transgressed and King Rama I tried to re-impose the old custom (SWC, 8:3776; KTS, 4:285–88).

body. This bad omen made him lose heart.

"Asking the king to delay would bring shame for the troops. No one born as a man can escape death." He steeled himself to go, whatever fate had in store.

As he urged the elephant to walk off, he saw a bird chick fall dead in front of his eyes. A barn owl[51] skimmed over his head. A vulture and crow alighted on his parasol.

barn owl

Thao Krungkan was full of apprehension. "Oh, my life is going to be crushed to dust!" Yet he had to leave as it was an auspicious time to march. With three cheers the army moved off.

Thao Krungkan saw the flags drooped instead of waving. Unusually, the wind did not blow. Even the sound of cheering did not echo but fell flat. Shaking and sighing, he entered the forest.

ఞ

Now to tell of Khun Phaen, great romancer, who was sitting along with Phlai Ngam, Phra Thainam, and Kueng Kamkong discussing the battle with their troops.

They saw a pall of dust cloaking the sky, and thought it was probably the Lao bringing a large army. Khun Phaen sat quietly with eyes closed, examining the path of his breath.

"The Lao are bringing an army of ten thousand through the forest." He commanded men to go immediately to cut giant reed and sugar reed, and plant them as an embankment across the end of the lake,

and as crow's wings on either side. Also to use sticks to mark out a moat on the ground, and to stack up reeds like flimsy toy models of fighting towers and watch towers.

When the army commander scattered enchanted rice, the reeds turned into hardwood, firmly fixed together all around, with the crow's wings more solid than true wood.[52]

---

51. นกแสก, *nok saek*, *Tyto alba*. Because of its ghostly white face and its call ("a loud screech," King, *Field Guide*, 189), the barn owl is believed to be a spirit, and considered inauspicious.

52. Rapidly constructed wooden fortresses were a staple of the era. The fortress built by the Lao at Nong Bua Lamphu in 1827 was among the most famous. "It was twelve hundred by 620 meters. . . . The ramparts were constructed by logs four meters high and seventy-five to one hundred centimeters in diameter, linked together by rope through holes bored at the ends of the logs. . . . Moats strengthened the external defense of the fortress, and the fortress was large enough to enclose an entire village and the river crossing it" (Mayoury and Pheuiphanh, *Paths*, 198, note 64).

Where the ground had been marked was now a deep-looking moat, stretching across from the banks of the lake to the forest. The fortifications could withstand even hits from large cannon. The fighting towers were also perfect.

Khun Phaen ordered his soldiers to prepare themselves quickly on all sides. Only the four commanders stayed up on a platform. Lookout units were sent to watch the Lao approach.

Let us leave Khun Phaen here and tell of Saentri Phetkla. He quick-marched the army to the Don Tabaek Forest[53] where the road forked.

Looking around thirty *sen*[54] ahead, they saw the extensive Thai camp with crow's wings spread to left and right, and a moat dug all the way across from the edge of the lake.

Arriving closer, they could see the field was set out according to the manual. They halted to establish a position, then raised flags, fired signal guns, and hollered three resounding cheers.

Khun Phaen, great soldier, heard the Lao cheer and announced, "As expected, the Lao have brought a large force.

My mighty son and I will lead our men out to engage them. You two wait here with the army and keep watch. We'll deal with the Chiang Mai Lao.

Gather all the Vientiane Lao men together inside a circle of sacred thread. Only the fierce Thai will all come out on horseback.

Phlai Ngam will lead the thirty-five tough men as the vanguard. I'll lead the main army in support. If we get an opportunity, we'll storm them.

Even if there are thousands of Lao troops, we'll attack them with the elephants and kill them all. Be resolute, don't fear, have courage."

Khun Phaen and his son dressed and decked themselves in imposing devices—lowercloths according to the battle manual, fine belts inscribed with yantra,

inner shirts with yantra, outer shirts with large

inner shirt with yantra

---

53. This could be a place name (unidentified), or could be descriptive: the upland with a *tabaek, Lagerstroemia calyculata*, forest.

54. A *sen* is 40 meters, hence 1.2 kms.

flowers in brilliant gold, glittering nine-jeweled and *mondop*
rings,[55] triple breast chains worn crosswise,

and golden beads around their necks.
Both father and son of brave military
lineage wore helmets edged with *tat*
silk, presented by the king. Standing
majestically holding Skystorm,

nine-jeweled ring and mondop ring

Khun Phaen prayed, peering intently, and saw an auspicious omen of a
four-armed Narai floating on a cloud.[56] He mounted on the neck of his robust
elephant,

with Nai Phetjetpan as rear mahout, wearing a shirt in a bright red pattern.
Phlai Ngam rode the horse Sijan. The order was given to sound a gong at an
auspicious time to move the troops.

Five shots were fired as a signal and a gong sounded. The troops replied
with three cheers. The commander unfurled an auspicious flag, and the army
moved off.

When the two armies came face to face, the Lao apprehensively split off as
crow's wings. Saentri Phetkla cast his eyes into the distance and saw the Thai
army was just a handful.

"It's like winged termites flying into a flame. Do they think they can survive?" He ordered the cavalry to advance at the head of his troops. "With one
hand, we'll crush the whole Thai army.

Take them, men! Grab them at will! Don't let them escape!" He spurred his
horse to lead his troops into the attack.

They surrounded the Thai at front and rear, slashing as they went. But the
Thai had been chosen for their bravery. Phlai Ngam ordered the troops to raise
three cheers, spurred his horse, and went swinging into the battle.

A Lao advanced, stabbing with a spear. A Thai parried the spear aside, and
slashed in retaliation. The Lao threw himself forward to block the Thai blow
but fell headlong down on his face.

A Thai attacked, struck, swung, and parried. A Lao stabbed but the Thai
leapt out of the way, not pierced by the blade. The Thai stamped on the ground
and advanced, slashing at the back of the Lao.

A Lao raised a long spear and thrust fiercely at a Thai, but the Thai batted

---

55. A มณฑป, *mondop*, Sanskrit *mandapam*, is a roof over a shrine with stacked layers diminishing to a peak. A *mondop* ring has gems arranged to give a similar pyramidical effect. The nine
jewels, นพเก้า, *nopphakao*, are: diamond, ruby, emerald, topaz, garnet, sapphire, moonstone,
zircon, and cat's eye (Chira, "Jewellery," 122).

56. See p. 621, note 15 above.

the spear away and stabbed back, sending the Lao tumbling headfirst from his horse. Yet however many died, even more galloped into the breach.

Phlai Ngam and the thirty-five swirled around like windmills. They saw the Lao had them surrounded, and were closing, hitting and slashing, but the Thai did not flee.

When the Lao stabbed, the Thai slashed them dead. Other Lao stepped over the bodies, and kept coming forward, surrounding them so completely in such numbers that the Thai began to feel weary in the shoulder.

Phlai Ngam rode Sijan into the fray, slashing like lightning with his yantra-inscribed sword. Though the Lao were decked in charms and had taken herbal medicine, they were scattered dead on the ground by this weapon.

The Lao regrouped and came at him, yelling and stabbing, but their spears broke and pikes crumpled. They advanced, chopping at him from both sides, but the blades did not pierce. Phlai Ngam slashed back, killing in droves.

The Lao backed away in fright, like a pack of dogs in face of a tiger. "Our swords don't pierce his flesh." "I slash him but it doesn't go through his shirt!"

Phlai Ngam raised his sword, flashing in the light. The Lao backed away, as daunted as if the mighty Lord of the Lions had pounced into the middle of a herd of cattle.

Wherever Phlai Ngam advanced, the Lao fled in uproar. All the Lao shook their heads in respect for his boldness, and did not dare approach him in fear of their lives.

At the head of his column, Saentri Phetkla was agitated at seeing the troops wavering in confusion. He charged angrily
up to the front, slapping his feet into his horse's flanks and bellowing loudly. He arrived in front of Phlai Ngam's horse
and noted the youth's attractive appearance. Going closer, he asked, "Here, my good officer, what's your name?
You're just a youth—slight, tiny. You're a pupil of what teacher? A member of whose lineage? Pray tell me."

Young Phlai Ngam replied boisterously, "I'm a soldier of Ayutthaya. My name is Phlai Ngam following the custom of our lineage.
My father is Phraya Phaen Phikhat, a name chosen and granted by the king. I'm a student of my father. The Phlai lineage extends over many generations.
And you, sir! What's your name? It's presumptuous to ask an elder who is not yet dead though very old, but what teacher did you study with?"

Phetkla was happy to reply. "I'll tell you what you ask. You southerners didn't know when you rushed up here.

I am Thao Kham Maen,[57] of royal descent, holding the rank of Saentri Phetkla, and I come from a lineage of powerful soldiers. In Lanna[58] nobody stands against me.

The teacher who gave me knowledge was the courageous and strong Si Kaeo Fa[59] who resides at Red Cow Cave on Gold Hill[60] and is truly famous and respected everywhere.

Your name, Phlai Ngam, suits you, young lad. You're very good-looking, like a statue. Your figure is pretty, like a girl's.

Compared to my children, you're younger than the youngest, younger than my grandchildren. You shouldn't fight with a grandfather. Go back and tell your father to come and do battle with me,

to be a treat for the troops, an example of soldiery. You're still a boy. Watch the exercise of knowledge. Hey, Grandson, where's your father? Tell him to come!"

Phlai Ngam called back to Saentri Phetkla, "Here, don't be too arrogant and defame my family name.

You're old like a grandfather buffalo while I'm young like a tiger cub. Through my handiwork, Lao have died in droves. Don't delude yourself that adults can't be defeated.

If I wasn't able, why would I have come? Let me try out my knowledge with you, oldster, so I can see whether your powers are as good as you say, or your mouth is mightier than your skill.

Forgive me, don't bother my father. Can you even triumph over his son? Come and try just this once so people will talk about it. Perhaps you're so tired you'd rather sully your name?"

Saentri Phetkla's eyes blazed red with anger like gleaming lacquer. "Mm! This fellow really won't listen. Boasting he can fight *me*!"

---

57. ท้าวคำแมน, "lord golden deity."

58. Name of the old kingdom centered on Chiang Mai. The name probably came into use in the fourteenth century, and its earliest dated appearance is in an inscription of 1553. The meaning has been debated but is now generally accepted as "million ricefields" (Sarassawadee, *History of Lan Na*, 11–12).

59. ศรีแก้วฟ้า, "sacred gem of the sky."

60. เขาคำ ถ้ำวัวแดง, *khao kham tham wua daeng*. There are caves of this name in Chaiyaphum, Udon Thani, Uttaradit, and Phitsanulok but none found around Chiang Mai. There's a village Ban Rong Wua Daeng to the east of Chiang Mai, a little beyond Sankamphaeng.

He dug in his heels and galloped over to the middle of the battlefield in a rage. Riding beautifully, he flourished his lance and prepared to charge.

Watching Saentri Phetkla on horseback, young and elegant Phlai Ngam rode his horse in a preparatory routine, then turned to approach with a nimble rhythm.

Phetkla flourished his lance, flashing in the light. Phlai brandished his sword, held two-handed. Both gestured rhythmically as their horses pranced round in a circle.

They drew up in the two-necked swan stance, feinting and slashing this way and that. Then they turned to the dragon-play-with-diamond stance, maneuvering deftly around each other without giving ground.

As Phetkla's lance was longer than his sword, Phlai Ngam darted in to slash then dodged away. Phetkla chased after him angrily. Phlai danced, letting him draw close.

Phetkla drew himself up and launched his weapon but Phlai dodged, the blow missed, and Phetkla tumbled headlong. Phlai Ngam closed on him, drew himself up, and delivered a slashing blow,

but it bounced off without piercing. Phetkla stepped forward and thrust in return. Phlai evaded the blow and slashed at Phetkla's shoulder but the flesh was as tough as laterite or stone.

Phetkla raised his lance high and hacked but Phlai Ngam's body was as hard as rock, and the blow was like a scratch on the back that made him stronger. Phlai leapt forward, slashing and chopping,

hitting and hacking several times with his sword but Phetkla was invulnerable and suffered no damage. Phetkla delivered a return blow with the lance handle but Phlai's flesh gave way and then expanded back, leaving no mark.

Wearily realizing that he could not win, Saentri Phetkla pondered quietly to himself, "Tcha! This Thai lad is really able.

He's stronger and more powerful than his body suggests. His looks and manner are like a girl but he can truly match an adult like me because of his tactics and real fighting skill.

I don't think there's any chance of victory using weapons. I must use the inner way of mantra to make him lose." He rode his horse to halt some distance away,

closed his eyes, chanted, and blew a formula given by his expert teacher for summoning the Great Waters.[61] Like a stream, water gushed down,

unnaturally flooding the whole area, while wind whipped the water into

---

61. มหาอาโป, *maha apo*, the water element. In Buddhism, there are four elements, ธาตุ, *that*, similar to the Western ones, namely earth, water, fire, and air. Their names are based on Pali.

sloshing waves. The Thai soldiers scrambled to swim off and scale trees in total confusion.

Horses were lifted off the ground and swept away by the swirling torrent. The troops desperately appealed to their commanders to counter the mantra.

The resourceful Phlai Ngam, whose fame was spreading everywhere, immediately chanted and blew a formula that drained the water, leaving the whole area dry.

Then he chanted and blew a mantra summoning the Fire Element.[62] Instantly, the whole plain burst into flames that licked towards the Lao troops.

On the fire's approach, the Lao spurred their horses away in all directions, shaking with fear, and calling out loudly to their leaders, "Help us!"

Seeing the fire crackling throughout the forest, Phetkla calmed his body and chanted a formula summoning the Great Precipitation.[63]

Clouds blanketed the sky, and torrential rains drenched the lofty forest, flooding the ground and extinguishing the fire.

The volunteers huddled together under the shelter of trees, shivering from unbearable cold, injured almost fatally by hits from huge hailstones.

Phlai Ngam drew on his expertise to chant a formula summoning the wind inside his body and blowing it out as the Wind Element.[64]

With this power, a howling gale gusted so hard that the streams of raindrops were scattered into thin air and the rain did not fall.

Phlai Ngam then hurled a lump of gravel into the sky, making it rain drops of sand and grit that splattered down on the Lao troops, who frantically ran to hide.

Some rode into the bushes to give cover for their heads. Others were hit by the sand rain and injured so severely that blood flowed. Unable to bear it, they took off their clothes to cover their heads.

Seeing his troops with faces bruised and chests swollen, Saentri Phetkla was as angry as raging fire. He joined his fingers above his head and blew.

A mesh appeared in the sky, blocking the sand drops from falling. Phetkla commanded his soldiers to dismount.

"It's no good attacking them on horseback because they just run away. For

---

62. เตโชธาตุ, *techothat*, the fire element (see note 61 above).
63. มหาวลาหก, *maha walahok*, from Phalahok (see p. 26, note 24).
64. วาโยธาตุ, *wayothat*, the water element (see note 61 above).

grappling with them at close quarters, it's quicker to go on foot.

Hide the horses in the bushes. Select only the long weapons—pikes, javelins, and spears—and advance to encircle the Thai.

We have over a thousand and they're very few. If we use our strength of numbers to stab them, even though they're invulnerable, their bones will break. We'll have them in an instant, men!"

The Lao soldiers dismounted and quickly formed up in groups. They surrounded the Thai at front and rear in large numbers, then fell on them, thrusting, stabbing, and hitting.

The volunteers slashed back, cutting Lao open from shoulder to hip. Heads fell and bodies dropped in splatters of red blood. Yet the Lao rearguard came up alongside to join the fight,

swarming over the Thai in waves, but their pike thrusts did not pierce the Thai. The volunteers hacked relentlessly but the more Lao that died, the more kept on coming.

The volunteers' shoulders drooped and they could hardly raise their arms. Wearily they called to their commander. "Phlai Ngam, sir, we've slashed them to the end of our strength but for every one dead, another five or six turn up."

Phlai Ngam was not disheartened but could see the volunteer troops were so tired that their shoulders drooped and they could scarcely raise their arms.

He pulled out three handfuls of tamarind leaves and enchanted them,[65] turning them into millions of wasps which buzzed around the forest, turning it all pitch black.

Each wasp was as long as a little finger. They did not sting the Thai, only the Lao, over and over again. The poison in the sting was like a blow. Those stung again and again tumbled down on top of one another,

dropping their weapons and frantically slapping with their hands. Unable to stand it, they got up, fell down, hid their faces in their hands, and dived into water to get away.

When they surfaced out of breath, they were stung again. If they did not dive back down, it was unbearable. Phetkla's eyes closed from the stings. Horses too were pestered by swarms of wasps,

and galloped off wildly with their faces smothered in stings. Both officers and men fled in defeat. The Thai chased after to grapple with them.

---

65. In chapter 5, Phlai Kaeo was taught by Abbot Khong of Wat Khae how to turn tamarind leaves into wasps.

Thao Krungkan saw Phetkla's troops fleeing away to hide in confusion and defeat. He urged his elephant to lead his own men forward.

Khun Phaen, great valiant, saw Krungkan coming to help the vanguard. He drove his elephant at the head of his troops, and came up in front of Krungkan,

shouting, "Ha, sir! Is this a royal army?" Then he advanced his elephant further into the middle of the troops. "Countless elephants and horses. Here, what country are you going off to fight?"

Krungkan was cut to the quick by this insult. "Someone who boldly asks such a question must be Phraya Phaen.

He's stolen elephants and horses, helped prisoners escape, killed many people, and posted an insulting message to boot. What a villain!

Doesn't Ayutthaya have any horses and elephants? Is that why you come to steal from Chiang Mai? This army has come to round up forest bandits. If you return the goods, you'll survive."

Khun Phaen, great valiant, smiled and laughed. "You can talk well when you don't think of your own shadow.[66] Though you try to hide the wrongdoing, there's no smoke without fire.

Lanchang sent the princess to the Thai capital. The King of Chiang Mai, intoxicated by delusions, had the princess abducted in the forest and the escort captured and punished.

The Thai royal servants escorting the princess were jailed, flogged, and mistreated, both officers and men. Violence was committed without due respect, and a challenge was issued for an elephant duel.

It's your king who's the forest bandit. Trading your life for this lady is senseless. If you love yourself and fear death, send the princess back, and live!"

Krungkan, the commander, was as angry as if struck by a thunderbolt. Knowing his king had acted badly, he felt as if a tree had fallen on him.

Yet he endeavored to cover things up. "Your words may go too far. The King of Vientiane is no good. He's always been a two-faced Phali.[67]

---

66. Spirits, i.e., the dead, don't have shadows.

67. A monkey in the *Ramakian*, called Vali in the *Ramayana*, who rules the land of Kiatkin. He promises his brother Sukrip (Sugriva) he will not violate Sukrip's wife, Dara, but then falls for her, forgets his promise, and marries her. Sukrip is forced into exile in the forest, where he meets Ram and Hanuman. Ram offers to take revenge on Phali. Sukrip challenges his brother to a fight, and lures him to a spot where Ram can shoot Phali with an arrow. Phali catches the arrow but then recognizes his opponent as Ram and thus realizes resistance is pointless, so stabs

A missive came offering the Princess Soithong to the King of Chiang Mai. Then Vientiane shifted his ground and offered her to the Thai. So we bear a grudge,

enough to lead to war. Why are you talking about us handing over this princess? Come for an elephant duel in the forest right now to see who's good enough to survive.

If I lose to you in this contest, Soithong will be handed over. If you're defeated, Soithong must stay in Chiang Mai."

With that, he commanded the left and right wings, and all the elephants and horses of the central brigade, to advance and surround the brave Thai. "Don't let anyone escape!"

Khun Phaen, great conjuror of spreading fame, called out orders to his troops. "Don't tangle with them. Make a defensive formation.

Sammayang, give support on the right wing. Phromson, provide cover on the left wing. Thammathian, hold the rearguard. I'll duel with him on elephants."

He rode Si Khotchadet[68] forward, chanting a formula and blowing it onto the elephant's forehead and tusks on both sides to make his whole head and body invulnerable. Then he rode the elephant towards Thao Krungkan.

Krungkan angrily drove Phlai Phlik Thorani forward, flourishing his lance-goad with expertise. The two elephants closed and their tusks clashed. The Lao elephant had been fed a great deal of liquor and was mad with intoxication. Khotchadet stood clear-eyed. He was in musth and had no fear of the other elephant.

Phlai Phlik Thorani closed. Khotchadet tossed his tusks. When the Lao elephant veered away, raising his head, the Thai elephant got in under his neck.

Nai Jetpan, manning the side strap, stabbed hard. The Lao elephant's head was thrown upwards, and its haunches dropped. Khun Phaen strongly urged the Thai elephant forward to press his advantage and push the opponent back.

The Lao elephant tried to fend Khotchadet away but could not hold his ground. The Thai elephant repeat-

lance-goads

himself. Sukrip becomes ruler of Kiatkin.

68. สีห์คชเดช, "lion elephant of power." คช, *khotcha*, is an elevated word for elephant from Sanskrit.

edly smashed into him hard, forcing the Lao elephant to retreat further and further.

Krungkan tried using the goad to make his elephant turn back to the attack but the Thai elephant pushed him beyond hope of recovery. The Lao elephant, crazed with liquor and in great pain, jerked his shoulders, trying to shake the opponent off.

Khun Phaen saw he had the advantage. He flourished his lance and slashed downwards, hitting Krungkan, who collapsed on the elephant's neck. But Krungkan's neck was not pierced by the blow, only bruised, oozing blood.

Krungkan recovered and raised himself up. Khun Phaen drove his elephant close, and slashed again. Krungkan lost his footing and fell dangling head downwards from the stirrup strap. Khun Phaen slashed again, and Krungkan plummeted to the ground.

Khun Phaen drove his elephant forward, crying, "Take him!" The elephant approached, trumpeting loudly, coiled up his trunk, closed his eyes, and smashed down with his tusks. He went on hitting and stabbing until Krungkan lay flat.

Withdrawing his tusks, he tossed the body up into the air so it fell back down onto the points. Krungkan's head shattered and his guts spewed out. Khotchadet trumpeted again. The Lao elephant fled away from the army.

Sammayang led his men to attack the brigade of Prap Mueang Maen on the right wing. Phromson led his troops to swarm into battle with Nai Kamkong on the left wing.

Both sides plunged into the attack, and the battle flowed back and forth at breakneck pace. When the Lao stabbed, the Thai defended. When the Thai slashed, the Lao parried.

Yet the Thai attacked hard, slashing first one side then the other without pause. Sammayang rushed on the opposing army commander, Nai Prap but it was like hitting iron or diamond.

Sammayang blew a Discharger[69] mantra, swung his sword, and lopped off his opponent's head, bathing his sword in blood like red paint. The Lao began to lose their stomach for the fight.

Phromson chanted an Annul-Ubosot[70] formula, and leapt forward, stab-

---

69. See p. 635, note 49 above.

70. ถอนโบสถ์, *thon bot*, another formula to cancel the powers of an enemy. Originally a prayer, *thon lak bot*, meaning to annul the principle of the *ubosot*, ordination hall. The prayer was offered prior to the construction of an ordination hall to remove the prior spiritual traces of any ordination hall or other sacred building that might have been on the spot in the past. Subsequently, the formula became more generally used to drive away spirits (SB, 393–94; PKW, 2:48).

bing Kamkong in the lower stomach. He pulled out his dagger and slashed the mahout, who toppled down on the body of his master.

Soi Dao saw the army commander was lost, and the officers on both the left and right wings were dead. He drove his tusker forward, thrusting with his pike at the Thai on all sides.

Thammathian watched from the middle of the fray then furiously drove his elephant, Phlai Kaeo Ming Mueang, forward at a gallop to plunge a tusk into Soi Dao's breast.

Soi Dao straightened himself up enough to pry out the tusk with his goad, and slashed in retaliation. Thammathian blew a Thunderer mantra[71] on the wind, and sunk his pike halfway through the Lao's neck,

then leapt over and slashed the rear mahout. Both the Lao servant and his master died, lopped off at the neck. The remaining troops shrank away into the forest.

Now to tell of Saentri Phetkla. When the wasp stings wore off, he opened his eyes, got up, and saw the army broken and scattered. In a rage, he rode off on his horse

and called out, "Ha! Phlai and Nai Phaen. Don't think that I fled away. Because my horse's eyes were stung by the wasps, I could not stop it dragging me off.

But I've come back so we may try out our strength. Don't imagine I'll retreat. If I defeat you and leave you dead, my name will be known all over the earth."

Khun Phaen, great master, heard Phetkla's reckless words and called out a reply for his ears. "You're still wagging your tongue and floating your face to challenge me.

I saw your powers against the infant. You had to raise a white flag and disappear off into the forest. Not ashamed at losing to my little son, now you want to fight the father.

Here we have the leader of all the Lao officers and men staggering up, intent on saving his face! Because there's no way out, you're steeling yourself to fight me. This time your life is up."

Phetkla was fiery-eyed with fury as if poked in the ear with a pike a hundred thousand times. Seething with rage, he rode straight into battle at the head of his troops without chanting any mantra.

---

71. โอ้ฟ้าผ่า, *o fa pha*, lightning strike, another very obscure formula to cancel the powers of an enemy (PKW, 2:48).

Khun Phaen bellowed a Power of Giants formula, rooting Phetkla to the spot, then raised his pike and slashed down on Phetkla's head and shoulder. The Lao collapsed onto his saddle.

Ta-Lo said, "Pa, allow me." He rushed over and chopped down with an axe. Ta-Rak said, "Me too." He poked a stave in Phetkla's stomach, knocking him down from the horse.

Nai Ho Sam Hok thrust with a spear but the metal buckled without piercing Phetkla. He threw away the spear, and hacked with a machete, while Nai Pan Khwan Fa slashed at Phetkla with a sword.

It was like hitting copper or stabbing rock. The weapons crumpled and broke off at the handles. Not even a single bone was broken. His whole body was invulnerable.

Ta-Lo said, "Pa and Phlai, sirs. This fellow Phetkla is shockingly able. However many time we slash and stab him, he doesn't die but lies there still breathing. Amazing."

Khun Phaen called, "Don't make a fuss. Hey, someone get a spear and stab his arse. Even though he's invulnerable, if you shove it up to his throat, he should die."

Ta-Lo and Ta-Rak hitched up their lowercloths and wrenched off Phetkla's clothes. Nai Mo and Nai Mao brought a spear and pushed it through the anus up his whole body.

Many people helped give a heave. They brought wooden poles and hammered them up to his head. Phetkla's face blanched. Blood leaked from the hole down to the ground like the slaughter of an ox.[72]

The surviving troops fled into the forest. Post horses raced to the city to inform the nobles and officials.

"Hail! The troops of all the five armies have been massacred, sir. I don't know how many have escaped with their lives."

After listening to the messengers, nobles picked up their prostration cloths, tied them round their waists, and rushed to the audience hall, trembling with alarm.

They found King Chiang In sitting on a jet-jeweled dais at the front. The officials prostrated, crawled in, made obeisance,

---

72. This killing resembles a form of execution by impalement witnessed by Gerrit Wuysthoff in Cambodia in 1642. In Alfons van der Kraan's summary: " . . . the executioner cut open the back of the crotch of the victim, inserted a stake into the wound and drove it upwards through the body, between the spine and the skin of the back, until the stake protruded from the neck" (*Murder and Mayhem*, 14–15).

and said, "Phetkla, Soi Dao, Thao Krungkan, Prap Mueang Maen, and the officers and men who marched out to fight with the Thai have been defeated and killed.

The remaining officers and men have fled into the forest and are still scattered to the winds. We don't know how many hundred there are."

Hearing the armies had been destroyed, King Chiang In felt as if the Lord of Darkness were about to annihilate him. His face was plunged in gloom.

But with the will of a king he gave orders to officials of all ranks to quickly organize the defense of the capital. "Set up camps around the city. Close the gates securely, and reinforce them with wooden barricades. Place defensive guns all around the boundary. Organize ranks of flintlocks. Around the camps, set up *jarong* cannon.[73] At the entrance of the central gate, place big cannons, wat sweepers[74] and victory umbrellas.[75] Block every opening.

flintlock gun

On the walls at the gate on the south side, suspend logs that can be cut with machetes to fall and crush enemy assailants.

Clear paths for walking on the ramparts, and make them big and broad. In the center, place guns and bonfires. Prepare hot gravel and sand for every brigade.

Have the city officer summon all gentlefolk and commoners from every village around. Set guards by the lamps. Make tours of inspection. Beat gongs. Check the recruitment.

---

73. จ่ารง, "a medium-sized cannon about three cubits long with shot four inches in diameter" (SB, 396). Lord Egerton called them "field pieces," and Captain Low in 1836 called them "field pieces with twenty men attached" (Egerton, *Indian and Oriental Armour*, 94; Low, "History of Tenasserim," 317).

74. ปะขาวกวาดวัด, *pa khao kwat wat*, "lay ascetic sweeps the wat," name of a heavy cannon firing shot almost 20 inches diameter, used in the 1767 defense of Ayutthaya (SB, 396; KCK, 244). The name may come from one of the stories about the legendary King Ruang that were collected into the *Phongsawadan nuea*, Northern Chronicles. Ruang wove a basket and sent it filled with water to the Khmer king who decided the giver of such a gift was too clever and hence sent an army to capture him. But Ruang escaped and went to stay as a monk in a Sukhothai wat. A Khmer tunneled through to Sukhothai and inquired after Ruang but the locals told him that Ruang had gone north. The Khmer inquired at Sawankhalok, and was sent back to Sukhothai where he accosted Ruang in the white robe of a lay ascetic sweeping the wat courtyard. Ruang turned the Khmer to stone. (*Phongsawadan nuea*, 28–29; KW, 572)

75. ฉัตรชัย, *chatchai*, another heavy cannon (SB, 396).

Set rosters to keep watch. If something happens, every house will face death. Have people accommodate the villagers brought into the city from outside the walls.

Dig out the ponds, wells, and streams of every house and fill them with water. Have any farm that has food bring everything to deposit here.

Only the local officials are to stay at their posts. If the enemy enters their territory, they are to slash and stab them at will."

The nobles took the orders, left at once, and frantically set to recruiting people. Cannons were dragged into position to defend the gates.

On the summons of the city officer, groups of men and women hurried in, some setting up camps on the perimeter of the moat, some conscripted to man the walls.

Kindling was brought, fires made, and braziers placed on them. Gravel and sand were heated in readiness at every spot. Supervisors went round to inspect. Gongs were beaten all over the town.

Villagers flocked in, carrying and dragging their children and grandchildren. In every house, betel boxes, bowls, footed trays, and salvers were buried in the earth.

Gold, rings, and other valuables were sewed into sacks and tied around the waist, sometimes in false pockets. Everyone hid important articles.

In fear of the Thai attack, widows and old folk bustled around wrapping things in cloth and hiding them in the cleft of their bottom, or under the chili and salt.

Possessions were hidden in chignons, in blankets, in pillows, in mats, or pasted with dammar under the hulls of boats. Not one little thing was left to be seized.

Unmarried young women, widows, and those who knew their menfolk had already died gave way to weeping and lamenting. With everyone swept inside the walls, the whole city was crowded and chaotic.

The palace was in uproar. All the royal family members down to the lower ranks were weeping and beating their chests red in desperation. Some hid their possessions under the palace buildings.

King Chiang In spoke with the royal kin and consorts to calm them. "Our few warriors took this little battle too lightly. They fought rashly and were defeated.

But, heigh! Wait till you see my skill. I'll chase them off into the forest. Their five hundred is puny compared to us. We'll crush them to dust under our feet.

Why weep and make a bad omen? Can an army of nobles rival me, a king? If they invade our city, we'll mobilize for a day and they'll be dead."

He walked out to the front and ordered officers to hasten all preparations. "Chiang Mai is our main camp.

If they storm the city, don't go out to repel them but stay secure here. We have a lot of food. They have nothing to eat.

Go and burn down all the rice granaries in the villages outside. That'll reduce these blackguards' strength. Just watch them flying around,

and when their supplies are finished, go out and put them to the sword. This handful of men is no match for us. We'll kill them in less than an eye blink."

The four-pillar officers prostrated and expressed their approval. "The king's words are appropriate as ordered on every point.

We'll gain victory because of the supplies. We can cut off their support so they starve. How many measures[76] of crisped rice do they have with them? Once their rice is finished, their strength will decline."

"Though they set a siege, we can surround them on the outside and prevent them from going for food. In a few days, they'll run up a white flag. Set an ambush at the entrance of the forest, and we'll catch them."

"No need to fight in our defense. Just cheer once and they'll run away to hide their heads. Capture alive all the five hundred who used to be our prisoners, both officers and men."

The nobles conferred together and reached agreement. They came to sit and give orders according to this strategy. They treated the walled city, with its moat and embankment, as their camp.

---

76. ทะนาน, *thanan*, a volume measure based on a half-coconut shell, a twentieth of a ถัง, *thang*, which was about 20 liters.

30: KHUN PHAEN AND PHLAI NGAM CAPTURE THE KING
OF CHIANG MAI

Now to tell of Khun Phaen, great romancer, unmatched in power. He watched the Lao army scatter in defeat and the Thai chase after the remnants to cut them down.

Nearing evening, the army was called back to camp. Buffaloes were killed and cooked. The soldiers ate, talked, and celebrated rowdily until sunset.

Khun Phaen spoke to his son Phlai Ngam, "We can't wait around here. We should take the troops to invest Chiang Mai immediately—

attack and crush them before they can get organized. Since we don't have supplies to feed the troops, we should engage the enemy within two days."

Phlai Ngam agreed with everything. "If we delay, we won't have any food because no Lao will give us anything.

Once they know the news, they'll shiver with fright and close the water-gates and port-gates.[1] If we don't go into the city but wait for them to come out, things will be difficult.

We must take the army to invest the city, and put them to sleep to enter at night. If we capture the King of Chiang Mai as we hope, it will bring an end to the war and our problems."

The father and son talked until the moon rose and shone brightly. They ordered the volunteers to cut wood for building an eye-level shrine,

then made a circle of sacred thread, enchanted yantra, and arranged offerings of duck, chicken, turtle, pig, liquor, and all kinds of food.

Khun Phaen gathered his powers and entered a trance.[2] He put a sacred thread around his head, enchanted rice, inserted an adept's knife in his belt, and walked over.

He lit candles, placed them on the shrine, and chanted a formula to summon all the spirits, sprites, and ghosts, including the ancestor spirits in the

---

1. ปิดประตูน้ำค้ำประตูท่า, *pit pratu nam kham pratu tha*, probably a proverbial phrase from Ayutthaya, a city ringed by watergates that had to be blocked when under siege (Phraya Boran-ratchathanin described excavating timbers probably used for this purpose; APA, 55–56).

2. ปลุกตัว, *pluk tua*, "activate oneself," to induce a trance by meditation, sometimes resulting in convulsions, "in which the actor flails the air with his arms and legs, writhes and wriggles uncontrollably, and often emits strange sounds and grunts" (Textor, *Patterns of Worship*, 298–99).

hills, to come and partake of
the offerings.

offerings

Now to tell of the spirits,
sprites, and ghouls from every
forest, saltlick, lair, and tree,
including the ancestor spirits
in every hill, cave, and stream.
All were touched by the mantra. The whole forest was in
turmoil.

The Thai spirits that had come
on campaign with Khun Phaen went around every wood, summoning the Lao
spirits that were intimidated by this power and all came to the rite.

Spirits from all around arrived in hundreds of thousands, and thronged
around the shrine in many layers, invisible to the people sitting there,

except for the masterful Khun Phaen who saw the whole crowd of formidable spirits showing off their tricks and transforming themselves into various
fierce animals.

Khun Phaen scattered enchanted rice, making the malevolent spirits prostrate all around the forest. He blew a Gem Wind[3] formula to make the mass
of them docile,

and said, "I beg you, guardian spirits of great power from every location,
to come with us as a spirit army to attack the principal protective guardians
of Chiang Mai.

As the King of Chiang Mai does not rule with righteousness, the city is
fated to fall apart. Please help us as volunteers of the realm. I invite all of you
to eat these offerings."

All the deities and spirits, touched by the Gem mantra, smiled and laughed.
They volunteered, saying "Have no fear. We'll help you, all of us."

They ate the offerings, drank the liquor, and took their leave, swarming away
through the forest, showing off their powers by transforming their bodies into
various forms, and making the earth shake as if on the brink of collapse.

They surrounded the city in a horde, creating as much commotion as if the
earth had been hit by a series of thunderbolts and the city would overturn
and crumble.

The principal guardians of Chiang Mai, including the Lord of the City's

---

3. ลมจินดา, *lom jinda*, a mantra blown to make spirits more amenable (KW, 685).

Lineage[4] and the Spirit Lord,[5] resided in the major and minor shrines of the city where they received offerings from King Chiang In.

Seeing the approach of the Thai spirits and forest spirits in force, they conscripted and swept up colleagues from every locality, including spirits under the ground in graveyards, to fight against the forest spirits.

All showed off their terrible powers. They flung awesome weapons. They tossed horses and elephants around. They grabbed flowers as big as logs and hurled them.

The forest spirits were knocked head over heels but the Thai spirits hurtled up as reinforcements, striking with clumps of camphorweed[6] as if with fire. The forest spirits threw themselves back into the battle.

King Chiang In had been a primary ruler[7] but was fated to decline back to the status of his ancestors and become a vassal state[8] of the Thai capital. Thus the city's protective aura[9] was weakened,

and as a result the city spirits were unable to compete with the strength and ferocity of the forest spirits. They retreated in defeat and disorder, and the forest spirits invaded the city.

---

4. *Phra suea mueang rueangchai.* Cities usually have two principal guardian spirits. The *phra suea mueang*, พระเสื้อเมือง, or lord of the city's lineage, represents the ancestors, especially the city's founder. The *phra song mueang*, พระทรงเมือง, is the spirit of the place (เจ้าที่, *jao thi*, lord of the place, here given as เจ้าผี, *jao phi*, spirit lord), and is often associated with a city pillar, *lak mueang*, an obelisk erected near the city center. At the Bangkok city pillar, the image of the *phra suea mueang* holds a sword in one hand and discus in the other, while the *phra song mueang* holds a sword in his left hand, and raises his right hand to head height. Here the Bangkok authors do not know much about Chiang Mai and are simply imposing what they know from Bangkok. (Anuman, *Phi sang thewada*, 36–38)

5. *Jao phi*, probably here a shorthand for the *phra song mueang* (see previous note).

6. หนาด, *nat*, *Blumea balsamifera*, camphorweed or camphor plant, a bushy herb with strong camphor smell and many medicinal properties, believed to be feared by some spirits.

7. เอกราช, *ekkarat*. Nowadays, the word means independent but is translated here to reflect the system of political relations of the time. It means a king who was not subordinate and tributary to another. Pallegoix gave as definition, "King superior to others" (PAL, 129).

8. ประจันตประเทศ, *prajantaprathet.* The ambition of Ayutthaya/Bangkok to control the Lanna capital is one of the long-running themes of the history of the Chaophraya Basin. In the early and mid-nineteenth century, when this passage was written, this ambition was close to being realized. In the wars of the late eighteenth century, Lanna had slipped free of subservience to Ava with the help of Thonburi-Bangkok. It was now a truculent tributary which would finally be absorbed from the 1870s onwards.

9. อาถรรพณ์, *athan*, from Atharava-veda, the Fourth Veda (see p. 125, note 34). At the foundation of a city, rituals are conducted to strengthen the place's *athan*. Possibly these rituals once included human and animal sacrifices. Subsequently, rituals are conducted regularly at a central shrine or city pillar to sustain the *athan*. The spirits that Khun Phaen's spirit army is attacking resided in these shrines, and were the agents providing the city's protection.

The deity of every shrine fled in disarray. The spirits of the conch, ceremonial umbrella, and Black Lord[10] bounded out of their sanctuaries. The Lord of the City's Lineage and the Lord of the City's Location made themselves scarce. The spirits of the royal treasure hall[11] and Jettakup[12] ran away.

As the forest spirits entered the city, all the minor spirits fled in all directions, some carrying their children in their arms or dragging them off by the hand into the woods. The whole city echoed with the sound of their cries.

At the time his spirit army was being destroyed, the King of Chiang Mai had a premonition in his sleep. His whole family and the city people had the same graphic dream

in which the Thai army fell on the Lao, and the king, nobles, and people of the city all fled into the wilds. In every household, people awoke and interpreted the dream, amazed to find all had had the same omen.

Some people said that when the gong sounded, they had heard a strange commotion "as if all our spirits were fleeing." Everybody trembled in fear.

The King of Chiang Mai awoke and got up apprehensively in the knowledge that the spirits of every house, ward, and wood had fled from the city.

He was very worried that the city would be in trouble and the people crushed to dust, "all because I acted badly and dragged an enemy up here."

But he recovered his royal will and again had aggressive thoughts. "My age is already sixty-five, and I won't rule this city much longer. I refuse to lose face and suffer the contempt of the Thai.

When one of tiger lineage dies, the stripes remain so people know the valor of the lineage. When one of royal lineage is crushed to death, he doesn't sully the lineage by showing fear to anyone.

Though life is lost, reputation is preserved, to be known throughout the

---

10. พระกาฬ, *phrakan*, another of the tutelary spirits of the city, full name พระกาฬไชยศรี, *phra-kan chaisi*, the black lord of holy victory. The spirit of the conch and umbrella guarded these two articles of royal regalia.

11. หอเครื่อง, *ho khrueang*, was the storehouse for valuables such as royal jewels. The spirit of this place was another of the main tutelary spirits of the city.

12. เจตคุก เจตคุปต์, *jettakhuk/p*, another of the city spirits, a Thai representation of Chi-tragupta. In Hindu tradition, Yama, the god of death, used to make mistakes in assigning people to heaven or hell so Shiva instructed Chitragupta to serve as Yama's registrar, keeping meticulous records of all humans from birth to death. Chitragupta probably arrived in Siam via Cambodia where he is depicted along with Yama in the galleries of Angkor Wat. In the Thai version, he rides on an owl, holding a *bailan*, palm leaf, in one hand and a stylus in the other. There is a figure of *jettakhup* at the entrance to the shrine of the Bangkok city pillar.

world, like the mighty ten-headed warrior of solar lineage[13] whose love was stolen and given to Ram.

If he had loved his own life and family, he would have handed over Sida. But he preferred to fight fearlessly to death so that his name and reputation would appear in stories set down in writing forever.

If I feared them, I'd send them Soithong and nothing major would happen. But like Thotsakan I'll fight to the death to retain my reputation so it may be known eternally throughout heaven and earth."

With these thoughts, he walked out to the front and ordered all the officers to be on guard for the enemy. "We take the city of Chiang Mai as the home where we die."

The officials took the orders, crawled out, and went to inspect every person, camp, moat, and fighting tower. They saw that every gate was closed, and that pans for heating sand were placed everywhere on the walls.

They ensured that men and women attended to their duties, that the fire department provided bright lighting, and that supervisors made arrangements to conscript people at every location and to inspect every department and unit.

෨

Apson Sumali, queen of Chiang In, paramount consort, understood that the country was in an unusual position. "This time, the city could fall.

I must go and beg the king to make a proper decision." With this thought, she went to attend on the king at once.

On arrival, she prostrated with clasped hands, and addressed the king with her head drooping and tears flowing. "Sire, by your grace,

I'm speaking honestly, not out of jealousy. I intend to depend on you until death. But the cause of our fate, the reason the enemy invests our city, is Soithong.

Why keep her here? It will make the people suffer and will bother the dust beneath the royal foot. Please think straight.

There are countless fair and cuddlesome consorts more beautiful than Soithong. You shouldn't fall into a dispute with the Thai country. If you send Soithong to their army commander,

the Thai will take their army home because that's what they came for—to

---

13. Thotsakan, the villain of the *Ramakian*, equivalent to Ravana in the Indian version. The Thai kings have identified strongly with Ram of the *Ramakian*, especially in the Bangkok era, so it is not surprising to find Bangkok court authors have the enemy King of Chiang Mai identify himself with Ram's rival, Thotsakan. However, this is again a Bangkok imposition. The *Ramakian* figures little in Lanna art and culture.

get her back. The palace and city of Chiang Mai will escape destruction, and you'll be like a god relieving your people's hardship.

Pry out this thorn and be happy. That would be the best ending. Please Sire, by your grace, spare the people of the realm this suffering."

King Chiang In uttered a great sigh. Concern for his queen softened his heart, but in a flash his anger returned.

"My dear, I've never let anyone insult me. The King of Vientiane deliberately crossed me. On top of that, the loathsome Ayutthayans came to invest the city.

If they'd asked for the princess properly, I'd have given her. But they showed no respect and used force first—stealing horses, seizing elephants, slaughtering people. News has spread to the whole three worlds.

They wrote a message with an insulting challenge. Even a monk in a wat wouldn't tolerate this. That's why we got involved in the battle and many Lao died.

It's past the time for sending them the princess now. I won't send her. I'd rather fight to the death. When karma wills it, anyone born a man must die."

Queen Apson Sumali was shocked that her husband was so stubborn, angry, and isolated but it was not fitting to protest too much.

She made obeisance, took leave of him, rushed away, and lay down on her bed in a state of turmoil and distress.

She hugged her daughter, Soifa, and said through sobs, "Your mother went to address the king but he's too stubborn and wouldn't listen.

All this has come about because of karma. It will make the whole Lao world collapse. For both men and women there'll be only tears and suffering as slaves of the Thai.

I'm so worried that you'll be their war prisoner, Mother's jewel. Fate led the king astray, made him see bad as good."

She beat her breast over and over, distressed enough to die. She and little Princess Soifa fainted with sadness.

Palace ladies brought fragrant water to revive them. Slowly they recovered and got up, but still beat their breasts in lamentation until they were red with bruising.

Now to tell of Khun Phaen, great romancer, whose reputation for mastery made all quail and submit. As the sun rose at dawn, he drew up the army under his command.

"Harness the horses and elephants. We'll march straight through the forest and invest the outskirts of Chiang Mai today."

The volunteers took the orders and went to harness horses and elephants. They rushed around finding their weapons and formed a column to march.

Phra Thainam was assigned to lead the army, riding Phlai Prakai Phruek,[14] followed by Phya Kueng Kamkong on Phlai Phlik Phasutha[15] in the middle of the column,

with Khun Phaen on Phlai Si Khotchadet and Phlai Ngam on Phlai Ket[16] at the rear. The volunteers were in high spirits and they marched quickly.

Their shouts echoed round the forest. In half a day they reached Chiang Mai and halted. Officers and men gathered together in a packed crowd.

They collected giant reed and sugar reed to stack on all sides, and scattered enchanted rice to transform the reeds into a camp with several layers at the front as protection against the city's cannon.

Outside the city walls, where people could see the Thai army had come to lay siege, there was a fearful hubbub. Throughout the city, the Lao applied themselves to their duties in fear for their lives.

They placed stoves on top of the walls to heat molten lead and burning sand. They set bonfires throughout the city to bathe the whole place in red light.

King Chiang In, eminence of the city, came out to command officers to keep close watch and make sure nobody entered and mingled with the people.

"Bring pikes, swords, guns, and other weapons. Prepare many strategic devices. Even cats, mice, dogs, and birds that enter the city are to be caught and killed."

He ordered four commanders to divide up inspection of the troops. The whole city was jammed with people and in uproar. Every road and path was lit with fires.

Khun Phaen, great romancer, whose famous powers shook the whole world, along with his son Phlai Ngam, found a favorable time by the manual at the third watch.

The sky was white with bright shining stars, and the waning moon had has-

---

14. พลายประกายพรึก, "Venus." This style of mentioning elephants by name appears in the accounts of the Naresuan era in the versions of the Ayutthaya royal chronicles probably written (or, at least, revised in this form) in the first Bangkok reign (see, for example, RCA, 108, 110, 117, 126–29, 151, 153, 176–77, 182).

15. พลายพลิกพสุธา, "earth overturner."

16. เกตุ, the ninth planet (see p. 132, note 10).

tened down, plunging the world into sleep. Father and son dressed and decked themselves out in black *pha-muang* lowercloths,

and tied a girdle round the waist, also in black. At the neck, they strung beads and golden *takrut*. They wore shirts with yantra of Lord Narai, spirit-skull belts,

and bandeaus bearing Buddha amulets, making them look fierce and strong. They applied powder instilled with yantra, and daubed their foreheads with enchanted sandal paste.

Both looked as robust and imposing as the Lord of the Lions, famous in battle. When ready, they made obeisance, picked up their war swords, and turned their faces according to the time of the sun.[17]

They went into the forest, entered a trance, and blew formulas and commands all around. They looked up for a cloud omen, and saw in the sky the figure of a powerful Narai

with four arms holding his weapons—diamond mace, discus, conch, and bow.[18] At the time to leave, they both sensed the breath flowing in their right nostril, and so set off on the right foot.

Spirits and sprites, including Goldchild, surrounded them as they walked along a road. They chanted a formula to stun others and conceal themselves.[19] Nobody greeted them with a single word.

As they passed the embankment, moat, and camp gate, many Lao officers and men hit by the mantra, were tumbled over one another in drowsy sleep. Khun Phaen led the way up to the walls.

They stood watching people bustling around the gate. Bonfires lit the place brightly. Artillerymen stood wearing red hats. Gongs chimed all around.

Khun Phaen and his son chanted special formulas to give orders to their spirits, then mounted the neck of the talented Goldchild who displayed his powers

by leaping over the city wall in a flash. Khun Phaen blew another Subduer mantra to put people to sleep all around the city.

They went to the palace of the ruler of Chiang Mai. Khun Phaen sent a Lao spirit in first to turn the locks and slide the bolts. Father and son entered the inner palace.

---

17. ตามยามอาทิตย์, *tam yam athit.* A day is divided into time periods, *yam*, of one and a half hours, each dominated by a certain heavenly body. Manuals prescribe auspicious and inauspicious directions, and other matters, for each period. They are in a period dominated by the sun, and are choosing the appropriate direction to set off.

18. See p. 621, note 15. This is a very good omen.

19. A simple version of such a formula is: อะวาคะภะโสปิอิติ, *a-wa-kha-pha-so-bi-i-ti* (*Phra khamphi khatha 108*, 84).

Lao women from royalty to sentinelles, including the queens, consorts, and servants, could not see Khun Phaen. Walking back and forth, shoulder to shoulder,

Khun Phaen and Phlai Ngam went to visit every nook and cranny, right and left, to see what palace people were like. They went up to the residence of the consort mothers.[20]

Some were gossiping about the enemy, some beating their breasts and sobbing, some clutching cowries and praying over and over to the spirits, and some sewing waist pouches to stuff with their gold and jewelry.

Everywhere there was panic, in every room more tears than sense. The pair crept around spying, feeling compassion for their pitiful misery.

Yet playful ones were still pairing off without a care, beautifying themselves for amusement, seeking out an old lover to fondle her cheeks and nuzzle her breasts,[21]

flirting with someone in the manner of a male lover with a clever line in chat, throwing fits of jealousy and spite, quarreling cattily with lots of noise,

or lying scratching their heads thinking, "If the city falls, we'll flee and probably die." One said, "Don't be upset, we still have property so we won't be poor for long."

Another asked, "If we finish up in the southern city, explain how to get on well." An outlandish lady told her the way. "Make an effort to treat everyone as they like."

A dumb one asked, "How to treat them? If a man keeps scolding and scolding, should we scold and scold back? I'm confused." "Who told you to argue with your mouth? Be risqué. Argue with your body!

You can't teach this sort of thing because every couple, every situation is different. If you treat him to his liking, before long he'll be stooping over to put himself at your service.

Now. People like us should not take a commoner as husband. It'd be like treading in chicken dung without knowing it. Meet a noble and behave suitably. Snuggle close, caress, and cuddle to his heart's content.

Fan him, massage him, comb his hair—do it well, and he'll fall for you in a trice. It's a better way to burrow into his heart than love potions. He'll chuck his ladyship away.

---

20. จอมมารดา, *jom manda*, a royal consort who has given birth to a child.

21. Love among ladies of the inner palace seems to have been common. The Ayutthaya Palatine Law had a clause specifying punishment: "Consorts or inner ladies who make love like man and woman shall be punished with fifty strokes of the lash, paraded around the palace for public shaming, then either put to work on frame embroidery or given to royal relatives" (KTS, 1:120–21).

The more doddery and broken-toothed, the more they love a young girl. They'll tumble for a Lao lover, no fear. Make the effort to attend to them, and use all your tricks. The older and uglier they are, the more they'll love you.

Just beware of the young lads. They're likely to enjoy a taste and then abandon you. If you can't help yourself, just don't go too far. If you get involved and your stomach swells up, your price will drop."

Khun Phaen, great conjuror, famous throughout the world, and his son looked up at the stars just at the time the Pleiades entered Taurus.[22]

The sky was clear and the moon had set. They could see the stars shining brightly and the Milky Way.[23] According to the manual, it was an auspicious time.

When they scattered enchanted rice, court ladies tumbled down with heads nodding. Some sitting with eyes open felt their heads spinning and collapsed, one after another.

One lady busily washing herself was hit by the mantra and fell headlong over the bowl. Another in the middle of trimming her hairline and applying oil dropped off holding a cotton bud.

Those embroidering lozenge patterns slipped into drowsy sleep with the silk in their hands. Those spinning cotton dropped the spindle and hugged the wheel. Those sitting guard by the lights lost consciousness.

Khun Phaen commanded Goldchild and the other spirits to go to the palace hall and put the Lao king, and his queen, daughter, and attendants to sleep.

The spirits saluted to acknowledge the order. In an eye blink, they went up to the royal residence and sat on everyone to put them to sleep.

Because the guardian spirits of the royal umbrella had been chased into the forest by the Thai spirits, Goldchild could enter and sit on the king to immobilize him.

Under the influence of the mantra and the spirits, the King of Chiang Mai blacked out as if his mind had been ripped out of his body. He lay asleep and motionless.

Khun Phaen and his powerful son chanted and blew a mantra in unison, then strode like tigers into a gilded chamber

crammed with palace maidens hit by the mantra and collapsed on top of

---

22. ดาวธง, *dao thong*, flag star, the Pleiades; ดาวรถ, *dao rot*, the chariot, Taurus, a constellation of five stars known in Thai astrology as *rohini* and sometimes as *achanai*, the horse (KW, 407–8; Prachak, *Prapheni*, 141–42).

23. คลองช้าง, *khlong chang*, the elephant canal, a good omen.

one another. All had alluring complexions and were fittingly beautiful to be royal consorts.

They slept on fine mattresses, pillows, and mats neatly arranged, covered by quilts in votive-deity pattern, under silk mosquito nets, fragrant and splendid. These were the attendants for every duty.

Father and son went into the second chamber which was brightly lit by torches. Inner ladies of superlative beauty lay sleeping inside

under scented silk coverlets, some revealing naked white breasts. Their cheeks looked as bright and smooth as the skin of a *maprang*. All were clearly more senior young ladies.[24]

They lay fast asleep on their pillows, looking softly pretty on velvet spreads. Their little mosquito nets had openings fringed with tassels. Everything around was fine silk in many colors.

Father and son went into the third chamber, resplendent with torches and lamps. They strode boldly ahead and saw petite palace ladies fast asleep.

jampa *flower*

All were just of age with superb figures in bloom and fair, sleek complexions like celestial maidens.[25] They wore uppercloths of colored silk, bracelets on their wrists, supple chains around their waists,

and earrings hanging from both ears. They were slightly built with thin waists and perfect breasts, firm like swelling lotus buds. A *jampa* flower tucked between them would not slip through.

Phlai Ngam walked behind, glancing around, mortified that these were the king's spare seats.[26] He slipped his hand among their budding breasts, as firm as tightly packed young petals.

Seeing his son fondling, Khun Phaen clenched his fist and thumped his son's back. "This is royal property! Don't touch! If you get carried away, we'll fail.

We shouldn't do this—you see, we're phrai. These are ladies who are forbidden to others. What's more, to be expert in warfare, you shouldn't dally with women."

Phlai Ngam replied, "I just came for a peek and a little feel while they're asleep. They're pretty. I'm not forgetting myself and getting carried away."

"Hey, we only have to sacrifice one night—just help one another to achieve success. When the war's over, whatever ladies you want, except for the princess, you're welcome to them."

---

24. สาวใหญ่, *sao yai*, probably meaning they were around twenty years old.

25. อัปสร, *apson*, Sanskrit *apsara*, heavenly maidens best known from portrayal on Angkor monuments.

26. A contemporary expression for women other than the major wife.

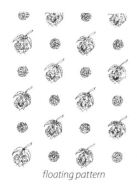

floating pattern

Father and son admired them, then went along to a gilded bedchamber where the king slept. They blew a Loosener to unlock and unbolt the door, and went up to the half-moon platform on the living level.

They entered under a golden spire and admired the palace hall, a bedchamber befitting a king's status. Two golden curtains were fastened with drawstrings. The walls were carved in a floating pattern,[27]

and the ceiling painted in golden stripes, with a glittering crystal chandelier suspended by a chain. Hanging lamps added to the dazzling brilliance of the light.

In front of the royal bed were many young palace ladies, the batch on forward duty. They were petite with stunning slight figures and a soft, adorable beauty.

Eyes, brows, cheeks, and hair were magnificent. Breasts nestled tightly together in beautiful pairs. Their mattresses, pillows, carpets, and bedspreads were all covered in colored silk with trimming.

They had gold bangles on their upper arms, rings on little fingers, soft chains wound round their tender ten fingers, and dangling ruby earrings. Their faces were as delicate as nutmeg.

Beside the bed was a group of musicians, all beautiful, graceful, and fair—as alike as dolls in the same costume.

The *ranat* player slept tumbled over the gong player, the singer on the lutist, the fiddler on the claves player, and the drummer on top—all lost to this world.

musicians asleep

---

27. ลายลอย, *lai loi*, a pattern with individual motifs, often flowers, painted or carved on a plain background so that they seem to float free of the surface. Often used on ceilings.

Father and son walked up to a room on the left. They pushed aside the magnificent golden curtains, entered the bedchamber,

and saw two ladies asleep. Caught by the lamplight, their skin glowed soft, luminous, and as fair as new cotton.

They examined the elder one. She had the supreme elegance of nobility, and her complexion was still clear and fine, but her bosom was no longer full.

They saw she was the mother, and the other young beauty was the royal daughter, just of age with a body as radiant as a shimmering star, and breasts like heavenly blooms,

red lotuses just peeping above the water, so inviting to pluck. Phlai Ngam stared unblinking. His father whispered to him to restrain himself.

She lay still on the pillow like a piece of crystal. Her radiant face had no wrinkle or blemish. Her elegant eyebrows curved softly and sweetly. Her eyes were strikingly pretty, even in sleep.

Her nose was like a royal goad, lips freshly gleaming as if painted with sappan, cheeks like the skin of *maprang*, neck and chin nicely rounded.

She was strikingly beautiful, neither too plump not too slender, lovely from head to toe. Her hair was drawn into an attractive chignon held by a gold cloisonné[28] hairpin.

She wore earrings sparkling with diamonds, a breast chain studded with jewels of many colors, gold bracelets in the shape of female nagas, and rings set with glittering colored gems.

Her lowercloth was embroidered in a *kanok* pattern, and her silk uppercloth was striped in brilliant gold. The queen wore a lowercloth with a flowing *kanok* pattern, and an uppercloth of yellow silk with a pattern of golden jasmine.

flowing kanok

"The queen has a daughter just of age. She looks around sixteen, if I'm not mistaken. She's slight, exquisite, and her skin is perfectly fine, just right to be cradled and caressed as a royal consort."

Phlai[29] Ngam's heart was thumping with desire to couple with her. He approached, torn by indecision, wanting a little touch, yet scared of his father.

---

28. ราชาวดี, *rachawadi*, from Persian *lazuverdi*, name for a chemical used to create enamelware of a light blue color. At Ayutthaya, cloisonné articles were among those reserved for families of the senior ministers—Kalahom, Mahatthai, four pillars. In late Ayutthaya, these sumptuary restrictions were widely breached, and King Rama I tried to re-impose them (KW, 686; KTS, 4:285–88).

29. The next two sections, down to "dragged him away," are taken from WK, 25:1004–6, absent from PD.

He trickily pretended to see something, and nudged his father to look at a screen beside the wall. When his father turned away as hoped, he made a grab but knocked over some worship offerings with a crash.

Khun Phaen turned and said, "Phlai Ngam, don't create trouble, damn you. She's a royal princess. Don't make a racket. A sword will jump up and take your neck."

Phlai Ngam mumbled an excuse, "She's just like Simala, Father." He stepped away and stood waiting. When his father walked off, he leapt back,

and came beside the bed where the princess was sleeping. Thinking of his father's warning not to bother her, he loosed a huge sigh. "She's the child of a king.

If her father loses his capital, she'll probably become a consort at Ayutthaya. Or perhaps this is Princess Soithong.

I volunteered to be a soldier. It's not fitting to couple." But he stayed there looking, with his mind in turmoil, the two towers thrusting upwards inviting his caress.

He stood sighing and groaning, itching to put out his hand. "Oh, lightning strike! If I didn't think of my king and his support, I wouldn't pass this up. Though Father scolds, I'm not taking any notice."

Khun Phaen looked over, "Ha, Phlai Ngam. You've already made a racket, you trickster. Though you stole a meal at Phichit, I can see you're not heeding my warning."

With this complaint, he walked over to look at his son. Phlai Ngam was so mesmerized, he did not notice his father was standing right beside him, watching,

as he laid his hand down on the princess. Khun Phaen rapped him on the head. "Mm! Phlai Ngam, you're not frightened. I should deal with you right now, you villain."

Phlai Ngam said, "I was about to go off for a pee. Why did you turn up here like a hungry ghost hit by a mantra? I hadn't been for the pee when you came."

"You're good at quick thinking. This is like your peeing at Phichit." Khun Phaen grabbed his son's hand and dragged him away.

They walked towards the master bed and wrenched the curtain aside. Everything was resplendent in gold. Beside the bed lay several swords.

Even in sleep, King Chiang In looked imposing. He was fair and had a full, rounded figure befitting the head of the city's royal dynasty.

His coverlet was of golden material in a splendid pattern of Garuda clutch-

offertory-rice pattern

ing a naga. His sleeping garments, in an offertory-rice[30] pattern on a red background, looked appropriately fine for the status of a king.

Phlai Ngam walked in on his left, and Khun Phaen on his right. They picked up the swords placed there so he would have no weapons to attack them.

As they stood beside him on left and right like bold Lords of the Lions, Khun Phaen blew a mantra to drive away Goldchild who crawled down and left the monarch.

Khun Phaen stepped up on the golden bed and bellowed a Power of Lord Garuda mantra at the top of his voice. The monarch started awake, struck fearful by the formula.

He opened his eyes, saw the Thai, and felt a shiver of deep fear. In the manner of a king, he resolved to fight and grasped around for his weapons, but found none.

He felt as if someone had come to lop off his head with a diamond trident. His mind seemed on the point of breaking apart. "My life has fallen into the hands of demons. They'll kill me before long for sure."

He was about to open his mouth and plead for his life but felt ashamed and changed his mind. He raised himself and sat, mute and unmoving, resigned to a probable death.

Khun Phaen, great romancer, seeing that King Chiang In was in despair yet maintained his royal manner and sat still and silent, bellowed out loud,

"Ha! Heigh! King and foe! You're an evil fellow, guilty of envy. His Majesty the King of Ayutthaya has not himself come to crush your city.

The King of Si Sattana was resolved to present his daughter to the Thai city but you, you blackguard, acted villainously, seized her, and ruined friendly relations.

You also captured the Thai who went to escort her, and had them imprisoned, flogged, and grievously mistreated. Then you sent a provocative missive with a challenge to bring up an army for an elephant duel.

You don't act humbly like a vassal state but are arrogant and devious in every way. Hence our king has sent us—just middle-ranking soldiers—to put an end to your life.

---

30. พุ่มเข้าบิณฑ์, *phum khao bin*, offertory rice, popped rice for offerings, a motif based on offertory rice in a folded leaf or heaped in an almsbowl in a shape resembling a lotus bud (SWC, 10:4559–61).

Don't sit there mute and still with your face bowed. Do you agree to die or will you have a change of heart? Who will this Lao country belong to? Whatever you have to say, then say it without delay."

The ruler of Chiang Mai felt his chest was being destroyed by a raging fire. Retaliation was unthinkable because the Thai soldiers were right upon him.

He wanted to fight but had no weapon. Any attempt at flight would be in vain. He restrained himself, feeling powerless, exasperated, and pitiable.

In fear of death, he decided to relax his royal manner and stifle his pride. After thinking, he said, "Now, you two gallant soldiers, I did make mistakes in my thinking.

If you have the mercy to spare my life, I'll be a servant of the crystal lord. I haven't had a whiff of Soithong. I haven't harmed her or coupled with her.

I agree to submit and offer myself to the king, along with my precious daughter and beloved wife, the queen. I also offer my capital and its people under the dust of the royal foot."

After hearing King Chiang In, Khun Phaen and Phlai Ngam could see he was overcome by fear of death and had agreed to submit because of fright.

Khun Phaen responded, "Are your words wholly honest and truthful, or are you accepting defeat because you're in a tight spot, but will later go astray, perhaps?"

The ruler of Chiang Mai replied, "I won't go back on my word as given. Everything is true. The word of a king is as solid as a tusker.

If in the future I crookedly retract like a turtle's head, may I lose my life and be consigned to suffer in the great Lokanta hell from the day of my death for a whole era.

If my courtiers, wife, or daughter press me to break my word, I won't listen but will uphold my promise until death. I beg you two officers to trust me."

King Chiang In's pledge overcame Khun Phaen's doubts. The two relaxed their hostility immediately, and went to sit close beside him for a talk.

"If you're straight and keep your oath, leave the matter of your offense to me. I'll plead your case with the king so you won't risk losing your life."

tusker

They gave him back his swords. "Please cheer up and don't be upset. We'll take our leave of Your Majesty and return to where the Thai army is staying."

King Chiang In saluted to accept the swords. His gloomy red face brightened up. "If you two have mercy as you say, I'll escape death because of you.

Let me entrust my life to you. Please plead with the king to pardon my fault so whether I live or die will be due to your grace."

Khun Phaen, great warrior, and Phlai Ngam felt compassion for the king, and so Khun Phaen replied, "Have no doubt or suspicion.

Everything we've told you is true. If you keep your word as you've said, you should be in no danger."

Father and son excused themselves, got up, took their leave, and walked down from the palace, glancing around. Khun Phaen whispered orders to their spirits, sprites, and Goldchild.

"Stay close to here and spy on the palace. Watch over the ruler of Chiang Mai in his room. Follow his tracks and keep an eye out. Let me know how he's thinking.

When his wife and daughter come to plead with him, if he holds firm, just stay here quietly. If he listens to his wife, breaks his word, and becomes an enemy, hurry to tell me."

He lifted the Subduer mantra from the people. Khun Phaen and Phlai Ngam became invisible, exited the gate through a keyhole, and returned to the Thai army.

Once released[31] from the mantra, Lao officials fled, trembling, shouting and screaming, pouring out through the gates,

crashing into one another in confusion, and falling flat on face and back. The Thai soldiers did not let them escape but grabbed some by the hair and dragged them off, still bleary and not fully conscious.

Some saw the Thai soldiers and tried acting dead but were still grabbed by the hair and elbowed with a lot of loud shouting. Phra Thainam's people joined in, crowding around to punch and beat.

Anyone who resisted or ran away was hit and elbowed in the back until they could not cry out. The soldiers besieging the city immediately ran to gather up goods and round up people.

---

31. The next two sections, down to "Get ready at once" on p. 669, are taken from WK, 26:1012–13, absent from PD.

One soldier caught a Lao, pulled his hair, and commanded, "Tell me where your silver and gold is kept or I'll set fire to your arse!" The Lao said, "Hold off! I can't stand heat. Take the money."

Muen At Narai got hold of an old lady and stuck her up on a frame[32] with legs splayed. She cried, "You can dig the money out of those jars of fermented fish." He whooped and hollered in joy.

Captives were made to sit in groups, "Now, don't be mean and try to hide your money and goods." The soldiers felt around in the twists of their lower-cloths, or went up into their houses and searched everywhere.

Ai-Phut dragged off a Lao girl and mounted her. "If you'd like to sleep, I'll sing you a lullaby. It's ages since I enjoyed a roll. I won't abandon you to be alone."

The Lao girl cried out, "I won't consent. This lullaby singer is an evil spirit with a head as high as the roof." Ai-Thong called out, "Oh damn! You're giving him such a hard time the rain's dried up."

Eventually people submitted and peace reigned. Every single Thai got some money. Some also carted off cloth,

or hauled away buffaloes and oxen by their harnesses. "I'm taking them as a gift for the mother of my little girl." Phra Thainam gave orders for building lodgings, and then sat to discuss with his phrai.

"Just now Khun Phaen and Phlai Ngam went into the palace. We haven't yet had any news. Be on alert until we hear.

If there's trouble in the palace, we'll have to surround it, capture people, and kill them to prevent the enemy besting us. Get ready at once."

Khun Phaen and Phlai Ngam walked smiling into the camp and sat down. Phra Thainam, Kamkong, the volunteers, and all the soldiers saluted their commander and asked about the fight.

Khun Phaen related how he went with Phlai Ngam, laid a Subduer mantra, crept up to the king, woke him, and could have taken his life.

"He was shocked senseless, and out of fear of death he agreed to offer Soi-thong and his daughter, along with all the officials and subjects of the Lao country, including the phrai, royalty, his wife, and the palace women.

He humbled himself as a servant and asked to be a vassal of the Ayutthaya capital. His only request was that he be spared death. He swore an oath that his word was true."

---

32. ขาย่าง, now usually ขาหยั่ง, *kha yang*, probably a tripod made of three sticks, used in the past to tie up offenders sentenced to public shaming. Nowadays the word is usually applied to an easel.

Hearing Khun Phaen's account, all the officers and men, Lao and Thai, felt they were flying. The war with Chiang In was over, and their hardship too. They would sing and dance with glee all the way home.

Officers and men talked and laughed until almost daybreak while Khun Phaen and Phlai Ngam retired to sleep.

꼭

At dawn the sun rose and shone in all ten directions. King Chiang In, eminence of the city, went to the residence of the queen.

He settled himself on a jeweled seat and told her, "While I was asleep last night, enemies came right up to me.

I was startled and my mind was racing. I grasped for my weapons but they'd disappeared. I was ashamed to run away so I offered the Lao city to the Thai king,

along with Princess Soithong, the main issue. I also presented Soifa, all the consorts and palace ladies, and the city people under the royal foot.

I admitted fault, humbled myself, offered tribute of gold, and begged only for my life. I've given my oath on everything.

I'm grateful to the enemy soldier who came. When I gave my promise, he went back to his main army. My love, don't be disheartened. This is the fruit of karma made in the past."

Listening to her husband, Queen Apson felt the Lord of Darkness was destroying her. She beat her breast in lamentation.

"My lord and master, I told you already but you wouldn't listen. I knew for sure there would be danger from the moment the Thai brought an army to our city.

They put everyone to sleep at the jail, released prisoners, stole horses and elephants, and killed people with only thirty-five of them! If they weren't able, they wouldn't have attacked so boldly.

Our five commanders who went to do battle were defeated, and the corpses were piled up like logs. Even our spirit army fled away and hid. But you were too stubborn.

If you'd just compromised and handed Soithong over in reconciliation, their army would have returned to the Thai city and Chiang Mai would have survived to flourish.

But how can we avoid disaster now? Though we may not die, we'll become vagabonds. Our people, both noble and commoner, will be battered about and suffer terrible hardship.

It'll be like the old episode about Sida. She was born to have Lanka devastated. The ten-faced one was so besotted with her that his own family members were slashed to death and the bodies mounted up in piles.

Queen Montho made the ten-faced lord so angry by challenging him that he let the people of the city die miserably.[33] Similarly here, you were so besotted by Soithong that you've led your family to their deaths.

Soithong is like Sida. She was born to devastate the city of Chiang Mai. When I opposed you, I was accused of jealousy, and at my wits' end." She sadly sobbed herself senseless.

Queen Apson's words made the King of Chiang Mai's heart burn as if on fire. He replied, "Why do you keep going on like this?

I wasn't besotted by Soithong. I was angry at Vientiane. That was the main issue. They showed no respect and gave her to the Thai to spite me, so I had her seized and brought here.

If I'd really fallen for her, how come I haven't made love to her? It's half a year now and I haven't gone to her. What a pity you keep going on at me.

I knew Ayutthaya would send an army, and I aimed to defeat them. It's like a gambling game. You play to see who's good, who'll win.

Against my hopes, I lost to them. And now you keep sticking a knife in to hurt me. But the error's been made and all this is too late. Why be sad when it doesn't achieve anything?

Even if you cry tears of blood, the mistake won't go away. We've come to this trouble in the course of fate. When you arrive at the time to die, you must die."

The king went out to the front with all the nobles, and related from start to end how the city had been offered to the Thai.

"Tell the officers and men to dismantle the camps, open the Chiang Mai city gates, drag the guns back to store, and disperse people from the palace.

Level the courtyard and build twenty good lodges and a rectangular central hall with walls. Make a bamboo fence around.

Prepare a playing field for elephants and horses. Decorate splendidly both

---

33. In the final part of the *Ramakian*, Thotsakan, the ten-faced lord, abducts Sida to Lanka where he suffers a fearful assault by Ram, his brother Lak, Hanuman, and his monkey army. Thotsakan's brother Kumphakan, son Inthorachit, and many others are killed. Thotsakan's queen, Montho, revives some of them with her magical mother's milk but is then tricked by Hanuman, who also steals Thotsakan's heart and thereby undermines his invulnerability. As matters are now hopeless, Montho pleads with Thotsakan to surrender Sida so that Thotsakan's family and the giants in Lanka might survive, but Thotsakan stubbornly refuses: "If I were to do this, my name would be scorned in all the three worlds." (See the episode "Suek Hanuman" in Premseri, *Ramakian*, 477–78).

outside and in, with white cloth for the ceiling, and curtains hanging. Then invite the two commanders and their men to come."

Phraya Jantharangsi took the command and awkwardly crawled out backwards. He gave orders to many officers to divide up the work.

They fetched the guns, decommissioned them, and put them in store. They opened the city gates, sent away people who came from outside the city, and built a row of lodges inside.

The ground was cleared and leveled, and twenty rectangular buildings constructed, enclosed by a high fence, with large and small stables for the elephants and horses.

Orders were given to officials to invite the two commanders and their army, including both officers and men, both Thai and Vientiane Lao, to stay at the lodges inside the city.

Old Thao Nu[34] and other nobles and officials arranged palanquins, and hurried along to the Thai army. They made obeisance to the two commanders,

saying, "His Majesty King Chiang In has sent us to invite you and all the Lao and Thai soldiers to stay in comfort in the city."

Khun Phaen, great romancer, whose powers were as strong as a lion, watched the officials crawl up, pay respect, and invite them to stay in the lodges.

He summoned Phlai Ngam, Phra Thainam, Kueng Kamkong, and all the volunteer troops. Khun Phaen and the two other officers sat in palanquins.

Kamkong rode his horse at the rear. The mass of troops reached the lodges and went to stay inside, billeted according to rank. They came out to sit and lie around, overflowing the area. Royal kitchens prepared a feast to feed the Thai army.

Lao ladies

Lao[35] nobles ordered, "Hey, bring in lots of food." Four Lao ladies of good appearance brought in water bowls and golden salvers.

---

34. ท้าวหนู, title of one of the leading officials in the traditional form of government of a *mueang* in the Lao world.

35. From here to the end of the chapter is taken from WK, 26:1018–20, absent from PD. The phrase "at every meal" has been deleted from the immediately preceding stanza to accommodate this insertion.

The King of Chiang Mai had food provided for Khun Phaen and his son to eat at a head table. Phra Thainam was seated further down.

Phlai Ngam sat beside his father while Lao brought trays of food for them. The volunteers got merrily drunk and chatted away, wreathed in smiles.

Phra Thainam ate at a big table, sitting cross-legged and speaking loudly with his head thrown back. Khun Phaen chatted and drank liquor. Phlai Ngam smiled sweetly the whole time.

All the soldiers drank liquor, and those that got drunk laughed and chattered away. Some enchanted liquor to give invulnerability and then bit bowls to display their lore. Others challenged their friends to slash and stab them.

Some gnashed their teeth and roared. Some showed off their mantra lore, leaping up and striking poses with red eyes, "I'll try out my strength riding a Lao girl!"

A Lao woman cried out, "I'm done for!"[36] and ran off white-eyed. Ta-Rak drew his sword and flashed it around. The Lao cried pitifully with staring eyes.

Some soldiers stabbed themselves for the Lao to see they were invulnerable to piercing. Chisel, drill, axe, and hoe were brought but their bodies were no more hurt than by being pinched with fingernails.

The Lao were shocked. Khun Phaen reprimanded his men. "Don't make so much noise. You're showing off so people will talk. Is that a good thing to do?"

Hearing Khun Phaen's words, the soldiers became embarrassed and trembled in fear. Those who had been drinking lost their drunkenness. Silence fell and nobody spoke.

The three officers sat comfortably on a low bench, and Lao served them attentively from left and right. Ladies were summoned to sing, dance, and let the guests gaze on their fair and lovely faces.

Ta-Rak nodded to his friends to watch. He pointed to a girl with an indigo uppercloth, breasts like sidebags, chubby cheeks, earrings, and a good singing voice. "If the boss didn't forbid it, I'd put it in her for several rounds."

Forgetting his body was old, Ta-Lo ran across and tripped over a water bowl, drenching his clothes like an infant. Ta-Plok got up and danced with a Lao girl,

tripping back and forth, then hugging her round the neck. His friends roared with laughter. They struck poses from the mask play and sang boat songs. With no room left for them to dance, the Lao girls sat down.

---

36. ข้อยตายเด, *khoi tai de*, in Lao.

31: KHUN PHAEN AND PHLAI NGAM TAKE
THE ARMY HOME

Khun Phaen, great warrior, sat discussing with Phra Thainam and Phlai Ngam that they should inform the capital, now that they had won a victory and taken the city.

"Give the king the news that we took Chiang Mai and captured its ruler, Chiang In, so the king may let us know his wishes."

Together they wrote a missive, affixed a seal of Hanuman the Expert Warrior,[1] attached a copy of a report on the affair, wrapped it three times, placed it in a bamboo cylinder,

closed the mouth with wax, and stamped it with a seal.[2] The cylinder was sent to Nai Jan Samphantueng[3] with the orders,

"Hasten down to Ayutthaya within fifteen days and deliver this missive without fail. Once it is delivered, wait to hear the reply."

Hanuman seal

Nai Jan Samphantueng made his farewell and plunged off. He dressed himself quickly, mounted a horse, slung a sidebag over his shoulder, and departed.

---

1. ตราหนุมานชาญสนาม, *tra hanuman chan sanam*, possibly a variant of ตราหนุมานแผลงฤทธิ์, *tra hanuman phlaeng-rit*, "Hanuman displaying his powers," an old military seal depicting Hanuman as a warrior, formerly the official seal of Phraya Decho, affixed to the appointments of military chiefs in provincial cities (KTS, 1:173). Since 1911, it has been the official emblem of Thailand's Second Army.

2. From here until "carrying a sidebag" on p. 675 is taken from WK, 26:1021–22. In PD, the messengers travel by land: Nai Pan Khwan Fa and Nai Khong Man were ordered to select good horses and leave on the following day / to cut straight down to Rahaeng, pass Kamphaeng, and make for Ayutthaya. "When you're done, return without delay. Be back here by the end of the month at the latest." / The two officers saluted and took the cylinder. They came out and promptly packed clothes, put dried rice in waist pouches, and went to choose fleet, well-paced horses to harness up. / They mounted Phan Phen Phajon and Dan Thorani, and gave the horses their heads. Cutting straight through the forest, they reached Ayutthaya in ten and a half days.

3. Nai Jan is one of the thirty-five volunteers. He was jailed for his part in the killing of Khun Siwichai, Khun Chang's father (see ch. 2), and led the vanguard on the march north from Phichit (see ch. 28).

Digging in his heels, he galloped furiously, speeding along at a powerful rate. Lao bowed and saluted him along the way.

He hastened into the deep forest, eating up the track with long strides. He passed through Thoen,

and in seven days arrived at Kamphaeng. He informed the local officials, who quickly made arrangements to receive him, and conscripted phrai to find a boat

while Nai Jan hit on liquor to the full, shouting "We fixed those northerners!" They seized a boat belonging to a Mon salt seller, I-Moei-Duea, who fell into the water with a splash.

Her cloth slipped off completely as she thrust her head above the surface. "Oh, my cunt! Lord fuck me! Oh mother![4] Damn you!" She doubled over with her bottom in the air, stark naked, shrieking "I'm drowning!"[5]

She was given two baht for the liquor. Officials took the boat, saying, "Let's go." It was a good *khon* boat with a canopy. They loaded rice, and ordered the oarsmen to paddle off,

singing boat songs loudly in chorus as they went. The officers sat in state under the canopy, pouring liquor in turns. Rowing strongly, they reached the city in seven days

and moored at the regular landing. Nai Jan washed and dressed, picked up the missive cylinder, put a cloth round his belly, and went off, trailed by servants carrying a sidebag.

He went straight to the inner official sala and informed all the nobles there, "Khun Phaen, great master, ordered me to bring you this sealed missive

to report on the course of the war. Please convey the news to the king that victory has been won over the Lao city. What are the king's wishes?"

Happy in the knowledge that the capital of Chiang Mai had been taken, the minister ordered a duty officer, "Copy the report quickly and bring it to me."

He put on a sompak of red silk with entwined naga kings, and wrapped a prostration cloth round his waist. Shortly before

entwined naga kings

---

4. แหงน บิชิ ตอก ขมิ อุ้ย ย่าย, *ngaen bi chi tok khami ui yai*, in Mon.

5. ทะแล(ต) อา, *thalae(t) a*, from Mon, *a* means "to go" but the previous word is unidentified and the translation guessed from context.

the king was due to appear for the morning audience, he hurried to wait on him.

Now to tell of the almighty king, resident of the Mahaisawan.[6] Late in the morning, he came to the resplendent audience hall

and was seated on a jeweled throne under a brilliant white tiered umbrella. All the senior officials bowed and prostrated together.

A minister addressed the king. "My liege, Your Majesty, my life is under the royal foot.

The volunteers, Khun Phaen Saensongkhram and Nai Phlai Ngam, have sent a report to the royal grace." The clerk of the seal[7] unfurled the report to read.

"This is the report of Khun Phaen Saensongkhram and Phlai Ngam who volunteered to the foot of Your Majesty to lead troops to war.

We marched the army up to the outskirts of Chiang Mai where we halted and made camp, then disguised ourselves and entered the city.

At nightfall we infiltrated the main jail and rescued every one of the Thai. Together we killed people, stole horses and elephants, and returned to our military camp.

Next morning the Lao came with five armies, flooding the whole forest with men. I led the troops to attack and engage them at close quarters.

Their commanders fell dead on the battlefield, and their troops scattered away in flight. All five armies retreated to the city where they closed and bolted all the gates,

posted guards around the boundaries to keep a strict watch, lit bonfires so it was like daytime, and waited to defend against the Thai army.

That night, Phlai Ngam and I infiltrated the palace of the Chiang Mai king and captured him while asleep. He awoke in shock and turmoil.

Fearing death, he pleaded to offer Princess Soithong, the royal family including his daughter and chief wife, and his consorts to be placed under Your Majesty's royal foot.

As for himself, he consented to submit as Your Majesty's servant and present royal tribute until death. He pleaded only for his life. He gave his word on everything.

---

6. มไหศวรรย์, great power, supremacy, great wealth. The name was given to the hill in Phetburi on which King Mongkut built a palace complex, and to one of the buildings there.

7. เสมียนตรา, samian tra, title of a department head in Kalahom, Khun Thip Akson, sakdina 600 (KTS, 1:279).

I judged that his word was acceptable and credible and so withheld from killing him. I pondered and consulted with others, then sent Nai Jan to carry this report

to inform under Your Majesty's royal foot. If I have made errors, please have mercy on my head. I wait to hear the royal command, by Your Majesty's grace."

Knowing they had taken Chiang Mai, the almighty king felt as if the hundred-eyed Lord of Suthat[8] had come to invite him to his heavenly palace.

His face was radiant and his mood joyful now that his desire was fulfilled. "Oh, is that so? Hearing this news dispels all my anger and vengeful feelings.

I have been sick at heart for over a year, and today this sickness is lifted because of Khun Phaen. For earning my appreciation, both father and son will be rewarded equally.

Chaophraya Jakri, send a sealed order to recall the army. As for the old ruler of Chiang Mai, state that he'll be punished most severely for his evil thoughts.

The provisions of the legal code must be followed, and he should be executed. All his officials and courtiers who colluded with their master should be punished by death without exception.

As for his daughter, wife, servants, and slaves, they must be sequestered as part of his punishment. Seize all the elephants, horses, buffaloes, cattle, families, silver, gold, and goods that they have.

Also, the men and women of the city must be swept down as war prisoners according to normal practice. Because the king submits and pledges loyalty, I will kindly grant him his life,

but sweep him and his family down here for all countries, great and small, to see as an example so nobody will act in such an improper way in the future.

As for the beautiful Princess Soithong, who he dared abduct to Chiang Mai, and his own daughter Soifa, have them sent here to be ladies of the palace.

Since the royal princess of Si Sattana was the original cause of this war with Chiang Mai, so it will be our honor to show that we were victorious and recovered her.

Arrange for royal barges to collect the princesses in the proper way. Also send two canopy boats to fetch Khun Phaen.

Father and son have done very well. It will be fitting for them to travel by

---

8. สุทัศน์, one of the mountain ranges surrounding Mount Meru (RR, 277). This phrase means Indra.

canopy boat so word spreads to every bend in the river that they defeated Chiang Mai and took their country.

As for the ruler of Chiang Mai and his family, put them in boats behind. Because he wanted to cause trouble, let people enjoy the sight."

The accomplished minister of Mahatthai took the royal order and placed it on his head.[9] He left the audience hall of victory, went to the sala, and had a sealed missive drafted immediately.

When[10] it was done, Nai Jan was ordered to hurry away. "Have the ruler of Chiang Mai brought under restraint. Let the army return immediately along with the Lao families."

Nai Jan took the sealed missive and went down to a boat. He made the oarsmen holler, shout, and sing boat songs while he poured liquor. They crashed into the boat of an old man

who leapt up and danced about naked, calling out, "A spirit has broken my neck!" The soldiers sat bent over watching him, forgetting all about paddling the boat.

Arriving at Bang Lang, they seized some liquor. Chinaman Kao shouted out "Cunts!"[11] as they hauled some over into the long boat, hollering. In shock the Chinaman cried, "Oh shit,[12] help me!"

At a river junction[13] they passed some fish nets and Nai Jan said, "I'm going on royal business. Let me have some fish." They slowed the boat, went close, and his men grabbed some. The villagers protested, "Oh, look here![14] We're finished!"

Reaching Chawai,[15] they went into a sugar plantation and carried off many sticks of cane. The guards of the plot ran away in fear, but they caught some and made them wrestle and dance to a *thon* drum.

thon *drum*

---

9. He raises his hands in wai, then moves them to touch his crown, as if placing the king's words there.

10. This account of the return journey, up to "handed over the cylinder" on p. 679 is taken from WK, 26:1027–30; PD has: Once it was set down on paper and the seal affixed, it was placed in a cylinder and closed securely. The two officers took the missive, prostrated to take leave, and left the capital immediately. / In ten days, they galloped through the forest to Chiang Mai, where they dismounted, crawled in, and delivered the sealed cylinder to Khun Phaen.

11. จีไบ๋, *ji bai*, from Hokkien.

12. ไส่บวย, *sai buai*, see p. 43, note 69.

13. ปาก น้ำ โพสพ, *pak nam phosop*, "river mouth junction." Probably this is where the Bang Lang Canal meets the Lopburi River close to Wat Sopsawan (see map 3).

14. อา อุมิ ชิ, *a umi chi*, in Mon.

15. In Ang Thong, 3 kms north of Chaiyo (see map 2).

Be forgiving, but this is customary for an army.[16] They create the kind of chaos you see in a mask play. Even though they think they're good, it's as crude as a robber getting a wife by capture and rape.

Description will take too much time and the story will be long and tiresome if you listen to every syllable and every line. They won't tell the wife they had a fling along the way.

In fifteen days they came to Rahaeng. The district officials flocked around. Nai Jan took his travel document to inform the governor seated in the central sala.

The governor arranged dried rice, betel, popped rice, and sweets for his waist pouch, and provided post horses as of old so he could hurry ahead as it was royal business.

Nai Jan Samphantueng took leave and hastened onward, accompanied by four phrai, all on horseback, with waist pouches and bags swaying and slapping a rhythm as they went.

They reached the outpost at Tha Kwian and stopped to rest.[17] The officers of the outpost shouted to Nai Jan in greeting, provided white liquor, and carried over food including fish and turtle.

As soon as they were full, they mounted and sped off with wind racing from their ears. At Thoen, where they turned in to be fed, snakeskin and liquor were sent over

along with elephant meat, fishcakes, and boiled eggs, carried by a line of people swaying to and fro. Once happily full, they mounted and went off, hollering,

drunk on the liquor and dribbling spittle. They blurrily saw elephants the size of pigs, "Let's fight!" They came across Lao walking on their own and dragged them along to sing and dance wild chicken songs.

Nai Jan arrived at Chiang Mai, found Khun Phaen, saluted him with a wai, and handed over the cylinder.

Khun Phaen saluted, took the cylinder, and cracked it open. He drew out the missive, read the contents, and reported everything to the Thai.

---

16. In old recitations of *KCKP*, performers probably inserted commentary like this quite often. Some other examples are found in chapter 1. That chapter, and the Wat Ko version of the Chiang Mai campaign, from which this passage is taken, are probably the oldest surviving parts of the text, dating back to the Ayutthaya era, transcribed from oral performance, and not subject to revision.

17. Again, the route in the north is muddled. A few stanzas above, he passed through Rahaeng on the Ping River but is now away to the east on the route coming from the Yom River valley.

Among[18] the soldiers, some sang, while others played flutes and banged drums in joy that the army was returning home and they would see their wives again.

Ta-Lo said, "Sir, I'm not sad. Though my old woman is sick and ailing, I've got a young Lao girl as wife." Giggling and jiggling his head, he stumbled away.

Khun Phaen told his son Phlai Ngam to inform the King of Chiang Mai that the King of Ayutthaya had ordered the families swept down to his capital.

"His Majesty has granted him his life. But he must collect all his property and inform all his people. We'll wait fifteen days."

Phlai Ngam took leave and went off, trailed by a crowd of volunteers. Entering the audience hall, he saluted and addressed King Chiang In.

"A sealed message has come from the capital. Because of your evil and misguided actions towards the realm, all the families are to be swept down, including you, your wife, and consorts.

Chiang Mai will be left in the care of officials. You will go down to the capital under guard. Ancient traditions must be upheld. The king grants you only your life."

Knowing he would be swept to the southern city, King Chiang In felt his chest was as hot as if he were lying in fire, and his face burned with dismay.

He spoke sweetly and plaintively with Phlai Ngam. "I knew already my punishment would be major. The fact that I survive this alive is due to you two army commanders."

Phlai Ngam responded, "Don't be upset that your punishment is very severe. You'll have to face hardship and discomfort but we'll help plead with the king to restore the city to you."

"Be praised! My hopes are with you two commanders. I've survived death because of your aid. If the city of Chiang Mai can be restored, I'll happily offer myself and present articles of tribute."

Phlai Ngam took leave, and returned to the army. The ruler of Chiang Mai ordered officials to summon the whole city population,

then walked back into his palace, feeling extremely miserable. He came to the golden bedchamber,

set himself on a jeweled seat, and said to his beloved Queen Apson, "The

---

18. This section, down to "stumbled away," is taken from WK, 26:1031, absent from PD.

King of Ayutthaya has sent a sealed missive to the army commander,

ordering that we and the families be swept down. We'll probably end up in the Thai city and not return. The people, great and small, will be crushed. There'll be piles of dead along the way.

Oh, a heap of karma made me take the wrong course and act badly! We must leave the palace where we have lived." The king grieved sadly.

Queen Apson responded in kind. "All the consorts and palace ladies are so distressed and dismayed.

Oh, just how terrible will it be in the southern city? We'll have to suffer as servants of the Thai. We'll end up dead and buried deep underground.

Children will be parted from parents, grandparents from grandchildren, king from the palace women, and consorts from the palace.

The lords and ladies of the court will weep and wail like horns and conches, writhe and shake to the end of their strength, and slump over one another as if stung by wasps."

The ruler of Chiang Mai spoke mournfully to all the consorts. "Please swallow your grief and cheer up. You should return to our city alive.

If I die in the southern country, you'll have to be their servants. But if by the power of merit my punishment is reduced, you probably won't stay in the Thai city.

This heap of karma that we've made between us has now caught up with us all. Don't cry. Face up to the karma first without fear. Weeping won't help you escape, so bear the pain."

The mass of the people beat their breasts in anger and distress as if pounding themselves to a tearful death. Everyone packed food and belongings to take with them.

They sawed bamboo cylinders and stuffed them with fermented fish, chili, salt, fish sauce, and grilled deer meat. They sewed waist pouches and filled them with crisped rice. They packed betel and pan,

mortar and pestle, fermented and dried fish, rice pots, curry pots, and skillets. With tears brimming, they rushed around gathering goods together, looking sadly at their wives' faces,

or beating their breasts and sobbing at the thought of their lovers. Newly weds, still madly sweet on each other, went into their apartments and wept.

Men who had just asked for their partner's hand and built a bridal house, were allowed by the parents to stay together. Widows left alone by the death of their husbands lay down in a stupor, curled up with weeping.

Playboy musicians got ready for a tough life
by packing their *khaen*, flute,[19] drum, claves,
lute, and fiddle so they would have means
to beg alms for food.

Some hid gold, dried food, and ornaments such as little gold rings with jet
gemstones in their lowercloths. Some
removed their hairpins and wrapped
them away.

Crude objects too difficult to carry
were hidden away in the hollows of big
trees. Other things were secreted in
ponds, wells, and water pipes, or buried as fake corpses at the wat.

Some people were too old to survive

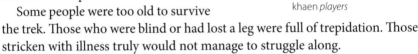

khaen *players*

the trek. Those who were blind or had lost a leg were full of trepidation. Those
stricken with illness truly would not manage to struggle along.

Some grandparents had to stay home while their children and grandchildren
left. The air was filled with the noise of lovelorn weeping, and the whimpering
and whining of little children. Some were too heavily pregnant to make it.

Some had just given birth and were still lying by the fire, while their husbands had gone with the army, died, and left them as widows. They could not
stay but were frightened about going. People boxed their heads and beat their
breasts all over the city.

Close to the time the army would leave, everyone was herded up. The roads
were crammed with people carrying goods on poles. In great distress, palace
ladies packed their silver, gold, food, and belongings.

King Chiang In commanded all the elephants to be harnessed, with one
mount for each consort. Howdahs were piled overflowing with goods.

Senior palace officials ordered sentinelles to mount and sit upfront to give
protection. Throngs of palace consorts were lined up in rank order all around.

The elephants of Soithong and Soifa each had a glittering golden canopy, a
red backcloth in offertory-rice pattern, and gold curtains to screen the princesses completely from view.

The elephants of the King and Queen of Chiang Mai had elegant golden
howdahs. Diligent and reliable mahouts brought the elephants alongside a
mounting platform.

---

19. ปี่อ้อ, *pi o*, a simple straight pipe, of folk origin, usually with a reed and seven stop holes.

Khun Phaen, great romancer, expert, masterful, and brave, and his powerful and beloved son, Phlai Ngam, each mounted the neck of a fine tusker.

Phra Thainam, Kamkong, and the standard bearer[20] also rode tuskers. Behind them, soldiers riding elephants and horses overflowed the road.

Khun Phaen ordered the Thai to divide into two detachments to march on each side of the road with the families in the middle. The elephant brigade was to march in line at the front.

The Lao of Vientiane were to march on the left and right sides to help guard the Lao soldiers from Chiang Mai. The volunteers were placed at the rear to watch over the families.

"There are more wild elephants than tame ones so take care. Keep a close watch on everything. If anyone starts a fight or sneaks off, catch them and chop off their heads without fail."

At an auspicious time, the army set off in a raucous, earth-shaking multitude. Soldiers cheered in unison. The air crackled with gunfire.

The King of Chiang Mai with his queen, consorts, and palace ladies mounted their elephants. The king gave orders to Thao Nu[21] to look after the palace.

As the elephants left through the east gate,[22] King Chiang In turned to look back at the golden spire of the royal palace, his eyes flooding with tears of parting.

herding war prisoners

"Oh, I grieve for the palace where we have lived for ages, since the ancestors. Now it will disintegrate day by day until it collapses, abandoned and overgrown like a graveyard.

The side pavilions[23] are like holy places, and the golden spire like a palace in a

20. ธงอาสา, *thong asa*, the militia flag, probably one of the guard officers whose official title includes the phrase ถือธง, *thue thong*, "hold the flag" (KTS, 1:281, 286, 288).

21. See p. 672, note 34.

22. Tha Phae Gate.

23. พระปรัศว์, *phra parat*, a Sanskrit-derived word for ancillary buildings beside a palace, often in flanking pairs.

heavenly city. Oh, from now on they'll disappear from sight. Everything will fall apart like a vulture's nest.

I grieve for our favorite trees in the garden of the right.[24] The crystal lotus ponds will run dry. The audience hall will be as empty as an open field, and the throne hall will crumble away.

Oh pity, pity! Where we used to sit in the evenings will be overgrown by elephant grass, brambles, and forest weeds.[25] All the residences of the consorts will crack and collapse. Their four lamp pillars will be in peril.

Oh, I grieve for the stables of the chariots, elephants, and horses which face ruin. Walls and fortifications will crumple, collapse, and be scattered all around the city.

I grieve for the moon garden where we used to play. Within days, it will decay into a flooded pit. The palace landing will become a waterless beach. The earth and sky will turn yellow[26] throughout the Lao country."

Queen Apson's breast burned with distress, as if she were being destroyed, her breast slashed open by a kris dipped in acid.

"Oh, while I lived in Chiang Mai, I enjoyed only happiness and good company. Wherever I went around the city, I was carried so pleasantly in an elegant palanquin,

trailed by throngs of senior female court officials,[27] and surrounded by lovely consorts from the palace. Oh, now I'll end up in the Thai city and have to walk among ordinary phrai.

Royal servants will order me around. I'll suffer as much pain as if I'd fallen into an abyss. I won't even have good cloth to wrap around my waist. My breast will feel shattered every day from now on.

Oh, while living in our city, the royal victuals were so refined, following the traditions of the queens of Chiang Mai. Now I must leave the city unhappily, and probably starvation and deprivation will follow."

She lamented, beat her body, pulled her hair, and shed floods of sad tears. All the consorts and palace ladies grieved along the way.

---

24. Within the palaces at Ayutthaya and Bangkok, the "garden of the right" was reserved for the king, and the "garden of the left" for the ladies of the palace. King Rama II created a famous garden of the right in Chinese style, replicated in Bangkok's "Ancient City" museum park.

25. ผักโหม, phak hom, "a class of forest vegetables which grow in waste places" (MC, 140), now more usually phak khom, a general term for plants of the Amaranthus family.

26. A yellow sky foretells a great disaster.

27. ชะแม่, chamae, female officers in the palace, ranking above consorts and attendants. Their responsibilities included overseeing the sentinelles, educating young royals, and taking parts in rites and entertainments (KTS, 1:124, 131, 137–38).

They marched out of Chiang Mai city, driven along by the Thai soldiers. The Lao families, fearful and subdued, carried goods on shoulder poles, hoisted young infants aloft, and dragged older children by the hand.

The old, lame, weak, and crippled were carried clumsily in litters. Gentlefolk who had no elephants mounted on cattle and buffaloes.

Ta-Rak, Ta-Ma, and Ta-Sai carried canes for herding people along with no mercy. Anyone trying to hide or slink away was whipped back into line, slipping and stumbling in turmoil.

Ta-Rak shouted, "Look, that's old Ai-Thi, one of the market people who was always abusing us. When Ta-Lo and me went to beg alms, he flogged me with a stick and almost broke my back.

I remember his face perfectly. Now it's my turn for revenge! I'll flog him so the forest echoes with his cries. There'll be only horns and skin left to give his master."

Reaching[28] Chomthong, the main army banged gongs to call a halt. The sound of gunfire echoed around. The whole army dismounted from horses and elephants.

Saen Kham Maen[29] cocked his head and sat shifting from side to side with mouth agape, then rushed off with his wife to meet the army and welcome their son-in-law.

The young women of Chomthong carried many presents along. Every single house brought something in a great crowd,

happy to see the son-in-law of the village head. The headman and his wife, dressed in their best, heaved themselves into litters, telling their servants to carry the gifts in an orderly fashion.

The village head reclined on the litter, looking intently ahead. Behind came phrai packed together in a big crowd as far as the eye could see. Khun Phaen lifted his head to look,

and saw his parents-in-law coming. He called out a welcome and walked to meet them. The two old folk clopped along in shoes and sat looking grand.

Khun Phaen and his son quickly prostrated. The couple greeted them and handed over gifts, asking questions one after another. Khun Phaen gave them many kinds of cloth,

two bowls of gold and silver, cartwheels, elephants, horses, cattle, buffaloes

---

28. This section on the visit to Chomthong, down to "crack of dawn" on p. 686, is taken from WK, 26:1044–45; PD has: At sunset, the army halted. People dismounted from horses, elephants, cattle, and buffaloes and left them in rows jamming the forest. The place looked crammed with people.

29. Laothong's father (see ch. 10).

for his mother-in-law, and five salvers of cloth along with a betel tray, a golden border cloth embroidered with circles,[30]

a footed and covered betel tray,[31] betel boxes in good-quality lacquerware,[32] pikes, swords, guns, spears, lances, rolled mats, and pillows embroidered with gold thread. His parents-in-law roared with laughter, showing their red mouths.[33]

"We heard you won victory and took the city. Son-in-law has given us so many things." The old man shook with laughter, slapping his thigh, "If I could fly, I'd go to a palace in the heavens!" Both sat jiggling with joy.

Towards evening, the old couple made their farewells. Khun Phaen and his son reciprocated. "We leave at the crack of dawn."

A pavilion was constructed for Soithong and Soifa with walls all around, a ceiling, and golden curtains to screen them from view. Guards were posted outside.

The families looked weak and pinched with hunger. Some just dropped their burdens and sprawled on the ground. The division head, Thammathian, called out orders to erect a circle of stakes and set bonfires.

The Thai had suffered deprivation for a long time. As soon as night fell, they went searching around everywhere. Where they saw young girls lying, they squeezed in beside them, or crawled off with them among the howdahs and harnesses.

When they felt a sagging breast, they immediately withdrew their hand. But if they touched a firm one, they gripped and held on tight. Lao girls awoke and realized it was the Thai. Some pretended to sleep and ignore them.

Some refused to play and cried out loud when they were grabbed. Those sleeping close by were alarmed and woozily thought a tiger or bear had come to bite them.

The division head, Thammathian, called out, "What's all that racket?" "Don't be alarmed. It's not a tiger with a long tail, just a two-legged beast with a teeny tail."

The tiger was abashed, and got out of there. But other tigers rambled about to court girls and make trouble. As soon as one unit was quiet, the next unit started up before there was time to go to sleep.

---

30. เชิง ทอง ปัก สัก สังเวียน, *choeng thong pak sak sangwian*. *Choeng* is a decorative strip of cloth often used as the border of a lowercloth, especially on the *pha sin* tubular lowercloths popular in Lanna and Lanchang.

31. ตะลุ่ม เชี่ยน, *talum chian*, a betel set with an onion-dome cover.

32. กำมะลอ, *kammalo*, which may mean lacquerware of Chinese or Japanese style, or something decorated with a pattern of the type used on such ware.

33. Stained from chewing betel.

Khun[34] Phaen and his troupe of famous spirits stood guard on the King of Chiang Mai. Thainam and the Lanchang Lao were put in charge of the two princesses and their people.

Phlai Ngam and the five hundred phrai stood guard all around, while the thirty-five volunteers went to lie down, keeping watch on the principal elephants.

Muen At Narai and two hundred phrai lay on watch as scouts in the forest. If anyone tried to enter or leave at the wrong time, they were captured and held by the troops.

In the evening at torch-lighting time after the sun set and darkness fell, the troops in charge of bonfires kept watch, beat gongs, and made inspections.

Phlai Ngam patrolled to check if any bonfires went out. As night fell, Thai soldiers who had got themselves wives went in to sleep

and called their wives into the mosquito net. "Come and take care of me." Some laid out mattresses and pillows, and massaged one another. One tried teaching his sulky young wife to pray saying "I-ii."[35]

The Lao girl said, "You're no young bull." "I used to teach I-Duek and she didn't complain." The Lao girl lowered her face and said "I-ii." The husband chuckled and cuddled her.

Ta-Lo said, "Oh, you two start early in the evening! This will make old folk like me unable to restrain ourselves. Young I-Toe, why are you lying quietly there? Come in and massage me for a bit."

Young Toe, who was deaf, replied sharply, "Tomorrow I can't walk, my legs are so stiff. If you can get me an elephant to ride, I'll love you. All of us have busted legs."

Ta-Lo was angry. "See here, I dislike you, you deaf bat, enough to throw up, to vomit, to heave." "Leaves?"[36] I-Toe cried, "I'd like leaves in a curry."

Friends laughed, "Oh Ta-Lo, don't bother her. This isn't your home ground. Whatever you say, she can't hear. Not everybody has gone to sleep yet, old fellow."

Ta-Lo laughed and cried out, "In a minute, I'm coming over and dragging her off." He got out of the mosquito net, walked over, grabbed I-Toe's hand, and pulled her along.

I-Toe screwed up her face and said, "I'm very hungry. Stop dragging me.

---

34. The next two sections, down to "Let their husbands come and collect them," is taken from WK, 26:1046–49, absent from PD.

35. Meaning humming, usually with eyes closed, as an exercise to still and concentrate the mind. Perhaps he is urging her to relax and be less sulky.

36. In the original, Toe mishears ฮวก (อ้วก, *uak*, vomit) as หยวก (*yuak*, banana pith).

I'm not willing." Ta-Lo said, "Get up in there." He went into the mosquito net and mounted her.

I-Toe shrieked and wriggled. Her lowercloth was ripped to pieces. Just when Ta-Lo was getting into position, I-Toe stood up. He said, "You're really uncontrollable. It's worse than herding buffaloes."

He gripped her neck with both hands. She kicked at Ta-Lo's throat, knocking him down. With bleary eyes, Ta-Lo readied to grab her. She shouted, "I'm scared to death!"[37] and sprawled down flat.

I-Toe could not match his strength. Ta-Lo said, "Wonderful, like jelly." Friends laughed, and Ta-Lo stabbed away until he reached the end of his strength and dozed off.

In the pitch dark of midnight, the Thai were fast asleep. Some lay embracing their wives and breathing softly. The Chiang Mai Lao were dead to the world.

Six women who had old husbands picked up their gold and valuables and sneaked away in a group with bodies trembling. They went outside the fence, found the entrance to a path,

and walked until they came across some people sitting on the road. Ai-Pu with the cauliflower ears leapt up and gave chase. His mates cried out, "Lao or Thai? Male or female? Where are you running to?"

The soldiers caught them and recognized their faces. "So the Lao from the main army are off to the fair! This is Ta-Lo's wife!" He laughed out loud. "Tie her up and put her in my mosquito net.

on the march

---

37. ยั่นตายพ่อแล้ว, *yan tai pho laeo*; in Lao.

It's our bonus payment. Why should we catch people for nothing. Let's give them a pounding through to dawn. Is this a moneybag or what tied round her belly?" He tugged an end, and the string came of its own accord.

The gang of friends laughed as the cloth slipped down. "Damnit, hair up to her ears." "Make her dance the forest dance." "That would be a sight!" They cheered in chorus.

In the morning they delivered the prisoners to the army officers. "Let their husbands come and collect them."

When the streaks of dawn lit the sky, people busily steamed rice, grilled fish, and ate their fill, then hoisted the carrying poles onto their shoulders and set off.

Buffaloes, cattle, elephants, and horses walked in file. The army commanders prodded and drove them along. The forest was full of the sound of the Lao crying.[38]

"Oh!

Oh, unending misery	roaming far from home
heavy poles bending	wending through the wood
tall grass, dense thicket	papyrus clumps and reeds
grimy sweat floods down	toil and trudge ahead
eat rice with salt alone	drink sweat not water
morning meal comes later	evening meal at nightfall
can't ever stop at all	Thai bash and thrash us
can't even have a pee	they seize us for a feel
knocked flat, goods fall	trawled into the trees
hump us if they can	thump us if we flee
by the road, by the track	jig-jig, jog-jog-jog
up-down, up-down-up	heart will crack, will die. Oh!"

"Oh!

Oh my love, my pet	when still in our city
we ate morn and eve	never to grieve for food
girls, young and old	flocked to the fields

---

38. Choomsai notes that this lament is not found in any of the *samut thai* manuscripts of *KCKP*, and suggests that it was probably a well-known song incorporated into the story by Prince Damrong's editorial team. The call "*aeo!*" แอ่ว, at the beginning and end indicates the song probably originates from Lanchang rather than Lanna, where the equivalent term would be "*khao!*" ค่าว. The lament is in four-syllable lines, with many rhymes in no regular pattern. The first part is obviously sung by a female, and the second by a male (CS, 91; Khwanmueang, "Lao nai *KCKP*," 96).

to pick water spinach	catch fish and catch prawn
apple snails, river snails	scoop all into a basket
go along the field bunds	hunting for holes of crabs
root out moles and mice	dig holes to trap lizards
nab beetles and cocoons	poke nests of spiders
catch long-legged frogs	little toads,[39] big bullfrogs
when one torch burns out	already half a basket's full
chili dip, sour salad	*jaeo ha* and *jaeo bong*[40]
going to the southern city	belly won't like the food
eat hot, eat mild	belly ache, belly swell
belly airy, belly bloated	bad belly will be the death! Oh!"

Khun Phaen, great romancer, powerful as the Lord of the Lions, rode his elephant at the front, impatient to avoid delay.

They slept at nightfall and set off again at dawn. The forest overflowed with people trailing behind. In fourteen and a half days of quick march, they reached the city of Phichit,[39]

and halted to let the troops rest. Everyone dismounted from their elephants and horses. The area behind Wat Jan was packed with hundreds and thousands of families.

The[40] mass of people swarmed down to bathe. Just before nightfall, people were rounded up to pitch camp. Huts and shelters were set up in rows. They busily steamed rice, grilled fish, and made curry.

Some went to collect vegetables and banana flower shoots, or snatch ducks and chickens from anywhere. "I'll go to spear a pig to give us some strength." A Jek protested noisily.

Orders were given to make pavilions for Soithong, Soifa, and the king of the Lao capital. Father and son stayed in a sala.

Now to tell of Phra Phichit and Busaba. They had learned from a missive with a royal lion seal[41] that Khun Phaen had taken the city. They had been happily waiting to receive him on his way home.

---

39. The Wat Ko version traces the route in more detail: Lampang, Thoen, through the defile, Tha Kwian, Sawankhalok, Phichit. By modern roads, the distance is 435 kms by that route, or 395 kms via Uttaradit, meaning they were covering 30 or 27 kms a day.

40. The next two stanzas, down to "A Jek protested noisily," are taken from WK, 27:1059, absent from PD.

41. Ratchasi, the seal of Mahatthai, the ministry that oversaw the territories to the north of Ayutthaya, including Phichit.

Royal barges had come up several days earlier, and were moored in a row along a landing. The oarsmen were being fed and lodged at a sala in front of Wat Jan.

In the wat itself, a large area had been cleared and leveled to order. Elephant grass, wood, and food of all kinds had been provided.

On the day the army reached Phichit, officials went to investigate, and rushed back to give the news. The governor and his wife were delighted and decided to go to Wat Jan.

They hurriedly changed clothes, and commanded servants to inform local officials to come quickly as they were going to welcome the army.

Phra Phichit and Busaba descended from the house and went along together with the deputy governor, magistrate, chief overseer, other local officials, and nobles.

Khun Phaen, great warrior, and Phlai Ngam were in front of the main sala when they saw Phra Phichit and Busaba approaching in the distance. They happily rushed to receive them,

and took them up to sit in the sala. Father and son greeted them, saying, "We've just arrived and things are still chaotic. We meant to come and prostrate at your feet,

but the place is overflowing with families, men and women, children and adults, commoners and royalty. If we're a bit slack, things get out of hand. If the Lao become spread out, we have to round them up.

Also we have to take care of two princesses, Soifa and Soithong. There's no other eye or ear we can trust. We'd thought of coming to see you tomorrow,

but you've been kind enough to make the effort to come out here. Have you been well all along? And how is Simala?"

Phra Phichit and Busaba smiled brightly and replied, "Both of us and our beloved daughter have been healthy and happy throughout.

But we've been very concerned about you every day, and waiting to give you every support. Since we knew you took the city, we've been expecting you each morning and night.

There are masses of families! How can two of you possibly look after them? We have local city officials who'll come to help. No problem."

He sent for the deputy governor, magistrate, and all the local officials. When they had arrived, he explained matters.

"Good sirs, there's a lot of official work to be done here. Khun Phaen has brought many Lao. If any incident happens in our city, we'll all be held responsible. Bear that in mind.

Deputy governor, assign our people to help them in every respect. As officials of this city, make sure there is no bothersome incident."

Khun Phaen, Phra Phichit, and the local officials discussed the division of work. The garrison commander would take care of the Thai army and Lanchang Lao.

The chief overseer would look after the feeding of elephants, horses, cattle, buffaloes, and various animals. The city officer[42] was to guard the families, watch the roads, barricade the entrances, and set bonfires.

The palace officer would build pavilions for royalty, including the ruler of Chiang Mai and his wife and daughter. The treasury officer would keep guard on all goods, including money.

The land officer was to coordinate the distribution of food and other supplies from granaries. Other people were kept in reserve for various duties. All the assignments were made.

The deputy governor and magistrate were to supervise. Boats were requisitioned and some selected to transport the army and families. In three days, they would all start out for the capital.

Once everything was properly arranged, Phra Phichit and Busaba returned home in the late afternoon.

Now to tell of the beloved Simala. She had been miserable after Phlai Ngam left, and had stayed in her room in floods of tears, thinking of him constantly, morning and night.

While eating, she sighed with longing. While sleeping, she dreamed fearful dreams. She did not smile or engage in conversation but hid away lying on her bed for almost a month.

Her parents suspected something was wrong, but when they asked their daughter, she was evasive. I-Moei was concerned. She went into the room and whispered warnings to her mistress. "Don't appear too sad.

Your father and mother will have an inkling. You're not badly sick. You must dress up, put on a happy face, and be sociable.

Try to appear like you used to be. Hide you sadness and don't let it show on your face. Though you have to suffer, it won't be long. He'll come as hoped and put you out of your misery."

Simala agreed and tried to be as cheerful as before. Only when going back to her inner room to sleep would she sigh and sob every night and day.

---

42. For details of the local officials mentioned here, see p. 537, note 8.

Her breast trembled with worry when she thought of him. "How will the war turn out?" She prayed and made offerings to the gods for his protection. She counted the days waiting for Phlai Ngam till they became many months.

When she heard the news that the army had returned, it was like receiving a peerless jewel. She summoned I-Moei into her apartment. "Don't delay. Find an opportunity to slip away.

If Phlai Ngam asks you, tell him that I've got a fever. Then listen to what he says. Don't make anyone suspicious."

I-Moei beamed. "Mistress, don't worry. If I don't get Phlai for you, you can bawl me out. But please leave this until tomorrow. I won't dawdle." They talked together until evening.

When the dawn sun brightened the heavens, Khun Phaen and his son conferred together, and made the necessary arrangements

to take gifts to Phra Phichit, Busaba, and—of prime concern—the fair Simala. They summoned servants and attendants to carry the gifts to the governor's residence.

On arrival, they went up to the house and saw Phra Phichit and Busaba in the sitting hall. Phlai had only Simala on his mind, and looked all round for her.

The servants unloaded the gifts in rows, filling the verandah of the cross-hall at the front. Father and son sat down to pay respect. "We've brought a few little things—

some Lao bowls, soft mats, triangular cushions, footed trays, salvers—everyday things from Chiang Mai. Also betel baskets, water bowls with drinking cups, tea, and sugar juice."

They prostrated at the feet of Phra Phichit and Busaba. "Just some presents from the forest. This valuable ruby ring is for dear Simala."

Phra Phichit said, "How kind of you to take the trouble. It's worthwhile to love you. Thank you. You're exceptionally generous."

Then he called, "Hey I-Moei! Go and tell Simala to come out here. Khun Phaen has come back to the city with Phlai Ngam.

He's been kind and thoughtful enough to bring some gifts. Don't be shy. Come see them." I-Moei smiled sweetly and went off to tell Simala in the inner room.

Fair Simala had already recognized the voices. "He's come! It's him and nobody else!" Love almost made her dash out,

but she thought twice because of feminine modesty, and because the adults did not know the truth. "If Phlai made an error and something slipped out, it could ruin things.

I must stifle my feelings and put off the meeting. At night he'll probably come to the house." She said to I-Moei quickly, "Tell them I'm sick. Help me."

She got up and spied through a gap in the wall. She saw Phlai looking plump and healthy but very sunburned.

He sat hidden behind his father with his eyes staring at the wall of her room, as if questioning. She felt elated to see him and could not tear her eyes away.

I-Moei, the tricky girl, put on a straight face, walked out of the room, and said to Phra Phichit, "Today, Mistress Simala's body is hot.

She's had a throbbing headache since midnight, and woke feeling weak and exhausted. She's still lying down, groggy and aching. She sent me to prostrate at their feet on her behalf."

Phra Phichit thought he understood perfectly—his daughter must be shy about coming out because of her betrothal to be married to Phlai Ngam.

He turned to smile at Khun Phaen. "She's got a high fever. We shouldn't force her. I'd like to consult you. Now that the war is successfully over,

we should discuss the marriage. I want to see a roof over our beloved daughter's head. While I'm still alive, I've got the means to make sure she's happy so I won't have to worry.

We parents are getting older, more like grandparents, and who knows whether we'll fall dead tomorrow. Please look for an auspicious date. Then we can find the timber to build a house."

Khun Phaen paid respect and replied, "I came here meaning to talk to you about the same thing. After we've taken the army home, we'll come back soon to plan the wedding here.

I calculated yesterday. On Tuesday the first waning in the fourth month, their fates coincide perfectly. It's up to you, sir, whether you agree."

Phra Phichit consulted with Busaba and replied, "The fourth month is good to fix the ceremony. The house should be finished in time."

Then he said to Khun Phaen. "Why stay at the wat? There are several days before you leave. Why not come and stay here with us?"

Khun Phaen, great romancer, thought quietly with concern. "Young Phlai has been apart from her. Now that he's back, he won't dawdle.

After dark he'll fumble around to find her. If the matter doesn't stay secret like the last time, but leaks out and spreads around, it'll bring shame and ruin to both sides."

He replied with the flow of conversation. "I'm in great difficulty, because the army we brought back is much bigger than on the outward journey.

Then there are Soithong, Soifa, the ruler of Chiang Mai, and his wives and children. On top of this, we have to guard the Lao families, forest people. If we don't stay close by, I fear it'll cause trouble.

Phra Thainam and people over there will report that we two neglected royal service and went to stay in creature comfort in your house.

I've had enough problems already. I don't want the slightest hint of any more risk. I'll have to drag my body along until we've finished what we undertook to do."

He took leave of the governor and his wife, and walked down from the house. Phlai Ngam trailed behind, mutely furious at his father.

"Pitiful! Father knows in his heart that I love her and have already had her as man and wife. I could put him to sleep with a mantra again with no fear but he still wants to obstruct me. What a joke!

Fine! Never mind. Let's see. Don't imagine I'm going to sit here and let him treat me like a monkey in a cage. After nightfall I'll go to see her."

He walked along, acting unconcerned. At some distance from the governor's residence, he saw I-Moei sitting smiling at the side of the road. He secretly signaled her to follow.

They reached Wat Jan in the late afternoon. Many local officials were waiting to see them. Khun Phaen talked to them earnestly. Phlai Ngam sneaked away to the side of the wat.

He looked for a hidden place with nobody around, and found a suitable big pupil tree with smooth sand underneath. He slipped in and sat hidden by the tree.

I-Moei walked up behind, sank down, and raised her hands in wai. Phlai Ngam smiled and said, "I hoped to run into you.

We have an urgent matter, as you know. Though my body went away from here, my heart remained. Every day and night I've been thinking of her. Is she happy?

This morning when we sat in there, I was hoping to see her face a little, but no sign. Is she angry for some reason? Is that why she pretended to be sick and wouldn't appear?

Before I left, I entrusted you to look after her and comfort her while waiting for me. You didn't keep your promise. What do you have to say for yourself?"

I-Moei tossed her head and said, "Oh Buddha! Why are you angry and blaming me? Don't you see my mistress's position? She doesn't want to meet you in front of people,

so she said she had a fever and wouldn't appear. She's not fibbing or pretending or going back on her word. After the day you led the army off, she was unwell for several months.

She wasn't sleeping or eating. She became weak. The streams of her tears never ran dry. I'm not making it up. I had to look after her all the time, and keep talking to jolly her along.

I'm glad you came back. Maybe you brought some medicine with you. I hurried over to hear what orders you'd give for nursing her.

I fear you don't remember the words you promised. You've brought piles of gifts for the noble folk but you seem to ignore a poor phrai girl."

"Tcha! Your mouth is as big as your body. Don't whine at me." He took out some money and offered it to her. "Here, for Moei as reward.

As for your mistress being unwell, I have some very good herbal medicine, but it's medicine enchanted with yantra. It can't be taken in daytime or the patient dies.

A little after dark, I'll come to the house. You work out how to let me in. I'll give your mistress the medicine, and it should cure her fever by tomorrow."

They agreed on a signal. I-Moei took leave. Phlai hurried back to the sala without raising any suspicion.

In the evening at sunset, Wat Jan was swarming with troops. Division and unit heads made inspections and kept watch.

Phlai Ngam, adept at devices and mantras, went around giving orders, inspecting this division and that division at all levels, as he did every day.

At the end of the watch, he wended his way to the kuti of Master Thai. He saw the light of torches where a chess circle was in session.

The volunteers had come to play in groups, while monks and novices watched for amusement. So many were sitting watching, squeezed in among the players, that a racket poured out of the kuti.

Phlai Ngam pondered quietly. "I must fool Father into thinking I'm here. I'll

playing chess

pretend to join the chess game until he's gone to sleep. Then I'll escape away to find her."

He went up to the kuti. "Hey! Let me make some moves." He banged down a piece. The soldiers let their commander sit in the middle. The noise on both sides was deafening.

Khun Phaen was waiting for Phlai Ngam. When his son failed to appear, he became worried. He stepped down from the sala and walked around. Seeing a light in a kuti, he hurried over.

When he got close, he could hear the commotion and knew his son was in there enjoying a game of chess, so he turned back to the sala.

Around the second watch, Phlai Ngam thought his father would be asleep. He left the chess circle, descended the stairway, and sneaked away to get dressed up.

He doused his body with fragrant water, powdered his face and forehead, and rubbed beeswax enchanted with a Beguiler mantra on his lips. He put on a flared[43] silk yok,

an uppercloth of colored wool given by the king, and a new ruby ring on his finger. In his right hand he carried an open fan with a tiny handle. He picked up a striped handkerchief and set off.

Coming to the middle of the wat, which was deserted, he chanted a Great Collection mantra, and his spirits came to surround him. He went into Phichit city

and before long reached the front of the governor's residence. There were spirits all round the front and back. The surrounding wall was solid and the gate bolted on the inside.

Phlai Ngam chanted a Great Loosener mantra. All the bolts sprung with a shudder. The gates of the house opened wide and he went through.

The Mon slave girl, I-Moei, was up in the house. She had drawn the bolt and was lying waiting. Hearing the locks on the house gates clack open, she rose to look and saw it was Phlai Ngam.

She opened the door, went down, and led him up to the house, threading her way through people scattered asleep. She took him up to her mistress's apartment and then deftly made herself scarce.

When Phlai Ngam reached the room, he was happy beyond compare. He tiptoed softly inside. By the fine bright lights of the room,

he saw his sweetheart, Simala. "Lying so quiet and still, you look perfect.

---

43. ไปล่ปลิว, *plai plio*, blown wide, a crisp silk cloth that flares outwards at the bottom.

Are you fast asleep or just pretending, my jewel?" He carefully sat beside her on the golden bed,

and gently kissed, stroked, and embraced her. "I'm here. Don't be miserable any more. I've been thinking of you constantly. My intention hasn't wavered for a single day.

At times to eat, I've had no taste for food. At times to sleep, I've dreamed of you. Had I not been afraid of the king, I'd have turned up here long ago.

By the power of our merit, my darling, we were victorious and returned here. I heard you hadn't been flourishing. I've been worried since this morning.

Sitting in front of your room, I was almost out of my mind. I looked everywhere but couldn't see you. I resolved, life or death, to find you tonight.

I had to wait until my father was fast asleep so I only just came at this late hour. Life's blossom, please turn your face this way for me to admire."

Simala pretended to lie still with her eyes closed under a coverlet. Listening to his sweet talk, she felt charmed and aroused with love, as he hoped.

She raised herself, sat beside him, then turned to prostrate on his lap. "I thought you'd still be very tired and would want to rest first rather than coming here.

You went to war, won a victory, and took a Lao city. I've heard Soifa's outstanding reputation. Didn't you grab something for yourself? There must be lots of girls among the war prisoners.

All[44] good lookers, not bad! Am I to think that you hate and fear girls so much you ignored them? Or could you restrain yourself like a barren monk?[45] I don't believe you. Don't try to fool me.

Why bother with the daughter of the Phichit governor? She's not worth romancing. Like a grassflower, she looks fine when you have nothing else, but once you have a real flower, you don't need her.

Maybe you're feeling some pity so you made the effort to break into the house. But now you've seen my face, you'll be bored and won't stay long. You'll get worried about the army and go back there."

"Look here! This taunting is pitiful. You can accuse me for nothing, if you like but I give you my word, I haven't courted any other woman, Lao or Thai, in the whole three worlds.

Since I left here, my heart has been with you, and I've missed you miserably.

---

44. This stanza is taken from WK, 27:1062–63, absent from PD.

45. อด ใจ ได้ อย่าง พระ เป็น กะเทย, *ot jai dai yang phra pen kathoei*. *Kathoei*, which now means transsexual or transgender, earlier meant sterile, unable to produce progeny, and could be applied to fruit that had no seeds.

Though I've been looking at Lao, I've been seeing only the sight of Simala, the ruler of my heart.

As for Princess Soifa, she's the daughter of the ruler of Chiang Mai, and has been offered to the King of Ayutthaya. So has Princess Soithong, both of them.

I've made the effort to control myself, as if I'd shaved my head, put on the triple robe, become a monk, and been religiously chanting prayers every morning and evening to share the merit with Simala.

But instead of the merit, I've brought a ring. Now it's the end of lent, and I'll disrobe tonight. You must make up your mind to be merciful."

Simala could not stop herself laughing. Phlai grabbed hold of her immediately. A[46] great storm blew in with a crash.

The sky exploded and rain sluiced down, though out of season and late at night. Thunder rumbled across the world, breaking with a great crack and gradually fading away.

Meeting after a long time, both joined in joy. Whirled around by the full force of love, they clung close together until both fell asleep.

Simala had prepared some food and left it beside a wall. She led him over there and they ate happily together,

chatting away. Simala was wreathed in smiles. Phlai teased her and would not leave her alone. They fondled away without sleeping

until the moon slipped from the sky and a coel called loud and clear. "It's almost morning. I have to go, my love. I'll come back to you every night.

After we've taken the army to Ayutthaya, I'll hurry back to you here. When we've had the marriage ceremony as planned, we won't be apart a single night."

He kissed and caressed her, then left the room. With I-Moei leading the way, he walked outside the wall

and cut quickly through to Wat Jan. It was still pitch dark when he arrived. He avoided his father, pulled covers over his head, and slept.

Khun Phaen woke in the morning and saw Phlai Ngam still fast asleep. He thought his son had enjoyed himself playing chess, and was not concerned over him.

That evening, Phlai Ngam again skipped off to show his face at the chess game, then late at night went to Simala. He was with his sweetheart every night.

---

46. From here until "both fell asleep" is taken from WK, 27:1063; PD has: They made love blissfully, lying together on the bed.

On the last night, the lovers got carried away talking, fell asleep, and did not wake in time. Only when dawn streaked the sky did Phlai wake up, wash his face, and leave.

Now to tell of the mother, Busaba. That night, she woke before the cock. Because Khun Phaen would depart at dawn, she was anxious about food.

She got up, opened a window to wash her face, and saw Phlai Ngam walking away. "Eh! This isn't right. He'll make trouble for our daughter."

Trembling, she woke her husband. "Sir! Phlai Ngam came into the house. He went down just now. What's been going on in here?

There's an ancient saying: When a dog shits, it makes a mess.[47] His tracks will lead straight to our dear daughter. We parents are dishonored without knowing it. Don't ignore this. What do you think?"

Understanding straightaway, Phra Phichit replied to his wife, "I thought something was wrong. How we view this comes down to Simala.

After the army left, she seemed sick and very upset. When I asked what the matter was, she didn't reply. I didn't know they'd sneaked off to make love already.

On the day the army returned, she was quiet and hid away as if she were afraid. He probably got to her, and she's spoiled. Why else would he have come up here?

But it's not right to get angry and punish our daughter. This is a very important fellow. He knows invisibility, stunning, concealment, and all kinds of love tricks.

Even if there were diamond walls, seven layers thick, he'd only have to chant and blow to blast them open. If he loves anybody, he just puffs some mantra and they all fall for him without exception.

But he's asked for Simala's hand in marriage. Whatever happens, he must become her husband. He just got impatient and showed no respect but why be angry?

If we get into a shouting match, it'll create scandal and hurt Khun Phaen, and that's not fitting. He's still faithful and loyal. We're parents and shouldn't be fickle.

If word gets around that Simala has had a lover, it'll shame her. It's like a sagging breast that slaps on your own chest.[48] Let it pass. Don't bring matters into the open."

---

47. หมาขี้ที่มูลฝอย, *ma khi thi munfoi*, a proverb meaning an action has consequences.

48. A stock saying meaning something that you cannot avoid and so have to live with.

The couple finished talking and got dressed to leave before it was late. They came out, summoned their servants, and walked to the front of Wat Jan.

The many boats that had come up were milling around the moorings. The place was teeming with local officials, boarding the boats and rafts. The courtyard of the wat was a hive of activity.

Phra Thainam and Kamkong went down to prepare the two golden royal barges. They called out urgently that they were short of this and that. The princesses' flotilla needed a lot of arrangements.

Phra Thainam's boat was to lead the way, with the volunteers' craft on both flanks, the royal barges in the center, and boats with the female servants behind.

Next was the flotilla of the army commanders. The two canopy boats that had come to collect them were resplendent, and their oarsmen were all skillful soldiers. Father and son had a boat each.

Then came craft carrying goods due to the king, and the boats for the Lao at the rear. The volunteers were to serve as guards, busily herding groups of people along without respite.

The boat of the ruler of Chiang Mai led the next group, followed by those of his daughter and wife, then those of their officials and servants. The boats of the volunteers came at the tail.

There were not enough craft remaining for the families, elephants, horses, cattle, weapons, and large quantity of military equipment. All had to be left in the keeping of Phichit.

When everything was loaded to take the army back to the southern city, Khun Phaen and his son went to prostrate to Phra Phichit and Busaba.

"I beg to take leave of your footsoles to go down to attend on King Phanwasa. After the audience, we'll definitely come back as promised."

royal barge

Phra Phichit and Busaba gladly gave their blessings and good wishes. "Go down to attend on the king, who will favor you with rank and rewards.

May you flourish and enjoy perfect prosperity. May both father and son live happily forever. May danger and trouble not intrude upon you.

When you've completed your royal service for the realm, come back here to discuss and finalize plans for the wedding."

Khun Phaen, great gallant, and Phlai Ngam prostrated to their elders, took their leave, and boarded the canopy boats in front of the wat.

Boats and rafts were crammed with officers and men. On a signal of three gunshots, the flotilla set off.

Khaek[49] drum, flute, *ranat*, and gong played in clear and sweet harmony. The oarsmen sang boat songs, all with strong voices. Entering the stream, the boats passed through Phichit,

where villagers and townsfolk massed to watch, standing packed together on the landings, chattering away to one another. "Never seen a water procession like this. My oh my!"

At Boraphet[50] while waiting for other boats, some Lao saw groups of villagers selling fish. Feeling hungry, they tried to snatch some. One grabbed at a catfish,

and fumbled around, trying to grip its tail, but the fish jumped up and flopped about. Granny Suk shouted out, "None of your tricks!" A hungry man with a head like a coconut shell took some fish anyway.

At Nakhon Sawan, *thon* drums, barrel drums, horn, and conch played magnificently. At Trok Phra they went downstream to Nam Song.[51] Villagers ran up noisily to make merit.

Through Hua Daen, Hua Dan, Khung Thaphao, and Chi Dat Khanon,[52] onlookers were packed together, pushing and shoving, rushing round in circles, and shouting at one another.

---

49. The passage from here to "got covered in mud" on p. 706 is taken from WK, 27:1067–73; PD has one stanza: The great mass of craft floated down with the current in line astern, passing villages and cities one after another until they entered the boundary of the capital.

50. A large lake and wetland immediately west of Nakhon Sawan town.

51. Now Krok Phra, an amphoe 8 kms south of Nakhon Sawan on the west bank of the river; and Nam Song, meaning water that maintains its level during tidal changes, 2 kms north of Phayuhakiri (see map 2).

52. Now Ban Sila Dan, on the east bank of the river just south of Uthai Thani town; Khung Samphao, 2 kms southeast of Uthai Thani on the east bank; and Dak Khanon on the east bank of the river 2 kms below Khung Samphao (see map 2).

They halted to spend a night at Chainat where a *klongyon*[53] was played by loud barrel drums, horn, conch, Khaek drum, and Java flute.

Rather late in the afternoon, they moored at a royal jetty. The governor and local officials came in a crowd to offer gifts to the princesses.

Villagers swarmed on both banks to catch a glimpse of the procession in all its beauty and variety. Young women sat at three rows of shops beside the governor's house, showing off their pretty figures.

Lao and Thai disembarked to go shopping. Vegetables and fish were available in profusion on both banks. Young Lao men went off to flirt, swaggering into the market, swishing their lowercloths to reveal their black legs.[54] One showed off his fine limbs to a southern lady but she turned her face away,

vendors

saying, "You villains with black legs and northern beads, babbling away and eyeing us up, with your dirty hair like clowns in a mask play." She looked over, saw his balls dangling, and ran slap into the shop of an old Mon lady.

"Oh mother, oh lord![55] You spilled a bowl of shrimp paste. You tousled-headed shit eater, why don't you look, bashing in like that all the time.[56] Opening your lowercloth is shameful."

Now to tell of the king at Ayutthaya. He summoned all the chaophraya. "Arrange for our city to be beautifully decked out to look splendid,

so that the Chiang Mai people fear our power as if this were the abode of the fatal Lord of Darkness. Have all the traders, great and small, moor their junks along the banks of the river

together with all the rafts, so that the place looks busy. On both sides of the roads, have rows of shops crammed together. Make sure all the troops are on duty.

Let them see the might of the Thai city so that they are as shocked as if they

---

53. กลองโยน, a type of Thai music usually played by a *piphat* ensemble, especially to accompany recitation of the *City* episode of the Mahachat (see p. 61, note 27).

54. See p. 611, note 45.

55. อุย ย่าย อุย ขมิ, *ui yai ui khami*, in Mon.

56. อะ ค่ำ ราว ยอง เนาะคะเมะ เคลิง, *a kha rao yong no khame khloeng*; from "bashing" in Mon, translation speculative.

were being killed by Lord Matjurat[57] and will all want to flee in panic."

The chaophraya took the order and made obeisance to take leave. Courtiers followed behind, chattering. Officials bustled around, intent on responding to the royal order promptly.

Call-up papers were issued. Elephants and horses were busily organized. Crowds of people rushed hither and thither to get everything arranged.

＜೯

Now to tell of Khun Phaen, in command of the Lao army. At dawn he set off to the sound of hollering, cheering, gongs, drums, and flutes.

The rows of oarsmen paddled in time with the beating of a staff. They came downstream through Ban Ngio[58] and Hua Wang, hollering loudly and making a great racket. To describe the journey in detail would take too long,

so we will hurry ahead with an economical account of places along the route. Everywhere, people rushed in great numbers to sit and watch.

The crowds were big at Mueang In, Mueang Phrom, Phla Mu, Ban Oi, and Phra Ngam.[59] All the way to the river mouth at Ban Phutsa, masses of people sat to watch them pass.

They went through Ban Kaeo and Ban Ri[60] without stopping. Villagers from the district of Tha To[61] came out to look. Mon people from around there powdered their faces, put on lowercloths, and rushed to watch.

The inhabitants of Ban Kup and Ban Tanim[62] collected in a fine crowd along the waterway. At the entrance to the Maha Sang River,[63] they went past

---

57. มัจจุราช, *matjurat*, a name for *yom*, Yama, the god of death.

58. There is a Ban Wat Ngio now in the south of Chainat town on the west bank of the river, and a Ban Ngio further south towards Inburi (see map 2).

59. Sanphaya is in the south of Chainat province, on the west bank, around 15 kms below Chainat town; Ban Oi is 10 kms southwest of Chainat, on the west bank; Phra Ngam may be Tambon Phra Ngam 4 kms south of Phromburi, but more likely Ban Tha Ngam, on the east bank just north of Inburi (see map 2).

60. The Bang Kaeo Canal branches east from the Chaophraya at Ang Thong. Bang Kaeo and Ban Ri are adjacent on the north bank of the canal, 2–3 kms west of Ang Thong. The journey leaves the river here and goes down this canal, one of the two northerly approaches to Ayutthaya at the time (see map 3 and its note).

61. Now Ban Tha To Tok, on the east bank of the Bang Kaeo Canal around 4 kms north of Maharat (see map 3).

62. Close to Maharat, the Ban Chaeng Canal branches from the Bang Kaeo Canal to the west. The journey follows this waterway. Ban Kup and Ban Tanim are on the Ban Chaeng Canal, south of the branch (see map 3).

63. มหาสังข์, possibly this means where the Ban Chaeng Canal rejoins the Ban Kaeo Canal close to Bang Pahan (see map 3).

hollering, and approached the river junction.[64]

Crowds of Mon called out "Oh lord!"[65] and ran down frantically. "Oh mother! Oh father!"[66] They knocked into one another and fell over, giving themselves black faces and bleary eyes.

The flotilla reached Three Bo Trees, where the crowds were raucous. The oarsmen sang boat songs and beat their paddles loudly on the water. At Ban Lao[67] they found themselves among woman traders who left their breasts bare, tying cloths only around their waists.

The traders crowded around to get a look, pushing and shoving, dropping betel and pan all around, climbing down the riverbanks with babes in arms strapped on their waists and wailing.

At Wat Rak Khae,[68] young men and women watched in crowds, pushing and shoving, shouting loudly, scolding at their parents, waving hands up and down with chopping movements.

elephant enclosure

They reached the elephant enclosure,[69] a Mon locality. The throng shouted, "Over there! Oh mother! Look at the boats."[70] Mon fell over, picked themselves up, ran off, and cursed one another. "Your mother![71] Your cane hit my arse."

---

64. See p. 678, note 13 above.

65. อุย แหล่ง, *ui laeng*, in Mon.

66. อุย ย่าย อีตา, *ui yai ita*, in Mon.

67. Now Ban Phut Lao, immediately south of Three Bo Trees (see map 3).

68. Officially Wat Khae, still known colloquially as Wat Rak Khae or Wat Tha Khae, on the west bank of the Old Lopburi River, half a kilometer above the elephant enclosure (see map 8). This area, called Ban Ko Khat, appears in the description of late Ayutthaya as a dense area with markets selling construction materials, cosmetics, metals, and paper. The wat was large, possibly dating back to the Sukhothai era, and may have been the center of a settlement of Lanna war prisoners, but was abandoned after 1767 (APA, 115; *Boranasathan*, 2: 67–70).

69. See p. 729, note 40.

70. อิเนาะ กะม่อน อุมิ ฉิ กำปั้น, *ino kamon u-mi chi kampan*, in Mon.

71. อ้ายตอก ขะย่าย, *ai tok khayai*, in Mon.

The leading boats moored at the landing of the Red Gate,[72] and others moored below the walls right up to the end. People packed every gate and landing, watching open-mouthed.

A jetty broke and crashed down into the water. Granny Mak was bewildered and looked as if she would throw up. Granny Sa, a nun, opened her mouth wide and screamed. Elder Duang cried, "My shoulder robe has been ripped off!"

Granny Ma Rattana, a nun, fell down. Novice Khong and Elder Ngok managed to escape but Nang Baen and Nang San were done for. Abbot Koeng looked on, jiggling his whole body around.

Jek Lok fell flat on his back, hitting Granny Phon. She grabbed him by mistake, thinking it was her husband, Old Leadhead. "Well, he'll do!" Others bashed their heads on stumps or got covered in mud.

Men and women ran up in crowds to see the army. Both banks were jammed. Shouts rang out and hands were raised in salute to celebrate the meritorious power of the victorious monarch.

"The might of our king could defeat the Lao city and the ruler of Chiang Mai!" "They're trailing masses of war prisoners!" "What city will oppose this power and merit?"

"Look, there are the boats of the army commanders." "This father and son are super-powerful." "Khun Phaen was good in the past. He's smart." "The Lord of Life granted him pardon."

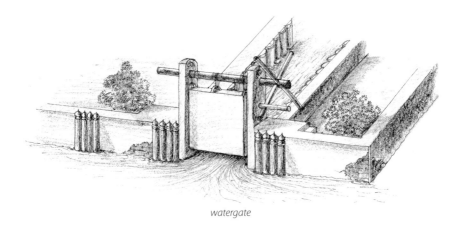

watergate

---

72. ท่า ประตูแดง, *tha pratu daeng*; at the western end of the north wall of the palace, there were four main gates and two ประตูสกัด, *pratu sakat*, probably tunnels through the base of the wall, known as *pratu daeng* (KCK, 205).

Some uninformed people asked, "Which is the boat of Phlai Ngam?" Those in the know said, "That one, the big one with the golden canopy.

Old Khun Phaen, the father, is in the boat in front. Phlai's boat is behind. Look, he's slender, lightly built, and fair." The watchers all stared.

The boats floated to the front of the royal cloister.[73] Seeing Phlai Ngam's good looks, the women were in turmoil. One enthused, "So slight but so much power!"

Another stared, captivated. "If I got him, I'd hug him tight." Another who used to be intimate with other women began to think she had made a mistake in the past.

One lady exaggerated. "See! Phlai is making eyes at me. Is he just trying to get me excited, or is he serious? He's only just got back and he wants a wife!"

Others said, "He wouldn't ask for the hand of people like us. He'd just flirt around, have a free one, and leave us ruined." "Don't be ambitious beyond your station and get mixed up with him. You'll weep and wail over him but he'll take no notice."

When Khun Phaen looked up from his canopy boat, he saw only widows and shy old maids who would be happy with either Phlai Ngam or his father.

The spectators—men and women, Thai and Jek, child and adult—swamped the riverbanks. Reaching the capital, the returning soldiers celebrated that their troubles were over and life would be good.

---

73. ฉนวน, *chanuan*, a covered corridor or cloister, especially for royal use. From Wasukri Landing (see p. 708, note 2), the royal landing in the center of the north wall of the palace, a cloister ran in a dogleg across the palace to Wat Si Sanphet. The gate leading into this passageway was called Chanuan Gate (see map 9).

32: THE PRESENTATION OF SOITHONG AND SOIFA

Khun Phaen, great commander, arrived at the capital feeling pleased at their achievement. He told his son that everybody, Lao and Thai,

should moor at Khan Landing,[1] including the boat of the ruler of Chiang Mai, while the two golden royal barges should moor at Wasukri Landing.[2]

He gave orders to lesser officials and attendants to assemble on the platform of the royal landing. Then he took his son into the inner official sala,

and made obeisance to Chaophraya Jakri. "The flotilla has brought the princesses and the ruler of Chiang Mai to the capital,

but the many Lao families, forest people, have been left in the care of Phichit town along with cattle, buffaloes, carts, horses, elephants, and various military equipment.

We feared that bringing all of that would slow us down so they are left there awaiting a sealed order from the king.

As for the Vientiane Lao who escorted the princess—over three hundred of them—only Kueng Kamkong has been brought down. We wait upon the royal grace."

Chaophraya Jakri was very pleased and had the statement recorded to be read to the king.

Then he turned with a smile and said in praise, "Sirs, you made no mistake in volunteering. Both father and son are wise, brave, and valiant beyond estimation.

You took the city of Chiang Mai in just one breath! The whole realm views you as supreme soldiers. You fulfilled the king's wishes and should be richly

---

1. ท่าคั่น, "boundary landing," so called because it marked the boundary of the palace at the northeast corner. This was the main jetty for nobles entering the palace, sometimes called *tha khoi*, waiting landing, or *tha khunnang*, nobles' landing as "it was the gate where officials moored to enter the palace" (KLW, 200; APA, 59; see map 8).

2. ท่าวาสุกรี, near the middle of the northern wall of the palace, was the jetty for royalty. It had a permanent *chanuan* or cloister to screen royal ladies from public view, and was also called the *tha phrachanuan*. Wasukri, Sanskrit Vasuki, is a lord of the naga. In some versions of the churning of the ocean of milk, including that in the Mahabharata, he forms the rope (KW, 435–6; KP, 298; KLW, 204; *Hindu Myths*, 275; see map 9).

rewarded for your achievement."

He summoned the minister of the capital and said, "Sir, as the Lao ruler's case has not yet been heard by the king, place him under arrest until such time as there's a royal order."

Minister Yommarat assigned royal punishers from the palace guard, and executioners, Jom Jai-at and Fat Jai Kla, to be ready to slash him dead.[3]

Both officers and men wore tight belts and carried Enforcer canes[4] tied in bundles as big as an arm. They brought chains, fetters, and cangue. "Whatever his title is, don't delay."

The ruler of Chiang Mai was clad in irons. Officers and men surrounded him, front and back. Ngam Mueang and Phetpani with their loud voices, Ratchasak, and a deputy of the palace were drafted to accompany them.[5]

King Chiang In's mind was numb, as if on the point of death. His face was pale with grief and he trembled in terror of his penalty.

Seeing the executioners and royal punishers, he thought he would not survive. His whole body streamed with sweat. In despair, he bowed his head and kept silent.

⊷

Chaophraya[6] Jakri, Chaophraya Yommarat, and the military chiefs greeted one another with smiles and conferred together on how to present the matter to the king.

nobles conferring in the palace

3. Yommarat is the name of the minister of the capital. ราชมัล, *ratchaman*, royal punishers, are officials who enforce royal punishments, two officers in the Ministry of the Palace with titles of Phan Phithakthiwa and Phan Raksaratri, *sakdina* 200. The two executioners have *muen* rank and also fearful names: Bold Attack, and Daring Slash. In the Wat Ko version, this list of intimidating guards also includes ประแดงจัน, Pradaengjan, a *samian tra* in the Ministry of the Capital, *sakdina* 600. (KP, 300; KW, 437; KTS, 1:230, 241; WK, 27:1075)

4. อ้ายถนัด, *ai thanat*, "the effective fellow," name of a type of cane (KP, 300).

5. จำเมือง, Khun Ngam Mueang, a court official under the Ministry of the Capital, *sakdina* 800; เพชรปาณี, Khun Phetpani, the deputy (*palat thun chalong*, see p. 510, note 52) under the Ministry of the Capital, *sakdina* 1,000; ราชศักดิ์, Khun Ratchasak, a *khun dap* officer in the left division of the main royal guard; the two deputies in the guard under the Ministry of the Palace were Nai Prakatmonthian and Nai Sathianraksa, both *sakdina* 600. Several units of guard participate in the imprisoning of such an important figure in order to display the king's power and to intimidate the victim. (KTS, 1:229, 237, 288; KW, 437)

6. This section, down to "bustled off," is taken from WK, 27:1076, absent from PD.

Khun Phaen, Phlai Ngam, and Phra Thainam, followed by their servants, came to pay respect. Khun Phaen bowed and crawled in. Reaching the senior officials, he spoke to them in a whisper.

"Please help the lord of Chiang Mai to avoid heavy punishment. Please arrange matters with the king so that he escapes the lash and is reprieved.

I'll provide thirty beautiful Lao girls as reward for your lordships' assistance." The ministers were pleased and laughed so hard

that they bent over double, bashing their heads together and bumping their bottoms into one another. They stopped whispering and spoke out loud, "So you say that royal horse is dead?"

Khun Phaen replied, "Indeed, sir." A minister said, "I'll tell His Majesty." As it was close to the time of the king's appearance, they put on their sompak and bustled off.

When the streaks of dawn marked the time, Chaophraya Jakri, Chaophraya Kalahom, and the four-pillar ministers entered the palace.

Civil and military officials were massed to left and right. Inside the palace, Chaophraya Jakri gave orders to Khun Phaen and his son.

"Wait in front of the golden audience hall. I'll report the matter to the king from start to finish. Then I'll present you to the royal foot.

The king will probably ask you about the war. Keep everything in mind. Don't forget the facts. Tell the truth.

My only worry is about Phra Thainam. The king will be critical of what he did but your victory should give him some help. Wait at the swordstore by the gate."

When it was almost time for the audience, all the officers, pages, and palace officials crowded into the resplendent audience hall of victory.

Now to tell of the king, preserver of the world, annihilator of the people's misery, the fount of happiness and prosperity, who resided under a brilliant jeweled spire,

with consorts and palace ladies waiting in attendance beside the royal bed. When the sun's rays pierced through the window, he left the bedchamber

and went to make his ablutions in fragrant water. He was arrayed in a lowercloth with a Garuda pattern on a red background, and a belt with a jeweled filigree buckle.

Holding a supreme short sword in his left

royal regalia

hand, and trailed by throngs of ladies carrying regalia, he walked out from the inner palace to the jeweled audience hall,

sat on a royal throne, looking as fine as the god-king of Traitrueng,[7] and gave orders for all the high officials and courtiers to enter the audience hall of victory.

Ministers and other officials of the departments all crawled in to attend on the king of the three worlds.[8] They prostrated and waited on their knees.

Chaophraya Jakri saluted and addressed the king. "My liege, Your Majesty, my life is under the royal foot.

Khun Phaen and Phlai Ngam, who went to war, have brought the troops back to the landing, along with the villainous lord of Chiang Mai, and two golden royal barges under close guard.

They bring royal levies of gold, silver, and other goods as follows: cash, 70 chests in total; Lao families, 5,000 in total; able-bodied young men, 1,150;

large cannons, 200; small guns, 3,000; spears with feather plumes, 1,000 exactly; swords belonging to the war prisoners themselves, 1,200; swords from the main arsenal, almost 500;

elephants, 305; horses, 800; cattle of all sizes in great numbers. There are no injuries among our officers and men owing to the meritorious power of Your Majesty.

The villainous ruler of Chiang Mai has been placed in chains under all five irons according to procedure. What is to be done or not done in his case awaits Your Majesty's wishes."

On hearing about Khun Phaen, the almighty king, eminence of the Ayutthaya realm, felt he had been transported to the heavenly city of sixteen levels.[9]

---

7. ไตรตรึงษา, the realm of the thirty-three gods, sometimes called Daowadueng, the second of the six heavens ruled by Indra, situated on the peak of Mount Meru. "Right at the peak of the royal Sumeru mountain there are gem palaces and gem *prangs*, and there are a great many places for play and amusement, which provide for a great deal of fun" (RR, 223). Indra's Wetchayan Palace is situated in this heaven.

8. ". . . a pair of Stairs of ten or twelve steps, by which we went up into the Hall of Audience at *Siam*, exceeded not two foot in breadth. They were of Brick joining to the Wall on the right side, and without any Rail on the left. But the *Siamese* Lords minded it not; they went up crawling on their Hands and Knees; and so softly, that they might have said that they would surprise the King their Master" (La Loubère, *New Historical Relation*, 31).

9. โสฬส, *solot*, a Pali word for sixteen. This phrase refers to the sixteen Brahma realms that constitute the "world with only a remnant of material factors," the middle section of the Three Worlds cosmology between the "world of sensual desire" and the "world without material factors." At the various levels of this sphere, beings are able to lift themselves upwards by mental application (RR, 49–50, 245–47).

"This Chiang In who insulted me badly will today show his face here. He used to be very boastful and disrespectful but now that we have him, his head has shrunk at once.

This war was no joke. On reflection, it was a major conflict. Because of the complex background, it was not an ordinary battle.

This fellow had captured our people, and it was known he would kill them if we attacked. The father and son infiltrated their city and deftly rescued them in time.

When it came to battle, it would have been wasteful to blunder into a siege of their city since their numbers were many times ours, and it would have been impossible to reduce them by killing.

The father and son were good at military ploys. They stole in and captured the ruler of Chiang Mai, thus cutting off the risk at source. Once he was caught, it was all over.

They must be praised and accorded royal appreciation. High rank should be conferred on them. Bring them in immediately. And bring that thick-faced Thainam too."

The minister turned to speak to a palace guard at the front. "Summon Thainam, Khun Phaen, and his son, Phlai Ngam—all three."

The palace guard crawled out backwards and conveyed the message first to Khun Phaen. "His Majesty, eminence of the world, has sent for you three."

Khun Phaen and Phlai Ngam happily put on sompak and hastened to enter the audience hall.

Only Phra Thainam was in a pitiful state. Hearing the words of the palace official, he felt seized by a fever. He put on his sompak, trembling with fear, and followed behind in a daze.

Khun Phaen and Phlai Ngam entered first, while Phra Thainam dragged his feet at the back. They prostrated, crawled along behind a palace guard, and crouched waiting for a royal command.

Pleased to see the father and son, the king roared like a lion, "Now, Khun Phaen and Phlai Ngam!

It's no bad thing that you're of military lineage, brave and expert on the field of battle. I sent you off to this war with only thirty-five soldiers.

Chiang Mai city has over a hundred thousand troops but when you attacked, the Lao warriors could not stand up to you and were pulverized. We recovered our men because of your handiwork.

On the spot, you thought out a smart and daring way to capture the ruler of Chiang Mai. Also they say there was a lot of fighting at the end of the lake. Don't hide and mumble. Tell us what happened."

Khun Phaen, great master, made obeisance and reported. "Owing to the power of Your Majesty, monarch of the three worlds, victory was gained and the city taken.

I volunteered to go with thirty-five able soldiers. We made use of powerful knowledge and the meritorious power of Your Majesty.

We went up to the great lake and made camp there. We talked and agreed together that just the two of us, Phlai Ngam and myself,

would enter disguised as Lao. We enchanted everybody to sleep and went up to the main jail at the third watch. We found Phra Thainam without difficulty, and all of them followed us out,

including the Vientiane people. Together we killed many guards, broke into the armory to seize weapons, stole horses for everybody from the stables,

and seized tuskers from their camp. That afternoon, when a horde of Lao troops came, we went out to give combat. The Lao armies broke and scattered.

That same day, Phlai Ngam and I enchanted everyone to sleep, entered the palace at nightfall, and captured the ruler of Chiang Mai. The ruler gave his word

that he would beg to be a servant under the dust of the royal foot, and offer his life and throne if required. Since that day, he has not wavered. I submit my report under the foot of Your Victorious Majesty."

The king was matchlessly happy at hearing this report. "This lineage of Khun Krai does not fail! Both his son and grandson are skillful and clever.

As for this old fellow, the ruler of Chiang Mai, I'll let him go. I won't execute him. Even though he acted arrogantly, it would be wrong to call it a revolt.

His city is of primary rank[10] and outside the dominion of the capital of Ayutthaya. Now that he's submitted and agreed to offer tribute, he should not be put to death.

If I were to execute him in revenge, who would trust Ayutthaya in the future? But if he acts improperly again, he should be punished with his life.

Khun Phaen and Phlai Ngam, you have won my appreciation, and I will reward you accordingly. Khun Phaen is appointed governor of Kanburi with fine insignia of rank—casket, saber,

umbrella, flask, golden betel box—and royal gifts of an elephant howdah

---

10. See p. 654, note 7.

and palanquin for use in war, all in keeping with the royal appreciation you have won.

I appoint you as the illustrious Phra Surintharuechai Mahaisunphakdi."[11] The king commanded the minister of the treasury[12] to give fifteen chang in cash as reward,

along with a sompak in flower-patterned silkwool and many royal gifts. "As for you, Phlai Ngam, you shall also have rank to show for it.

You're still a youth, very quick and strong, and should be retained for service close at hand. I'll give you an appointment that will be to your liking, and fitting for someone who took a city.

You become Muen Wai Woranat, lieutenant of the royal pages, guard of the right side,[13] and will receive royal gifts of insignia, cash, silkwool, and various cloth."

Then the king said, "This Wai who has done so well doesn't have a house. A lieutenant on his own is not good. I must set him up in a house.

Minister Yommarat! Send a requisition to the district officer to acquire land for a house for Wai in the city. Make sure it's close to the palace."

The king then gave orders to a department head of the palace guard, "Build a house of around five units including a kitchen and fence around the compound. Make it befitting with his appointment as Phra Wai."

Turning to find Phra Thainam, the king looking angry enough to slaughter him. He roared like a lion, "Mm! Thainam, you did a fine job!

It was a waste of my time to like you and promote you to high rank. I didn't know you'd be a coward from a tribe of cowards. I wrongly trusted you as a soldier but the Lao trussed you up like a monkey.

You didn't even fight back to scare them off. Pah! A heart like a woman! A

11. พระสุรินทฤๅไชย มไหสูรย์ภักดี, great Indra loyal to the great power. According to the Three Seals Law, the title for the governor of Kanburi, a third class city, was Okphra Phichaiphakdi Simahaisawan, *sakdina* 800. However, the title here may have a trace of the title found in an older document, Okphra Kanchanaburi Mahaisawan. Khun Wichitmatra notes the title given to Khun Phaen is similar to titles used for various posts in late Ayutthaya (KTS, 1:324; Suphawat, "Phra aiyakan kao," 342; KW, 439).

12. พระคลัง, *phrakhlang*, originally meaning the royal warehouse. From mid Ayutthaya onwards, this department oversaw trade and foreign relations. The title of the minister was Chaophraya Kosathibodi, *sakdina* 10,000 (KTS, 1:233).

13. Wai Woranat is the title of one of the four deputy heads of the royal pages (see p. 16, note 75). A former holder of this title appeared in chapter 13. Here the exact wording is Jamuen. His title oscillates between Muen, Jamuen, Phramuen, and Phra in the text, but he is referred to as Phra Wai in the translation. หัวหมื่น, *hua muen*, "head ten thousand," lieutenant, is a rank derived from old Thai decimal-based systems, used for both military and civilian officials. The right division was on duty at night (KW, 439).

terrible failure, truly abominable! Sitting there and letting yourself be captured was shameful.

If Khun Phaen had not come to help, you'd still be tied up in jail, being thrashed with two canes. For causing his master to lose face, this atrocious fellow is reduced to phrai status and put to work as a gatekeeper."

The king commanded a department head of the front guard to fetch the ruler of Chiang Mai, and sent Phraya Thamma[14] to escort the two princesses to the inner palace.

The guard rushed to tell the jail governor that the king had summoned the ruler of Chiang Mai. The ruler was lifted by both upper arms and carried in. He prostrated, trembling in fear.

The king roared loudly like a lion, "Heigh! Lord[15] of Chiang Mai, you black-guard! Your actions have displeased me.

You seized a princess, imprisoned some Thai, and even sent a missive with a challenge to war. What should be the punishment for such arrogance? Don't remain quiet. Answer right now."

The ruler of Chiang Mai dripped with sweat and shivered in every pore, feeling his chest was on fire and his body buried under the earth.

He replied with a confession. "Your Victorious Majesty has given favor over my head. The errors committed in the past by this servant of the royal foot deserve punishment with his life.

If, by your grace, I am not executed but receive royal pardon for my wrong-doing, let me be a servant of the foot of Your Majesty, and keep my word to act with rectitude until death.

Let me present my kingly wealth and the great territory of Lanna to be placed under the royal foot, and let me depend on the bo-tree shelter of your accumulated merit from now on."[16]

The king heard the ruler of Chiang Mai out. "Now that you show proper awareness and fear, I will pardon you this time,

and send you back to rule Chiang Mai. Make sure you keep your word to

14. Phraya Thammathibodi, minister of the palace, one of the four pillars, *sakdina* 10,000 (KTS, 1:237).

15. King Phanwasa avoids addressing the Chiang Mai ruler with a clearly regal title. Here he addresses him as Phraya. When referring to him in the third person, King Phanwasa usually uses *jao chiang mai*, translated as "ruler of Chiang Mai."

16. See p. 19, note 86.

Ayutthaya and maintain friendly relations forever according to the example of other countries' rulers."

The king ordered senior officials of Mahatthai and the military to take the ruler of Chiang Mai to swear loyalty and drink the waters of allegiance.

He had a lodging prepared to accommodate the ruler as an official guest, with walls dividing inner from outer sections[17] so that he and his entourage would feel comfortable.

"Distribute supplies of food, clothing, and bedding. Provide a place for the soldiers and servants to sleep. Minister of the capital, make sure no one bothers them."

Next, the king ordered rewards of cash and cloth for the thirty-five soldiers who went to war, and to the porters following the army.[18]

"They are exempt from royal service, city work, and all other duties. They will be attached to *athamat*, and will be called up in the future if an army threatens.

Give each of them a sealed order exempting them from farmed taxes, customs levies, and market dues. Draw up a list of all of them with unit heads, and place them under Phra Wai.

As for the Lanchang Lao officers and men who escorted Princess Soithong, requisition silver and cloth to give them, and send them all back to Vientiane."

Coming to the end of his words, the king left the glittering audience hall, and walked up to the palace of victory.

Phraya Thammathibodi went promptly to a palace gate and told the governesses[19] inside to assign people

palace governesses

to fetch the two princesses,

---

17. That is, in the style befitting a king, with an inner section for private life and an outer section for public affairs. This phrase indicates that Chiang In is now recognized as a monarch and guest of the city (KW, 440).

18. Schedules of rewards for success in war were listed in the Law on Revolt and Warfare, for example clause 36: "for ordinary soldiers who killed enemy soldiers, defeated their army, or put them to flight, gift of one chang, a golden tray of cloth, and the rank of *khun asa*; anyone who engaged and defeated an enemy soldier, five tamlueng; anyone who fought two enemies and survived, a golden bowl and cloth, with elevation to the rank of *khun* if he also captured the enemy's weapons" (KTS, 4:141–42).

19. ท้าวนาง, *thao nang*, "lady lords," the general term for senior officials in the ladies' inner quarters of the palace.

and arrange for golden palanquins with curtains embroidered in golden silk appliqué. The two princesses came, looking handsome, along with a throng of old palace governesses.

The beautiful Princess Soithong was invited to enter the leading palanquin, with Princess Soifa behind. The governesses led the way into the inner palace,

and hastened to arrange a residence and attendants so that Soithong and Soifa could stay without any inconvenience while awaiting the king's orders.

∽

Now to tell of the king, auspicious crown of the heavenly abode of Ayutthaya, who resided in a crystal and golden palace, surrounded by consorts and palace ladies making obeisance.

After the passing of the sun, the moon's chariot glided aloft, stars glittered in the sky, and moonlight bathed the earth in a cool glow.

Inside the palace was as bright as a heavenly city under the moonlight. A gentle breeze blew. The king's thoughts turned to the two princesses.

"Word has already spread to the lower city that Soithong, daughter of the ruler of Vientiane, is the supreme beauty of Lanchang, desired by everyone in the three worlds.

Then there's young Princess Soifa, the illustrious daughter of the ruler of Chiang Mai. How splendid are her looks?" With these thoughts, he gave orders to the head royal governess.

On the king's command, Thao Worajan[20] went to tell the two princesses to be dressed. Their faces were powdered to have complexions like moonlight,

their hair was coiled into chignons to suit their faces, fastened with hairpins of sparkling crystal filigree, and embellished with beautiful flowers. They were decked with glittering tasseled earrings in both ears,

gold bangles on each arm, and rings on every finger of both hands. They wore yok woven with dazzling gold, and uppercloths of silk embroidered with gold.

Looking as supremely beautiful as *kinnari*, the two walked in file, led by the head governess, to the golden spire to attend on the royal foot.

The head governess made obeisance with clasped hands. "Princess Soithong is the one prostrating on the right, while Princess Soifa is on the left."

---

20. See p. 315, note 23.

The almighty king looked at them. Both were suitably attractive to be royal daughters but the manner of each was different.

He examined Soithong. She had a superb, radiant face, and a gentle, graceful loveliness in every respect—fitting to be the cynosure of the Lao country.

She seemed quiet and reserved, with a youthful beauty and friendly manners befitting a young lady. "So this was why she became so famous in the Lao country that Chiang Mai heard and tried to seize her."

Then he turned to examine Soifa, and saw she had an affected manner. "Her poise and bearing are truly good. Her only fault is that she looks sulky.

Her eyes are very sharp, and they dart around. After a quick glance, I feel bored straightaway. With her beautifully slim and curvy waist, she's like a drama actress.[21]

She has the slenderness and elegance of a racing boat. A clumsy oarsman would come close to capsizing." He looked at her thin lips and rounded chin. "These are an indication that she's talkative for sure.

If she were a horse, you'd be wary of mounting her; if an elephant, the type that must be pleased. Even if decked with a golden harness as a royal mount, a careless rider could get hurt.

Soithong, the daughter of Lanchang, has both rank and good manners. But this Princess Soifa looks frightening." The king whispered to Thao Worajan,

"Governess, what do you make of the manner of these two young ladies? Do they look as if they'll please me or not? Soithong's manner looks good but Soifa has the bearing of a drama actress.

I could keep her as an inner elephant[22] and have a trial ride to see first. But on second thoughts, I'm not so sure. I fear I'm getting old. How should I resolve this?"

Knowing the king's disposition, the head governess prostrated and said, "I think your appraisal is correct.

Princess Soithong has the right attributes. Her appearance is beautiful in every way but Soifa looks affected and unsuitable to be beside the royal foot.

Her manner looks like a boat hit by waves, pitching and tossing and spinning around. I'm afraid she'll displease Your Majesty like a bucking horse that needs to be controlled.

Though her figure with no sagging flabbiness will appeal to you, she will

---

21. In late Ayutthaya, actresses were associated with prostitution. "At the back of Ban Jin market at the mouth of the Khlong Khun Lakhonchai Canal, actress-prostitutes have set up four halls where they provide men with sex for hire" (KLW, 175).

22. ช้างระวางใน, chang rawang nai, an elephant adopted as a royal elephant and given a title (SB, 466).

be the source of royal displeasure and will not make you bloom with joy.

She's not like the lovely Princess Soithong, who merits praise and the king's desire. Her manner seems suitable to support the foot of Your Victorious Majesty.

If Princess Soifa is to enter royal service, the level of lady attendant seems adequate.[23] May Your Majesty, ruler of the three worlds, make the appropriate decision."

After hearing the head governess, the king smiled. "I'm bored with difficult women and sick of being displeased.

But if I keep her only as an attendant, she'll feel it's a debasement and loss of face since she's the daughter of a ruler. Better to have her married off.

Now then! Phlai Ngam has won royal favor and has gained rank in a big way, along with property, a house, and servants, but he still has no wife to carry water.[24]

I'll keep him under my patronage, and I'd already thought of finding him a wife. If we leave him unattached, he might seize upon some low person who'll prejudice his good knowledge.

He's now Muen Wai Woranat, lieutenant of the royal pages in close service to me. The ruler of Chiang Mai at this moment is indebted to him for his support.

I don't think it'll anger the ruler. If I make the request, he should grant her accordingly. That will settle the issue of Soifa and give face to Phra Wai.

It seems a wholly appropriate solution. How do you feel, governess? If Phra Wai gets Soifa, will it benefit me?"

The head royal governess prostrated at the royal foot and showed respect for the royal consideration. She responded following the king's gist. "It is fitting for Your Majesty to give her to Phra Wai.

Since he has taken the Lao city, news has spread throughout the domain. If Your Majesty grants him Soifa as wife, it will strengthen his loyalty."

The almighty king, supreme eminence of the capital, listened to the governess endorsing his own wishes, and said, "Mm. This Wai is right for Soifa."

He turned to talk with Princess Soithong. "Don't be sad. I will keep you in a state befitting a royal daughter of Si Sattana, bestowed on me by your father in friendship."

---

23. นางพนักงาน, *nang phanak ngan*, a general term for staff rather than consorts in the palace.

24. ถือน้ำ, *thue nam*, meaning to attend the ceremony of drinking the water of allegiance. The major wife of a noble attended this ceremony with her husband, and thereby reaffirmed her status as the major wife.

He commanded attendants of the Inner Treasury[25] to arrange suitable royal gifts of a gold cloisonné betel box, twenty chang of silver, golden bowl,

wasp-nest ring, snake ring, tasseled diamond earrings, bodice[26] with ornamental glass, golden yok, silk yok, and embroidered sabai. He also gave gifts to her ladies-in-waiting

and arranged a residence in the large group of brick buildings,[27] along with servants to provide for her every happiness. Then he talked to Princess Soifa. "Don't be upset.

Although your father rashly made me angry, I have pardoned him. When his royal service is over, he'll return home, and I'll be father to young Soifa.

bodice

I'll look after you so you're not ashamed before your peers. In the future I'll arrange a good marriage for you so that you have face and nobody can cavil about me.

You'll stay in the inner palace. The head governess will arrange a residence for you. See to this matter, governess, including a retinue to ensure she's comfortable.

If you miss your father and mother, have a palace matron[28] escort you over." When the king had given his orders, the head royal governess led Soifa away.

---

25. คลังใน, *khlang nai*, one of the "twelve treasuries" (see p. 563, note 59). The Three Seals Law lists Inner Treasuries of the left and right headed by Phra Rachaiyamahasuriyathibodi and Phra Sombathiban, both *sakdina* 3,000. The left one stored paper, oil for umbrellas, tea, thread, soap, sugar, black tin, blinds, benzoin, saltpeter, alum, copper sulfate, kapok, candles, beeswax, mortars, salt, and gum in earthenware containers. The right one stored metal items and teak items including barrels, trays, and planks. The Inner Treasury was adjacent to the outer palace wall by the Crystal Pond, สระแก้ว, *sa kaeo*, on the south side of the palace, close to Wat Si Sanphet. (KTS, 1:270–71; APA, 132; SWC, 14:6769; see map 9, area 7)

26. ก้อง, *kong*, an ornamental bodice, now usually associated with costume for traditional dance.

27. There were several *tamnak* (residences) around the palace compound. However, the wording here recalls the particular group known as the *phra tamnak thuek (yai),* the (large) brick residence. This was in the inner part of the palace, to the south of the pool surrounding the Banyong Rattanat Throne Hall. It was originally built for King Narai's queen and daughter, Yothathip and Yothathep, and later used for the Inner Treasury. The foundations can still be seen. (APA, 70; *Phraratchawang lae wat boran*, 7; see map 9)

28. เฒ่าแก่, *thao kae*, an official of the inner palace. Both components of the name mean old.

In the bright shining light of dawn, the king went out to the jeweled audience hall.

The officers and courtiers of every grouping gathered. Now that he had escaped punishment, the ruler of Chiang Mai came to attend on the royal foot.

The king pondered on the border territories. "As the ruler of Chiang Mai has set his mind, he should be allowed to keep his rank."

So he said, "Ha! Heigh! Ruler of Chiang Mai, I'm sending you back home along with your servants, phrai, and palace women. You can take everything back.

Return to look after your palace and territory. Protect them against military threats from north and south. If an enemy beyond your powers appears in any direction, send word down here."

The ruler of Chiang Mai felt he was flying in the sky with happiness. He bowed and prostrated to the king. "May I serve the royal foot until death.

If in the future I break my word and incur your anger, have me executed. As guarantee that I will not lapse, may I offer my daughter under the royal foot."

The almighty king smiled and laughed. "Go to your city, ruler of Chiang Mai. You and your daughter may travel to visit each other without hindrance.

I'm very grateful that you've bestowed on me your beloved child. But when I saw her face, I made up my mind to ask for Soifa to be given to Phlai Ngam.

They're very compatible. The daughter of Chiang Mai is enchanting, while Phlai Ngam excels in knowledge. They'll make a happy couple.

Don't be disappointed about his low rank. I love Phlai Ngam like my own son, and he is now lieutenant of the royal pages, so you may consider the two of us connected."

The ruler of Chiang Mai's heart sank in mortification over the honor of his solar lineage. He sighed, trembled, and was too choked to speak.

He thought of Soifa. "Oh what a pity. She shouldn't descend to mixing with servants but if I object, it'll irritate the royal foot." Out of necessity, he prostrated in gratitude.

"I've presented you with my daughter to be a servant of the royal foot until death. If the king wishes to grant her to Phra Wai, that is the royal privilege.

This Phra Wai has gained honor. He's a shrewd, talented fellow of military lineage and should remain in royal service in the future. I'll depend on him from now on."

The king, ruler of the world, said, "If there's any crisis, I'll make use of the services of young Wai.

Return to your city where your family is waiting forlornly so that both lords and phrai may be happy every night and day." The king went into the inner palace.

King Chiang In, eminence of his people, returned to his lodging and related the royal order to his wife.

Queen Apson was happy about going home but sad about her daughter, her life's jewel.

She sent I-Mai to tell Soifa to come quickly. Soifa took leave of the governess and was escorted over by an old retainer and sentinelles.

At her father's residence, Soifa raised her hands in wai and prostrated at his feet. The ruler of Chiang Mai hugged his daughter and sadly said, "Your father and mother will leave you and return home.

Because we had you to present to the king, his anger abated and our city was restored, but you will stay in his capital. He wishes to present you to Phra Wai. I'm beyond grief, my jewel."

Soifa felt she would writhe to death. She lowered her face, embraced her father's feet with both arms, and lamented.

"Oh my lord and master, you'll leave your child and flee away. Though we'd fallen on bad times, being close to Mother and Father gave me some warmth and affection.

Since I'm being presented in order to save lives, I've no thought of deviating from your wish. Even if you had me fetch water or carry a palanquin, I would not refuse but would repay your kindness.

I'm unhappy about only one matter—having a husband. My lord, I'm not used to such a thing! How can I manage a household in the Thai style when I don't know the customs?

I'll be blamed, mocked, and shamed before the people of Ayutthaya. They'll criticize me all year round. I'll suffer ignominy and humiliation.

The main point is that the person who'll be my husband does not love me. I'm given by the king.[29] If my husband has no mercy, he'll curse and mistreat me at will.

If he tramples over me, even hitting and slapping, how can I fight back or

---

29. A wife granted by the king was one of four categories of wives recognized in the Law on Inheritance along with a wife by regular ceremony, a wife requested from the king, and a slave wife. In this law, a wife granted by the king has superior rights (KTS, 3:26–27).

where can I flee? I'll be on my own among the Thai with nobody to depend on in difficult times.

I'll cry myself to death, and my father and mother will be too far away to help. How can I survive this? I'll probably die." Soifa was bathed in tears of sorrow.

Filled with regret over his daughter, the ruler of Chiang Mai sat shaking and sighing deeply. Then he braced himself, swallowed his tears, and consoled her with a caress.

"It's our karma, my darling. Since your birth, I've never forced you against your will, but this time I'm at my wits' end. You're like a patron to your father,

also to our kinsfolk, and to the common people, who are in great difficulty as war prisoners captured by their army. You're helping them survive.

If we didn't have you to present to the king, all would probably die in this southern city. But you are enough to win the king's trust so he allows us to return up to our city.

The king asked for your hand for Phra Wai. I wasn't happy to consent, but opposing the king's command would have seemed insulting so I had to follow his order and agree.

One thing—the king has undertaken to support you in a befitting manner. As he's gracious towards you, you must depend on him.

If there's any trouble in the future, you can attend in audience and address him. As for Phra Wai, when he went up to trample our city,

he was our enemy and used force because he was acting on behalf of his king. Now that we've submitted, he should also relax and you two can become intimate.

He should view matters with the friendship that existed before. Also, you're being presented to him as wife by the king. If a point of conflict should arise, I don't think he'll shame you by beating or cursing.

Anyway, to protect you against danger, I'll give you Elder Khwat, who's adept with lore and exceptional powers, and also another junior official, Khanan Ai.

Your mother will probably select some women who've been with you from the start and who you can truly trust to be your close attendants. Though I'm going back to the northern city, you won't be neglected.

As for being a housekeeper, just follow the example of your own mother. She's truly good. Anything you've never done, just ask her, my sweet."

Queen Apson called Soifa into the main apartment. Pitying her daughter, she caressed and consoled her. "Don't cry too much, dear child.

Nobody born as an ordinary human being can escape sorrow. It depends on karma made in the past. When a time for happiness is over, sorrow begins.

When a time for sorrow passes, then happiness returns again. This has been the nature of things forever. There's no need for fear.

Your father presented you to gain pardon. In effect, you made it possible for him to recover the country, just like the two children, Kanha and Chali, helped their father to gain enlightenment.[30]

Your good deed will earn great merit and benefit you in the future. Don't be reluctant and disheartened. Bow your face and repay your father's kindness.

Don't be afraid because the king is arranging for you to have a husband. There should be nothing wrong. Women everywhere have husbands because sensual desire is part of human nature.

Though your partner is from far away and speaks a different language, and you're not even familiar with each other's faces, the main thing is that he's a good person. So you will have happiness not sorrow.

Phra Unnarut and Nang Usa were foreign to each other—from different cities far apart. While Usa slept, the god took her to Unnarut, and the couple loved each other intimately.[31]

When I was in the bloom of youth, I lived far away in the city of Chiang Tung.[32] When your grandfather was ruler of Chiang Mai, he went to ask for my hand, and I saw your father's face only on the wedding day.

He hadn't seen me either, only heard about my appearance. We've now lived

---

30. In the Wetsandon Chadok (Vessantara Jataka), these are the two children that Phra Wetsandon gives away and thereby achieves the "perfection of giving," the last of the ten perfections, which enable him to be reborn as the Buddha in his next life (see p. 61, note 27).

31. Anirut or Unnarut is a romance based on the Krishna stories from India. It was composed as a Thai poem in the seventeenth century and subsequently adapted to many forms, especially as a drama by King Rama I, tentatively dated to 1787. In this episode, which occurs in chapters 15–16 of the Rama I version, Unnarut, the grandson of Vishnu, follows a golden deer into the forest and falls asleep at the foot of a large banyan tree. Upon waking, he orders his servants to make a sumptuous offering to the spirit of the tree. To return this gratitude, the spirit puts a charm on Unnarut and conducts him to Nang Usa, the beautiful daughter of a giant, Thao Krung Phan. To avoid complications that might arise from their respective human and divine origins, the spirit also casts a mantra to render them both dumb. They make love, then fall asleep. The spirit transports Unnarut back to where he had been, but Usa's father resolves to kill him. Unnarut defeats and kills the father and takes Usa back to his kingdom.

In Indian versions, Aniruddha ("without obstacles") is an associate or grandson of Krishna, or another avatar of Vishnu like Krishna himself. Usa is a princess who has Aniruddha magically lured to her city, where he is abducted by a rival deity, Bana, provoking a grand battle ending with Bana defeated and Aniruddha marrying Usa.

32. The old capital of the Tai Yai or Shan, sometimes called Kengtung or Jengtung, now in northeastern Burma. The cities of Chiang Mai and Chiang Tung have been closely related back to the beginning of their recorded histories in the thirteenth century.

together for a long time without any falling out.

The matter of lovemaking depends on the love in the heart. When you're together with him, you'll be moved by the passion inside. Once you know the taste, you'll shed any fear.

The first time a young man and woman are intimate as husband and wife, usually they get carried away in kisses and caresses as if they'd gone up to the Traitrueng[33] level of heaven.

elephant and mahout

When you lie beside him on the pillow for the very first time, don't be fearful or you'll make him tense and angry. After many days, when all the caressing dwindles, that's when you'll know each other.

Men by nature are like elephants. If the mahout knows how to treat them, they're hardworking. But at times when they're in musth, the mahout must know how to make allowances for the sake of harmony.

It's normal that a woman with a husband must defer to him in fear he may use force. As long as that husband still protects her, it doesn't matter if other people laugh.

But if a husband leaves the wife lonely and forlorn, it's like the end of her life, her name, her flesh and blood. Women deserted by their husbands are smirked at by people wherever they go.

Finding a new husband to repair the loss, a suitable one, is very difficult because you've lost the specialness of your virginity. As with something hollowed out by beetles, people don't like it.

For this reason, when you have a husband, don't be negligent. If you make a mistake, it's like life is over. You must please him every day so you win his undying affection.

Show him respect. Don't alienate him by your manner or words. If you want to arouse him, or if there's something annoying you, deal with it in secret when there are no people around.

Observe what he likes—in food and everything else—and then do what you can without him having to force you. Make him feel you're a truly good housekeeper.

The most important thing for a wife in pleasing her husband is her own body. If she makes him happy, he won't abandon her. The next thing to win his heart is food.

If she can cook to please his palate, he won't abandon her even when she's

---

33. See p. 711, note 7 above.

old and no longer pretty, but will be pleading to eat her food every day. Make sure you prepare a variety of dishes.

Know how to make delicious boiled pig's trotters, for example. Take trouble over fresh chicken eggs, fish, and *tomyam*. Chop up spleen, loin, and testicle into tiny pieces the way the Jek do.

Try to feed him to his liking. He may find himself a pretty new wife but if she doesn't have a cook's touch,[34] he'll get over the infatuation before too long.

Your father has about three hundred forbidden ladies. No matter. I don't let him slip away easily. He gets these girls and goes gaga over them, but as soon as he's bored, he misses me every time.

Why is he stupid over these Lao girls? Though they're beautiful, they're dumb as corpses. I still admire your grandmother's cleverness. She was not in my situation until she was very old.

Being a woman is about ministering to men's needs. Anyone who does it well finds the husband loves her greatly. If you do as I tell you, it's better than a love charm buried the whole year round.[35]

Soifa raised her hands to her head to accept her mother's words. "When you go away, Mother, may you be well. When a year has passed, send someone to let me know you're happy, as that knowledge will lessen my sorrow." The two of them grieved enough to faint away.

The sun descended and weakened in the late afternoon. The King and Queen of Chiang Mai were distraught at leaving their daughter. "It's almost time for you to go into the palace."

The queen took off a nine-peak ring and gave it to her daughter. "Even sold very cheap, it'll fetch ten chang. Keep it to pawn in the palace when you face helpless poverty."

She selected Lao girls to be her daughter's retinue—first young Mai as her nursemaid, then four others who were just of age with good appearance. "Keep them as your friends, dear child."

Then she gave strict orders to Mai. "Don't consider yourself as a servant but think of her as your younger sister from the same womb. Try to look after each other and teach each other.

It's almost time they close the gate, Mother's jewel. Hurry back into the palace. May you be eternally happy. May danger and evil not cross your path."

---

34. Literally, the charm at the end of the ladle.
35. See chapter 37 in *Companion* on burying love charms.

Soifa felt her breast would break apart. She prostrated at the feet of her mother and father with tears flowing down in despair.

It was very late with no time for delay but she was loath to rush into the palace. As the sun had almost set, others were worried about her reluctance to go.

The palace matrons warned it was getting dark. Soifa shuddered and sighed at having to leave her parents. She kept on grieving until she entered the palace.

The King of Chiang Mai's tears flowed with the sorrow of parting. His eyes followed Soifa until she disappeared behind a wall. Then he sat quietly sobbing.

Queen Apson wept so much that the whole group of palace ladies gave way to grief.

After they had gradually recovered, the king summoned his officers and said, "The King of Ayutthaya has pardoned me and allowed us to return to our city.

Give orders to the Lao soldiers and servants to make preparations for the return. Be ready from tomorrow. At an auspicious time on the day after, we'll leave."

The Lao officers and lords were happy to learn that they could return to the north. They hastened to organize boats, find chili and salt, and prepare food supplies.

All the Lao soldiers and servants busied themselves attending on their masters. They caulked boats and rafts, collected goods together in piles, and went to buy clothes and food. Those who had debts hurried to repay. Everyone rushed around to be ready in time. Even when exhausted and bathed in sweat, they were not unhappy.

Hearing that the Lao would leave, traders arrived in crowds, carrying goods on shoulder poles. They pressed the Lao to buy things to take home, and happily sold goods worth one fueang for one salueng.[36]

Worried about their property, Lao ladies in royal service scurried around to find

woman trader

---

36. A salueng, equivalent to one fourth of a baht, was double the value of a fueang.

chests for packing. They folded their lowercloths and sabais, and packed as much powder and oil as could be carried.

All of those returning home were beaming, but those who had to stay in Ayutthaya were red-eyed and down in the mouth. When spoken to, they did not reply.

The King of Chiang Mai took pity on them and handed out many gratuities. "Bear up! Stay here with Soifa and next year I'll arrange to bring you home."

At dawn, crowds of officials came from Kalahom, Mahatthai, the Department of the Arsenal,[37] and the Inner Treasury. People carried goods this way and that. Concerning the property that had been confiscated,

there was a royal order for the palace ladies and goods sent to the capital to be returned. On the homeward journey, they were to stop by at Phichit to collect

the elephants, horses, carts, servants, and people left there. Officials would go along to check items against a manifest, hand them over according to a royal order, and then return forthwith.

The Lao officials, nobles, and people of Chiang Mai carried goods in file. Boats were summoned to moor in a line, and all were crammed to the gunwales.

Porters bustled about carrying properties belonging to the king and nobles. Once loaded, craft were backed out to moorings. The water echoed with the sound of Lao voices.

The boat of the ruler of Chiang Mai was moored at a landing below Ban Taphan.[38] Just behind came boats of the palace staff, with those of the phrai downstream.

When everything was ready, the King and Queen of Chiang Mai boarded near nightfall. The boats of the nobles were arrayed in lines waiting to depart.

Near the break of dawn, the moon slid down below the tree line, the morning star still shone brightly, and the city sounded with cockcrows and birdsong.

The Lao awoke, steamed rice, and grilled fish as needed. When the sun rose and flooded sky, earth, and water with light,

they went down to board the boats. The ruler of Chiang Mai came outside

---

37. กรมแสง, *krom saeng*, a department of the palace under the royal chamberlain, *phrasadet*, headed by two *jao krom* with the titles Khun Samret-phrakhan and Khun Sanphawut, *sakdina* 800 (KTS, 1:246).

38. Perhaps a place name, unidentified, but could mean just the house, or village, at the jetty. Judging from the account of their departure below, they are near the northwest corner of the city.

the curtains. At an auspicious moment when the sun's rays appeared, he ordered his boat to leave the jetty.

Oarsmen paddled in time, churning the water noisily. Entering the deep channel, they passed in front of the main palace. The king missed his daughter even more. He sat quietly in the stern with tears flowing.

When his boat wended its way upstream to the elephant enclosure,[39] he was disheartened at the sight of elephants tied to posts in rows. "You bull elephants followed the herd and got lured into a trap.

Now you stand lonely at these *jalung* posts with trunks resting on tusks, eyes looking at nothing in gloom, and tears flooding your faces. You no longer charge with your tusks,

as you used to charge around in the wilds with courage and fear of no one. Oh elephants, you were carried away by the pride in your own strength and got lured into the lasso.

Love for cow elephants clouded your eyes.[40] You joined the herd and simply followed along. It was lust that led you into the trap, and now you're tied up all the time.

jalung *posts*

You think of your friends, just as I do. In the past, there were all kinds of pleasures and dazzling possessions. Every city quailed before me.

Falling in love with Soithong was a mistake that brought enormous misfortune. I lost my home, lost my city, and gained torment. My beloved child cannot return with me.

The more I think, the more I feel lonely and low in spirits." He sat weeping. At the Mon

---

39. To the northeast of the city, beside the main northward waterway. Captured herds of wild elephants were kept in this enclosure for the king to view. The enclosure was originally in the northeast of the island near the later site of the Front Palace but was moved when the city walls were expanded to enclose the whole island in 1580. The enclosure was destroyed in the Burmese attack of 1767 and rebuilt in the Bangkok Third Reign (SWC, 10:4607; APA, 87–88; see map 3).

40. After accompanying King Naresuan on an elephant hunt in 1595, Jacques de Coutre wrote this description: "The entry of the enclosure was about half a mile wide, and inside were narrow lanes of trees. We saw many cow elephants, trained for this purpose, enter. Some men, camouflaged with branches sat on them and guided them to the lanes. Their genital parts were smeared with certain herbs whose odor made the bull elephants follow them, enraptured. After they had entered one after the other in the small alleys, many men surrounded them. With forks they pricked them so that they would put themselves in the narrowest parts of the small lanes. They surrounded them so that they could not backtrack nor turn around. After they were so restrained, the men put many logs between each elephant, and they attached their feet with green Bengal cane as fetters" (Coutre, *Andanzas asiáticas*, 125).

village,[41] he saw a Mon standing on a log and poling it along the shallows.

Mon

At Three Bo Trees, he saw three trees standing tall and fine in a row. The leaves of the middle tree looked sparse, withered, and sad, while the other two were lush and beautiful. "Those two bo trees are like us two going back to govern the city, while our daughter mopes like the middle one. What misfortune!" They came to where two rivers meet.[42] "When will we meet our daughter again?" He lamented along the journey. At Ban Khwang Tha,[43] he felt heartbroken.

Looking ahead towards the queen, he saw her sobbing sadly. Feeling bored by the villages and districts along the way, he took no delight in admiring birds and plants.[44]

Close to evening they halted and found somewhere to stay. In the morning they continued on. In the heat of the sun, they rested in the shade. They passed villages and districts—Inburi, Phromburi, Chainat, and Manorom, in order.

After Nakhon Sawan they switched to the main channel, and entered a tributary by the river mouth at Koeichai. At Bang Khlan,[45] they did not stop but poled ahead until they arrived in front of Phichit.

The governor and local officials, informed by a sealed order, came out to receive them. They handed over all the various goods that had to be returned by royal command according to the manifest.

---

41. Mon had been settled along the waterways north of Ayutthaya for a long time. In 1766–67, the Burmese chose Three Bo Trees as the site of their camp to attack Ayutthaya because there were many Mon in this area. After Ayutthaya fell, this camp was left in charge of a Mon called Suki. The wat is still called the Wat Khai Raman, wat of the Mon camp. Probably the "Mon village" here means the area around that wat.

42. Probably at Wat Sopsawan (see map 3).

43. About 5 kms east of Ang Thong where there is a Ban Khwang and Ban Wat Tha next to each other (see map 3).

44. This is an anti-*nirat*; he feels so bad, he cannot respond to the landscape in the conventional way.

45. The main channel means the Nan River, and this "tributary" is now the main channel of the Yom River which joins the Nan River just south of Chumsaeng. Bang Khlan is along the old course of the Nan River around 15 kms above Chumsaeng (see map 4).

Families and goods required by the king were dispatched down to Ayutthaya. Arrangements were completed in a few days, and a report sent on what had taken place.

The ruler of Chiang Mai ordered one group to go in advance by land, taking families, cattle, horses, and elephants to wait before Sawankhalok.[46]

All the boats entered the Phing Canal,[47] passed Kong Landing,[48] and went up the Yom River past Ban Mai[49] to the boat landing.

The governor and local officials of Sawankhalok, who guarded the capital's northern boundary, had heard that the ruler of Chiang Mai was released to return home. They prepared chili, salt, rice, and fish.

When all the Lao arrived, they distributed supplies of food, and checked the manifest of men, elephants, horses, and arms allowed to proceed.

Luang Phon Songkhram[50] was deputed to send them off at the border and entry to the forest. Then a post horse was dispatched to inform Thoen.

When the column was all ready, the ruler of Chiang Mai happily disembarked and led the troops in seven days from Sawankhalok to the district of Lampang.[51]

The governor and nobles of Lampang all came out in welcome, as had been the former practice. Growing gradually more cheerful, the ruler of Chiang Mai ordered a halt to recover from fatigue.

The lords and servants attending the ruler sent a detachment ahead to inform people that their city had been restored to the king and queen.

The Lao of Chiang Mai all came out in happy crowds. A splendid procession was arranged, decked with green and yellow flags,

including the royal litter and golden palanquin, gongs, drums, and all kinds of musical instruments, to tell the city people to go and make a welcome at Lamphun,

---

46. Here called Satchanalai but changed to avoid confusion.

47. See p. 538, note 13.

48. Kong Krailat.

49. "New village," possibly Sukhothai, relocated 13 kms east of the ancient site after the Yom River shifted its course.

50. In an old listing of provincial officials, Luang Phon Songkhram was the garrison commander, หลวงพล, *luang phon*, of Sukhothai, while the title of his counterpart in Sawankhalok was Luang Phet Songkhram, both *sakdina* 1,000 (Suphawat, "Phra aiyakan kao," 335–36).

51. Here called Nakhon. The distance from Sawankhalok to Lampang by modern roads, following much the same route, is 182 kms.

so that when the King of Chiang Mai arrived there, everybody including officials and royal relatives would attend on him and welcome him with joy.

On an auspicious day, all came to salute the king and invite him to return and rule the nine-jeweled city as a sheltering umbrella of victory.[52]

The king and queen mounted golden palanquins and traveled in procession from Lamphun to Chiang Mai on that day.

On both sides of the procession route, royal balustrades[53] and umbrellas were set up at intervals. House owners sat in rows to receive the king's blessing as he passed.

Masses of people scattered flowers and raised their hands in wai. The king entered the city like Phra Wetsandon in the past.[54]

"Hail! May you have victory and good fortune, oh lord!" "May the king be forever happy!" All the cityfolk gave their blessings.

When the king arrived at the palace, a large number of monks were sitting waiting with many

balustrade

---

52. Is this account of the return to Chiang Mai, and some of the preceding tale, loosely based on historical events? In the Smith/Wat Ko edition, the return is much simpler. There is no big entourage. They travel by boat to Rahaeng, and then by elephant and horse. There is no grand procession from Lampang. This version was recomposed, probably in the Fourth Reign, and might be based on King Kawilorot's journey in 1866. After the death of the Chiang Mai king in 1854, the succession was disputed. Four members of Lanna royalty were summoned to Bangkok to decide the issue. Kawilorot was chosen as king but this did not quell the rivalry. A year later, leading nobles informed Bangkok that Kawilorot was consorting with Burma, and had presented two white elephants to the ruler in Ava. Kawilorot and the nobles were called to Bangkok in 1866. Kawilorot presented gifts he had received from Ava to King Mongkut but Mongkut accepted only one ruby ring and returned the rest. Kawilorot was acquitted of charges and allowed to return to Chiang Mai, while his accusers were detained at Bangkok. The sources do not describe Kawilorot's journey. The missionary Daniel McGilvary traveled from Bangkok to Chiang Mai in the following year, taking three months, including four weeks by boat to Rahaeng, and another month up the thirty-two rapids through the mountains into the Chiang Mai valley. (*Phongsawadan Yonok*, 497–500; Sarassawadee, *History of Lan Na*, 145–48; McGilvary, *A Half Century*, 71–76)

53. แผงราชวัติ, *pheng ratchawat*, which can mean a railing or balustrade placed to mark the boundary of an area used for a ritual, but also a temporary barrier made with a lattice of bamboos bound with bamboo lath (SWN, 11:5680).

54. A reference to Phra Wetsandon's return to his city in the finale of the Mahachat (see p. 61, note 27).

different kinds of offerings used in the past for ceremonies to mark the passing of misfortune.

The holy patriarch invited the King of Chiang
Mai to sit under one arch of banana plants, and
the queen under another.[55] The monks chanted
in unison to dispel misfortune.

The holy patriarch took a water bowl, pronounced a mantra to concentrate power, and
then poured the water to dispel misfortune
to the strains of loud and joyful music.

In the late afternoon when the sun was
about to set, many royal relatives, officials,
courtiers, and palace staff gathered to sit in
the jeweled audience hall.

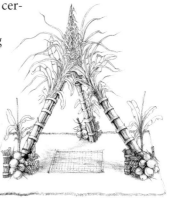

arch of banana plants

They invited the King and Queen of Chiang Mai to be seated on royal
thrones, then placed *baisi*, and set out food and various other articles.

High officials and village heads gave blessings to
strengthen the royal souls and invite them to return
there. They tied sacred thread on each of their wrists
according to custom.

When the ceremony was over, the king went
out to a pavilion. People came in a noisy crowd.
Some boxers, the best from all around, staged a
contest in the palace courtyard.

The hubbub continued until evening, when the
celebration ended and everybody returned home.
King Chiang In was bursting with joy. He ruled
Chiang Mai with happiness, day after day.

boxer

---

55. Probably this is a สืบชะตา, *suep chata*, prolonging fortune or life-enhancement ceremony,
an all-purpose rite for well-being, similar to calling back the soul (see p. 11, note 59), characteristic of Lanna. The participants sit under arches or tripods made of banana plants and other
foliage, said to imitate the wood placed to prop up branches of aging bo trees, along with various
offerings. Monks chant prayers, then sprinkle the participants with water. Sacred threads are
tied on the participants' wrists.

33: THE MARRIAGE OF PHRA WAI

Now to tell of the almighty king, crown of the Ayutthaya capital, who resided in a resplendent palace with throngs of consorts making obeisance with clasped hands.

When the sun descended behind golden mountains and a brilliant moon raced aloft and shone brilliantly, he took his diamond-encrusted regal sword in hand and went out to the audience hall.

Crystal lamps flickered brightly. Nobles prostrated, arrayed in order of rank. The king decided cases in a righteous way, faithfully following ancient practice.

He turned to find Phra Kanburi,[1] and became more joyous because of his wish to give away Princess Soifa. He said, "Ha! Heigh! Kanburi,

I've given Phra Wai rank, title, and a complete retinue. All he lacks is a wife. I'll give him Soifa.

That befits his rank and the royal favor he's won. To be a noble and have no wife is a waste. I'll make sure he has at least one."

Phra Kanburi prostrated elegantly three times and addressed the king. "Your Majesty's kindness is boundless.

But I cannot lie. Phra Wai is not single. When he went with the army, he got Simala, the daughter of Phra Phichit.

They're in love but haven't yet married. The ceremony was postponed until the fourth month but they have already been betrothed in the traditional way. May I inform the dust beneath the royal foot."

The king, upholder of the teachings, heard Khun Phaen say that Phra Wai's spouse was named Simala, daughter of Phra Phichit.

He said, "Phlai Ngam is now Phra Wai. However many wives he has is fitting. If he had ten, it would be even better." He commanded Chaophraya Jakri,

"Send a sealed order to Phra Phichit to come together with his daughter, and I'll marry her to Wai. Do it quickly today."

---

1. This is the form of address for Khun Phaen as governor of Kanburi, appointed in the last chapter.

The king went up inside. All the nobles left. Chaophraya Jakri went to sit in the sala and issue commands.

A sealed order was prepared and handed to Nai Sawat.[2] "Hasten up to Phichit." Nai Sawat prostrated, took the order, boarded a canopy boat, and set off with long strokes.

Arriving at Phichit, he delivered the order to the governor, as required. Phra Phichit received the order, and local officials came to hear its contents.

Phra Phichit learned from the order sent by Chaophraya Jakri that Simala would be married. He told his wife and daughter to make preparations.

Along with their servants, they boarded boats, set off from home, and came straight down the Bang Khlan route,[3] passing many places along the way.

At the city, they moored at Chaophraya Jakri's house.[4] Phra Phichit went up to find the astute senior official, and was informed about the matter.

"The royal order was issued to fetch you because the marriage will be arranged between your daughter, Simala, and Phra Wai. Hurry to see Phra Kanburi."

Phra Phichit took leave and went straight to find Khun Phaen, who prostrated and happily invited him into a sitting hall to talk.

Khun Phaen related the story to Phra Phichit. "His Majesty the King said that, as Phra Wai had no wife, he would give Soifa to him.

I told the king that Wai already had a wife named Simala. The king said he could have more, and had an order sent to fetch you to the capital for Simala's marriage.

It turns out there'll be two wives. I don't like that but I dare not oppose the king's wishes. Sir, please have mercy and don't blame my son for being unfaithful."

Phra Phichit said, "The king's power is great. We are his servants and must follow whatever he wishes."

river boat

2. Nai Sawat Mueang Maen, a messenger in Mahatthai, *sakdina* 150 (KTS, 1:227; KW, 453).

3. Meaning down the Nan River (see map 4).

4. In 1767, Chaophraya Jakri's house was beside Wat Rong Khong, the wat of the gong store, on the outer bank of the river along the northern side of the city, to the east of the palace (KLW, 173; see map 8).

They both agreed that Phra Wai should be informed immediately. Phra Phichit and his wife boarded a boat to go to Phra Wai's house.

Phra Phichit, Busaba, and their beloved daughter went to stay in this new house provided by the king. A kitchen was busily arranged, and servants bustled around performing their duties.

When dawn brightened the sky, Phramuen Si arrived at Phra Wai's house, went up inside, and planned arrangements for having it decked out.

Carpets, mats, and felt rugs[5] were laid down. Rows of cushions were placed for reclining. Sets of crystal were arrayed on half-moon tables. Curtains and folding screens were spread across.

Lamps with oil wicks were placed in rows to be lit at nightfall. Spittoons and water bowls were set out. At midday, all was finished.

Phra Phichit said to Phramuen Si, "Please help me over this matter. Today there's to be a water sprinkling ceremony and nobody will be there. Please find about ten young women,

all palace ladies who you know and who could be bridesmaids on this occasion. Have them huddle around the bride to sit and listen to the prayer chanting. Many people makes it warmer."

Phramuen Si said, "No problem. I'll arrange it for you this afternoon. My house is full of young women. Don't worry, sir."

At Phramuen Si's house, Phra Wai was busy choosing nine good-looking pages to bring along as the groom's party. He arranged for them to dress up smartly.

They bathed, powdered, and put on yok with a brilliant cross-branch pattern, and uppercloths in glittering gold meshwork. Jamuen Samoe Jai[6] was to lead the groom's party.

When ready, they left Phramuen Si's house and went along the street, attracting a lot of attention. They reached the house and went up to listen to a sermon and the monks chanting prayers in unison.

yok in cross-branch pattern

༄

---

5. เจียม, *jiam*, a floor covering, originally from northern China, made with matted animal hair, usually of a deer (KP, 315).

6. Jamuen Samoe Jai Rat, one of the four lieutenants of the pages along with Phramuen Si and Muen Wai (KTS, 1:223).

Now to tell of the beautiful Wanthong who was living lovingly with Khun Chang, an important man in Suphan. That day, she heard the news being passed around

that her son Phlai Ngam had won royal favor and been raised to much higher rank. The king had graciously given him Princess Soifa, and he would marry Simala also on this occasion.

"As a parent, I must go to give some help and have the honor of making myself known to the nobles." With this thought, she went to take leave of her husband. "Tomorrow I'll go to the city.

The news is all over town that Phlai Ngam is getting married. If I don't go, it might cause some offense and make the common people gossip."

Khun Chang sat with a broad smile. "Eh! If you'd like to go, I won't complain. He's an officer of the pages. In the future we can depend on such a noble.

Don't go empty-handed. Take some money, and some food to help them out. I won't sit still here while you're gone. I'll follow later by elephant.

Precious, I'd like to ask one favor. If you meet Khun Phaen and he greets you, don't talk with this sex-mad fellow, and if he takes any liberties, give him an earful."

Wanthong said, "Don't order me around. I'm not going to sit talking with him." She commanded servants to get things together quickly. She went into her room, unlocked a trunk,

and picked out some good quality yok in pink. She selected snake rings, ornamental rings,[7] and four or five gold bars. The gold was to give to Phra Wai.

The good pink yok and rings were to be given to the daughters-in-law when they wai-ed her. "One each, as much as we can afford, so my daughters-in-law won't mock me."

Then she arranged for various gourds, young rice, ordinary rice, and fresh palm fruit to be carried along. "Also those good pumpkins I planted. Cut and pack them, I-Jo."

Servants carried everything down to a big boat with a crowd of retainers trailing behind. Wanthong boarded the boat and the phrai paddled off with long strokes and loud shouts.

They cut through to Bang Yihon, and soon come out at Ban Jao Jet.[8] At the

---

7. The snake ring is for the groom, and the ornamental ring (*waen pradap*) for the bride (KW, 455).

8. Bang Yihon is 10 kms south down the Suphan River, at present-day Bang Plama. From here Jao Jet Canal runs east towards Ayutthaya. Ban Jao Jet is just before Sena (see map 2).

city, they moored at the jetty of the house at Wat Takrai, and had the servants carry things up.

Wanthong walked ahead along the road and went up to the big house of Phra Wai,[9] who welcomed his mother with clasped hands and invited her in.

Ten bridesmaids had been brought over, all of them pretty.[10] In the late afternoon, Phra Phichit and Busaba told them

to bathe, powder, and get dressed. They wore patterned lowercloths, and silk uppercloths in various colors. Simala powdered her cheeks to be fair, and put on a lowercloth in *nok yang* pattern,[11] and uppercloth in moon yellow.

Adults walked at the front with the bridesmaids following in rows. They each brought a citrus thorn hidden in their cloth to protect themselves against importunate young men.

Outside the house, they huddled around the bride.[12] Every face was as fair as that of a palace lady. The fragrance on their cloth hung in the air. Simala walked in the center of the procession.

On arrival, they sat down to listen to a sermon. Monk Sadam[13] took a sacred thread to connect Simala and Phra Wai. When a big gong resounded loudly, they chanted the Chayanto blessing.

The young men and women sat crowded tightly beside one another. Monks held their palm-leaf fans

monks with palm-leaf fans

9. This passage suggests Phlai Ngam's house is close to Wat Takrai. In chapter 32, the king ordered his house built close to the palace. In chapter 35, Phlai Ngam listens at night to the tolling of the palace gong from this house.

10. The bride's party should be an even number (Anuman, *Prapheni kiao kap chiwit taeng ngan*, 128).

11. นอกอย่าง, *nok yang*, "outside the type," meaning cloth imported from India that did *not* conform to patterns prescribed by the Siamese court. The latter were called ผ้าลายอย่าง, *pha lai yang*, "patterns of the type." *Nok yang* cloth was considered of lower quality. Often the pattern was based on a Thai original but less well executed and sometimes clearly influenced by Indian style (Wibun, *Saranukrom pha*, 252–53; *Pha phim lai boran*, 119, 121).

12. In this ceremony, unlike at the wedding of Phim and Phlai Kaeo, the bride comes to the groom's house. This was the practice among the nobility. The bride's party huddles around the bride, partly because she may be shy, but partly as horseplay to confuse the groom who might not know the bride well enough to identify her within the group. Members of the bridal party may dress similarly to add to the confusion. (KW, 456; Anuman, *Prapheni kiao kap chiwit kan taeng ngan*, 127–30)

13. สดำ, *sadam*, which may mean the monk on the right, but more probably is a proper name, possibly a famous monk at the time of composition. The sacred thread would be looped into two circles, placed on the head of bride and groom, with one end attached to a bowl of sacred water (Anuman, *Prapheni kiao kap chiwit taeng ngan*, 129).

and sprinkled water, pouring five or six bowls on the side with the women. At the front, Granny Pho got water in her eyes.

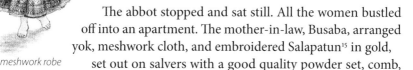

They all jostled and squeezed close together in a tight circle.[14] Thorns were stabbed into bellies, making people yelp. Some pushed in but others got booted out. Granny Sa came over to get in the way.

The pages mischievously banged into her. "Oh! I'm going to foul myself. I can't stand it!" Granny Sa got out of the way, leaving Phra Wai and Simala next to each other.

The abbot laughed and sprinkled more water. The adults were chilled and shivering. "No more water, Master Jan!" "Enough already, Your Lordship."

The abbot stopped and sat still. All the women bustled off into an apartment. The mother-in-law, Busaba, arranged yok, meshwork cloth, and embroidered Salapatun[15] in gold,

meshwork robe

set out on salvers with a good quality powder set, comb, and mirror. She also prepared sandalwood fans as gifts for those in the party of the groom, and gold *talap* caselets[16] for those in the party of the bride, and had people take them to Phra Wai.

The groom's party went to change clothes. The abbot gave an offertory blessing. When they saw it was time to leave, all the monks went off to their kuti.

The groom's party entered the sitting hall. Footed trays were carried in and set out with spittoons, water bowls, and salvers placed neatly alongside.

All the salvers were fine silverware, set with bowls of food. The groom's party was invited to eat. When they were happily full, low tables of sweets were carried in and placed around.

Everything was very good, served on four-level pedestal trays,[17] carefully

---

14. The water splashing was the climax of the ceremony. The presiding monk would start pouring water during the thread ritual, and would pour a large amount, soaking the participants and creating an atmosphere of hilarity. Under this shower, the two parties would push the groom and bride towards each other, breaking down any barrier or reluctance. As part of this horseplay, a fun-loving elder (here, Granny Sa) would stand in the middle and be the last to get out of the way. (KW, 456–57; Anuman, *Prapheni kiao kap chiwit kan taeng ngan*, 127–30)

15. สะละปะตุ่น, a contraction of Machilipatnam (Masulipatam), a port on India's east coast that traded cloth through Mergui to Siam. Since at least the late sixteenth century, some of the cloth was made specifically for the Siamese market with Siamese designs (KW, 457–58; Guy, "Painted to Order").

16. ตลับ, *talap*, a small container, either square or round, of any material.

17. เทียบสี่ชั้น, *thiap si chan*, pedestal serving trays that can be stacked to four levels, probably for sweets (KW, 460, 687).

arranged and placed. When they were finished, the tables were carried back inside, and betel trays in nak and gold set out.

Orders were given to take ordinary food to the phrai, and the whole group happily ate their fill. Lamps were lit and shone brightly. A *mahori* ensemble played a tune with a fiddle accompaniment,

filling the hall with gently plaintive music. The fiddle was joined by the rhythm of round gongs and a tinkling *ranat*, making the music flow.

musicians

The melody was loud and rousing, then sweetly plaintive and lamenting. Listening to a wistful *thayoi*,[18] Phra Wai was carried away by the enjoyment and drifted off to sleep.

When sunrise lit the heavens, servants awoke and aroused their fellows. They arranged rows of tables for feeding the monks,

chopped firewood, fetched water, ground chili and ginger, cleaned rice in pots, lit fires to heat skillets, carried trays and ladles, and washed crockery. All was a noisy bustle.

⚬

Now to tell of the king, ruler of the world, eminence of excellence in all three worlds, resident of a lofty gilded palace where thousands of ladies prostrated in order of rank.

In the presence of all his officials, he gave thought to Phra Wai's marriage. "Why delay over this matter of Soifa? Send her to him today.

Let it be a dazzling spectacle in public view of all the nobles." With this thought, he ordered an official of the Inner Treasury to requisition twenty sets of cloth;

combs, mirrors, and powder sets; rings of emerald, nine-jeweled, snake, and ornamental types; two sets of betel trays in nak and gold; along with five chang of money, footed trays, and salvers.

"Have her ride over there in a palanquin with patterned curtains. Head governess, escort her to the house. Hurry to be there in time. Have the royal gifts carried along behind."

The king said to Soifa, "Don't be sad. If there's a calamity in the future, I won't abandon you. Look after each other well and be without peril. If there's any difficulty, come to tell me."

---

18. ทยอย, *thayoi*, a genre of songs played to accompany sad scenes of drama performances.

palanquin with curtains

Soifa bowed her face, bathed in tears. She summoned up her courage, and prostrated to take leave.

Governess Si Satja[19] took her off to a beautiful palanquin that was already waiting. Soifa got in, and the governess led the way out of the palace.

Soifa sat in the palanquin. Young ladies and sentinelles carried the presents behind. Mai walked along, glancing warily around.

Phra Wai's house was packed with people. Many nobles, big and small, had come. Monks had chanted prayers up in the hall. The novices had readied the almsbowls in a row.

Two golden ladles were brought and placed in the middle of the verandah. Wanthong called the servants to fill a bowl around half full with white rice.

Phramuen Si went into the apartment to tell Simala, "Come out to give alms, my dear child." Simala was extremely shy of the people. She hid behind a curtain, looking listless, and would not come out.

Wanthong called out to her daughter-in-law, "Please pluck up some courage and just go out there. Make merit and don't lose your faith. I'll accompany you."

Simala could not oppose her mother-in-law. She daubed her hairline with a cotton bud, and strung on a slender breast chain.

She knew how to make herself up lightly so it looked like the natural fair sheen of her complexion rather than powder. She put on emerald and nine-gem rings, an uppercloth in *attalat*, and a lowercloth with gold stripes.

Her fine figure matched her elegant face. She followed her mother-in-law out of the room, walking carefully to steady herself. Moei walked beside, ready to support her.

Simala came out to the terrace with heart fluttering. Phra Wai had scooped a ladle of rice and was waiting. He proffered the ladle towards Simala. When their eyes met, she gently lowered her face.

---

19. One of the four deputies, *nang chalong phra-ot*, of Thao Worajan overseeing the inner palace, each with *sakdina* 600. The others were Thao Somsak, Thao Sopha, and Thao Insuriya. Satja was in charge of the female palace guard (KTS, 1:221; KP, 319–20; KW, 462).

She was shyly reluctant to take a hold. Wanthong took her elbow and guided Simala to clasp Phra Wai's hand firmly and tip the rice carefully into a monk's bowl.[20]

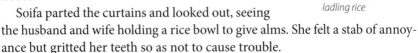

While Simala and Phra Wai were still giving alms, a palanquin arrived. Phra Wai called his father to welcome the palace ladies into the house.

ladling rice

Soifa parted the curtains and looked out, seeing the husband and wife holding a rice bowl to give alms. She felt a stab of annoyance but gritted her teeth so as not to cause trouble.

Phra Kanburi came to receive Soifa, the palace governess, and sentinelles. He led Soifa in, and invited the governess to sit over at the back.

Simala finished giving alms and came into the apartment. Phra Wai ordered food for the sentinelles. Cooks rushed around setting out food trays, spittoons, and water jugs so busily that they bumped their heads together.

Phra Kanburi had the task of looking after the royal party and making sure there were no problems. Phramuen Si took care of the nobles. Phra Phichit saw to feeding the monks and novices.

When the monks had eaten and their pupils had packed the remains, they were presented with robes of good quality ochre-dyed cloth, and Phra Phichit organized the distribution of offering hampers.[21] Just before the forenoon mealtime, the monks took leave and returned to the wat.

༄

Now to go back and tell of Khun Chang. Earlier, when the streaks of dawn brightened the sky, he had ordered a handsome tusker harnessed with ropes encased in fine red cloth.

He bathed, went inside, and picked up his mirror and comb. Feeling furious about his awful head, he ran to get as much soot as he could find,

mixed it with oil, and shaped his hair into a wing. He put on more soot, yet light spots still showed through even when he had used up more than one cockleshell. He powdered himself liberally,

---

20. See p. 257, note 53.

21. กระจาดอังคาส, *krajat angkhat*. *Krajat* are basketwork containers, traditionally used for offerings. *Angkhat* is a Khmer-derived word for offering food or other articles to monks. Here the hamper would contain everyday necessities.

and put on a yok lowercloth in an ancient-style cross-branch pattern and an uppercloth of brilliant red wool. Seeing the sun was bright, he mounted the bull elephant and left with a crowd of servants trailing behind.

Khun Chang's lofty elephant, with baldheaded old Bua as the mahout, ambled along the edge of the forest. The crowd of servants tagged along behind.

They crossed a marsh and climbed a knoll. The bald old mahout sat astride the rear, bumping and jolting along, his body soaked in sweat and his head gleaming.

Khun Chang rode on the neck, his shiny pate swaying to and fro. He wielded the goad to make the elephant trot along with its rear end jiggling this way and that. They took a direct route to the city across the open plain,

down to the crossing at Kopjao, through Ban Mahaphram, turning right to Golden Mount,[22] then across the paddy fields to reach Ayutthaya while still daylight.

He[23] dismounted from his elephant and went up to the central hall where all the nobles and pages were gathered. Acquaintances among the nobles greeted him. Phra Wai welcomed him immediately,

Golden Mount

offered him a golden betel tray, and chatted away as was fitting. Khun Chang asked after Phra Kanburi. "Is he here at present or has he gone to attend on His Majesty?"

---

22. Kopjao is 6 kms west of Ayutthaya, at the crossing of the Chaophraya River (now the Bang Ban Canal). Ban Mahaphram is 3 kms west of Ayutthaya on the Mahaphram Canal. Wat Phukhaothong, the golden mount, is a massive stupa and major landmark just to the northwest of the city (see maps 3 and 8).

23. From here to "You forget I'm your elder" on p. 745 is taken from KJ, 11–14; PD has: Khun Chang went up to the central hall where all the nobles were gathered, and greeted those he knew. Phra Wai looked away in embarrassment and only cast him a sidelong look. / To feed all the nobles and pages, food trays were placed in rows around the central hall with kit for drinking liquor placed beside each. Khun Chang walked over, tossing his wool uppercloth over his shoulder, and took the last place. / He repeatedly took big helpings including triple-strength liquor. Everybody noticed and tingled in every pore. Khun Chang finished off the pork and then the chicken like a naughty child, chewing even the bones into powder.

Phra Wai said, "Father is in the central hall." Khun Chang stooped in feigned deference, saying, "My dear lord, you glow with such youth and plumpness, befitting your merit. Your skin looks as radiant as if painted with gold."

Khun Chang crawled in to pay respect to Phramuen Si, who said, "Tcha! I saw you just recently. You didn't appear for your duty round but were intent on drinking liquor. I'll have you tied by the neck and dragged off one of these days."

Phra Kanburi came out of the room and called out in greeting to Khun Chang. "My, you're truly fat, my old friend, like a great pig. How come your skin looks so clear?"

Khun Chang crawled closer in deference, stroked his knee, and said unctuously, "We were once friends but it went wrong because of ill fortune. Don't prolong the enmity but remember we once loved each other."

Phra Kanburi said, "Don't worry, Khun Chang. I'll invite you to our house to dine sometime." When a noble acquaintance greeted him, Khun Chang turned his rotund body and made a wai.

Then he crawled in to pay respect to Thong Prasi. "What a pity you're getting a little old." Thong Prasi replied cordially, "Mm. Mm." She shaded her eyes to peer at him,

and called out, "Oh Khun Chang! Why is your head so bald?" She carried on by asking, "How are Thepthong and Siprajan?

Are they healthy and happy or sick and troubled? I'm full of aches and pains. I keep breaking wind, coughing, and wheezing. I'm not so healthy so I haven't been to visit friends in Suphan."

Khun Chang replied, "Mother Thepthong is still active and her eyesight is good, but Siprajan is old and very rickety."

He took his leave of Thong Prasi and came to the sitting hall. The servants busily arranged his table. The meal was of high quality in the Farang style. Brandy and whisky were set out for each circle of guests.

The nine in the groom's party sat looking splendidly grand. Luang Sak, Sit, Rit, Det, Ja Ret, Ja Rong, Ja Yong, and Ja Yuat[24]

had all come to help the lieutenant of the pages. Muen Sanphetphakdi, Muen Si Saowarak, and Muen Samoe Jai were also there.[25] Both seniors and juniors were all gentlemen of rank.

---

24. All members of the pages. The first four had the title of Nai and *sakdina* of 800. The second four had title of Nai Ja and *sakdina* of 600 (KTS, 1:224).

25. The three other lieutenants (*hua muen*) of the pages besides Phra Wai Woranat, all *sakdina* 1,000 (KTS, 1:223).

Acquaintances greeted Khun Chang. Seeing the nobles altogether, he sat close to them, chatting, teasing, flattering nonstop, and chuckling with shoulders jiggling.

Servants brought in the sets of food—whole duck, chicken *phanaeng*, curried sliced pork, and *kaolao* soup[26]—all lined up on tiered trays along with brandy, anise, and triple-strength liquor.[27]

Khun Chang sat in the middle with his bald head shining and nobles sitting all around. Servants set out food in rows including sweet, savory, and liquor.

Eating at the central table surrounded by his friends, Khun Chang became thoroughly drunk. He laughed uproariously, and wanted to chant a story.

The nobles played up to him. "Sir, please let us hear the part where Inao enters the cave."[28] Khun Chang cried out, and set his face like a dancer. He called for the *mahori* ensemble to play a *klongyon*.

The more people egged him on, the more playful he became, leaping outside the circle and miming a mask play. He could not dance but jumped up and down to the drum, and chanted to the rhythm.

Phra Kanburi got up in embarrassment to stop him. "Drink moderately. When drunk you lose your dignity." Khun Chang said. "I'm not drunk. The liquor's no good. Bring the anise over and I'll do a somersault."

He assumed the pose of Thotsakan about to take the stage, clicking his tongue and hopping from one leg to the other like a mask-play dancer. He fell over flat, got up with his tuck-tail lowercloth all askew, and shouted, "I want the triple-strength!"

In embarrassment, Phra Wai came over to stop him. "You've had enough to drink. Go and sleep it off." Phra Wai took the liquor and hid it away. Khun Chang replied, "I'm not drunk!

Shame on you, Phra Wai Woranat, for claiming I'm drunk and shaming me improperly in front of guests. It's demeaning. You forget I'm your elder."

The nobles cheered him, "What a glutton!" Getting more excited, Khun Chang squatted on his haunches to upend a liquor jar, picked up a trumpet-

---

26. เกาเหลา, a soup base of Chinese origin.

27. บ้าหรั่น, *baran*, an elided pronunciation of brandy; อะหนี, more usually อาหนี, *ani*, from the French anise, liquor flavored with aniseed; สามทับ, *sam thap*, strong liquor, distilled three times (KW, 678).

28. See p. 588, note 12.

mouth spittoon, rushed out to the middle, put it on his head, and staggered around

liquor jars

with his hands on his bottom, his face pushed forward, and his eyes half-closed. "Hey! Look at me. I'm the Lord of the Lepers." Phra Wai felt ashamed and rebuked him, but Khun Chang did not hear. He staggered around and collapsed unconscious.

Wanthong heard laughter and came to look. So ashamed she wanted to disappear into the earth, she came out of the room and shouted, "You awful man! How can you do this without any shame?"

trumpet-mouth spittoon

Khun Chang looked at her through half-closed eyes. "Eh! Ah! I'm not ashamed." He leapt up and danced around even more wildly. "Hey, mother of this Wai! Come and be Wanarin, and I'll be Lord Hanuman.[29] The tail that used to hang past my feet has shrunk to nothing. I used to be the lord of many lands." He stuck out his tongue, scratched his leg,[30] and grabbed at Wanthong.

She pushed him away. Phra Wai cursed him, "You arrogant fellow! Coming here to call me 'this Wai.'[31] Were I not thinking of my mother, I'd put a lock on your neck and elbow you half to death."

Khun Chang stood drunkenly scratching his bottom. "Pah! You dog, you can curse so easily. Are you arrogant enough to elbow me, Phlai? You think a lot of yourself as an officer of the pages, don't you?

You don't remember my kindness, you ungrateful creature. Who kept you in line since you were a child? Who raised you when you were little? Yet you rebuke your father, you Jek-heart."

---

29. หัวละมาน, hualaman, a colloquial pronunciation of Hanuman. In the *Ramakian*, Wanarin, วานรินทร์, is a deity and lamplighter in Siva's audience hall. She allows a lamp to be extinguished and is hence banished to take human form and live in the mountains with a troop of monkeys as her retainers. She can return to the heavens only by helping Hanuman. In pursuit of a *yak* giant named Wirun Chambang, Hanuman enters Wanarin's cave, is entranced by her beauty, and woos her. When she tells him her story, Hanuman reveals his identity. Wanarin shows him the way Wirun Chambang went, and earns the right to be restored to the heavens. (See the episode "Suek satthasun lae wirun chambang," Premseri, *Ramakian*, 409–21; Olsson, *Ramakien*, 259; KW, 687)

30. The tongue and scratching are standard gestures of actors playing Hanuman and other monkey characters.

31. He is angry because Khun Chang has disrespectfully omitted his title.

Phra Wai was so angry at this insult that his body shook and his scalp crawled. "This baldy wants to hurt me with insults, slandering my good name as a noble.

Enough! What will be will be." In fury, he clenched his fist and hit Khun Chang in the mouth. Wanthong shrieked and ran between them. Khun Chang tumbled down head over heels.

Nobles came and roughly pulled him upright. Phra Wai cursed him mercilessly. Wanthong cried, "Wai, don't get upset at a drunk.

Please grant him forgiveness, dear son. He's not fully himself so he was speaking nonsense. Restrain yourself and you'll gain merit. Don't be rash. Have some consideration for your mother."

Phra Wai fumed, "Oh Mother, he always acts so shamelessly like this. If I wasn't thinking of you, I'd finish him off with ease."

Phra Kanburi wagged his finger at Wanthong. "Eh? Are you an angel like Wanarin? You're not ashamed, not hurt even a tiny bit. You're all over him, creating a scandal in full public view.

Your husband insulted my son, yet you didn't tell him off even once. When they hit your husband, you danced around like a puppet.[32] My son is ashamed in front of these people, but you don't care."

Wanthong tossed her head angrily. "If you want to kill me, then kill me. You close your eyes and ears and make assumptions about who's creating the scandal for people to gossip over.

Yes! I'm the angel in a mask play, the bawdy one. Didn't you see me playing the part? You talk like a little thumb-sucking child. You're a good person but as stubborn as a drunk.

You accuse me of loving my husband and hating my son. Do you think I approve of what Chang just did? He shouldn't have insulted Wai but he only did it because he was drunk. He got hit in public because he deserved it."

Khun Chang began to recover from his daze. He got up, hitching up his lowercloth Khmer-style, but so high that it exposed his bottom. He wagged his finger and said, "Hey, you evil fellow. You hit me in the mouth because you're overexcited.

You're like Thoraphi,[33] you slave. You come butting your own father. Do you remember when you were tiny? I dragged you by the hair, split your head, and buried you under logs.

---

32. เป็นชักยนต์, *pen chakyon*, meaning "without stopping."
33. See p. 464, note 5.

If you don't believe me, Phlai, feel the back of your head. Round the hairline there's a scar where it was split by the wood. I thought you died out of sight. I didn't know you'd come back to rough me up."[34]

Hearing matters from deep in the past, Phra Wai trembled with rage. "Beg pardon, Mother." He rushed up into the hall. "Let me tell all of you what happened.

This monstrosity tried to break my neck. Because of merit, I was able to escape and survive." Phra Wai hitched up his cloth, drew himself up tall, and called his men. "Take him! Don't spare his life!"

His young retainers crowded around, elbowing Khun Chang until he could not cry out, and kicking him down writhing on the ground. Some nobles came between them to stop it.

Wanthong jumped down from the sitting hall, and ran over to bend down and embrace Khun Chang. He was motionless and seemed not to be breathing. She wept and wailed, "Oh my lord!

You came here because you love your wife, but now this has happened and you'll die under this house. They pounded you mercilessly like pounding a fish. Maybe your merit is all used up."

She had him carried into the middle of the house. Some people tried massaging him by standing on his upper legs with both feet, but no matter how much, his eyes did not open. Wanthong lay down beside him.

"Oh little bo tree shelter of your darling wife, you're dead and I think I'll die too. There was no goodwill to be found in the city except you, my golden bo.

We lived together fifteen or sixteen years without a single word to distress me. When I gave birth, you sat gently supporting my back. When you saw me crying, you grieved too.

When I had fever and couldn't eat, you sat beside me and fed me for a long while. When you saw I couldn't sleep, neither would you. In the hot season you fanned me.

In the cool season when a chill gripped my whole breast, you covered me with a blanket and hugged me to sleep. When rain poured down in the monsoon, you closed the windows all round the house and made me stay inside.

There's no man on the surface of the earth who loved his wife as much as you. Though your looks are not fine, your heart shines like the moon. Karma made you follow your wife here to die.

Oh pity, pity! Before coming here, I had you as company. Now I'll return

34. Dredging up past events to provoke a quarrel was an offence (see p. 416, note 39).

home alone and you'll be gone." She flailed around with anguish as if about to die.

When her grief eased, she felt his body and found it was still soft, and his pulse still beating. His chest began to lose its chill and warm up. "Oh! His drunkenness seems to be easing."

She ordered servants to bring hot water and wipe his whole body to help him recover. She went to pour some water in his mouth but could not pry his jaw open. Suddenly, he let out a groan and began breathing strongly.

Khun Chang revived. Fiery-eyed with fury, he gritted his teeth and bellowed, "Hey! Even if I don't complain, have no doubts I'll beat down walls before I depart this life.

Even if my body dies, my bones will talk. Don't think you can elbow me around with no consequences. Even though there are many of you, watch out, Phlai. If the king ceases to keep me, no matter."

Trembling uncontrollably, he called his servants, and hauled Wanthong out of the big house by her hand. "You go home first, and don't be upset. I'll go to attend on the Lord of Life."

Wanthong warned him through tears. "If you bring up the matter with the king, aren't you worried you could be in the wrong? At this moment, Phlai is in the king's intimate favor. Stop and think carefully."

Khun Chang said, "I'm not drunk now, my jewel, so don't say anything to oppose me." He sent her off to Suphan straightaway, and hurried into the palace.

Now that the quarrel had passed, Phra Wai brightened up. All the nobles took their leave. Phra Wai went to sit with Thao Si Satja.

The palace governess said, "His Majesty the King entrusted me to bring Soifa from the palace and send her to you."

Phra Wai was very happy to hear this. He prostrated to pay respect to the king, and ordered presents for the governess's party—

white woolen cloth in floral and *nok yang* pattern[35] for Si Satja, thin white cloth in parrot's-eye design for the sentinelle officers, cloth in a *chalang* pattern with a Vietnamese stripe for the ordinary sentinelles,

and silk for all the thirty-five young ladies who came in the retinue. Everybody great and small received something suitably beautiful. They took leave and returned to the palace.

---

35. See p. 738, note 11 above.

Phra Wai arranged the house so that Soifa occupied two apartments with a sitting room, bedroom, bathroom, and curtains and screens to conceal them from view.

He divided the house into halves by making a wall enclosing the area for Soifa's people so that Simala's people would not mix with them.

Now that the wedding was over, he distributed cash and foreign white cloth to the royal cooks so that nobody would gossip and criticize. Even the house servants received gifts.

᪥

After the wedding, Phra Phichit and Busaba took leave to return home. They came to see Phra Wai. "There's a great deal of government business.

If I leave it to the officials for too long, some disaster will happen. We've come to say farewell but our concern for Simala remains.

Since birth, she's not been apart from us. Now she'll be very far away in this southern city, and forlorn, having no kinsfolk around. If she makes a mistake, please have concern for me,

Also, you now have two wives. I think there'll be jealousy for sure. I fear the two will choose to antagonize each other. Please think carefully at all times, and don't act rashly.

There's an old saying that you shouldn't have four houses or two wives. You may not be comfortable, Phlai Ngam, having to manage matters between them all the time.

Even if you lever my daughter's mouth open with a machete, she won't speak out. Living in the provinces, she never argues with anybody. No matter how much her friends curse and criticize her, she just weeps and cannot argue back.

Like two fierce elephants in one forest, two wives with one husband means trouble. The slow-witted one will end up in tears. You have to be as even-handed as a pair of weigh scales."

Phlai Ngam bowed his head and wai-ed. "My lord, please travel safely. Don't worry about Simala.

Though I'm young and foolish and make mistakes, I'll remember the kindness of both you and your wife. I like people who don't talk too much, and I don't like those who are glib and obsequious.

I won't forget your words. You've been very kind, and a patron of my parents since long ago. I'll repay your kindness as I have promised."

"It's good that you show gratitude to those who have been kind to you. May you earn merit. We two will take our leave." They went off to see their daughter.

Phra Phichit embraced his beloved daughter and said. "I'm taking leave. Don't be miserable. Make up your mind to be loyal. Put yourself in your husband's hands from now on."

Simala clasped her father's feet in tears. "Who will I turn to in times of trouble? When Mother and Father were close, you looked after me.

However much my husband loves me, it's not the same as parents. If he's not fair, things will change and I'll be unhappy every night."

Busaba consoled her daughter. "Don't cry. Your father and I made sure your husband swore an oath to be steadfast.

Yet I'm still worried about one thing. I fear jealousy will cause trouble and shame in public. According to ancient practice, having two wives is forbidden. It always creates trouble without exception.

Since you were little, I've taught you over a thousand times that nothing is more important than forbearance. Don't act badly because you're the poorer one and people will make comparisons. Show forbearance and be deferential.

If anyone riles you, ignore them and bear with it. Don't complain to your husband. Good people take time to gain recognition but someone bad is easy to spot.

If[36] they see you stay passive, they'll become ruder. If they see you don't fight, they'll bully you. Don't answer back to your husband but show deference. Let him hear the others for himself. That's the best way.

Then if there's a violent quarrel in the future, he'll take your side and chew them to dust. Obey him without stubbornness for half a year, and you should be able to ride on his neck from then on.[37]

One other thing, minister to his needs. Anyone good at lovemaking does very well. There's one thing that will make your husband merciful. Make the midday meal without fail.

---

36. The next seven stanzas, down to "he won't leave the house," are taken from KJ, 20–21; PD has: Make an effort to be humble and restrained. Don't let anybody bully you. Be honest to your husband and show him respect. Don't sound off about him with the servants. / Minister to him, and don't forfeit his goodwill. Put your heart into management of the household. Look after all the property carefully and don't be negligent.

37. See p. 272, note 25.

Take the effort to boil longan, make sweet eggs,[38] and simmer bird nests[39] in granular sugar until perfect. Boil cow's milk with sugar until it's really sweet, and give him a jar every day.

If he eats nothing else, it doesn't matter. At mealtimes, serve him quickly. Along with rice, try to find a tasty fish for *tomyam*. That's the important thing.

Make chili dip and *tomyam* very well. Use good shrimp paste, and find some Japanese fish sauce. Boil until thick and whitish like jelly, add coriander and crispy garlic, and he'll love it.

As long as he always has a full mouth and a full stomach, you'll have no need to fear your husband will forsake you. Give him generous amounts of sweet and savory, and even if you push him away he won't leave the house."

Turning from her daughter, she said to I-Moei, "You and I-Ju must be her companions, and must give the orders to I-Mi and I-Rak. You've been in charge of a household for a long time."

Then she summoned the trusty male servants, Ai-Thit and Ai-Tao, to stay with her. "Hey! Far away from home and city, don't trust anyone easily. If any trouble happens, don't abandon your mistress."

She embraced her daughter. "It's getting late. I'll take my leave." Both parents got up and went down from the house. Phra Wai followed to send them off to their boat.

Phra Kanburi and Simala also came to see them off with tears streaming down their faces. They sat watching until Phra Phichit disappeared behind a promontory, then went to their rooms to sleep.

From now on, Phra Wai had two wives. His heart shone as brightly as the moon. He was eternally blessed with abundance.

When the sun dropped and disappeared behind the mountains, the moon rose, shining brightly, and stars twinkled.

Cicadas and crickets, which slept quiet through the day, trilled a melody, loud and clear. Fireflies flickered. Around the rows of flowerpots,

bees and other insects flitted, fondling the flowers, and fluffing up soft clouds of pollen. Phra Wai was befuddled thinking about the two women.

"Right now Simala will be lying there thinking despondently that my love for her has faded. She'll be so hurt she can't get it out of her mind.

Then there's Soifa to consider. She's sleeping on her own and will be feeling

---

38. ไข่หวาน, *khai wan*, eggs poached in a syrup made with palm sugar and floral water.

39. Nests made from saliva by certain swiftlets, *Collocalia fuciphaga/maxima*, are harvested from seaside caves and made into a soup believed, especially by the Chinese, to be rich in nutrients which improve health and libido.

lonely since she's never yet been intimate with a man. But if I go to her first, I'll have Simala on my mind.

The day I left Phichit, I had to give many promises." He dithered and agonized back and forth while time passed to the end of the second watch.

A haloed moon shone brilliantly in a cloudless sky. Phra Wai bathed and went into Simala's room.

He found the gentle soul fast asleep, with the lamplight catching her fair face. Her beautiful figure matched her fine demeanor. She looked as radiant as if lustrated with gold.

Phra Wai was so overcome with passion he almost lost his mind. He lay down close and embraced her, gently kissing and caressing her supine form. "Why are you still fast asleep?"

Simala opened her eyes and raised herself from the pillow. Seeing Phra Wai, she felt angry and turned to him with a sharp, hooded look.

"Why do you come here over halfway through the night? Did you wake from sleep and decide to slip over? Before you left, did you take leave from her nicely, or did you sneak off while she was asleep?"

"What a pity, eye's jewel. Don't be too catty, precious. I'll tell you the truth. Just now I was sitting in the central hall,

enjoying the sight of my favorite plants. A scented breeze aroused me. I was yawning sleepily so I came to find you. You shouldn't be suspicious and use hurtful words.

That day I left Phichit, I promised I wouldn't act improperly and shame you. Picking at me for no reason is hurtful. I've come to fine you a kiss on each cheek."

"Oh, don't play around with me so. This wrestling and pestering isn't funny. As they say, a bandit who's been caught but not thrashed will admit to nothing.

Your lordship pops his face up here because she's too lazy to catch you. You believe nobody else will see, so you presume you can come here in secret.

Don't pretend you have to be here. My looks can't please you as much. Where there's good talking, go bill and coo. Where there's good kissing, go wallow till the taste fades."

"You're so eloquent, Simala, good at being cutting, playful—everything. I surrender. I can't compete with your fine words." He spread his arms and hugged her against his body.

"I'm[40] willing, sir. Don't bully me." "Let me hug you a little. Don't try to escape." "The more I complain, the more you persist." "Surely you can stand it just once."

"I'm hot, sir. Please release me." "My love, bear it for a bit." "I'm really angry at you." "Don't push me away. You'll bruise your hand."

"Don't play around or I'll pinch you hard." "Oh love, aren't you worried about breaking a fingernail?" "Oh sir, your hands are making me shy." "What? It's pitch dark. Who is there to be shy of?"

Nose pressed to cheek. Hand grasping hand. Leg pressed on leg so she could not move. Belly against belly. Breast hugged against breast.[41] Like a pair of fighting cocks of great skill,

strutting up and down on the leash[42] in all directions, then each pecking, picking, and parrying back. The lower one sprang into an attacking stance. The upper one closed and clashed, banging together.

The lower ducked, kicked, bucked, smacked. The upper rode every blow without fail. After the long, white, sharp, serum-loaded spur stabbed, spilling blood, they slept.

fighting cocks

In the dead of night, when the whole household was fast asleep, a cold dew descended like strands of hair. Flowers opened their petals and new leaves budded.

Bees flew around to take pollen from blooming lotuses. Beasts slumbered quietly and peacefully. Phra Wai lay thinking of Soifa.

---

40. From here to the end of the chapter is taken from KJ, 23–27; PD omitted the tryst with Soifa and ends with a shorter tryst with Simala: The skies erupted in confusion. Lightning streaked. Thunder crashed and crashed. Rain spattered, sprinkled, spurted, and splashed. The wind blew hard enough to overwhelm the world. / Waves swirled, stormed, and smashed. Foaming spume overflowed the shore. The banks were shaken, swamped, and shattered. When the rain poured down, the wind dropped, and they drifted off to sleep.

41. Compare *Samuthakot khamchan* (70–71): His regal face against her fragrant face. / His royal belly against her rounded belly. / His chest pressed against hers. And *Lilit Phra Lo*: Flesh against flesh. "Oh soft fulfilling flesh!" / Radiant, fresh face against face. "Oh his fitting face!" / Breast against her soft breast. Belly against belly. "Oh her lithe belly, her breast!"

42. เดินมัด, *doen mat*, a cockfighting term, and เดินผูก, *doen phuk*, a chess term, both literally meaning "walking tied." The chess term means guarding a piece so that it cannot be taken without a costly exchange.

"Right now, is my jewel asleep or is she lying awake and waiting? Perhaps she complains I pay her no attention. It would be a pity if she feels slighted and sad.

In a moment I'll go to find how she performs. Is she truly good, like a Thai, or somehow different? This is a fine time to make an examination."

He turned to look at Simala sleeping soundly, and carefully slid away. He closed the curtain good and tight, and walked out of the apartment.

Coming to the room of Soifa, he saw masses of servants lying asleep. Lanterns cast light as bright as the moon. He slowly slid his body down onto the bed,

and sat examining Soifa. Her face glowed with a flawless beauty. In the light of the lamp, her delicate complexion shone as if just powdered.

Her lips seemed on the point of breaking into a sweet smile. Her neck fell in three circlets. Her two breasts were like golden lotuses pushing up beside each other, looking adorable.

He was beyond the point of restraining his body. He lifted Soifa onto his lap. "Wake up, gentle soul, don't stay asleep." He hugged her to his chest and kissed her.

When Soifa opened her eyes and saw Phra Wai, she panicked as she had never tasted love with a man. She trembled in the fullness of shyness and fright,

drew back and turned away, full of fear and foreboding in her breast. When he touched her, she flinched like a fledgling, overcome with distress.

Realizing she was stricken by fear, Phra Wai pronounced a mantra to ease her mind, sat close to her, and spoke intimately.

"Oh my soft flesh, my golden nugget, why are you turning away? Who is there to be shy about in this room? I've come to hug you to sleep."

Soifa was struck by the force of the mantra. Her fear and anxiety abated. She bent forward, turned her face and glanced at him from the corner of her eye. "I slept soundly over half the night and just woke up,

hot and running with sweat so I'm all clammy. Please go to sleep." With these words she got up. Phra Wai stood up too and held her tight.

"Ow, don't hurt me! You're squeezing so tight my fingers have lost any feeling already. Let me go. I'll sit here and not run away. Oh, I'm upset that the more I complain the more you hold on."

"Why are you so angry? Just touching your hand upsets you. I hold you very gently. There was no need to come outside the net.

If my darling isn't merciful, I'll stay here hugging you until dawn, letting the mosquitoes torment you. By morning your body will be covered in bumps."

He embraced and caressed her, "Please come into the net for relief and let me gently hug and kiss you. I pity your gold-like skin will be tarnished.

What's this black thing on your breast?" He groped with his hand and laughed. "Oh, it's a speck of dust." He pretended to look closely, then caressed and kissed. "Oh, here's a beauty spot too."

Soifa turned away and tossed her head. "I didn't invite you to sit inspecting me. Stop teasing like this. You should know it's not funny.

Even though a mosquito bites my cheek, don't bother brushing it off. My skin and yours are not the same. I don't care about my own flesh and blood. I'll sit and let the mosquitoes feed until morning."

"But I feel sorry for your cheeks, so fair and firm and smiling. Lit by the flickering light of the lamps, they seem fashioned from gold and nine jewels.

I wish to defend their softness and fragrance." He kissed her gently on both cheeks. "Only my nose is touching and that doesn't hurt, but the bites of these mosquitoes are sharp.

It's up to you. If my devout darling intends to make a charitable donation of her flesh and blood to the mosquitoes, I won't interfere with her wishes. But I can't allow your cheeks and breasts to be given as alms."

"Why not? Cheeks and breasts belong to someone, and if the owner wants to give them away, who are you to object? Don't hinder my charity. Let them be sliced up for the crows. I don't fear the pain.

If someone comes begging for a cheek as alms, I'll open the window and offer my face with a smile. Whether the cheeks get kissed or pinched, I'll close my eyes. If anyone scolds me, I'll shout to shoo them away."

"Oh, why do you say they cannot be mine? Don't play around with words. The king presented you as my partner, as everyone knows. If someone else kisses you and you don't resist, then look out.

I feel sorry for these breasts, so full, soft, and round. I'm worried about slicing them up for nothing." Pretending to be shocked, he cradled them gently. "Stop it. Take your hands off."

She shook him off and twisted away. "Oh, don't play around like this. It annoys me. The king presented me to you as a servant. He didn't order me to be your wife.

I won't consent so cease kissing and fondling. I'll serve only as a slave. Stop kissing and caressing my precious parts. Don't bother them so much they lose their fair sheen."

Soifa tried to squirm her way free. Phra Wai held onto her breasts and squeezed. She brushed him away sulkily. Passion stirred passion. Battle commenced.

She backed. He nudged. She trotted. He thrust. She recoiled. He pressed. She broke. He drove. She started and writhed. He thrust at full force. She responded with the style of a fine-bred filly,

only just harnessed for training, mouth still soft, unruly, and not yet used to a rider. He gave the filly her head for a while to watch her performance, till she slackened and slowed down,

lowering her haunches and turning her neck aside. He covered her, slapping her side so she sprang. Easy, easy. He pounded along at a pumping pace. Her bucking slowed to a graceful rhythm.

Once she knew the way, she was as good as a trained steed. Now that they knew each other, there was no limit to their energy, no need for him to urge her onwards, just follow the rhythm, until the sweat soaked down to her hooves, and he unharnessed her.

Both were overjoyed by the delicious, sweet taste of love. Sated as if they had soared to heaven, they slept sweetly and soundly.

Now to tell of the almighty king, supreme pillar of the world, resident of the heavenly palace. When the chariot of the sun rose and the orb shone,

he awoke from sleep, came down from his bed, and walked out of the chamber. Inner ladies attending on the king prostrated and waited to perform their regular duty.

The king was bathed in fragrant water and anointed with sweet perfumes. He grasped his glittering nine-jeweled regal sword, went out to the audience hall,

and seated himself on a royal throne. Large numbers of officials prostrated. The king pronounced on government matters, and then cast a glance towards the pages.[1]

Khun Chang saw an opening. "My liege, dust over my head, my life is beneath the royal foot. Since I became a servant below the dust,

in the pages for over eight years, I have not felt the crack of the rattan. Just now, this excitable Phra Wai almost elbowed me to death.

Not content with beating me, he said provocatively, 'I'm not afraid even of your master.' Over a hundred of his men hit me again and again. Some nobles came between us or else I'd have died.

While elbowing me, they also cursed me in front of all the nobles. Many witnessed this event and tried to stop them. If this is untrue, may I offer my life."

The king, upholder of the teachings, quietly pondered what Khun Chang had said. "It may be true that they beat him up,

but the provocative reference to his master is probably invented to create a big issue. The reason the incident blew up so messily is because this fellow thinks he's the stepfather,

---

1. The word มหาดชา, *mahatcha* is used several times in the *sepha*. It is assumed that the authors meant *dekcha* who were one type of pages on duty at the throne and royal residence, and also during government meetings. In the Fifth Reign, a department of *dekcha* was formed with the duty to look after the Jakri Mahaprasat throne, to provide the oil and light the lamps throughout the palace, to look after various royal properties associated with the throne during ceremonies, and to carry things at night. [A footnote from the PD edition]

and when he's full of liquor, he becomes insulting. Wai was shamed so he argued and started a quarrel. Each went a bit too far and it gradually got out of hand. Khun Chang cursed him, and Wai turned and beat him to his satisfaction.

If I ignore this matter and don't conduct an interrogation, Phra Wai will become even rougher. He'll think the king loves him, and he'll be overbearing. If anyone angers him, he'll abuse them badly and beat them up."

With these thoughts, the king gave orders to a palace guard to fetch Phra Wai. The guard ran off to Phra Wai's house and informed him.

"The king has sent for you immediately. Khun Chang has put his case to the king so it's a big issue." Phra Wai called his servants, descended the stairway, and dashed to the palace.

He quickly put on a sompak, wrapped a prostration cloth round his waist, and hurried along to the royal audience. He made obeisance and waited for the king's command.

prostration cloth

The king roared like a lion. "Heigh! Wai, at your marriage, why did you highhandedly commit violence on Khun Chang—

kicking, beating, and even making a provocative reference to his 'master'? Exactly who is the 'master' of this Chang that you claim you don't fear? Who?

Some nobles came between you but you still didn't listen—went on kicking, elbowing, and punching him down the stairs. What's true and what's false? Tell me."

Phra Wai addressed the points raised. "My liege, I do not lie. Everything that Khun Chang has conveyed to Your Majesty is concocted to put himself in a good light.

The allegation about insulting him is serious. If it's true, execute me. Khun Chang went to the wedding yesterday. After drinking liquor, he got tight

and said many insulting things. I tried to stop him several times. He teased my mother and tugged her around in front of people. I couldn't tolerate that so we quarreled.

He began spewing out many insults, and addressed me improperly. I was greatly shamed in front of people. Then he made things up about the past to slander me in public.

When I was seven years old,[2] Khun Chang took me off to a forest to beat me to death. When I collapsed on the ground, he worried I might not die and his deed would be exposed,

so he kept on slapping and hitting me, even after I fainted. He hit my forehead, chopped my head with a stick, dragged my body into undergrowth, and piled logs on top. Then he went home.

By the power of merit, I did not die. I recovered and staggered off to find a monk.[3] I hid with Master Non, in fear for my life.

Yesterday Khun Chang referred to the past. He spoke very loudly so all could hear. I've told everybody everything. If it's not true, let me offer my life."

After listening to Phra Wai's testimony, the king thought, "The early part seems to be a criminal matter but the latter part becomes a matter for the city court.[4]

The defendant's plea makes it a major crime. It'll be necessary to cross-examine the plaintiff to clarify matters." "Heigh! Khun Chang, Phra Wai has given evidence that when he was around seven years old,

you lured him into a forest, piled logs on him, and ran off. This case has lain hidden for over eight years—until yesterday when you made it public.

---

2. In chapter 24, where this incident happens, he is nine or ten years old.

3. In Phra Wai's version, Wanthong's role has been deleted. In chapter 24, she came searching in the forest, found him, and took him to stay with a monk in a wat.

4. The jurisdiction of different courts is defined in the *Phra thammanun*, Code of Procedure, in the Three Seals Law. Section 3 stated: "Any case in which, without deed of authorization, someone commits violence to seize, assault, tie up, beat, put in chains and cangue by force and without consent, or takes any property for his own benefit, or intimidates the party to a lawsuit, is a matter for the Department of Criminal Justice." The dispute and assault at the wedding was thus a matter for the criminal court which at that time came under Kalahom. Section 5 of the same law states: "Any case in which someone commits robbery of property or gold and silver, or kills a householder by day or night, or steals wives, children, phrai, servants, elephants, horses, boats, carts, cattle, buffaloes, cloth, noodles, vegetables, ducks, chicken, or anything else, or commits adultery with a wife, or commits murder, or uses filth-eating spirits, or makes love philters or abortion medicines causing death, is a matter for the Ministry of the Capital." The "latter part," meaning the accusation of attempted murder in the forest, thus fell under the jurisdiction of a court under the Ministry of the Capital. (KTS, 1:162–63; KW, 473)

As Khun Wichitmatra points out, the account of legal process in this chapter and the next, and the case in chapter 22, can only have been written by someone in the court with detailed knowledge of law and judicial procedure. The Three Seals Law, compiled for King Rama I in 1805 from earlier texts, existed only in very few copies. When Dan Beach Bradley and Mot Amatayakul printed an edition in 1850, King Rama III ordered the copies seized and burned. Bradley was finally allowed to print an edition in 1862–63. Khun Wichitmatra surmises that this segment was revised in the Second Reign salon, possibly by Chaophraya Mahasak Phonlasep who he thinks also revised chapter 22. But Khun Wichitmatra also wonders if the future King Rama III was involved, especially in view of one passage (KW, 510–13).

This incident is the original reason for your quarrel. That is what he told everybody. And he denies the allegation about making a grave insult. So, heigh! What is the real reason?"

Khun Chang realized the king's question meant the old incident had resurfaced. He was truly taken aback, and his body was bathed in sweat for fear of punishment.

He steeled himself to address the king. "Great power over my head. Everything Phra Wai told Your Majesty is invention and falsehood.

It's not true that I tried to beat him to death. If I had done so, there would be evidence. Why then did he keep the matter hidden and not inform Your Majesty? He's made this up to create a big issue.

Since I accused him of assault, he's trying to cover up his evil deeds by making things up and petitioning Your Majesty on the basis of lies and supposition.

I can state this is untrue. Phra Wai deliberately got me drunk, lured me to speak under the influence, and now wants to smear me with wrongdoing.

His provocative reference to Your Majesty is a grave matter. If I am not honest, may Your Majesty punish me. If things are not true as I say, punish me with death."

The king, ruler of the world, slapped his thigh. "I'll get to the bottom of this. Heigh! Nobles attending in audience, don't take sides. Those of you who went to the wedding yesterday

and saw what happened, speak out. Don't be biased towards the rich and noble. Khun Chang says Phra Wai assaulted him and made an improper reference to the king.

Phra Wai says Khun Chang referred to a past incident, and spoke so loudly everyone could hear—that when he was tiny, Khun Chang took him off to do away with him but, by his merit, he survived.

When Khun Chang mentioned trying to kill Phra Wai, was he or was he not totally drunk? Don't take sides. Speak out without deference to anybody."

A noble who had attended the wedding responded to the king. "I can recall, as can everybody. It began when Khun Chang arrived at the wedding.

He drank until he was drunk and then spoke rashly. He got up and danced around, saying he was Hanuman and speaking flirtatiously with Wanthong.

Phra Wai felt ashamed and told him off, but Khun Chang didn't listen. Tempers flared and they had an exchange of blows. Khun Chang blurted about matters in the past. He was raving

that when Phra Wai was living with his mother, Khun Chang took him off to kill him in a deep forest, split Phra Wai's head at the hairline with a stick, piled logs on him, and left him to die.

In a rage, Phra Wai summoned his men to beat Khun Chang until he fell down flat on his back. As for the improper comment about his master, none of us heard that.

But Khun Chang was totally drunk. He even stripped off his clothes quite shamelessly. I'm not telling untruths, taking sides, or playing tricks. I beg to inform the royal foot."

The king, upholder of the teachings, astutely appraised the testimony of the witnesses in his mind. "The important point is the improper reference.

The plaintiff's allegation is serious. If true, it's punishable by death.[5] If not true, the plaintiff is liable to the same penalty. On the other point about beating to death,

if the testimony goes against him, Khun Chang must be executed for the wrongdoing. But some allowance may be made on grounds he was totally drunk and not fully sensible when he spoke.

It'll be necessary to interrogate Phra Wai for clarification. Khun Chang cannot yet be found guilty." Thus the king said, "Ha! Heigh! Phra Wai, back then when Khun Chang tried to beat you to death,

why did you sit on the case and bring it out only now when he accuses you? It doesn't look right. In what forest did it happen? Are there people who know anything about this?"

"My liege, over my head. I was only a little boy when he did this, and I can't recall anything except that the forest was beyond Suphan. Also no one was around to be a witness.

I shouted out but there were no houses nearby. I couldn't escape as it was deep in the forest. I survived by the power of merit, and was too young to consider bringing a charge.

I didn't know what district it was, what officials to see, or where a court was, so I didn't speak of this matter for a long time, until guardian deities prompted me.

---

5. Probably under clause 1 of the Law on Revolt and Warfare: "Anyone who has ideas above his station and by revolt or violence drags the king down from his golden umbrella" is liable to a penalty of death (KTS,1:14). Possibly under clause 1 of the Code of Crimes Against Government: "Anyone who covetously elevates himself above his rank, acts beyond his station, and, unmindful of the kindness of king, speaks words that should not be spoken in *ratchasap* or appropriates undeserved insignia, is guilty of vainglory and subject to punishment of eight grades," of which the first was to be severed at the neck and have the house seized (KTS, 4:6).

Since it happened in a forest, there were no witnesses. It's beyond my ability to prove it properly. Should I be found in the wrong in an ordeal by water, let me offer my life to Your Majesty."[6]

The king, ruler of the earth, heard Phra Wai out, and then roared like a lion. "What Wai says sounds right.

Ha! Heigh! Khun Chang, relate the matter from the start without concealment. If you confess you did wrong, I'll be lenient. Tell everything without lying or withholding information."

The king's question made Khun Chang greatly distressed. He raised his clasped hands and bowed his head. Sweat poured down him, front and back. After a pause, he addressed the king.

"My liege, dust under the royal foot, holy patron. Phra Wai's words are untrue, invention, all of it.

I didn't beat him as claimed. He brought this matter up to smother the charges I made. All the nobles are siding with Phra Wai because they are colleagues.

I've no allies so I'm at a loss. To stay alive, I must prove my case to the king. If I lose, do away with me. Let me offer my life."

The king carefully reviewed the evidence. "Khun Chang is telling lies. His account is suspicious on every point.

Even if he produced witnesses, I'd have doubts. This is not the sort of case for the courts.[7] Right now the evidence is against Khun Chang. His claims conflict with everybody else.

Though he spoke in the manner of a drunk, his words can still give rise to suspicion. If I ordered officials of the capital to use the cane, we'd sort truth from falsehood in no time.

But at present, Phra Wai is in royal favor, and the common people talk about that. If I side with Phra Wai and accuse Khun Chang, who'll know what's true and what's false?

---

6. A case could be decided by ordeal if either: the two parties' claims conflicted, and they challenged one another to an ordeal; or the evidence was insufficient; or the evidence was hopelessly conflicting (Ishii, "Thai Thammasat," 169). Here Phra Wai issues a challenge. However, in what follows Khun Chang does not accept the challenge and eventually the king commands the ordeal on grounds of insufficient evidence.

7. ผิดวิสัยความหลวงกระทรวงศาล, *phit wisai khwam luang krasuang san*. Parties in conflict could either mutually agree on an independent arbitrator, or submit the case to the courts. If submitted to the courts, the case became a royal case, *khwam luang*, as all courts were considered subdivisions of the king's court. Here the king appears to appoint himself as arbitrator (Law on Judgment, preface, KTS, 2:124).

The case must be examined by due process to get to the bottom of the competing claims and let people see who's telling the truth and who's not. That way I'll escape criticism."

Thus the king said, "Ha! Heigh! Khun Chang, you cited royal officials as witnesses. I've questioned them on the matter of improper comments, and all said they heard nothing.

This is a serious offense, yet all of the witnesses for the plaintiff turned out to be for the defendant. When they didn't support you, you changed your tune and cast doubt on your own witnesses.

I think your case is a pack of lies. If I went by the book, your head would be cut off. You've lied about the improper comment without fear, and wrongly defamed Phra Wai.

I accept the charge that he assaulted you. On the matter of defaming him, the two of you could reach a settlement. On the improper comment, you're guilty and condemned to death. Yet I pardon you, Khun Chang.

The charge of beating to death has lain hidden for a long time. There are no witnesses, no clear proof, nothing certain either way—for Phra Wai or for Khun Chang."

Having made his pronouncement, the king gave orders to the four chief judges.[8] "Arrange the equipment for the plaintiff and defendant to undergo ordeal by water.[9] Have the posts set up in front of the Floating Pavilion.[10]

Have both of them enter confinement tomorrow for seven nights until

---

8. สี่พระครู, *si phra khru*, meaning the two Phra Maharatchakhru in charge of the two sets of judges, and their two respective deputies, Phra Ratchakhru Phrakhruphichet and Phra Ratchakhru Phrakhruphiram (KTS, 1:265).

9. Several seventeenth century European visitors who wrote about Siam mentioned trial by fire or water (Schouten, *True Description*, 133; *Van Vliet's Siam*, 112, 153–54; Gervaise, *Natural and Political History*, 62; La Loubère, *New Historical Relation*, 86–87).

Possibly the last usage of trial by fire took place in 1770 when King Taksin tried the rebellious monks of Fang. According to the eighteenth century description of the Ayutthaya palace, there was a pit for the ordeal by water outside the inner official sala inside the palace. However, Phraya Boranratchathanin, who excavated the area, doubted whether there was a place large and deep enough for the ordeal inside the palace walls, and suspected that such trials took place, as in *KCKP*, in the river. In 1991, excavation of the eight-sided pond to the west of the old Ayutthaya jail found two large posts which might have been used for the ordeal. In the new capital of Bangkok, the necessary pond and pit were prepared beside the law courts. Though never used, the pond was not filled in until a century later. (KLW, 200; Boranratchathanin, *Tamnan krung kao*, 104; *Boranasathan*, 1:50; Wales, *Divination*, 113–14)

10. ตำหนักแพ, *tamnak phae*, literally the raft royal residence, according to Khun Wichitmatra, a name for the pier called *Phrachanuan nam* at Wasukri Landing on the north of the palace (KW, 638; see map 9).

the day of the ordeal. Keep them under guard, and have them ready by one o'clock in the afternoon.[11]

Officials from every department will come to watch. Chief judges, issue the requisition orders. Detain the two of them in the palace." Having given these commands, the king went inside.

The chief judges came out and sat in the main swordstore to prepare and distribute the various requisition orders. They sent for the posts belonging to the Ministry of the Capital,

and had the prison warders store two of them. They defined the zone, made shrines, had clerks write out the charges and testimony, and found judges to serve as neutral observers.

"Do not allow any food sent from their homes. The court officers will prepare food for both of them. Get both the plaintiff and defendant to provide some thin white cloth to spread at the two shrines for placing offerings,

betel and pan in a well-made leaf basket, along with incense, candles, flowers, and *baisi*, all to be offered to Krung Phali. Arrange to have kaffir lime, soap nut,[12] krajae-sandal,

upper and lower cloths in white, carpet and mat, sacred thread, new pots for rice and curry, water pitcher, spittoon, and water bowl under a shade,

along with a new stove, mortar and pestle, ladle, flagon of liquor, rice, galangal, lemongrass, onion, garlic, dry chili, and chicken *phanaeng*. Arrange the same things in the two places."

water pitcher

Khun Chang and Phra Wai took the command and sent for their servants who promptly arrived with all the requirements.

They went into confinement for seven nights. Workmen set up the posts at the boat dock of the Floating Pavilion. Prison warders found a gong to be beaten,

---

11. This passage follows closely the procedure laid out in detail in the Law on Trial by Ordeal in the Three Seals Law. The law went to great lengths to ensure that the two parties would prepare for the ordeal in the same way: "The judges (*tralakan*) will detain both parties; buy chickens from the same place; buy beeswax, undyed thread, soap nut, kaffir lime, new rice pot, new curry pot, uppercloth, lowercloth, all from the same place, and materials for a *baisi*, also from the same place. The judges will detain both parties; have them dress in white upper and lower cloths; remain in confinement for three days without walking outside; have the judges cook rice for them, and look after them. . . . . Do not allow anyone to talk with either party, or else that party loses. If either party goes outside, that party loses." The quarantine and other procedures were intended to prevent the use of mantra or other forms of lore to affect the result (KTS, 2:106–7; KW, 477; Saowalak, *Wannakam ek*, 186).

12. ส้มป่อย, *sompoi*, *Acacia concinna*. The pods are powdered and used as shampoo—perhaps the intended usage here.

Chinese

scribes to pronounce the oath,[13] judges to read the full court record, and ropes for tying their waists. Everything was in place awaiting the arrival of the king.[14]

Crowds of people rushed to see the ordeal—young men and women, adults and children, Chinese, Farang, Khaek, Kha, Mon, and Lao.

Young girls in their homes saw their friends on the way and jumped up to join them. Striding[15] off, one fell headlong down the stairs.

Her cloth flopped over her face, exposing her big thighs. A new Chinese[16] onlooker danced around in excitement. He took off his hat and used it like trousers. Young men roared with laughter.

Gay ladies in the palace called out to their partners, "We're going to see the ordeal by water, loves." Some were pleased, "Let's go, Mae Ampha." "Yes, yes, let's all go down to the jetty, Mae Arun."

Those still cuddling together came out of the mosquito net and hid the sac[17]

---

13. The oath calls on a very long list of Brahmanical gods and protective spirits to ensure a fair result (KTS, 2:115–22; KW, 479–80).

14. The Law on Trial by Ordeal stated: "In case of trial by water, a scribe will read out the two testimonies to the gods. Then the plaintiff and defendant will wash their heads and present their bodies. The posts will be placed six cubits apart. Judges will tie a rope round the waist of plaintiff and defendant, and attach it to the post, place a plank on their shoulders, strike a gong three times, then press their necks under water and pay out the rope. Each will submerge together to the base of each post. A clock will be placed. Once they have submerged, the first to emerge will have a rope placed round his neck, and the other's rope will be tugged to bring him up. If after 6 *bat* [*bat*=6 minutes], neither plaintiff or defendant has emerged, the ropes will be tugged to bring them up" (KTS, 2:112–13; KW, 479).

15. The next four and a half stanzas, down to "raced after the others," are taken from KJ, 34–35; PD has: They called on other friends to hurry along with them to see Phra Wai and Khun Chang undergo the ordeal by water. / Old folks who wanted to watch left their homes, dragging and carrying their children and grandchildren. The boat dock was overflowing with people chaotically crammed together. / In the palace, all the lords and ladies, sentinelles, royal retainers, and everyone else knew that Khun Chang and Phra Wai would undergo the ordeal that afternoon. / They bathed, powdered, combed their hair, and put on smart lower and upper cloths. Some popped two or three mouthfuls of betel in a packet. Some dragged their friends along by the hand.

16. จีนใหม่, *jin mai*, a newly arrived Chinese migrant.

17. ถุง, *thung*, bag. Possibly this is a tubular bag filled with seeds of hoary basil, แมงลัก, *maenglak*, *Ocimum canum*, which swell and become slippery when wet. This device was used in lesbian love play in the novel *Khang paet*, Prison No. 8, written by Daosawai Paichit in the 1970s and made into a film in 2002.

in a basket of kapok. Ampha said, "I'm coming too, loves. Come along, Mae Yisun. Don't delay."

"Hey! Can't you wait just a little?" She parted her hairline so hurriedly that the stick broke. She swiped on a black pencil, dashed a comb through her hair, and raced after the others.

When they reached the Floating Pavilion, it was packed with people jostling together. Rafts were swarming all over the surface of the river, waiting for the time of the ordeal.

Boatmen had moored everywhere, upstream and down. Smaller boats floated around. The whole river was chock-full and raucous.

Now to tell of King Phanwasa, eminence of Ayutthaya, the great heaven, who resided in a glittering crystal palace where throngs of inner ladies made obeisance.

He thought back to the big case involving Phlai Ngam. "How will the ordeal by water with Khun Chang turn out?" Close to three o'clock in the afternoon,

he was bathed, arrayed in a brilliant nine-jeweled costume, and left the golden royal residence, gripping a glittering filigree regal sword.

He stepped into a royal palanquin, accompanied by senior officers and royal poets. To the sound of horn, conch, and drum, he came along the cloister down to the river.

On arrival, the king ascended a throne while senior officials bowed and prostrated. The main guard boarded canopy boats, and went to lay buoys and stand with guns to ward away people.

Many craft were moving up and down the river in confusion. Prison warders boarded boats and went upstream to push away anything floating dead in the water so it would not disturb the proceedings.

The king, eminence of the earth, issued a royal order to the chief judges to have the parties submerge promptly at sunset.

The chief judges acted on the king's order. "Following the ancient manual of judicial procedure, Phra Wai should take the upstream side and Khun Chang the downstream.[18]

It's true that originally Khun Chang was the plaintiff but after thorough interrogation with supporting evidence, this trial by ordeal is for Phra Wai.

---

18. Normally the plaintiff, i.e., Khun Chang, would be upstream but the story of his attempt to kill Phra Wai as a child has converted the case into a trial of Khun Chang.

Besides, he is a noble. Khun Chang must take the downstream side." Having agreed on this point, the two were brought out from confinement

and led along under heavy guard. They washed head and body,[19] faced off against each other,[20] and went down into the water.

Clocks were placed at the water's edge.[21] At each side, guards grasped the end of a rope, held a bamboo across the shoulders, and waited ready to force the head under water.

ordeal by water

When a gong sounded, both submerged. But as soon as he ducked under, Khun Chang shot back up again. The onlookers jeered and booed. Guards put a large chain around his neck,

and crowded around to hustle him away. Khun Chang called out, "Please have mercy, Sire. This fellow, Phra Wai, has knowledge. He blew something onto me.

The power of a formula gripped my heart. I couldn't stand it. My hair stood on end. Giving the defendant the upstream side allowed him to blow a mantra down to affect me."

---

19. Possibly to avoid the upstream person having some substance secreted which could float down on his rival (KW, 481).

20. This part of the procedure was called ชนไก่, *chon kai*, cockfight, and perhaps was a chance to check whether the two were in a fit state for the ordeal (KTS, 2:112; KW, 688; SB, 495).

21. Half coconut shells were pierced with holes so that, when floated on water, they sank after a specified time (KW, 485).

After hearing Khun Chang, the king exclaimed, "Damn this loudmouth! He loses but tries to turn it round by dribbling on about Wai using lore.

Because he's beyond hope, he twists things in front of everybody, and forces another submersion. Such a great, slippery-tongued liar should be thrashed to dust.

But what he says about the defendant being upstream is fair. The decision will not be untainted, given that the case arose because of him.

Let him go upstream and submerge again. Arrange it immediately. If he loses again, I won't listen. Just take him away for the chop he deserves."

The chief judges took the order from the king. "Come and submerge again at once, Chang." They tied the rope round Phra Wai's waist, led both of them to the posts,

and put the wood on their shoulders. The gong sounded. They pushed their necks down, and paid out the rope. Onlookers crowded around in excitement. Boats jostled to get a view.

Because Khun Chang was in the wrong, when he had been under for only half his breath, he imagined snakes were twining round his body. He shot above the surface shaking with fear.

Phra Kanburi jumped into the water and lifted Phra Wai out in front of everybody. The city guards clapped the baldy in irons and dragged him off.

The king stamped his foot in anger. "Yommarat! Throw him in jail! This danger to the realm has a fast tongue.[22] It's no small thing to kill someone without a thought.

He was crooked and mendacious even with me. He seemed to imagine there was no authority. He showed off, issued challenges, and offered his life, but now he's proved to be in the wrong twice over.

He made bold to kill someone and dared lie even to me. Don't leave him to pollute the earth. Cleave open his breast as an example to deter others.

He took Wai off to kill in a forest. Go and impale him in that same forest." The king left his throne and returned by palanquin to the inner palace.

Minister Yommarat issued orders to all the officials. "Don't trust someone who's been condemned to death. Send him to the head of the Department of Royal Corrections.[23]

---

22. ลิ้นลังกา, *lin langka*, a Lankan tongue; a reference to South Asians' rapid speech (KW, 688).

23. กระทรวงหลวงพัศดี, *krasuang luang phatsadi*, usually ขุนพัศดี, *khun phatsadi*, one of two deputies overseeing the prisons, *sakdina* 800 (KTS, 1:229).

Have warders put him in all five irons immediately so he can't escape. Chains, yoke, cangue—have no mercy." Four warders dragged Khun Chang off to jail.

Though he used to walk with long strides, chained three times over, just a small step made him tumble down. Guards crowded around hustling him, but he would not get up. He pretended to be winded in the stomach, and wailed loudly.

In anger, the warders grasped canes, punched him down, and kept on beating him back and front. "Die. See if we care! If we're in the wrong, we'll just pay one fueang to disown responsibility."

Khun Chang understood but ignored them. He leapt up and pretended to be crazy, gaping his mouth open, lolling his tongue, and rolling up his eyes. He threw off his lowercloth and ran dangling.

He picked up a lump of dogshit, chased after people, and threw it at them. He bashed his head against a post and danced wildly, knocking onlookers with the cangue. His chains clanked on the ground and his mouth shouted a song.

Warders threatened him, "You mongrel! I'll cure your madness with this cane." "You abominable wretch, throwing shit at people and letting it all hang out."

Women averted their faces and ran away, crying, "He's done for." "I'm fed up with him." "Worse than a beggar." Young men ragged him, "Why don't you tie it in tuck-tail style?"

The servants who had come with Khun Chang felt ashamed. They ran over to pick up his cloth and wrap it round him. The warders dragged him off and clapped him in jail.

They put on a proper wooden cangue fixed securely with nails, chains fastened tightly, a brick under his rear, his head bent over the cangue, and fetters fastened tightly on his hands.

Khun Chang was severely manacled. His hands were trussed, and he was suspended from the waist with his head lolling. He could not move and his heart shuddered. "Oh, I've reached my dying day!"

He spoke a prayer but it came out muddled.[24] "*Pattisangkha ye play ply, karanang yang mura kusalai, papaya cock cry khat chai mi,*
hirupakka hirapakke, samtan sante ye tasi, mut takang pan matter can curry, hit batter box hungry break mouth die." The warders cursed him angrily.

"What kind of prayer is that, you disaster?" "Officers are making an inspec-

---

24. This is gibberish but in the rhythm of a prayer chant. It starts with a Pali word for merit, becomes nonsense that sounds a bit like a Pali prayer, and finally becomes recognizable words.

tion. Why are you making a racket?" "You're too noisy. Don't you know the power of the cane?"

Khun Chang called out, "Beg pardon. Don't be angry. I'll give you seven tamlueng, ten salueng. Please loosen the chains so I can breathe. I'll give you ten tamlueng for the reduction fees."[25]

"Fine. Don't be angry. You're condemned to death. So as not to annoy the overseers, keep quiet until the inspection. Then we'll turn the key to loosen them a bit."

◈

Now to tell of the beautiful Wanthong. At home, she could not sleep but tossed and turned because her husband was involved in a court case with her son, and she did not know the outcome as he had not returned.

Ai-Phlap came back, bent over with crying. "The master lost the case, mistress. He's been sent to jail, and manacled, including a cangue. King Phanwasa was angry and sentenced him to death.

They put him at the end of the row of people with rears suspended. He's chained so he has to sit from dawn to dusk, hanging with his bottom off the bench. I feel sorry for the master. When I left, they hadn't loosened him at all."

Hearing news of her husband, Wanthong lay down choked with tears, on the point of fainting away, writhing around as if her life would end.

The servants beat their breasts in dismay, and crowded around to help Wanthong—massaging, kneading with their feet, giving smelling salts, and bathing her with floral water. Gradually she returned to her senses,

raised herself, and awkwardly crawled into her room. She brought the key to unlock a trunk, opened the lid, and took out two or three bars of gold. Using a bowl with a carved rim, she scooped cash

into several baskets, covered their tops with handfuls of cowries, and handed them for I-Khiat to carry on her waist. She put food in a large bowl,

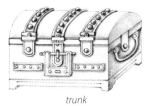

and prepared presents including venison and half a pitcher of honey. She sent servants off to buy

trunk

---

25. Fees to have constraints reduced or removed were detailed in the laws, for example: "Anyone condemned to the cane or five restraints may pay reduction fees of 2 baht 7 tamlueng to the department head, 2 tamlueng to the deputy, 1 baht to the head of the imprisoning unit, 2 baht to the guard and registrar of people, 2 baht to the registrar of boats, and 1 baht 2 salueng to the five guard officers on duty to share" (KTS, 5:45–53).

blackear catfish, then loaded a watermelon boat[26] and hurried off.

On arrival, she moored the boat and went along trailed by many servants carrying trays of presents and bowls of food. At the jail, she went up to find the chief governor

and gave him presents. "Sir, have some mercy on me. I've had no experience of how things are in jail. May I send food to Khun Chang?"

The governor summoned warder Niam. "Take this good lady to see her husband." The warder led her away through the slip gate[27] into the inner prison.

Wanthong appealed to the warder, "Please release him to come down and eat something, can you?" The warder said, "You may go in to see him, Wanthong, but there's no release for a punishment like this."

Wanthong steeled herself to enter the jail. She saw people suffering gruesomely, with thin bodies like creatures in hell.[28] They looked ugly and frightful, making her scalp crawl.

No food passed through the gut of those locked in the cangue. Seeing Wanthong coming, they wai-ed her imploringly. She threw bananas and they shakily fought over them, the strongest hitting the others and eating them,

taking whatever they could get with no choice, not bothering to peel the bananas but chewing them whole. They had scabies, boils, running sores, stench like corpses,

and hairy lice crawling on their skulls. Wanthong could not look and stepped awkwardly away. She struggled to bear it until she reached the end of the inner jail. Khun Chang saw her and wailed out loud.

Wanthong saw him, threw herself down, and cried. He was bent over, exhausted, and covered in snot and tears like a calf. "Oh, you abandoned me with no pity!

liquor seller

---

26. เรือแตงโม, *ruea taengmo*, now the name of a drum barge in the royal barge procession but here a boat hollowed from wood, but of shape now unknown. Perhaps it was the boat usually known as เรือป๊าบ, *ruea pap*, or เรือแตะ, *ruea tae*, a small boat with a slightly bowed shape and upcurving bow and stern which resembles a segment of watermelon (Phuthon, *Ruea nai phak klang*, 27).

27. *Hap phoei*, the same gate where Khun Phaen and Kaeo Kiriya lived in chapter 23.

28. Gruesome pictures of people suffering in hell are a staple of wat murals based on the Three Worlds cosmology.

Go and hand out bribes wherever you can, quickly! Have mercy. Don't let me die in chains. Put money in big, big sacks, and go to Jek Lo to buy some liquor for me.

Oh, I forgot. Please help me out of this. Go around inside and at the front.[29] Choose some presents and bring them. Also food, liquor, knick knacks, pork, and Vietnamese sausage."

Wanthong was angry. "You stumblebum! You're so brainless your head will be lopped off soon. Drinking liquor is what got you into these chains, and you're still drooling after some more."

Seeing her anger, Khun Chang begged forgiveness. "Hit me on the head, I won't complain. I'm so miserable. I didn't watch what I was doing and blundered badly.

Scold me as much as you like, I won't object. But bring me cash to pay the jail fees, and ten tamlueng for the reduction charges. Whatever expense is needed to please them, pay it, my dear."

Wanthong replied. "Don't babble. We have loads of money. I'll take it to distribute among the officers, don't worry. Though you're a provincial, they should be kind."

A warder had Ai-Rot remove the cangue. "Eat, brother Chang. Stop moaning. Why be afraid whether you live or die? You can't escape by disappearing into the earth."

Khun Chang grasped a bowl of rice and put a handful in his mouth, but his throat was too dry. Chewing turned the rice into flour and he could not swallow. He had to moisten his throat with water first.

Each mouthful had to be mixed with water. Thinking of his situation, he put down the bowl and sobbed. Wanthong consoled him. "Try to swallow some. Force yourself to eat in order to have some strength."

Seeing he was just sitting and grieving, she fed him spoonfuls of lizard curry to ease his dry throat, and then spicy meat, eels, and chicken *phanaeng*. Khun Chang managed to finish the whole large basin.

Shaking his head, he said, "That's enough. It's very awkward. Don't force me." Thinking of his plight, tears welled up. He threw himself round his wife's neck and pleaded,

"My dear, hurry off with the money and bribe the inner officials to talk to the king to petition for my pardon so I can get out of this."

Wanthong said, "I can't do it myself. If I run after people, I'll probably fall

---

29. "Inside" means in the palace, while "at the front" means among officials.

flat on my face. To extract a thorn, you must use another thorn to pry it out. I'll plead with Wai to see to it."

Khun Chang said, "Truly, my dear? If so, I'll survive because you help me. If I'm pardoned and stay alive, wherever you go, you can ride me instead of an ox!"

Wanthong said, "Don't be too obsequious. My kinsfolk never ride on their husband's neck. Should I die, I won't mind. Don't worry. I won't abandon you, no matter what."

She took money from the baskets, distributed it to the warders from senior to junior ranks, and gave alms to every one of the convicts.

She entrusted her husband to their care, went out of the main cells, gave money to the prison governor, and hurried off to Phra Wai's house.

She threw herself into Phra Wai's arms, and cried on his shoulder until she almost collapsed. Phra Wai felt very sorry for her. He paid respect and asked,

"What's troubling you, Mother? Don't cry. Speak up. Has one of the grandparents died? Were you so upset that you burst out crying before you could tell me?"

Wanthong said, "My dear sir, my problem is as bad as dying. I can't see anyone to turn to for help so that I may survive this time.

I think only my beloved Phra Wai can solve the problem. Khun Chang is so crooked and evil that he's a danger to himself.

He's like a sagging breast that weighs on my chest.[30] I suffer. For better or worse, he became my husband. If I stand by and let him die, the shame will follow me, and I'll have a bad name for a whole era.

For this reason alone, I can't abandon him. I'm at a loss, so I've reluctantly come to you. Dear son, please have mercy on your mother. Please request the king to spare Khun Chang's life.

The king is merciful. He should not refuse you. Khun Chang respectfully asks to beg your forgiveness. Don't create sin for yourself.

Apart from you, there's no one else I can ask. Please help save his life so he may be your servant. He did wrong in the past but please don't bear a grudge from now on."

Phra Wai replied immediately, "Why do you come pleading to me, Mother? I didn't lay charges against Khun Chang.

Rather, it was he who wanted me dead. He went and told everything

---

30. See p. 700, note 48.

to the king to get me on a capital charge, but I got off because there were witnesses.

In the past he took me to beat to death but I recovered and survived. You know full well about that. Don't you have some concern for me?

You don't think about the times your son nearly died. You care only about the life of your husband, and so you come around here weeping helplessly because you're afraid he'll die.

The king is angry. What can I get from asking for a pardon? It'll be like throwing myself on a fire. Hopeless, Mother!"

Wanthong embraced Phra Wai, racked with tears. "What you say is true. When Khun Chang almost killed you, I knew all about it.

I took you and entrusted you to a wat, and offered them cloth to make into flags so no one was suspicious. Not seeing you for just one day, I was on the point of death. Every night I lay crying out of love.

To have a loving husband is not as important as having a child. A husband can disappear just going down three steps.[31] Even if I loved him enough to swallow, it would not be like you, my son.

You're angry at him for trying to kill you but that was a long time ago. Make some merit. Don't wish him dead and harbor vengeance. If you ignore this now, the king will soon execute him for certain.

For your mother's sake, help him get out of this, like releasing fish or turtles to make merit.[32] I've taken the trouble to feed and look after you since you were still in my womb.

When you were born, I took care of you—pounding rice three times a day to feed you, bathing you, putting you in a cradle, singing you to sleep—from when you were tiny until you grew up.

Khun Chang found some little servants for you, gave gold to make bracelets and a *sema* chain, and a single nielloware *takrut*—all good quality.

At new year, at Songkran, he dressed you up and took you to the wat grounds, with your crowd of little servants tailing along, and a wet nurse, Nang Si, to carry you in her arms.

When Khun Chang loves someone, there's nobody like him. The only thing he cannot give is the moon and the stars. If you took a liking to anything available in Suphan, he wouldn't deny you and make you unhappy.

---

31. Kukrit claimed a husband could divorce a wife by walking down three stairways from his house and making a public declaration, but he offers no evidence for this claim, and there is no such provision in the Law on Marriage. Kukrit added, "The world of that era truly belonged to men. Too bad I wasn't born in time" (KP, 333–34).

32. A common form of merit making is to release captive animals, especially fish or birds.

He may be bad but he's also good, very good. You were a child and won't remember. Don't bear a grudge. Please let him live. It'll be like repaying the debt of gratitude to your mother."

Phra Wai was softened by his mother's plea. "I pity her enormously. If I do nothing and let Khun Chang die,
 where will she find happiness? She'll just become sadder and sadder until she falls ill, and might even hang herself. Then the sin and karma will really be mine.
 Though Khun Chang is as bad as a pig or dog, it's known everywhere that he's my mother's husband. If I just stand by, showing no concern, people will gossip."
 With these thoughts, he said to his mother, "It's hopeless because it's the king. But refusing will seem like I have no consideration for my mother. I'll try to make the king take pity on me.
 So stifle your tears and don't cry. I'll petition for a review. If the king pardons him, he'll be released alive, but if he's fated to die, it's beyond my power."

"Oh my dear son, please secure this mercy. I'll give you two chang as payment for the petition. If you help, I truly believe he won't die. The punishment should be eased because you're in royal favor."

"What's this you're saying, Mother? Do you think I'm a chicken that can be tempted with rice? You think your poor son will make the plea because your rich man has lots of money,
 because with this two chang I can build a house of five rooms with wooden walls, and can keep lots of wives and servants, all because of a bribe from my mother!"

"Oh my beloved son, don't get angry. Your mother's like a lunatic. My mind deserted me. I spoke terribly without thinking. I made a slip.
 Don't delay. Go and ask for the pardon as if you were helping your mother go to heaven.[33] You'll gain merit that will last a whole era. Most beloved, don't delay."
 Phra Wai's tears flowed out of pity for his mother. He consoled her, "Don't lose heart. I'll make the petition and then it's up to merit."
 He called out to Simala to fetch a betel box, cloth for wrapping, nak ket-

---

33. An allusion to the belief that a son entering the monkhood creates merit for the parents.

tle, Japanese umbrella, red pipe tipped with gold which a servant filled with tobacco, and water pipe.[34]

Phra Wai bathed his body, went into the house, took off his old clothes, and put on a *pha-muang* lowercloth of olive green imported silk, and uppercloth of plain chicken-skin silk, genuine Pakthao.[35]

He pinched Simala's cheek with a smile, went to take leave of his mother in the sitting hall, then hurried out of the house followed by a crowd of servants.

He soon arrived at the palace where many government officials were gathered. At the appropriate time in the light of dawn, they went in to wait on the king.

Now to tell of the king emperor, ruler of Ayutthaya, the great heaven, who resided in a glittering crystal palace where throngs of palace ladies,

all just of age, radiant, fair, and beautiful, with figures like those in a painting, serviced the royal footsoles. The king slumbered in the golden palace

until dawn streaked the sky, when he woke from sleep and came to bathe in cool rosewater and be arrayed in splendid raiment.

Grasping a diamond sword in his left hand, he went out to the main audience hall to sit on a glittering crystal throne, surrounded by senior officials and royal poets.

throne

Chaophraya, phraya, and lesser nobles from all the ministries paid respect and waited silently in the audience hall to hear royal commands.

The king inquired about petitions from the people on matters great and small. Nobles holding relevant positions in various departments responded to the king.

34. อุดเตา, *ut-tao*, a word that usually means an iron but here probably is some smoking equipment, and possibly a pipe which, like an iron, uses charcoal (SB, 502).

35. ปักเถา. Suphon thinks this is a weaving center in China (SB, 502). In the eighteenth-century description of Ayutthaya, along Yan Pa Chomphu Street was sold "belts in chicken-skin from Kai-eng and Pakthao, ordinary pink cloth, ordinary printed cloth . . ." (KLW, 191). Kai-eng is an old rendering of Kaifeng in Henan province of northeast China. Kaifeng has a textile industry that developed from Jewish traders bringing cloth along the Silk Road. Pakthao may be another Chinese textile center but is difficult to identify. Alternatively, the word might mean "embroidered with a vine pattern."

Seeing the government business was over, Phra Wai prostrated three times. "My liege, dust under the royal foot, the royal power is fathomless.

Whether or not it may gain approval, allow me to seek a royal pardon. May Your Majesty grant favor over my head. Khun Chang has been condemned to death and is now in the main jail.

My mother is so distressed she is almost at the point of death. She grieves morning and night. She does not eat.

If I did not agree to address the dust beneath Your Majesty's foot, she'd certainly die or go mad. I'm extremely concerned for her. Since I was born,

I have not yet repaid my debt of gratitude to her in full measure. From the age of seven years, we were parted from each other. Please pardon Khun Chang this once. It will be equivalent to saving my mother's life."

Knowing the meaning behind Phra Wai's words, the king quietly weighed up both sides. "If I don't spare Khun Chang's life,

Wanthong will waste away to death with grief, and her son will be miserable and resentful. He'll feel awkward and shamed among his fellow nobles, and will become increasingly detached, day by day.

I was hoping to rely on him for service. He's only slight but a strong fighter, a true offspring of a valiant military lineage. I shouldn't make him sad and dispirited."

So the king said, "Ha! Heigh! Phra Wai, I greatly detest this mother of yours. She didn't think of your reputation when she took this dreadful Chang as her husband.

If Chang dropped dead, she could make up with your father, yet you're whining at me to pardon this evil-minded, foulmouthed fellow,

who'd even beat his stepson to death. Aren't you angry about that? The life you're asking for will be a burden on the earth. I wish to execute him as an example to deter others."

"My liege, dust under the royal foot, lord of all power and creation. I was very angry at Khun Chang for trying to do away with me,

and I intended to take revenge, but my mother has made a big issue of preventing me. To leave her to grieve to death would be the same as ignoring my debt of gratitude to her.

So I've suppressed my anger and addressed the royal foot. May Your Majesty pardon Khun Chang's crime. May Your Majesty have mercy for me, his loyal servant."

The king looked at Phra Wai. "Khun Chang's punishment is death but I grant a reprieve. Because I care for you, he won't be executed.

Your mother's sorrow will disappear because her child has done well and is someone she can depend on. For a criminal who is deeply guilty and under penalty of death,

I'm not happy about giving a reprieve, but because you want to repay the debt of gratitude to your mother, I grant the pardon." He ordered the city deputy[36] to have Khun Chang released immediately.

"Send him to Phra Wai. Don't let anyone charge reduction fees." The king left the audience hall and walked elegantly into the inner palace.

The city deputy took the royal order and rushed out, followed by a crowd of servants. He invited Phra Wai to go along to the slip gate of the jail.

A retainer was sent inside to summon the governor who ordered warders to release Khun Chang. They crowded around, cutting his chains

and breaking the cangue by hitting it noisily with pieces of wood. Before long, everything had fallen off Khun Chang's body. The warders supported him to limp along with crossed feet.

Arriving before the slip gate, he raised his face and saw the city deputy and Phra Wai sitting close together. Trembling, he prostrated and crawled forward.

In love and fear, he lowered himself down until his head rested on the thigh of Phra Wai, who was too embarrassed to speak. He took leave of the city deputy at once.

Khun Chang was in a daze and could not walk. Phra Wai had a litter made for his servants to carry along behind. Khun Chang sat with his bushy beard,

looking like a potbellied Cantonese doll. The bald top of his head glistened red in the sunlight. Crowds came to watch all along the way.

They soon arrived at Phra Wai's residence. Wanthong was overjoyed to see them. She supported her husband to walk. Khun Chang hugged his wife and babbled.

Wanthong said, "You survived because of him, didn't you?" "Oh, yes! I'm alive because your lord helped me survive.

From today into the future, I offer myself as his servant until my dying day. If he goes to war, to north or south, I'll follow along to attend on him closely for any service."

---

36. พระรองเมือง, *phra rong mueang*, head of the right division of the city patrol, with title Luang Intharabodi-sirat, *sakdina* 1,000 (KTS, 1:229).

Phra Wai ordered Simala and Soifa to arrange food, which arrived in an instant. He invited Wanthong to eat,

and Khun Chang also. Trays of food were placed in a row. They happily ate their fill, and trays of sweets arrived immediately.

When both Khun Chang and Wanthong were satisfied, they went into the house to see Phra Wai. Khun Chang said, "May you be eternally happy. In time, you should become a very important person.

May you be enormously joyful, free of care and royal punishment. May your good name rise higher and higher, and be known throughout the land in the future so we can depend on you like the shelter of a great bo tree."

Phra Wai acknowledged the blessing. Khun Chang took out a pile of money to give him. "I hope twenty chang will repay your kindness, Phra Wai. Use it to buy new rice."

Phra Wai said, "Keep it! At present I've enough for my needs. It's not good to give money like this. It'd be like taking a bribe from my mother."[37]

Wanthong knew his character. She scooped the money into a basket and passed it to a servant. As evening was approaching, they took their leave and boarded a boat crammed with their servants.

With both men and women paddling strongly, they reached Suphan before nightfall. Granny Thepthong danced in joy at seeing them. "I'm truly happy he's out of jail."

She rushed to welcome them up into the house. Neighbors came to visit and sat jam-packed in the hall, talking noisily from evening until the last watch.

Khun Chang sent Sonphraya to fetch some sacred water and pour it over him to dispel evil. Monks were asked to come for three days. They chanted to get rid of bad fortune, and sprinkled water to cleanse his body.

---

37. In Khru Jaeng's version of this chapter, this scene of Khun Chang offering a bribe to Phra Wai and being rebuffed does not appear, while a rather different scene is inserted just before the meal: Khun Chang said, "I will offer respect to Phra Wai as if he were my father for saving my neck." He spoke to Wanthong, "My dear, are those two sacks of silver around somewhere? / Please take them to Simala. We cannot be tardy about this." Wanthong replied, "Don't talk too loud. I'll take care of it." (KJ, 48)

35: KHUN CHANG PETITIONS THE KING

Now to tell of Phlai Ngam. After winning the case against Khun Chang, he went back to living contentedly at home with his two wives.

While all his other relatives were around, his mother alone was missing. Pondering on this made him plaintive. "Oh Mother, Wanthong, you must be miserable. You shouldn't be partnered with Khun Chang.

Bad karma has led things astray. It's shameful you haven't got over the falling out with Father. He now has the merit to become a noble but you're stuck fast beside that villain.

Khun Chang looks strange and inhuman. He's ugly, evil, and ill-intentioned. His heart is vicious and cruel. How could you fall for him?

On the day he lost to me in the ordeal by water, the king was angry enough to have Khun Chang executed. I'm furious that Mother had pity on him, and made me beg for his life.

And if I'm furious at Mother, I must make this fury disappear by repaying Khun Chang in some way. I had intended him to die but have not succeeded because his luck has still been good.

No more! I'll pry Mother away from that evil fellow and bring her back to live here happily with Father." The more he thought about this, the angrier he got.

"When will the sun set?" He went into his room, fuming with rage and frustration, and waited restlessly until the sun had disappeared behind the mountains.

Animals all fell silent. The moon shone and stars came out. A cool dew fell. No sound of voices disturbed the quiet.

He heard the tolling of the palace gong floating on the wind over to his house, and counted until the third watch. He checked that the time was free of any trouble or inauspiciousness.[1]

The sky was white and free from clouds. Stars sparkled brightly, and a brilliant haloed moon shone. He made offerings of liquor, rice, and fish to the spirits. He enchanted a potion of turmeric and herbs, and applied it to his body.

---

1. See p. 100, note 21; p. 319, note 23; and p. 563, note 61.

He put a yantra on his chest, tied a sacred thread around his head, blew a mantra upwards into the darkness to urge his spirits to go along,

and picked up a sword once used in battle. When everything was ready, he chanted a formula, descended from the house, and hastened to Khun Chang's compound.[2]

He saw a fence, gates securely bolted, bonfires shedding light as bright as daytime, and people sleeping all around. He made straight for the gate,

and chanted a Great Subduer mantra. The *athan* buried there lost its power. Khun Chang's spirits all fled. People in the house collapsed, befuddled.

Men and women were overtaken by dull drowsiness, nodded dozily, fumbled around dopily, and dropped asleep, tumbled on top of one another. Oil leaked from fish left grilling on the fire.

Phlai Ngam sent his spirits to pull bolts and remove battens. Latches slipped out of place. He walked in without being challenged.

Everyone slept, dreamed, murmured, and mumbled in their sleep. At the bonfires protecting every opening, the only sound from the people was snoring. He arrived at the house of Khun Chang,

lit a candle, enchanted rice, and scattered it. All the spirits jumped away from the house, shaking it with a bang. He used a Loosener formula to open

the windows wide, and walked up to a frame for plants.

Fragrance billowed from the shrubbery. Flowers bloomed. Branches intertwined. Twigs trembled. Pollen wafted. He walked ahead silently.

Servants lay asleep, tumbled over one another. He sprung the bolts into the third stage.[3] Light danced off many mirrors and screens. A flickering glow from crystal lamps caught his eye.

bedroom

---

2. As he is in Ayutthaya and Khun Chang's house is in Suphan, he must have been carried by his spirits, though this is not explicit. More likely this is a continuity error. Did this scene originate as an alternative version of Khun Phaen's abduction in chapters 17–18? Or was it composed, a little carelessly, as a pastiche of that scene?

3. The "stages" here are not stories but barriers. The first was the wall and gate of the compound; the second, the entrance into the house; and this third is the door from the terrace into an apartment.

He walked through, glancing around to admire the curtains, blinds, screens, half-moon tables, and abundance of crystal. He opened a mosquito net and saw the face of his mother, Wanthong,

fast asleep on the bed. She and Khun Chang were embracing as a couple. Phlai Ngam felt hurt enough for his heart to burst. He drew his sword and raised it with the wish to chop Khun Chang dead.

He wanted to kick Khun Chang in his middle but feared he would hit Wanthong. He sank down, wai-ed to pay respect, and sobbed in anger and frustration with tears flowing.

"Oh Mother, mistress of your child! You shouldn't have been separated from Father. Ill fate led you on with no hesitation but it's not right that you and he must be apart.

This baldy dragged you here by force with no respect. I'll repay him in full for the wrong done to me." He asked his mother's forgiveness, drove his spirits away,

and blew a formula to wake her. Sheathing his sword, he stood motionless while Wanthong regained her senses and opened her eyes.

sword in sheath

Very drowsy from the mantra, Wanthong awoke, looked around, and saw someone standing beside the bed.

Fearing it was a criminal, she clutched her husband, cried out at the top of her voice, and huddled down into a crouch, peeping out. Phra Wai went up beside her and said,

"Why are you filling this bedroom with shouting, Mother? I was feeling upset so I came to see you. Why take fright and cry out? I'm not a thief. Let's talk."

Knowing it was her son, Wanthong was not afraid. She got up, and Phra Wai went to clasp her feet.

She embraced her son gently, weeping, with her head buried in his shoulder. "Why did you come at this time, my son? There are guards everywhere,

bolts on the doors, and bonfires all round. How did you sneak in here so bold and fearless? Did your father send you or did you come yourself?

If Khun Chang wakes up, there'll be trouble. He'll attack violently, and I fear something bad will come out of this. If there's a fight and you slip up, it won't be good.

What's on your mind? Please tell me and then go home. You shouldn't be doing this. Don't make me upset by being impetuous like your father."

Phra Wai prostrated at her feet in apology. "It was wrong to come. I don't dispute that. I've no wish to get myself into trouble, but I've come anyway because I love my mother, Wanthong.

At present I'm comfortable with my rank, two lovely wives, servants at my bidding, money, and all Father's relatives around.

The only thing missing is you, Mother. You're alive but might as well be dead and gone. This single point is a source of great sorrow. If you were there too, my happiness would be complete.

I came here to take you away, to invite you back to the house. If any bad consequences arise, that's a matter of fate.

Why stay with this ill-intentioned, jealous-minded lowlife? You're like a gold rim on a coconut shell. He looks as black as soot.

He's like a fly that buzzes around garbage and then bothers a sweetly fragrant lotus. Does a fig go well with a *phayom*?[4] My words must be making you miserable.

You brought me up until I was seven. Then, as fate would have it, we were separated. Do you think of your son sometimes? Maybe you don't at all.

If you care for your child, come home without delay. Then I'll lose this moodiness and be as happy as when you were raising me."

Wanthong felt very distressed for her son. "Oh Phlai Ngam, Mother's beloved, I'm sad almost to death.

It's not true that I'm wallowing in money. These things here haven't been mine for long. Among all these elephants, horses, and servants, there's nothing I love like you.

It's not true that I'm happy. Every day now I feel sad and wounded as if I were stuck with thorns. I have to bear the karma I've accumulated. I can't overcome this thought.

When your father went to jail, I was heavily pregnant. Khun Chang dragged me off. Don't harbor suspicions that I ran away with him. As for your father, I didn't know whether things went well or badly. It's now many years since I came to live with Khun Chang.

When your father came back from Chiang Mai, he didn't make any petition to the king. At the time when I was in the middle between them, the king gave a ruling returning me to your father.

You've become a lieutenant of the pages. You're not a child so listen to my words. Please go back and think it over with your father. Make a case to the king.

---

4. *Phayom* has spectacular yellow blooms, while the *madue* fig is associated with evil because flies lay eggs in the fruit which are consequently often full of worms.

He should rule in your favor because of your rank and valor. Don't talk about abducting me. I'm not willing to go that way."

Phlai Ngam thought his mother was putting up evasive arguments against leaving because she loved Khun Chang more than his father,
so he said, "What a pity. I took the trouble to fetch you but you won't go. You're resisting strongly as if you don't love your son at all.

I don't care about being a gentleman, accepted by my peers. I'm taking you home, no matter what. If you won't go nicely, that's up to you. Whatever the sin and karma, come what may.

I'll cut off your head and take that, leaving only the body to remain here. Don't be slow to answer. It's almost light and we must hurry away."

Wanthong saw her son was gritting his teeth in frustration and waving his sword, Skystorm,[5] to and fro. She was scared he would slash her dead,
and so she pacified him. "Phlai Ngam, my beloved, don't get riled and do something rash. Try to see the main point. I'm only afraid this will create an issue.

All this abducting back and forth will cause trouble in the future, so I oppose it. But if you think it'll be fine and won't get out of hand, then I'll go along with you."

She left the room in sorrow with tears flowing. Phra Wai took her, reaching the house as dawn streaked the sky.

Now to tell of Khun Chang. As he lay asleep, snoring loudly, a strange dream crept over him. His whole body was leprous.

A doctor treated him with a medicine of mercury which ate away his lungs, liver, kidney, large intestine, small intestine, and appendix. His teeth broke and fell out of his mouth.

In fright, he awoke and fumbled for Wanthong, calling out, "Help me, my dear!" He got up trembling in fear that the mercury would kill him.

He opened his eyes and turned to find Wanthong but she was not there. The sun was high and the room bright. He was taken aback to see a curtain was damaged. His cloth slipped from his body.

---

5. Another sign that this scene was adapted from Khun Phaen's abduction of Wanthong in chapters 17–18. Khun Phaen was carrying Skystorm in that scene but Phra Wai should not have it here as he does not receive the sword until chapter 36. A few stanzas below, a damaged curtain is mentioned, "things have disappeared," and a post is damaged—all true of chapter 17 but not the earlier part of this scene.

He shouted out, "Oh Wanthong!" No familiar word came in reply. Several things had disappeared. The gate was unbolted and open wide.

He frantically summoned servants. "I-Un, I-Im, I-Chim, I-Son, I-Mi, I-Ma, I-Sakhon! Why are you asleep? Come to me!"

The female servants ran up trembling, and found their master naked with his legs splayed. They all sank down aghast, hidden behind a door, looking but not entering.

Seeing his servants would not come close, Khun Chang got up angrily and stood naked with his legs apart and his bleary face in the air. He walked forward in a daze.

Granny Jan shakily raised her hands in wai. "Why do you come here dangling like that, master?[6] With nothing on, you look frightful." Khun Chang peered down at his body in alarm.

He covered his legs with his two hands like a hungry ghost. "Who came and took my cloth?" He sat down doubled over, feeling ashamed.[7] "Granny Jan, come and fetch me a cloth."

In shock, Granny Jan went in, grabbed a cloth, unfolded it, and quickly passed it to him, then ran out, averting her face, too embarrassed to look at her master.

With his body shaking, Khun Chang said to the servants, "Where's Wanthong gone? Why has she disappeared? Find what's happened to her, and ask her to come here without any fuss."

On Khun Chang's order, the servants busily tried to please their master by searching the whole house from top to bottom—inner rooms, outer rooms, and grounds—but did not find her.

They saw the gate in the fence open wide, people sleeping upright, and the first post damaged.[8] In consternation, they returned to Khun Chang,

told him they could not find her, and related all the details. "I think it's very strange that Wanthong has disappeared."

After he had heard the servants, Khun Chang's shiny bald skull was bathed in sweat. He felt angry and very hurt. "Truly she can do all kinds of everything. Two times, three times now, she's been intent on running off. This is a mis-

---

6. This sentence is taken from WK, 30:1178; PD has : "Where are you going, master?"

7. This sentence is taken from WK, 30:1178; PD has: He felt ashamed in front of the servants.

8. The main post, which would have been invested with protective lore at the time of building. Damage to this post is a sign that this protection has been undermined. Khun Phaen damaged the post on entering Khun Chang's house in chapter 17 but there is no mention of Phlai Ngam damaging the post earlier in this scene.

take the fine lady won't get away with. That time, Khun Phaen seized her. This time, who's she gone after?

I didn't think this would happen now that she's old, but she still goes out of her way to make off somewhere. Well, what will be will be. If I don't get her back, then I'm not Khun Chang."

⁊

Now to tell of Phlai Ngam who had begun to have second thoughts. "Khun Chang is our enemy in every way. If he knows I abducted Mother,

he'll send spies, make up stories, and inform King Phanwasa. We'll be suspected of wrongdoing, and Mother will be punished."

He summoned Muen Wisetphon. "You're someone who gets along with people. Please go immediately to Khun Chang's house, and appease him so he doesn't get angry.

Say that I've had a fever for many days, and that I feared Mother wouldn't come in time to see me before I died. Last night the fever was worse so I sent someone to fetch her.

Just when he arrived, Mother came out to relieve herself. He called to the room to wake Khun Chang, then hurried back as ordered. Mother tended me until daybreak.

Instead of dying, I recovered. I've asked her to stay here so I can see her face for several days until the fever abates. Then I'll send her back."

Muen Wiset took leave and hurried to Khun Chang's residence. On arrival, he hid and spied from afar, seeing people hustling and bustling all over the house.

He saw Khun Chang sitting at a window, looking bitter and vexed. Muen Wiset thought walking in would not work, so he got down and crawled through a gate.

From the window, Khun Chang saw someone crawling in and glancing around. "Is he coming to play tricks on me or what?

In broad daylight too. Servants! Catch him and elbow him at will." He leapt up, tucked up his cloth Khmer-style, and shouted, "Tcha! These phrai slaves try to fool gentlefolk!"

The smart Wisetphon stood his ground and quickly raised his hands in wai. He called out in reply, "I'm not a criminal.

I'm a servant of Phra Wai, a supervisor in his house. He sent me to pay respect and tell you that last night he suddenly had a stomachache, and didn't think he could be cured. He was writhing and wailing on the point of death so he sent me here to give the news.

I ran into his mother when she came out to relieve herself. I called to wake you in the house, but going back up into the house would have wasted time, so she hurried off in the middle of the night.

She nursed Phra Wai to allay the fever. He gives you his word for certain that when he's cured, she'll return without delay. Don't be suspicious that matters are otherwise."

Khun Chang was angry enough for blood to spurt from his eyes, but he hid his rage and said, "I don't complain. It's all for the good.

At present this fatal and remorseless fever is all over the capital. If there's anything you need, please come and take from here. Don't be shy to ask."

He banged the window shut. With his stomach seething, he lay down on a pillow and sighed. "Oh no! Can this be, Wanthong?

Because I lost the case to Phra Wai, he's acting high and mighty. Like father, like mother, like son. Now this has happened twice!

The father won a victory in Chiang Mai and now carries himself like the Lord of the Lions. His son became Phra Wai and now thinks I'm a condemned criminal.

He can bully me without respect. Who can I depend on over this? All the nobles will stick together. I could lay charges but they'd get smothered.

Let matters fall according to the merit and karma I've made. I may get thrashed or executed but I'm not thinking of my own life." The more he pondered, the more he seethed and raged. Fetching a slate,

he drafted a charge at some length, then put it down on paper and folded it up. After bathing and changing his clothes, he set off.

That day the king had gone lotus viewing[9] and had not yet returned.[10] When

---

9. Lotus viewing in the rainy season was a popular pastime for kings and common people. The main destination for the kings of Ayutthaya was along Khlong Sa Bua, Lotus Pond Canal, running northwards from opposite the palace (see map 8). In Bangkok in the Second and Third Reigns, when this chapter was probably composed, the popular places were Sam Khok to the north, and an area in the east of the city. These were later named Pathumthani, "abode of lotuses," now a Bangkok suburb; and Pathumwan, "lotus grove," a central ward where the police headquarters now occupies the site of the lotus pond (KW, 503).

10. Most of the time the king remained within the palace and hence was inaccessible to petitioners. The Palatine Law, clause 21, specified that the king may receive petitions when traveling: "When the king is traveling by boat, accompanied by guards, boatmen, gate-boats and *dang*-boats, whether stationary or in motion, should a criminal, rebel, drunk, madman, or someone presenting a gift or petition enter past the Mahatthai, soldiers, or guards up to the *dang*-boat, wave cloth as warning; if this is ignored, obstruct them with bricks, sticks, and

Khun Chang arrived at the palace, he found a place to wait below the Floating Pavilion.

Now to tell of the almighty king. Close to nightfall, he was returning to the palace, speeding along with a full boatload of oarsmen and the usual flotilla following noisily behind.

When the king's craft arrived, Khun Chang rushed down to the foot of the pier, and waded doggedly out with the letter held above his head. He popped up his face and gripped a gunwale of the boat,

right by the coxswain at the front of the boat's canopy. The coxswain thought the bald head was a water monster spirit[11] and hit it with a coconut shell. Some pages on fanning duty fell out of the boat, shouting, "A big tiger is swimming towards us!"

king's oarsman

Khun Chang hung on to the boat and said, "It's not a tiger. It's just my bald head. I'm desperate. Let me present a petition. I'm angry beyond endurance."

King Phanwasa was furious. "Tcha! This villain is inhuman. On land, on shore, there's no one like him.

This is not the way or the place to do it. Maybe this Chang is mad? Heigh! Someone take this fellow's petition. Give him thirty strokes, then let him go."[12]

A page took the petition. Guards took a firm grip on Khun Chang and delivered the punishment as ordered. The king then issued an edict.

---

swords; and if this is ignored, swim over to take the boat away; *if the king sees and calls the boat to approach, the service boat will receive them*; but if anyone enters without obstruction, the soldiers, guards and boatmen will be punished by slashing their necks and seizing their houses" (KTS, 1:78–79, emphasis added). The main occasions for travel were *kathin* journeys to present robes to monks, but then the procession would be large and difficult to approach. Khun Chang was "lucky" to find the king traveling in a small party. An announcement from the Fourth Reign stated: "There was only a time, once a year in the *kathin* season, when the king traveled a long distance by boat. Presenting a petition from the riverbank would not be heard. It had to be on land but when the king traveled in the capital, every opening around was guarded. People could not approach. The only place they could sneak up to make a petition was by the hall in front of the Thewaphirom Gate" (KW, 502–4).

11. See p. 475, note 26.

12. Around 1800, King Rama I decreed that anyone wishing to submit an appeal to the king must first agree to thirty lashes. The provision was to discourage malicious accusations (Flood and Flood, *Dynastic Chronicles*, 2:115).

"Henceforth from today, should anyone on guard duty neglect their government service by allowing people into the vicinity,

that person shall be liable to punishment of seven grades[13] including execution, under this edict for the protection of the king." He disembarked and entered the palace.

⤙

Now to tell of Khun Phaen, great romancer, whose powers were known throughout the world. He was living happily at home with his two beloved wives.

Laothong and Kaeo Kiriya ministered closely to his needs, making him cheerful all the time. In the middle of that night,

when both Laothong and Kaeo Kiriya were asleep, he woke with a start. The moon was shining brightly, and a breeze wafted the fragrance of flowers.

His thoughts turned to his old partner. "It's a pity Wanthong has been far apart and lacking in love. Twice she was separated from me as if my heart had been plucked from my body.

It was bad of me to get lost in love with two others, and abandon her to sorrow. When I took Chiang Mai and won royal favor, had I petitioned the king it would have gone smoothly.

Whatever I said, Khun Chang would not have been able to answer. I shouldn't have neglected her. Now that Wai has been to fetch her,

I must go to make love to her. Wanthong will be waiting for me with longing." He dressed, doused himself in fragrant water,

left the room, and walked to his son's apartment. He went into Wanthong's room and found her fast asleep.

Lowering himself down to sit beside her, he touched her lovingly, "Do wake up. I've come to see you. Don't sleep."

Wanthong was awake and realized it was her husband. She feigned sleep to see whether his manner was truly loving or he was just going through the motions.

She lay still, assessing his mood for a long time, unable to find a reply because both love and anger choked her heart, both longing and disquiet churned her soul.

---

13. Khun Wichitmatra cites the seven grades of punishments as follows: "First, reprimand; second, single fine; third, double fine; fourth, quadruple fine; fifth, plough on neck according to rank for public mockery; sixth, seize property and put to work cutting grass for the elephants; seventh, execution; according to the severity of the crime." Khun Wichitmatra gives no source. There are several similar lists in the *Phra aiyakan aya luang*, Code of Crimes against Government, but none matches this one (KW, 503; KTS, 4:6–33).

"Oh my eye's sparkling jewel, why are you so fast asleep. You seem cross and distant. Are you angry that I abandoned you?

My breast is heavy with love and longing. My love for you hasn't lessened even a little. Truly I've been in the wrong, but why lie still and hold a grudge?"

He lay close beside her, kissing to kindle her love, and fondling to soothe and please her. "What's wrong? Why don't you wake from sleep?"

Wanthong rose from the bed and agreed to talk, making her case. "Are you annoyed that I won't talk? It's not me that's carping and complaining.

What's right or wrong, you please think for yourself. This body of mine is completely tainted. It seems Wanthong is two-minded. Wherever you go, that's what you hear.

The truth is, though I went to stay in another house, I always thought of returning to you for certain because I love my child and my husband very much. I went away then because I had to.

I was angry because my partner didn't love me. When he had others to enjoy, he ignored me completely. It was a waste to have gone through hardship together in the forest, eating fruit instead of rice every morning and evening.

As soon as you found happiness, you forgot the hard times because you already had what you wanted. But I'm saying too much. I'll annoy you. Have a care for me, and don't make me ashamed again."

"Truly I was in the wrong, Wanthong. I seemed to forget and neglect you. But it's not true that I was carried away because of other loves. Raise your face and I'll tell you. Don't harbor resentment.

When I was in jail, I grieved for you every day and night. I had to swallow enormous sadness. Besides, Khun Chang took a crooked revenge, and looked down on me as poor and ruined.

I missed you as much as my own heart. I thought of escaping and coming to get you back but I feared that would pile up another problem. I hesitated up to the time of going to Chiang Mai.

On return I meant to come after you but Wai's case caused more delay. Nobody else in this land has been wronged and tormented as much as you and me.

I thought of appealing to King Phanwasa but knew it would be a long time before we lived in the same room again. If there's a court case, it has its own pace. So I sent our son to fetch you home.

Dead or alive, easy or hard, I won't be apart from my love. I'll cherish you just like the times when we were in the wilds. I beg forgiveness. I was in the wrong, I can't deny. My friend in love, please have a care.

I made a mistake so I've come to admit fault. How long will you harbor resentment? My love for you is still a passionate love. Don't break it off and make me die of despair."

He hugged her to his chest, and gently cradled her breasts. "Heavenly flesh, fulfill a man's feelings. Please comfort me a little without anger."

"My heart doesn't wish to hurt your feelings or disappoint your love. If I'd expelled you from my heart already, I wouldn't have come. Don't say that I have no thought of returning to you.

Though my body went away, my heart still counted you as my husband. But I worry the sin will weigh on me when I die. One woman, two husbands! Unless this can be wiped away, I won't fall in with your wishes.

Back then when I followed you into the forest, my face was black as if smeared with soot. After you won the case, my face was as bright as a victory candle. But he dragged me off, like going deep under the sea.

Phlai Ngam came and brought me back but here my face will be as black as ink—worse, because Wai is impetuous, and he'll drag me down so deep I must die.

You're not a young man. Don't be tormented by love. Think of your sins and simmer down. If you love me, shield me from shame. If I shift again, you can slash me dead.

Go and petition the king. I'll arrange a *baisi* to summon back the soul. Stop pleading to sleep together. I'm having none of that. You'll get too used to it."

"Oh pity, pity. You're hurting me like you're cutting open my breast with a kris. You have fears about wrongdoing and sin. I was bad to have insulted you carelessly.

Were it anyone less close, I'd give up, but it's you so I'm not listening to your resistance. It's no use pleading so please be amenable, and don't try to hinder or delay our love."

He hugged her close, kissing and caressing to soothe her, his body twining around hers. Wanthong blocked him and would not consent.

He pulled her close, urging her to intimacy. Trembling with fright, she twisted to obstruct him and refused to make love. A breeze wafted the fragrance of flowers.

Bees caressed plants in the deep forest. But the flowers wilted, the stalks withered, and the pollen wept. Celestial waters sprinkled only the sky.

Thunder rumbled and crashed but the shower shied from the flowers and splashed around the ocean shore. After the heartquake, they slept.

Late at night, only a rustle of dry leaves disturbed the silence. A wind wafted luscious scents, and a luminous moon shone.

A coel called clearly. Bells tolled in the royal palace. As Wanthong slept deeply, her drowsy mind drifted.

She dreamed she was transported into a wild forest where she wandered, twisting and turning, until she was lost in the depth of the *rang* woods, not knowing how to return. Fierce tigers came to attack her.

Two crouched watching at the edge of her path. When she came upon them, one pounced, picked her up in its jaws, and dragged her away into the forest.

At the end of the dream, she woke in fright with a shriek, and hugged her husband, sobbing. Fearfully she related the reverie to him. "So strange. I'm startled to dream something so disturbing."

Under the bed, a mouse chattered. By the wall, a spider beat its chest.[14] She became even more frightened to death, as if her soul would leave her body.

Khun Phaen, great romancer, was shocked by the omen. "This foretells danger. The dream is seriously bad according to the manual."

He examined by the Eight Phases[15] and found an extremely strong force but

---

14. See p. 22, note 9, and p. 311, note 19.

15. อัฐกาล, or อัฐเคราะห์, *atthakan*, *atthakhro*, a form of astrological reckoning, sometimes called ทักษา, *thaksa* or *mahathaksa*, based on eight planets, the day planets plus Rahu, placed in a nine-cell diagram. Each person has a dominant planet. In the simpler version, this is the planet corresponding to the day in week of the day of birth, e.g., the moon for Monday. In a more complex version, the calculation is a sum of the animal year, the lunar month, and the day in week of the birth day, e.g., (ox = 2) + (month = 5) + (Friday = 6) = 13, divide by 8 and take the remainder which is 5 meaning Jupiter.

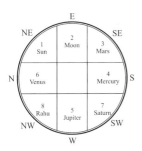

The eight planets are positioned around the diagram in the sequence: Sun, Moon, Mars, Mercury, Saturn, Jupiter, Rahu, Venus. Eight aspects, ประการ, *prakan*, are then distributed clockwise around the diagram, beginning from the location of the dominant planet. These eight aspects are: บริวาร, *boriwan*, personal relations; อายุ, *ayu*, age; เดช, *det*, power; สรี, *sri*, prosperity; มูละ, *mula*, security; อุตสาหะ, *utsaha*, effort, work; มนตรี, *montri*, protection; กาลกรรณี/กาลกิณี, *kalakanni/kalakini*, adversity. For that person, each planet is thus associated with one aspect. In addition, the two planets associated with prosperity and adversity operate as qualifiers. These associations are then used to help read the disposition of the stars in the *rasi*, houses, at any point in time. The important conjunctions occur when either the prosperity or adversity qualifier falls in the same *rasi* as one of the other stars. For example if the adversity qualifier, *kalakanni*, falls in the same *rasi* as the star associated with age, then that person will face extreme adversity, even death. Possibly that is the case here. (Thep, *Horasat nai wannakhadi*, 286–94; Eade, *Calendrical Systems*, 108)

did not want to tell her the full story. He hugged her, averting his face welling tears,

and fabricated an interpretation. "A dream like this doesn't foretell trouble. It came because you're very unsettled. Stay with me and don't fear, my darling.

Tomorrow I'll remedy the inauspiciousness[16] of the dream so that no calamity arises, and so my darling cheers up. Don't be troubled. Relax."

᭫

When the sun touched the hilltops and streaks of dawn brightened the sky, the victorious king, who lived in a jeweled palace

where throngs of consorts and palace ladies making obeisance were on duty to fan and attend on him, had been feeling angry about Khun Chang since the middle of the night.

"Is there anyone as vile as this vilest of men? Everything about this slippery-headed fellow is bad. Hardly a night has passed since his last charge, and now he presents another, even standing in water out of his depth.

Last time he sued over Wanthong. Who's this slave suing about this time?" He went out to the Chakkaphat Throne Hall,[17]

which was crowded from front to rear. A curtain was drawn back to reveal the royal presence. Nobles all prostrated, crammed tightly together in rows.

The king looked round and saw Khun Chang. "Who's brought his charge?" Phramuen Si presented it to the king, who opened it and read.

When he knew the points of the case, he lost his temper. "What is so urgent about this? Don't these people know that Wanthong isn't the only woman?

They seem to be fighting over her as if there were no others, or as if she were a precious jewel. Chang looks terrible with his vacant eyes. I can't see the faintest reason why she'd love him.

Anyone taking him as husband would face shame. His head looks like a buffalo fallen into a bog. At the time of the old case, I conducted an interrogation and the blame fell heavily on old Siprajan.

I sent Wanthong to be with Phaen. Why did she rush off to live with Chang?

---

16. แก้เสนียด, *kae saniat*, a ritual to overcome adversity.

17. The Chakkaphat Phichaiyon Throne Hall was built in 1632 in the reign of King Prasat Thong. Originally it was outside the old palace area but the king subsequently expanded the palace to the east, enclosing the parade ground and this building. The hall was originally called Siyasothonmaha Phiman Banyong, but was changed to "Great Palace and Residence of the World Conqueror Indra" on the court seer's advice after the king dreamed Indra had descended to sit on his bed. The hall was set into the eastern inner wall of the palace, and its upper levels were used for the king to view processions, entertainments, and military exercises on the parade ground (as in chapter 27). The base of the building still exists. (RCA, 216; KLW, 208–9; APA, 59; *Phraratchawang lae wat boran*, 5–6; *Boranasathan*, 1: 232–33; see map 9)

Phramuen Si, fetch Wanthong, Khun Phaen, and Phra Wai immediately!"

Phramuen Si promptly backed out, and gave orders to a palace guard, who rushed off.

At Phra Wai's house, he told them of the order. "Khun Chang has petitioned the king. All three of you are sent for."

Wanthong and Phra Wai were frightened to hear the order. Khun Phaen called Wanthong into an inner room. Because of the uncertainty, he used lore.

He put beeswax on her lips, and made her eat a betelnut treated by mantra to overcome various difficulties. He enchanted a mixture of spirit oil[18] and sandal oil that had helped give protection in the past.

He made *itthije* powder[19] and daubed it on her forehead so anyone she met would love her. He enchanted krajae-cinnamon-sandal oil and applied it. When he had finished, he led Wanthong off.

Thong Prasi heard about the case and could not sit still. "Servants! Run along with me. Quick!" She went down the stairs shakily, and fell over on the terrace.

Phlai Chumphon[20] hugged her bottom. "I'm not an elephant for you to ride, Grandson." She raised herself up, bottom in air, and crawled along, wheezing through her open mouth.

When they arrived at a gate of the palace, officials hustled them along without stopping. Khun Phaen, Wanthong, and Phra Wai went in to attend on the king.

---

18. Oil extracted from a corpse by various methods. Khun Wichitmatra gives this version. The spirit doctor takes two or three acolytes to a graveyard and puts in stakes around the grave of a newly dead corpse to make a sanctified area with sacred thread and yantra cloths at the eight directions. The acolytes dig up the corpse and place it in a sitting position. The spirit doctor sits in meditation pose opposite the corpse, chants a mantra to activate the soul of the corpse, lights a candle, and holds it under the corpse's chin. The oil drips down and is collected in a bowl. The spirit doctor may first have to quell a fierce spirit in the grave of the corpse. To do so, he chants a mantra and the spirit comes out as tall as a sugar palm. The spirit doctor must then chant mantras to reduce him to normal human size and quiet him down. If the spirit is still too strong, the spirit doctor may die when he applies the candle to the corpse. The diggers also risk being dragged down into the grave. The process is thus only attempted by very skilled spirit doctors, and the resulting oil is credited with great powers, especially in love magic (KW, 549–50; Francis Giles, "About a Love Philtre" describes in English a similar method with some variations).

19. Meaning he wrote a device or word such as ปุริโส, *puriso*, "man," in whiteclay powder while intoning an *itthije* formula (see p. 483, note 43), then collected the powder to smear on her forehead. The powder induces love.

20. Phlai Chumphon Ronnarong, son of Khun Phaen and Kaeo Kiriya, born on the day Khun Phaen left with troops to Chiang Mai in chapter 27. He is a little short of two years old.

When the almighty king, eminence of the resplendent city, saw the three arrive and pay respect, his mood improved and he took pity on them as he would children in the womb.

Because of the force of the powerful lore, the king's attitude became warmer and more sympathetic. He interrogated in the manner of a common case.[21] "Ha! Heigh! Look here, Wanthong,

when you came out of the great forest, I ordered you to live with Khun Phaen as a couple. Then I was angry and had him jailed. Where did you go?

Why didn't you stay with Phaen but rush off to live with Chang again? Earlier you loved Phaen and chased after him. Then when I gave you to Phaen, you danced back, flaunting yourself, to stay with Chang. But then you began to hate him because of his awful head, and couldn't

palace gate

stay. You seem to switch and swap husbands, back and forth. You've become bad and uncaring."

The king's question made Wanthong nervous. With face bowed, hands clasped above her head, and hair standing on end, she addressed the king.

"My liege, dust under the royal foot, divine protector, ruler and creator. When I came out of the forest, Your Majesty granted me to Khun Phaen.

After a time, Khun Phaen was imprisoned. I was heavily pregnant and staying at the house in front of Wat Takrai. Khun Chang came and said that Your Majesty

had given an order granting me to him. I didn't want to go but he used force and dragged me off—a despicable act. Neighbors wanted to help but it seemed hopeless.

Because Khun Chang claimed there was a royal order,[22] the neighbors feared

---

21. In case of a dispute, the parties involved could either agree on the selection of arbitrators, or submit the case to the courts. A case submitted to the courts was considered a royal case or king's case, เนื้อความหลวง, *nuea khwam luang*, as the king was deemed the fount of justice and all courts were considered subdivisions of an original royal court. A case submitted to arbitrators was called a common case, เนื้อความราษฎร, *nuea khwam ratsadon*. One major difference was that a plaintiff who sued in the royal courts and lost was liable to retribution, often equivalent to the punishment that would have been imposed on the defendant if found guilty. Here the king seems to unilaterally constitute himself as the arbitrator, but the eventual judgment belies this arrangement (KTS, 2:102, 199; KTS, 4:243).

22. In chapter 23, Khun Chang's people seized Wanthong and gave onlookers the impression

they would be in the wrong if they made any obstruction. I was at a loss. It was beyond my power not to go with him. My life is under the royal foot."

After hearing her out, the king was furious at Khun Chang. He roared like a lion. "You madman! Tugging a woman back and forth. You obscene monkey!

It turns out I'm not the Lord of Life. You think I'm just a lord in a mask play with no authority. You have a stubborn mind, and go around acting in an arrogant fashion like a thief.[23]

I can't keep you, you villain. You should be thrashed with a pair of canes down your whole spine." The

Lord Ram in mask play

king switched and asked Wanthong, "Eh, the time he dragged you off was a long time ago, around eighteen years. How were you able to come back now? Did you run away from Chang, or did someone fetch you?"

The question alarmed Wanthong. She bowed and raised clasped hands above her head. "My liege, Your Majesty, holy power over my head.

I returned now because Phra Wai fetched me, but I did not sneak off to be unfaithful. Khun Phaen hasn't made love with me.

Because I came around the second watch, Khun Chang is trying to make a case that I ran away. May Your Majesty have mercy. My life is under the royal foot."

---

there was a dispute over a debt but there was no direct mention of a royal order.

23. โจร, *jon*, meaning robber or bandit, is a crucial term in the Three Seals Law. It implies not only an offense against an individual but also potentially a threat to public order. In the political philosophy of the time, the first duty of the king was to provide the protection that enabled the populace to escape suffering of all kinds. This protection included ensuring public order. Kukrit called this "the king's peace." The Law on Theft has a detailed categorization of offenses, with higher punishments for those which affect public order. The Law on Conflict, พระไอยกานลักษณวิวาทตีด่ากัน, *phra aiyakan laksana wiwat ti da kan*, literally the law on quarreling, beating, and cursing, takes this concept further. The preamble states that the law was passed "to alleviate the sufferings of the people" (KTS, 3:184; Ishii, "Thai Thammasat," 165–66).

The law provides penalties, including caning, for quarreling that causes public disorder. Here, the king is clearly concerned that the conflict between Khun Phaen and Khun Chang is a threat to public order but he is probably more bothered by the allegation that Khun Chang—or his people, which would amount to the same thing in law—had invented a nonexistent royal order giving Wanthong to Chang. This offense would fall under the Code of Crimes against Government. Under clause 3, persons falsely claiming to be acting on government order are liable to punishments ranging from a fine and fifteen lashes to execution (KTS, 4:7–8).

The almighty king was greatly enraged. "Phra Wai has acted arrogantly. It seems the country has no master.

People don't pay attention to the law but do whatever they like. If they slash and kill one another, it'll be a danger to the populace. That angers me.

I gave Wanthong to Phaen but Chang acted rashly by dragging her off on an elephant, citing my name, and shouting threats to frighten her.

He deserves to be knocked unconscious right here, thrashed countless times, and have a ripe coconut stuffed in his mouth.[24] Phra Wai has also committed a serious crime.

You think that because Wanthong is your mother you can act wildly without fear or hesitation. Why didn't you fetch her in daytime? Your father Phaen is behind this.

He's like an ox or horse that knows its rider too well.[25] Whatever you tell me now is not believable. Chang has laid charges with two accusations—that Wai abducted his mother, and that he did so on behalf of his father.

This is a serious crime and a major blemish on his record. If Wai wanted to fetch his mother, he should have asked his father to make a case in the proper way.

There are courts and codes of law. Or perhaps you think I can't make a judgment. You should be whipped painfully with a lash, and be fined on par with an adulterer. [26]

This whole affair arose because of a woman, and grew through jealousy and rivalry. To have fruit and flowers on a single branch, many big roots have to be pruned away.

Wanthong is like a taproot. If its base is cut, the leaves will wither. Who she should be coupled with in partnership must be known for certain today.

---

24. Clause 1 of the Code of Crimes against Government, which prescribes punishments for defaming the king or infringing on the prerogatives of the king, includes this punishment, phrased in exactly the same words, มะพร้าวห้าวยัดปาก, maphrao hao yat pak, as the second of the eight punishments. This clause, and the preamble to the same law, are the only place where this punishment appears in these words in the Three Seals Law, although mutilation of the mouth, sometimes to death, appears as punishment for other crimes, such as defamation of a government official (Ishii, "Thai Thammasat," 162; clause 58, KTS, 4: 5–6, 51).

25. Literally, you're like an ox used to the leg, and a horse used to its rider. This is a proverbial simile about two people who have done things together so long that they know each other well. It is often used in reference to sexual relations. Here the king is accusing Wai of presuming on his relationship with the king.

26. ลวด, luat, more fully ลวดหนัง, luat nang, leather strips plaited into a lash. Probably this was more painful than the rattan as the commutation fee was higher: 100,000 cowries for three lashes, as against 100,000 cowries for five to ten strokes of the rattan. Several clauses of the Law on Marriage prescribe fines and the lash for an adulterer and any accomplices (e.g., KTS, 2: 232–33; Seni, Pathakatha rueang kotmai, 7–8).

Heigh! Wanthong, what do you say? Make a final decision right here and now. Don't be irresolute. It taints you. Your having two husbands angers me.

If you love the second one, go and live with Chang. If you love the old one, go to the side of Khun Phaen. Don't spin round in circles and earn people's contempt. If you love either, then say so."

The king's order made Wanthong very agitated. If she spoke, she feared the king's authority. Khun Chang looked across, winking and raising his eyebrows.

Phra Wai signaled to his mother by pursing his lips towards his father several times. Wanthong's head spun in confusion. At a loss, she remained silent and did not address the king.

Hearing no reply from Wanthong, the king asked, "Do you love neither? Then say so.

If you reject the husband and go with the lover, you fear shame. If you want to be with your son, there's no objection. Whatever you wish I will command, and from now onwards that will be final!"

Hearing the king's order, Wanthong's mind went blank, and she could not think. Her demerit clouded her reason because she had reached the years for which she was born.

She was stunned like someone who had fallen down a mountain. Her breast was choked with confusion. She was so afraid of putting herself in the wrong, her mind swam.

"How can I say I love Khun Chang when in truth I don't love him even a little? I love Khun Phaen and my son like my own life. If I say the wrong thing, the king will rage and have no mercy.

Don't do it! Be neutral. Let the king dispose at will." With these brief thoughts, she bowed her head and said,

"My love for Khun Phaen is a great love because we shared such hardship going into the forest together. We lacked everything but loved and cherished each other.

All the time I lived with Khun Chang, he said not one harsh word, heaped money on me and me alone, and placed servants at my beck and call as if they were my own.

Phra Wai is my own flesh and blood. I brought him up, and love him as much as my husband." As she spoke, her body began to tremble in terror of the king's authority.

junks

The king, ruler of the world, erupted in anger like gunpowder sparked by flame. "Oh Wan-thong, how can you be like this?

You cannot say which one you love! Your heart wants both of them so you can switch back and forth, having a reserve deeper than the deep sea.

Fill it with rafts, masts, weeds, and great junks. No amount will make any impression— like a great ocean, so deep the floor is beyond fathoming.[27]

Bring bricks and rocks and dump them in, and all will sink from sight. You're base, evil, and black of heart like a jet gem in a pile of feces.

You have a beautiful appearance and a sweet sounding name, yet your heart is not as loyal as a strand of hair. Even animals know what they want and mate only in season.

You're baser than base, the dregs of the city,[28] lustful, insatiable, oily-eyed. Anything new, you'll take. Hundreds or thousands, you'd not be satisfied.

Even a harlot has only one man at a time. Nobody has so many sniffing around as you. Why should you remain a burden on my land? Wai, don't count her as your mother.

I raised you to be a lieutenant of the pages. If others know she's your mother, you'll be shamed. Khun Chang and Khun Phaen, don't miss her. I'll find wives for both of you.

There are plenty of suitable beauties. This scourge,[29] this slut, is not suitable for loving. Cut her out of your hearts.

---

27. A *phleng yao* by King Rama III includes the following passage: "For example, like Wan-thong of two husbands, / who both wanted to hold her tight / until Khun Chang was intent on spiriting her away. / As comparison, she is like a great river, / fed by many tributaries, / mooring for junks and rafts / that pass up and down busily." Khun Wichitmara noted the parallel simile used in this stanza, and wondered if King Rama III had composed this section, or if Chaophraya Mahasak Phonlasep had composed it on Rama III's command (KW, 512–13).

28. ท้ายเมือง, *thai mueang*, the end of the city. Towns have a "head," which means the original settlement and often the location of the political authority, and an end or tail which is the later expansion, often an area occupied by newcomers and migrants (Pornpun, "Environmental History," 49–51).

29. กาลกิณี, *kalakini*, evil, inauspiciousness, probably from the Sanskrit *kalagni*, era fire, a conflagration that will destroy the world at the end of an era, but also with an echo of the fearful goddess Kali. *Kalakini* is also the aspect of adversity or inauspiciousness in systems of astrology (Stutley and Stutley, *Dictionary of Hinduism*, 135; see p. 793, note 15 above).

Heigh! Phraya Yommarat, execute her immediately! Cleave open her chest with an axe without mercy. Don't let her blood touch my land.

Collect it on banana leaves for feeding to dogs.[30] If it touches the earth, the evil will linger. Execute her for all men and women to see!" Having given the order, the king returned to the palace.

---

30. This sentence, specifying that the blood should not fall on the land, appears only once in the Three Seals Law, in clause one of the Law on Revolt and Warfare. In summary, the law reads: Anyone who attempts to dethrone the monarch, or who attempts to do damage to the monarch with weapons or poison, or who refuses to submit tribute as a governor, or who encourages enemies to attack, or who gives information to enemies, is liable to punishment of death and seizure of property for 1) the entire clan; 2) seven generations of the clan; or 3) the whole clan, ensuring no successors; with the executions to linger over seven days "without letting the blood or corpse fall on the realm but having it put on a raft and floated with the current 240,000 *yojana* to the next country" (KTS, 4:124).

36: THE DEATH OF WANTHONG

Wanthong trembled in terror and her scalp crawled. Khun Chang, Khun Phaen, and Phra Wai were shocked and stunned.[1]

Officials in audience felt their heads swell and hair bristle in dismay. Nobody knew how to address the king as they were in awe of his authority.

Phraya Yommarat gave orders for Wanthong to be led away and detained out front. Phra Wai and Khun Phaen rushed after her, both brimming with tears of grief.

Khun Chang stood up, slipped, banged into a pillar, and fell flat on his face. Picking himself up, he stumbled after Wanthong in tears.

Thong Prasi, who had been waiting to hear the verdict, beat her breast and hung her head in shock. She too hurried after them on wobbly legs, her body trembling, her tears flowing.

News was sent to Laothong, Kaeo Kiriya, Soifa, and Simala, who all arrived in a state of shock, beating their chests and blubbering like chicks.

Khun Chang tripped over a brick and fell headfirst into a pile of dogshit. He got up and dashed ahead without wiping it off. A swarm of flies buzzed around the stench.

A servant called, "Master, wipe off the dogshit first, I beg you." Khun Chang turned round and said, "You villain, where is there any dogshit on me?"

The servant pointed it out. "It's all over your face and the top of your head. You're swarming with flies." Khun Chang would not listen. "Leave me be!" People following behind cried out, "What a stink!"

They arrived at the execution ground.[2] Men and women came to watch. Wan-

---

1. Khun Wichitmatra: "There is no sadder scene to be found in all Thai literature" (KW, 514).

2. ตะแลงแกง, *talaengkaeng*, "four ways," a crossroads close to the center of the Ayutthaya island, near to the drum tower, shrines for the guardian spirits of the city, city pillar, jail, and a market. It appears first in the chronicles in the account of a fire in 1545, and is first mentioned as the site of execution and impalement in the purge after the failed revolt of Prince Si Sin in 1561, and again for executions after the succession struggles at the start of the Narai and Borommakot reigns (1656, 1733). Currently it is the junction of Pa-tong and Pa-thon roads. (RCA, 21, 42, 221, 417–19; *Boranasathan*, 1:51; KLW, 187, 189, 192; APA, 97; see map 8)

thong sank down, at the end of her strength. Phra Wai ran up and embraced her.

Khun Phaen sat beside, streaming tears, overwhelmed with pity, and struck speechless by the shock.

Kaeo Kiriya, Laothong, Soifa, and Simala were consumed by sorrow. They went

onlookers

off to gather flowers for begging forgiveness.

A wall of onlookers surrounded them. No standing room was left in the execution ground. Khun Chang pushed his way through the crowd saying, "I beg you sir, for your merit."

People started away from him. "You stink to death of dogshit, sir!" Young men were so appalled at the stench, they shoved him forward. He stumbled up to Wanthong.

Looking up and seeing Khun Chang, Phra Wai leapt up angrily, hit Khun Chang with an elbow, and put a lock on his head, getting both hands mired in shit. He picked up a stave and hit down with a thud.

Phraya Yommarat said, "Don't, Phra Wai. Why beat this lost fellow?" He grabbed Khun Chang to drag him outside the circle, then sat down, enraged at getting the stink on his own hands.

"You villain! My hands are covered in dogshit. If I'd known, I wouldn't have stopped Phra Wai." He stood up and kicked Khun Chang out of the circle. Khun Chang cried out, "This time I'm done for!"

Khun Phaen rushed across and repeatedly hit Khun Chang, who fell down, banging his head on Thong Prasi. She cried out angrily, "Oh, this is impossible!" Khun Chang got up and ran off.

Wanthong sobbed sadly, hugging her beloved son with yearning, tears trickling down.

"Today I say farewell to Phlai Ngam. I must be parted from you forever. By evening I'll be dead and covered with earth. Turn your face. Mother wants to look at you.

From birth, your life hasn't been like that of others. You didn't savor the sweetness of love and intimacy. When tiny, you we're blown away to float on the wind. Sadly, you were severed from me since seven years old.

All I could do was yearn, fearing I wouldn't even see your dead body. But now instead of you losing your life, you've come to cremate your mother's corpse.

It was worthwhile carrying you in my womb, trekking across ridge, swamp, and forest stream. With you in my belly as companion, I could put up with the hardship of the wilds,

the heat of the sun, the rain, leeches, gnat bites, and thorns. As we wended our way, I had to be careful with you in my womb.

Your father didn't gallop the horse but rode gently for fear you might be frightened. When the sun was burning hot, we found the shade of hills. When he saw I was tired, we'd rest and drink water,

but only a little, every morning and evening, enough to refresh me, not a lot for fear you might choke. When we were sent down to Ayutthaya and jailed, I was very worried about sitting or lying down.

Out of concern for you, I feared that walking too much would disturb my belly, sitting too much might discomfort you, and lying too much might make poor you tired.

Then I gave birth safely and felt relieved. I rocked you, lullabied you, and cared for you for seven happy years. But Khun Chang wickedly kidnapped you out of my sight.

He beat you and abandoned you in the forest. By merit, you recovered and I saw you again. But immediately we were separated, and it was a long time before we were reunited.

Good deeds from the past helped give my darling child added merit. You traveled to find your father and mother and bring us together again. Yet now it turns out you must arrange my cremation.

It's like struggling to find a way out of a deep forest, seeing the moon shining brightly in the sky, and thinking you'll be happy forever. Then the lightning strikes and you fall, buried deep in the earth.

You have only half a day to set eyes on me. After that there'll be nothing but cinders and ash. You'll have only the memory for a long time. Go home, my son. Don't wait for evening.

When they sever my neck it'll be a pitiful sight you shouldn't witness. Look on my face while I'm still alive so that is what you see when you think of your mother."

She hugged Phra Wai with her face lowered and tears flowing. Her mind swam and she collapsed onto the earth, lying motionless with arms around her beloved son.

Sitting weeping beside his mother, Phra Wai was shocked at seeing her collapse. He desperately massaged to revive her. Little by little she came round, and he spoke to her sorrowfully.

"Oh Mother, mistress of your child, you raised me and taught me, tied me a cradle,[3] and lullabied me to sleep, fed me, bathed me, suckled me,

cuddled me and kissed my forehead, washed my hair and coiled a topknot, daubed turmeric, laid me to bed, and told me to beware of dangers.

When I was sick, you worried over me, and took great care about food and medicine. You strung up a net so little me wouldn't be bothered by flies, bugs, and mosquitoes.

When I'd grown to seven years, bad fortune loomed. Khun Chang lured me into a forest and loaded logs on top of me.

My whole body ached with pins and needles. I thought I'd die and become prey for wild animals to gnaw. But the gods of the forest had mercy.

They dragged away the logs that Khun Chang had piled on me, and I managed to return alive.[4] But I had to part from you from then, and I walked in misery through the thorny forest

all on my own from Suphan to Kanburi. By merit, I survived the wild animals. Grandmother brought me up, which is why I'm still alive.

Nobody has suffered as much hardship as your little child—a hundred thousand times worse than anyone. Nobody has been poor in quite the same way as me, starved of the sight of both Father and Mother.

I saw you only when I was a child. And Father's face I didn't see when I was small. I had to ask Grandmother to understand why. Then I ran away from her through the hills and forest,[5]

thick with elephants and tigers, and swarming with biting mosquitoes, midges, and flies. I went without food and suffered the scratches of branches and thorns by the hundreds.

At night in the deep forest I felt wretched when a chill dew fell and a strong wind blew the leaves. I was alone and lonely walking to the city.

I found Father in a terrible state—in jail and so poor he had nothing, not even a lowercloth. So I applied myself to study and improve myself through knowledge. I went to war, won victory, and prospered.

---

3. A simple hammock made by tying a length of cloth between two posts.

4. In the account of this incident in chapter 24, Wanthong came into the forest and rescued Phlai Ngam. In Phra Wai's account here, and his account during the trial in chapter 34, Wanthong is not mentioned. During the trial, it could be argued that Phra Wai is cleverly keeping Wanthong out of the account told to the king. But here it is obvious that the author of this chapter is working with a different version of chapter 24 in which Phlai Ngam finds his own way out of the forest. See also the difference over the role of Thong Prasi (note 5 below). These changes suggest that there was an earlier version of chapter 24, and that Sunthon Phu adjusted details of the story in his revision.

5. The chapter on "The birth of Phlai Ngam" stated that Thong Prasi brought Phlai Ngam to find Khun Phaen but this chapter says Phlai Ngam ran away from Thong Prasi. This is because the authors of each chapter did not know the other chapter. [Note in PD edition]

I gained piles of money, servants, a house, rank, and happiness. I saw Father's face every night. The only thing missing was Mother, living far away.

I longed for you, and so I went to fetch you. I meant to make you happy. I didn't know I was leading you to your death—like a child killing his own mother."

Phra Wai turned and said, "Hey, executioner! Better to come and chop me. Don't take my mother's life but let me die in her place.

It's because I brought her back that the king handed her a grave punishment." He sobbed, shook, and flailed about at his mother's feet.

Recovering himself, he asked for forgiveness. "Mother, please grant pardon on my head. When I was a child, I didn't know anything. I annoyed you by overstepping the mark,

by pinching, biting, swiping, hitting, and answering back. Mother, please forgive me so your son doesn't carry this karma into the future." He wai-ed her over and over again in sadness.

"Oh sun, why are you hurrying across the sky, hastening the time my mother will be dead and gone? If you were sick, Mother, I could find the medicine to treat you and ease any discomfort.

I could sell off bowls,[6] betel boxes, and other goods, or take all the servants, oxen, and buffaloes to pledge against the doctors' fees, even pledge myself and my wives.

I've never nursed and tended you, and now karma has caught up and you'll perish by execution." Feeling his breast being licked by fire, Phra Wai grieved as if he too would die.

Khun Phaen felt great pity for Wanthong. He sat listening quietly and feeling helpless. She turned to clasp his feet, weeping. Khun Phaen buried his face on his wife's back,

shaking with sobs and sighs, mouth straining open, and tears streaming down. "It was a waste for us to have gone through such suffering, scratching the earth to feed like birds,

living in the deep forest, warding off the mosquitoes with only a lowercloth, digging up taro and potatoes in the wilds. Yet however hard the hardship, we were together.

We crossed streams, crags, ravines. We gathered leaves to make shelters. I destroyed an army of thousands to protect you, and we weren't apart for a single day.

---

6. Bowls, normally made of silver, were valuable items included among goods presented to nobles as marks of rank.

Though the hardships were heavy, you bore them to be with your husband, even eating lotus roots when other food was hard to find, and not a single grain of rice.

For eight months we saw no house. Hiding away caused you great grief. Then you became pregnant and we had to take special care of the dear child that had come to join us.

I rode the horse at walking pace in fear of upsetting your womb. Every morning and evening I cradled you with care. When your belly became big, I feared a disaster.

So I took you to Phra Phichit and we all survived. If they'd killed us both in the forest, I wouldn't have felt as bad as I feel now.

At that time, we were suffering so much we could have bowed our faces and gone to our deaths. As it happened, we stayed alive, came to Ayutthaya, and faced trial.

We won, and the king granted you to me. I felt happy that our troubles were over, and all the effort had been worthwhile. But ill fate caught up with me and I was put in jail.

Again I had to suffer day and night, and was troubled about your pregnancy too. Khun Chang seized you, redoubling my pain, as if some six fires were burning in my breast.

You seem to have died and left me once already. For you, there was the torment of parting from me; for me in jail, the grief of longing for you. Sorrow piled on sorrow piled on sorrow—

the sorrow of separation from my companion in suffering. When you gave birth, I didn't know whether it went well or badly, whether the child was boy or girl, alive or dead. For many years I was in the dark.

Only later, Phlai Ngam found me and told me, so I knew you were still alive. When I got out of jail, I meant to come after you so we could try again, come what may.

By the power of merit, Phlai Ngam came to ask for my release. I was not unmindful of you but I went to Chiang Mai. On return I found comfort, and happened to forget you for almost a year.

Then our son brought you to this room—as if you were born again for me. I felt relieved that our troubles were behind us. I thought we could live together happily until our dying day.

We met and talked in the middle of the night, went to sleep, and didn't wake until the sun was high. Then the case blew up in terrible turmoil, and in the end my beloved has to die.

What troubles I've had! In many battles, even against armies of hundreds and thousands, I was never at a loss, and my troops were not destroyed.

Even though the sky rained spears, I could protect my men unscathed. The Chiang Mai Lao had skills unsurpassed but they broke and scattered because of my lore.

Their weapons didn't even pierce my horse. Their fire I could put out on the spot. My reputation spread throughout the land. What's happening now is pitiful.

I've protected the lives of tens and hundreds of thousands. Only my greatest love I can't protect. My very own heart alone must be pruned and plucked away. Why is it beyond my power to prevent?

If armies came to besiege the city, they shouldn't harbor any illusion they could seize the throne. I'd volunteer to fight single-handed, and not quail in the face of tens or hundreds of thousands.

But here I'm at a loss because His Crystal Majesty has given his command without allowing any petition. He went back into the palace immediately. Your neck will be severed at royal command.

Oh my king and lord! Why were you so enraged? If you would pardon her life, whatever cities Your Majesty desires—

Khaek, Farang, Lao, Lue, Mon, or Burmese—I'd truss them up and present them to you. I would ask only for my beloved Wanthong, and leave the result to fate.

Stay here. I'll go to petition the king." Wanthong said, "Don't! Don't be rash! The time you begged for Laothong, you were clapped in irons. This time, I'm condemned to die.

You'll pile a new problem on top of those we already have.[7] You'll be condemned along with me and we'll both die. Don't imagine that your wife can survive.

If you die too, when will you be born again? Live on and make merit for me, my beloved. Hell is a dark place and I fear it. If you live on, you can send me the merit you've made."

Hearing these words, Khun Phaen could say nothing more. Feeling hopeless and helpless, overwrought and overwhelmed, he collapsed flat on the ground.

The crowds of onlookers could not smother their own sadness. Everyone wept, young and old, streaming with tears. The only sound heard was weeping and wailing,

---

7. She says: You'll bring up the matter of the buffaloes while the matter of the cattle has not yet been resolved. This is a variation on a saying, ความวัวไม่ทันหาย ความควายเข้ามาแทรก, *khwam wua mai than hai khwam khwai khao ma saek*, "The buffalo matter has not yet disappeared but the cattle matter intervenes," a stock saying from a time when disputes over livestock were endemic.

like a forest blasted by a fierce gale that blows leaves, branches, and twigs into trembling turmoil. The weak-hearted fell down in a faint, seeing the sun dipping towards the trees.

Kaeo Kiriya, Laothong, Simala, and Soifa grieved for Wanthong. Setting a salver with *miang* and betel, they crawled up to pay respect and ask forgiveness.

Kaeo Kiriya said, "I beg your forgiveness so that I will not carry any ill karma into the future. We gave ourselves to the same husband. If there's any matter that has angered you,

I beg you to pardon me so it will not be added to my karma." Wanthong said, "I hold nothing against you, Kaeo Kiriya. If I offended you in any way, please forgive me."

Kaeo Kiriya acknowledged the apology with tears flowing. Laothong sorrowfully went forward. "If I've offended you in the past, please absolve me of blame from today."

Wanthong accepted Laothong's apology. "I abused you a great deal. I beg your forgiveness too. Don't bear resentment." All were in tears.

Soifa and Simala sobbed and sadly sought her forgiveness. "Whatever wrongs we've done you, from the past until the end of your life today,

don't let them be our ill karma." They bowed their faces and wept. Wanthong accepted their apologies, growing ever more sorrowful, her face bathed in tears of compassion.

Wanthong called for flowers, and crawled over to pay respect to Thong Prasi. "Your child will take leave of you today, Mother. Please forgive me. Don't let there be any wrong between us.

If I've made you angry in any way, since I was with Khun Phaen until the time they execute me, let the karma lapse, Mother."

Thong Prasi raised her trembling hands in acceptance, and fell down faint in the dust. When she recovered, she said, "Don't abandon merit. Be intent on prayer, dear daughter.

Find some flowers for your mother, dear Wai. It's better to remember the goodness of the Buddha. Why are you crying, Phaen? Go and find a bowl to pour water on the ground.[8]

Simala, fetch some raw and cooked rice to make offerings to the spirits. It's nearly nightfall. Then we can make merit." Thong Prasi mumbled and grumbled on.

Her grandson, Chumphon, crawled over to her. She lifted him onto her

---

8. See p. 58, note 18.

shoulder with tears flowing. Thinking of Wanthong, she wept while cradling
Chumphon to suckle her breast.

"She'll fall dead, my little Phlai. Don't cry, little thing. Have some sweets."
She took betel from her mouth, gave it to her grandson to suck, and cuddled
him in a daze.

Khun Chang sat some distance away on his own, blubbering and babbling unhappily with his face white as a ghost. "This time you'll die for sure,
beloved.

Oh Buddha! We were together until a moment ago. Oh Wanthong, now
you'll die because of me. Your flesh will turn to dust because this stupid mole
went to petition the king.

Your son was sick so you went to see him, and I wrongly thought you'd run
away. They came to tell me what had happened but this hairless chalkhead
took issue with them,

even told the king the whole story from beginning to end. In truth, I'm not
the reason you'll die. The king asked who you loved but you were two-minded
and couldn't think straight.

The king was angry at your befuddlement. If you loved Chang and Chang
alone, it would be sweet bliss.[9] You could stay in a house with huge pillars, eat
blackear catfish curry, and live a life of ease.

But you're going to die in full public view. Oh, my heaven's peak, my holy
bowl, my huge hamper![10] Where will I find another like you? If I can't, I'll have
no wife.

I'll donate my house and possessions to the monks, give up this world, shave
my head, and be ordained. Even if a noble's daughter would consent to be my
wife, why have someone who's not the same?

I'll pray fervently, count my beads, and grieve from nightfall until cockcrow
for a hundred lives, a thousand lives, with not one day's relief. Just my own
five fingers, until death."

Thong Prasi heard him raving. "Why are you weeping, you disaster, you
baldheaded, cockle-skulled lowlife? She's going to die and you malign her.

It's not a fitting way to weep—raving over a holy bowl, a huge hamper." Phra

---

9. Literally, ขนมโก้, *khanom ko*, a Chinese sweet made with rice flour.

10. แม่ยอดฟ้าฝาบาตรกระจาดใหญ่, *mae yot fa fa bat krajat yai*, literally, mistress peak of heaven,
lid of begging bowl, big basket. The basket here is the large *krajat* used for carrying the Mahachat offerings (see p. 67, note 49) and other acts of almsgiving, so the image conveys bountiful-
ness (Anuman, *Prapheni kiao kap chiwit taeng ngan*, 135). *Krajat* can also be a metaphor for
the vagina.

Wai strode over in a rage. "You insulted me, you bald lowlife,

speaking like a dog spraying its shit around. Go away, or prepare for a beating. If you stay I'll elbow you, so watch out." He dragged Khun Chang away
by his ear.

Khun Chang squirmed and screamed. "I truly love her absolutely, Phra
Wai, sir." Phra Wai elbowed him down to the ground. "You slave, haven't you
gone away yet?"

Khun Chang loped off, barging into some onlookers who drew back and
kicked him on his way. Khun Chang leapt out of the circle, crying, "Never in
my life!

I love my wife. I weep for her. And he elbows me for nothing, people. I'll
contest this again. I won't let this pass." Phra Wai called out, "Hey baldy!

Get yourself out of here. Go and press more charges somewhere." Khun
Chang said, "Why? I'm going home." But he skulked back, and trod on I-Tan,
the daughter of I-Tae, who shrieked,

stormed at Chang, and scratched him. "This baldy has come back, I tell you!"
Khun Phaen called out, "Stop it, Wai!" He tugged his son back into the sala.

Grief-stricken over his mother, Phra Wai tried to ease his distress by talking
with his father. "I'd like your opinion.

Though we weep and wail, she'll be executed. What should we do? Father,
please stay here to protect her. I'm going to petition His Majesty.

I'll plead with him to moderate his anger and pardon her. I don't care about
the consequences. When she is this close to death, I must repay my debt of
gratitude. That's my idea. What do you think, Father?"

Khun Phaen, great valiant, considered his son's words and agreed, but he
looked at the horoscope and got a clear picture, so said to Phra Wai,

"There's a lot of obstruction in the Eight Phases."[11] He spoke as if to deter his
son. "Even if you go and appeal to the king, the position says His Majesty

should grant the pardon that you request for sure, but your mother will not
escape death. See her face. She looks white and close to death. It's nearly time,
almost four o'clock."

He scratched the horoscope on the ground for Phra Wai to see. "She's ill
fated. It looks like a violent death. Saturn is in conjunction with her ascendant,
and the Crow appears in the Coffin. This is a time when the monkey reaches
into a hole and is eaten by a crocodile.[12]

---

11. See p. 793, note 15.

12. The ascendant, ลักขณา, ลักนา, *lakhana*, lagna, the planet rising on the eastern horizon at

Someone with this position cannot survive." Phra Wai saw the whole picture, and tears trickled down his face. He turned to say to his father, "It's up to karma.

I can see it all—bad fate, life, and death. But I must still repay her kindness and my upbringing. I'll say a couple of words in appeal for her, then it depends on her own merit and karma.

Father, please stay and protect her. Don't let them kill her first." With these words, he went up to Phraya Yommarat and paid respect.

"Sir, please hold off the punishment. I'm going to attend on King Phanwasa to beg a reprieve for my mother. Have mercy and don't let her die."

Phraya Yommarat was pleased. "Go! Don't delay. Hurry. If you take too long beyond the time, I'll fear the king's authority too much to hold off."

Phra Wai heard him and took leave. With his servants, he rushed to the palace and sat waiting for the time. Composing his mind, he turned his face to the east,

chanted[13] a Great Beguiler mantra to charm and inspire love, put a Phakhawam with a powerful face in his mouth, pronounced a sacred mantra of Kasak[14] displaying mastery and another of Narai transforming into a floating omen,[15]

and recited prayers to his powerful teachers for the king's anger to recede. He waited until he felt the breath passing through his left nostril,[16] and then

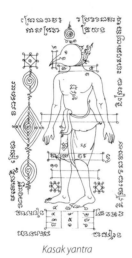

Kasak yantra

---

the time of birth, the most influential planet in that person's horoscope, is occupying the same sign as Saturn. Also, ก, *ka*, the Crow, a triangular constellation like a beak, known in Western astronomy as Delphinus, the Dolphin, is appearing within โลง, *long*, the Coffin, a square constellation, known in Western astronomy as Aquila, the Eagle. In some astrology manuals, portents are described by similes with scenes from Jataka stories or other folktales, in this case an unidentified tale of a monkey and crocodile, clearly a very bad portent.

13. This stanza is taken from WK, 31:1201; PD has: chanted the Great Beguiler mantra to charm and inspire love, made a Thepnimit yantra from powder, then closed his hand and wiped it away, leaving no trace.

14. กาสัก ประจักษ์ ฤทธิ์, *kasak prajak rit. Kasak* is a fabulous bird, sometimes depicted with a human body and a bird's head, believed to be invisible, depicted in certain yantra. Possession of a *kasak's* feathers conveys the power of becoming invisible.

15. นารายน์ แปลง รูป นิมิตร์ ประจักษ์ ลอย, *narai plaeng rup nimit prajak loi.* "Narai Transforming" is a well-known mantra and yantra for invulnerability. The Beguiler is to induce the king's compassion, while the other devices are to protect Wai himself from possible consequences of the king's anger.

16. See p. 101, note 23.

crawled into the jeweled audience hall.

He saw the king was in a good mood and speaking with a merry smile. Phra Wai prostrated elegantly three times, and crouched, waiting and glancing around.

The[17] holy lord, crown of Ayutthaya, whose power and might resembled the Lord of the Lions, saw Phra Wai prostrating to the dust. He watched quietly without speaking,

feeling love and concern for Phra Wai on account of the power of the lore. He said, "Heigh! Wai, why have you come? Have they executed your mother yet?"

Narai Transforming yantra

Thepnimit yantra

Phra Wai listened to the king's questions with tears flowing. He saw that his lore was working and that the king was not badly disposed. He prostrated to pay respect and said,

"My liege, Your Majesty, most excellent in all worlds, great and small, whatever pleases or displeases,[18] my life is beneath the royal foot.

Your Majesty raised me to be a lieutenant of the pages. Every morning and night your goodness is over my head. I am happy every succeeding day, and have never betrayed the royal foot.

Your humble servant's mother is a very bad woman who has gone astray as a result of excessive carnal desire. Your Majesty has rightly shown her no favor.

If this were a sister, aunt, or grandmother, I'd leave her to die without pity. But this is the mother who suffered to carry me in her womb. Because of her, I was born and live long.

Her benevolence is manifold and boundless. It would be most unbefitting to abandon her. In addition, since birth I've not had the chance to tend her at all.

Now that she faces the ending of her life, I appeal to Your Majesty to bestow

17. These two stanzas down to "executed your mother yet" are taken from WK, 31:1201; PD has: The mighty king, eminence of the holy city, saw Phra Wai come in to pay respect. He felt merciful. / "How come this fellow is so persevering? They're executing his mother but he still comes round to see me." He asked, "Why have you come, Wai? Have they executed Wanthong yet?"

18. A formula acknowledging absolute royal authority (see p. 497, note 12).

on me a favor, so word may spread that Phra Wai repaid his debt of gratitude to his mother.

I beg Your Majesty to pardon her life. Instead of execution, have her thrashed and confined in pitiful circumstances as is appropriate to her improper conduct."

The king heard Phra Wai out and was inclined to be compassionate. "I have sympathy for you, Phra Wai.

You did well and gained royal favor. I've already compensated you in many ways but I've not yet exhausted my gratitude. I'll lift your mother's punishment as a reward.

If it were anyone else but you, I wouldn't grant this. Whoever pleaded would die along with her. Heigh! Thainam, go quickly with Phra Wai.

Tell Minister Yommarat not to execute Wanthong because I've pardoned her for Phra Wai. Hurry before the sword falls."

Phra Wai was delighted to have achieved his wish. He prostrated in front of the throne to receive the royal command, and rushed off.

He spoke with Phra Thainam. "It's evening, almost nightfall. We can't delay or Phraya Yommarat will execute her. Call the servants to harness horses."

They mounted a horse apiece and galloped along the middle of the road, waving a white flag as a signal, with servants and phrai flocking behind.[19]

Phraya Yommarat thought something was unusual, and trembled in fear. Because the fruit of Wanthong's karma was to be executed, he misconstrued what was happening.

"Phra Wai went away on foot and now someone is coming on horseback, flying a white flag. That's suspicious. It can't be Phra Wai returning.

It must be like this: Phra Wai went to petition the king, and His Majesty was angry to find she hadn't yet been executed. I'll be in the wrong because of the delay. Quick, there! Bring her and carry out the sentence!"

The executioner and royal punishers[20] dragged Wanthong over. Shaking with terror, she turned to call her husband, "I fear they're going to chop me!" Khun Phaen barged his way in front of the guards,

gnashing his teeth, and embracing Wanthong as protection. Khun Chang called out, "Seize her!" The executioner strode up with a long sword. Khun Phaen threw himself on top of his wife.

---

19. From Khan Gate of the palace to the execution ground was around 1 km.
20. See p. 709, note 3.

They pushed and pulled, grabbed and grappled. The executioner chopped down, hitting Khun Phaen, but the sword bent and crumpled without piercing him. Guards crowded in and hauled Khun Phaen off her.

He gnashed his teeth in fury, twisted his body into a coil, and shouted, "Let me go!" The executioner brandished a sword, glinting in the light, stepped forward, raising his arm, and struck down,

severing Wanthong's neck. In an instant, her life turned to dust. At that moment, Phra Wai galloped up, leapt down from his horse, and embraced the feet of his mother's motionless body.

Khun Phaen collapsed down flat, as if he would never rise again alive. Khun Chang fell rolling on the ground at a distance. All the servants were in turmoil.

Thong Prasi flailed in agony. Soifa and Simala fell flat on their backs. Kaeo Kiriya crumpled, dropping her son. Everyone without exception was shocked senseless.

In the packed crowd of onlookers, some collapsed in a faint, some ran off, and others busily tried to help their friends by massaging.

Royal doctors treated Phra Wai and Khun Phaen with snuff, and bathed them with water to revive them. All slowly recovered their senses.

In grief, Khun Phaen, Phra Wai, Laothong, the two daughters-in-law, Thong Prasi, and Kaeo Kiriya each went to embrace the body and lament.

Khun Phaen said, "Oh Wanthong, it's pitiful you had to die. However much I tried to prevent it, this was the karma you had made."

Phra Wai said, "I was determined you should not die. I appealed to the king and rushed here but—Oh Buddha!—I didn't arrive in time for the execution."

Kaeo Kiriya's tears fell. "Oh, my own breast feels severed!" Laothong wept miserably. Simala was smothered in tears.

Soifa flailed in agony. Thong Prasi stood up and let forth a keening wail. The whole circle resounded with grief. Khun Phaen bent down to embrace the body.

Everyone wept and wailed. Everyone stumbled and staggered. Everywhere was stained red with blood. Phra Wai hugged Wanthong, his heart leaden and his mind maddened.

Seeing his father, he flew into a rage. "I left you and you alone to look after her but you carelessly let this happen. I'm blaming you even though it'll make you angry.

You won't miss her because you have a fine flock of other wives. If you had some compassion for her, she need not have been killed.

You're so skilled in lore that you face hundreds of thousands of Lao without fear. You have stunning mantras, powerful enough to immobilize people in droves.

Why didn't you blow one to stun this executioner and stop him? She died because you didn't help her. Or have you lost your powers?

You're crying only because you see me here. Otherwise you'd just look the other way." The more he spoke, the more he felt choked with anger. He turned to Minister Yommarat.

"What happened to your promise? Did you have to sever my mother's neck? You worried we'd return so you rushed to chop her first. Have you some reason for revenge on me?

Maybe you loathe me but why take it out on my mother? Do you enjoy chopping women dead? What war are you waging on women?

When I was leaving, I asked you not to carry out the execution. You agreed to take care of it. I appealed to the king and he granted the pardon.

Yet just now my mother died! What do you have to say? You had her killed to show off your attention to duty. You saw me empty-handed[21] and acted big with fear of nobody.

On top of that, they chopped at my father too. He survived only because the blows didn't pierce him. What was he being punished for? Was there a royal command to execute him too?

I'm your sworn enemy until my dying day. My wish for revenge will never weaken—ever! Enough! You've probably heard news of my skill. If I don't kill my enemy, I agree to die myself."

Phra Wai turned to see the executioner who dispatched her, and rushed upon him, kicking him down flat on the ground and drawing his sword to kill him. Crowds of people ran off in turmoil.

Khun Chang was shocked when Phra Wai confronted him too. He raised his hands and shouted, "Why me?" Phra Wai kicked him down and put a foot on his neck. In fear, Phraya Yommarat bowed to ask forgiveness.

Khun Phaen rushed over and pulled Phra Wai away. "Listen to me. Don't lose your temper. She had to die as fruit of her karma. I was sitting close by but I forgot to think.

I leapt up to cover Wanthong and so I was too late to undo anything. They swarmed over me and dragged me off. It was beyond my powers. Wanthong's life had reached its end."

---

21. Presumably meaning without a weapon.

Phra Wai angrily pushed his hand away and growled, "I'm going to slash him." His father wrested the weapon out of his hand. Phra Wai collapsed down beside his mother's body.

"Oh mistress of your darling child, you're asleep now and cannot see my face. I went against royal authority to appeal to the king with no thought for my own life.

The king granted a pardon. I was happy that you wouldn't be done away with, and my reputation would spread. I didn't know you'd die as the fruit of fate.

I rushed here with Phra Thainam, riding horses like we were flying. But in truth, karma had to lead to this result alone, and I saw them sever your neck."

He hugged his mother's body in grief, his heart trembling in turmoil, until he lost control of his senses and collapsed in a mute faint.

Khun Phaen, great valiant, felt huge pity for Phra Wai as he watched him weeping over the loss of his mother and sorrowfully hugging her body
until he collapsed and lost consciousness. In shock, Khun Phaen massaged his son to revive him.

As Phra Wai gradually came round, Khun Phaen consoled him. "Listen to your father. A dead person never rises again. It's no use to keep grieving.

Try to still your heart, dear Wai. Don't weep, and listen to my advice. It's natural that all of us born in any shape or form must die, one after another.

Men and women have a life, but when they reach their line of destiny,[22] they cannot stay. Even the earth, sky, and oceans are annihilated in the era-destroying fire.

There's no point wallowing in tears. Think about making some merit to send to her. Your mother's body is still lying in the circle. Think about putting her to rest, my son."

Phra Wai agreed with his father's soothing words. Smothering his sadness and tempering his tears, he turned to give orders to servants.

"Bring the required white cloth and wrap the body without delay. Cut planks to make a coffin, and line it with banana fronds.

Then lift the body, place it on the wood, and have it carried for burial in

---

22. พรหมลิขิต, *phromlikhit*, inscription of Brahma, written by Brahma on a child's face either prior to birth or immediately after the infant is first washed, and controlling the course of life. The belief is especially strong among the Mon who prepare fruit, powder, pencil, and paper for Brahma to use at the time of birth (Phlainoi, *Wannakhadi aphithan*, 223–24).

the graveyard. Assign people to guard the body closely."[23] They all returned home in tears.

The whole house was as chilly as a graveyard. The only sound throughout was people grieving in anguish and despair. The neighbors and townsfolk shared the sadness.

❦

After he saw Wanthong executed, Khun Chang could not stay. He promptly called his servants and boarded a boat to go to Suphan.

Moving quickly, they reached the house just before dawn. Khun Chang feared his mother-in-law would hear about the case so he quickly sneaked into the house, sobbing tears from glistening eyes.

❦

Khun Phaen, great romancer, thought deeply about his beloved wife. When dawn lit the sky, he sent a servant to find Siprajan,

and tell her that Wanthong was dead. Ai-Sa hastened across the plain to Suphan and went into Siprajan's house.

Just at that moment, Saithong[24] was walking out. Ai-Sa sank down and raised his hands in wai. Saithong asked why he had come. "Khun Phaen sent me to convey the news

that in the middle of the night before last, Phra Wai very rashly abducted Wanthong. In anger, Khun Chang went to tell the king,

who was enraged and ordered her execution. Wanthong is no more." Feeling she was being burned by fire, Saithong collapsed in grief.

She lay motionless, just sobbing as if her heart would break with sorrow. Servants tried to help but she would not recover. Everybody was stunned.

Just then, Siprajan saw Saithong. Her body trembled as if possessed by a ghost. She shouted, "Hey you, what did you do to her?

Saithong fell down headlong with a crash. Did you hit her or what?" Ai-Sa cried out, "Mistress Wanthong has died."

Siprajan heard "is to die." In shock she collapsed back onto a tray, then raised herself and feverishly prayed to the spirits and the Buddha. "Lord, let her survive and not die.

When did she get sick? I didn't know. Well, well! That disaster Khun Chang

---

23. Newly dead bodies were considered to have special power which could be transferred into objects or potions for application of magic.

24. Saithong has disappeared from the story since chapter 14. We can imagine from this reappearance that she has been living with Siprajan all along.

is too embarrassed to tell me until she's almost dead." She blundered off to the house of her son-in-law,

and was surprised to find the stairway was pulled up. She got Ai-Bia to lean a ladder on a window, and climbed up into the central hall. Khun Chang sat bent over, weeping.

Siprajan saw his face. "Eh, something's up. So bleary eyed." Khun Chang said, "Wanthong shouldn't have died.

It happened because Phlai Ngam abducted her and the king became enraged. I didn't lay charges with the king. He knew and had her executed. That's the truth."

Siprajan realized her daughter was dead. She collapsed flat on her back and lay still. Khun Chang tended to her but she did not move. He sent his servants to fetch doctors.

Both doctors of massage and doctors of medicine arrived in a crowd and sat huddled around her. They massaged, applied smelling salts, and squeezed her jaw, but it was a long time before she recovered her senses.

Old Siprajan was in a pitiful state. Her body shook, and her face was as white as a ghost. Tears splashed down in torrents as she raved over the loss of her child.

Khun Chang sat tending to her for more than a watch, then had her borne home on a litter. When they carefully but awkwardly carried her up the stairs and put her down, she was still wailing on and on.

"Oh my Wanthong! You shouldn't have gone to the city and let them execute you. If you were sick at home with your mother, I could nurse you.

After your father died, I hoped you'd be my companion, staying here in this house until my old age. As it happened, karma and ill fate got you an outcaste husband who destroyed you.

If I'd known it'd come to this, I'd have had the abbot ordain you as a nun, and not let myself be carried away by money, even piles of it. I wouldn't have allowed any man to enjoy you as husband.

But both Phaen and that shiny baldy became my sons-in-law. I'd never seen anything like it. The villains fought like pig and dog until this disaster happened and you lost your life.

When Phlai Ngam was a little child, I thought of him tenderly as a grandson. I didn't know he'd grow up so heartless that he could be the cause of his mother's death.

Oh, I'll be lonely in my dotage! My husband and my child have gone and left me alone. Why should I live to suffer?" She wept and wailed in torrents of tears.

Saithong, who had been like an elder sister to Wanthong, recovered her senses and got up. She thought of Wanthong forlornly and tears splashed down in streams.

She took leave of Siprajan, and went to board a boat, lost in grief. Reaching the capital, she walked straight to the house of Khun Phaen.

On arrival she entered his room and asked, "Where's Wanthong's body?" Khun Phaen said, "Buried at Wat Takrai."[25] He told someone to take Saithong there.

She descended from the house in tears, and pushed herself along in a daze. At the graveyard, her sobbing worsened and she collapsed down in a sad heap.

The accompanying servants helped her recover. After a moment, Saithong breathed a sigh and began to come round.

She called out in grief, "Oh dear Wanthong, you stay so still and don't greet me. Why did you come to lie in this earth, to make a little tunnel and flee away by yourself?[26]

It was a waste to have loved you from long ago. We shared one house, one heart, one husband. We faced good and bad in happiness and harmony. We've loved and looked after each other since we were little.

Now Wanthong, my beloved, you've run away and abandoned me to sorrow. Don't expect me to live long. I'll die and follow so we can go together.

For years from now, I won't see you. For months, I'll mourn in misery. Every day, I'll grieve for you. When will I meet you again?"

She flailed around as if she were about to die on top of Wanthong's body. Racked by sobs, she slumped down and lay limp, beating her chest and wailing.

She tried to still her mind and pull herself together. Nightfall was coming and she needed to return quickly. Grieving over her loss, she walked back to the house of Phra Wai,

and gave orders to the accompanying servants to return to Suphan forthwith. She alone would stay to help Phra Wai with the ceremony.

At dawn, when a bright sun lit up the whole world, the valiant Phra Wai's thoughts turned to the cremation of his mother.

---

25. Wat Takrai was probably a crematory wat. It is sited outside the city of Ayutthaya, off the island, as was the usual practice for crematory wat, and had large enough grounds of 25 *rai* extended down to Khlong Sa Bua. Besides a main stupa, the ordination hall is surrounded by sixteen other stupas of various sizes. Possibly these were built to enshrine crematory remains. Further up Khlong Sa Bua is Wat Phraya Maen which appears below in chapters 37, 40–41 with a graveyard, suggesting this whole area may have had some specialization in cremation.

26. A variation on ตัดช่องน้อยแต่พอตัว, *tat chong noi tae pho tua*, cut a channel only big enough for yourself, a proverbial saying meaning, saving oneself alone.

"Let's make it very grand. I must go to approach King Phanwasa." He dressed and went to attend on the king.

Now to tell of the almighty king, who slumbered in the golden palace, attended by throngs of palace ladies of exceptional beauty and charm.

Every face was fair and adorable. Every group paid him respect. Ladies-in-waiting performed their duties inside, some singing and playing music.

An orchestra of *ranat*, gong, plucked instruments, and bowed instruments played and sang in melodious tones. At the time to discuss affairs of state, the king went out to preside in the golden audience hall.

Quailing in fear of committing mistakes, those attending on regular government service presented their addresses, taking care not to provoke the king's irritation on government affairs.

The king noticed Phra Wai. "Eh! How was it with your mother yesterday? You sought and gained my favor but didn't return. What did your father say?"

Phra Wai listened with tears flowing. He raised his clasped hands and addressed the king. "I wasn't in time to help my mother.

When I arrived, they'd severed her head down onto the ground. She was dead." He sobbed fitfully in front of the royal throne.

The king felt as if thunder had struck, making the palace quake. His mind was in utter consternation, and he was too stunned to say anything.

It was a little time before he recovered his voice. "I feel great pity for you, Phra Wai. You secured your mother's reprieve but she did not escape punishment. That was her fate.

Don't be too troubled. I'll provide money and equipment to arrange an appropriate cremation. Let it be a lively affair lasting many days and nights. Don't be hesitant about asking for whatever you need.

Come and take from the treasury. I'll order officials to release everything for you. Make it as splendid as you want. If you need anything, don't hide.

Let there be mask plays, dramas, Mon dances,[27] boxing, wrestling, and shadow plays after nightfall. Let the gongs and drums play loudly. I'll provide a casket for the body—everything,

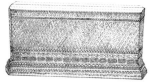

casket presented by king

---

27. มอญรำ, *monram*. Since the Narai reign (1656–1688), dances by Mon women had been popular at court, especially at ceremonial occasions such as cremations and welcomes for state guests. The dances are in the Southeast tradition of Indic origin and differ from Thai versions mainly in the details of dress and adornment of the dancers.

including a bier,[28] all the necessary decorations, all kinds of entertainments, and the frames and fireworks for a display. Get everything done in time. Don't be hesitant to ask."

Phra Wai was overjoyed to hear the king's favor. He prostrated to the royal foot and said, "The royal kindness is great beyond estimation.

Your humble servant is happy as no other. The word will spread through every land and river that Your Majesty bestowed such favor on the head of his servant, Phra Wai.

For those condemned to death, nobody dares to petition. I was resigned to losing my life but have been favored by royal grace.

Though I was unable to fulfill my wish and my mother has passed away, let this servant of the royal foot repay her kindness. I request leave to enter the monkhood for seven days."

The king was very happy to hear this. "I'm pleased with you, Wai. You show filial devotion in recognition of her goodness with a full heart."

The king gave orders to the staff of the Monastic Treasury.[29] "Provide triple robes of mine. I'll gain merit and send it to help her." Phra Wai prostrated and took leave.

The requirements for arranging the cremation—all of very good quality—were carried to the wat. Relatives all gathered around.

Mekhala and Ramasun

Old Siprajan also came to attend Wanthong's cremation. Close to the sun's descent, the body was dug up, cleansed, and placed in a casket provided by the king. Decorations were placed at intervals. Java flute and victory drum played. Monks were invited to chant.

Phlai Chumphon, wearing a white lowercloth and a conical hat, scattered puffed rice in front

---

28. ร้านม้า, *ran ma*, a frame with six posts on which the coffin is placed for cremation.

29. คลังศุภรัต, *khlang supharat*, a building used for storing monks' robes, carpets, pillows, curtains, and monks' seating. It was situated in the area of the palace known as the Phaichayon Benjarat Garden (number 5 on map 9; SWC, 14:6767–68; KLW, 204).

of the procession.[30] The relatives, all gentlefolk wearing white lowercloths, followed behind in mourning.

Her mother, Siprajan, eyes glistening with tears, walked with Thong Prasi. The body was taken into a crematory pavilion,[31] and raised onto a bier.

Crematory articles were placed all around. The site was fashioned as a mountain, so artfully painted and ornamented that those not in the know thought it was rock.[32]

There were steep slopes, cliffs, ravines, streams, and a ledge for a rishi's kuti. At the corner of a cliff, Mekhala played with her gem, and Ramasun threw his axe to clash on the rock.[33]

On a cliff, an overhang created a shallow cave in which was placed the image of an *orahan*.[34] A tiger and bear were bit-

orahan

30. Puffed rice is scattered as an offering to any malevolent spirits in the vicinity to dissuade them from stealing food from the corpse. Puffed rice is used a lot in Tamil Vaishnavite Brahman ceremonies which seem to have been a major source of Siamese court ritual.

31. โรงทึม, *rong thuem*, a roofed shelter where the coffin is placed while people come to pray and pay respect (Woranan, "Kan sueksa sangkhom," 262).

32. "The corpse is placed on a very high platform beneath a gilded pyramid and is taken in this order to a spot near the pagoda where the dead are customarily cremated. It is placed in the middle of a great pyre made specially for the occasion of flammable materials, decorated in a manner similar to our theatres and containing jars full of fireworks, which the Siamese know how to prepare in a special way of their own" (Gervaise, *Natural and Political History*, 144).

In normal cremations, the pyre is a simple affair. Wanthong's pyre is unusually grand because of the role of the king in arranging the ceremony. Resplendent funerary ceremonies are a long-established tradition of kingship in Hindu- and Buddhist-influenced Southeast Asia. Beginning with the funeral of King Naresuan in 1605, the Ayutthaya chronicles devote considerable space to describing the grandeur of royal cremations. In these royal ceremonies, the *meru* is decorated with reference to the description of Mount Meru and its surroundings in the Three World cosmology (RCA, 200, see also 233–34, 319–20, 369, 380, 398–90, 422–23, 466).

The decoration for Wanthong's pyre also resembles the artificial mountains that became a popular feature of wat decoration, especially in the mid-nineteenth century (see, for example, Wat Suthat and Wat Pho). These Chinese-inspired creations were originally designed to represent Wutai Shan and other sacred peaks in China. They are built with natural stones and then decorated with plants, model temples, and figures of humans and animals, as in the case here.

33. A folktale of Indian origin about the origin of thunder and lightning. Mekhala/Manimekhala is a celestial being, and Asura/Ramasun is a giant. Mekhala has a crystal gem. Ramasun covets both the crystal and Mekhala. When he gives chase, Mekhala directs the rays reflected from the crystal (lightning) to blind Ramasun who throws his axe but misses and it clatters against a rock (thunder). The scene is a popular theme of dance. A variation of the story appears in the *Ramakian* and other literary works.

34. According to Khun Wichitmatra, the original PD edition had อรหัน *orahan*, a mythical animal from the Himaphan Forest with a bird's head on a human body but the Khurusapha

ing at each other, rearing up and baring their teeth as if alive.

A deer gamboled where a forest huntsman hid unseen among trees, wearing a mule's head as disguise and loping forward with his eyes fixed on the deer.

Nearby was a figure of a forest dweller, goggling his eyes and pulling faces like a ghost. Many gaur stood motionless in various poses, some bent down as if eating grass.

Between the rock cliffs was a clearing, made from paper cut neatly and stuck on a board in a combination of green, black, and red, with a surrounding of much nak and gold.

Parts were made as ponds and islands with indented edges painted in colors of unmatched freshness. Other parts were piled up higgledy piggledy in the strange shape of a cave chimney.

Down inside, the abyss looked very deep and murkily black. Above, birds posed with wings outspread, and a fish-owl perched on a lush *krathum*.

The area around was very neat and clean, placed with pots of topiary and decorated with a ritual balustrade, *jamon*,[35] and fine jeweled umbrellas.

The base for the casket was fashioned in the shape of a golden lotus.[36] Above, three sharp peaks made with gold and glass filigree rose up to three levels. Fragrant garlands of threaded flowers hung down, along with glittering crystal pendants.

Standing screens were painted with the story of Inao.[37] Brightly shining mirrors were placed on the arches above the pillars. White curtains glittered with fine gold embroidery. Crystal lanterns were lined up along with rows of candles.

A neat four-cornered dais had boards at the back and lines drawn to indicate the spaces where monks would sit to chant. Handsome mats were laid on the floor.

jamon

In the evening after sunset, performers of many languages came to present their overtures, all shouting at the same time in a noisy hubbub.

---

edition added an extra character making it อรหันต์ *arahan*, a Buddhist saint. Since the scene is based on Mount Meru, the site of Himaphan, the original would seem correct (KW, 526). Both the Smith and Wat Ko editions have *arahan*.

35. จามร, a long-handled standing piece of regalia, modeled on a flywhisk of yak hair, usually made of hide encased in silk embroidered with gold thread (SWC, 3:1172–74).

36. Coffins with gold, glass, and gem filigree were provided by the king for cremations of high nobility in the First Reign (KW, 527).

37. See p. 588, note 12.

shadow play

After sunrise, at around seven, the stages opened, competing against one another merrily. There were mask plays, dramas, and Mon dances to enjoy. Choruses sang in time to the rhythm of clacking claves.

Puppets moved from pose to pose. Pairs of performers exchanged repartee back and forth. Clowns brought in a hunchback who peered around. The stages echoed with the sounds of chatter and laughter.

At a Chinese opera, actors with faces made up magnificently in red and white entered holding spears and lances, and engaged in fights, wrestling and boxing. Some returned backstage, and others came forward, pulling faces.

Nai Jaeng[38] came to play chicken-flapping songs, jiggling his shoulders up and down and singing "cha, cha." He danced and sang with Granny Ma, each trying to outdo the other with flirtatious repartee, making people laugh uproariously.

Many different performances played at the same time, and throngs of people walked around to watch. Gentlefolk, ordinary people, and paupers all jostled shoulder to shoulder.

Young country girls with powdered faces came wearing flimsy white upper-cloths and lowercloths in peeled-lotus design. They kept bumping into people and making others laugh. Their faces looked afraid and embarrassed at their carelessness.

Unruly drunks staggered around, raising their fists to challenge passersby for a fight. They abused anyone who got in their way until they were clapped in the stocks, red-eyed.

Chinese opera

38. Later known as Khru Jaeng, the author of several chapters of *KCKP*. This passage was probably written in the Third Reign, when he was known as a performer of chicken-flapping songs with Granny Ma as his performing partner (see *Companion*, 1351–52).

tree of plenty

firework tower

Many groups of playboys circulated around on the prowl, some with their hair cut handsomely short *en brosse*, preening themselves and courting girls by throwing flowers.

In the afternoon sunlight came the throwing of alms. People climbed up to trees of plenty, removed the cloth covers, picked off the limes, and hurled them in all directions.[39]

Waiting crowds of Khaek and Thai, men and women, scrambled to catch the limes, chasing, hitting, and elbowing one another. Some people sneaked away to the rear to avoid the mayhem.

Strong ones were ready to pounce. They jumped up to grab the limes, and gripped them tight. Others squeezed their hands to make them release their hold. Rowdily they pushed and pulled, back and forth.

At dusk, fireworks were lit for entertainment. Candle-showers[40] whizzed and rockets popped from tall towers.[41] Shadow players were called over to set up their screens.

When a group of Khaek shadow players came on, everyone watched with eyes a-goggle. Their puppets looked grotesque

---

39. This is a form of playful almsgiving, based around the *kalapaphruek*, a mythical tree of plenty which provides people in the Himaphan Forest with everything they wish for (see RR, 133, 191, 200, 233–34, where it is called "the wishing tree" and sometimes equated with the Parichat tree, see p. 173, note 22). At royal or royally sponsored cremations, such trees figured in rituals of almsgiving, as described here. The artificial trees were made with a central bamboo post, topped with a bulbous frame of bamboo laths, and mounted on a base of around human height. Money was inserted in limes which were impaled on spikes fixed to the bamboo lath, and the whole construction was covered with a white cloth. This configuration is known from early Bangkok-era wat murals. The Great Treasury, *khlang mahasombat*, was responsible for making the trees, and an official of this office distributed the alms by prying the limes off the tree with a spiked stick and hurling them far away into the crowd. A record from the Second Reign describes a funeral at which four trees were erected, each with around twenty limes inserted with one salueng. The practice is mentioned in the chronicles at the royal funerals of King Narai in 1688, King Phetracha in 1703, and Princess Yothathip in the 1710s. In 1638, King Prasat Thong had such trees set up at 20-meter intervals around the city, and made a circuit, scattering alms from elephant back while officials dispersed alms from the trees. In early Bangkok, this form of alms giving featured in the celebration of the capital after King Rama I's coronation, and the dedication of Wat Pho. (SWC, 1:254–57; RCA, 223–24, 324, 380, 400, 407; Flood and Flood, *Dynastic Chronicles*, 1:84–85, 237–38)

40. พะเนียง, *phaniang*, a firework which shoots up showers of sparks, like a Roman candle (Sittha, *Dokmai phloeng boran*, 80–81).

41. *Ratha*, see p. 49, note 80. As these are provided by the king, they would be more substantial than those at the cremation in chapter 2.

with curly hair, curved noses, and necks jutting like suffering ghosts.[42]

Relatives went to sit with the body, all sobbing because they loved her enough to swallow her, all in a state of collapse from unrelenting grief.

Weeping beside the body, Thong Prasi and Siprajan got into an argument. Thong Prasi said, "I've never seen anything like it. All because you colluded with that Chang."

Siprajan said, "He's a rich man. For better or worse, we've depended on him in many ways." Thong Prasi replied, "My dear, that was a mistake. Because you depended on Chang, your child was chopped dead."

Siprajan said, "What rubbish! It was your child that caused the calamity." Phra Wai called on his grandmothers to desist. The pair brimmed over with tears, on and on.

༄

Now to tell of Khun Chang. He knew the cremation was taking place and he could not stay away, but he feared that walking straight in would cause trouble. "Phra Wai might use violence.

His father Phaen would go along with him, and if I made a mistake, things might come to a head. Now that I've lost my beloved Wanthong, why get myself hurt unnecessarily?"

He ordered his servants to bring a boat in front of the house, and packed monk's robes, alms offerings, and various items of worship to take along.

On arrival he went to Wat Takrai, moored his boat, and entered from the landing. He went up to find the abbot and paid respect. "Lord Abbot, please give me some assistance this once.

I've come for Wanthong's cremation, and I've brought all the requirements along. But the host has been my enemy for many years. I fear he'll attack me and make a scene.

Please help speak to him and settle the matter that is causing the rift. May I invite you to receive our alms?[43] Think of me as your son."

After listening to Khun Chang's plea, the abbot sighed. "A cremation ceremony is for making merit.

robes for offering

---

42. The description suggests the *wayang* puppets of the Malay world.

43. เป็นหัวทาน, *pen hua than*, to be the head of a group of monks receiving alms. Khun Chang is asking the abbot to act as conciliator. His words mean that he is asking to present the quarrel to the abbot as alms, which cannot be returned. The abbot then goes to Phra Wai and asks him to "put something in my almsbowl," meaning Wai's agreement to give up the quarrel. Wai agrees by "offering up" the quarrel, using the word for a donation, ถวาย, *thawai*.

Why quarrel and create trouble?

Fine! Leave the matter to me. As the other party was my pupil, I can talk to him." He went down the stairs, sought out Phra Wai at the hall for the ceremony,

and said to him, "I wish to bother you to put something in my almsbowl.[44] You've been in conflict with the bald fellow for a long time.

Today you're making merit. It would be better to put an end to this karma as a good deed to make merit for your mother. Just now, Khun Chang came to make merit.

He's still afraid to come in. He fears the host will make trouble. He asked for compassion, and said he'd remember your kindness until death."

Phra Wai paid respect and replied as hoped. "I wish to make merit without any trouble. Let this old matter be offered up today.

Whatever gave rise to my mother's misfortune, now that she's dead and gone, let the matter stop right here. Don't let the ill karma linger into the future.

Lord Abbot, please tell Khun Chang that if he wishes to make merit, he may. I'll not make any obstruction. It's up to his love and devotion."

The abbot of Wat Takrai was pleased at this answer, and laughed, saying, "May you be blessed with happiness and joy!" He returned to his kuti

and told Khun Chang, "I went down below just now and explained as you told me. He agreed to end the matter

in order to extinguish the ill karma for the one who's died. On your side, reconcile and be happy. Don't leave any legacy of this trouble. Let the ill karma end from now on."

Feeling very happy, Khun Chang paid respect to the abbot and said, "I've made up my mind to be careful. I'll not make you lose faith in me."

He went down to find Phra Wai who welcomed him in a spirit of peace. Both sides patched up their differences.[45] Khun Chang made merit by presenting dedicatory robes[46] and giving alms.

---

44. ขอบิณฑ์บาต, *kho binthabat*, see note 43 above.

45. This whole scene is not present in the Wat Ko edition where there is no reconciliation.

46. บังสุกุล, *bangsukun*, Pali *pamsukula*, "stained, dirty," originally meant discarded cloth, especially the wrapping of corpses left in charnel grounds, that monks used as robes as a signal of detachment from worldly matters. The name was used for a length of white cloth which was attached to the binding of the corpse and draped over the edge of the coffin for the presiding monk to hold while chanting the *abhidhamma* funeral prayer. At the end of the chant, the *bangsukun* was pulled free, and worn by some monks, especially forest monks, allowing the dead person

After three days of ceremonies, including presenting dedicatory robes to all the monks, the decorations were taken down.
Phra Wai went to the graveyard,

sat in a meditation pose, and composed his mind. When
he was focused, he pronounced a formula and blew it
onto sesame oil, making it boil, then applied the oil
to his body,

monk in meditation

clothes, and head. He quickly returned, climbed
up onto the pyre, and had the body lifted and laid on top of him.

The relatives who had come to attend the cremation brought decoratively
carved pieces of sandalwood,[47] incense, candles, and flowers. The fire was lit.
Khun Phaen and other relatives wept in lamentation.

Flames blazed up. Flute, drum, and a whole ensemble played. Firecrackers
were lit by fuse. Women ran off in confusion.

Some said that Phra Wai was lying in the fire to be burned to death with
his mother for nothing. Others said to them, "Don't worry. In a moment the
fire will die down."

The firewood and coffin were consumed. Amazingly, Phra Wai came back
out. The circle of people watching were impressed that he was invulnerable
even to fire.

When it was over, Phra Wai changed into new upper and lower cloths.
Monks from Wat Takrai were asked to shave his head.

He went into the ordination hall, and a monk initiated him into the monkhood. Relatives and servants loudly cried "*Sathu!*" Khun Chang wanted to
make his devotion. He rushed in to find Phra Wai

---

to make merit by this gift. Ordinary monks' robes were also placed on the coffin so the dead
person could make merit by offering them to a monk who removed them from the coffin before
cremation. These also were known as *bangsukun*, as in the passage here. In the early nineteenth
century, both the connecting white cloth and the removal of the robes from the bier were practiced. Between the early and mid-twentieth century, the white cloth draped from the cotton has
disappeared, and *bangsukun* now refers solely to the robes removed from the bier (Pattaratorn,
"Chanting for the Dead"). The cloth of *bangsukun* robes has high spiritual value. *Phirot* rings,
yantra cloths, and flags to display at wat ceremonies should ideally be made with this cloth.

47. ท่อนจันทน์ฟั่นประดับ, *thon jan fan pradap*. In the past, when sandalwood was more plentiful, it was used for cremation, partly to mask the smell, and partly in the belief that the fragrance
would waft the spirit to a happy life in heaven. Alternatively, thin sheets of the wood were used,
sometimes carved into the shapes of flowers—as here. Nowadays, for royal cremations, the pyre
is still built with logs of sandalwood. At ordinary cremations, the symbolic kindling given for
each mourner to place on the pyre is still known as *dok mai jan*, sandalwood flowers, though it
is usually now made from dried maize leaves.

and[48] said, "I want to be ordained. Forgive me but please initiate me. I want to be ordained as a novice for Wanthong. I'd be ordained as a monk but that's impossible,

because I can't go without eating, and I don't have the thirty-two attributes."[49] Phra Wai said, "It's up to you, goggle eyes. I don't know."

Khun Chang left Phra Wai and rushed in to pay respect to Abbot Nu. "Please help me, Your Lordship. Please shave my head."

Abbot Nu looked at Khun Chang and said, "You're always a laugh, disciple. I don't have a shaving knife, and there's no one I can borrow from." Khun Chang rushed into the wat,

and searched here and there for a shaving knife. The place was packed with bareheaded novices. Thinking he recognized one, he asked, "Novice That, may I respectfully borrow a shaving knife?"

Elder Ruang said, "You fool! There's only a dirty rusty knife in the spittoon." Khun Chang said testily, "These bald elders!" and ran back to find the abbot.

He sank down and wai-ed, "It's hopeless, Abbot Nu. A machete or a sickle will have to do." The abbot said, "There's only this blunt blade? Well, sharp or blunt, I'll give it a try."

He took the huge cleaver and sharpened it on a stone. "The rust hasn't all gone, disciple." With two strokes, the head was good and bare. He scraped at the nape and lip,

but the knife would not cut the soft hair, leaving clumps here and there. He had Khun Chang lie on his back, and, with eyes popping out of his head, scraped away the whole tangled mat on Khun Chang's cheeks and chest.

The abbot was not very meticulous. "I'm tired of this. It goes all the way down to the ankles. I don't think I can shave that." He bent Khun Chang's head

---

48. This whole scene of Khun Chang's ordination and sermon, down to "as huge as a yogi" on p. 833, is taken from WK, 31:1225–30; PD has: and said, "I want to enter the monkhood. Please initiate me as a novice." Phra Wai said, "I can't. I've just entered myself, and I don't know the chants." / Khun Chang left Phra Wai and went to pay respect to Abbot Nu. "Please show me consideration, Your Lordship. Please initiate me as a novice." / Abbot Nu looked at Khun Chang. "You still have a little bit of hair, devotee. And even if we tonsure you, you still have no triple robe. Go and have your head shaved and bring a triple robe." / Khun Chang got the robes and had his head shaved. Holding the robes with his hands in wai, he went in, opened his mouth, rolled his eyes and cried "*uka.*" Then he trembled with nerves and mumbled. / He could not remember and got everything mixed up. "Please tell it to me, Abbot Nu. I've never "*uka*" before. Please help." He raised the triple robe to hide his face, and followed the recitation. / At the end, he put on the robes, rolled the upper one on his shoulder, took the precepts, and came out. He stayed in the kuti at Wat Takrai for three nights, then disrobed and went to Suphan.

49. อาการสามสิบสอง, *akan samsip song*, thirty-two elements or constituent parts of the body, mentioned in the Buddha's teachings on self-awareness. This is a conventional saying similar to "being all there."

forward and tried to pull out the clumps at his nape by hand.

Khun Chang cried in pain, "Hey! Hasn't it all gone yet? Please put a little lime paste on your hands first." People walking past had a good laugh, saying, "Why don't you use a Mon cleaver instead?"

When it was done, Khun Chang quickly bathed and rubbed himself with turmeric mixed with lots of lime and tamarind.

A servant said, "That's one whole fueang's worth of turmeric but his skin is still not a bit yellow." Khun Chang daubed his body and head to gleam, and went off, followed by his retinue.

When they reached Abbot Nu, Khun Chang raised his hands, holding the robes, opened his mouth, rolled his eyes, and cried "*Uka*,"[50] then trembled with nerves and mumbled.

He called out in Thai, "Please recite and I'll follow, Abbot Nu. I don't know how to *uka*." Khun Chang raised his shaking hands in wai.

The abbot grasped a betel-stem fan[51] to hold before his face, raised himself into a squat, and give the six precepts. He wound a girdle round Khun Chang's neck with shaky hands, fumbling about and saying, "I'll put it on you."

Khun Chang said, "No matter. I'll take off my other clothes first. When I go on my almsround in the market, I'll bring something for you." He took the girdle off his neck, and put on the upper robe very hastily,

getting the cloth tangled round his body. Carrying a walking stick, he paced away with face down, trying to hold in the bulges and look composed.

Thong Prasi and Siprajan shakily lowered themselves down and raised their clasped hands. "May we invite you to give a sermon? Can you give a sermon or not, Novice Chang?"

The novice said, "I can't read but I can give a sermon, willingly." Siprajan said, "Please do so!" and promptly set down a salver of offerings.

Novice Chang lurched up to the pulpit, sat cross-legged, and gave the four precepts. Then he announced the date, "This year and month are the hibernal season.

---

50. At the ordination ceremony, the ordinand first pronounces the *pabbajja*, which expresses his desire for admission to the monkhood, and then utters the *upasambada* or oath of ordination. The Pali *pabbajja* opens "*okasa vandami bhante*." Khun Chang's *uka* is an attempt at the start of this formula. The formula begins: "[Grant me the] chance. I salute the master with respect, May the master pardon all my faults. May the merit I have gained be accepted by the master. May the master transfer to me the merit he has gained. Salutations! I accept." (Bizot, *Les traditions de la pabbajja*, especially 24–26, 106)

51. พัดกาบหมาก, *phat kapmak*, a traditional form of fan. On many palms, including the betel, each leaf grows on a stem which ultimately separates from the trunk and falls away. This fan was fashioned from the base of a stem.

Two rains retreats have passed. The present is the semolina era[52] when cocks crow. The religion will be complete at five thousand. There's still a remnant of three hours."

offering to the monks

Holding her hands clasped, Thong Prasi said, "Pitiful. Please give a sermon that makes sense, damn you." Novice Chang bent his body forward, thrust out his neck, and started shouting at the top of his voice.

He read a Pali extract[53] and verse, "*Thoso kosa ta kesi*,"[54] then translated the content of the Pali. "There were thirty women.

What all their names were, I don't know. The one with the swollen eyes and stubby legs was the first. Each had six children. They built a house by a cow-itch tree."

With her hands still clasped, Thong Prasi spat and said, "This sermon isn't worth hearing, you muddlehead." Khun Chang spluttered loudly, "Whoever spits on a sermon will turn into a suffering ghost."

Siprajan prostrated and said, "Yes, yes. May you give sermons more wonderful and hauntingly beautiful than I have ever heard!" People around laughed out loud.

pulpit

Novice Chang turned the leaves of a Pali text and read, "*Ko ka ki ke kae kai.* The lotus lady was the wife of Sangsinchai. Suwannahong flew to Lanka.

Nang Montho was the wife of the conch shell.[55] There are many true tales from the past. Follow whatever you can, oh disciples." Having finished what he wanted to say, he mumbled a blessing.

The men and women in the wat said to one another, "Does anyone know what this is about?" Novice Chang said, "I don't care about you." He rolled up the text and came down the staircase.

---

52. In the original, Chang says *sangkhaya*, สังขยา, which sounds like a word from a Pali prayer but means "egg custard."

53. จุลนีบท, *julanibot*, see p. 68, note 55 where the word is spelt *junniyabot*. A common practice in sermons is to read a passage from a Pali text, translate it, and then expound on its meanings.

54. Meant to sound like a Pali verse, but could mean "Grandpa Kesi is furious."

55. Montho is the wife of Thotsakan in the *Ramakian*; the conch shell refers to the story of *Sangthong* (see p. 258, note 56); Suwannahong and Sangsinchai are both stories adapted as outer dramas (see p. 78, note 84; p. 102, note 25). As usual, Khun Chang is muddling everything.

A boy spoke to his friends too loudly, "The awful old gourd is leaving. Phew!" Novice Chang turned back angrily, "Mm! What did you say about me, you slave child?"

The boy said, "I was praising the fine sermon but your ear didn't catch it." Novice Chang laughed in glee. "Hey, go and fetch some sweets."

The boy shouted, "Ah, just what I wanted. Cheers to you, sir. Let's have something to nibble." Thong Prasi said, "I have no faith. I'd rather feed dogs than make merit.

The boy was making fun of you but then he lied. He made a fool of you, you baldy, you tenderhead with a face as huge as a yogi."

After Wanthong's cremation was over, Phra Wai joyfully stayed in the monkhood for seven days. After disrobing, he went to attend on the king.

In the evening, the king, famous in continents great and small, came out to the audience hall of victory. Phra Wai prostrated.

"My liege, dust under the royal foot. Allow me to offer to Your Majesty the merit from my time in the monkhood, such as I was able, to repay my debt of gratitude to my mother."[56]

The king smiled and laughed. He joined his hands together and said, "May you be blessed," and presented cloth to Phra Wai.

The king thought about matters on the frontier? "How is your father, Khun Phaen? I had him govern Kanburi. Why is he still skulking here? Go and tell him, Wai."

Phra Wai returned home and spoke to Khun Phaen. "The king has instructed you

to go and live in Kanburi. Suppose something was to happen on that frontier?" Khun Phaen understood, and so looked for an auspicious day.

He prepared incense, candles, and flowers for paying respect to the king. As he was pondering matters at dusk, he became concerned,

and so went to talk to Thong Prasi. "I've been worried for some time that the king would have me go to Kanburi.

Wai went to audience this morning, and the king commanded exactly that. I feel sorry for you as you're getting much older, and my departure will upset you.

---

56. As a servant of the king, Phra Wai was obliged to ask permission from the king before entering the monkhood and to offer him the resulting merit.

I'm also worried about Phra Wai. My heart feels burned with fire. Just my concern for you is boundless. I wish to ask you to go too."

Thong Prasi listened with tears falling. She thought quietly and then said, "I'm not against this at all. You've no choice because you fear royal authority.

But if I go along with you, I'll be very anxious about Wai. Being here on his own, he'll be lonely and in low spirits—orphaned in every way.

My heart is split between my concerns for son and for grandson. I don't know which way to turn. I think I must stay with Wai. If he has nobody, his tears won't stop trickling down.

Since his mother died, the sadness hasn't left him. His father's departure will make things worse. But if I don't go with you, I'll miss little Chumphon." She sighed wearily from indecision.

"Oh lord and master of your mother! Have a care for an old person. Don't leave me feeling bruised and bathed in tears. Please let me have Chumphon, can you?

When I feel heavy-hearted, I'll be able to look at the face of my little grandson, and it'll help dispel the gloom. Kaeo Kiriya, please don't miss him. Have a care for me. I wai you."

Her mother-in-law's words threw Kaeo Kiriya into confusion. She would miss her dear son, and feel sorry for him being parted from his mother's warmth.

But if she refused the request, she feared it would displease her mother-in-law, so she steeled herself and said, "As you wish. If you want to take him, then let it be so."

She got up and took leave with tears flowing and misery deepening. As evening turned to night, she took her child to suckle and put to sleep.

"Oh what a pity, jewel of Mother's eye. I'll be far apart from you and miserable." She hugged her child, weeping and not sleeping until the rising sun brightened the sky.

Khun Phaen awoke and came out to wash his face. He ate, changed clothes, called his servants, and went off to the palace as planned.

Now to tell of the mighty, illustrious, excellent, and sublime king. He commanded Khun Phaen, "Proceed to Kanburi
to look after government affairs, take care of the capital's frontier, and inspect the forest guard posts. Go well, and have no trouble."

Khun Phaen took the royal blessing and put it on his head. The king returned inside forthwith. Khun Phaen came home and ordered servants to prepare food supplies.

Kaeo Kiriya and Laothong found everything needed. Elephants were prepared to carry it all. Carts were sent ahead in advance.

At dawn on a Sunday, at a conjunction of great success,[57] Khun Phaen brought Kaeo Kiriya and Laothong to take leave of his mother.

Thong Prasi was pounding betelnut. She dropped the pestle with a bang, stared in a daze of grief, and mumbled blessings through her tears. "May none of you three suffer sickness.

May your ages stretch to ten thousand years. May you be eternally hale and healthy. May you have a thousand children, one a day. Little Chumphon, come over here.

Why are you crying to go with your mother? Don't you fear the macaque and *tukkae* in the forest? Stay with Grandmother. I'll give you a doll, and buy sweets and citron to eat."

Kaeo Kiriya grieved over leaving her beloved child. She flailed around with floods of tears flowing down. She turned her face to talk to the child, feeling forlorn.

Khun Phaen hugged her gently in consolation. "Where will all this weeping and wailing get you? The journey isn't so long. Whenever you think of him, then come."

Kaeo Kiriya stifled her sorrows. She held her son in her arms and passed him to the grandmother. She was so upset she could not walk away, and her tears streamed down.

Khun Phaen gave instructions to Phra Wai and his two daughters-in-law. He brought Skystorm and handed it to Phra Wai. He drew a yantra on the palm of his hand,

put his palm against Phra Wai's forehead, and gave a blessing. Phra Wai inclined his head with joy, wai-ed to accept his father's blessing, and paid respect at his feet.

Soifa and Simala sadly wai-ed their husband's father. Tears welled up and they sobbed, grieved, and wept some more.

Kaeo Kiriya entrusted Phlai Chumphon to their care. "Please look after him, both of you, without any prejudice or ill feeling. Drum into him what's right and what's wrong."

palm yantra

---

57. See p. 319, note 23.

They mounted elephants. The two wives rode together on a cow elephant, and Phra Kanburi on a bull elephant, Jamlong. Servants and phrai followed in a crowd.

A jumble of cases and baskets swayed back and forth. Men raised their loads and staggered along, weaving unsteadily. The troop went straight into the forest, and admired the fine trees along the way—

clumps of lush dense thicket, budding leaves, sprays of flowers blooming aloft, *samo thale*, *pheka*, and *khanang*. An egret flew to perch on a *phayom*.

A dove cooed from a paperwood. Carpenter bees swarmed around the fragrant flowers of a *pradu*. Sandal fruit were so plentiful the branches were bowed down low, and they happily picked them.

Many animals ran around the forest, darting through the undergrowth. Gaur galloped off in all directions. A great tiger slunk away and crouched, watching,

intent on catching a young gaur. The tiger pounced, one on one, swiped its paw, sunk its teeth, and hung on, making blood flow. The gaur bellowed.

When people approached the spot, the tiger took fright, abandoned the gaur, and loped away towards the deep forest. The gaur, almost mortally wounded, ran off to hide from danger and travail.

They made a way with all good speed
sun dipping and dropping, colors pale,
A mother gibbon, swinging from a tree,
He thought of his wife, more distressed,
Oh Wanthong, these are woods we knew
to play in a stream, cool-skinned bride.
Wanthong, my love, how can this be,
Some karma made in time's domain
So surely, the learned abbot saw it all.
As predicted, so indeed it happened.
Along the way, as the elephants drove,
Three nights slept in a forest clearing
Mounts unroped, goods handed down,
raised men to cut timber, and speedily
At Kanburi, they made a happy household.
The home hummed in joy and merriment,

through grass and reed, by hill and dale,
cock and quail flying to find their nest.
whooped plaintively, piercing his breast.
"You'd be in this forest, had you not died.
when I took you from Khun Chang's side,
This place again spied deepens my pain.
never to see your bright beauty again?
did foreordain this unfortunate end.
I still recall what omens did portend.
Dull death did descend, unrelenting."
he strove to still his spirit's seething.
before riding straight into Kanburi.
officials of the town welcomed merrily,
build a residency with every ornament.
On matters manifold, he gave fair judgment.
content and cheerful every night and day.

PRONUNCIATION GUIDE FOR KEY PROPER NAMES

This guide gives the pronunciation for the most frequent names in the text using the IPA phonetic system and an approximation using sample English words. For simplicity, neither of these takes account of tone.

In multi-syllable words, the stress is always on the first syllable, and only slight. In the combinations *kh, ph,* and *th,* the *h* indicates aspiration. These are pronounced much like the initial sounds in *kin, pin,* and *tin,* respectively.

The *r* sound is trilled.

Ayutthaya	ʔajutʰajaː	*a* as in *pa; yu* like *you; ta* with short vowel; *ya* to rhyme with *pa*
Chang	tɕʰaːŋ	with vowel in *pa*
Chaophraya	tɕawpʰrajaː	*chao* to rhyme with *cow; pra* with short vowel; *ya* to rhyme with *pa*
Chiang Mai	tɕʰiaŋ maj	*chiang* like *ia* in *India; mai* like *my*
Chumphon	tɕʰumpʰɔːn	*ch* as in *child; um* as in *oomph; pon* to rhyme with *don*
Jakri	tɕakriː	*jak* to rhyme with *luck; ri* to rhyme with *see*
Kaeo	kɛːw	with vowel in *air* (British) or *man* (American) followed by the vowel in *cow*
Kanburi	kaːnburiː	*gan* with vowel in *pa; bu* short like *book; ri* to rhyme with *see*
Khun	kʰun	*(ra)coon,* but with shorter vowel
Kiriya	kirijaː	*gi* like the start of *give; ri* as in *rip; ya* to rhyme with *pa*
Lanchang	laːntɕʰaːŋ	both syllables with the vowel in *pa*
Laothong	lawtʰɔːŋ	*lao* to rhyme with *cow; tong* to rhyme with *song*
Nang	naːŋ	with vowel in *pa*
Ngam	ŋaːm	*ng* as in *singer,* with vowel in *pa*
Palelai	paːleːlaj	*pa* like *pa* (father); *le* like *lay; lai* like *lie*
Phaen	pʰɛːn	with vowel in *air* (British) or *man* (American)
Phanwasa	pʰanwasaː	*pan* like *pun; wa* with short vowel; *sa* to rhyme with *pa*
Phichit	pʰitɕit	*pi* to rhyme with *see; chit* to rhyme with *sit*

Phim	pʰim	*pim* to rhyme with *dim*
Phlai	pʰlaːj	*ply*
Saithong	sajtʰɔːŋ	*sai* like *sigh*; *tong* to rhyme with *song*
Siprajan	siːpʰratɕan	*si* like *see*; *pra* with short vowel, *jan* to rhyme with *fun*
Soifa	sɔːjfaː	*soi* as in *soya*; *fa* to rhyme with *pa*
Sukhothai	sukʰoːtʰaj	*su* like *sue*; *ko* to rhyme with *go*; *tai* like *tie*
Suphanburi	supʰanburiː	*su* like *sue*; *pan* to rhyme with *fun*; *bu* short like *book*; *ri* to rhyme with *see*
Thainam	tʰajnaːm	*tai* like *tie*; *nam* with vowel in *pa*
Thepthong	tʰeːptʰɔːŋ	*tep* to rhyme with *tape*; *tong* to rhyme with *song*
Thong Prasi	tʰɔːŋ pʰrasiː	*tong* to rhyme with *song*; *pra* with short vowel; *si* like *see*
Wanthong	wantʰɔːŋ	*wan* like *one*; *tong* to rhyme with *song*

A long time ago in the kingdom of Ayutthaya, three children were born in Suphanburi and became childhood friends. Phim grew up to be the beauty of the town. Khun Chang was rich and well-connected, but bald from birth, ugly, and crass. Phlai Kaeo was handsome and clever but poor because his father was executed for a blunder on royal service, and the family had to flee to remote Kanburi. (1–2)

Phlai Kaeo was ordained as a novice to study. Later he moved to Wat Palelai and Wat Khae in Suphanburi. When Phim put food in his almsbowl at Songkran, Phlai Kaeo recognized his childhood friend, and was smitten. He sneaked out of the wat to court her in a cotton field. Phim succumbed, but insisted he ask for her hand. Phlai Kaeo dragged his feet, saying he wanted to finish his study first.

Khun Chang was also smitten by the lovely Phim. She rejected his advances, but Khun Chang tempted Phim's mother with his wealth. In desperation, Phim gave Phlai Kaeo enough money to fetch his mother from Kanburi to ask for her hand. Phlai Kaeo and Phim were married and moved into a newly built bridal house. (3–7)

Two days later, Phlai Kaeo was conscripted to lead a military campaign in the north. Left on her own, Phim sickened almost to death, but recovered after the abbot of Wat Palelai advised her mother to change her name to Wanthong.

Khun Chang renewed his campaign to snare Wanthong. He spread a rumor that Phlai Kaeo had been defeated and killed, and that his family would be seized as punishment—unless she married Khun Chang. Greedy for Khun Chang's wealth and protection, Wanthong's mother consented. The old bridal house was knocked down, and Khun Chang built an enormous replacement on the site. Wanthong was forced to undergo the marriage ceremony, but resisted going into Khun Chang's bridal house.

In the meantime, Phlai Kaeo had won victory in the north. A village headman presented him with his beautiful daughter, Laothong, to save the whole village from being swept down as slaves. On return to Ayutthaya, Phlai Kaeo was appointed to a post in the royal guard with the title of Khun Phaen Saensathan.

Khun Phaen reached Suphanburi a week after the second wedding. But instead of a joyful reunion, he and Wanthong fell into a bitterly jealous quarrel. Khun Phaen threatened to kill Wanthong, severed relations, and left for Kanburi with Laothong. Wanthong tried to hang herself but was rescued. Bereft of hope, she was no longer able to resist Khun Chang. At first she pined sadly for Khun Phaen, but gradually came to enjoy the comforts of Khun Chang's wealth and loving attention. (8–14)

Khun Chang and Khun Phaen were summoned for training as royal pages in the palace. When Laothong fell gravely ill, Khun Phaen returned to Kanburi to nurse her. Khun Chang agreed to cover for him, but then deviously informed the king that Khun Phaen had climbed over the palace wall—a grave offense. The king sent Khun Phaen to patrol the frontier, and seized Laothong to serve as a palace embroiderer.

Khun Phaen brooded over Khun Chang's perfidy, and resolved on revenge. In preparation, he traveled around the country to find the equipment he needed—a sword instilled with great power, an exceptional horse, and a spirit son, Goldchild, created from the body of an unborn child that died along with its mother. (15–16)

One night, Khun Phaen climbed into Khun Chang's house. He chanced upon Kaeo Kiriya, a noblewoman fallen on hard times, and enjoyed a tryst. Coming upon three curtains embroidered by Wanthong, he slashed them to pieces in anger. He woke Wanthong and the couple fell into mutual recriminations. Wanthong was torn between the security and comforts offered by Khun Chang, or the romance but uncertainty offered by Khun Phaen. Eventually she agreed to leave with him, but also left a letter imploring Khun Chang to rescue her. Khun Phaen and Wanthong rode out of Suphanburi towards the western hills. Once alone and together, their love quickly rekindled, even amid the hardships of life in the forest.

Khun Chang raised a troop of forest dwellers to give chase, but Khun Phaen easily dispersed them. Khun Chang went to Ayutthaya, informed the king that Khun Phaen was raising a revolt, and asked for an army to go after him. Khun Phaen also defeated this force and killed its two noble officers. Now a wanted man, he fled deeper into the forest where he and Wanthong lived frugally off lotus roots and love. (17–20)

After some months, Wanthong became pregnant. Khun Phaen decided to leave the forest for the sake of the baby. They surrendered to the governor of Phichit, who had a reputation for compassion. A month later they decided to return to Ayutthaya and face trial. In the court case, Khun Phaen was cleared, while Khun Chang was found guilty of seizing Wanthong and falsely accusing Khun Phaen of revolt. The king imposed a heavy fine on Khun Chang, and restored Wanthong to Khun Phaen. But Khun Phaen rashly asked for the release of Laothong too. Angered by this presumption, the king threw him into jail where he festered for over a decade.

Again Khun Chang saw a chance, and abducted Wanthong. Again Wanthong grew to enjoy the comforts of living with Khun Chang. She gave birth to Phlai Ngam, who grew up very like his father, Khun Phaen, rousing Khun Chang's lingering jealousy. One day, Khun Chang took him off into the forest and tried to beat him to death. But Wanthong discovered him alive, and sent him off to live in safety with his grandmother in Kanburi where he was educated, using his father's library. (21–24)

When war broke out against Chiang Mai, Phlai Ngam volunteered to lead the army, and petitioned for Khun Phaen to be released to assist him. Instead of a large conscript force, Khun Phaen asked for only thirty-five of his fellow jailbirds, all versed in the military arts. On the way north, they called at Phichit, where Phlai Ngam was betrothed to Simala, the daughter of the governor. At Chiang Mai, they infiltrated the jail, freed the Ayutthaya soldiers held captive, and seized the king, who capitulated and agreed to become a vassal of Ayutthaya. The army returned south with a great hoard of booty and prisoners. As reward, Khun Phaen was appointed governor of Kanburi. Phlai Ngam became a lieutenant in the royal pages with the title Phra Wai, and was presented with the daughter of the Chiang Mai king. (25–32)

At Phra Wai's wedding, Khun Chang became badly drunk, clashed with Phra Wai, and went off to lodge a complaint with the king. At the ensuing trial, the story of Khun Chang's attempted murder of Phra Wai as a child was revealed. As there were no witnesses to this event, the king commanded an ordeal by water. Khun Chang lost in the ordeal and was sentenced to death. Wanthong begged Phra Wai to use his current favor with the king to plead for Khun Chang's pardon. Phra Wai was reluctant but could not refuse his mother. Understanding the subtlety of the situation and wishing to keep Phra Wai's loyalty, the king granted the pardon.

Now blessed with rank, fortune, and two wives, Phra Wai decided that he needed his mother with him to make his happiness complete. He broke into Khun Chang's house in Suphanburi and took Wanthong away at sword point. Reunited with Khun Phaen in Ayutthaya, Wanthong resisted his attempt at lovemaking in fear of the old problems multiplying. Sure enough, Khun Chang again petitioned the king for redress. Out of patience with these squabbles, the king summoned all the parties, and berated Khun Chang, Khun Phaen, and Phra Wai for flouting the law and threatening peace and public order. The king identified Wanthong as the root of the problem, and insisted she choose finally between Khun Chang and Khun Phaen. As the two had such different meaning for her—Khun Phaen as her great love and Khun Chang as her source of security—she was unable to respond. In anger, the king condemned her to death.

Phlai Ngam secured a reprieve from the king, but before he reached the execution ground there was a misunderstanding and Wanthong was tragically excuted. (33–36)

TIMELINE

As different chapters were composed by different authors, there is some variation in the reported ages of characters and the times between incidents. This table shows the "best fit" of the various and sometimes conflicting evidence.

Year	Animal	Events	Notes
1	tiger	Births of Phlai Kaeo and Khun Chang.	Phlai Kaeo is born in a tiger year (ch. 1). The animal years of other characters do not match.
2	hare		
3	dragon	Birth of Wanthong. Birth of Laothong.	Laothong is fifteen when she meets Khun Phaen.
4	snake		
5	horse	Death of Khun Krai.	Phlai Kaeo is variously described as five or seven years old at the time of his father's death.
15	dragon	Phlai Kaeo becomes a novice in Kanburi.	
16	snake	Phlai Kaeo moves to Wat Palelai.	
17	horse	Phlai Kaeo and Phim meet at Songkran. Mahachat recitation.	
18	goat	Phlai Kaeo and Wanthong romance and wed. Chomthong campaign.	
19	monkey	Phim becomes Wanthong. Quarrel. Abduction. Flight to forest.	Phim is sixteen (ch. 11).
20	cock	Surrender. Court case. Khun Phaen is jailed. Khun Chang seizes Wanthong. Birth of Phlai Ngam.	If fulfilling the prediction in ch. 2, the jailing would be five years later. The time between the quarrel and abduction is variously reported as two months (ch. 22) and a year (ch. 28).

28	snake	Khun Chang tries to kill Phlai Ngam, who flees to Kanburi.	Phlai Ngam's age at this incident is variously described as seven (ch. 34), nine (ch. 24), and ten (ch. 28).
29	horse	Phlai Ngam visits Ayutthaya.	
30	goat		
31	monkey		
32	cock	Phlai Ngam's topknot ceremony, moves to Ayutthaya.	Phlai Ngam is thirteen at the topknot ceremony (ch. 24).
33	dog		
34	pig	Khun Phaen is released from jail.	Khun Phaen's time in jail is described as "over ten" or fifteen years. He is predicted to be released in a year of the pig (ch. 24). Phlai Ngam has been in Ayutthaya "over a year" when he volunteers and asks for his father's release (ch. 27).
35	rat	Chiang Mai campaign. Marriage of Phra Wai. Birth of Phlai Chumphon.	
36	ox	Trial by ordeal. Death of Wanthong.	Wanthong lived with Khun Chang for fifteen to sixteen years (ch. 33). Khun Chang says eighteen years had elapsed since the first abduction (ch. 36). Her death is a year after the army's return from Chiang Mai.
42	goat	Simala and Soi Fa quarrel. Phlai Chumphon flees to Sukhothai.	Phlai Chumphon is seven (ch. 39 reports he is fifteen and came to Sukhothai eight years earlier).
50	hare	Phlai Chumphon returns with the army.	Phlai Chumphon is fifteen (ch. 39).

MAP 1 THE REGION

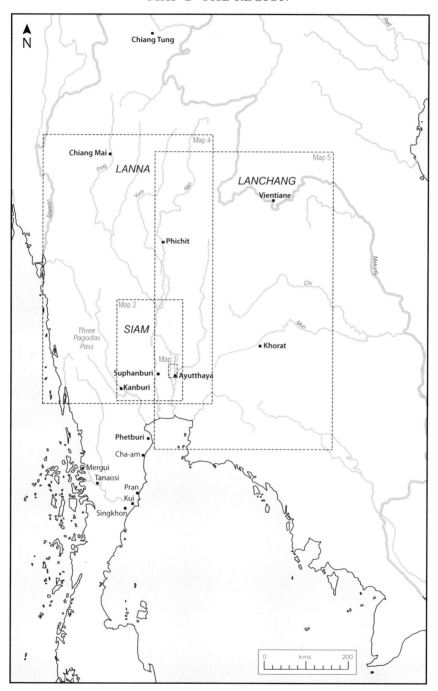

N

Chiang Tung

Red

Map 4

Chiang Mai

LANNA

Ping

Salween

Yom

Nan

Map 5

LANCHANG

Vientiane

Phichit

Mekong

Chi

Map 2

SIAM

Three
Pagodas
Pass

Mun

Khorat

Map 3

Suphanburi

Ayutthaya

Kanburi

Phetburi

Cha-am

Mergui
Tanaosi

Pran
Kui

Singkhon

0   kms   200

MAP 2 CENTRAL SIAM

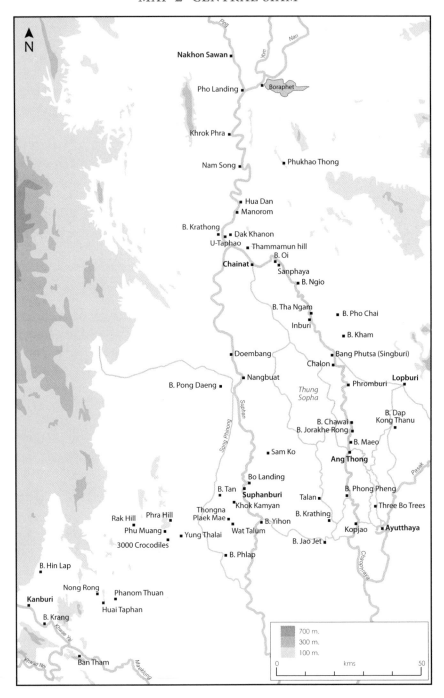

N

Nakhon Sawan

Pho Landing

Boraphet

Khrok Phra

Nam Song

Phukhao Thong

Hua Dan
Manorom

B. Krathong
Dak Khanon
U-Taphao
Thammamun hill
B. Oi
Chainat
Sanphaya
B. Ngio

B. Tha Ngam
B. Pho Chai
Inburi
B. Kham

Doembang
Bang Phutsa (Singburi)
Chalon

Nangbuat
Phromburi
Lopburi

B. Pong Daeng
Thung
Sopha
B. Dap
Kong Thanu
B. Chawai
B. Jorakhe Rong
B. Maeo
Sam Ko
Ang Thong

Bo Landing
B. Tan
Suphanburi
Khok Kamyan
Talan
B. Phong Pheng
Three Bo Trees
Rak Hill
Phra Hill
Thongna
Plaek Mae
B. Krathing
Phu Muang
Wat Talum
B. Yihon
Kopjao
Ayutthaya
Yung Thalai
3000 Crocodiles
B. Jao Jet
B. Phlap
B. Hin Lap

Nong Rong
Phanom Thuan
Kanburi
B. Krang
Huai Taphan

Ban Tham

Ping
Nan
Yom
Maeklong
Suphan
Song Phnong
Pasak
Chaophraya
Khwae Yai
Khwae Noi
Maeklong

700 m.
300 m.
100 m.

0   kms   50

JOURNEYS FROM SUPHAN

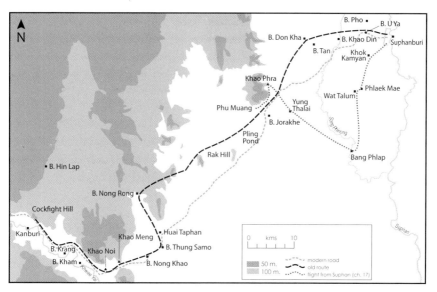

The several journeys between Suphanburi and old Kanburi in *KCKP* take a route shown on early nineteenth-century maps recently found in the Bangkok palace (Santanee and Stott, *Royal Siamese Maps*, 92–93, 101). The old route runs closer to a line of rocky outcrops, the first ripples of the Tenasserim range. Following this line was probably the simplest way to navigate the route between the two towns. The area along the route is now mostly hardscrabble farmland and some open-cast mining, but is shown as forest on the military maps of fifty years ago.

Fleeing from Suphanburi in chapter 17, Khun Phaen and Wanthong went south to a crossing of the Song Phinong Canal, then northeast to the nearest outcrop of the western hills at Khao Phra (both the hill and crossing are also on the old maps). Suphon Bunnag suggested the tryst at Banyan Landing was in the present-day Phu Muang National Park, but the area now is very dry, possibly because of the massive deforestation of the surrounding area, and difficult to associate with the scene. The rest of their journey cannot be traced.

MAP 3 AROUND AYUTTHAYA

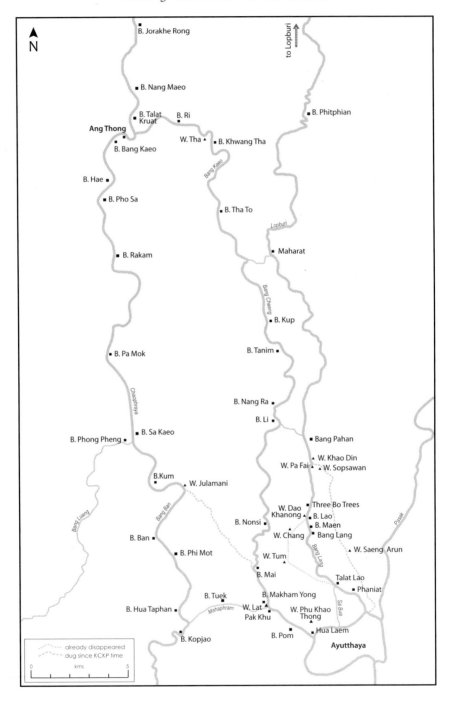

WATERWAYS ABOVE AYUTTHAYA

At the time of *KCKP*, waterways north of Ayutthaya differed from today. The main route branched east from the Chaophraya River at Singburi, passed Lopburi, and came south through Maharat, Wat Khao Din, and Three Bo Trees. At Wat Dao Khanong, the old waterway looped to the west past Wat Chang and Wat Tum, then curved eastwards to the northeast corner of the city. This route was shortened by digging the Bang Lang Canal, perhaps in the Narai reign (Gervaise, *Natural and Political History*, 35). The customs post for the north was sited at Bang Lang, indicating this was the main northbound route. The course of the canal is still lined with old wat, testament to its importance in the past. Most journeys in *KCKP* take this route. The route was later shortened further, probably in the nineteenth century, along the channel past Wat Saeng Arun. The loop past Wat Chang has now almost disappeared, while the Bang Lang Canal is very small.

A second route branched east from the Chaophraya River at Ang Thong along the Bang Kaeo Canal, and wound southward through Ban Kup, Ban Nang Ra, and Ban Mai to the northwest corner of the city. This is the route taken in some journeys during the Chiang Mai campaign in the latter part of *KCKP*.

François Valentijn's maps of the river, printed in 1724–26, clearly show these two northerly approaches to the city (Thawatchai, *Krung Si Ayutthaya*, 102).

A third route came down the Chaophraya River to Kopjao, then east along the Mahaphram Canal past Pak Khu (the western customs post) to the city. In *KCKP*, this route is taken only by the King of Chiang Mai returning home. The eastern end of the Mahaphram Canal is still visible just north of Wat Lat, which occupies the site where the customs post once stood. Most of the canal's course is now under paddy fields.

Prior to the nineteenth century, the Chaophraya River passed some five kilometers to the west of Ayutthaya. In 1813, a dam was built at Ang Thong to divert the river along the Bang Kaeo Canal past Ban Nang Ra and Ban Mai to the northwest corner of Ayutthaya, but flood waters repeatedly burst the dam, and the project was abandoned. In 1857, a five-kilometer canal was dug from Wat Julamani to Ban Mai, bringing the Chaophraya onto its current route, and reducing the stretch of the old river south of Wat Julamani to the status of Bang Ban Canal. (Boranratchathanin, *Tamnan krung kao*, 132–35; Van Beek, *Chao Phya*, 11–12)

MAP 4 THE NORTH

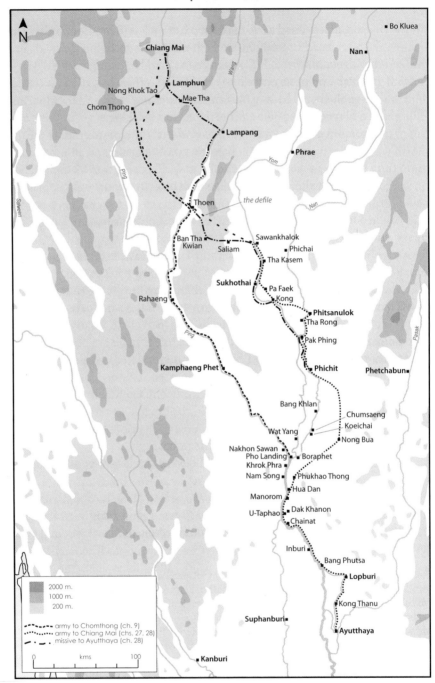

N

Bo Kluea

Nan

Chiang Mai

Lamphun

Nong Khok Tao

Mae Tha

Chom Thong

Lampang

Wang

Phrae

Ping

Yom

Salween

Thoen

the defile

Nan

Ban Tha Kwian

Sawankhalok

Saliam

Phichai

Tha Kasem

Sukhothai

Pa Faek

Kong

Rahaeng

Phitsanulok

Tha Rong

Pak Phing

Ping

Pasak

Kamphaeng Phet

Phichit

Phetchabun

Bang Khlan

Chumsaeng

Koeichai

Wat Yang

Nong Bua

Nakhon Sawan

Pho Landing

Boraphet

Khrok Phra

Nam Song

Phukhao Thong

Hua Dan

Manorom

Dak Khanon

U-Taphao

Chainat

Inburi

Bang Phutsa

Lopburi

Kong Thanu

Suphanburi

Ayutthaya

Kanburi

2000 m.
1000 m.
200 m.

army to Chomthong (ch. 9)
army to Chiang Mai (chs. 27, 28)
missive to Ayutthaya (ch. 28)

0   kms   100

THE LOCATION OF CHIANG THONG

Chiang Thong, which figures in chapters 8 to 10, has disappeared. Its old site has been a matter of debate, but most likely it was just south of present-day Tak/Rahaeng.

On his travels to Sukhothai in 1908, the future King Vajiravudh wrote, "Found an old city about 200 *sen* [8 kms] north of Kamphaeng Phet, of medium size with wall and moat. Local people called it Thoen Thong or Kong Thong. . . . Probably this is the Chiang Thong mentioned many times in the chronicles and in *KCKP*" (*Thiao mueang phraruang*, 19–20). We cannot locate this site.

In Sukhothai Inscription 11, Si Sattha visits Chiang Thong, which Griswold and Prasert annotated as "a riverine port on the Ping (perhaps near the present town of Tak) used by travelers wishing to continue their journey overland, via Mè Sòt, to Martaban" (*Epigraphical and Historical Studies*, 410, fn. 20). In an early Ayutthaya list of provincial towns, Chiang Thong appears between Chiang Ngoen and Tak in a group of towns under Kamphaeng Phet (Suphawat, "Phra aiyakan kao," 337). In a document carried by Siamese envoys to Portugal in 1684, "Mueang Chieng Thong" is one of ten towns under Kamphaeng Phet (Smithies and Dhiravat, "Instructions," 129). La Loubère mentioned "Tian-Tong" immediately after Tak and before Kamphaeng Phet in a list of places along the river (*New Historical Relation*, 4). In *Khamhaikan chao krung kao*, Chiang Thong appears in a list of towns under Tak, along with Rahaeng and Chiang Ngoen, now a tambon adjacent to Tak town (KCK, 191).

Chiang Thong appears several times in the chronicles in the sixteenth century. King Chairacha (r. 1534–1547) camped there on a march from Kamphaeng Phet to Chiang Mai. Around 1574, Naresuan went from Kamphaeng Phet through Chiang Thong to Pegu; and returned via Chiang Thong to Sawankhalok. Two years later, the King of Chiang Mai led an army south through Chiang Thong to Nakhon Sawan. Another few years later, the King of Pegu marched through Chiang Thong to attack Kamphaeng Phet (RCA, 20, 87, 92, 102, 113). These routes all intersect around Tak/Rahaeng.

There is still a village named Khlong Chiang Thong on the west bank of the Ping River five kilometers south of Tak. The location (and name) of the major river crossing around Tak/Rahaeng has shifted many times over the centuries. Possibly this village is a remnant of the sixteenth-century location.

In *KCKP*, however, Chiang Thong is clearly north of Thoen. Possibly the authors used the name Chiang Thong precisely because it was known as an ancient place name but no longer existed.

MAP 5 TO VIENTIANE

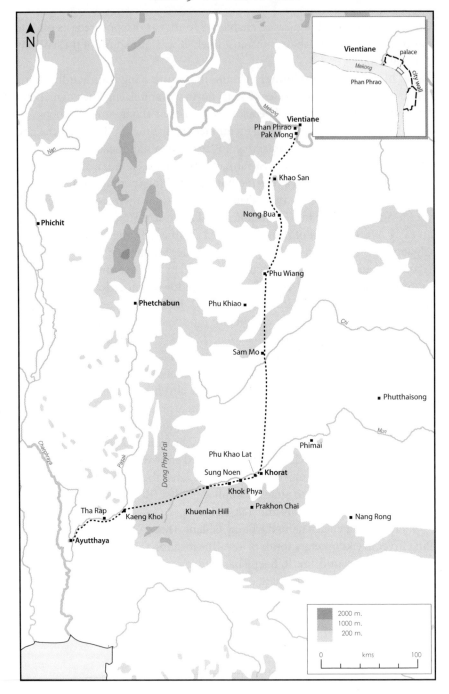

THE GEOGRAPHY OF THE KHORAT PLATEAU

In the first collection of *KCKP* manuscripts, later published as the Smith and Wat Ko editions, the geography of the Khorat Plateau is very vague. Only one toponym is mentioned—Wiang Khiri, a variant of Phu Wiang. The Lanchang princess leaves Vientiane en route to Ayutthaya mounted on an elephant with no realization that the Mekong River was in the way. This version probably predates the war between Bangkok and Vientiane in the late 1820s. Indeed, other evidence suggests it may have origins in the Ayutthaya era.

By going to war with Vientiane, Bangkok learned more about the Khorat Plateau. In the revised version of the Chiang Mai campaign in *KCKP*, probably composed in the mid-nineteenth century and included in the Damrong edition, the geography is more detailed and accurate. The Lanchang princess begins her southward journey in a grand royal flotilla across the Mekong. Strikingly, the route traveled between Bangkok and Vientiane follows the tracks taken by Bangkok armies during the crucial 1829 war, and many of the places mentioned were sites of key battles.

Sam Mo was a gathering point for Lao forces in the early stages of the war. Phu Wiang and Phu Khiao were both Lao advance posts that fell to the Siamese forces in early May. Nong Bua (Lamphu) was the site of a major battle, falling to the Siamese forces on 6 May. The Khao San gap fell to the Bangkok forces on 26 May after a struggle lasting two weeks. (Mayoury and Pheuiphanh, *Paths*, 145, 197–99, 203–11)

MAP 6 SUPHANBURI

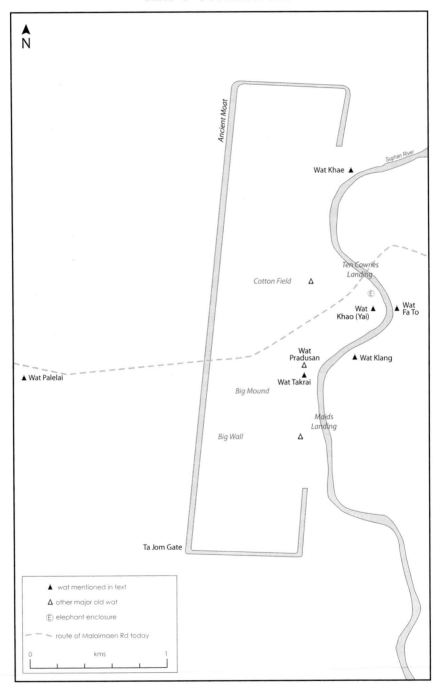

N

Ancient Moat

Suphan River

Wat Khae ▲

Ten Cowries
Landing

Cotton Field △

Ⓔ

Wat ▲
Khao (Yai)

▲ Wat
Fa To

Wat
Pradusan
△

▲ Wat Klang

▲ Wat Takrai

▲ Wat Palelai

Big Mound

Maids
Landing

Big Wall △

Ta Jom Gate

▲ wat mentioned in text

△ other major old wat

Ⓔ elephant enclosure

– – route of Malaimaen Rd today

0   kms   1

LOCATIONS IN SUPHANBURI

Names derived from *KCKP* are used for wards and streets in present-day Suphanburi. But the locations of Ten Cowries Landing and Maids Landing may have moved with the changing layout of the town.

At present, Ten Cowries Landing is a ward on the eastern bank of the Suphan River north of the city center. By local Suphanburi tradition, the home of Phim's parents was close to Wat Fa Tho. In *Nirat suphan* (1836), Sunthon Phu wrote: "I stayed by ancient Ten Cowries Landing / near Wat Fa Tho, now abandoned / its great bo tree, preaching hall, and ordination hall collapsed / built by Phim Philalai as heritage of Suphan" (stanza 138). Wat Fa Tho subsequently disappeared due to erosion of the riverbank. The site was opposite today's main police station.

However, some believe that Ten Cowries Landing was originally located on the west bank, between Wat Khae and Wat Khao. As a child, Phim plays regularly at Wat Khao. Siprajan returns home from Wat Khae "in no time." Wanthong and Saithong walk to Wat Palelai "in a short time."

At present, Maids Landing is a ward on the east bank where the central market now stands. However, some argue that the original location was on the west bank in the south of the city, close to Khun Chang's residence.

All or most of the action of *KCKP* in Suphanburi seems to take place on the west bank. The three wat which appear often—Wat Khao, Wat Khae, Wat Palelai—are all on the western side. According to local legend, Khun Chang's house was in the spot known as *Khok yai*, "big mound," close to Wat Pratusan—a site high enough to keep elephants above any flooding. Until recently, the remains of an elephant enclosure were still visible close by.

In all the journeys between the houses of the main characters and the three wat, there is no mention of any ferry, bridge, or river crossing. The only location mentioned that is definitely on the eastern side of the river is Wat Klang. Khun Phaen's old bridal house is sent there, possibly so it would be well out of sight.

In ancient times, the city of Suphanburi was on the west bank. Possibly at the time *KCKP* developed this was still true. From the late eighteenth century, the city was abandoned for several decades. The modern town has grown with its center on the east bank. Possibly the two landings that figure in *KCKP* have crossed the river with this shift. (Somchai, *Suphanburi*, 29, 33; Winyu, *Tam roi*, 158).

MAP 7 OLD KANBURI

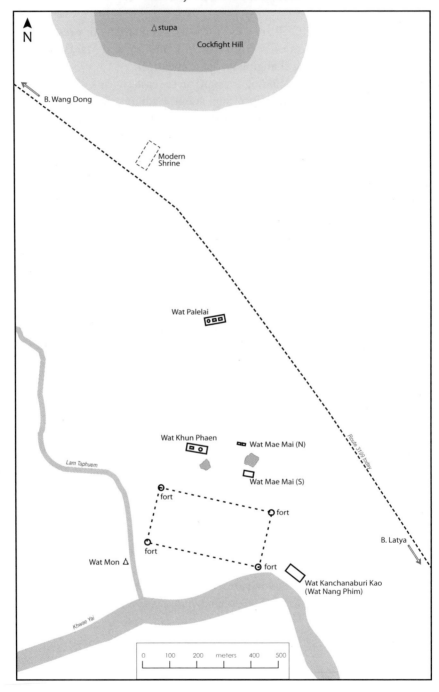

THE REMAINS OF OLD KANBURI

None of the places in Kanburi mentioned in *KCKP*—Wat Chon Kai, Wat Soeng Wai, Wat Som Yai, Thong Prasi's house—can be identified today. The old town was abandoned at the end of the eighteenth century, and a new town subsequently founded eighteen kilometers to the east.

The site of Old Kanburi languished. In the early 1900s, there were only four or five houses surrounded by forest teeming with deer, gaur, boar, elephant, and tiger. In 1924, Phra Khru Juan, a monk from nearby Ban Wang Dong, settled in a ruined wat. He identified the sites of seven wat in the area, and gave them names, several derived from the poem: Wat Nang Phim (where he stayed), Wat Khun Phaen, Wat Khun Krai, Wat Mae Mai (widow), Wat Pha Ok (split chest, a description of the ruined image), Wat Mon, and Wat India (which he claimed had been built by Indian settlers). He also claimed to identify the sites of Khun Phaen and Thong Prasi's house, Thong Prasi's market, and Khun Phaen's jetty on the river. The house and market sites, and Wat India, have now completely disappeared.

In the 1920s, a Chinese, Jek Khim, planted tobacco in the area. He unearthed many artifacts, including a cache of bullet money, and gave them to Khru Juan and his successor who sold them to finance the gradual restoration of Wat Nang Phim and the construction of a school beside it. One of the collectors who bought from Khru Juan became a spirit medium, channeling Wanthong. Wat Nang Phim was renamed as Wat Kanchanaburi Kao, and several new buildings now supplement the original stupa and preaching hall beside the river.

Wat Khun Phaen has remains of a ten-meter *prang* with a style that suggests an early Ayutthaya origin. In 1974, local villagers had the damaged Buddha in Wat Pha Ok repaired and remodeled on the image in Wat Palelai, Suphanburi, complete with attendant monkey and elephant. The site was renamed as Wat Palelai. In 1989, the Fine Arts Department adopted and restored the four remaining ruined wat (Wat Palelai, Wat Khun Phaen, and Wat Mae Mai, south and north) as monuments. Wat Mon has disappeared except for some brick rubble but had the remains of a stupa until a few years ago.

The fortification was simple—four small towers at the corners of a rectangle of 355 by 168 meters. Each tower is around ten meters in diameter and originally two meters high, built crudely of rock, brick, and mud. There is absolutely no trace of the connecting walls, suggesting they were timber palisades. (This account is based on Sathaphon, *Mueang Kanchanaburi kao*, and research at the site in 2009.)

MAP 8 AYUTTHAYA

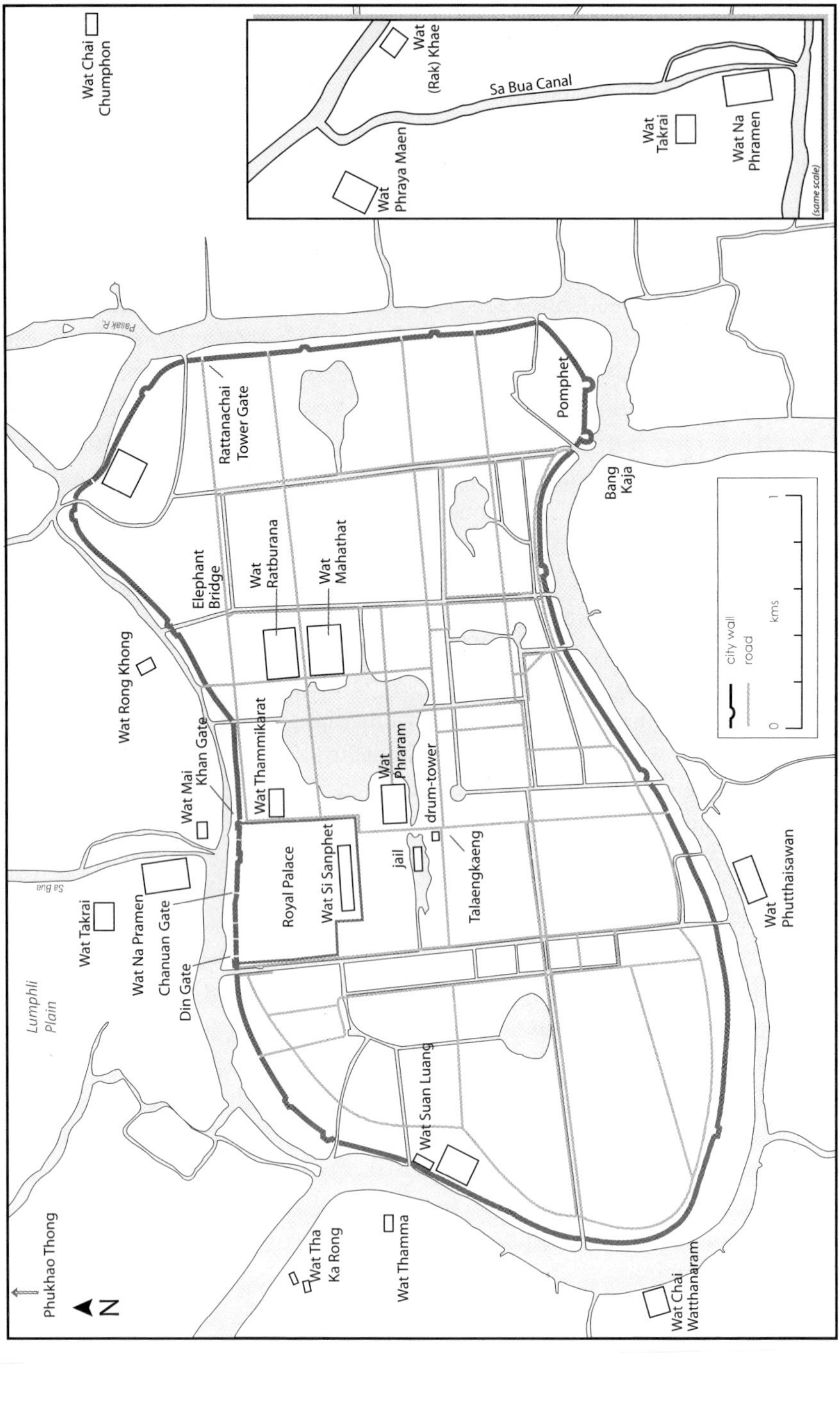

Wat Chai Chumphon

Wat (Rak) Khae

Sa Bua Canal

Wat Phraya Maen

Wat Takrai

Wat Na Pramen

(same scale)

Pasak R.

Rattanachai Tower Gate

Pomphet

Bang Kaja

Elephant Bridge

Wat Ratburana

Wat Mahathat

Wat Rong Khong

Wat Mai Khan Gate

Wat Thammikarat

Wat Phraram

drum-tower

Royal Palace

Wat Si Sanphet

jail

Talaengkaeng

Wat Takrai

Wat Na Pramen

Chanuan Gate

Din Gate

Lumphli Plain

Sa Bua

Wat Phutthaisawan

Wat Suan Luang

Phukhao Thong

N

Wat Tha Ka Rong

Wat Thamma

Wat Chai Watthanaram

City wall

road

kms

0   1

WAT TAKRAI

Wat Takrai lay north of Ayutthaya, across the river from the palace in an area probably popular for residence because of proximity to the palace. Close by was a large market that stretched along Sa Bua Canal. The wat covered 25 *rai* enclosed by two sets of walls. The ruins today are all brick with only a very small amount of stucco. A Buddha image found on this site is kept in Wat Thammikarat. Thep Sukrattani argued on grounds of style that the wat was built in the late fifteenth or early sixteenth century, but such dating is no longer considered reliable. It was not a royal wat but may have been patronized by a prominent family and the many small stupas constructed for their crematory remains.

Wat Takrai was probably destroyed in 1767 as it was directly in the line of fire between the main Burmese camp and the palace. Monks subsequently reoccupied the wat, but it was never repaired and finally abandoned in the early twentieth century. The last abbot, Bun, was famous for his knowledge of lore. Army recruits drank or bathed in water from the wat pool, believed to be sacred. Amulets from the wat "with a Garuda face" (actually a Buddha subduing a beak-faced Mara) are still popular for protection against wild animals. (KLW, 175; *Phraratchawang*, 129–33; Nikhom, "Silapa," 155)

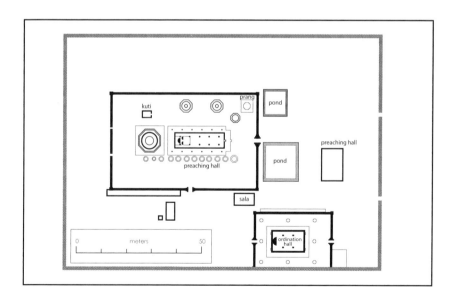

MAP 9 THE AYUTTHAYA PALACE

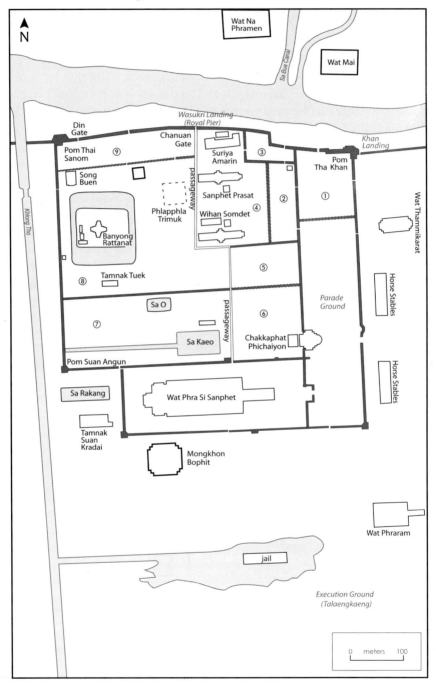

INSIDE THE PALACE

After the city was sacked in 1767, materials were removed to build Bangkok. Only substantial buildings with solid foundations can now be located. Other buildings can be assigned to areas of the palace on the basis of a verbal description in the testimonies taken down from prisoners in Ava (KLW, 200–207; APA, 65–70).

Area 1: Parade ground, northern end
  Along the outer wall
    inner official sala, twin buildings
    tamnak (residence)
    translation hall
    two armories
    carriage store
    four armories
  Along the inner wall
    stables for eight elephants
    two three-roomed buildings

Area 2
  four elephant stables
  two horse stables
  store for horse tack

Area 3
  swordstore for palace staff
  swordstore for guard
  medical hall
  carriage store
  jewelry store
  carpet and mat store
  two craft workshops (needlework)
  stable for white elephant

Area 4: Audience halls
  two *tamnak*, each with five rooms
  Suriya Amarin Audience Hall
  statue of King Naresuan
  Sanphet Prasat Audience Hall
  Wihan Somdet Audience Hall
  two swordstores
  Great Treasury
  mint
  Cardinal Treasury

Area 5: Phaichayon Benjarat Garden
  Ho Phra Monthiantham, in a pond

  Annex of Great Treasury
  mint
  Monastic Treasury (monk robes)
  Phiman-akat Treasury (glassware, foreign items)
  shrine to King U Thong
  cannon store

Area 6
  Chakkaphat Phichaiyon Audience Hall
  tamnak (in front of above)
  Saeng Treasury (craft tools)

Area 7: Sa Kaeo and Suan Angun
  Tamnak Sa Kaeo

Area 8: Banyong Rattanat
  Benjarat Mahaprasat Hall
  Banyong Rattanat Audience Hall
  Song Buen Audience Hall
  medical hall
  tamnak, 2-room
  swordstore for monks, 5 rooms
  swordstore for off-duty pages
  regalia store for pages
  waiting hall for royalty
  clock store
  store for elephant gear
  store for horse gear
  store for regalia
  craft workshop
  scribes' hall, library
  tamnak, 5-room, in Rabbit Garden
  Tamnak Kohasawan (*tamnak tuek*)

Area 9: Thai Sanom (female section)
  Tamnak Prathom Phloeng
  Sandal Garden
  tamnak, 5-room

MAP 10 OLD PHICHIT

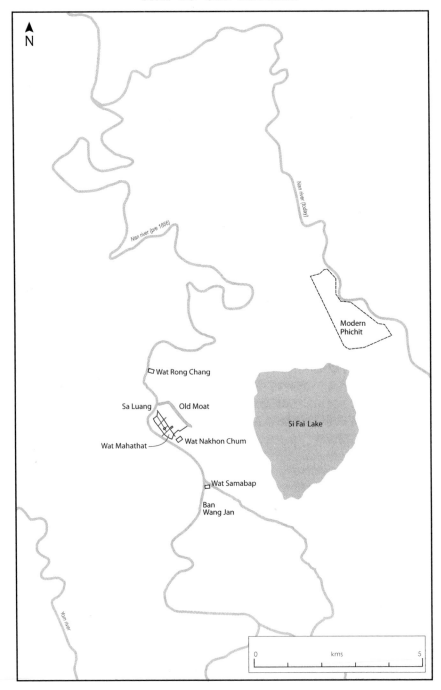

OLD PHICHIT AND WAT JAN

Phichit in *KCKP* is the old town, now a small historical park about nine kilometers to the southwest of the modern town along Route 1068.

According to the *Phongsawadan nuea* (Northern Chronicles), this city was founded by Jao Kanjanakuman in the twelfth century and had a wall measuring 400 x 1400 meters. Under the name Sa Luang (great lake) it became a leading dependency of Sukhothai. The moat and walls are still clearly visible. The only significant surviving monument, Wat Mahathat, has a moderate-sized bell-shaped stupa and the base of a preaching hall. The Fine Arts Department found both Sukhothai and Ayutthaya era periods on the site.

Immediately to the southeast of the ancient town site is Wat Nakhon Chum, which has a beautiful ordination hall with inward sloping walls and slit windows. In the nineteenth century its brick and stucco Buddha image, probably Sukhothai era, was taken away to the new provincial capital to "preside" at the annual ceremony for drinking the water of allegiance to the king. After devotees complained bitterly, a replica was installed in the wat. Possibly this was an important wat of the town that appears in *KCKP*.

The Nan River used to run a hundred meters in front of the wat. In 1866, after Chinese settlers had removed soil to fertilize their cotton fields, the river in flood broke its banks to the north of Phichit and established a new course to the east. Because the old river became too narrow for transport, the governor relocated Phichit to its modern site in 1881. The diminished old river is now a canal alongside Route 1068.

Wat Jan where Khun Phaen billets the army is probably Wat Sama Bap (วัดสมาบาป), the monastery to atone for sin, around two kilometers south of Wat Nakhon Chum in Ban Wang Jan. In one corner, there is a small restored preaching hall with wooden pillars, and a handful of small brick and stucco stupas, claimed to be remnants of a wat that goes back seven hundred years. Wat Sama Bap would be the right distance from the old town of Phichit to fit the role of Wat Jan, and big enough to have camped Khun Phaen's modest army. Perhaps Wat Jan was its old name, or the *KCKP* text collapsed "Wat Sama Bap, Ban Wang Jan" into "Wat Jan."

King Narai billeted an army near here in the 1660s, and King Sorasak/Suea (r. 1703–1709) was born in the camp. Further up the road is Wat Rong Chang (monastery of the elephant shed), further suggesting that this was a strategic area where armies often made camp. (Somchai, "Jangwat Phichit," 184–86; Pornpun, "Environmental History," 27, 242; RCA, 381)

RANKS AND TITLES

People in the official nobility had names that belonged to their posts, not to them personally. As they changed posts, their names changed too. In the upper nobility, this name consisted of three parts: *yot*, a prefix denoting rank; *rajathinnanam*, a name, usually derived from Sanskrit, assigned to that post; and *tamnaeng*, a description of the post. For example, the full name of the head of the Ministry of the Capital was: Chaophraya (*yot*); Yommarat-intharathibodi-siwichai-borirak-lokakon-thantharathon (*rajathinnanam*); kromphra-nakhonban-bodi-aphaiphiriyabara-krom-phahu (*tamnaeng*, describing him as *nakhonban*, from Sanskrit *nagarapala*, guardian of the city). In everyday usage, this was reduced to Chaophraya Yommarat, or shorter still to Phraya Yom. Lower ranks had only the prefix and simpler assigned name, e.g., Khun (prefix) Phaen Saensathan (assigned name).

Each post also had a numerical ranking, known as *sakdina*. The posts are listed in two codes in the Three Seals Law (KTS, 1:219–327). Because departments used these ranking systems in different ways, and because the importance of posts changed over time, there is no precise matching between titles and *sakdina* values. Those with *sakdina* of at least 400 were counted as *khun nang*, nobles. The hierarchy ran roughly as follows:

Chaophraya, *sakdina* 10,000, reserved for the ten most senior ministers
Phraya, *sakdina* 3,000–5,000, minor ministers, provincial governors
Phra, *sakdina* 1,000–5,000
Luang, *sakdina* 500–3,000, department heads
Muen, Jamuen, Phramuen (*muen*=10,000), *sakdina* 400–600
Phan (*phan*=1,000), *sakdina* 200–900
Khun, *sakdina* 200–900
Nai, *sakdina* 100–500, a general term of address for males

Commoners often have a prefix defining age and hierarchical position: Yai- (Granny), for an older woman; Ta- (Grandpa), for an older man; Ai-, for male subordinates; I-, for female subordinates. Nang is a prefix for females of all ranks. Thao, meaning elderly or senior, is a prefix for senior females in the palace administration, and for senior males in the provincial cities.

GLOSSARY

adept's knife มีดหมอ *mit mo*—A knife that has been made with special materials, inscribed with yantra, and instilled with power by an adept. It is used in spirit ceremonies, and carried for invulnerability.

aiya ไอ๊ย่า—An expression of dismay, used to indicate a Chinese is speaking.

almsbowl บาตร *bat*—A bowl carried by a monk to collect alms.

amphoe อำเภอ—A modern term for a subdivision of a province, and its head town.

appliqué หักทองขวาง *hak thong khwang*—"Break-gold-athwart," an embroidery technique used on royal regalia such as fans and umbrellas. A pattern is made by laying cut lengths of golden silk thread perpendicular to the weave, and attaching them by overstitching.

athamat อาทมาต—Probably a word used to describe spies, especially those working across the border into Burma.

athan อาถรรพณ์—Protective magic, especially protection for a house or city provided by foundation rituals and devices such as a city pillar.

attalat อัตลัด—A satin fabric, originally from Persia.

avatar อวตาร—The incarnation of a Hindu god in visible form, especially Ram, hero of the *Ramakian*, an incarnation of Vishnu.

Ayutthaya อยุธยา—Capital of Siam, founded according to its chronicle in 1351, sacked by the Burmese in 1767.

back-basket กระทาย, *krathai*—An openmouthed, tapering basket, usually carried on the back with straps.

baisi บายศรี—A representation of a food offering, crafted from folded banana leaves and flowers, used in many ceremonies.

balustrade ราชวัติ *ratchawati*—A fence or railings to demarcate a ritual area for a cremation or other ceremony, often made of wood or metal in lattice design, with ritual umbrellas at the corners, and a covering of paper or cloth.

bandeau ประเจียด *prajiat*—A piece of cloth inscribed with a yantra design, worn to convey invulnerability.

banphap บานพับ—An ornament, often a lozenge shaped piece of brocade, that accompanies the *sangwan* breast chain, hanging at the waist, especially as part of drama costume.

barrel drum ตะโพน *taphon*—A barrel drum with a body carved from teak or jackfruit wood, and two heads of different sizes, tensioned by leather thongs, played with the hands.

Beguiler (มหา)ละลวย *(maha)laluai*—A mantra to induce love.

benjarong เบญจรงค์—"Five colors," name of a pattern and style of pottery.

betel box ล่วม *luam*—A small chest with compartments for carrying betelnut, pan, and tobacco.

betel(nut) หมาก *mak*—Areca nut, chewed as a mild stimulant.

black belly พุงดำ *phung dam*—A Siamese name for the people of Lanna, where men tattooed the abdomen, in distinction from the white-bellied Lao from Lanchang who tattooed only their legs.

blinds มู่ลี่ *muli*—Blinds made with strips of material, hung vertically.

Bodhisatta โพธิสัตว์ *photisat*—A Buddha to be.

Brahman พราหมณ์—A Hindu priest.

breast chain สังวาล *sangwan*—A long chain or sash worn either around the neck, looped over the shoulders, or crosswise on the breast, as a mark of status for gods, kings, or nobles.

britches สนับเพลา *sanap phlao*—Close-fitting trousers ending below the knee, often with a flared cuff, now seen mostly as part of the costume for traditional dance.

buffalo charm ควายธะนู *khwai thanu*—A buffalo-shaped amulet, made from woven bamboo, earth, beeswax, metal, or lac, for protection or doing harm.

canopy boat เรือกัญญา *ruea kanya*—A long boat with prow and stern curved up, and an area amidships sheltered by a *kanya*, canopy, usually roofed with woven bamboo. Such boats were used by officials, and in royal processions, and conveyed status.

caselet ตลับ *talap*—A small container, either square or round.

casket เจียด *jiat*—A small lidded container, often octagonal, for keeping handkerchiefs or similar items, often made of silver or woven cane, sometimes part of the regalia of rank.

casumunar ไพล *phlai*—A tuberous root, *Zingiber casumunar/purpureum*, used for treating wounds, nausea, and headaches.

chalom ฉะลอม, ชะลอม—A container made of loose basketwork, often used for fruit or vegetables.

chalang **pattern** ลายฉลาง *lai chalang*—A type of patterned cloth, possibly from Thalang, Phuket.

chaophraya เจ้าพระยา—The highest rank in the official nobility, reserved for ministers and governors of first-class towns.

Chayanto ชยันโต—A prayer widely used for victory or success.

chicken-flapping ปรบไก่ *prop kai*—A popular entertainment in which two groups of singers improvise verses in a challenge-response style, trying to outdo one another for innuendo and humor, while dancing and clapping with exaggerated elbow movements like chickens flapping their wings.

chicken-skin silk แพรหนังไก่ *phrae nang kai*—A fine silk that creases like chicken skin.

chili dip แจ่ว *jaeo*—A characteristically Lao dip, usually made with a base of red onion, fermented fish, chili, and lime juice.

claves กรับ *krap*—Two pairs of wooden cylinders, around six inches long, tapped together to provide rhythm and stress during the recitation of *sepha* and other performances.

cone pattern กรวย, กรวยเชิง *kruai, kruaichoeng*—A pattern of elongated cones, used as a border on cloth or other decorations such as wat pillars.

conical hat ลอมพอก *lomphok*—A tall, tapering conical hat with an upturned brim decorated with golden flowers. Originally from Persia, it became part of court and ceremonial attire.

creel ข้อง *khong*—A pot-shaped basket for keeping fish with a lid made from strips of bamboo that let the fish slip in but not escape.

cross-branch ก้านแย่ง *kanyaeng*—A pattern with lines of intertwined flowers and stems dividing the area into a grid of squares or diamonds.

cross-hall หอขวาง *ho khwang*—A building on the short side of the oblong plan of a Thai house. Usually houses were built on an east-west axis, and a *ho khwang* ran north-south.

crow's wings ปีกกา *pik ka*—A military formation with both wings spread like a crow. The term is used today for a curly bracket (}) which gives an idea of the shape.

crupper ซองหาง *song hang*—A strap from the saddle under a horse's tail.

department head เจ้ากรม *jao krom*—A mid-ranking official title held mainly by the heads of guard units under Mahatthai or the palace, with *sakdina* between 400 and 1,000.

deputy ปลัด *palat*—A deputy, especially to a minister or governor.

duty officer นายเวร *nai wen*—"Head of a duty shift," a low-ranking post in Kalahom, *sakdina* 200 to 500.

Dvaravati ทวารวดี *thawarawadi*—A polity that may have existed in the Chao-phraya Basin between the fifth and twelfth centuries CE.

eaglewood ไม้กฤษณา *mai kritsana*—A tree, *Aquilaria agallocha/crassna*, that secretes a fragrant resin to counter a parasite. The resinous wood was highly prized as an aromatic, especially in China.

era-destroying fire ไฟกัลป์ *fai kan*—A fire that consumes the world at the close of an era in the Three Worlds cosmology. The fire starts after seven suns rise in succession, and burns not only the realm of mankind, but all four realms of loss and woe below, and ten of the realms above.

eye-level shrine ศาลเพียงตา *san phiang ta*—A temporary shrine for making offerings to gods or spirits. Four wooden or bamboo posts are planted in a square of one meter or less, with a shelf suspended between them at eye level to hold the offerings, and a cloth stretched over the top of the posts.

Farang ฝรั่ง—Foreigners of western appearance.

fathom วา *wa*—Approximately two meters.

fiddle ซอ *so*—General name for fiddles, two- or three-string, played upright.

flanchard แผงค้าง *phaeng khang*—Panels of cow or buffalo leather to protect a horse's flanks.

flask คนโท *khontho*—A jug, often with an elaborate spout like an extended goose's neck, an item of regalia, probably of Persian origin.

Floating Pavilion ตำหนักแพ *tamnak phae*—Literally the raft royal residence, a name for the pier called *Phrachanuan nam* at Wasukri Landing on the north of the palace.

flower tassel พู่กลิ่น *phuk lin*—A fragrant ornament made with fresh flowers.

fluid metal เหล็กไหล *lek lai*—A naturally occurring metal-like compound that becomes malleable under a little heat such as a candle, believed to convey invulnerability to piercing by making blades bend, or by making the skin elastic and impenetrable.

flute ปี่ *pi*—A general name for a range of double-reed pipes of varying length with six holes for fingers and one for thumb.

footed tray โต๊ะ, โตก *to, tok*—A round tray, made of wood and often lacquered, on a raised base, for eating while seated on the floor.

forbidden lady นางห้าม *nang ham*—A term for ladies of the palace.

fore harness ผ่านหน้า *phan na*—A strap passing under the neck and over the back of an elephant.

forenoon meal เพล *phen*—The main daily meal that monks take between 11 a.m. and noon.

four pillars จตุสดมภ์ *jatusadom*—Four leading ministers of city, palace, treasury, and lands, and equivalent officials in a provincial city.

Garuda ครุฑ *khrut*—A mythical bird with a human body and the head, wings, and talons of an eagle; the mount of Vishnu.

gaur กระทิง *krathing*—*Bos gaurus*, a massive wild buffalo of dark grey or black color, weighing around a ton when fully grown.

God-Arouser เทพรำจวน *thep-ranjuan*—A mantra to induce love.

grassflower ดอกหญ้า *dok ya*—Literally "flower of grass," not a genus but a metaphor for a plain woman.

Great Collection mantra มุขใหญ่ *muk yai*—A mantra for invulnerability that combines the key portions of several other mantra.

guard ตำรวจ *tamruat*—General word for security officers.

hair quill ไม้สอย *mai soi*—Wood splints or hedgehog quills used for styling hair.

half-moon tables อัฒจันทร์ *attajan*—A set of tables of diminishing sizes for displaying articles.

hamper กระจาด *krajat*—A basketwork receptacle woven from bamboo with a small round or square base and much wider mouth. They are used especially for carrying offerings.

Hanuman หนุมาน—Chief of Ram's monkey warriors in the *Ramakian*.

heart formula หัวใจ *hua jai*—Abbreviated mantras used for purposes of memorization, and for quick application. Often these were two or three syllables, each of which represented a complete prayer.

heron-leg gun ปืนขานกยาง *puen kha nok yang*—A gun with a barrel over a meter long and a tripod to support it.

Himaphan หิมพานต์—In the Three Worlds cosmology, the area beyond human habitation, populated by animals, many of them fantastic, and visited by deities; modeled on the Himalayas.

Ho ฮ่อ—A Thai name for Chinese from southern China, especially Yunnan

ho mok ห่อหมก—"Wrap and bury," fish and herbs, wrapped in banana leaves, covered with mud, and baked with charcoal in a hole in the ground.

Hongsa, Hongsawadi หงสา, หงสาวดี—Hamsawati, city of swans, the Thai term for the Mon capital of Pegu.

horse-stool ม้า *ma*—"Horse," a stool used for sitting or placing things.

hungry ghost ผีกระสือ *phi krasue*—A female spirit, usually old, that goes out at night to eat dirt, rubbish, and feces.

inner official sala ศาลาลูกขุนใน *sala luk khun nai*—A working hall for the senior officials inside the palace.

Isuan อิศวร—Sanskrit Iswara, the usual Thai name for Siva, a Hindu god.

jalung จะลุง—Post for tethering elephants, or making a stockade for them.

jap-ping จับปิ้ง—A protective ornament tied round an infant girl's hips.

Jataka ชาดก *chadok*—"Birth story," previous lives of the Buddha recounted as moral tales.

Java flute ปี่ชวา *pi chawa*—A long reeded instrument that usually accompanies the Khaek drum, especially nowadays at boxing matches.

Jek เจ๊ก—Chinese, nowadays pejorative, but neutral in *KCKP*.

jingjok จิ้งจก—Small common house lizard, gecko.

Kalahom กลาโหม—One of the two major ministries, overseeing the south, and later the military.

Kaliyuga กลียุค *kaliyuk*—In Hindu cosmology, the fourth of four eras, a time when human virtue progressively diminishes, leading to eventual destruction. In Thai the word is used to mean a calamity.

Kamnan กำนัน—A village headman.

kanok กนก, กระหนก—A motif, based on a flame, with many variants.

Karen กะเหรี่ยง *kariang*—General name for a collection of ethnic groups that mainly live in the hills separating Siam and Burma.

karma wind กัมมัชวาต *kammachawat*—An old belief that there is a wind in a woman's body that blows at the time the child is ready for delivery, turning the child's head downwards.

kathom กะท่อม—A leaf chewed as a narcotic.

Kha ข่า—Term applied to many non-Thai groups; considered pejorative.

Khaek แขก—Term for foreigners of Malay, Indian, or Arabian origin.

Khaek drum กลองแขก *klong khaek*—Two double-headed drums of different diameter, with calfskin heads and thongs to adjust the pitch, struck by two players. Similar drums are found in Malaysia, Java, and India.

khaen แคน—Lao musical instrument with multiple bamboo pipes.

Khanan ขนาน—Title for a former monk, especially one who takes a leading role in ceremonies at the wat.

Khmer-style ถกเขมร *thok khamen*—A way of hitching up a lowercloth by tucking the lower edge in the waist and rolling up the sides.

khon **boat** โขน, โขลน—A decorative prow or stern, usually carved from wood, and hence a boat with such decoration, particularly ceremonial craft.

khonthan คนธรรพ์—Sanskrit *gandharva*, celestial musician.

Khun ขุน—Title for holders of low rank in the official nobility.

kimkhab เข้มขาบ *khemkhap*—Silk with gold thread in the warp, and longitudinal brocade patterns made with strands of flattened metal wound over a core of silk; originally from Persia but made extensively in northern India.

kinnari กินรี—Mythical female creature, half-bird, half-human.

kinnon กินร—Mythical male creature, half-bird, half-human.

klon กลอน—A verse form, used for *sepha*.

klongyon กลองโยน—A type of music usually played by a *piphat* ensemble, especially to accompany the *City* episode of the Mahachat.

krajae กระแจะ—Fragrant water made by steeping bark of the *krajae* tree, used like eau de cologne. It might come as a powdered extract for dissolving, sometimes combined with sandal and other ingredients.

krajang กระจัง—A motif like a lotus petal used in horizontal frieze designs.

kris กริช—Malay word for a dagger with a distinctive wavy blade.

Krung Phali กรุงพาลี—A spirit who presides over all the spirits of the place.

kuti กุฏิ—The residential quarters for monks in a wat.

Kwan กวาน—Title for a noble or village head.

lady attendants สนมกรมวัง *sanom krom wang*—Ladies in close attendance on the king and other royalty.

lance ง้าว *ngao*—A curved blade around eighteen inches long mounted on a long handle, wielded with a slashing movement; primarily a foot-soldier's weapon, but also used on horse or elephant.

Lanchang ล้านช้าง—A Lao polity, once with capital at Luang Prabang, but in *KCKP* at Vientiane.

Lanna ลานนา—Polity centered on Chiang Mai, covering upper valleys of the Chaophraya Basin, absorbed by Siam in the late nineteenth century.

lantern อัจกลับ *atjaklap*—A hanging brass lantern, in various forms including a globe suspended by four chains.

Lao ลาว—Language and ethnicity closely related to Thai. The term was applied by Ayutthaya and Bangkok to both Lanchang and Lanna.

Lawa ละว้า—Name of a Mon-Burmese ethnic group, often used as a catch-all descriptor of non-Thai groups.

leaf basket กระทง *krathong*—A cup or small basket sewn from banana or other leaves, used especially for containing offerings or presents.

li-ke ลิเก—A genre of folk performance with drama and music.

Lokanta โลกันต์ *lokan*—The lowest hell in the Three Worlds cosmology, devoid of light, destination of those who have harmed parents, monks, or Brahman teachers.

longan ลำไย *lamyai*—A tropical fruit with a thin skin and translucent flesh.

looking glass คันฉ่อง *khanchong*—A mirror with a standing base.

Loosener (มหา)สะเดาะ *(maha)sado*—A mantra for opening locks, easing childbirth, and other forms of release.

Lord of Darkness พระกาฬ *phra kan*—The black lord, sometimes identified as *yom*, the god of death, and sometimes described as *yom*'s retainer.

Lord of the Lions พญาไกรสรราชสีห์ *phya kraison ratchasi*—Lord of the mythical lions in the Himaphan Forest; a simile for power.

Lord of the Swans พญาราชหงส์, *phya ratchahong*—A golden swan in the Mahahamsa Jataka; a simile for beauty.

lowercloth นุ่ง *nung*—Any cloth worn on the lower body by men or women, usually a simple oblong wrapped around and tucked at the waist.

Lue ลื้อ—A Tai language and ethnic group, now mostly living in Yunnan, southern China.

lute กระจับปี่ *krajap-pi*—A plucked lute with four gut strings and eleven frets.

Mahatthai มหาดไทย—One of the two major ministries, overseeing the north, and later the civilian administration.

mahori มโหรี—A musical ensemble. The old form, *mahori boran*, had a three-string fiddle, lute, *thon* drum, and *krap* claves, along with a singer.

Malay drums กลองมลายู *klong malayu*—A pair of double-ended drums carved from wood and tensioned with leather thongs, played by two people in sitting position using curved wooden drumsticks.

mantra มนตร์ *mon*—A formula or prayer. The term is sometimes used more generally to mean supernatural, supernaturalism.

maprang มะปราง—A fruit, the size and shape of a small chicken egg, with a fine smooth skin that turns from yellow to orange when ripe; common simile for a good complexion.

mastermind วิทยา, วิทยาธร *withaya, withayathon*—"Upholder of (special) knowledge," a non-human being, ranked below deities, with the ability to fly through the air; attendants on Siva.

Meng เม็ง—Synonym of Mon.

meru เมรุ *men*—Funeral pyre, modeled on Mount Meru, the mountain at the center of the Three Worlds cosmology.

meshwork กรอง *krong*—Fine loosely woven cotton, often woven or embroidered with gold thread, tailored as a robe, or draped over the shoulder as adornment on auspicious occasions.

miang เมี่ยง—Fermented tea, or a snack made with various chopped foods wrapped in a leaf.

Mon มอญ—A language and ethnic group, mostly found in southern Burma.

montha มณฑา—A tree of the Magnolia family with large yellow flowers and a strong morning fragrance.

mot โหมด—A check fabric of Indian origin, in Siam woven with silk, silver and gold thread, and silver and gold paper.

Mount Meru เขาพระสุเมรุ *khao phra sumen*—In Buddhist cosmology, the center of the universe.

mounting platform เกยชัย *koeichai*—A general name for platforms used by royalty to board conveyances such as elephants, horses, and boats.

Muen หมื่น—"Ten thousand," a component of many titles of rank.

Mujalin มุจลิน—A lake or river in the Himaphan Forest.

musth ซับมัน *sap man*—A frenzied state of male elephants.

naga นาคา *nak*—A mythical snake, modeled on a cobra.

nak นาก—Alloy of gold, silver, and copper with an appearance similar to silver, known among European traders as tutenague.

namya jin น้ำยาจีน—A curried fish sauce, often eaten with *khanom jin*, a form of rice noodles.

Nang นาง—Title for females.

Narai นารายณ์—The usual Thai name for the Hindu god, Vishnu.

netherworlder อสุรกาย *asurakai*—A spirit stranded in the netherworld between the human world and the realms of hell.

Ngo เงาะ—A negrito hunter-gatherer group, who call themselves Samang and live in the forests on the hills of the peninsula.

nielloware ถม, ถมยา *thom, thomya*—Metal decorated by incising, filling the incisions with a black compound, and polishing.

nine jewels เนาวรัตน์, นพรัตน์, นพเก้า *naowarat, noppharat, nopphakao*—A combination of diamond, ruby, emerald, topaz, garnet, sapphire, moonstone, zircon, and lapis lazuli.

nirat นิราศ—"Parting," a poetic form, recalling a loved one, often structured around a journey.

norasing นรสิงห์—A mythical creature with the upper body of a man and the lower body of a hoofed animal like a deer, similar to a satyr, or with a lion's head on a human body.

offertory blessing ยถาสัพพี *yatha sapphi*—A Pali formula chanted after monks have been fed or received offerings.

offertory-rice pattern พุ่มเข้าบิณฑ์ *khao bin*—A motif based on popped rice in a folded leaf or almsbowl in a shape resembling a lotus bud.

olive สมอ *samo*—Fruits of trees in the Terminalia genus, especially *Terminalia chebula*. The oval pithy stoned fruit resembles an olive.

open style ห่มดอง *hom dong*—A way of wearing monk's robes, usually only inside the wat at ceremonies and formal occasions. The *jiwon* is worn over the left shoulder with the right shoulder left bare; the *sangkati* is draped over the left shoulder and fastened with a belt around the waist.

orahan อรหัน *orahan*—A mythical beast with a bird's body and human head.

pack basket โพล่ *phlo*—Twin containers made of basketwork with a shoulder pole, used for transporting food, cloth, weapons, etc.

palace governess ท้าวนาง *thao nang*—"Noble lady," general term for senior administrators of the inner palace, often consorts from a prior reign.

palm-leaf fan ตาละปัตร *talapat, talipot*—A monk's fan, originally made from a sugar-palm leaf.

pan พลู *phlu*—Leaf of the betel vine, used for wrapping betelnut for chewing.

pannier แฟ้ม *faem*—Containers made of thick cloth, hide, or basketwork, hung on shoulder poles, slung on the back, or hitched on horses or elephants.

parot ปรอท *parot*—A small enclosed metal cylinder filled with mercury, believed to convey invulnerability by flowing to any part of the body that is threatened with piercing.

pathamang ปถมัง—Writing initial characters in Khmer script as devices of lore.

patriarch สังฆราช *sangkharat*—Head of the monkhood in a city or territory.

pavilion พลับพลา *phlab-phla*—A temporary residence for royalty.

peeled-lotus ตาบัวปอก *ta bua pok*—A printed cloth with a square pattern, popular in the court.

persimmon พลับ *phlap*—A fruit, not the well-known *Diospyros kaki* but a relative in the Diospyros family, probably *Diospyros malabarica*.

phakhaoma ผ้าขาวม้า—Originally a waist sash from Persia, now a general-purpose cloth for bathing, but in *KCKP* an uppercloth of high value.

Phakhawam ภควำ—An image of Gavampati, an early disciple of the Buddha, usually depicted covering his eyes and perhaps other bodily orifices with extra hands; a powerful, protective amulet, often very small.

Phalahok พลาหก—"Cloud," name of the gem horse, one of the attributes of the Buddhist emperor in the Three Worlds cosmology.

pha-muang ผ้าม่วง—Silk woven with stiff yarn in dark colors (blue, purple, or green), generally worn in tuck-tail (*jongkraben*) style.

Phan พัน—"Thousand," a low-ranking title in the official nobility.

phanaeng พะแนง—A thick red curry, probably named after Penang.

phimsen พิมเสน—A crystallized herb used like smelling salts, sometimes called *patchouli*, borneol, or Barus camphor.

phirot พิรอด—Cloth or paper inscribed with yantra, then rolled and twisted into something that can be worn, usually a ring.

phleng เพลง—A genre of singing or recitation in challenge-response style between two people or groups of performers.

phrai ไพร่—Commoner with obligations of labor service to a king or noble.

phrakhlang พระคลัง—Minister of the treasury, from mid Ayutthaya onwards, overseeing trade and foreign relations.

phraya พระยา—High rank in the official nobility.

pike หอก *hok*—A stabbing weapon with a straight metal blade like a twin-edged knife on a long, usually wooden handle; a foot-soldier's weapon.

pipe ขลุ่ย *khlui*—A woodwind instrument rather like a recorder.

pipe flag เทียว *thiao*—A flag in the form of a cylinder.

pomade มุหน่าย *munai*—A hair dressing made with coconut oil mixed with soot and lime.

post horse ม้าเร็ว, ม้าใช้ *ma reo, ma chai*—Horse for delivering messages.

precept ศีล *sin*—The rules of conduct in Theravada Buddhism. The Five Precepts define a basic code of ethics. Novices are trained to follow ten precepts, while monks are expected to follow 277 as required in the Patimokkha code.

prostration cloth ผ้ากราบ, *pha krap*—Originally a cloth for placing on the ground for prostration by nobles and monks, it evolved into a narrow sash tied around the waist or chest as a mark of status.

Rahu ราหู—A demon-god, and an imaginary planet positioned at the north lunar node, where the paths of the sun and moon intersect.

rains retreat พรรษา *phansa*—A period of three lunar months from July to October, when forest monks "retreat" to a wat because of the rains.

Ramakian รามเกียรติ์—The Thai adaptation of the Indian epic, the *Ramayana*.

ranat ระนาด—A musical instrument, resembling a xylophone. The lead version, *ranat ek*, has twenty-one keys made of hardwood or bamboo strung on cords in a boat-shaped cradle.

Ratchasi ราชสีห์—Lord of the mythical lions in the Himaphan Forest; symbol on the seal of Mahatthai.

regal sword พระแสง *phrasaeng*—A double-edged short sword, part of the royal regalia, often carried by the king at audience.

retainer ทนาย *thanai*—A substitute attending court for a plaintiff or defendant, or a member of a noble's retinue.

rishi ฤษี *ruesi*—Ascetic, holy man.

robe ครุย *khrui*—A light robe worn as a sign of office, often made of muslin or similar light fabric, knee-length with long arms, open at the front, perhaps with decoration denoting rank on the collar, cuffs, and lower hem.

sabai สไบ—Uppercloth, worn by both men and women.

saber กระบี่ *krabi*—A one-handed sword with a single-edged curving blade.

sakdina ศักดินา—A numerical system of ranking status ranging from 10,000 for a chaophraya to 5 for a slave.

sala ศาลา—Hall, especially one without walls, often in a wat.

salver พาน *phan*—A pedestal tray used for offerings.

sappanwood ฝาง *fang*—A timber, *Caesalpinia sappan*, source of a red pigment used for dyeing textiles, also for cosmetics. Large quantities were exported to Japan.

sathu สาธุ—Pali word uttered to show appreciation at sermons, etc.

scribe อาลักษณ์ *alak*—An official with responsibility for documents.

sema เสมา—Stone boundary-marker, especially for an ordination hall, and anything with a similar, inverted-shield shape.

sentinelle โขลนจ่า *khlon ja*—Female guards in the inner palace.

sepha เสภา—A genre of tales in verse form (like *KCKP*) and their performance by oral recitation.

sesame-seed pattern เมล็ดงา *malet nga*—An intricate flower pattern on dark cloth, imported from India or brought by cart traders from Khorat.

shenai ปี่ไฉน *pi chanai*—A reed instrument with a distinctive squawking tone.

shoulder cloth อังสะ *angsa*—A cloth worn by a monk over the shoulder.

Si Sattanakhannahut ศรีสัตนาคนหุต—Pali version of Lanchang, Vientiane.

Sida สีดา—Heroine of the *Ramakian*, equivalent to Sita.

sidebag ย่าม *yam*—A simple cloth bag with a shoulder strap.

silkwool ปูมส่าน *pumsan*—A high-quality fabric used for sompak presented to nobles by the king.

sin ซิ่น—A tubular style of lowercloth, worn in Lanna and the Lao country.

Sithandon สีทันดร—Pali Sithantara, the ocean surrounding Mount Meru and all the ranges around Mount Meru.

six militia units อาษาหกเหล่า *asa hok lao*—A collective term for six permanent military units whose main role was to guard the city.

sompak สมปัก—A lowercloth worn by nobles while attending at court.

Songkran สงกรานต์—Thai new year, in mid April.

soul ขวัญ *khwan*—In traditional belief, the body and its thirty-two elements each have a *khwan* or spiritual representation that may desert the body in times of illness or trouble, and have to be recalled by ceremony.

spear ทวน, หลาว *thuan, lao*—A simpler, lighter form of pike. *Thuan* is usually a bamboo shaft tipped with a cone of metal, while *lao* is a wooden staff with a sharpened point.

spectral โขมด *khamot*—A spirit with an internal source of light, that disappears when approached, rather like a will-o'-the-wisp.

spirit-skull belt ปะขะมองพราย *pa khamong phrai*—A belt made from the skull of a corpse of someone who died a violent death, sawn into strips, woven in a checkered pattern, and inscribed with formula.

stupa เจดีย์ *jedi*—Monument to enshrine a relic of the Buddha or ashes after cremation.

Subduer สะกด *sakot*—A mantra for immobilizing or putting people to sleep.

suffering ghost เปรต *pret*—One form of spirit stranded in the netherworld. It is as tall as a sugar palm tree, with long hair, elongated neck, dark body, protruding belly, and a mouth as small as a needle hole as a result of which such spirits are emaciated and constantly hungry.

Surat สุหรัด—A port and weaving center in Gujarat, western India, which became a major supplier of printed cotton textiles designed specifically for the Siamese market in the eighteenth and nineteenth centuries.

swan หงส์ *hong*—Sanskrit *hamsa*, a mythical swan.

swordstore ทิมดาบ, *thim dap*—Literally a storehouse for swords, but in practice working space for officials inside the palace walls.

takrut ตะกรุด—A protective device made from thin metal, inscribed with yantra, rolled around a cord, and worn around the neck, waist, or arm.

Tani oil ตานี—A type of coconut oil, usually applied to hair or skin, originally from Pattani.

tat ตาด—A silk brocade of Middle Eastern origin, reserved for higher nobility.

Ten Royal Virtues ทศพิธราชธรรม *thotsaphit ratchatham*—A code of conduct for kings, based on Buddhist principles: munificence, moral living, sacrifice, honesty, gentleness, self-restraint or austerity, non-hatred, non-violence or not causing harm, patience or tolerance, and non-oppressiveness.

thian **sweets** ขนมเทียน *khanom thian*—A dough of rice flour and sugar, rolled into a cylinder in a banana leaf, and steamed.

thon **drum** โทนทับ *thon thap*—A drum, possibly of Arabic or Persian origin, with a body of clay or wood shaped like a goblet, struck with the right hand while the left influences the tone by covering the open end.

Thorani ธรณี—Goddess of the earth.

Thotsakan ทศกรรฐ์—"Ten-faced," villain of the *Ramakian*, equivalent to Ravana.

Three Worlds ไตรภูมิ *traiphum*—The cosmology of Theravada Buddhism.

toasting spirit ชัยบาน *chaiyaban*—"Victory liquor" for toasting and feasting.

tomyam ต้มยำ—A spicy and sour soup.

tuck-tail โจงกระเบน *jongkraben*—A lowercloth with a long "tail" passed between the legs and tucked in the waist at the back, giving a pantaloon-like appearance.

tukkae ตุ๊กแก—A lizard with a distinctive call captured in the name.

Upahat, Uparat อุปฮาด, อุปราช—A deputy or second king.

uppercloth ห่ม *hom*—Any cloth worn on the upper body by men or women.

victory candle เทียนขัย *thian chai*—A candle used in offerings.

victory drums กลองชนะ *klong chana*—A double-ended drum played slung around the neck.

votive deity เทพพนม *thep-phanom*—A motif with a deity sitting with crossed legs and hands in wai.

wai ไหว้—Gesture of greeting and respect by joining the palms in front of the chest or face.

waist pouch ไถ้ *thai*—A tubular pouch tied around the waist.

wak วรรค—Hemistich, a half-line of verse.

war prisoner/slave เชลย, เชลยศึก *chaloei(suek)*—A prisoner captured in war and enslaved.

wasp-nest ring รังแตน *rang taen*—A ring with stones arranged in a hexagonal shape like a wasps' nest.

Wasukri วาสุกรี—A mythical serpent king used as the rope for churning the ocean of milk to create the world in the Mahabharata. He is often portrayed in conflict with Garuda.

wat วัด—Buddhist temple.

watch ยาม *yam*—A unit of time. The night is counted in three three-hour watches, the first running from 6 to 9 p.m., the second from 9 p.m. to midnight, and the third from midnight to 3 a.m.

water of allegiance น้ำพระพิพัฒน์สัจจา *nam phra phipat satcha*—A ceremony of swearing allegiance to the king by drinking sacred water.

waving flowers ดอกไม้ไหว *dok mai wai*—Artificial flowers made from paper, cloth, or metal with pliable stalks so that they wave; used to decorate the hair or elsewhere.

whiteclay ดินสอ *dinso*—A fine powdered clay, used to cool the body, and also to write in sticks, like chalk.

wicker basket กระบุง *krabung*—A basketwork container with a square base widening to a round opening.

yak ยักษ์—Sanskrit *yaksa,* originally nature spirits in Indic mythology, transformed in Buddhist cosmology into attendants on Vaisravana, guardian of the north, and in Thai tradition fearful giants or monsters.

Yama ยม *yom*—The Hindu god of death.

yang, yung ยาง, ยูง—Two dipterocarp trees, used to denote deep forest.

yantra ยันต์, เลขยันต์ *yan, lekyan*—A graphic device, made by an adept, combining several powerful symbols, usually to provide protection.

yok ยก—A high-quality lowercloth, usually brocade, worn by both men and women.

CURRENCY

| cowry | เบี้ย *bia*; small shell used as currency; 1/800th of a baht |

		baht	cowries
fueang	เฟื้อง 100 cowries	1/8	100
salueng	สลึง 2 fueang	1/4	200
baht	บาท 4 salueng	1	800
chang	ชั่ง 80 baht	80	64,000
dun	ดุลย์ 20 chang	1,600	1,280,000

LENGTH

inch	นิ้ว	*nio*; 2.5 centimeters
fist	กำ	*kam*; 10 centimeters
cubit	ศอก	*sok*; 50–60 centimeters
fathom	วา	*wa*; 2 meters
sen	เส้น	40 meters
yojana	โยชน์	*yot*; 400 sen, 16,000 meters

Khun Chang Khun Phaen (*KCKP*) counts among a handful of great classical works in the Thai language, but it differs from the others in some key ways. It was developed locally rather than being adapted from sources in Indian, Chinese, Persian, or Javanese literature. It deals with relatively ordinary people with some striving after realism rather than relating the heroic and fantastic exploits of gods and kings. It also differs from the genres with which most western readers will be familiar. It was developed in oral tradition over a long period. It was not designed for reading but for performance by stylized recitation.

This afterword provides background information to aid a better understanding of the poem. The first three sections trace how the poem developed. The next four sketch key features of the physical, social, geopolitical, and mental landscape in which the poem is set. In the last section, we explain how we have approached the translation.

1 THE STORY OF *KHUN CHANG KHUN PHAEN*

KCKP is not the product of a single author or a precise time. The poem "grew" over several centuries with contributions from many people, all but a handful unknown and unnamed. Prior to the early nineteenth century, there are almost no external sources about the story or its telling, only some elusive clues buried in the text. What follows is our reconstruction of the history of *KCKP*, based mainly on these clues.[1]

In old Siam, there was a tradition of storytellers reciting folktales (*nithan*) to entertain local audiences.[2] Most likely, *KCKP* began in this tradition. In the first chapter, the narrator tells us "This story comes down from ancient times, and there is a text in Suphan" (15). *KCKP* then far outgrew this tradition, becoming so popular that performers lengthened it to meet demand. A story once told at a single sitting grew into many episodes that were each recited separately. By the eighteenth century, these recitations were the most

---

1. For a more detailed version of this argument, see Baker and Pasuk, "Career of *KCKP*."
2. See Damrong in *Companion*, 1341–42 Sujit, *KCKP*, 49–60.

popular form of local entertainment, and the court had begun to adopt, adapt, and further extend the tale.

Origins

Nobody knows for sure when the story and its telling originated. The only external reference appears in the *Testimony of the Inhabitants of the Old Capital*, a document which surfaced in the early twentieth century. The *Testimony* is a compilation of information taken down from prisoners swept away to Ava after the sack of the old Siamese capital of Ayutthaya by the Burmese in 1767. The information covers the history of Siam, the geography of Ayutthaya, and details on government and ritual. In the historical material, there is an account of a war with Chiang Mai that is clearly the same story as the campaign described in chapters 25–32 of *KCKP*, including a "Khun Phaen" as the army commander.[3] On the basis of this document, Prince Damrong Rajanubhab concluded that *KCKP* "is a true story," and dated it around 1500 on grounds of the story's position in the *Testimony*'s historical narrative and his interpretation of the date "147" in the opening stanzas of the poem.[4]

There are many reasons to be cautious about Damrong's conclusion. The prisoners were recalling information from memory. The events of 1500 were as distant from them as the sack of Ayutthaya is from us today. The early part of the *Testimony*'s historical narrative is generally problematic. U Thong, founder of Ayutthaya, reigns for forty-five years, rather than the sixteen given in the chronicles. He visits a Buddha's Footprint in Saraburi not found until three hundred years later. After U Thong, there is no name or details about any king of the next two centuries except for "King Phanwasa," which is a general honorific for a king, not a specific name. The Khun Phaen tale is related in parallel with an account of an Ayutthaya diplomatic mission to Ava which seems unlikely at this date but would make sense following the conflicts of the late sixteenth century.[5] The Khun Phaen tale, a long story about a commoner

---

3. KCK, 57–63, 66–67.

4. Damrong interpreted this date as a copyist's miswriting of 847 in the Chula Sakkarat calendar, equivalent to CE 1485/86, and thus identified King Phanwasa with King Ramathibodi II (r. 1491–1529) (*Companion*, 1345–46). Phiset Jiajanphong suggested that 147 appears in the Singhonawat (Singhanavati) chronicle from Lanna as the year in which the Buddha died, an old era of dating was closed, and the Buddhist era began (this old era was subsequently named the Anchana Sakkarat). Phiset argued that 147 was a known date with sacred significance, and was inserted into *KCKP* to denote nothing more exact than "once upon a time" (Phiset, unpublished, summarized in Sujit, *KCKP*, 51–54). Choomsai suggested that 147 was originally C.S. 1147 (AD 1785/86), the year of Bangkok's official foundation, but was truncated to fit the meter ("Sakkarat 147").

5. After "King Phanwasa," the *Testimony* relates the story of Sudachan and Chinnarat, and from that point the *Testimony* and the chronicles roughly correspond. Damrong found that

soldier, is also out of character with the rest of the *Testimony*, which focuses closely on the exploits of kings.

The later part of the *Testimony*'s historical account matches closely with the chronicles, but the early part seems to have been padded rather haphazardly. Possibly, the episode of Khun Phaen leading an army to Chiang Mai went from *KCKP* into the *Testimony* rather than vice versa. This episode seems to be based on historical events which occurred in 1564 and appear in both the Thai and Lao chronicles.[6] Perhaps these events were adapted into an episode in *KCKP* which then somehow found its way into the *Testimony*. Perhaps the tale seemed real to the prisoners giving the testimony in Ava; or those taking the testimony down misunderstood what they were being told; or the tale was inserted when the document found its way back from Burma to Siam in the late nineteenth century—a process which is still mysterious. Two variant versions of the *Testimony* do not include the Khun Phaen tale.[7] The original text of the *Testimony*, supposedly in an archive in Burma, has never been located.

There are two hints which in combination suggest the *KCKP* tale may have emerged around 1600.

Someone called "Khun Phaen Saensathan" appears three times in other documents around this date. He appears in the chronicles commanding a brigade during King Naresuan's siege of Toungoo in the late 1590s, and again in 1604 carrying out an enemy-cursing ceremony when King Naresuan is setting out to march on Ava.[8] In an epic poem, *Lilit Taleng Phai* (Defeat of the Mon), set in the 1590s, Khun Phaen is the name of a messenger sent from Kanchanaburi to inform Ayutthaya of a Burmese incursion.[9] "Khun Phaen Saensathan" is the official title of a lowly guard officer. The title would have been held by a succession of people over time. Individuals of such modest rank do not often figure by name in the royal chronicles or heroic poetry. These references suggest there was a prominent soldier holding this title around 1600.

The second hint is a mention in *KCKP* of the Chinese emperor making a gift of crystal to Ayutthaya for something to do with Burma. At the time of Khun

---

the gazetteer portion of the *Testimony* was very muddled, perhaps because "the original *bailan* sheets were mixed up," and he re-sequenced the gazetteer portion in his edition, but not the historical part (KCK, preface).

6. RCA, 49–51; Stuart-Fox, *Lao Kingdom*, 80–81.

7. These other versions are known as *Khamhaikan khun luang ha wat* (Testimony of the king who sought a wat) and *Khamhaikan khun luang wat pradu songtham* (Testimony of the king of Wat Pradu Songtham).

8. RCA, 177, 193. In the chronicles the name appears as Khun Phlaeng Sathan (ขุนแผลงสท้าน) and Khun Phaen Sathan. Such spelling variations were common.

9. *Lilit Taleng Phai*, 46. As this work was composed by Kromphra Paramanuchit Chinorot in the 1840s, the use of the name could be influenced by *KCKP*.

Phaen (Phlai Kaeo)'s birth, his grandfather advises:

> His birth-time is three by the shadow on Tuesday in the fifth month of a
> year of the tiger. The Chinese emperor has presented glittering crystal to the
> King of Ayutthaya
>   for placement on the pinnacle of the great stupa built since the time of
> Hongsa and called Wat Chaophraya Thai in the past. Give him the name Phlai
> Kaeo, the brilliant. (10)

Neither the Thai chronicles nor the Chinese annals mention such gifts at
this or any other time. But such a gift might well have figured in the political
circumstances around 1600.

Through the late sixteenth century, the Chinese imperial court was concerned that the expansion of the aggressive Toungoo state in Burma would
create problems on China's southern frontier. At times, China called on other
rulers in Southeast Asia to help contain this threat. In 1604, Peking sent agents
to "Siam and Bo-ni to arrange the combining of forces" against Ava, promising rewards if Ava were destroyed. It also sent a missive to the commander of
Guang-dong/Guang-xi "to notify the countries of Siam, Bo-ni and Champa
to join forces in a pincer attack" against Ava.[10] Earlier, in February 1593, the
Chinese court received an offer from Siam to attack Japan. This extraordinary
proposal makes no sense unless it was an expression of Siamese support for
China in the hope of some reciprocal assistance against their common Burmese enemy.[11]

Perhaps this gift was sent in recognition of King Naresuan's victories against
Ava in the 1590s. There is no other historical moment when China was quite as
concerned at Burmese expansion, and when Siam's own efforts at self-defense
provided assistance to China. The stupa mentioned is the Chaiyamongkhon
which Prince Damrong suggested was built to commemorate Naresuan's victory of 1593.[12] The first tiger year after that victory was 1602/3.

---

10. Wade, *Southeast Asia in the Ming Shi-lu*, records 2907, 3130, 3013.

11. Wolters, "Ayudhya."

12. Damrong imagined that Abbot Phanarat advised Naresuan to follow the example of King
Dutthagamani who in Sri Lanka in 205 BC commemorated victory in a similar elephant duel
by building one victory stupa at the battle site, and another in his capital; and that as a result
Naresuan built a commemorative stupa at the battle site of Nong Sarai in Don Chedi, and the
Chaiyamongkhon in Ayutthaya (Damrong, *Biography of King Naresuan,* 125). Montri Limpa-
phayom has argued that Don Chedi was not the site of the battle, and that the commemorative
stupa is actually Wat Phu Khao Thong. Piset Jiajanphong and Sisak Wallipodom doubt there
were any commemorative stupas built at all. This debate was collected in Sujit, *Jedi yutthahatthi.*
Yet, the name of the Chaiyamongkhon stupa clearly suggests it was built to commemorate a vic-

There is one other hint on when the tale was developed. At every appearance of the king in *KCKP* there is an invocation. These passages portray the monarch surrounded by the best of everything as proof of his supreme merit. In the first and most elaborate of these invocations, the king is "bathed in water flowing in a stream from a showerhead" (18). To appear in this context, a showerhead must have been new and very special—something available only to the king. The word used is *surai*, which derives from the Persian *surahi*. This suggests the invocation may have been composed in the middle or late seventeenth century, most probably in the Narai reign (1656–1688), when the court adopted architecture, dress, regalia, vocabulary, and much else through trade and diplomatic contacts with Persia. Prince Damrong also surmised that the tale began to be told in the Narai era.[13]

Original Story

The original folktale of *KCKP* is long lost. We can only guess what it might have been. The core story is a love triangle which ends with the death of the heroine. This death makes the story special—both dramatic and enigmatic. Possibly a true story of a young woman's death was the original spark for the tale.

In the early part of the tale there is a series of episodes which remain among the most famous. As we shall see below, even when *KCKP* was lengthened, the basic narrative of these episodes remained unchanged, probably because they were so well-known as to be sacrosanct. This sequence of episodes possibly maps the original tale, which may have gone like this:

> Khun Phaen, Khun Chang, and Wanthong were childhood friends in Suphanburi. Khun Chang was ugly but rich, while Khun Phaen was handsome but poor. When they reached mid teens, Khun Phaen and Khun Chang competed for Wanthong's love. Khun Phaen wooed her in a cotton field and wed her, but was then sent away to war. In his absence, Khun Chang seized Wanthong. On his return, Khun Phaen quarreled with Wanthong, and abandoned her, but returned soon after and abducted her away from Khun Chang's house into the forest. Khun Phaen killed men sent after him, thus becoming an outlaw. When Khun Phaen decided to give himself up, there was a court case in which Wanthong was condemned to death.[14]

---

tory. There is no evidence on the date of its construction.

13. See *Companion*, 1346. Damrong wrote a sketch imagining *KCKP* being related as a folktale in a riverside sala at Ayutthaya in 1538 (Damrong, *Rabiap*).

14. Recently, a Mon version of *KCKP* has been published in Burma. The story is quite short, around seventy pages. We have not seen a translation or summary, but the chapter headings suggest that the story is roughly as outlined here.

This Original Story[15] may have become so popular because it combined two classic themes. The first is the situation of women. Wanthong becomes a tragic victim because she is unable to control her own life, because she lives in a society which vests all power in men. While the love triangle begins as a classic contest between a handsome pauper and a rich oaf, it develops into a much deeper discussion of what man offers to woman. Khun Phaen gives Wanthong romance, adventure, and children but is utterly unable to provide her with the crucial function of protection (on which more below) because he is always disappearing off to the army, to the wilds, or to prison. Khun Chang gives Wanthong protection and comfort, but their relationship is loveless and barren. In the crucial final scene, Wanthong states clearly that she cannot choose between the two men because they mean such different things to her.

> My love for Khun Phaen is a great love because we shared such hardship going into the forest together. We lacked everything but loved and cherished each other.
> All the time I lived with Khun Chang, he said not one harsh word to me, heaped money on me alone, and placed servants at my beck and call as if they were my own. (799)

Women probably formed a majority in the audiences for recitations of stories as many men were absent from local society because of military duty, corvée service, or adventure. The core of the Original Story would have had great appeal for this female majority in the audience, and the storytellers probably developed the tale to enhance this appeal. Several storytellers may have been women.[16] In this part of *KCKP*, Wanthong is the most complex character, and has many of the best lines.

The second classic theme of the Original Story is an ordinary man pitted against wealth and power. Khun Phaen is poor and powerless because his father fell foul of the king. To court Wanthong, he even has to borrow the bride price from her. Khun Chang competes for Wanthong by tempting her mother with money. He also undermines Khun Phaen by manipulating his connections at court. Khun Phaen articulates the resentment of the underdog when he vents his anger against Wanthong's mother for giving Wanthong to Khun Chang:

---

15. The division of the poem into an Original Story and sequels is our invention, and the terms are capitalized to denote that they are terms of art.

16. The performer of a recitation of *KCKP* recorded in 1950 was a middle-aged woman (Simmonds, "Thai Narrative Poetry," 282). Women figure strongly as performers in other recitation and chanting genres.

Perhaps you thought I had only low rank and little of any kind of property, so you could act highhandedly and I wouldn't have the standing to pursue you in court.

Your new son-in-law is such a big fellow, overflowing with so much property, and so many elephants and horses, that you conspired together to treat me roughly with no respect. . . .

You think I deserve to be cut to pieces like this just because I'm poor. (292)

Khun Phaen overcomes his disadvantages by arming himself with weapons from the liminal tradition of lore (supernaturalism, on which more below). Khun Chang then increases the stakes by accusing Khun Phaen of revolt—of intending to use these weapons to oust the king. Wanthong's death sentence is a penalty for revolt which seems to have been transferred from Khun Phaen to her.[17]

These twin classic themes of woman's lot and everyman against wealth and power probably account for *KCKP*'s exceptional popularity in a tradition of tales recited for local audiences. In this part of *KCKP*, the setting, supporting roles, concerns, and style of storytelling have a very distinctive character, molded by its development in this tradition.

The setting for the Original Story is the provincial towns of Suphanburi, Kanburi, and Phichit, and the wild periphery of the forests, with only short excursions to the royal capital of Ayutthaya. The minor characters of the Original Story are drawn from local society—neighbors, relatives, domestic servants, petty officials, incompetent doctors, monks, hunters, boatmen, and tribal villagers. The plot is wound around the notable events of everyday life—births, weddings, cremations, temple festivals, crime, house building, travel, sickness. The storytelling is very fast-paced, with a rapid-fire mixture of romance, tragedy, bawdy comedy, violence, sex, and supernaturalism, typical of many varieties of popular entertainment. Much of the text consists of dialogue, particularly the argumentative dialogue found in other Thai folk performance genres.

In sum, this is classic popular culture with themes of universal relevance, a setting, characters, and background events that are familiar to the audience, and a style of telling designed to entertain through pace and variety.

---

17. For a fuller discussion of this theme, see Baker and Pasuk, "Revolt of Khun Phaen." See also Cholthira, "Kan nam wannakhadiwijan phaen mai," 76–123.

Growing with the telling

Recitation or unaccompanied singing—variously called *lam*, *khap*, and *phleng*[18]—has had a large role in popular culture in Siam and adjacent areas for a long time. These forms are mentioned in old legends and chronicles.[19] News was spread in this way. In *Lilit Phra Lo*, a poem possibly composed in the Narai era, the handsomeness of the hero is "broadcast by recitation to every city of the realm."[20] Calls to revolt were issued by itinerant singers. Extemporized counterpoint singing was both a local pastime and an entertainment offered by professional performers.[21] To this day, Suphanburi, the home of *KCKP*, is a center of such performance genres. The early phase of *KCKP*'s development probably took place in this milieu. Prince Damrong thought *KCKP* "was passed on orally as a folktale" for at least a century.[22] Nidhi Eoseewong argues that the distinctive meter of *sepha* was adapted from a form found in *phleng* performance (see below).

Improvisation was a key element of this genre of performance. The oldest account of *sepha* performance is found in the text of *KCKP* itself—in chapter 24 at the tonsure ceremony of Khun Phaen's first son (see p. 486). The performers mentioned were the famous players of the era.[23] The scene emphasizes that each had a very distinctive style, and one "was a comedian good at bawdy improvisation" (487). When written texts of *KCKP* became available, improvisation declined, but slowly, because the quality of improvisation was highly prized in this tradition. When E. H. S. Simmonds recorded a performance of *KCKP* in Suphanburi's neighboring province, Ang Thong, in 1950, the text followed the general outline of the printed version but with a great deal of improvised variation in the detail.[24]

The importance of improvisation in this performance tradition is key to

---

18. These terms seem originally to have been different regional words for describing the whole broad genre. *Phleng* has since come to mean music. *Lam* is especially associated with forms of counterpoint singing. *Khap* is closely associated with *sepha* and similar forms of performance.

19. Sujit, *KCKP*, 57–60.

20. ขับซอยอราชเทียรทุกเมือง, *khap so yo rat thian thuk mueang (Lilit Phra Lo)*.

21. "The rhymes are usually sung by at least two parties (male and female) in opposition; there is much controversy in the substance of the rhymes, each trying to defeat its opponents; amorous advances are made and registered, grave mock charges stated and defended; there is much sneering and leg-pulling, often plenty of vulgarity on the part of the men, and positive rudeness on the part of the women" (Bidyalankarana, "The Pastime," 108).

22. *Companion*, 1374.

23. Damrong also related that *sepha* was popular at tonsure, marriage, and other ceremonies (see *Companion*, 1375–77). Damrong recounts in detail the use of *sepha* by the court and capital elite, but pays no attention to popular entertainment.

24. Simmonds, "Thai Narrative Poetry."

understanding how *KCKP* grew from a simple story into a rambling epic. Poet-performers embroidered their own distinctive versions of the major episodes in the Original Story of *KCKP*—the cotton field, jealous quarrel, abduction, etc. In this milieu, the text grew in length by three processes: elaboration, recycling of passages, and incorporation of outside tales.

Performers lengthened the tale by constantly improvising extra content and detail to meet the audience's demand for novelty. For one scene—Khun Phaen's abduction of Wanthong from Khun Chang's house—there are three surviving versions which show this process in action. The first two are fragments known as *Samnuan kao*, the "old version," that may date from the first Bangkok reign or earlier, and were originally published in 1925 (see below). The third, composed in the Second Reign salon, appears in the Damrong edition. The three form a sequence, with the second developed from the first, and the third from the second. The first may be in a form transcribed from performers in the late eighteenth century. Khun Phaen arrives at Khun Chang's house, climbs in, dallies with another woman, Kaeo Kiriya, and then enters Wanthong's bedroom. Most of the telling is narrative, with only a moderate amount of dialogue and minimal description. In the second version, the same content has grown to over three times the length. A few scenes have been added, but most of the expansion comes from greater density. The house and its contents are described in much greater detail. The dialogue between the characters is much longer, allowing more depth in the characterization. In many places, a single line in the first version has been converted into a sub-scene in the second, or a short exchange has lengthened into a more elaborate conversation. Compare the example of Kaeo Kiriya's protest in the two versions:

Version 1

Once you've had me you'll rush away.

While you float off and disappear, Kaeo Kiriya will be left waiting here, looking but seeing nothing, eyes unblinking.

Version 2

Once you've had me, you'll cast me away, not caring which direction the wind will blow me. On my part, it'll be like hoisting a sail and letting the wind blow me astray. I'll be hurt.

Once you've had a taste, you'll abandon me. A lotus wilts away from the stream. Bees take the pollen, and the bloom is battered and bruised.

My breast will be consumed with sorrow, as mournful as a gem that's lost its hue. I shouldn't get myself hurt, but this will. I shouldn't invite shame, but this will.

Friends will hurt me with their criticisms and insinuations. My lord and bene-
factor will pick at me critically. I'll join the ranks of the shamed forever.

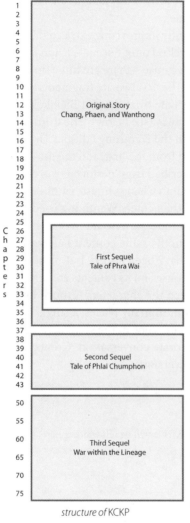

structure of KCKP

Another way that the poem expanded was through recycling. In the oral tradition, different storytellers or schools of storytellers elaborated the story in their own directions, leading to widely differing versions. For instance, among surviving manuscripts there are different versions of Khun Chang's wedding, some straightforward and respectful, and some deliberately hilarious. In a few cases, a variant version seems to have been recycled as an additional episode of the poem.

For example, the story which appears in chapter 14 of the Damrong edition probably began life as an alternative version of the abduction in chapters 17–18. It opens in exactly the same way with Khun Phaen missing Wanthong, riding to Khun Chang's house, and climbing in. It then diverges into a different, comic tale of Khun Phaen tormenting Khun Chang and other members of his household. It is building towards a similar climax as the abduction scene when Khun Phaen abruptly and illogically leaves and returns home. Most probably, storytellers had developed two versions of this abduction scene—one romantic (Kaeo Kiriya), the other comic. The Kaeo Kiriya version came to be preferred, but the other version had its own charm. Performers were reluctant to throw it away, so the ending was cut off, and the episode moved earlier in the story.[25]

---

25. We suspect the Kaeo Kiriya tale was a late addition. The introduction of her in chapter 17, her reappearance in chapter 21, and her later appearances, are rather clumsily pasted into the story. The two skirmishes in the forest in chapters 19 and 20 are probably another example of the

At some point in the poem's history, this process of recycling seems to have resulted in a major addition to the work, rather like a sequel.

The story of Khun Phaen's son, Phra Wai, closely follows the story of Khun Phaen himself. Just like his father, he is separated from his family in childhood, grows up in Kanburi, becomes expert in lore, is sent by the king to fight in the north, gains a splendid victory, is rewarded with a noble title, and has the pleasures and problems of two wives. Possibly large parts of the Phra Wai story began as alternative versions of the Khun Phaen story. At some point, these were recycled as an extension of the story with the son as hero. This sequel was not placed at the end, but inserted in the middle of the Original Story, probably in order to retain Wanthong's death as the climax. To accommodate this insertion, Khun Phaen is consigned to jail for over a decade while his son grows up. To get back to the ending of the Original Story, Phra Wai abducts his mother from Khun Chang's house, just as his father did earlier, provoking a court case and the tragic finale.[26]

An old version of this First Sequel is found in the earliest printed versions of *KCKP* (the Smith and Wat Ko editions, see below). As in the Original Story, the narrator sometimes addresses his audience as "listeners," and editorializes about the plot. Also the telling has a very folksy feel. The military campaign to Chiang Mai is viewed from the perspective of the common soldier. The soldiers live off the land during the march north, start looting Chiang Mai even before victory is won, and return south celebrating among the female war prisoners. Prince Damrong slated this text as "clearly a vulgar (*chaloeisak*) version in a style unsuitable for performance in the court."[27]

This folksy feel, as well as some hints in the text, suggests this First Sequel was initially developed in the late Ayutthaya period. Two other sequels were also developed, probably at a later date. The Second Sequel is another retelling of the Khun Phaen story, this time with Khun Phaen's second son, Phlai Chumphon, in the leading role. This again has the outline structure of the son leaving home, getting educated, volunteering to serve the king, and winning favor. Posi-

---

same process of recycling. The structure of both episodes is the same: Khun Chang follows after Khun Phaen and finds him in the forest; Khun Phaen uses stunning mantras, animates grass dummy troops, and wins the skirmish; Khun Chang flees; Khun Phaen returns to Wanthong; they bathe in a stream; the defeated army falls to recriminations.

26. There is internal evidence that parts of Phra Wai's abduction (in chapter 35) may have been reworked from a version of Khun Phaen's abduction (in chapters 17–18). Phra Wai is carrying Skystorm which Khun Phaen was carrying in the earlier abduction and which he does not give to Phra Wai until chapter 36. After Wanthong has left in chapter 35, Chang refers to a destroyed curtain, damage to the house's first post, and the disappearance of valuables—all of which are part of the story in chapter 17, but do not figure in chapter 35.

27. *Companion*, 1386.

tioned after the original ending of Wanthong's death, this Second Sequel is much less elegantly crafted, strewn with continuity errors and narrative illogicality. A Third Sequel has a very different structure and form. Taking cues from conflicts between the characters in the first two sequels, the Third Sequel develops these conflicts down through the next two generations of Khun Phaen's lineage.

A third way in which the story was lengthened was by incorporating other tales. This is a common characteristic of sagas that develop in oral tradition, including the Robin Hood tale, with which *KCKP* has many parallels. These external tales appear especially in the sequels, probably because the storytellers were striving to provide a mix of familiarity and novelty. Some of these stories are adapted from historical events that can be found in the chronicles. The Chiang Mai campaign in the First Sequel seems based on events dated to 1564. One incident in this campaign—a rescue from the Chiang Mai jail—seems modeled on a similar rescue that took place in a campaign in Burma in 1662.[28] The Chiang Thong campaign shares many details with an incident in 1660.[29] The reception of a Lanchang embassy at Ayutthaya in chapter 25 is strikingly similar to the account of a Tavoyan embassy to Bangkok in 1791.[30] Other external stories incorporated into *KCKP* were popular pieces of fiction. These include the Buakhli episode, and the tale of a giant crocodile terrorizing the Chaophraya River.

Adoption by the court

By late Ayutthaya, *KCKP* was also adopted in court circles. Eventually this court interest would lead to a major transformation of the poem.

It is not possible to determine when the court became interested in *KCKP*. The fifteenth-century Palatine Law has a timetable of the king's daily activities

---

28. In *KCKP*, Phra Thainam and five hundred soldiers are imprisoned but not killed in Chiang Mai. In the chronicles, Phraya Siharat Decho and five hundred soldiers are imprisoned but not killed in Ava. In *KCKP*, Khun Phaen arrives and uses supernatural powers to enter the jail and release all the prisoners from their chains. In the chronicles, a relief force under Phraya Surin Phakdi arrives and begins to attack the stockade. "Meanwhile, Phraya Siha Ratcha Decho, bound in fetters, thereupon examined the clouds and shadows in the sky, saw a propitious omen, and recited a holy Buddhist mantra spell and magically managed to make all his fetters fall off from his body." In *KCKP*, the freed prisoners kill the guards and steal weapons, horses and elephants. In the chronicles, the freed prisoners kill the guards and capture "Burmese prisoners, elephants, horses and weapons" (RCA, 281).

29. In 1660, a border town pledged allegiance to Ayutthaya but then changed its mind, in fear of the power of its old overlord, Ava. Ayutthaya sent an army. Some clever monks came out to negotiate, pledging secret allegiance to Ayutthaya, and promising to cooperate against the old overlord (RCA, 250–60). In chapters 8 and 9 of *KCKP*, Chiang Thong pledges allegiance to Ayutthaya, changes its mind after a visit by a Chiang Mai army, is attacked by Khun Phaen at the head of an Ayutthayan force, and sends out three clever monks to negotiate.

30. Flood and Flood, *Dynastic Chronicles*, 1:176–82.

which specifies "at midnight, *sepha* and music; at 1 o'clock, folktales."[31] But the meaning of *sepha* in this context is not clear, and the reference cannot be dated because the laws may have been modified during copying. Foreign visitors in the seventeenth century described witnessing several court entertainments, but none identifiable as *sepha*, though La Loubère mentioned recitation.[32] Two hints in the *KCKP* text and one external source suggest the court interest in *KCKP* may date to the early eighteenth century.

In the late Ayutthaya era, the king went on an annual pilgrimage to the Buddha's Footprint on Phra Phutthabat Hill in Saraburi. Among the articles the king presented as offerings at the site were "a Phra Narai cloth, a Wanthong tapestry (*man wanthong*), and a gold model junk."[33] This fact emerged when a group of Ayutthaya-era officials was convened in 1784/85 to record the old practice on this pilgrimage. The "Wanthong tapestry" had presumably acquired this name by reference to the three pieces of embroidery which appear in the abduction scene in *KCKP*. According to legend, after Wanthong's death, Khun Chang presented one of her embroideries to King Songtham (r. 1610/1–1628) who in turn presented it at the footprint shrine, hence founding the tradition.[34] For a "Wanthong tapestry" to figure in such an important royal rite, *KCKP* must have acquired some status in court culture already.

A second hint on the timing of the court's interest in *KCKP* is found in the text. The Banyong Rathanat throne hall is one of only two major buildings of the Ayutthaya palace mentioned directly by name in the poem. This hall was built late in the Narai reign, used as the principal audience hall from 1688 to 1733, then repaired by King Borommakot and used again between 1744 and 1758.[35] Most likely this reference appeared in *KCKP* at the time the hall was in use.

In a note published in his journal *Siam Prabheth* in 1900, K. S. R. Kulap[36] wrote:

---

31. KTS, 1:131.

32. "They sometimes accompany the Voice with two short sticks, which they call *Crab* [กรับ, claves], and which they strike one against the other; and he that sings thus is stiled *Tchang cap* [ช่างขับ, reciter]. They hire him at Weddings with several of those instruments I have mentioned" (La Loubère, *New Historical Relation*, 68; see also 46–49, and Choisy, *Journal,* 178; Gervaise, *Natural and Political History*, 88–89).

33. "Khamhaikan khun khlon," 57.

34. Chotchuang and Khru Sepha, *KCKP chabap yon tamnan*, 89.

35. On the Banyong Rathanat, see p. 540, note 22.

36. Kulap Kritsananon (1834–1921), son of a Siam-born Chinese married to the daughter of a minor official, was educated on the fringes of the court, worked fifteen years in Western companies, moved back to Bangkok in the 1880s, and started an independent press. His journal *Siam Prabheth* gained a circulation of 1,500 for articles on history and culture, often reworked from texts in the palace library (Reynolds, "Mr. Kulap").

> Concerning *sepha KCKP*, I'm not sure whether it is true or false but I found an old government text saying that King Suea of the old capital composed nine volumes of *samut thai,* not completing the task before he passed away. Subsequently, Jaofa Jit, Chaophraya Yommarat (Kun), and Phra Siphuripri-chasalaksana (Thongduang) composed further between the three of them until the story was complete. These three composed in the reign of King Thaisa.[37]

King Suea or Sorasak (r. 1701–1708) is not usually associated with literary pursuits, but "composed" in this extract may mean that the composition was done at his bidding or in his reign. It is not clear where Kulap got this information. He had access to manuscripts in the palace library, and other old manuscripts purloined from noble houses. A year later, he was found guilty of imaginatively embroidering on these sources in his journalism.[38] Kulap's information is uncertain, but it fits with the impression that the court took up *KCKP* in the early eighteenth century, and it raises the possibility that written versions did exist in the Ayutthaya era and may have been the basis for later revisions.

This court interest in *KCKP* increased markedly in the early Bangkok period. From the First Reign (1782–1809), there was a deliberate effort to rescue surviving documents from the Ayutthaya era including laws, religious texts, histories, and literature. *KCKP* was not among the texts rescued under royal auspices, but seems to have attracted the interest of others. Khun Wichitmatra believed that Chaophraya Phrakhlang (Hon), the most prominent court litterateur of the Bangkok First Reign, contributed to the project of recording *KCKP*.[39]

In his preface, Damrong shows that the only storyteller from the Ayutthaya era known to be still performing in early Bangkok was a gatekeeper, a lowly commoner. By the Second Reign, there were many other performers, all with minor official titles, possibly of commoner birth but now under the patronage of the court nobility.[40] The ownership of the poem had begun to shift.

Revision by the court

Over the nineteenth and early twentieth century, there were three major

---

37. *The Siam Prabheth*, 2:20 (16 Sept. 1900): 1029. Many thanks to Niyada Laosunthorn. Jaofa Jit was born to a son of King Phetracha and daughter of King Thaisa (Busakorn, "Ban Phlu Luang Dynasty," 158). Phra Siphuripricha was the title of the head of the legal drafting department in the palace administration (KTS, 1:272).

38. Reynolds, "Mr. Kulap."

39. KW, 166–69. In the Thonburi era (1767–1782), Hon was a customs official in Uthai Thani who met the future King Rama I on his northern military expeditions. He became the head of the treasury in the First Reign, translated *Three Kingdoms* and *Rachathirat* into Thai, and died in 1805.

40. *Companion*, 1350–53.

projects of revising sections of *KCKP* within the court. The first, concentrating on the latter part of the Original Story, was undertaken by the salon of King Rama II (r. 1809–1824). The second, involving a complete revision of the Chiang Mai campaign in the First Sequel, took place around mid century. The third was Prince Damrong's compilation and editing for his standard book edition, published in 1917–18.

King Rama II was born and grew up in Amphawa, a region known for *sepha* recitation. The revision by his salon focused especially on the abduction episode, the ensuing trial, and the birth of Khun Phaen's son. Some idea of the extent and nature of this revision can be gained by comparing the salon version of the abduction scene (included in the Damrong edition) with the earlier version in the second fragment. Unlike the comparison between the first and second fragments, there is no increase in length. In fact, the salon version is slightly shorter (comparing the equivalent passages) as some sub-scenes have been pruned. Again, the outline story is unchanged.[41] The salon authors regularized the meter, elevated the language, and inserted passages of outstanding verse. For example, Wanthong's exit from Khun Chang's house is simple in the second fragment, but in the salon version has become one of the most famous passages of nineteenth-century Thai poetry.

Version 1

With that, he led Wanthong away, feeling cheerful,
    and took her out through the main gate. She was crying pitifully. "Oh, I was happy here. I sat embroidering curtains for display.
    You stay here, Kaeo Kiriya. Don't be sorrowful like me. All the guardian spirits and lords of this house, I salute you and bid you farewell.

Version 2

On the terrace she stopped and turned to look back at the house with pangs of regret. She walked to the fish pond, leaned over and slid in her hand to feel
    the smooth, round, sculpted shapes of the fish as they wheeled and whirled. She glanced her eyes over the pot plants, paired in couples with pretty blooms,
    and a hollow-trunked tamarind, bent like an elbow, its seedpods parched, split, and peeling. "I say farewell, my fragrant sandalwoods. Stay and flourish, double jasmine and hiddenlover.

---

41. This is important to emphasize because it is easy to find statements that King Rama II or Sunthon Phu "wrote" these passages, or perhaps the whole of *KCKP*, in the manner of a Western author.

Oh *lamduan*, I lament having to hurry away. Milkwood, pupil tree, gem jasmine, and damascene, I'll miss the scent of your falling flowers. Dear *jampi*, till I see you, how many years?

Oh fragrant friends, your flooding scent will sadly fade and fail. Oh flowering friends, your blooms will wither, wilt, and fall." (359)

There is no clear evidence of which members of the salon worked on which episodes. Chapter 24, *The Birth of Phlai Ngam*, is generally attributed to Sunthon Phu on grounds of his very distinctive style. Prince Damrong asked one of King Rama II's sons whether the king was involved in the salon project and was told, "Yes, he composed, but not openly, and several other people helped."[42] Damrong surmised that King Rama II had worked on chapters 17–18, and the future King Rama III on chapter 19. Even though these were only surmises, and Damrong changed the attribution in his revised preface in 1925, these attributions have now acquired the status of fact. Khun Wichitmatra proposed that other parts of the revision were done by Krommuen Mahasak Phonlasep, a son of King Rama I and half-brother of King Rama II, who authored a drama based on an episode from *KCKP*.[43] The salon also seems to have tinkered with earlier parts of the romance between Khun Phaen and Wanthong, but only rewriting particular scenes and speeches.[44] The salon probably also reworked parts of the poem's climax.[45]

The revision of the Chiang Mai campaign in the First Sequel was more thoroughgoing. The timing is unknown but was probably around the mid-nineteenth century. Khru Jaeng was responsible for parts of the revision, but other contributors are not identified. Little is known about Khru Jaeng except that he was a famous performer who became an author. Several reasons probably prompted the revision. First, as Damrong noted, the old version was "clearly a vulgar version in a style unsuitable for performance in the court." Second, through waging a war against Vientiane in 1827, Bangkok had learned a lot about the Lao country, and authors of the revision were able to correct many

---

42. *Companion*, 1353.

43. KW, 267–81.

44. Prince Damrong thought King Rama II had also revised parts of chapter 4 and 13, while King Rama III had revised parts of chapter 5. Some have detected Sunthon Phu's hand in parts of chapter 3, and attribute parts of chapter 13 to King Rama III (see the video presentation in Suphanburi museum).

45. The account of judicial proceedings in chapter 34–35 must have been written by a court author with knowledge of legal procedure and access to law texts. Khun Wichitmatra suspects it was Krommuen Mahasakdi or the future King Rama III (KW, 410–13).

errors of culture and geography in the old version of *KCKP*.[46] A third reason for the revision may have been political. The older version made the King of Chiang Mai appear a buffoon. The revision restored some of his dignity. Possibly this reflected Bangkok's more subtle approach to Chiang Mai in the mid-nineteenth century (see below).

This revision entailed the rewriting of a long section—over six chapters. Although the outline story remained the same and some key passages remained untouched (e.g., the roll call of the thirty-five soldiers), many details of the plot were changed. Most significantly, the view of the campaign from the perspective of the common soldier completely disappeared, and the revised narrative focused closely on the key political and military figures.

Unlike these two earlier revisions, the project overseen by Prince Damrong in 1915–18 did not set out to revise or recompose any of the story but rather to assemble existing texts and edit them as a printed book. Yet there were still many changes. Damrong's team continued the work of regularizing the meter and elevating the language in passages which had not been touched in earlier Bangkok-era revisions. More significantly, Damrong's project was part of a larger concern at the time to create a "national literature" as part of Siam's emergence as a nation of the modern world in an era influenced by Victorian morality. Damrong was intent on overcoming "the old view that women should not read *KCKP* because it is an obscene book."[47] To this end, he deleted or toned down several sex scenes, and removed "comic passages [that] were probably improvised during recitation, but are not funny on the printed page."

Court style

Although the court writers worked from the old texts and made no significant change to the plot of the Original Story, the net result of the court revisions was a major overhaul of the balance and character of *KCKP* as a whole.

The compositions by court writers are very different in setting and style from those developed in the folk tradition. This distinction is most clearly on display in the sequels—in the revised version of the First Sequel, and in the Second and Third Sequels which were probably developed from scratch in the court tradition.

---

46. Bangkok dubbed both Vientiane/Lanchang and Chiang Mai/Lanna as "Lao" regions even though their languages and cultures were significantly different. This confusion led to mistakes in the old version of this passage of *KCKP*: Lanna people sometimes speak Lanchang Lao, wear costume more appropriate to Lanchang than Lanna, and play the *khaen* which is the emblematic instrument of the Lao, unknown in Lanna. Also, the geography of the Isan plateau is very vague in the old version. In the revision, some of these errors were corrected.

47. *Companion*, 1391.

The setting for these passages is the capital city of Ayutthaya or an army on campaign. Visits back to the provincial towns, the major setting of the folk portions of *KCKP* developed in the storyteller tradition, are rare and short. The minor characters are all officials, soldiers, and members of the court in Ayutthaya or other capitals, with almost no sign of the monks, hunters, neighbors, and other local characters in the folk passages. The events which carry the plot along are battles, royal audiences, court cases, and diplomatic negotiations rather than the festivals and family events of the folk portions. The authors delight in showing off their technical knowledge of court protocol, government practice, legal proceedings, and military affairs, not the details of festivals and lifecycle ceremonies in a provincial town. The narrative is measured and linear unlike the fast-paced storytelling and rapid succession of styles found in the folk portions.

In addition, the court authors inserted elements that conformed to the canons of "good literature" of the time. These included formal exercises in poetry, passages of didactic advice, and cross references to other literary works.

"Admiring the forest" was one of the stock exercises of court poetry. In the eighteenth and nineteenth centuries, this exercise was elaborated into *nirat*, poems built around a journey where birds, trees, and places trigger associations with a loved one left behind.[48] In such passages, the emphasis is on the aural effect not any natural realism. Names of plants and animals are strung together to enable the poet to show off skill at alliteration, rhyming, and onomatopoeia with no attention to their likely association in nature. Trees are clustered together because they rhyme, alliterate, or sound euphonious, not because they might exist in the same ecosystem. Birds perch on certain trees because of affinities between their Thai names. Whenever the characters travel in *KCKP*, there is an exercise in this genre.

Another favorite exercise of court poesy was laments, especially on death or parting. Such passages figure prominently in romantic court poetry and drama scripts of the era. The court-authored sequels of *KCKP* have many examples.

Manuals of correct behavior became a popular genre in nineteenth-century Bangkok. Sunthon Phu wrote two famous examples. Probably their popularity reflected the emergence of a new middling social stratum that wanted to learn genteel behavior in the hope of upward mobility. The sequels of *KCKP* contain several passages of didactic advice that resemble these manuals. The queen of

---

48. On the *nirat*, see Manas, "Emergence and Development." Because of the key role of wordplay in the format, translation of *nirat* is a forlorn task, but two brave attempts are *Nirat Muang Klaeng*, translated by Prince Prem, and the excerpts in *Sunthorn Phu: An Anthology*, translated by Montri Umavijani.

Chiang Mai lectures her daughter on the arts of being a wife and a royal wife. Khun Phaen receives from his mother a long and highly formal lecture on the ten principles for succeeding in royal service. Later, when he is about to set out on the Chiang Mai campaign, she gives him a lecture on military technique. In the Second Sequel, Wanthong returns as a ghost in order to instruct her son on the same subject.

The court-composed passages are also sprinkled with allusions to other literary works. The largest number of these refer to the *Ramakian, Inao*, and *Anirut*—the three "inner" works which were reserved for performance at court, and which were all composed in versions by King Rama I. Other references are to "outer" dramas made popular by the Second Reign salon: *Sangthong, Khawi, Kaki, Suwannahong, Chaiyachet*, and *Manora*. There are also many references to the Three Worlds cosmology, a key text of the Siamese royal tradition, consciously revived in the early Bangkok court.

Whereas the Original Story developed in the folk tradition is a romantic tragedy which strives hard for realism, the sequels composed in the court tradition are tales about war not love, larded with formalism and fantasy, closer to traditional heroic poetry than to the Original Story. It is easy to imagine the passages developed in the folk tradition being performed for local audiences, eliciting empathy for the characters, familiarity with the setting, tears, laughter, and great acclaim, but it is impossible to imagine the same about the passages crafted in the court. Conversely, it is possible to imagine passages developed in the court being appreciated by a court audience precisely because of their formal elegance, their range of allusions, and their political and didactic concerns, but it is impossible to imagine them entertaining a local audience.

Changes in theme and characterization

The court revisions also subtly changed the character of the principal actors, and shifted the meanings of the plot.

Through the cumulative effect of the various court revisions, the contrast between Khun Chang and Khun Phaen as rich and poor, foolish and clever, villainous and heroic was greatly diluted. Several direct references to Khun Chang's riches were deleted, and many passages showing his crassness were removed or toned down, especially a hilarious version of his wedding, and a long scene of Khun Chang getting drunk at Phra Wai's marriage. In the case of Khun Phaen, several direct references to his poverty were cut, while the addition of the sequels raised him to noble rank and the governorship of Kanburi.[49]

---

49. Chapter 15, in which Khun Phaen becomes a page, is clearly a late insertion with several inconsistencies. In particular, this chapter "forgets" that Khun Chang has been a royal page

At the same time, Khun Phaen's claims to heroic stature were diminished by making him more violent. In the old version, he kills only on the battlefield. After the revisions, he murders two defenseless peasants, butchers a wife, and attempts to kill one of his own sons. He is also much more aggressive in his relationship with Wanthong, particularly in the two key scenes of the jealous quarrel and the abduction. As a result, he becomes much more responsible for his own downfall, rather than being a victim of Khun Chang's manipulation of wealth and power.

The changing role of Wanthong, and of women in general, is even more far-reaching. In the Original Story, Wanthong and her dilemma are very much the focus of the plot. In the First Sequel, she hardly appears, and she dies before the remaining sequels. No other female character inherits her prominence. Indeed, the sequels are male-centered war stories in which women figure mostly as prizes for victory.

In surviving old versions, women are portrayed as sexually confident, even aggressive. In a folk version of the first meeting between Phlai Kaeo and Phim, she takes the lead, flirting even though he is in a novice's robe, then teasingly blocking his responses with a reminder that he is forbidden from talking to a woman on almsround.[50] At their first meeting, Simala appraises Phlai Ngam enthusiastically in her inner thoughts, concluding "If he came to lie with me for one night, I'd gobble him up." When he comes to her bed, her only resistance is a token suggestion that they wait until the servants go to sleep. In Khru Jaeng's version of the Buakhli story, she gazes at the handsome stranger with as much interest as Khun Phaen looks at her. Whenever armies march north in the Wat Ko version, women in the crowd ogle the soldiers lustily ("I'd like to jump up in his saddle for a ride").

Through the various revisions in the nineteenth century, the roles of women were rewritten to conform to a court ideal of women as secluded, passive, and innocent. Even Laothong is brought up in total seclusion, highly unlikely for a headman's daughter in a modest northern village. At their first meeting in the Damrong version, Phlai Kaeo takes the lead and Phim demurely lowers her face. At the first encounter of Phlai Ngam and Simala, we no longer hear her thoughts because she rushes shyly away into a room. Buakhli's appraisal of Khun Phaen, and the scenes of women lustily ogling soldiers, have disap-

---

since childhood. By chapter 34, the positions of the two are almost reversed, with Khun Chang complaining that the nobles are ganging up to support Khun Phaen against him.

50. "Santiwan" (Somdet Phra Ariyawongsathotayan, Pun Punsirimahathen, later Supreme Patriarch) recounted the scene in an article on Wat Palelai first printed in 1970. Probably his variant came from a local version, though he does not explain that (see Sithawatmethi, *Luang Pho To*, 29–31).

peared. In all the sexual encounters, women are portrayed as passive innocents whose shy resistance has to be overcome by violence, giving all these encounters a touch of rape.

The revisions also changed the balance of the plot, in particular by reducing the importance of the second major theme—of Khun Phaen as the ordinary man, pitted against wealth and power, and drawn by the logic of his position to resistance and revolt.

The insertion of the First Sequel interposes some twelve chapters and fifteen years between Khun Phaen's flight to the forest as an outlaw, and the denouement of Wanthong's death sentence. The connection between Khun Phaen's equipping himself with lore to defy authority, and Wanthong's sentence to a penalty for revolt, is almost totally lost by this distancing. In the king's words during the court scene, the implication of the sentence is still perfectly clear. But in the modern interpretation of *KCKP*, this second theme of the story, and particularly its significance for the ending, have gone totally without comment. All the attention has been on Wanthong's dilemma over her two husbands, none on Khun Phaen's challenge to royal authority.[51]

Folk and court

Let us sum up our argument about the development of the text.

KCKP may have roots around 1600 in a dramatic and possibly true story of the death of a very beautiful young woman. The tale became exceptionally popular because it captured two classic themes—the dilemmas of women in a male-dominated society, and the struggle of everyman against wealth and power. In response to popular demand, the storytellers lengthened the tale by adding plot detail, description, and dialogue, by recycling duplicate versions into new episodes, and by absorbing other tales, both historical and fictional. The resulting Original Story forms most of chapters 1–13, 16–22 and 35–36. Although parts of this were later overwritten, the plotline remained largely unchanged, the setting, characters and background events stayed rooted in the reality of small-town provincial society, and the narrative retained the fast-paced and kaleidoscopic style of popular entertainment.

The court adopted the story from at least the early eighteenth century, and court authors devoted considerable energies to revising the tale to suit court

---

51. In the old version, there are four points where the issue is raised whether Khun Phaen's lore is stronger than the king's power. In two of the cases, the lore is shown to be superior, and in the other two Khun Phaen explains why he chose not to use it. All four instances were either deleted or modified to become less explicit in the Damrong edition (Baker and Pasuk, "Career of *KCKP*," 35–37)

tastes over the nineteenth and early twentieth centuries. They rewrote a sequel focused on Khun Phaen's son which had originated in the folk tradition, and added two more sequels. In contrast to the Original Story, these were war stories set in and around the court, with strong affinities to traditional heroic poetry. The court writers also revised the Original Story, especially its later parts, improving the meter, elevating the language, and sprinkling the story with laments, travel poetry, didactic advice, and literary cross references. Along the way, they also changed the characterization—making Khun Chang less foolish, Khun Phaen less heroic, Wanthong more submissive—and obscured the theme of everyman against wealth and power.

The result is a highly complex work with roots in two very different traditions.

2 FROM TALE TO BOOK

In its early development, *KCKP* may have been totally an oral work. Prince Damrong believed no texts had survived from the Ayutthaya era, and suspected that was because there were few or even none,[52] though Kulap's note suggests otherwise. Sakda Bannengphet has argued that one manuscript of chapter 25 may date from Ayutthaya.[53] Damrong also surmised that initially only the major episodes were recorded. The oldest surviving manuscripts from the early Bangkok era are *samut thai*, accordion books made from a long sheet of paper folded into around thirty strips, each around 8 x 22 centimeters, written on both sides.[54] The text is written continuously, with space-breaks between each *wak* (hemistich or half line), and circular marks (*fong man*, "oil bubble") at paragraph breaks. Short synopses were often written on the cover of each volume. Almost three hundred of these volumes have been collected by the National Library.

Prince Damrong thought the whole story was assembled for the first time in the palace during the Fourth Reign (1851–1868).[55] The episodes were copied in sequence into a set of thirty-eight *samut thai* volumes. The text continued

---

52. *Companion*, 1348–49.

53. Cited in Choomsai, "Kan sueksa priapthiap," 9.

54. *Samut thai* used *sa* paper made from the bark of the *khoi* tree (*Streblus asper*). The size varies in width from 10 to 20 cms and in length from 30 to 60 cms. Most of the *KCKP* manuscripts are on black *sa* paper, made by adding soot to the soaking bark (Choomsai, "Kan sueksa priapthiap," 10–11).

55. In his first version of the preface he estimated the Third Reign, but revised this judgment in the second version (see *Companion*, 1361, 1386, note 74).

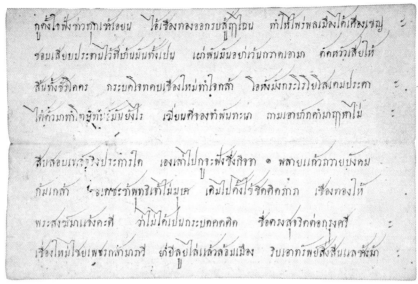

samut thai *accordion book of* KCKP

from one volume to another, and the break between volumes was arbitrary. There was no division into chapters and no titling of chapters or episodes. This collection included the old version of the Chiang Mai campaign, and went beyond Wanthong's death to include the story of Phlai Chumphon, Phaen's second son.[56] Four more volumes were later added. Some copies of this collection seem to have been made for senior members of the court, including Chuang Bunnag.[57]

The ex-missionary Samuel Smith published the first printed version of *KCKP* in 1872.[58] Smith borrowed Chuang Bunnag's text, which in turn was a copy of

56. This is the coverage of the Smith and Wat Ko editions, which were based on Chuang Bunnag's text, which in turn was copied from the palace text.

57. *Companion*, 1361, 1366. Descended from a prominent family of Persian origin, Chuang (Chaophraya Sisuriyawong) was the most powerful noble of the Fourth Reign, and architect of the succession to the Fifth.

58. Samuel Jones Smith was born in Cannanore, southern India, in 1820. After his parents died in Burma, he was adopted by John Taylor Jones and arrived in Siam in 1833. Jones set up a Baptist mission and church in Bangkok, and printed parts of the Bible translated into Thai. Smith went to the US to study at Brown and Amherst, and learn printing, returning in 1849. In 1851, Jones died and the Baptist mission and press were burned down. In 1853, Smith married Jones' widow, his own foster mother, left the mission, and established an independent printing press at Bang Ko Laem. He published religious works but also a Thai-English dictionary, the *Siam Repository*, a periodical of news and information, and newspapers, *Siam Daily Advertiser* (from 1868) and *Siam Weekly Advertiser* (from 1869). When he printed a Thai edition of *Sam*

the palace collection.[59] He published the text in installments which followed the arbitrary division into *samut thai* volumes found in the manuscripts. He retained most of the conventions from the *samut thai* including continuous text, circular markers for paragraph breaks, synopses at the start of the volume, and no chapter divisions or titles. His one innovation was to put spaces between individual words. He sold the work in ten volumes, each containing the text of four *samut thai*, and priced at one baht.[60]

According to Prince Damrong, the edition was popular, and was quickly copied by other printing houses. The press at Wat Ko[61] printed an edition in 1890, following the same layout and conventions including spaces between words, and selling it in forty-two smaller volumes each containing only one *samut thai* and priced at one salueng.[62]

---

kok (The Three Kingdoms), Bradley, who had already printed the same work, complained to Chuang Bunnag about unnecessary competition. Chuang brokered an agreement that Bradley would concentrate on prose works, and Smith on verse. Smith subsequently published versions of *Phra Aphaimani, Anirut, Inao, Singhatraiphop, Laksanawong*, and *Ramakian*, as well as *KCKP*. He also engaged in "selling presses and fonts of types to Siamese and Chinese job-printers who opened presses everywhere" (McFarland, *Historical Sketches*, 33), as well as the first manual of printing in Thai. Bradley reprimanded him for printing Buddhist works. In 1887, he was sued by some missionaries for printing frivolous works, and had closed the press by 1890. He died in Bangkok in 1908. So Phlainoi summarized, "Smith's press set the model for verse publications, and later printing houses almost all used Smith's originals." (Matichon, *Sayam phimphakan*, 22–23, 68–69; McFarland, *Historical Sketches*, 32–33; Lord, *Mo Bradley*, 45, 60, 100, 172; Phlainoi, *Samnak phim*, 17–20, 31)

59. In his first version of the preface, Damrong wrote that Chuang's text was "thought to be" the text that Smith used, but in the revised preface he states this as a fact (*Companion*, 1361, 1389).

60. We have not found a copy of Smith in any library, or seen an original. We were kindly given a partial photocopy consisting of chs. 2, 17–42. This has only one cover page, reproduced on p. 905, which reads: Khun Chang Khun Phaen / volumes 21 to 24 / the *sepha* / priced at one baht per volume / printed for the first time / in Bangkok / at the press of Khru Smith / at Bang Ko Laem, year of the chicken fifth of the decade / Julasakkarat 1235. Each volume is around 66 pages measuring 120 x 175mm.

61. Wat Ko is the familiar name for Wat Samphanthawong in Sampheng. The area opposite the wat's gate was one of the first markets for books in Bangkok. Ratcharoen Printers, commonly known as Wat Ko Printers, was founded in 1889 when Nai Sin Somunsap, who had earlier been an agent for selling Smith's publication through his glassware shop, installed a manual printing press in a shophouse on Wanit 1 Road opposite the wat. The press was probably founded soon after Smith's press closed (see note 58 above), and took the opportunity to take over some of Smith's successful titles. The press became famous for its cheap editions of classics and popular works. (Matichon, *Sayam phimphakan*, 24–28; Phlainoi, *Samnak phim*, 32–35)

62. There is a complete copy of the Wat Ko text in the William Gedney collection in the Michigan University Library. The title pages (example reproduced on p. 906) have the title, volume number, the place and date of publication as "Wat Ko, Rattanakosin So Ko 108," and the price of 25 satang contained in a paean to the benefits of reading. One volume (number

title page from the Smith edition   *title page from the Wat Ko edition*

After Prince Damrong resigned from government service in 1915 and devoted himself to literary works, one of his first projects was to produce a definitive edition of *KCKP*. He used four sets of *samut thai* in the Wachirayan Library:[63]

31) in the Gedney-Michigan set comes from a different printing. Its cover reads: Fourth printing, 1,000 volumes, Panit Suphaphon [พานิช ศุภผล] Press, 205 Sampheng Road, Bangkok, BE 2460 [1917]. There are some individual volumes of the Wat Ko edition (or copies) in the Prince Damrong Library and the Rare Books Room of Chulalongkorn University Library, but they have lost their cover pages with all the publication information, and are not properly identified in the catalogs.

The Smith and Wat Ko texts are not exactly the same but have clearly come from a common original. The wording is almost exactly the same, except for some typical copyist's errors and omissions. The division between *samut thai* volumes differs between the two sets, and the spelling is often widely different. This suggests that an original manuscript (perhaps the palace text) was copied into two different sets by copyists with different handwriting size, different views on spelling, and different susceptibility to error. These two sets were then the basis of the Smith and Wat Ko publications respectively.

63. The Wachirayan Library, named after King Mongkut's monastic name, was founded by several senior princes as a membership library inside the Bangkok palace in the early 1880s. After King Chulalongkorn had visited the British Museum and other national libraries on his European visit in 1897, the Wachirayan Library was amalgamated with other libraries as the Wachirayan Library for the Capital, often shortened to the Capital Library, and moved in 1916 to a building on Na Prathat Road (now part of Silpakorn University). In 1933, the library was transformed into the National Library under the control of the new Fine Arts Department, and in 1962 moved to its current location in Thewet.

1. a set that came from the palace, written in the orthography of the Third Reign; 2. a set from Somdet Chaophraya Borommaha Phichaiyat [That Bunnag], written in the Fourth Reign; 3. a royal collection from the Fifth Reign, written in 1869; 4. a set belonging to Somdet Chaophraya Borommaha Sisuriyawong [Chuang Bunnag] written in the Fifth Reign in 1869, thought to be the version that Dr Smith printed.[64]

He replaced the long passage on the Chiang Mai campaign with the version revised by Khru Jaeng and others (discussed above), and also adopted three shorter passages by Khru Jaeng.[65] His edition has around 21,000 lines.

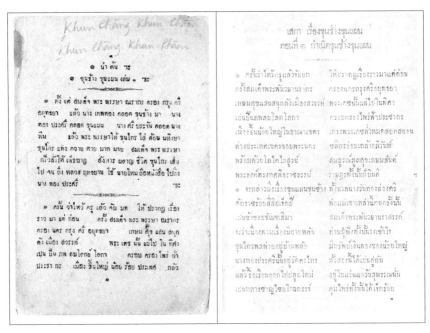

first pages of Wat Ko and Damrong editions

Prince Damrong's edition of 1917–18 is a book rather than a replication of the *samut thai* text. He divided the narrative into chapters on the basis of the story, and invented chapter headings. He dispensed with the opening synopses (but retained them in his table of contents). In place of the continuous text of

---

64. *Companion*, 1361.

65. These passages are: forging the Skystorm sword; Buakhli and the Goldchild: and Crocodile Khwat. For Skystorm and Khwat, Khru Jaeng's versions were revisions of older versions of the story, while the Buakhli story was a new import into the *sepha*.

the manuscripts, he arrayed the text in a two-column format used for drama scripts and other forms of poetry. He retained the paragraph divisions from the original.[66]

The conversion from oral transmission to printed book was also a transition from a tradition of change through improvisation to a static form. Prince Damrong created a canonical version, a definitive text. His second edition (1925) has been constantly reprinted without any modification, not even correction of the (very few) obvious errors. There has been no attempt to produce an alternative selection from the many texts available. All of the many subsequent commentaries, prècis versions, and prose renderings are based on his publication.

Only a handful of fragments from alternative texts have been published. The two fragments of the abduction scene known as *Samnuan kao* were printed by the Fine Arts Department in 1925 using texts from the Wachirayan Library, and republished in 1990 and 1998, copying the 1925 printed text.[67]

Khru Jaeng's contributions to *KCKP* were printed around 1890 by Bangkok Prasit Press. This is known from an advertisement on the cover of another publication by the same press.[68] By 1935, according to the Fine Arts Department, the book was already "hard to find."[69] Kukrit Pramoj had lost his copy before he wrote his articles on *KCKP* in the 1980s.[70] Khun Wichitmatra had the book but his library was destroyed by fire. We have been unable to locate a copy. The National Library has five chapters by Khru Jaeng in typescript.

title page from Prince Damrong's first edition

---

66. Prince Damrong's detailed account of this publication is translated in *Companion*, 1361–70, 1390–92. The first edition was printed by Phim Thai Press, and a second edition was produced in 1925. The government textbook publisher, Khurusapha, continues to print this three-volume edition. Subsequently a one-volume version was printed by Bannakhan Press, and a two-volume version by Sinlapa Bannakhan Press. The content of these three editions is the same. All three have gone through many reprints and are intermittently still available.

67. *KCKP chabap khwam kao* (1925); Atsiri et al., *KCKP chabap nok thamniap* (1990); Chotchuang and Niranam, *KCKP chabap yon tamnan* (1998). Choomsai suspects the original manuscripts of these fragments have since disappeared ("Kan sueksa priapthiap," 12).

68. Matichon, *Sayam phimphakan*, 35–36. This press was probably owned by the Bunnag family.

69. KJ, preface.

70. KP, 92–95.

The Fine Arts Department printed one of these (*The marriage of Phra Wai*) in 1935, and Sujit Wongthet printed another (*Khun Phaen forges a sword, buys a horse, finds a spirit son*) in 2002.[71]

Life after book

Damrong noted that the tradition of improvising the *sepha* diminished as soon as written manuscripts were available, and diminished even further after the appearance of Smith's printed edition. *KCKP* continued to be developed in other genres with more opportunity for variation. Excerpts were performed in the stylized drama known as *li-ke,* including a different and possibly older version of the segment from the jealous quarrel to the abduction.[72] In recent times, all or parts of *KCKP* have been adapted into films, novels, television series, cartoons, and manga, with some authors and directors adding their own improvisations for contemporary relevance.[73] The great popular novelist, Po Intharapalit, penned a version of the whole *KCKP* story in 1972 with several adjustments to the plot.[74] A television series on Channel 7 in the 1970s added another sequel to the tale with five hundred episodes on the exploits of Khun Phaen as governor of Kanburi. A handful of feminist novels and films have countered the "victimization" of Wanthong by explicitly mak-ing her the focus.[75] A 2002 film, *Khun Phaen,* directed by Thanit Jitnukun, portrayed Wanthong welcoming her own death as a form of penance.

KCKP also retains a large presence in everyday popular culture. Most schoolchildren learn to recite short passages by heart. The name "Khun Phaen" has the same usage and resonance as Romeo or Casanova, as well as being slang for a chopper motorcycle. Many popular amulets are given his name. The poem is the source of several proverbs, including

Khun Phaen amulet

---

71. "For eighty-four years, ordinary people had not read this, and could not read it, because the government officials in charge refused permission for anyone to read it by writing a notice 'Closed [ห้ามบริการ, no service]' on the *samut thai* and not allowing printing. Luckily the People's Constitution of 1997 makes it possible to read Khru Jaeng's original" (Sujit, *KCKP*, 166). The other three chapters in typescript in the National Library are: the Chiang Mai campaign, Phra Wai affected by a love charm, and Crocodile Khwat (see KJ, preface). However the Chiang Mai chapter is almost certainly not Khru Jaeng's version, but an earlier version, different from WK too.

72. Sukanya, "'Khun Chang plaeng san.'"

73. Narongsak, "Rueang *KCKP* nai rup baep tangtang" has a wide-ranging catalog of the renderings of *KCKP* into different forms and media.

74. Discussed in Narongsak, "Kan sueksa priapthiap."

75. See especially Jan Sijarun Anderson, *Nang phim* (2001), which sets the story in the present day.

"No pursuit surpasses the pursuit of knowledge," "You die from no food, you don't die from no lovemaking," and several everyday similes such as being as two-minded as Wanthong. Many extracts have been converted to songs. In Suphanburi and Phichit, streets and wards are named after characters, as are several wat in the Chaophraya Plain. At certain locations featured in the poem, there are shrines to the characters including Simala in old Phichit, Buakhli at Ban Tham, and Khun Phaen and his father at Cockfight Hill.

3 GENRE, POETRY, PERFORMANCE

Sepha

The poem is usually called *Sepha Khun Chang Khun Phaen*, as if *sepha* (เสภา) was a genre like an ode or ballad. Yet nobody is sure what the word means or where it came from. Key to decoding the term is a realization that its meaning may have changed over time.

There is a musical form of the same name but it has no connection to the poem.[76] Kukrit argued that *sepha* was a genre developed in prison on grounds that the old titles of some prison officials contained the word *sepha*, and that prison figures strongly in *KCKP*, but his argument has garnered little support.[77] The most convincing derivation links the word to *sewa*, an Indian, Sanskrit-derived word meaning service, including religious rituals. As such it would be one of many religious, literary, and political terms resulting from the court's employment of Brahmans from India. Separated from their cultural context, such loan words can easily drift in meaning.

Perhaps because of the role of chanting in religious rites, *sepha* came to be associated with recitation. The phrase "*sepha* and music," which appears in an old timetable of the king's activities (see above, pp. 892–93), might then indicate a time for entertainment, either music or recitation. In late Ayutthaya, *sepha* came to mean verse recitation, and particularly recitation of episodes of the *KCKP* story since they so dominated this popular genre. No other tale has survived from the Ayutthaya era with a title as *sepha*, and perhaps *sepha* in late Ayutthaya simply meant the various episodes of *KCKP*. In the nineteenth century, three other works were composed as *sepha* on royal command but failed to win popularity and were largely lost.[78]

Over the nineteenth century, the court performance of *sepha* underwent

---

76. *Companion*, 1341.
77. See KP, 10–12.
78. *Companion*, 1371–72.

many changes. Initially music was introduced as a supplement to recitation, but subsequently music became the focus of the performance while the text was shortened and demoted in importance. As a result, today one of the major meanings of the term *sepha* is a recitation which introduces and explains a musical performance.

Klon

KCKP is written throughout in a verse form called *klon* (กลอน), with the rhyming scheme sustained from start to finish, even bridging chapter boundaries. The *klon* meter is not mentioned in *Chindamani*, a manual of prosody usually dated to the Narai reign, indicating that it was unknown at the time or not adopted by the court. *Klon* became widely used in the eighteenth and nineteenth centuries.

The Thai language lends itself well to rhyme and alliteration. The language is tonal and largely monosyllabic. The grammar is simple with no conjugation or declension. Shades of meaning are created through syntax, by the addition and ordering of words. The language has absorbed a large number of words from other tongues. Many everyday words have been imported from the neighboring languages of Khmer, Mon, and Malay, while specialist terms have been adapted from Persian, Arabic, Chinese, and Western languages, and much of the elevated language of religion, philosophy, poetry, and politics from Pali and Sanskrit. As a result, Thai has many synonyms. Poets can "paint" with words drawing on a very rich palette with little hindrance from grammatical constraints. Rhyming and alliteration are relatively easy, and are constantly used in the expressiveness of everyday speech.[79]

Traditional court poetry favored verse forms adapted from Indian and Chinese originals.[80] These forms impose constraints on the number of syllables in a line, position of rhymes, and tone values of certain syllables within a line—forcing the court poets to display ingenuity and economy of expression.

In popular culture, there were many styles of singing or chanting, known collectively as *phleng*. They included lullabies, boating songs, harvest songs, courting songs, and humorous repartee. Many involved pairs or groups of players, singing back and forth, and improvising the words within rules of rhyme and length. These rules were not too strict or demanding in order to give scope for improvisation.[81]

---

79. Gedney suggested that *klon* became so popular because its use of rhyme and alliteration was "close to the structure of ordinary Siamese speech" ("Siamese Verse Forms," 53).

80. Hudak, *Indigenization*, ch. 1.

81. Bidyalankarana, "The Pastime."

Klon seems to have emerged as a rap-prochement between the folk tradition of chanting and the court tradition of poetry. The basic rhyming rules for *klon* are the same as those for the final verse in boating and har-vesting songs, and in certain lullabies.[82] The *sepha* seems to have developed through sto-

diagram of klon *meter*

rytellers adopting this rhythm found in *phleng* singing to recite a folktale.

This particular snatch of *phleng* meter was probably adopted for narrative recitation because it has great forward momentum. The basic unit is a *wak* (hemistich, half line) of around seven to nine syllables. This is made up of three phrases, two of which are usually linked by a rhyming syllable or alliteration, creating an underlying rhythm. Two *wak* form a line, with a rhyme linking the last syllable of the first with a mid syllable of the second (anywhere between the first and fifth syllable). Two lines form a stanza with a rhyme that has not two points but four. It starts on the final syllable of the previous stanza, falls next on the end of the first line of the stanza, then picks up the two rhymes in the second line of the stanza—on the end of the first hemistich, and finally midway through the last hemistich. The rhyme is like a bouncing ball, with the gap shortening between successive bounces. The last syllable of the stanza, instead of concluding the main rhyme sequence and thus requiring a stop and restart in the following stanza, is "thrown" to become the anchor rhyme for the next stanza, creating a chain of interlinked rhymes.

In the original form used for *sepha*, the *klon* seems to have had no more constraints than these. The only passage of printed versions of *KCKP* remaining in this form is chapter 1 in the Wat Ko edition. The number of syllables per hemistich varies between six and eleven, with no constraints on the tonal values of certain syllables, and great variation in the position of the mid-hemistich rhyming points. The reciters do not seem to have placed great store on adding extra rhymes and alliterations. In short, they gave themselves a lot of space to tell a story.

Because of its flexibility and rhythmic appeal, *klon* was soon used for many different forms of writing including stage dramas, *nirat* poetry, and manuals such as the *Manual on Victorious Warfare*. At some point in the last decades of the Ayutthaya era, the rules for *klon* were formalized in a treatise, *Siriwibunkiti.*

The court adopted *klon* but also changed it by applying the court litterateurs' liking for rules and standardization. By the early Bangkok era, a form known as

---

82. Nidhi, *Pen and Sail*, 26–29.

klon suphap, genteel verse, had become the most favored. It requires a regular number of syllables per hemistich between six and nine, with eight the most favored (*klon paet*). The rhyming scheme allows fewer choices for the mid-hemistich points. Words at certain positions in the stanza must have certain tones.[83] This form was favored for stage dramas and for poetry designed to be read rather than performed.

In the revisions of *KCKP* in the nineteenth century, the poetry was refined in line with court taste, but *klon sepha* was allowed more flexibility than *klon suphap*. Lines vary within a range of seven to nine syllables. Tonal requirements are lax. Poets were free to add extra rhymes or other aural associations such as alliteration. Sunthon Phu is famous for his facility in adding extra rhymes and alliterative touches, often of great complexity.

Khap

The term for performing *sepha* is *khap* (ขับ), usually translated as "recite." This term covers many varieties of chanting or singing without musical accompaniment.

The earliest description of *khap sepha* is found at the tonsure ceremony of Phlai Ngam in *KCKP*. The different performers are shown to have very different styles, often drawing on other types of music or chanting. One uses *oei cha*, a phrase used to mark a pause in *phleng* singing. Another imitates *kroei choet*, rousing music once used for marching and now the prelude to boxing contests. Another is proficient in the use of the claves for percussion. The *sepha* performance recorded by Simmonds in 1950 was similarly varied. One segment was sung to a traditional tune, another was chanted in a form in which the tone value of the syllable dictated the pitch and length of its vocalization, and another segment resembled *phleng* singing with a distinct pause after the initiation of a rhyming sequence, presumably to allow the performer to improvise the rest of the sequence.[84]

These two examples show that folk performance of *sepha* allowed great latitude to the player to entertain the audience through variety and to bring out the different textures of the tale.

Again adoption by the court brought greater standardization. By the early nineteenth century, there was a recognizable court style of *khap* recitation

---

83. The last syllable of the first hemistich can be any tone, with the mid tone least preferred; the last syllable of the second hemistich can be any tone except mid, with rising preferred; the last syllable of the third hemistich can be any tone except that of the prior hemistich, with mid preferred; the last syllable of the fourth hemistich can be any tone except rising, with mid preferred (Hudak, *Indigenization*, 14–15; Gedney, "Siamese Verse Forms," 531–32).

84. Simmonds, "Thai Narrative Poetry."

which did not draw on other styles and tunes, or allow the pitch and length to be dictated by the words, but which concentrated heavily on bringing out the rhyming structure. Performers were admired for showing off their vocal powers by drawing out the lines with scales of ululation.

The court gradually de-emphasized the storytelling in *KCKP* as against the quality of its poetry and the experience of its performance. As already noted, music came to overshadow recitation. Damrong confessed that his publication had "the aim of preserving poetic works that are good examples of Thai language, rather than trying to preserve the story of *KCKP*."[85] An extreme form of court recitation was developed, known as the "beggar style," in which each line is drawn out into a minute or more of ululation, losing the meaning behind the sound.

4 PHYSICAL SETTING

The composition of *KCKP* stretched across several centuries. The versions that have come down to us have all undergone some revision in the nineteenth century, and as a result some have argued that the poem should be set in the context of that period.[86] Yet the genesis of the tale and the development of the Original Story—as well as the explicit setting of the poem itself—are all in the late Ayutthaya era. Hence the background ranges across the period from mid Ayutthaya to the mid-nineteenth century.

KCKP is set in the floodplain formed by the Chaophraya River. Four tributaries which rise in what is now northern Thailand, flow south to unite at Paknam Pho (Nakhon Sawan), then split again into several branches meandering south to empty into the Gulf of Siam. Over centuries, these rivers have created a flat plain sloping gently to the south, interrupted by only a few rocky outcrops. To east, north, and west this plain is bounded by hill ranges which define the area as a geographical, social, and political unit. In the time of *KCKP*, this plain was virtually identical with the political unit known as Siam.

Today the Chaophraya Plain is a lattice of paddy fields. At the time of *KCKP*, most was covered by forest. European visitors in the seventeenth century all commented on the wildness. Schouten found much of the country "mountainous, woody and moorish."[87] Gervaise noted that "The forests of this kingdom are so enormous that they cover over half of its area and so dense that it is

---

85. *Companion*, 1362.
86. For example, Woranan, "Kan sueksa sangkhom."
87. Schouten, *True Description*, 95.

almost impossible to cross them."[88] La Loubère found the territory "almost wholly incultivated and cover'd with woods."[89]

The forest figures prominently in the geographical and mental landscape of the poem. In the many journeys described, characters leave the towns and plunge straight into a forest thick with trees and teeming with animals—monkey, langur, gibbon, treeshrew, wild dog, buffalo, gaur, deer, boar, elephant, crocodile, and the occasional tiger. In all the poem mentions around sixty species of bird, fifty land animals, thirty aquatic species, twenty-five insects, and three hundred varieties of plant. This forest is both beautiful and fearful. Among the fathers of the three leading figures, one is executed in the forest, another is felled by a forest fever, and another murdered by a band of forest robbers.

The population of the Chaophraya Plain was sparse—probably less than half a million people, about a fortieth of the number today. People were not spread evenly across the landscape, but concentrated in the major towns and along the rivers. Gervaise noted that the banks of the Chaophraya "are densely populated and permanently covered with the most beautiful greenery in the world."[90] Outside Ayutthaya, Choisy saw "broad landscapes of rice."[91] Traveling from Ayutthaya to Lopburi, Tachard saw "vast plains reaching out of sight covered with rice."[92] But away from the rivers, as Gervaise also noted, "there are fearful deserts and vast wildernesses where one only finds wretched little huts, often as much as 7 or 8 leagues distant from one another."[93] In the 110 kilometers between Suphan and Kanburi traversed several times in the poem, only three villages are mentioned. When Wanthong instructs her son on this route, the landmarks are ponds, streams, and hills, not settlements.

Beyond the plain lie the hills that separate Siam from its neighbors. Whenever the scene of KCKP moves into this liminal region, the text emphasizes the physical, social, and political difference. The landscape becomes striking, marked by rocky hills and crags, towering dipterocarp forest, and splashing streams with beds of brightly colored rock—all a contrast to the unremitting flatness of the plain and its sluggish, muddy rivers. The forests, hills, upland villages, and their cultivation are described in detail because they offer a contrast to the plain's landscape of paddy fields, so familiar that it is not once described in the poem. The peoples of the hills are given ethnic descriptors which mark them as different. Some are Lawa, a catch-all term

---

88. Gervaise, *Natural and Political History*, 23.

89. La Loubère, *New Historical Relation*, 11.

90. Gervaise, *Natural and Political History*, 12

91. Choisy, *Journal*, 172.

92. Tachard, *Voyage to Siam*, 193.

93. Gervaise, *Natural and Political History*, 45.

for people of Mon-Khmer origin, possibly descendants of the oldest settlers in the region. Others are Karen who had migrated southward along the hills ranges since the sixteenth century. At Ban Tham in the Buakhli episode, the area is not only physically separate but also politically separate—a lair ruled by a bandit chief who offers refuge for people fleeing the social controls of plains society.

The difference of the hills helps to define what is the physical character of the plains, the society of the Thai, the polity of Siam.[94]

Suphanburi and Kanburi

Most of the population of old Siam lived off agriculture, and yet many of them resided in and around towns. The classical pattern of settlement in the Tai world was a *mueang*, a political and trading center surrounded by a penumbra of cultivating villages. The Original Story mostly takes place in two of these.

Suphanburi was one of the major towns of the Chaophraya Plain outside the capital. It is located on the westerly-most branch of the Chaophraya delta system. The tract along this river was an important area of settlement and trade going back to the early Common Era. Suphanburi rose to prominence in the twelfth century CE when the city of U Thong, 27 kilometers to the southwest, went into decline, probably because of a shift in the river course. The rectangular wall and moat of the main settlement measured 900 by 3500 meters. A subsidiary moated area to the east, probably a later expansion, was almost as large again. Suphanburi was prominent in the politics surrounding the founding of the Ayutthaya kingdom in the fourteenth century. At the death of the king-founder of Ayutthaya in 1369, a Suphanburi lord took over the throne, and his family remained part of Ayutthaya court politics until the end of the fifteenth century.[95]

With the rise of the Phitsanulok dynasty in the sixteenth century, Suphanburi's political role declined, but the town remained prominent in other ways. Wat Palelai may be one of the oldest Buddhist centers of worship in the Chaophraya Plain. Enthusiasts trace its history back to the seventh or eighth century (the Dvaravati era), though the documentation is shaky.[96] The massive 23-meter Buddha image known as Luang Pho To, which originally stood in the open air, was one of the largest images in the region. Suphanburi was studded with other

---

94. See Suvanna, "Characters in Thai Literary Works." For a brilliant exposition of the role of the forest in *KCKP*, see Atherton, "Space, Identity, and Self-Definition."

95. Charnvit, *Rise of Ayudhya*, 106–114.

96. Sithawatmethi, *Prawat Wat Palelai*; Sithawatmethi, *Luang Pho To*; Manat, *Prawatisat mueang Suphan*.

wat almost as densely as the capital city of Ayutthaya. Though most have now completely disappeared, remembered only by name, several substantial ruins remain. A Persian visitor who passed through the town in 1685 described the area as "extremely fertile and beautiful."[97]

The wealth and prominence of Suphanburi probably depended greatly on the elephant. These animals were a main vehicle for land transport, and important to kings for military use and public display in processions. By the fifteenth century, elephants with special characteristics—including the color tone of the hide, length and shape of tusks, texture of tail hair, and shape of genitals— were considered auspicious for kings and kingdoms. Kings of this era devoted time to elephant hunts,[98] and the laws demanded that anyone chancing upon an albino "white" elephant had to render it to the monarch. The first mention of the Ayutthaya king acquiring a white elephant appears in the chronicles in 1471/72.[99] King Chakkaphat (r. 1548–1569) acquired seven.

A few kilometers to the west of Suphanburi, the flat plain ends and the foothills rise. The deep forests here were the nearest to the capital of Ayutthaya. The area was known as *Pa ton*, the primary or royal forest, similar to the royal demesne forests of Europe, areas reserved for hunting by the king. There are remains of old elephant enclosures in the forest some thirty-five kilometers southwest of Suphanburi.[100] At least two of the white elephants acquired by King Chakkaphat were found in the forest stretching from here into Kanchanaburi.[101]

In 1595, Jacques de Coutre, an adventurer from Bruges, accompanied King Naresuan on an elephant hunt. They stayed at "Sapampur," Coutre's attempt to render Suphanburi. He described the town as follows.

> We arrived in the city of Sapampur, which was very large and in ruins. In that city the king kept more than three thousand elephants in a half mile long street. The elephants were in large equerries on each side of the street, as if they were horses. Between each elephant a log was buried in the ground where they rubbed themselves. The place was only inhabited by mahouts who took

---

97. O'Kane, *Ship of Sulaiman*, 49–50. The "rajah" of Suphanburi at the time was Chelebi from Rum in Anatolia.

98. Gervaise reckoned King Narai hunted at least three hundred elephants a year, and employed thirty thousand men on the expeditions (*Natural and Political History*, 177).

99. RCA, 17.

100. In the Phu Muang National Park.

101. The place names are difficult to identify. One was found at Kanchanaburi; another at Saento, which may be 10 kms to the east of Kanchanaburi; and another at Wat Kai, which might be Wat Chon Kai, Cockfight Hill (RCA, 30–31).

care of the elephants. These men, whom they called *cornecas*,[102] slept in high places, surrounded by thorn because of the tigers. These were in such numbers that we slept safely in our boats. The king took lodging in a mosque or pagoda [probably a wat], with his guard around it. The temple was fenced in with scarlet cloth. At night they made big fires to defend themselves against tigers and mosquitoes.[103]

As this was only a couple of years after a Burmese invasion, the description of the town as "in ruins" and inhabited only by elephants and their keepers rings true, though Coutre's estimate of "three thousand" elephants is certainly a massive exaggeration. Suphanburi was an elephant town.

The forests and elephants help us to understand the wealth and prominence of Khun Chang. His father was "an officer in the provincial division of the Department of Elephants" (2), organizing royal elephant hunts and overseeing royal elephants kept in the area. The name "Khun Chang" was probably a nickname, meaning "Mr. Elephant" or "the elephant man," which was passed on to his son. Such high officials were also in a position to trade. The forests were the source of many materials valued by the court and sold in overseas trade including timbers, lacquer, aromatics, medicines, hides, horn, and bone. Khun Chang dealt with "Karen and Lawa who came to sell eaglewood from the great forest" (373). He also owned paddy lands, had chests stuffed with wealth, and engaged in money-lending. The family's wealth and status were sufficient for the father to present his son at court in the hope he would be adopted as a page—a position which gave direct access to the king and other contacts in the court circle. With his combination of official status, trading wealth, and political connections, Khun Chang was possibly not just a rich man of Suphanburi, but one of its most prominent citizens.

Kanburi was a key frontier outpost. The passage westward up the Khwae (Kwai) River and over the Three Pagodas Pass has long been a trade route, attested by archaeological finds ranging from Roman lamps to Dongson drums. Old Kanburi was sited at the point where the hills and gorges along the Khwae Yai River (the northern of two branches) give way to the plain. The junction of Taphuem Creek with the Khwae Yai created a natural moat to north and west (see map 7). The remains of the town, abandoned since the late eighteenth century, suggest it was a modest place. The fortification was simple

---

102. This term appears as *cornaque* in Gervaise, and John Villers hazarded it derived from Singhalese, *kurawa-nayaka*, meaning "chief of the elephant stud" (Gervaise, *Natural and Political History*, 207).

103. Coutre, *Andanzas asiáticas*, 126.

(see p. 859). The five remaining wat were relatively modest in size,[104] built of brick and stucco with small amounts of stone, and "very local in style."[105] The artifacts retrieved by excavation include votive tablets in metal and earthenware, roof tiles and finials, burial pots, and construction nails—nothing sophisticated and valuable, though partly that may be a result of looting. The ordination hall of one wat and the preaching hall of another show signs of being extensively rebuilt in late Ayuttaya, possibly after damage in war.[106] While Suphanburi was a sizable commercial and political center, Kanburi was a simple frontier garrison.

From the mid-sixteenth century, Suphanburi and Kanburi became of great strategic importance for Ayutthaya. In 1548–49, a Burmese army from Pegu crossed over the Tenasserim range at the Three Pagodas Pass, marched down the Khwae Yai River past Kanburi, captured Suphanburi, and invested Ayutthaya.[107] Although there were several other passes across the Tenasserim Range, this route was especially sensitive because it was the shortest. A Burmese army could march from the Three Pagodas watershed to Ayutthaya in fifteen days. Kanburi became an outpost for collection of intelligence, and Suphanburi a center for assembling armies. When a Burmese army crossed the Three Pagodas Pass in 1584, a blocking army was sent from Ayutthaya to Suphanburi by boat. Between 1590 and 1594, three Burmese armies crossed the pass, Suphanburi served as a staging center for the Siamese defense, and much of the fighting took place around Suphanburi, including possibly the famous elephant duel of 1593. In 1663–64, a Burmese army again invaded through the pass, and a Siamese army counterattacked along the same route in the following year. In the sack of Ayutthaya of 1765–67, one of the Burmese armies crossed via the pass, and most of the withdrawal seems to have taken this route. Between 1548 and 1786, Burmese armies invaded through the Three Pagodas Pass eleven times in all, and Siamese armies attacked in the opposite direction four times.

These attacks made Suphanburi and Kanburi both important and vulnerable. After the 1548 raid, the Ayutthaya king decided to raze the walls of

---

104. Wat Palelai, with an outer wall of 25 x 70 meters, and Wat Khun Phaen, with an outer wall of 32 x 90 meters, are larger and more complex. The two sites of Wat Mae Mai (really two wat) are smaller and simpler. Wat Nang Phim was originally only the ordination hall and stupa in the southeast corner of present-day Wat Kanchanaburi Kao, near the river. Wat Mon, on the north bank of Taphuem Creek, may have been only a small stupa and has now completely disappeared except for a few brick fragments.

105. Sathaphon, *Mueang Kanchanaburi kao*, 56.

106. The two are Wat Khun Phaen and Wat Mae Mai (Sathaphon, *Mueang Kanchanaburi kao*, 50–51, 56–72).

107. RCA, 27–28, 32.

Suphanburi (and other towns) to prevent the city serving as a base for an invading Burmese army. In the 1593 clash, Burmese scouts fell on Suphan, "killing people in great numbers and seizing food supplies."[108] In the fighting that sputtered on for forty years after the 1767 fall of Ayutthaya, this area suffered badly. In 1774, an invading Burmese army "split into parties capturing people and families in every village in Kanburi, Ratburi, Nakhon Chaisi, and Suphanburi."[109] During the massive Burmese attack of 1785, one of the major battles was fought at Latya, beside Kanburi, and the town was in the path of a long artillery battle between the two camps. The clash in 1786 was a little beyond, at Saiyok.[110]

Old Kanburi was abandoned in this era, fell into ruins, and was never reoccupied on the same site. After 1767, Burmese armies chose to attack along the Khwae Noi River to the south rather than along the Khwae Yai. As a result, the strategic point for defense shifted to Pak Phraek, eighteen kilometers southeast of the old Kanburi site, where the two Khwae branches meet. The army camp there expanded into a town which was eventually renamed as the new site of Kanchanaburi and fortified with a city wall in 1831, when the town was reported to have eight hundred houses.[111]

Suphanburi was also abandoned and its many temples ruined by attack or neglect. In the lists of major towns (*hua mueang*) during the Bangkok first and second reigns, Suphanburi does not appear, suggesting it had not yet been reoccupied.[112] When the poet Sunthon Phu visited in 1836, he encountered a tiger close by, found the place still "ruined," and lamented over the decay of its old monuments.[113] Yet in his description, the town had a governor and local officials, as well as a distillery, and boats moored along the riverbank. When Nai Mi, a poet and tax collector, visited in 1844, he found the town "looking ruined, ragged, pitiful, like some country in the forest, with plant life pressing in everywhere, trees big and small of every description." But he noted "there are many rich people and many poor," and he managed to collect taxes from several.

Most of the people seen by the early travelers in this area were not Thai.

108. KCK, 87.

109. *Phraratcha phongsawadan krung Thonburi*, 80.

110. Flood and Flood, *Dynastic Chronicles*, 1:52, 126–27; Phasakon, *Prawatisat songkhram kao thap*, 32–36.

111. Sathaphon, *Mueang Kanchanaburi kao*, 42–43, 109–113.

112. Julathat, "Botrian," 6.

113. *Chiwit lae ngan khong Sunthon Phu*, 183–86, especially stanza 139: "I pity the wat and houses, ruined and scattered /with only the sound of birds, morn and eve." See also Waruni, "Nirat mueang Suphan." In 1840, Slafter reckoned Suphanburi's population was around 10,000 but this may have been an exaggeration (Terwiel, *Through Travelers' Eyes*, 100, 112).

Many were Chinese settlers who had arrived up the Suphan and Maeklong rivers. Some were Mon who had fled from southern Burma. Others were Lao and Khmer war prisoners that the Bangkok government had imported to revitalize this strategically important region.

Ayutthaya

According to its chronicle, Ayutthaya was founded in the mid-fourteenth century. When Europeans visited the city over two centuries later, they described it as one of the greatest ports and most distinctive cities of Asia. Ayutthaya's rise was based on a good defensive position, access by river to a rich interior, and integration into maritime trade.

The city was located in the center of the Chaophraya delta on a slight rise above the surrounding swamps. With a little engineering of the rivers, the site was turned into a moated island, and further defended by walls. Each year for three to four months in the monsoon rains, the surrounding countryside was flooded under several feet of water, forming another line of defense. Until 1767, the city was taken only once, and then partly because of internal dissension. The rivers also gave the city its distinctive water-borne character. Much of the population lived in rafts and houseboats. Houses on land were elevated on stilts. Boats were the main form of transportation around the city and into the hinterland. As Choisy recorded in the 1680s, "One goes through limitless watery passages under green trees, to the sound of 1,000 birds, between two rows of wooden houses on piles, very uncouth externally, very clean within."[114]

The waterways were key to the city's growing wealth. Its early prosperity was based on trade in exotic goods found in the forests and hills of the interior, brought to the markets of the city by river and canal, and sold to markets in China and Japan. In the 1590s, Ayutthaya gained firm control over a portage route across the neck of the Thai peninsula from the Gulf of Thailand to the Mon port of Marit/Mergui. This route provided a shorter and less dangerous alternative to the pirate-infested Malacca straits for linking east and west. At a time when the Moghul, Ottoman, and Abbasid empires flourished to the west, and the Ching and Shogunate to the east, Ayutthaya acted as an entrepot for the exchange of goods between them. Siam also began to export rice, timber, and ships. In the seventeenth century, the city became large, rich, and cosmopolitan. Early European maps show the Ayutthaya island surrounded by settlements of Chinese, Vietnamese, Malays, Indians, Japanese, Dutch, and Portuguese. Colloquially, it was host to "forty different nations."[115] European

---

114. Choisy, *Journal*, 169.
115. La Loubère, *New Historical Relation*, 10–11.

visitors estimated the population at two hundred thousand or more, and per-haps "as big as London."[116]

With its wealth and population, Ayutthaya became a great market, drawing in goods and services from a broad hinterland. The central area was "full of shops of Tradesmen, Artificers, and Handicraftmen,"[117] and "The throng of people there is so great that it is sometimes very difficult to make one's way through,"[118] A detailed verbal description of the city in the eighteenth century lists forty markets around the island, four on the rivers, thirty-two in the outskirts, and another twenty specialist craft settlements where people from far-flung places offered services ranging from rope making to cloth dying to metalwork.[119]

In *KCKP*, we glimpse this cosmopolitan economy at work. Chinese appear as market gardeners, liquor sellers, and settlers embroiled in marital problems with their Thai wives. Khaek—a term applied to people from the Middle East, India, or modern Indonesia—are familiar figures who sell exotic imports from the junk trade. Vietnamese ply petty items from boats. Mon settlements line the waterways northward. Lao and Cham appear in the crowds.

In this picture, the Farang (Westerners) are conspicuous by their near absence. A few Farang articles appear including a portrait, a helmet, and glass-ware. But Farangs figure as characters only in a jokey description of battle (in the Wat Ko version), and as official guests at a ceremony in a passage probably written in the mid-nineteenth century. Partly this may be because much of *KCKP* developed in the period after a political crisis in 1688, when many Euro-peans left, and before 1855 when the Bowring Treaty was signed as a foundation for colonial trade. But partly it is because the focus of *KCKP* is on Ayutthaya as a royal capital.

The city was divided geographically into its two major functions as a trad-ing port and political capital. The foreign traders arrived up the river, moored around Pomphet, and did business at the markets in the southeast corner of the city. In the maps and paintings of the city by Europeans, this area is depicted in some detail, while elsewhere only major landmarks are shown.

All the facilities and functions of the official city were arrayed around the palace in the opposite northwest corner (see map 8). Streets lined with the

116. The estimates are summarized in Reid, *Southeast Asia in the Age of Commerce*, 2:71. Gervaise noted, "The city is so densely populated that, when the king is there, it could easily supply him with sixty thousand men of an age to bear arms, and this number could be doubled, if the inhabitants of the villages on the other side of the river, which can be considered as sub-urbs, were included" (*Natural and Political History*, 33).

117. Kaempfer, *Description*, 44.
118. Gervaise, *Natural and Political History*, 33.
119. APA, 94–95, 110–14.

stables of royal elephants stretched eastwards from the palace along the city's northern strip. The residences of the principal nobles were scattered here and along the opposite northern bank of the moat. Most of the city's major wat and protective shrines were ranged around the southern and eastern sides of the palace. Immediately beyond them to the south was the jail and execution ground. All the action of *KCKP* takes place in a quadrant stretching from the northwest corner to the northeast corner of the city. All the named places and all the river crossings are in this quadrant. All the journeys leave towards the north or northwest. No place name from the southeast part is mentioned, except when Khun Chang is groping for a rhyme in his clumsily improvised verse. In the accounts by foreigners, the most prominent minister at Ayutthaya is the Phrakhlang who oversaw foreign trade, often mistakenly called the "prime minister." In *KCKP*, he is almost invisible.[120]

In 1767, Burmese armies captured Ayutthaya and, as the Burmese chronicle states, "The city was then destroyed."[121] The Burmese aimed to obliterate the city as a rival capital by destroying not only its physical resources but also its human resources, ideological resources, and intellectual resources. Any of these which were movable were carted away to Ava including nobles, skilled people, Buddha images, books, weapons, and (reportedly) two thousand members of the royal family. Resources that were immovable were destroyed. The walls were flattened and the arsenals trashed. The palaces and wat that distinguished the city as a royal and religious center were reduced to "heaps of ruins and ashes."[122]

The new rulers of Siam chose to relocate the capital further south at Bangkok. Ayutthaya was further depleted as building materials were looted for the new city. But Ayutthaya remained important as memory—both as heritage and as a warning to be watchful. The focus on Ayutthaya in the later parts of *KCKP*, composed or recomposed in the Bangkok era, indulges that nostalgia.

5 SOCIAL LANDSCAPE

Across Southeast Asia, the sixteenth century was a time of warfare as rival cities and ambitious dynasts competed for precedence with the help of new military technology, including firearms and much greater use of elephants. Societies were geared for warfare. Some areas were devastated. Population probably

---

120. He appears only once, in chapter 32.
121. Phraison Salarak, "Intercourse," 54.
122. Turpin, *History of the Kingdom of Siam*, 109.

decreased. In the transition from the sixteenth to the seventeenth century, this era of warfare petered out in a series of stalemates. For the next century, there was very little warfare and a lot more trade. Cities prospered. Societies reoriented to commerce and more peaceful pursuits. Population probably increased. The military campaigns in the Original Story of *KCKP* may belong to the final phase of the sixteenth-century age of warfare, while the story may have developed in the following age when peace and prosperity created a demand for new forms of entertainment.

Siam was not a poor society. Seventeenth-century European visitors were struck by the sheer abundance of produce.[123] Van Vliet concluded that "Siam is a country that has more than most other countries of everything that the human being needs."[124] La Loubère added that with rice and fish so cheap, and arrack available at two sous for a Parisian pint, "it is no wonder if the Siameses are not in any great care about their Subsistence, and if in the Evening there is heard nothing but Singing in their Houses."[125]

But of course some lived much better than others. The social setting of *KCKP* is a society of personal relationships and steep hierarchy, in which those at the bottom had to work on behalf of others, sometimes forcibly and sometimes in return for protection.

Protection

Throughout *KCKP*, people seek protection against threats in order to ward off sorrowful hardship and achieve peaceful content. They look for someone who they can depend on, and who will feed or support them. When Khun Siwichai dies, his servants lament "We have lost our protector," and fear harassment by local officials. When Wanthong is told that Khun Phaen has died in the north, her first thought is "Who will protect us?" When Khun Phaen comes under attack by Khun Chang, he asks himself, "How can I protect myself?" and goes off to acquire his sword, horse, and personal spirit.

The second chapter defines the spectrum of danger by recounting the deaths of the three main characters' fathers. One type of danger lies in nature, especially in the wild forest. Wanthong's father dies from a fever contracted on a trading expedition. A second form of danger arises from human wickedness. Khun Chang's father is killed by a professional bandit gang that conducts its raids like military operations. The third form of danger comes from authority. Khun Phaen's father is executed by the king.

---

123. For example, *Van Vliet's Siam*, 168; Gervaise, *Natural and Political History*, 12.
124. *Van Vliet's Siam*, 107.
125. La Loubère, *New Historical Relation*, 35.

Individuals protect themselves against these dangers in various ways. They use methods of divination in order to locate dangers in time and space so they may be avoided. They adorn themselves with protective devices that have the power to block weapons or discourage spirits. The major role of Buddhist monks in the poem is to provide services of divination and protection, and teaching in these skills.

The model for the role of protector is a parent's custodianship of children, and especially the male in the combined role of father, husband, and householder. Good parents protect their children from all dangers, even the menace of sun, wind, and insects. Husbands shelter their wives like the spreading branches of a bo tree ("Oh, little bo tree shelter of your darling wife…," 748). Marriage is a transfer of the daughter from the protection of the father to that of the husband.

The role of a father is a metaphor for other relations of protection. The word for father, *pho*, is used as a pronoun between ward and protector. Wives address their husbands as *pho*. Khun Phaen addresses his official patrons, Phramuen Si and Phra Phichit, as *pho*, and they reciprocate by addressing him as a child. The thirty-five soldiers released from jail address Khun Phaen as *pho*.

The ability to serve as a protector depends on personal qualities, wealth, and political connections. Wanthong's mother prefers Khun Chang over Khun Phaen as a suitor-protector because Khun Chang has wealth and connections in the Ayutthaya court. Khun Phaen's attraction as a protector increases after he wins a military victory and gains title and royal favor. Laothong's parents present Khun Phaen with their daughter in anticipation that Khun Phaen will gain royal favor and thus be a good protector.

Viewed from below, the social order of late Ayutthaya and early Bangkok is a system that offered protection, especially against the danger imposed by official authority. People seek a patron in the hierarchy to serve as a shield against the authority of higher levels. Khun Phaen's father is an effective patron in Suphanburi because he has a reputation as a soldier and recognition from the king. As a result, "local officials shook their heads and knew never to cross him" (8). After the father is killed, his servants lament that, "nobody dared bully us, because everyone feared Khun Krai. But now they'll all come and push us around" (35). An abbot urges Khun Phaen to stay in the monkhood because the robe is protection against the dangers of conscription. A bandit lair provides protection for people who have offended their overseers. After becoming an outlaw, Khun Phaen gives himself up to the governor of Phichit because he has a reputation for offering shelter to those in trouble.

The king is at the apex of this official pyramid of protection. Two of the main items of royal regalia, the sword and multi-tiered umbrella, are symbols of protection. In the invocations that preface the king's appearances in the poem, he shields the populace from enemies so well that other territories eagerly seek the same shelter. The young Khun Chang is taken to be presented as a royal page so that he will enjoy royal protection. But the king's role is complex because he is also a threat. All the major characters, and many of the minor ones, lose life, liberty, property, rank, spouse, or kin at the hands of the king. Although the monarch is also a giver of rank and property, particularly to those who bring him victory in war, in the folk portions of *KCKP*, this aspect receives much less emphasis than his capacity to deprive.

Official nobility

The major division in the society ran between those who were in service to others and those who had others in their service. In *KCKP*, this division is clearly present in the conventions of naming. Those below the line are addressed with prefixes that imply subordination (I-, Ai-, Ta-, Yai-). Those above have a title as Khun, Nang, or one of the ranks of the official nobility.

The principal way to rise above this line was by *rap ratchakan*, literally "taking up the business of the king," entering royal service. Youths entered by being "entrusted" (*thawai tua*) to the king or a noble who accepted the role as patron. In the case of the king, this system operated through the corps of royal pages (*mahatlek*). Within this corps, there was an elite contingent which actually served as personal attendants on the king, but also other lesser contingents who were trainees in government service. Only families with some position at court had access to this route. Khun Chang's father can put forward his son as a page because he himself has an important government position. Khun Phaen can put forward his son because he has the patronage of Phramuen Si, head of the corps of pages. The king might occasionally elevate someone into royal service on account of a special talent or service, especially success in war. Beyond this charmed circle, even the nouveau riche were excluded. A law of 1740 forbade recruitment into the pages of "young men of humble birth or slaves who, having made a fortune by gambling, would offer bribes."[126]

In the ministries and their subsidiary departments, the procedure was the same. Youths were presented to the head of the department or ministry. At first they might serve in the noble's household, as the line between public and private affairs was very blurred. Whether in the royal pages corps or the ministries, future promotion depended on both talent and patronage. Patriarchs already ensconced in the higher ranks of the bureaucracy politicked to help their sons and wards move up the ladder, and hence sustain the family's

---

126. KTS, 5:150; Busakorn, "Ban Phlu Luang Dynasty," 222.

importance. Office tended to be hereditary, perhaps even more so in the provinces. Khun Chang seems to inherit his father's important role even though he
has little talent. When the king needs a successor to Khun Krai, his immediate
reaction is to seek out Khun Krai's son.

The official nobility was a finely graded hierarchy. Each job had both an
official title and an official name. As an individual moved up the hierarchy,
he changed both title and name. The hierarchy was defined by both a ladder
of titles—khun, phan, muen, luang, phra, phraya, chaophraya—but also a
numerical ranking known as *sakdina*. As the last syllable of this word means
rice field, it is often assumed that *sakdina* was once a system of land grants,
similar to a feudal system. But there is no evidence of such grants, while
similar systems of purely numerical ranking are known from old Tai polities and from China. The important part of the word is the first two symbols
meaning "dignity," and the word may mean something like "dignity value."
A chaophraya at the top of the official nobility had *sakdina* of ten thousand,
while a slave had five. In the middle levels, the matching of title and *sakdina*
varied somewhat across ministries, indicating that each ministry had some
independence in such matters.

Rather than land, what nobles received along with their title were goods
which served as signals of rank including distinctive styles of cloth, betel boxes,
swords, flasks, and caskets. Nobles displayed their status by parading through
the city wearing such cloth and trailed by a crowd of retainers, carrying their
insignia of office.

Nobles were not remunerated by government, but expected to support themselves from their office. Legitimately they were allowed to charge fees for some
services, especially legal adjudication, and to keep some proportion of taxes
they collected and fines they levied. They also leveraged the power of their office
for profit in other ways. Holding a governor's post was conventionally known
as "eating the province." King Phanwasa explodes at his courtiers, "Fighting
wars doesn't interest you at all. You're only good at cheating your own men for
corrupt gain, and using fancy words to get blood out of a crab." (418)

Nobles who became wealthy and powerful risked provoking the suspicion
of the king. Kosa Lek, the Phrakhlang and most prominent general in the
1670s,was found guilty of accepting bribes to avoid corvée work, flogged so
severely that he was "rendered prostrate," died soon after, and had his estate
seized by the king.[127] His brother, Kosa Pan, the most resplendent official of
Narai's reign, had his nose cut off, his family members arrested and tortured,
his property seized, and his body buried at night after he had possibly com-

---

127. Bèze, "Memoir," 13–15.

mitted suicide.[128] La Loubère noted that grandsons or even sons of the greatest nobles were often reduced to oarsmen. In *KCKP*, Khun Phaen's family is ruined because of his father's mistake on a buffalo hunt. Phra Thainam, commander-in-chief of the army, is reduced to phrai status and a gatekeeper's job as penalty for military failure. Wealth and status were far from secure.

Servitude

At the bottom of the social order were slaves (*that, kha, lek*), meaning people who were considered the property of their owners. Many had been captured in war. On both of the northern campaigns in *KCKP*, the rewards for the commanders and soldiers of the victorious army are property looted from the defeated, and people who are swept down to become their slaves. In the 1680s, Chaumont observed Malay slaves "in great numbers," and reckoned that Mon captives and immigrants "are as numerous in the country as the originary Siamese."[129]

Others were sold or mortgaged into slavery. A household head had the right to sell or mortgage himself, his wife, and his children into slavery, just as Kaeo Kiriya is mortgaged by her father. Others were forced into slavery by creditors when they failed to pay their dues. Slaves of this kind could be redeemed by paying off the outstanding amount, just as Khun Phaen redeems Kaeo Kiriya, and Thong Prasi redeems several slaves in Kanburi so they can work for her benefit. Slave status was also hereditary. There are no reliable estimates of the number of slaves in late Ayutthaya or early Bangkok, but it was clearly substantial. The Kalahom minister in 1629 had two thousand slaves, and Kosa Lek in the 1680s had eight thousand.[130] Although there was no slave market, people were bought and sold, and had monetary value. When La Loubère showed a picture of a French woman to some Siamese nobles, "One of them reply'd, that a Woman like this would be worth an hundred *Catie*, or fifteen thousand Livres."[131]

Slavery was more varied than the English-language term implies. Some slaves were unfree personal retainers who worked on their master's household or landholding, and accompanied their master in public as a demonstration of status. They were remunerated in both kind (paddy and clothing) and cash. Women might become "slave wives," a distinct category in the law codes. But other slaves were a source of income rather than of service for their masters.

---

128. Launay, *Histoire*, 2:45.
129. Chaumont and Choisy, *Aspects*, 84.
130. Bèze, "Memoir," 13–15.
131. La Loubère, *New Historical Relation*, 28.

They worked for a living, and delivered a portion of their income in cash to their master, sometimes as a daily release fee, sometimes for an annual sum of half their earnings.[132]

Most of the remaining population had the legal status of phrai, meaning roughly commoner as against a member of the official nobility. They were not, however, freemen but had to work for a master for part of the time. Some put themselves under a noble or "big man" in return for protection, and perhaps a better chance to earn a living. Some were attached to government departments and had to work for the department on a rota. Khun Krai commands five hundred phrai who are probably farmers or other workers who have to do guard duty in Suphanburi at certain times. At the capital, most phrai were attached to the major ministries. According to the laws, they were liable to be called up for service every other month in late Ayutthaya, reduced to every third month in early Bangkok. They might have to serve as troops, row boats, clear paths through the jungle, construct and repair temples, or work as "earth-carriers, brickmakers, woodcutters and miners."[133]

Government conducted censuses in the capital and provincial towns to compile recruitment rolls. A similar system is known from old Tai polities. It first appears in the Ayutthaya records in the late fifteenth century, and was probably elaborated and enforced most strictly in the era of warfare in the sixteenth century. Over the seventeenth century, as war gave way to commerce, the system had begun to decline.

As is clear from *KCKP*, corvée service was hated. Throughout the poem, there is a recurring joke about how phrai are deliberately bad at rowing boats. Abbot Khong of Wat Khae warns Phlai Kaeo about leaving the novitiate and becoming a phrai:

> Once your wrist is black, it's all hard times—carrying pack baskets on your shoulder until you collapse.
> If the overseer likes you, things are a bit easier. He can look after you and find work that's not too heavy. But if he hates you, he'll use you until you ache—sawing wood, dragging big logs, anything. (132)

Military service was especially hated and resisted, obliging the government to introduce a guarantor system and often use brute force. Evasion was widespread. Many hid in the monkhood. Some sold themselves into slavery as a way to raise money and avoid the corvée at the same time. Some bought their

---

132. *Van Vliet's Siam*, 149; Gervaise, *Natural and Political History*, 97
133. Gervaise, *Natural and Political History*, 98–99.

way out. La Loubère commented on the minister of the rolls, "Tis an Office, very subject to Corruption, by reason that every particular person endeavors to get himself omitted out of the Rolls for money."[134] More and more phrai seem to have placed themselves under the protection of individual nobles in order to escape serving the government. In late Ayutthaya and early Bangkok, government passed several laws on corvée in desperate efforts to shore up a crumbling system.

Although the categories of slave and phrai seem quite distinct in law and definition, in *KCKP* the two terms are constantly lumped together to describe the retinue of a noble. Some characters, such as I-Moei, are sometimes described as phrai, sometimes as slave. Perhaps this was poetic license, but perhaps it indicates that the two statuses were not so different in practice. Comparing phrai and slaves, La Loubère commented "Liberty is oftentimes more burdensome than servitude," and quoted a local proverb that the Siamese found liberty so "abject" that they would sell it to eat a durian.[135] Both phrai and slaves exchanged some of their labor for the protection of a patron.

Women

In law and in politics, women in the Ayutthaya era were at a great disadvantage. As children, they were virtually the property of their father (as were sons, too), and at marriage they became virtually the property of their husband. They could be sold or mortgaged into slavery without their own consent, as Kaeo Kiriya is mortgaged by her father to defray a debt. If a woman was found guilty of adultery, the husband could kill her—a right that was not reciprocal. They also ran the risk of being punished for their menfolk's transgressions—a fate that befalls several characters in *KCKP*. After her husband is executed by the king, Thong Prasi has to flee to avoid being seized in punishment. Laothong is imprisoned as a menial worker in the palace because of Khun Phaen's error on royal service. Wanthong believes she will suffer a similar fate because of Khun Phaen's rumored defeat and death on campaign. Although the law is not perhaps as brutal as Khun Chang pretends, Wanthong believes she is going to be enslaved because her husband has been killed—"Sorrow piled on sorrow piled on sorrow," indeed.

Women are vulnerable because their male protectors may leave to do corvée work, serve in the army, go on trading expeditions, or philander. After Khun Phaen marries Wanthong but then goes away to war and is presumed dead, Wanthong's mother urges her to marry Khun Chang to avoid the dangers of

134. La Loubère, *New Historical Relation*, 84.
135. La Loubère, *New Historical Relation*, 77, 107.

being without a protector. After Khun Phaen abandons Wanthong for another wife, she berates him for leaving her unprotected using the simile of a birds' nest which is looted and destroyed by crows because of the male's negligence. When Khun Phaen's second wife, Laothong, is taken to do menial labor in the palace, Khun Phaen urges her to ingratiate herself with the palace governesses so she will have protection. Mothers advise their daughters to minister to their husbands well in order to avoid the danger of being abandoned without a protector. Faced with the prospect of being swept down to Ayutthaya as prisoners, the palace ladies of Chiang Mai discuss how to find new protectors: "Meet a noble and behave suitably. Snuggle close, caress, and cuddle to his heart's content. . . . The older and uglier they are, the more they'll love you." (661)

Women without the protection of a father or husband were especially vulnerable. Saithong, Mai, and Moei are all single women in slavery. Mai is the daughter of a slave in the Chiang Mai palace, while Moei is Mon and perhaps a war prisoner or an immigrant assigned as a slave by the king. Saithong's only remark about herself—"If I didn't [love you, Wanthong], I'd probably have gone off roaming all over the place, maybe got myself arrested and killed, or else survived unscathed. That's the way things go" (84)—hints that she chose servitude rather than the risks of an unprotected life.

Political authority is entirely a male preserve. In the listing of officeholders in the *Three Seals Law*, there are no women except in the administration of the inner palace. Outside the capital in *KCKP*, governors, town officials, and village heads are all male. Of course, some women might wield considerable power in the background, particularly in the politics of the palace, but for the majority of women, powerlessness was sadly real. When Wanthong wants to check Khun Chang's information on her husband's rumored death, she laments, "But it's beyond poor me to find out. There are so many obstacles, checkmate on every square. I don't know how things are in Ayutthaya. Ever since I was born I've never once been to Ayutthaya" (230). In the final condemnation scene in the Ayutthaya audience hall, Wanthong would have been the only female present (other than palace attendants) among a mass of men.

Women are spiritually disadvantaged too. The monkhood is a male preserve. The practice of lore is not only limited to males, but women may be a threat to its efficacy. Khun Phaen is careful to remove all his protective devices before making love. He warns his son against touching women in the Chiang Mai palace as it will compromise his martial ability. The only spiritual function that women play in *KCKP* is to distract the spirits during childbirth. Beneath these attitudes is a sense of differential spiritual value. When Khun Phaen pretends he might hang himself, Saithong exclaims, "Are you mad enough to kill yourself so easily? It's very difficult to be born a man." (142)

But the tyrannies of the law codes and official rules were fiercest at the political center, and perhaps more relaxed at a distance. La Loubère made the general point: "the Yoke thereof is less heavy...on the Populace than on the Nobles. ... The more one is unknown to the Prince [i.e., king], and further from him, the greater ease he enjoys."[136] It is unknown to what extent the laws prescribed in the Three Seals code were enforced beyond the capital. In *KCKP*, Suphanburi seems to fall fairly strictly under Ayutthaya's authority, but Phichit is more remote, and the governor is prepared to defy the capital's commands.

Moreover, while women were severely disadvantaged in law, politics, and matters spiritual, the economy was a different matter. One result of corvée was that much of the labor and enterprise devolved upon women. La Loubère observed, "The women plough the Land, they sell and buy in the Cities."[137] Van Vliet wrote "the women, (who are well built and pretty), do most work in the fields. These women also row the boats on the river and besides many other things."[138] The scribe of a Persian embassy to Ayutthaya in 1685 observed, "It is common for women to engage in buying and selling in the markets and even to undertake physical labour. ... Thus you can see the women paddling to the surrounding villages where they successfully earn their daily bread with no assistance from the men."[139] Gervaise added on the subject of legal process, "Since the women are more lively and more articulate than the men, they almost always receive a more favourable hearing, and they know better how to defend their interests."[140]

In *KCKP*, women work and trade. After Thong Prasi is widowed and goes to Kanburi, "She redeemed some slaves and phrai so they could farm. She bought land, elephants, horses, cattle, and buffaloes. She acquired property through trading. People looked up to her with respect" (39). When Kaeo Kiriya is redeemed from slavery, "She did good business selling low-price goods such as fruit, sweets, oranges, and lychees from a dry goods store" (432). Buakhli oversees her father's workers in the fields. Most of the servants who go to harvest Siprajan's cotton are female. At the Lawa village visited by Khun Phaen and Wanthong, there is not a single man in sight, and an old woman is in charge. Along the rivers we meet many female vendors. In the street-side shops and markets in Chiang Mai and Phichit, most vendors are female.

---

136. La Loubère, *New Historical Relation*, 106.
137. La Loubère, *New Historical Relation*, 50.
138. *Van Vliet's Siam*, 162.
139. O'Kane, *Ship of Sulaiman*, 139.
140. Gervaise, *Natural and Political History*, 61–62.

The passage of *KCKP* on the *Mahachat* performance in Suphanburi gives a hint of status in local society. The chanting was a major local event. The sponsors would be those with wealth and local standing. Of the six episodes where the sponsor is identified, three are men, two are women, and one is a couple. Despite her youth, Phim carries off this role with great confidence.

Wanthong's tragedy is a complex mix of gender and politics. At the outset, she is in command of her life. She chooses the match with Phlai Kaeo (Khun Phaen) by giving him the money that makes the marriage possible. She is captured by Khun Chang because Khun Phaen fails as a protector—by being sent to war, by going off with another woman, by being thrown in jail. Still, at this stage she fears only the public shame of being branded "two-minded." There is no hint of anything worse. Her situation becomes much more dangerous when she is drawn towards Ayutthaya, the seat of power. Tellingly, she visits the capital only twice in the poem, the first time for her son's marriage which revives the fatal conflict, and the second time for the final trial and her execution. Her vulnerability as a woman is multiplied manifold by the danger of drawing close to the center of royal authority.

Trade and change

The transition from war to commerce in the seventeenth century sparked great social changes. Noble office and royal preferment were no longer the only or even the major routes to riches and social distinction. The changes were evident by the time Europeans visited in the late seventeenth century. Gervaise noted that, "The majority of the population is engaged in trade," and pointed to "the inordinate passion for amassing wealth, which is the dominant vice of the country."[141] A minted coinage was created in the seventeenth century to meet the demands of rising trade. Gervaise observed that, "When they [nobles] have amassed a sufficient quantity of minted money, they put it out to usury, and the interest they earn on it is so great that it already exceeds the value of the original investment after three or four years."[142] La Loubère found that "The most general Professions at Siam are Fishing for the common People, and Merchandizing for all those that have wherewithal to follow it. I say all, not except the King himself."[143] He described King Narai's investments in the cloth trade, including importing from India and retailing in the local markets.

From the early seventeenth century, the kings tried to resist these new forces by preventing the accumulation of wealth. They imposed death duties which

141. Gervaise, *Natural and Political History*, 61, 98.
142. Gervaise, *Natural and Political History*, 98.
143. La Loubère, *New Historical Relation*, 71.

foreign observers thought were administered punitively to disperse wealth.[144] Some of the most successful trader mandarins were arraigned for corruption, and had their property seized, and their houses open for public looting. Late seventeenth century European visitors commented that prominent people owned little property because they feared seizure, and preferred diamonds which were easy to secrete.[145]

But this repression could not last. In the eighteenth century, expanding commerce, especially with China, gradually created what Nidhi Eoseewong has described as a "bourgeois culture" among the old nobility and immigrant Chinese.[146] The development was interrupted by the fall of Ayutthaya in 1767 and the subsequent remilitarization, but only temporarily. European visitors in the early nineteenth century found Bangkok's upper class reveling in possessions, novelty, and display. The court-authored passages of *KCKP* show signs of having been developed against this background. Khun Chang is portrayed as a classic rich provincial, flaunting his wealth and struggling to ape the manners and tastes of the court. The text dwells lovingly on details of dress and domestic furnishings, on the abundance of produce in the markets, on the variety of peoples attracted to the capital. The embedded criticism of absolute royal power and old institutions such as conscription and *kin mueang* ("eating the province") is founded on emerging bourgeois values. The exemplary character of this section of *KCKP* is Pramuen Si, the established senior noble who combines courtly manners with a humanistic outlook.

Because of its long development, the narrative of *KCKP* spans this change of eras. In the early part, Khun Phaen trains as a soldier in order to advance through the spoils of war and the patronage of the king. His mentality is rooted in the age of Naresuan, however much the text has been overwritten since. In the later part, when Phlai Ngam rides north on campaign, he daydreams not about glory or rank but about furnishing his house. His mentality belongs to the bourgeois court culture of the mid-nineteenth century.

144. *Van Vliet's Siam*, 164–65; Gervaise, *Natural and Political History*, 97.

145. La Loubère, *New Historical Relation*, 52–53.

146. Nidhi, *Pen and Sail*, ch. 1. Nidhi argued that this development was a product of early Bangkok society when the old elite had been destroyed in 1767, and a more fluid society had emerged with a growing trading economy. Subsequent research, especially by Saichon Satyanurak, has shown that the conditions Nidhi placed in early Bangkok were also true of late Ayutthaya as a result of the growing Siam-China trade, the dynastic disruptions from the seventeenth century onwards, and consequent changes in society and mentality (Saichon, *Phutthasasana*, ch. 1).

KCKP in context

The development of *KCKP* was itself a product of these social and cultural changes in late Ayutthaya and early Bangkok. With growing trade and prosperity, the society was becoming more fascinated by itself, by its own vitality and variety. Nowhere is this better on display than in wat mural painting and in the *sepha*.

The few examples of murals which survive from mid Ayutthaya focus almost exclusively on the image of the Buddha, executed with a limited palette (red, black, yellow, gilding), no perspective, and mainly graphical rather than naturalistic background. But those which were painted from the Narai reign (1656–1688) onwards, show many distinct differences. While the thematic focus is still on the Buddha's life, Jataka stories, and the Three Worlds, the execution has more realism and humanism. The palette expands to include green and other natural shades. Interstitial areas are crowded with flora and fauna. Houses are drawn with perspective. Panels are broken up into sections telling various parts of a single story. Scenes of wat festivals are drawn into the illustrations of Buddha's cremation, complete with drama performances and acrobats. Vignettes of everyday life—housewives pounding rice, kids chasing chickens, goats scavenging—appear as the backdrop of Jataka tales. Erotic glimpses pop up in the marginalia. Episodes of the Buddha's life are watched by crowds showing great variety of dress, hairstyle, facial type, and skin color—Thais, pigtailed Chinese, bearded Moors, head-shaven Japanese, and the occasional westerner as trader, soldier, or missionary. The overall impression is of a varied and busy society—all sorts of people doing all sorts of things.[147]

KCKP shows the same spirit. The narrative rambles all over the geography of Siam. As in the murals, the interstices of the story are painted with vignettes of Vietnamese vendors, Mon boatman, avuncular abbots, liquor-loving hunters, gay palace women, Jek vendors, and countless old crones and groping old men. The crowd scenes on the riverbanks teem with life. Weddings, funerals, and local festivals are described with an anthropologist's love of detail. A society is looking at itself.

---

147. The best known examples are from Ayutthaya's Wat Pradu Songtham, where King Borommakot was ordained. The paintings were redone in Mongkut's reign, but the overall style and many of the details indicate these renovations were based on earlier works. Other examples are Wat Chong Nonsi in Bangkok, and Wat Ko Kaeo Suttharam in Phetchaburi (Muang Boran, *Wat Pradu Songtham*; Ringis, *Thai Temples*, esp. 101–102; Santi and Mermet, *Temples of Gold*).

6 POLITICAL GEOGRAPHY

In today's versions of Siam's history, the main external antagonist is Burma. But this rivalry figures only peripherally in *KCKP*. Both of the military campaigns in *KCKP* are attacks on Chiang Mai, the capital of Lanna. The second campaign also involves Lanchang.

Siam, Lanna, and Lanchang all emerged in the fourteenth and fifteenth centuries. Siam was a coalition of trading towns close to the coast of the Gulf, while Lanna and Lanchang were landlocked groupings of valley lordships among the hills. Siam gradually became the dominant polity.

The crucial difference was maritime trade. Siam grew richer on trade, particularly to China and later Japan. In the mid-fifteenth century, the coastal coalition centered on Ayutthaya merged with the "northern cities" centered on Phitsanulok to create a polity encompassing roughly all the Chaophraya Plain below the hills. With the rivers as highways—supplemented by canal digging—Ayutthaya was able to exert control over this large area. In the interests of the trade, which was its lifeline, Ayutthaya established an outpost at Khorat to gain access to the forest products of the Isan plateau, took control of a portage route across the neck of the peninsula to the Indian Ocean, and tried to control northern areas which were the source of many trade goods.

Lanna and Lanchang were less expansive. Chiang Mai was founded according to its chronicle in 1296 but truly emerged as a political center around a century later. Its ambitious rulers imposed their authority over petty lords ruling in the upper valleys of the four tributaries of the Chaophraya, and some stretches of the Mekong to the north. But the fractured geography of the hills ensured that this control was always loose, and constantly disrupted by the ambitions of individual valley lords.

Lanchang emerged as a similar coalition of valley centers along the Mekong River and its tributaries, with an initial capital at Luang Prabang, and with the same problem of control. In the early eighteenth century, the warring between subordinate lords deteriorated to the point that Lanchang split into two, and Vientiane became the more important of the two capitals. Except in the reigns of a handful of remarkable rulers, Chiang Mai, Luang Prabang, and Vientiane were more prominent as cultural rather than political capitals—famous for the learning of their monks, beauty of their wat, skills of their craftsmen, and their output of religious texts and fine Buddha images.

From the mid-fourteenth to mid-sixteenth centuries, Ayutthaya sent several military expeditions northwards. But while these armies could often defeat the northern rulers and sometimes take their capitals, they could not impose any permanent dominion. Again, geography was key. Above the points where each falls onto the plain, the Chaophraya tributaries are not navigable over any distance because of shallows and rapids. As in the northward journeys in *KCKP*, travelers had to transfer from water to land. Onward travel was slow because of the terrain, difficult because of the lack of settlements and food supplies, and dangerous because of forest robbers and fevers.

In the sixteenth century, the emergence of the powerful Toungoo state in Burma changed the geopolitics of the region. The Toungoo capital of Ava extended its influence over Chiang Mai, and imposed a form of indirect rule. At the same time, Ayutthaya became more than ever absorbed in overseas trade. Spheres of political influence were now layered horizontally. Burma's power extended eastward across Lanna, and occasionally into Lanchang. Siam's power extended westward into the Mon towns, eastward into Cambodia, and down the peninsula. Between 1600 and 1767, Ayutthaya sent only two military expeditions north against Lanna and two against Lanchang, none with much result.[148]

The portrayal of political relations between Siam, Lanna, and Lanchang in *KCKP* is rather complex. Firstly, if there is any historical reality behind the Chomthong and Chiang Mai campaigns, it belong to the sixteenth century. As noted above, the story of the Chiang Mai campaign seems to have been adapted from incidents that took place in the 1560s. Between 1600 and the late eighteenth century, Siam had very little to do with these two northern states.

Secondly, these portions of *KCKP* were most likely developed during this era of separation. The telling evidence is the ignorance these passages display about Lanna and Lanchang. The geography is all wrong. The culture is muddled. The political systems are imagined as the same as Ayutthaya.

Thirdly, the political messages buried in these passages belong to yet another period, beginning in the late eighteenth century, when Siam was again trying to impose its authority over its northern neighbors. Although Ayutthaya was destroyed in 1767, Siam revived under King Taksin (r. 1767–1782) and King Rama I (r. 1782–1809) by reverting to something like the warrior state that had existed prior to 1600. Citizens again became soldiers, nobles generals, and the king the commander-in-chief. After beating back Burma's follow-up invasions, this new military might was redirected into an expansion of Siam's power far beyond its earlier limits—both down the peninsula and up into the northern

---

148. In the early 1660s, Narai heard that Ava was threatened by Chinese armies, and twice sent armies north to Chiang Mai, but had to backtrack when the Chinese threat to Ava faded. In the 1670s, two or three expeditions were dispatched to Vientiane, probably to coerce trade, but were so unsuccessful that they are omitted from all the Thai chronicles. In the 1710s, a Thai army helped to enforce the formal split between Luang Prabang and Vientiane.

hills. This was possible because other states were even more weakened than Siam by Burmese attacks. Lanna was especially damaged. People scattered away. Chiang Mai was abandoned for twenty years. Other valley centers did not revive for half a century. Lanchang remained crippled by internal divisions.

Lanna and Lanchang looked to resurgent Siam to help fend off Burmese aggression. In 1774, King Taksin led a Siamese army north with the future King Rama I serving as his principal general. The new ruler of Lanna presented them with a niece and sister respectively, and Vientiane presented Taksin with a daughter (though the delivery was never completed). But these alliances came at a cost. Bangkok demanded that both Lanna and Lanchang become tributary states. Their rulers had to drink the water of allegiance regularly, send annual tribute to Bangkok, request Bangkok's approval of royal succession, and allow Bangkok to place spies in their capitals. On top, Siam was a ruthless competitor for the scarce resource of the age—manpower. On their northern expeditions, the Bangkok armies swept away people to be resettled in Siam, just as portrayed in the *KCKP* passage on the ending of the Chiang Mai campaign. Lanna was a rival for the same manpower to repopulate the valleys. The competition for manpower eventually brought Bangkok and Vientiane into conflict in the 1820s.

The politics of the northern episodes in the Wat Ko edition belongs to the early Bangkok period. At this time, the scions of the Lanna and Lanchang ruling houses were brought to Bangkok for education and acculturation (besides serving as hostages for good behavior). The rulers had to make occasional visits to show loyalty. Possibly these portions of *KCKP* were developed to instruct these visitors by warning of the perils of over-ambition. Of the two states, Lanna was the most truculent under Bangkok's yoke. In the Wat Ko version of *KCKP*, the Lanna king is described as "leader of the Lao people of the forest, brutish of manner, prepared to leap into a fire and die for nothing" (1325). He is a buffoon who is punished for his over-ambition, and returns home like a vagabond. Lanchang is portrayed rather differently. For four decades from 1782 onwards, Lanchang was generally a good ally of Siam. Three successive rulers were educated in Bangkok and gave military help to defend Bangkok against the Burmese and clear the Burmese out of Lanna. In the Wat Ko version, Lanchang is portrayed as a properly obedient ally.

These politics changed in the 1820s. Vientiane rebelled against Bangkok's efforts to control the manpower of the Khorat Plateau, and Bangkok responded by attempting to eradicate Vientiane, just as Burma had eradicated Ayutthaya a half-century earlier. Lanna, which had gradually been repopulated, became more important as an ally for Bangkok. This new situation is reflected in the revised version of the Chiang Mai campaign composed in the mid-nineteenth century. The portrayal of Lanchang is unchanged, but the King of Chiang Mai becomes more kingly. He is still punished for his over-ambition, but he is allowed to return home in some dignity.

7 SPIRITS, KARMA, AND LORE

The mental landscape of *KCKP* is framed by Theravada Buddhism, but also by older beliefs in spirits and forces in the natural world.

In old Southeast Asia, as in much of the world, people believed in spirits that resided in nature, and spirits of the ancestors who continued to serve as guardians. From the early Common Era, many new ideas were brought to the region from India by traders and adventurers. Hinduism as a system of worship never took root. Instead, the Vedic gods were incorporated into local beliefs as a superior form of spirits. Buddhism of several schools arrived in this wave. From the fourteenth century, a more vital strain of Theravada Buddhism, with its distinctive institution of monks who serve as teachers and as exemplars of good conduct, was brought from Sri Lanka by itinerant monks and gained an enthusiastic welcome according to the monastic chronicles. Although some Theravada teachers ridiculed old beliefs in spirits and Hindu deities, and demanded renunciation from their followers, the old beliefs and practices were too deeply embedded in everyday life. Instead of driving these beliefs and practices away, the Theravada monks eventually embraced them, decorating their wat with tales of the Hindu deities alongside the life of the Buddha, and carrying out ceremonies to propitiate spirits alongside their Buddhist teaching.

In *KCKP*, there are two main sets of belief that appear constantly. The first is the concept of karma as a cumulative accounting of good and bad actions that determines the fate of people through successive lives. The second is the existence of forces hidden in nature which determine natural events, and which can be understood, divined, and manipulated by adepts with the right skills and tools.

Karma

In their everyday conversation, the characters of *KCKP* constantly refer to the laws of karma which underlie their own happiness and sorrow, and their passage from past through present to future.

Each person has an account of merit (บุญ, *bun*), fortune (เวร, *wen*), or karma (กรรม, *kam*). This account is credited for doing good deeds towards others, for following the Buddhist precepts, and for performing ritual acts which "make merit," such as feeding monks or sponsoring wat events like the *Mahachat* recitation. Merit may be transferred to others, for example into the accounts of deceased kin to assist their rebirth. The account is debited for bad deeds, particularly offenses against the precepts such as killing. The karma of bad deeds can be canceled if the wronged party grants forgiveness, as shown in the scene immediately preceding Wanthong's execution.

Both the balance in the account, and the nature of particular actions, shapes events in this and future lives. Phlai Kaeo speculates that some merit made in the past caused him to acquire Laothong as a wife. Seeing her husband's ugly death, Thepthong speculates "Maybe in a previous life you skewered a fish, and so in this life you've been skewered to death too" (47).

At death, the person becomes a spirit (the terms for corpse and spirit are identical), and the balance in the karma account determines the afterlife and rebirth. The possibilities are set out in treatises on Buddhist cosmology, especially the *Three Worlds*. Those with a credit balance are on a ladder which may lead to eventual enlightenment and release from the world of suffering. Those in deficit will sink into one of many hells, the "realms of loss and woe." The characters of *KCKP* might not know this text but would be aware of its geography of heavens and hells from sermons and wat murals.

The length of time spent in the "realms of loss and woe," and the intensity of suffering there, eventually draw down the karma account to the point where rebirth is possible.[149] In *KCKP*, the process of birth is accomplished by a "molding spirit" which catches the spirit ready for rebirth, forms the physical human creature, and slips this handiwork into a womb ready to be born.

Spirits

Yet many of the dead do not ascend to the upper regions or descend into the many hells, but remain stranded in this world or in a netherworld between hell and the human world from where they can pay visits to the human world. This is the origin of the many varieties of spirits, ghosts, and ghouls.

A special category of these stranded spirits are those resulting from a sudden, violent, and unexpected death. Perhaps because the person was not able to prepare for such a death, perhaps because of the unrealized potential of the unlived portion of the life, these *phi tai hong* are especially powerful and potentially very malicious.[150] The extreme form of such a spirit is the unborn

---

149. The action of karma in this life works on similar accounting principles. When the thirty-five prisoners are released from jail, the text explains, "For their karma, they had been imprisoned a long time. But now the ending of that karma caused a change for the better." (553)

150. Also, the unnatural death is proof of some other problem: "But they never burn [cremate] those that Justice cuts off, nor Infants dead-born, nor Women that die in Child-bed, nor those which drown themselves, or which perish by any other extraordinary disaster, as by a

child of a woman who dies while pregnant. In the past, pregnant women may have been sacrificed and buried in the foundations of city pillars or city gates in order to create fierce guardian spirits. These *hong* and the less malevolent *phrai* can be recruited and directed by adepts with the right skills, such as Khun Phaen. Besides serving as guardians of people, villages, or cities, they can provide transport, deliver messages, and serve as soldiers. They are rewarded by being fed with food and liquor.

Other spirits are more benign, as long as properly propitiated. The most important fall into one of two categories: the spirits of ancestors and the spirits of a place. Ancestors include the forebears of a family and also the founders of a village, city, or realm. They need to be propitiated to ensure that they continue to act as guardians for their descendants. Most villages have a shrine to the ancestor spirits, usually a rock, tree, or other natural feature at the entrance or center of the settlement. As *KCKP* shows, a capital such as Ayutthaya or Chiang Mai had not one but a contingent of these guardians, some overseeing such important facilities as the treasury.

Spirits of the place run through a spectrum from the naga spirits that represent the physical earth in general, to spirits that live in a particular place, tree, or mountain. At Khun Chang's house building, ceremonies are held to apologize to the spirit of the earth for digging the postholes, to the spirit of the trees for cutting the timber, and to the locally resident spirits for being displaced by the house.

Inner ways

Khun Phaen is educated in the "inner ways," a phrase which nicely captures the depth of the knowledge, its arcane origins, and its reliance on the innate talent of the practitioner. The skills he learns are primarily for use in war, but have wider application. He learns both how to divine the hidden forces which determine natural events, and to manipulate them.

The main technique for divination depends on astrology, signs read from the position of celestial bodies. In Siam, the royal court imported the Indian system of astrology known as Jyotisha, meaning "light, heavenly body," probably via Sri Lanka.[151] It also imported Brahmans to use the technique, and rewarded

---

Thunderbolt. They rank these unfortunate persons amongst the guilty, because they believe that such Misfortunes never happen to innocent Persons" (La Loubère, *New Historical Relation*, 125).

151. The standard modern work with details of two methods of calculation is Luang Wisantharunakon (An Sarikabut), *Khamphi horasat thai matrathan*. This manual was originally prepared for the court in 1923 using new methods of calculation. It was republished in 1965 and presented to the king.

them with high posts in the nobility. The Jyotisha system plots the path of nine heavenly bodies (sun, moon, five planets, and two imaginary planets) against a map of the sky divided into twelve houses named after constellations. Each house represents a certain mental aspect (stability, tolerance, love, judgment, etc.), and each heavenly body represents a certain aspect of life (ego, wealth, mind, etc.). A reading taken at birth determines which of the heavenly bodies will influence which aspects of that life. Readings of the position of these influential bodies at a future time can then be used to divine events.

This technique can be applied to individuals, cities, kingdoms, anything for which a "birth" time can be identified. But the calculations are extremely taxing, given that the heavenly bodies are not moving evenly across the sky map, but orbiting other bodies, and hence capable of accelerating, decelerating, and even reversing, when seen from earth. Moreover, the method allows for the introduction of infinite complexity by giving meaning to subdivisions of measurement, and to various interactions between the heavenly bodies in play. The court had probably imported this system precisely because it was so difficult to use and so redolent with complexity that it gave the court a monopoly on the most sophisticated and most flexible divination.[152]

The divinations made by Khun Phaen and his teachers and battle foes do not use fully fledged Jyotisha, but other systems which are based on the same principle of locating heavenly bodies within a map but which require much simpler forms of calculation. Several of their predictions seem to use the method known as (*maha*)*thaksa*. To construct the birth chart, all that needs to be known is the *lagna*, the body rising on the eastern horizon at that time, or (in an even simpler variant) the day of the week. The other bodies are assigned to their spheres of influence in simple sequence. To examine the forces acting at any future point, another chart can be made in the same way. Alternatively, the calculation of which bodies are influential at any time is made through a simple arithmetical progression from the birth chart.[153]

Other divination systems appearing in *KCKP* are even simpler. The Circles method depends on the intersections between lunar and solar calendars. The conjunction of certain days in the week and certain dates in the (lunar) month are prescribed as auspicious, and others as inauspicious.[154] The Three-

152. In Siam in 1687–88, Simon de La Loubère acquired a document describing the calculations for the sun and moon. He had it translated into French and examined by M. Cassini of the Royal Academy of Sciences, who pronounced the technique "ingenious." The calculations appear similar to those used in Thai astrology today. The document is not found in the English translation of La Loubère, but in Jacq-Hergoualc'h, *Etude historique et critique*, 488–503.

153. See p. 793, note 15.

154. See p. 319, note 23.

Tiered Umbrella uses the birth year and age to locate a certain position on a chart where each segment is associated with a legendary episode (mostly from the *Ramakian*) with metaphorical meaning.[155] Nowadays, charts setting out the results of these and similar methods are published in manuals such as *Phrommasak*. Possibly something similar is indicated when manuals are mentioned in *KCKP*. La Loubère wrote that an "Almanac which he [the king] causes Annually to be made by a *Brame* [Brahman] Astrologer, denotes to him and his Subjects the lucky or unlucky days for most of the things they used to do."[156]

Besides these divinations based on aspects of time, Khun Phaen and others in *KCKP* gather many different omens from nature. They look at the clouds, examine the breath through their nostrils, listen to the sounds of insects and animals, read meanings from the brightness of the stars and the halo of the moon, and tease predictions out of dreams. Many of these omens and signs are documented in old manuscripts of the *Manual on Victorious Warfare*.

Khun Phaen is also educated in methods to manipulate the hidden forces in the world using formulas, substances, command over the spirits, and other devices. These methods have roots in several traditions, many of which originated in India but have been adapted and rearranged over many centuries in Southeast Asia.

The first of these origins goes back around three thousand years when the Vedas, the great texts of Hinduism, were compiled. Besides their three volumes of philosophical texts, the compilers put together a fourth volume with a catalog of local beliefs and practices in north India at the time.[157] This catalog includes ways to influence natural forces in the world, particularly to achieve protection against threats from disease, natural disasters, and the perfidies of fellow man. The methods include natural substances with supernatural powers, formulas for recitation, and devices constructed by adepts. They influence events through two pairs of forces: *repulsion*, warding off danger or, in its most complete form, providing invulnerability; *attraction*, inducing love, sympathy, or good fortune; *constraint*, preventing an event or action; and *release*, removing constraints, such as undoing locks and chains, or ensuring a smooth delivery at birth. The scope of the catalog, and many of the methods detailed, are very similar to the repertoire of supernatural beliefs and practices found in *KCKP*, to those recorded by Robert Textor in central Siam half a century ago,[158]

155. See p. 208 note 4.
156. La Loubère, *New Historical Relation*, 66.
157. Witney, *Atharva-Veda Samhita*; Whitaker, "Ritual power."
158. Textor, "An Inventory," and Textor, *Patterns of Worship*.

and to those still practiced today. The story of how they made their way from northern India to Siam is unknown. The title of the compilation as *Atharva Veda*, the Fourth Veda, survives in Thai as อาถรรพณ์, *athan* (sometimes *athap*, *athanpawet*), meaning protection, particularly the convoking of supernatural forces to protect a city, palace, or other location. The word is used several times in *KCKP* with this meaning.

Khun Phaen and his rival adepts use substances that are found in nature and believed to be intrinsically powerful (ขลัง, *khlang*) because of some unusual property. Mostly these are carried to convey protection or invulnerability. An example is mercury, a metal that acts like a liquid, which conveys protection by flowing to any part of the body threatened by penetration.

Khun Phaen also uses spoken formulas, especially four which match the two pairs of forces found in the *Atharva Veda*. The Great Collection formula provides protection or invulnerability. The Beguiler induces love and is used not only to charm women but to win sympathy from those in authority. The Subduer and other stunning formulas are used to immobilize people. The Loosener is used to open locks and chains, and induce a smooth childbirth.

A second major origin, also from Indic tradition, is a belief that mastery over oneself conveys mastery over natural processes. Through mental control and ascetic practices, a rishi or yogi attains supernatural abilities. This tradition became enshrined within Buddhism. According to one interpretation, the Buddha was schooled in such ascetic practice which he used not only to attain enlightenment but also to perform various "miraculous" acts. He forbade his followers to use such practices on grounds of danger, but after his death, some followers continued to use them and pass them on by teaching. In some Buddhist cultures, these practices were outlawed but continued in unorthodox sects.[159]

The third origin lies in the local belief in the pervasive presence of spirits that determine actions in the natural world. Khun Phaen has the skill to raise and direct spirits. He has a personal team of spirits and adds a particularly powerful one made from the fetus of an unborn child. These spirits provide him with personal protection, and also are able to attack and remove similar protection from opponents. In addition, Khun Phaen has the ability to summon up spirits in the surrounding area for special uses ranging from emergency transport to attacking his enemies. Finally he has the ability to convert grass into spirit warriors—considered one of the most difficult skills in the repertoire.

In the Siamese tradition, the methods of *athan*, the idea of mastery, and the belief in spirits have become closely intertwined. Mastery of oneself gives

159. Fic, *Tantra*, 42–44.

the adept the ability to control spirits and activate natural forces using *athan*'s repertoire of formulas, unusual substances, and other devices. In the manufacture of his sword, Khun Phaen draws on all three of these techniques. He first collects an array of unusual metal substances, then combines them to the accompaniment of many incantations, and finally convokes the spirits to instill the weapon with exceptional power.

The conflation of these different traditions is dramatized in yantra, the single most prominent device used in *KCKP*. By origin, yantra were geometric designs to aid meditation. One of the simplest is a pair of interlocking triangles to aid concentration on duality. In the Southeast Asian tradition, these devices have been developed by the addition of several other elements. The geometrical shapes have acquired symbolic meaning; for example, a circle or oval signifies the Buddha. Pictures of powerful figures have been added, including Hindu deities, legendary figures such as Hanuman, imaginary creatures from the Himaphan Forest, and fierce animals such as lion, tiger, and snake. Written formulas are also included, usually in Pali language in old Khmer script, and often in abbreviated form. Sequences of numbers may be added, again in Khmer script, with individual numbers signifying a deity or a formula, and longer sequences having supernatural significance. Yantras must be made by an adept under very strict conditions, and activated by pronouncing formulas.

Yantras bring together devices from several traditions including ascetic mastery, the Hindu pantheon, Buddhism, spirit beliefs, and number magic. Their primary function is to provide protection, but they are also a means to transfer the intrinsic power of the adept to another person, animal, or thing. For this purpose they can be tattooed on the skin; drawn on wearable articles such as shirts, bandanas, or cloth fashioned into belts and rings; inscribed on metal and strung round the arm, neck, or waist; or written with powder that is then daubed on the forehead or poured into the haft of a weapon.[160]

In modern Thai, this complex of practices to influence the hidden forces in nature is called *sai* or *saiyasat*, derived from a Khmer word for excellence or expertise. But in *KCKP*, this word appears only twice. Throughout *KCKP*, these skills are described with a particular vocabulary: มนตร์, *mon* is the Thai rendering of mantra, meaning a Buddhist prayer or formula; คาถา, *khatha* is a verse in a Buddhist text; อาคม, *akhom*, from Sanskrit *agama* meaning "that which has come down," refers especially to prescriptions of pre-Vedic learning, including those collected into the *Atharva Veda*;[161] เวท, *wet* derives from

160. Bizot, *Les traditions*; PKP, especially vol. 1; YS, passim; Becchetti, *Le mystère*; Bunce, *Yantras*.

161. Sharma, *Kalpacintāmanih*, xviii.

Veda. In *KCKP*, these four individual words are used almost interchangeably for a specific exercise of skill, such as intoning a formula. They are also used in various conjoined forms (*wet mon, khatha akhom,* etc.) to refer to the practice of these skills in general. Alternatively, these skills are called วิชา, *wicha,* meaning knowledge. This is the same word which, via Indo-European, gives us "witch" and the fashionable modern version, "wican." This vocabulary suggests exceptional forms of knowledge authenticated by age, exotic Indic origins, and textual recording—lore.

In Siam, this tradition of lore is closely integrated with the everyday practice of the Buddhist monkhood. Khun Phaen's teachers are all abbots. His curriculum at Wat Som Yai includes the Buddhist scriptures, astrology, and the formulas and mantras of lore, with no sense of incompatibility. In some Buddhist cultures, these practices have been isolated as a specific tradition. François Bizot has argued this was the case in Cambodia where tantric practice seems to have become mainstream at the height of the Angkorian era, but subsequently continued as a distinct, heretical, and covert sect.[162] In Siam, however, practices of self-mastery seem always to have been part of the mainstream Buddhist tradition. Ascetics with miraculous powers have prominent roles in old legends and chronicles, and are integrated into the iconography of wat decoration. The introduction of a purer form of Buddhism from Sri Lanka in the fourteenth to sixteenth centuries failed to overwhelm the old practice. King Mongkut's reforms in the mid nineteenth century and, more importantly, the bureaucratization of the *sangha* by his successor, have since shifted the balance, but far from completely. To this day, monks carry out *athan* rites for house building, and bless amulets which are the modern-day equivalent of yantra. "Forest" monks imitate the Buddha's life, including extreme forms of asceticism, and are accredited with supernatural powers.[163] Royalty, politicians, and generals endeavor to associate themselves with these figures in order to draw on their power.

The power of lore is circumscribed by the law of karma. The divinations furnished by astrology and other omens allow the adept to glimpse the operation of karma in advance, but the techniques of lore are powerless to prevent the law of karma operating. When Khun Phet, Khun Ram, and Saentri Phetkla see omens predicting their death, they conclude that karma determines their life is over, and have no illusion that they can avoid their fate. At the death of Wanthong, Khun Phaen divines that her karma means certain death, and that

---

162. Bizot, *Le figuier à cinq branches*; Bizot, "Notes sur les yantras bouddhiques."
163. Tambiah, *Buddhism and the Spirit-cults,* 49–51; Tambiah, *Buddhist Saints of the Forest,* 45, 315.

although Phra Wai may successfully use lore to extract a pardon from the king, this will not disrupt the law of karma one bit.

8 THIS TRANSLATION

> A friend once consulted me on the idea he had in mind of translating *Khun Chang Khun Phan* into English. I found myself unable to promise much help; it would take more time than a lazy man can afford. Many of you know Burton's translation of the *Arabian Nights*, unexpurgated edition, with footnotes everywhere explaining the significance of words and phrases—on religion, customs, beliefs, social practices, and so on. This is my conception of an adequate translation of *Khun Chang Khun Phan*, footnotes and all.[164]

The author of this passage, Prince Bidyalankarana (Krommuen Phitthayalongkon),[165] was a talented author in both Thai and English. He wrote an article summarizing the plot of *KCKP* and explaining the poetic form. Prince Prem Purachatra began a condensed version of the story in English, but completed only half.[166] J. Kasem Sibunruang summarized the story in French with some commentary.[167] Klaus Wenk sternly transliterated chapter 24 word for word into German.[168] E. H. S. Simmonds recorded recitation of a short passage of *KCKP* in Ang Thong in 1950, and wrote an article comparing the recitation text to Damrong's version.[169] William Gedney wrote enthusiastically about the quality and significance of *KCKP*.[170] In Western-language publication, that seems to be it. This edition is the first complete translation into any language.

Sources

Anyone who reads *KCKP* today owes an enormous debt to Prince Damrong Rajanubhab. He managed the transition of *KCKP* from manuscript to book,

---

164. Bidyalankarana, "*Sebha* Recitation," 12.

165. Prince Bidyalankarana (1876–1945), son of Prince Wichaichan, the last *upparat* or Front Palace king at the center of the "Front Palace Crisis" of King Chulalongkorn in 1875, was an author, editor, and translator, often under the alias "No Mo So."

166. Prem Chaya, *Story*.

167. Sibunruang, *La femme*. The total length is 159 pages.

168. Wenk, *Studien*, 30–89.

169. Simmonds, "Thai Narrative Poetry." Unfortunately the tapes in SOAS library have deteriorated.

170. "I have often thought that if all the other information on traditional Thai culture were to be lost, the whole complex could be reconstructed from this marvellous text" (Gedney, "Problems in Translating," 23).

creating a classic edition which will last forever. Yet *KCKP* is not a specific text but a tradition. The story has developed with contributions by unknown numbers of storytellers, poets, copyists, and editors over several hundred years. As Damrong described in his preface to *KCKP*, he selected passages from various alternative manuscripts, and made many editorial changes, with two specific aims in view—to make the book acceptable within the moral standards of the time, and to highlight its literary quality. In preparing this translation, we are working in this same fluid tradition. We have used Prince Damrong's edition as the basis for our translation, but we have been alerted by William Gedney, Khun Wichitmatra, Choomsai Suwannachomphu, Atsiri Thammachot, Sujit Wongthet, and others that there are alternative versions worth considering. We have added or substituted roughly a hundred passages from older versions, especially from the Wat Ko/Samuel Smith printed editions, but also from Khru Jaeng's compositions, the *Samnuan kao* fragments, and some *samut thai* texts in the National Archives. We have not attempted to read all the manuscript texts of *KCKP*. There are almost three hundred volumes in the National Archives and we judged that if we got too far into those, we would probably never complete the translation. We have included some passages that were judged obscene or unsuitable over a century ago, but are differently assessed by today's values. We have included some passages, such as a funeral chant and house-building ceremony, which seem valuable as cultural record.

The proper finale of the *KCKP* story is the death of Wanthong in chapter 36 which concludes with an explicit "they all lived happily ever after" ending. From that point forward, two of the three main characters no longer appear, and the subsequent chapters are sequels about the lineage of Khun Phaen. Prince Damrong included seven of these chapters before ruling that the others "are not considered to have value as literature."[171] In truth, the quality falls off after Wanthong's death, though episodes such as the giant crocodile spreading panic along the Chaophraya River are deservedly popular. We have set the ending at Wanthong's death, but we have included translations of Damrong's extra seven chapters in the *Companion* volume. Another 11,000 lines of sequel chapters have been published since Damrong's edition. We include a brief summary of these in the *Companion* volume.

The major excision we have made from the Damrong edition is the Buakhli story on the creation of the Goldchild. This story was not part of the manuscript text of *KCKP* which was first assembled in the mid-nineteenth century, and does not appear in the Smith and Wat Ko printed editions. It was probably an independent tale that became popular with storytellers and was adapted into

---

171. *Companion*, 1362.

KCKP by Khru Jaeng. It was included in the assembled version for the first time in the Damrong edition. The Buakhli story is so powerful that it strongly affects the reader's impression of the whole work. Yet Prince Bidyalankarana noted that "the old version is more in accord with general belief as to the method of procuring the spirit of an unborn infant."[172] We have used this old version. A translation of the Buakhli episode is found in the *Companion* volume.

On the same grounds, we perhaps ought to substitute the version of the Chiang Mai campaign from the Wat Ko edition. Damrong used a new version, also partly composed by Khru Jaeng, which tells the same outline story but with many differences in detail, atmosphere, and angle of vision. But substituting the older version here would be more difficult because there are several links from Damrong's version to later incidents in the plot. Besides, the new version does not affect the overall meaning of the poem in the same way as the Buakhli episode does. Hence we have retained the Damrong version, but imported several passages from the older Wat Ko text where this can be done without disruption. We have also included a full translation of the Wat Ko version of the Chiang Mai campaign in the *Companion* volume.

The passages we have imported appear in older texts but were either deleted or rewritten in the nineteenth-century revisions. In his preface, Damrong related that he deleted material that he considered obscene, and comic scenes, probably improvised by storytellers, that he judged were not funny on the printed page.[173] Probably most of our restorations are these excisions. The replacements range in length from half a line to around a hundred lines. The two longest are the "twelve language chant" in chapter 2, and the account of Khun Chang's ordination in chapter 36. In every case where we have deviated from the Damrong text there is a footnote which indicates what material has been inserted, and which provides any text that has been removed. Hence, there is a full translation of the Damrong text in this edition, but some is in the notes and some in the *Companion* volume. We have not composed any material, and have added only a handful of words for clarity.

Style

Our overriding principle in compiling the translation has been to provide a full and accurate rendering of the story. Our second objective has been to make it fun and easy to read. For this second reason, we have not translated word by word, hemistich by hemistich, or line by line, as the result would be stilted and clumsy. Instead, we have treated the two-line stanza as a unit. In the Thai

---

172. Bidyalankarana, "*Sebha* Recitation," 20.
173. *Companion*, 1363.

original, the order of words and clauses within a stanza is sometimes strange. In some cases, the order was probably suitable for recitation, but contradicts the linear logic expected by a reader. In others, the order may be dictated by the metrical form. We may reorder words and clauses within a stanza in the interests of readability, but we never move words or clauses across stanzas.[174] We have kept the stanza divisions in the layout. This does not reflect the traditional layout, but serves as a reminder that the original was a poem not prose.

In the original there are paragraph breaks marked by a circular symbol. In the older passages, probably transcribed from recitation, these were points where the focus shifts from one character to another. The first stanza of the paragraph usually names the new focal character, and often fills out the stanza with epithets. Perhaps the storyteller adopted a new vocal style or stance to dramatize the change of character. In passages composed later, this convention is looser. There are more passages of dialogue which would be clumsy or impossible to break into paragraphs in the same way. The division becomes more like a modern paragraph. Generally speaking we have kept these paragraph breaks as in the original, but have not treated them as sacrosanct. In old texts, the positioning of these breaks sometimes differs across different versions. Very occasionally (maybe a dozen places), we have inserted, moved, or deleted a break. At some points in the story where there is a leap of time or place, we have inserted a symbol (✺). These do not appear in the original.

In three places we have rearranged whole passages. The most important of these is in the opening chapter. In the original, the three families are introduced; then the dreams of the three wives are related; and then the three births are described. For a reader who is not familiar with the story and the characters, this is very confusing. We have rearranged the material to treat each family (introduction, dream, birth) in sequence. In chapter 19 we have moved two stanzas, and in chapter 21, we have moved a small passage about Kaeo Kiriya.

Prince Damrong inserted chapter divisions and chapter titles into the previously continuous text. We have retained all of his chapter divisions but have changed a few titles. We have shortened some because they are long and clumsy in English translation, and we have occasionally substituted a title based on the way this passage is traditionally known (for example, *Khun Phaen meets Phim in a cotton field*).

---

174. We sometimes omit words which we judge have been inserted for euphony or to conform to the demands of the metrical form. Quite often, a stanza will end with various phrases which mean "soon" or "quickly," but which seem to be there to serve as the anchor for the next rhyming sequence, not because of their meaning.

We have used as few Thai words as necessary. Sometimes that has meant using a translation that experts may find too simple (e.g., "soul" for *khwan*). Ten words that appear very often (e.g., *wat, wai*) have been treated as naturalized. We have invented some English words, including terms like "sentinelle" for the female palace guard, and the names of several plants that in the original Thai have metaphorical meanings that would be lost if the words were romanized or rendered with their usual English name. The invented terms for flora and fauna are explained in tables in the *Companion* volume. Other inventions are explained in the glossary.

We have not tried to render the text in poetic form.[175] Given the difference in the structure of Thai and English, it would be very difficult to convert the Thai text into an English poetic form without substantially modifying the content. However, we have been very aware that *KCKP* originated as a text for recitation and have tried to retain some of that character in the translation.

---

175. Where the characters recite a poem, song, or chant, we have generally tried to approximate the rhyming scheme found in the Thai original. Some, however, are impossible. We have also rendered the opening and closing stanzas of the story in an approximation of the *klon* meter, as a sample.

BIBLIOGRAPHY

Texts of *KCKP*, dictionaries, and other key sources are referenced with abbreviations.

1. Texts of KCKP

KJ   *Bot sepha rueang Khun Chang Khun Phaen ton taeng ngan Phra Wai (samnuan Khru Jaeng)* [Khru Jaeng's version of the marriage of Phra Wai]. Bangkok: Fine Arts Department, printed for distribution at the royal *kathin* at Wat Sangwet-witsayaram, 3 April 1935. Printed from a manuscript in the Thailand National Archives.

PD   *Sepha Khun Chang Khun Phaen.* Edited by Prince Damrong Rajanubhab. 3 vols. Bangkok: Khurusapha, 2003 [1917–18].

SK1   "Sepha rueang Khun Chang Khun Phaen samnuan kao thi 1." [*KCKP,* old version 1].

SK2   "Sepha rueang Khun Chang Khun Phaen samnuan kao thi 2." [*KCKP,* old version 2]. First printed in: *Khun Chang Khun Phaen chabap khwam kao,* Bangkok: Sophon Phiphannathanakon, 1925. Pagination here from: Chotchuang Nadon and Khru Sepha Niranam, *Khun Chang Khun Phaen chabap yon tamnan* [*KCKP,* the legendary version], Bangkok: Phloi Tawan, 1998.

SS   *Khun Chang Khun Phaen.* 40 vols. Bangkok: Rong phim Khru Smit thi Bang Ko Laem [Samuel Smith press at Bang Ko Laem], 1872. Incomplete copy provided by Choomsai Suwannachomphu.

TNA   Manuscripts in the Thailand National Archives.

WK   *Khun Chang Khun Phaen.* 40 vols. Rattanakosin [Bangkok]: Wat Ko, 1890. Complete copy in William Gedney collection, University of Michigan library, PL 4206 .K46, FILM 30292(15).

2. Dictionaries (cited only for obscure words)

MAT   *Phojananukrom chabap matichon* [Matichon dictionary]. Bangkok: Matichon, 2004.

MC   McFarland, G. B. *Thai-English Dictionary.* Stanford: Stanford University Press, 1944.

PAL   Pallegoix, Jean-Baptiste. *Sapha phajana phasa thai: Sive Dictionarium Linguae Thai.* Paris: Jussu Imperatoris Impressum, 1865. Entries only in the second edition, Bangkok 1896, are referenced as PAL2.

RI   *Phojananukrom chabap ratchabanditsathan pho so 2542* [Royal Institute dictionary, 1999 edition]. Bangkok: Royal Institute, 2003.

3. Other key sources, cited as abbreviations

APA Boranratchathanin, Phraya. *Athibai phaen thi phranakhon Si Ayutthaya* [Descriptive map of Ayutthaya]. Bangkok: Ton Chabap, 2007 [1926]. Believed to be a description of Ayutthaya transcribed from prisoners taken to Ava in 1767. This edition is a facsimile of the 1926 edition, including extensive commentary by Phraya Boranratchathanin, the official responsible for the first archaeological work, and a facsimile of *Phumisathan krung Si Ayutthaya* [Geography of Ayutthaya], an appendix which Phraya Boranratchathanin added in 1939.

CK Choti Kalyanamit. *Phojananukrom sathapattayakam lae sinlapa kiao nueng* [Dictionary of architecture and related arts]. Bangkok: Muang Boran, 2005.

CS Choomsai Suwannachomphu. "Kan sueksa priapthiap sepha rueang Khun Chang Khun Phaen chabap ho phrasumut Wachirayan samrap phranakhon kap chabap samnuan uen" [Comparative study of the Wachirayan Capital Library edition of *KCKP* with other versions]. M.A. diss., Silpakorn University, 1991.

KCK *Khamhaikan chao krung kao* [Testimony of the inhabitants of the old capital]. Edited by Prince Damrong Rajanubhab. Bangkok: Chotmaihet, 2001 [1924]. Believed to be testimony of Ayutthaya prisoners taken to Ava in 1767.

KLW *Khamhaikan khun luang ha wat* [Testimony of the king who sought a wat]. Bangkok: Sukhothai Thammathirat University, 2004. A variant version of KCK.

KP Kukrit Pramoj. *Khun Chang Khun Phaen: Chabap an mai* [*KCKP*, a new reading]. Bangkok: Dokya, 2000 [1989]. A telling of the story with commentary and asides, originally serialized in *Siam Rath* from 20 August to 5 November 1988.

KTS *Kotmai tra sam duang* [Three Seals Law]. 5 vols. Bangkok: Khurusapha, 1994 [1805]. Surviving laws of the Ayutthaya period, collected on the bidding of King Rama I.

KW Kanchanakphan (Sanga Kanchanakphan, Khun Wichitmatra) and Nai Tamra na Muang Tai (Plueang na Nakhon). *Lao rueang Khun Chang Khun Phaen* [Telling the story of *KCKP*]. Bangkok: Amarin, 2002 [1961]. A summary of the story with extensive commentary on words, customs, and historical matters, mostly by Khun Wichitmatra.

PKW Thep Sarikabut. *Phra khamphi phrawet* [Manuals of lore]. 6 vols. Bangkok: Utsahakam kan phim, n.d. A massive collection of mantras, yantras, and other aspects of lore.

RCA *The Royal Chronicles of Ayutthaya*. A synoptic translation by Richard D. Cushman. Edited by David K. Wyatt. Bangkok: Siam Society, 2000. A translation of most known versions of the chronicles.

RR *Three Worlds According to King Ruang: A Thai Buddhist Cosmology*. Translated and edited by Frank E. Reynolds and Mani B. Reynolds. Berkeley: University of California Press, 1982. Translation of a key work in Thai Buddhist cosmology.

SB Suphon Bunnag. *Sombat kawi chut Khun Chang Khun Phaen* [Poetic treasure of *KCKP*]. Printed for the cremation of the author, 15 June 1975 [original two-volume edition, 1960]. A telling of the story with commentary and appreciation.

SW? *Saranukrom watthanatham thai* [Thai cultural encyclopaedia]. Bangkok: Siam Commercial Bank, 1994. Printed in multiple volumes for each region; SWC denotes central, SWN north, SWI northeast, SWS south. A massive encyclopaedia of Thai objects and practices.

YS Yanchot, Achan Hon (Chayamongkhon Udomsap). *Khamphi saiyasat chabap sombun* [The complete manual of supernaturalism]. Bangkok: Sinlapa Bannakhan, 1995. A recent and extensive collection.

4. Other works cited

Akin Rabibhadana. *The Organization of Thai Society in the Early Bangkok Period, 1782–1873.* Bangkok: Amarin, 1996.

Anuman Rajadhon, Phya. "The Khwan and its Ceremonies." In Anuman, *Essays on Thai Folklore.* Bangkok: Thai Inter-Religious Commission for Development and Sathirakoses Nagapradipa Foundation, 1968.

Anuman Rajadhon, Phya. *Essays on Thai Folklore.* Bangkok: Thai Inter-Religious Commission for Development and Sathirakoses Nagapradipa Foundation, 1968.

Anuman Rajadhon, Phya. *Phi sang thewada* [Spirits and deities]. Bangkok: Printed for the cremation of Rawin Sisanphang, Wat Khruewanworawihan, 22 April 1961.

Anuman Rajadhon, Phya. *Prapheni kiao kap chiwit taeng ngan* [Life customs: marriage]. Bangkok: Sayam, 1996.

Anuman Rajadhon, Phya. *Prapheni bet set* [Miscellaneous customs]. Bangkok: Social Science Association of Thailand, 1965.

Anuman Rajadhon, Phya. *Prapheni kiao kap thesakan* [Customs associated with festivals]. Bangkok: Social Science Association of Thailand, 1963.

Anuman Rajadhon, Phya. *Prapheni nai kan sang ban pluk ruean* [Customs of house building]. Bangkok: Sayam, 1996.

Anuman Rajadhon, Phya. *Prapheni nueang nai kan koet* [Birth customs]. Bangkok: Sayam, 1996.

Anuman Rajadhon, Phya. *Prapheni nueang nai kan tai* [Death customs]. Bangkok: Sayam, 1996.

Anuman Rajadhon, Phya. *Some Traditions of the Thai and Other Translations.* Bangkok: Thai Inter-religious Commission for Development and Sathirakoses Nagapradipa Foundation, 1987.

Anuman Rajadhon, Phya. *Thet Maha Chat* (in English). Bangkok: Fine Arts Department, 1969.

Atherton, David C. "Space, Identity, and Self-definition: The Forest in *Khun Chang Khun Phaen.*" M.A. diss., University of Wisconsin-Madison, 2006.

Atsiri Thammachot, Chotchuang Nadon, and Khru Sepha Niranam. *Khun Chang Khun*

Phaen chabap nok thamniap [*KCKP*, the unofficial version]. Cremation volume of Nang Samnuan Intharawat. Bangkok: Bai Bua, 1990.

Baker, Chris and Pasuk Phongpaichit. "The Career of *Khun Chang Khun Phaen.*" *Journal of the Siam Society*, vol. 97 (2009): 1–42.

Baker, Chris and Pasuk Phongpaichit. In *New Frames of Analysis in Thai Literary Studies*, edited by Rachel Harrison, forthcoming.

Barnes, Ruth, Steven Steven, and Rosemary Crill. *Trade, Temple and Court: Indian Textiles from the Tapi Collection*. Mumbai: India Book House, 2002.

Bastian, Adolf. *A Journey in Siam* (1863). Translated by Walter E. J. Tips. Bangkok: White Lotus, 2005.

Battye, Noel Alfred. "The Military, Government and Society in Siam, 1868–1910: Politics and Military Reform During the Reign of King Chulalongkorn." Ph.D. diss., Cornell University, 1974.

Becchetti, Catherine. *Le mystère dans les lettres*. Bangkok: Edition des Cahiers de France, 1991.

Bèze, Claude de. "The Memoir of Father de Bèze." In *1688 Revolution in Siam*, translated by E. W. Hutchinson. Bangkok: White Lotus, 1990.

Bickner, Robert J. *An Introduction to the Thai Poem 'Lilit Phra Law'—The Story of King Law*. DeKalb: University of Northern Illinois, 1991.

Bidyalankarana, Prince. "*Sebha* Recitation and the Story of *Khun Chang Khun Phan.*" *Journal of the Thailand Research Society*, vol. 33 (1941): 1–22.

Bidyalankarana, Prince. "The Pastime of Rhyme-making and Singing in Rural Siam." *Journal of the Siam Society*, vol. 20 (1926): 101–129.

Bizot, François. "Notes sur les yantras bouddhiques d'Indochine." In *Tantric and Taoist Studies in Honour of R. A. Stein*, edited by Michael Strickmann. Brussels: Institute Belge des Hautes Études Chinoises, 1981. Vol I (*Mélanges Chinois et Bouddhiques*, vol. xx): 155–91.

Bizot, François. *Le figuier a cinq branches: recherche sur le bouddhisme Khmer*. Paris: École française d'Extrême-Orient, 1976.

Bizot, François. *Les traditions de la pabbajja en Asie du Sud-East. Recherches sur le bouddhisme Khmer, iv*. Abhandlungen der Akademie der Wissenschaften in Göttingen. Göttingen: Vandenhoeck & Ruprecht, 1988.

Boonsong Lekagul. *Nok mueang thai* [Birds of Thailand]. Bangkok: Dr Boonsong Lekagul Group, 2007.

Boranasathan nai jangwat phranakhon Si Ayutthaya [Monuments in Ayutthaya Province]. 2 vols. Bangkok: Fine Arts Department and James H. W. Thompson Foundation, 2008.

Boranratchathanin, Phraya Boranburanurak (Phon Dechakup). "Tamnan krung kao" [Annals of the old city]. In *Prachum phongsawadan* [Collected chronicles, history series], part 63; reprinted as vol. 37 in the Khurusapha edition (1969).

Bot lakhon nok phraratchaniphon ratchakan thi 2 [Outer dramas of King Rama II]. Bangkok: Sinlapa Bannakhan, 2002.

"Bot lakhon rueang Unarut roi rueang" [Drama script of Unarut]. In *Bot lakhon Phramalethethai lae Unarut roi rueang khong Khun Suwan bot lakhon rueang Raden Landai khong Phramahamontri (Sap)* [Dramas of Phra Malethai and Unarut by Khun Suwan, and Inao by Phra Mahamontri (Sap)]. Bangkok: Kasembannakit, 1967

Bunce, Frederick W. *The Yantras of Deities and their Numerological Foundations: An Iconographic Consideration.* New Delhi: DK Printworld, 2001.

Bunce, Frederick W. *An Encyclopaedia of Hindu Deities, Demi-Gods, Godlings, Demons and Heroes with Special Focus on Iconographic Attributes.* Vol. I. New Delhi: DK Printworld, 2000.

Bunnak Phayakmet. *Sepha rueang Khun Chang Khun Phaen ton to chak chabap ho samut haeng chat* [*KCKP* following on from the National Library version]. Sinlapa Bannakhan, n.d.

Busakorn Lalilert. "The Ban Phlu Luang Dynasty 1688–1767: A Study of the Thai Monarchy during the Closing Years of the Ayutthaya Period." Ph.D diss., SOAS, University of London, 1972.

Cadet, J. M. *The Ramakien: The Stone Rubbings of the Thai Epic.* Bangkok: Central Department Store, 1970.

Chandra, Moti. "Costumes and Textiles in the Sultanate Period." *Journal of Indian Textile History*, vol. 6 (1961).

Chang ratchaphahana [Royal elephant mounts]. Bangkok: Project to Sustain Thai Cultural Heritage, n.d. (?2000).

Chang Surin, http://www.surin.net/elephant/

Charnvit Kasetsiri. *The Rise of Ayudhya: A History of Siam in the Fourteenth and Fifteenth Centuries.* Kuala Lumpur: Oxford University Press, 1976.

Chatraphon Jindadet, "Kan borihan ratchasamnuek fai nai ratchasamai Phrabat Somdet Phra Chulachomklao Jaoyuhua" [The inner court administration in the reign of King Chulalongkorn]. *Warasan ruam botkhwam prawatisat* [Journal of the Historical Society], no. 25 (2003): 145–200.

Chatri Prakitnonthakan. *Phraphutthachinnarat* [The Chinnarat Buddha]. Bangkok: Sinlapa Watthanatham, 2008.

Chatthip Nartsupha. *The Thai Village Economy in the Past.* Translated by Chris Baker and Pasuk Phongpaichit. Chiang Mai: Silkworm Books, 1999.

Chaumont, Chevalier de, and Abbé de Choisy. *Aspects of the Embassy to Siam in 1685.* Edited by Michael Smithies. Chiang Mai: Silkworm Books, 1997.

Chawalit Withayanon. *Pla nam juet* [Fresh water fish]. Bangkok: Sarakadee, 2004.

Chawdri, L. R. *Secrets of Yantra, Mantra and Tantra.* New Delhi: Sterling, 1992.

Chew, Katherine Liang. *Tales of the Teahouse Retold: Investiture of the Gods.* New York: Writers Club Press, 2002.

Childers, R. C. *A Dictionary of the Pali Language*, 1971, available online at http://dsal.uchicago.edu/dictionaries/pali/frontmatter.html

Chira Chongkol, "Jewellery and Other Decorative Arts in Thailand." *Arts of Asia*, vol. 12, no. 6 (December 1982): 82–91.

Chira Chongkol, "Textiles and Costumes in Thailand." *Arts of Asia,* vol. 12, no. 6 (December 1982): 121–31.

Chiwit lae ngan khong Sunthon Phu [Life and works of Sunthon Phu]. Revised edition, ninth printing. Bangkok: Khurusapha, 2000.

Choisy, Abbé de. *Journal of a Voyage to Siam 1685–1686*. Translated by Michael Smithies. Kuala Lumpur: Oxford University Press, 1993.

Cholthira Satyawadhna. "Kan nam wannakhadiwijan phaen mai baep tawan tok ma chai kap wannakhadi thai" [Application of modern western literary criticism to Thai literature]. MA diss., Chulalongkorn University, 1970.

Choomsai Suwannachomphu. "Kan sueksa priapthiap sepha rueang Khun Chang Khun Phaen chabap ho phrasumut Wachirayan samrap phranakhon kap chabap samnuan uen" [Comparative study of the Wachirayan Capital Library edition of *KCKP* with other versions]. MA diss., Silpakorn University, 1991.

Choomsai Suwannachomphu. "Sakkarat 147 phi thi pen panha nai bot sepha rueang Khun Chang Khun Phaen" [The problem date of 147 in *KCKP*]. *Sinlapa watthanatham* [Art and culture], vol. 23, no. 6 (May 2002).

Chotchuang Nadon and Khru Sepha Niranam. *Khun Chang Khun Phaen chabap yon tamnan* [*KCKP*, the legendary version]. Phloi Tawan, 1998.

Chulalongkorn, King. *Sadet praphat saiyok* [Visiting Saiyok]. Bangkok: Khurusapha, 1998 [1888].

Coutre, Jacques de. *Andanzas asiáticas* [Asian adventures]. Edited by Eddy Stols, B. Teensma, and J. Werberckmoes. Cronicas de America 61 series, Historia 16. Madrid: Información y Revistas, 1990.

Cowell, E. B., ed. *The Jataka or Stories of the Buddha's Former Births*. Translated by Robert Chalmers. 6 vols. Cambridge: Cambridge University Press, 1895.

Daeng Kaosaen et al. *Leklai mi jing* [Fluid metal truly exists]. Nonthaburi: Busarakham, 2006.

Damrong Rajanubhab, Prince, *A Biography of King Naresuan the Great.* Translated and edited by Kennon Breazeale. Bangkok: Toyota Thailand Foundation and the Foundation or the Promotion of Social Science and Humanities Textbooks Project, 2008.

Damrong Rajanubhab, Prince. *Athibai raya thang long lamnam Ping tang tae mueang Chiang Mai jon tueng Paknampho* [Journey down the Ping River from Chiang Mai to Paknampho]. Bangkok: Sophonphiphat-thanakon, 1927.

Damrong Rajanubhab, Prince. *Khwam songjam* [Memories]. Bangkok: Phra Chan, 1946.

Damrong Rajanubhab, Prince. *Nithan borankhadi* [Historical tales]. Bangkok: Phra Chan. 11th printing, Bangkok: Kaona, 1962 [1944].

Damrong Rajanubhab, Prince. *Our Wars with the Burmese*. Translated by Phra Phraison Salarak, edited by Chris Baker. Bangkok: White Lotus, 2001.

Damrong Rajanubhab, Prince. *Phraratchaphongsawadan krung Rattanakosin ratchakan thi 2* [Chronicle of the Bangkok second reign]. Ninth edition, Bangkok: Fine Arts Department, 2003 [1916].

Damrong Rajanubhab, Prince. *Rabiap kan len tamnan sepha* [Dramatized history of *sepha*]. Printed for the cremation of Nai Chuan Manyanon, Wat Somnatwihan, 31 March 1956.

Damrong Rajanubhab, Prince. *Tamnan sepha* [History of *sepha*], for the second edition of the Wachirayan Library edition of *KCKP*. Bangkok: Thai Press (Thanon Rong muang), 1925.

Dhani Nivat, Prince. "Siamese Versions of the Panji Romance." In *India Antiqua. A Volume of Oriental Studies Presented by his Friends and Pupils to Jean Philippe Vogel.* Leyden: E. J. Brill, 1947.

Dhiravat na Pombejra, *Siamese Court Life in the Seventeenth Century as Depicted in European Sources.* Bangkok: Chulalongkorn University, 2001.

Eade, J. C. *The Calendrical Systems of South-East Asia*. Leiden and New York: E. J. Brill, 1995.

Egerton of Tatton, Lord. *Indian and Oriental Armour*. London: Arms and Armour Press, 1968 [facsimile of 1896 second edition, original from 1880].

Englehart, Neil A. *Culture and Power in Traditional Siamese Government.* Ithaca: Cornell Southeast Asia Program Publications, 2001.

Farrington, Anthony and Dhiravat na Pombejra. *The English Factory in Siam, 1612–1685.* 2 vols. London: British Library, 2007.

Fic, Victor. *The Tantra. Its Origins, Theories and Diffusion to Nepal, Tibet, Mongolia, Japan and Indonesia.* New Delhi: Abhinav, 2003.

Flood, Thadeus and Chadin Flood, tr. and ed. *The Dynastic Chronicles, Bangkok Era, The First Reign, Chaophraya Thiphakorawong Edition.* Tokyo: Center for East Asian Cultural Studies, Vol. I, Text, 1978; Vol II, Annotations and Commentary, 1990.

Floor, Willem. *The Persian Textile Industry in Historical Perspective 1500–1925.* Paris: L'Harmattan, 1919.

Forbin, Count Claude de. *The Siamese Memoirs of Count Claude de Forbin 1685–1688.* Introduced and edited by Michael Smithies. Chiang Mai: Silkworm Books, 1996.

Gardner, Simon, Pindar Sidisunthorn, and Vilaiwan Anusarnsunthorn. *A Field Guide to Forest Trees of Northern Thailand.* Bangkok: Kobfai, 2000.

Gedney, William J. "Problems in Translating Traditional Thai Poetry." In *William J. Gedney's Thai and Indic Literary Studies,* edited by Thomas J. Hudak. Michigan Papers on South and Southeast Asia, 446. Ann Arbor: University of Michigan Press, 1997.

Gedney, William J. "Siamese Verse Forms in Historical Perspective." In Gedney, *Selected Papers on Comparative Tai Studies,* edited by R. J. Bickner et al. Ann Arbor:

University of Michigan, 1989.

Gerini, G. E. "On Siamese Proverbs and Idiomatic Expressions." *Journal of the Siam Society*, vol. 93 (2005): 147–264 [1904].

Gerini, G. E. *The Thet Mahachat Ceremony*. Bangkok: Sathirakoset-Nagapradipa Foundation, 1976 [1892].

Gervaise, John. *The Natural and Political History of the Kingdom of Siam*. Translated by John Villiers. Bangkok: White Lotus, 1998 [1688].

Giles, Francis H. "About a Love Philtre." *Journal of the Siam Society*, vol. 30, no. 1 (1938): 25–28.

Griswold, A. B. and Prasert na Nagara. *Epigraphical and Historical Studies*. Bangkok: Historical Society, 1992.

Guy, John. "Painted to Order: Commissioning Indian Textiles for the Court of Siam." In *Proceedings of the International Symposium "Crossroads of Thai and Dutch History" 9-11 September, 2004,* edited by Dhiravat na Pombejra et al. Bangkok: SEAMEO-SPAFA, 2007.

Guy, John. *Woven Cargoes: Indian Textiles in the East*. London: Thames and Hudson, 1998.

Halliday, R. "Immigration of the Mons into Siam." *Journal of the Siam Society,* vol. 10, no. 3 (1913): 1–15.

Hindu Myths: A Sourcebook Translated from the Sanskrit. With an introduction by Wendy Doniger O'Flaherty. London: Penguin Books, 1980.

Hogg, Ian V. *Encyclopedia of Weaponry*. Enfield: Guinness Printing, 1992.

Hora Purajan. *Tamra phrommachat chabap sombun* [Complete Phrommachat manual]. Bangkok: Liang Chiang, 2006.

Hudak, Thomas J. *The Indigenization of Pali Meters in Thai Poetry*. Monographs in International Studies, Southeast Asia Series No. 87. Athens: Ohio University Press, 1990.

Ishii Yoneo. "The Thai Thammasat (with a Note on the Lao Thammasat)." In *The Laws of South-East Asia, Vol. I, The Pre-Modern Texts*, edited by M. B. Hooker. Singapore: Butterworth, 1986.

Ishii, Yoneo. *Sangha, State and Society: Thai Buddhism in History*. Translated by Peter Hawkes. Monographs of the Center of Southeast Asian Studies, Kyoto University, 16. Honolulu: University of Hawaii Press, 1986.

Jacq-Hergoualc'h, Michel. *Etude historique et critique du livre de Simon de La Loubère "Du Royaume de Siam," Paris 1691*. Paris: Editions recherche sur les civilisations, 1987.

Jamison, Stephanie W. *The Ravenous Hyenas and the Wounded Sun: Myth and Ritual in Ancient India*. Ithaca and London: Cornell University Press, 1991.

Jory, Patrick. "The *Vessantara Jataka, barami,* and the *Boddhisatta*-kings: The Origin and Spread of a Thai Concept of Power." *Crossroads*, vol. 16, no. 2 (2002): 36–78.

Julathat Phayakharanon, "Botrian: rueang jedisathan nai Suphanburi" ["Learnings on religious monuments in Suphanburi." In Thai Studies Institute, *Suphanburi: Prawatisat sinlapa lae watthanatham* [Suphanburi: History, art, and culture]. Proceedings of a seminar, Suphanburi, 12–20 November 1987.

Julathat Phayakharanon. "Asawa-alongkan kochasan-alongkan" [Decoration of horses and elephants]. In *Sichamaiyachan* [Two illustrous teachers], edited by Winai Pongsripian and Pridi Phitphumiwithi. Bangkok: Ministry of Culture, 2002.

Kaempfer, Engelbert. *A Description of the Kingdom of Siam.* Bangkok: Orchid Press, 1998 [facsimile of 1727 edition].

Kan taeng kai thai: Wiwatthanakan jak adit su patjuban [Thai costume: From past to present]. Bangkok: Committee to Celebrate His Majesty the King's 6th Cycle, 1999.

Kasem Sibunruang, J. *La femme, le héros et le vilain. Poème populaire thai. Khun Chang, Khun Phen.* Paris: Presses Universitaires de France, 1960.

"Khamhaikan khun khlon" [Testimony of officials]. In *Prachum phongsawadan phak thi 7* [Collected chronicles, vol. 7]. Cremation volume of Luang Chamni Bannakom (Ma Jarurat), 30 March 1918.

Khun Chang Khun Phaen chabap khwam kao [*KCKP*, the old version]. Bangkok: Sophon Phiphannathanakon, 1925.

Khwanmueang Jantharot, "Lao nai Khun Chang Khun Phaen" [Lao in *KCKP*]. *Warasan aksonsat* [Arts journal], vol. 26, no. 2 (1993): 91–97.

King, Ben, Martin Woodcock, and E.C. Dickinson, *A Field Guide to the Birds of South-East Asia.* London: Collins, 1975.

La Loubère, Simon de. *A New Historical Relation of the Kingdom of Siam.* Translated by A. P. Gen. London, 1793.

Lagirarde, François. "Devotional Diversification in Thai Monasteries: The Worship of the Fat Monk." In *The Buddhist Monastery: A Cross-Cultural Survey*, edited by Pierre Pichaud and François Lagirarde. Paris: École française d'Extrême-Orient, 2003.

Lagirarde, François. "Gavampati et la tradition des quatre-vingts disciples du Buddha: Texte et iconographie du Laos et de Thaïlande." *Bulletin de l'École française d'Extrême-Orient*, vol. 87, no. 1 (2000): 57–78.

Launay, Adrien. *Histoire de la mission de Siam. Documents historiques.* 2 vols. Paris: Société des Missions étrangères, 1920.

Lilit Taleng Phai [Defeat of the Mon]. Printed for the cremation of Prof. M.L. Kaset Sanitwong, Wat Thepsirin, Bangkok, 2 September 1995.

Lingat, R. *L'Esclavage privé dans le vieux lois Siamois.* Paris: Les Editions Domat-Montchrestien, 1931.

Lord, Donald C. *Mo Bradley and Thailand.* Grand Rapids: William B. Eerdmans, 1969.

Low, James. "Captain Low's History of Tennasserim." *Journal of the Royal Asiatic Society,* vol. 4 (1836): 25–54.

Malalasekara, G. P. *Dictionary of Pali Proper Names.* London: Luzac, 1960.

Manas Chitakasem. "The Emergence and Development of the Nirat Genre in Thai Poetry." *Journal of the Siam Society*, vol. 60, no. 2 (1972): 135–68.

Manat Ophakun, *Prawatisat mueang Suphan* [History of Suphanburi]. Bangkok: Sinlapa Watthanatham, 2004.

Manat Ophakun. *Prawat wat khae* [History of Wat Khae]. 8th printing, n. p., 1 August 2001.

Matichon. *Sayam phimphakan: Prawatisat kan phim nai prathet thai* [Siamese printing: History of printing in Thailand]. Bangkok: Matichon Press, 2006.

Mattani Mojdara Rutnin. *Dance, Drama, and Theatre in Thailand: The Process of Development and Modernization.* Tokyo: Toyo Bunko, 1993.

Maxwell, Robyn. *Textiles of Southeast Asia: Tradition, Trade and Transformation.* Melbourne, Oxford, etc: Oxford University Press, 1990.

Mayoury Ngaosyvathn and Pheuiphanh Ngaosyvathn, *Paths to Conflagration: Fifty Years of Diplomacy and Warfare in Laos, Thailand, and Vietnam, 1778–1828.* Ithaca: Cornell University Press, 1988.

McFarland, George Bradley, ed. *Historical Sketch of Protestant Missions in Siam.* Bangkok: White Lotus, 1999 [1928].

McGilvary, Daniel. *A Half Century Among the Siamese and the Lao: An Autobiography.* Bangkok: White Lotus, 2002 [1912].

Miller, Anthony and Preecha Juntanamalaga, "Thai Time." Australian National University, 2000. http://dspace.anu.edu.au/bitstream/1885/41890/3/thai_time.html

Miller, Terry E. and Sean Williams, ed. *The Garland Encyclopedia of World Music. Vol. 4, Southeast Asia.* New York and London: Garland Publishing, 1998.

Montri Umavijani. *Sunthorn Phu: An Anthology.* UNESCO Series of Representative Authors. Bangkok: Office of National Culture Commission, 1990.

Muang Boran. *Wat Pradu Songtham.* Bangkok: Muang Boran, 1985.

Munro-Hay, Stuart. *Nakhon Si Thammarat: The Archaeology, History and Legends of a Southern Thai Town.* Bangkok: White Lotus, 2001.

Murphy, Veronica and Rosemary Crill. *Tie-Dyed Textiles of India: Tradition and Trade.* London: Victoria and Albert Museum/Mapin, 1991.

Naritsaranuwattiwong, Prince and Prince Damrong Rajanubhab. *San somdet: Lai phrahat khong Somdet Jaofa Kromphraya Naritsaranuwittiwong lae Somdet Kromphraya Damrong Rachanuphap* [Princely matters: correspondence between Prince Naritsaranuwittiwong and Prince Damrong]. Bangkok: Khurusapha, 1961.

Narongchai Pitkorat. *Saranukrom phleng thai* [Dictionary of Thai music]. Bangkok: Rueankaeo, n.d. (?1991).

Narongsak Sonjai, "Kan sueksa priapthiap bannakam that plaeng rueang Khun Chang Khun Phaen" [Study of adaptations of *KCKP*]. MA diss., Silpakorn University, 2002.

Narongsak Sonjai. "Rueang Khun Chang Khun Phaen nai rup baep tangtang" [*KCKP* in various forms]. *The Journal* (Mahidol University), No. 1 (January 2005): 71–90.

Natthan Manirat. *Lek yan: Phaen phang an sakdisit* [Yantra: Powerful diagrams]. Bangkok: Discovery Museum Institute, 2010.

Natthaphat Janthawit. *Chang ton: Sat mongkhon phrajakaphat lem 1* [Major elephants: The emperor's auspicious animals, vol. 1]. Bangkok: Krom Sinlapakon, 1996.

Nidhi Eoseewong. *Kan mueang thai nai samai phrachao krung Thonburi* [Thai politics in the Thonburi reign]. 2nd ed. Bangkok: Sinlapa Watthanatham, 1993.

Nidhi Eoseewong. *Pen and Sail: Literature and History in Early Bangkok.* Chiang Mai: Silkworm Books, 2005.

Nikhom Musikakama. "Sinlapa lae phumisathan Ayutthaya" [Art and geography of Ayutthaya]. In *Athibai phaen thi phranakhon Si Ayutthaya kap kham winichai khong Phraya Boranratchathanin rueang sinlapa lae phumisathan Ayutthaya krung Phichit* [Description of the map of Ayutthaya with commentary by Phraya Boranratchathanin on the art and geography of Ayutthaya, and Phichit City]. Printed for the cremation of Nang Daeng Khaewattana at Wat Makut-kasattriyaram, 20 September 1971.

Nirat Suphan (by Nai Mi). www.reurnthai.com/w/index.php?title=นิราศสุพรรณ

Nirat Suphan. In *Chiwit lae ngan khong Sunthon Phu* [Life and works of Sunthon Phu], revised edition, ninth printing. Bangkok: Khurusapha, 2000.

Nirat Thalang. At: www.tv5.co.th/service/mod/heritage/nation/nirad/talang/talang.htm

Niyada Lausoonthorn. *Phinit wannakam: Ruam botkhwam wichakan dan wannakhadi lae phasa* (sueksa jak ton chabap tua khian) [Literary investigations: Collected academic articles on literature and language (studied from manuscripts)]. Bangkok: Maekhamphang, 1992.

Niyada Thasukhon. *Tamra phap thewarup lae thewathanophakhro* [Manual of deity images and poses]. Bangkok: National Library, 1992.

Noranit Setthabut. *Sanuk kap Khun Chang Khun Phaen* [Fun with *KCKP*]. Bangkok: Suksaphan, 2002.

O'Flaherty, W. D. *Karma and Rebirth in Classical Indian Traditions.* Delhi: Motilal Banarsidass, 1983.

O'Kane, John, tr. *The Ship of Sulaiman.* London: Routledge and Kegan Paul, 1976.

Olsson, Ray A. *The Ramakien: A Prose Translation of the Thai Ramayana.* Bangkok: Phrae Phitthaya, 1968.

Paitoon Mikusol. "Social and Cultural History of Northeastern Thailand from 1868–1910: A Case Study of the Huamuang Khamen Padong (Surin, Sangkha and Khukhan)." Ph.D. diss., University of Washington, 1984.

Pallegoix, Jean-Baptiste. *Description of the Thai Kingdom or Siam.* Translated by Walter E. J. Tips. Bangkok: White Lotus, 2000.

Pant, G. N. *A Catalogue of Arms and Armours in Bharat Kala Bhavan.* Delhi: Parimal Publications, 1995.

Parr, John W. K. *Large Mammals of Thailand.* Bangkok: Sarakadee, 2003.

Pattaratorn Chirapravati, ML. "Chanting for the Dead: Illustrations of the Pamsukula Ceremony in Thai Manuscripts." In Pattaratorn, *Thai Funeral Culture: Studies of Images and Texts in Thai Art,* forthcoming.

Pha phim lai boran nai phiphitaphansathan haeng chat [Ancient chintz fabrics in the national museums]. Bangkok: Krom Sinlapakon, 2002.

Phanomphon Niranthawi. "Khwam ru thang horasat khong Sunthon Phu nai rueang Phra Aphaimani" [Sunthon Phu's knowledge of astrology in Phra Aphaimani]. In *Julasan lai thai chabap phiset*. Bangkok: Department of Thai Language, Faculty of Arts, Thammasat University, 29 July 2002.

Phasakon Wongtawan. *Prawatisat songkhram kao thap samai ton krung Rattanakosin* [History of the nine-army war in the early Bangkok period]. Bangkok: Yipsi Press, 2009

Phiset Jiajanphong. "Sakkarat nai rueang Khun Chang Khun Phaen" [Dating in *KCKP*]. Unpublished paper.

Phlainoi, S. *Samnak phim samai raek* [Printing houses of the first era]. Bangkok: To Nangsue, 2005.

Phlainoi, S. *Wannakhadi aphithan* [Literature lexicon]. Bangkok: Phim Dam, 2006.

Phojananukrom kham wat [Dictionary of wat terms]. Bangkok: Sathaban Banluetham, 2008.

Phongsawadan Yonok [Yonok chronicle], edited by Phraya Prachakitkorachak (Chaem Bunnag). Bangkok: Phrae Phitthaya, 6th ed., 1972 [1898–99].

Phongsawdan nuea [Northern chronicles]. Printed for the cremation of Mahasawektho Phrayathonratanabodi (Sengiam Singhonka), Bangkok, Wat Thepsirin, 1931.

Phra khamphi khatha 108 [Manual of 108 verses]. Printed by Luk So Thammaphakdi, n.p, n.d.

Phra khamphi na 108 phisadan [Manual of 108 *na* formulas]. Printed by Luk So Thammaphakdi, n.p, n.d.

Phraison Salarak, Luang. "Intercourse Between Burma and Siam as Recorded in Hmannan Yazawindawgyi." *Journal of the Siam Society*, vol. 11, no. 3 (1915): 1–67.

Phraratcha phongsawadan krung Thonburi [Royal chronicles of Thonburi, Dr Bradley edition], edited by Sinin Noibunnaeo. Bangkok: Kosit, 2008.

Phraratchawang lae wat boran nai jangwat nakhon Si Ayutthaya phrom thang rup thai lae phaen phang [Old palaces and temples in Ayutthaya province with images and plans]. Bangkok: Fine Arts Department, 1968.

Phrasaeng ratchasastra [Royal weapons]. Cremation volume for General Mongkhon Phromyothi. Bangkok, Wat Thepsirin, 29 June 1966.

Phuthon Phumathon. *Ruea nai phak klang* [Boats of central Thailand]. Sold at the Boat Museum, Wat Yang na Rangsi, Lopburi. n.p., 1990.

Phutthasasanakhadi lae ruam rueang mueang Kanchanaburi [Buddhist sites and related matters in Kanchanaburi]. Cremation volume of Phra Thepmongkhonrangsi, Wat Thewasangkharam, Kanchanaburi, 7 April 1968.

Pinyo Sijamlong. *Thong lok kawi thoet akson Sunthon Phu* [The world of Sunthon Phu]. Bangkok: Ban Pinyo, 2004.

Pornpun Futrakul. "The Environmental History of Pre-Modern Provincial Towns in Siam to 1910." Ph.D. diss., Cornell University, 1989.

Prachak Praphaphithayakon. *Prapheni lae saiwetwitthaya nai Khun Chang Khun Phaen* [Customs and supernaturalism in *KCKP*]. Privately published, 1976.

Prem Chaya (Prince Prem Purachatra). *The Story of Khun Chang Khun Phaen*, told in English by Prem Chaya with illustrations by Hem Vejakorn. 2 vols. Bangkok: Chatra Books, 1955, 1959.

Premseri. *Khun Chang Khun Phaen: Chut wannakhadi amata khong thai samnuan roi kaeo* [*KCKP*: Series of immortal Thai literature in prose versions]. Bangkok: Ruamsat, 11th printing, 2003.

Premseri. *Ramakian samnuan roi kaeo* [Ramakian in prose]. Bangkok: Ruam Sasin, 2004.

Reid, Anthony. *Southeast Asia in the Age of Commerce.* 2 vols. Chiang Mai: Silkworm Books, 1993.

Reynolds, Craig. J. "Mr. Kulap and Purloined Documents." In Reynolds, *Seditious Histories: Contesting Thai and Southeast Asian Pasts.* Seattle and London: University of Washington Press, 2006 (originally published in *Journal of the Siam Society*, vol. 61, no. 2, 1973).

Rhys Davids, T. W., and C. A. F. Rhys Davids. *Dialogues of the Buddha.* 3 vols. London: Pali Text Society, 1965.

Ribeyro de Sousa, Salvador. "A Brief Account of the Kingdom of Pegu in the East Indies with the Story of its Conquest." *Journal of the Burma Research Society*, vol. 16, no. 2 (August 1926): 99–138.

Ringis, Rita. *Thai Temples and Temple Murals.* Singapore, Oxford, New York: Oxford University Press, 1990.

Robinson, H. Russell. *Oriental Armour.* London: Herbert Jenkins, 1967.

Robson, Stuart. "Panji and Inao: Questions of Cultural and Textual History." *Journal of the Siam Society*, vol. 84, no. 2 (1996): 39–54.

Rueang mahatlek khong krom sinlapakon [On the royal pages by the Fine Arts Department]. Bangkok: Phrajan press, printed for the cremation of General Nai Worakan Bancha, Wat Thepsirin, 4 November 1974.

Saichon Satyanurak. *Phutthasasana kap thit thang kan mueang nai ratchasamai Phrabatsomdet Phraphutthayotfachulalok (pho so 2325–2352)* [Buddhism and political trends in the reign of King Rama I, 1782–1807]. Bangkok: Matichon, 2003.

Santanee Phasuk and Philip Stott. *Royal Siamese Maps: War and Trade in Nineteenth Century Thailand.* Bangkok: River Books, 2004.

Santi Leksukhum and Gilles Mermet. *Temples of Gold: Seven Centuries of Thai Buddhist Paintings.* Bangkok: River Books, 2000.

Saowalak Anantasan. *Wannakam ek khong thai (Khun Chang Khun Phaen)* [Leading Thai literature: *KCKP*]. Ramkhamhaeng University, 1980.

Sarassawadee Ongsakul. *History of Lan Na.* Chiang Mai: Silkworm Books, 2005.

Sathaphon Khwanyuen. *Mueang Kanchanaburi kao* [Old Kanchanaburi]. Bangkok: Fine Arts Department, 1991.

Schouten, Joost. *A True Description of the Mighty Kingdom of Siam*. In Caron and Schouten, *The Mighty Kingdoms of Japan and Siam (1671)*. Edited by John Villiers. Bangkok: Siam Society, 1986.

Seni Pramoj. *Pathakatha rueang kotmai samai Si Ayutthaya* [A lecture on law in the Ayutthaya era], delivered 8 April 1957. Bangkok: Committee for the Ayutthaya Memorial, 1957.

Sharma, Narendra Nath. *Kalpacintāmanih of Damodar Bhatta, an Ancient Treatise on Tantra, Yantra, and Mantra*. Delhi: Eastern Book Publishers, 1979.

Simmonds, E. H. S. "Thai Narrative Poetry: Palace and Provincial Texts of an Episode from *Khun Chang Khun Phaen*." *Asia Major*, vol. 10, no. 2. (1963): 279–99.

Singto Suriya-arak. *Horasat thai: Rian duai ton eng lem diao jop* [Thai astrology for self study in a single volume]. Bangkok: Kasem Bannakit, n.d.

Sirindhorn, Princess Mahachakri. *Banthuek rueang kan pokkhrong khong thai samai Ayutthaya lae ton Rattanakosin* [Record of administration in the Ayutthaya and early Bangkok periods, from the lectures of MR Kukrit Pramoj]. Bangkok: Chulalongkorn University, 2006.

Sithawatmethi, Phra, ed. *Luang Pho To Wat Palelaiworawihan* [The Luang Pho To image at Wat Palelai]. Suphanburi: Wat Palelai, 2007.

Sithawatmethi, Phra, ed. *Prawat Wat Palelaiworawihan* [History of Wat Palelai]. Volume distributed at the royal *kathin* on 13 December 2002. Bangkok: Chulalongkorn University Press.

Sittha Salakkham. *Dokmai phloeng boran: Mahatsajan haeng phumpanya thai* [Ancient fireworks: Marvel of Thai wisdom]. Bangkok: Sakakhadi, 1997.

Skilling, Peter. "Compassion, Power, Success: Notes on Siamese Buddhist Liturgy." Paper presented at the United Kingdom Association of Buddhist Studies Day Conference, School of Oriental and African Studies, London, Wednesday, 3 July 2002.

Smithies, Michael and Dhiravat na Pombejra. "Instructions Given to the Siamese Envoys Sent to Portugal, 1684." *Journal of the Siam Society*, vol. 90 (2002): 125–35.

Somchai Phumsa-at. "Jangwat Phichit" [Phichit province]. In *Athibai phaen thi phranakhon Si Ayutthaya kap kham winichai khong Phraya Boranratchathanin rueang sinlapa lae phumisathan Ayutthaya krung Phichit* [Description of the map of Ayutthaya with commentary by Phraya Boranratchathanin on the art and geography of Ayutthaya, and Phichit City]. Printed for the cremation of Nang Daeng Khaewattana at Wat Makut-kasattriyaram, 20 September 1971.

Somchai Phumsa-at. *Suphanburi nai samai Sunthon Phu lae Suphanburi nai samai patjuban* [Suphanburi in the era of Sunthon Phu and the present]. Cremation volume of Khun Mae Son Chutikun, Wat Trithosathep, Bangkok, 10 April 1974.

Somphop Jantharaprapha, *Ayutthaya aphon* [Ayutthaya ornamentation]. Bangkok: Krom Sinlapakon, 1983.

Souneth Phothisane. "The Nidān Khun Borom: Annotated Translation and Analysis." Ph.D. diss., University of Queensland, 1996.

Strong, John S. "Gavampati in Pali and Sanskrit Texts: The Indian Background to a Southeast Asian Cult." Paper presented at the Fifteenth Conference of the International Association of Buddhist Studies, SOAS, London, August 2005.

Stuart-Fox, Martin. *The Lao Kingdom of Lan Xang: Rise and Decline.* Bangkok: White Lotus, 1998.

Stutley, Margaret and James Stutley. *A Dictionary of Hinduism.* London and Henley: Routledge and Kegan Paul, 1977.

Sujit Wongthet, ed. *Jedi yutthahatthi mi jing rue?* [Does the stupa commemorating the elephant duel truly exist?]. Bangkok: Sinlapa Watthanatham, 1994.

Sujit Wongthet. *Khun Chang Khun Phaen saensanuk* [*KCKP*, lots of fun]. Bangkok: Sinlapa Watthanatham, 2002.

Sukanya Pathrachai. "'Khun Chang plaeng san' ton thi hai pai jak sepha Khun Chang Khun Phaen chabap ho samut." ['Khun Chang changes the letter': A passage missing from the library edition of *KCKP*]. *Phasa lae wannakhadi thai* [Thai language and literature], vol. 8, no. 1 (1991): 29–37.

Sunthorn Phu. *Nirat Muang Klaeng.* Translated by Prem Chaya (H.H. Prince Prem Purachatra). Bangkok: Khurusapha, 2001.

Suphawat Kasemsi, MR. "Phra aiyakan kao tamnaeng na huamueang chabap Ayutthaya" [An old registrar of official positions in provincial towns of Ayutthaya]. In *Sichamaiyachan* [Two illustrious teachers], edited by Winai Pongsripian and Pridi Phitphumiwithi. Bangkok: Ministry of Culture, 2002.

Suphon Ocharoen. "Chao mon nai prathet thai: Wikhro thana lae botbat nai sangkhom thai tang tae samai Ayutthaya ton klang thueng samai Rattanakosin ton ton" [Mon in Thailand, a study of their social role in Thai society from mid Ayutthaya to early Bangkok]. MA diss., Department of History, Chulalongkorn University, 1976.

Suwit Phuangsuwan. *Ratchasap chabap sombun* [Royal language, complete edition]. Bangkok: Waen Kaeo, 2006.

Tachard, Guy. *Voyage to Siam Performed by Six Jesuits Sent by the French King to the Indies and China in the Year 1985.* Bangkok: White Orchid, 1981 [1688].

Tambiah, S. J. *Buddhism and the Spirit Cults in North-East Thailand.* Cambridge: Cambridge University Press, 1970.

Tambiah, S. J. *The Buddhist Saints of the Forest and the Cult of Amulets: A Study in Charisma.* Cambridge: Cambridge University Press, 1984.

Tamra chang chabap ratchakan thi 1 [Manual of elephants, First Reign edition]. Committee for Memorial Books and Records for Celebration of the King's Age Equalling that of King Rama I in 2000. Bangkok: Ruansin, 2002.

Tamra phichai songkhram chabap ratchakan thi 1 [Manual of victorious warfare, First Reign edition]. Committee for Memorial Books and Records for Celebration of the King's Age Equalling that of King Rama I in 2000. Bangkok: Ruansin, 2002.

Terwiel, B. J. *Monks and Magic: An Analysis of Religious Ceremonies in Central Thailand.* Scandinavian Institute of Asian Studies Monograph Series 24. London: Curzon Press, 1975.

Terwiel, B. J. *Through Travelers' Eyes: An Approach to Early Nineteenth Century Thai History.* Bangkok: Duang Kamol, 1989.

Textor, Robert B. "An Inventory of Non-Buddhist Supernatural Objects in a Central Thai Village." Ph.D. diss., Cornell University, 1960.

Textor, Robert B. *Patterns of Worship: A Formal Analysis of the Supernatural in a Thai Village.* 4 vols. Human Relations Area Files, New Haven, Connecticut, 1973.

Thai Textiles: Threads of a Cultural Heritage. Bangkok: National Identity Board, 1994.

Thawatchai Tangsirivanich. *Krung Si Ayutthaya nai phaenthi farang* [Ayutthaya in western maps]. Bangkok: Matichon, 2006.

Thep Sarikabut, *Khamphi na 108* [108 "na" formulas]. Bangkok: Soemwit Bannakhan, n.d.

Thep Sarikabut. *Horasat nai wannakhadi* [Astrology in literature]. Bangkok: Sinlapa Bannakhan, 1963.

Thep Sarikabut. *Khamphi hua jai 108* [108 "heart" formulas]. Bangkok: Soemwit Bannakhan, n.d.

Thep Sarikabut. *Wicha athan* [The study of protection]. Bangkok: Soemwit Bannakhan, n.d.

Thirabhand Chandracharoen, "Royal Brocades in the Siamese Court." In *The Secrets of Southeast Asian Textiles: Myth, Status and the Supernatural*, edited by Jane Puranananda. The James H. W. Thompson Foundation Symposium Papers. Bangkok: River Books, 2006.

Turpin, F. H. *A History of the Kingdom of Siam.* Translated by B. O. Cartwright. Bangkok: White Lotus, 1997 [1771].

Turton, Andrew. "Invulnerability and Local Knowledge." In *Thai Constructions of Knowledge,* edited by Manas Chitkasem and Andrew Turton. London: SOAS, 1991.

Untracht, Oppi. *Traditional Jewelry of India.* London: Thames and Hudson, 1997.

Vajiravudh, King. *Thiao mueang Phra Ruang* [Visiting King Ruang's city]. Cremation volume of Prasuthi-athonrimon (Sut Lekyanon), Bangkok, 1938.

Van Beek, Steve. *The Chao Phya: River in Transition.* Oxford: Oxford University Press, 1995.

Van Der Kraan, Alfons. *Murder and Mayhem in Seventeenth-Century Cambodia: Anthony van Diemen vs. King Ramadhipati I.* Chiang Mai: Silkworm Books, 2009.

Van Vliet's Siam. Edited by Chris Baker, Dhiravat na Pombejra, Alfons van der Kraan, and David K. Wyatt. Chiang Mai: Silkworm Books, 2005.

Vickery, Michael. "The Constitution of Ayutthaya: The Three Seals Code." In *Thai Law: Buddhist Law. Essays on the Legal History of Thailand, Laos and Burma,* edited by A. Huxley. Bangkok: White Orchid, 1996.

Wachari Romyanan. "Khun Chang Khun Phaen roem taeng nai ratchakan dai?" [Composition of *KCKP* began in what reign?] *Phasa lae wannakhadi thai* [Thai language and literature], vol. 7, no. 3 (1990): 13–18.

Wade, Geoff, translator, *Southeast Asia in the Ming Shi-lu: An Open Access Resource,* Singapore: Asia Research Institute and the Singapore E-Press, National University of Singapore, http://epress.nus.edu.sg/msl/

Wales, H. G. Quaritch. *Ancient South-East Asian Warfare.* London: Bernard Quaritch, 1952.

Wales, H. G. Quaritch. *Divination in Thailand: The Hopes and Fears of a Southeast Asian People.* London: Curzon Press, 1983.

Waruni Osotharom. "Nirat mueang Suphan khong Sunthon Phu lae Samian Mi: banthuek kan doenthang lae kan an phuea khao thueng rueang lao thongthin" [*Nirat Suphan* by Sunthon Phu and Nai Mi: record of travel and reading on the locality]. *Rathasatsat,* vol. 28, no. 2 (May–July 2007): 323–84.

Wat Khao Phra sisanphetyaram. Booklet distributed at Wat Khao Phra, U Thong, in 2005. n.p., n.d.

Wenk, Klaus. *Studien zur Literatur der Thai: Texte und Interpretationen von und zu Sunthon Phu und seinem Kreis.* Hamburg and Bangkok: DK, 1985.

Whitaker, Jarrod L. "Ritual Power, Social Prestige, and Amulets (mani) in the Atharvaveda." In *The Vedas: Texts, Language and Ritual,* edited by Arlo Griffiths and Jan E. M. Houlson. Groningen: Egbert Forsten, 2004.

Wibun Lisuwan. *Phojananukrom hattakam khrueang mue khrueang chai phuen ban* [Dictionary of handicrafts and local household articles]. Bangkok: Mueang Boran, 2003.

Wibun Lisuwan. *Saranukrom pha khrueng thak tho* [Encyclopedia of cloth and weaving]. Bangkok: Mueang Boran, 2007.

Wilkinson, F. *Flintlock Guns and Rifles.* London: Arms and Armour Press, 1971.

Winyu Bunyong. *Tam roi Khun Chang Khun Phaen* [Following the tracks of *KCKP*]. Bangkok: Ton Or Grammy, 1996.

Wira Thantharanon. *Sapthanukrom chang* [Dictionary of elephants]. Bangkok: Chulalongkorn University Press, 2001.

Wirot Nutaphad. *The Turtles of Thailand.* Bangkok: Siamfarm, 1979.

Wisantharunakon, Luang (An Sarikabut). *Khamphi horasat thai matrathan chabap sombun* [Standard Thai astrology, complete edition]. 2nd ed., Bangkok: Sinlapasan, 1997 [1965].

Witney, William Dwight. *Atharva-Veda Samhita.* 2 vols. Cambridge: Harvard University Press, 1905.

Wolters, O. W. "Ayudhya and the Rearward Part of the World." *Journal of the Royal Asiatic Society*, 3–4, 1968: 166–78. Reprinted in Wolters, *Early Southeast Asia: Selected Essays*, edited by Craig J. Reynolds. Ithaca: Cornell University Press, 2008.

Woranan Aksonphong. "Kan sueksa sangkhom lae watthanatham thai nai samai Rattanako-sin ton ton jak rueang Khun Chang Khun Phaen" [Study of Thai society and culture in the early Bangkok era from *KCKP*]. M.A. diss., Faculty of Arts, Chulalongkorn University, 1972.

Woraphon Phuphongphan. "Kan borihan ratchakan krom wang sueksa jak phra aiyakan tamnaeng na phonlaruen nai kotmai tra sam duang" [The administration of the palace studied from the civil list in the Three Seals Law]. *Warasan ruam botkhwam prawatisat* [Journal of the Historical Society], vol. 27 (2005): 37–77.

Wyatt, David. K. and Aroonrut Wichienkeeo, tr. and ed. *The Chiang Mai Chronicle*. Chiang Mai: Silkworm Books, 1995.

Yai Nophayon. "Suat kharuehat jam-uat" [Lay chanting]. *Muang Boran*, vol. 27, no. 1 (January–March 2001): 108–12.

ACKNOWLEDGMENTS

The first and deepest of our many debts are to the greats. Prince Damrong Rajanubhab chose to edit *Khun Chang Khun Phaen* as one of his first projects when he retired from his extraordinary career as an administrator and devoted himself fully to historical, literary, and cultural pursuits. The great Thai linguist, William Gedney, sparked our interest by his enthusiastic writing on the poem. He also alerted us to the importance of reading older editions, and made it possibly by acquiring an old copy of the Wat Ko edition, now in the Michigan University Library. Khun Wichitmatra wrote an enthusiastic and erudite commentary on the poem which forms the basis of many of our footnotes. Without these three, we would probably have never started the project, and certainly never have finished.

Cholthira Satyawadhna, who wrote a pioneering study of the poem in 1970, spent hours helping us to understand difficult passages. Peter Skilling and Justin McDaniel answered a stream of questions on arcane matters. Choomsai Suwannachomphu pointed our way to old texts, and provided the only copy of the Smith edition we have found. Among our several readers, Bonnie Brereton read the whole thing and crowded the margins with corrections, queries, and suggestions. Lom Pengkaeo and Niyada Laosunthorn helped to decode the most obscure words, phrases, and allusions.

The James H. W. Thompson Foundation provided a very generous grant to support this publication. We are very grateful to the Foundation, and especially to Bill Klausner and Bill Booth.

We owe a very large debt to Chakrabhand Posayakrit, national artist, who very kindly allowed us to reproduce his beautiful oil painting, done in 1989–90, for the cover.

Kriangkrai Sampatchalit, director-general of the Fine Arts Department, provided invaluable assistance. At the National Library, the staffs of the manuscript room and reproductions department were very helpful, and kindly provided the reproductions of *samut thai* texts which illustrate our Afterword. We are also grateful to the librarian and staff of the Siam Society, the Prince Damrong Library, and the Rare Books Room in Chulalongkorn University Library.

We owe a special debt to the Center of Southeast Asian Studies at Kyoto University. We started the translation during a fellowship at the Center. We are grateful for use of the library, and the database of the Three Seals Law on the Center's website.

For help in translating passages in Chinese, Lao, Mon, Tavoyan, Vietnamese, Khmer, and "Indian," we would have been lost without Diem Trang, Do Thien, Jacques Leider, Kasian Tejapira, Khoo Boo Teik, Kyaw Minn Htin, Li Tana, Mathias Jenny, Michael Vickery, Montira Rato, Ong Bunjoon, Paphatsaun Thianpanya, Patrick McCormick, Phra Maha Jarun Yanjari, Somchai Phatharathananunth, Sriram Natrajan, Swai Wiswaman, Wanna Buthasane, and Worasak Mahatthanobon. Karl Weber translated and interpreted Klaus Wenk's studies and translations in German. Weerachai Nanakorn, Thawatchai Wongprasert, and Prachaya Srisanga helped us to identify plant species.

Many people read early drafts and helped us to avoid many crimes of style and understanding. We are very grateful to Bonnie Brereton, Fritz Goss, Natalie Baker, Nilubol Nikki Phanichkarn, Richard LePage, and Susan Morgan.

We have bothered several people with queries on a host of issues. We owe thanks to Bas Terwiel, Charles Keyes, Chatthip Nartsupha, Cholada Ruengruglikit, Constance Wilson, David Atherton, David Wyatt, Dhiravat na Pombejra, Domnern Garden, Geoff Wade, Grant Evans, HRH Princess Maha Chakri Sirindhorn, John S. Strong, Junko Koizumi, Kennon Breazeale, Leedom Lefferts, Marc Askew, Maryvelma O'Neill, ML Pattaratorn Chirapravati, Mushtaq Khan, Nopporn Suwanpanich, Patrick Jory, Pattana Kitiarsa, Phuthorn Bhumadhon, Pornpilai Lertvicha, Praphat Chuvichean, Prapod Assavavirulhakarn, Renoo Wichasin, Rungroj Piromanukul, Santanee Phasuk, Santi Pakdeekham, Soumhya Venkatesan, Steve Van Beek, Sujit Wongthet, Sunait Chutintharanond, Susan Kepner, Susan Morgan, Tamara Loos, Trisilpa Boonkhachorn, Warunee Osatharom, and Woraporn Promjairak.

We are grateful to Allen Hicken, Lara Unger, and Joel Selway who helped us to acquire the microfilm of the Wat Ko edition from Michigan, and to Peter Laverick who loaned the GPS used for making maps.

Finally we owe a lot to a select group who provided us with a very undervalued commodity—encouragement—particularly in the early stages. Special thanks to Ben Anderson, Craig Reynolds, Eiichi Hizen, Jane and Charles Keyes, MR Chakrarot Chitrabong, and Thongchai Winichakul.

Throughout this project, Silkworm Books, and especially Trasvin Jittidecharak and Susan Offner, have been more like partners than publishers. We thank them for their professionalism and their enthusiasm.

We would be very grateful if readers who identify errors—in translation, style, or explanation—would please let us know at kckp@silkwormbooks.com.